ALSO EDITED BY OTTO PENZLER

The Black Lizard Big Book of Pulps

The Vampire Archives

Agents of Treachery

Bloodsuckers

Fangs

Coffins

The Black Lizard Big Book of Black Mask *Stories*

The Big Book of Adventure Stories

ZOMBIES! ZOMBIES! ZOMBIES!

EDITED AND WITH AN INTRODUCTION BY

OTTO PENZLER

VINTAGE CRIME/BLACK LIZARD

VINTAGE BOOKS

A DIVISION OF RANDOM HOUSE, INC.

NEW YORK

A VINTAGE CRIME/BLACK LIZARD ORIGINAL, SEPTEMBER 2011

Introductions and compilation copyright © 2011 by Otto Penzler

Owing to limitations on space, permissions to reprint previously published material appear on pages 807–810.

Library of Congress Cataloging-in-Publication Data
Zombies! zombies! zombies! / [selected by] Otto Penzler.
p. cm.—(Vintage crime/Black Lizard original)
ISBN: 978-0-307-74089-2 (pbk.)
1. Zombies—Fiction. 2. Zombiism—Fiction. 3. Horror tales, American.
I. Penzler, Otto.
PS648.Z64Z66 2011
813'.0873808—dc23
2011026525

Book design by Christopher M. Zucker

www.blacklizardcrime.com

Printed in the United States of America
10 9 8 7 6 5 4 3 2 1

For Steve Stilwell

Who, like me, will live forever

CONTENTS

CONTENTS

INTRODUCTION

OTTO PENZLER

ZOMBIES AIN'T WHAT they used to be. Not so long ago, they were safely ensconced on Haiti so the rest of the world could merely scoff at the bizarre myth of the living dead on one relatively small Caribbean island. Well, they have proliferated at an alarming rate, invading the rest of the world, and it seems unlikely that they have any intention of going away anytime soon.

W. B. Seabrook, in his 1929 book, *The Magic Island*, recounted "true" tales of voodoo magic on Haiti bringing the recently dead back to life as slow-moving, virtually brain-dead creatures who would work tirelessly in the fields without pay and without complaint. These stories introduced the zombie to much of the world, though most national folklores have similar

tales and legends. A decade after Seabrook's groundbreaking volume, Zora Neale Hurston researched Haitian folklore and told similar stories of eyewitness accounts of zombies, as have subsequent anthropologists, sociologists, and others not prone to imaginative fancies.

If zombie literature began with the reportage of Seabrook, it had powerful ancestral works on which to draw. Stories of the living dead, or ghouls, or reanimated people, have existed since the *Arabian Nights* tales and borrowed from other horror story motifs, from the lurching reanimated monster of Mary Shelley's *Frankenstein* to the undead vampires of John Polidori's *The Vampyre* and Bram Stoker's *Dracula*.

Several of the most distinguished short-story

writers of the nineteenth century turned to figures who had been dead but then, uh-oh, were alive. Edgar Allan Poe was almost relentless in his use of the dead coming back to life, most famously in "The Fall of the House of Usher" but most vividly in his contribution to this volume, "The Facts in the Case of M. Valdemar." Guy de Maupassant's poignant "Was It a Dream?" lingers in the memory as an example of how a corpse leaving a grave can destroy the living without a single act or thought of violence. Ambrose Bierce's famous "The Death of Halpin Frayser" may be interpreted as a ghost story, a vampire story, or a zombie story, and is equally terrifying as any of them; it is not included in this volume because I selected it for inclusion in *The Vampire Archives*.

Now a staple of horror fiction, zombies, as we know them today, have a very short history. Tales of resurrected corpses and ghouls were popular in the weird menace pulps of the 1930s, but these old-fashioned zombies had no taste for human flesh. For that, we can thank George Romero, whose 1968 film *Night of the Living Dead* introduced this element to these undead critters. Writers, being writers, took to this notion as a more extreme depiction of reanimation and have apparently made every effort to outdo one another in the degree of violence and gore they could bring to the literature.

While this incursion into the realm of splatterpunk may be welcomed by many readers, I have attempted to maintain some balance in this collection and have omitted some pretty good stories that, in my view, slipped into an almost pornographic sensibility of the need to drench every page with buckets of blood and descriptions of mindless cruelty, torture, and violence. Of course, zombies *are* mindless, so perhaps this behavior is predictable, but so are many of the stories, and I have opted to include a wider range of fiction. While the characters in early stories are not called zombies, they are the living dead (or, occasionally, apparently so), and they qualify for inclusion.

Inevitably, some of the most popular writers and their best stories will have been collected in other anthologies, so will seem familiar. For a definitive collection like this one, I wanted them to be included, so if you've already read the stories by H. P. Lovecraft, Poe, and Stephen King, skip them if you must, though they became popular because they are really good and bear rereading. On the other hand, you will find in these pages some stories that you've never read by authors of whom you've never heard, and you are in for a treat.

To cover the broad spectrum and significant history of zombie literature required a good bit of research, and I am indebted to the welcome and needed assistance of numerous experts in the genre, most notably John Pelan, Robert Weinberg, John Knott, Chris Roden, Joel Frieman, Michele Slung, and Gardner Dozois.

DEAD MEN WORKING IN THE CANE FIELDS

W. B. SEABROOK

W(ILLIAM) B(UEHLER) SEABROOK (1884–1945) was the type of adventurer, explorer, occultist, and author more frequently encountered among the British eccentrics of the Victorian era although he was an American born in Westminster, Maryland. He began his career as a journalist for the *Augusta Chronicle* in Georgia, became part owner of an advertising agency, and joined the French army when World War I broke out, receiving the Croix de Guerre. After recovering from being gassed in the trenches, he became a reporter for *The New York Times* before setting out on a series of travels that provided subject matter for his immensely successful books.

His first book, *Diary of a Section VIII* (1917), told of his war experiences. This was followed by *Adventures in Arabia* (1927), about his time with various desert tribes, and then *The Magic Island* (1929), which explored the voodoo practices and black magic of Haiti; he claimed to be the first white man to witness the rituals, songs, and sacrifices of the islanders. This adventure was succeeded by a trip to the Ivory Coast and what was then Timbuktu, where he again witnessed native sorcery and magic, as well as cannibalism, in which he willingly participated, describing the various cuts of human flesh and comparing them to veal. These travels inspired *Jungle Ways* (1934) and *The White Monk of Timbuctoo* (1934). Drawn to witchcraft, Satanism, and other occult practices, and for a time befriending Aleister Crowley, he wrote frequently on the subject, notably in *Witchcraft: Its Power in the World Today* (1940).

Seabrook spent a year and a half in a rehabilitation clinic to treat his alcoholism, writing *Asylum* (1935) about the experience. He committed suicide with a drug overdose a decade later.

"Dead Men Working in the Cane Fields" purports to be entirely true, without "fiction or embroidery," as he said of his many books. It was originally published in *The Magic Island* (New York, Harcourt Brace, 1929).

W. B. SEABROOK

DEAD MEN WORKING IN THE CANE FIELDS

PRETTY MULATTO JULIE had taken baby Marianne to bed. Constant Polynice and I sat late before the doorway of his *caille,* talking of fire-hags, demons, werewolves, and vampires, while a full moon, rising slowly, flooded his sloping cotton-fields and the dark rolling hills beyond.

Polynice was a Haitian farmer, but he was no common jungle peasant. He lived on the island of La Gonave, where I shall return to him in later stories. He seldom went over to the Haitian mainland, but he knew what was going on in Port-au-Prince, and spoke sometimes of installing a radio. A countryman, half peasant born and bred, he was familiar with every superstition of the mountains and the plain, yet too intelligent to believe them literally true—or at least so I gathered from his talk.

He was interested in helping me toward an understanding of the tangled Haitian folk-lore. It was only by chance that we came presently to a subject which—though I refused for a long time to admit it—lies in a baffling category on the ragged edge of things which are beyond either superstition or reason. He had been telling me of fire-hags who left their skins at home and set the cane fields blazing; of the vampire, a woman sometimes living, sometimes dead, who sucked the blood of children and who could be distinguished because her hair always turned an ugly red; of the werewolf—*chauché*, in Creole—a man or woman who took the form of some animal, usually a dog, and went killing lambs, young goats, sometimes babies.

All this, I gathered, he considered to be pure

superstition, as he told me with tolerant scorn how his friend and neighbour Osmann had one night seen a grey dog slinking with bloody jaws from his sheep-pen, and who, after having shot and exorcised and buried it, was so convinced he had killed a certain girl named Liane who was generally reputed to be a *chauché* that when he met her two days later on the path to Grande Source he believed she was a ghost come back for vengeance, and fled howling.

As Polynice talked on, I reflected that these tales ran closely parallel not only with those of the negroes in Georgia and the Carolinas, but with the medieval folk-lore of white Europe. Werewolves, vampires, and demons were certainly no novelty. But I recalled one creature I had been hearing about in Haiti, which sounded exclusively local—the zombie.

It seemed (or so I had been assured by negroes more credulous than Polynice) that while the zombie came from the grave, it was neither a ghost nor yet a person who had been raised like Lazarus from the dead. The zombie, they say, is a soulless human corpse, still dead, but taken from the grave and endowed by sorcery with a mechanical semblance of life—it is a dead body which is made to walk and act and move as if it were alive. People who have the power to do this go to a fresh grave, dig up the body before it has had time to rot, galvanize it into movement, and then make of it a servant or slave, occasionally for the commission of some crime, more often simply as a drudge around the habitation or the farm, setting it dull heavy tasks, and beating it like a dumb beast if it slackens.

As this was revolving in my mind, I said to Polynice: "It seems to me that these werewolves and vampires are first cousins to those we have at home, but I have never, except in Haiti, heard of anything like zombies. Let us talk of them for a little while. I wonder if you can tell me something of this zombie superstition. I should like to get at some idea of how it originated."

My rational friend Polynice was deeply astonished. He leaned over and put his hand in protest on my knee.

"Superstition? But I assure you that this of which you now speak is not a matter of superstition. Alas, these things—and other evil practices connected with the dead—exist. They exist to an extent that you whites do not dream of, though there is evidence everywhere under your eyes.

"Why do you suppose that even the poorest peasants, when they can, bury their dead beneath solid tombs of masonry? Why do they bury them so often in their own yards, close to the doorway? Why, so often, do you see a tomb or grave set close beside a busy road or footpath where people are always passing? It is to assure the poor unhappy dead such protection as we can.

"I will take you in the morning to see the grave of my brother, who was killed in the way you know. It is over there on the little ridge which you can see clearly now in the moonlight, open space all round it, close beside the trail which everybody passes going to and from Grande Source. For four nights we watched there, in the peristyle, Osmann and I, with shotguns—for at that time both my dead brother and I had bitter enemies—until we were sure the body had begun to rot.

"No, my friend, no, no. There are only too many true cases. At this very moment, in the moonlight, there are zombies working on this island, less than two hours' ride from my own habitation. We know about them, but we do not dare to interfere so long as our own dead are left unmolested. If you will ride with me tomorrow night, yes, I will show you dead men working in the cane fields. Close even to the cities there are sometimes zombies. Perhaps you have already heard of those that were at Hasco . . ."

"What about Hasco?" I interrupted him, for in the whole of Haiti, Hasco is perhaps the last name anybody would think of connecting with either sorcery or superstition. The word is American-commercial-synthetic, like Nabisco, Delco, Socony. It stands for the Haitian-American Sugar Company—an immense factory plant, dominated by a huge chimney, with clanging machinery, steam whistles, freight cars. It is like a chunk of Hoboken. It lies in the eastern suburbs of Port-au-Prince, and beyond it stretch the cane fields of the Cul-de-Sac. Hasco makes rum when the sugar market is off, pays low wages, a shilling or so a day, and gives steady work. It is modern big business, and it sounds it, looks it, smells it.

Such, then, was the incongruous background for the weird tale Constant Polynice now told me.

The spring of 1918 was a big cane season, and the factory, which had its own plantations, offered a bonus on the wages of new workers. Soon heads of families and villages from the mountain and the plain came trailing their rag-tag little armies, men, women, children, trooping to the registration bureau and thence into the fields.

One morning an old black headman, Ti Joseph of Colombier, appeared leading a band of ragged creatures who shuffled along behind him, staring dumbly, like people walking in a daze. As Joseph lined them up for registration, they still stared, vacant-eyed like cattle, and made no reply when asked to give their names.

Joseph said they were ignorant people from the slopes of Morne-au-Diable, a roadless mountain district near the Dominican border, and that they did not understand the Creole of the plains. They were frightened, he said, by the din and smoke of the great factory, but under his direction they would work hard in the fields. The farther they were sent away from the factory, from the noise and bustle of the railway yards, the better it would be.

Better, indeed, for these were not living men and women but poor unhappy zombies whom Joseph and his wife Croyance had dragged from their peaceful graves to slave for him in the sun—and if by chance a brother or father of the dead should see and recognize them, Joseph knew that it would mean trouble for him.

So they were assigned to distant fields beyond the crossroads, and camped there, keeping to themselves like any proper family or village group; but in the evening when other little companies, encamped apart as they were, gathered each around its one big common pot of savoury millet or plantains, generously seasoned with dried fish and garlic, Croyance would tend *two* pots upon the fire, for, as everyone knows, the zombies must never be permitted to taste salt or meat. So the food prepared for them was tasteless and unseasoned.

As the zombies toiled day after day dumbly in the sun, Joseph sometimes beat them to make them move faster, but Croyance began to pity the poor dead creatures who should be at rest—and pitied them in the evenings when she dished out their flat, tasteless *bouillie.*

Each Saturday afternoon Joseph went to collect the wages for them all, and what division he made was no concern of Hasco, so long as the work went forward. Sometimes Joseph alone, and sometimes Croyance alone, went to Croix de Bouquet for the Saturday night *bamboche* or the Sunday cockfight, but always one of them remained with the zombies to prepare their food and see that they did not stray away.

Through February this continued, until Fête Dieu approached, with a Saturday-Sunday-Monday holiday for all the workers. Joseph, with his pockets full of money, went to Port-au-Prince and left Croyance behind, cautioning her as usual; and she agreed to remain and tend the zombies, for he promised her that at the Mardi Gras she should visit the city.

But when Sunday morning dawned it was lonely in the fields, and her kind old woman's heart was filled with pity for the zombies, and she thought, "Perhaps it will cheer them a little to see the gay crowds and the processions at Croix de Bouquet, and since all the Morne-au-Diable people will have gone back to the mountain to celebrate Fête Dieu at home, no one will recognize them, and no harm can come of it." And it is true that Croyance also wished to see the gay procession.

So she tied a new bright-coloured handkerchief round her head, aroused the zombies from the sleep that was scarcely different from their waking, gave them their morning bowl of cold, unsalted plantains boiled in water, which they ate dumbly uncomplaining, and set out with them for the town, single file, as the country people always walk. Croyance, in her bright kerchief, leading the nine dead men and women behind her, passed the railroad crossing, where she murmured a prayer to Legba, passed the great white-painted wooden Christ, who hung life-sized in the glaring sun, where she stopped to kneel and cross herself—but the poor zombies prayed neither to Papa Legba nor to Brother Jesus, for they were dead bodies walking, without souls or minds.

They followed her to the market square before the church, where hundreds of little thatched, open shelters, used on weekdays for buying and selling, were empty of trade, but crowded here and there by gossiping groups in the grateful shade.

To the shade of one of these market booths, which was still unoccupied, she led the zombies, and they sat like people asleep with their eyes open, staring, but seeing nothing, as the bells in the church began to ring, and the procession came from the priest's house—red-purple robes, golden crucifix held aloft, tinkling bells and swinging incense-pots, followed by little black boys in white lace robes, little black girls in starched white dresses, with shoes and stockings, from the parish school, with coloured ribbons in their kinky hair, a nun beneath a big umbrella leading them.

Croyance knelt with the throng as the procession passed, and wished she might follow it across the square to the church steps, but the zombies just sat and stared, seeing nothing.

When noontime came, women with baskets passed to and fro in the crowd, or sat selling little sweet cakes, figs (which were not figs but sweet bananas), oranges, dried herring, biscuit, casava bread, and *clairin* poured from a bottle at a penny a glass.

As Croyance sat with her savoury dried herring and biscuit baked with salt and soda, and provision of *clairin* in the tin cup by her side, she pitied the zombies who had worked so faithfully for Joseph in the cane fields, and who now had nothing, while all the other groups around were feasting, and as she pitied them, a woman passed crying:

"*Tablettes! Tablettes pistaches! T'ois pour dix cobs!*"

Tablettes are a sort of candy made of brown cane sugar (*rapadou*); sometimes with *pistaches*, which in Haiti are peanuts, or with coriander seed. And Croyance thought, "These *tablettes* are not salted or seasoned, they are sweet, and can do no harm to the zombies just this once." So she untied the corner of her kerchief, took out a coin, a *gourdon*, the quarter of a *gourde*, and bought some of the *tablettes*, which she broke in halves and divided among the zombies, who began sucking and mumbling them in their mouths. But the baker of the *tablettes* had salted the *pistache* nuts before stirring them into the *rapadou*, and as the zombies tasted the salt, they knew they were dead and made a dreadful outcry and rose and turned their faces toward the mountain.

No one dared to stop them, for they were corpses walking in the sunlight, and they themselves and everyone else knew that they were corpses. And they disappeared toward the mountain.

When later they drew near their own village on the slopes of Morne-au-Diable, these men and women walking single file in the twilight, with no soul leading them or daring to follow, the people of their village, who were also holding *bamboche* in the market-place, saw them drawing closer, recognized among them fathers, brothers, wives, and daughters whom they had buried months before. Most of them knew at once the truth, that these were zombies who had been dragged dead from their graves, but others hoped that a blessed miracle had taken place on this Fête Dieu, and rushed forward to take them in their arms and welcome them.

But the zombies shuffled through the market-place, recognizing neither father nor wife nor mother, and as they turned leftward up the path leading to the graveyard, a woman whose daughter was in the procession of the dead threw herself screaming before the girl's shuffling feet and begged her to stay; but the grave-cold feet of the daughter and the feet of the other dead shuffled over her and onward; and as they approached the graveyard, they began to shuffle faster and rushed among the graves, and each before his own empty grave began clawing at the stones and earth to enter it again; and as their cold hands touched the earth of their own graves, they fell and lay there, rotting carrion.

That night the fathers, sons, and brothers of the zombies, after restoring the bodies to their graves, sent a messenger on muleback down the mountain, who returned next day with the name of Ti Joseph and with a stolen shirt of Ti Joseph's which had been worn next to his skin and was steeped in the grease-sweat of his body.

They collected silver in the village, and went with the name of Ti Joseph and the shirt of Ti Joseph to a *bocor* beyond Trou Caiman, who made a deadly needle *ouanga*, a black bag *ouanga*, pierced all through with pins and needles, filled with dry goat dung, circled with cock's feathers dipped in blood. And in case the needle *ouanga* be slow in working or be rendered weak by Joseph's counter-magic, they sent men down to the plain, who lay in wait patiently for Joseph, and one night hacked off his head with a machete . . .

WHEN POLYNICE HAD finished this recital, I said to him, after a moment of silence, "You are not a peasant like those of the Cul-de-Sac; you are a reasonable man, or at least it seems to me you are. Now, how much of that story, honestly, do you believe?"

He replied earnestly: "I did not see these special things, but there were many witnesses, and why should I not believe them when I myself have also seen zombies? When you also have seen them, with their faces and their eyes in which there is no life, you will not only believe in these zombies who should be resting in their graves, you will pity them from the bottom of your heart."

Before finally taking leave of La Gonave, I did see these "walking dead men," and I did, in a sense, believe in them and pitied them, indeed, from the bottom of my heart. It was not the next night, though Polynice, true to his promise, rode with me across the Plaine Mapou to the deserted, silent cane fields where he had hoped to show me zombies labouring. It was not on any night. It was in broad daylight one afternoon, when we passed that way again, on the lower trail to Picmy. Polynice reined in his horse and pointed to a rough, stony, terraced slope—on which four labourers, three men and a woman, were chopping the earth with machetes, among straggling cotton stalks, a hundred yards distant from the trail.

"Wait while I go up there," he said, excited because a chance had come to fulfil his promise. "I think it is Lamercie with the zombies. If I wave to you, leave your horse and come." Starting up the slope, he shouted to the woman, "It is I, Polynice," and when he waved later, I followed.

As I clambered up, Polynice was talking to the woman. She had stopped work—a big-boned, hard-faced black girl, who regarded us with surly unfriendliness. My first impression of the three supposed zombies, who continued dumbly to work, was that there was something about them which was unnatural and strange. They were plodding like brutes, like automatons. Without stooping down, I could not fully see their faces, which were bent expressionless over their work. Polynice touched one of them on the shoulder and motioned him to get up. Obediently, like an animal, he slowly stood erect—and what I saw then, coupled with what I had heard previously, or despite it, came as a rather sickening shock. The eyes were the worst. It was not my imagination. They were in truth like the eyes of a dead man, not blind, but staring, unfocused, unseeing. The whole face, for that matter, was bad enough. It was vacant, as if there was nothing behind it. It seemed not only expressionless, but incapable of expression. I had seen so much previously in Haiti that was outside ordinary normal experience that for the flash of a second I had a sickening, almost panicky lapse in which I thought, or rather felt, "Great God, maybe this stuff is really true, and if it is true, it is rather awful, for it upsets everything." By "everything" I meant the natural fixed laws and processes on which all modern human thought and actions are based. Then suddenly I remembered—and my mind seized the memory as a man sinking in water clutches a solid plank—the face of a dog I had once seen in the histological laboratory at Columbia. Its entire front brain had been removed in an experimental operation weeks before; it moved about, it was alive, but its eyes were like the eyes I now saw staring.

I recovered from my mental panic. I reached out and grasped one of the dangling hands. It was calloused, solid, human. Holding it, I said, *"Bonjour, compère."* The zombie stared without responding. The black wench, Lamercie, who was their keeper, now more sullen than ever, pushed me away—*"Z'affai' nèg paz 'z'affai' blanc"* (Negroes' affairs are not for whites). But I had seen enough. "Keeper" was the key to it. "Keeper" was the word that had leapt naturally into my mind as she protested, and just as naturally the zombies were nothing but poor ordinary demented human beings, idiots, forced to toil in the fields.

It was a good rational explanation, but it is far from being the end of this story. It satisfied me then, and I said as much to Polynice as we went down the slope. At first he did not contradict me, even said doubtfully, "Perhaps"; but as we reached the horses, before mounting, he stopped and said, "Look here, I respect your distrust of what you call superstition and your desire to find out the truth, but if what you were saying now were the whole truth, how could it be that over and over again people who have stood by and seen their own relatives buried, have, sometimes soon, sometimes months or years afterwards, found those relatives working as zombies, and have sometimes killed the man who held them in servitude?"

"Polynice," I said, "that's just the part of it that I can't believe. The zombies in such cases may have resembled the dead persons, or even been 'doubles'—you know what doubles are, how two people resemble each other to a startling degree. But it is a fixed rule of reasoning in my country that we will never accept the possibility of a thing being 'supernatural' so long as any natural explanation, even far-fetched, seems adequate."

"Well," said he, "if you spent many years in Haiti, you would find it very hard to fit this reasoning into some of the things you encountered here."

As I have said, there is more to this story—and I think it is best to tell it very simply.

In all Haiti there is no clearer scientifically trained mind, no sounder pragmatic rationalist, than Dr. Antoine Villiers. When I sat with him in his study, surrounded by hundreds of scientific books in French, German, and English, and told him of what I had seen and of my conversations with Polynice, he said:

"My dear sir, I do not believe in miracles nor in supernatural events, and I do not want to shock your Anglo-Saxon intelligence, but this Polynice of yours, with all his superstition, may have been closer to the partial truth than you were. Understand me clearly. I do not believe that anyone has ever been raised literally from the dead—neither Lazarus, nor the daughter of Jairus, nor Jesus Christ himself—yet I am not sure, paradoxical as it may sound, that there is not something frightful, something in the nature of criminal sorcery if you like, in some cases at least, in this matter of zombies. I am by no means sure that some of them who now toil in the fields were not dragged from the actual graves in which they lay in their coffins, buried by their mourning families!"

"It is then something like suspended animation?" I asked.

"I will show you," he replied, "a thing which may supply the key to what you are seeking," and standing on a chair, he pulled down a paperbound book from a top shelf. It was nothing mysterious or esoteric. It was the current official *Code Pénal* (Criminal Code) of the Republic of Haiti. He thumbed through it and pointed to a paragraph which read:

Article 249. Also shall be qualified as attempted murder the employment which may be made against any person of substances which, without causing actual death, produce a lethargic coma more or less prolonged. If, after the administering of such substances, the person has been buried, the act shall be considered murder no matter what result follows.

The strangest and most chimeric story of this type ever related to me in Haiti by Haitians who claimed direct knowledge of its essential truth is the tale of Matthieu Toussel's mad bride, the tale of how her madness came upon her. I shall try to reconstruct it here as it was told to me—as it was dramatized, elaborated, perhaps, in the oft re-telling.

An elderly and respected Haitian gentleman whose wife was French had a young niece, by name Camille, a fair-skinned octoroon girl whom they introduced and sponsored in Port-au-Prince society, where she became popular, and for whom they hoped to arrange a brilliant marriage.

Her own family, however, was poor; her uncle, it was understood, could scarcely be expected to dower her—he was prosperous, but not wealthy, and had a family of his own—and the French *dot* system prevails in Haiti, so that while the young beaux of the élite crowded to fill her dance-cards, it became gradually evident that none of them had serious intentions.

When she was nearing the age of twenty, Matthieu Toussel, a rich coffee-grower from Morne Hôpital, became a suitor, and presently asked her hand in marriage. He was dark and more than twice her age, but rich, suave, and well-educated. The principal house of the Toussel habitation, on the mountainside almost overlooking Port-au-Prince, was not thatched, mud-walled, but a fine wooden bungalow, slate-roofed, with wide verandahs, set in a garden among gay poinsettias, palms, and Bougainvillaea vines. He had built a road there, kept his own big motorcar, and was often seen in the fashionable cafés and clubs.

There was an old rumour that he was affiliated in some way with Voodoo or sorcery, but such rumours are current concerning almost every Haitian who has acquired power in the mountains, and in the case of men like Toussel are seldom taken seriously. He asked no *dot*, he promised to be generous, both to her and her straitened family, and the family persuaded her into the marriage.

The black planter took his pale girl-bride back with him to the mountain, and for almost a year, it appears, she was not unhappy, or at least gave no signs of it. They still came down to Port-au-Prince, appeared occasionally at the club soirées. Toussel permitted her to visit her family whenever she liked, lent her father money, and arranged to send her young brother to a school in France.

But gradually her family, and her friends as well, began to suspect that all was not going so happily up yonder as it seemed. They began to notice that she was nervous in her husband's presence, that she seemed to have acquired a vague, growing dread of him. They wondered if Toussel were ill-treating or neglecting her. The mother sought to gain her daughter's confidence, and the girl gradually opened her heart. No, her husband had never ill-treated her, never a harsh word; he was always kindly and considerate, but there were nights when he seemed strangely preoccupied, and on such nights he would saddle his horse and ride away into the hills, sometimes not returning until after dawn, when he seemed even stranger and more lost in his own thoughts than on the night before. And there was something in the way he sometimes sat staring at her which made her feel that she was in some way connected with those secret thoughts. She was afraid of his thoughts and afraid of him. She knew intuitively, as women know, that no other woman was involved in these nocturnal excursions. She was not jealous. She was in the grip of an unreasoning fear. One morning, when she thought he had been away all night in the hills, chancing to look out of a window, so she told her mother, she had seen him emerging from the door of a low frame building in their own big garden, set at some distance from the others and which he had told her was his office where he kept his accounts, his business papers, and the door always locked . . . "So, therefore," said the mother relieved and reassured, "what does all this amount to? Business troubles, those secret thoughts of his, probably . . . some coffee combination he is planning and which is perhaps going wrong, so that he sits up all night at his desk figuring and devising, or rides off to sit up half the night consulting with others. Men are like that. It explains itself. The rest of it is nothing but your nervous imagining."

And this was the last rational talk the mother and daughter ever had. What subsequently occurred up there on the fatal night of their first wedding anniversary they pieced together from the half-lucid intervals of a terrorised, cowering, hysterical creature, who finally went stark, raving mad. But what she had gone through was indelibly stamped on her brain; there were early periods when she seemed quite sane, and the sequential tragedy was gradually evolved.

On the evening of their anniversary Toussel had ridden away, telling her not to sit up for him, and she had assumed that in his preoccupation he had forgotten the date, which hurt her and made her silent. She went away to bed early, and finally fell asleep.

Near midnight she was awakened by her husband, who stood at the bedside, holding a lamp. He must have been some time returned, for he was fully dressed now in formal evening clothes.

"Put on your wedding dress and make yourself beautiful," he said; "we are going to a party." She was sleepy and dazed, but innocently pleased, imagining that a belated recollection of the date had caused him to plan a surprise for her. She supposed he was taking her to a late supper-dance down at the club by the

seaside, where people often appeared long after midnight. "Take your time," he said, "and make yourself as beautiful as you can—there is no hurry."

An hour later when she joined him on the verandah, she said, "But where is the car?"

"No," he replied, "the party is to take place here." She noticed that there were lights in the outbuilding, the "office" across the garden. He gave her no time to question or protest. He seized her arm, led her through the dark garden, and opened the door. The office, if it had ever been one, was transformed into a dining room, softly lighted with tall candles. There was a big old-fashioned buffet with a mirror and cut-glass bowls, plates of cold meats and salads, bottles of wine and decanters of rum.

In the centre of the room was an elegantly set table with damask cloth, flowers, glittering silver. Four men, also in evening clothes, but badly fitting, were already seated at this table. There were two vacant chairs at its head and foot. The seated men did not rise when the girl in her bride-clothes entered on her husband's arm. They sat slumped down in their chairs and did not even turn their heads to greet her. There were wine-glasses partly filled before them, and she thought they were already drunk.

As she sat down mechanically in the chair to which Toussel led her, seating himself facing her, with the four guests ranged between them, two on either side, he said, in an unnatural, strained way, the stress increasing as he spoke: "I beg you . . . to forgive my guests their . . . seeming rudeness. It has been a long time . . . since . . . they have . . . tasted wine . . . sat like this at table . . . with . . . so fair a hostess . . . But, ah, presently . . . they will drink with you, yes . . . lift . . . their arms, as I lift mine . . . clink glasses with you . . . more . . . they will arise and . . . dance with you . . . more . . . they will . . ."

Near her, the black fingers of one silent guest were clutched rigidly around the fragile stem of a wine-glass, tilted, spilling. The horror pent up in her overflowed. She seized a candle, thrust it close to the slumped, bowed face, and saw the man was dead. She was sitting at a banquet table with four propped-up corpses!

Breathless for an instant, then screaming, she leaped to her feet and ran. Toussel reached the door too late to seize her. He was heavy and more than twice her age. She ran still screaming across the dark garden, flashing white among the trees, out through the gate. Youth and utter terror lent wings to her feet, and she escaped . . .

A procession of early market-women, with their laden baskets and donkeys, winding down the mountainside at dawn, found her lying unconscious far below, at the point where the jungle trail emerged into the road. Her flimsy dress was ripped and torn, her little white satin bride-slippers were scuffed and stained, one of the high heels ripped off where she had caught it in a vine and fallen.

They bathed her face to revive her, bundled her on a pack-donkey, walking beside her, holding her. She was only half-conscious, incoherent, and they began disputing among themselves as peasants do. Some thought she was a French lady who had been thrown or fallen from a motor car; others thought she was a *Dominicaine,* which has been synonymous in Creole from earliest colonial days with "fancy prostitute." None recognised her as Madame Toussel; perhaps none of them had ever seen her. They were discussing and disputing whether to leave her at a hospital of Catholic sisters on the outskirts of the city, which they were approaching, or whether it would be safer—for them—to take her directly to police headquarters and tell their story. Their loud disputing seemed to rouse her; she seemed partially to recover her senses and understand what they were saying. She told them her name, her maiden family name, and begged them to take her to her father's house.

There, put to bed and with doctors sum-

moned, the family were able to gather from the girl's hysterical utterances a partial comprehension of what had happened. They sent up that same day to confront Toussel if they could—to search his habitation. But Toussel was gone, and all the servants were gone except one old man, who said that Toussel was in Santo Domingo. They broke into the so-called office, and found there the table still set for six people, wine spilled on the table-cloth, a bottle overturned, chairs knocked over, the platters of food still untouched on the sideboard, but beyond that they found nothing.

Toussel never returned to Haiti. It is said that he is living now in Cuba. Criminal pursuit was useless. What reasonable hope could they have had of convicting him on the unsupported evidence of a wife of unsound mind?

And there, as it was related to me, the story trailed off to a shrugging of the shoulders, to mysterious inconclusion.

What had this Toussel been planning—what sinister, perhaps criminal necromancy in which his bride was to be the victim or the instrument? What would have happened if she had not escaped?

I asked these questions, but got no convincing explanation or even theory in reply. There are tales of rather ghastly abominations, unprintable, practised by certain sorcerers who claim to raise the dead, but so far as I know they are only tales. And as for what actually did happen that night, credibility depends on the evidence of a demented girl.

So what is left?

What is left may be stated in a single sentence:

Matthieu Toussel arranged a wedding anniversary supper for his bride at which six plates were laid, and when she looked into the faces of his four other guests, she went mad.

AFTER NIGHTFALL

DAVID A. RILEY

IN ADDITION TO writing fantasy, horror, and science fiction, David A. Riley (1951–) works for a law firm as a legal cashier and runs a charming bookshop in Lancashire, England, the eponymous Riley's Books, which specializes in the genres in which he writes, but also carries first editions and out-of-print books in numerous other fields, as well as folio art and photographic books.

He is currently the editor of *Prism*, the magazine of the British Fantasy Society. In 1995, he coedited, with his wife, Linden, the fantasy and science fiction magazine *Beyond*. His first novel, *Goblin Mire*, was published as an original electronic book by Renaissance. Riley has also written under the pseudonym Allan Redfern (a story titled "Gwargens"). His first short-story collection, *The Lurkers in the Abyss* (2010), includes the title story and such other frequently anthologized tales as "The Farmhouse," "The Urn," "The Satyr's Head," "Out of Corruption," and "After Nightfall," of which Hugh Lamb, in *The Penguin Encyclopedia of Horror and the Supernatural*, wrote, ". . . the nearest literature has yet come to creating George Romero's cinematic effects in words."

"After Nightfall" was first published in *Weird Window* (1970), then in *The Year's Best Horror Stories*, edited by Richard Davis (London: Sphere, 1971).

DAVID RILEY

AFTER NIGHTFALL

I

ELIOT WILDERMAN NEVER struck anyone as a person possessing that necessary instability of character which makes men in a sudden fit of despair commit suicide. Even Mrs. Jowitt, his landlady, never had even the vaguest suspicions that he would ever do anything like this. Why should she? Indeed, Wilderman was certainly not poor, he was in good health, was amiable and well liked in the old-fashioned village of Heron. And in such an isolated hamlet as this it took a singularly easygoing and pleasant type of person to be able to get on with its definitely backward, and in many cases decadent, population.

Civilisation had barely made an impression here for the past two hundred years. Elsewhere such houses as were common here and lived in by those not fully sunken into depraved bestiality were thought of as the slums, ancient edifices supporting overhangs, gables, high peaked roofs, bizarrely raised pavements three feet above the streets and tottering chimneys that towered like warped fingers into the eternally bleak sky.

Despite the repellant aspect of the village Wilderman had been enthusiastic enough when he arrived early in September. Taking a previously reserved room on the third floor of the solitary inn he soon settled down and became a familiar sight wandering about the wind-ravaged hills which emerged from the woods in barren immensities of bracken and hardy grass, or visiting various people, asking them in his tactful and unobtrusive manner about their local folklore. In no way was he disappointed and the volume he was writing on anthropology soon had an abundance of facts and information. And yet in some strangely elusive way he felt the shadow of dissatisfaction. It was not severe enough to worry him or even impede his creative abilities and cheerfulness, but all the same it was there. Like some "imp of the perverse" it nagged at him, hinting that something was wrong.

After having been here a month his steadily growing hoard of data had almost achieved saturation point and little more was really needed. Having done far better than he had expected prior to his arrival he decided that he could now afford to relax more, investigating the harsh but strangely attractive countryside and the curious dwellings about it, something he had only been able to do on a few brief occasions before.

As he had heard from many of his antiquarian friends Heron itself was a veritable store of seventeenth and early eighteenth century buildings, with only a few from later periods. Except for the ramshackle huts. Even these, though, were perversely fascinating. None exhibited any features suggesting comfort; sanitation and ventilation were blatantly disregarded and hampered to an unbelievable extent. Roughly constructed from wood veneered with mould, with murky insides infested with the humid and sickening stench of sweat, they were merely dwellings to sleep and shelter in, nothing more.

In fact the only feature which he noticed in common with the other buildings was that each had heavy wooden doors reinforced from outside with rusted strips of iron, barred by bolts or fastened with old Yale locks from within. Apart from the plainly obvious fact that there was nothing inside them to steal Wilderman was puzzled at such troublesome if not expensive precautions against intruders.

Finally when an opportunity presented itself Wilderman asked Abel Wilton, one of the degenerates inhabiting these huts, a thick set man with a matted beard and cunningly suspicious eyes, why such precautions were taken. But, despite his fairly close acquaintance with this man, for whom he had previously bought liquor and shared tobacco with for information about local legends, all the response he got was a flustered reply that they were to keep out the wild animals that "run 'n' 'ide in th' 'ills where none but those pohzessed go, where they wait for us, comin' down 'ere at night, a 'untin' "; or so Wilton claimed. But his suddenly narrowed eyes and obvious dislike of the subject belied him, though Wilderman tactfully decided to accept this explanation for the moment. After all it would do him no good, he reasoned, to go around accusing people of being liars. It could only result in his drawing onto himself the animosity of Wilton's kinfolk who, ignorant though they were, were extremely susceptible to insult.

However, after having noticed this point about the clustered huts on the outskirts of Heron, Wilderman realised that all the other houses that he had entered also had unusually sturdy locks. Not only on their doors; most had padlocks or bolts across the shutters on their windows, too, though they were already protected by bars. But, when he questioned someone about this, he again received a muttered reply about wild beasts, as well as the danger of thieves, and again he did not believe it. He could have been convinced of the possibility of thieves, even in the worthless huts, but how could he accept the wild animals, when he had never seen a sign of them during his now frequent rambles across the hills? Certainly none that were of any danger at all to man. And so, realising then that any further approaches on this subject would probably only bring similar results he did not pursue it any further, though he fully intended to keep it in mind. Perhaps, he thought, this was what had been troubling him all along.

It was at this time in late October, when he was beginning to pay closer attention to his surroundings, that he first realised that no one ever left their houses after dusk. Even he himself had never gone out after nightfall since he had first arrived. He had not been particularly conscious of this before since it had kept light until late, but as the nights became longer, creeping remorselessly into the dwindling days, this universal peculiarity in Heron became apparent to him, adding yet another mystery to be solved.

The first time he had this brought to his attention was one evening when he tried to leave the inn and failed, both the front and back doors being locked. Irritably he strode up to Mrs. Jowitt, an elderly woman, grey of face and hair with needle-like fingers and brown teeth that seemed to blend in with the gloom of the sitting-room where she sat knitting a shawl. Without preamble he asked why the inn had been locked at so early an hour.

For a moment she seemed to have been stunned into silence by his outburst and immediately stopped her work to turn towards him. In that brief instant her face had paled into a waxen mask, her eyes, like Wilton's, narrowing menacingly—or were they, Wilderman conjectured in surprise, hooded to hide the barely concealed fear he felt he could glimpse between the quivering lids?

"We always lock up at night, Mr. Wilderman," she drawled at length. "Always 'ave an' always will do. It's one of our ways. P'raps it's foolish—you might think so—but that's our custom. Any'ow, there's no reason to go out when it's dark, is there? There's nowt 'ere i' the way of entertainment. Besides, can't be too careful. More goes on than you'd suspect, or want to. Not only is there animals that'd kill us in our sleep, but some o' them in the 'uts—I'm not sayin' who, mind you—wouldn't think twice o' breakin' in an' takin' all I've got if I didn't lock 'em out."

Her reply left little with which Wilderman could legitimately argue, without seeming to do so solely for the sake of argument: and he was loath to antagonise her. Always he was aware that he was here only on the townspeople's toleration; they could very easily snub him or even do him physical damage and get away with it. Justice, a dubious word here, was at best rudimentary, depending for a large part on family connections and as good as open bribery; or at its worst and most frequent on personal revenge, reminding Wilderman distastefully of the outdated duelling system of latter day Europe, though with less notice here taken of honour.

Convinced that fear of wild animals was not the reason for Mrs. Jowitt's locking of the doors after dusk Wilderman became determined to delve further into this aggravating mystery.

The next morning, rising deliberately at dawn, he hurried noiselessly down the staircase to find his landlady busy unlocking the front door. So engrossed was she in the seemingly arduous task that she did not notice his presence.

Finally succeeding in turning the last of the keys she cautiously prised the door open and peered uneasily outside. Evidently seeing nothing to alarm her she threw the door open and knelt down to pick up an enamel dish from the worn doorstep outside. Filled with curiosity Wilderman tried to see what was on it but could only glimpse a faint red smear that might have been a reflection of the sun now rising liquescently above the hills.

Before Mrs. Jowitt could turn and see him he retraced his steps to the second floor, walking back down again loudly and calling a greeting to her. After a few brief but necessary comments about the weather he left, stepping out into the cold but refreshing early morning air to see the narrow streets still half obscured by mists through which beams of sunlight shone against the newly unshuttered windows like drops of molten gold.

As he slowly made his way down the winding street he could not help but notice the plates and dishes left on many of the doorsteps. Some others had been shattered and left on the stagnant gutter that ran down the centre of the street to a mud-clogged grate at the end.

It was immediately obvious to Wilderman that these dishes had contained meat, raw meat, as shown by the watery stains of blood still on them. But why should the villagers leave food out like this, he asked himself, every one of them, including those in the fetid huts, though they themselves had little enough to eat at the best of times? Such behaviour as was evident here seemed ludicrous to him. Why, indeed, should they have left food out like this, presumably for animals, when they dared not go out after nightfall for fear of those very creatures which the meat would only attract? It didn't make sense! That people in Heron were not exceptionally kind and generous to animals he knew; quite the opposite, in fact. Already he had seen what remained of one dog—a wolf hound with Alsatian blood in its savage veins—that made a nuisance of itself one Saturday on Market Street. Its mangled carcass, gory and flayed to the bone, had almost defied description after some ten or so heavy boots backed by resentful legs had crushed it writhing into the cobbles. Then why, if they had no other feelings but contempt for their own animals, should they be so unnaturally benevolent to dangerous and anonymous beasts?

Obviously, though, no one would tell him why they did this. Already he had tried questioning them about their heavily locked doors with only the barest of results. There was, he knew, only one way in which he would have the slightest chance of finding out anything more, and that was to see for himself what came for the food.

Preparing himself for the nocturnal vigil he returned to his room and spent the rest of the day re-reading several of his notes and continuing his treatise from where he had left off the previous day.

Nightfall soon came, and with it an all-penetrating fog that tainted even the inside of his room with an obscuring mist. Sitting on a high backed chair by the window he cursed it, but was adamant that the fulfilment of his malign curiosity would not be foiled by a mist.

Almost as soon as the sun had disappeared beneath the fog-hidden mountains Wilderman heard several doors nearby being opened,

though no one called out. The only sound was the indistinct clatter of plates being placed on the pavements, before the doors were hastily slammed shut and locked. Following this came an absolute silence in which nothing stirred on the fog-shrouded street. It was as though all life and movement had come to an end, disturbed only by the clock atop the hearth within his room as it slowly ticked out the laboured seconds and minutes. Then something caught his attention.

Looking out over the worn windowsill he stared down at the street, trying to penetrate the myopic mist. Some thing or things were coming down the street. But the noises were strange and disturbing, not the anticipated padded footfalls of wild cats or dogs gone ferile from neglect or cruelty. No, the sounds that reached his ears were far from expected, like a sibilant slithering sound, as of something possessed by an iron determination dragging itself sluggishly across the cobbles.

A tin plate was noisily up-ended and went clattering down the street, coming to a halt at the raised pavement beneath his window. As he leaned out further to look he saw a darkish, shadowy thing, a hulking shape, appear. For several moments following this intrusion he heard no more until the creature found its food and began to devour it.

Pulling himself together Wilderman shouted to scare whatever was beneath him away; but as his cry echoed dismally down the street to the clock tower in the square at the end, sounding even more hysterical at each dinning repetition, more forlorn and pathetic, there was only an instant's pause before he heard the other milling creatures on the street begin to drag themselves across and along it, deserting their food to make their way to the inn.

And with them came a fiendish tittering, ghoulish in its overtly inhuman form, devoid of all but the foulest of feelings: hatred, lust, and surprising Wilderman in his interpretation of it, an almost insatiable greed. So clear was it in the vague sounds shuddering below that he felt the tremors of panic growing inside him, sweat streaming down his face. Again, after an inner struggle, he called out, his voice rasping with fear.

In answer came a scratching at the base of the inn beneath his window as though something sought to surmount the decaying barrier.

More shapes were gathering on the street, slithering towards the inn and scratching at it. Trembling fiercely he realised why the villagers took such precautions as they did, and why none spoke or left their houses at night, leaving the village as though deserted. But the facade had been broken. They knew he was here, they had heard him!

Picking up a heavy fore-edged book he hurled it down at the creatures below. As it struck them there was the sound as of a large stone falling into mud, and then a series of cracks like breaking bones, thin, brittle ones shattered by the copper-bound book. At this the horrid sounds increased into a crescendo of fiendish glee. A shriek as inhuman as the others, yet still possessing the wretched qualities of agony and terror, echoed down the street. But loud and terrible though this was no one in any of the neighbouring houses appeared to see what was happening. All shutters and doors remained closed.

As a sudden breeze that died almost as soon as it came sent the fog floundering from the street in scattering wisps Wilderman saw the shapes more clearly though blurred even now by the gloom. For a time he had thought them to be animals, hybrids of some sort, but what he now saw was neither wholly bestial nor human, but possessed, or seemed to be possessed, in the shadow world they inhabited, of the worst features of each. Hunched, with massive backs above stunted heads that hung low upon their chests, they dragged themselves along with skeletal arms which, when outstretched above their shoulders into the diffused light from his room, proved white and leprous, crumbling as though

riddled with decay. Tapering to gangrenous stumps their fingers opened slowly, painfully, and closed again before the mist returned and resealed them in a spectral haze.

When once more half hidden in the fog Wilderman saw that the shadows were converging upon one spot which then became progressively clearer, more distinct. And suddenly with the self-consuming quick-lime of fear he realised why; slowly, inevitably they were climbing upon each to form a hillock, a living hillock to his window.

Again he threw a book at them, and then another and another, each one more savagely than the last, but though they seemed to crash into and through the skulking bodies, the mound still continued to grow. And from the nethermost extremes of the mist-filled street he could make out others slithering and shuffling towards the inn.

In alarm Wilderman threw himself back from the window, slamming and fastening its shutters as he did so. Then in a fit of nausea he staggered to a basin on his dresser and was violently sick. Outside the tittering was continuing to grow louder, nearer. Awful in its surfeit of abhorrence it filled Wilderman with increasingly more dread at every passing instant. With movements strained from forcing himself to resist the panic he felt growing in him, he crept behind the writing desk in the centre of the room until, with his hand clenched tightly on it, he faced the shuttered window, his face shivering uncontrollably as his eyes stared harder and harder at the window . . . waiting, dreading the end of his wait, fearing the expected arrival.

And still from outside, the gibbering, the hellish inhuman giggling increased in volume until suddenly it ended and a scratching of claws on wood took its place. The shutters shook and rattled on their creaking hinges so violently that they threatened to give way at any moment. And then they did.

A myriad shrieks of fiendish glee flooded Wilderman's room, shrieks that mingled with and then utterly overpowered and drowned the tortured screams of anguish, terror and then agony that were human, and which ended as the slobbering tearing sounds of eating took their place.

II

The next day as a reluctant sun reared itself in a blood-red crescent above the pale pine forests to the east the locked door to Wilderman's room was forced open by two of Mrs. Jowitt's permanent guests after her unsuccessful attempt to rouse him earlier. As the men pushed and beat at the old oak panels she waited behind them, shivering as she remembered the cries of the night when she lay locked in her room down the passageway, wide eyed in fear and dread. So had, as she could tell by their red-rimmed eyes and fearful expressions, the two men.

With a mournful rending of wood the door fell inwards. As the men were contorted with disgust and nausea she looked into the room, and screamed. Inside, the room was cluttered with shattered and overturned furniture, scratched till the wood was bare, sheets torn into shreds, and a skeletal thing that lay amidst a bloody upheaval of tattered books, manuscripts, pens and cloth, bones scattered to every corner of the room.

III

Though the circumstances surrounding Wilderman's death did not show even the vaguest trace of suicide this was the verdict solemnly reached by the coroner, a native of Heron, four days later in the poorly lit village hall.

All through the hastily completed inquest Wilderman's various relatives from Pire were refused permission to view his remains before they were interred in the cemetery on the outskirts of the village, the coroner saying that his mode of self destruction—drowning himself in a nearby river—and the fact that it had taken nearly a week to find him, had left him in a state that was most definitely not wise to be seen.

"It would be better to remember him as he was," said the wrinkled old man, nervously cleaning his wire-framed bifocals, "than like he is now."

While outside, unnoticed by the visitors, the church warden completed his daily task of beating down the disrupted earth on the graves in the wild and tawny burial ground, whispering a useless prayer to himself before returning to his home for supper.

MISSION TO MARGAL

HUGH B. CAVE

HUGH B(ARNETT) CAVE (1910–2004) was born in Chester, England, but his family moved to Boston when World War I broke out. He attended Boston University for a short time, taking a job at a vanity publishing house before becoming a full-time writer at the age of twenty. At nineteen, he had sold his first short stories, "Island Ordeal" and "The Pool of Death," and went on to produce more than a thousand stories, mostly for the pulps but also with more than three hundred sales to national "slick" magazines such as *Collier's*, *Redbook*, *Good Housekeeping*, and *The Saturday Evening Post*. Although he wrote in virtually every genre, he is remembered most for his horror, supernatural, and science fiction. In addition to the numerous stories, he wrote forty novels, juveniles, and several volumes of nonfiction, including an authoritative study of voodoo. His bestselling novel *Long Were the Nights* (1943) drew on his extensive reportage of World War II in the Pacific and featured the adventures of PT boats and those who captained them at Guadalcanal. He also wrote several nonfiction books chronicling World War II in the Pacific theater.

Cave was the recipient of numerous awards, including the Living Legend Award from the International Horror Guild, the Bram Stoker Lifetime Achievement Award from the Horror Writers Association, and the World Fantasy Life Achievement Award.

"Mission to Margal" was first published in the anthology *The Mammoth Book of Zombies*, edited by Stephen Jones (London: Robinson Publishing, 1993).

HUGH B. CAVE

MISSION TO MARGAL

I

"OH-OH." KAY GILBERT jabbed her foot at the jeep's brake pedal. "Now what have we got, *ti-fi?*" She spoke in Crèole, the language of the Haitian peasant.

In the middle of the road stood a man with his arms outthrust to stop them. Beyond him, at the road's edge, was one of the big, gaudy buses the Haitians called *camions.* Crudely painted orange and red and resembling an outsized rollercoaster car, it was pointed north in the direction they were going. Disembarked passengers stood watching two men at work under it.

The man who had stopped them strode for-ward as the jeep came to a halt. He was huge. "*Bon soir*, madame," he said with a slight bow. "May I ask if you going to Cap Haïtien?"

"Well . . ." The hesitation was caused by his ugliness. And, being responsible for the child, she must be extra careful.

"I beg you a lift," the fellow said, one heavy hand gripping the edge of the windshield as though by sheer force he would prevent her from driving on without him. "I absolutely must get to Le Cap today!"

She was afraid to say no. "Well . . . all right. Get in."

Stepping to the rear, he climbed in over the tailgate and turned to the metal bench-seat on her side of the vehicle. "May I move this, madame?" He held up a brown leather shoulderbag that she had put there.

"Give it to me!" Turning quickly, Kay snatched it from his hand and placed it on the floor in front, at little Tina's feet.

"*Merci*, madame." The man sat down.

When the jeep had finished descending through hairpin turns to the Plaisance River valley, Kay was able to relax a little. Presently she heard their passenger saying, "And what is your name, little girl?"

Evidently the child did not find him intimidating. Without hesitation she replied brightly, "My name is Tina, m'sieu."

"Tina what, if I may ask?"

"Anglade."

A stretch of rough road demanded Kay's full attention again. When that ended, the child at her side was saying, "So you see, I have been at the hospital a long time because I couldn't remember anything. Not my name or where I lived or *anything*. But I'm all right now, so Miss Kay is taking me home."

"I am glad for you, *ti-fi*."

"Now tell me *your* name and where *you* live."

"Well, little one, my name is Emile Polinard and I live in Cap Haïtien, where I have a shop and make furniture. I was on my way back from Port-au-Prince when the *camion* broke down. And I'm certainly grateful to *le Bon Dieu* for causing you to come along when you did."

Darkness had fallen. Kay cut her speed again so as not to be booby-trapped by potholes. Lamps began to glow in scattered peasant *cailles*. Now and then they passed a pedestrian holding a lantern or a bottle-torch to light his way. As the jeep entered the north coast city of Cap Haïtien, rain began to fall.

In the wet darkness, Kay was unsure of herself. "I have to go to the Catholic church," she said to their passenger. "Can you direct me?"

He did so, remarking that he lived near there, himself. She stopped under a street lamp near the church entrance, the rain a silvery curtain now in the glare of the jeep's headlights. "For us, this is the end of the road, M'sieu Polinard. Tina and I will be staying here tonight with the sisters."

Their passenger thanked her and got out. To the child Kay said, frowning, "Where do the sisters live, Tina?"

"I don't know."

"But you stayed here almost a month before you came to the hospital!"

"I didn't know what was happening then."

Kay gazed helplessly at the church, a massive dark pile in the rain, then saw that Emile Polinard had stopped and was looking back at them. He returned to the jeep.

"Something is wrong, madame?"

"Well, I—I thought Tina would know where to find the sisters, but she doesn't seem to."

"Let me help. Is there a particular sister you wish to see?"

She felt guilty, keeping him standing there in the downpour. But if she did not accept his help, what would she do? "It was a Sister Simone who brought Tina to the hospital. But if she isn't there, someone else will do, I suppose."

"I know her. She should be here."

He was back in five minutes holding aloft a large black umbrella under which moved a black-robed woman not much taller than Tina. Saying cheerfully, "Hello, you two! Tina, move over!" she climbed into the jeep. Polinard handed her the umbrella and she thanked him. "Just drive on," she instructed Kay. "I'll show you where to go."

Kay, too, thanked "ugly man" Polinard, who bowed in reply. Driving on, she turned a corner at the sister's direction, turned again between the back of the church and another stone building.

"Come," the sister commanded, and they hurried into the building. But once inside, the sister was less brisk. Giving the umbrella a shake, she closed it and placed it in a stand near the door, then hunkered down in front of Tina and put out her arms. "And how *are* you, little one?" She was Haitian, Kay noticed for the first time. And remarkably pretty.

"It's a good thing I phoned you yesterday," Kay said. Actually, she had phoned only to say that she and Tina would be passing through Le Cap on their way to the town of Trou and would stop for a few minutes. "I'm afraid I'll have to ask you to put us up for the night. Can you?"

"Of course, Miss Gilbert. What happened? Did you have car trouble?"

"We got off to a late start. Tina had one of her headaches."

"Ah, those headaches." The sister reached for Tina's hand. "Come upstairs, both of you. First your room, then we'll see about something to eat."

She put them both in the same room, one overlooking the yard where the jeep was, then disappeared. "We'll need our gear," Kay told the child. "I'll go for it while you wash up." The brown leather shoulder-bag she had brought with her, and before leaving the room she carefully slid it out of sight under a bed. Then on the stairs she met Sister Simone and a second nun coming up, each with a backpack from the jeep.

They supped on soup and fish in a small dining room: Kay and Tina, Sister Simone, Sister Anne who had helped with the backpacks, and Sister Ginette who at sixty or so was the oldest. What little conversation there was concerned only the journey. "That road is not easy, is it? . . . It so badly needs repairing . . . And the Limbé bridge is closed, so you had to come through the river . . ."

Why don't they ask about Tina—what we've been doing with her all this time at the hospital, and how she's coming along? They did talk to the youngster, but asked no personal questions. It almost seemed a conspiracy of silence.

But when the meal ended and Kay took Tina by the hand to walk her back upstairs, little Sister Simone said quietly, "Do come down again when she is in bed, Miss Gilbert. We'll be in the front room."

She found the three of them waiting there on uncomfortable-looking wooden chairs. It occurred to her that perhaps Polinard had built them. An empty chair was in place for her.

On a small table in the centre of the circle lay a wooden tray on which were mugs, spoons, a pitcher of milk, a bowl of sugar. A battered coffee pot that might have been silver was being kept warm over an alcohol flame.

The nuns rose and waited for Kay to sit, managing somehow—all but Simone—to sit again precisely when she did. "Coffee, Miss Gilbert?" Simone asked.

"Please."

"Milk and sugar?"

"Black, please." It was a crime to tamper with Haiti's marvellous coffee.

Simone served the others as well—perhaps this was an aftersupper ritual—then seated herself. "Now, Miss Gilbert, please tell us how Tina regained her memory. If it won't tire you too much."

She told them how Dr. Robek had hit on the idea of reading map names to Tina and how, on hearing the name Bois Sauvage, the child had snapped out of her long lethargy. "Like Snow White waking up when the prince kissed her."

They smiled.

"Then she remembered her own name. If, of course, Tina Louise Christine Anglade really is her name. We can't be sure until I get her to Bois Sauvage, can we? Or even if that's really where she came from."

The oldest sister, frowning deeply, said, "Bois Sauvage. Isn't that up in the mountains near the Dominican border?"

"According to the map, yes."

"How in the world will you get there?"

"I've been promised a guide at Trou."

"But you can't *drive* to such a place! There aren't any roads."

"I suppose we'll walk, or ride mules. I really won't know until tomorrow." Kay waited for them to sip their coffee. "Now will you tell *me* something, please? How did Tina come into your care in the first place? All we've ever heard is that she was brought to you by a priest."

"By Father Turnier," Simone said, nodding. "Father Louis Turnier. He was stationed at Vallière then and had a number of chapels even farther back in the mountains. We have a picture of him." She put her coffee mug down and went briskly, with robe swishing, to a glass-doored bookcase. Returning with a large photo album that smelled of mildew, she turned its pages, then reversed the book and held it out to Kay. "That's Father on the right, in front of the Vallière chapel. Those big cracks in the chapel were caused by an earthquake just a few days before this picture was taken. Can you imagine?"

Kay saw a husky-looking white man with a cigarette dangling from his lips. French, she guessed. Most of the white priests in the remote areas were French. He wore no clerical garment; in fact, his shirt was neither buttoned nor tucked into his pants. The way he grinned at the camera made her instantly fond of him.

"He was coming back from some far-off chapel one day," Simone said, "and stopped at this isolated native *caille* beside a little stream. He had never passed that way before, he said, but a landslide had carried away part of the usual trail and forced him to detour. He was on a mule, of course. And the animal was weary, so he thought he would just stop and talk with these people a while."

Kay gazed at the photo while she listened.

"Well, there was the child lying on a mat inside the *caille*, and the people asked Father to talk to her. She had wandered into their clearing a few days before and couldn't remember who she was or where she had come from."

"I see."

"That photo shows you the kind of man Father Turnier is. He ended up staying the night there and deciding the child must have been through some really traumatic experience and ought to have help. In any case, she couldn't remain there with those people. They didn't want her. So at daybreak he lifted her up on his mule and carried her out to Vallière, still not knowing her name or where she came from."

"Then what happened?"

"Well, he kept her there for about three weeks—he and young Father Duval who was stationed there with him—but she didn't respond as they hoped, so he brought her here to us." Sister Simone paused to finish her coffee, then leaned toward Kay with a frown puckering her pretty face. "You haven't found any *reason* for her lapse of memory?"

"None."

"On hearing the name of her village she just suddenly snapped out of it?"

"That's what happened. We've always thought there was nothing much wrong with her physically. Of course, when you brought her to us she was underweight and malnourished—not your fault; you didn't have her long enough to change that," Kay hurriedly added. "But she seemed all right otherwise."

"How strange."

"I wonder if her people in Bois Sauvage have been looking for her all this time," Ginette said. "It's been how long? Father Turnier had her for three weeks. We had her a month. You've had her for nearly six months."

Simone said, "It could be longer. We don't know that she went straight from her village to that *caille* where Father found her. Maybe *that* journey covered a long time." Life was full of puzzles, her shake of the head said. "Miss Gilbert, we can only bless you for taking her home. None of us here would be able to do it, I'm sure. But have you thought of leaving her here and having us send for the father in that district to come for her?"

"Father Turnier, you mean?"

"Well, no, it wouldn't be Father Turnier now. He's no longer there."

"It would be someone Tina doesn't know, then?"

"I'm afraid so. Yes."

Kay shook her head. "I'd better take her myself."

All the sisters nodded and looked at her expectantly. It was close to their bedtime, Kay guessed. She rose.

"I'd better make sure Tina is all right, don't you think? She has nightmares sometimes."

"And the headaches, poor thing," Simone said.

"Like this morning. Well then—until tomorrow?"

"Tomorrow," they responded in chorus, and little Simone added, "Sleep well, both of you."

Kay climbed the stairs. As she went along the corridor to their room, she heard a drumming sound overhead that told her the rain was still falling. *Please, God, let it stop soon or those mountain trails will be hell.* The room itself was a steam bath. Tina slept with her face to the wall and her arms loosely clasping an extra pillow.

In no time at all, Kay was asleep beside her.

WEARING A MUCH-PATCHED carpenter's apron this morning, Emile Polinard stepped back to look at a table he was working on. It was a large one of Haitian mahogany, crafted to order for a wealthy Cap Haitian merchant. The time, Emile noted, was twenty past eight. The rain had stopped just before daybreak and now the sun shone brightly on the street outside the open door of his shop.

His helper, 17-year-old Armand Cator, came from the back room and said, "I've finished the staining, M'sieu Polinard. Should I start on Madame Jourdan's chairs now?" Armand was a good boy, always respectful.

"Do that, please."

Glancing out the door at the welcome sunshine, Polinard saw a familiar vehicle coming down the street and voiced a small "Ha!" of satisfaction. He had been expecting it. To get from the church to the main north-coast highway, it would have to pass his shop. Hurrying out onto the cracked sidewalk, he waited.

Just before the jeep reached him, he waved both arms vigorously and called out, "*Bonjour,* good friends! Be safe on your journey!"

"Why, that must be Mr. Polinard," said little Tina Anglade to Kay Gilbert. "That must be the furniture shop he told us about." She returned Polinard's wave.

Kay waved, too, but did not stop. They had got off to a late start again. She had overslept, and then the sisters had insisted on giving them a big breakfast.

The jeep sped on. Polinard stood on the sidewalk, hands on hips, smiling after it.

"You know those people, sir?" Armand asked from the doorway.

"Indeed, I do. They gave me a lift yesterday when the *camion* broke down. She's a charming woman. And the little girl . . . well, Armand, there's a curious story. You know what it means to lose your memory?"

"Huh?"

The jeep had disappeared from sight. Polinard re-entered the shop. "The little girl you just saw has been at that hospital in the Artibonite for a long time—months—because she could not remember her name or where she came from. She is such a bright child, too. But she has at last remembered and is going home."

"That's good."

"Yes. Provided, of course, that what she told them is not just her mind playing tricks again. By the way, don't you have a pal who came from a place called Bois Sauvage not long ago?"

"Yes, sir, I do. Luc Etienne."

"You see him often?"

"Two or three times a week."

"Ask him, then—because I am curious—if he knows of a girl about eight or nine years old who used to live there until, say, six or seven months ago. Her name is Tina Anglade."

"I'd better write it down." Armand stepped to a bench and reached for paper and a carpenter's pencil. "I may see Luc tomorrow at the cockfights."

"You spend your Saturdays at the fights, risking your hard-earned wages on chickens?"

"Only a few cobs now and then. But Luc— now there's a fellow who bets big and almost never loses. Everybody wonders how he does it."

"I don't approve of cockfights and wagering," Polinard said sternly. "But ask him about the little girl, please."

THE COCKFIGHTS ARMAND at-

tended were held near the coastal village of Petite Anse, just east of the city. A fight was in progress as Armand approached. A white bird and a black-and-red one made the grey sand of the enclosure fly like rain as they tried to kill each other. Spectators leaned over the wall of knee-high bamboo stakes, yelling encouragement.

The white was getting the worst of it. Even as Armand located his friend across the pit, the battle suddenly ended in a spurt of blood. There was a rush to collect bets.

Armand worked his way around to his friend and was not surprised to find Luc Etienne clutching a fistful of gourde notes. Luc must have a sixth sense, he so seldom lost a wager! "Hi," said Armand, grinning. "You've done it again, hey?"

Chuckling, the tall young man stuffed the notes into a pocket of his expensive, multicoloured shirt. He offered Armand a cigarette—another expensive item these days—and the two stayed together through the remainder of the morning. With his friend's help, Armand tripled the money he had brought.

When at last they boarded a tap-tap to the city, Armand remembered to inquire about the little girl and consulted the paper on which he had written her name. "Did you know her when you lived in Bois Sauvage?" he asked.

The little bus clattered along the highway through shimmering waves of heat that rose from the blacktop. Luc gazed at Armand with an expression of incredulity.

Puzzled, Armand said, "What's the matter? All I asked was if you knew—"

"I didn't know her! No!"

"Well, don't get sore with me. What's wrong with you, anyway? I only asked because my boss told me to."

The look of incredulity faded. What took its place was the shrewd one that appeared on Luc's face when he was about to make a wager at the cockfights. "You say this girl is on her way to Bois Sauvage *now*?"

"That's right. With a nurse from the hospital where her memory came back. That is, if it really did come back. You say you never knew her, so I guess it didn't."

"When do they expect to get there?"

"How would I know? They left here yesterday morning. All I want to know for M'sieu Polinard is, was there really a Tina Anglade in your village or is she going there for nothing?"

"She is going there for nothing," Luc said, and then was silent.

Luc was the first to get off. For a moment he stood frowning after the bus as it went on down the street. Then he turned and walked slowly up a cobbled lane to a small house he shared with his latest girlfriend. The girl was not at home. Going into their bedroom, Luc climbed onto the bed and assumed a sitting position there with his back against the headboard and his arms looped about his knees. Then he closed his eyes and fixed his thoughts on a face.

Only twice before had he attempted this, and on both occasions he had only partially succeeded. The second time had been better than the first, though, so maybe he was learning, as Margal had predicted. Aware that he was sweating, he peeled off his expensive shirt and tossed it to the foot of the bed, then resumed the position and closed his eyes again. After a while the sweat ran down his chest in rivers.

The face was beginning to come, though, and there was a difference.

Before, the image had appeared only inside his head, in his mind. But not this time. This time the face of the *bocor* was floating over the lower part of the bed, out of reach.

"Margal, you've come!" Luc whispered.

The eyes stared back at him. No one but Margal had eyes as terribly piercing as those.

"I am not asking for your help at the fights," Luc said then. "This time I have something important to tell you."

The head slowly moved up and down.

"You remember that little girl, Tina Louise Anglade?"

The reply—"Of course!"—seemed to come from a great distance.

"Well, she is on her way back to Bois Sauvage right now. After she disappeared from Dijo Qualon's house she could not remember her name or where she came from, but now she has remembered. A nurse from the Schweitzer hospital is bringing her home!"

The eyes returned his stare with such force that he felt they would stop his breathing. He heard a question and replied, "Yes, I am sure." Then another question and he said, wagging his head, "No, there is nothing I can do. It's too late. They left here yesterday morning."

The floating image slowly faded and was gone. After a while Luc sank down on the bed and lay there shivering in his own sweat until he fell asleep.

II

Standing alone in a clearing, the house was a small one of wattle and clay, roofed with banana-leaf thatch. Only moments before, Kay Gilbert had wondered if her guide, Joseph, really had a stopping place in mind or was merely hoping to chance on one. Glad to have reached any kind of destination after so many hours of sitting on a mule, she gratefully swung an aching leg over the saddle and dropped to the ground.

And stumbled. And sat down hard on her bottom. And then just sat there with her arms looped about her knees, embarrassed at having made herself look foolish in the eyes of the man and woman who had just emerged from the house.

Joseph leaned from his mule to lower Tina to the ground, then leaped down himself and ran to help.

Joseph. Thank God for Joseph. She had encountered enough Haitian young men at the hospital to know the good ones. Clean, intelligent, mild of speech and manner, he was exactly the sort of guide she had hoped for. The corporal at the police post in Trou had produced him.

She had hoped to sleep in Vallière tonight. There was a church and the priest would put them up. The late start from Cap Haïtien had put that village out of reach, though. And the trail. The trail had been a roller-coaster that made every mile a misery.

Steady climbing was not so bad; you got used to leaning forward and more or less wrapping your arms around your mule's neck. Descending was all right, too, after you accustomed yourself to leaning back, clinging for dear life to the pommel, and hoping to heaven the leather stirrups would not snap under the strain. But the constant shift from one to the other was pure hell, scaring the wits out of you while subjecting your poor tired body to torment. More than once she had envied little Tina, so confidently perched there in the crescent of Joseph's sturdy arms without a care in the world.

As she sat on the ground now, gazing up at the man and woman from the house, Joseph reached her and began helping her to her feet. "M'selle, I know these people," he said. "They will put us up for the night."

He introduced the couple as Edita and Antoine, no last names. She shook their hands. They were in their late sixties, she guessed. Both were barefoot and nearly toothless; both wore slight facial disfigurements indicating long-ago bouts with yaws.

That curse was pretty well wiped out in Haiti now, thank God.

"Please go into the house," Antoine said. "I will attend to your animals."

"Wait." No stranger must handle the brown leather bag! Lifting it from a saddle-bag, she slung it over her shoulder.

There were two small rooms. The front one contained four homemade chairs and a table; the other, a homemade bed. No connecting door. No kitchen. Cooking was done under a thatch-roofed shelter outside.

"You and the child will use the bed," Edita said in a manner that forbade any protest. "My man and I will sleep here in the front room, as will Joseph. Joseph is my sister's son."

"Thank you." It would not be the first time she had slept in a peasant *caille*. Nurses at the Schweitzer often did things their sisters in more advanced countries might think extraordinary. The bed could harbour bedbugs, of course. More likely, the swept-earth floor was a breeding ground for the little beasties called *chigres*, which got under your toenails and laid eggs there.

"Tina should rest before supper," she said. "I'll help you with the cooking, Edita."

The woman seemed pleased. The child fell asleep as soon as she climbed onto the bed.

Supper was to be a chicken stew, Kay saw when she joined the woman in the kitchen. First, kill the chicken. Edita attended to that with a machete, then cleaned the severed head and put it into the pot along with the rest of the bird. Kay prepared malangas, leeks, and carrots. While working, they talked.

"Where are you going, M'selle, if I may ask?"

"Bois Sauvage. Tina lives there."

"Oh?"

Kay explained, stressing the child's loss of memory.

"Stranger things than that happen around Bois Sauvage," Edita said with a shake of her head. "Do you know the place?"

"No. I don't know these mountains at all. What do you mean by 'stranger things'?"

"Well . . . unnatural things."

"Voodoo?" Any time a country person talked this way, the underlying theme was likely to be voodoo. Or associated mysteries.

"I think not voodoo, M'selle. Rather, sorcery or witchcraft. Do you know about a man named Margal in that district?" More than yaws were responsible for the depth of Edita's frown.

"Margal? No. Who is he?"

"A *bocor*. You know what a *bocor* is?"

"A witch doctor?" Admit you know something and you may learn more.

Edita nodded. "Margal is a powerful one, it is said. Perhaps the most powerful one in all Haiti. Much to be feared."

"And he lives in Bois Sauvage?" Kay was not happy at the prospect of taking Tina to a village dominated by such a man.

"In Legrun, a few miles from there." The frown persisted. "Perhaps you will not encounter him. I hope not."

"I hope not, too."

Night fell while the stew was cooking. The woman used a bottle lamp in the outdoor kitchen but called on her man to bring a lantern when the food was ready to be carried to the house. Kay woke Tina and the five of them sat at the table in the front room where, with the door shut, there was a strong smell of kerosene from the lantern now hanging from a soot-blackened wall peg.

After a few moments of eating in silence, Edita looked across the table at her man and said, "These people are going near to where the crippled *bocor* is, Antoine." The frown was back on her pocked face.

"So Joseph has been telling me."

The nurse in Kay was curious. "Crippled, you say?"

They nodded. "He cannot walk," Antoine supplied. "Different tales are told about the cause of it. One is that he was hurt when a *camion* he was riding in overturned and crushed him. Another is that he became involved in politics and had his legs broken by enemies from the capital. Still another tale is that his mule fell from the cliff at Saut Diable."

"You will be seeing Saut Diable tomorrow," Edita interjected, "and can judge for yourself whether one could survive a fall from there. At any rate, Margal cannot walk but is very much alive."

"And very much to be feared," Antoine said.

SLEEP FOLLOWED THE supper. In these remote mountain districts no one stayed up much after nightfall. For one thing, kerosene for illumination had to be transported long distances and was expensive.

But falling asleep on that peasant bed was not going to be easy, Kay discovered. At least, not with all her aches. The mattress was stuffed with some kind of coarse grass that had packed itself into humps and hollows. Each time she sought a more comfortable position, the stuff crackled as though on fire. Tina slept, thank heaven, but in the end Kay could only lie there.

The *caille* was far from quiet, too. One of the three sleepers in the front room snored loudly. In the thatch overhead, geckos croaked and clicked and made rustling sounds. Outside, other lizards sounded like people with sore throats trying to cough, and tree frogs whistled like toy trains. But the outside noises were muffled; the room had no windows. At this altitude, the problem at night was to keep warm, not cool.

A roachlike fire beetle, the kind the peasants called a *coucouyé*, came winging in from the front room, pulsing with green light as it flew. Landing on the wall, it climbed to the thatch and pulsed there like an advertising sign that kept winking on and off.

In spite of it, Kay felt herself dozing off.

Suddenly Tina, beside her, began to tremble.

Was the child dreaming? If so, it must be another of her bad ones. She had been sleeping with her hands pressed palm to palm under one cheek, and now turned convulsively on her back and began moaning.

Damn! I don't want to wake her but I'll have to if she doesn't stop. Propping herself on one elbow, Kay peered at the twitching face, glad now for the pulsing light of the beetle above them.

Something dropped with a dull plop from the thatch onto the foot of the bed. A gecko, of course, but she glanced down to make sure. The gecko lizards were small and harmless. Kind of cute, in fact.

The nightmare was causing Tina to thrash about in a frenzy that made the whole bed shake. Kay reached for her to wake her. There was a second plop at the foot of the bed. Kay turned her head again.

The fire beetle had fallen from the thatch. Still glowing, it struggled on its back with its legs frantically beating the air, six inches from the gecko.

The lizard's head swivelled in the bug's direction and its beady eyes contemplated the struggle. Its front feet, looking like tiny hands, gripped the blanket. Its slender brown body moved up and down as though doing pushups.

Mouth agape, it suddenly lunged.

Crunch!

With the light gone, the room was suddenly dark as a pit. The child at Kay's side sat bolt upright and began screaming in a voice to shake the mountains.

The rest of what happened was so terrifying that Kay felt a massive urge to scream along with the child.

At the foot of the bed the beetle-devouring gecko had become larger. Was now, in fact, a great black shape half as big as the bed itself. Its feet spread out to grip the blanket, and its huge reptilian head turned toward Kay and the screaming child. Its enormous dragon body began to do pushups again.

It was about to leap, to open its awful jaws and crunch again!

Scarcely aware of what she was doing, Kay grabbed the child and rolled with her off the bed, onto the swept-earth floor near the doorless doorway. Not a second too soon. As she scrabbled for the doorway, pulling the shrieking youngster along with her, she heard the creature's awful jaws snap together. Then, still on hands and knees, still pulling the child after her, she reached the front room.

The screaming had aroused the sleepers there. Antoine was lighting the lantern. His woman caught hold of Tina and hugged her, telling her to stop screaming, she would be all right. Joseph, helping Kay to her feet, peered strangely at her, then turned to look into the back room as Antoine stepped to the doorway and held the lantern high to put some light in there.

Tina stopped screaming.

Kay stepped to the doorway to look into the room she had just frantically crawled out of.

Nothing.

But I saw it! It was there! It was huge and leaped at us!

After a while Antoine said, "M'selle, what frightened you?"

"I don't know."

There was nothing on the bed. Not even the small lizard that had eaten the fire beetle.

You imagined it, Gilbert. But Tina had become frightened first. Tina, not she, had done the screaming.

She looked at her watch. In an hour or so, daylight would replace the frightening dark. Backing away from the bed, she returned to the front room where Edita was now seated on a chair with Tina on her lap.

"Are you all right, M'selle?"

"I guess so. But I know I can't sleep anymore. Just let me sit here and wait for morning."

The woman nodded.

Kay sat. She had gone to bed in her clothes, expecting the night to be cold. She looked at Tina, then up at the woman's disfigured face. "Is she asleep?"

"I believe so, yes."

The silence returned.

Joseph and Antoine came back into the room. Both glanced at the child first, then focused on Kay, no doubt awaiting an explanation.

Don't, she warned herself. *If you even try, Joseph might decide to go back.*

But they were not willing just to stand there staring at her. "M'selle, what happened, please?" Joseph said.

He had to be answered somehow. "Well . . . I'm ashamed, but I believe I just had a bad dream and woke Tina up, poor thing, and she began screaming."

"That is all?"

"I'm afraid so."

By the way they looked at her, she knew they had not bought it.

III

In the village of Vallière the expedition was stalled for a time while Joseph talked with peo-

ple he knew. But not for long. Beyond, the trail continued its slow, twisting climb and the stillness returned.

The mountain stillness. No bird cry or leaf rustle could have much effect on a silence so profound, nor could the muffled thumping of the mules' hoofs over the layers of leaf mold. She felt as though she were riding through another world.

Now at last the trail was levelling off and she saw Joseph ten yards ahead, looking back and waiting for her. As usual, Tina sat snugly in front of him, fenced in by his arms. Kay pulled up alongside.

"For a little while it will be hard now, M'selle," Joseph said. "Should we stop a while?"

"I'm not tired."

"Well, all right. Perhaps we should get this place behind us, anyway."

Remembering something the woman had said last night, Kay frowned. "Is this the place they call Saut Diable?" It meant, she knew, Devil's Leap.

He nodded.

She strained to see ahead. The track, mottled with tree shadows, sloped down into a kind of trench where seasonal rains had scored it to a depth of eight or ten feet. Riding through such a place, you had to remove your feet from the stirrups and lift them high. Otherwise, if the mule lurched sideways, you could end up with a crushed leg.

"You must make your animal descend very slowly, M'selle," Joseph solemnly warned.

She nodded, feeling apprehensive.

"But don't even start to go down," he said, "until I call to you from below."

"Until you call to me?"

"At the bottom, the trail turns sharply to the right, like this." Dramatically he drew a right angle in the air. "I will be waiting there to help you."

She was not sure she understood, but watched him ride on and noticed how carefully he put his mule to the trench. Waiting at the top, she saw him disappear around a curve. It seemed a long time before she heard him calling her, from below.

Scared, she urged her own mule forward.

It was the worst stretch they had encountered, not only steep but slippery. The red-earth walls were barely far enough apart to permit passage. Her mule took short, mincing steps, stumbling at times. At one twist of the trail he went to his knees, all but pitching her over his head, then was barely able to struggle up again. With her feet out of the stirrups, she marvelled that she was able to stay on the animal's back.

Luckily, the walls were a little farther apart at the bottom of the trench, and her feet were back in place. Joseph waited for her with feet apart and hands upraised, clutching a dead stick as long as his arm. Behind him was only empty blue sky.

"Come slowly and hang on!" he shouted at her.

As she reached him, he swung the stick. *Whap!* It caught her mule across the left side of the neck and caused the animal to wheel abruptly to the right. As she clung to the pommel to keep from falling, she got the full picture and promptly wet herself.

Joseph had been standing on the edge of a sheer drop, to make sure her mule didn't take one step too many before turning. Had the animal done so, both she and it—and Joseph, too, no doubt—would have gone hurtling down into a valley hundreds of feet below!

Her mule stopped. A little distance ahead, Joseph's animal was waiting, with Tina aboard and looking back. The trail was a ribbon of rock no more than six feet wide, winding along a cliff face for a hundred yards or more with awesome heights above and those terrifying depths below. Joseph, still clutching his stick, caught up with her and gave her mule a pat on the shoulder, as if to apologize for clubbing it.

"You are all right, M'selle?"

"I'll never be all right again."

He chuckled. "Actually, I was not worried.

This grey beast of yours has been here before and is not stupid. I only wanted to be sure he would remember that place. Just give him his head now and let him follow my animal along here. Okay?"

"Okay," she said, hoping he would not notice her wet pants.

He walked on ahead and swung himself into the saddle, saying something to Tina that made the child look at him with adoring eyes. His mule started forward, and Kay's clop-clopped along behind it.

Then the trail began to go dark.

Kay looked up to see what had happened to the sun. It was there but fading, and the sky began to look like a thick sheet of overexposed photographic film, becoming blacker every second.

She looked down. A dark mist rose from the valley which only a moment ago had been green. But *was* it a mist? Distinctly, she smelled smoke and saw flames. Then, like an exhalation from the earth itself, the darkness swirled up to engulf her.

Suddenly she could see nothing in front of her, nothing above or below, nothing behind. All creation was black and boiling.

Her mule stopped. Why? Because in her sudden terror she had jerked the reins, or because he, too, was now blind? What was happening was unreal. It was no more real than the harmless gecko that had become a ravenous dragon last night.

Margal, she thought. *The* bocor *who can't walk. We're getting closer and he doesn't want us to.*

The sky, the valley, the trail snaking along the cliffside—all had disappeared now. The darkness had engulfed them and was furiously alive, shot through with flames and reeking of smoke. The smoke made her cough and she had to cling to the saddle as she struggled to breathe.

And now the thunder. Peal upon peal of thunder, filling the fiery darkness in the valley and bouncing off the cliff in front of and behind her. Only it wasn't thunder she was hearing, was it? It was a booming of drums, ever so many drums. The sound assaulted her head and she wanted to scream but knew she must not. A scream might frighten the grey mule.

The animal wasn't easily frightened. More than once he had proved that. But he was still standing motionless, waiting for her to urge him forward again.

Should she do that? Had his world, too, gone mad? Or did he still see the trail in front of him, Joseph and Tina on the mule ahead, and the green valley below?

I can't stay here. Can't risk it. But there is no way to turn and go back.

Should she try to dismount and walk back? No, no! The world was so dark, she might as well be blind. If she tried to slide from the saddle on the cliff side, the mule might step away to make room for her. Might take a step too many and go plunging over the edge. And if she tried to dismount on *that* side without knowing where the edge was, she might drop straight into space.

She clucked to the grey as Joseph had taught her. Touched him, oh so gently, with her heels. "Go on, fella. But slow, go slow."

He gave his head a shake and moved forward through the smoke and drum-thunder, while she prayed he could see the trail and would not walk off the edge or grind her into the wall.

If he does grind me into the wall, I'll know he can't see any better than I. Then I can pull him up and at least wait. But if he goes wrong on the outside, God help me.

The mule plodded on through the unreal darkness. The drums thundered. Tongues of scarlet leaped high from the valley—high enough to curl in over the trail and stab at her feet, as if to force her to lift them from the stirrups and lose her balance. Fighting back the panic, she clutched the saddle with both hands and ground her knees into the mule's sides for an added grip.

What—oh God!—was happening to Joseph and Tina? She could not even see them now.

Saut Diable. The Devil's Leap. *Had* the man named Margal been crippled in a fall from here?

She didn't believe it. No one could survive such a fall.

Dear God, how much longer?

But the grey could see! She was convinced of it now. He trudged along as though this journey through the nightmare were all in the day's work. Not once did he brush her leg against the cliff, so she had to assume that not once did he venture too close to the drop on the other side. Was the darkness only in her mind, then? Was Margal responsible for it?

Never mind that now, Gilbert. Just hang on. Pray.

It almost seemed that the one creating the illusion knew his grisly scheme was not working. Knew she had not panicked and spooked the mule into plunging over the edge with her. The thunder of the drums grew louder. She thought her skull would crack under the pounding. The darkness became a gigantic whirlpool that seemed certain to suck her into its vortex. She tried shutting her eyes. It didn't help.

I'm not seeing these things. I'm thinking them.

The big grey walked on.

The whirlpool slowed and paled. The flames diminished to flickerings. The sky lightened and let the sun blur through again. Slowly the image of the other mule took shape ahead, with Joseph and Tina on its back.

She looked down and saw darkness leaving the valley, the smoke drifting away in wisps, the green returning. It was like the end of a storm.

Ahead, Joseph had stopped where the cliff passage ended and the trail entered a forest again. Dismounting, he swung Tina down beside him. The child clung to his legs. On reaching them, Kay slid from the saddle, too.

She and Joseph gazed at each other, the Haitian's handsome face the hue of wood ash, drained of all sparkle, all life. Trembling against him, the child, too, stared at Kay, with eyes that revealed the same kind of terror.

The nightmare wasn't just for me. They rode through it, too.

Kay felt she had to say something calming. "Well . . . we're here, aren't we? Saut Diable is behind us." *Brilliant*, she thought. *Just what we didn't need.*

"M'selle . . . what happened?"

"What do *you* think happened?" *Get him talking. Get that ghastly look off his face. Off Tina's, too.*

"Everything went dark, M'selle. The valley was on fire. The flames reached all the way up to the trail and the smoke made me cough."

She only looked at him.

"Drumming," he continued hoarsely. "I heard all three drums—the manman, the seconde, the bula. And I think even a fourth. Even the giant assotor."

"It was all in our minds," Kay said. "It wasn't real."

"M'selle, it *happened*." He turned his ashen face to look at Tina. "Didn't it, *ti-fi?*"

Still too frightened to speak, the child could only nod.

"No." Kay shook her head. "The drumming was only thunder, and there was no real fire. Walk back and look."

He refused to budge. When she took him by the hand to lead him back, he froze.

"Just to the cliff," she said. "So we can see."

"No, M'selle!"

"It didn't happen, Joseph. I'm telling you, it *did not* happen. We only imagined it. Now come."

His head jerked again from side to side, and she could not budge him.

At the hospital she was known to have a temper when one was called for. "Damn it, Joseph, don't be so stubborn! Come and see!" Her yank on his wrist all but pulled him off his feet.

He allowed himself to be hauled far enough back along the trail so that he could peer into the valley. It was frighteningly far down but in no way marked by fire.

"You see? If there had really been a fire raging down there, you would still see and smell smoke. Now will you believe me?"

"I know what I *saw*!"

"You know what you think you saw, that's all." Oh God, if only there were words in Creole

for this kind of discussion, but there were not. It was a bare-bones language, scarcely adequate even for dealing with basics. So few words to *think* with.

Well, then, stick to basics. Stop trying to explain things.

"All right, Joseph. There was a fire, but it's out now. Let's go, hey?"

He shook his head. "No, M'selle. Not me. I am turning back."

"*What?*"

"These things that have happened are a warning. Worse will happen if we go on."

Guessing her face was telltale white, she confronted him with her hands on her hips. "You can't do this to me, Joseph. You agreed to guide me to Bois Sauvage. I've already paid you half the money!"

"I will give it back. Every cob."

"Joseph, stop this. Stop it right now! I have to take Tina home, and you have to help me. These crazy things that have happened don't concern us. They were meant for someone else. Who would want to stop Tina from returning home?"

"I am going back, M'selle. I am afraid."

"You can't be such a coward!"

He only shrugged.

She worked on him. For twenty minutes she pleaded, cajoled, begged him to consider Tina, threatened him with the wrath of the police who had hired him out to her. Long before she desisted, she knew it was hopeless. He liked her, he was fond of the child, but he was terrified.

"All right. If you won't go any farther, you can at least tell me how to get there. Because I'm going on without you."

"M'selle, you must not!"

"Does this trail lead to Bois Sauvage, or can I get lost?"

In a pathetic whisper, with his gaze downcast, he said, "It is the only road. You will not get lost."

"Please rearrange our gear then, so Tina and I will have what we need." Extracting the brown leather shoulder-bag from her mule's saddle-bag, she stepped aside with it.

He obeyed in silence, while she and Tina watched him. The child's eyes were enormous.

"Now lift Tina onto my mule, please. I know I'll have to do it myself from now on because of your cowardice, but you can do it one more time."

He picked the child up. Before placing her on the grey mule, he brushed his lips against her cheek. His own cheeks were wet.

Kay carefully swung herself into the saddle, then turned and looked down at him. "You won't change your mind?"

"M'selle, I will wait for you at my aunt's house, where we stayed last night."

"Don't bother," she retorted bitterly. "A lizard might eat you."

Tight-lipped and full of anger, she rode on.

AFTER THE FIRST hour, her fear began to subside. It had been real enough earlier, despite the bravado she had feigned for Joseph's benefit. But the trail was not so formidable now. At least, they had not encountered any more Devil's Leaps.

Mile after mile produced only bird-song and leaf-rustle. She and the child talked to push back the stillness.

"Will you be glad to see your mother and father, baby?"

"Oh, yes!"

"What are they like? Tell me about them."

"Maman's pretty, like you."

"Bless you. And your father?"

"He works all the time."

"Doing what?"

"Growing things. Yams, mostly. We have goats and chickens, too."

"What's his name?"

"Metellus Anglade."

"And your mother's?"

"Fifine Bonhomme."

Not married, of course. Few peasants married. But many living in *plaçage* were more faithful than "civilized" people in other countries who *were* married.

"Will you be glad to see your sister and two brothers too?"

"Yes, Miss Kay."

"Are they older than you?"

"Only Rosemarie. The twins are younger."

"Your brothers are twins? I didn't know that. It must make your family very special." In voodoo, twins played important roles. There were even special services for the spirits of *marassas*.

"Would you like to know about my village, Miss Kay?" Tina asked.

"I certainly would. Tell me about it."

"Well, it's not as big as the one we rode through this morning. Vallière, I mean. But it has a nice marketplace, and a spring for water . . ."

Just talk, to pass the time. Then, as the afternoon neared its end, the trail ascended to a high plateau, levelled off, and began to widen. Wattle and mud *cailles* appeared on either side, and people stood behind bamboo fences gazing curiously at the strangers. Had they ever seen a white woman before?

But she was not the main object of their attention, Kay presently realized. They were staring mostly at the child who sat in front of her.

Tina stared back at them. This was her village.

THE ROAD DIVIDED, and Kay reined the grey mule to a halt. "Which way, Tina?"

"That way!" The child's voice was shrill with excitement.

Kay reined the mule to the left, looked back, and saw the trailing crowd of villagers turn with her.

What did they want? And if they recognized the child, why in heaven's name weren't they calling her name and waving to her? Could the hunch that had prompted her to bring along the brown shoulder-bag be valid, after all?

The trail they followed now was only a downhill path through a lush but unkempt jungle of broad-leafed plantains and wild mangoes. More *cailles* lined its sides. More people stared from yards and doorways, then trooped out to join the silent and somehow sinister procession.

Oh God, don't tell me things are going to go wrong now that I've finally got here! What's the matter with these people?

"There it is!" Bouncing up and down on the mule, Tina raised a trembling right arm to point.

Standing by itself near a curve of the path, behind a respectable fence of hand-hewn pickets, the *caille* was a little larger than most of the others, with a roof of bright new zinc. "We're home! That's my house!" the child shrilled, all but out of her mind with excitement.

End of the line, Kay thought with relief. We made it. Be proud, gal.

She turned to look at the crowd behind them and was not proud. Only apprehensive. Worse than apprehensive. Downright scared.

At the gate in the fence she reined in the mule, slid wearily from the saddle, and reached up for Tina. Out of the house came a slender, good-looking woman of thirty or so, wearing a dress made of feed bags. Staring at Kay, she walked to the gate. Then her gaze shifted from Kay to Tina, and she stopped as though she had walked into a stone wall. And began screaming.

The sound tore the stillness to shreds and brought a man from the house, stumbling as he ran. He reached the woman in time to catch her under the arms as she sank to her knees. Standing there holding her, he too looked at the strangers and began to make noises. Nothing as loud as the woman's screaming but a guttural "huh huh huh huh" that seemed to burble, not from his mouth alone, but from his whole convulsed face.

From the crowd came a response like a storm roar, with words flashing in and out like jabs of lightning. *Mort! Mort! Li Mort!*

Clasping the youngster's hand, Kay pushed the gate open and walked to the kneeling woman. There was nothing she could do to stop the nightmare sounds. *Don't listen to it, Gilbert. Just do what you have to.*

"Is this your mother, Tina?"

For answer, the child threw her arms around the kneeling woman's neck and began sobbing, "Maman! Maman!"

The woman wrenched herself free and staggered erect. She looked at her daughter in horror, then turned and ran like a blinded, wild animal across the bare-earth yard, past a cluster of graves at its edge, into a field where tall stalks of *piti mi* swallowed her from sight.

The man continued to stand there, gazing at Tina as though his eyes would explode.

The child looked up at him imploringly. "Papa . . ."

"Huh huh huh . . ."

"It's me, Papa. Tina!"

He lurched backward, throwing up his arms. "You're dead!"

"No, Papa!"

"Yes you are! You're dead!"

"Papa, please . . ." Reaching for him, the child began to cry. And Kay's reliable temper surged up to take over.

She strode to the man and confronted him, hands on hips and eyes blazing. "This is nonsense, M'sieu Anglade! Because the child has been missing for a while doesn't mean she's dead. You can see she isn't!"

As he stared back at her, his heavy-lipped mouth kept working, though soundlessly now. His contorted face oozed sweat.

"Do you hear what I'm saying, M'sieu? Your daughter is all right! I'm a nurse, and I know."

"You—don't—understand."

"What don't I understand?"

As though his feet were deep in the red-brown earth and he could move them only with great difficulty, he turned in the direction the child's mother had fled. Lifting his right arm as though it weighed a ton, he pointed.

"What do you mean?" Kay demanded, then looked down at the weeping child and said, "Don't cry, baby. I'll get to the bottom of this."

Metellus Anglade reached out and touched her on the arm. "Come." He began walking slowly across the yard, his bare feet scraping the earth. Beyond the cluster of graves toward which he walked was the field of kaffir corn.

What could there be in such a field that would make him afraid of his own daughter?

Kay followed him, but looked back. Tina gazed after them with her hands at her face, obviously all but destroyed by what had happened. The crowd in the road was silent again. The whole length of the fence was lined with starers, the road packed solid, but no one had come into the yard even though the gate hung open. She had neglected to tie the grey mule, she realized. Should she go back and do so, to make sure the crowd wouldn't spook him? No. It could wait.

Metellus Anglade reached the edge of the yard and trudged on through the gravestones— not stones, really, but crudely crafted concrete forms resembling small houses resting on coffin-shaped slabs of the same material. Nothing special. You saw such grave markers all over Haiti. Kay looked beyond to the corn field.

Where was the woman?

Suddenly the leaden feet of her guide stopped and, preoccupied as she was, Kay bumped into him. He caught her by the arm to steady her. With his other hand he pointed to the last of the graves, one that was either new or had been newly whitewashed.

"Look."

The name was not properly carved. Like those on the other markers, it had merely been scratched in with a sharpened stick before the concrete hardened. It was big and bold, though. Kay had no difficulty reading it.

TINA LOUISE CHRISTINE ANGLADE.
1984–1992.

Kay's temper boiled to the surface again as she turned on him. "You shouldn't have done this! Graves are for people you've buried, not for someone you only think might be dead!"

He looked at her now without flinching, and she saw how much he resembled Tina. About thirty, he was taller than most mountain peasants and had good, clean features. "M'selle, you don't understand. My daughter *is* buried here."

"What?"

"She died. I myself made the coffin. Her own mother prepared her for burial. I put her into the coffin and nailed it shut, and when we put it into this grave and shovelled the earth over her, this yard was full of witnesses. All those people you see standing in the road were here. The whole village."

Kay got a grip on herself. *Watch it, Gilbert. Don't, for God's sake, say the wrong thing now.* "M'sieu, I can only say you must have made a mistake."

With dignity he moved his head slowly from side to side. "There was no mistake, M'selle. From the time she was placed in the coffin until the earth covered her, the coffin was never for one moment unguarded. Either my wife or I was with her every moment."

We can't stand here talking, Kay thought desperately. Not with that mob in the road watching us. "M'sieu, can we go into the house?"

He nodded.

"And Tina? She is not dead, I assure you. All that happened was that she lost her memory for a time and could not recall who she was."

He hesitated, but nodded again.

They walked back across the yard to Tina, and Kay put a hand on the child's shoulder. "Come, baby. It's going to be all right." Metellus Anglade led the way to the house. Kay followed with Tina. The villagers by the fence still stared.

If they actually think they buried this child, I don't blame them. I'd probably do the same.

The house seemed larger than the one Tina and she had slept in the night before. But before attempting an appraisal or even sitting down, she said, "M'sieu Anglade, will you please see about my mule? He should be unsaddled and given some water, and tied where he can eat something."

He did not seem eager to comply.

"You'll have to put me up for the night or find someone nearby who will," she went on firmly. "So please bring in the saddle-bags, too." Especially the one with my shoulder-bag in it, she added mentally.

He frowned at her. "You wish to spend the night *here?*"

Kay made a production of peering at her watch, though she knew the time well enough. "I can't be expected to start back to Trou at this hour, can I? That's where my jeep is. I've brought your daughter all the way from the Schweitzer Hospital, M'sieu Anglade. Do you know how far that is?"

"All that way?" He peered at her with new respect, then looked again at Tina. What was he thinking? That if the child had been at the Schweitzer, she must not be a ghost, after all?

"The mule, please," Kay repeated. "Tina and I will just sit here until you return. Believe me, we're tired." As he turned to the door, she spoke again. "And try to find her mother, will you? I must talk to you both."

While he was gone, she asked Tina to show her around. In addition to the big front room, which was crowded with crude but heavily varnished homemade furniture, there were three bedrooms. But despite the zinc roof, which indicated a measure of wealth in such a village, the floors were of earth, hard-packed and shiny from years of being rubbed by bare feet. At least there would be no lizards dropping from the thatch.

As they waited for Metellus to return, Tina began to cry again. "Come here, baby," Kay said quietly.

The child stepped into the waiting circle of her arm.

"Listen to me, love. We don't know what's going on here, but we're not going to be afraid of it. You hear?"

"I hear, Miss Kay."

"You just concentrate on being brave and let me do the talking. For a while, at least. Can you do that?"

Tina nodded.

Kay patted her on the bottom. "Good girl. Now go sit down and try to relax. The big thing is, you're home."

It took Metellus Anglade a long time to attend to the mule. Or perhaps he spent much of that time trying to locate his woman. Daylight was about finished when at last he came through the door, lugging the saddle-bags and followed by Tina's mother.

Having already decided how to handle the situation, Kay promptly rose and offered her hand. "Hello, Fifine Bonhomme, how are you? I'm Nurse Gilbert from the Schweitzer Hospital."

Tina had said her mother was pretty, hadn't she? Well, she was, or might be if she could get over being terrified. A certain firmness was called for at this point, Kay decided.

"Sit down, Fifine. I must talk to you."

The woman looked fearfully at her daughter. She had not spoken to the girl, and obviously had no intention of embracing her. But then, she actually thought she was staring at a child who was buried in that grave outside, didn't she?

Suddenly the door burst open and three children stormed into the room: a girl who resembled Tina but was a little older, and two peas-in-a-pod boys a year or so younger. Rosemarie and the twins, Kay thought. All three were out of breath but remarkably clean for country kids. Barefoot, of course, but decently dressed. And handsome.

At sight of Tina, they stopped as though they had been clubbed. Their eyes grew bigger and bigger. The girl backed up a step. The twins, as if they were one person, took two steps forward and whispered Tina's name in unison.

Tina lurched from her chair and stumbled to her knees in front of them. Wrapping her arms around their legs, she cried so hard she must have been blinded by her own tears.

Reassured, Rosemarie dared to advance again. Dared to sink to *her* knees and press her face against her sister's.

"Let the children go into another room," Kay said to their mother. "I would like to talk to you and Metellus alone."

Fifine Bonhomme only gazed at her brood in a silence of apprehension. It was their father who told them what to do.

"Now listen, both of you," Kay said. "I'm going to tell you what I know about your daughter, how she was found by Father Turnier and—" She paused. "Do you know Father Turnier?"

"The priest who used to be in Vallière?" Metellus said. "We know of him."

"All right. I'm going to tell you how he found her and what happened afterward. Then *you* are going to tell *me* why her name is on that grave out there. You understand?"

They nodded.

"After that," Kay said, "we'll decide what's to be done here."

She took her time telling it. Had to, because her Creole was not that good. She even included a brief lecture on amnesia, because it was so terribly important for them to understand that the youngster was perfectly normal.

In telling of her journey with Tina from the hospital to Bois Sauvage, though, she was very, very careful not to mention the dragon lizard or the strange occurrence at Devil's Leap.

"Now then," she said firmly in conclusion, "*you* do the talking, please. Explain that grave to me."

"Tina became ill and died," said Metellus.

"What made her ill?"

"We don't know. We asked her if she had eaten anything the rest of us had not. Only a mango, she said. A boy named Luc Etienne gave her two of them when she was passing his yard on her way home from a friend's house. One was for her, one for the twins. But nobody was at home when she got here, so she ate hers and when we returned an hour or so later, she was not well."

"How do you mean, not well?"

"Her stomach hurt and she had *la fièv*. A really high fever. I went at once for the *houngan*. He is a good man. He came and did things. Brewed a tea for her and used his hands on her—things like that. He stayed the whole night trying to make her well. But in the morning she died."

"Who said she was dead? This *houngan*?"

"All of us." Metellus returned her gaze without flinching. "It is not in dispute that she was dead when we buried her. When someone dies, the people we call in may not be as learned as your doctors at the hospital, but they know how to determine if life has ended. Tina was dead."

"And you think this mango that was given her by—by whom?—"

"Luc Etienne."

"—might have caused her death? Poisoned her, you mean?"

"*Something* made her ill. She had not been sick before."

"There were two mangoes, you said."

"Yes."

"Did anyone eat the other?"

He shook his head.

"What became of it?"

"After the funeral we opened it up, I and some others, to see if it had been tampered with. It seemed to be all right, but, of course, you can't always be sure. Some people are wickedly clever with poisons. Anyway, we buried it."

"Did you talk to this Luc Etienne?"

"Yes, M'selle."

"What did he say?"

"Only that the mangoes were from a tree in his yard, perfectly innocent, and he gave them to Tina for herself and the twins because he was fond of children. Especially of them."

Speaking for the first time, Tina's mother said, "Our children liked him. He was a nice young man."

"What do you mean, *was*?"

"He is not here now."

"Oh? When did he leave?"

"Soon after the funeral, didn't he, Metellus?"

Metellus nodded.

"Where did he go?" Kay asked.

Metellus shrugged. "We heard to Cap Haïtien, where he makes a lot of money betting on cockfights."

Feeling she had sat long enough, Kay rose stiffly and walked to the door. It was open, but would soon have to be closed because the yard was turning dark. There were still people at the fence. Turning back into the room, she frowned at Tina's father. "And there is no doubt in your mind that Tina was in the coffin when you buried it?"

"None at all. No."

"Are you saying, then, that the child I've

brought back to you is not your daughter but someone else?"

He looked at his woman and she at him. Turning to meet Kay's demanding gaze again, he shrugged. "M'selle, what can we say?"

With her fists against her hips for perhaps the fourth time that day, Kay faced them in a resurgence of anger. "You can admit there's been a mistake, that's what you can say! Because, look. When the name Bois Sauvage was read to this child by a doctor reading a map, she clapped her hands and cried out, "That's where I live!" And then she remembered her name—her full name, just as you've got it inscribed on that grave out there. Tina Louise Christine Anglade. And she remembered *your* names and her sister's and the twins'. So if she isn't your Tina, who in the world do you think she is?"

The woman whispered something.

"What?" Kay said.

"She is a zombie."

"What did you say?"

"*Li sé zombie,*" the woman stubbornly repeated, then rose and turned away, muttering that she had to begin preparing supper.

ONLY BECAUSE KAY insisted did the woman allow her "zombie" daughter to sit at the supper table with her other children. After the meal, Kay stubbornly tried again to break down her resistance, and again failed.

She probably could have convinced Metellus had the child's mother been less afraid, she told herself. The father was strong and intelligent but unwilling, obviously, to make trouble for himself by challenging this woman he slept with. It was a tragic situation, with no solution in sight.

Go to bed, Gilbert. Maybe during the night Metellus will find himself some guts.

She lay with her right arm around Tina, the child's head on her breast. A lamp burned low on a chest of drawers made mostly of woven sisal.

"Miss Kay?" Tina whispered.

"What, baby?"

"They think I'm dead. Did I die, Miss Kay?"

"Of course not."

"Why do they say I did, then? Even Rosemarie and the twins."

"Because they . . ." *Oh, Christ, baby, I don't know why! I'm way out of my depth here and don't know what to do about it.*

She was so tired, so very tired. All day long on a mule, most of the time scared because Joseph had left her alone with the child in an unknown wilderness. Her knees ached, her thighs burned, her arches must be permanently warped from the stupid stirrups, even her fingers were cramped from holding the reins. And now this impasse with the child's mother.

She listened to Tina's breathing and it calmed her a little. After a while she dozed off.

THERE WAS A tapping sound at the room's only window. The window had no glass in it, and she had decided not to close the shutters lest the smell of the kerosene lamp give her more of a headache than she already had. The tapping was on one of the open shutters, and she sat up in bed and turned her head in that direction, still half asleep. The voice of Metellus Anglade whispered to her from the opening.

"M'selle . . . M'selle . . . I have to show you something!"

She looked at the watch on her wrist. Why, on this crazy pilgrimage, was she always trying to find out the time in the middle of the night?

Three-ten. Well, at least she'd been asleep for a while and would be rested tomorrow for whatever might happen.

"What do you want?"

"Come out here, please. Be careful not to wake anyone!"

"All right. Just give me a minute."

She had worn pyjamas to bed and was damned if she would get dressed at this idiot hour just to go into the yard to see what the man wanted. Pulling on her sneaks, she left the bedroom, walked silently across the dim front room with its clutter of chairs, stepped outside, and found him waiting.

"Come!" he whispered, taking her by the arm.

He led her across the yard, through moonlight bright enough to paint the ground with dark shadows of house, fence, trees, and graves. He walked her to the graves. Next to the one with Tina's name on it was a hole now, with a spade thrust upright in the excavated dirt piled at its edge.

"Look, M'selle!"

Peering into the hole, she saw what he had done. Unable to move the concrete slab that covered the grave, he had dug down beside it, then tunnelled under. Far enough under, at least, to find out what he wanted to know.

"You see? The coffin is gone!"

She nodded. There was nothing to argue about. He hadn't dug enough dirt out to risk having the slab sag into the excavation, but had certainly proved there was no wooden box under it. She stood there hearing all the usual night sounds in the silence.

"How could anyone have stolen it without moving the slab?" she asked, but knew the answer before finishing the question. Let him say it anyway.

"M'selle, we don't do the tombing right away. Not until the earth has settled. In this case, more than six weeks passed before I could go to Trou for the cement."

Which you brought back on a mule, she thought, walking the whole way back yourself so the mule could carry it. And then you built this elaborate concrete thing over the grave to show your love for a daughter whose body had already been stolen.

"Metellus, I don't understand." Let him explain the whole thing, though she guessed how he would do that, too.

"There can be only one answer, M'selle. I know I put my daughter into a coffin and buried her here. The coffin is not here now. So . . . she was stolen and made into a zombie."

"Meaning she was not really dead."

"Well, there are two kinds of zombies, as per-haps you know. Those who truly die and are re-stored to life by sorcery; that is one kind. Others are poisoned in various ways so they only seem to die, then are taken from their graves and re-stored."

"You think Tina was poisoned?"

"Now I do. Yes."

"With the mango you told me about?"

He reached for the spade and, holding it in both hands, turned to frown at her. "Luc Etienne gave her two mangoes, one for herself and one for the twins to share. Do you know what I think? I think that on the way home she got them mixed up, and when she found no one at home and ate her mango, the one she ate was the one she had been told to give to the twins."

"I don't know what you mean." This time she really did not.

"Twins are different from ordinary people," Metellus said. "He wanted them for some spe-cial purpose."

"Who? This fellow Etienne?"

"No, not Etienne." With a glance toward the house, he began quietly putting the earth back into the hole. "At least, not for himself. Luc was friendly with a much more important person at that time. With a *bocor* named Margal, who lives in Legrun. There are people here who say Luc Etienne was Margal's pupil."

"The one who can't walk," Kay said.

He stopped the spade in mid stroke. "You know of him?"

"I think he tried to stop me from coming here."

"Very likely. Because do you know what I believe happened after he stole the coffin from this grave? I think he brought Tina back to life the way they do—with leaves or herbs or what-ever—and then sold her to someone in some distant place where she would not be known. He had hoped for the twins, but even Tina was worth something as a servant."

"And she wandered away from whoever bought her."

"Yes. And the priest found her."

"How could Margal have known I was bringing her back here?"

"Who can say, M'selle? But he probably knows we are standing here this very minute, discussing him." Metellus plied the spade faster now, obviously anxious to get the job finished. But again he stopped and faced her. "M'selle, Tina must not stay here. Margal will surely kill her!"

"You think so?"

"Yes, yes! To protect himself. To save his reputation!"

She thought about it, and nodded.

The hole refilled at last, he turned to her. "M'selle, I love my daughter. You must know that by now."

"I'm sure you do."

"Fifine, too, loves her. But things can never be the same here now."

Kay gazed at him in silence.

Thoughtfully he said, "I have a brother in Port-au-Prince, M'selle, who is two years younger than I and has only one child. He would give Tina a good home, even send her to school there. She must not stay here. Everyone here in Bois Sauvage knows she died and was buried in this yard and must now be a zombie. Even if Margal did not destroy her, she would forever be shunned."

"You want me to take her to your brother? Is that what you're saying?"

"Will you? I will ride out with you to where your jeep is."

Kay thought about it while he stood before her, desperately awaiting her reply. A white owl flew across the yard from the road to the field of kaffir corn. Time passed.

"I will do it on one condition," Kay said at last.

On the verge of tears, he seemed to hold his breath. "And—that is?

"That before we leave here you take me to Legrun, to visit this *bocor* who can't walk, this Margal. Will you do that?"

Trembling, he stared at her with bulging eyes. But at last he nodded.

IV

The grey mule carried no saddle-bags this time, but Kay had slung the brown leather bag over her shoulder before leaving the Anglade house in Bois Sauvage. As her animal plodded along after the one ridden by Tina's father, she realized she would have had a difficult time attempting the trip by herself.

It was only four miles to Legrun, Metellus had said, but the road was difficult. That had been his word: difficult. Just beyond the Bois Sauvage marketplace, which was deserted because today was not the weekly market day, a path to the right had been marked by a cross to Baron Samedi. When asked why he had stopped and dismounted there for a moment, her guide had replied with a shrug, "It is sometimes well to ask the baron for protection, M'selle."

"You think this Margal is into voodoo, then?"

"No, no, M'selle. He is an *evil* man, a *bocor*!"

Not the same thing at all, of course. Voodoo was a religion. A *bocor* was a sorcerer, a witch doctor, a loner. And the one they were about to confront was also a monster.

For an eternity the mules toiled up a ladder of boulders, with the high-mountain forest walling them in on both sides. At times even the sky was hidden by massed tree limbs. Then the path straggled over a rocky plateau painted gold by the sun, and plunged down through a trench.

The trench gradually widened into a grassy clearing dotted with thatch-roofed huts. Kay counted five of them. From a vertical cliff on the right tumbled a forty-foot waterfall that filled the vale with sound. Beyond the peasant huts stood a substantial, metal-roofed house painted bright red.

Margal's, she supposed. And she was looking at the first painted house she had seen since leaving Vallière. Margal the Sorcerer apparently believed in being different, and was wealthy enough to indulge his whims.

Red houses were not common in Haiti. This one brought to mind a poem, or part of a poem, she had read in a volume of verse by a Haitian writer known to be deeply interested in the occult.

> High in a mountain clearing
> In a red, red house
> In the wilds of Haiti,
> Black candles burn
> In a room of many colors.

Had the poet visited this place? If so, he must be a brave man to have dared write about it. But the book was in French, and Margal, being a peasant, could probably not read French. Or even any of the versions of written Creole.

In front of her, Metellus had reined his mule to a halt. As she caught up to him, he lifted an arm to point. "Margal lives there in the red house, M'selle," he said without looking at her. "I will take the mules and wait for you by the waterfall."

She drew in a breath to slow the beating of her heart. "You mean you're not going to confront him with me?"

"M'selle, no." He shook his head. "I do not have your courage."

"Very well." Disappointed but not angry, she dismounted and walked her mule the few steps to where Metellus could lean from the saddle and grasp its reins. Then, with her head high, she strode the last hundred yards alone.

On reaching the door, she lifted a hand to the brown leather bag to make sure it was still in place. Throughout the journey it had been a nuisance; now it was a comfort. She knocked. In a moment the door swung open. A boy about twelve years old, wearing only ragged khaki pants, stood gazing up at her.

She went through the usual peasant formalities. *"Honneur, ti-moun."*

"Respect, M'selle."

"I would like to speak with M'sieu Margal, if you please. I have come a long way to see him."

Motioning her to enter, the boy silently stepped back from the doorway.

The room in which she found herself surprised her, and not only for its large size. Its floor was of tavernon, the close-grained cabinet wood that was now even rarer and more expensive than Haitian mahogany. Tables and chairs, one of the latter strangely shaped, were of the same wood. Did it grow here? Probably, but Margal must have paid a small fortune to have the trees felled and cut up. The walls of the room were of clay, but each was a different colour—aquamarine, rose, black, green—and intricately decorated. The effect was startling.

"Please be seated," the boy said. "I will ask my master if he wishes to see you. Not there!" he added quickly when Kay, out of curiosity, moved toward the oddly shaped chair. "That is my master's!"

"Sorry." She veered away, but not before noticing what a really remarkable chair it was. Its back was vertical, its extra-wide seat littered with varicoloured cushions. It had wide, flat, slotted arms. Fit a board across those arms, using the slots to anchor it, and the chair could be a desk, a work table, even a dining table.

She remained standing. The boy disappeared into a connecting room, leaving the door open.

In a moment the youth reappeared pushing a kind of wheeled platform on which was seated a man. Wearing a bright red nightshirt—if that was the word for it—the man weighed perhaps a hundred and fifty pounds, and would have been about five foot six had he been able to stand erect.

Apparently he could not do that. His legs, crossed in front of him, looked to Kay as though they had been broken and allowed to heal without benefit of medical attention.

The boy pushed the wheeled platform to the odd-shaped chair. Reaching behind him, the man placed both hands on the chair's arms, hoisted himself up, and worked his crippled body backward into position. After squirming to make himself as comfortable as possible, he lifted his head. It was awrithe with a thick, stringy mass that resembled the dreadlocks of Jamaican Rastafarians.

His stare was totally innocent. "I bid you welcome, M'selle. My name is Margal. Please tell me who you are and why you have come here."

It was the moment of truth. Kay took in a breath to steady herself.

"M'sieu Margal, my name is Kay Gilbert, and I am a nurse. A hospital nurse. I came here—as I think you already know—to return a lost child to her home in Bois Sauvage. A child whom you, M'sieu, turned into a zombie but whom we at the hospital were able to restore to health. And I have a proposition for you."

The man who could not walk only stared at her with unblinking eyes, saying nothing.

"I know what you are," Kay continued, using words she had silently rehearsed on the way to this place. "I also know you cannot walk. So I have come to make you an offer."

Those eyes! She could not even decide what colour they were, they were so frightening. And they were doing things to her mind. She was losing her power of concentration.

"As I say—M'sieu Margal—I am from the hospital. That hospital—in the Artibonite—which everyone in Haiti, including you, I am sure—knows about and respects. And I promise you this—that if you—if you will stop doing to people what you—what you did to Tina Anglade—if you will give me your word of honor never to—never to do such a thing again—we at the hospital will do our best to—to repair your legs so that you will be able to—to walk again."

She paused, struggling desperately to maintain control. Dear God, those eyes were making it so hard for her to think straight! Then when he did not answer her, except for a downward, ugly twist of his mouth, she added weakly, "I—I am not fluent in your—your language, M'sieu. Do you understand what—what—I—just—said?"

Something like a laugh issued from that ugly mouth, and the stare intensified. Suddenly Kay was back in the *caille* where the harmless gecko

had become a giant dragon intent on devouring her and the child. And then she was sitting on a grey mule, clutching its saddle, while an unreal darkness full of smoke and flames swirled up from a far-below valley to engulf her. And she knew what Margal was doing.

Her offer of help meant nothing to him. He was bent on controlling her, perhaps destroying her. Perhaps the prospect of creating a white female zombie intrigued him. With only one move left to her, she grabbed at the brown leather bag dangling from her shoulder.

Tearing it open, she thrust her hand in and snatched out the one thing it contained—the shiny black automatic her boyfriend, a doctor at the hospital, had insisted she keep with her for safety's sake on this mad mission to the realm of Margal.

But before she could even level the weapon, that room with its multicoloured walls became something else. No longer was she standing there in a house, struggling to point a deadly weapon at another human being. All at once she was in an outdoor place of idyllic beauty where any thought of killing seemed a kind of blasphemy.

There were no weirdly painted walls here. No man with twisted legs sat on a chair in front of her, gazing at her with hypnotic eyes that merely mirrored the awful powers of his incredible mind.

What she saw was a broad valley shimmering in sunlight—a lovely, dreamlike valley carpeted with green grass and colourful wild flowers. And where Margal's chair had been was a young tulip tree with a soft, wide-eyed dove perched on one of its branches, gazing at her with pretty head atilt.

But this isn't Eden and that isn't a dove, Gilbert! You know it isn't! For God's sake, don't let him do this to you!

She still had the gun in her hand. With every ounce of will power she possessed, she forced the hand to lift it, made her eyes and mind take aim, and commanded her finger to squeeze the trigger.

In that idyllic setting there was but one living thing to aim at. The dove.

The sound of the shot shattered the illusion and jolted her out of the hypnotic spell the man on the chair had not quite finished weaving about her. She came out of it just in time to see the bullet pierce his forehead and slam his head against the back of the chair. Still in a partial daze, she pushed herself erect and stumbled forward to look at him.

He was dead. Not even Margal the Sorcerer could still be alive with such a hole in his head and most of his brains splattered over the back of the chair. Never again would he do what he had done to little Tina Anglade—and probably more than a few others.

Probably it had been a foolish notion, anyway, to think he might change his ways if given the ability to walk again.

Her trembling had subsided. In full control of herself again, she looked for the boy, who perhaps, like Luc Etienne, had hoped by serving the master to absorb some of Margal's evil knowledge. When she called to him, there was no answer. Apparently he had fled.

With a last glance at the dead man on the chair, she put the gun back into the brown leather bag and walked out of the house. At the waterfall, the father of little Tina Anglade was waiting for her, as promised. He stepped forward, frowning.

"I heard a noise like a gunshot," he said, his frown asking the unspoken question.

She shrugged. "That man made a noise to frighten me, the way he made the thunder at Saut Diable that I told you about." With his help, she climbed onto the grey mule. "I'm finished," she added. "I've done what I was sent here for. Now we can go home."

THE CAIRNWELL HORROR

CHET WILLIAMSON

IN ADDITION TO being a prolific author, mainly of horror and supernatural fiction, Chet Williamson (1948–) has had a successful career as a musician and as an actor with a lifetime membership in Actors' Equity. Born in Lancaster, Pennsylvania, he received his B.A. from Indiana University of Pennsylvania and became a teacher in Cleveland before becoming a professional actor. He turned to full-time freelance writing in 1986 and has written more than a hundred short stories for such publications as *The New Yorker, Playboy, The Twilight Zone, The Magazine of Fantasy and Science Fiction, Alfred Hitchcock's Mystery Magazine,* and *Esquire.* He has also written twenty novels, beginning with *Soulstorm* (1986), and a psychological suspense play, *Revenant.* Among his numerous awards are the International Horror Guild Award for Best Short Story Collection for *Figures in Rain: Weird and Ghostly Tales* (2002), two nominations for the World Fantasy Award, six for the Bram Stoker Award by the Horror Writers Association, and an Edgar Allan Poe Award nomination by the Mystery Writers of America for Best Short Story for "Season Pass" (1985). Many readers believe that Williamson's finest work was in his Searchers trilogy: *City of Iron* (1998), *Empire of Dust* (1998), and *Siege of Stone* (1999), an *X-Files*–type series with the basic premise being that three CIA operatives are asked by a rogue CIA director to investigate paranormal activities—not to find out the truth, but to debunk the claims.

"The Cairnwell Horror" was based on the infamous Glamis Castle in Scotland and its horrifying secrets, said to be known only by male members of the royal family, who learn them on their eighteenth birthday but are sworn to secrecy. It was first published in *Walls of Fear,* edited by Kathryn Cramer (New York: William Morrow, 1990).

CHET WILLIAMSON

THE CAIRNWELL HORROR

"A MONSTER, DO you suppose? A genetic freak that's remained alive for centuries?"

"Undoubtedly, Michael. With two heads, three sets of genitals, and a curse for those who mock." George McCormack, sole heir to Cairnwell Castle, raised a three-by-five-inch card on which lay a line of cocaine. "I propose a toast—of sorts—to it then. Old beast, old troll, nemesis of my old great-however-many-times-granddad, whom I shall finally meet next week." A quick snort, and the powder was gone.

George smiled, relishing the rush, the coziness of his den, the company, and found himself thinking about asking Michael to spend the night. He was about to make the suggestion when Michael asked, "Why twenty-one, do you suppose? If it's all that important, why not earlier?"

"Coming of age, Michael. As you well know, all males are virgins until that age, and no base liquors or, ahem, controlled substances have passed their pristine lips or nostrils. Other than that, I can't bloody well tell you until after next week, and even then, according to that same stifling and weary tradition, I must keep the deep, dark family secret all to my lonesome."

"Yes, but if you don't pay any more attention to *that* tradition than you do to the others, well . . ."

"Ah, will I tell, you're thinking? In all likelihood, if there's a pound to be made on it, yes, I damned well will. I've thought the whole thing was asinine ever since I was a kid. And the five thousand pounds your little rag offers can pay for an awful lot of raped tradition."

"So when'll you be leaving London for the bogs?"

"The *bogs*?" George snorted. "Careful, mate. That's my castle you're speaking of."

"I thought it was your father's."

"Yes, well." George frowned. "It doesn't appear he'll be around much longer to take care of things."

"You've asked him what the secret is, I suppose."

"Christ, dozens of times. Always the same answer: 'You're better off not knowing until the time comes.' Yeah. Pardon me while I tremble with fear. Bunch of shit anyway. When I was a kid, I spent hours looking for secret panels, hidden crypts, all that rubbish, and not a thing did I find. After a while, I just got bored with it."

"Ever see any ghosts?"

George gave Michael a withering glare. "No," he said flatly. "Whatever plagues the Mc-Cormacks, it's not ghosts." He hurled a soft pillow at his friend. "*Jesus*, will you stop jotting down those notes—it's driving me mad!"

"George, this *is* an interview, and you *are* being paid."

"I'm just not used to being grilled."

"You knew I was a journalist when we became . . . friends."

"You were about to say lovers." George smiled cheekily. "And why not?"

"We haven't been lovers for months."

"No fault of mine."

Michael shook his head. "I'm here to do a job, not . . . rekindle memories. I didn't suggest your bogey story to David because I wanted to start things up again."

"And I didn't agree to talk to you because I wanted to start things up either," George lied. "I agreed to it because of the money. We're having a lovely little hundred-pound chat. And if I decide to spill the beans after next week, we'll have an even lovelier five-thousand-pound chat." George stood and stretched, bending his neck back and around in a gesture that he hoped Michael would find erotic.

"And I'm happy to keep it on those terms," Michael said.

George stopped twisting his neck. "Bully for you. Do you want to go up to Cairnwell with me next week?"

"I didn't know I was invited."

"Of course you are." George grinned. "And I'll tell them exactly what you're there for—to expose the secret of Cairnwell Castle, should I care to reveal it to the whole drooling world. That should make old Maxwell shit his britches. You'll come?"

"Wouldn't miss it. Thank you."

"I assume then you'll foot my traveling expenses? My taste for the finer things has laid me low financially once again, and that damned Maxwell won't send a penny. Once I'm laird of the manor, let me tell you the first thing I'm doing is finding a new solicitor."

CAIRNWELL CASTLE WAS as ungainly a pile of stones as was ever raised. Even though George had grown up there, he always felt intimidated by the formidable gray block that heaved itself out of the low Scottish landscape like a megalithic frowning head. Often when he was a child, he awoke in the middle of the night and, realizing what it was that he was within, would cry until his mother came and held him and sang to him until he fell asleep. His father had not approved of his behavior, but his mother always came when he cried, right up until the week that she died, and was no longer able. From then on, he cried himself back to sleep.

"Dear God, that's an ugly building," Michael remarked.

"Isn't it. You see why I came down to London as quickly as my little adolescent legs would carry me."

As they drove into the massive court, charmlessly formed by two blocky wings of dirty stone, they saw an older man dressed in tweeds standing at the front door. "Maxwell," George said. "Richard Maxwell."

The man looked every day of his sixty-odd years, and wore the constant look of mild disapproval with which George had always associated him. His eyebrows raised as he observed George's spiky blond hair and the small diamond twinkling in his left ear. They raised even higher when he learned Michael Spencer's profession, and he asked to speak to George alone.

Leaving Michael in the entryway, Maxwell led George into a huge, starkly furnished antechamber, and closed the massive door behind them. "What do you think you're doing bringing a journalist with you?" he said.

"I think I'm doing the world a favor by sharing the secret of the lairds of Cairnwell, so we can stop living in some Gothic storybook, Maxwell, *that's* what I'm doing."

Maxwell's ruddy complexion turned pale. "You'd expose the secret?"

"If it turns out to be as absurd as I think it will."

"You cannot. You *dare* not."

"Spare me the histrionics, Maxwell. I'm sure you've been practicing your lines for months now, looking forward my birthday tomorrow, but it's really getting a bit thick."

"You don't understand, George. It's not the nature of the secret itself that will keep you from exposing it—though I daresay you'll want to keep it as quiet as all your ancestors have. Rather, it's the terms of the inheritance that will ensure your silence." Maxwell smiled smugly. "If you ever reveal what you see tomorrow, you lose Cairnwell and all your family's holdings. All told, it comes to half a million."

"Lose it! How the hell can I lose it? I'm sole heir."

"You can lose it to charity, as stipulated in the document written and signed by the seventeenth laird of Cairnwell and extending into perpetuity. I've made you a copy, which you'll receive tomorrow. It further states that you're to spend nine months out of every year at Cairnwell, and, *if* you have a male heir"—here Maxwell curled his lip—"the secret's to be revealed to him on his twenty-first birthday. Any departure from these stipulations means that you forfeit the castle. Understood?"

George smiled grimly. "Thought of everything, haven't you?"

"Not me. Your four-times great-grandfather."

"Sly old bastard."

"Now," Maxwell went on, ignoring the comment, "I would like you to dismiss that journalist and come see your father. He's been waiting for you."

George walked slowly out to the entryway, where Michael was waiting. "I'm afraid I've rather bad news," he said, and watched Michael's lips tighten. "You can't stay. I'm sorry."

"I can't *stay?*" The last word leapt, George thought, at least an octave.

"No. It's part of the . . . tradition, you see."

"Oh, for Christ's sake, George, you mean I motored all the way up to this godforsaken pile for nothing?"

"I'll be in touch as soon as it's over," George said quietly, fearing that Maxwell would overhear.

"Christ . . ."

"I didn't *know.* But I'll call you, I swear. I said I was sorry."

Michael gave him the same look as when he had told George that he didn't think they should see each other anymore. "All right then. Come and get your bloody bags."

Michael opened the boot, roughly handed George his luggage, and drove away with no words of farewell. George watched the car disappear over the fields, then went to visit his father in the largest bedchamber of the castle.

The twenty-second laird of Cairnwell was propped up on an overstuffed chaise, and George was shocked at the change in his father since his last visit over six months before.

The cancer had been progressing merrily along. At least another thirty pounds had been sucked off the old man's frame. What was left of the muscles hung like doughy pouches on the massive skeleton. The skin was a wrapping of faded parchment, a lesion all of its own. There was no hope in the eyes, and the smell of death—of sour vomit and diseased bowels, of bloody mucus coughed from riddled lungs—was everywhere.

His father was the castle. What the man had become was nothing less than Cairnwell itself, a massive tumor of the soul that grew and festered like the lichen on the gray stone.

Then, just for a moment, trapped within the rotting hulk, George glimpsed his father as he had been when George was a boy and his father was young. But the moment passed, and, expressionless, he walked to his father's side, leaned over, and kissed the leathery cheek, nearly choking at the smell that rose from the fresh stains on the velvet dressing gown.

They talked, shortly and uncomfortably, saying nothing of the revelation of the secret the next day except for setting the time when the three of them should meet in the morning. Eight thirty-five was the appointed hour, the time of George's birth.

That night, George could not sleep, so he sat by the fireplace long past midnight, thinking about Cairnwell and its hold on his father, its unhealthy, even cancerous hold on all the McCormacks. He thought about the way the castle had sapped his father's strength, and, years before, his mother's. Although she had never known the secret, she nonetheless had shared the burden of it with her husband, and, being far weaker than he, she had been quickly consumed by it, just after George's eighth birthday.

Then he thought about his debts, about nine months of every year spent at Cairnwell, about the horror that he was to see tomorrow.

When sleep finally came, it was dreamless.

The next morning dawned gray and misty, with no sunlight to banish the shadows that hung in every cold, high-ceilinged room. George rose, showered, and put on a jacket and tie rather than one of the sweaters he usually wore. In spite of his anger over the hereditary charade, he felt the situation demanded a touch of formality. He even removed the diamond from his ear.

His father and Maxwell were already breakfasting when George arrived in the dining hall: Maxwell on rashers and eggs, his father on weak tea and toast cubes. George took the vacant chair.

"Good morning, George," his father said in a thin, reedy tone. The old man wore a black suit that hung on him like a blanket on a scarecrow. The white shirtfront was already stained in several places. "Have some breakfast?"

George shook his head. "A cup of coffee, that's all," he said, and poured himself some from a silver teapot.

Maxwell smiled. "Off your feed today? Can't say I blame you. It's a difficult thing."

"Enough, Richard," said George's father. "No need to upset him. He'll see soon enough."

"I'm not upset, Father," said George, with a cool glance at Maxwell. "I'll wait to hear Mr. Maxwell's bogey story. I hope he won't disappoint me."

Maxwell flushed, and George hoped he was about to choke on a rasher, but he cleared his throat and smiled again. "I don't think you'll be disappointed, *Master* George."

"I said enough—both of you." The elder McCormack looked at the pair with disapproval. "This is not to be treated lightly. Indeed, Richard, this may be the most serious moment of George's life, so please conduct yourself as befits your position. You also, George. You shall soon be laird of Cairnwell, so start behaving as such." The voice was pale and weak, but the underlying tone held a rigid intensity that wiped the sardonic smiles from the other two faces.

"Now," McCormack went on, "I think it's time."

Maxwell rose. "Are you sure you don't want the wheelchair?"

"What'll you do, carry it down the stairs? No, I'll walk today as my father walked in front of me nearly forty years ago."

"But your health . . ."

"Life holds nothing more for me, Richard. If death comes as a result of what happens today, so much the better. I'm very tired. It's made me very tired."

At first George thought that his father was referring to the cancer, but something told him this was not the case, and the implications made him shiver.

He rose and followed his father and Maxwell as they left the room, passed down the hall, through a small alcove, and into a little-used study. Maxwell drew back the curtains of the room, allowing a sickly light to enter through grimy beveled panes. Then he dragged a wooden chair over to a high bookcase, stepped up on it, removed several volumes from the top shelf, and turned what George assumed was a hidden knob. Then he descended, flipped back a corner of a faded Oriental rug, and scrabbled with his fingers for a near-invisible handhold. Finding it, he pulled the trap door up so easily that George assumed it must be counterweighted.

"Good Christ," said George with a touch

of awe. "It's just like a thirties horror film. No wonder I never found it."

"Don't feel stupid," said Maxwell, not unkindly. "No one has ever discovered it on their own." He then opened a closet, inside which were three kerosene lamps.

"No flashlights?" asked George.

"Tradition," said Maxwell, lighting the lamps with his Dunhill and handing one each to George and his father, keeping the third for himself. Looking at McCormack, he said in a voice that held just the hint of a tremor, "Shall I lead the way?"

McCormack nodded. "Please. I'll follow, and George, stay behind me." There was no trembling in McCormack's voice, only a rugged tenacity.

Maxwell stepped gently into the abyss, as if fearing the steps would collapse beneath him, but George saw that they were stone, and realized that Maxwell, for all his previous bravado, was actually quite hesitant to confront whatever lay below.

They descended for a long time, and, although he did not count them, George guessed that the steps numbered well over two hundred. The walls of the stairway were stone, and appeared to be quite as old as the castle itself.

Halfway down, Maxwell explained briefly: "This was built during the border wars. If the castle was stormed, the laird and retainers could hide down here with provisions to last six months. It was never used for that purpose, however."

He said no more. By the time they reached the bottom of the stairs, the temperature had fallen ten degrees. The walls were green with damp mold, and George started as he heard a scuffling somewhere ahead of them.

"Rats," his father said. "Just rats."

For another thirty meters they walked down a long passage that gradually grew in width from two meters to nearly five. George struggled to peer past Maxwell and his father, trying to make forms out of the shadows their lanterns cast. Then he saw the door.

It appeared to be made of one piece of massive oak, crisscrossed with wide iron bands like a giant's chessboard. Directly in the center of its vast expanse was a black-brown blotch of irregular shape, looking, in the dim light, like a huge squashed spider. Maxwell and McCormack stopped five meters away, and turned toward George.

"Now it begins," said McCormack, and his eyes were sad. "Go with your lantern to the door, George, and look at what is mounted there."

George obeyed, walking slowly toward the door, the lantern held high in front of him protectively, almost ceremonially. For a moment he wished he had a crucifix.

At first he could not identify the thing that was nailed to the oaken door. But he suddenly realized that it was a skin of some kind, a deerskin perhaps, that centuries of dampness and decay had darkened to this dried and blackened parody before him.

But deer, he told himself, do not have pairs of breasts that sag like large, decayed mushrooms, or fingers that hang like rotted willow leaves. Or a face with a round, thick-lipped gap for a mouth, a broad flap of bulbous skin for a nose, twin pits of deep midnight in shriveled pouches for eyes. And he knew beyond doubt that mounted on that door with weary, rusting nails was the flayed skin of a woman.

He struggled to hold it back, but the bile came up instantly, and he bent over, closed his eyes, and let it rain down upon the stone floor. When it was over, he spit several times and blew his nose into a handkerchief, then looked at the two older men. "I'm sorry."

"Don't be," his father said. "I did the same thing the first time." He looked at the skin. "Now it's just like a wall-hanging."

"What the hell is it?" asked George, repelled yet fascinated, hardly daring to look at the thing again.

"The mortal remains," said Maxwell, "of the first wife of the sixteenth laird of Cairnwell." The words were mechanical, as if he had been practicing them for a long time.

"The wife . . ." George looked at the skin on the door. "Was she a black? Or did the tanning—"

Maxwell interrupted. "Yes, she was an African native the laird met as a young man on a trading voyage, the daughter of a priest of one of the tribes of Gambia. The ship traded with the tribe, and the laird, Brian McCormack, saw the woman dance. Apparently she was a great beauty as blacks go, and he became infatuated with her. Later he claimed she had put a spell on him."

George was shaking his head in disbelief. "A spell?" he asked, a confused and erratic half-smile on his lips. "Are you serious, Maxwell? Father, is this for real?"

McCormack nodded. "It's real. And under the circumstances, I believe that she *did* bewitch him. Let Maxwell continue."

"Spell or no," Maxwell went on smoothly, "he brought her back with him, she posing as a servant he'd taken on. The captain of the ship—and Brian's employee—had secretly married them on board, and by the time they docked in Leith, she was, technically, Lady Cairnwell."

A low, rich laugh of relief started to bubble out of George. "My God," he said, while his father and Maxwell stared at him like priests at a defiler of the Host. "That's the secret then? That's what kept this family shamed for over three hundred years, that we've some black blood in the line?" His laughter slowly faded. "Back then I can understand. But now? This is the 1990s—no one cares about that anymore. Besides, whatever genetic effect she would have had is long gone, and this 'Cairnwell Horror' isn't anything more than racial paranoia."

"You're wrong, George," said Maxwell. "I've not yet told you of the horror. That was still to come. Will you simply listen while I finish?" His voice was angry, yet controlled, and George, taken aback, nodded acquiescence.

"Brian McCormack," Maxwell went on, "once back in Scotland, quickly realized his mistake. Whether through diminished lust or the failure of the spell, we can't know. At any rate, he wanted a quiet divorce, and the woman

returned to Gambia. She refused to be divorced, but he made arrangements to have her transported back to Africa anyway. She overheard his plan and told him that if she was forced to leave him, she would expose their marriage to the world. Why he didn't have her killed immediately is a mystery, as it was well within his power. Perhaps he still felt a warped affection for her.

"So he locked her away down here, entrusting her secret to only one servant. The others, who had thought her Brian's mistress, were told she had been sent away, and were greatly relieved by the fact.

"Brian then wooed and married an earl's daughter, Fiona McTavish, and the world had no reason to suspect that it was his second wedding. There was a problem with the match, however. Fiona was barren, and no doctor could rectify the situation. After several years of trying to sire a son, Brian asked his first wife to help with her magic. She offered to do so with an eagerness that made him suspicious, and he warned her that if Fiona should suffer any ill consequences from the magic, he would not hesitate to painfully kill the woman. Then he brought her the things she asked for, and secretly gave Fiona the resulting potion.

"Within two months she was pregnant, and the laird was delirious with joy. But his happiness soured when Fiona became deathly ill in her fifth month. It was only then he realized that the black woman had increased his hopes so that they should be dashed all the harder by losing both mother and child.

"In a fury he beat the woman, demanding that she use her powers to reverse the magic and bring Fiona back to health. She told him that the magic had gone too far to save both—that he could have either the mother or the child. Brian continued to beat her, but she was adamant—one or the other.

"It must have been a hard choice, but he finally chose to let the child live." Maxwell cleared his throat. "There was a great deal of pressure on him, as on any nobleman, to leave an heir, so we can't criticize him too harshly for his decision. At any rate, the witch was true to her word. The child was born, but under rather . . . bizarre circumstances."

Maxwell paused and looked at McCormack, as if for permission to proceed.

"Well?" said George, angry with himself for the way his voice shook in the sudden silence. "Don't stop now, Maxwell, you're coming to the exciting part." He had wanted the forced levity to relax him, but instead it made him feel impatient and foolish. He tried in vain to keep his gaze from the pelt fixed to the door. It had been difficult enough when it was simply the skin of a nonentity. But now that it had an identity, it was twice as horrifying, twice as fascinating. He wondered what her name was.

Maxwell went on, ignoring George's comment. "Fiona McCormack died in her seventh month of pregnancy. But the child lived."

"Born prematurely then? Convenient."

"No," answered the solicitor quietly. "The child came to term. He was born in the ninth month."

"But . . ." George felt disoriented, as if all the world was a step ahead of him. "How?"

"The black woman. She kept Fiona alive."

"I thought you said she was dead."

"She was. It was an artificial life, preserved by sorcery, or, as we would think today, by some primitive form of science civilization has not yet discovered. Call it what you will, no heart beat, no breath stirred, but Fiona McCormack lived, and was somehow able to nourish her child *in utero.*"

"But that's *absurd*! A fetus needs . . . *life,* its respiratory and circulatory system depends on its mother's!" He laughed, a sharp, quick bark. "You're having me on."

"God damn you, George, shut *up*!" The old man's words exploded like a shell, and sent him into a fit of coughing blood-black phlegm, which he spit on the floor. He rested for a moment, breathing heavily, then raised his massive head to look into George's eyes. "You be silent. And at the end of the story, at the *end,* then you laugh if you wish."

"I don't know how it occurred, George," said Maxwell, "but it has been sworn to by the sixteenth laird and his servant, as has everything I've told you. You shall see further evidence later." He took a deep breath and plunged on.

"She gave birth to the child, and it suckled at his dead mother's breast for nearly a year, drawing sustenance from a cup that was never filled. A short time after the birth, Brian McCormack, with his own hands, flayed his first wife alive, and tanned the hide himself. He must have been quite mad by then. As you can see, he worked with extreme care."

He was right, George thought. For all of the abomination's hideousness, it was extraordinarily done, as if a surgeon had cut the body from head to toe in a neat cross section, like a plastic anatomical kit he had once seen. George looked at Maxwell and his father, who were both staring quietly at the mortal tapestry on the door. It seemed that the story was ended.

"That's it, then," George said, with only a trace of mockery. "That's the legend." He turned to his father with pleading eyes. "Is that all that's kept us in a state of fear from cradle to grave? That's become as legendary as the silkie or the banshee? Dear God, is the Cairnwell Horror only a black skin nailed to a cellar door?"

The expressions of the two men in the lantern light added years to their faces. For a second George thought his father was already dead, a living corpse like the sixteenth Lady Cairnwell, doomed to an eternity of haunting the dreams of McCormack children.

"There's more," said Maxwell, in such a way that George knew immediately that they had not been looking at the door as much as what was behind it.

Maxwell fumbled in the pocket of his suit coat and withdrew a large iron key, which he handed to McCormack. The old man hobbled to the massive door and fitted the key into a keyhole barely visible in the dim light. It rattled, then turned slowly, and McCormack pressed against the iron-and-oak panel. The door did not move, and the dying man leaned tiredly against it. Maxwell added his weight to the task. Though George knew he should have helped, he could not bring himself to touch the tarry carcass the older men seemed to be obscenely caressing. The door began to move with a shriek of angry hinges, and George thought of a wide and hungry mouth with teeth of iron straps, and wondered what it had eaten and how long ago. Then the smell hit him, and he reeled back.

It was the worst smell he had ever known, worse than the sour tang of open sewers, the sulfur-rich fumes of rotten eggs, worse even than when he had been a boy and found that long-dead stag, swarming with maggots. He would have vomited, but there was nothing left in his stomach to bring up.

His father and Maxwell picked up their lanterns. "Do you want to come with us," Maxwell asked, "or would you rather watch from here at first?"

George was impressed by Maxwell's objectivity. It was as if the man were viewing the situation far outside, watching a shocker on the telly. George wished he could have felt the same way. "I'll come," he said, and jutted his weak chin forth like a brittle lance.

Holding the lanterns high, the three entered the chamber. It was a small room six meters square. A rough-hewn round table with a single straight-backed chair was to their right as they entered, another chair, less stern in design, to their left. It was the bed, however, that dominated the room, a massive oaken piece with a huge carved headboard and high footboard, over which George could not see from the door. Maxwell and McCormack moved to either side of the bed, and the old man beckoned for his son to join him.

The woman in the bed reminded George of the mummies he had seen in the British Museum. The skin was the yellow of dirty chalk, furrowed with wrinkles so deep they would always remain in darkness. The same sickly shade sullied the hair, which spread over the pillow fanlike, a faded invitation to a lover now dust. She wore a night-gown of white lace, and her clawed fingers interlocked over her flattened breasts, bony pencils clad in gloves of the sheerest silk. She had been dead a long, long time.

"The Lady Fiona," whispered McCormack huskily. "Your five-times great-grandmother, George."

Again George felt relief. If this was the ultimate, if this dried and preserved corpse was the final horror, then he could still laugh and walk in the world without bearing the invisible curse all McCormacks before him bore. He held his lantern higher to study the centuries-old face more closely. Then he saw the eyes.

He had expected to see either wrinkled flaps of skin that had once been eyelids, or shriveled gray raisins nesting loosely in open sockets. What he had not expected was two blue eyes that gazed at the smoke-blackened ceiling, insentient but alive.

"She's . . . alive," he said half-wittedly, so overcome by horror that he no longer cared what impression he gave.

"Yes," said his father. "So she has been since the spell was put on her." George felt the old man's arm drape itself around his shoulder. "The sixteenth laird wanted her undead misery ended when the son was weaned, but the witch said it could not be done. He tortured her—in this very room—but she would not, possibly could not, relent. It was then that he killed her by skinning. He kept his wife upstairs as long as he could, but the . . . odor grew too strong, and the servants started to whisper. So he brought her down here, and here she has been ever since, caught in a prison between life and death.

"She neither speaks nor moves, nor has she since she died. Giving birth and feeding her child were her only acts, and even then, records the document, she was like an automaton."

George's head felt stuffed with water, and his words came out as thick as a midnight dream. "What . . . document?"

"The record Brian McCormack left," answered his father, "and that the servant signed as witness. The history of the event and the charge put on every laird of Cairnwell since—to preserve the tale from outside ears and to care for his poor wife 'until such time as God sees fit to take her unto Him.' It is the duty of the eldest son, such as I was, and such as you are, George."

The liquid in his brain was nearly at a boil. "Me?" He lurched away from his father's cloying embrace. "You want me to mind *that* the rest of my life?"

"There is little to care for," Maxwell said soothingly. "She requires no food, only . . ."

"What? *What* does she require?"

"Care. A wash now and again . . ."

George laughed desperately, and knew he was approaching hysterics. "A wash! Good Christ, and perhaps a permanent, and some nail clipping . . . !"

"Care!" bellowed McCormack. "What you would do for *anyone* like this!"

"There *is* no one *like this*! She is . . . she is *dead*." The word had stuck in his throat. "I'm not going to have any part of this, nor of Cairnwell. *You* chose this, not me! I won't rot here like the rest of you did. *Keep* Cairnwell—give it away, burn it, *bury* it, for Christ's sake—that's what suits the dead!"

"No! She is *not* dead! She is alive, and she *needs* us! She needs . . ." McCormack paused, as if something had stolen his words. A pained look grasped his features, and before George or Maxwell could leap to his side, he toppled like a tree, and his head struck the stone floor with a leaden thud.

Maxwell swept around the bed, pushed George aside, and knelt by McCormack. "The lantern!" he said, and George moved the flickering light so that he and Maxwell could see that his father's face wore the gray softness of death.

MUCH LATER, in the study, Maxwell poured George another glass of sherry. "I shouldn't have let him go down there," the older man said, almost to himself. He turned back to the cold fireplace. "After the last operation . . . it left his heart so weak . . ."

"It was better," George said quietly. "Better that way than for the cancer to finish him."

"I suppose."

They sat, sipping sherry and saying nothing. George rose and walked to the window. The sun, setting over the ridge of the western fields, slashed a thin blade of orange-red through the beveled panes. He looked at a flock of blackbirds pecking in the damp earth for grain.

"I shouldn't have upset him," said George.

"He hadn't been down there for quite a while," Maxwell said. "I shouldn't have let him go."

"You couldn't have stopped him," George said, still gazing out of the window.

"I suppose not. He felt it . . ."

"His duty," said George.

"Yes." Maxwell turned from the dead fire toward George's tall figure, outlined in the sun's flame. "Will you go then? Leave Cairnwell?"

George kept watching the birds.

"It's not . . . there's really very little to it," said Maxwell, with the slightest trace of urgency. "You don't have to see her at all, you know, not ever, if you wish it. Just so long as you stay here."

In the field, the blackbirds rose in formation, turned in the wind like leaves, and settled once more. George looked at Maxwell. "May I have the key?"

THE DOOR OPENED more easily this time, and George walked into the room, holding the lantern at his side without fear. He knew there were no ghosts. There was no need for ghosts.

His earlier exposure to the smell made it much more palatable, and he thought about fumigants and disinfectants. He pulled the straight-backed chair over to the bedside and looked at the woman's face.

Strange he hadn't noticed before. The resemblance to his father was so strong, particularly about the eyes. They were so sad, so sad and tired, open all these years, staring into darkness.

"Sleep," he whispered. "Sleep for a bit." He hesitated only a moment, then pressed with his index finger upon the cool parchment of the eyelids, first one, then the other, drawing them down like tattered shades over twilight windows.

"There," he said gently, "that's better now, isn't it? Sleep a bit." He started to hum a tune he had not thought of for years, an old cradle song his mother had crooned to him on the nights when the terrors of Cairnwell made sleep come hard. When the last notes died away, caught by the smooth fissures of the chamber walls, he rose, laid a hand of benediction on the wizened forehead, and started upstairs where his brandy waited.

The twenty-third laird of Cairnwell had come home.

CRAWLING MADNESS
ARTHUR LEO ZAGAT

ONE OF THE most common adjectives that sits next to the name of a pulp writer is "prolific," and few have earned the sobriquet more richly than Arthur Leo Zagat (1895–1949). Born in New York City, he went to Europe to serve in the signal corps in World War I, staying on in Paris to study after his discharge. He returned to New York and received a law degree from Fordham University in 1929 but began writing for the pulps instead of going into legal practice. His first story sold and he quickly established himself as a force in various literary genres, but most successfully as a master of weird menace. His specialty was the long story, approximately twenty thousand words, which magazines described on their covers as "feature-length novels." Zagat was one of the first of "the electric typewriter boys" whose "novels" often appeared on three or four magazine covers a month, with a few short stories thrown in, written under his own name or pseudonyms (he wrote as Grandon Alzee, among others). He became a popular regular contributor to *The Spider* magazine with his series about Doc Turner, and enjoyed success with his Red Finger spy series in the pages of *Operator #5*. For the new magazine *Bizarre Detective Mysteries*, he appeared in the debut issue with the warmhearted Dr. John Bain, who bears a striking resemblance to his Doc Turner character, always ready to help those in need. All contributed to making him one of the highest-paid pulp writers of all time until his sudden death of a heart attack at the age of fifty-three.

"Crawling Madness" was first published in the March 1935 issue of *Terror Tales*.

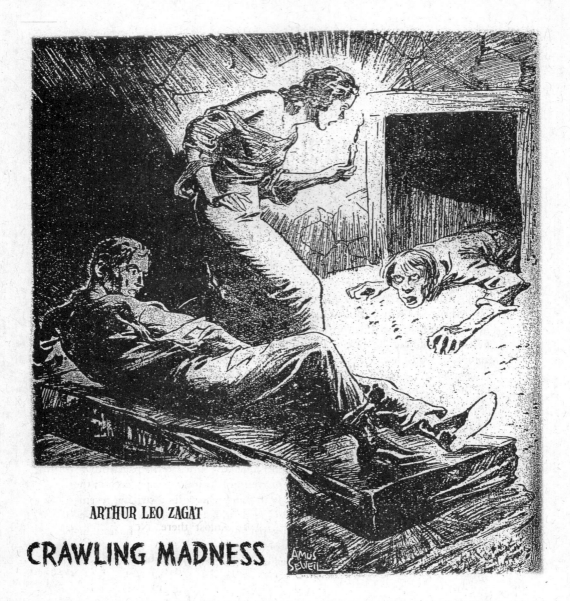

ARTHUR LEO ZAGAT

CRAWLING MADNESS

THE MEN WHO WERE TO HAVE HELPED ANN TRAVERS AND HER INJURED, HELPLESS HUSBAND HAD DRIVEN MADLY AWAY, FEAR'S CLUTCHING FINGERS AT THEIR THROATS. NOW ANN WAS ALONE IN THE DESERT—ALONE WITH HIM OF THE GAUNT, SATANIC FEATURES, AND WITH THE CRAWLING HORRORS THAT SLITHERED UP FROM THE GREY MOONLIGHT TO FEED ON HUMAN FLESH!...

ANN TRAVERS AWOKE with a start. She lifted her head from the rough tweed of Bob's overcoat shoulder and looked dazedly around. The roadster's motor still thrummed the monotonous song that seldom had been out of her ears in the long week since they had left New York. Her husband's blunt-fingered, capable hands still gripped the steering wheel. The

desert still spread—bare, utterly lifeless—from horizon to horizon; and running interminably under the hood there were still the two faint ruts in the sand which the thin-lipped filling-station attendant in Axton had pointed out as the road to Deadhope. Yet Ann was uneasy, oppressed, aware of a creeping chill in her bones that matched the anomalous chill of the desert night.

"Awake, hon?" Bob broke the silence. "We're almost there. Not much over a mile more."

Ann's lips smiled, but her weary eyes were humorless. "I don't believe it. This trip is never going to end. We're going on and on . . ."

"Wrong again. A mere five thousand feet from here, the gang I sent ahead to get things ready is waiting to greet their boss—Mrs. Travers."

How Bob loved to mouth that title. She hadn't gotten used to it yet—one doesn't identify a new name with oneself in a week. . . .

All at once now, Ann realized what change had occurred to weigh her down with vague fear since she had drifted off to sleep. The stars that had been close and friendly, their myriads a vast, coruscating splendor in the velvety black bowl of the heavens, now were pale, infinitely distant in a sky suffused with heatless, silvery radiance, forerunner of a not-yet-risen moon. The spectral luminance silted down to paint the undulating, gaunt plain with weird mystery, and long flat shadows of mesquite bush and cactus barred the vibrant glow with a network strangely ominous.

Bob leaned forward, flicked a switch on the dashboard. The headlights boring the night dimmed. "Save battery," he muttered, in explanation. Then, grinning, "Show my employer how economical her mine-superintendent can be."

Ann twisted to him. "Bob! I don't want to hear that sort of talk any longer. The silver mine Uncle Horvay left is as much yours as mine. More, because it's just so much dirt except for your wonderful process. There hasn't been anything taken out of it for years."

The man threw an arm up in mock defense against her vehemence. "All right. All right. I'll be good. Give me a kiss."

Even while Bob's lips clung warmly to hers, Ann's eyes strayed past him. Ahead, the horizon was close, much too close, as if the road ended abruptly in a vast uncanny nothingness. It was just the crest of a rise, she told herself fiercely; but she could not rid herself of the eerie sensation that they were plunging on to a jumping-off place, a Land's End over which the car would hurtle to fall eternally into some abysmal chasm.

Under the steady thrum of the roadster and the sough of its tires there was a hissing sound, like the breathing of some unseen monster. It was the whispering of countless grains of sand sifted along the desert by the wind, but it added to the spine-prickling certainty of impending disaster in Ann's mind. This strange, grim land resented their intrusion, their intention to re-open the old wounds in its bosom that long ago had healed. Once before it had lured men with

false promise into its deadly gullet, had spewed them out broken in pocket and health, grey with the patina of defeat. Now it was warning them to turn back—before it was too late.

Ann started at a new sound that filled her ears. It was a roaring from ahead from the secret region beyond the ridgecrest. It was the thunder of an approaching engine, a ponderous engine plunging through moon-hazed night at breakneck speed.

The tremendous apparition on that too-close skyline was startling despite the trumpeted warning of its approach. The huge truck lurched over the ridge, careened down the road, hurtled straight at them. Bob's horn blared raucous warning. Ann glimpsed his pallid, lined face, his blanched hands fighting the wheel. The truck blasted down upon them like a juggernaut, an avalanche of destruction. Ann screamed. . . .

THE GIGANTIC FRONT of the bellowing projectile loomed right above her. In that age-long, frozen instant of imminent demolition Ann saw the utterly white countenance of its high-perched driver his eyes that bulged with a terror blinding him to the presence of the other car, of anything but some stark inner vision from which he fled; his twitching, bitten lips. She screamed again, more in horror at that which she read in the contorted visage than from her own peril.

Her shrill keening penetrated the brain of the truck driver. His big-thewed arms jerked, the careening vehicle swerved, scraped past the edge of the roadster's fender. The swaying body of the dirt-truck, altitudinous above her, .was crowded with husky, brute-jawed men. They were rigid in the grip of the same terror that invested their chauffeur. Their livid faces were color-drained masks straining through the dust-cloud that swirled after them. Their eyes were deep-pitted coals ablaze with black flame. The truck skidded. . . .

The picture of soul-shattering, fearful flight

flashing on Ann's vision exploded in a grinding crash, a thunderous detonation of metal on metal, of bursting tires and smashing glass. She hurtled, asprawl, through a whirling world, thudded down on stinging, breath-expelling grit.

She looked up through dazed eyes. The truck was already yards away, its breathless haste not slackened at all, the red eye of its tail-light penduluming in short arcs as panic speed magnified the slight inequalities of the desert road. The sideward, yellow spray of the tiny lamp spattered, not on a license plate, but on an incredible figure hanging by clenched, bony fingers from a bracing truss under the truck's tailboard and hidden by it from the terror-stiffened men above.

Ann saw the man clearly. The grisly fingers by which the rag-garmented, dust-greyed apparition was suspended from the catapulting vehicle seemed to probe her brain with horror. Skeleton-thin, he streamed out behind the hurtling lorry like a bedraggled pennant; whatever of clothing had covered his pipe-stem, bounding legs was torn away and they were greyed to the hue of putrescent bone. His feet, flesh-stripped as they dragged through the dirt of the turnpike, trailed two lines of scarlet blood.

Then the truck was gone. Only a low-lying band of drifting dust-cloud and two scars on the desert's silvered surface showed that it had even been. Two scars between which thirsty sand drank red moisture, till no trace remained to testify that the grisly figure she had seen, or thought she had seen, was real.

The truck was gone! The meaning of that impacted on Ann's bewildered mind. As on the trackless sea, so in the desert waste the unwritten law of Man's obligation to his fellow in distress is stringent, inflexible. To have ignored it as the occupants of the lorry had, in rushing heedless from the wreck they had caused, stamped them as utterly vile—or inflamed by such devastating panic as had stripped humanity from them. . . .

The sound of a groan cut into Ann's consciousness. She rolled toward it.

THE ROADSTER WAS on its side, smashed to a jumble of twisted metal, burst rubber. Ann realized that only by the miracle of a lowered top had she been thrown free. Threshing arms, a body twisting up from chaos, falling back into it, showed her that Bob had not been so fortunate.

A sob tightened her throat. She pawed sand, pushed herself to her knees, heaved erect. The ground rolled like a tidal swell, staggered her, reeled her to a grip on the crumpled car-side. Bob groaned again, and she saw his twisted torso, the pale, tortured oval of his face.

"Ann!" His voice was a husked, hoarse whisper, pain-edged. "Ann! You're—you're all right?"

"Yes," the monosyllable squeezed from between her icy lips. "But you—you're hurt, darling. You're terribly hurt."

"A—little." Bob gasped and collapsed to the sickening sound of grating bone. "I—can't—get free."

His eyes sought Ann's face. Agony flared in them, was obscured by drooping, bloodless lids. Suddenly he was so motionless, so filmed over by the spectral moonlight with the very hue of death, that Ann's heart stood still and her skin was an icy sheath constricting her trembling body. But his cheek was warm to her darting palm; his nostrils quivered with pain, and a muscle twitched across the taut cords of his stretched-back neck.

Ann's teeth gritted. Her lips tightened to a grim, thin line. Her husband's right leg was strangely askew. Its ankle, making a nauseatingly awkward angle with its calf, already was swollen to twice normal size and the foot was caught between gear-lever and emergency brake. No wonder he had groaned in anguish, no wonder he had fainted!

The next few minutes greyed to a blur of feverish activity, of muscle-tearing effort. How Ann accomplished it she never knew, but somehow she extricated Bob, somehow she lifted his hundred-eighty pounds free of the wreck. At last he was stretched out on the sand. Ann loosened his shoe, got it off. Then, staggering back to the car to pull seat-cushions out, she improvised a bed for him. She tugged and pushed at his inert frame till he was as comfortable as she could make him. She paused then, stared down at his big-boned face, appallingly white against the black leather.

Bob's eyelids flickered open, revealing hot torment. "My boy," Ann sobbed. "My poor boy."

There was something besides pain in those queerly glittering eyes—an appeal, an urgent demand. "What is it, dear?" the girl gasped. "What do you want?"

The croak that came from him was unintelligible. But his arm lifted, motioned waveringly to the breast pocket of his coat.

Ann realized what worried him. She slipped a hand between the warm roughness of the fabric and his pounding heart. Paper crackled at the tips of her searching fingers. She pulled it out, the envelope containing the essential formulae for the process that would make profitable the working of low-grade ore from the abandoned mine at Deadhope. She pulled it out and held it up for Bob to see.

His mouth twisted, and his eyes signaled imperatively. Ann slid the envelope into her bosom, felt it crackle against her breast. After he had proved the worth of his process, Bob had told her he could sell it for vast sums. Until then he must keep it secret. There were interests. . . .

But her husband was once more unconscious. Her own limbs were water weak. She sank down beside him, squatted there, holding his hand in hers. Exhaustion welled up in her like a dark sea.

CHAPTER TWO

THE CRAWLERS

The moon was risen now over the ridge whence had catapulted the juggernaut of terror and destruction. It hung low in the sky, a great orange globe. It was so close, yet so infinitely far. It watched Ann's distress with an impersonal stolidity and she was small, terribly small, in the unpeopled immensity of the desert, in the hush weirdly emphasized by the whispering of the restless sand. What else did the moon watch, there on the hill, there where the ghost town of Deadhope had spawned horror which had sent hard-faced, stolid men careening through the night in a paroxysm of terror?

Ann tried to wrench her mind away from fear, tried to tell herself that she ought to see what she could do for Bob's broken ankle; that she ought to bathe his face, pimply with the cold sweat of pain even in his coma. In a minute she would—in a minute, but just now she must rest. She was so tired, so tired, and her body was one gigantic ache. And she was terribly afraid. Not only because of the breath of death's wings that had brushed so close. Not only because of Bob's hurt, his helplessness. But because of that which she had read in the faces of the men on that truck—because of that which had trailed behind the vehicle as it rushed away!

Recalling these, a pall of dread closed down, somehow visible in the sheeted moonlight lying spectrally on the limitless, lifeless waste around her. Lifeless? Was it some trick of the half-light, of her tired eyes, or was that shadow, that one way off there on the horizon, moving? . . .

It *was* moving. It was something gruesomely alive, undiscernible, flat against the sand, something that slithered slowly, that slithered over that ridge to the east, that vanished over the earthfold beyond which was—what?

Ann's scalp was a tight cap on her throbbing skull. That which had crawled along the desert surface, how long had it lain there? How long had its shadow lain immobile like the other shadows, shorter now, of the water-starved, grotesque foliage of the barrens? How long had it watched there, buzzard-like? Had it now gone to call its fellows, certain that there would soon be carrion here for them to feed upon?

"Ten thousand men laboring an hour apiece!

That slide rule's warped. . . ." Gibberish in a hoarse, parched voice pulled her head around to Bob's sweat-wet face, to his open, staring eyes. *"DX over DY multiplied by cosine thirty degrees and you get two kilograms of Ag O Cl."* His hand was a burning coal in hers, his lips were black, cracked. He jerked up to a sitting posture, his other arm flung up over his head, and he screamed: *"Ann! I've got it! I've got it, Ann! We're rich. We're rich!"*

"Bob. Bob, dear. Lie down. Be quiet." The young wife had both hands on the delirious man, was trying to wrestle him down. But fever-madness contorted his face, and with the strength of madness he tossed her about, fighting her.

"You can't have it!" he screeched, in that awful voice that was not Bob's voice. *"You can't have my secret. It's for Ann. For Ann, I tell you. I won't give it to you!"*

The desert silence took his shrill cries and quenched them, but they rang on in Ann's ears, and in her veins the blood ran cold with fear for her husband, her lover. Even as she fought to save him from his fever-demented self, tears streamed down her face, and sobs racked her. Oh, God! What was she to do? What could she do for him? If he got away from her . . .

As suddenly as it had come, the paroxysm of delirium passed. Bob slumped down. One word, one word more rasped from him. "Water . . ."

Water! He was burning with fever. Water would relieve him, water for his dry throat, water to bathe his torrid brow. Ann clawed to her feet, fought weakness, fought exhaustion to get to the car.

Water! The cans had torn loose from their straps on the crumpled running-board, the cans all travelers in the desert must carry. Here they were. Here in the sand was the red-painted one for gas, there the blue one for oil. The white one! Good Lord! Where was the white can, the water can? Breath sobbed from between Ann's lips as she spied it, flung farther than the others, blending with the silver of the sands.

She tottered to it, bent to it, got hands on it and lifted it. It was light! *Too light!* Oh, God! Oh, merciless God! The depression it left in the sand was wet, though rapidly drying, and a gash in the white side of the round can showed where the water, more precious than a thousand times its weight of silver or platinum, had run out. *There was no water!*

THERE WAS NO water, and on the pallet she had improvised for him Bob, her Bob, tossed and rasped out his agonized demand for—water. "Ann," he husked. "Ann. I'm burning. Water. Ann, give me water."

The distracted girl licked her own dry lips, let the mocking canteen slip from her powerless fingers, stood statuesque, rigid, numbed by a disaster more overwhelming than all the intangible fears crowing around her had foreshadowed. To be waterless in the desert! Even now the fever-racked, thirst-tormented man was thrashing on his bed of pain, was crying for cooling liquid to assuage the fire within him. What would it be when the sun came blazing up over the horizon to pour down its torrid beams on the shadeless, waterless waste? What would it be when the air, so chill now, quivered with insupportable heat and the sands became a fiery furnace, a searing hell?

Water! Old tales crawled out of the past to trail their awful warning through her anguish. Tales leathery-visaged Uncle Horvay had told, come from the Purgatory of his depleted mine to find a year or two of brooding sanctuary in her home. They had haunted her dreams, those stories of men creeping, creeping through the thirsty, interminable miles of the desert, black tongues hanging from blackened mouths— stark, staring mad after hopeless struggle and ripping their own veins to drink relieving death at last. One gibbering, skull-like visage seemed to form in the ambient sheen of the vacant night as it had gibbered at her in nightmares then. It changed to Bob's square-jawed, bronzed countenance, changed back again to a mask of horror. Her larynx constricted to a soundless scream.

"Ann!" Bob's cry came like the cry of a frightened child, through the shell of despair encompassing her. "Ann! Where are you? *Ann!*" He was sitting up, was staring about him with glittering, frightened eyes. He stared right at her and did not see her.

She got to him, knelt to him. Her arms were around him. "Bob!" she sobbed. "Bob, dear. Here I am. Right here."

"Ann," he whimpered, clinging to her. "Ann. Why don't you give me some water? I'm so thirsty. So terribly thirsty. And my foot hurts so."

Fever and pain had made of her strong, brawny husband a little, frightened child. Agony tore at her heart, clawed her brain.

"Help me, Ann. Help me."

"Of course I'll help you." The girl got steadiness into her voice. "But you will have to be brave." She loved him. Only now did she know how love strained in her every nerve, in her every sinew, how it yearned to him. She got his head down to her palpitant breast, held it there. He was quieter, his upturned eyes more reasonable. She would have to chance telling him. "Listen, dear. Our water is spilt. I'll have to go and get some more. I'll have to go and get help. I'll have to leave you, but it will be only for a little while."

"Leave me! Alone?" Fear flared in the pain-filled orbs that were fastened on her face. Then it died away. The lines of Bob's face hardened, the lines of his mouth firmed. "Of course. Deadhope is only over the hill." He lay more heavily against her breast. The fever was sapping what little strength he had left. "Kane . . . foreman. Tell him . . . hurry. I'll be—all right—till he—comes." Bob's voice trailed into silence. His eyes were closed. He was asleep.

Ann slid him gently off her lap, onto the seat cushions, pulled his overcoat together, buttoned it with shaking fingers. She stood up and slipped out of her own warm garment to roll it and push it under his head for a pillow. Her lips brushed his and he smiled in his sleep. Muttered, "Ann. Darling."

Then she was erect, was walking away from him, the desert sands clogging her footsteps. Walking toward the crest of the road-rise that now was silver-edged, shimmering as though it were the crest of a long sea-swell. Deadhope was over the hill. Deadhope from which two-fisted, hard-faced brawlers had fled in an extremity of blood-curdling terror. Deadhope where some awful menace lurked, more fearful because she could not know, could not guess its nature.

Deadhope where water must be, water and some conveyance, perhaps, that would enable her to carry Bob to shelter.

Behind lay mile upon mile of unpopulated, barren country. Only in the mystery ahead was there any reachable possibility of help for Bob. And so, although apprehension lay a leaden weight within her, and fear clawed her with gelid talons, and her veins were a network lacing her shuddering form with icy dread, Ann Travers stalked like a lonely specter through the ghost-grey moonlight. And far out on the desert another shadow that had lain motionless and watching, moved imperceptibly and slithered over the edge of the ground-swell to carry ahead word of her coming. . . .

ANN CLIMBED THE ground-swell as though she were moving through some transparent, thick liquid. Though quite invisible, it resisted her slow advance so that she had to force through it, fighting for every inch of progress. It was barely a hundred yards to the summit of the rise, yet it was an endless journey as within her fear shrieked, "Look out! Danger ahead! If those men could not fight it, how can you hope to? Turn back. Turn back before it is too late!" Thus fear. And love answered, "Go on! Go on! At whatever peril to yourself, you must go on. Bob will die if you do not. Bob will die." Love, conquering fear. *"Go on before it is too late."*

She reached the last tiny rise at last, hesitated a moment, shuddering with cold dread, took the final step that brought her up and over the summit. Stopped again.

The desert pitched more steeply than it had

climbed, so that it descended into a vast hol-low filled with moonglow, ghostly, evanescent. It seemed brighter here, and momentarily Ann could see nothing but that all-pervading, silver-grey radiance investing sky and earth alike with brooding mystery. Then she made out the grey bowl of sand merging with the grey bowl of the heavens so that their joining was indiscern-ible. Far at the other side of the hollow, a maze of darker lines resolved themselves into gaunt, shattered timbers hazily outlining what once had been houses, dwellings.

Like silhouetted skeletons they rose, those ghastly beams, like stripped skeletons of a dead town. Here a tall chimney leaned askew, still faithful to a hearth that never again would gather about itself laughter and merriment. There the collapsed roof-poles of a more am-bitious structure stabbed through a space that must have been a dance-hall, perhaps the very dance-hall Dan Horvay had cleaned out one mad and brawling night. . . .

Ann's gaze pulled away from the ghostly town, pulled nearer. Midway across the lower plain an angular-edged black blot lay athwart the shifting, luminous sands, somehow in-congruous to the color-drained, incorporeal, dreamlike scene. This was the long barracks, Ann guessed, erected by the men Bob had sent to prepare the mine for its reopening, the men who had been driven away from here by some supernal terror. And her heart leaped as she saw, in the ebony side of it facing her, a yellow oblong flash out, an oblong of light, and across it shadow move.

Someone had been left behind! Someone alive! Someone who could help her! The girl for-got her dread in exultation, sprang into motion. She was running down the side of the hill, her lips formed to a call. . . .

The call was never uttered. Ann's heels dug into the sand, braked her to a halt. Her hand came up to her frozen lips, stifling that cry. A nightmare paralysis held her rigid on the hill-side, and the affrighted blood fled the surfaces of her body, sought the warmth of her pound-ing heart. Only her eyes were alive, only her fear-widened, aching eyes that were focused on something that moved, there ahead of her in the phantasmal sand, something that crawled slowly toward her with loathsome life.

It was movement only, at first, and the length-ening shadow of a mesquite bush. Then an arm writhed into the lunar luminance, a long, shud-deringly emaciated arm, livid and ghastly. It lifted inches from the ground, dropped, and the tentacular, fleshless fingers of its hand hooked into the dirt, dug deep, pulled, pulled head and body after it, out of the shadow.

A head! But it was a gargoylesque mask, livid, hatchet-edged, sunken-socketed. The head of a thing long dead, of a woman long dead, crawling out from the shadow on her belly, crawling with slow malevolence toward the staring, motionless Ann.

Bedraggled, grey hair was stringy about that dreadful countenance. Clearly in the moonglow Ann saw saliva drool from between lips drawn back to reveal blued and toothless gums. In the awful visage there was no expression, no sign of human intelligence, so that that which slithered toward her seemed a soulless imbecile thing, ut-terly brainless. But then the dragging, prostrate body came fully out into such light as there was, and a vagrant beam struck deep into the abysmal pits under the livid brow, and red hate stared out at Ann.

Power over her limbs came back to the girl in that moment, power to whirl, to run from the inexorable advance of that crawling, hateful, mindless thing. Sand spurted from beneath her feet. She plunged back up the slope down which she had come with hope and relief flaring within her. A queer low wail rose from behind her. . . .

Abruptly the hillcrest before her changed form, took on an outline that halted her in her tracks and wrenched a groan of ineffable fear from her parched throat. For another crawling creature seethed over the ridge, rustled slowly through the sand! Another gargoyle face peered at her with mad hate, the face of a man this time, pitted and scarred and with its flesh sloughed away as though the owner had been rejected from a nameless grave! . . .

CHAPTER THREE

THE WHIP

The horror slithered fearsomely down with a dread leisureliness that told how sure it was of its prey, how certain it was that it had cut her off. The woman behind, the man ahead—and Ann knew, knew without looking, without daring to look, that more of the crawling things were closing in on her from all sides, that they had enclosed her in a ring from which there was no escape!

Terror was a living thing in her breast, a thing that tore upward to her throat and burst from her mouth, in a piercing, shrill shriek she had not willed. Again she screamed. . . .

A shout from below whirled her around, a deep-throated shout that somehow she knew had responded to her outcry. The woman who crawled was nearer, fearfully nearer, though Ann had been certain she had outsped the creature's slow advance. But beyond her, whence the resonant shout came again, a second oblong of light broke the black expanse of the barracks, an opened door—and in it was framed a tall thin figure that stood there peering out.

That *stood*! The girl's whirling brain seized on that fact to distinguish the newcomer from the ringing grey creepers who closed about to capture her for an unguessable fate. *He was erect!*

"Help!" she shrieked. "Help!"

The man's head jerked to her. Though he was only a slim black silhouette against the saffron luminance, Ann knew he must see her plainly. "Help!" she cried again.

He was motionless, and the woman was crawling always closer, and behind her Ann could hear the approach of the snaking man as sand sifted away from beneath his crawling advance. Oh, Mother of Mercy! "Help! Save me!"

An ululation of sound burst over the desert,

a long-drawn crescendo filled with threat, with unspeakable menace. It stabbed the girl's brain with new terror, chilled her, rocked her with a veritable apotheosis of fear. It rose to an apex of quivering sound, cut short—and the silence that followed it was aquake with the awful recollection. . . .

Good Lord! Ann came up out of the bottomless sea of horror into which that cry had plunged her and was startlingly aware that the desert crawlers no longer advanced upon her, that they were gone, completely gone as though they had been figments of her own distorted imaginings! Oh, Mother of Mercy! Was that truly what they had been? She shuddered at the appalling thought. They had seemed real, so real, and now they were vanished. Was she . . . ?

No! She would not even phrase that question to herself. They had been real, too real. And there was covert enough for them to have hidden now, covert enough in the black pools of shadow cast by mesquite and cactus, in the rolling, uneven terrain. That's what it was, of course. They were hiding. . . .

Let it be enough that they no longer slid toward her, that their dreadful bodies writhed no longer toward her, that their skinny arms no longer reached for her with soul-shattering menace.

The man in the doorway beckoned to her. Had the strange outcry that had banished the grey creepers come from him? Ann started to him—froze once more. Who was he? What was he? Why was he here in this camp from which terror had driven all others? What mastery did he hold over the crawling people? Was he one of them? Fear flamed within her. She whipped around to run away, to run back to Bob. . . .

But slowly she turned back. Bob was injured, dying perhaps. Down there was water for Bob, help for him. She must go down there, whatever the peril, to get it for him. She had promised him to return with help.

She drew a long breath into her tortured, aching lungs, and willed herself to move. Then she was running down the hill, through the sand, running the gauntlet of the weird creatures she knew must be all about her, though she could see no trace of them. She was running interminably while the very soul within her cringed with fear that this instant, or *this,* would bring the clutch of bony fingers at her ankle, would see a crawling, slimy creature spring up at her out of the very ground.

INCREDULOUSLY, Ann reached the open door, plunged through. She whipped around as it banged shut behind her, as the tall man rattled a bolt into its socket. She stood gasping, shuddering, as he turned to her—and smiled.

"Hello," the man said. "You're Mrs. Travers, I know. I'm Haldon Kane, your foreman. Where is Mr. Travers?"

Ann gasped, catching her breath. "He's out on the desert, hurt. We've got to get help to him, quickly. A truck came over the hill, driven by a maniac, and wrecked us, broke Bob's ankle. He's—"

"A truck. That must have been ours. Damn those fellows!" The oath ripped from between thin lips in a long, horse face. "When they've got their skins full of white mule they *are* a bunch of raving maniacs. I sent them down to Axton to get them away from here so you wouldn't have to hear their caterwauls your first night in camp, and that's what they've done."

"They—they looked scared to me." The explanation had been too pat. "As if they were running away from something."

"Sure they were," Kane responded smoothly. "Running away from the beatings I'd promised them if they were here when you and Mr. Travers arrived."

A dark suit, complete with coat and vest and white collar, clothed his slender frame. Ann could not quite picture him victorious in a hand-to-hand tussle with the stalwarts of the truck. "But we oughtn't to leave Mr. Travers alone any longer than necessary," he said. "I'll jump in the flivver and fetch him."

"You have a car! How lucky! Come on." Ann started to the door. "He was delirious when I left him. We've got to get to him quickly."

Kane was somehow in her way, though he had not seemed to move. "It won't take the two of us, Mrs. Travers. Hadn't you better stay here and get things ready? Put up water to heat on the range?" He gestured vaguely toward the end of a long door-walled corridor that appeared to bisect the barracks. "Tear up some sheets into bandages and so on? From what you tell me he's going to need plenty of attention, and we ought to be ready to act quickly."

"But I can't stay here alone." Panic flared up in Ann once more. "Those awful creatures—"

"Won't bother you here!" The smile was wiped from the foreman's face, and momentarily a grim ferocity came into it that made the narrow countenance with its pointed chin somehow Satanic. "Not here . . ."

His insistence seemed somehow sinister. "I'm going with you," the girl gulped. "I won't stay away from Bob that long."

She tried to shove past him. But his hand was on her arm, his long-fingered bony hand. It stopped her. His black glittering eyes took hers, were gimlets of black flame boring into her brain.

"I said you are safe in here. I'll go bond for that. But if you put one foot over this threshold—" Kane's voice dropped to an ominous, fearful whisper—"I could not protect you if I were the devil himself. The moon and the desert have spawned evil, prowling things out there, and they have scented you, and they are waiting for you.

"It will do your Bob no good if I save him and he wakes up to find you—what you will be when they get through with you."

Shudders of icy dread shook Ann's slender frame. Kane whipped around, was through the door. Momentarily Ann was rigid, incapable of movement, and in that moment the door slammed behind him, footsteps pounded on hard sand, a motor roared. The girl fought her hand to the doorknob. The car she heard roared away. . . .

It was too late. He was gone, Kane was gone. And she was alone, alone in the hollow with— the foul spawn of the desert! Surging terror jerked her hand to the bolt, rattled it home. . . .

FOR A LONG time Ann remained in the grip of a nightmare paralysis, staring unseeingly at the rough-planed panels of the door. What was Kane? What was his power over the crawling horrors of the sands . . . ?

Or had he any such power? Was she sure, dead sure, that the eerie cry that had cleared them from her path had come from him? It had seemed sourceless, had seemed to invest the atmosphere from all directions at once. . . .

But when he returned—*if* he returned— he would bring Bob with him. She must get ready. . . .

The light here came from a lantern hanging on a hook beside the entrance. Ann lifted it off, turned to locate herself. The structure was hastily thrown together; the walls and partitions were of rough, unpainted lumber, joists and studding not covered. Angular shadows moved as she moved the lantern, slithered menacingly. The sharp odor of new-sawed wood stung her nostrils, mingled with the stench of man-sweat, the rubbery aroma of boots, the stench of machine-grease, of strong soap, of stale tobacco. The place was alive with the aura of occupancy, yet it was deathly silent.

Had Kane pointed to left or right when he spoke of heating water on the range? Ann could not remember. She would have to look. A curious reluctance slowed her movements as she reached for the driven nail serving as knob to the nearest door. What was behind it? What would she find behind it? She pulled it open.

Light struck into a big room, showed an overturned table, cards strewn over the floor, a lumberjacket in a heap in the corner, a smashed chair. Chaos. Had a drink-maddened brawl done this, bearing out Kane's glib explanation of the flying truck? It might have, except for one thing. There was no smell of alcohol here, there were no flasks emptied or full, no glasses of any kind. . . .

The nape of Ann's neck prickled. Something *had* happened here. Something that had disrupted an orderly gathering into hasty, disorganized flight. *Something about which Haldon Kane had lied.*

But Bob would soon be here. Time later to investigate; now she must get a bed ready for him, hot water, bandages. A bed! Sheets to rip for bandages! None here. Maybe in this next room.

No. This was an office, the foreman's office. A rude desk told her that, a small safe with its door open. Here too were signs of panicky departure. Blueprints spilling from a rude cupboard in the corner, a pen stuck point down in the floor, ink blotching the place where it had stabbed. Papers disorderly on the desk, held down by— What *was* it?

Ann took a step nearer, lifting her lantern to throw a stronger light. The black, slender thing coiled ominously on the table-top, ended in a thicker, wire-wound handle. It was a whip, a short-handled, cruel whip. A bull-whip such as she had seen mule-freighters use, in the borax mines on the journey here. But they had no mules here, no oxen. . . . The end of the lash trailed over the further edge of the desk, was hidden by it. Oddly fascinated, the girl circled till she could see it.

The long lash ended in a snapper, a barbed thing such as she had seen raise weals on the tough skin of a mule. This one glistened in the light. A drop formed, dripped off, splashed on the floor. It was a frayed disk of red on the planed board. It was a splotch of blood!

An iron band constricted Ann's temples, and the floor heaved under her feet.

CHAPTER FOUR

WHERE HORROR FED

From somewhere came a muffled roar. Ann's head jerked up. It was the sound of a motor laboring, pounding against the clogging desert sand. Kane was coming back. Had he found Bob? Was he bringing Bob back with him?

The girl whirled, her feet pounded wood. She reached the outer door, rattled the bolt free, grabbed for the knob, twisted it and pushed. . . .

The door would not open. Somehow it had jammed. The car sound was louder now, was right outside. Ann pushed again, threw her weight against the portal. It was immovable.

Good God! It hadn't jammed. It was locked! Locked from the outside!

The car didn't stop! Mother of Mercy, it hadn't stopped! It had passed; its noise was growing fainter, was dying down. Was it some other car than Kane's, perhaps? Or . . . ?

Ann beat small fists on the wood, pounded till her hands were bruised and bleeding. "Bob!" she screamed. "Bob!"

Something like a laugh answered her, a mocking laugh, muffled by wall and by distance. There was a window somewhere on this side of the structure, a window from which light had glowed. The frantic girl twisted away from the locked door, toward it.

Then she was at it, was peering out through glass. Her own face stared back at her from blackness. The lantern glared behind it. The lantern! Of course! Its light was stronger than that outside, was making a mirror of the pane.

Whimpering, Ann smashed the lamp to the floor, reckless of fire. She could see through now, could see the desert spectral in the moonlight, could just see a dilapidated, open flivver plowing toward the gaunt timbers of the ghost town. Someone was hunched over the wheel, and beside him a body folded limp over the car side, its arms hanging down, its hands just touching the running-board. Bob!

The window was framed glass; its sash did not lift. The girl flailed at it with her bare hands. Glass splintered, crashed. Her fingers were bloody, her knuckles gashed. She plucked shards from their hold in the frame, uncaring. She lifted to the high sill, squirmed through. Jagged edges of broken glass caught at her, tore her frock. She

dropped to the sand outside, sprawled. Then she exploded to her feet and was running toward the ruins of Deadhope.

Down there, where those skeleton timbers affronted the sky, nothing stirred. Nothing at all. While she had battered at the window the laboring car had vanished into nothingness as the crawlers had vanished. She could see it no longer, could no longer hear it. But she could see the tracks it had left in the desert, long tracks reaching clear into the mazed shadows of the skeleton village. She could follow them. Staggering, stumbling, reeling, she could follow them to where Bob had been taken.

The soft sand sifted from beneath her flying feet, gave no footing. Even through her desperation, her frenzy of anxiety for her husband, her soul-sapping fear for him and for herself, the feeling of eerie unreality flooded back on her that first had manifested itself when she awoke in the car to see a world flooded by ghostly moonlight. The naked timbers ahead seemed to retreat as she ran, as if she were spinning a treadmill beneath her, an eternally wheeling treadmill on which she would run forever and make no headway. Pain strapped her leg muscles, stabbed her bursting lungs. Yet somehow she seemed no nearer her goal. No nearer . . .

THE PALLID DESERT all about her was blotched by shadows that weirdly were other than shadows. The sands shimmered like water under the moonlight, like water furrowed by the wind, swirling into a whirlpool. Ann gasped, halted her headlong rush, her heels digging into the silt, her eyes staring. There was a circular, wide wallow here where the desert had been plowed up, torn, trampled by some terrific struggle. As though some great beast—or some man—had fought here long and unavailingly against a ravening something that had dragged him down at last.

Yes, here was the mark of shod feet and here—blood-darkened—the depression his body had made when it had come down. The shifting sand had kept the shape of the impact because it had been wetted—wetted red by life-fluid spurting from severed veins. And from this spot a long furrow started to run along with the tire-tracks Ann followed! Vividly, as if the tragedy were being reënacted before her pulsing eyes, the girl could see what had made it: the gore-bathed corpse pouring blood; the slimy, crawling things dragging their victim to their lair. . . .

The record was plainly written—too plainly—in the sand. No wonder they had fled in crazed terror from this dire hollow, the half-mad men in the truck. No wonder they had not dared to stop when Bob—

Bob! Oh, God! He was somewhere in there, somewhere in the ruined town ahead to which the crawlers had dragged their prey! Ann's larynx clamped on a scream, and she was running once more, was following the twin tracks of the flivver in which Bob's limp body had been, was following the blood-darkened furrow that gibbered at her an awful promise of what it was to which her lover had been taken.

On and on, endlessly, she ran, till—suddenly—barred shadows fell across her and she leapt aside, panting. . . .

It was only the shadow of a tumbledown house, stripped of its siding. Others clustered around, the rotted skeletons of a vanished town, the fleshless bones of Deadhope! But where was the flivver? Where was Bob?

The girl reeled, paused, gasping for breath. She staggered against a rotting beam, clung to it, gagging, retching. Her heart pounded against her heaving ribs as though it would break through the thin confining wall of her chest. She lifted a hand to her breast to still it, felt paper rustle under her hand. Paper! The formulae of Bob's process. Bob's secret.

Bob's secret! Dizzy, nauseated, afraid, the thought pounded into Ann's brain. BOB'S SE-CRET. *She must keep it safe.* She glanced around with eyes crafty, not wholly sane. No one was in sight. The jumbled beams against which she leaned screened her from observation. Here were two that made a cross, an *inverted cross,* and beneath them was another that lay close to the ground so that there was only a slit beneath it. Ann clawed at her bosom, clawed out the precious envelope, shoved it under that beam. There was no sign of digging to betray that cache, but the envelope was out of sight and it was marked by a sign she would not forget. The sign of the inverted cross. *The sign of Satan.*

The momentary rest somewhat restored her. She could breathe again and her vision had cleared. There were the tracks, the rutted tracks of the car that had carried her Bob, winding among the strewn timbers of the ghost town. And there, still marching with them, was the grim furrow dug by that which had been dragged here. Ann's eyes followed that grisly spoor, probed a pool of shadow, some fifty feet ahead, to which it led.

It wasn't a shadow! It was a grey-black shapeless mound in the barred moonglow, a mound that heaved restlessly, a mound that was animate with gruesome life. Through the desert hush sounds came clearly to Ann, smacking sounds, low whimperings, *the scrape of a gnawing tooth on bone.* That gruesome shape was feeding! *On what?*

A hand squeezed Ann's heart, and an awful fear sheathed her with quivering cold. The furrow of the dragged corpse led straight to that squirming pile, and the tracks of the car in which Bob had been brought here! *What was it that composed that grisly meal?*

Sound rasped through the girl's cramped larynx. A whine, a whimper—it was not a word. It was not anything one could have recognized as human speech. But perhaps *He* understood it, He to whom that prayer of a woman's tortured soul was spoken. Perhaps He knew that the racked brain of the devoted wife was saying, over and over: "God! Dear God! It isn't Bob. It isn't. It can't be. Please, God, don't let it be Bob."

PERHAPS HE HEARD and touched that loathly tumulus with His finger. Perhaps Ann's sob of agony and dread reached the ghastly feeders. At any rate, the heaving mass split apart. Grey, earth-hugging forms slithered away from it, like satiated vermin from their putrid feast, slithered through the sand, out of range of Ann's vision. She did not see where they went, saw nothing but the motionless something to which her burning gaze clung, that which they had left behind. A nausea retched her stomach, but she could not see—she could not be certain what it was at which she stared.

She could not be certain, and she had to be. She pushed herself away from the beam against which she leaned, took a reeling step toward—toward the motionless, awfully motionless *debris* ahead. Her legs, water-weak, buckled, and she tumbled headlong into the sand.

She moaned, and then was crawling toward *it*, was shoving palms down into gritty, cutting sand, was lifting herself on breaking arms, dragging herself onward little by little. And all the while the dread question grew in her shaken mind like a bubble blown in acid, burst so that she did not know why she crawled, and grew again.

Time was a grey nothingness that flowed over her. The anguish of her ripped hands, of her torn knees, was a pulsing torment she did not feel. She was mumbling, "Not Bob. God. Not Bob," and she did not know what it was she said nor why she said it. But she kept going, eternally, hitching through the sand, dragging the agony of her body and her soul to a destination she had forgotten but that she knew she must reach.

The pallid desert must have pitied her then, the desert and the shadows that moved on its spectral breast and were not shadows. Even They must have pitied her, the leprous-faced horrors that crawled—or did They think her one of them, this tatter-clothed, crawling woman with the contorted features of dementia and the eyes glowing red with madness? At any rate they let her pass unscathed until her outreaching hand fell upon something that was not sand, something that rolled and left a red, wet stain on the sand where it had lain.

The clammy, shuddersome feel of the thing upon which Ann's hand had fallen shocked her back to reason. To reason and the flooding horror of her search. She shoved up on extended arms, arching her back; she looked dazedly about her.

Madness pulsed in her once more as she stared at that which the crawlers had left—at tattered, gnawed flesh; at a torso from whose ribs meat hung in frayed strips, at a skull that had been scraped quite clean so that the grinning bone glowed whitely in the lunar rays. And everywhere on the pitiful remnants that once had been human were the marks of teeth, of *human teeth*!

But even through the swirling blackness that mounted in her brain, the gibbering question still screamed its query. *Who was it? Bob? Was it Bob? How could she tell? How could she tell when there was no face left on this, no skin?*

Whimpering, Ann looked hopelessly down at that upon which her hand still rested. It was a bone that had been torn loose, a thigh-bone. Hanging to it by a shred of ligament was the long calf-bone, bits of flesh still adhering, and the foot was quite untouched. The foot! The *right* foot!

Ann remembered. It was Bob's *right* ankle that had been broken!

And this—right ankle was—whole!

Oh, God! Oh, thank God!

Something gave way within Ann and she slid down and down into weltering, merciful blackness.

SOMEONE WAS SHAKING her. Someone was whispering, "Mrs. Travers. Mrs. Travers. Wake up."

Someone was bending over her. Ann's eyes came open, and she saw Kane's narrow face in the moonlight, its lips writhing. Somehow she was on her feet. Bone crunched under her heel, but she did not notice it. Her hands shot out, gripped the lapels of Kane's coat.

"Where is Bob?" she shrilled. "What have you done with him?"

Strong fingers clutched her wrists, tore them away. "Come out of here," Kane said. "Quickly."

A howl sliced across the words, a howl of animal threat. Arms went around her and lifted her, cradled her. The man was running, breathing hard, was plunging through the vague moonlight that glowed around them. Ann twisted around in the arms that carried her, saw Kane's face above her, sharper, more Satanic than ever as its eyes slitted dangerously, as lips curled away from dull-white, huge teeth in a narrow mouth.

She beat at his breast with futile thrusts. "Where's Bob?"

He carried her across the silvered desert, carried her toward the black bulk of the barracks. "I don't—know," he gritted. "I don't know."

Ann squirmed, fighting to get free. The grip of his arms was unrelenting, inescapable. "You lie," she spat at him. "What have you done with him?"

"I'm not lying," the man grunted. "He wasn't there when I found the wreck. He was gone."

Fury was a red flame swirling in Ann's brain. "You lie," she screeched again. "You've got him somewhere in there, somewhere in Deadhope. I saw your flivver pass the house and I saw him in it."

"My—flivver?" The nostrils of his tremendous hooked nose flared, and white spots showed in the thin-drawn skin on either side of it. "Not mine. I have no flivver. Look, this is my car."

They had reached the entrance to the barracks. A car puffed before it, the engine running. It was an old Dodge sedan! A Dodge! A sedan! But the car Ann had seen dart past and vanish into the barred shadows of the ghost town had been a Model T. It had been a touring car in which Kane had brought back Bob's horribly limp body. . . .

Wait! She had not seen the driver clearly. Was it Kane? She could not be certain. Oh, God! She *was not* certain it had been Kane.

"He was gone when I got there," Haldon Kane said again. Ann had ceased struggling. He set her down. But he had to support her as they took the few further steps to the barracks door, so weak she was from exhaustion, from terror and wild anxiety. "I found the overturned roadster, the cushions by its side on which he had lain. But no one. No one living . . ."

There was a curious emphasis on the last word. Ann twisted to him. "Living! Then there was . . ."

A veil dropped across the glitter of his eyes. His free hand made a curious gesture, as if he were pushing something away from him, something revolting. "Never mind that." His lips seemed to move not at all. "It isn't—important." Then, "Mr. Travers was not there. But I don't understand—you said you saw him in a flivver, saw someone taking him down to the old town?"

"Yes." The monosyllable hissed from between Ann's compressed lips, as she fought to expel a grisly speculation from the maelstrom of her mind. "I heard it, saw it. But it disappeared down there—as though it were—something unreal." They had reached the barracks door. She twisted to Kane, fear of the crawlers forgotten in a greater fear. "But you must have seen it, too! It had to pass you.

"No." A muscle twitched in his hollow cheek. "No. I saw nothing. Nothing passed me." The response dripped dully into a crystal sphere of heatlessness that seemed suddenly to enclose the girl. "Nothing. No one."

A shadow moved out in the desert, sand slithered. Kane's pupils flickered to it. His hand darted to the doorknob—and the portal swung open effortlessly. But it had been locked—locked—minutes before!

He shouldered Ann through, came into the dark hallway himself and had the barrier shut in one smooth flow of movement. Red worms of fear crawled in his eyes.

"That's better," he breathed. A pale, eerie luminance sifted in through the window Ann had smashed, flowed over him, showed a toothy smile that was palpably forced on his narrow face. "Better. But where's the lantern?"

Ann jerked a pointing hand to it, where it had guttered out. "I—dropped it."

Kane flashed a curious glance at her, then at the lantern. From that to the smashed window. "Have to get that fixed," he snapped. "At once."

Then he was gone!

THE GIRL WAS startled. Then she realized that as she automatically had followed the direction of his glance he had soundlessly taken the one necessary step into the foreman's office, had closed its door. She heard his footsteps moving about, heard the rasp of a pulled-out drawer, heard a dull thud as if something heavy had dropped. Then there was no sound in there, no sound at all. . . .

Minutes dragged past as Ann stared with widened eyes at the blank wood. Coils seemed to tighten about her, gelid coils of nameless dread. Certainty grew upon her that something had happened to Kane in there—something that all the time he had feared. It was her fault. *Hers!* In breaking the window to gain exit she had breached his defenses, had made a way for something to enter—something that had lurked in the darkness of that room. . . .

She backed, inch by slow inch, till she felt the outer door pressing against her. Her hand lifted behind her, her fingers found and closed about the knob. She turned it, pushed, her apprehensive gaze still fixed ahead.

A faint breath of air stirred in through the slitted opening she had made, and with it came a vague, hissing sound. The whispering voice of the desert? *Or the sound of the crawlers, closing in?* Panic scorched her breast, was a living flame in her brain. She pulled to the door, shot its bolt with shaking, bloodless fingers. Fearful, horribly fearful as she was of what *might* lie in the secret silence of the room from whose entrance her gaze had never wavered, she was more terrified still of the creeping things she *knew* prowled the sands. She dared not go out there again. She dared not stay here, not knowing with what peril she was housed.

Ann whimpered, far back in her throat. She could not remain forever rigid in the grip of an icy fear. She must—do something—or in minutes she would—go mad.

There was no sound in the darkly brooding barracks. No movement. There couldn't be anything, living, in there. She must know what had happened to Kane. At all costs she must know. Or—give herself over to gibbering madness.

She forced unwilling limbs across the narrow corridor. Its nail-handle was hot to her frigid clutch. The door came creakingly open. Her body blocked light from the obscurity within, but something lumped on the floor ahead, a shapeless something that was fearfully still. Ann fought herself over that dread threshold, into the gloom. . . .

A shadow came alive, swooped down on her, engulfed her! Not a shadow, but cloth, black cloth enveloping her, smothering her, clamping her threshing arms, her flailing legs, clamping tight and holding her immobile. She was being lifted from her feet, was being carried off. And through the thick, blinding folds of the shrouding fabric a laugh sounded, a hollow mocking laugh, *the laugh that she had heard while a battered flivver had chugged past with Bob, with her limp and broken husband.*

CHAPTER FIVE

DESPAIR UNDERGROUND

Ann could fight no longer. Bruised, battered, her soft flesh torn, her brain a whirl of agony and terror, she sagged, strengthless, flaccid. Consciousness shrank to a minute spark in the vast, dark limbo of her fear. Terror piled on terror, fear on fear, had brought her at last to that ultimate point where her distracted mind must find refuge within an enclave of numbed, despairing acceptance of horror or be wholly shattered.

She was only dimly aware that the arms encircling the bundle they had made of her were so powerful that they handled her weight with utter ease. Only vaguely did she feel shambling, level progress. It did not matter now what became of her, now that Bob was dead. . . .

But she did not *know* that Bob was dead. Perhaps he was still alive. Perhaps she was being taken to him now, to the place where he had been taken. Hope stirred within her—a faint thread of pitiful hope that again she might be near him, might see his face, might for an instant press her lips to his dear mouth before she died. But *was* it to death she was being borne? To merciful death?

And once more she was awake to ineffable fear, to grueling terror. If that which was carrying her off, human or ghoul, desired only death of her, he could easily have killed her in the same unguarded moment that he had overcome her. He had not. *Why?*

Neither this searing, dreadful query nor the faint hope that preceded it was destined yet to be answered. Quite suddenly Ann felt herself deposited on some soft, high pallet. A slow chuckle came muted to her ears, and the shambling footfalls faded away. Then silence enfolded her once more, and helpless dread.

The girl lay lax, straining to catch some murmur of sound. She heard only the *pud, pud* of her own pulse. Had her captor gone off? Was whatever doom that lay in store for her postponed?

Ann chanced tentative movement, held her breath as she waited for its effect. Nothing happened. Strangely, this was more frightening than a heavy-handed rebuke, a threatening voice, would have been. She was alone. He had left her alone. How sure he must be of his power to have done that, of the impossibility of her rescue!

Rescue! Who was there to rescue her? Kane? Haldon Kane lay dead on the office floor. She had seen him, had seen in the gloom a mound of blacker black that must have been he, lying lifeless.

Even in her extremity of dread, Ann found time to regret her suspicions of the man, her certainty that it had been he who had vanished with Bob into the ghost town, that he was the master of the creepers. She realized now that the crawling fear she had felt in his presence had been the contagion of *his* fear. The man had been afraid, had been as terror-stricken as those who had careened in mad flight from this doomed hollow in the desert. But he had remained, faithful to his charge—had remained here to guard the mine for herself and Bob and had met the death he feared in doing so.

WHAT WAS THAT sound? During interminable minutes Ann had tossed, had struggled unavailingly to free herself of the muffling fabric which held her rigid, had twisted, jerked, fought until sheer exhaustion had forced her to quit. Then for an endless time she had lain quiescent, gathering strength to struggle again. . . .

It was close at hand—the slow slither of a heavy body through sand, the almost imperceptible hiss of labored breathing. It came closer, and Ann was quivering, the cold sweat of terror dewing her forehead, her breasts aching with its agony. They had her at last, the crawlers, the belly-creeping, snaking Things with the form of humans and the dead eyes of the damned. At last they had come for her, and she was helpless to escape them.

A hand prodded her, fumbled along the fabric within which she was muffled. Ann drew in breath through the constricted cords of her throat. The sound it made was a screeching, sharp-edged squeal.

"Hush," a muted voice hissed warningly. "Hush."

Fever ran hotly through Ann's veins, exploded within her skull. Good—Lord! Who was it that warned her to silence? Whose hands were they that groped down her flanks, that pulled, tugged at the lashings about her ankles? Bob's? Oh, Merciful God! Could it be Bob, escaped somehow, come somehow to find her, to release her from terror? . . .

The bag pulled up over her ankles, her knees, stripped up over her torso, caught momentarily under her chin and then was entirely gone. Ann squirmed, twisted about, gasped. Closed her lips on the glad "Bob!" that had almost escaped them.

This wasn't Bob's face, this gaunt, long countenance silhouetted against dim moonglow in a broken-arched aperture across which a shattered beam sprawled. It—wasn't—Bob's. Hope seeped out of her, almost life itself.

"Oh!" she gulped. "I thought it was my husband."

"Quiet," Kane breathed. "Quiet, Mrs. Travers, or we may be heard." His lips were paler, tighter, his eyes more narrowly slitted, more piercing. A curious excitement danced in them. "I've taken an awful chance tracing you here. We're both in terrible danger and you must not make it worse."

"What is it? Who is it that's doing all this? What terrible things are happening here?" Pushing herself up, Ann whispered the questions. "I won't move till I know."

"For God's sake!" he groaned, his pupils flicking into the darkness beyond her. "If it is known that I am still alive, that I have freed you . . ." His gesture finished the sentence. "We've got to get out of here." His skin was fish-belly grey with—was it fear . . . ? "Come. Hurry."

The urgency of his speech, his evident terror, got through to Ann. Once more he had risked his life to save her. She had no right to impede him now. And yet . . .

"Can you walk?" His left arm reached for her. Odd how long and slender his hand was, how it clawed vulture-like. Odd that his right should be concealed behind his back. *What was it he hid from her?*

Ann avoided his grasp. He had fought for her, sided with her. He was her only hope for safety. She must be mad indeed to shudder with revulsion from his touch as though he were something unclean.

"I can walk," she muttered. "You needn't help me."

"Go ahead, then." He turned toward the radiance-silvered opening, pointed with a preternaturally long, straight finger: "I'll follow."

A tocsin of alarm sounded deep within Ann at the thought of letting him get behind her. But she could not refuse. She slid by him, shrinking; she almost reached the light.

"Wait!" Kane spat. "Wait."

Ann twisted. "What . . . ?" she gasped. "What is it?"

He was startlingly close, towered gauntly gigantic above her. "We may not get through." His voice was a husked whisper. "If you have anything you wouldn't want found, any—papers, for instance, give them to me. I'll hide them here."

"Papers!" the girl blurted. "I—" She bit off the words. Good Lord! Why should he ask that now? Her mouth was suddenly dry. "I—I don't know what you're talking about." *How would he know that she carried any papers unless he had wrung the information from Bob?* "What do you mean?"

THERE WAS A subtle change in Kane's face. Through their slits his eyes were ablaze with a strange eagerness; the long lines from their corners to his strangely pointed chin had deepened. "Travers was bringing out the formulae for his new process. They weren't in the luggage in your car, and—" He checked himself, tried again. "And . . ."

"And he didn't have them on him!" Ann almost shrieked the accusation. "You've searched him! It *was* you that brought him in." She leaped at him, her hooked fingers clawing at his saturnine eyes. "What have you done with him?"

Kane's hidden hand leaped into view. In midspring Ann saw the whip in it, butt reversed. The wire-wound handle crashed across the side of her head, sent her down.

She sprawled, half-stunned, and Kane bent to her. His whip hand pinned her to the ground; the other was on her thighs, was scrabbling frantically over her body, was violating the privacy of her breasts. "Where are they?" he snarled. "Where are they?"

"Where you can't get them," Ann mouthed. "Murderer!"

His countenance now was utterly Satanic.

"You've hidden them, damn you," he spat. "You've hidden them."

"Yes." There was nothing left to her now but defiance. "Yes. I've hidden them where you'll never find them."

His hands gripped her shoulders, shook her, worried her as a terrier a rat. "Tell me where they are," he snarled. "Where are they?"

"I'll—never—tell," Ann said as he shook her. "You can—kill me—and I won't—tell."

"You'll tell!" Kane surged erect. The whip in his hand lashed up, swished above his head. "You'll tell." It whistled down, coiling, writhing like a thing alive.

Screaming, Ann rolled from under just as it pounded down on the spot where she had been. Dust spurted as the snapper at the lash's end dug dirt. Kane snarled once more and jerked his terrible weapon up again.

Terror exploded in Ann, blasted her to her feet in a lightning-swift splurge of effort that had its impetus from something other than her will. The snakelike lash whipped around her legs, seared from her a shriek of purest agony. It jerked, swept her footing from under her. The girl crashed down. The whip jerked free and curled above Kane's head for another blow. Savagely his arm arced down.

But the lash did not descend. It tautened, jerked the whip butt from Kane's hand. The button-like snapper had caught in some inequality of the dark roof. A bestial snarl spat from Kane's twisted mouth; he whirled savagely and snatched at the thong as it swung from some hidden fastening. It pendulumed, avoided his first rage-blinded grab. Ann writhed away into the darkness, pitched over the edge of a steep incline.

Somehow she was on her feet. An animal bellow from behind catapulted her into hurtling speed. Footsteps pounded behind her. The descent pitched steeply and now she was more falling than running. Her footing was no longer sliding sand. It was a flooring of small stones that rolled beneath her, that threw her suddenly sidewise.

One flailing arm struck a wall; she gathered herself for the crash of her body against it. That crash never came and she was really falling now. She pounded down on—on something alive that squealed, that slid out from under her and scuttered away in the darkness.

The rattling thump of pursuit pounded above her. Passed. Ann lay in pitch darkness, dazed by the shock of her fall, quivering from the stinging torment of the whip blows, shuddering with revulsion at the cold and clammy feel of that upon which she had thumped down, retching with terror at the prospect of Kane's return. He must soon realize that she had avoided him by tumbling into some side passage off the lightless tunnel. He would come back to seek her. And he would find her there helpless to escape his fury. She was done, completely exhausted. She could flee no further.

But his pounding footsteps kept on, faded into distance, into silence. Slow, timorous hope began to grow in the dizzy turmoil of the girl's mind, matured into certainty. Her blood ran a little more warmly; strength commenced to seep back, and the ability to think.

But thought brought despair blacker than the Stygian gloom in which she lay. Bob was dead, undoubtedly he was dead. Kane had only half lied when he had said he had found nothing alive at the wreck. He had *left* nothing alive! It was Bob's corpse that had slumped over the side of his flivver, Bob's corpse he had hidden somewhere here. Somewhere in this underground maze that must be the workings of the old mine. Somewhere . . .

A noise cut off thought. A tiny noise, sourceless, almost inaudible. A sensation of movement rather than of sound, of furtive movement paralyzingly near. There it was again! The flicker of a breath. A moan so low that only in the breathless hush of the underground could it have been heard.

The knowledge that she was not alone, that something alive was here in the dark with her, brought no fear to Ann. She was beyond fear. She was beyond emotion. With the conviction that her husband, her lover, was dead, she too seemed to have died. Only her body was left— her aching, torn body—and her senses. But something like a dull, dazed curiosity made her strain to locate that sound, made her wonder what it was that produced it.

The low moan came again, firmed into a word. A name! *Her* name! "Ann." And then, "Oh, Ann. I'm so sick. So sick."

"Bob!" The girl screamed into reverberating darkness. "Bob! Where are you? Oh, God! Where are you?"

CHAPTER SIX

THE CRAWLERS CLOSE IN

"Ann!" The voice was so weak, so terribly weak. "I thought—you would never—come back." There was no longer delirium in Bob's voice, but evidently he was unaware he was no longer beside the wreck in the desert.

Ann managed speech. "Where are you, Bob? It's so dark I can't see you." Then he didn't know what was happening. He didn't know that anything was happening. "Keep on calling."

Pangs of excruciating agony rewarded the girl's effort to turn, to get going toward him.

"Ann. Here I am." It didn't matter. Nothing mattered except that Bob was alive, that Bob was restored to her. "I'm here, Ann." She gritted her teeth, choked to silence a scream of anguish, twisted over on hands and knees. "Come to me, Ann."

"I'm coming, dear. I'm coming as fast as I can." There was nothing in her tone to betray the network of fiery pain that meshed her body. "But it's so dark I can't see you. Keep calling, Bob. . . ."

There was torture in Bob's accents, torment to match her own. "I've been calling for hours, Ann. Hours." Sharp stones across which she crept cut her knees. Her hands were sticky with the blood oozing from their gashed palms. "Why is it so dark, darling? Where are the stars?"

Ann's arm reached out for another torturous advance, rasped against vertical stone. An iron band constricted about her temples, and a sudden fear tightened her scalp. Her other hand found the rock-face. She squatted, felt wildly to left and right, groped above her head. Apprehension firmed to certainty. This was a wall, a wall of stone right across her path. But Bob's voice came from right ahead, from beyond that wall!

"Are you coming, Ann?" It sounded clearly, apparently unmuffled by anything intervening!

"Just a minute, dear. I'm resting." Bob was hurt, weakened by the awful fever that had swamped his mind in delirium. On no account must he be frightened. "I must rest, I'm awfully tired." It took indomitable courage, steel-nerved grit to keep out of her call the despair that knotted her stomach, the panic that twisted her breast.

Ann found projections in the rock-face before her, gripped them and dragged herself erect while all her maltreated body screamed protest. Leaning against the stone, she groped above her head, high as she could reach. The barrier was still there, the barrier from beyond which Bob's voice still sounded with uncanny clearness. "Ann!"

From the unholy dark that clamped almost tangible oppression around her, madness once more gibbered its mopping threat at the tormented girl. This wasn't real! It couldn't be real! Her ears told her that Bob was right here, right in front of her, so near that she had only to reach out a hand to touch him—but that reaching hand found only cold, damp, immovable stone.

But what was this? Her fingers, clawing sidewise, touched something cylindrical, greasy. A candle! Great God! A candle stuck in a niche. And a match next to it. A single match! Light!

Ann clutched the candle, the match. She was shaking, trembling as with an ague. By striking this match, by touching its flame to the wick of this candle, she would be able to see again. To see what it was that barred her way to Bob! But there was only one match. One only. And her hands were ripped, bleeding, numb with cold and weakness. . . .

THE UNIVERSE ITSELF stood by with bated breath as Ann licked a finger and held it up to discover if any draft wandered here to blow out the precious flame in the moment of its birth, as she felt with a quivering hand for a dry spot on the rock before her, as she placed the head of the match against one that she found and rubbed it slowly across the rough surface.

Phosphorus spluttered, flared. The girl's whole soul was in her eyes as she watched that tiny flare, as she watched the blue spark ignite the splinter of wood. Her heart missed a beat as the glow flickered, pounded wildly when it grew stronger again and became a robust flame she dared move the all-important inch to the charred fiber of the wick. And no detonation that meant the collapse of a city's wall ever fired a besieger's heart with greater exultation than the ignition of that candle-end did hers.

Light guttered, steadied, drove back darkness. It revealed a chamber hollowed out of rock by human hands, human tools. It showed, some ten feet high in the farther wall, the aperture through which she had tumbled into this artificial cavern. Below this, and to one side, the growing illumination fell across a great mound of burlap bags, some of which had burst to spill forth jagged fragments of ore. The burlap of which the bags were fashioned was new and fresh! How could that be when the mine had not been worked for decades?

"Ann! I can see your light." Bob's cry struck across the wild surmise springing to the girl's consciousness. "Ann!"

She turned. There was the rocky wall touch had told her about, unbroken. And always, as though he were right here in front of her, she could hear Bob. "Ann! You're almost here. What are you waiting for?"

It was nightmarish, fantastic. "Ann!" Then she saw where the voice was coming from. Above her, right above her, there was another break in the surface of the rock, an arched opening like the one through which she had so fortuitously entered, except that it was barely two feet high and not much more across. It gaped blackly at her, and the stone that edged it was slightly blacker for inches than the rest of the wall, and from it Bob's whimper came as though out of an old-fashioned speaking tube. "Please come to me, dear. Please hurry."

A speaking tube. That's what it was! A tube, the orifice of a small tunnel boring into rock! And somewhere within it, not far away, Bob lay, weak and sick, and in need of her! The thought sloughed exhaustion and pain from Ann like a discarded garment. She got a foot on an outjutting knob of rock, lifted, slid her candle into the hole she could just reach, got her fingers onto its edge and was scrambling, was lifting herself up that sheer rock-face. She had one knee up, another, was squirming into the narrow tunnel.

"Coming, Bob," she said. "I'm coming now." She had to snake through here on her stomach, for the roof of the passage was not high enough even for her to lift to hands and knees. But Bob was somewhere in there, and even had the tunnel been narrower still she would somehow have squeezed through.

The flickering luminance of the candle Ann pushed ahead of her showed damp-blackened stone, slimy, scummed over by the blanched small fungi of the regions where the sun never reaches. Stalactites ripped long gashes in her clothing, tore her skin. Ahead there was the scutter of the eyeless creatures of the dark. But here and there Ann saw the mark of a pickaxe, a tooled groove, and knew she was not the first human to crawl through this tight gallery, knew that it was man-formed, man-driven through the bowels of the earth, knew that it was the old mine through which she crept. But . . .

The ground slanted upward, beneath her, the tunnel opened out. "Ann!" Bob's face was suddenly before her, pallid, bloodless, Bob's body recumbent on the same auto cushions that so long ago—years, it seemed—she had dragged from the crumpled remains of their car.

"Bob! My dear! My dearest!" She had her arms around him, was kissing him. "My sweet."

His hand came up, feebly, stroked her face. "Ann! I've been dreaming—the most horrible . . . Good Lord! . . . Where is this? What place is this. I thought . . ."

"Don't think, Bob. Don't think. Things have happened, all kinds of things. But everything's all right now. I have you back and everything must be all right."

"But, Ann—Holy Jumping Jehosaphat— *what's that?*"

ANN TWISTED IN the direction of his startled gaze, saw across the low, irregularly circular chamber where they were the orifices of a number of such tunnels as that through which she had come, saw a clawed, skeleton hand writhe from one of them, an emaciated arm. And it was followed by a face!

The face looked at her, broke into a loathsome grin. That is, the livid gash that was its mouth widened to expose rotted, black teeth in a grimace that might have been intended for a grin. But there was no humor in the concave, grey countenance above it, no humor in the blank, imbecile eyes. There was only menace, lewd menace that brought back all the horror of that dreadful night and multiplied it a thousandfold.

Breath hissed from Bob's lips, close against her face, and Ann felt his body stiffen to the rigidity of terror. That same terror ran molten through her own frame. . . .

The Thing moved gruesomely, and a sound came from it, a chattering, mindless howl, hollow and horrible. It echoed— No! It was being repeated from the other openings into this low, flat chamber, and from them came the rustling dry rasp of fabric dragged along stone. Skeleton fingers clutched the edge of a second hole. . . .

Realization burst like black flame in Ann's skull. They were closing in! The loathsome crawlers were closing in on her and on Bob! *On Bob!*

Breath gusted from her throat in a shriek the more poignant because it was soundless. Ann threw herself over the prostrate form of her husband to blanket him, to shield him from the obscene menace closing inexorably in. Her hand struck the candle, struck the light from it. Blackness swept down, blanking out the monstrous faces peering in, blanking out the grotesque half-human masks and the reptilian, snaking arms that writhed out of the rock in a constricting circle of doom. But it did not quench the slithering noises of the crawlers' coming, their voiceless husked cries, the pungent, fetid odor of their foul bodies.

Bob's cheek against hers was icy cold. Ann hitched to cover him more completely, to cover him with her own quivering flesh from the Things that came slowly nearer, nearer. . . . Perhaps they would be satisfied with her. Perhaps possession of her would sate them. Perhaps she yet might save him from them.

It was feeling, not thought, that curdled in her brain with this last thread of hope, and reason gibbered to her how futile it was. They would take her, and they would take him, and there was utterly no hope for either.

Something touched her outstretched, bare arm, slithered gruesomely down its length. Ann's skin crawled to the bloodless, lusting touch. A fleshless hand fastened about her ankle. . . .

Rock grated, thunderously. The darkness paled suddenly to the color-drained spectral luminance of moonlight. For one reason-devastating moment Ann was aware of a grotesque, leprous mask thrust close against her face, of lecherous eyes in which hell-fire glowed. Then an enormous, batlike shadow fell across the twisted, prone form behind it, fell across her. Shrill, horrible sound burst like a tornado in the confined space—the piercing, weird ululation that had answered her cry for help and banished the crawlers when first she had glimpsed them. It crescendoed to its blasphemous apex of soul-shattering threat, held that topmost note till Ann knew that in another instant it would blast reason from her brain and leave her forever mad. . . .

Abruptly it ended. The nerve-racked girl was aware that the crawlers had pulled away, that they were writhing on ground-scraping bellies to their holes, that they were sliding into them like so many rats. Above her, someone chuckled.

Ann rolled, thanksgiving bursting in her heart, trembling on her lips, rolled over to see who it was that twice had saved her from the fearful threat of the crawlers. Who was this unknown unseen friend that alone in the weltering horror of Deadhope had aided her?

Gaunt, black and gigantic in the silting moonglow, Haldon Kane loomed above her. In his Luciferean countenance huge teeth showed, grinning with demonic triumph, and about that head of Satan his black whip whistled and writhed!

"You," Ann sobbed. "You!"

THE WHIP-LASH WRITHED down, flicked her chin, lifted again. The dextrous play of Kane's thin wrist kept it in hissing, ominous motion. "Of course," he snarled. "You didn't think you could get away from me, in this place whose every nook and cranny I know? After ten years one should be more familiar with even a maze like this than another who had known it for ten minutes."

"Ten years! But you haven't been here that long! Bob hired you only last week." Clutching at straws, Ann was trying to keep him in play, was desperately trying to stave off the final moment.

A mocking hideous laugh mingled with the whir of the whip. "Travers didn't lure me, I was here long ago, ever since it was deserted by fools who thought they must pay for labor to work it, who thought they must dig five times as much dirt as the thin vein occupied so that that labor might have a place to stand at its work . . . Who do you think I am?"

"You said—Haldon Kane, the—"

The circling whip-lash rippled in time to the chuckle that dripped from its wielder's mouth. "Kane is miles away from here, still running from the one sight I allowed him and his men of my pets. How do *you* like them?"

Ann shuddered, could not keep her eyes from the menace of the black thong snaking above her. "They—they're horrible . . ." she whimpered. "They—"

"They're not pretty, but useful. I don't have to pay them, you know, and their food costs little. They find it themselves. . . ."

"They find food—in this desert? How . . ." A gruesome speculation formed in Ann's mind, added a new horror to that which encompassed her, was answered by the grinning fiend.

"There were more of them when I brought them here. Many more. And it was not disease that killed them. Do you understand?" Hell itself quivered in his sardonic smile. "Queer," he mused. "How simply this State can be persuaded to farm out its convicts to anyone who will engage to board and clothe them. It saves the taxpayers money, you see, especially if the contractor engages also to guard them himself. And then—even guards are not necessary when a simple inoculation will make the prisoners amenable, very amenable to orders from one who has a brain. . . ."

His voice trailed away, leaving behind it a slimy smear of horror, then came again. "But they're hungry. My pets are hungry now." Again that slow, Satanic smile and the whip's hissing. "Shall I let them feed?" His slitted eyes flickered to Bob's pallid figure, came back to her and seemed to strip the clothes from her in one lewd glance. "In the presence of such juicy morsels I have already had quite a little difficulty restraining them."

Nausea retched bitterness into Ann's throat at the ultimate horror he implied. "No. Oh God, no!" she whimpered. "Kill us but don't let—" Terror choked her.

"Perhaps I may. Perhaps I may even let you— and Travers—live. . . . Your husband's formulae—what did you do with them?"

The man was no longer smiling, but his whip

seemed to chuckle as somehow he managed to evoke a rattling sound from the snapper at its end. The choice he offered was clear.

Ann's lips twitched. Gelid fingers clutched her throat. She contrived to squeeze out speech. "I'll show you. Promise to let us go and I'll show you."

"Get up, and take me to where you have hidden them." The whip stopped its eternal whir, floated down to his side, hung there, tense and ready. "Then, if you will sign this mine over to me I will—let you live."

"And Bob?"

"And your husband. I swear it."

Ann had to drag herself up by his leg, had to hold onto his arm, while the nausea of repugnance retched her, or she could not have remained standing. Her head came above the roof of the chamber, and she saw that the desert stretched, away from it, shimmering in the moonlight. Something like a trapdoor fashioned of rock lay to one side. When that was in place there would be no sign of what lay below.

"Come," the man who was not Kane said. "I don't know how long my pets can restrain themselves."

The skeleton town was to one side, silhouetted against a moon across whose face luminous clouds drifted. "Over there," Ann husked.

ANN STUMBLED OVER to the spot, with the man close behind her. Here were the beams in the form of an inverted cross, below them the other beneath which she had slid the envelope. Ann managed to stoop over, to slide her hand into the recess. . . .

A cold chill took her. There was nothing there! Oh God! The envelope was not there, the envelope that was to ransom Bob from horror!

"Well?"

She turned haunted, lifeless eyes to her tormentor. Her lips moved soundlessly.

He needed no words to understand. Livid fury leaped into his eyes. His lash surged up.

Ann shrank against the stripped framework of timber, horror staring from her twisted face.

"You've tricked me!" the man screamed. "You've dared to trick me!" The black thong spat at her, spat across her face. "I'll flay you alive."

Agony seared through to Ann's brain. Her body was a shell of ice enclosing agony, seething with terror. The whip hissed up, stopped.

"No. That's too good for you," the man squealed. "*They* shall have you!" His chest swelled, and an ululation burst from between his colorless, writhing lips—a sound somehow like the warning cry she had heard twice before, but somehow different, somehow more horrible.

They were coming! Past the quivering passion-shaken figure of the fiend she could see them squirming up out of the hole where Bob still was. Verminous grey shadows in the silver of the moon-bathed desert, spectral shadows of uttermost horror from a living grave, they were crawling loathesomely toward her.

"*Take her!*" their master shrieked. His long left hand jerked a pointing finger across his quivering body, his whip curled above his head, lashing air, hissing a song of doom. "Take her! Her flesh is sweet, her blood is warm."

They slithered along the sand, coming fast now, faster than ever before they had moved. Ann could see their drooling mouths now, their devastated faces, their mindless eyes in which glowed the fires of damnation. "*Take her!*" the maddened voice shrilled again, and grey talons writhed out, grey hands gripped the hem of her dress.

She held onto the splintered timbers behind her, she kicked out at them with her small feet. But they were dragging her down. They were dragging her down to their seething, foul mouths.

And most horrible of all was the silence with which they attacked her, and the spectral glow of the moon on their contorted forms, more horrible even than the crackling of the man's whip, and the shrillness of his mad voice as he screamed, "*Take her!*"

The grip of Ann's hands on the beams behind

her was torn away. She was on her knees. Twisting, she grabbed again at the shattered timbers, still frantically fighting, still desperately struggling against the inevitable horror that tore at her. A fanged tooth sank into her thigh, ripped. She jerked convulsively.

Above her there was a grinding crash! Light was blotted out. Cataclysmic sound burst all about her. Behind her there was a thunderous crash, a high-pitched scream of agony. Dust was in her nostrils, her eyes. It choked and blinded her. Coughing, spluttering, she flailed out frenzied arms, struck wood close on either side, wood above her.

Her knees, her legs were queerly wet. But hands no longer plucked at her, teeth no longer ripped her flesh. And there was no longer a shrill voice in her ears, keening, "Take her."

The dust settled. Upheld by shattered timbers, Ann moaned. Her brain cleared. Silvery light splotched shadow around her, and slowly she became aware that she was penned in a pyramidal space of shattered, jagged timbers, that beneath her the ground was soaked, muddy with blood, that behind her there were small whimperings, tiny noises of infinite suffering. The whimperings faded at last to silence. Her bewildered mind struggled with these things, and realization finally dawned on her. That last, hopeless grab of hers, that last frenzied clutch, somehow had seized upon the key beam of a precariously balanced heap of timbers. It had collapsed, and missing her, by some miracle had fallen upon and crushed the crawlers behind her, and their master. . . .

A miracle? Perhaps. And then again . . . *"Oh God!"* Ann sobbed. *"Oh God, I thank Thee."* Perhaps she was right. Perhaps He in whose sight no sparrow's fall is unnoted . . .

THE SUN MAY have warmed them to courage again, the men whom the crawlers had routed from Deadhope and sent careening away in marrow-melting fear. At any rate, it was they, bristling with automatics and borrowed rifles,

who returned, when that desert sun was already blazing high in the sky, to dig Ann out from under the blood-spattered beams, and fetch her again delirious husband from the strange pit where he lay. They carried them to the room prepared for them in the bunkhouse and aided them with rude surgery till a doctor and nurse could be summoned from Axton to take over the job.

But it was not till a week later that Ann came sufficiently out from the shadows to talk to Bob. "It's all like a horrible nightmare," she said. "I still don't understand what it was all about."

"We've pieced it together from what we've been able to find here, and the things he said to you, and what little was known about him." Travers' mouth was still lined with pain, his eyes somber. "The man's real name was Grandon Rolfe. He knew your Uncle Horvay in the old days, knew that his silver vein had petered out till it was unprofitable to work the mine.

"After Deadhope was abandoned he moved in. He got convicts from the prison camp at Pimento, got them out here and made imbeciles of them with an injection extracted from loco weed, that grows wild all through this desert. Then he worked the mine with them, starving them and whipping them into submission. With free labor, with no cost for equipment, it still could be made to pay. . . ."

"But why did they crawl like that?"

"Because to further save expense and time, he excavated only the narrow vein of silver ore and made them work on their bellies, like snakes crawling in their burrows, till they no longer were able to walk erect."

"Oh, horrible—"

"Not more horrible than some coal mines of which I know, in this country and abroad, where the miners work stooped over all day long, and tiny children are used for any task that requires quickness of movement. Greed inspires horrible things, my dear, and it is only in degree that Rolfe was worse than a great many highly-respected industrialists.

"However, he knew the jig was up when our

men came in. He stopped operations, covered over all signs of them, and pretending to be a friendly neighbor, wormed out of them the reason for their activity, my discovery of the new process. He made up his mind to get hold of that and—"

"And his twisted brain conceived the idea of using his crawling idiots to scare them away, and then to frighten the process out of us."

"Yes. It was only your bravery that defeated him, my dear."

"Not bravery, Bob. I was scared to death. But all your work, all your hopes would have been ruined." Then a new thought leaped to her brain, stinging her with anxiety. "Bob! The envelope. The papers with your formulae. They're gone!"

"No, dear. They had only slipped into a little hole farther back than you could reach. I have them." His hand reached across the space between their beds, found hers. An electric circuit seemed to close. Its current tingled between them, made them one. "I don't deserve you, Ann."

"Silly," Ann said dreamily. "Someday I shall go through worse things than that for you. . . ."

Bob's eyes shone. "You mean . . ."

"I think so— Oh Bob, I love you so much!"

TREADING THE MAZE
LISA TUTTLE

LISA TUTTLE (1952–) was born in Houston, Texas, and received her B.A. in English literature from Syracuse University. She has lived in the United Kingdom since 1980 and currently lives in Scotland with her husband. When still quite young, she joined the Turkey City Writer's Workshop in Austin, Texas, and was the cowinner of the John W. Campbell Award for Best New Writer in Science Fiction in 1974.

Her first novel, *Windhaven* (1981), was written with George R. R. Martin after they collaborated on a short story, "The Storms of Windhaven," which won a Hugo Award in 1975; she wrote a young adult fantasy novel illustrated by Una Woodruff (*Catwitch,* 1983) and coauthored a novel with Michael Johnson *(Angela's Rainbow,* 1983). She has written ten novels on her own, including *Familiar Spirit* (1983), *Gabriel* (1987), *Lost Futures* (1992), and *The Silver Bough* (2006).

In 1981, as the Guest of Honor at Microcon, she was awarded the Nebula for Best Short Story, but turned down the honor. In 1989, she won the British Science Fiction Association Award for short fiction, which she accepted. Outside the fantasy and horror genres, she wrote *Encyclopedia of Feminism* (1986).

"Treading the Maze" was originally published in the November 1981 issue of *The Magazine of Fantasy and Science Fiction.*

LISA TUTTLE

TREADING THE MAZE

WE HAD SEEN the bed and breakfast sign from the road, and although it was still daylight and there was no hurry to settle, we had liked the look of the large, well-kept house amid the farmlands, and the name on the sign: The Old Vicarage.

Phil parked the Mini on the curving gravel drive. "No need for you to get out," he said. "I'll just pop in and ask."

I got out anyway, just to stretch my legs and feel the warmth of the late, slanting sunrays on my bare arms. It was a beautiful afternoon. There was a smell of manure on the air, but it wasn't unpleasant, mingling with the other country smells. I walked towards the hedge which divided the garden from the fields beyond. There was a low stone wall along the drive, and I climbed onto it to look over the hedge and into the field.

There was a man standing there, all alone in the middle of the field. He was too far away for me to make out his features, but something about the sight of that still figure gave me a chill. I was suddenly afraid he would turn his head and see me watching him, and I clambered down hastily.

"Amy?" Phil was striding towards me, his long face alight. "It's a lovely room—come and see."

The room was upstairs, with a huge soft bed, an immense wooden wardrobe, and a big, deep-set window, which I cranked open. I stood looking out over the fields.

There was no sign of the man I had just seen, and I couldn't imagine where he had vanished to so quickly.

"Shall we plan to have dinner in Glastonbury?" Phil asked, combing his hair before the mirror inside the wardrobe door. "There should still be enough of the day left to see the Abbey."

I looked at the position of the sun in the sky. "And we can climb the tor tomorrow."

"*You* can climb the tor tomorrow morning. I've had about enough of all this climbing of ancient hills and monuments—Tintagel, St. Michael's Mount, Cadbury Castle, Silbury Hill—"

"We didn't climb Silbury Hill. Silbury Hill had a fence around it."

"And a good thing, too, or you'd have made me climb it." He came up behind me and hugged me fiercely.

I relaxed against him, feeling as if my bones were melting. Keeping my voice brisk, mock-scolding, I said, "I didn't complain about showing you all the wonders of America last year. So the least you can do now is return the favour with ancient wonders of Britain. I know you grew up with all this stuff, but I didn't. We don't have anything like Silbury Hill or Glastonbury Tor where I come from."

"If you did, if there was a Glastonbury Tor in America, they'd have a lift up the side of it," he said.

"Or at least a drive-through window."

We both began laughing helplessly.

I think of us standing there in that room, by

the open window, holding each other and laughing—I think of us standing there like that forever.

Dinner was a mixed grill in a Glastonbury café. Our stroll through the Abbey grounds took longer than we'd thought, and we were late, arriving at the café just as the proprietress was about to close up. Phil teased and charmed her into staying open and cooking for two last customers. Grey-haired, fat, and nearly toothless, she lingered by our table throughout our meal to continue her flirtation with Phil. He obliged, grinning and joking and flattering, but every time her back was turned, he winked at me or grabbed my leg beneath the table, making coherent conversation impossible on my part.

When we got back to the Old Vicarage, we were roped into having tea with the couple who ran the place and the other guests. That late in the summer there were only two others, an elderly couple from Belgium.

The electric fire was on and the lounge was much too warm. The heat made it seem even smaller than it was. I drank my sweet milky tea, stroked the old white dog who lay near my feet, and gazed admiringly at Phil, who kept up one end of a conversation about the weather, the countryside, and World War II.

Finally the last of the tea was consumed, the biscuit tin had made the rounds three times, and we could escape to the cool, empty sanctuary of our room. There we stripped off our clothes, climbed into the big soft bed, talked quietly of private things, and made love.

I hadn't been asleep long before I came awake, aware that I was alone in the bed. We hadn't bothered to draw the curtains, and the moonlight was enough to show me Phil was sitting on the wide window-ledge smoking a cigarette.

I sat up. "Can't you sleep?"

"Just my filthy habit." He waved the lit cigarette; I didn't see, but could imagine, the sheepish expression on his face. "I didn't want to disturb you."

He took one last, long drag and stubbed the cigarette out in an ashtray. He rose, and I saw that he was wearing his woollen pullover, which hung to his hips, just long enough for modesty, but leaving his long, skinny legs bare.

I giggled.

"What's that?"

"You without your trousers."

"That's right, make fun. Do I laugh at you when you wear a dress?"

He turned away towards the window, leaning forward to open it a little more. "It's a beautiful night . . . cor!" He straightened up in surprise.

"What?"

"Out there—people. I don't know what they're doing. They seem to be dancing, out in the field."

Half-suspecting a joke, despite the apparently genuine note of surprise in his voice, I got up and joined him at the window, wrapping my arms around myself against the cold. Looking out where he was gazing, I saw them. They were indisputably human figures—five, or perhaps six or seven, of them, all moving about in a shifting spiral, like some sort of children's game or country dance.

And then I saw it. It was like suddenly comprehending an optical illusion. One moment, bewilderment; but, the next, the pattern was clear.

"It's a maze," I said. "Look at it, it's marked out in the grass."

"A turf-maze," Phil said, wondering.

Among the people walking that ancient, ritual path, one suddenly paused and looked up, seemingly directly at us. In the pale moonlight and at that distance I couldn't tell if it was a man or a woman. It was just a dark figure with a pale face turned up towards us.

I remembered then that I had seen someone standing in that very field, perhaps in that same spot, earlier in the day, and I shivered. Phil put his arm around me and drew me close.

"What are they doing?" I asked.

"There are remnants of traditions about dancing or running through mazes all over the country," Phil said. "Most of the old turf-mazes have vanished—people stopped keeping them up before this century. They're called troy-towns, or mizmazes . . . no one knows when or why they began, or if treading the maze was game or ritual, or what the purpose was."

Another figure now paused beside the one who stood still, and laid hold of that one's arm, and seemed to say something. And then the two figures fell back into the slow circular dance.

"I'm cold," I said. I was shivering uncontrollably, although it was not with any physical chill. I gave up the comfort of Phil's arm and ran for the bed.

"They might be witches," Phil said. "Hippies from Glastonbury, trying to revive an old custom. Glastonbury does attract some odd types."

I had burrowed under the bedclothes, only the top part of my face left uncovered, and was waiting for my teeth to stop chattering and for the warmth to penetrate my muscles.

"I could go out and ask them who they are," Phil said. His voice sounded odd. "I'd like to know who they are. I feel as if I *should* know."

I stared at his back, alarmed. "Phil, you're not going out there!"

"Why not? This isn't New York City. I'd be perfectly safe."

I sat up, letting the covers fall. "Phil, don't."

He turned away from the window to face me. "What's the matter?"

I couldn't speak.

"Amy . . . you're not crying?" His voice was puzzled and gentle. He came to the bed and held me.

"Don't leave me," I whispered against the rough weave of his sweater.

"Course I won't," he said, stroking my hair and kissing me. "Course I won't."

But of course he did, less than two months later, in a way neither of us could have guessed then. But even then, watching the dancers in the maze, even then he was dying.

In the morning, as we were settling our bill, Phil mentioned the people we had seen dancing in the field during the night. The landlord was flatly disbelieving.

"Sure you weren't dreaming?"

"Quite sure," said Phil. "I wondered if it was some local custom . . ."

He snorted. "Some custom! Dancing around a field in the dead of night!"

"There's a turf-maze out there," Phil began.

But the man was shaking his head. "No, not in that field. Not a maze!"

Phil was patient. "I don't mean one with hedges, like in Hampton Court. Just a turf-maze, a pattern made in the soil years ago. It's hardly noticeable now, although it can't have been too many years since it was allowed to grow back. I've seen them other places and read about them, and in the past there were local customs of running the maze, or dancing through it, or playing games. I thought some such custom might have been revived locally."

The man shrugged. "I wouldn't know about that," he said. We had learned the night before that the man and his wife were "foreigners," having only settled here, from the north of England, some twenty years before. Obviously, he wasn't going to be much help with information on local traditions.

After we had loaded our bags into the car, Phil hesitated, looking towards the hedge. "I'd quite like to have a look at that maze close-to," he said.

My heart sank, but I could think of no rational reason to stop him. Feebly I tried, "We shouldn't trespass on somebody else's property . . ."

"Walking across a field isn't trespassing!" He began to walk along the hedge, towards the road. Because I didn't want him to go alone, I hurried after. There was a gate a few yards along the road by which we entered the field. But once there, I wondered how we would find the maze. Without an overview such as our window had provided, the high grass looked all the same, and from this level, in ordinary daylight, slight alterations in ground level wouldn't be obvious to the eye.

Phil looked back at the house, getting in alignment with the window, then turned and looked across the field, his eyes narrowed as he tried to calculate distance. Then he began walking slowly, looking down often at the ground. I hung back, following him at a distance and not myself looking for the maze. I didn't want to find it. Although I couldn't have explained my reaction, the maze frightened me, and I wanted to be away, back on the road again, alone together in the little car, eating apples, gazing at the passing scenery, talking.

"Ah!"

I stopped still at Phil's triumphant cry and watched as he hopped from one foot to the other. One foot was clearly on higher ground. He began to walk in a curious, up-down fashion. "I think this is it," he called. "I think I've found it. If the land continues to dip . . . yes, yes, this is it!" He stopped walking and looked back at me, beaming.

"Great," I said.

"The grass has grown back where once it was kept cleared, but you can still feel the place where the swathe was cut," he said, rocking back and forth to demonstrate the confines of the shallow ditch. "Come and see."

"I'll take your word for it," I said.

He cocked his head. "I thought you'd be interested. I thought something like this would be right up your alley. The funny folkways of the ancient Brits."

I shrugged, unable to explain my unease.

"We've plenty of time, love," he said. "I promise we'll climb Glastonbury Tor before we push on. But we're here now, and I'd like to get the feel of this." He stretched his hand towards me. "Come tread the maze with me."

It would have been so easy to take his hand and do just that. But overriding my desire to be with him, to take this as just another lark, was the fearful, wordless conviction that there was danger here. And if I refused to join him, perhaps he would give up the idea and come away with me. He might sulk in the car, but he would get over it, and at least we would be away.

"Let's go now," I said, my arms stiff at my sides.

Displeasure clouded his face, and he turned away from me with a shrug. "Give me just a minute, then," he said. And as I watched, he began to tread the maze.

He didn't attempt that curious, skipping dance we had seen the others do the night before; he simply walked, and none too quickly, with a careful, measured step. He didn't look at me as he walked, although the pattern of the maze brought him circling around again and again to face in my direction—he kept his gaze on the ground. I felt, as I watched, that he was being drawn further away from me with every step. I wrapped my arms around myself and told myself not to be a fool. I could feel the little hairs standing up all along my arms and back, and I had to fight the urge to break and run like hell. I felt, too, as if someone watched us, but when I looked around, the field was as empty as ever.

Phil had stopped, and I assumed he had reached the centre. He stood very still and gazed off into the distance, his profile towards me. I remembered the man I had seen standing in the field—perhaps in that very spot, the centre of the maze—when we had first arrived at the Old Vicarage.

Then, breaking the spell, Phil came bounding towards me, cutting across the path of the maze, and caught me in a bear hug. "Not mad?"

I relaxed a little. It was over, and all was well. I managed a small laugh. "No, of course not."

"Good. Let's go, then. Phil's had his little treat."

We walked arm in arm back towards the road. We didn't mention it again.

IN THE MONTHS to come those golden days, the two weeks we had spent wandering around southwest England, often came to mind. Those thoughts were an antidote to more recent memories: to those last days in the hospital, with Phil in pain, and then Phil dead.

I moved back to the States—it was home, after all, where my family and most of my friends lived. I had lived in England for less than two years, and without Phil there was little reason to stay. I found an apartment in the neighbourhood where I had lived just after college, and got a job teaching, and, although painfully and rustily, began to go through the motions of making a new life for myself. I didn't stop missing Phil, and the pain grew no less with the passage of time, but I adjusted to it. I was coping.

In the spring of my second year alone I began to think of going back to England. In June I went for a vacation, planning to spend a week in London, a few days in Cambridge with Phil's sister, and a few days visiting friends in St. Ives. When I left London in a rented car and headed for St. Ives, I did not plan to retrace the well-remembered route of that last vacation, but that is what I found myself doing, with each town and village a bittersweet experience, recalling pleasant memories and prodding the deep sadness in me wider awake.

I lingered in Glastonbury, wandering the peaceful Abbey ruins and remembering Phil's funny, disrespectful remarks about the sacred throne and King Arthur's bones. I looked for, but could not find, the café where we'd had dinner, and settled for fish and chips. Driving out of Glastonbury with the sun setting, I came upon the Old Vicarage and pulled into that familiar drive. There were more cars there, and the house was almost full up this time. There was a room available, but not the one I had hoped for. Although a part of me, steeped in sadness, was beginning to regret this obsessional pilgrimage, another part of me longed for the same room, the same bed, the same view from the window, in order to conjure Phil's ghost. Instead, I was given a much smaller room on the other side of the house.

I retired early, skipping tea with the other guests, but sleep would not come. When I closed my eyes I could see Phil, sitting on the window ledge with a cigarette in one hand, narrowing his eyes to look at me through the smoke. But when I opened my eyes it was the wrong room, with a window too small to sit in, a room Phil had never seen. The narrowness of the bed made it impossible to imagine that he slept beside me still. I wished I had gone straight to St. Ives instead of dawdling and stopping along the way—this was pure torture. I couldn't recapture the past—every moment that I spent here reminded me of how utterly Phil was gone.

Finally I got up and pulled on a sweater and a pair of jeans. The moon was full, lighting the night, but my watch had stopped and I had no idea what time it was. The big old house was silent. I left by the front door, hoping that no one would come along after me to relock the door. A walk in the fresh air might tire me enough to let me sleep, I thought.

I walked along the gravel drive, past all the parked cars, towards the road, and entered the next field by the same gate that Phil and I had used in daylight in another lifetime. I scarcely thought of where I was going, or why, as I made my way to the turf-maze which had fascinated Phil and frightened me. More than once I had regretted not taking Phil's hand and treading the maze with him when he had asked. Not that it would have made any difference in the long run, but all the less-than-perfect moments of our time together had returned to haunt me and given rise to regrets since Phil's death—all the opportunities missed, now gone forever; all the things I should have said or done or done differently.

There was someone standing in the field. I stopped short, staring, my heart pounding. Someone standing there, where the centre of the maze must be. He was turned away, and I could not tell who he was, but something about the way he stood made me certain that I had seen him before, that I knew him.

I ran forward and—I must have blinked—suddenly the figure was gone again, if he had ever existed. The moonlight was deceptive, and the tall grass swaying in the wind, and the swiftly moving clouds overhead cast strange shadows.

"Come tread the maze with me."

Had I heard those words, or merely remembered them?

I looked down at my feet and then around, confused. Was I standing in the maze already? I took a tentative step forward and back, and it did seem that I was standing in a shallow depression. The memory flooded back: Phil standing in the sunlit field, rocking back and forth and saying, "I think this is it." The open, intense look on his face.

"Phil," I whispered, my eyes filling with tears.

Through the tears I saw some motion, but when I blinked them away, again there was nothing. I looked around the dark, empty field, and began to walk the path laid out long before. I did not walk as slowly as Phil had done, but more quickly, almost skipping, hitting the sides of the maze path with my feet to be certain of keeping to it, since I could not see it.

And as I walked, it seemed to me that I was not alone, that people were moving ahead of me, somehow just out of my sight (beyond another turn in the winding path I might catch them up), or behind. I could hear their footsteps. The thought that others were behind me, following me, unnerved me, and I stopped and turned around to look. I saw no one, but I was now facing in the direction of the Old Vicarage, and my gaze went on to the house. I could see the upper window, the very window where Phil and I had stood together looking out, the point from which we had seen the dancers in the maze.

The curtains were not drawn across that dark square of glass this night, either. And as I watched, a figure appeared at the window. A tall shape, a pale face looking out. And after a moment, as I still stared, confused, a second figure joined the first. Someone smaller—a woman. The man put his arm around her. I could see—perhaps I shouldn't have been able to see this at such a distance, with no light on in the room—but I could see that the man was wearing a sweater, and the woman was naked. And I could see the man's face. It was Phil. And the woman was me.

There we were. Still together, still safe from what time would bring. I could almost feel the chill that had shaken me then, and the comfort of Phil's protecting arm. And yet I was not

there. Not now. Now I was out in the field, alone, a premonition to my earlier self.

I felt someone come up beside me. Something as thin and light and hard as a bird's claw took hold of my arm. Slowly I turned away from the window and turned to see who held me. A young man was standing beside me, smiling at me. I thought I recognized him.

"He's waiting for you at the centre," he said. "You mustn't stop now."

Into my mind came a vivid picture of Phil in daylight, standing still in the centre of the maze, caught there by something, standing there forever. Time was not the same in the maze, and Phil could still be standing where he had once stood. I could be with him again, for a moment or forever.

I resumed the weaving, skipping steps of the dance with my new companion. I was eager now, impatient to reach the centre. Ahead of me I could see other figures, dim and shifting as the moonlight, winking in and out of view as they trod the maze on other nights, in other centuries.

The view from the corner of my eyes was more disturbing. I caught fleeting glimpses of my partner in this dance, and he did not look the same as when I had seen him face to face. He had looked so young, and yet the light, hard grasp on my arm did not seem that of a young man's hand.

A hand like a bird's claw . . .

My eyes glanced down my side to my arm. The hand lying lightly on my solid flesh was nothing but bones, the flesh all rotted and dropped away years before. Those peripheral, sideways glimpses I'd had of my dancing partner were the truth—sights of something long dead and yet still animate.

I stopped short and pulled my arm away from that horror. I closed my eyes, afraid to turn to face it. I heard the rustle and clatter of dry bones. I felt a cold wind against my face and smelled something rotten. A voice—it might have been Phil's—whispered my name in sorrow and fear.

What waited for me at the centre? And what

would I become, and for how long would I be trapped in this monotonous dance if ever I reached the end?

I turned around blindly, seeking the way out. I opened my eyes and began to move, then checked myself—some strong, instinctual aversion kept me from cutting across the maze paths and leaping them as if they were only so many shallow, meaningless furrows. Instead, I turned around (I glimpsed pale figures watching me, flickering in my peripheral vision) and began to run back the way I had come, following the course of the maze backwards, away from the centre, back out into the world alone.

RED ANGELS

KAREN HABER

THE MULTIFACETED KAREN HABER (1955–) works in numerous areas within the science fiction and fantasy genres. She is the author of nine novels, including *Thieves' Carnival* (1990), the four-volume Fire in Winter series (*The Mutant Season*, 1989, written in collaboration with her husband, noted science fiction author Robert Silverberg; *The Mutant Prime*, 1990; *Mutant Star*, 1992; and *Mutant Legacy*, 1992), which chronicles the struggle between mutants and humans for the fate of Earth; *Bless the Beasts* (1996) in the Star Trek Voyager series; the War Minstrels trilogy (*Woman Without a Shadow*, 1995, *The War Minstrels*, 1995, and *Sister Blood*, 1996), about an underground mining colony on the planet Styx; and *Crossing Infinity* (2005), a young adult novel. She has also produced nearly twenty short stories for such magazines as *The Magazine of Fantasy and Science Fiction* and *Asimov's Science Fiction Magazine*, as well as anthologies.

Among Haber's most important nonfiction work as a writer and editor are as a reviewer of art books for *Locus;* a writer of artists' profiles for *Realms of Fantasy;* editor of *Kong Unbound* (2005), a collection of essays about various views and elements of the significance of King Kong as a cultural icon; and editor or coeditor of numerous anthologies, including four years of *Fantasy: The Best of (2001–2004)* and three years of *Science Fiction: The Best of (2003–2005)*. She was nominated for a Hugo Award for editing *Meditations on Middle Earth* (2001), an essay collection celebrating the life and work of J. R. R. Tolkien.

"Red Angels" was first published in *The Ultimate Zombie*, edited by Byron Preiss and John Betancourt (New York: Dell, 1993).

KAREN HABER

RED ANGELS

THE DRUMS.

They were the first thing David Weber heard—felt, really, a steady pulsing beat—as he stepped from the gleaming seaplane onto Port-au-Prince's sunny Bowen Field.

"Passports, please, passports." The immigration agent chanted his mantra in lilting French-accented English.

Weber stepped up to the sagging metal table and stared beyond it at the murals decorating the walls, scenes of local frolic and revelry. Probably Philome Obin's work or Castera Bazile's, Weber thought, and his heart beat faster. Hadn't he come to Haiti to buy the best native artwork he could find for his gallery? If it was right here in the customs shed then it was probably all over the island, his just for the asking. The drums

beat behind him, through his pale skin, and right into his blood—boombadaboombadaboom.

"USA?" The agent had a dark, genial face. His smile was ragged, with crooked incisors.

"Yes."

"Welcome. Not many Americans come here anymore. Purpose of your visit?"

"Business."

"Really?" The man looked at him in surprise. "Perhaps you're a trade inspector from Miami? Looking for smugglers?" He chuckled and Weber forced a smile.

"How'd you guess?" he said. "My cover story is that I'm a gallery owner from Los Angeles looking for art. For Ti Malice, the famous Haitian artist."

The man gave him a sly, knowing glance.

Weber's hopes leaped high: perhaps he would get his first lead here, right now.

"Ti Malice?"

Weber nodded eagerly.

"Ti Malice. Heeheehee." The immigration agent bent double with laughter. "Ti Malice. Ti Malice. Hoohoohoo. You really came here to find him?"

"Yeah. To find him and buy paintings from him."

The passport-control agent laughed yet again, a quick mocking snort this time.

Weber began to get annoyed. He shuffled his feet and wondered just what was so funny. Should he ask? He hated being laughed at.

"Ti Malice won't want to do business with you, my friend. Trust me."

The drums were getting louder now.

"We'll see." Weber shrugged. "Maybe he will, and maybe he won't. What's that drumming? Some voodoo thing?" He tried to sound casual, but deep inside he trembled at the thought of actual voodoo rites taking place nearby. Grainy images from ancient movies floated to his mind. He pushed them aside.

The official was stiff now, even a bit contemptuous. "That's not vodou. There's a festival, a combite, someplace. Probably the hill farmers are building a barn up there."

"But the drums—"

"It helps them to work. They sing." The agent stamped his passport and handed it back without looking at him. "Next."

Weber stumbled out into the bright sunshine, dragging his suitcase. He was just trying to make a living but it certainly brought him to some odd places, he thought. Now here he was in the nutty world of voodoo drums, witch doctors, and zombies. It was funny, really, where a guy with a master's degree in fine arts from UCLA could find himself.

Suddenly, a small, wiry man was at his side.

"Taxi?"

"Uh, yeah."

"Hotel Jolly?"

"No. Hotel L'Ouverture."

"You're not Swiss?" The driver seemed surprised.

"No."

"German, then."

"Guess again."

"But the blond hair, the blue eyes—all Swiss and Germans stay at the Jolly."

"I'm American."

"Oh. Good. Big tippers, Americans." The driver chuckled deep in his throat. "Not many of you here now."

"So I've heard."

The car was an old gray Ford daubed with pinkish primer paint, sagging on its rusting suspension. It bounced as the driver stowed his bags in the yawning trunk, and again when Weber climbed into the back. The seat was black vinyl patched by red and gray tape whose edges had curled in the heat. He pitched and slid across it as the driver took off.

Weber grabbed the door handle and braced himself as the cab made the first of several sharp turns away from the empty fields of the airport and into the winding maze of Port-au-Prince's potholed streets. After the third near-collision, Weber leaned over the front seat and tapped the cabbie on the shoulder. "Can't you drive any slower?"

The man barely glanced at him. "You don't want me to go fast? Americans always do. Americans and Japanese, forever in a rush, in a big hurry."

Weber felt a warning tingle of suspicion: his biggest rival for collectors was an aggressive gallery owner in Tokyo, Hideo Tashamaki. "Japanese? Here? What do they come here for?"

"The puffer fish. And whores." The cabbie giggled.

Whores. That was the last thing Weber wanted here. He settled against his seat-back in silence and wondered why anyone would risk his life eating poisonous fish or screwing diseased prostitutes.

With a squeal of tires and brakes, the cab stopped in front of a six-story wooden building. The upper three floors sported balconies with graceful wrought-iron supports. From the lowest balcony hung a sign in faded gilt that read: "Hotel L'Ouverture."

A statue of the Haitian revolutionary Toussaint L'Ouverture stood nearby the porte-cochère. It was green with age, surrounded by a circle of dead brown grass. White and gray pigeons roosted on L'Ouverture's tricornered hat, on his outstretched hand, and along the eaves of the hotel that bore his name.

Weber stood on the stained front steps holding his suit bag as the taxi roared off. No bellboys swept him up in a welcoming bustle. Well, what did you expect? Weber thought. He elbowed his way past the stiff paint-flecked double door into the dim, cool lobby. His footsteps echoed. A clerk sat behind the wide mahogany desk, head propped on his hand, reading a creased and tattered comic book. He didn't look up until Weber had put his bag down across the top of the desk. His expression was mildly hostile but mostly sleepy.

"I have a reservation," Weber said.

The clerk didn't budge. "The room isn't ready."

"When will it be ready?"

"I don't know. The maid didn't come in today."

Weber looked around the lobby. Empty, dark, and quiet. "Oh, come on. Do you mean the entire hotel is full? It doesn't seem that way to me."

The clerk shrugged and gazed wistfully at his comic book.

Weber sighed, pulled out his wallet, and carefully removed a five-dollar bill which he ostentatiously slapped into his passport. "Here, you might want to see this."

The clerk perked right up. He took the passport, nodded, and opened the guestbook. "Lucky for you we've had a cancellation. Room 37. This way."

Room 37 had obviously not been occupied in some time. The air was hot and musty, and a thin layer of dust coated the dresser and the old-fashioned black phone on the nightstand.

The clerk lingered in the doorway. Obviously, this was even more entertaining than his comic book. Weber slung his bag onto the sagging bed, and the bedsprings groaned rustily. He brushed off the phone, picked up the receiver, and, after checking a card in his pocket, dialed the number of Jean Saint-Mery, a local art dealer who had been highly recommended.

The gallery number was busy. Weber double-checked the card and dialed again. Still busy.

"Damn," he said. "Is there a phone book here?"

"No," said the clerk. "Sorry."

Weber forced himself to smile. After all, hadn't he been warned by more than one friend in the business not to have any expectations? Well, perhaps he'd have better luck with Mrs. Dewey—the old woman who was said to have a terrific collection of Haitian art. "Do you know where I can find the Dewey house?"

"The art teacher's widow?"

"That's right."

"Go to Rue Macajoux and, when it narrows, take the first alley on the right. Fifth house."

"Is it far?"

"You can walk."

Following the scrawled map the clerk gave him, Weber walked across the street from the hotel, made a right, a left, and found himself on a bustling street crisscrossed overhead with a web of electrical wires. Bicycles and cars fought for space on the narrow pavement, and the pedestrians outnumbered both, swarming in the hot sunlight in their brightly colored clothing. Tattered baskets of laundry and vegetables were balanced upon their heads like huge inverted hats.

The air was thick with humidity. Weber's shirt began to stick to his back and arms. He dodged an orange-and-yellow-striped bus, swearing. Why hadn't he taken a taxi, he wondered, or hired a guide? There had to be an easier way to reach Mrs. Dewey and her potential gold mine.

Alex Dewey's widow was in her eighties and blind, but reports tagged her as sharper than many sighted people half her age. Her husband had helped to popularize Haitian folk art and the family collection was rumored to be worth millions. If Weber couldn't charm Mrs. Dewey into releasing some of her stock, at the very least he would make her acquaintance. And maybe, just maybe, she could put him on the trail of a few artists—including Ti Malice.

Finally, after much doubling back, he found the alley and the house. It was a dilapidated two-story wooden structure with a sagging balcony, its silvered walls spotted with age. The paint, where it still showed on the door and window shutters, was a faded ghostly red. In the Caribbean manner, Weber stood outside and clapped his hands sharply three times. When there was no response, he repeated the action. On his third attempt, a shutter on the first floor cranked open and a woman with a guarded, sleepy expression peered out at him.

"Is Mrs. Dewey in?"

"She's not seeing anybody."

"I've come all the way from Los Angeles."

The woman shrugged and made as if to shut the window.

"Please," Weber called. "Tell her Roland Gunther sent me."

The woman paused, stared at him wordlessly, and retreated into the house. Weber could hear voices, but could not make out what they were saying or in what language they spoke.

Weber felt the sweat trickle slowly down his back in a maddening itch. Would he stand out here all day, melting? Suddenly he heard the sound of footsteps. Then the front door shuddered as a bolt was thrown back. The sullen maid stood blinking in the sunlight. "She says okay."

The floorboards creaked under Weber's weight. He was surprised to see that the house was lit by candles and hurricane lamps. A fire seemed imminent. As they made their way down a narrow corridor, Weber asked, "Isn't there any electricity?"

The maid said nothing, merely gestured for him to enter a doorway at his right.

He stooped to avoid the low lintel and emerged in a broad, dim room. By the window sat a small figure enthroned upon a wide wooden chair. Her feet dangled above the floor, and she stared at him fixedly.

"Did I hear you ask about the electricity?" she said. "I only use it in the kitchen. Otherwise, I certainly don't need it." The voice was firm and crisp, with a distinct upper-class English accent.

"Given that argument," said Weber, "why bother using candles, either?"

"For Sarah, here." There was amusement in Mrs. Dewey's voice, mild but unmistakable. "Besides, it's cheaper than the electricity. More reliable, too." She smiled and held out her hand. "If Roland sent you then you must be worth talking to. Roland hardly ever sends anybody."

Weber grasped her tiny hand. It felt dry and papery, as though it would crumble in his grip. "It took me a long time to win his trust," he said.

"I'm sure." Again, the smile in the voice. "Sarah, bring more light for Mr.—what is your name?"

"Weber. David Weber."

"Sarah, bring more light for Mr. Weber. And some lemonade."

"No lemons," the maid said.

"Then cold water." Mrs. Dewey paused. "Or would you prefer sugar water?"

"Plain would be fine, if it's safe." Weber stared at her in fascination. No one in L.A. would believe him when he described this dark place and the old crone who lived here.

"Bottled, of course," she said. "Oh, I can tolerate the local stuff. But you'd be doubled over with stomach cramps in fifteen minutes." She chuckled, a deep witchy sound, and gestured toward a straight-backed chair. "Sit down, Mr. Weber. Make yourself as comfortable as possible."

He sat down carefully on an old easy chair and heard the stiff leather upholstery creak. A maddening tickle on the back of his neck made him jump—some tropical insect? He swatted at it in a panic, but his hand came away clean and empty.

Sarah returned with a chilled bottle, two glasses, and a hurricane lantern. Weber decided that she had memorized the location of everything in the room—otherwise, how could she avoid bumping into things in the near-darkness? With practiced skill she set the lantern upon a small table and lit the wick.

Weber gasped.

The room had come to life around him. Every wall was covered with paintings of lively figures rendered in vigorous brushstrokes. The chamber that he had taken for some dark, enclosed snuggery was a high-ceilinged cathedral, a chapel of Haitian art. Red-cloaked angels danced in a royal blue sky while, below, men and women arrayed in rainbow colors gamboled in fields of gold and green.

"I see you've noticed the paintings," said Mrs. Dewey.

"Hard to miss, once you've got a little light in here."

"I miss them constantly."

Weber felt his cheeks heating with embarrassment and anger. Why was the old woman still harping upon her disability? Did she want to throw him off balance? "Have you been blind a long time?" he asked.

"Thirty years. I've only had the glass eyes for five. The new doctor insisted. Said the old ones were rotting because of diminished blood supply."

Glass eyes. No wonder she stared. Despite Mrs. Dewey's matter-of-fact attitude, Weber shuddered. "If you can't see the paintings any longer, how can you bear to keep them around?"

She leaned back against her throne, obviously amused. "You must want these paintings very badly."

Weber took a deep breath. "I'm here to buy paintings for my gallery," he said. "That's why I came to Haiti."

"You're not the first art dealer to come calling."

"You must love these paintings very much."

Mrs. Dewey tapped her skeletal fingers against a padded armrest. "On the contrary, I don't give a bloody damn about them." She grinned. Her teeth looked too large, like white tombstones crowding her mouth.

"What?"

"It's true. It was always Alex, my husband, who was completely obsessed by the art. Mad for it. I tolerated his whims because, well, one must in a marriage, yes?"

"I wouldn't know. I'm single."

"Well, I suppose there is less baggage that way," Mrs. Dewey said. "But less comfort as well."

The art dealer stirred restlessly. "Ma'am, I'm having trouble understanding you. If you don't actually care about these works, then why keep them? Why didn't you sell them to the first gallery owner who looked you up? There's a fortune in artwork here. You could be living in London like a queen."

"Hate the climate. Absolutely hate it. At its best, English weather is fair to poor."

"The Riviera, then."

"The local snobs there would find my Haitian French hilarious. And I'm too old to learn Italian."

"California?"

She sniffed disdainfully. "The culture, my dear."

"You know what I'm saying."

"Yes, of course. But it's such fun to play with you and it's been so very long since I've had a playmate. Forgive me. The reason I didn't—and won't—sell the paintings is simple. There's a curse on them."

"I beg your pardon?" Weber felt as though he had been punched in the stomach.

"A vodou curse. If I sell them, I'll die."

At the mention of the word voodoo, his hands and feet had turned to ice. They all take this stuff so seriously, he thought.

"You must be joking." He told himself she was deranged, floating in and out of lucidity the way old folks sometimes did.

"I know that it must seem absurd to someone from Los Angeles to whom freeways and electricity and budget deficits are normal and expected. But I assure you that here, in Haiti, vodou is very much alive and very much something to be respected and even feared."

Weber played along, pretending to be cynical and amused. "Well, who cursed the paintings?"

"The artist."

"The artist?" Weber said. "Why in the world . . . ?"

"He was also a vodou priest. Somehow he got the impression that my husband had cheated him and paid more for some other artist's work. It wasn't true, of course, but nothing could be done. Once we had the paintings, we were forced to keep them. Alex defied the curse and sold two paintings to a wealthy Frenchman on vacation. A week later the buyer was dead. Drowned off his yacht."

"An accident. A tragic coincidence."

"Two weeks later, Alex died."

"But I'd heard he had chronic heart problems. That his death was natural."

"The reports were in error. I begged him to wear the *ouanga* I'd had made—the countercharm—but he just laughed."

Weber stared at her inscrutable raisin face in disbelief. "Are you certain that you're not reading too much into this? I don't know much about voodoo, but I didn't think that curses could be placed upon inanimate objects." At least I hope not, he thought.

"I assure you, Mr. Weber, that vodou is a religion that can be used for most anything." Mrs. Dewey's voice grew sharp with impatience. "I've had almost a decade to consider this and nothing has changed my mind yet." She plunged her hand down the front of her dress, fished around for a moment, and brought forth a rawhide pouch tied to a leather cord. From the stained look of it, Mrs. Dewey had worn it for a long, long time. "This is my *ouanga*. It keeps me safe. It was made by the top *papaloi*, and I wear it everywhere."

Weber stared at the ugly little bag. After a moment he decided not to pursue the subject. This talk of charms and death was all bullshit

anyway. Maybe the tropical sun drove everybody crazy down here.

"You won't sell me your paintings, then."

"No."

"Will you at least help me locate some of the local artists?"

"You mean to say that you actually like the work?"

"Of course," he said. "The gaiety, the colors, the freedom from convention. It's joyful, a celebration of life." He didn't bother to add that his clients, most of whom couldn't tell kindergarten finger-paintings from Renaissance masterworks, would buy whatever was the latest, hottest item. And Caribbean art was hot, hot, hot.

"*Now* you do sound like a dealer. And a collector. Who are you looking for?"

"Ti Malice, for starters."

Mrs. Dewey's hands flew to the charmed bag around her neck. "But he was the very artist whose curse killed my husband! Please, Mr. Weber, stay away from him. You don't want Ti Malice. Really, you don't."

"I'm not afraid."

"You should be."

Despite the heat, Weber felt strangely chilled. He stood up to get the blood moving in his veins.

"Ma'am, if you won't tell me where he is, would you please be so kind as to direct me to someone who will? Or at least to some of the other artists."

"There are several artists whose work you should see. But please, stay away from Ti Malice."

Her instructions were thorough. Weber made several notes, thanked her copiously, and left.

He was halfway down the street when he heard a hissing sound and looked down, thinking: snakes?

But the sound had come from behind him. Someone tugged the back of his sweaty shirt. He spun around, heart pounding, to meet the insolent stare of Mrs. Dewey's maid, Sarah.

"I can help you, blanc."

Her voice was flat, studiedly uninterested.

But she had followed him and Weber suspected that her insolence masked some inner urgency.

"What do you mean?"

"You want to find Ti Malice? I can take you to him."

"You can?" Weber stared at her suspiciously. "For how much?"

"Fifty."

"Are you out of your mind? I'll pay you ten."

"Twenty."

"Fifteen."

Sarah nodded, satisfied. "Meet me by the fountain in the main plaza of Rue St. Raphael, tonight. At sunset."

"Fine." Weber turned to go, but her hand on his arm held him there.

"You pay me, blanc. Pay me first."

"Now?"

She nodded. Suddenly there was fierceness and hunger in her gaze.

"No way," Weber said. "I'll pay you *after* you take me to Ti Malice." He pulled free of her grip and moved quickly down the street.

AT SUNSET THE fountain at Place St. Raphael was crowded with young and old women sitting together in the cool air, gossiping and drinking fermented palm wine out of hollowed gourds. Despite the sight of the badly eroded faceless statue at the center of the fountain, Weber found the tableau rather pleasing: the soothing splash of falling water, the bright colors of the women's dresses and bandanas, their laughing eyes and friendly smiles, the purple sky. Not for the first time he wished that he could really paint. The fate of failed painters, he mused, was to become art directors or gallery owners.

"Hsst. Blanc!"

Sarah was at his side, sullen as ever. Weber felt as though a shadow had passed over him: why should he trust her? What if it was some sort of setup? But why would she be going to all the trouble to trap one jet-lagged art dealer?

Despite his misgivings he followed Sarah away from the plaza, the splashing water, and the laughing women. She set a surprisingly quick pace and never once looked back at him.

The paintings, he thought. Remember, the paintings.

Within minutes she was leading him down a deserted alley. They wound their way out of the alley and up a hilly street toward the Rue Turgeau. Fine homes, many-storied, with elaborate balconies, began to appear behind hedges. Weber suspected they were heading for the houses where the remnants of the expatriate colony lived. But Sarah made a sudden turn and the fine villas were left behind. Silently Weber followed her through a neighborhood of tin-roofed shacks. The longer they walked the greater the distance became between each shack. Now they were trampling dry glass in an empty lot overgrown with tangled thorny weeds, in a sparsely inhabited area where massive thickets of palms and wild jungle pressed right up against the city limits.

Darkness had fallen with tropical swiftness, and there were no street lamps to illuminate their way. Weber began to wish he had packed his pocket flashlight. You were too eager, he told himself. Too greedy. Too quick to trust. What if she leaves you here in the middle of nowhere? And now that he was beyond the sounds of the city, he could hear the drums, steady, incessant, summoning him closer. Closer. But where and to what?

"Sarah! Where the hell are we headed?"

"Where you asked to go. To see Ti Malice. And maybe to see the *houngan*."

Weber knew that meant the voodoo priest and his neck prickled anew. "That's a witch doctor, isn't it? I don't want to see a witch doctor. I just want to see Ti Malice, understand? Where the hell are we? In the middle of nowhere?"

Sarah laughed sharply. "There are people all around, all around us, but you must know where to look. Be patient, blanc, and you will see."

They pushed through a thick grove of palms and emerged into a clearing in which a small, white-washed building stood. The sides of it bore sinuous arabesques painted with a bold hand. The roof was partially thatched. A pierced tin can lantern hung by the door, casting a pool of yellow light.

"Inside," Sarah said. Her face was more animated than ever before. Weber thought she looked excited, almost gleeful, and it made him nervous.

He hesitated at the door. "I guess I should pay you."

"I can wait until you've seen him."

"Should I knock?"

"Go inside. He's waiting for you."

"Ti Malice?"

Sarah nodded and smiled a ferocious smile.

Weber told himself that he had come too far to stop now. Boldly he pushed his way into the house. There appeared to be two rooms leading away from the main entrance. The house was quiet, lit by a single candle. It felt deserted.

"Hello?"

There was no reply. Weber called once more, then backed out of the hut. "Sarah?"

She was gone. All he heard was the liquid trill of birds, the whisper of wind, and the murmur of insects seeking animal blood. How could she have left him here? He hadn't paid her yet. Surely she would come back.

He shook his head, feeling foolish and more than a little frightened. There was nothing for him to do but go back into the deserted house. He couldn't just stand outside in the middle of the Haitian wasteland after sunset and be eaten alive by mosquitoes.

Weber stepped inside again and heard something strange: as though fingernails were being scraped against smooth wood, over and over.

"Hello?"

Still there was no response.

Weber stalked the sound, heart pounding. Was it an animal? A hillside spirit? Don't be ridiculous, he told himself.

In the farthest room of the house a single candle burned. Weber drew closer and closer to its feeble light and the scratching grew louder.

He entered the room and saw the source of the noise.

A thin black man in a stained shirt sat with his back to the door, oblivious to his surroundings, painting steadily upon a stretched canvas propped against the wall. Under his brush a peculiar scene was taking shape: a great eye floated in the center of a blue-black sky, casting a golden searchlight upon kneeling figures below. To the right and left of the floating eye were red-gowned angels, their golden wings and halos glowing brightly. The colors were bold, the style assured and masterful. The painting seemed three-quarters finished. The patient hand of the artist painted on, and the long brush scratched against canvas.

"Ti Malice?"

He didn't move, didn't even nod to acknowledge Weber. In fact, aside from the hand holding the brush, there was a curious stillness about his entire body, as though he were meditating and painting at the same time.

"Excuse me," Weber said loudly. "I'm looking for Ti Malice."

Still the painter painted.

"Hello?"

The man was ignoring him. His arrogance inflamed Weber.

"Hey, I'm talking to you!" He grabbed Ti Malice by the shoulder and spun him around.

Eyeballs rolled up in their sockets until the white showed. The slack mouth drooled a ribbon of saliva.

"What the hell?" Weber dropped his hand and stepped back, aghast.

A low, guttural moan came forth from the loose, wet lips, and then Ti Malice turned slowly, blindly, back to the canvas. The emaciated hand which had never dropped the brush dipped once again into the paint upon his palette and rose to the canvas once more.

Weber made it out of the room, out of the house, but just barely. He bent over, retching noisily between two hibiscus bushes in the yard.

When he was finished, Weber found Sarah waiting for him. She looked at the traces of vomit on his chin and smiled. "Have you found what you were looking for? The great Ti Malice?"

Weber straightened up and wiped his mouth with the back of his hand. "What's wrong with him?" he said. "Is he retarded? Some sort of an idiot savant?"

"No. He's a zombie."

Weber's stomach spasmed again but he managed to control it. "That's not possible. There are no zombies."

She waggled a finger at him in reproach. "Who says? You're not in Los Angeles anymore, Mr. Weber. This is Haiti. He is Ti Malice—and Ti Malice is a zombie."

"Oh, come off it. You don't really believe it, do you?"

Sarah gazed at him gravely but said nothing.

"Okay, so you say he's a zombie," Weber said. "Then why haven't you at least told Mrs. Dewey about it? That way she could stop wearing her smelly old magic bag."

Another shrug. "I tried. But she won't believe me. And I can't bring her here: she can't walk anymore." Sarah gave him a sly look. "I've done what you asked, blanc. Brought you to see Ti Malice. You must pay me now."

It was too easy to imagine her melting away into the jungle with his money in her pocket, leaving him here with a drooling, vacant-eyed idiot. "I'll pay you when we're back in town."

Sarah frowned. "Now."

"Half now," Weber said. He handed her some bills. "You get the rest after we're safe in Port-au-Prince."

Reluctantly she nodded.

"Let's go." Weber was eager to get away, to be out of the jungle, far from the sound of that awful scratching brush. He imagined he could still hear it even though he was outside of the house.

As they walked, Weber began to feel better. Soon the house was out of sight and they were most of the way down the hill which led back to town.

Drums, primal and compelling, began to pound from nearby.

"What's that?"

"Vodou," Sarah said. "A *petro*. Blood sacrifice. I might be able to get you in—for a price."

"No!" Weber could imagine the ghastly rites only too well.

"Nothing bad will happen to you. It won't be very expensive. Good price."

"Sarah, if you don't take me back to town right now, I won't pay you the rest of the money."

She stared at him in surprise. "But most blancs want to see the vodou."

"I came here for art, not magic."

"It's a religion, not magic."

"Call it what you want. Just take me back."

"All right, blanc. But you'll pay me what you owe me."

WEBER AWAKENED TO find sunlight streaming in the open window of his hotel room. The faded drapes danced gently in the breeze, sending motes of dust dancing into the air. A breezy morning to dispel the ugly phantoms of the night. The image of Ti Malice's slack face came into his mind and he shuddered.

A zombie, he thought. The best artist in Haiti is some sort of undead thing that just drools and paints. It made him shiver despite the sunshine and warm breeze, and for a moment he wanted to pack his bags and take the next plane back home. But nobody would believe him in L.A. They would just laugh.

Well, at least it'll make a good story.

Weber dressed carelessly, and didn't bother with breakfast, save for coffee. As he toyed with his half-empty cup, he wondered if he should call somebody about Ti Malice. But who? And tell them what? He didn't even know where that cabin was.

But it's a man's life—an artist—at stake. What should I do?

By nine o'clock he was on the street in the already searing heat, dodging piles of garbage and wondering where to go.

Jean Saint-Mery, that's who he should go see.

Yes, he thought, Saint-Mery knew Haiti—hell, he was a native. Besides, Weber didn't know where else to turn.

He passed a green park where a dozen gray geese grazed serenely between the red bougain-villea and pink crape myrtle, but he didn't see them. He passed a group of women singing and swaying in slow rhythm and never heard them. He had but one thought, one goal: find Jean Saint-Mery and do whatever Saint-Mery told him to do.

Rue Charpentier was a narrow street filled with houses shuttered against the hot sun-shine. But Weber was in luck: Jean Saint-Mery was just unlocking his gallery door. The dealer, a trim light-skinned black man with a pencil moustache and goatee, gave him a courteous but remote greeting, as though somehow he sensed trouble.

"Can I help you?"

"My name's Weber. I'm a dealer from Los Angeles. I need to talk to you."

Saint-Mery raised a thin eyebrow as he looked him over. "Come in, Mr. Weber," he said, just a beat or two too late.

The gallery was cool, with a scrubbed pine floor and white-washed walls. To Weber it was a welcome shelter from the merciless morning sunlight.

Saint-Mery settled himself in a padded swivel chair behind a broad oak desk and lit a cigarette. "I'd heard an American dealer was in town," he said. "Why didn't you come to see me right away?"

"I tried calling, but I couldn't get through."

"The famous Haitian phone system." Saint-Mery nodded and blew a cloud of smoke away from Weber. His expression warmed a bit. "Normally, I would be in France by now. But I decided to stay on in Haiti a while longer this year. Sit down. Would you care for some cof-fee?"

"Please."

Saint-Mery gestured carelessly to a boy lin-gering in the doorway of the shop. *Deux cafés au lait. Vite.*

The child nodded and slinked off out of sight.

"So how is the art market in Los Angeles?"

"Volatile, as always. I have a few regular buy-ers. Thank God for the movie business and its newly rich who decide they need a big house and art to cover its blank walls."

"Thank all the gods," Saint-Mery said.

The coffee arrived on a wooden tray, bowl-sized cups filled with steaming golden brown liquid. Saint-Mery ground his cigarette butt into half of a coconut shell, handed the boy a coin, and shooed him away.

"You said you had something urgent to dis-cuss?"

"Well, I'm worried about an artist here."

"Who?"

"Ti Malice."

Saint-Mery stared at him as though aston-ished. "Ah, Ti Malice. Yes. But why would you be worried about him in particular?"

"I saw him, and he's in terrible shape."

"He is?"

"He's been drugged." Weber shook his head helplessly. "I don't know what's going on. Someone told me he was, well, a zombie." He half-expected Saint-Mery to laugh at him. But the dealer merely nodded.

"All this is true. Ti Malice is a zombie. The *houngan* Coicou made him one."

Weber's jaw worked for a moment as though he were searching for a word. "So you know, too?"

"Everybody knows."

"And done nothing?"

"What's to be done?" The dealer seemed genuinely confused.

Weber wanted to put his head down upon the polished surface of the desk and weep. He felt like a ticket-holder who had missed the first act of a play and therefore can't understand anything that follows. "Am I the only person in Haiti who cares that a great artist has become some drug victim? There's nothing supernatural about this. He's not a zombie—he's stoned out of his mind."

"My dear Weber, calm yourself, please." Saint-Mery's voice held a note of pity. "Ti Malice was a strutting peacock, a braggart, a drunkard, and a troublemaker. He gloried in creating difficulties. Many people, myself included, feel he got no more than he deserved." The art dealer nodded sanctimoniously. "Please, drink your coffee before it cools."

"No one, no matter what kind of bastard he is, deserves to be treated that way."

"You mustn't judge unfamiliar things too harshly."

"Do you actually believe in voodoo? In zombies?"

Saint-Mery looked at him as if he were simpleminded. "Of course. I couldn't live here otherwise."

"Do the police believe in it, too?"

"*Everybody* who lives here believes. And visitors are well-advised not to worry about things they don't understand." The dealer's tone was polite but final. Despite his genial expression his dark eyes were cold, and in them Weber saw the rebuttal of every argument or appeal he might make.

"I'm pleased you came to see me," Saint-Mery continued. "How long will you be staying in Haiti?"

"I'm leaving tomorrow."

"Ah. A short visit. Often the best. Why don't you examine my inventory while you're here? I'd be honored to assist you in any way I can."

Dutifully, feeling a bit numb, Weber leafed through the nearest stack of paintings leaning against the wall. "Who's the blue one by?"

"A new artist, quite a fine talent—Henri Damian."

"He's not a zombie?"

Saint-Mery gave a hearty bellow of false laughter. "No, no. The rest of my artists are all quite alive."

After much negotiation and hand-shaking, Weber left Saint-Mery's shop with two small paintings for which he had paid twice as much as they were worth. The acrylics were lively and he would make some sort of profit on them, but

they were nothing compared with Ti Malice's work. Not that he would be bringing home any of Ti Malice's paintings, the way things were shaping up.

But the longer he thought about it the less good Weber felt about taking Saint-Mery's advice.

It's a horror, he thought, not just party talk. A life is being destroyed here. And Saint-Mery just condones the whole thing because he makes a profit out of it. But meanwhile Ti Malice slaves away, drugged and half-dead. He can't be a zombie—he's just in some drugged state induced by . . . I don't know what. Toad sweat and puffer fish venom and stuff like that. Eye of newt. Lark's tongue. Goddamn Haiti. Goddamn voodoo.

He stumbled out of Rue Charpentier and up the wide main street that led to the Iron Market. The putrid smell of sewage was appalling, but Weber barely noticed. The street bustled with people hawking their wares and shopping. Despite the din, Weber was oblivious to the merchants and their sagging tires, rusty tin cans, moldy rice, and cheap bright cotton cloth.

"Mister, you want?"

"Look here, mister. Here."

"Here, mister, look. You like?"

Their repeated cries finally broke through Weber's fog. He gazed in amazement at the welter of stuff being sold: an entire economy built upon the theory of recycling and contraband. You could buy anything here. Cigarettes. Bottle caps. Pieces of string. Parts of old cars.

Weber froze. You could buy anything you wanted here, he thought. What about a man's freedom?

Oh, right, he told himself. And you'll come riding up with the cavalry, to save him? Come off it. You're no hero. You're a gallery owner in a strange place.

But there's a life at stake.

He rubbed his jaw, feeling sheepish but oddly determined. If he were to try and save Ti Malice, how would he do it? Pay ransom? To whom, Coicou? No. He couldn't imagine negotiating with him.

I'll free him, Weber thought wildly. Yes, I'll break down the door of that hut and bring Ti Malice down from the mountainside to the Albert Schweitzer Clinic. That place was run by Americans. Surely they'll be able to cure him, regardless of the poison Coicou used against him. To keep an artist of his caliber in mindless servitude like that—it was criminal.

It was easier than Weber could have imagined. He told the clerk at his hotel that he wanted to hire a group of strong young men for one night.

The clerk smiled knowingly and nodded. "Twenty dollars," he said.

Sarah wanted twenty-five to lead him back to Ti Malice.

"Your price has gone up," said Weber.

"It's another trip, yes? And you pay me first this time."

THE CABIN SAT in its pool of light. The tin can lantern still hung by the door.

"Here we are," said Weber. "Inside, quickly."

Ti Malice sat on his pallet in the back room, painting, endlessly painting. The brush and the scenes that sprang into being beneath it were alive, vibrant and glowing. Every stroke painted was confident, even compelling.

"Grab him and let's go."

His assistants stared at one another and, for a moment, Weber feared they would all refuse to help him. But one made a face, another shrugged, and they reached for Ti Malice's arm.

The zombified artist turned slowly, neither resisting nor helping his would-be liberators. He was a dead weight in their arms, motionless save for the hand that held the brush and went on painting upon the open air.

"Hey, he's going to be painting my shirt next," one of the men whispered.

"If he does, save it," said another. "You'll be able to sell it and retire."

It was slow work to carry Ti Malice through the hut and out the door. They had gone per-haps a dozen steps toward a thick stand of palms when a voice rang out.

"Don't move." The voice spoke in Creole and was so coolly authoritative that even Weber froze in his tracks.

A searchlight pinned down each member of the party in turn.

"Coicou," one of the men gasped.

Weber heard the thump of a heavy burden hitting the ground, and the sound of running feet, but he was blinded by the light in his eyes. It took a moment for his vision to clear and another after that to ascertain that he was alone, with Ti Malice, and Coicou. Even Sarah had deserted him.

Coicou's broad face was impassive. Light from his electric torch glinted off the round lenses of his eyeglasses and the brutal barrel of his handgun. "Take Ti Malice back," he said to two of the men with him. "Blanc, you come with me."

Weber's heart began pounding madly. "Where?"

"Back to town, of course. Or would you like to stay out here all night?"

"You can't do this."

"I'm not doing anything. Please, lower your voice. People are sleeping nearby."

Coicou led him downhill through scrub brush and thickets of palms, past ghostly huts and shanties, and into a neighborhood filled with well-tended houses and gardens. Expensive cars sat in every driveway.

"Where are we going?" Weber demanded.

"To my house."

Coicou's dwelling was a two-story building with a thatched roof and graceful wrought-iron supports for his balcony. A lantern glowed beside every window, and the path to the front door was lit by torches hanging from curving metal poles.

"Inside, please, Mr. Weber," Coicou said. "The rest of you wait here."

Weber and Coicou were alone in the house. Weber looked around, half expecting to see shrunken heads and animal parts strewn across the floor. Instead, he saw a blue velvet couch, two padded wing chairs, and a glass-topped coffee table upon which sat a marble bust of a Roman emperor. The witch doctor's living room looked like something out of an interior decorator's magazine.

"Look," Weber said. "This is really just a misunderstanding. Can't we talk about it?"

"Sit down," said Coicou. "Would you like a drink?"

Weber badly wanted something to drink, but he eyed the dusty bottle that Coicou held out to him with suspicion. "No."

"Don't be ridiculous. It's a first-rate rum. Take it. You look like you need a hit of alcohol."

A glass was thrust into his hand, half-full of rich amber liquid. Weber took a sip. It tasted like rum, all right. He took a gulp, and another. A small glow kindled in his stomach. He sank down onto the soft cushions of the sofa.

Coicou sat opposite him in one of the wing chairs. He raised his glass in mock salute, and took a generous swallow. "I see you're interested in zombies."

"There's no such thing," Weber said.

"No?" Coicou gave him a shrewd, calculating look. "I suppose your scientists wouldn't say so. They don't believe in vodou."

"Come on, of course they don't. Neither do I."

"Perhaps you'd like a firsthand experience? I'm sure I could convert you." Suddenly Coicou had a golden amulet in his hand. He swung it like a pendulum, back and forth, in steady hypnotic rhythm.

Weber stared, fascinated. It took a great deal of effort to tear his gaze away. "No! Hey, knock it off."

"I think you may believe more than you think you do," Coicou said, sardonically. "But a man should be free to choose his fate, yes?"

"Just like Ti Malice?"

Coicou ignored him. "And I'll give you a choice, Mr. Weber. You caused me much trouble just now, and I've half a mind to make a zombie out of you and be done with it."

"Please, God, don't. . . ."

"I thought you didn't believe in it?"

"What's there to believe in?" Weber cried. Despite his terror, sweat ran down his face. "A bunch of transplanted African mumbo jumbo accompanied by drums and aerobics in the night? That man, Ti Malice, he's suffering from a nerve poison, that's all. I read about that zombie stuff in the newspaper. He needs a doctor. A real doctor, not some witch doctor."

Coicou wasn't smiling any longer. "My beliefs are my concern," he said. "Don't be so quick to criticize what you don't understand. Besides, Ti Malice brought it upon himself."

"How? What did he do, anyway, that was so terrible?"

"He mocked my family. Despite my warnings, he wouldn't stop. And he was a public nuisance, always drunk, picking fights. Finally, he angered the *loas*—the gods."

"What did he do to you?"

"It's none of your concern. Besides, if I were you, I would be worried about my own fate just now."

Despite the night's humidity and the liquor's warmth, Weber felt icy cold begin to creep up from his toes along his feet and legs, toward his heart.

"As I said," Coicou continued. "I really should turn you into a zombie, too. To punish you for your meddling. But I think there's an alternative. One that will please me even more." And he grinned broadly, displaying a mouthful of perfect white teeth. "We'll be partners."

"In what?"

"We'll split the profits fifty/fifty," Coicou said. "And a resourceful blanc like you should do very well with this."

Weber pulled back deeper into the cushions. "What the hell are you talking about?"

"Ti Malice's paintings. You wanted to buy them, Mr. Weber. That's why you came down here. You may have them. All you want. Take a planeload home with you to Los Angeles and build a new vogue for him."

"I don't want his work anymore."

"But you'll take it, nonetheless."

"And if I don't."

Coicou said nothing, merely swung the pendulum until it glittered in the lamplight.

THE WEBER GALLERY was aglow and golden, each towering floral centerpiece in place, every wineglass polished, every bottle iced and waiting for the opening of "Caribbean Spice."

At six sharp, Weber unlocked the doors for his guests. They glittered with jewelry and fine silks dyed in jewel tones. Like a group of chattering tropical parrots they filled the room, eager to see, to buy, to be seen buying.

As though in a dream, Weber wandered among his customers, listening to them ooh and aah.

"Fabulous."

"I love the color."

"God, they're so free with their work. Their lives are so natural, much more in touch with the basics than ours."

"David! Buddy, this is great." It was Fred Lovell, the well-heeled producer. "I had no idea this work by Tu Malice—"

"Ti Malice," Weber said.

"Right, Ti. Anyway, I didn't know his stuff would be so exciting. You sure know how to pick 'em."

Weber smiled wanly. "Thanks, Fred."

"I can't resist it. I shouldn't do it, but I've gotta have some. Especially that one with the red angels in it."

"A marvelous choice," Weber said, a bit too heartily. "I'll just put a red dot on it. And Fred, I've got an even better painting to show you, one I hung with you in mind."

Docile with two glasses of champagne in him, Lovell followed him across the room. "Really? Wow." He gawked at the white, green, and gold canvas, which showed a voodoo ritual taking place. "It's terrific. I'll take this one, too." He patted Weber on the jaw. "Babe, you always know what I like."

Weber smiled his party smile and made a note on his inventory sheet.

"What's that necklace you're wearing, Dave?"

Weber touched the small rawhide bag on its leather cord. He fingered the bag lightly, twice. "This? Just something I picked up in Haiti."

Lovell sniffed loudly. "Boy, I'll bet it keeps the mosquitoes away."

"Among other things."

Before the night was over, red dots had sprouted next to almost every painting in the gallery. Weber gazed at them, bleary-eyed from writing sales receipts. The show was a huge success.

Guests crowded around him, patting him on the back and shaking his hand.

"Terrific party, Dave!"

"You've really got an eye for art."

"Dave, it's another winning show. You always know where to find the best talent, don't you?"

"What's your secret? Magic?"

Weber knew he was surrounded, everybody yammering congratulations at him. But instead of the crowd he heard only one sound, the slow scratch of brush against canvas. Instead of the gallery walls, Weber saw a man's dark emaciated hand locked in a death grip around a paintbrush, constantly moving. The brush against the canvas, the blind eyes, the slack, drooling mouth.

"Yeah," Weber said. "Black magic."

LATER

MICHAEL MARSHALL SMITH

MICHAEL MARSHALL SMITH (1965–), who also writes as Michael Marshall, was born in Knutsford, Cheshire. When he was a child his family moved to the United States, South Africa, and Australia before settling in England when he was ten; he attended King's College, Cambridge. His professional career began as a comedy writer and performer under the name Michael Rutger for the BBC Radio 4 series *And Now in Colour,* which ran for three seasons.

He has been nominated for and won numerous awards, notably a 1991 British Fantasy Award for his first published short story, "The Man Who Drew Cats"; he won the award for best newcomer the same year. The same organization honored him for Best Short Story for "The Dark Land" in 1992, Best Novel (*Only Forward*) in 1995, and Best Short Story in 1996 for "More Tomorrow." He has also been nominated for four World Fantasy Awards: for short story ("To Receive is Better"), 1995; novella (*More Tomorrow*), 1996; novella (*Hell Hath Enlarged Herself*), 1997; and best collection (*More Tomorrow and Other Stories*), 2003.

As Michael Marshall, he wrote the brilliant Straw Men series, switching from science fiction and horror to the crime novel with a literary style more elevated than most contributions to the serial-killer genre, achieving even greater success than he had previously enjoyed. His crime novels are *The Straw Men* (2002), *The Upright Man* (released in the United Kingdom as *The Lonely Dead* (2004), *Blood of Angels* (2005), *The Intruders* (2007), and *Bad Things* (2009).

"Later," which was nominated for the best short story of the year by the British Fantasy Society, was originally published in the anthology *The Mammoth Book of Zombies,* edited by Stephen Jones (London: Robinson Publishing, 1993).

MICHAEL MARSHALL SMITH

LATER

I REMEMBER STANDING in the bedroom before we went out, fiddling with my tie and fretting mildly about the time. As yet, we had plenty, but that was nothing to be complacent about. The minutes had a way of disappearing when Rachel was getting ready, early starts culminating in a breathless search for a taxi. It was a party we were going to, so it didn't really matter what time we left, but I tend to be a little dull about time. I used to, anyway.

When I had the tie as close to a tidy knot as I was going to be able to get it, I turned away from the mirror, and opened my mouth to call out to Rachel. But then I caught sight of what was on the bed, and closed it again. For a moment I just stood and looked, and then walked over towards the bed.

It wasn't anything very spectacular, just a dress made of sheeny white material. A few years ago, when we started going out together, Rachel used to make a lot of her clothes. She didn't do it because she had to, but because she enjoyed it. She used to trail me endlessly round dress-making shops, browsing patterns and asking my opinion on a million different fabrics, while I half-heartedly protested and moaned.

On impulse I leant down and felt the material, and found I could remember touching it for the first time in the shop on Mill Road, could remember surfacing up through contented boredom to say that yes, I liked this one. On that recommendation she'd bought it, and made this dress, and as a reward for traipsing around after

her she'd bought me dinner too. We were poorer then, so the meal was cheap, but there was lots and it was good.

The strange thing was, I didn't even really mind the dress shops. You know how sometimes, when you're just walking around, living your life, you'll see someone on the street and fall hopelessly in love with them? How something in the way they look, the way they are, makes you stop dead in your tracks and stare? How for that instant you're convinced that if you could just meet them, you'd be able to love them for ever?

Wild schemes and unlikely meetings pass through your head, and yet as they stand on the other side of the street or the room, talking to someone else, they haven't the faintest idea of what's going through your mind. Something has clicked, but only inside your head. You know you'll never speak to them, that they'll never know what you're feeling, and that they'll never want to. But something about them forces you to keep looking, until you wish they'd leave so you could be free.

The first time I saw Rachel was like that, and now she was in my bath. I didn't call out to hurry her along. I decided it didn't really matter.

A few minutes later a protracted squawking noise announced the letting out of the bath water, and Rachel wafted into the bedroom swaddled in thick towels and glowing high spirits. Suddenly I lost all interest in going to the party, punctually or otherwise. She marched up to me, set her head at a silly angle to kiss me on the lips and jerked my tie vigorously in about three different directions. When I looked in the mirror I saw that somehow, as always, she'd turned it into a perfect knot.

Half an hour later we left the flat, still in plenty of time. If anything, I'd held her up.

"Later," she said, smiling in the way that showed she meant it. "Later, and for a long time, my man."

I remember turning from locking the door to see her standing on the pavement outside the house, looking perfect in her white dress, looking happy and looking at me. As I walked smiling down the steps towards her she skipped backwards into the road, laughing for no reason, laughing because she was with me.

"Come on," she said, holding out her hand like a dancer, and a yellow van came round the corner and smashed into her. She spun backwards as if tugged on a rope, rebounded off a parked car and toppled into the road. As I stood cold on the bottom step she half sat up and looked at me, an expression of wordless surprise on her face, and then she fell back again.

When I reached her blood was already pulsing up into the white of her dress and welling out of her mouth. It ran out over her makeup and I saw she'd been right: she hadn't quite blended the colours above her eyes. I'd told her it didn't matter, that she still looked beautiful. She had.

She tried to move her head again and there was a sticky sound as it almost left the tarmac and then slumped back. Her hair fell back from around her face, but not as it usually did. There was a faint flicker in her eyelids, and then she died.

I knelt there in the road beside her, holding her hand as the blood dried a little. It was as if everything had come to a halt, and hadn't started up again. I heard every word the small crowd muttered, but I didn't know what they were muttering about. All I could think was that there wasn't going to be a later, not to kiss her some more, not for anything. Later was gone.

When I got back from the hospital I phoned her mother. I did it as soon as I got back, though I didn't want to. I didn't want to tell anyone, didn't want to make it official. It was a bad phone call, very, very bad. Then I sat in the flat, looking at the drawers she'd left open, at the towels on the floor, at the party invitation on the dressing table, feeling my stomach crawl. I was back at the flat, as if we'd come back home from the party. I should have been making coffee while Rachel had yet another bath, coffee we'd drink on the sofa in front of the fire. But the fire was off and the bath was empty. So what was I supposed to do?

I sat for an hour, feeling as if somehow I'd slipped too far forward in time and left Rachel behind, as if I could turn and see her desperately running to try to catch me up. When it felt as if my throat was going to burst I called my parents and they came and took me home. My mother gently made me change my clothes, but she didn't wash them. Not until I was asleep, anyway. When I came down and saw them clean I hated her, but I knew she was right and the hate went away. There wouldn't have been much point in just keeping them in a drawer.

The funeral was short. I guess they all are, really, but there's no point in them being any longer. Nothing more would be said. I was a little better by then, and not crying so much, though I did before we went to the church because I couldn't get my tie to sit right.

Rachel was buried near her grandparents, which she would have liked. Her parents gave me her dress afterwards, because I'd asked for it. It had been thoroughly cleaned and large patches had lost their sheen and died, looking as much unlike Rachel's dress as the cloth had on the roll. I'd almost have preferred the bloodstains still to have been there: at least that way I could have believed that the cloth still sparkled beneath them. But they were right in their way, as my mother was. Some people seem to have pragmatic, accepting souls, an ability to deal with death. I don't, I'm afraid. I don't understand it at all.

Afterwards I stood at the graveside for a while, but not for long because I knew that my parents were waiting at the car. As I stood by the mound of earth that lay on top of her I tried to concentrate, to send some final thought to her, some final love, but the world kept pressing in on me through the sound of cars on the road and some bird that was cawing in a tree. I couldn't shut it out. I couldn't believe that I was noticing how cold it was, that somewhere lives were being led and televisions being watched, that the inside of my parents' car would smell the same as it always had. I wanted to feel something, wanted to sense her presence, but I couldn't. All I could feel was the world round me, the same old world. But it wasn't a world that had been there a week ago, and I couldn't understand how it could look so much the same.

It was the same because nothing had changed, and I turned and walked to the car. The wake was worse than the funeral, much worse, and I stood with a sandwich feeling something very cold building up inside. Rachel's oldest friend Lisa held court with her old school friends, swiftly running the range of emotions from stoic resilience to trembling incoherence.

"I've just realized," she sobbed to me, "Rachel's not going to be at my wedding."

"Yes, well she's not going to be at mine either," I said numbly, and immediately hated myself for it. I went and stood by the window, out of harm's way. I couldn't react properly. I knew why everyone was standing here, that in some ways it was like a wedding. Instead of gathering together to bear witness to a bond, they were here to prove she was dead. In the weeks to come they'd know they'd stood together in a room, and would be able to accept she was gone. I couldn't.

I said goodbye to Rachel's parents before I left. We looked at each other oddly, and shook hands, as if we were just strangers again. Then I went back to the flat and changed into some old clothes. My "Someday" clothes, Rachel used to call them, as in "someday you must throw them away." Then I made a cup of tea and stared out of the window for a while. I knew damn well

what I was going to do, and it was a relief to give in to it.

That night I went back to the cemetery and I dug her up. What can I say? It was hard work, and it took a lot longer than I expected, but in another way it was surprisingly easy. I mean yes, it was creepy, and yes, I felt like a lunatic, but after the shovel had gone in once the second time seemed less strange. It was like waking up in the mornings after the accident. The first time I clutched at myself and couldn't understand, but after that I knew what to expect. There were no cracks of thunder, there was no web of lightning and I actually felt very calm. There was just me and, beneath the earth, my friend. I just wanted to find her.

When I did I laid her down by the side of the grave and then filled it back up again, being careful to make it look undisturbed. Then I carried her to the car in my arms and brought her home.

The flat seemed very quiet as I sat her on the sofa, and the cushion rustled and creaked as it took her weight again. When she was settled I knelt and looked up at her face. It looked much the same as it always had, though the colour of the skin was different, didn't have the glow she always had. That's where life is, you know, not in the heart but in the little things, like the way hair falls around a face. Her nose looked the same and her forehead was smooth. It was the same face, exactly the same.

I knew the dress she was wearing was hiding a lot of things I would rather not see, but I took it off anyway. It was her going away dress, bought by her family specially for the occasion, and it didn't mean anything to me or to her. I knew what the damage would be and what it meant. As it turned out the patchers and menders had done a good job, not glossing because it wouldn't be seen. It wasn't so bad.

When she was sitting up again in her white dress I walked over and turned the light down, and I cried a little then, because she looked so much the same. She could have fallen asleep, warmed by the fire and dozy with wine, as if we'd just come back from the party.

I went and had a bath then. We both used to when we came back in from an evening, to feel clean and fresh for when we slipped between the sheets. It wouldn't be like that this evening, of course, but I had dirt all over me, and I wanted to feel normal. For one night at least I just wanted things to be as they had.

I sat in the bath for a while, knowing she was in the living room, and slowly washed myself clean. I really wasn't thinking much. It felt nice to know that I wouldn't be alone when I walked back in there. That was better than nothing, was part of what had made her alive. I dropped my Someday clothes in the bin and put on the ones from the evening of the accident. They didn't mean as much as her dress, but at least they were from before.

When I returned to the living room her head had lolled slightly, but it would have done if she'd been asleep. I made us both a cup of coffee. The only time she ever took sugar was in this cup, so I put one in. Then I sat down next to her on the sofa and I was glad that the cushions had her dent in them, that as always they drew me slightly towards her, didn't leave me perched there by myself.

The first time I saw Rachel was at a party. I saw her across the room and simply stared at her, but we didn't speak. We didn't meet properly for a month or two, and first kissed a few weeks after that. As I sat there on the sofa next to her body I reached out tentatively and took her hand, as I had done on that night. It was cooler than it should have been, but not too bad because of the fire, and I held it, feeling the lines on her palm, lines I knew better than my own.

I let myself feel calm and I held her hand in the half light, not looking at her, as also on that first night, when I'd been too happy to push my luck. She's letting you hold her hand, I'd

thought, don't expect to be able to look at her too. Holding her hand is more than enough: don't look, you'll break the spell. My face creased then, not knowing whether to smile or cry, but it felt alright. It really did.

I sat there for a long time, watching the flames, still not thinking, just holding her hand and letting the minutes run. The longer I sat the more normal it felt, and finally I turned slowly to look at her. She looked tired and asleep, so deeply asleep, but still there with me and still mine.

When her eyelid first moved I thought it was a trick of the light, a flicker cast by the fire. But then it stirred again, and for the smallest of moments I thought I was going to die. The other eyelid moved and the feeling just disappeared, and that made the difference, I think. She had a long way to come, and if I'd felt frightened, or rejected her, I think that would have finished it then. I didn't question it. A few minutes later both her eyes were open, and it wasn't long before she was able to slowly turn her head.

I still go to work, and put in the occasional appearance at social events, but my tie never looks quite as it did. She can't move her fingers precisely enough to help me with that anymore. She can't come with me, and nobody can come here, but that doesn't matter. We always spent a lot of time by ourselves. We wanted to.

I have to do a lot of things for her, but I can live with that. Lots of people have accidents, bad ones: if Rachel had survived she could have been disabled or brain-damaged so that her movements were as they are now, so slow and clumsy. I wish she could talk, but there's no air in her lungs, so I'm learning to read her lips. Her mouth moves slowly, but I know she's trying to speak, and I want to hear what she's saying.

But she gets round the flat, and she holds my hand, and she smiles as best she can. If she'd just been injured I would have loved her still. It's not so very different.

WHITE ZOMBIE

VIVIAN MEIK

THE LIFE OF Vivian (Bernard) Meik (1894–1955) is as filled with adventure and mystery as his fiction. Born either in Calcutta or, as he claimed, on a British ship, he pursued careers in engineering and journalism as well as writing suspense and horror fiction. During World War II, he passed himself off as a member of the British intelligence staff and obtained documents, undoubtedly with journalistic enthusiasm rather than traitorous intent, but served two years in prison for violating the Official Secrets Act. As a noted war correspondent, he was wounded in both World Wars. He lived in Germany after the war but moved to America permanently in 1947. His extensive travels in Africa, India, and the Far East provided weird stories, as well as flavor, for his fiction. Among his published work is the short-story collection *Devils' Drums* (1933), which contains mostly horror tales but also some that feature mystery and crime; the episodic novel (five connected novellas) *Veils of Fear* (1934), which is a sequel of sorts to *Devils' Drums,* with several of the characters returning; and *The Curse of the Red Shiva* (1936), a "Yellow Peril" tale of Oriental villains and a curse that strikes every five generations.

In addition to producing fiction, Meik wrote a once-important book, *The People of the Leaves* (1931), a factual report on a very primitive and obscure tribe located in Orissa, India, with whom he lived for several months.

"White Zombie" was first published in *Devils' Drums* (London: Philip Allan, 1933).

VIVIAN MEIK

WHITE ZOMBIE

GEOFFREY AYLETT, acting commissioner of the district of Nswadzi, was frightened. During his twenty years of Africa never before had he experienced the sensation of being so definitely baffled. He felt as if something was pressing against him, something that he could neither see nor locate, but, nevertheless, something that seemed to envelop him, and, in some inexplicable way, threaten to stifle him. Lately he had begun to wake suddenly at nights, struggling for breath and almost overcome by a feeling of nausea. After the nausea had disappeared there still remained a strange suggestion of some nameless horrible odour, an odour that was strongly reminiscent of the aftermath of the earlier battles of the Mesopotamia campaign.

Those had been days of foul disease, when cholera and dysentery, sunstroke, typhoid and gangrene had raged unchecked; where hundreds had lain where they had fallen; when, pressed by enemies and forgotten by friends, the survivors were forced to let even the elementary decencies of death go by the board. . . . He remembered the flies and the corruption, and the temperature of a hundred and twenty degrees. . . .

And now, eighteen years later, that same smell of fetid corruption seemed to hover about him like some evil presence when he woke at nights.

Aylett was, first and foremost, a rational man, accustomed to face facts. His knowledge of the mystery of Africa, of its depths and jungles, of its eerie atmosphere, was as complete as that of any white man—he smiled whimsically as he emphasised to himself how little that was—and he looked for some concrete reason that would explain the bridging of the years by this horrible harmonic. Failing a satisfactory solution he would be forced to conclude that it was about time he went home on long leave.

Carefully, as befitted a man of his experience of the ways of the dark gods, he searched his innermost soul, but failed to find the answer he sought.

There was only one connection in the district between him and the Mesopotamia of 1915—a certain John Sinclair, late of the Indian Army—but that connection was already a broken link long before the first occurrence of these nauseating nightmares.

Sinclair had been a brother officer in the old days, and, mainly on Aylett's advice, had taken up a few thousand acres of virgin country in the comparatively unknown Nswadzi district immediately after the War. But he had died more than a year previously—and, what was more to the point, had died a natural death. Aylett himself had been present at the passing of his friend.

Being both a mystic as the result of his knowledge of Africa, and a logician as a result of his Western upbringing, Aylett methodically considered the platitudinous truth that there are more things in heaven and earth than are dreamed of in our philosophy, and went over the entire period of his association with Sinclair in every detail.

At the end of it all he was forced to admit failure, and, indeed, judged either logically or mystically, there was no adequate reason for linking Sinclair with his present troubles. Sinclair had died peacefully. He even remembered the utter content of the last sigh . . . as if some great burden had been lifted.

It was true that before this, Sinclair—and Aylett himself for that matter—during the first two years of the War, had been through a hell that only those who had experienced it could appreciate. It was also true that Sinclair had saved Aylett's life at a great risk to his own, on a certain memorable occasion, when Aylett, left for dead, had been lying badly wounded in the sun. Aylett had, naturally, never forgotten that, but being a typical Englishman, had done very little more than shake his friend's hand, and mumble something to the effect that he hoped that one day there would be an opportunity to repay. Sinclair had waved the matter aside, with a laugh, as one of no account—merely a job in the day's work. There the incident had ended, and each went about his own lawful occasions.

As a settler Sinclair had been a complete success. In due course he had married a very capable woman, who, it appeared to Aylett, whenever he had broken journey at the homestead, was eminently suited to the hard existence of a planter's wife.

At first Sinclair had seemed very happy, but as the years went by Aylett had not been quite so sure. He had had occasion more than once to notice the subtle change for the worse in his old friend. Staleness, he diagnosed, and recommended a holiday in England. Lonely plantations, far from one's own kind, are apt to get on the nerves. Nothing came of his suggestion, however, and the Sinclairs stayed on. They had grown to love the place too well, they said, though he thought that Sinclair's enthusiasm did not ring true. Anyway, it had not been his business.

That was all that he could recall in his contemplation, and he repeated again how it had all finished over a year ago. But old memories cling. He found himself living over again that ghastly day after Ctesiphon when Sinclair had literally brought him back to life.

He began to wonder—idly, fantastically. The afternoon dimmed to sundown, sundown gave way to the magic of the night. Still Aylett made no move to leave the camp-chair under the awning of his tent and go to bed. After a while the last of his "boys" came up to ask him whether he might retire. Aylett answered him absently, his eyes on the glowing logs of the camp-fire.

As the hours wore on he could hear the sound of the night drums more distinctly. From all the points of the compass the sounds came and went, drum answering drum . . . the telegraph of the trackless miles that the world calls Africa. Lazily he wondered what they were saying, and how exactly they transmitted their news. Strange, he thought, that no white man has ever mastered the secret of the drums.

Subconsciously he followed their throbbing monotony. He gradually became aware that the beat had changed. No more were simple news or opinions being transmitted. That much he could understand. There was something else being sent out, something of importance. He suddenly realized that whatever this something was, it was apparently regarded as being of vital urgency, and that, for at least an hour, the same short rhythm had been repeated. North, south, east and west, the echoes throbbed and throbbed again.

The drums began to madden him, but there was no way to stop them. He decided to go to bed, but he had been listening too long, and the rhythm followed him. Eventually he dropped off into a listless disturbed sleep, during which the implacable staccato throbbing kept hammering away its unreadable message into his subconsciousness.

It seemed only a moment later that he awoke. A malarious mist had rolled up from the swamps below and had pervaded his camp. He found himself gasping for breath. He tried to sit up, but the mist seemed to be pressing him down where he lay. No sound issued from his lips when he endeavoured to call his "boys." He felt himself being steadily submerged—down, down, down and still down. Just before he lost consciousness he realized that he was being suffocated, not by the heavy mist, but by a foul miasma reeking with all the horror of corruption. . . .

Aylett looked about him in a bewildered fashion when he opened his eyes again. A kindly bearded face was bending over him, and he heard a voice that seemed to be coming from a great distance encouraging him to drink something. His head was throbbing violently, and his breath came in deep gasps. But the cool water

cleared in some measure the foul odour that seemed to cling to his brain.

"Ah, *mon ami, c'est bon*. We thought you were dead when the 'boys' brought you in." The bearded face broke into a grin: "But now you will be well, *hein?* You are—what you say?—a tough, *hein?*"

Aylett laughed in spite of himself. Why, of course, this was the mission station of the White Fathers, and his old friend, Padre Vaneken, placid and reliable, was looking after him. He closed his eyes happily. Now there was nothing more to fear, everything would soon be well. Then, as suddenly as it had come, that terrible clinging odour of death and decay left him. . . .

"But, padre man," he discussed his horrible experience later, "what could have happened? We are both men of some experience of Africa—"

The missionary shrugged his shoulders. "*Mon ami*, as you imply, this is Africa . . . and I have no evidence that the curse on Ham, the son of Noah, has ever been lifted. The dark forests, they are the stronghold of such whose unconscious spirits have rebelled and have not yet come out to serve as was first ordained. Who knows? . . . We—I—do not look too deeply there. When I first came out, in my early idealism I sought but the convert, now I—I am content to do mostly the cures for fevers and wounds, and hope that *le bon Dieu* will understand. It is the same everywhere where the curse of Noah carries. Civilisation counts not. Regard Haiti—I spent twelve years there—Sierra Leone, the Congo, and here. What can I say about your attack by the mist? Nothings, *hein?* You—you thank God you live, for here, *mon ami*—here is the cradle of Africa, the oldest stronghold of the sons of Ham. . . ."

Aylett regarded the missionary intently. "Padre," he spoke deliberately, "what exactly are you trying to make me understand?"

The two men, old in the ways of the black jungle, faced each other steadily. "*Mon ami*," the priest said quietly, "you are my old friend. On the forms of religion we think differently, you and I, but this is not conventional Europe, thank God, and, side by side, we have done our best according to our lights. God himself cannot do more. So I will tell you. *I have seen the mist before . . . twice. Once in Haiti and once in this district.*"

"Here?"

The padre nodded. "I was in camp at the catechumen's school by Mrs. Sinclair's estate—"

"Go on." Aylett's voice was low.

"As you know, Mrs. Sinclair has run the plantation since her husband's death. She refused to go home. At first you, I—all the countryside— thought she was mad to stay there alone, but—" the missionary shrugged his shoulders—"*que voulez-vous?* A woman is a law unto herself. Anyway, she has made it a greater success than ever, and we are silenced, *hein?*"

"But the mist?"

"I was coming to that. It caught me by the throat that night. I was living at the house, as we all do who pass that way—Central Africa is not a cathedral close—but beyond not knowing anything of what happened for several hours nothing happened to me." He touched the emblem of his faith on the rosary that was part of his dress. "Mrs. Sinclair said that I had been overcome by the heat, but to me that explanation would not do. . . ."

"But that doesn't explain anything."

"Perhaps not—*but Mrs. Sinclair said that she had not noticed anything peculiar . . . !*"

"How was that?"

The priest shrugged his shoulders. "I am not Mrs. Sinclair," he said abruptly, and Aylett knew that not another word about her would the missionary say.

"Tell me about Haiti, padre," he asked.

The priest replied quietly. "We understood it there to mean that it was artificially produced by *voodoo* black magic—a very real thing, *mon ami,* which my church readily admits, as you probably know—and there they call it 'the breath of the dead.' Why? . . ." He shrugged his shoulders again.

Aylett turned away and looked out steadily into the distance. For a long time he fixed his gaze on the line of distant hills, thinking deeply. He recalled a picture where just such hills appeared in the background—a photograph taken by a man who had been almost beyond the borderline to give the truth to the world. But he had failed. The picture showed a group of figures. That was all until one studied them, and even then no one would believe that this was a photograph of dead men—*who were not allowed to die.*

For hours the two men sat silently, each busy with his own thoughts. Night mantled the tiny mission station, and from afar the sound of drums came through on the soft breeze. Aylett turned suddenly to the missionary. "Padre man," he said quietly, "it's only twenty miles from here to the Sinclairs' estate. . . ."

The padre nodded. "I understand, *mon ami,*" he replied. Then after a moment, "Would you think it an impertinence if I asked you to keep this in your pocket—till you come back?" He produced a small silver crucifix.

Aylett held out his hand. "Thank you," he said simply.

The sun had set when Aylett's *machila** was set down on Mrs. Sinclair's verandah. She came forward to welcome him. "I wondered if I should ever see you again." She looked at him quietly. "You haven't been here since—for over a year now." Then she changed her tone. She laughed. "As a district officer," she said, "you've neglected your duties shamefully!"

Aylett smilingly pleaded guilty, excusing himself on the ground that everything had gone so well in this section, that he had hesitated to intrude on perfection.

"Has it fallen from perfection now?" she countered.

"Not at all," he replied, "this visit is merely routine."

"Er—thank you," she said dryly, "Anyway, come in and make yourself comfortable, and to-morrow I'll show you a perfect estate."

Aylett studied his hostess carefully through

---

*Machila—a stretcher slung on a pole—the standard means of transport in the "bush."

dinner. He felt uneasy at what he saw whenever he caught her off her guard. He could hardly believe that this was the same woman whom he had welcomed as a bride only a few years ago. The lonely life had hardened her, but he had expected that. There was something more, though—a kind of bitter hardness, he called it, for want of a better term.

After her formal welcome Mrs. Sinclair spoke very little. She seemed preoccupied with the affairs of the plantation. "My very own stake in Africa," she said. "Oh, how I love the country, its magic and mystery and its vast grandeur." She reminded him how she had refused to go home. But tomorrow, she said, when he saw *her* Africa—the plantation—he would understand.

Aylett retired early, distinctly puzzled. He had noticed her looking over the swept and garnished tidiness of the plantation before she had said goodnight. She had unconsciously stretched out her hands to it in a kind of adoring supplication and yet, in the brilliant moonlight under this sensual adoration, he distinctly noticed the contrast of the hard lines on her face and the bitterness of the mouth. Africa . . .

Exhausted as he was, he slept well. Whether the little cross the padre had given him had anything to do with it or not, he did not know, but in the morning he had waked more refreshed than he had been for weeks. He looked forward to the visit over the estate.

Mrs. Sinclair had not exaggerated when she had used the word perfection. Fields had been hoed till not a stray blade of grass grew among the crops; barns stood in serried rows; wood fuel was stacked in the neatest of "cords"; the orchard and the kitchen garden were luxurious, and the pasture in the miniature home farm was the greenest he had seen in the tropics.

"For what?" his subconscious brain kept hammering at him. "Why—and above all, *how?*"

Aylett had noticed what only an expert would have seen. There was a great shortage of labour, though such workers as were dotted about seemed to be very busy.

As if she divined his thoughts, Mrs. Sinclair answered them. "My 'boys' *work*," she said, in even tones as she flicked the hippo hide whip she carried.

Aylett raised his eyebrows. "Portuguese methods?" he asked quietly, and looked at the whip.

Mrs. Sinclair turned to him. For the first time he noticed her deliberate antagonism. "Not at all," she said evenly. "A knowledge of how to get the most out of a native, a faculty which I notice officialdom has not yet acquired."

The district officer took the rapier-like thrust without faltering. "*Touché,*" he answered, but nevertheless he knew he had not been wrong about the labour. "Queer," he thought, "damnably queer . . ."

Mrs. Sinclair took no notice of his acknowledgement of her point. Her lips were set hard and she spoke coldly. She continued, "It's only a matter of getting to the heart of Africa—the throbbing beating heart below all this—Africa has no use for those who do not join their own souls." Suddenly she realized what she was saying, but before she could change the subject Aylett took up the question. He matched her tone.

"Very interesting . . ." he said, "but we don't encourage Europeans, especially European women, to go 'native.'"

The last word, however, was with the woman. "All the perspicacity of officialdom!" she murmured. Then she looked Aylett full in the face. "Do I sound native," she said harshly, "or *look* native?"

Aylett was hardly listening. He was staring at her. Her eyes belied her words, for if ever he saw an expression of masterful, baleful perversion in any human face, he saw it then. He began to understand. . . .

He was thankful when the inspection was over, and felt relieved that she did not offer the formal suggestion that he should stay a little longer.

Five miles beyond her boundary he had a bivouac tent pitched behind a thorn-bush, and stored two days' rations in its shade. He sent his *safari* on at the double to the mission station, and watched it till it was out of sight. Then he sat down to wait for the night.

"The heart of Africa . . ." he repeated to himself, but his voice was grim, and his eyes flashed in cold anger.

It was not till he heard the news drums throb that Aylett retraced his steps along the ill-defined track to the plantation. At the edge of the estate he merged himself in the shadows of the forest fringe, and gradually worked his way along the eucalyptus wind breaks. He crawled noiselessly as far as the tree which grew in the garden before the homestead.

In a little while he saw Mrs. Sinclair come out on to the verandah. Beside her stood a gigantic native who looked like some obscene devil, a witch doctor, sinister and grotesque, and naked but for a necklace of human bones dangling and rattling on his enormous chest. Daubs of white clay and red ochre plastered his face.

Only partly covered by a magnificent leopard skin, the white woman stepped down into the clearing and snapped the whip she had in her hands. It sounded like a revolver shot. As if it were a signal Aylett heard the roll of drums near at hand. From one of the barns began the most grotesque procession he had ever seen. The drums throbbed malevolently—the short staccato throb that had preceded the fetid mist which had almost suffocated him. Louder they grew and louder. The message rolled through the jungles, was caught up and answered again. There was no doubt as to its meaning.

He crouched lower as the drums approached, his eyes fixed on the macabre scene before him. Following the drums, as regularly as a column on the march, moved the men who worked the perfect plantation. In columns of four they moved, heavy footed and automatic—but they moved. Every now and then the crack of that terrible whip sounded like a pistol-shot through the roll of drums, and every now and then Aylett could see that cruel thong cut through naked flesh, and a figure drop silently, only to pick itself up again and rejoin the column.

They marched round the garden. As they came near Aylett held his breath. He had to strain every nerve in his body to prevent himself screaming. Almost as if he were hypnotised he looked on the dull expressionless faces of the silent, slow-moving automatons—faces on which there was not even despair. They simply moved to the command of that merciless whip, as they would shortly move off to their allotted task in the fields. Bowed and crushed they passed by him without a sound.

The nervous tension almost broke Aylett. Then the realisation came to him—*these pitiful automatons were dead—and they were not allowed to die. . . .*

The figures in the unbelievable photograph came back to him; the padre's words; the magic of the *voodoo*, acknowledged as fact by the greatest Christian Church in history. The dead . . . who were not allowed to die . . . Zombies, the natives called them in hushed voices, wherever the curse of Noah was borne . . . and *she* called it knowing Africa.

A cold terror came over Aylett. The long column was nearing its end. Mrs. Sinclair was walking down the line, her whip cracking mercilessly, her face distorted with perverted lust, the foul witch doctor leering over her naked shoulder. She stopped by the tree behind which he crouched. A single bent figure followed the column. With a gasp of horror Aylett recognized Sinclair. Then the whip crashed across the poor thing who had once died in his arms.

"My God!" Aylett muttered helplessly. "It's not possible—" but he knew that the witch doctor's *voodoo* had thrown the impossibility in his face. The whip cracked again, hurling the lone white Zombie to the ground. Slowly it picked itself up—without a sound, without expression—and automatically followed the column. He heard, as in a nightmare, unbelievably foul obscenities fall from the woman's lips—cruel taunts. . . . And the whip cracked and bit and tore, again and yet again. At the head of the column the drums throbbed on.

Horror gave way at last. Aylett found himself desperately clutching the tiny cross the padre had given him. With the other hand he found his revolver and took aim with icy coolness. . . . Four times he fired at a point above the leopard skin and twice into the ochred face of the witch doctor. . . . Then he leapt forward, cross in hand, to what had once died as Sinclair.

The figure was standing silently, bent and expressionless. It made no sign as Aylett approached, but as the crucifix touched it a tremor shook the frame. The drooping eyelids lifted and the lips moved. "You have repaid," they whispered gently. The body swayed slightly and toppled over. "Dust to dust . . ." Aylett prayed. In a few moments all that remained was a little greyish powder. A tropical year had passed, Aylett remembered with a shudder. . . . Then he turned, and, crucifix in hand, walked along the column. . . .

WAS IT A DREAM?

GUY DE MAUPASSANT

GUY DE MAUPASSANT (1850–1893) was born in Normandy, France, to an old and distinguished family. His parents divorced when he was eleven and his mother was befriended by Gustave Flaubert, who took an interest in her elder son, becoming his literary mentor. Immediately after graduating high school, Maupassant served with distinction in the Franco-Prussian War, then took a job as a civil servant for nearly ten years. He was beginning to write, first poetry, which was undistinguished, then short stories, most of which Flaubert forced him to discard as unworthy. When his first story was published in a collection with such literary lions of the day as Émile Zola, it outshone them all and his future was secured. Over the next decade, he wrote more than three hundred short stories, six novels, three travel books, poetry, several plays, and more than three hundred magazine articles.

His naturalistic style was a powerful influence on other great short-story writers, including O. Henry and W. Somerset Maugham. Unfortunately, Maupassant died before his forty-third birthday. As an ardent womanizer, he had contracted syphilis when he was quite young and suffered from other ailments as well. His brother died in an insane asylum, and when Maupassant felt he was losing his mind, he twice attempted suicide; he died a lunatic.

"Was It a Dream?" was first collected in the United States in *Pierre and Jean, Ball-of-Tallow: The Complete Works of Guy de Maupassant* (Boston: C. D. Brainard, 1910).

GUY DE MAUPASSANT

WAS IT A DREAM?

"I HAD LOVED her madly! Why does one love? Why does one love? How queer it is to see only one being in the world, to have only one thought in one's mind, only one desire in the heart, and only one name on the lips; a name which comes up continually, which rises like the water in a spring, from the depths of the soul, which rises to the lips, and which one repeats over and over again which one whispers ceaselessly, everywhere, like a prayer.

"I am going to tell you our story, for love only has one, which is always the same. I met her and loved her; that is all. And for a whole year I have lived on her tenderness, on her caresses, in her arms, in her dresses, on her words, so completely wrapped up, bound, imprisoned in everything which came from her, that I no longer knew whether it was day or night, if I was dead or alive, on this old earth of ours, or elsewhere.

"And then she died. How? I do not know. I no longer know; but one evening she came home wet, for it was raining heavily, and the next day she coughed, and she coughed for about a week, and took to her bed. What happened I do not remember now, but doctors came, wrote and went away. Medicines were brought, and some women made her drink them. Her hands were hot, her forehead was burning, and her eyes bright and sad. When I spoke to her, she answered me, but I do not remember what we said. I have forgotten everything, everything, everything! She died, and I very well remember her slight, feeble sigh. The nurse said: 'Ah!' and I understood, I understood!

"I knew nothing more, nothing. I saw a priest, who said: 'Your mistress?' and it seemed to me as if he were insulting her. As she was dead, nobody had the right to know that any longer, and I turned him out. Another came who was very kind and tender, and I shed tears when he spoke to me about her.

"They consulted me about the funeral, but I do not remember anything that they said, though I recollected the coffin, and the sound of the hammer when they nailed her down in it. Oh! God, God!

"She was buried! Buried! She! In that hole! Some people came—female friends. I made my escape, and ran away; I ran, and then I walked through the streets, and went home, and the next day I started on a journey."

"YESTERDAY I RETURNED to Paris, and when I saw my room again—our room, our bed, our furniture, everything that remains of the life of a human being after death, I was seized by such a violent attack of fresh grief, that I was very near opening the window and throwing myself out into the street. As I could not remain any longer among these things, between these walls which had enclosed and sheltered her, and which retained a thousand atoms of her, of her skin and of her breath in their imperceptible crevices, I took up my hat to make my escape, and just as I reached the door, I passed the large glass in the hall, which she had put there so that she might be able to look at herself every day from head to foot as she went out, to see if her toilet looked well, and was correct and pretty, from her little boots to her bonnet.

"And I stopped short in front of that looking-glass in which she had so often been reflected. So often, so often, that it also must have retained her reflection. I was standing there, trembling, with my eyes fixed on the glass—on that flat, profound, empty glass—which had contained her entirely, and had possessed her as much as I had, as my passionate looks had. I felt as if I loved that glass. I touched it, it was cold. Oh! the recollection! sorrowful mirror, burning mirror, horrible mirror, which makes us suffer such torments! Happy are the men whose hearts forget everything that it has contained, everything that has passed before it, everything that has looked at itself in it, that has been reflected in its affection, in its love! How I suffer!

"I went on without knowing it, without wishing it; I went towards the cemetery. I found her simple grave, a white marble cross, with these few words:

" *'She loved, was loved, and died.'*

"She is there, below, decayed! How horrible! I sobbed with my forehead on the ground, and I stopped there for a long time, a long time. Then I saw that it was getting dark, and a strange, a mad wish, the wish of a despairing lover seized me. I wished to pass the night, the last night in weeping on her grave. But I should be seen and driven out. How was I to manage? I was cunning, and got up, and began to roam about in that city of the dead, I walked and walked. How small this city is, in comparison with the other, the city in which we live: And yet, how much more numerous the dead are than the living. We want high houses, wide streets, and much room for the four generations who see the daylight at the same time, drink water from the spring, and wine from the vines, and eat the bread from the plains.

"And for all the generations of the dead, for all that ladder of humanity that has descended down to us, there is scarcely anything afield,

scarcely anything! The earth takes them back, oblivion effaces them. Adieu!

"At the end of the abandoned cemetery, I suddenly perceived the one where those who have been dead a long time finish mingling with the soil, where the crosses themselves decay, where the last comers will be put to-morrow. It is full of untended roses, of strong and dark cypress trees, a sad and beautiful garden, nourished on human flesh.

"I was alone, perfectly alone, and so I crouched in a green tree, and hid myself there completely among the thick and somber branches, and I waited, clinging to the stem, like a shipwrecked man does to a plank.

"When it was quite dark, I left my refuge and began to walk softly, slowly, inaudibly, through that ground full of dead people, and I wandered about for a long time, but could not find her again. I went on with extended arms, knocking against the tombs with my hands, my feet, my knees, my chest, even with my head, without being able to find her. I touched and felt about like a blind man groping his way, I felt the stones, the crosses, the iron railings, the metal wreaths, and the wreaths of faded flowers! I read the names with my fingers, by passing them over the letters. What a night! What a night! I could not find her again!

"There was no moon. What a night! I am frightened, horribly frightened in these narrow paths, between two rows of graves. Graves! graves! graves! nothing but graves! On my right, on my left, in front of me, around me, everywhere there were graves! I sat down on one of them, for I could not walk any longer, my knees were so weak. I could hear my heart beat! And I could hear something else as well. What? A confused, nameless noise. Was the noise in my head in the impenetrable night, or beneath the mysterious earth, the earth sown with human corpses? I looked all around me, but I cannot say how long I remained there; I was paralyzed with terror, drunk with fright, ready to shout out, ready to die.

"Suddenly, it seemed to me as if the slab of

marble on which I was sitting, was moving. Certainly, it was moving, as if it were being raised. With a bound, I sprang on to the neighboring tomb, and I saw, yes, I distinctly saw the stone which I had just quitted, rise upright, and the dead person appeared, a naked skeleton, which was pushing the stone back with its bent back. I saw it quite clearly, although the night was so dark. On the cross I could read:

" *'Here lies Jacques Olivant, who died at the age of fifty-one. He loved his family, was kind and honorable, and died in the grace of the Lord.'*

"The dead man also read what was inscribed on his tombstone; then he picked up a stone off the path, a little, pointed stone, and began to scrape the letters carefully. He slowly effaced them altogether, and with the hollows of his eyes he looked at the places where they had been engraved, and, with the tip of the bone, that had been his forefinger, he wrote in luminous letters, like those lines which one traces on walls with the tip of a lucifer match:

" *'Here reposes Jacques Olivant, who died at the age of fifty-one. He hastened his father's death by his unkindness, as he wished to inherit his fortune, he tortured his wife, tormented his children, deceived his neighbors, robbed everyone he could, and died wretched.'*

"When he had finished writing, the dead man stood motionless, looking at his work, and on turning round I saw that all the graves were open, that all the dead bodies had emerged from them, and that all had effaced the lies inscribed on the gravestones by their relations, and had substituted the truth instead. And I saw that all had been tormentors of their neighbors— malicious, dishonest, hypocrites, liars, rogues, calumniators, envious; that they had stolen, deceived, performed every disgraceful, every abominable action, these good fathers, these faithful wives, these devoted sons, these chaste daughters, these honest tradesmen, these men and women who were called irreproachable, and they were called irreproachable, and they were all writing at the same time, on the threshold of their eternal abode, the truth, the terrible and the holy truth which everybody is ignorant of, or pretends to be ignorant of, while the others are alive.

"I thought that *she* also must have written something on her tombstone, and now, running without any fear among the half-open coffins, among the corpses and skeletons, I went towards her, sure that I should find her immediately. I recognized her at once, without seeing her face, which was covered by the winding-sheet, and on the marble cross, where shortly before I had read: *'She loved, was loved, and died,'* I now saw: *'Having gone out one day, in order to deceive her lover, she caught cold in the rain and died.'*

"It appears that they found me at daybreak, lying on the grave unconscious."

BODIES AND HEADS

STEVE RASNIC TEM

STEVE RASNIC TEM (1950–) was born in Jonesville, Virginia, in the middle of Appalachia. He went to college at Virginia Polytechnic Institute and State University, and Virginia Commonwealth, receiving a B.A. in English education. He later earned a master's in creative writing from Colorado State University. He lives in Denver with his wife; they have four children and three grandchildren.

Tem's first work was poetry, followed by short fiction. Since 1980, he has produced more than two hundred short stories of mystery, science fiction, dark fantasy, horror, and many that are difficult to categorize; they have been published in such magazines as *The Saint, Twilight Zone, Asimov's Science Fiction, The Magazine of Fantasy and Science Fiction,* and *Crimewave.* His stories have been nominated for a World Fantasy Award ("Firestorm") in 1983 and three Bram Stoker Awards ("Bodies and Heads," 1990; "Back Windows," 1991; and "Halloween Street," 2000). He also had Bram Stoker nominations for Best Novelette (*The Man on the Ceiling,* 2001) and Best Collection (*City Fishing,* 2001). He has written four novels: *Excavation* (1987), which was nominated for the Bram Stoker Best First Novel Award; *Daughters,* written with Melanie Tem (2001); *The Book of Days* (2003), nominated for the International Horror Guild Award; and *The Man on the Ceiling* (2008).

"Bodies and Heads" was first published in the anthology *Book of the Dead,* edited by John Skipp and Craig Spector (New York: Bantam, 1989).

STEVE RASNIC TEM

BODIES AND HEADS

IN THE HOSPITAL window the boy's head shook no no no. Elaine stopped on her way up the front steps, fascinated.

The boy's chest was rigid, his upper arms stiff. He seemed to be using something below the window to hold himself back, with all his strength, so that his upper body shook from the exertion.

She thought of television screens and their disembodied heads, ever so slightly out of focus, the individual dots of the transmitted heads moving apart with increasing randomness so that feature blended into feature and face into face until eventually the heads all looked the same: pinkish clouds of media flesh.

His head moved no no no. As if denying what was happening to him. He had been the first and was now the most advanced case of something they still had no name for. Given what had been going on in the rest of the country, the Denver Department of Health and Hospitals had naturally been quite concerned. An already Alert status had become a Crisis and doctors from all over—including a few with vague, unspecified governmental connections—had descended on the hospital.

Although it was officially discouraged, now and then in the hospital's corridors she had overheard the whispered word *zombie*.

"Jesus, will you look at him!"

Elaine turned. Mark planted a quick kiss on her lips. "Mark . . . somebody will see . . ." But she made no attempt to move away from him.

"I think they already know." He nibbled down her jawline. Elaine thought to pull away, but could not. His touch on her body, his attention, had always made her feel beautiful. It was, in fact, the only time she ever felt beautiful.

"You didn't want anyone to know just yet, remember?" She gasped involuntarily as he moved to the base of her throat. "Christ, Mark." She took a deep breath and pushed herself away from him. "Remember what you said about young doctors and hospital nurses? Especially young doctors with administrative aspirations?"

He looked at her. "Did I sound all that cold-blooded? I'm sorry."

She looked back up at the boy, Tom, in the window. Hopelessly out of control. No no no. "No—you weren't that bad. But I'm beginning to feel a little like somebody's mistress."

Some of the other nurses were now going into the building. Elaine thought they purposely avoided looking at the head-shaking boy in the window. "I'll make it up to you," Mark whispered. "I swear. Not much longer." But Elaine didn't answer; she just stared at the boy in the window.

There was now a steady stream of people walking up the steps, entering the hospital, very few permitting themselves to look at the boy. *Tom*, she thought. *His name is Tom.* She watched their quiet faces, wondering what they were thinking, if they were having stray thoughts about Tom but immediately suppressing them, or if they were having no thoughts about the boy at all. It bothered her not knowing. People led secret lives, secret even from those closest to them. It bothered her not knowing if they bore her ill will, or good will, or if for them she didn't exist at all. Her mother had always told her she cared far too much about what other people thought.

"I gather all the Fed doctors left yesterday afternoon," Mark said behind her.

"What? I thought they closed all the airports."

"They did. I heard this morning the governor even ordered gun emplacements on all the runways. Guess they left the city in a bus or something."

Elaine tried to rub the chill off her arms with shaking hands. The very idea of leaving the city in something other than an armored tank terrified her. It had been only a few months since the last flights. Then that plane had come in from Florida: all those dead people with suntans strolling off the plane as if they were on vacation. A short time later two small towns on Colorado's eastern plains—Kit Carson and Cheyenne Wells—were wiped out, or apparently wiped out, because only a few bodies were ever found. Then there was another plane, this one from Texas. Then another, from New York City. "It's hard to believe they could land a plane," had been Mark's comment at the time. But there were still more planes; the dead had an impeccable safety record.

"I'm just as glad to see them go," Mark said now. "Poking over that spastic kid like he was a two-headed calf. And still no signs of their mysterious 'zombie virus.'"

"No one knows how it starts," she said. "It could start anywhere. It could have dozens of different forms. Any vague gesture could be the first symptom."

"They haven't proven to me that it *is* a virus. No one really knows."

But Denver's quarantine seemed to be working. No one got in or out. All the roads closed, miles of perimeter patrolled. And no zombie sightings at all after those first few at the airport.

The boy's head drifted left and right as if in slow motion, as if weightless. "I missed the news this morning," she said.

"You looked so beat, I thought it best you sleep."

"I *need* to watch the news, Mark." Anger had such a grip on her jaw that she could hardly move it.

"You and most everybody else in Denver." She looked at him but said nothing. "Okay, I watched it for you. Just more of the same. A few distant shots of zombies in other states, looking like no more than derelicts prowling the cities, and the countryside, for food. Nothing much to tell you what they'd really be like. God knows what the world outside this city is really like anymore. I lost part of it—the reception just gets worse and worse."

Elaine knew that everything he was saying was true. But she kept watching the screens just the same, the faces seeming to get a little fuzzier every day as reception got worse, the distant cable stations disappearing one by one until soon only local programming was available, and then even the quality of that diminishing as equipment began to deteriorate and ghosts and static proliferated. But still she kept watching. Everybody she knew kept watching, desperate for any news outside of Denver.

And propped up in the window like a crazed TV announcer, young Tom's head moved no no no. At any moment she expected him to scream his denial: "No!" But no words ever passed the blurring lips. Just like all the other cases. No no no. Quiet heads that would suddenly explode into rhythmic, exaggerated denial. Their bodies fought it, held on to whatever was available so that muscles weren't twisted or bones torqued out of their sockets.

His head moved side to side: no no no. His long blond hair whipped and flew. His dark pebble eyes were lost in a nimbus of hair, now blond, now seeming to whiten more and more the faster his head flew. His expressionless face went steadily out of focus, and after a moment she realized she couldn't remember what he looked like, even though she had seen him several times a day every day since he had been admitted into the hospital.

What is he holding on to? she wondered, the boy's head now a cloud of mad insects, the movement having gone on impossibly long. His body vibrated within the broad window frame. At any moment she expected the rhythmic head to levitate him, out the window and over the empty, early-morning street. His features blurred in and out: he had four eyes, he had six. Three mouths that gasped for air attempting to scream. He had become a vision. He had become an angel.

"IT'S GOING TO take more than a few skin grafts to fix that one," Betty said, nervously rubbing the back of her neck. "My God, doesn't he ever stop?" They were at the windows above surgery. He'd been holding on to a hot radiator; it had required three aides to pull him off. Even anesthetized, the boy's head shook so vigorously the surgeons had had to strap his neck into something like a large dog collar. The surgeries would be exploratory, mostly, until they found something specific. It bothered Elaine. Tom was a human being. He had secrets. "Look at his eyes," Elaine said. His eyes stared at her. As his face blurred in side-to-side movement, his eyes remained fixed on her. But that couldn't be.

"I can't see his eyes," Betty said with sudden vehemence. "Jeezus, will you look at him? They oughta do something with his brain while they're at it. They oughta go in there and snip out whatever's causin' it."

Elaine stared at the woman. *Snip it out. Where?* At one time they had been friends, or almost friends. Betty had wanted it, but Elaine just hadn't been able to respond. It had always been a long time between friends for her. The edge of anger in Betty's voice made her anxious. "They don't know what's causing it," Elaine said softly.

"My mama don't believe in 'em." Betty turned and looked at Elaine with heavily-shadowed eyes, anemic-looking skin. "Zombies. Mama thinks the zombies are something the networks came up with. She says real people would never do disgustin' things like they're sayin' the zombies do." Elaine found herself mesmerized by the lines in Betty's face. She tried to follow each one, where they became deeper, trapping dried rivers of hastily applied makeup, where pads and applicators had bruised, then covered up the skin. Betty's eyes blinked several times quickly in succession, the pupils bright and fixed like a doll's. "But then she always said we never landed on the moon, neither. Said they filmed all that out at Universal Studios." Milky spittle had adhered to the inside corners of Betty's mouth, which seemed unusually heavy with lipstick today. "Guess she could be right. Never read about zombies in the Bible, and you would think they'd be there if there was such a thing." Betty rubbed her arm across her forehead. "Goodness, my skin's so *dry*! I swear I'm flakin' down to the *nub*!" A slight ripple of body odor moved across Elaine's face. She could smell Betty's deodorant, and under that, something slightly sour and slightly sweet at the same time.

That's the way people's secrets smell, Elaine thought, and again wondered at herself for thinking such things. *People have more secrets than you could possibly imagine.* She wondered what secret things Betty was capable of, what Betty might do to a zombie if she had the opportunity, what Betty might do to Tom. "Tom's not a zombie," she said slowly, wanting to plant the idea firmly in Betty's head. "There's been no proof of a connection. No proof that he has a form of the virus, if there is a virus. No proof that he has a virus at all."

"My mama never believed much in *coincidences,*" Betty said.

Elaine spent most of the night up in the ward with Tom and the other cases that had appeared: an elderly woman, a thirty-year-old retarded man, twin girls of thirteen who at times shook their heads in unison, a twenty-four-year-old hospital maintenance worker whose symptoms had started only a couple of days ago. As in every other place she'd worked, a TV set mounted high overhead murmured all evening. She couldn't get the vertical to hold. The announcer's head rolled rapidly by, disappearing at the top of the screen and reappearing at the bottom. But as she watched she began thinking it was different heads, the announcer switching them at the rate of perhaps one per second. She wondered how he'd managed the trick. Then she wondered if all newscasters did that, switching through a multitude of heads so quickly it couldn't be detected by the average viewer. She wanted to turn off the TV, but the doctors said it was best to leave it on for stimulation, even though their charges appeared completely unaware of it. Dozens of heads shaking no no no. Heads in the windows. Heads exploding with denial. Heads like bombs.

Two more nurses had quit that day. At least they had called; some had just stopped showing up. All the nurses were on double shifts now, with patient loads impossible to handle. Betty came in at six to help Elaine with feeding some of the head shakers.

"Now buckle the strap," Elaine said. She had the "horse collar," a padded brace, around the old woman's neck, her arms around the woman's head to hold it still. Betty fiddled with the straps.

"Damn!" Betty said. "I can't get it to buckle!"

"Hurry! I can't hold her head still much longer." Holding the head still put undue pressure on other parts of the system. Elaine could hear the woman's protesting stomach, and then both bladder and bowel were emptied.

"There!" Elaine let go and the old woman's head shook in her collar. Betty tried to spoon the food in. The woman's body spasmed like a lizard nailed to a board. Sometimes they broke their own bones that way. Elaine held her breath. Even strapped down, the old woman's face moved to an amazing degree. Like a latex mask attached loosely to the skull, her face slipped left and right, led by an agonized mouth apparently desperate to avoid the spoon. Elaine thought it disgusting, but it was better than any other

method they'd tried. The head shakers choked on feeding tubes, pulled out IVs, and getting a spoon into those rapidly moving mouths had been almost impossible.

"I know it's your turn, but I'll go feed Tom," Elaine said.

Betty glanced up from the vibrating head, a dribble of soft brown food high on her right cheek. "Thanks, Elaine. I owe you." She turned back, aiming the spoon of dripping food at the twisting head. "I don't know. If I had to be like them . . . I don't know. I think I'd rather be dead."

Tom had always been the worst to feed. Elaine fixed a large plastic bib around his neck, then put one around her neck as well. He stared at her. Even as the spasms pulled his eyes rapidly past, she could see a little-boy softness in those adolescent eyes, an almost pleading vulnerability so at odds with the violent contortions his body made.

She moved the spoon in from the side, just out of his peripheral vision. But every time the metal touched the soft, pink flesh of the lips, the head jerked violently away. Again and again. And when some food finally did slip into the mouth cavity, he choked, his eyes became enormous, the whites swelling in panic, and his mouth showered it back at her. It was as if his mouth despised the food, reviled the food, and could not stand to be anywhere near it. As if she were asking him to eat his own feces.

She looked down at the bowl of mushy food. Tom reached his hand in, clutched a wet mess of it, then tried to stuff it into his own mouth. The mouth twisted away. His hand did this again and again, and still his mouth rejected it. Eventually his hands, denied the use of the mouth, began smearing the food on his face, his neck, his chest, his legs, all over his body, pushing it into the skin and eventually into every orifice available to receive it. He looked as if he had been swimming in garbage.

Tom's face, Tom's eyes, pleaded with her as his hands shoved great wet cakes of brown, green, and yellow food up under his blue hospital pajama top and down inside his underwear. Finally, as if in exasperation, Tom's body voided itself, drenching itself and Elaine in vomit, urine, and feces.

Elaine backed away, ripping off her plastic gloves and bib. "Stop it! Stop it! Stop it!" she screamed, as Tom's head moved no no no, and his body continued to pat itself, fondle itself, probe itself lovingly with food-smeared fingers. Elaine's vision blurred as she choked back the tears. Tom's body suddenly looked like some great bag of loose flesh, poked with wet, running holes, some ugly organic machine, inefficient in input and output. She continued to stare at it as it fed and drained, probed and made noises, all independent of the head and its steady no no no beat.

She ran into Betty out in the corridor. "I have to leave *now*," she said. "Betty, I'm *sorry!*"

Betty looked past her into the room where Tom was still playing with his food. "It's all right, kid. You just go get some sleep. I'll put old Master Tom to bed."

Elaine stared at her, sudden alarms of distrust going off in her head. "You'll be okay with him? I mean—he didn't *mean* it, Betty."

Betty looked offended. "Hey! Just what kind of nurse do you think I am? I'm going to hose him off and tuck him in, that's all. Unless you're insisting I read him a bedtime story, too? Maybe give him a kiss on the cheek? If I could *hit* his cheek, that is."

"I'm sorry. I didn't mean . . ."

"I know what you meant. Get some rest, Elaine. You're beat."

But Elaine couldn't bear to attempt the drive home, searching the dark corners at every intersection, waiting for the shambling strangers who lived in the streets to come close enough that she could get a good look at their faces. So that she could see if their faces were torn, their eyes distant. Or if their heads were beginning to shake.

Mark had been staying in the janitor's apartment down in the basement, near the morgue. The janitor had been replaced by a cleaning service some time back as a cost-cutting measure.

Supposedly it was to be turned into a lab, but that had never happened. Mark always said he really didn't mind living by the morgue. He said it cut the number of drop-in visitors drastically.

Elaine went there.

"SO DON'T GO back," Mark said, nibbling at her ear. He was biting too hard, and his breath bore a trace of foulness. Elaine squirmed away and climbed out of bed.

"I have to go to the bathroom," she said. After closing the bathroom door, she ran water into the sink so that she would be unable to hear herself pee. People reacted to crisis in different ways, she supposed. Mark's way was to treat all problems as if they were of equal value, whether it was deciding what wattage light bulb to buy or the best way to feed a zombie.

Elaine looked down at her legs. They'd gotten a little spongier each year; her thighs seemed to spread a little wider each time she sat down. Here and there were little lumps and depressions which seemed to move from time to time. Her belly bulged enough now that she could see only the slightest halo of dark pubic hair when she looked down like this. And the pubic hair itself wasn't all that dark anymore. There were streaks of gray, and what had surprised and confused her, red. By her left knee a flowery pattern of broken blood vessels was darkening into a bruise. She tried to smell herself. She sometimes imagined she must smell terrible.

It seemed she had always watched herself grow older while sitting on the toilet. Sitting on the toilet, she found she couldn't avoid looking at her legs, her belly, her pubic hair. She couldn't avoid smelling herself.

She stood up and looked at herself in the mirror. She looked for scars, bruises, signs of corruption she might have missed before. She pretended her face was a patient's, and she washed it, brushed her hair. As a child she'd pretended her face was a doll's face, her hair a doll's hair. She'd never trusted mirrors. They didn't show the secrets inside.

"I have to go back," Elaine said coming out of the bathroom. "We're short-handed. They count on me. And I can't let Betty work that ward alone."

But Mark was busy fiddling with the VCR. "Huh? Oh yeah . . . well, you do what you think is right, honey. Hey—I got us a tape from one of the security people. The cops confiscated it two weeks ago and it's been circulating ever since." Elaine walked slowly around the bed and stood by Mark as he adjusted the contrast. "Pretty crudely made, but you can still make out most of it."

The screen was dark, with occasional lighter shadows floating through that dark. Then twin pale spots resolved out of the distortion, moving rapidly left and right, up and down. Elaine thought of headlights gone crazy, maybe a moth's wings. Then the camera pulled back suddenly, as if startled, and she saw that it was a black man's immobile face, but with eyes that jumped around as if they were being given some sort of electrical shock. Frightened eyes. Eyes moving no no no.

But as the camera dwelled on this face, Elaine noticed that there was more wrong here than simple fright. The dark skin of the face looked torn all along the hairline, peeled back, and crusted a dark red. A cut bisected the left cheek; she thought she could see several tissue layers deep into the valley it made. And when the head moved, she saw a massive hole just under the chin where throat cartilage danced in open air.

"That's one of them," she said in a soft voice filled with awe. "A zombie."

"The tape was smuggled in from somewhere down South, I hear," Mark said distractedly, moving even closer to the screen. "Beats me how they can still get these videos into the city."

"But the quarantine . . ."

"Supply and demand, honey." As the camera moved back farther, Elaine was surprised to see live, human hands pressing down on the zombie's shoulders. "Get a load of this," Mark said, an anxious edge to his voice.

The camera jerked back suddenly to show the zombie pressed against gray wooden planks— the side of a barn or some other farm building. The zombie was naked: large wounds covered much of its body. Like a decoration, an angry red scar ran the length of the dangling, slightly paler penis. Six or seven large men in jeans and old shirts—work clothes—were pushing the zombie flat against the gray wood, moving their rough hands around to avoid its snapping teeth. The more they avoided its teeth, the more manic the zombie became, jerking its head like a striking snake, twisting its head side to side and snapping its mouth.

An eighth man—fat, florid, baggy tits hanging around each side of his bib overalls—carried a bucket full of hammers onto the scene and handed one to each of the men restraining the zombie. Then the fat man reached deeper into the bucket and came out with a handful of ten-penny nails, which he also distributed to the men.

Mark held his breath as the men proceeded to drive the nails through the body of the zombie—through shoulders, arms, hands, ankles— pinning it like a squirming lizard on the boards.

The zombie showed no pain, but struggled against the nails, tearing wider holes. Little or no blood dripped from these holes, but Elaine did think she could detect a clear, glistening fluid around each wound.

The men stared at the zombie for a moment. A couple of them giggled like adolescent girls, but for the most part they looked dissatisfied.

One of the men nailed the zombie's ears to the wall. Another used several nails to pin the penis and scrotum; several more nails severed it. The zombie pelvis did a little gyration above the spot where the genitals had become a trophy on the barn wall.

The zombie seemed not to notice the difference. The men laughed and pointed.

There were no screams on this sound track. Just laughter and animalistic zombie grunts.

"Jesus, Mark." Elaine turned away from the TV, ashamed of herself for having watched that long. "Jesus." She absentmindedly stroked his hair, running her hand down his face, vaguely wondering how she could get him away from the TV, or at least to turn it off.

"Damn. Look, they're bringing out the ax and the sickle," Mark said.

"I don't want to look," she said, on the verge of tears. "I don't want *you* to look either. It's crazy, it's . . . pornographic."

"Hey, I know this is pretty sick stuff, but I think it tells us something about the way things *are* out there. Christ, they won't show it to us on the news. Not the way it *really* is. We need to know things like this exist."

"I know goddamn well they exist! I don't need it rubbed in my face!"

Elaine climbed into bed and turned her back on him. She tried to ignore the static-filled moans and giggles coming from the TV. She pretended she was sick in a hospital bed, that she had no idea what was going on in the world and never could. A minute or two later Mark turned off the TV. She imagined the image of the zombie's head fading, finally just its startled eyes showing, then nothing.

She felt Mark's hands gently rubbing her back. Then he lay down on the bed, half on top of her, still rubbing her tight flesh.

"They're not in Denver," he said softly. "There's still been no sightings. No zombies here, ma'am." The rubbing moved to her thighs. She tried to ignore it.

"If there were, would people here act like those rednecks in your damn video? Jesus, Mark. Nobody should be allowed to behave that way."

He stopped rubbing. She could hear him breathing. "People do strange things sometimes," he finally said. "Especially in strange times. Especially groups of people. They get scared and they lose control." He resumed rubbing her shoulders, then moved to her neck. "There are no zombies in Denver, honey. No sightings. All the news types keep telling us that. You *know* that; you're always watching them."

"Maybe they won't look the same."

"What do you mean?"

"Maybe they won't look the same here as

they do everywhere else. Maybe it'll take a different form, and we won't know what to look for. They think it's a virus—well, viruses mutate, they have different forms. Maybe the doctors and the Health Department and all those reporters aren't as smart as they think they are. Christ, it might even be some form of venereal disease."

"Hey. That's not funny."

"You think I intended it to be?" She could feel her anger bunching up the shoulder muscles beneath his hands. She could feel all this beginning to change her; no way would she be the same after it all stopped. If it ever stopped.

"I know. I know," he said. "This is hard on all of us." Then he started kissing her. Uncharitably, she wondered if it was because he'd run out of things to say to her. But she found her body responding, even though her head was sick with him and all his easy answers and explanations.

His kisses ran down her neck and over her breasts like a warm liquid. And her body welcomed it, had felt so cold before. "Turn out the light, please, Mark," she said, grudgingly giving in to the body, hating the body for it. He left silently to turn out the light, then was back again, kissing her, touching her, warming her one ribbon of flesh at a time.

In the darkness she could not see her own body. She could imagine away the blemishes, the ugly, drifting spots, the dry patches of skin, the small corruptions patterning death. And she could imagine that his breath was always sweet smelling. She could imagine his hair dark and full. She could imagine the image of the zombie's destroyed penis out of her head when Mark made love to her. And in this darkness she could almost imagine that Mark would never die.

His body continued to fondle her after she knew his head had gone to sleep.

MARK'S KISS WOKE her up the next morning. "Last night was wonderful," he whispered. "Glad you finally got over whatever was bothering you." That last comment made her angry, and she tried to tell him that, but she was too sleepy and he'd already left. And then she was sorry he was gone and wished he would come back so his touch would make her body feel beautiful again.

She stared at the dead gray eye of the TV, then glanced at the VCR. Apparently Mark had taken his video with him. She was relieved, and a little ashamed of herself. She turned the TV on. The eye filled with static, but she could hear the female newscaster's flat, almost apathetic voice.

". . . the federal government has reported increased progress with the so-called 'zombie' epidemic . . ." Then this grainy, washed-out bit of stock footage came on the screen: men in hunters' clothing and surplus fatigues shooting zombies in the head from a safe distance. Shooting them and then moving along calmly down a dirt road. The newscaster appeared on the screen again: silent, emotionless, makeup perfect, her head rolling up into the top of the cabinet.

It was after four in the morning. Betty had handled the ward by herself all night and would need some relief. Elaine dressed quickly and headed upstairs.

Betty wasn't at the nurse's station. Elaine started down the dim-lit corridor, peeking into each room. In the beds dark shadows shook and moved their heads no no no, even in their dreams. But no sign of Betty.

The last room was Tom's, and he wasn't there. She could hear a steady padding of feet up ahead, in the dark tunnel that led to the new wing. She tried the light switch, but apparently it wasn't connected. Out of her pocket she pulled the penlight that she used for making chart notations in patients' darkened rooms. It made a small, distorted circle of illumination. She started down the darkened tunnel, flashing her small light now and then on the uncompleted ceiling, the holes in the walls where they'd run electrical conduit, the tile floor streaked white with plaster dust, littered with wire, pipe, and lumber.

She came out into a giant open area that hadn't yet been divided into rooms. Cable snaked out of large holes in the ceiling, dangled by her face. Streetlight filtered through the tall, narrow windows, striping piles of ceiling tile, paint cans, and metal posts. They were supposed to be finished with all this by next month. She wondered if they would even bother, given how things were in the city. The wing looked more like a structure they were stripping, demolishing, than one they were constructing. Like a building under autopsy, she thought. She could no longer hear the other footsteps ahead of her. She heard her own steps, crunching the grit under foot, and her own ragged breath.

She flashed her light overhead, and something flashed back. A couple of cameras projected from a metal beam. Blind, their wires wrapped uselessly around the beam. She walked on, following the connections with her light. There were a series of blank television monitors, their enormous gray eyes staring down at her.

Someone cried softly in the darkness ahead. Elaine aimed her light there, but all she could see were crates, paneling leaned against the wall and stacked on the floor, metal supports and crosspieces. A tangle of sharp angles. But then there was that cry again. "Betty? Tom?"

A pale face loomed into the blurred, yellowed beam. A soft shake of the face, side to side. The eyes were too white, and had a distant stare.

"Betty?" The face shook and shook again. Betty stumbled out of a jumble of cardboard boxes, construction and stored medical supplies breaking beneath her stumbling feet.

"No . . ." Betty's mouth moved as if in slow-motion. Her lipstick looked too bright, her mascara too dark. "No," she said again, and something dark dripped out of her eyes as her head began to shake.

Elaine's light picked up a glint in Betty's right hand. "Betty?" Betty stumbled forward and fell, keeping that right hand out in front of her. Elaine stepped closer thinking to help Betty up, but then saw that Betty's right arm was swinging slowly side to side, a scalpel clutched tightly in her hand. "Betty! Let me help you!"

"No!" Betty screamed. Her head began to thrash back and forth on the litter-covered floor. Her cheeks rolled again and again over broken glass. Blood welled, smeared, and stained her face as her head moved no no no. She struggled to control the hand holding the scalpel. Then she suddenly plunged it into her throat. Her left hand came up jerkily and helped her pull the scalpel through muscle and skin.

Elaine fell to her knees, grabbed paper and cloth, anything at hand to dam the dark flow from Betty's throat. After a minute or two she stopped and turned away.

There were more noises off in the darkness. At the back of the room where she'd first seen Betty, Elaine found a doorless passage to another room. Her light now had a vague reddish tinge. She wondered hazily if there was blood on the flashlight lens, or blood in her eyes. But the light still showed the way. She followed it, hearing a harsh, wet sound. For just a moment she thought that maybe Betty might still be alive. She started to go back when she heard it again; it was definitely in the room ahead of her.

She tried not to think of Betty as she made her way through the darkness. *That wasn't Betty. That was just her body.* Elaine's mother used to babble things like that to her all the time. Spiritual things. Elaine didn't know what she herself felt. Someone dies, you don't know them anymore. You can't imagine what they might be thinking.

The room had the sharp smell of fresh paint. Drop cloths had been piled in the center of the floor. The windows were crisscrossed by long stretches of masking tape, and outside lights left odd patterns like angular spiderwebs on all the objects in the room.

A heavy cord dropped out of the ceiling to a small switch box on the floor, which was in turn connected to a large mercury lamp the construction crew must have been using. Elaine bent over and flipped the switch.

The light was like an explosion. It created strange, skeletal shadows in the drop cloths, as if she were suddenly seeing *through* them. She walked steadily toward the pile, keeping an eye on those shadows.

Elaine reached out her hand and several of the cloths flew away.

My god, Betty killed him! Betty killed him and cut off that awful, shaking head! The head was a small, sad mound by the boy's filthy, naked body. A soft whispering seemed to enter Elaine's ear, which brought her attention back to that head.

She stopped to feel the draft, but there was no draft, even though she could hear it rising in her head, whistling through her hair and making it grow longer, making it grow white, making her older.

Because of a trick of the light the boy's—Tom's—eyes looked open in his severed head. Because of a trick of the light the eyes blinked several times as if trying to adjust to that light.

He had a soft, confused stare, like a stuffed toy's. His mouth moved like a baby's. Then his naked, headless body sat up on the floor. Then the headless body struggled to its feet, weaving unsteadily. *No inner ear for balance,* Elaine thought, and almost laughed. She felt crazed, capable of anything.

The body stood motionless, staring at Elaine. Staring at her. The nipples looked darker than normal and seemed to track her as she moved sideways across the room. The hairless breasts gave the body's new eyes a slight bulge. The navel was flat and neutral, but Elaine wondered if the body could smell her with it. The penis—the tongue—curled in and out of the bearded mouth of the body's new face. The body moved stiffly, puppet-like, toward its former head.

The body picked up its head with one hand and threw it out into a darkened corner of the room. It made a sound like a wet mop slapping the linoleum floor. Elaine heard a soft whimpering that soon ceased. She could hear ugly, moist noises coming from the body's new bearded mouth. She could hear skin splitting, she could see blood dripping to the dusty floor as the body's new mouth widened and brought new lips up out of the meaty darkness inside.

The sound of a wheelchair rolling in behind

her. She turned and watched as the old woman grabbed each side of her ancient-looking, spasming head. The head continued its insistent no no no even as the hands and arms increased their pressure, the old lady's body quaking from the strain. Then suddenly the no no no stopped, the arms lifted up on the now-motionless head, and pulled it away from the body, cracking open the spine and stretching the skin and muscle of the neck until they tore or snapped apart like rotted bands of elastic. The old woman's fluids gushed, then suddenly stopped, both head and body sealing the breaks with pale tissues stretched almost to transparency.

The new face on the old woman's body was withered, pale, almost hairless, and resembled the old face to a remarkable degree. The new eyes sagged lazily, and Elaine wondered if this body might be blind.

The old woman's head gasped, and was still. The young male body picked up the woman's dead head and stuffed it into its hairy mouth. Its new, pale pink lips stretched and rolled. Elaine could see the stomach acid bubbling on those lips, the steadily diminishing face of the old lady appearing now and then in the gaps between the male body's lips as the body continued its digestion. The old woman's denuded skull fell out on the linoleum and rattled its way across the floor.

Elaine closed her eyes and tried to remember everything her mother had ever told her. Someone dies and you don't know them anymore. It's just a dead body—it's not my friend. My friend lives in the head forever. Death is a mystery. Stay away from crowds. Crowds want to eat you.

She wanted Mark here with her. She wanted Mark to touch her body and make her feel beautiful. No. People can't be trusted. No. She wanted to love her own body. No. She wanted her body to love her. No. She tried to imagine Mark touching her, making love to her. No. With dead eyes, mouth splitting at the corners. No. Removing his head and shoving it deep inside her, his eyes and tongue finding and eating all her secrets.

No no no, her head said. Elaine's head moved no no no. And each time her vision swept across the room with the rhythmic swing of her shaking head, the bodies were closer.

DEATH AND SUFFRAGE

DALE BAILEY

BORN IN PRINCETON, West Virginia, Dale Bailey (1968–) began writing as a very young child, producing his stories in booklet form to give to family and friends. After receiving his Ph.D. in English, he taught that subject at Lenoir-Rhyne College in North Carolina but continued to write. Most of his work has been in the weird menace category, combining elements of science fiction, fantasy, and horror. Many of his twenty-five or so short stories have been published in *The Magazine of Fantasy and Science Fiction*, but other publications in which his work has appeared include *Amazing Stories* and *Pulphouse*.

Bailey won the International Horror Guild Award for his novelette *Death and Suffrage* in 2003, the same year that he was nominated in the Best First Novel category for *The Fallen*. He has written two other novels, *House of Bones* (2003), which is reminiscent of Shirley Jackson's *The Haunting of Hill House*, and *Sleeping Policeman* (2006), written with Jack Slay Jr. The title story of his collection *The Resurrection Man's Legacy and Other Stories* (2003) was nominated for a Nebula Award and has been optioned by 20th Century Fox for a motion picture. His doctoral thesis was slightly rewritten and published by Bowling Green University's Popular Press as *American Nightmares: The Haunted House Formula in American Popular Fiction* (1999), the theme of which inspired his novel *House of Bones*.

Death and Suffrage was originally published in the February 2002 issue of *The Magazine of Fantasy and Science Fiction*.

DALE BAILEY

DEATH AND SUFFRAGE

IT'S FUNNY HOW things happen, Burton used to tell me. The very moment you're engaged in some task of mind-numbing insignificance—cutting your toenails, maybe, or fishing in the sofa for the remote—the world is being refashioned around you. You stand before a mirror to brush your teeth, and halfway around the planet flood waters are on the rise. Every minute of every day, the world transforms itself in ways you can hardly imagine, and there you are, sitting in traffic or wondering what's for lunch or just staring blithely out a window. History happens while you're making other plans, Burton always says.

I guess I know that now. I guess we all know that.

Me, I was in a sixth-floor Chicago office suite working on my résumé when it started. The usual chaos swirled around me—phones braying, people scurrying about, the televisions singing exit poll data over the din—but it all had a forced artificial quality. The campaign was over. Our numbers people had told us everything we needed to know: when the polls opened that morning, Stoddard was up seventeen points. So there I sat, dejected and soon to be unemployed, with my feet on a rented desk and my lap-top propped against my knees, mulling over synonyms for *directed*. As in *directed a staff of fifteen.* As in *directed public relations for the Democratic National Committee.* As in *directed a national political campaign straight into the toilet.*

Then CNN started emitting the little overture that means somewhere in the world history is happening, just like Burton always says.

I looked up as Lewis turned off the television.

"What'd you do that for?"

Lewis leaned over to shut my computer down. "I'll show you," he said.

I followed him through the suite, past clumps of people huddled around televisions. Nobody looked my way. Nobody had looked me in the eye since Sunday. I tried to listen, but over the shocked buzz in the room I couldn't catch much more than snatches of unscripted anchor-speak. I didn't see Burton, and I supposed he was off drafting his concession speech. "No sense delaying the inevitable," he had told me that morning.

"What gives?" I said to Lewis in the hall, but he only shook his head.

Lewis is a big man, fifty, with the drooping posture and hangdog expression of an adolescent. He stood in the elevator and watched the numbers cycle, rubbing idly at an acne scar. He had lots of them, a whole face pitted from what had to be among the worst teenage years in human history. I had never liked him much, and I liked him even less right then, but you couldn't help admiring the intelligence in his eyes. If Burton had been elected, Lewis would have served him well. Now he'd be looking for work instead.

The doors slid apart, and Lewis steered me through the lobby into a typical November morning in Chicago: a diamond-tipped wind boring in from the lake, a bruised sky spitting something that couldn't decide whether it wanted to be rain or snow. I grew up in Southern California—my grandparents raised me—and there's not much I hate more than Chicago weather; but that morning I stood there with my shirt-sleeves rolled to the elbow and my tie whipping over my shoulder, and I didn't feel a thing.

"My God," I said; and for a moment, my mind just locked up. All I could think was that not two hours ago I had stood in this very spot

watching Burton work the crowd, and then the world had still been sane. Afterwards, Burton had walked down the street to cast his ballot. When he stepped out of the booth, the press had been waiting. Burton charmed them, the consummate politician even in defeat. We could have done great things.

And even then the world had still been sane.

No longer.

It took me a moment to sort it all out—the pedestrians shouldering by with wild eyes, the bell-hop standing dumbfounded before the hotel on the corner, his chin bobbing at half-mast. Three taxis had tangled up in the street, bleeding steam, and farther up the block loomed an overturned bus the size of a beached plesiosaur. Somewhere a woman was screaming atonally, over and over and over, with staccato hitches for breath. Sirens wailed in the distance. A t.v. crew was getting it all on tape, and for the first time since I blew Burton's chance to hold the highest office in the land, I stood in the presence of a journalist who wasn't shoving a mike in my face to ask me what had come over me.

I was too stunned even to enjoy it.

Instead, like Lewis beside me, I just stared across the street at the polling place. Dead people had gathered there, fifteen or twenty of them, and more arriving. Even then, there was never any question in my mind that they were dead. You could see it in the way they held their bodies, stiff as marionettes; in their shuffling gaits and the bright haunted glaze of their eyes. You could see it in the lacerations yawning open on the ropy coils of their guts, in their random nakedness, their haphazard clothes—hospital gowns and blood-stained blue jeans and immaculate suits fresh from unsealed caskets. You could see it in the dark patches of decay that blossomed on their flesh. You could just see that they were dead. It was every zombie movie you ever saw, and then some.

Gooseflesh erupted along my arms, and it had nothing to do with the wind off Lake Michigan.

"My God," I said again, when I finally managed to unlock my brain. "What do they want?"

"They want to vote," said Lewis.

THE DEAD HAVE been voting in Chicago elections since long before Richard J. Daley took office, one wag wrote in the next morning's *Tribune, but yesterday's events bring a whole new meaning to the tradition.*

I'll say.

The dead had voted, all right, and not just in Chicago. They had risen from hospital gurneys and autopsy slabs, from open coffins and embalming tables in every precinct in the nation, and they had cast their ballots largely without interference. Who was going to stop them? More than half the poll-workers had abandoned ship when the zombies started shambling through the doors, and even workers who stayed at their posts had usually permitted them to do as they pleased. The dead didn't threaten anyone—they didn't do much of anything you'd expect zombies to do, in fact. But most people found that inscrutable gaze unnerving. Better to let them cast their ballots than bear for long the knowing light in those strange eyes.

And when the ballots were counted, we learned something else as well: They voted for Burton. Every last one of them voted for Burton.

"IT'S YOUR FAULT," Lewis said at breakfast the next day.

Everyone else agreed with him, I could tell, the entire senior staff, harried and sleep-deprived. They studied their food as he ranted, or scrutinized the conference table or scribbled frantic notes in their day-planners. Anything to avoid looking me in the eye. Even Burton, alone at the head of the table, just munched on a bagel and stared at CNN, the muted screen aflicker with footage of zombies staggering along on their unfathomable errands. Toward dawn, as the final tallies rolled in from the western dis-

tricts, they had started to gravitate toward cemeteries. No one yet knew why.

"*My* fault?" I said, but my indignation was manufactured. About five that morning, waking from nightmare in my darkened hotel room, I had arrived at the same conclusion as everyone else.

"The goddamn talk show," Lewis said, as if that explained everything.

And maybe it did.

The goddamn talk show in question was none other than *Crossfire* and the Sunday before the polls opened I got caught in it. I had broken the first commandment of political life, a commandment I had flogged relentlessly for the last year. Stay on message, stick to the talking points.

Thou shalt not speak from the heart.

The occasion of this amateurish mistake was a six-year-old girl named Dana Maguire. Three days before I went on the air, a five-year-old boy gunned Dana down in her after-school program. The kid had found the pistol in his father's nightstand, and just as Dana's mother was coming in to pick her up, he tugged it from his insulated lunch sack and shot Dana in the neck. She died in her mother's arms while the five-year-old looked on in tears.

Just your typical day in America, except the first time I saw Dana's photo in the news, I felt something kick a hole in my chest. I can remember the moment to this day: October light slanting through hotel windows, the television on low while I talked to my grandmother in California. I don't have much in the way of family. There had been an uncle on my father's side, but he had drifted out of my life after my folks died, leaving my mother's parents to raise me. There's just the two of us since my grandfather passed on five years ago, and even in the heat of a campaign, I try to check on Gran every day. Mostly she rattles on about old folks in the home, a litany of names and ailments I can barely keep straight at the best of times. And that afternoon, half-watching some glib CNN hardbody do a stand-up in front of Little Tykes Academy, I lost the thread of her words altogether.

Next thing I know, she's saying, "Robert, Robert—" in this troubled voice, and me, I'm sitting on a hotel bed in Dayton, Ohio, weeping for a little girl I never heard of. Grief, shock, you name it—ten years in public life, nothing like that had ever happened to me before. But after that, I couldn't think of it in political terms. After that, Dana Maguire was personal.

Predictably, the whole thing came up on *Crossfire*. Joe Stern, Stoddard's campaign director and a man I've known for years, leaned into the camera and espoused the usual line—you know, the one about the constitutional right to bear arms, as if Jefferson had personally foreseen the rapid-fire semi-automatic with a sixteen-round clip. Coming from the mouth of Joe Stern, a smug fleshy ideologue who ought to have known better, this line enraged me.

Even so, I hardly recognized the voice that responded to him. I felt as though something else was speaking through me—as though a voice had possessed me, a speaker from that broken hole in the center of my chest.

What it said, that voice, was: "If Grant Burton is elected, he'll see that every handgun in the United States is melted into pig iron. He'll do everything in his power to save the Dana Maguires of this nation."

Joe Stern puffed up like a toad. "This isn't about Dana Maguire—"

The voice interrupted him. "If there's any justice in the universe, Dana Maguire will rise up from her grave to haunt you," the voice said. It said, "If it's not about Dana Maguire, then what on Earth is it about?"

Stoddard had new ads in saturation before the day was out: Burton's face, my words in voice-over. *If Grant Burton is elected, he'll see that every handgun in the United States is melted into pig iron.* By Monday afternoon, we had plummeted six points and Lewis wasn't speaking to me.

I couldn't seem to shut him up now, though.

He leaned across the table and jabbed a thick finger at me, overturning a Styrofoam cup of coffee. I watched the black pool spread as he shouted. "We were up five points, we had it won before you opened your goddamn—"

Angela Dey, our chief pollster, interrupted him. "Look!" she said, pointing at the television.

Burton touched the volume button on the remote, but the image on the screen was clear enough: a cemetery in upstate New York, one of the new ones where the stones are set flush to the earth to make mowing easier. Three or four zombies had fallen to their knees by a fresh grave.

"Good God," Dey whispered. "What are they doing?"

No one gave her an answer and I suppose she hadn't expected one. She could see as well as the rest of us what was happening. The dead were scrabbling at the earth with their bare hands.

A line from some old poem I had read in college—

—*ahh, who's digging on my grave*—

—lodged in my head, rattling around like angry candy, and for the first time I had a taste of the hysteria that would possess us all by the time this was done. Graves had opened, the dead walked the earth. All humanity trembled.

Ahh, who's digging on my grave?

Lewis flung himself back against his chair and glared at me balefully. "This is all your fault."

"At least they voted for us," I said.

NOT THAT WE swept into the White House at the head of a triumphal procession of zombies. Anything but, actually. The voting rights of the dead turned out to be a serious constitutional question, and Stoddard lodged a complaint with the Federal Election Commission. Dead people had no say in the affairs of the living, he argued, and besides, none of them were legally registered anyway. Sensing defeat, the Democratic National Committee countersued, claiming that the sheer *presence* of the dead may have kept legitimate voters from the polls.

While the courts pondered these issues in silence, the world convulsed. Church attendance soared. The president impaneled experts and blue-ribbon commissions, the Senate held hearings. The CDC convened a task force to search for biological agents. At the UN, the Security Council debated quarantine against the United States; the stock market lost fifteen percent on the news.

Meanwhile, the dead went unheeding about their business. They never spoke or otherwise attempted to communicate, yet you could sense an intelligence, inhuman and remote, behind their mass resurrection. They spent the next weeks opening fresh graves, releasing the recently buried from entombment. With bare hands, they clawed away the dirt; through sheer numbers, they battered apart the concrete vaults and sealed caskets. You would see them in the streets, stinking of formaldehyde and putrefaction, their hands torn and ragged, the rich earth of the grave impacted under their fingernails.

Their numbers swelled.

People died, but they didn't *stay* dead; the newly resurrected kept busy at their graves.

A week after the balloting, the Supreme Court handed down a decision overturning the election. Congress, meeting in emergency session, set a new date for the first week of January. If nothing else, the year 2000 debacle in Florida had taught us the virtue of speed.

Lewis came to my hotel room at dusk to tell me.

"We're in business," he said.

When I didn't answer, he took a chair across from me. We stared over the fog-shrouded city in silence. Far out above the lake, threads of rain seamed the sky. Good news for the dead. The digging would go easier.

Lewis turned the bottle on the table so he could read the label. I knew what it was: Glenfiddich, a good single malt. I'd been sipping it from a hotel tumbler most of the afternoon.

"Why'n't you turn on some lights in here?" Lewis said.

"I'm fine in the dark."

Lewis grunted. After a moment, he fetched the other glass. He wiped it out with his handkerchief and poured.

"So tell me."

Lewis tilted his glass, grimaced. "January fourth. The president signed the bill twenty minutes ago. Protective cordons fifty yards from polling stations. Only the living can vote. Jesus. I can't believe I'm even saying that." He cradled his long face in his hands. "So you in?"

"Does he want me?"

"Yes."

"What about you, Lewis? Do you want me?"

Lewis said nothing. We just sat there, breathing in the woodsy aroma of the scotch, watching night bleed into the sky.

"You screwed me at the staff meeting the other day," I said. "You hung me out to dry in front of everyone. It won't work if you keep cutting the ground out from under my feet."

"Goddamnit, I was *right*. In ten seconds, you destroyed everything we've worked for. We had it won."

"Oh come on, Lewis. If *Crossfire* never happened, it could have gone either way. Five points, that's nothing. We were barely outside the plus and minus, you know that."

"Still. Why'd you have to say that?"

I thought about that strange sense I'd had at the time: another voice speaking through me. Mouthpiece of the dead.

"You ever think about that little girl, Lewis?"

He sighed. "Yeah. Yeah, I do." He lifted his glass. "Look. If you're angling for some kind of apology—"

"I don't want an apology."

"Good," he said. Then, grudgingly: "We need you on this one, Rob. You know that."

"January," I said. "That gives us almost two months."

"We're way up right now."

"Stoddard will make a run. Wait and see."

"Yeah." Lewis touched his face. It was dark, but I could sense the gesture. He'd be fingering his acne scars, I'd spent enough time with him to know that. "I don't know, though," he said.

"I think the right might sit this one out. They think it's the fuckin' Rapture, who's got time for politics?"

"We'll see."

He took the rest of his scotch in a gulp and stood. "Yeah. We'll see."

I didn't move as he showed himself out, just watched his reflection in the big plate glass window. He opened the door and turned to look back, a tall man framed in light from the hall, his face lost in shadow.

"Rob?"

"Yeah?"

"You all right?"

I drained my glass and swished the scotch around in my mouth. I'm having a little trouble sleeping these days, I wanted to say. I'm having these dreams.

But all I said was, "I'm fine, Lewis. I'm just fine."

I WASN'T, THOUGH, not really.

None of us were, I guess, but even now—maybe *especially* now—the thing I remember most about those first weeks is how little the resurrection of the dead altered our everyday lives. Isolated incidents made the news—I remember a serial killer being arrested as his victims heaved themselves bodily from their shallow backyard graves—but mostly people just carried on. After the initial shock, markets stabilized. Stores filled up with Thanksgiving turkeys; radio stations began counting the shopping days until Christmas.

Yet I think the hysteria must have been there all along, like a swift current just beneath the surface of a placid lake. An undertow, the kind of current that'll kill you if you're not careful. Most people looked okay, but scratch the surface and we were all going nuts in a thousand quiet ways.

Ahh, who's digging on my grave, and all that.

Me, I couldn't sleep. The stress of the campaign had been mounting steadily even before my meltdown on *Crossfire,* and in those clos-ing days, with the polls in California—and all those lovely delegates—a hair too close to call, I'd been waking grainy-eyed and yawning every morning. I was feeling guilty, too. Three years ago, Gran broke her hip and landed in a Long Beach nursing home. And while I talked to her daily, I could never manage to steal a day or two to see her, despite all the time we spent campaigning in California.

But the resurrection of the dead marked a new era in my insomnia. Stumbling to bed late on election night, my mind blistered with images of zombies in the streets, I fell into a fevered dream. I found myself wandering through an abandoned city. Everything burned with the tenebrous significance of dreams—every brick and stone, the scraps of newsprint tumbling down high-rise canyons, the darkness pooling in the mouths of desolate subways. But the worst thing of all was the sound, the lone sound in all that sea of silence: the obscurely terrible cadence of a faraway clock, impossibly magnified, echoing down empty alleys and forsaken avenues.

The air rang with it, haunting me, drawing me on at last into a district where the buildings loomed over steep, close streets, admitting only a narrow wedge of sky. An open door beckoned, a black slot in a high, thin house. I pushed open the gate, climbed the broken stairs, paused in the threshold. A colossal grandfather clock towered within, its hands poised a minute short of midnight. Transfixed, I watched the heavy pendulum sweep through its arc, driving home the hour.

The massive hands stood upright.

The air shattered around me. The very stones shook as the clock began to toll. Clapping my hands over my ears, I turned to flee, but there was nowhere to go. In the yard, in the street—as far as I could see—the dead had gathered. They stood there while the clock stroked out the hours, staring up at me with those haunted eyes, and I knew suddenly and absolutely—the way you know things in dreams—that they had come for me at last, that they had always been coming for me, for all of us, if only we had known it.

I woke then, coldly afraid.

The first gray light of morning slit the drapes, but I had a premonition that no dawn was coming, or at least a very different dawn from any I had ever dared imagine.

STODDARD MADE HIS run with two weeks to go.

December fourteenth, we're 37,000 feet over the Midwest in a leased Boeing 737, and Angela Dey drops the new numbers on us.

"Gentlemen," she says, "we've hit a little turbulence."

It was a turning point, I can see that now. At the time, though, none of us much appreciated her little joke.

The resurrection of the dead had shaken things up—it had put us on top for a month or so—but Stoddard had been clawing his way back for a couple of weeks, crucifying us in the farm belt on a couple of ag bills where Burton cast deciding votes, hammering us in the south on vouchers. We knew that, of course, but I don't think any of us had foreseen just how close things were becoming.

"We're up seven points in California," Dey said. "The gay vote's keeping our heads above water, but the numbers are soft. Stoddard's got momentum."

"Christ," Lewis said, but Dey was already passing around another sheet.

"It gets worse," she said. "Florida, we're up two points. A statistical dead heat. We've got the minorities, Stoddard has the seniors. Everything's riding on turnout."

Libby Dixon, Burton's press secretary, cleared her throat. "We've got a pretty solid network among Hispanics—"

Dey shook her head. "Seniors win that one every time."

"Hispanics *never* vote," Lewis said. "We might as well wrap Florida up with a little bow and send it to Stoddard."

Dey handed around another sheet. She'd orchestrated the moment for maximum impact,

doling it out one sheet at a time like that. Lewis slumped in his seat, probing his scars as she worked her way through the list: Michigan, New York, Ohio, all three delegate rich, all three of them neck-and-neck races. Three almost physical blows, too, you could see them in the faces ranged around the table.

"What the hell's going on here?" Lewis muttered as Dey passed out another sheet, and then the news out of Texas rendered even him speechless. Stoddard had us by six points. I ran through a couple of Alamo analogies before deciding that discretion was the better part of wisdom. "I thought we were gaining there," Lewis said.

Dey shrugged. I just read the numbers, I don't make them up.

"Things could be worse," Libby Dixon said.

"Yeah, but Rob's not allowed to do *Crossfire* anymore," Lewis said, and a titter ran around the table. Lewis is good, I'll give him that. You could feel the tension ease.

"Suggestions?" Burton said.

Dey said, "I've got some focus group stuff on education. I was thinking maybe some ads clarifying our—"

"Hell with the ads," someone else said, "we've gotta spend more time in Florida. We've got to engage Stoddard on his ground."

"Maybe a series of town meetings?" Lewis said, and they went around like that for a while. I tried to listen, but Lewis's little icebreaker had reminded me of the dreams. I knew where I was—37,000 feet of dead air below me, winging my way toward a rally in Virginia—but inside my head I hadn't gone anywhere at all. Inside my head, I was stuck in the threshold of that dream house, staring out into the eyes of the dead.

The world had changed irrevocably, I thought abruptly.

That seems self-evident, I suppose, but at the time it had the quality of genuine revelation. The fact is, we had all—and I mean everyone by that, the entire culture, not just the campaign—we had all been pretending that nothing much had changed. Sure, we had UN debates and a CNN feed right out of a George Romero movie, but the implications of mass resurrection—the spiritual implications—had yet to bear down upon us. We were in denial. In that moment, with the plane rolling underneath me and someone—Tyler O'Neill I think it was, Libby Dixon's mousy assistant—droning on about going negative, I thought of something I'd heard a professor mention back at Northwestern: Copernicus formulated the heliocentric model of the solar system in the mid-1500s, but the Church didn't get around to punishing anyone for it until they threw Galileo in jail nearly a hundred years later. They spent the better part of a century trying to ignore the fact that the fundamental geography of the universe had been altered with a single stroke.

And so it had again.

The dead walked.

Three simple words, but everything else paled beside them—social security, campaign finance reform, education vouchers. *Everything.*

I wadded Dey's sheet into a noisy ball and flung it across the table. Tyler O'Neill stuttered and choked, and for a moment everyone just stared in silence at that wad of paper. You'd have thought I'd hurled a hand grenade, not a two-paragraph summary of voter idiocy in the Lone Star State.

Libby Dixon cleared her throat. "I hardly thin—"

"Shut up, Libby," I said. "Listen to yourselves for Christ's sake. We got zombies in the street and you guys are worried about going negative?"

"The whole . . ." Dey flapped her hand. ". . . zombie thing, it's not even on the radar. My numbers—"

"People *lie*, Angela."

Libby Dixon swallowed audibly.

"When it comes to death, sex, and money, everybody lies. A total stranger calls up on the telephone, and you expect some soccer mom to share her feelings about the fact that grandpa's rotten corpse is staggering around in the street?"

I had their attention all right.

For a minute the plane filled up with the muted roar of the engines. No human sound at all. And then Burton—Burton smiled.

"What are you thinking, Rob?"

"A great presidency is a marriage between a man and a moment," I said. "You told me that. Remember?"

"I remember."

"This is your moment, sir. You have to stop running away from it."

"What do you have in mind?" Lewis asked.

I answered the question, but I never even looked Lewis's way as I did it. I just held Grant Burton's gaze. It was like no one else was there at all, like it was just the two of us, and despite everything that's happened since, that's the closest I've ever come to making history.

"I want to find Dana Maguire," I said.

I'D BEEN IN politics since my second year at Northwestern. It was nothing I ever intended—who goes off to college hoping to be a Senate aide?—but I was idealistic, and I liked the things Grant Burton stood for, so I found myself working the phones that fall as an unpaid volunteer. One thing led to another—an internship on the Hill, a post-graduate job as a research assistant—and somehow I wound up inside the beltway.

I used to wonder how my life might have turned out had I chosen another path. My senior year at Northwestern, I went out with a girl named Gwen, a junior, freckled and streaky blond, with the kind of sturdy good looks that fall a hair short of beauty. Partnered in some forgettable lab exercise, we found we had grown up within a half hour of one another. Simple geographic coincidence, two Californians stranded in the frozen north, sustained us throughout the winter and into the spring. But we drifted in the weeks after graduation, and the last I had heard of her was a Christmas card five or six years back. I remember opening it and watching a scrap of paper slip to the floor. Her address and phone number, back home in Laguna Beach, with a little note. *Call me sometime*, it said, but I never did.

So there it was.

I was thirty-two years old, I lived alone, I'd never held a relationship together longer than eight months. Gran was my closest friend, and I saw her three times a year if I was lucky. I went to my ten year class reunion in Evanston, and everybody there was in a different life-place than I was. They all had kids and homes and churches.

Me, I had my job. Twelve hour days, five days a week. Saturdays I spent three or four hours at the office catching up. Sundays I watched the talk shows and then it was time to start all over again. That had been my routine for nearly a decade, and in all those years I never bothered to ask myself how I came to be there. It never even struck me as the kind of thing a person ought to ask.

Four years ago, during Burton's re-election campaign for the Senate, Lewis said a funny thing to me. We're sitting in a hotel bar, drinking Miller Lite and eating peanuts, when he turns to me and says, "You got anyone, Rob?"

"Got anyone?"

"You know, a girlfriend, a fiancée, somebody you care about."

Gwen flickered at the edge of my consciousness, but that was all. A flicker, nothing more.

I said, "No."

"That's good," Lewis said.

It was just the kind of thing he always said, sarcastic, a little mean-hearted. Usually I let it pass, but that night I had just enough alcohol zipping through my veins to call him on it.

"What's that supposed to mean?"

Lewis turned to look at me.

"I was going to say, you have someone you really care about—somebody you want to spend your life with—you might want to walk away from all this."

"Why's that?"

"This job doesn't leave enough room for relationships."

He finished his beer and pushed the bottle away, his gaze steady and clear. In the dim light

his scars were invisible, and I saw him then as he could have been in a better world. For maybe a moment, Lewis was one step short of handsome.

And then the moment broke.

"Good night," he said, and turned away.

A few months after that—not long before Burton won his second six-year Senate term—Libby Dixon told me Lewis was getting a divorce. I suppose he must have known the marriage was coming apart around him.

But at the time nothing like that even occurred to me.

After Lewis left, I just sat at the bar running those words over in my mind. *This job doesn't leave enough room for relationships*, he had said, and I knew he had intended it as a warning. But what I felt instead was a bottomless sense of relief. I was perfectly content to be alone.

BURTON WAS DOING an event in St. Louis when the nursing home called to say that Gran had fallen again. Eighty-one-year-old bones are fragile, and the last time I had been out there—just after the convention—Gran's case manager had privately informed me that another fall would probably do it.

"Do what?" I had asked.

The case manager looked away. She shuffled papers on her desk while her meaning bore in on me: another fall would kill her.

I suppose I must have known this at some level, but to hear it articulated so baldly shook me. From the time I was four, Gran had been the single stable institution in my life. I had been visiting in Long Beach, half a continent from home, when my family—my parents and sister—died in the car crash. It took the state police back in Pennsylvania nearly a day to track me down. I still remember the moment: Gran's mask-like expression as she hung up the phone, her hands cold against my face as she knelt before me.

She made no sound as she wept. Tears spilled down her cheeks, leaving muddy tracks in her make-up, but she made no sound at all. "I love you, Robert," she said. She said, "You must be strong."

That's my first true memory.

Of my parents, my sister, I remember nothing at all. I have a snapshot of them at a beach somewhere, maybe six months before I was born: my father lean and smoking, my mother smiling, her abdomen just beginning to swell. In the picture, Alice—she would have been four then—stands just in front of them, a happy blond child cradling a plastic shovel. When I was a kid I used to stare at that photo, wondering how you can miss people you never even knew. I did though, an almost physical ache way down inside me, the kind of phantom pain amputees must feel.

A ghost of that old pain squeezed my heart as the case manager told me about Gran's fall. "We got lucky," she said. "She's going to be in a wheelchair a month or two, but she's going to be okay."

Afterwards, I talked to Gran herself, her voice thin and querulous, addled with pain killers. "Robert," she said, "I want you to come out here. I want to see you."

"I want to see you, too," I said, "but I can't get away right now. As soon as the election's over—"

"I'm an old woman," she told me crossly. "I may not be here after the election."

I managed a laugh at that, but the laugh sounded hollow even in my own ears. The words had started a grim little movie unreeling in my head—a snippet of Gran's cold body staggering to its feet, that somehow inhuman tomb light shining out from behind its eyes. I suppose most of us must have imagined something like that during those weeks, but it unnerved me all the same. It reminded me too much of the dreams. It felt like I was there again, gazing out into the faces of the implacable dead, that enormous clock banging out the hours.

"Robert—" Gran was saying, and I could hear the Demerol singing in her voice. "Are you there, Ro—"

And for no reason at all, I said:

"Did my parents have a clock, Gran?"

"A clock?"

"A grandfather clock."

She was silent so long I thought maybe *she* had hung up.

"That was your uncle's clock," she said finally, her voice thick and distant.

"My uncle?"

"Don," she said. "On your father's side."

"What happened to the clock?"

"Robert, I want you to come out he—"

"What happened to the clock, Gran?"

"Well, how would I know?" she said. "He couldn't keep it, could he? I suppose he must have sold it."

"What do you mean?"

But she didn't answer.

I listened to the swell and fall of Demerol sleep for a moment, and then the voice of the case manager filled my ear. "She's drifted off. If you want, I can call back later—"

I looked up as a shadow fell across me. Lewis stood in the doorway.

"No, that's okay. I'll call her in the morning."

I hung up the phone and stared over the desk at him. He had a strange expression on his face.

"What?" I said.

"It's Dana Maguire."

"What about her?"

"They've found her."

EIGHT HOURS LATER, I touched down at Logan under a cloudy midnight sky. We had hired a private security firm to find her, and one of their agents—an expressionless man with the build of an ex-athlete—met me at the gate.

"You hook up with the ad people all right?" I asked in the car, and from the way he answered, a monosyllabic "Fine," you could tell what he thought of ad people.

"The crew's in place?"

"They're already rigging the lights."

"How'd you find her?"

He glanced at me, streetlight shadow rippling across his face like water. "Dead people ain't got much imagination. Soon's we get the fresh ones in the ground, they're out there digging." He laughed humorlessly. "You'd think people'd stop burying 'em."

"It's the ritual, I guess."

"Maybe." He paused. Then: "Finding her, we put some guys on the cemeteries and kept our eyes open, that's all."

"Why'd it take so long?"

For a moment there was no sound in the car but the hum of tires on pavement and somewhere far away a siren railing against the night. The agent rolled down his window and spat emphatically into the slipstream. "City the size of Boston," he said, "it has a lot of fucking cemeteries."

The cemetery in question turned out to be everything I could have hoped for: remote and unkempt, with weathered gothic tombstones right off a Hollywood back lot. And wouldn't it be comforting to think so, I remember thinking as I got out of the car—the ring of lights atop the hill nothing more than stage dressing, the old world as it had been always. But it wasn't, of course, and the ragged figures digging at the grave weren't actors, either. You could smell them for one, the stomach-wrenching stench of decay. A light rain had begun to fall, too, and it had the feel of a genuine Boston drizzle, cold and steady toward the bleak fag end of December.

Andy, the director, turned when he heard me. "Any trouble?" I asked.

"No. They don't care much what we're about, long as we don't interfere."

"Good."

Andy pointed. "There she is, see?"

"Yeah, I see her."

She was on her knees in the grass, still wearing the dress she had been buried in. She dug with single-minded intensity, her arms caked with mud to the elbow, her face empty of anything remotely human. I stood and stared at her for a while, trying to decide what it was I was feeling.

"You all right?" Andy said.

"What?"

"I said, are you all right? For a second there, I thought you were crying."

"No," I said. "I'm fine. It's the rain, that's all."

"Right."

So I stood there and half-listened while he filled me in. He had several cameras running, multiple filters and angles, he was playing with the lights. He told me all this and none of it meant anything at all to me. None of it mattered as long as I got the footage I wanted. Until then, there was nothing for me here.

He must have been thinking along the same lines, for when I turned to go, he called after me: "Say, Rob, you needn't have come out tonight, you know."

I looked back at him, the rain pasting my hair against my forehead and running down into my eyes. I shivered. "I know," I said. A moment later, I added: "I just—I wanted to see her somehow."

But Andy had already turned away.

I STILL REMEMBER the campaign ad, my own private nightmare dressed up in cinematic finery. Andy and I cobbled it together on Christmas Eve, and just after midnight in a darkened Boston studio, we cracked open a bottle of bourbon in celebration and sat back to view the final cut. I felt a wave of nausea roll over me as the first images flickered across the monitor. Andy had shot the whole thing from distorted angles in grainy black and white, the film just a hair overexposed to sharpen the contrast. Sixty seconds of derivative expressionism, some media critic dismissed it, but even he conceded it possessed a certain power.

You've seen it, too, I suppose. Who hasn't?

She will rise from her grave to haunt you, the opening title card reads, and the image holds in utter silence for maybe half a second too long. Long enough to be unsettling, Andy said, and you could imagine distracted viewers all across the heartland perking up, wondering what the hell was wrong with the sound.

The words dissolve into an image of hands, bloodless and pale, gouging at moist black earth. The hands of a child, battered and raw and smeared with the filth and corruption of the grave, digging, digging. There's something remorseless about them, something relentless and terrible. They could dig forever, and they might, you can see that. And now, gradually, you awaken to sound: rain hissing from a midnight sky, the steady slither of wet earth underhand, and something else, a sound so perfectly lacking that it's almost palpable in its absence, the unearthly silence of the dead. Freeze frame on a tableau out of Goya or Bosch: seven or eight zombies, half-dressed and rotting, laboring tirelessly over a fresh grave.

Fade to black, another slug line, another slow dissolve.

Dana Maguire came back.

The words melt into a long shot of the child, on her knees in the poison muck of the grave. Her dress clings to her thighs, and it's a dress someone has taken some care about—white and lacy, the kind of dress you'd bury your little girl in if you had to do it—and it's ruined. All the care and heartache that went into that dress, utterly ruined. Torn and fouled and sopping. Rain slicks her blond hair black against her skull. And as the camera glides in upon Dana Maguire's face, half-shadowed and filling three-quarters of the screen, you can glimpse the wound at her throat, flushed clean and pale. Dark roses of rot bloom along the high ridge of her cheekbone. Her eyes burn with the cold hard light of vistas you never want to see, not even in your dreams.

The image holds for an instant, a mute imperative, and then, mercifully, fades. Words appear and deliquesce on an ebon screen, three phrases, one by one:

The dead have spoken.
Now it's your turn.
Burton for president.

Andy touched a button. A reel caught and reversed itself. The screen went gray, and I realized I had forgotten to breathe. I sipped at my drink.

The whiskey burned in my throat, it made me feel alive.

"What do you think?" Andy said.

"I don't know. I don't know what to think."

Grinning, he ejected the tape and tossed it in my lap. "Merry Christmas," he said, raising his glass. "To our savior born."

And so we drank again.

Dizzy with exhaustion, I made my way back to my hotel and slept for eleven hours straight. I woke around noon on Christmas day. An hour later, I was on a plane.

BY THE TIME I caught up to the campaign in Richmond, Lewis was in a rage, pale and apoplectic, his acne scars flaring an angry red. "You seen these?" he said, thrusting a sheaf of papers at me.

I glanced through them quickly—more bad news from Angela Dey, Burton slipping further in the polls—and then I set them aside. "Maybe this'll help," I said, holding up the tape Andy and I had cobbled together.

We watched it together, all of us, Lewis and I, the entire senior staff, Burton himself, his face grim as the first images flickered across the screen. Even now, viewing it for the second time, I could feel its impact. And I could see it in the faces of the others as well—Dey's jaw dropping open, Lewis snorting in disbelief. As the screen froze on the penultimate image—Dana Maguire's decay-ravaged face—Libby Dixon turned away.

"There's no way we can run that," she said.

"We've got—" I began, but Dey interrupted me.

"She's right, Rob. It's not a campaign ad, it's a horror movie." She turned to Burton, drumming his fingers quietly at the head of the table. "You put this out there, you'll drop ten points, I guarantee it."

"Lewis?" Burton asked.

Lewis pondered the issue for a moment, rubbing his pitted cheek with one crooked finger. "I agree," he said finally. "The ad's a frigging nightmare. It's not the answer."

"The ad's revolting," Libby said. "The media will eat us alive for politicizing the kid's death."

"We *ought* to be politicizing it," I said. "We ought to make it mean something."

"You run that ad, Rob," Lewis said, "every redneck in America is going to remember you threatening to take away their guns. You want to make that mistake twice?"

"Is it a mistake? For Christ's sake, the dead are walking, Lewis. The old rules don't apply." I turned to Libby. "What's Stoddard say, Libby, can you tell me that?"

"He hasn't touched it since election day."

"Exactly. He hasn't said a thing, not about Dana Maguire, not about the dead people staggering around in the street. Ever since the FEC overturned the election, he's been dodging the issue—"

"Because it's political suicide," Dey said. "He's been dodging it because it's the right thing to do."

"Bullshit," I snapped. "It's *not* the right thing to do. It's pandering and it's cowardice—it's moral cowardice—and if we do it we deserve to lose."

You could hear everything in the long silence that ensued—cars passing in the street, a local staffer talking on the phone in the next room, the faint tattoo of Burton's fingers against the Formica table top. I studied him for a moment, and once again I had that sense of something else speaking through me, as though I were merely a conduit for another voice.

"What do you think about guns, sir?" I asked. "What do you really think?"

Burton didn't answer for a long moment. When he did, I think he surprised everyone at the table. "The death rate by handguns in this country is triple that for every other industrialized nation on the planet," he said. "They ought to be melted into pig iron, just like Rob said. Let's go with the ad."

"Sir—" Dey was standing.

"I've made up my mind," Burton said. He picked up the sheaf of papers at his elbow and shuffled through them. "We're down in Texas and California, we're slipping in Michigan and Ohio." He tossed the papers down in disgust. "Stoddard looks good in the south, Angela. What do we got to lose?"

WE COULDN'T HAVE timed it better.

The new ad went into national saturation on December 30th, in the shadow of a strange new year. I was watching a bowl game in my hotel room the first time I saw it on the air. It chilled me all over, as though I'd never seen it before. Afterwards, the room filled with the sound of the ball game, but now it all seemed hollow. The cheers of the fans rang with a labored gaiety, the crack of pads had the crisp sharpness of movie sound effects. A barb of loneliness pierced me. I would have called someone, but I had no one to call.

Snapping off the television, I pocketed my key-card.

Downstairs, the same football game was playing, but at least there was liquor and a ring of conversation in the air. A few media folks from Burton's entourage clustered around the bar, but I begged off when they invited me to join them. I sat at a table in the corner instead, staring blindly at the television and drinking scotch without any hurry, but without any effort to keep track either. I don't know how much I drank that night, but I was a little unsteady when I stood to go.

I had a bad moment on the way back to my room. When the elevator doors slid apart, I found I couldn't remember my room number. I couldn't say for sure I had even chosen the right floor. The hotel corridor stretched away before me, bland and anonymous, a hallway of locked doors behind which only strangers slept. The endless weary grind of the campaign swept over me, and suddenly I was sick of it all—the long midnight flights and the hotel laundries, the relentless blur of cities and smiling faces. I wanted more than anything else in the world to go home. Not my cramped apartment in the District either.

Home. Wherever that was.

Independent of my brain, my fingers had found my key-card. I tugged it from my pocket and studied it grimly. I had chosen the right floor after all.

Still in my clothes, I collapsed across my bed and fell asleep. I don't remember any dreams, but sometime in the long cold hour before dawn, the phone yanked me awake. "Turn on CNN," Lewis said. I listened to him breathe as I fumbled for the remote and cycled through the channels.

I punched up the volume.

"—unsubstantiated reports out of China concerning newly awakened dead in remote regions of the Tibetan Plateau—"

I was awake now, fully awake. My head pounded. I had to work up some spit before I could speak.

"Anyone got anything solid?" I asked.

"I'm working with a guy in State for confirmation. So far we got nothing but rumor."

"If it's true—"

"If it's true," Lewis said, "you're gonna look like a fucking genius."

OUR NUMBERS WERE soft in the morning, but things were looking up by mid-afternoon. The Chinese weren't talking and no one yet had footage of the Tibetan dead—but rumors were trickling in from around the globe. Unconfirmed reports from UN Peacekeepers in Kosovo told of women and children clawing their way free from previously unknown mass graves.

By New Year's Day, rumors gave way to established fact. The television flickered with grainy images from Grozny and Addis Ababa. The dead were arising in scattered locales around the world. And here at home, the polls were shifting. Burton's crowds grew larger and more enthusiastic at every rally, and as our jet winged down through the night toward Pittsburgh, I watched Stoddard answering questions about the crisis on a satellite feed from C-SPAN. He looked gray

and tired, his long face brimming with uncertainty. He was too late, we owned the issue now, and watching him, I could see he knew it, too. He was going through the motions, that's all.

There was a celebratory hum in the air as the plane settled to the tarmac. Burton spoke for a few minutes at the airport, and then the Secret Service people tightened the bubble, moving us en masse toward the motorcade. Just before he ducked into the limo, Burton dismissed his entourage. His hand closed about my shoulder. "You're with me," he said.

He was silent as the limo slid away into the night, but as the downtown towers loomed up before us he turned to look at me. "I wanted to thank you," he said.

"There's no—"

He held up his hand. "I wouldn't have had the courage to run that ad, not without you pushing me. I've wondered about that, you know. It was like you knew something, like you knew the story was getting ready to break again."

I could sense the question behind his words—*Did you know, Rob? Did you?*—but I didn't have any answers. Just that impression of a voice speaking through me from beyond, from somewhere else, and that didn't make any sense, or none that I was able to share.

"When I first got started in this business," Burton was saying, "there was a local pol back in Chicago, kind of a mentor. He told me once you could tell what kind of man you were dealing with by the people he chose to surround himself with. When I think about that, I feel good, Rob." He sighed. "The world's gone crazy, that's for sure, but with people like you on our side, I think we'll be all right. I just wanted to tell you that."

"Thank you, sir."

He nodded. I could feel him studying me as I gazed out the window, but suddenly I could find nothing to say. I just sat there and watched the city slide by, the past welling up inside me. Unpleasant truths lurked like rocks just beneath the visible surface. I could sense them somehow.

"You all right, Rob?"

"Just thinking," I said. "Being in Pittsburgh, it brings back memories."

"I thought you grew up in California."

"I did. I was born here, though. I lived here until my parents died."

"How old were you?"

"Four. I was four years old."

We were at the hotel by then. As the motorcade swung across two empty lanes into the driveway, Gran's words—

—*that was your uncle's clock, he couldn't keep it*—

—sounded in my head. The limo eased to the curb. Doors slammed. Agents slid past outside, putting a protective cordon around the car. The door opened and cold January air swept in. Burton was gathering his things.

"Sir—"

He paused, looking back.

"Tomorrow morning, could I have some time alone?"

He frowned. "I don't know, Rob, the schedule's pretty tight—"

"No, sir. I mean—I mean a few hours off."

"Something wrong?"

"There's a couple of things I'd like to look into. My parents and all that. Just an hour or two if you can spare me."

He held my gaze a moment longer.

Then: "That's fine, Rob." He reached out and squeezed my shoulder. "Just be at the airport by two."

THAT NIGHT I dreamed of a place that wasn't quite Dana Maguire's daycare. It *looked* like a daycare—half a dozen squealing kids, big plastic toys, an indestructible grade of carpet—but certain details didn't fit: the massive grandfather clock, my uncle's clock, standing in one corner; my parents, dancing to big band music that seemed to emanate from nowhere.

I was trying to puzzle this through when I saw the kid clutching the lunch sack. There was an odd expression on his face, a haunted heartbroken expression, and too late I understood

what was about to happen. I was trying to move, to scream, anything, as he dragged the pistol out of the bag. But my lips were sealed, I couldn't speak. Glancing down, I saw that I was rooted to the floor. Literally *rooted*. My bare feet had grown these long knotted tendrils. The carpet was twisted and raveled where they had driven themselves into the floor.

My parents whirled about in an athletic foxtrot, their faces manic with laughter. The music was building to an awful crescendo, percussives bleeding seamlessly together, the snap of the snare drums, the terrible booming tones of the clock, the quick sharp report of the gun.

I saw the girl go over backwards, her hands clawing at her throat as she convulsed. Blood drenched me, a spurting arterial fountain— I could feel it hot against my skin—and in the same moment this five-year-old kid turned to stare at me. Tears streamed down his cheeks, and this kid—this child really, and that's all I could seem to think—

—*he's just a child he's only a child*—

—he had my face.

I woke then, stifling a scream. Silence gripped the room and the corridor beyond it, and beyond that the city. I felt as if the world itself were drowning, sunk fathoms deep in the fine and private silence of the grave.

I stood, brushing the curtains aside. An anonymous grid of lights burned beyond the glass, an alien hieroglyph pulsing with enigmatic significance. Staring out at it, I was seized by an impression of how fragile everything is, how thin the barrier that separates us from the abyss. I shrank from the window, terrified by a sense that the world was far larger—and immeasurably stranger—than the world I'd known before, a sense of vast and formless energies churning out there in the dark.

I SPENT THE next morning in the Carnegie Library in Oakland, reeling through back issues of the *Post-Gazette*. It didn't take long to dig up the article about the accident—I knew the date well enough—but I wasn't quite prepared for what I found there. Gran had always been reticent about the wreck—about everything to do with my life in Pittsburgh, actually—but I'd never really paused to give that much thought. She'd lost her family, too, after all—a granddaughter, a son-in-law, her only child—and even as a kid, I could see why she might not want to talk about it.

The headline flickering on the microfilm reader rocked me, though. *Two die in fiery collision*, it read, and before I could properly formulate the question in my mind—

—there were three of them—

—I was scanning the paragraphs below. Disconnected phrases seemed to hover above the cramped columns—bridge abutment, high speed, alcohol-related—and halfway through the article, the following words leaped out at me:

Friends speculate that the accident may have been the product of a suicide pact. The couple were said to be grief-stricken following the death of their daughter, Alice, nine, in a bizarre shooting accident three weeks ago.

I stood, abruptly nauseated, afraid to read any further. A docent approached—

"Sir, are you all—"

—but I thrust her away.

Outside, traffic lumbered by, stirring the slush on Forbes Avenue. I sat on a bench and fought the nausea for a long time, cradling my face in my hands while I waited for it to pass. A storm was drifting in, and when I felt better I lifted my face to the sky, anxious for the icy burn of snow against my cheeks. Somewhere in the city, Grant Burton was speaking. Somewhere, reanimated corpses scrabbled at frozen graves.

The world lurched on.

I stood, belting my coat. I had a plane to catch.

I HELD MYSELF together for two days, during our final campaign swing through the Midwest on January 3 and the election that followed, but I think I had already arrived at a decision. Most of the senior staff sensed it, as well, I think. They congratulated me on persuading Burton to run the ad, but they didn't come to me for advice much in those final hours. I seemed set-apart somehow, isolated, contagious.

Lewis clapped me on the back as we watched the returns roll in. "Jesus, Rob," he said, "you're supposed to be happy right now."

"Are you, Lewis?"

I looked up at him, his tall figure slumped, his face a fiery map of scars.

"What did you give up to get us here?" I asked, but he didn't answer. I hadn't expected him to.

The election unfolded without a hitch. Leaving off their work in the graveyards, the dead gathered about the polling stations, but even they seemed to sense that the rules had changed this time around. They made no attempt to cast their ballots. They just stood behind the cordons the National Guard had set up, still and silent, regarding the proceedings with flat remorseless eyes. Voters scurried past them with bowed heads, their faces pinched against the stench of decay. On *Nightline*, Ted Koppel noted that the balloting had drawn the highest turnout in American history, something like ninety-three percent.

"Any idea why so many voters came out today?" he asked the panel.

"Maybe they were afraid not to," Cokie Roberts replied, and I felt an answering chord vibrate within me. Trust Cokie to get it right.

Stoddard conceded soon after the polls closed in the west. It was obvious by then. In his victory speech, Burton talked about a mandate for change. "The people have spoken," he said, and they had, but I couldn't help wondering what might be speaking through them, and what it might be trying to say. Some commentators speculated that it was over now. The dead would return to the graves, the world would be the old world we had known.

But that's not the way it happened.

On January 5, the dead were digging once again, their numbers always swelling. CNN was carrying the story when I handed Burton my resignation. He read it slowly and then he lifted his gaze to my face.

"I can't accept this, Rob," he said. "We need you now. The hard work's just getting under way."

"I'm sorry, sir. I haven't any choice."

"Surely we can work something out."

"I wish we could."

We went through several iterations of this exchange before he nodded. "We'll miss you," he said. "You'll always have a place here, whenever you're ready to get back in the game."

I was at the door when he called to me again.

"Is there anything I can do to help, Rob?"

"No, sir," I said. "I have to take care of this myself."

I SPENT A week in Pittsburgh, walking the precipitous streets of neighborhoods I remembered only in my dreams. I passed a morning hunting up the house where my parents had lived, and one bright, cold afternoon I drove out 76 and pulled my rental to the side of the interstate, a hundred yards short of the bridge where they died. Eighteen wheelers thundered past, throwing up glittering arcs of spray, and the smell of the highway enveloped me, diesel and iron. It was pretty much what I had expected, a slab of faceless concrete, nothing more.

We leave no mark.

Evenings, I took solitary meals in diners and talked to Gran on the telephone—tranquil gossip about the old folks in the home mostly, empty of anything real. Afterwards, I drank Iron City and watched cable movies until I got drunk enough to sleep. I ignored the news as best I could, but I couldn't help catching glimpses as I buzzed through the channels. All around the world, the dead were walking.

They walked in my dreams, as well, stirring memories better left forgotten. Mornings, I woke with a sense of dread, thinking of Galileo,

thinking of the Church. I had urged Burton to engage this brave new world, yet the thought of embracing such a fundamental transformation of my own history—of following through on the article in the *Post-Gazette*, the portents within my dreams—paralyzed me utterly. I suppose it was by then a matter mostly of verifying my own fears and suspicions—suppose I already knew, at some level, what I had yet to confirm. But the lingering possibility of doubt was precious, safe, and I clung to it for a few days longer, unwilling to surrender.

Finally, I could put it off no longer.

I drove down to the Old Public Safety Building on Grant Street. Upstairs, a grizzled receptionist brought out the file I requested. It was all there in untutored bureaucratic prose. There was a sheaf of official photos, too, glossy black-and-white prints. I didn't want to look at them, but I did anyway. I felt it was something I ought to do.

A little while later, someone touched my shoulder. It was the receptionist, her broad face creased with concern. Her spectacles swung at the end of a little silver chain as she bent over me. "You all right?" she asked.

"Yes, ma'am, I'm fine."

I stood, closing the file, and thanked her for her time.

I LEFT PITTSBURGH the next day, shedding the cold as the plane nosed above a lid of cloud. From LAX, I caught 405 South to Long Beach. I drove with the window down, grateful for the warmth upon my arm, the spike of palm fronds against the sky. The slipstream carried the scent of a world blossoming and fresh, a future yet unmade, a landscape less scarred by history than the blighted industrial streets I'd left behind.

Yet even here the past lingered. It was the past that had brought me here, after all.

The nursing home was a sprawl of landscaped grounds and low-slung stucco buildings, faintly Spanish in design. I found Gran in a garden overlooking the Pacific, and I paused, studying her, before she noticed me in the doorway. She held a paperback in her lap, but she had left off reading to stare out across the water. A salt-laden breeze lifted her gray hair in wisps, and for a moment, looking at her, her eyes clear in her distinctly boned face, I could find my way back to the woman I had known as a boy.

But the years intervened, the way they always do. In the end, I couldn't help noticing her wasted body, or the glittering geometry of the wheelchair that enclosed her. Her injured leg jutted before her.

I must have sighed, for she looked up, adjusting the angle of the chair. "Robert!"

"Gran."

I sat by her, on a concrete bench. The morning overcast was breaking, and the sun struck sparks from the wave-tops.

"I'd have thought you were too busy to visit," she said, "now that your man has won the election."

"I'm not so busy these days. I don't work for him anymore."

"What do you mean—"

"I mean I quit my job."

"*Why?*" she said.

"I spent some time in Pittsburgh. I've been looking into things."

"Looking into things? Whatever on Earth is there to look *into*, Robert?" She smoothed the afghan covering her thighs, her fingers trembling.

I laid my hand across them, but she pulled away. "Gran, we need to talk."

"Talk?" She laughed, a bark of forced gaiety. "We talk every day."

"Look at me," I said, and after a long moment, she did. I could see the fear in her eyes, then. I wondered how long it had been there, and why I'd never noticed it before. "We need to talk about the past."

"The past is dead, Robert."

Now it was my turn to laugh. "Nothing's dead, Gran. Turn on the television sometime. Nothing stays dead anymore. *Nothing*."

"I don't want to talk about that."

"Then what do you want to talk about?" I waved an arm at the building behind us, the ammonia-scented corridors and the endless numbered rooms inhabited by faded old people, already ghosts of the dead they would become. "You want to talk about Cora in 203 and the way her son never visits her or Jerry in 147 whose emphysema has been giving him trouble or all the—"

"All the what?" she snapped, suddenly fierce.

"All the fucking minutiae we always talk about!"

"I won't have you speak to me like that! I raised you, I made you what you are today!"

"I know," I said. And then, more quietly, I said it again. "I know."

Her hands twisted in her lap. "The doctors told me you'd forget, it happens that way sometimes with trauma. You were so *young*. It seemed best somehow to just . . . let it go."

"But you lied."

"I didn't choose any of this," she said. "After it happened, your parents sent you out to me. Just for a little while, they said. They needed time to think things through."

She fell silent, squinting at the surf foaming on the rocks below. The sun bore down upon us, a heartbreaking disk of white in the faraway sky.

"I never thought they'd do what they did," she said, "and then it was too late. After that . . . how could I tell you?" She clenched my hand. "You seemed okay, Robert. You seemed like you were fine."

I stood, pulling away. "How could you know?"

"Robert—"

I turned at the door. She'd wheeled the chair around to face me. Her leg thrust toward me in its cast, like the prow of a ship. She was in tears. "Why, Robert? Why couldn't you just leave everything alone?"

"I don't know," I said, but even then I was thinking of Lewis, that habit he has of probing at his face where the acne left it pitted—as if someday he'll find his flesh smooth and handsome once again, and it's through his hands he'll know it. I guess that's it, you know: we've all been wounded, every one of us.

And we just can't keep our hands off the scars.

I DRIFTED FOR the next day or two, living out of hotel rooms and haunting the places I'd known growing up. They'd changed like everything changes, the world always hurrying us along, but I didn't know what else to do, where else to go. I couldn't leave Long Beach, not till I made things up with Gran, but something held me back.

I felt ill at ease, restless. And then, as I fished through my wallet in a bar one afternoon, I saw a tiny slip of paper eddy to the floor. I knew what it was, of course, but I picked it up anyway. My fingers shook as I opened it up and stared at the message written there, *Call me sometime,* with the address and phone number printed neatly below.

I made it to Laguna Beach in fifty minutes. The address was a mile or so east of the water, a manicured duplex on a corner lot. She had moved no doubt—five years had passed—and if she hadn't moved she had married at the very least. But I left my car at the curb and walked up the sidewalk all the same. I could hear the bell through an open window, footsteps approaching, soft music lilting from the back of the house. Then the door opened and she was there, wiping her hands on a towel.

"Gwen," I said.

She didn't smile, but she didn't close the door either.

It was a start.

THE HOUSE WAS small, but light, with wide windows in the kitchen overlooking a lush back lawn. A breeze slipped past the screens, infusing the kitchen with the scent of fresh-cut grass and the faraway smell of ocean.

"This isn't a bad time, is it?" I asked.

"Well, it's unexpected to say the least," she told me, lifting one eyebrow doubtfully, and in the gesture I caught a glimpse of the girl I'd known at Northwestern, rueful and wry and always faintly amused.

As she made coffee, I studied her, still freckled and faintly gamine, but not unchanged. Her eyes had a wary light in them, and fresh lines caged her thin upper lip. When she sat across from me at the table, toying with her coffee cup, I noticed a faint pale circle around her finger where a ring might have been.

Maybe I looked older too, for Gwen glanced up at me from beneath a fringe of streaky blond bangs, her mouth arcing in a crooked smile. "You look younger on television," she said, and it was enough to get us started.

Gwen knew a fair bit of my story—my role in Burton's presidential campaign had bought me that much notoriety at least—and hers had a familiar ring to it. Law school at UCLA, five or six years billing hours in one of the big LA firms before the cutthroat culture got to her and she threw it over for a job with the ACLU, trading long days and a handsome wage for still longer ones and almost no wage at all. Her marriage had come apart around the same time. "Not out of any real animosity," she said. "More like a mutual lack of interest."

"And now? Are you seeing anyone?"

The question came out with a weight I hadn't intended.

She hesitated. "No one special." She lifted the eyebrow once again. "A habit I picked up as a litigator. Risk aversion."

By this time, the sky beyond the windows had softened into twilight and our coffee had grown cold. As shadows lengthened in the little kitchen, I caught Gwen glancing at the clock.

She had plans.

I stood. "I should go."

"Right."

She took my hand at the door, a simple handshake, that's all, but I felt something pass between us, an old connection close with a kind of electric spark. Maybe it wasn't there at all, maybe I only wanted to feel it—Gwen certainly seemed willing to let me walk out of her life once again—but a kind of desperation seized me.

Call it nostalgia or loneliness. Call it whatever you want. But suddenly the image of her wry glance from beneath the slant of hair leaped into mind.

I wanted to see her again.

"Listen," I said, "I know this is kind of out of the blue, but you wouldn't be free for dinner would you?"

She paused a moment. The shadow of the door had fallen across her face. She laughed uncertainly, and when she spoke, her voice was husky and uncertain. "I don't know, Rob. That was a long time ago. Like I said, I'm a little risk aversive these days."

"Right. Well, then, listen—it was really great seeing you."

I nodded and started across the lawn. I had the door of the rental open when she spoke again.

"What the hell," she said. "Let me make a call. It's only dinner, right?"

I WENT BACK to Washington for the inauguration.

Lewis and I stood together as we waited for the ceremony to begin, looking out at the dead. They had been on the move for days, legions of them, gathering on the Mall as far as the eye could see. A cluster of the living, maybe a couple hundred strong, had been herded onto the lawn before the bandstand—a token crowd of warm bodies for the television cameras—but I couldn't help thinking that Burton's true constituency waited beyond the cordons, still and silent and unutterably patient, the melting pot made flesh: folk of every color, race, creed, and age, in every stage of decay that would allow them to stand upright. Dana Maguire might be out there somewhere. She probably was.

The smell was palpable.

Privately, Lewis had told me that the dead had begun gathering elsewhere in the world, as well. Our satellites had confirmed it. In Cuba and North Korea, in Yugoslavia and Rwanda, the dead were on the move, implacable and slow, their purposes unknown and maybe unknowable.

"We need you, Rob," he had said. "Worse than ever."

"I'm not ready yet," I replied.

He had turned to me then, his long pitted face sagging. "What happened to you?" he asked.

And so I told him.

It was the first time I had spoken of it aloud, and I felt a burden sliding from my shoulders as the words slipped out. I told him all of it: Gran's evasions and my reaction to Dana Maguire that day on CNN and the sense I'd had on *Crossfire* that something else, something vast and remote and impersonal, was speaking through me, calling them back from the grave. I told him about the police report, too, how the memories had come crashing back upon me as I sat at the scarred table, staring into a file nearly three decades old.

"It was a party," I said. "My uncle was throwing a party and Mom and Dad's babysitter had canceled at the last minute, so Don told them just to bring us along. He lived alone, you know. He didn't have kids and he never thought about kids in the house."

"So the gun wasn't locked up?"

"No. It was late. It must have been close to midnight by then. People were getting drunk and the music was loud and Alice didn't seem to want much to do with me. I was in my uncle's bedroom, just fooling around the way kids do, and the gun was in the drawer of his nightstand."

I paused, memory surging through me, and suddenly I was there again, a child in my uncle's upstairs bedroom. Music thumped downstairs, jazzy big band music. I knew the grown-ups would be dancing and my dad would be nuzzling Mom's neck, and that night when he kissed me good night, I'd be able to smell him, the exotic aromas of bourbon and tobacco, shot through with the faint floral essence of Mom's perfume. Then my eyes fell upon the gun in the drawer. The light from the hall summoned unsuspected depths from the blued barrel.

I picked it up, heavy and cold.

All I wanted to do was show Alice. I just wanted to show her. I never meant to hurt anyone. I never meant to hurt Alice.

I said it to Lewis—"I never meant to hurt her"—and he looked away, unable to meet my eyes.

I remember carrying the gun downstairs to the foyer, Mom and Dad dancing beyond the frame of the doorway, Alice standing there watching. "I remember everything," I said to Lewis. "Everything but pulling the trigger. I remember the music screeching to a halt, somebody dragging the needle across the record, my mother screaming. I remember Alice lying on the floor and the blood and the weight of the gun in my hand. But the weird thing is, the thing I remember best is the way I felt at that moment."

"The way you felt," Lewis said.

"Yeah. A bullet had smashed the face of the clock, this big grandfather clock my uncle had in the foyer. It was chiming over and over, as though the bullet had wrecked the mechanism. That's what I remember most. The clock. I was afraid my uncle was going to be mad about the clock."

Lewis did something odd then. Reaching out, he clasped my shoulder—the first time he'd ever touched me, really *touched* me, I mean— and I realized how strange it was that this man, this scarred, bitter man, had somehow become the only friend I have. I realized something else, too: how rarely I'd known the touch of another human hand, how much I hungered for it.

"You were a kid, Rob."

"I know. It's not my fault."

"It's no reason for you to leave, not now, not when we need you. Burton would have you back in a minute. He owes this election to you, he knows that. Come back."

"Not yet," I said, "I'm not ready."

But now, staring out across the upturned

faces of the dead as a cold January wind whipped across the Mall, I felt the lure and pull of the old life, sure as gravity. The game, Burton had called it, and it was a game, politics, the biggest Monopoly set in the world and I loved it and for the first time I understood *why* I loved it. For the first time I understood something else, too: why I had waited years to ring Gwen's doorbell, why even then it had taken an active effort of will not to turn away. It was the same reason: *because* it was a game, a game with clear winners and losers, with rules as complex and arcane as a cotillion, and most of all because it partook so little of the messy turmoil of real life. The stakes seemed high, but they weren't. It was ritual, that's all—movement without action, a dance of spin and strategy designed to preserve the status quo. I fell in love with politics because it was safe. You get so involved in pushing your token around the board that you forget the ideals that brought you to the table in the first place. You forget to speak from the heart. Someday maybe, for the right reasons, I'd come back. But not yet.

I must have said it aloud for Lewis suddenly looked over at me. "What?" he asked.

I just shook my head and gazed out over the handful of living people, stirring as the ceremony got under way. The dead waited beyond them, rank upon rank of them with the earth of the grave under their nails and that cold shining in their eyes.

And then I *did* turn to Lewis. "What do you think they want?" I asked.

Lewis sighed. "Justice, I suppose," he said.

"And when they have it?"

"Maybe they'll rest."

A YEAR HAS passed, and those words— *justice, I suppose*—still haunt me. I returned to D.C. in the fall, just as the leaves began turning along the Potomac. Gwen came with me, and sometimes, as I lie wakeful in the shelter of her warmth, my mind turns to the past.

It was Gran that brought me back. The cast had come off in February, and one afternoon in

March, Gwen and I stopped by, surprised to see her on her feet. She looked frail, but her eyes glinted with determination as she toiled along the corridors behind her walker.

"Let's sit down and rest," I said when she got winded, but she merely shook her head and kept moving.

"Bones knit, Rob," she told me. "Wounds heal, if you let them."

Those words haunt me, too.

By the time she died in August, she'd moved from the walker to a cane. Another month, her case manager told me with admiration, and she might have relinquished even that. We buried her in the plot where we laid my grandfather to rest, but I never went back after the interment. I know what I would find.

The dead do not sleep.

They shamble in silence through the cities of our world, their bodies slack and stinking of the grave, their eyes coldly ablaze. Baghdad fell in September, vanquished by battalions of revolutionaries, rallying behind a vanguard of the dead. State teems with similar rumors, and CNN is on the story. Unrest in Pyongyang, turmoil in Belgrade.

In some views, Burton's has been the most successful administration in history. All around the world, our enemies are falling. Yet more and more these days, I catch the president staring uneasily into the streets of Washington, aswarm with zombies. "Our conscience," he's taken to calling them, but I'm not sure I agree. They demand nothing of us, after all. They seek no end we can perceive or understand. Perhaps they are nothing more than what we make of them, or what they enable us to make of ourselves. And so we go on, mere lodgers in a world of unpeopled graves, subject ever to the remorseless scrutiny of the dead.

THE GRAVEYARD RATS

HENRY KUTTNER

CONSIDERING THE FACT that he died at the age of only forty-three, Henry Kuttner (1915–1958) was not only a prolific writer but a remarkably influential one. Born in Los Angeles to a bookseller and his wife, he became interested in horror and supernatural fiction by reading the legendary pulp magazine *Weird Tales* and sold his first story, "The Graveyard Rats," to it at the age of twenty-two. Except for his military service, his entire career was spent as a freelance author. The Great Depression forced him to abandon his education, but in the 1950s he returned to school to study for a master's degree. In 1940, he married the writer Catherine L. Moore and thereafter much of their work was collaborative, producing stories and novels under their own names and more than a dozen pseudonyms. Among the authors who have dedicated books to him are Marion Zimmer Bradley (*The Bloody Sun*), Richard Matheson (*I Am Legend*), and Ray Bradbury (*Dark Carnival*).

As Lewis Padgett, he wrote two excellent mystery novels, *The Day He Died* (1947) and *The Brass Ring* (1946). As Kuttner, he wrote *Man Drowning* (1952) and a popular series about a lay psychoanalyst, Michael Gray: *The Murder of Eleanor Pope* (1956), *The Murder of Ann Avery* (1956), *Murder of a Mistress* (1957), and *Murder of a Wife* (1958). Several of his works have been filmed, including *The Twonky* (1953), a comic science fiction movie starring Hans Conreid, based on "The Twonky" (published in the September 1942 issue of *Astounding Science Fiction*); *Timescape* (1992), a science fiction film starring Jeff Daniels and Ariana Richards, based on the Kuttner/Moore novella *Vintage Season* (published in the September 1946 issue of *Astounding Science Fiction*); and *The Last Mimzy* (2007), starring Rhiannon Leigh Wryn, Chris O'Neil, and Timothy Hutton, based on the couple's short story "Mimsy Were the Borogoves" (published in the February 1943 issue of *Astounding Science Fiction*).

"The Graveyard Rats" was first published in the March 1936 issue of *Weird Tales*.

HENRY KUTTNER

THE GRAVEYARD RATS

OLD MASSON, THE caretaker of one of Salem's oldest and most neglected cemeteries, had a feud with the rats. Generations ago they had come up from the wharves and settled in the graveyard, a colony of abnormally large rats, and when Masson had taken charge after the inexplicable disappearance of the former caretaker, he decided that they must go. At first he set traps for them and put poisoned food by their burrows, and later he tried to shoot them, but it did no good. The rats stayed, multiplying and overrunning the graveyard with their ravenous hordes.

They were large, even for the *mus decumanus*, which sometimes measures fifteen inches in length, exclusive of the naked pink and gray tail. Masson had caught glimpses of some as large as good-sized cats, and when, once or twice, the grave-diggers had uncovered their burrows, the malodorous tunnels were large enough to enable a man to crawl into them on his hands and knees. The ships that had come generations ago from distant ports to the rotting Salem wharves had brought strange cargoes.

Masson wondered sometimes at the extraordinary size of these burrows. He recalled certain vaguely disturbing legends he had heard since coming to ancient, witch-haunted Salem—tales of a moribund, inhuman life that was said to exist in forgotten burrows in the earth. The old days, when Cotton Mather had hunted down the evil cults that worshipped Hecate and the dark Magna Mater in frightful orgies, had passed; but dark gabled houses still leaned perilously toward each other over narrow cobbled streets, and blasphemous secrets and mysteries were said to be hidden in subterranean cellars and caverns, where forgotten pagan rites were still celebrated in defiance of law and sanity. Wagging their gray heads wisely, the elders declared that there were worse things than rats and maggots crawling in the unhallowed earth of the ancient Salem cemeteries.

And then, too, there was this curious dread of the rats. Masson disliked and respected the ferocious little rodents, for he knew the danger that lurked in their flashing, needle-sharp fangs; but he could not understand the inexplicable horror which the oldsters held for deserted, rat-infested houses. He had heard vague rumors of ghoulish beings that dwelt far underground, and that had the power of commanding the rats, marshaling them like horrible armies. The rats, the old men whispered, were messengers between this world and the grim and ancient caverns far below Salem. Bodies had been stolen from graves for nocturnal subterranean feasts, they said. The myth of the Pied Piper is a fable that hides a blasphemous horror, and the black pits of Avernus have brought forth hell-spawned monstrosities that never venture into the light of day.

Masson paid little attention to these tales. He did not fraternize with his neighbors, and, in fact, did all he could to hide the existence of the rats from intruders. Investigation, he realized, would undoubtedly mean the opening of many graves. And while some of the gnawed, empty coffins could be attributed to the activities of the rats, Masson might find it difficult to explain the mutilated bodies that lay in some of the coffins.

The purest gold is used in filling teeth, and this gold is not removed when a man is buried. Clothing, of course, is another matter; for usually the undertaker provides a plain broadcloth suit that is cheap and easily recognizable. But gold is another matter; and sometimes, too, there were medical students and less reputable doctors who were in need of cadavers, and not overscrupulous as to where these were obtained.

So far Masson had successfully managed to discourage investigation. He had fiercely denied the existence of the rats, even though they sometimes robbed him of his prey. Masson did not care what happened to the bodies after he had performed his gruesome thefts, but the rats inevitably dragged away the whole cadaver through the hole they gnawed in the coffin.

The size of these burrows occasionally worried Masson. Then, too, there was the curious circumstance of the coffins always being gnawed open at the end, never at the side or top. It was almost as though the rats were working under the direction of some impossibly intelligent leader.

Now he stood in an open grave and threw a last sprinkling of wet earth on the heap beside the pit. It was raining, a slow, cold drizzle that for weeks had been descending from soggy black clouds. The graveyard was a slough of yellow, sucking mud, from which the rain-washed tombstones stood up in irregular battalions. The rats had retreated to their burrows, and Masson had not seen one for days. But his gaunt, unshaved face was set in frowning lines; the coffin on which he was standing was a wooden one.

The body had been buried several days earlier, but Masson had not dared to disinter it before. A relative of the dead man had been coming to the grave at intervals, even in the drenching rain. But he would hardly come at this late hour, no matter how much grief he might be suffering, Masson thought, grinning wryly. He straightened and laid the shovel aside.

From the hill on which the ancient graveyard lay he could see the lights of Salem flickering dimly through the downpour. He drew a flashlight from his pocket. He would need light now. Taking up the spade, he bent and examined the fastenings of the coffin.

Abruptly he stiffened. Beneath his feet he sensed an unquiet stirring and scratching, as though something was moving within the coffin. For a moment a pang of superstitious fear shot through Masson, and then rage replaced it as he realized the significance of the sound. The rats had forestalled him again!

In a paroxysm of anger Masson wrenched at the fastenings of the coffin. He got the sharp edge of the shovel under the lid and pried it up until he could finish the job with his hands. Then he sent the flashlight's cold beam darting down into the coffin.

Rain spattered against the white satin lining; the coffin was empty. Masson saw a flicker of movement at the head of the case, and darted the light in that direction.

The end of the sarcophagus had been gnawed through, and a gaping hole led into darkness. A black shoe, limp and dragging, was disappearing as Masson watched, and abruptly he realized that the rats had forestalled him by only a few minutes. He fell on his hands and knees and made a hasty clutch at the shoe, and the flashlight incontinently fell into the coffin and went out. The shoe was tugged from his grasp, he heard a sharp, excited squealing, and then he had the flashlight again and was darting its light into the burrow.

It was a large one. It had to be, or the corpse could not have been dragged along by it. Masson wondered at the size of the rats that could carry away a man's body, but the thought of the loaded revolver in his pocket fortified him.

Probably if the corpse had been an ordinary one Masson would have left the rats with their spoils rather than venture into the narrow burrow, but he remembered an especially fine set of cufflinks he had observed, as well as a stickpin that was undoubtedly a genuine pearl. With scarcely a pause he clipped the flashlight to his belt and crept into the burrow.

It was a tight fit, but he managed to squeeze himself along. Ahead of him in the flashlight's glow he could see the shoes dragging along the wet earth of the bottom of the tunnel. He crept along the burrow as rapidly as he could, occasionally barely able to squeeze his lean body through the narrow walls.

The air was overpowering with its musty stench of carrion. If he could not reach the corpse in a minute, Masson decided, he would turn back. Belated fears were beginning to crawl, maggot-like, within his mind, but greed urged him on. He crawled forward, several times passing the mouths of adjoining tunnels. The walls of the burrow were damp and slimy, and twice lumps of dirt dropped behind him. The second time he paused and screwed his head around to look back. He could see nothing, of course, until he had unhooked the flashlight from his belt and reversed it.

Several clods lay on the ground behind him, and the danger of his position suddenly became real and terrifying. With thoughts of a cave-in making his pulse race, he decided to abandon the pursuit, even though he had now almost overtaken the corpse and the invisible things that pulled it. But he had overlooked one thing: the burrow was too narrow to allow him to turn.

Panic touched him briefly, but he remembered a side tunnel he had just passed, and backed awkwardly along the tunnel until he came to it. He thrust his legs into it, backing until he found himself able to turn. Then he hurriedly began to retrace his way, although his knees were bruised and painful.

Agonizing pain shot through his leg. He felt sharp teeth sink into his flesh, and kicked out

frantically. There was a shrill squealing and the scurry of many feet. Flashing the light behind him, Masson caught his breath in a sob of fear as he saw a dozen great rats watching him intently, their slitted eyes glittering in the light. They were great misshapen things, as large as cats, and behind them he caught a glimpse of a dark shape that stirred and moved swiftly aside into the shadow; and he shuddered at the unbelievable size of the thing.

The light had held them for a moment, but they were edging closer, their teeth dull orange in the pale light. Masson tugged at his pistol, managed to extricate it from his pocket, and aimed carefully. It was an awkward position, and he tried to press his feet into the soggy sides of the burrow so that he should not inadvertently send a bullet into one of them.

The rolling thunder of the shot deafened him, for a time, and the clouds of smoke set him coughing. When he could hear again and the smoke had cleared, he saw that the rats were gone. He put the pistol back and began to creep swiftly along the tunnel, and then with a scurry and a rush they were upon him again.

They swarmed over his legs, biting and squealing insanely, and Masson shrieked horribly as he snatched for his gun. He fired without aiming, and only luck saved him from blowing a foot off. This time the rats did not retreat so far, but Masson was crawling as swiftly as he could along the burrow, ready to fire again at the first sound of another attack.

There was a patter of feet and he sent the light stabbing back of him. A great gray rat paused and watched him. Its long ragged whiskers twitched, and its scabrous, naked tail was moving slowly from side to side. Masson shouted and the rat retreated.

He crawled on, pausing briefly, the black gap of a side tunnel at his elbow, as he made out a shapeless huddle on the damp clay a few yards ahead. For a second he thought it was a mass of earth that had been dislodged from the roof, and then he recognized it as a human body.

It was a brown and shriveled mummy, and with a dreadful unbelieving shock Masson realized that it was moving.

It was crawling toward him, and in the pale glow of the flashlight the man saw a frightful gargoyle face thrust into his own. It was the passionless, death's-head skull of a long-dead corpse, instinct with hellish life; and the glazed eyes swollen and bulbous betrayed the thing's blindness. It made a faint groaning sound as it crawled toward Masson, stretching its ragged and granulated lips in a grin of dreadful hunger. And Masson was frozen with abysmal fear and loathing.

Just before the Horror touched him, Masson flung himself frantically into the burrow at his side. He heard a scrambling noise at his heels, and the thing groaned dully as it came after him. Masson, glancing over his shoulder, screamed and propelled himself desperately through the narrow burrow. He crawled along awkwardly, sharp stones cutting his hands and knees. Dirt showered into his eyes, but he dared not pause even for a moment. He scrambled on, gasping, cursing, and praying hysterically.

Squealing triumphantly, the rats came at him, horrible hunger in their eyes. Masson almost succumbed to their vicious teeth before he succeeded in beating them off. The passage was narrowing, and in a frenzy of terror he kicked and screamed and fired until the hammer clicked on an empty shell. But he had driven them off.

He found himself crawling under a great stone, embedded in the roof, that dug cruelly into his back. It moved a little as his weight struck it, and an idea flashed into Masson's fright-crazed mind. If he could bring down the stone so that it blocked the tunnel!

The earth was wet and soggy from the rains, and he hunched himself half upright and dug away at the dirt around the stone. The rats were coming closer. He saw their eyes glowing in the reflection of the flashlight's beam. Still he clawed frantically at the earth. The stone was giving. He tugged at it and it rocked in its foundation.

A rat was approaching—the monster he had already glimpsed. Gray and leprous and hideous it crept forward with its orange teeth bared, and in its wake came the blind dead thing, groaning as it crawled. Masson gave a last frantic tug at the stone. He felt it slide downward, and then he went scrambling along the tunnel.

Behind him the stone crashed down, and he heard a sudden frightful shriek of agony. Clods showered upon his legs. A heavy weight fell on his feet and he dragged them free with difficulty. The entire tunnel was collapsing!

Gasping with fear, Masson threw himself forward as the soggy earth collapsed at his heels. The tunnel narrowed until he could barely use his hands and legs to propel himself; he wriggled forward like an eel and suddenly felt satin tearing beneath his clawing fingers, and then his head crashed against some thing that barred his path. He moved his legs, discovering that they were not pinned under the collapsed earth. He was lying flat on his stomach, and when he tried to raise himself he found that the roof was only a few inches from his back. Panic shot through him.

When the blind horror had blocked his path, he had flung himself into a side tunnel, a tunnel that had no outlet. He was *in a coffin*, an empty coffin into which he had crept through the hole the rats had gnawed in its end!

He tried to turn on his back and found that he could not. The lid of the coffin pinned him down inexorably. Then he braced himself and strained at the coffin lid. It was immovable, and even if he could escape from the sarcophagus, how could he claw his way up through five feet of hard-packed earth?

He found himself gasping. It was dreadfully fetid, unbearably hot. In a paroxysm of terror he ripped and clawed at the satin until it was shredded. He made a futile attempt to dig with his feet at the earth from the collapsed burrow that blocked his retreat. If he were only able to reverse his position he might be able to claw his way through to air . . . air . . .

White-hot agony lanced through his breast,

throbbed in his eyeballs. His head seemed to be swelling, growing larger and larger; and suddenly he heard the exultant squealing of the rats. He began to scream insanely but could not drown them out. For a moment he thrashed about hysterically within his narrow prison, and then he was quiet, gasping for air. His eyelids closed, his blackened tongue protruded, and he sank down into the blackness of death with the mad squealing of the rats dinning in his ears.

THE FACTS IN THE CASE OF M. VALDEMAR

EDGAR ALLAN POE

WHEN ASSESSING A body of work that includes "The Purloined Letter," "The Pit and the Pendulum," "The Cask of Amontillado," and "The Tell-Tale Heart," few would claim that "The Facts in the Case of M. Valdemar" is the greatest short story written by Edgar Allan Poe (1809–1849), but there can be little doubt that it is one of the most disturbing.

Born in Boston, Poe lost both of his parents when he was two and was taken in, though never formally adopted, by the prosperous John Allan and his wife, who adored the young orphan. Most of his life was turbulent and, after his foster mother died in 1830, Poe was dismissed from the family by Allan's second wife and he became impoverished. His wife, Virginia Clem, not yet fourteen when Poe married her, died at twenty-four. After a series of briefly held jobs, he turned to journalism as a writer and editor, quickly becoming the country's foremost literary critic as well as its greatest poet. After three volumes of poetry, beginning with *Tamerlane and Other Poems* (1827), failed, he found modest success with short fiction, mostly horror stories of unsurpassed suspense that remain highly readable today. He is noted for having invented the detective story, complete with most of the major tropes of the genre, with "The Murders in the Rue Morgue" (1841).

"The Facts in the Case of M. Valdemar" has inspired many imitations, including Fritz Leiber's "The Dead Man" (*Weird Tales*, 1950), which served as the basis for an episode of the television series *Night Gallery* that aired on December 16, 1970. Poe's story, which in turn was highly reminiscent of his own story "Mesmeric Revelation" (published in the August 1844 issue of *Columbian Magazine*), was originally published in the December 1845 issue of *The American Review;* it was published as a separate pamphlet in London in 1846 under the title *Mesmerism "In Articulo Mortis."*

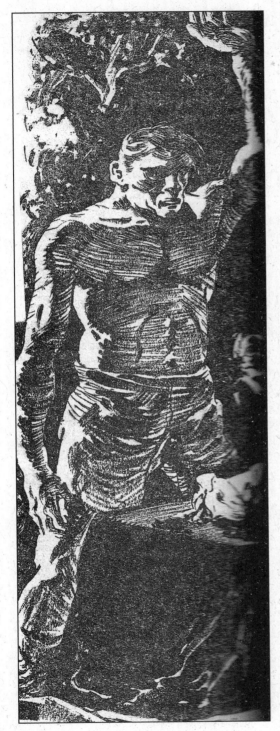

EDGAR ALLAN POE

THE FACTS IN THE CASE OF M. VALDEMAR

OF COURSE I shall not pretend to consider it any matter for wonder, that the extraordinary case of M. Valdemar has excited discussion. It would have been a miracle had it not—especially under the circumstances. Through the desire of all parties concerned, to keep the affair from the public, at least for the present, or until we had farther opportunities for investigation—through our endeavors to effect this—a garbled or exaggerated account made its way into society, and became the source of many unpleasant misrepresentations, and, very naturally, of a great deal of disbelief.

It is now rendered necessary that I give the facts—as far as I comprehend them myself. They are, succinctly, these:

My attention, for the last three years, had been repeatedly drawn to the subject of Mesmerism; and, about nine months ago it occurred to me, quite suddenly, that in the series of experiments made hitherto, there had been a very remarkable and most unaccountable omission:—no person had as yet been mesmerized in articulo mortis. It remained to be seen, first, whether, in such condition, there existed in the patient any susceptibility to the magnetic influence; secondly, whether, if any existed, it was impaired or increased by the condition; thirdly, to what extent, or for how long a period, the encroachments of Death might be arrested by the process. There were other points to be ascertained, but these most excited my curiosity—the last in especial, from the immensely important character of its consequences.

In looking around me for some subject by whose means I might test these particulars, I was brought to think of my friend, M. Ernest Valdemar, the well-known compiler of the "Bibliotheca Forensica," and author (under the nom de plume of Issachar Marx) of the Polish versions of "Wallenstein" and "Gargantua." M. Valdemar, who has resided principally at Harlaem, N.Y., since the year 1839, is (or was) particularly noticeable for the extreme spareness of his person—his lower limbs much resembling those of John Randolph; and, also, for the whiteness of his whiskers, in violent contrast to the blackness of his hair—the latter, in consequence, being very generally mistaken for a wig. His temperament was markedly nervous, and rendered him a good subject for mesmeric experiment. On two or three occasions I had put him to sleep with little difficulty, but was disappointed in other results which his peculiar constitution had naturally led me to anticipate. His will was at no period positively, or thoroughly, under my control, and in regard to clairvoyance, I could accomplish with him nothing to be relied upon. I always attributed my failure at these points to the disordered state of his health. For some months previous to my becoming acquainted with him, his physicians had declared him in a confirmed phthisis. It was his custom, indeed, to speak calmly of his approaching dissolution, as of a matter neither to be avoided nor regretted.

When the ideas to which I have alluded first occurred to me, it was of course very natural that I should think of M. Valdemar. I knew the steady philosophy of the man too well to apprehend any scruples from him; and he had no relatives in America who would be likely to interfere. I spoke to him frankly upon the subject; and, to my surprise, his interest seemed vividly excited. I say to my surprise, for, although he had always yielded his person freely to my experiments, he had never before given me any tokens of sympathy with what I did. His disease was of that character which would admit of exact calculation in respect to the epoch of its termination in death; and it was finally arranged between us that he would send for me about twenty-four hours before the period announced by his physicians as that of his decease.

It is now rather more than seven months since I received, from M. Valdemar himself, the subjoined note:

My DEAR P——,
You may as well come now. D—— and
F—— are agreed that I cannot hold out
beyond to-morrow midnight; and I think
they have hit the time very nearly.

VALDEMAR

I received this note within half an hour after it was written, and in fifteen minutes more I was in the dying man's chamber. I had not seen him for ten days, and was appalled by the fearful alteration which the brief interval had wrought in him. His face wore a leaden hue; the eyes were utterly lustreless; and the emaciation was so extreme that the skin had been broken through by the cheek-bones. His expectoration was excessive. The pulse was barely perceptible. He retained, nevertheless, in a very remarkable manner, both his mental power and a certain degree of physical strength. He spoke with distinctness—took some palliative medicines without aid—and, when I entered the room, was occupied in penciling memoranda in a pocketbook. He was propped up in the bed by pillows. Doctors D—— and F—— were in attendance.

After pressing Valdemar's hand, I took these gentlemen aside, and obtained from them a minute account of the patient's condition. The left lung had been for eighteen months in a semi-osseous or cartilaginous state, and was, of course, entirely useless for all purposes of vitality. The right, in its upper portion, was also partially, if not thoroughly, ossified, while the lower region was merely a mass of purulent tubercles, running one into another. Several extensive perforations existed; and, at one point, permanent adhesion to the ribs had taken place. These appearances in the right lobe were of comparatively recent date. The ossification had proceeded with very unusual rapidity; no sign of it had discovered a month before, and the adhesion had only been observed during the three previous days. Independently of the phthisis, the patient was suspected of aneurism of the aorta; but on this point the osseous symptoms rendered an exact diagnosis impossible. It was the opinion of both physicians that M. Valdemar would die about midnight on the morrow (Sunday). It was then seven o'clock on Saturday evening.

On quitting the invalid's bed-side to hold conversation with myself, Doctors D—— and F—— had bidden him a final farewell. It had not been their intention to return; but, at my request, they agreed to look in upon the patient about ten the next night.

When they had gone, I spoke freely with M. Valdemar on the subject of his approaching dissolution, as well as, more particularly, of the experiment proposed. He still professed himself quite willing and even anxious to have it made, and urged me to commence it at once. A male and a female nurse were in attendance; but I did not feel myself altogether at liberty to engage in a task of this character with no more reliable witnesses than these people, in case of sudden accident, might prove. I therefore postponed operations until about eight the next night, when the arrival of a medical student with whom I had some acquaintance, (Mr. Theodore L——l,) relieved me from farther embarrassment. It had been my design, originally, to wait for the physicians; but I was induced to proceed, first, by the urgent entreaties of M. Valdemar, and secondly, by my conviction that I had not a moment to lose, as he was evidently sinking fast.

Mr. L——l was so kind as to accede to my desire that he would take notes of all that occurred, and it is from his memoranda that what I now have to relate is, for the most part, either condensed or copied verbatim.

It wanted about five minutes of eight when, taking the patient's hand, I begged him to state, as distinctly as he could, to Mr. L——l, whether he (M. Valdemar) was entirely willing that I should make the experiment of mesmerizing him in his then condition.

He replied feebly, yet quite audibly, "Yes, I wish to be. I fear you have mesmerized"—adding immediately afterwards, "deferred it too long."

While he spoke thus, I commenced the passes which I had already found most effectual in subduing him. He was evidently influenced with the first lateral stroke of my hand across his forehead; but although I exerted all my powers, no farther perceptible effect was induced until some minutes after ten o'clock, when Doctors D—— and F—— called, according to appointment. I explained to them, in a few words, what I designed, and as they opposed no objection, saying that the patient was already in the death agony, I proceeded without hesitation—exchanging, however, the lateral passes for downward ones, and directing my gaze entirely into the right eye of the sufferer.

By this time his pulse was imperceptible and his breathing was stertorous, and at intervals of half a minute.

This condition was nearly unaltered for a quarter of an hour. At the expiration of this period, however, a natural although a very deep sigh escaped the bosom of the dying man, and the stertorous breathing ceased—that is to say, its stertorousness was no longer apparent; the intervals were undiminished. The patient's extremities were of an icy coldness.

At five minutes before eleven I perceived unequivocal signs of the mesmeric influence. The glassy roll of the eye was changed for that expression of uneasy inward examination which is never seen except in cases of sleep-waking, and which it is quite impossible to mistake. With a few rapid lateral passes I made the lids quiver, as in incipient sleep, and with a few more I closed them altogether. I was not satisfied, however, with this, but continued the manipulations vigorously, and with the fullest exertion of the will, until I had completely stiffened the limbs of the slumberer, after placing them in a seemingly easy position. The legs were at full length; the arms were nearly so, and reposed on the bed at a moderate distance from the loin. The head was very slightly elevated.

When I had accomplished this, it was fully midnight, and I requested the gentlemen present to examine M. Valdemar's condition. After a few experiments, they admitted him to be in an unusually perfect state of mesmeric trance. The curiosity of both the physicians was greatly excited. Dr. D—— resolved at once to remain with the patient all night, while Dr. F—— took leave with a promise to return at daybreak. Mr. L——l and the nurses remained.

We left M. Valdemar entirely undisturbed until about three o'clock in the morning, when I approached him and found him in precisely the same condition as when Dr. F—— went away—that is to say, he lay in the same position; the pulse was imperceptible; the breathing was gentle (scarcely noticeable, unless through the application of a mirror to the lips); the eyes were closed naturally; and the limbs were as rigid and as cold as marble. Still, the general appearance was certainly not that of death.

As I approached M. Valdemar I made a kind of half effort to influence his right arm into pursuit of my own, as I passed the latter gently to and fro above his person. In such experiments with this patient I had never perfectly succeeded before, and assuredly I had little thought of succeeding now; but to my astonishment, his arm very readily, although feebly, followed every direction I assigned it with mine. I determined to hazard a few words of conversation.

"M. Valdemar," I said, "are you asleep?" He made no answer, but I perceived a tremor about the lips, and was thus induced to repeat the question, again and again. At its third repetition, his whole frame was agitated by a very slight shivering; the eyelids unclosed themselves so far as to display a white line of the ball; the lips moved sluggishly, and from between them, in a barely audible whisper, issued the words:

"Yes;—asleep now. Do not wake me!—let me die so!"

I here felt the limbs and found them as rigid as ever. The right arm, as before, obeyed the direction of my hand. I questioned the sleep-waker again:

"Do you still feel pain in the breast, M. Valdemar?"

The answer now was immediate, but even less audible than before: "No pain—I am dying."

I did not think it advisable to disturb him farther just then, and nothing more was said or done until the arrival of Dr. F——, who came a little before sunrise, and expressed unbounded astonishment at finding the patient still alive. After feeling the pulse and applying a mirror to the lips, he requested me to speak to the sleep-waker again. I did so, saying:

"M. Valdemar, do you still sleep?"

As before, some minutes elapsed ere a reply was made; and during the interval the dying man seemed to be collecting his energies to speak. At my fourth repetition of the question, he said very faintly, almost inaudibly:

"Yes; still asleep—dying."

It was now the opinion, or rather the wish, of the physicians, that M. Valdemar should be suffered to remain undisturbed in his present apparently tranquil condition, until death should supervene—and this, it was generally agreed, must now take place within a few minutes. I concluded, however, to speak to him once more, and merely repeated my previous question.

While I spoke, there came a marked change over the countenance of the sleep-waker. The eyes rolled themselves slowly open, the pupils disappearing upwardly; the skin generally assumed a cadaverous hue, resembling not so much parchment as white paper; and the circular hectic spots which, hitherto, had been strongly defined in the centre of each cheek, went out at once. I use this expression, because the suddenness of their departure put me in mind of nothing so much as the extinguishment of a candle by a puff of the breath. The upper lip, at the same time, writhed itself away from the teeth, which it had previously covered completely; while the lower jaw fell with an audible jerk, leaving the mouth widely extended, and disclosing in full view the swollen and blackened tongue. I presume that no member of the party then present had been unaccustomed to death-bed horrors; but so hideous beyond conception was the appearance of M. Valdemar at this moment, that there was a general shrinking back from the region of the bed.

I now feel that I have reached a point of this narrative at which every reader will be startled into positive disbelief. It is my business, however, simply to proceed.

There was no longer the faintest sign of vitality in M. Valdemar; and concluding him to be dead, we were consigning him to the charge of the nurses, when a strong vibratory motion was observable in the tongue. This continued for perhaps a minute. At the expiration of this period, there issued from the distended and motionless jaws a voice—such as it would be madness in me to attempt describing. There are, indeed, two or three epithets which might be considered as applicable to it in part; I might say, for example, that the sound was harsh, and broken and hollow; but the hideous whole is indescribable, for the simple reason that no similar sounds have ever jarred upon the ear of humanity. There were two particulars, nevertheless, which I thought then, and still think, might fairly be stated as characteristic of the intonation—as well adapted to convey some idea of its unearthly peculiarity. In the first place, the voice seemed to reach our ears—at least mine—from a vast distance, or from some deep cavern within the earth. In the second place, it impressed me (I fear, indeed, that it will be impossible to make myself comprehended) as gelatinous or glutinous matters impress the sense of touch.

I have spoken both of "sound" and of "voice." I mean to say that the sound was one of distinct—of even wonderfully, thrillingly distinct—syllabification. M. Valdemar spoke—obviously in reply to the question I had propounded to him a few minutes before. I had asked him, it will be remembered, if he still slept. He now said:

"Yes;—no;—I have been sleeping—and now—now—I am dead."

No person present even affected to deny, or attempted to repress, the unutterable, shuddering horror which these few words, thus uttered, were so well calculated to convey. Mr. L——l (the student) swooned. The nurses immediately left the chamber, and could not be induced to return. My own impressions I would not pretend to render intelligible to the reader. For nearly an hour, we busied ourselves, silently—without the utterance of a word—in endeavors to revive Mr. L——l. When he came to himself, we addressed ourselves again to an investigation of M. Valdemar's condition.

It remained in all respects as I have last described it, with the exception that the mirror no longer afforded evidence of respiration. An attempt to draw blood from the arm failed. I should mention, too, that this limb was no farther subject to my will. I endeavored in vain to make it follow the direction of my hand. The only real indication, indeed, of the mesmeric influence, was now found in the vibratory movement of the tongue, whenever I addressed M. Valdemar a question. He seemed to be making an effort to reply, but had no longer sufficient volition. To queries put to him by any other person than myself he seemed utterly insensible—although I endeavored to place each member of the company in mesmeric rapport with him. I believe that I have now related all that is necessary to an understanding of the sleep-waker's state at this epoch. Other nurses were procured; and at ten o'clock I left the house in company with the two physicians and Mr. L——l.

In the afternoon we all called again to see the patient. His condition remained precisely the same. We had now some discussion as to the propriety and feasibility of awakening him; but we had little difficulty in agreeing that no good purpose would be served by so doing. It was evident that, so far, death (or what is usually termed death) had been arrested by the mesmeric process. It seemed clear to us all that to awaken M. Valdemar would be merely to insure his instant, or at least his speedy dissolution.

From this period until the close of last week—an interval of nearly seven months—we continued to make daily calls at M. Valdemar's house, accompanied, now and then, by medical and other friends. All this time the sleeper-walker remained exactly as I have last described him. The nurses' attentions were continual.

It was on Friday last that we finally resolved to make the experiment of awakening or attempting to awaken him; and it is the (perhaps) unfortunate result of this latter experiment which has given rise to so much discussion in private circles—to so much of what I cannot help thinking unwarranted popular feeling.

For the purpose of relieving M. Valdemar from the mesmeric trance, I made use of the customary passes. These, for a time, were unsuccessful. The first indication of revival was afforded by a partial descent of the iris. It was observed, as especially remarkable, that this lowering of the pupil was accompanied by the profuse out-flowing of a yellowish ichor (from beneath the lids) of a pungent and highly offensive odor.

It was now suggested that I should attempt to influence the patient's arm, as heretofore. I made the attempt and failed. Dr. F—— then intimated a desire to have me put a question. I did so, as follows:

"M. Valdemar, can you explain to us what are your feelings or wishes now?"

There was an instant return of the hectic circles on the cheeks; the tongue quivered, or rather rolled violently in the mouth (although the jaws and lips remained rigid as before;) and at length the same hideous voice which I have already described, broke forth:

"For God's sake!—quick!—quick!—put me to sleep—or, quick!—waken me!—quick!—I say to you that I am dead!"

I was thoroughly unnerved, and for an instant remained undecided what to do. At first I made an endeavor to re-compose the patient; but, failing in this through total abeyance of the will, I retraced my steps and as earnestly struggled to awaken him. In this attempt I soon saw that I should be successful—or at least I soon fancied that my success would be complete—and I am sure that all in the room were prepared to see the patient awaken.

For what really occurred, however, it is quite impossible that any human being could have been prepared.

As I rapidly made the mesmeric passes, amid ejaculations of "dead! dead!" absolutely bursting from the tongue and not from the lips of the sufferer, his whole frame at once—within the space of a single minute, or even less, shrunk—crumbled—absolutely rotted away beneath my hands. Upon the bed, before that whole company, there lay a nearly liquid mass of loathsome—of detestable putridity.

FEEDING THE DEAD INSIDE

YVONNE NAVARRO

YVONNE NAVARRO (1957–) was born in Chicago but now lives in Arizona. She has written more than a hundred short stories and twenty novels in the genres of horror, fantasy, science fiction, and thriller. Although several of her novels are original, including *AfterAge* (1993), *Deadrush* (1995), *Final Impact* (1997), *Red Shadows* (1998), *DeadTimes* (2000), *That's Not My Name* (2000), *Mirror Me* (2004), and *Highborn* (2010), she has established a following for her seven works in the Buffyverse series. These books are based on the universe in which the characters in the *Buffy the Vampire Slayer* and *Angel* television series reside, with its own set of rules. Created by Joss Whedon, this is a world in which supernatural phenomena are accepted as part of normal life, and in which supernatural evil may be fought and defeated by humans willing to wage the battle. There are scores of novels in this young adult series, written by nearly thirty authors, including numerous novelizations of episodes from the television programs, as well as original stories using many familiar characters. Navarro's contributions to the canon are *The Darkening, Shattered Twilight, Broken Sunrise, Paleo, Tempted Champions,* and *The Willow Files,* volumes 1 and 2, all published between 1999 and 2004. Other movie tie-ins include *Species* (1995), *Music of the Spears* (1996), and *Hellboy* (2004). Among other honors, she frequently has been nominated for Bram Stoker Awards for Short Story, as well as First Novel, Novel, and Work for Young Readers.

"Feeding the Dead Inside" was originally published in *Mondo Zombie,* edited by John Skipp and Craig Spector (Baltimore: Cemetery Dance, 2006).

YVONNE NAVARRO

FEEDING THE DEAD INSIDE

"GOTCHA!"

Metal sweeps the air as the silver handcuffs arc down and around the woman's thin wrists. There is a quiet *thunk* as the steel lodges against fragile bones, then a ratcheting as the circlet snaps closed next to several thousand dollars' worth of gold Cartier watch. More than the actual noise, Carmen *sees* the sound reflected in the woman's eyes.

"What's the meaning of this?" the woman demands. There is no fear in her voice, not yet. Outrage and puzzlement, but not fear.

Not yet.

Carmen Valensuela keeps her face bland, her smiling eyes hidden behind the mirrored shades that are so crucial to her image—dark blue uniform, sharply creased slacks, sky blue shirt, the heavy leather belt with its implements comfortably girdling her hips. All this would mean nothing had Carmen's eyes been anything more than emotionless silver pools.

"Come with me, ma'am." Carmen's voice is cool and controlled. Her existence, the whole world, *her* world, is built on *control*. In the microsecond before the woman can protest again, the hand holding the sister cuff pulls sharply to the left and binds the woman's other wrist, that same harsh noise so much louder now that the imprisonment is complete.

The woman, whose name Carmen will later learn is Susan McDunnah Atgeld, watches, stunned and helpless, as Officer Valensuela

plucks her leather briefbag from the cart and ignores the intended purchase, the pink teddy puddled untidily on the counter. There is a sharp nudge in the small of her back, a poke just a shade short of pain, as the policewoman turns her and directs her forward, sweeping the briefbag along and pausing only to muscle the cart next to the counter and out of the aisle. Anger momentarily pocks Mrs. Atgeld's vision with small yellow sparkles, then she finds her voice, that small but self-assured soprano that had retreated from the brazen sound of the locking police handcuffs. "I'm not going anywhere until you tell me what's going on!" she snaps. Her knees lock and the policewoman nearly collides with her back; damn this cop and all her family, too, if she actually has any. She looks as if she is smiling. Not outright, but smiling just the same.

"You are being detained on suspicion of shoplifting, ma'am." Indignation spirals through Susan Atgeld's clenched fists, then relief. "That's ridiculous. Look in my bag—there's no merchandise inside!"

Carmen tips a finger to an arched eyebrow in a mock salute. "No ma'am. Your belongings will be searched by store personnel."

Two scarlet circles appear on Mrs. Atgeld's cheeks as she realizes this woman, this blue-collar, uneducated female *cockroach*, means to lead her through Lord & Taylor in handcuffs, parade her past the cosmetics counter where Ms. Loreen has set aside a jar of body sloughing cream for her to pick up on her way out, and even past the salon, where Jacob had tried to convince her with his pretty-boy smile to cut and perm those feathery blond locks.

Carmen is not oblivious to the woman's embarrassment; rather, she revels in it as she guides her detainee through the busy store, the woman's slender form stepping beside her like a jerky wooden doll. The woman tenses and Carmen smiles without moving her mouth because she knows what is coming.

"I'm an important person," her prisoner hisses. "I've never been so embarrassed in my life, and I'll have your job for this farce. I hope you like cruising the midnight shift at the Robert Taylor Homes, because that's where you'll be next week." Her capped teeth form each word briskly, clipping the end of each *S* with scissor-like precision.

Officer Valensuela acknowledges this prediction with a calm nod; she has no doubt whatsoever that this woman is important. In fact, the woman looks even more important in person than she has on the videotapes her brother-in-law has given Carmen to study over the past three months. On the tapes Susan Atgeld is a grainy black and white spectre; a two-dimensional smudge of shadowy grays without personality or vibrance, a *non*-person. In the flesh she is brittle and sharp and smooth all at once, like a long crystal knife; she smells of Chanel perfume and wears hundred-dollar designer jeans topped by a tee shirt that costs nearly as much and which moves across the woman's taut flesh like lotion. "Don't you have something better to do than harass me?" Carmen's prisoner demands furiously. "There's bound to be a Dead Thing for you to play with somewhere!" She yanks at her bonds, but it is a petulant, futile effort.

Carmen's unseen smile widens as the woman's words flash ignorantly into a more personal arena and her stomach curls around itself in pleasurable anger as she gives her prisoner another bland nod. She has exquisite *control*, the same control which this scented and powdered woman feels sliding so swiftly away as Officer Valensuela steers her toward a door marked SECURITY/HOLDING in red block letters. Her trained grip around the woman's elbow is strong and hard but stops short of physical pain. Carmen pulls open the door and hustles the woman inside.

Her brother-in-law sits behind a sand-colored Steelcase desk, his expression unreadable above a sheaf of papers. He is blond and pale, like the woman Carmen has cuffed; his last name is Rodgers and there is no picture of his wife, Carmen's sister, who is dark and Latino-looking like her, on the desk that he keeps professionally free of clutter. His eyes are small and blue and bright and they fix on Carmen's charge with interest. "Yes, Officer?"

"Shoplifter." Carmen pushes the woman forward, just enough to make her stumble against the edge of the desk.

"Take your hands off of me!" The woman jerks aside, hair flying into her face and sticking across the bridge of her nose. Her eyes, brown and rimmed carefully with expensive cosmetics, have metamorphosed into hard, dirty-looking stones. "I haven't stolen anything," she declares. "There's been an . . ." she shoots a nasty glance at Carmen, "*unfortunate* error."

The store has given her brother-in-law a title and a tag which actually says *Lt. Rodgers* but Carmen mostly thinks of him as *That Fucking Pervert*, or at best just plain old Walter. Now Walter stands with a grunt—he is six-two and over the two-forty mark—and comes around the desk, his lungs making little wheezy squirts with each exhalation. Carmen wonders idly if he sounds like that when he is playing with one of the Dead Things she occasionally makes available to him in the lock-up of the sub-basement at 12th and State. Most of the Dead Things are destroyed on sight, but the CPD keeps a supply of the freshly dead for justice purposes. It's still obscenely easy to find one, despite federal health regulations mandating decapitation. Carmen turns the thought over in her mind with lazy curiosity; Walter has his Dead Things muzzled and cuffed, then covers the head with a plastic bag to keep the smelly drool off of his face. It doesn't bother her that he likes cold, dead cunt—lots of the guys were going for that since viruses died with the corpses—but it . . . *annoys* her to think that he might make the same sound over a molding, lifeless piece of fly food that he makes while he is poking her sister.

And while he makes these noises—if he really does—does Walter, this failed, lazy student of film and video school, videotape what he does with Carmen's sister like he videotapes his Funtime with Dead Things?

Walter is looking at Carmen quizzically, the angles of the woman's haughty face peering around his chubby jowls. "Officer?" Wordlessly Carmen hands him the woman's briefbag, an expensive, softly tanned leather thing. As he lifts the outer flap the smell of good leather drifts from its interior, floating above the milder scents of hand lotion and face powder. Stuffed atop an illegal alligator wallet from which a thick wad of bills peeks is the pink silk teddy the woman had been fingering when Carmen cuffed her, its edging of creamy Irish lace smashed between the wallet and a red suede checkbook. Walter lifts it out with one finger, as though it has become something he doesn't want to touch. The woman gasps once—twice—and begins to talk, her voice razored and fast and dripping with the first hint of panic.

"I didn't take that, I swear to God I didn't. She put it there, she *did,* and I demand to see my attorney right now, you—"

Carmen isn't just smiling inside now, she is *grinning,* like a big, happy slice is curving inside her chest from lung to lung.

"You have the right to remain silent," Carmen interrupts. "Anything you say can and will be held against you. You have the right to have an attorney present—"

"You're damned *right* I'm going to have an attorney present, you evil little bitch!" Snarling and incredulous, the woman's cheeks are now a rich shade of magenta. "You *planted* that in my purse, and if you think a judge is going to take your word over mine, you've got another thing coming, you stupid, mindless—"

"Anything you say can and will be held against you," Carmen continues patiently. She finishes the Miranda above the woman's raving and Walter stays as she calls for a transport squad to take the woman to lock-up. Despite her shock, the woman is still self-righteous, hurling insult after insult at Carmen, who has been nothing but polite during the entire situation. Only once had a perpetrator been polite throughout the arrest process, never raised her voice or fabricated an insult. That woman's security had been of a different kind, self-secure but not self-*smug,* and Carmen had let her go due to a . . . "mix-up" in the evidence room and the disappearance of the stolen merchandise; thus the alleged perpetrator had walked from the station a free, whole woman, a little wiser and able to pat herself on the back and say "Courtesy pays, by God." But this one . . . ah.

Carmen so loves to discipline people, especially the rude ones. There is little else left. As a child, quiet and unremarkable; a mediocre teenager; a dull young woman, barely above the poverty line as she worked in a factory like a small, automated robot, doing what, when and where she was told—through all that she dreamed of reversing the roles, being able to tell others what to do, how to do it, to reprimand them when they were wrong or acting incorrectly, to control their very *destiny.*

Then had come The Change, and the world was filled with Dead Things and the cops and the National Guard and the Army had their hands full, then overflowing. As people died by the thousands then came back as Dead Things themselves, a panicked nation withdrew into itself, as did the rest of the world, and restructured its forces, replenishing them from every possible source. And suddenly Carmen had a chance to lift herself out of factory work and into law enforcement as it had been redefined, and it was so *exciting,* nearly orgasmic in its first, fiery intensity as she and her co-graduates burst from the Academy and joined to wipe out the hordes of Dead Things prowling the city. All that bloodshed and downed flesh, the *permission* to annihilate using the intense, vicious training she had so taken to at the Academy.

Finally the Dead Things were not so numerous, and though times were a little stricter and a little faster, it might as well have been *before,* with its legal doubletalk and loopholes and the frustration of watching the same slimes, white- *and* blue-collar, walk free, again and again. And so Carmen, with the help of That Fucking Pervert, had devised a system with which she could occasionally tip the scales in favor of justice, and if the perpetrator wasn't an *outright* criminal, what difference did it make? Money still bred injustice, greed, envy, all those undesirable attributes, and there lay her justification. Society had become three-tiered: the rich, like the woman Carmen had just arrested; the blue-collars, like Carmen, her brother-in-law and all these clerks who slobbered over the rich like adoring puppies; and . . . Everyone Else. "Everyone Else" was a phrase that, like the cheap polyester shirts Walter wore off duty, covered the ugly but didn't quite hide it all away. Everyone Else was the poor, the homeless, the sick, the old—all those wretches who had no place to go and no way to escape the Dead Things. And Everyone Else included the Dead Things themselves.

Carmen and Walter watch the transport pull away and Carmen glances at her watch; the woman will be put in holding and Carmen has plenty of time before she must report to the booking sergeant at the station—legally the woman can be held for twenty-four hours before charges are filed, although Officer Valensuela wants to get to the station as quickly as possible. Beside her Walter shoves a cigarette between dry lips—a habit Carmen despises—then touches a match to it. He sucks in, then exhales, and she closes her lungs against the smoke that circles her head. There is a restaurant in the American National Bank Building on LaSalle and Wacker, and the smell reminds her of the heavy, foul air

it leaks into the building's hallway after a full crowd. She thinks again of her petite sister and is granted a vision of this pig of a man grunting over her, with his thick, smoky breath and Dead Thing–dirtied cock; she resists the urge to spit, steeling herself because she knows he will take her by the elbow and turn her toward the store. He always does.

His hand is cold and damp, but she will not flinch. Seeing his nicotine-stained teeth bothers her more than his touch. Does he kiss the flesh of the Dead Things he plays with? Does he give them love bites? The thought makes her want to gag.

"Come on back to my office and we'll check the videotape." This is what he always says, in case someone else is within earshot or monitoring the arrest process. If Carmen did not need the tape for the arraignment and trial, she would not go with him; as such, she has no choice and this gives her brother-in-law, That Fucking Pervert, a measure of control over *her,* and it eats at her insidiously, like a splinter embedded under a fingernail. Behind her cool-blue exterior the grin inside her has abruptly turned upside down but she follows him anyway, watching him lumber through the aisles of china and crystal perfume bottles, slightly amazed that the air pushed in front of his massive body does not tremble the fragile containers, wishing it would tumble a few from the shelves. As they reach the door to SECURITY/ HOLDING, Carmen's secret frown twists briefly into a snarl, but she bites the tip of her tongue hard enough to bring blood and clear her mind, a technique she uses often when she must deal with Walter. For the two days following a trial she is usually unable to eat salted food.

But that's okay. It's all worth it.

He leaves the door open and she does not sit. He settles onto his chair with an appreciable wheeze and picks up a videotape lying by the VCR and security monitor, then shoves it into the machine with a practiced flick. One thick finger stabs the PLAY button and the autosweep of the jewelry and silver department's camera is cracked apart by a lookalike shot of lingerie.

Carmen watches critically, looking for jump-cuts or cracked celluloid, an arm that angles unnaturally, but there is nothing; the fade-ins are smooth and undetectable to the naked eye. The scene ends and Walter looks at her expectantly.

"Again," she orders.

His snort is the only hint of rebellion, then the machine rewinds, stops and begins to play again. It is a well-practiced routine, and he knows to run it on slow motion the second time. At the scene's end, he looks up at her, his florid face hopeful. If he expects her to compliment his work, he is a fool; she will not give him the satisfaction of praising the skills that support his perversity. "It'll do," she says shortly.

Her brother-in-law ejects the tape and hands it to her, his grip leaving a nasty slick print on the case; Carmen plucks it from his hand by the edge, loathing the thought of getting this man's body oil on herself. She turns on her heel and walks out.

She makes her way to the station and the booking sergeant sets the trial for two o'clock tomorrow and instructs her to turn in her evidence no later than noon; she nods but does not hand over the videotape; he does not care enough to ask why. He is blue-collar like herself and while on the surface he is unconcerned about the Susan McDunnah Atgelds of the world, Carmen instinctively glimpses the resentment behind the bottle-thick lenses of his glasses. Mrs. Atgeld will spend the night in the upper holding cell, sharing quarters with two to four other criminals. Shoplifters, robbers, perhaps a rapist or murderer; it is a different world now and criminals have attained a startling, deadly equality among themselves. Ten years ago a white-collar shoplifter would have been out on bail within an hour and would never have seen the inside of a smelly cell where the toilet was in full view of other men and women. Today things move a lot quicker and the word "bail" no longer exists.

Carmen clocks out and goes to the women's locker room, carefully holding the tape by the edges that Walter hasn't touched. She changes into street clothes, slips her gun into the leather holster under her left breast, then dons a short jacket to conceal it. The walk to the fingerprint lab on the second floor gives her a chance to run a mental check and make sure she isn't screwing up; by the time she pulls open the door, she is confident everything is covered.

"Afternoon, Stan," she says serenely. She pushes the tape across the counter. "I need fingerprint photos on this, with a full blow-up. The tape's due in evidence on a different case by noon tomorrow. Can you handle it?"

Bernick, the little man behind the counter, grunts noncommittally but bags the tape and pushes a form at her. "Fill it out," he rasps. "And don't forget the TIME DUE box. Use red." Carmen completes the form obediently, marking the TIME DUE as eleven a.m.; she's worked with Bernick before and knows she will have her tape and print photos back on time.

Outside the air is clean and crisp, with only the faintest scent of burning flesh drifting from the old stockyards southwest of the station where the Dead Things who are too far gone to be of any use are burned. She has smelled it too long and too often for it to affect her, and even the sight of them twisting beneath the flames does nothing anymore, not since she and her older brother (himself dead and burned eight months ago) had hauled their parents' struggling corpses to the burnyards and pitched them in. In a way Carmen is a Dead Thing herself, with a dead *place* inside which no one on the force can see and do anything about. But that is okay, because she can do something about other people, people who have Dead Places inside that bleed outside and dirty others, either with their attitudes, as with those like Susan Atgeld, or with their mere physical presence. Like Walter, for instance. His loss will cost her the security connection at Lord & Taylor, but that's played out anyway, growing into too much of a pattern to be safe. There are always other ways to break the parchment pedestals that people build for themselves and foolishly think elevate them above the common man. Walter has made it easier to knock down a few, but she has been studying his books and a few of her old surveillance texts from the Academy, and adjusting to his absence will not be that difficult. Besides, it is better for her sister in the long run.

Carmen's studio apartment is stark and clean, a monk's quarters but for the television and video equipment, the piles of film books and mini-towers of videotapes with neat, carefully coded labels that no one can decipher but her. So many old tapes, so many arrests, the streamlining of procedures as mankind struggled to adapt and survive in the face of a predator surpassing him in numbers, if not intelligence. There is no time or desire for red tape now, carboned forms, juries and the archiving of bygone evidence. Now there is an arrest, an arraignment and trial within twenty-four hours, and immediate punishment if guilty—and that's it. It's amazing how crime has declined, with only the craziest white-collars doing it out of greed and the sick thrill of gambling with their lives—or the poor and homeless, so desperate that being caught and executed means losing little beyond the misery of their day-to-day existence.

By now Susan McDunnah Atgeld has called her attorney, who is preparing a case of planted evidence or mistaken assumption. What Ms. Atgeld does not consider is that unless her lawyer is a relative, when he loses the case he will raise an eyebrow, then go out to lunch on a crab salad croissant after depositing his check ("Payment in advance, please"). Carmen feels sure her evidence will hold up, and it will, of course, be a surprise to the defendant; appeals have gone the way of juries, red tape and lawsuits, and there will be no second chance. It is a hard world now, a world where children run in packs and not just for protection, where outsiders foolishly traveling alone are thrown into rings with Dead Things for sport by gangs of kids. And the games go on, unchecked, because one bite, one *scratch* from a Dead Thing is damnation within an hour, and where is the crime without a complaining witness?

Carmen studies the older tapes, paying careful attention to Mrs. Atgeld's clothes and hairstyle in each until she is satisfied; there is no discrepancy, the original tapes chart everything. After an hour she bundles the old tapes, nine in all, into a bag which she sets by the door. She will drop the tapes in her locker at the beginning of her shift until after the Atgeld trial; then she will combine the trial tape with the fingerprint photos from Bernick. This will be a double week.

She takes a shower, hot at first to wash away the dirt and Dead Thing stink, then cold, standing rigid as the icy water works away the fiery spaces inside her. She is shivering when she shuts off the water but at least she is exhausted and able to sleep, to elude the warmth of anticipation, the bolts of need that hum through her veins and tease her stomach. There is little to excite her anymore, but tomorrow and her plans for later this week have her teetering on the edge of a rarely satisfied lust.

In the morning Carmen is up early. The sun is a hot, spiky ball in the eastern sky; at six o'clock the bodyfires have been burning for almost an hour, the smoke tendrils curling around the sunbeams which slice through the dirty morning air and bake the fried flesh aroma more thoroughly into the low, desolate buildings surrounding the old stockyards. Her apartment is not air-conditioned, but she throws its single window wide so the day's heat and stench can join her in this hellpit of a home, momentarily hooking her fingers through the steel mesh that keeps her in and the Dead Things out. After a minute she turns away and dresses in a clean uniform, then cooks herself a poached egg before leaving for the station ahead of schedule. No one comments at her arrival.

The morning drags but Carmen does not mind. No one from evidence or IA comes to question her on the Atgeld case and she knows, with a sudden gut-freeing rush, that no one will. The only surprise at the trial will be for the defendant. She thinks of what the woman is doing now, biding her time, fuming and flinching away from the filth with whom she must share the holding cell, inspecting her nails with disgust even as she slaps away the advances of one of her inmates and wishes she could urinate in private. Carmen grins to herself; the woman should count herself lucky that the precinct has the manpower to keep a guard posted to protect the inmates from one another; less than a year ago she would've been a tasty diversion for her cellmates.

Twenty to twelve. Carmen picks up the tape and fingerprint photos from Bernick, then takes the tape to the evidence desk without stopping at her locker and hands them to the clerk. The case is white with print powder but the evidence sergeant says nothing as he logs it in. Carmen drops the photos in her locker and goes back to her desk to wait; she has a one day on, one day off schedule and is forbidden to pound the pavement today.

Finally, ten to two. Time for the trial.

The courtroom is moderately full, friends and family come to attend the trials—about one every ten minutes—and lend support, old women clutching their purses and muttering, a few white-collars with grim faces, pale expressions witness to this incredible intrusion on otherwise normal lives. Interspersed among the visitors are the attorneys, coolly shuffling papers and secure in their safety. Susan McDunnah Atgeld stands with her own counsel and her husband, a tall, lanky man dressed in an Armani suit designed to mock the starvation of the lower classes. Carmen can see he wishes to touch Susan but cannot because a prison guard separates them; instead he whispers something to the lawyer, then flashes Susan a smug smile that makes Carmen's eyes narrow behind her mirrored sunglasses as she joins the other officers along the church-like seats.

Carmen's arrest is eighth on the call and she sits for almost an hour and a half, anticipation heating her belly and dampening the soft skin beneath her arms. The judge is not in a good mood today, and that is to the Atgeld woman's detriment; perhaps his wife rejected his advances this morning, or he stepped in dog shit on the way to his car. Whatever his reason the magistrate is more heavy-handed than usual,

and tension mounts as case after case is found guilty and the defendants are unceremoniously hauled away as family members wail and stumble out of the courthouse. By the time she is called, excitement nearly makes Carmen hyperventilate and the cop next to her glances at her in amusement, then frowns and looks away from the unsettling twin lakes of her gaze.

A ratty-looking clerk steps forward and wastes no time. "People v. Atgeld," he snaps. He retreats as the group moves in front of the judge.

"Your honor," Susan's attorney begins, "my client is an important woman in the community. Her husband is Tyler Wilhelm Atgeld, owner of—"

"Important people steal too, counselor," the judge interrupts irritably. "Get on with it. You have five minutes."

"Yes sir, of course." The attorney rushes on: his client is wealthy and store records show numerous charges on her account, all paid, and no complaint has ever been registered—

"She probably wouldn't be here if there had, would she?" the judge asks wryly. He rolls his eyes. "You're wasting the court's time."

"Mrs. Atgeld contends that the clothing found in her bag was placed there by the arresting officer, Patrolwoman Valensuela," the lawyer announces. "My client states that the item was implanted during her initial detention."

"A fairly common accusation, I'm afraid." The judge peers at Carmen. "Officer Valensuela, what is your response?"

Carmen steps forward, jaw rigid to prevent the telltale shake of pleasure in her voice. "I submit as evidence, sir, the security videotape from the store."

"Oh, by all means," Susan Atgeld says sarcastically, "let's look at *that*!"

"No one gave you permission to speak," the magistrate snaps. "If you're out of order again, I'll end this trial prematurely. Do you understand?"

She nods, shocked as realization finally seeps into her senses; all the money in the world will not buy her special treatment in this courtroom.

The ruddy tan on her husband's cheeks goes gray around the edges.

"All right." The judge motions to his clerk and the ratty man obediently rolls a small cart forward with a thirteen-inch television and a small VCR on it. He powers both on and steps away. "Plug it in, Officer."

Carmen slides the tape into the VCR without hesitation and hits PLAY, then fast forwards for a few seconds before pausing. She glances at Susan and her lawyer, then at the judge. "This is it." Her finger jabs the PLAY button again.

The snowy background of the screen is replaced by a grainy black-and-white shot of Lord & Taylor's lingerie department from a ceiling viewpoint. A woman strolls into view with her back to the camera and fingers a few items, then turns and picks up a lace teddy; the camera gives a full shot of a woman who is unmistakably Susan Atgeld. Across from Carmen, the defendant thrusts out her chin defiantly, confident the tape will prove her innocence. But the woman on the videotape turns back, then hastily stuffs the lingerie into her bag; Susan McDunnah Atgeld's eyes bulge and she chokes and sways. Her husband reaches for her but the prison guard shoves a billyclub between them and forces Mr. Atgeld back.

"That's a lie," Susan shrieks. "I've never stolen anything!" She is restrained by the guard and her attorney speaks frantically to her in a low voice; abruptly she shuts up.

"Your honor," the attorney says smoothly, "you must realize how out of character this behavior would be for Mrs. Atgeld." He looks pointedly at Carmen and she keeps her face carefully impassive. "I allege this tape has been doctored."

Carmen's heart pounds with exhilaration as the judge taps his finger impatiently. "Did you take this tape home with you, Officer?" His eyes are large and brown; there is no resemblance whatsoever to a doe or any other soft animal.

"No sir." She stands straight, impeccably attired, a model of professional police work. "I obtained the tape from the store security lieu-tenant. After the arrest I returned immediately to the station. The tape was in the fingerprint lab until noon today, then it was logged in with the evidence sergeant."

The judge looks at her quizzically. "Fingerprint lab?"

"Another matter, sir."

He shuffles quickly through the small file, noting the police department's time punches on the forms. "It all checks out." He wastes no further time.

"Guilty."

Susan's husband gasps as the judge's gavel makes its final descent; Susan herself faints and Mr. Atgeld is detained, helpless as another guard hooks a hand under each arm and drags his wife away without comment. One of her prison slippers comes off and lies in the middle of the floor until the clerk kicks it aside. Watching, Carmen thinks the woman is a fool for wasting what little time she has left by being unconscious. She turns back to the clerk and he nods and hands her the judgment slip. She turns it over and reads where the judge has written six o'clock in the ENFORCEMENT TIME box.

Carmen wouldn't miss it for anything.

WITH LITTLE TIME for red tape and no money or manpower for prison, the system has restructured dramatically. Justice is swift and sure, and what crime exists in the city is born of size and sheer desperation. The Code of Law is simple, ancient and vicious: An Eye for an Eye. Because Susan McDunnah Atgeld has been convicted of shoplifting the Code of Law will claim her hands. Still, the legislators had been unable to agree on the appointment of workers to perform such barbaric tasks as were needed—after all, could a person who was willing to commit such atrocities actually be allowed to roam freely within society? Was not such a person basically like one of the . . .

Dead Things?

But everything has a function now, nothing is wasted. Even the Dead Things have their roles.

Enforcement #3 is a concrete room in the second level basement with rigid security; anyone, alive or dead, attempting to escape is shot on sight. Because she is the convicting officer, Carmen must witness the punishment, the flames inside her flaring with ecstasy at the sight of the hold-down device. Consisting of matched pieces of steel with cut-outs for hands, the device is set into the wall below an unbreakable slab of one-way mirror that looks into a narrow cubicle which sports a steel sliding door of its own. Near the ceiling is a small speaker. The device has been cleaned but the stains of former thieves remain, dark, ominous blots around the openings as though it has been splattered with rust-colored ink. Revived, Mrs. Atgeld is led into the room and at the sight of the device begins screaming anew, gibbering with fright and foreknowledge. Her pleas fall upon deaf ears as two guards force her forward and shove her flailing hands through the openings, then lock them in place and wind a complex series of leather straps around her upper body and arms. When they retreat, Susan Atgeld is bound to the hold-down device so tightly that her chest is pressed to the device's steel front and her straining elbows jut backwards past the ribs of her back. Although her right cheekbone is plastered against the cold mirror, her words are still understandable.

"Lying bitch!" she screams. "You framed me! Burn in hell, you whore—"

Her words choke away as the door beyond the mirror makes a ratcheting sound and slides open; a snarling Dead Thing, trussed by steel poles with loops, is pushed inside. Grunting and stumbling, the Dead Thing, once a woman, falls to its knees, then pitches forward as the cable looped around its neck yanks it forward, then expands and lifts. Freed, the Dead Thing is too slow to successfully turn before the poles are withdrawn and the door shuts behind it. It finds its footing and stands uncertainly, wobbling and looking around the cubicle. Its eyes are runny and white and blank; still they sweep the empty room until they fixate on the only thing that stands out.

Susan McDunnah Atgeld's hands and wrists.

As the Dead Thing begins to salivate, Susan whimpers, her eyes glassy and spit smearing the mirror and dribbling down to one shoulder as she bucks futilely within the leather harness.

It is over quickly though not quietly, barely lasting long enough to satisfy the hunger within Carmen. Susan Atgeld is unconscious, her grayed skin already streaming perspiration from the parasitic invasion caused by the Dead Thing's bite. Her bleeding stumps are tied off with rubber bungee cords as the Dead Thing in the other room chews on its delicate, manicured meal with single-minded determination. Mrs. Atgeld is left to die beneath the holding device; in under an hour she will rise with her own hunger, then die a second time. CPD will not decapitate and burn the body until it ensures that Susan McDunnah Atgeld has become a Dead Thing herself, but when this happens, she will be dispatched even quicker the second time around. As Carmen leaves the department preacher to mutter his harried prayer over the pre-corpse, the two Enforcement guards are readying their poles and running a leather sharpening strap along the length of the machete that will bring a final end to the Atgeld shoplifting case. Hurrying to the next Enforcement room, the preacher pushes past Carmen before she is two steps outside the door; when she glances back, she notes that the so-called man of God has not even closed Susan's eyes.

Carmen returns to her locker with lazy steps, moving slowly like a snake made sluggish by a full belly, collecting the evidence tape on her way. She takes the fingerprint photos out and studies them momentarily, then drops them off at Records and Research. All service workers are fingerprinted and by tomorrow morning the only prints on the tape, as well as the others she brought to the station this morning, will be identified as belonging to her brother-in-law. She has been very careful and while Walter is certain to claim he was framed, she knows there is no written record of the Dead Things she has given him to play with, while he has left a blatantly traceable legacy to tie him to the deaths of nearly a dozen women. Susan McDunnah Atgeld was the last of those, and the sense of nearly orgasmic fulfillment Carmen felt will be refilled to a new level when Walter is charged with premeditated murder, the Enforcement for which will be particularly fine and grisly. The law mandates a punishment equal to the crime, thus her brother-in-law will meet his final end locked weaponless in a cell with eleven Dead Things, and Officer Valensuela hopes they will all be dead *women*. At least he will leave a sizeable pension for Carmen's sister.

And Carmen will find other ways in which to feed the Dead Inside.

CHARLES BIRKIN

SIR CHARLES LLOYD BIRKIN, 5th Baronet (1907–1986), was the son of Colonel Charles Wilfred Birkin and Claire Howe of a historic old family. He was educated at Eton College and served in the Sherwood Foresters during World War II.

Although a short-story writer of great repute in the world of horror fiction, both under his own name and the pseudonym Charles Lloyd, he is mostly remembered today as the editor of the legendary Creeps series published in London by Philip Allan, beginning in 1932. Most of the books in the series were anthologies, but there were also a few novels and single-author collections as well, including Birkin's own *Devil's Spawn* (1936) as Charles Lloyd. Although this very successful series of books has largely been dismissed as second-rate, collectors and aficionados of old-fashioned tales of terror avidly seek them. The first book was titled simply *Creeps,* giving the series its unofficial name. After his deep immersion in the horror genre for less than a decade, other commitments forced him to retire from it in 1936, but he returned to it in 1964 with the short-story collections *Kiss of Death* (1964) and *Smell of Evil* (1964). His stories are so dark, and his own worldview so bleak, that a critic once said that "five minutes with him and the most devoutly practicing Pollyanna would have cheerfully slit her own throat."

"Ballet Nègre" was first published in *The Smell of Evil* (London: Library 33, 1964); it was reprinted in 1965 by Tandem Books, which is usually cited as the first edition.

CHARLES BIRKIN

BALLET NÈGRE

THEIR SEATS WERE in the eighth row of the stalls, well placed in the exact center. Simon Cust and David Roberts had arrived early, earlier than they had intended, for the traffic had been less heavy than they had anticipated, and they had misjudged the timing.

The theatre was filling up, but although it lacked only five minutes to the rise of the curtain, the audience continued to obstruct the foyer rather than take their places. It was the premiere of the Emanuel Louis' "Ballet Nègre

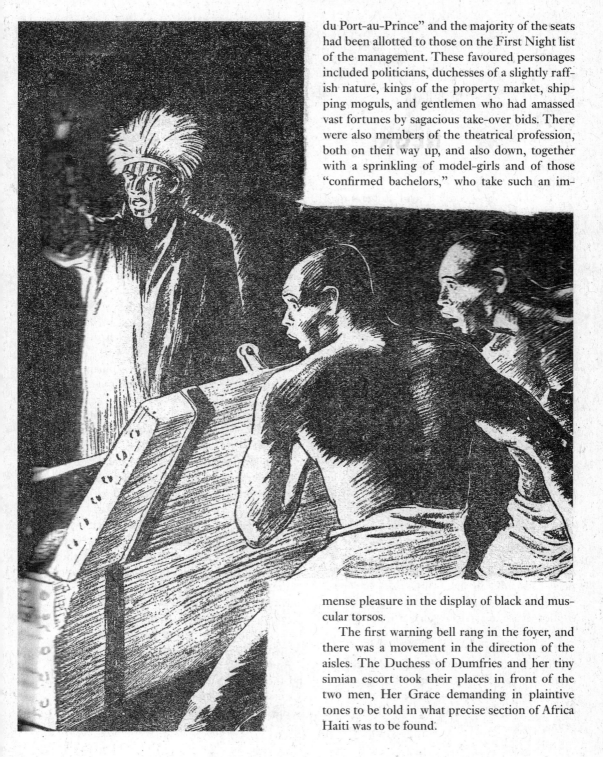

du Port-au-Prince" and the majority of the seats had been allotted to those on the First Night list of the management. These favoured personages included politicians, duchesses of a slightly raffish nature, kings of the property market, shipping moguls, and gentlemen who had amassed vast fortunes by sagacious take-over bids. There were also members of the theatrical profession, both on their way up, and also down, together with a sprinkling of model-girls and of those "confirmed bachelors," who take such an im-

mense pleasure in the display of black and muscular torsos.

The first warning bell rang in the foyer, and there was a movement in the direction of the aisles. The Duchess of Dumfries and her tiny simian escort took their places in front of the two men, Her Grace demanding in plaintive tones to be told in what precise section of Africa Haiti was to be found.

Simon Cust looked up from his programme. "What language do these people speak?" he asked David.

"In the country districts, a kind of French-Creole patois."

"Intelligible to a Wykhamist?" the young man asked.

"Yes, if you try and take it slowly," said David. Simon gave a sigh of relief. He was covering the evening for a colleague who was away on holiday.

"It should be good," David Roberts said comfortingly. "They're natural dancers and absolutely uninhibited. Or they used to be when I was there before the war. Of course it's more than possible that their travels have degutted them," he said, surveying the sophisticated audience.

The token orchestra, which was white, and composed largely of earnest ladies, was playing a spirited selection from recent American musicals which sounded oddly at variance with the evening which lay ahead. The bell gave a second and more imperious summons and the audience began a belated jostling in the gangways to claim their places. In order that they might be able to do so, the music continued for a further period before the house lights dimmed.

A tall young man stalked to a seat near to the front, stepping as delicately as a flamingo, and David nodded in his direction. "James Lloyd," he said, "the impresario."

The curtain rose on a riot of color. The backcloth was of a nebulous plantation, sugar-cane or banana. The front of the stage was a clearing in the jungle. At either side a group of musicians squatted in loin cloths crouched over their drums and primitive instruments. After a studied pause to erase the former tinklings, the drums began to throb.

The first number was spectacular but unexciting, a dance concerning the cultivation of the crops, stylized and formal, and accompanied by muted chanting. Next came a homage to "Papa Legba," one of the more benevolent of the voodoo hierarchy. This was succeeded by

a tribute to "Agoue," the God of the Sea, with a magnificently-built Negro playing the part of the deity, a scene during which the company warmed up, and which ended to considerable applause.

The final item of the first half of the bill was devoted to the propitiation of "Ogoun Badagris," the most feared and powerful of all the Powers of Darkness in the sinister cult of Voodoo. The scene had been changed to the interior of a "houmfort" or temple. Against one wall stood a low wooden altar bearing feathered ouanga bags, a pyramid of papiermache skulls, and a carved symbol of a hooded serpent in front of which burned coconut-shell lamps with floating flames. On the floor before the altar were calabashes brimming with fruit and vegetables, adding a deceptively peaceful note.

Simon had been able to study the programme with its explanatory notes, and so recognized the characters as they appeared, such as "Papa Nebo," hermaphroditic and the Oracle of the Dead, dressed as part man, part woman, top-hatted and skirted and carrying a human skull. This figure was accompanied by "Papaloi," crimson-turbaned and sporting a richly embroidered stole, and by "Mamaloi," glorious in her scarlet robes, and surrounded by their male and female attendants and by dancers disguised in animal masks as the sacrificial victims, sheep, kids, goats and a black bull, that had surely but recently taken the place of human beings.

The stage was crowded with a motley of old and young, weak and strong, and the tom-tom drums increased the pace of their rhythm and their volume, building up into a crescendo. "Damballa oueddo au couleuvra moins." It came as a mighty cry.

Simon glanced sideways at David. "Damballa Oueddo, who is our great Serpent-God." He whispered the translation.

And now came the offerings of the sacrifices and the complicated ritual of voodoo worship, in which terrified animals had been substituted for the boys and girls of yesterday. The propitiation over, there came the celebration dances to the deafening clamour of the drums and gourd rattles, the tempo ever increasing, ever mounting, until the scene was awhirl with lithe black bodies, some practically nude, others with flying white robes and multi-coloured turbans centred round "Papa Nebo," curiously intimidating, the smoked spectacles which were worn emphasizing the significance of the blind and impartial nature of death.

The dancers were becoming completely carried away, shrieking and sweating, degenerating into a beautifully controlled but seemingly delirious mob, maddened into a frenzied climax of blood and religion and sex.

The curtain fell to a thunder of appreciation, and the house lights went up. As they struggled towards the bar, David Roberts said: "I have to admit that they still appear to be totally uninhibited!"

The second and final half of the programme consisted of a narrative ballet based on a legend lost in folk lore. The story was that of an overseer who, with the help of his younger brother, hired out workers to till the fields. In order to augment his labour force he took to robbing the graves of the newly dead to supplement the quota of the living men with zombies, their identity being no secret to their fellow workers, who were themselves little better off than slaves and so too afraid to inform.

After a while the younger brother, overcome by pity for the zombies' misery, for his former love had been included in their ranks, broke, from the softness of his heart, the strictest rule which all must observe, that which forbade the use of salt in their spartan diet, for having partaken of salt the zombies would at once be conscious of their dreadful state and rush back to the cemetery in an effort to regain the lost peace of their violated graves.

Included in this saga was a stupefying dance, when a man and a woman swayed and postured in a lake of red-hot ash and, so far as the audience could see, this is precisely what they did, in fact, do.

It was the crux of the ballet, which was itself

the high spot of the evening, and the leading players had not appeared during the previous act. Their extraordinary performance and gaunt and ghastly make-up was breathtaking, and they seemed indeed to have strayed from another world, filling the most blasé of the spectators with a profoundly disquieting sense of unease.

Simon struck a match to see who they might be. Mathieu Tebreaux and Helene Chauvet. At curtain fall he turned to David. "This is it!" he said. "It's quite incredible. Don't you think so? How in God's name did they fake the fire?"

"Perhaps they didn't." David smiled. "They were probably drugged or doped. Narcotics are not unusual in those voodoo rites; and the soles of their feet are as tough as army boots," he finished prosaically.

"Be that as it may," Simon said with enthusiasm, "I'm off to get an interview and," he glanced at his watch, "I'd better be jet propelled about so doing or I'll be given no more of these assignments. Not that I've designs on Baring's job. Don't think that! But I must get back to the office. Will you come along with me to interpret?"

"If you'd like me to do so," said David. "My Creole dialect may be a bit rusty. It's been a long time since I've used it."

Simon presented his Press card to the stage doorkeeper and, after a few minutes' wait, the two men were escorted up to a dingy functional room where the manager of the ballet company was awaiting them.

He was a short fat Negro, and was wearing a dinner jacket with a yellow carnation in his buttonhole. He advanced to greet them, his gold teeth gleaming. "Mr. Cust?" he asked, looking from one to the other, Simon's card clutched in his left hand and with his right outstretched. "Mr. Lloyd has already left. He will be sorry to have missed you."

"I am Simon Cust. This is David Roberts, who knew your country well at one time. We were both of us deeply impressed by the performance tonight."

"My name is Emanuel Louis," said the Negro. He shook their hands in turn. "Shall we speak in French? I regret that my English is very halting. I cannot express myself as I would desire."

"By all means," Simon agreed. "You will have noticed from my card that I represent the *Daily Echo*. I would like to have the pleasure of meeting some of your cast, in particular Monsieur Tebreaux and Mademoiselle Chauvet."

Emanuel Louis gave an apologetic smile. "I am afraid, Monsieur, that that is not possible. My dancers give no interviews. I discourage strongly the star system. We work as a team. Personal publicity is strictly against my rules. I would have liked to co-operate but I cannot make exceptions. In any case it would be useless, for neither Mademoiselle Chauvet nor Mathieu Tebreaux speaks one word of English, and very few of French." He shrugged apologetically. "They come from a remote and backward part of my island."

"Mr. Roberts," said Simon, "could translate. He could talk to them in their own patois."

Monsieur Louis seemed taken aback by this suggestion and the look he gave David was speculative. "In the patois of La Gonave?" he inquired incredulously. "That is indeed unexpected."

David shook his head. "La Gonave? I'm sorry. No."

"And I regret, Monsieur, that I can make no variations to the regulations. It is not in my province to do so. You will understand. It is to me a great pleasure that you have enjoyed the show. My poor children are exhausted by their efforts. It is very tiring. Haiti is one thing. A large capital city is another thing altogether." He was shepherding them towards the door.

"I feel still," said Simon obstinately, "that I might get somewhere with them by mime, despite the language barrier. I could telephone my copy through to you for your approval."

Emanuel Louis' face set. "I have already told you, Monsieur Cust, that what you ask of me is absolutely impossible. May I wish you both a good evening?" His dismissal was curt. Simon

opened his mouth, but decided against further argument.

"I'll drop you off," David volunteered as they stood waiting for a taxi.

As they neared Fleet Street Simon said: "I wonder just why that fat little bastard wouldn't let me go back-stage. I've half a mind to double back and have another try at reaching them by by-passing the so-and-so."

"I don't think you'd succeed," said David as he lit a cigarette. "And how about your deadline?"

"Bugger my deadline," said Simon robustly, "and the same thing goes for Monsieur Louis."

David laughed. "*Chacun a son gout,*" he said, agreeably, as the taxi drew up at Simon's office.

THE "BALLET NÉGRE du Port-au-Prince" received fantastic notices, and by the afternoon all bookable seats had been sold out for the six weeks' season, for the telephones of the agencies had been ringing since early morning. Overnight it had become a "must" for London's theatregoers.

More than ever Simon fretted about his failure with Emanuel Louis, nor was he at all mollified when he learned that the representatives of rival papers had been equally unsuccessful. During the day he telephoned David Roberts, finally locating him at his club. "After the performance tonight," he told him, "I'm going to follow that loathsome black beetle back to where they're all staying. He can't possibly stick with them every moment, and tomorrow I'll shadow the place and wait my chance. Care to come?"

"Certainly not," said David. "The wretched fellow has a perfect right to run his own business according to his own views. And you must be aware," he added in an over-polite voice, "of my feelings regarding newspaper men, yourself included, and their thrusting ubiquity!"

Simon delivered himself of a few blistering remarks on the subject of the lack of helpfulness of the public in general and of David Roberts in particular, to struggling journalists, and rang off before David could have a chance to elaborate his theme.

At eleven o'clock that night, having contrived to fold his long length behind the driving seat of his turquoise blue Mini-Minor, and with his lights turned off, he sat watching the stage entrance of the Princess Theatre.

He had learned from the doorman, after a friendly talk and a cigarette and the passing of a pound note between them had created the right atmosphere, that the company was called for each night by two buses, but the man did not know, or had been unwilling to divulge, their destination, beyond the fact that it was an hotel somewhere in the Notting Hill direction which catered for "coloureds." "Accommodation is always their problem," he had said. "We had the same thing when the 'Hot Chocolates' were here, and a nicer bunch you couldn't wish to meet."

Simon peered at his watch. It was nearly half-past eleven, and the transport, two thirty-seater charabancs, was in the process of backing in to the narrow cul-de-sac. The dancers, on cue, were coming out into the street, some in their native clothes hidden under coats, others in European dress, and were starting to climb into the vehicles. They talked softly among themselves.

Emanuel Louis stood by one door checking a list, and a gigantic Negro in a light grey suit was similarly engaged by the other. When the buses were full they both jumped in and the vehicles moved off.

Simon had no difficulty in trailing such a convoy and kept at a discreet distance. In Holland Park they left the main road, and after five minutes or so came to a halt before an hotel, which had been made by knocking together two lofty Victorian houses. It had "The Presscott" painted in brown letters on the glass of the fanlights, and was sorely in need of renovation.

He was unable to pick out either Mathieu Tebreaux or Helene Chauvet. Louis and his giant aide-de-camp were the last to enter, the latter slamming the door behind him.

There was nothing more that he could do to-

night. Simon drove away, making a note of the name of the road as he turned the corner. He would be back in the morning.

ALICE LINLEY WAS always glad of a talk, especially with nice-looking young gentlemen who had the time and inclination to spare to take her for a Guinness. She was established by Simon's side in the private bar of the Cock Pheasant, perched on a high stool.

"They get all sorts at the Presscott," she said. "This district isn't what it was, not at all it isn't. Gladys, that's my friend, Gladys and I are seriously thinking about leaving our flat and moving to somewhere more select. Those Jamaicans started it. The whole place is becoming just like the Congo if you ask me. Not that I've got any personal feelings against coloured boys. Some of them are very nice really, but it's no longer such a good address, if you see what I mean."

Simon drained his bitter and ordered another round of drinks. "That Presscott lot," he asked, "do they get around much?"

"Thanks," said Alice. "It's hard to say, I'm sure. They moved in last Friday, I believe it was. Stacks of baggage they brought. Props and things, I expect. Great boxes and I don't know what. They're theatricals. Seem to keep pretty much to themselves. There's a short chap, the head one he seems to be. He does go out sometimes with a big fellah, black as coal. They've got a limousine car." She compressed her lips in mock disappointment. "Wish I had! Maybe some day I will. It's a long lane, I always say."

"Where do you suppose they go?" asked Simon. "I heard somewhere that they were French Colonials," he added inconsequentially.

"Couldn't really say." Alice sounded disinterested. She smoothed the cream silk of her blouse over her full breasts and Simon could not but observe that she had dispensed with a brassiere. "It's usually in the afternoon," she went on. "Being theatricals, I'd say they'd need their rest in the mornings." Her eyes travelled with approval over Simon's athletic and square-shouldered figure. "Like to come back to my place?" she asked pleasantly.

"I'd like to very much," he said, "but I'm afraid I can't. My office calls."

"Oh well," acquiesced Alice obligingly, "perhaps another day. I'm nearly always there until the evening, and you'd be welcome." She smiled at him. "It might even be 'on the house.' I think you're sweet. Most of my . . . my boy friends are such weeds," she said, "or else they're grandpas with pot bellies. It would make a change. I've quite fallen for you. Really I have." They emptied their glasses and stood up, going together into the street. "Ta-ta," Alice said. "Thanks ever so for the Guinness. Don't do anything I wouldn't do! I live round the corner over the paper shop if you want to find me." She walked away, swinging her orange plastic handbag, the beehive of her peroxide hair glinting in the sunshine.

Simon went back into the pub and purchased a pork pie which he took with him into the car as he settled down to begin his vigil.

The day was bright and warm. Soon after two o'clock a limousine stopped at the Presscott, and shortly afterwards Monsieur Louis and the large Negro came out of the hotel and drove away. Simon watched the car until it was out of sight, deciding to remain where he was for a spell longer.

Presently, in twos and threes, other members of the company emerged to take the air. The girls were mostly in flowered or patterned dresses, the men in tight suits with elaborately decorated shoes or sandals; but neither of the dancers for whom he was searching was among them.

And now a woman came out by herself. She was taller and broader than the other girls, and her carriage was splendid, and Simon thought that it had been she who had taken the role of "Papa Nebo" in the principal ballet. He pulled the crumpled programme from his pocket, scanning the names of the cast. Here it was: "Papa Nebo" . . . Marianne Dorville.

She was standing on the pavement at the foot of the stone steps enjoying the sunshine that was hardly more than a vitiated version of her own. Simon swung his long legs out of the tiny car and straightened up. Casually he walked towards her. As he drew level with her he stopped and raised his hat. "Mademoiselle Dorville?" he asked.

The woman glanced up at him in some surprise that he should know her name; or could it have been in fear? "Monsieur?"

"You speak French?" asked Simon, using that language.

"I do," she admitted, still ill at ease.

"I much admired your performance," Simon said. "I was at your opening night."

"You are very kind."

"I was," said Simon, "enchanted. I am the drama critic of the *Daily Echo*," he went on untruthfully, "which is the most powerful of the English papers, and I have come here by arrangement with Monsieur Louis to interview Mathieu Tebreaux and Helene Chauvet . . . and naturally yourself," he finished gallantly.

Marianne regarded him with some doubt. "That is not possible, Monsieur. We never give interviews. It is not permitted." She turned away.

"I assure you that it is all arranged," said Simon. "Monsieur Louis has made a rare exception in my case. If you will take me to him he will tell you so himself."

"He is not here. He has gone out."

"Not here?" repeated Simon in dismay. "He must be." He pulled back his cuff to look at his watch. "But that is a disaster. I have to turn in my copy by four o'clock. My paper is giving your show a tremendous boost. I would be greatly obliged if you would be so kind as to lead me to Monsieur Tebreaux. Otherwise," he said, relapsing into English, "there will be hell to pay. Hell for us all."

Marianne's large black eyes clouded. "Monsieur," she said, "you are talking nonsense. No interviews are permitted, particularly with Tebreaux and Chauvet. They would be unable to answer you." She hesitated and went on: "They are talented, yes—but they are also dumb, and comprehend nothing of the outside world."

"Dumb?" He searched her face. "How do you mean, dumb? Stupid?"

She shook her head and indicated her own tongue. "They cannot speak. They have suffered from this affliction since their birth. Unhappily there are many such in my country." Her gaze was as impassive as that of an image.

"I see," said Simon. So they were dumb, were they? And Louis had told him that they could speak only some obscure dialect. It didn't tie up. It didn't tie up at all. Regarding her pensively, Simon realized that she was beautiful. She hailed from Byzantium or from the land of the Pharoahs or from the drowned continent of Atlantis. She came entirely from the past. "Where are they?" he shot the question at her abruptly.

"In the room next to Monsieur Louis'," said Marianne before she could stop herself. "But you will not be admitted. You can spare yourself the trouble."

"I thank you," said Simon. He ran past her and up the steps into the lobby of the sleazy hotel. Marianne watched him go in a state of considerable distress. Then she followed him into the house, and darted into the telephone booth which stood in the hall.

Simon took the stairs two at a time. He had no way of knowing when Emanuel Louis would be back. Halfway up he nearly collided with a child that was on its way to the street. It could not have been more than ten years old. Simon took a shilling from the pocket of his trousers. "Monsieur Louis?" he inquired. The information would confine his quest to the two adjoining rooms.

The little boy took the coin, regarding him seriously out of huge dark eyes. "You will find him in room 12, Monsieur."

"Thank you." He found himself on a landing crowded with doors. Their positioning made it clear that the big rooms of the old house had been divided and sub-divided again. The numbers ranged from one to ten. He listened, but the house was quiet save for a muted crooning from a room on his left and the murmur of women's voices from further down the passage.

He tiptoed to the floor above, which was a replica of that which he had just left. The same walls of arsenic green, the same cocoa-brown dados and surrounds, and all around like incense was the sweetish smell of coloured people, which was vaguely reminiscent of musk. Simon found it at once both repugnant and exciting.

From the end of the corridor came the sound of imprecations and the rolling of dice. The ejaculations were agitated and guttural. He knocked on the door of number 11. There was no answer. He knocked again. Dead silence. He tried the door-knob and rather to his astonishment it opened at his touch. There was no one there. So it must be number 13. Twice he knocked and once more there was no sign of occupation. There were footsteps coming up the stairs. He could not risk discovery. He went in. The room was high and narrow. At one end an altar had been erected, a twin of that which he had seen in the "houmfort" at the theatre, except that he had an idea that the skulls which he was seeing were not made of papiermache.

There were two mattresses thrown on to the floor, and lying upon them were the couple for whom he had been searching. They lay there motionless, arms to their sides, and their eyes, turned to the ceiling, were filled with sadness and desolation. They made no movement at his entrance nor gave any acknowledgement of his presence. Their clothes were those which they had worn in the ballet in which they had danced.

Simon froze where he stood, unwilling to go further. "My apologies," he said, "if I am disturbing you. I am a Press reporter and have come here at the request of Monsieur Emanuel Louis. I represent the *Daily Echo*." Still there was no reply nor reaction and he stepped forward. "You do not understand French?" he asked. Only their eyes registered that they possessed a semblance of life. At closer quarters their faces were hideous and heart-breaking, the lips drawn back from prominent teeth, the skin taut over jutting cheek bones. "You are ill," he said gently. "Shall I get you a doctor?" He received no answer and walked forward once more until he stood gazing down at the emaciated forms. "You are hungry?" he suggested. "Is that it? You are hungry?"

And now the girl spoke, and her voice was as soft as the wind blowing through willow trees. "Yes," she whispered. "We are hungry. Oh, so hungry." Her jet black hair hung in ragged pennants to her shoulders. Simon dropped to his knees beside her and groped for her pulse. The grey skin of her wrist was as cold as that of a dead fish.

At his back the door was pushed open unobtrusively, but it gave a slight creak which was sufficient to make him turn his head. The doorway appeared to him to be filled and crowded with people. Emanuel Louis, who was grasping a revolver in his hand, the immense Negro in the pale suit, Marianne Dorville, saucer-eyed with apprehension, and behind her the craning necks and dusky terror-stricken faces of a tableau of other men and women.

Emanuel Louis' face was stiff and contorted by rage. "Get out!" he said. "Leave this room immediately. I will not have my artistes upset by such behaviour. If you must know, they are suffering from fever, from grippe, but it is not serious. It has happened before, and they are under my personal supervision. You are committing a trespass, and if you refuse to take yourself off at once, I will summon the police. Your actions are insupportable—beyond all reason. Get out! Get out! Will you leave, or must we throw you into the street?"

Simon got to his feet. "That will not be necessary, Monsieur Louis," he said. "And you can put that thing away," he added, pointing to the revolver. "I must warn you, however, that it is illegal to carry weapons in this country. And also that you have two very sick people on your hands."

"Go," said Louis, "and should you try to return I warn *you* that I will not hesitate to have you arrested." He was so choked by his fury that he could scarcely speak.

Simon said no more. He walked over to the doorway, and the rows of black faces divided to let him pass. He was shaking as he got into his car.

In the evening he visited the Princess Theatre for a second time, standing at the back of the dress circle. Both Tebreaux and Helene Chauvet were dancing, and their performance was as good as the one which they had given on the first night.

David Roberts must have been right. Perhaps, after all, they were dope addicts. But Simon was by no means satisfied. There was a story here, and he was determined to get it.

IT WAS AFTER midnight when Simon reached the Presscott. No lights showed, and he walked round to the tradesmen's entrance and down a flight of steps leading to an area. Here there was a glow from a curtained window of what he took to be the kitchen. There was a bell in the surround and he pressed it.

It was opened by a mulatto in his shirt sleeves and a tattered pullover, who stood there waiting for him to speak.

"I know it's very late," Simon said, "but I wondered if you could by any chance oblige me by letting me have a room? It would be for tonight only. I arrived from Cornwall an hour or so ago and I can't get a bed anywhere."

The mulatto stared at him with mistrust. "No," he said, "I can't. I am full up. This hotel is for coloured people." He made as if to shut the door in Simon's face.

"I don't mind that at all," Simon said. He produced his wallet, from which he extracted a five-pound note. "I only want somewhere to sleep, and perhaps a cup of coffee in the morning."

The man eyed the note. Then he turned away. "Olive!" he called. "Come here a second, will you? There's a bloke out here who wants a bed. He's a white feller." He pushed the door nearly shut once more, and Simon could hear a muttered colloquy coming from behind it. There was a lighter step, and through the crack he was aware that a fair-haired woman was inspecting him.

Apparently satisfied by what she saw, she

said: "Come in, won't you? As my husband told you, we are full up, but if it's only for one night, and you don't mind roughing it, I daresay we could let you have Ivy's room. She's my living-in maid, and a lazy slut. Her mother's been taken poorly, or so she says, so she won't be coming back until tomorrow afternoon. 'Clinging Ivy' I calls her, the way she throws herself at those black chaps. She'll get what's coming to her one of these fine days if she doesn't look out. They're only human, aren't they, same as the rest of us? Girls are so inconsiderate these days. But you can't pick and choose, more's the pity, you can't by any manner of means, and well they know it! No luggage?" she finished sharply, looking at his empty hands.

"I'm afraid not." Simon thrust the note towards her. "Will that do instead?"

"Not on the run, are you?" she asked him suspiciously. "We don't take that sort here."

"No," said Simon, "I'm not on the run."

Olive's hand closed on the five pounds. "It's just to oblige," she said. "We don't usually accept men without any luggage. Certainly not at this time of night. If you'll follow me, I'll show you your room. It's nothing very grand."

He went up behind her to the top floor, and to a door that had no number. "The bed's not bad," said the woman defensively. "And it's clean. You'll find no bugs in my house. What time would you be wanting calling in the morning?" They had encountered no one on their way up.

"Half-past seven?" Simon suggested, knowing that long before that he would be gone.

"Righty-oh. Whatever you say." She glanced around her. "Ivy's left her things, I see. Still, you won't be needing cupboard space, having brought no luggage. Well, good night." Her pin heels clattered away down the staircase.

Simon took off his coat and removed his shoes, and stretched out on the bed, which protested loudly under the weight of his fourteen stone. He would give his landlady and her husband half an hour in which to retire. He must have dozed, for when he looked at his watch it pointed to a quarter to three.

Jumping up he crossed in his stockinged feet to the peg on which he had hung his coat, and took from its bulging pocket a packet of sandwiches, which had been thickly stuffed with nearly raw beef. He had remembered the whisper of the girl in room 13. "We are hungry. Oh, so hungry."

Their room must be on the floor below his own. He stuck his head over the stair-well. There was a dim bulb burning on each landing. Cautiously he made his way down, hoping that there would be no loose treads. On the landing he stood listening. From behind the door nearest to him came the noise of rhythmic snoring.

He reached number 13 and slipped inside, for it was not locked. It was in darkness, but he could hear no breathing. He might have been in a tomb. He had satisfied himself that there was no transom, so he fumbled for the switch and turned on an unshaded light.

The man and the girl were lying just as he had last seen them. "Do not be afraid," he said in a whisper. "I was here to see you yesterday and this time I have brought you food. There is no reason for you to be afraid of me." He leant down and closed first the girl's cold fingers and then those of the man round the gift that he had brought them.

Their fingers gripped like pincers into the soft bread, and slowly they raised it to their mouths. Simon looked at them with compassion. Drugs, he thought, that is what it is. The pupils of their eyes had dwindled to pin-points. They were chewing on the meat convulsively, their mouths crammed.

And now they were stirring and raising themselves up from the mattresses, and their eyes were changing. The sadness and hopelessness was fading, and a fierce intense hatred was taking its place. Appalled by what he saw Simon jack-knifed to his feet, but quick as he had been, they too had leaped up and were upon him.

Mathieu closed with him and his scrawny arms had in them all the strength of steel. Exerting every ounce of his considerable force Simon was barely holding his own with his assailant.

And then the girl, uttering a piercing shriek of passionate and diabolical rage, snatched up a curved knife from the altar and clawed herself up upon his back.

Simon knew that he was being overpowered and had no chance and, weak with fear for the first time in his life, started to shout for help. The girl had twisted her hand into his hair and was forcing back his head, exposing his throat. And the knife flashed once in the light from the unshaded bulb. Simon's cries ceased, silenced by the bubbling blood that gushed into his windpipe.

There came the patter of running feet, and of calling, and amid a great confusion and tumult the door was burst open and Emanuel Louis ran into the room. Almost at his feet lay the body of Simon Cust, the throat from which his lifeblood was pouring had been slit from ear to ear like that of a sacrificial animal.

Emanuel's eyes passed on to the dirty matting on the floor where a beef sandwich was oozing from its torn wrapping. It was clear to him what had taken place. His charges had been fed meat. Meat and salt; those were the forbidden foods of zombies, the keys which would give them back their memories, and the interfering fool had not known it. So they had turned and rent the first man they had seen, judging him to have been responsible for their final degradation.

The two occupants of the shabby room, blood spattered and with their arms hanging loosely by their sides and nearly to their knees, brushed past him blindly. Along the passage, lined with horrified Negroes, they went, and passed unmolested down the stairs and out into the deserted street.

Emanuel Louis let them go, for it was useless to try to stop them, and then in his turn he paced through the waiting and watching men and women and went down to the hall and to the telephone. As he reached it a woman began to wail from above and soon all had taken it up in a weird and uncanny lament.

Having made his call, Emanuel Louis sat on a hard chair by the booth and waited. He had not long to wait. In a very few minutes there was a screech of tyres as a squad car braked to a halt in front of the house and there was a roar of motor bicycles, and the hall became filled with policemen, two of them middle-aged and in plain clothes, and a uniformed constable, and a young Hercules in crash helmet and leather-encased legs who stood behind them with his hands planted on his belt. From the street more men could be heard arriving.

Emanuel Louis led them up to the room where Simon Cust was lying, and for a moment the men stood in a shocked semi-circle eyeing the body. The smaller of the plain clothes men was the first to speak. "Stop those damned niggers making such a bloody din, can't you?" he said. "It's enough to turn your stomach."

His companion also swivelled round to face Emanuel Louis. "Well," he said, "are you going to tell me which one of you is responsible?"

The plump little man stared back at him sorrowfully. "I am going to tell you," he said. "Those who have done this thing have gone. They have gone I do not know where, but it will be to the west."

"What's that?" demanded the police officer. "You admit that you know the identity of the murderers? Why the hell did you let them get away?"

"They will be making for the west," said Emanuel Louis once again, scarcely seeing the stern and stolid faces that surrounded him, "for when the Living Dead realize what they really are, they always head for the graves from which they have been dragged."

DEAD RIGHT

GEOFFREY A. LANDIS

AN ASTONISHINGLY DISTINGUISHED and demanding career as a physicist and aeronautical scientist has not prevented Geoffrey A. Landis (1955–) from producing eighty short stories, fifty poems, a novel, and more than three hundred learned papers on scientific subjects. His fiction has been translated into twenty-one languages.

Born in Detroit, Michigan, Landis led a peripatetic life as a child before attending the Massachusetts Institute of Technology, receiving degrees in physics and electrical engineering, then receiving a Ph.D. in solid-state physics from Brown University. He has worked for the National Aeronautics and Space Administration on such projects as planetary (particularly Mars and Venus) exploration and interstellar propulsion.

His first published short story, "Elemental," appeared in the December 1984 issue of *Analog,* and his fiction, mainly in the area of hard science fiction but extending to fantasy and horror as well, has enjoyed exceptional success. He has been nominated for six Hugo Awards, winning in the short-story category in 1992 for "A Walk in the Sun" and again in 2002 for "Falling onto Mars." He also has been nominated for six Nebula Awards, winning for Best Short Story in 1989 for "Ripples in the Dirac Sea." His first novel, *Mars Crossing* (2000), won the Locus Award.

"Dead Right" was first published in *The Ultimate Zombie,* edited by Byron Preiss and John Betancourt (New York: Dell, 1993).

GEOFFREY A. LANDIS

DEAD RIGHT

ALI DANCED LEFT, right, but I had his number, I had the unbeatable combination; I hit him where he dodged and dodged him where he hit. Not even the Champ at his prime could stand against me. He danced back—as expected—and I started into the knockout sequence, counting under my breath (Left! Left! Duck!) to keep the timing (Cross! Half pace back!) and *there*!

Muhammad Ali froze in mid-punch and the lights came on. I took off the glasses and looked at the tally screen: *Ali by knockout.* "What?"

Jim Mallok was standing in the door. "You were a quarter-second late on the A3 sequence, and a half-second on the C3. A fighter like Ali, you have to be right in the groove; the bandwidth is too tight for anything else." He flipped a switch, and the video image of Muhammad Ali vanished into the sweat-filled air. A punching bag stood forlorn where he had been. "What the hell you doing fighting Ali, Dave? You got real work to do."

"Yeah, I know. Just sharpening up my moves."

"Can't you sharpen 'em up on your own time? This is business, not a video arcade. We got work to do."

I shrugged. "Can't train against this Sobo guy until you get some videos of him fighting."

"You can still practice your basics. Forget the fancy stuff; you're not going up against Ali. Practice knocking down some real human beings like you might see in the ring."

"Yow-SUH, Mr. Boss-Man suh! Ah's working, Ah's working jes as hard as I can."

Jim smiled.

I USED TO fight golden-gloves when I was in high school. I was pretty good, but—let's face it—golden-gloves Minneapolis isn't quite the same league as golden-gloves New York or Chicago. The kids who hung out at the gym were dead-enders from the projects, kids whose only ways to leave the inner city were with their fists or on a slab. I liked it anyway; the jive talking and no-nonsense attitudes were a welcome change from the suburban intellectuals of high school. And besides, there is a pure visceral satisfaction in going into the gym and beating the hell out of a speed bag, walloping the thing until you fall into the flow, a rhythm that goes on effortlessly, until suddenly you wake up covered with sweat and tired right down to your kneecaps.

I boxed at the Naval Academy, too, at least until they told me I was too tall to go into flight training and I opted out to finish my degree at Cleveland State. State didn't have boxing, so while I still kept in shape working out at the Y, I stopped fighting. I didn't think I missed it. Boxing is a young man's sport anyway.

I figured that was the end of my fighting career. Just goes to show how wrong you can be.

I met Mallok during my first, and last, year in grad school, the year I spent slowly discovering that I didn't have any desire to spend the rest of my life as an electrical engineer. I used to go over to the west side to the bouts down on Worthing Street every Saturday afternoon. Alone, of course: the girl I was dating considered any hint of macho something unutterably gauche and the fights absolutely barbaric. One of those Saturdays—a welterweight match—I ran into Mallok. I'd seen him around the fights, but never really noticed what he'd been doing. He was sitting right up by the ring, flicking his attention from the fight to his laptop computer and back, tapping frenetically at the keyboard. I came over to watch, and soon we got to talking fights. By the end of the evening Kid Rutano had downed Corregio with an overhand right, and Mallok had invited me back into his place, a gym and computer lab in one, to look over his fight analysis software.

Until he'd failed to get tenure and dropped out of academia, Jim Mallok had had all the Air Force contracts he could handle. He'd been big in computer conflict modeling, based on a network theory of games. Network theory says that every sufficiently complicated system must have poles and zeros. Put simply, this means that every strategy has a weakness, every opponent has a blind spot. If he knew the physiology and the tactics of a boxer, Mallok said, he could find a strategy that would put him down as easily as tapping him on the shoulder.

I tried a couple of rounds with the video-boxing simulator he'd hacked together, and tried some of the combinations he showed me. It wasn't as realistic as the one he trained me on later, but it was still surprisingly effective. The computer pulled images from a CD-ROM library, and twin video projectors put a separate image onto each eyepiece of a set of special glasses. Anybody looking at me would see me circling around a video projector, but to me it looked like the video image had puffed up and started throwing punches.

We made a peculiar pair, Mallock and I; him short and dapper and full of enthusiasm, dark hair slicked back; me the ex-jock in faded sweatshirts, stocky and slow speaking, but always moving. We complemented one another perfectly.

WE WERE AT the ring, and Mallok still hadn't gotten any videos of this Sobo. I was ready for him, though, limbered up and ready with a hatful of winning combinations.

I was dressing down when Sal walked back to the car to get his kit and Jim had gone to talk business with some backers. An old black man in a beat-up felt hat sidled up to me, grabbed my biceps, and looked me earnestly in the eye. "This Sobo, he bad *baka*," he said, with an odd lilting accent that it took me a few seconds to understand. "You understand? He not person. No heart. You fight him, he going kill you. Better you drop out, you sick."

I yanked away, disgusted. "Thanks, guy. I'll do okay." A lot of weird stuff goes on in the fight game. Drugs, legal and illegal, and bribes of all kinds, of course, but not just that. Anything for an edge. Had Sobo's trainer put this guy up to this, or did he have money on the fight? Either way, I wasn't going to buy into it.

"I serious." His look was intense, almost fearful. Maybe he owed money to the mob, needed to win a bet. "Sobo, he different. You not know his type in America. He once dead man, no can die."

Jim had promised that we would be different, we wouldn't play those games, and I wasn't going to be played with, either. "Go away, old man, or I call security. You shouldn't be here."

"I just ignorant man, sir," he said. "But, please, you think it, okay? You be smart."

Sal pushed through the door and stopped. He took one look at me, then threw the tape down on the floor in disgust, and grabbed the man with one hand on his collar and the other on the seat of his pants. "You. Out." He shuffled the man toward the door and gave him a boost outward, then turned to me. "You shouldn't let guys like that talk trash to you, kid. What did he want, ask you to throw the fight?"

I held out my hands to be taped up, and shook my head slightly. "Just trying to scare me, I think," I said. "Didn't work. We don't play those games."

THE DAMN RING was too hot, and I was sweating before I'd even stood up. Sobo looked tough. He was a tall, stringy guy, skin black as graveyard dirt, thin as a cadaver, but with plenty of reach. He sat there unmoving as his trainer fussed over him, staring straight forward as if he'd forgotten how to use his eyelids. I've seen 'em like that before, brain damaged from too many punches, but still, something about the complete emptiness in his eyes unnerved me. What the old black man had said still ran through my head. "You heard anything about this guy Sobo?" I whispered to Sal.

He didn't look up. "Not much." He continued to rub oil into my back, loosening me up for the bout. "Hasn't been in the country long. Fought twice, won 'em both by wearing the other guy down."

"Umm." I probably knew more than he did; I'd read the dossier. But Sal had street smarts, and we didn't have a good lock on this guy. I'd been hoping for something better.

Sal slapped me on the back. "You can take him, kid. Show him how a red-blooded American fights."

The trainer was muttering to him. From across the ring I could barely hear it, unusual, urgent cadences in a whispered, distorted Creole. At the same time he was wiping Sobo down. I squinted. What was that fluid he was wiping him with? It glistened with an evil shine on Sobo's preternaturally black skin.

The ref made the announcement and I stood up. We looked at each other for a moment, and then the bell rang. Sal punched me softly. "Kill 'im, kid."

Sobo moved out slowly, with a trace of hesitation between movements giving him a jerky look. I memorized that. If he moved with the same rhythm in the ring, I'd have to compensate, or I'd be punching in places where he wasn't.

He had a slow guard, and barely even tried to duck punches. I did the basic sequence: one, two, pause, three, four, down! I stepped back to let the ref in as he fell.

Sobo was still on his feet.

Whap, whap, whap; I licked out a few fast lefts to the face. He raised his guard. Whap, whap; I hit him a couple of times in the stomach. He lowered his guard. He didn't seem to notice, just kept plugging away with his right, pumping like a slow piston. Mostly I blocked 'em, but he put in a couple every now and then.

In the clinches his skin felt cool and squishy. I was breathing hard now, and sweating like a horse. Sobo didn't seem to be sweating at all. Nor breathing, either, as far as I could tell. And he had that same dead, impassive expression on his face. His eyes were funny—flat, almost dusty. No matter where I dodged, he stared straight ahead. I was wearing myself out hitting him, and he didn't even seem to notice it.

This was no projection. This was the real thing, and I didn't like it.

I hate these sleazy, second-rate arenas. The lights hang down low, the air is stagnant and full of smoke; you get hot and soaked in sweat in no time. I was beginning to tire, but Sobo hadn't slowed down a whit. He didn't seem to notice any of my blows, though I was landing three for every one he hit me with. My hands were beginning to hurt. I was sweating rivers, but he hadn't started to sweat at all. The bell rang, at last. I gave him one final lick where the ref couldn't see, then headed back to my corner.

"I gotta talk to Mallok, Sal." When Jim came over, I said, "Got anything new?"

Jim shook his head.

"I got a bad feeling about this one, Jim. He's not responding right."

"Keep on it, Dave. We'll get a make on him yet. We got the technology, dig it? Hang in there."

"I got a bad feeling, Jim." Then the bell rang, and I was back in the ring.

Second round was worse. I was killing him on points, but he was wearing me down. The combinations I used had been optimized and fine-tuned and should have been able to knock over a horse, but he kept on moving. I'd gotten in one good one to the face and cut him bad over one eye, but instead of blood, the open edges of the wound oozed a sickly pale yellow fluid, and he took no notice. My throat was raw from panting; bile like stale piss burned in the back of my mouth. I couldn't stand up any longer, and then the bell came.

Third round was worse yet. Sal was yelling advice—"Hands high! Head down!"—but I was too tired to keep up. My hands were too heavy, sliding down of their own will. My nostrils were clogged with the tang of sweat and linament, but under those familiar smells was another, a rank odor of decay, like a whiff of rotten meat. I was beginning to feel an awful certainty about the word the old man had been too frightened to say. The bell rang, and I called for Jim.

"He's a zombie, Jim! I mean, a real, live zombie! I mean, a dead one! From Haiti. He's not alive!"

In the opposite corner Sobo stared unmoving, unblinking, the voodoo man chanting over him and rubbing his skin with fresh blood.

Jim didn't even blink. "Isn't that some sort of blowfish poison they use? Should slow him down—what's the problem?"

"No, Jim. I don't mean some poor drugged-out crazy. I mean, he's a zombie. Dead, and I mean D-E-A-D, dead."

"Zombie, like the walking dead? I don't think I believe in zombies, kid."

"You've been updating the program, right? What have you come up with?"

He shook his head. "According to my model, he should be dead twice over by now. Just keep hitting him in the same places, and sooner or later—"

"Negative, Jim. It's voodoo. He *is* dead. Feed it into the computer. Tell me—how can you knock out a fighter who's *already dead?*"

The bell rang. He blinked, and nodded. "I'll try."

THE JOB MARKET for people to play around with computers, the only profession I was decently prepared for, had quietly gone soft while I was wasting time flunking out of grad school. My girlfriend had drifted off with a vague, "We'll stay friends, okay?"; my second-hand Plymouth vanished when the bank noticed I hadn't made any payments for six months. I didn't have any idea of what to do next. I certainly hadn't planned to go back into the fight scene, never even considered going pro. But that summer there was nothing, not even any openings flipping burgers, and I was getting desperate. I'd been hitting the bags at the Y when Jim caught up with me and made his offer. Jim believed that fighting was a thinking man's sport, and he wanted a partner who could think as well as fight.

I could barely believe him. Unless you're up there with Ali, prizefighting is a lousy way to make a living. On the bottom of the card it's hard work and constant training for a shot at a hundred, maybe two hundred dollars. He wasn't even a trainer, not a real trainer, he was an ex-professor with a theory.

His theory was simple. He claimed that net-work theory guaranteed that for any system, there was an input that it couldn't respond to. For every fighter there exists some combination of moves that he can't respond to, that leaves him waltzing right into the knockout blow. He could input videotapes of a fighter's past fights into the computer, and have it model the fighter and tell us the moves.

With a piece of software that could train any boxer to beat anybody, he could just name his price, right?

Wrong. An out-of-work college professor? Just who was he trying to scam, anyway? Before he could win fights, he had to win some fights. He needed a demo model.

Me.

I was in no condition for extended bouts, but that made little difference to his strategy.

The computer was programmed with all the great fighters of the past . . . and videos of all the fighters I was going to meet. I was pro-grammed, too: programmed with the moves to beat them.

It was crazy to accept it, but what else did I have? I told him I'd think it over. The next day he'd hired Sal, an old guy who'd been work-ing the corner since the forties, until he got squeezed out by the mqb. Sal came in for noth-ing but a cut of the prize and Mallok's prom-ise that we were going to play straight. When I came by that afternoon to tell him I was in, he was already setting up for the first bout.

The first few fights were upsets—surprise victory by knockout in the first round. It had been so easy it surprised even me; I knew what they were going to do before they did, and they walked into my knockout punch like they were following a script. Suddenly we were getting the attention Mallok needed. With one more win to show that the first two were more than a fluke, I'd be able to get out of the ring and the money would start rolling in. But we were sty-mied with Sobo. No videos. Most boxers were glad to supplement their income with the little bit of money they'd get from selling videos, but

there was a wall of secrecy about the new Hai-tian fighter. We were going in blind.

No big deal, since we still had the physiology, the nerve connections and blood flow. If you hit him right, not even necessarily very hard, just *right,* any fighter would have to go down. Any fighter alive.

We had never counted on meeting a fighter who wasn't.

HIS SMELL WAS making me retch; something in my hindbrain said that it was wrong, evil, unclean. I was in shape for a sprint, and the match had turned into a marathon. I'd barely stayed upright last round, much less done any damage, and he'd been impassive, steady as a stiffened corpse. As I collapsed onto the stool, I could hear the voodoo man start to mutter his chant in the opposite corner. Jim's voice seemed to come from far away. "I've got it set. Get him off balance to the left, and then knock him over with an A3-A3-B13 combination."

I blinked. A3-A3 was a classic feint combina-tion, footwork opposite to left jab, which would certainly get him off balance—this guy Sobo was no Fred Astaire when it came to dancing—but a B13 wouldn't do anything. Knock him over? Possible, even likely, but tripping him wouldn't hurt him any. What was the point, when he would just get back up again punching? I started to say something when the bell rang.

"Go!" Sal lifted me up off the bench and pushed me toward the ring. Somewhere I found enough energy to stagger forward.

Sobo stepped forward, pistoning away tire-lessly. I stepped left, he stepped left, I crossed and jabbed, and then whacked him. It was a soft blow, I was too tired; I had no power left to put behind it. He tripped over his misplaced feet, and his own momentum carried him down. He started to get up—

"Stop the fight!"

The ring medic jumped the rope and ran to Sobo. Sobo was already stumbling to his feet, his right still pumping away, even though I wasn't anywhere in range. "Stop the fight!" The ref looked confused, and then the medic pulled out a hypodermic.

Sobo's trainer shrieked.

The ring medic had to hold Sobo down to examine him. He didn't have a pulse, and his flesh was cold as a shock victim, but he was still trying to get up when the medic jabbed him full of adrenaline to restart his heart.

SOBO MAY OR may not have been clinically dead when he entered the ambulance. For certain, though, after the paramedics tried adrenaline injections, CPR, electroshock, and all the rest in a frantic effort to restart his heart, he was good and dead by the time he got to the hospital.

There was a big commotion for a while—that's how I picked up the nickname "Killer"—but the coroner's statement said Sobo had been in such bad shape that he never should have been in the ring in the first place. "I don't understand why he was even walking, much less fighting," the doctor said, and nobody ever quite figured out how he'd ever won his first two fights. His trainer was deported back to Haiti as an undesirable alien.

I was feeling nothing: no triumph, no pity, no pain. Just weary. Jim came in as Sal was cutting the tape off my hands. I looked up slowly. "So?"

"So he was already dead. It wasn't exactly illegal, kid. We heard what you said. We figured, if he was a zombie, he couldn't stand up to even a cursory med exam. Sal had to bribe the ring medic to get him to jump in in the middle of the fight, but once he got close to Sobo, the show was over. We didn't intend to kill the guy, but, hell, he was already dead. Should of figured it. Stands to reason, if he was dead to start with, starting his heart wouldn't do him any good."

"What do you mean, not exactly legal?"

"So, new philosophy: if you can't win by the rules," he shrugged, "bribe an official."

I winced as Sal touched up a ripening bruise. "I thought we didn't play that way."

"Hell, kid, you think they were playing by the rules? They must of paid to get somebody to look the other way."

"Then the program's wrong." I just looked at him.

There's a lot of weird stuff that goes down. Fighting a dead man was a new one, but it wouldn't be the weirdest thing to happen in the ring, or outside of it.

"Well, of course. I mean it's not exactly *wrong*, it's just . . . it's that it couldn't . . . it . . ." He paused. "Yeah. Wrong. Dead wrong."

I nodded. "So you know."

We looked at each other, but I was tired, too dead tired to think now, too tired to make fine moral distinctions. In the morning I'd see it clearly.

"I think," Jim said, slowly, "we have some work to do." And, after a long while, he began to laugh.

THE TAKING OF MR. BILL

GRAHAM MASTERTON

BORN IN EDINBURGH, Graham Masterton (1946–) began his career as a journalist, first as a newspaper reporter, then as editor of the men's magazine *Mayfair,* followed by the same position for both *Penthouse* and *Penthouse Forum* in Great Britain. This led, perhaps inevitably, to a prolific career as a writer of sex books, with more than two dozen titles published, including *How to Drive Your Man Wild in Bed* (1976), which sold more than three million copies worldwide.

Masterton also became a prolific author of horror, adventure, thriller, and historical fiction, publishing more than a hundred books, beginning with *The Manitou* (1975), which he claims to have written in ten days. The story of a Native American shaman who is reborn in the present day to wreak revenge on white people, it became a bestseller and has had five sequels. It was filmed in 1978, produced and directed by William Girdler; it starred Tony Curtis, Susan Strasberg, Burgess Meredith, Michael Ansara, Stella Stevens, and Ann Sothern. Three of his stories were filmed for the television series *The Hunger.* His novel *Charnel House* (1979) was nominated for an Edgar Allan Poe Award. Two historical sagas, *Rich* (1979) and *Maiden Voyage* (1984), were *New York Times* bestsellers. He has frequently written for children, and the seven books in the Rook series for young adults have an avid following.

"The Taking of Mr. Bill" was originally published in *The Mammoth Book of Zombies,* edited by Stephen Jones (London: Robinson Publishing, 1993).

GRAHAM MASTERTON

THE TAKING OF MR. BILL

IT WAS ONLY a few minutes past four in the afternoon, but the day suddenly grew dark, thunderously dark, and freezing-cold rain began to lash down. For a few minutes, the pathways of Kensington Gardens were criss-crossed with bobbing umbrellas and au-pairs running helter-skelter with baby-buggies and screaming children.

Then, the gardens were abruptly deserted, left to the rain and the Canada geese and the gusts of wind that ruffled back the leaves. Marjorie found herself alone, hurriedly pushing William in his small navy-blue Mothercare pram. She was wearing only her red tweed jacket and her long black pleated skirt, and she was already soaked. The afternoon had been brilliantly sunny when she left the house, with a sky as blue as dinner-plates. She hadn't brought an umbrella. She hadn't even brought a plastic rain-hat.

She hadn't expected to stay with her uncle Michael until so late, but Uncle Michael was so old now that he could barely keep himself clean. She had made him tea and tidied his bed, and done some hoovering while William lay kicking and gurgling on the sofa, and Uncle Michael watched him, rheumy-eyed, his hands resting on his lap like crumpled yellow tissue-paper, his mind fading and brightening, fading and brightening, in the same way that the afternoon sunlight faded and brightened.

She had kissed Uncle Michael before she left, and he had clasped her hand between both of his. "Take good care of that boy, won't you?" he had whispered. "You never know who's watching. You never know who might want him."

"Oh, Uncle, you know that I never let him out of my sight. Besides, if anybody wants him, they're welcome to him. Perhaps I'll get some sleep at night."

"Don't say that, Marjorie. Never say that. Think of all the mothers who have said that, only as a joke, and then have wished that they had cut out their tongues."

"Uncle . . . don't be so morbid. I'll give you a ring when I get home, just to make sure you're all right. But I must go. I'm cooking chicken chasseur tonight."

Uncle Michael had nodded. "Chicken chasseur . . . ," he had said, vaguely. Then, "Don't forget the pan."

"Of course not, Uncle. I'm not going to burn it. Now, make sure you put the chain on the door."

Now she was walking past the Round Pond. She slowed down, wheeling the pram through the muddy grass. She was so wet that it scarcely made any difference. She thought of the old Chinese saying, "Why walk fast in the rain? It's raining just as hard up ahead."

Before the arrival of the Canada geese, the Round Pond had been neat and tidy and peaceful, with fluttering ducks and children sailing little yachts. Now, it was fouled and murky, and peculiarly threatening, like anything precious that has been taken away from you and vandalized by strangers. Marjorie's Peugeot had been stolen last spring, and crashed, and urinated in, and she had never been able to think of driving it again, or even another car like it.

She emerged from the trees and a sudden explosion of cold rain caught her on the side of the cheek. William was awake, and waving his arms, but she knew that he would be hungry by now, and that she would have to feed him as soon as she got home.

She took a short cut, walking diagonally through another stand of trees. She could hear the muffled roar of London's traffic on both sides of the garden, and the rumbling, scratching noise of an airliner passing overhead, but the gardens themselves remained oddly empty, and silent, as if a spell had been cast over them. Underneath the trees, the light was the colour of moss-weathered slate.

She leaned forward over the pram handle and cooed, "Soon be home, Mr. Bill! Soon be home!"

But when she looked up she saw a man standing silhouetted beside the oak tree just in front of her, not more than thirty feet away. A thin, tall man wearing a black cap, and a black coat with the collar turned up. His eyes were shaded, but she could see that his face was deathly white. And he was obviously waiting for her.

She hesitated, stopped, and looked around. Her heart began to thump furiously. There was nobody else in sight, nobody to whom she could shout for help. The rain rattled on the trees above her head, and William let out one fitful yelp. She swallowed, and found herself swallowing a thick mixture of fruit-cake and bile. She simply didn't know what to do.

She thought: there's no use running. I'll just have to walk past him. I'll just have to show him that I'm not afraid. After all, I'm pushing a pram. I've got a baby. Surely he won't be so cruel that he'll—

You never know who's watching. You never know who might want him.

Sick with fear, she continued to walk forward.

The man remained where he was, not moving, not speaking. She would have to pass within two feet of him, but so far he had shown no sign that he had noticed her, although he must have done; and no sign at all that he wanted her to stop.

She walked closer and closer, stiff-legged, and mewling softly to herself in terror. She passed him by, so close that she could see the glittering raindrops on his coat, so close that she could *smell* him, strong tobacco and some dry, unfamiliar smell, like hay.

She thought: thank God. He's let me pass.

But then his right arm whipped out and snatched her elbow, twisted her around, and flung her with such force against the trunk of the oak that she heard her shoulder-blade crack and one of her shoes flew off.

She screamed, and screamed again. But he slapped her face with the back of his hand, and then slapped her again.

"What do you want?" she shrieked. "What do you want?"

He seized the lapels of her jacket and dragged her upright against the harsh-ribbed bark of the tree. His eyes were so deep-set that all she could see was their glitter. His lips were blue-grey, and they were stretched back across his teeth in a terrifying parody of a grin.

"What do you want?" she begged him. Her shoulder felt as if it were on fire, and her left knee was throbbing. "I have to look after my baby. Please don't hurt me. I have to look after my baby."

She felt her skirt being torn away from her thighs. Oh God, she thought, not that. Please not that. She started to collapse out of fear and out of terrible resignation, but the man dragged her upright again, and knocked her head so hard against the tree that she almost blacked out.

She didn't remember very much after that. She felt her underwear wrenched off. She felt him forcing his way into her. It was dry and agonizing and he felt so *cold*. Even when he had pushed his way deep inside her, he still felt cold. She felt the rain on her face. She heard his breathing, a steady, harsh *hah! hah! hah!* Then she heard him swear, an extraordinary curse like no curse that she had ever heard before.

She was just about to say, "My baby," when he hit her again. She was found twenty minutes later standing at a bus-stop in the Bayswater Road, by an American couple who wanted to know where to find Trader Vic's.

The pram was found where she had been forced to leave it, and it was empty.

JOHN SAID, "WE should go away for a while."

Marjorie was sitting in the window-seat, nursing a cup of lemon tea. She was staring across the Bayswater Road as she always stared, day and night. She had cut her hair into a severe bob, and her face was as pale as wax. She wore black, as she always wore black.

The clock on the mantelpiece chimed three. John said, "Nesta will keep in touch—you know, if there's any development."

Marjorie turned and smiled at him weakly. The dullness of her eyes still shocked him, even now. "Development?" she said, gently mocking his euphemism. It was six weeks since William had disappeared. Whoever had taken him had either killed him or intended to keep him for ever.

John shrugged. He was a thick-set, pleasant-looking, but unassertive man. He had never thought that he would marry; but when he had met Marjorie at his younger brother's 21st, he had been captivated at once by her mixture of shyness and wilfulness, and her eccentric imagination. She had said things to him that no girl had ever said to him before—opened his eyes to the simple magic of everyday life.

But now that Marjorie had closed in on herself, and communicated nothing but grief, he found that he was increasingly handicapped; as if the gifts of light and colour and perception were being taken away from him. A spring day was incomprehensible unless he had Marjorie beside him, to tell him why it was all so inspiring.

She was like a woman who was dying; and he was like a man who was gradually going blind.

The phone rang in the library. Marjorie turned back to the window. Through the pale afternoon fog the buses and the taxis poured ceaselessly to and fro. But beyond the railings, in Kensington Gardens, the trees were motionless and dark, and they held a secret for which Marjorie would have given anything. Her sight, her soul, her very life.

Somewhere in Kensington Gardens, William was still alive. She was convinced of it, in the way that only a mother could be convinced. She spent hours straining her ears, trying to hear him crying over the bellowing of the traffic. She felt like standing in the middle of Bayswater Road and holding up her hands and screaming, "Stop! Stop, for just one minute! Please, stop! I think I can hear my baby crying!"

John came back from the library, digging his fingers into his thick chestnut hair. "That was Chief Inspector Crosland. They've had the forensic report on the weapon that was used to cut your clothes. Some kind of gardening-implement, apparently—a pair of clippers or a pruning-hook. They're going to start asking questions at nurseries and garden centres. You never know."

He paused, and then he said, "There's something else. They had a DNA report."

Marjorie gave a quiet, cold shudder. She didn't want to start thinking about the rape. Not yet, anyway. She could deal with that later, when William was found.

When William was found, she could go away on holiday and try to recuperate. When William was found, her heart could start beating again. She longed so much to hold him in her arms that she felt she was becoming completely demented. Just to feel his tiny fingers closing around hers.

John cleared his throat. "Crosland said that there was something pretty strange about the DNA report. That's why it's taken them so long."

Marjorie didn't answer. She thought she had

seen a movement in the gardens. She thought she had seen something small and white in the long grass underneath the trees, and a small arm waving. But—as she drew the net curtain back further—the small, white object trotted out from beneath the trees and it was a Sealyham, and the small waving arm was its tail.

"According to the DNA report, the man wasn't actually alive."

Marjorie slowly turned around. "What?" she said. "What do you mean, he wasn't actually alive?"

John looked embarrassed. "I don't know. It doesn't seem to make any sense, does it? But that's what Crosland said. In fact, what he actually said was, the man was dead."

"*Dead?* How could he have been dead?"

"Well, there was obviously some kind of aberration in the test results. I mean, the man couldn't have been *really* dead. Not clinically. It was just that—"

"Dead," Marjorie repeated, in a whisper, as if everything had suddenly become clear. "The man was *dead*."

JOHN WAS AWAKENED by the telephone at five to six that Friday morning. He could hear the rain sprinkling against the bedroom window, and the grinding bellow of a garbage truck in the mews at the back of the house.

"It's Chief Inspector Crosland, sir. I'm afraid I have some rather bad news. We've found William in the Fountains."

John swallowed. "I see," he said. Irrationally, he wanted to ask if William were still alive, but of course he couldn't have been, and in any case he found that he simply couldn't speak.

"I'm sending two officers over," said the chief inspector. "One of them's a woman. If you could be ready in—say—five or ten minutes?"

John quietly cradled the phone. He sat up in bed for a while, hugging his knees, his eyes brimming. Then he swallowed, and smeared his tears with his hands, and gently shook Marjorie awake.

She opened her eyes and stared up at him as if she had just arrived from another country. "What is it?" she asked, throatily.

He tried to speak, but he couldn't.

"It's William, isn't it?" she said. "They've found William."

THEY STOOD HUDDLED together under John's umbrella, next to the grey, rain-circled fountains. An ambulance was parked close by, its rear doors open, its blue light flashing. Chief Inspector Crosland came across—a solid, beef-complexioned man with a dripping mustache. He raised his hat, and said, "We're all very sorry about this. We always hold out hope, you know, even when it's pretty obvious that it's hopeless."

"Where was he found?" asked John.

"Caught in the sluice that leads to the Long Water. There were a lot of leaves down there, too, so he was difficult to see. One of the maintenance men found him when he was clearing the grating."

"Can I see him?" asked Marjorie.

John looked at the chief inspector with an unspoken question: how badly is he decomposed? But the chief inspector nodded, and took hold of Marjorie's elbow, and said, "Come with me."

Marjorie followed him obediently. She felt so small and cold. He guided her to the back of the ambulance, and helped her to climb inside. There, wrapped in a bright red blanket, was her baby, her baby William, his eyes closed, his hair stuck in a curl to his forehead. He was white as marble, white as a statue.

"May I kiss him?" she asked. Chief Inspector Crosland nodded.

She kissed her baby and his kiss was soft and utterly chilled.

Outside the ambulance, John said, "I would have thought—well, how long has he been down there?"

"No more than a day, sir, in my opinion. He was still wearing the same Babygro that he was wearing when he was taken, but he was clean and he looked reasonably well nourished. There were no signs of abuse or injury."

John looked away. "I can't understand it," he said.

The chief inspector laid a hand on his shoulder. "If it's any comfort to you, sir, neither can I."

ALL THE NEXT day, through showers and sunshine, Marjorie walked alone around Kensington Gardens. She walked down Lancaster Walk, and then Budge's Walk, and stood by the Round Pond. Then she walked back beside the Long Water, to the statue of Peter Pan.

It had started drizzling again, and rainwater dripped from the end of Peter's pipes, and trickled down his cheeks like tears.

The boy who never grew up, she thought. Just like William.

She was about to turn away when the tiniest fragment of memory scintillated in her mind. What was it that Uncle Michael had said, as she left his flat on the day that William had been taken?

She had said, "I'm cooking chicken chasseur tonight."

And *he* had said, "Chicken chasseur . . ." and then paused for a very long time, and added, "Don't forget the pan."

She had assumed then that he meant saucepan. But why would he have said "don't forget the pan"? After all, he hadn't been talking about cooking before. He had been warning her that somebody in Kensington Gardens might be watching her. He had been warning her that somebody in Kensington Gardens might want to take William.

Don't forget the Pan.

HE WAS SITTING on the sofa, bundled up in maroon woollen blankets, when she let herself in. The flat smelled of gas and stale milk. A thin sunlight the colour of cold tea was straining through the net curtains; and it made his face look more sallow and withered than ever.

"I was wondering when you'd come," he said, in a whisper.

"You expected me?"

He gave her a sloping smile. "You're a mother. Mothers understand everything."

She sat on the chair close beside him. "That day when William was taken . . . you said 'don't forget the Pan.' Did you mean what I think you meant?"

He took hold of her hand and held it in a gesture of infinite sympathy and infinite pain. "The Pan is every mother's nightmare. Always has been, always will be."

"Are you trying to tell me that it's not a story?"

"Oh . . . the way that Sir James Barrie told it—all fairies and pirates and Indians—*that* was a story. But it was founded on fact."

"How do you know that?" asked Marjorie. "I've never heard anyone mention that before."

Uncle Michael turned his withered neck toward the window. "I know it because it happened to my brother and my sister and it nearly happened to me. My mother met Sir James at a dinner in Belgravia, about a year afterwards, and tried to explain what had happened. This was in 1901 or 1902, thereabouts. She thought that he might write an article about it, to warn other parents, and that because of his authority, people might listen to him, and believe him. But the old fool was such a sentimentalist, such a fantasist . . . he didn't believe her, either, and he turned my mother's agony into a children's play.

"Of course, it was such a successful children's play that nobody ever took my mother's warnings seriously, ever again. She died in Earlswood Mental Hospital in Surrey in 1914. The death certificate said 'dementia,' whatever that means."

"Tell me what happened," said Marjorie. "Uncle Michael, I've just lost my baby . . . you have to tell me what happened."

Uncle Michael gave her a bony shrug. "It's difficult to separate fact from fiction. But in the late 1880s, there was a rash of kidnappings in Kensington Gardens . . . all boy babies, some of them taken from prams, some of them snatched directly from their nannies' arms. All of the babies were later found dead . . . most in Kensington Gardens, some in Hyde Park and Paddington . . . but none of them very far away. Sometimes the nannies were assaulted, too, and three of them were raped.

"In 1892, a man was eventually caught in the act of trying to steal a baby. He was identified by several nannies as the man who had raped them and abducted their charges. He was tried at the Old Bailey on three specimen charges of murder, and sentenced to death on June 13, 1893. He was hanged on the last day of October.

"He was apparently a Polish merchant seaman, who had jumped ship at London Docks after a trip to the Caribbean. His shipmates had known him only as Piotr. He had been cheerful and happy, as far as they knew—at least until they docked at Port-au-Prince, in Haiti. Piotr had spent three nights away from the ship, and after his return, the first mate remarked on his 'moody and unpleasant mien.' He flew into frequent rages, so they weren't at all surprised when he left the ship at London and never came back.

"The ship's doctor thought that Piotr might have contracted malaria, because his face was ashy white, and his eyes looked bloodshot. He shivered, too, and started to mutter to himself."

"But if he was hanged—" put in Marjorie.

"Oh, he was hanged, all right," said Michael. "Hanged by the neck until he was dead, and buried in the precincts of Wormwood Scrubs prison. But only a year later, more boy babies began to disappear from Kensington Gardens, and more nannies were assaulted, and each of them bore the same kind of scratches and cuts that Piotr had inflicted on his victims.

"He used to tear their dresses, you see, with a baling-hook."

"A baling-hook?" said Marjorie, faintly.

Uncle Michael held up his hand, with one finger curled. "Where do you think that Sir James got the notion for Captain Hook?"

"But I was scratched like that, too."

"Yes," nodded Uncle Michael. "And that's what I've been trying to tell you. The man who attacked you—the man who took William—it was Piotr."

"What? That was over a hundred years ago! How could it have been?"

"In the same way that Piotr tried to snatch me, too, in 1901, when I was still in my pram. My nanny tried to fight him off, but he hooked her throat and severed her jugular vein. My brother and my sister tried to fight him off, too, but he dragged them both away with him. They were only little, they didn't stand a chance. A few weeks later, a swimmer found their bodies in the Serpentine."

Uncle Michael pressed his hand against his mouth, and was silent for almost a whole minute. "My mother was almost mad with grief. But somehow, she *knew* who had killed her children. She spent every afternoon in Kensington Gardens, following almost every man she saw. And—at last—she came across him. He was standing amongst the trees, watching two nannies sitting on a bench. She approached him, and she challenged him. She told him to his face that she knew who he was; and that she knew he had murdered her children.

"Do you know what he said? I shall never forget my mother telling me this, and it still sends shivers down my spine. He said, 'I never had a mother, I never had a father. I was never allowed to be a boy. But the old woman on Haiti said that I could stay young for ever and ever, so long as I always sent back to her the souls of young children, flying on the wind. So that is what I did. I kissed them, and sucked out their souls, and sent them flying back to Haiti on the wind.'

"But do you know what he said to my mother? He said, 'Your children's souls may have flown to a distant island, but they can still live, if you wish them to. You can go to their graves, and you can call them, and they'll come to you. It only takes a mother's word.'

"My mother said, 'Who are you? *What* are you? And he said, 'Pan,' which is nothing more nor less than Polish for 'man.' That's why my mother called him 'Piotr Pan.' And that's where Sir James Barrie got the name from.

"And here, of course, is the terrible irony—Captain Hook and Peter Pan weren't enemies at all, not in real life. They were one and the same person."

Marjorie stared at her uncle Michael in horror. "What did my great-auntie do? She didn't *call* your brother and sister, did she?"

Uncle Michael shook his head. "She insisted that their graves should be covered in heavy slabs of granite. Then—as you know—she did whatever she could to warn other mothers of the danger of Piotr Pan."

"So she really believed that she could call her children back to life?"

"I think so. But—as she always said to me—what can life amount to, without a soul?"

Marjorie sat with her uncle Michael until it grew dark, and his head dropped to one side, and he began to snore.

SHE STOOD IN the chapel of rest, her face bleached white by the single ray of sunlight that fell from the clerestory window. Her dress was black, her hat was black. She held a black handbag in front of her.

William's white coffin was open, and William himself lay on a white silk pillow, his eyes closed, his tiny eyelashes curled over his deathly-white cheek, his lips slightly parted, as if he were still breathing.

On either side of the coffin, candles burned; and there were two tall vases of white gladioli. Apart from the murmuring of traffic, and the occasional rumbling of a Central Line tube train deep beneath the building's foundations, the chapel was silent.

Marjorie could feel her heart beating, steady and slow.

My baby, she thought. My poor sweet baby.

She stepped closer to the coffin. Hesitantly, she reached out and brushed his fine baby curls. So soft, it crucified her to touch it.

"William," she breathed.

He remained cold and still. Not moving, not breathing.

"William," she repeated. "William, my darling, come back to me. Come back to me, Mr. Bill."

Still he didn't stir. Still he didn't breathe.

She waited a moment longer. She was almost ashamed of herself for having believed Uncle Michael's stories. Piotr Pan indeed! The old man was senile.

Softly, she tiptoed to the door. She took one last look at William, and then she closed the door behind her.

She had barely let go of the handle, however, when the silence was broken by the most terrible high-pitched scream she had ever heard in her life.

IN KENSINGTON GARDENS, beneath the trees, a thin dark man raised his head and listened, and listened, as if he could hear a child crying in the wind. He listened, and he smiled, although he never took his eyes away from the young woman who was walking towards him, pushing a baby-buggy.

He thought, *God bless mothers everywhere.*

THE GRAVE GIVES UP

JACK D'ARCY

JACK D'ARCY IS one of the pseudonyms used by D.('Arcy) L.(yndon) Champion (1902–1968), who was born in Melbourne, Australia, and fought with the British army in World War II before immigrating to the United States. He wrote a few horror and weird menace stories, but is best known for his mystery and detective series in the pulps. His first published work was a serialization under the pseudonym G. Wayman Jones, a house name, of *Alias Mr. Death* in the February–October 1932 issues of *Thrilling Detective;* it was published in book form later in the same year. In 1933, he created the character of Richard Curtis Van Loan, better known as the Phantom Detective, under another house name, Robert Wallace. He wrote most of the early episodes of what was the second hero pulp (after *The Shadow*). It ran for 170 issues between 1933 and 1953, the third-most of any of the hero pulps after *The Shadow* and *Doc Savage*. Under his own name and as Jack D'Arcy, he created several other memorable characters. Mariano Mercado, a hypochondriac detective, appeared in eight novelettes between 1944 and 1948 in *Dime Detective*. Inspector Allhof, a former New York City policeman who lost his legs while leading a botched raid, is retained by the NYPD because of his brilliance and in spite of his arrogance. Allhof appeared in twenty-nine stories from 1938 to 1945, mainly in *Dime Detective;* twelve of the tales were collected in *Footprints on a Brain: The Inspector Allhof Stories* (2001). Perhaps his most popular series featured Rex Sackler, known as the "Parsimonious Prince of Penny Pinchers." The hilarious series began in *Dime Detective*, then moved to *Black Mask*.

"The Grave Gives Up" was originally published in the August 1936 issue of *Thrilling Mystery*.

THE GRAVE GIVES UP

CHAPTER I

A VOICE FROM THE DEAD

IT WAS A melancholy night. Dampness impregnated the sultry autumn air. The light of the moon filtered faintly through a huge black cloud that hung over the face of the heavens. Somewhere from the great swamp near the graveyard a whippoor-will sobbed; and the throbbing sound echoed the anguish in the heart of Gordon Lane.

He sat alone in his small bachelor apartment in the eastern end of the town. A fire crackled on the hearth, and a book lay upon his lap. Yet he could not see the type for the tears that dimmed his vision.

For two weeks now he had seen none of his friends. Mechanically, he had gone about his daily duties with that numbing pain in his heart that pumped a deadly emotional opiate to his brain.

Once he had sworn that he could not live without Janice and she had laughed at him. Now he knew that his words were not mere lover's rhetoric. Since that awful day a fortnight ago, something within him had died. When Janice

"Slay him! Slay the thing you hate!"

had been killed in the automobile accident, the soul of Gordon Lane had been slain with her.

The overwhelming love that he had borne her had evolved into a great sorrow which gnawed like the Spartan fox at his heart. Despite the heat of the fire, he shuddered as he thought of Janice's slim white body lying in the coldness of the dank earth.

Within his breast he could feel that coldness as surely as if he had been lying in the grave with her. Within his brain was a deadness, a lifelessness, as if his body, too, was interred in a mossy stone crypt on the other side of town.

And if Death himself had entered the room at that moment, he would have been a welcome visitor to Gordon Lane.

For the first time in a week, the phone bell jangled. Lane did not stir at its metallic summons. Again and again it shrilled until it finally hammered into his consciousness.

He turned slowly to the table at his side and lifted up the instrument. In a dull listless voice, he said, "Hello."

A sound came over the wire as if from a great distance. It was tired and dispirited as a weary breeze that stirred sere autumn leaves. Yet the words it uttered crashed into Lane's ear like a thunder clap.

"Gordon? Is that you, Gordon?"

Lane's pulse leaped, and for the first time since the funeral his heart pumped surging vibrant life through his veins. But what slew his lethargy was the stimulating toxin of stark terror.

Like a fluttering kite it rose in his pulses; like the wings of a black bat it beat against his brain. For the rustling voice that had come to him over the wire was the voice of Janice!

Lane's hand was hot as he clutched the phone to his breast. His face was white and there was a tremor in his tone as he answered.

"Yes, this is Gordon. Janice! Janice, where are you? Where—"

Again Lane heard the voice of the woman he had loved more than life itself; and it seemed to come from a great distance as if it had been projected from the borderland of the netherworld from which no man has ever returned.

"Gordon— Gordon—" For an instant the dreariness left her tone and her words came pantingly like a hot wind over hell. "Gordon! Come to me— I need you! I need you. I—"

THE NEXT SYLLABLE was an inarticulate, strangled fragment in her throat. From somewhere in the realm of infinity Lane heard a stifled scream—a scream that caused the black bat in his brain to beat its dark wings more furiously. Then there was silence.

"Janice!" Lane rasped her name into the mouthpiece. "Janice!"

But there was no answer. If that voice had come from the grave, it had returned to its awful prison once more. If, for a fleeting moment, the other world had opened its locked doors, they were sealed again now. The complete silence of the receiver seemed to mock him.

Lane dropped the telephone upon the table and fell into his chair. Diamonds of sweat were on his brow.

His face, far whiter than the glacial snows, was painted a ghastly hellish red by the licking flames of the fire. He resembled a phantom before the gates of hell.

Two facts seared themselves into his throbbing brain. He had heard HER voice; and she was dead. For a long time he stared into the fire as if in those flickering yellow tongues he would read the awful mystery which confronted him.

Was it madness that assailed him? Had the burden of grief he had borne for the past two weeks, caused a delicate hairline between sanity and madness to break? Was the phone call an illusion which existed only in his own tortured mind?

Two distinct fears met and clashed within him—fear for his own sanity and fear that he had for a moment communicated with that unknown uncharted world beyond the grave.

Slowly his mind began to function logically through the maelstrom in his head. Slowly his thoughts became translated to action. He moved toward the telephone; picked it up with trembling fingers. A moment later the operator's voice was in his ear.

"Operator." He made a desperate effort to make his tone casual. "This is Gordon Lane of the County Attorney's office. I believe my phone rang a few minutes ago. Have you a record of the call?"

There was a moment's silence.

"Yes, sir. You were called at nine-sixteen. We have the record here."

Lane could feel his heart pound up against his breast like a pendulum weighted with ice.

"And can you tell me where the call originated?"

Again there was a short silence; a heavy ominous silence in which shadowy phantoms bred in Lane's mind. Then the operator's voice rasped on the wires again.

"Why yes, Mr. Lane. That call was made from one-eighty-one Lenora Street."

Lane's hand gripped the phone with all its strength. It was as if he had to cling to something material, to anchor himself against the terrifying nebulae of his thoughts.

"One-eighty-one Lenora," he said and his voice was dry as a cactus stalk. "That's the Gaunt Hill cemetery."

"That's right."

There was a dull click at the other end of the wire as the operator broke the connection. But Gordon Lane did not replace the phone immediately. His hot, perspiring hand held the receiver clutched hard against his breast as if it was an aegis against the incredible thing which he must now believe.

Janice had called him. It had been her voice. And the call had come from Gaunt Hill on the other side of town. Gaunt Hill, where Janice's lovely tender body lay buried in a cold marble crypt!

TWENTY MINUTES LATER, Lane's coupé slithered to a halt before a rectangular two-story building. His nervous finger jerked against a bell in the doorway. An immaculate butler opened the door.

"Dr. Ramos," said Lane pantingly. "Is he in?"

"Hello, Lane," a voice greeted him from the foyer. The doctor, wearing his hat and coat had spoken. "I was just going out. What can I do for you?"

Lane crossed the threshold. His eyes were brilliant with a shining fever. His hair was rumpled and his face was a dirty, ashen grey. As he spoke his voice was hoarse and thick with feeling.

"I've got to see you a moment," he said. "At once. Privately."

Ramos regarded him with a professional eye. Then quietly he replaced his hat on the hall tree.

"All right. Come on into the office."

He led the way to a book-lined sanctuary, and took a seat beside his desk. Lane threw himself in a huge overstuffed chair and stared with his glassy eyes at the doctor.

Already he felt somewhat better. For the doctor symbolized everything that was reasonable. Ruddy-faced and solid, he held the respect of

the ancient town. He was firmly opposed to all that might even be suspected of mysticism.

He was a complete atheist, a crass materialist, fond of good food and better wines. If anyone in town could explain away the mad thing that had happened to Lane that night, the man was Dr. Ramos.

Lane's white knuckles gripped the sides of the chair.

"Listen, Doctor," he said slowly. "It's about Janice."

Ramos raised his eyebrows.

"Janice," he said. "Now listen, Lane. You've got to steady yourself on that score. Death comes to us all. You've got to get hold of yourself. I—"

"Wait a minute, Doctor. It's not that. It's—Well, you signed her death certificate, didn't you?"

Ramos' eyes narrowed. A peculiar expression was on his face as he nodded at the younger man.

"Well," went on Lane and there was a terrible tenseness in his tone, "was she dead? Are you sure that she was really dead? Are you sure?"

He had risen from his chair and now he pounded excitedly on the smooth top of the desk. Ramos made no reply until Lane's outburst had exhausted itself in a fit of words.

"My boy," he said at last, in a grave sympathetic voice, "I know what suffering must have gone on in your heart. But you must fight it with your reason. You must. Janice is dead. I saw her dead. You saw her interred. There can be no doubt about it."

"Then," said Lane, and his voice was the voice of a man who fears the words he speaks, "how did she speak to me tonight? Where did her voice come from if she is dead? Is my ear so attuned that I can hear a voice from Beyond?"

A shadow, almost imperceptible, flickered into the doctor's eyes. The ruddiness of his face grew a shade lighter. He leaned forward slightly in his chair.

"What's that you say?" he breathed. "You heard her voice?"

"From the grave, I heard it. She telephoned

me. Said she needed me. And the call came from Gaunt Hill cemetery."

RAMOS' FACE WAS dark for a fleeting instant. Then it became normal again. He rose and crossed the room. He flung a fraternal arm about Lane's shoulder.

"My boy," he said, "there's a simple explanation. You would have thought of it yourself if you hadn't been so overwrought. It's a joke. A cruel practical joke, played by some unfeeling fool who is trying to frighten you. Janice died here in my sanitarium. Of that I can assure you. Here, I'll give you a sedative. Take it and go to bed."

Gordon Lane came to his feet. It seemed that in that single instant, the cobwebs of fear had been brushed from his brain. There was something within him that was stronger than the terror that had held him in its icy thrall. Something stronger than any other emotion he had ever experienced.

Now the thing was clear at last. Now he knew where his duty lay. Now he knew what he must do.

"No," he said and his voice was resolute, "I want no sedative. No matter what hideous thing is behind that call tonight, I *know* that it was the voice of Janice. I know further that she needs me. I shall go to her. She spoke to me from Gaunt Hill. That is all I know. So it is to Gaunt Hill that I must go. She needs me."

He turned on his heel and strode toward the door. Ramos' voice, pitched oddly, came to him on the threshold.

"Wait a minute, Lane. Now don't be a fool. Janice is dead, I tell you. Don't go to Gaunt Hill tonight."

As Lane turned to face the doctor, it seemed to him that there was a cloud of apprehension in Ramos' eyes.

"I'm going," he said simply. "Now."

Ramos crossed the room and stood in the doorway facing Lane. He put his hands on the younger man's shoulders and gazed squarely into his eyes. An odd sensation came over Lane in that moment. He could feel the blood mount to his face, feel its swift rhythmic beat in his temples.

"Don't go to Gaunt Hill tonight," said Ramos, speaking each word in a measured spondee beat. "Don't go."

Again Lane was aware of that odd lulling throb in his temples, but the knowledge of Janice's need was a strong impelling force in his breast. Roughly he took the doctor's hands from his shoulders.

"I must go," he said quietly.

He strode past the other, through the hall and out of the sanitarium. A moment later his coupé raced, a shadowy phantom through the deserted streets; it sped, a ghostly vehicle through the town, toward the marshy swamp on whose sloping bank reposed that city of the dead—the Gaunt Hill cemetery.

CHAPTER II

THE DEAD ALIVE

The tombstones were white, motionless specters in the night. Overhead the stark leafless branches of the trees waved in the breeze like the naked arms of some black Lorelei beckoning to disaster. The lethal silence which hung over the graveyard was not the silence which occurs through mere lack of sound. Rather it was a positive thing, a throbbing silence which assailed the senses as surely as the beat of savage drums.

On the right, near the entrance, a squat building loomed against the faint, clouded moonlight. That, Lane knew, was the caretaker's lodge. No light shone in its windows. Lane walked past the place on quiet feet. He had no wish to disturb the men at this hour.

He realized the explanation for his presence here would sound ridiculous in another's ears. As he moved noiselessly through the steles, it seemed as if the directing portion of his brain was a detached part of him. Quite clearly he knew what he must do.

He walked directly toward the Lansing mausoleum where Janice was buried. Dead or not dead, whether she were in the crypt, whether she were in Hell or Heaven, she had said she needed him. And he had come.

Yet despite his grim resolve, despite his firm purpose, he was not entirely unafraid. That uncanny telephone call had pricked his delicate nervous system with the pin of fear. And now in this ancient graveyard that had spread its earthy cloak over decayed corpses since the days of the Spaniards, there was an eerie electric atmosphere.

What it was he did not know. Normally he had not the weak man's fear of death and dead things. But here tonight he felt that some intangible horror stalked him; that some invisible monster strode at his side.

He started for a moment as he saw a black rectangular shape rise from a tombstone, flap black wings and fly off in the face of the moon. An involuntary shudder ran through his body, for at that moment it seemed as if the bat presaged some dire happening; as if it were a forerunner of the evil thing that was destined to happen.

On his left, some forty feet this side of the Lansing tomb, stood a square marble edifice. Lane recognized it as the burying place of the Cervantes family, the old clan of the town who could trace their ancestry back to the brave days of Balboa.

Then, abruptly, he halted. A sound had broken that deathly silence. A faint creaking noise had reached his eardrum. And it had come from the tomb of the Cervantes!

For a long moment Gordon Lane stood motionless. But inside him there was no stillness. Fear swirled like a misty cloud within his heart. The vague apprehension that had been with him suddenly crystallized into a definite horror that the unknown thing which he had feared was at last imminent.

Again he heard the creaking sound. Long-

drawn-out and undulating it crawled into his hearing. Then it ended, punctuated by a lower note like the grunt of a wallowing swine.

GORDON LANE'S WILL held him where he was, held him firmly from obeying all his screaming instincts to run from this place of evil. His face was white and in his eyes shone a mighty resolve as he deliberately turned his face toward the tomb.

His hand reached out and touched the handle on the crypt door, and his fingers were colder than the metal which they clasped.

He turned the handle and pushed his weight against the massive oaken door. Slowly it swung inward. The darkness that poured into his eyes was almost a material thing. Dank air seeped into his nostrils. The frightful odor of decaying flesh filtered into his lungs.

His cold fingers groped in his vest pocket, and found a package of matches. Then as he was about to strike the match, he heard a sigh—a human sigh!

It was a weary, discouraged exhalation like the last whisper of a damned soul. With effort Lane held his fingers steady as he struck the match.

The tiny light flared eerily in the chamber. Ghostly flickering shadows danced on the damp stone walls as the little flame burned unevenly. Lane's eyeballs pained him as he stared strainingly into the gloom. The walls were lined with coffins of ancient wood. A rat scurried across the floor at his feet.

The match burned low and seared his fingers. Hastily he lit another. Then as he stood there, holding that tiny inadequate light in his hand, he felt a cold snake of terror crawl along his spine. Wings of panic beat in his brain.

His eyes stared straight ahead of him, and in their depth was a glazed expression of fearful doubt as if he trembled to believe the thing he saw.

For directly opposite him the lid of a coffin was rising. The rotted, dust-covered wood made an odd creaking sound as it moved, a sound like the off-key note struck on a ghostly violin.

Then as it lifted higher, Lane saw the hand that was moving it. It was a grey and bony hand with long prehensile fingers. Tightly they grasped the edge of the coffin lid and thrust it upward.

Then an arm appeared, a tenuous, naked arm like the ashen tentacle of some fiendish octopus. Lane's eyes dropped from the ghastly sight for a moment and focused upon the tarnished silver nameplate of the coffin. Then as the words engraved there registered on his mind, a white madness froze his nerves.

For the man who was rising from the tomb had been dead for over a hundred years!

The creaking noise increased. Wildly Lane glanced about him. On all sides the lids were moving. Thin, emaciated arms appeared pushing, pushing up the covers which sealed the corpses in their tombs. Verily, the grave was yielding up its dead.

It was no longer the human concept of fear that coursed through Lane's arteries. It was now an overwhelming dread; that awful paralyzing force which deluges man when he witnesses the violation of all natural law; of all the things that he has been taught to believe.

THE DEAD WERE rising up around him! The dead who never returned were rising from their coffins, coming back to an earthly sphere. They were bursting the inviolate bonds of the grave, shattering all natural law in one unholy manifestation.

Gordon Lane's heart cried, "Flee!" His brain reeled dazedly before the incredible sight he witnessed. But his muscles were beyond his control. Some unseen vise held his sinews in mighty thrall. His legs were rooted to the spot where he stood.

Again the match burned his finger. His shaking hands essayed to light another. For darkness redoubled the terror of the tomb. Again the match flickered to jerky light.

Glassy eyes stared at Lane. The lifeless gaze of the dead stared at the intruder who had blasphemed their tomb with his presence. Their faces were horrible things over which the white hand of death had passed, leaving its indelible mark.

They were blank, expressionless faces, devoid of all intelligence, sans all life and animation. Gaunt, bony chests thrust themselves from filthy, ragged shreds which hung about their unearthly shoulders. But their eyes held the most awful thing of all.

They were the eyes of men who have gazed upon the unholy mysteries of the netherworld; eyes which have traveled across the Styx itself and witnessed the iniquitous evil of the banks of Hell.

And behind all this lay an insufferable pain, an agony of the soul which even Death's great power had been unable to release.

Lane never knew how long he stood there, exchanging scrutiny with these Things that had climbed back from the abyss. It seemed that infinity ticked past and the muscles of his body remained completely beyond his control.

Then came the thing that broke the paralysis. A scream ripped through the air; a scream pregnant with terror and agony. And despite its unnaturally high-pitched tone, Gordon Lane recognized the voice.

Janice!

That single fact smashed into his numbed consciousness with a force that precluded all else. The blood surged through his arteries once more.

He flung the burning match to the floor. He spun around on his heel and raced like one possessed from the dank interior of this frenzied vault of death.

The cool fresh air of the night hit his face like a wave of cold water. As he ran he once again heard that awful scream hammer with dreadful force through the fetid atmosphere of the graveyard.

He changed his direction slightly. Now he knew whence that scream came. It had emanated from the Lansing crypt. There was no doubt of that.

Despite the terrific strain under which he was laboring, relief pumped into his heart. If that voice was Janice's—and he knew it was—she was alive! Alive! She had returned from the tomb to him!

He crashed up against the door of the mausoleum. His trembling fingers found the handle and turned it. He raced into the tomb.

"Janice!" he cried. "Janice!"

There was no reply save the mocking reverberations of his own voice hurled back at him by the stone walls of the vault. Once again he groped for his matches, struck one and stared about him.

There was no sign of life here. Death was indicated by the solid line of coffins which flanked the wall.

SWIFTLY, LANE WALKED about the cavernous chamber. Swiftly his eyes glanced at the silver nameplates on the coffins. Then at last he came to a halt at the rear end of the room. Reposing on a marble slab lay a bier, and on the gleaming argent at its base was written the name of the woman that Gordon Lane had loved above life itself.

He fell to his knees beside the coffin, murmuring her name. Then as his hands gripped the coffin lid to wrench it off, his match went out. Feverishly he struck another. He held it, flickering and dancing in his left hand, while he jerked the lid up with his right.

With a hollow thud the cover fell back. Lane leaned forward, lowering his match. A vague relief had temporarily banished the dread he had felt. Janice had needed him; even in death she had needed him. And now he was here.

He bent lower over the bier, staring into the little pool of light cast by the match. Slowly his eyes dilated, slowly the old fear seeped back into his veins. Slowly he became conscious once again of the gnawing horror inside him.

For the coffin was empty!

CHAPTER III

ZOMBIES

Gordon Lane let the match go out. He stood there in the thick darkness. Was this madness that assailed him? Had he taken leave of his normal physical world and through some unholy device been transported to a realm of evil paradox?

Janice was not there. Janice had broken her tomb, had slashed through the fetters of death even as had those ghastly things in the crypt of the Cervantes.

What unearthly things were happening here? Was this a case for the blue uniformed officer of the police, or the black robed servant of the church?

Then he moved. He strode swiftly toward the still open door of the vault. If a few moments ago he had taken care to avoid the keeper of the cemetery, he was seeking him now. Perhaps the caretaker could clear up the ghastly mysteries of the night.

He raced from the tomb and headed toward the distant gate of the graveyard.

With his fists he hammered on the wooden door of the lodge. After a while he heard a creaking footstep within the building. Then the door opened, and an old man in pajamas stood upon the threshold.

A pair of grey, rheumy eyes stared at Lane. A twisted, distorted mouth snarled at him.

"Why do you wake me at this hour? Are you a ghoul? Are you—?"

"No, no!" cried Lane. "But there's hell abroad in this cemetery. Dead men are walking. Dead men are rising from their tombs. And a girl is missing. Gone from the Lansing crypt."

Something flickered in the old man's eyes. Something evil and calculating. A frown corrugated his brow. Then he stepped aside.

"Come in," he said, and his voice was soft, slimy. "Come in. Perhaps we should telephone the police."

He stepped aside and Lane entered the

house. A telephone stood on a table near the window. The old man indicated it.

"Go on," he said. "Call. If there is evil here we two cannot cope with it. Call the police."

LANE NODDED. THIS, of course, was the sane thing to do. Supernatural or human, the pair of them could not cope with the terrifying forces which had been unleashed this night. He picked up the receiver.

He did not see the expression of sadistic triumph which had crawled into the old man's eyes. He did not see the contorted grey, feral lips as the caretaker took a step toward him. He did not see the solid metal object that the old man held firmly in his right hand.

True, he heard the faint hissing sound as the blackjack hurtled down through the air toward his temple. But then it was too late. The club smashed hard against his skull. A streak of dancing light flashed across his vision.

Then blackness seeped in—total blackness that was even darker than the sable atmosphere of the tomb where he had seen the grave give up its dead.

Gordon Lane had no way of knowing how much later he opened his eyes. Directly above him a grotesque shadow danced on a rocky ceiling. His head throbbed achingly. With an effort he raised his head and looked about him. He blinked dully as he stared at the uncanny scene which met his eyes. His first thought was that he had been struck down by the Reaper's scythe and that now he lay in some dank tomb of the underworld.

The rocky chamber was illuminated by a score of candles, which cast their unsteady light dispiritedly in the room. Far over to the left a half dozen creatures worked with pick and shovel.

They moved in their task like robots. Their thin arms swung mechanically through the air as they dug. No expression was on their drawn faces.

And as Lane stared at them, he inhaled sibi-

lantly as he realized what they were. They were the Things he had seen resurrected from the Cervantes tomb!

Zombies! Snatched by some unholy hand from their surcease of the grave to slave for some iniquitous force. Lane felt the skin on the back of his neck tighten. Then he was aware of an ugly chuckle behind him.

Slowly he turned his aching head. There, standing directly over him, was the caretaker of the cemetery. His face was a twisted, ugly thing and in his hand the naked blade of a knife gleamed eerily in the flickering light of the candles.

Lane looked at him and beyond him. Needles seemed to prick his eyeballs. His throat was suddenly dry. His heart stood still. For there, at the other end of the cavern, clad in a single diaphanous garment, was Janice Lansing!

Unsteadily Lane got to his feet.

"Janice," he cried and his voice was like a hollow echo in the rocky room. "Janice!"

But she did not look at him. Her usually vivacious, lovely face was drab and blank. Her eyes were turned toward a dark-garbed figure who sat some little distance from her.

Her full red lips were drawn thin and taut across her teeth, and in her eyes was a gleam of ineffable anguish. Shocked by her appearance, Lane cried out again.

"Janice! Janice! It's Gordon. Janice, can't you hear me?"

FOR A LONG moment there was a tense silence, broken only by the metallic clang of pick and shovel against the shale-filled earth. Then through the chamber there sounded a voice— a voice which was vaguely familiar to Gordon Lane's ears. Yet which somehow seemed to hold a malignant threat.

"No, you fool, she cannot see you. She can see only what I will her to see. But you, you shall see death before another dawn. You were warned not to come here tonight."

Lane lifted his eyes. He stared through the

murkiness of the chamber. Slowly the figure was limned before him. Then as recognition dawned he uttered a gasp of utter astonishment.

For the speaker was Dr. Ramos!

Yet it was not the Ramos that Lane had once known. The bluff ruddiness of the man's face now seemed to be the crimson stain of blood. The hearty, solid voice had lost its affable tone and it now held an awful note of doom.

The doctor's casual atheism which the village had tolerated suddenly became a fearful thing to Gordon Lane. It was a black unholiness—a defy to the very God who had created him.

From the other side of the room, Lane noticed that the sounds of shoveling had ceased. He was aware of a low, animal-like rumble of voices. He turned his head to see the six emaciated Things that had once been men, standing stock still, their tools in their hands.

Their eyes were fixed on the dark figure of Dr. Ramos and in the depths of their gaze was the most appalling menace of evil that Lane had ever seen.

Ramos' flashing dark eyes turned to them. He fixed them with a satanic gaze.

"Work, you dogs," he snarled. "You, Cataran!"

The caretaker stepped forward. He thrust his knife in his belt and snatched up a crimson-stained whip which lay on the rocky bottom of the cavern. The doctor's eyes were still fixed, glittering obsidian marbles, upon the creatures that had crawled from their tombs.

Cataran lifted the whip. Its rawhide sang a bitter *ziraleet* in the air. The lash bit deep into flesh. Blood, black and terrible, streaked down the cadaver's body and ran onto the fresh earth.

The man opened his ashen lips and his vocal cords vibrated in a terrible cry of affliction. Yet, Lane noted, the Thing made no move to attack its torturer. The others seized their tools and resumed their arduous labor.

The flicker of life which had registered on their faces a moment ago was gone now. They had returned to the lifeless life which seemed to hold them in its awful thrall.

Gordon Lane was frozen with horror. Janice, too, must be held fast in this overwhelming power of Ramos. She had not even glanced at him, Gordon. Her eyes were fastened to the dark figure of the doctor who sat upon a shelf of rock, for all the world like some wicked monarch surveying his wretched subjects.

"That'll do, Cataran," said Ramos. "Let them work. There is much to be done tonight. This shall be our night of nights. The treasure we've recovered thus far will be as nothing if we can find the Grail. It must be here. We've searched everywhere else that I can think of."

LANE TURNED TO Ramos. No longer could he control the potent wrath that welled within him as he gazed at Janice. He rushed toward the doctor.

"You swine!" he roared and the echoes of his anger filled the catacomb. "What have you done? What evil thing have you wrought? Curse you, lift your evil spell off Janice or I'll tear you to pieces with my own hands!"

Ramos smiled evilly as he looked down at him. Even as he finished the sentence Lane was aware of the cold steel of Cataran's blade pressed against the flesh of his neck.

"You are a fool," said the doctor. "You have blundered in here. You shall never blunder out. You know too much. Your girl knew too much. That is why she is here. That is why my spell is upon her."

He indicated the laboring creatures with a wave of his hand. "Those," he said contemptuously, "shall die, too, when I am done with them. They mean little. I needed bodies for my work and I took them. But Janice pried into my affairs. She shall never do so again. When I am finished with her, when her beauty tires me, she, too, shall join those creatures in the grave once more."

Despite the threat of the knife at his jugular, Gordon Lane hammered against the rock with impotent fists.

"In God's name, man—" he began.

Ramos rose from his seat, and it was as if the devil himself had etched the expression on his face.

"God!" he said. In the single syllable was all the hate, all the contempt and loathing that a voice can muster, and in his eyes there had crawled a look that had been born in the eyes of Lucifer on the day he had damned his Master.

"God," said Ramos again. Then he spoke rapidly and terribly. A torrent of horrible blasphemy poured from his bitter lips. Words evil and ugly as a Black Mass poured in Lane's shocked ears.

"God," said Ramos again. "What has your God done for me? On my distaff side my people were Indians, Incas. The men of the Christian God slew them, slaughtered them, robbed them. I curse your God, and from Him I take back what is rightfully mine—the treasures He has taken from me."

Panting he resumed his seat. His eyes fell upon the graven image of lifeless beauty at his side. Then a smile crept across his mouth, a ghastly, ugly smile.

"You shall die, Lane," he said more quietly. "And it is fitting that you die by Janice's hand. Because of her love for you, I have been unable to control her will completely. There is some deep emotion for you within her that thwarts me. But in time I shall shatter it and she shall be mine, all mine. When you are dead the power within her that withstands me shall crumble. I shall have your girl, Lane. And she shall slay you with her own hands. She shall drive a knife through your heart."

He turned to the girl and thrust a dirk into her slim hand. "Janice," he said.

CHAPTER IV

A DISEASED BRAIN

A wave of jealous loathing rippled through Gordon Lane's body as he saw how completely submissive the girl was to the beast in whose thrall she was inexorably held. Yet a flicker of hope went through him. She still loved him! And that love had kept her from submitting entirely to the mad doctor. The depth of that love had resisted his black arts.

"Janice," said Ramos again, and the quiet menace in his tone was more threatening than his roaring demands of a moment ago. "You will take that dirk. You will plunge it into the heart of that man there." He pointed a finger at Lane and for the first time since he had come to this chamber, Janice looked at him. "You will slay him," said Ramos again. "Because you hate him. You loathe him. You shall kill him. Cataran, stand back."

The caretaker's voice rose in protest.

"He will overpower her," he said in a cracked, hysterical tone. "I shall slash with my knife, too."

"Stand back, you fool! It is not her strength she is using. Stand back."

Cataran stood back. His knife's blade no longer touched the flesh of Lane's neck. And now Janice advanced upon him.

At that moment, Gordon Lane knew that he would rather have gazed into the heart of Hell itself than behold the sight which he confronted then.

The woman he had loved beyond all else had metamorphosed into a snarling, savage beast. Her beauty had evolved into a satanic evil thing. Hate and loathing were in her face as she approached to slay the man she had once pledged to love until death.

Until death! The phrase struck Lane's mind ironically. Perhaps she had obeyed that vow literally. Perhaps she was now beyond death, and had come from the grave to slay, to kill.

Slowly she came toward him. Lane took a step forward and stretched out his arms.

"Janice," he said, a suppliant appeal in his tone. "Janice, it's Gordon. You must know me!"

For a moment it seemed to him that Janice wavered in her death-dealing march. But then

Ramos' voice cracked like an icy whip through the room.

"Slay him! Slay the thing you hate!"

Lane essayed to catch the girl's eye. Yet even when their gazes met no sign of recognition shone in her face. Closer and closer she came, like a crazed tigress stalking her prey. Then, in an instant she was upon him.

Lane had no desire to harm her. It seemed a simple matter to take the weapon away from this fragile girl. Why Ramos had permitted this farce to begin he did not understand. He reached out his hand to take the dirk from her slim hand as easily as possible.

And then a moment later he was fighting with all his strength for his life.

The thing that grappled with him was not Janice Lansing. It was possessed of the strength of a terrible fiend. Lane seized her right wrist in his hand. Her left clawed like a beast's talon at his face and blood streaked in rivulets down his chin.

NEVER HAD WOMAN been born who possessed such terrible strength. And then as Lane glanced over her shoulder he saw the countenance of the doctor. It was taut and dripping with sweat as if the man was undergoing some awful strain.

Then in an instant the significance of Ramos' words came to him. "It is not her strength she is using!" Dear God! It was not her own strength. It was Ramos'!

In a blazing flash Lane understood part of the enigma. Janice was held fast in the invisible tentacles of Ramos' mind. Lane had heard of the doctor's proficiency at hypnotism. Janice was at the complete mercy of Ramos' brain. And somehow, through some devilish refinement of mesmerism, he was pouring his own strength into her body.

Desperately Lane grappled with the girl. The power of an Amazon was in her arms. He could feel her hot breath on his face, could see the bared teeth as she snarled at him, and all the while, her terrible might was bringing her arm down—bringing that gleaming blade closer to his heart.

Sweat, cold and glistening as drops of ice, stood on Gordon Lane's brow. The demoniac power which the girl derived from the evil force in Ramos' head drove the knife down closer and closer to his body.

Lane leaned his face over toward the girl, and spoke to her softly.

"Janice—Janice— This is Gordon. Gordon, who loves you. Janice, you must remember."

There was a pleading agony in his tone. Their eyes met. It seemed to him that for an infinitesimal fraction of a second the driving force of her arm abated. For a fleeting moment he thought he saw a glimmer of intelligence, of recognition in her eyes.

And it was then that he made his move. Beyond her the veins were standing out on the doctor's forehead. He seemed under a great strain.

Lane's hand tightened on the girl's wrist, wrenched it hard. He brought up his right and seized the hilt of the dirk. Then he snatched it from her.

He thrust her away from him and took a step backward. Cataran's cry of alarm echoed staccato through the catacomb. In an instant, Ramos rose to his feet. His hand dropped to his coat pocket.

The flickering candlelight danced crazily on the blue steel barrel of the revolver he jerked from his coat. It came up to aim at Lane's heart.

But Gordon Lane did not hesitate. With a serpentlike movement he drew back his arm, then he hurled it forward with all his strength. The dirk hurtled through the air.

Even as Ramos' revolver spoke the blade ate its way avidly into his shoulder. The doctor uttered a cry of pain, and stumbled forward. His foot slipped and he fell with a crash.

Janice Lansing fell forward into Lane's arms. Then Lane heard a slithering footfall at his side. Grinning evilly, Cataran approached with his own blade, prepared to slay. Lane sidestepped, swinging the girl around. Then his right lashed out. It cracked with a sickening sound on the point of the other's jaw. Cataran dropped to the floor.

TIGHTLY GORDON HELD the girl in his arms. Now she looked up at him, wonder and bewilderment in her face.

"Gordon," she whispered. "Gordon. I knew you'd come. How did you find me? What had he done? Don't let him take me again, Gordon! Don't!"

"He won't," said Lane grimly. "Nor will he ever take *them*. . . . Look!"

He indicated the six workmen. Since Ramos had fallen it seemed that the spell which held them had been broken, too. Exhausted they had fallen to the fresh earth they had dug. They stared at each other with wondering, bewildered eyes.

"For God's sake," cried Lane, "why did he do this to you?"

A shudder ran through the girl's slim body.

"For two reasons," said Janice. "First, he made violent love to me and I refused him. Second, I learned his awful secret."

Lane indicated the prostrate emaciated Things which lay on their backs at the rear of the cavern.

"You mean the secret of that?"

She nodded. "It was when I was convalescing. He permitted no one to see me, telling people I was much worse than I was. That was when he was making love to me. Then one day I came upon him and Reeves, the undertaker, talking to Cataran. I didn't mean to eavesdrop. But after hearing the first few words, I had to listen to the rest.

"They—" She shivered as she glanced toward the exhausted creatures behind her. "They were patients of his over a period of time—who had no immediate relatives or friends. Or at least whose people didn't care much what happened to them. He used to advertise in weekly country papers offering to take care of indigent relatives. He treated them with a preparation of *Cannabis Indica*. That stupefied them, rendered their wills supine to his devilish hypnotism."

Lane shook his head. "He must be mad."

"I think he is. He boasted of all this to me when he warned me what he would do if I refused him. Reeves, the undertaker, would bury his 'dead' live men. Ramos would sign the death certificate and with his reputation in the town there was no suspicion."

"But," said Lane. "What if these distant relatives had wanted to see the body laid out? What if I had not been out of town when you were supposed to have been at the undertaker's? If I had learned of your supposed death early enough to have viewed your body as well as have attended the funeral?"

"He had that worked out, too," said Janice. "You see, it was arranged that when Reeves laid out a corpse, he was to arrange the coffin so that the body was completely covered. The head seen through thick glass was the only thing visible."

"THE DRUG REDUCED respiration. The thick glass would also screen the almost imperceptible movement of slow breathing. Of course, I was buried in the family vault. But the others took the places of the dead Cervantes whose bodies Ramos burned. When he put them into the coffin in the mornings, he would order them in their hypnotic spell to arise at a certain hour. They were so obedient to his will that they awoke and reported to the catacombs ready for labor on the stroke of midnight."

Lane nodded. "And with Cataran in his pay that would explain why the Cervantes tomb was unlocked. So that the 'dead' men could get out. But, darling, why? For God's sake, why? Is the man merely mad that he did these incredibly evil things?"

"I'm certain he's mad," she said slowly. "Yet there was one completely sane motive for what he did. Ramos had always hated the Church. Far back he was descended from the persecuted Incas. He hated Christianity. One day when cleaning out the Cervantes tomb, Cataran found an old map that revealed the whereabouts of buried Church treasures that the Spaniards had taken from the Indians five hundred years ago.

"Ramos wanted them. Apparently they were worth a great deal of money and they were buried in the catacombs of the graveyard. He dared not let anyone know. For then they would have become the property of the Church. Neither his blasphemous views nor his cupidity would permit that.

"Those poor creatures were his laboring slaves. They dug at night for the treasure. During the day they returned to their coffins, held there by Ramos' drug and by hypnosis. He did the same thing to me, fighting to dominate me completely."

"But tonight," said Lane. "The phone call."

"I suddenly awoke in my coffin. For a short while I was in complete possession of my faculties. He had always had more trouble keeping the spell on me than he did with the others."

Lane's arm tightened about her shoulder. "And I know why," he said.

"Anyway, I ran from the crypt. Ran to Cataran's house and phoned you. Cataran found me and dragged me away."

She lifted her eyes, glanced across the room and uttered a little moan.

"Look! He moved. He's not dead."

"No," said Lane. "But after this he'll be where he can do no harm."

She clung to him.

"Oh, Gordon, I'm afraid. I shall always be afraid while he's alive. To know that someone can have such power over me."

FOR A LONG moment they held each other. Then Gordon Lane knew what he must do.

"Darling," he said, "go to Cataran's cottage. Phone the police. Bring them here at once. I'll wait here and keep guard. Hurry, darling."

She smiled at him bravely and ran out of the dank catacomb.

Lane glanced around the room. The six emaciated Things lay almost unconscious on the ground. Perhaps they would live; perhaps they would pay with their lives for the ghastly thing that Ramos had done to them.

Cataran lay motionless on the floor. Ramos stirred uneasily. Lane crossed the room and picked up the revolver that the doctor had dropped. In his head there burned Janice's words. "I shall always be afraid while he lives!"

He bent down over the prostrate figure of the fiend and leveled the gun. There was no compunction in his heart as he sent two bullets crashing into Ramos' diseased brain.

HERBERT WEST—REANIMATOR & PICKMAN'S MODEL
H. P. LOVECRAFT

IN MANY WAYS, H. P. Lovecraft (1890–1937) lived a paradoxical life. Known today as one of the greatest of all horror writers, with numerous books in print and the model against whom other authors of dark fantasy are compared, he was a pitiful failure while alive.

His first book, *The Shunned House,* written in 1924, was never published, merely privately printed and circulated among a small circle of friends in unbound pages in 1928. His next, *Weird Shadow over Innsmouth* (1926), had a painfully small printing of four hundred copies, of which only two hundred were bound, the remaining sheets destroyed some years later when there was no call for them. No other book was published in his lifetime.

Although a frail recluse with few friends, he carried on a lively, almost pathologically relentless correspondence with other writers, fans, and, indeed, anyone who wrote to him, resulting in an estimated hundred thousand letters (according to his biographer, L. Sprague de Camp), an impressive total for an author who produced a mere sixty stories in his entire career.

Lovecraft was asked to write a series of connected short stories for a new magazine, *Home Brew,* which he did for a quarter of a cent per word, and the inferiority of the work reflects the pittance of five dollars per story he was paid. The publisher titled the series, about a man who revives corpse after corpse and the consequences he endures, *Grewsome Tales,* but it was retitled *Herbert West— Reanimator* when reprinted. The first story, "From the Dark," was published in the debut issue of *Home Brew* (January 1922), and five further installments followed through June. It was first collected in *Beyond the Wall of Sleep* (Sauk City, WI: Arkham House, 1943).

The idea for "Pickman's Model" came when Lovecraft heard of a series of tunnels that connected cellars of old houses in Boston, probably built for smugglers. It was originally published in the October 1927 issue of *Weird Tales;* its first book appearance was in an anthology edited by Christine Campbell Thomson, *By Daylight Only* (London: Selwyn & Blount, 1929); it later was collected in Lovecraft's first short-story collection, *The Outsider and Others* (Sauk City, WI: Arkham House, 1939).

H. P. LOVECRAFT

HERBERT WEST—REANIMATOR

I.

FROM THE DARK

OF HERBERT WEST, who was my friend in college and in after life, I can speak only with extreme terror. This terror is not due altogether to the sinister manner of his recent disappearance, but was engendered by the whole nature of his life-work, and first gained its acute form more than seventeen years ago, when we were in the third year of our course at the Miskatonic University Medical School in Arkham. While he was with me, the wonder and diabolism of his experiments fascinated me utterly, and I was his closest companion. Now that he is gone and the

spell is broken, the actual fear is greater. Memories and possibilities are ever more hideous than realities.

The first horrible incident of our acquaintance was the greatest shock I ever experienced, and it is only with reluctance that I repeat it. As I have said, it happened when we were in the medical school, where West had already made himself notorious through his wild theories on the nature of death and the possibility of overcoming it artificially. His views, which were widely ridiculed by the faculty and his fellow-students, hinged on the essentially mechanistic nature of life; and concerned means for operating the organic machinery of mankind by calculated chemical action after the failure of natural processes. In his experiments with various animating solutions he had killed and treated immense numbers of rabbits, guinea-pigs, cats, dogs, and monkeys, till he had become the prime nuisance of the college. Several times he had actually obtained signs of life in animals supposedly dead; in many cases violent signs; but he soon saw that the perfection of this process, if indeed possible, would necessarily involve a lifetime of research. It likewise became clear that, since the same solution never worked alike on different organic species, he would require human subjects for further and more specialised progress. It was here that he first came into conflict with the college authorities, and was debarred from future experiments by no less a dignitary than the dean of the medical school himself—the learned and benevolent Dr. Allan Halsey, whose work in behalf of the stricken is recalled by every old resident of Arkham.

I had always been exceptionally tolerant of West's pursuits, and we frequently discussed his theories, whose ramifications and corollaries were almost infinite. Holding with Haeckel that all life is a chemical and physical process, and that the so-called "soul" is a myth, my friend believed that artificial reanimation of the dead can depend only on the condition of the tissues; and that unless actual decomposition has set in, a corpse fully equipped with organs may with suitable measures be set going again in the peculiar fashion known as life. That the psychic or intellectual life might be impaired by the slight deterioration of sensitive brain-cells which even a short period of death would be apt to cause, West fully realised. It had at first been his hope to find a reagent which would restore vitality before the actual advent of death, and only repeated failures on animals had shewn him that the natural and artificial life-motions were incompatible. He then sought extreme freshness in his specimens, injecting his solutions into the blood immediately after the extinction of life. It was this circumstance which made the professors so carelessly sceptical, for they felt that true death had not occurred in any case. They did not stop to view the matter closely and reasonably.

It was not long after the faculty had interdicted his work that West confided to me his resolution to get fresh human bodies in some manner, and continue in secret the experiments he could no longer perform openly. To hear him discussing ways and means was rather ghastly, for at the college we had never procured anatomical specimens ourselves. Whenever the morgue proved inadequate, two local negroes attended to this matter, and they were seldom questioned. West was then a small, slender, spectacled youth with delicate features, yellow hair, pale blue eyes, and a soft voice, and it was uncanny to hear him dwelling on the relative merits of Christchurch Cemetery and the potter's field. We finally decided on the potter's field, because practically every body in Christchurch was embalmed; a thing of course ruinous to West's researches.

I was by this time his active and enthralled assistant, and helped him make all his decisions, not only concerning the source of bodies but concerning a suitable place for our loathsome work. It was I who thought of the deserted Chapman farmhouse beyond Meadow Hill, where we fitted up on the ground floor an operating room and a laboratory, each with dark curtains to conceal our midnight doings. The place was far from any road, and in sight of no other house, yet precautions were none the less necessary; since rumours of strange lights, started by chance nocturnal roamers, would soon bring disaster on our enterprise. It was agreed to call the whole thing a chemical laboratory if discovery should occur. Gradually we equipped our sinister haunt of science with materials either purchased in Boston or quietly borrowed from the college—materials carefully made unrecognisable save to expert eyes—and provided spades and picks for the many burials we should have to make in the cellar. At the college we used an incinerator, but the apparatus was too costly for our unauthorised laboratory. Bodies were always a nuisance—even the small guinea-pig bodies from the slight clandestine experiments in West's room at the boarding-house.

We followed the local death-notices like ghouls, for our specimens demanded particular qualities. What we wanted were corpses interred soon after death and without artificial preservation; preferably free from malforming disease, and certainly with all organs present. Accident victims were our best hope. Not for many weeks did we hear of anything suitable; though we talked with morgue and hospital authorities, ostensibly in the college's interest, as often as we could without exciting suspicion. We found that the college had first choice in every case, so that it might be necessary to remain in Arkham during the summer, when only the limited summer-school classes were held. In the end, though, luck favoured us; for one day we heard of an almost ideal case in the potter's field; a brawny young workman drowned only the morning before in Sumner's Pond, and buried at the town's expense without delay or embalming. That afternoon we found the new grave, and determined to begin work soon after midnight.

It was a repulsive task that we undertook in the black small hours, even though we lacked at that time the special horror of graveyards which later experiences brought to us. We carried spades and oil dark lanterns, for although electric torches were then manufactured, they were not as satisfactory as the tungsten contrivances of today. The process of unearthing was slow and sordid—it might have been gruesomely poetical if we had been artists instead of scientists—and we were glad when our spades struck wood. When the pine box was fully uncovered West scrambled down and removed the lid, dragging out and propping up the contents. I reached down and hauled the contents out of the grave, and then both toiled hard to restore the spot to its former appearance. The affair made us rather nervous, especially the stiff form and vacant face of our first trophy, but we managed to remove all traces of our visit. When we had patted down the last shovelful of earth we put the specimen in a canvas sack and set out for the old Chapman place beyond Meadow Hill.

On an improvised dissecting-table in the old farmhouse, by the light of a powerful acetylene lamp, the specimen was not very spectral looking. It had been a sturdy and apparently unimaginative youth of wholesome plebeian type—large-framed, grey-eyed, and brown-haired—a sound animal without psychological subtleties, and probably having vital processes of the simplest and healthiest sort. Now, with the eyes closed, it looked more asleep than dead; though the expert test of my friend soon left no doubt on that score. We had at last what West had always longed for—a real dead man of the ideal kind, ready for the solution as prepared according to the most careful calculations and theories for human use. The tension on our part became very great. We knew that there was scarcely a chance for anything like complete success, and could not avoid hideous fears at possible grotesque results of partial animation. Especially were we apprehensive concerning the mind and impulses of the creature, since in the space following death some of the more delicate cerebral cells might well have suffered deterioration. I, myself, still held some curious notions about the traditional "soul" of man, and felt an awe at the secrets that might be told by one returning from the dead. I wondered what sights this placid youth might have seen in inaccessible spheres, and what he could relate if fully restored to life. But my wonder was not overwhelming, since for the most part I shared the materialism of my friend. He was calmer than I as he forced a large quantity of his fluid into a vein of the body's arm, immediately binding the incision securely.

The waiting was gruesome, but West never faltered. Every now and then he applied his stethoscope to the specimen, and bore the negative results philosophically. After about three-quarters of an hour without the least sign of life he disappointedly pronounced the solution inadequate, but determined to make the most of his opportunity and try one change in the formula before disposing of his ghastly prize. We had that afternoon dug a grave in the cellar, and would have to fill it by dawn—for although we had fixed a lock on the house we wished to shun even the remotest risk of a ghoulish discovery. Besides, the body would not be even approximately fresh the next night. So taking the solitary acetylene lamp into the adjacent laboratory, we left our silent guest on the slab in the dark, and bent every energy to the mixing of a new solution; the weighing and measuring supervised by West with an almost fanatical care.

The awful event was very sudden, and wholly unexpected. I was pouring something from one test-tube to another, and West was busy over the alcohol blast-lamp which had to answer for a Bunsen burner in this gasless edifice, when from the pitch-black room we had left there burst the most appalling and daemoniac succession of cries that either of us had ever heard. Not more unutterable could have been the chaos of hellish sound if the pit itself had opened to release the agony of the damned, for in one inconceivable cacophony was centred all the supernal terror and unnatural despair of animate nature. Human it could not have been—it is not in man to make such sounds—and without a thought of our late employment or its possible discovery both West and I leaped to the nearest window like stricken animals; overturning tubes, lamp, and retorts, and vaulting madly into the starred abyss of the rural night. I think we screamed ourselves as we stumbled frantically toward the town, though as we reached the outskirts we put on a semblance of restraint—just enough to seem like belated revellers staggering home from a debauch.

We did not separate, but managed to get to West's room, where we whispered with the gas up until dawn. By then we had calmed ourselves a little with rational theories and plans for investigation, so that we could sleep through the day—classes being disregarded. But that evening two items in the paper, wholly unrelated, made it again impossible for us to sleep. The old deserted Chapman house had inexplicably burned to an amorphous heap of ashes; that we could understand because of the upset lamp. Also, an attempt had been made to disturb a new grave in the potter's field, as if by futile and

spadeless clawing at the earth. That we could not understand, for we had patted down the mould very carefully.

And for seventeen years after that West would look frequently over his shoulder, and complain of fancied footsteps behind him. Now he has disappeared.

II.

THE PLAGUE-DAEMON

I shall never forget that hideous summer sixteen years ago, when like a noxious afrite from the halls of Eblis typhoid stalked leeringly through Arkham. It is by that satanic scourge that most recall the year, for truly terror brooded with bat-wings over the piles of coffins in the tombs of Christchurch Cemetery; yet for me there is a greater horror in that time—a horror known to me alone now that Herbert West has disappeared.

West and I were doing post-graduate work in summer classes at the medical school of Miskatonic University, and my friend had attained a wide notoriety because of his experiments leading toward the revivification of the dead. After the scientific slaughter of uncounted small animals the freakish work had ostensibly stopped by order of our sceptical dean, Dr. Allan Halsey; though West had continued to perform certain secret tests in his dingy boarding-house room, and had on one terrible and unforgettable occasion taken a human body from its grave in the potter's field to a deserted farmhouse beyond Meadow Hill.

I was with him on that odious occasion, and saw him inject into the still veins the elixir which he thought would to some extent restore life's chemical and physical processes. It had ended horribly—in a delirium of fear which we gradually came to attribute to our own overwrought nerves—and West had never afterward been able to shake off a maddening sensation of being haunted and hunted. The body had not been quite fresh enough; it is obvious that to restore normal mental attributes a body must be very fresh indeed; and a burning of the old house had prevented us from burying the thing. It would have been better if we could have known it was underground.

After that experience West had dropped his researches for some time; but as the zeal of the born scientist slowly returned, he again became importunate with the college faculty, pleading for the use of the dissecting-room and of fresh human specimens for the work he regarded as so overwhelmingly important. His pleas, however, were wholly in vain; for the decision of Dr. Halsey was inflexible, and the other professors all endorsed the verdict of their leader. In the radical theory of reanimation they saw nothing but the immature vagaries of a youthful enthusiast whose slight form, yellow hair, spectacled blue eyes, and soft voice gave no hint of the supernormal—almost diabolical—power of the cold brain within. I can see him now as he was then—and I shiver. He grew sterner of face, but never elderly. And now Sefton Asylum has had the mishap and West has vanished.

West clashed disagreeably with Dr. Halsey near the end of our last undergraduate term in a wordy dispute that did less credit to him than to the kindly dean in point of courtesy. He felt that he was needlessly and irrationally retarded in a supremely great work; a work which he could of course conduct to suit himself in later years, but which he wished to begin while still possessed of the exceptional facilities of the university. That the tradition-bound elders should ignore his singular results on animals, and persist in their denial of the possibility of reanimation, was inexpressibly disgusting and almost incomprehensible to a youth of West's logical temperament. Only greater maturity could help him understand the chronic mental limitations of the "professor-doctor" type—the product of generations of pathetic Puritanism; kindly, conscientious, and sometimes gentle and amiable, yet always narrow, intolerant, custom-ridden, and lacking in perspective. Age has more char-

ity for these incomplete yet high-souled characters, whose worst real vice is timidity, and who are ultimately punished by general ridicule for their intellectual sins—sins like Ptolemaism, Calvinism, anti-Darwinism, anti-Nietzscheism, and every sort of Sabbatarianism and sumptuary legislation. West, young despite his marvellous scientific acquirements, had scant patience with good Dr. Halsey and his erudite colleagues; and nursed an increasing resentment, coupled with a desire to prove his theories to these obtuse worthies in some striking and dramatic fashion. Like most youths, he indulged in elaborate daydreams of revenge, triumph, and final magnanimous forgiveness.

And then had come the scourge, grinning and lethal, from the nightmare caverns of Tartarus. West and I had graduated about the time of its beginning, but had remained for additional work at the summer school, so that we were in Arkham when it broke with full daemoniac fury upon the town. Though not as yet licenced physicians, we now had our degrees, and were pressed frantically into public service as the numbers of the stricken grew. The situation was almost past management, and deaths ensued too frequently for the local undertakers fully to handle. Burials without embalming were made in rapid succession, and even the Christchurch Cemetery receiving tomb was crammed with coffins of the unembalmed dead. This circumstance was not without effect on West, who thought often of the irony of the situation—so many fresh specimens, yet none for his persecuted researches! We were frightfully overworked, and the terrific mental and nervous strain made my friend brood morbidly.

But West's gentle enemies were no less harassed with prostrating duties. College had all but closed, and every doctor of the medical faculty was helping to fight the typhoid plague. Dr. Halsey in particular had distinguished himself in sacrificing service, applying his extreme skill with whole-hearted energy to cases which many others shunned because of danger or apparent hopelessness. Before a month was over the fearless dean had become a popular hero, though he seemed unconscious of his fame as he struggled to keep from collapsing with physical fatigue and nervous exhaustion. West could not withhold admiration for the fortitude of his foe, but because of this was even more determined to prove to him the truth of his amazing doctrines. Taking advantage of the disorganisation of both college work and municipal health regulations, he managed to get a recently deceased body smuggled into the university dissecting-room one night, and in my presence injected a new modification of his solution. The thing actually opened its eyes, but only stared at the ceiling with a look of soul-petrifying horror before collapsing into an inertness from which nothing could rouse it. West said it was not fresh enough—the hot summer air does not favour corpses. That time we were almost caught before we incinerated the thing, and West doubted the advisability of repeating his daring misuse of the college laboratory.

The peak of the epidemic was reached in August. West and I were almost dead, and Dr. Halsey did die on the 14th. The students all attended the hasty funeral on the 15th, and bought an impressive wreath, though the latter was quite overshadowed by the tributes sent by wealthy Arkham citizens and by the municipality itself. It was almost a public affair, for the dean had surely been a public benefactor. After the entombment we were all somewhat depressed, and spent the afternoon at the bar of the Commercial House; where West, though shaken by the death of his chief opponent, chilled the rest of us with references to his notorious theories. Most of the students went home, or to various duties, as the evening advanced; but West persuaded me to aid him in "making a night of it." West's landlady saw us arrive at his room about two in the morning, with a third man between us; and told her husband that we had all evidently dined and wined rather well.

Apparently this acidulous matron was right; for about 3 a.m. the whole house was aroused by cries coming from West's room, where when they broke down the door they found the two of us unconscious on the blood-stained carpet, beaten, scratched, and mauled, and with the broken remnants of West's bottles and instruments around us. Only an open window told what had become of our assailant, and many wondered how he himself had fared after the terrific leap from the second story to the lawn which he must have made. There were some strange garments in the room, but West upon regaining consciousness said they did not belong to the stranger, but were specimens collected for bacteriological analysis in the course of investigations on the transmission of germ diseases. He ordered them burnt as soon as possible in the capacious fireplace. To the police we both declared ignorance of our late companion's identity. He was, West nervously said, a congenial stranger whom we had met at some downtown bar of uncertain location. We had all been rather jovial, and West and I did not wish to have our pugnacious companion hunted down.

That same night saw the beginning of the second Arkham horror—the horror that to me eclipsed the plague itself. Christchurch Cemetery was the scene of a terrible killing; a watchman having been clawed to death in a manner not only too hideous for description, but raising a doubt as to the human agency of the deed. The victim had been seen alive considerably after midnight—the dawn revealed the unutterable thing. The manager of a circus at the neighbouring town of Bolton was questioned, but he swore that no beast had at any time escaped from its cage. Those who found the body noted a trail of blood leading to the receiving tomb, where a small pool of red lay on the concrete just outside the gate. A fainter trail led away toward the woods, but it soon gave out.

The next night devils danced on the roofs of Arkham, and unnatural madness howled in the wind. Through the fevered town had crept a curse which some said was greater than the plague, and which some whispered was the embodied daemon-soul of the plague itself. Eight houses were entered by a nameless thing which strewed red death in its wake—in all, seventeen maimed and shapeless remnants of bodies were left behind by the voiceless, sadistic monster that crept abroad. A few persons had half seen it in the dark, and said it was white and like a malformed ape or anthropomorphic fiend. It had not left behind quite all that it had attacked, for sometimes it had been hungry. The number it had killed was fourteen; three of the bodies had been in stricken homes and had not been alive.

On the third night frantic bands of searchers, led by the police, captured it in a house on Crane Street near the Miskatonic campus. They had organised the quest with care, keeping in touch by means of volunteer telephone stations, and when someone in the college district had reported hearing a scratching at a shuttered window, the net was quickly spread. On account of the general alarm and precautions, there were only two more victims, and the capture was effected without major casualties. The thing was finally stopped by a bullet, though not a fatal one, and was rushed to the local hospital amidst universal excitement and loathing.

For it had been a man. This much was clear despite the nauseous eyes, the voiceless simianism, and the daemoniac savagery. They dressed its wound and carted it to the asylum at Sefton, where it beat its head against the walls of a padded cell for sixteen years—until the recent mishap, when it escaped under circumstances that few like to mention. What had most disgusted the searchers of Arkham was the thing they noticed when the monster's face was cleaned—the mocking, unbelievable resemblance to a learned and self-sacrificing martyr who had been entombed but three days before—the late Dr. Allan Halsey, public benefactor and dean of the medical school of Miskatonic University.

To the vanished Herbert West and to me the disgust and horror were supreme. I shudder tonight as I think of it; shudder even more than I did that morning when West muttered through his bandages,

"Damn it, it wasn't *quite* fresh enough!"

III.

SIX SHOTS BY MIDNIGHT

It is uncommon to fire all six shots of a revolver with great suddenness when one would probably be sufficient, but many things in the life of Herbert West were uncommon. It is, for instance, not often that a young physician leaving college is obliged to conceal the principles which guide his selection of a home and office, yet that was the case with Herbert West. When he and I obtained our degrees at the medical school of Miskatonic University, and sought to relieve our poverty by setting up as general practitioners, we took great care not to say that we chose our house because it was fairly well isolated, and as near as possible to the potter's field.

Reticence such as this is seldom without a cause, nor indeed was ours; for our requirements were those resulting from a life-work distinctly unpopular. Outwardly we were doctors only, but beneath the surface were aims of far greater and more terrible moment—for the essence of Herbert West's existence was a quest amid black and forbidden realms of the unknown, in which he hoped to uncover the secret of life and restore to perpetual animation the graveyard's cold clay. Such a quest demands strange materials, among them fresh human bodies; and in order to keep supplied with these indispensable things one must live quietly and not far from a place of informal interment.

West and I had met in college, and I had been the only one to sympathise with his hideous experiments. Gradually I had come to be his inseparable assistant, and now that we were out of college we had to keep together. It was not easy to find a good opening for two doctors in company, but finally the influence of the university secured us a practice in Bolton—a factory town near Arkham, the seat of the college. The Bolton Worsted Mills are the largest in the Miskatonic Valley, and their polyglot employees are never popular as patients with the local physicians. We chose our house with the greatest care, seizing at last on a rather run-down cottage near the end of Pond Street; five numbers from the closest neighbour, and separated from the local potter's field by only a stretch of meadow land, bisected by a narrow neck of the rather dense forest which lies to the north. The distance was greater than we wished, but we could get no nearer house without going on the other side of the field, wholly out of the factory district. We were not much displeased, however, since there were no people between us and our sinister source of supplies. The walk was a trifle long, but we could haul our silent specimens undisturbed.

Our practice was surprisingly large from the very first—large enough to please most young doctors, and large enough to prove a bore and a burden to students whose real interest lay elsewhere. The mill-hands were of somewhat turbulent inclinations; and besides their many natural needs, their frequent clashes and stabbing affrays gave us plenty to do. But what actually absorbed our minds was the secret laboratory we had fitted up in the cellar—the laboratory with the long table under the electric lights, where in the small hours of the morning we often injected West's various solutions into the veins of the things we dragged from the potter's field. West was experimenting madly to find something which would start man's vital motions anew after they had been stopped by the thing we call death, but had encountered the most ghastly obstacles. The solution had to be differently compounded for different types—what would serve for guinea-pigs would not serve for human beings, and different human specimens required large modifications.

The bodies had to be exceedingly fresh, or the slight decomposition of brain tissue would render perfect reanimation impossible. Indeed, the greatest problem was to get them fresh enough—West had had horrible experiences during his secret college researches with corpses of doubtful vintage. The results of partial or imperfect animation were much more hideous than were the total failures, and we both held fearsome recollections of such things. Ever since our first daemoniac session in the deserted farmhouse on Meadow Hill in Arkham, we had felt a brooding menace; and West, though a calm, blond, blue-eyed scientific automaton in most respects, often confessed to a shuddering sensation of stealthy pursuit. He half felt that he was followed—a psychological delusion of shaken nerves, enhanced by the undeniably disturbing fact that at least one of our reanimated specimens was still alive—a frightful carnivorous thing in a padded cell at Sefton. Then there was another—our first—whose exact fate we had never learned.

We had fair luck with specimens in Bolton—much better than in Arkham. We had not been settled a week before we got an accident victim on the very night of burial, and made it open its eyes with an amazingly rational expression before the solution failed. It had lost an arm—if it had been a perfect body we might have succeeded better. Between then and the next January we secured three more; one total failure, one case of marked muscular motion, and one rather shivery thing—it rose of itself and uttered a sound. Then came a period when luck was poor; interments fell off, and those that did occur were of specimens either too diseased or too maimed for use. We kept track of all the deaths and their circumstances with systematic care.

One March night, however, we unexpectedly obtained a specimen which did not come from the potter's field. In Bolton the prevailing spirit of Puritanism had outlawed the sport of boxing—with the usual result. Surreptitious and ill-conducted bouts among the mill-workers were common, and occasionally professional talent of low grade was imported. This late winter night there had been such a match; evidently with disastrous results, since two timorous Poles had come to us with incoherently whispered entreaties to attend to a very secret and desperate case. We followed them to an abandoned barn, where the remnants of a crowd of frightened foreigners were watching a silent black form on the floor.

The match had been between Kid O'Brien—

a lubberly and now quaking youth with a most un-Hibernian hooked nose—and Buck Robinson, "The Harlem Smoke." The negro had been knocked out, and a moment's examination shewed us that he would permanently remain so. He was a loathsome, gorilla-like thing, with abnormally long arms which I could not help calling fore legs, and a face that conjured up thoughts of unspeakable Congo secrets and tom-tom poundings under an eerie moon. The body must have looked even worse in life—but the world holds many ugly things. Fear was upon the whole pitiful crowd, for they did not know what the law would exact of them if the affair were not hushed up; and they were grateful when West, in spite of my involuntary shudders, offered to get rid of the thing quietly—for a purpose I knew too well.

There was bright moonlight over the snowless landscape, but we dressed the thing and carried it home between us through the deserted streets and meadows, as we had carried a similar thing one horrible night in Arkham. We approached the house from the field in the rear, took the specimen in the back door and down the cellar stairs, and prepared it for the usual experiment. Our fear of the police was absurdly great, though we had timed our trip to avoid the solitary patrolman of that section.

The result was wearily anticlimactic. Ghastly as our prize appeared, it was wholly unresponsive to every solution we injected in its black arm; solutions prepared from experience with white specimens only. So as the hour grew dangerously near to dawn, we did as we had done with the others—dragged the thing across the meadows to the neck of the woods near the potter's field, and buried it there in the best sort of grave the frozen ground would furnish. The grave was not very deep, but fully as good as that of the previous specimen—the thing which had risen of itself and uttered a sound. In the light of our dark lanterns we carefully covered it with leaves and dead vines, fairly certain that the police would never find it in a forest so dim and dense.

The next day I was increasingly apprehensive about the police, for a patient brought rumours of a suspected fight and death. West had still another source of worry, for he had been called in the afternoon to a case which ended very threateningly. An Italian woman had become hysterical over her missing child—a lad of five who had strayed off early in the morning and failed to appear for dinner—and had developed symptoms highly alarming in view of an always weak heart. It was a very foolish hysteria, for the boy had often run away before; but Italian peasants are exceedingly superstitious, and this woman seemed as much harassed by omens as by facts. About seven o'clock in the evening she had died, and her frantic husband had made a frightful scene in his efforts to kill West, whom he wildly blamed for not saving her life. Friends had held him when he drew a stiletto, but West departed amidst his inhuman shrieks, curses, and oaths of vengeance. In his latest affliction the fellow seemed to have forgotten his child, who was still missing as the night advanced. There was some talk of searching the woods, but most of the family's friends were busy with the dead woman and the screaming man. Altogether, the nervous strain upon West must have been tremendous. Thoughts of the police and of the mad Italian both weighed heavily.

We retired about eleven, but I did not sleep well. Bolton had a surprisingly good police force for so small a town, and I could not help fearing the mess which would ensue if the affair of the night before were ever tracked down. It might mean the end of all our local work—and perhaps prison for both West and me. I did not like those rumours of a fight which were floating about. After the clock had struck three the moon shone in my eyes, but I turned over without rising to pull down the shade. Then came the steady rattling at the back door.

I lay still and somewhat dazed, but before long heard West's rap on my door. He was clad in dressing-gown and slippers, and had in his hands a revolver and an electric flashlight. From the revolver I knew that he was thinking more of the crazed Italian than of the police.

"We'd better both go," he whispered. "It wouldn't do not to answer it anyway, and it may be a patient—it would be like one of those fools to try the back door."

So we both went down the stairs on tiptoe, with a fear partly justified and partly that which comes only from the soul of the weird small hours. The rattling continued, growing somewhat louder. When we reached the door I cautiously unbolted it and threw it open, and as the moon streamed revealingly down on the form silhouetted there, West did a peculiar thing. Despite the obvious danger of attracting notice and bringing down on our heads the dreaded police investigation—a thing which after all was mercifully averted by the relative isolation of our cottage—my friend suddenly, excitedly, and unnecessarily emptied all six chambers of his revolver into the nocturnal visitor.

For that visitor was neither Italian nor policeman. Looming hideously against the spectral moon was a gigantic misshapen thing not to be imagined save in nightmares—a glassy-eyed, ink-black apparition nearly on all fours, covered with bits of mould, leaves, and vines, foul with caked blood, and having between its glistening teeth a snow-white, terrible, cylindrical object terminating in a tiny hand.

IV.

THE SCREAM OF THE DEAD

The scream of a dead man gave to me that acute and added horror of Dr. Herbert West which harassed the latter years of our companionship. It is natural that such a thing as a dead man's scream should give horror, for it is obviously not a pleasing or ordinary occurrence; but I was used to similar experiences, hence suffered on this occasion only because of a particular circumstance. And, as I have implied, it was not of the dead man himself that I became afraid.

Herbert West, whose associate and assistant I was, possessed scientific interests far beyond the usual routine of a village physician. That was why, when establishing his practice in Bolton, he had chosen an isolated house near the potter's field. Briefly and brutally stated, West's sole absorbing interest was a secret study of the phenomena of life and its cessation, leading toward the reanimation of the dead through injections of an excitant solution. For this ghastly experimenting it was necessary to have a constant supply of very fresh human bodies; very fresh because even the least decay hopelessly damaged the brain structure, and human because we found that the solution had to be compounded differently for different types of organisms. Scores of rabbits and guinea-pigs had been killed and treated, but their trail was a blind one. West had never fully succeeded because he had never been able to secure a corpse sufficiently fresh. What he wanted were bodies from which vitality had only just departed; bodies with every cell intact and capable of receiving again the impulse toward that mode of motion called life. There was hope that this second and artificial life might be made perpetual by repetitions of the injection, but we had learned that an ordinary natural life would not respond to the action. To establish the artificial motion, natural life must be extinct—the specimens must be very fresh, but genuinely dead.

The awesome quest had begun when West and I were students at the Miskatonic University Medical School in Arkham, vividly conscious for the first time of the thoroughly mechanical nature of life. That was seven years before, but West looked scarcely a day older now—he was small, blond, clean-shaven, soft-voiced, and spectacled, with only an occasional flash of a cold blue eye to tell of the hardening and growing fanaticism of his character under the pressure of his terrible investigations. Our experiences had often been hideous in the extreme; the results of defective reanimation, when lumps of graveyard clay had been galvanised into morbid, unnatural, and brainless motion by various modifications of the vital solution.

One thing had uttered a nerve-shattering

scream; another had risen violently, beaten us both to unconsciousness, and run amuck in a shocking way before it could be placed behind asylum bars; still another, a loathsome African monstrosity, had clawed out of its shallow grave and done a deed—West had had to shoot that object. We could not get bodies fresh enough to shew any trace of reason when reanimated, so had perforce created nameless horrors. It was disturbing to think that one, perhaps two, of our monsters still lived—that thought haunted us shadowingly, till finally West disappeared under frightful circumstances. But at the time of the scream in the cellar laboratory of the isolated Bolton cottage, our fears were subordinate to our anxiety for extremely fresh specimens. West was more avid than I, so that it almost seemed to me that he looked half-covetously at any very healthy living physique.

It was in July 1910, that the bad luck regarding specimens began to turn. I had been on a long visit to my parents in Illinois, and upon my return found West in a state of singular elation. He had, he told me excitedly, in all likelihood solved the problem of freshness through an approach from an entirely new angle—that of artificial preservation. I had known that he was working on a new and highly unusual embalming compound, and was not surprised that it had turned out well; but until he explained the details I was rather puzzled as to how such a compound could help in our work, since the objectionable staleness of the specimens was largely due to delay occurring before we secured them. This, I now saw, West had clearly recognised; creating his embalming compound for future rather than immediate use, and trusting to fate to supply again some very recent and unburied corpse, as it had years before when we obtained the negro killed in the Bolton prize-fight. At last fate had been kind, so that on this occasion there lay in the secret cellar laboratory a corpse whose decay could not by any possibility have begun. What would happen on reanimation, and whether we could hope for a revival of mind and reason, West did not venture to pre-dict. The experiment would be a landmark in our studies, and he had saved the new body for my return, so that both might share the spectacle in accustomed fashion.

West told me how he had obtained the specimen. It had been a vigorous man; a well-dressed stranger just off the train on his way to transact some business with the Bolton Worsted Mills. The walk through the town had been long, and by the time the traveller paused at our cottage to ask the way to the factories his heart had become greatly overtaxed. He had refused a stimulant, and had suddenly dropped dead only a moment later. The body, as might be expected, seemed to West a heaven-sent gift. In his brief conversation the stranger had made it clear that he was unknown in Bolton, and a search of his pockets subsequently revealed him to be one Robert Leavitt of St. Louis, apparently without a family to make instant inquiries about his disappearance. If this man could not be restored to life, no one would know of our experiment. We buried our materials in a dense strip of woods between the house and the potter's field. If, on the other hand, he could be restored, our fame would be brilliantly and perpetually established. So without delay West had injected into the body's wrist the compound which would hold it fresh for use after my arrival. The matter of the presumably weak heart, which to my mind imperiled the success of our experiment, did not appear to trouble West extensively. He hoped at last to obtain what he had never obtained before—a rekindled spark of reason and perhaps a normal, living creature.

So on the night of July 18, 1910, Herbert West and I stood in the cellar laboratory and gazed at a white, silent figure beneath the dazzling arc-light. The embalming compound had worked uncannily well, for as I stared fascinatedly at the sturdy frame which had lain two weeks without stiffening I was moved to seek West's assurance that the thing was really dead. This assurance he gave readily enough; reminding me that the reanimating solution was never used without careful tests as to life; since it could have no effect if any of the original vitality were present. As West proceeded to take preliminary steps, I was impressed by the vast intricacy of the new experiment; an intricacy so vast that he could trust no hand less delicate than his own. Forbidding me to touch the body, he first injected a drug in the wrist just beside the place his needle had punctured when injecting the embalming compound. This, he said, was to neutralise the compound and release the system to a normal relaxation so that the reanimating solution might freely work when injected. Slightly later, when a change and a gentle tremor seemed to affect the dead limbs, West stuffed a pillow-like object violently over the twitching face, not withdrawing it until the corpse appeared quiet and ready for our attempt at reanimation. The pale enthusiast now applied some last perfunctory tests for absolute lifelessness, withdrew satisfied, and finally injected into the left arm an accurately measured amount of the vital elixir, prepared during the afternoon with a greater care than we had used since college days, when our feats were new and groping. I cannot express the wild, breathless suspense with which we waited for results on this first really fresh specimen—the first we could reasonably expect to open its lips in rational speech, perhaps to tell of what it had seen beyond the unfathomable abyss.

West was a materialist, believing in no soul and attributing all the working of consciousness to bodily phenomena; consequently he looked for no revelation of hideous secrets from gulfs and caverns beyond death's barrier. I did not wholly disagree with him theoretically, yet held vague instinctive remnants of the primitive faith of my forefathers; so that I could not help eyeing the corpse with a certain amount of awe and terrible expectation. Besides—I could not extract from my memory that hideous, inhuman shriek we heard on the night we tried our first experiment in the deserted farmhouse at Arkham.

Very little time had elapsed before I saw the attempt was not to be a total failure. A touch of colour came to cheeks hitherto chalk-white, and spread out under the curiously ample stubble of sandy beard. West, who had his hand on the pulse of the left wrist, suddenly nodded significantly; and almost simultaneously a mist appeared on the mirror inclined above the body's mouth. There followed a few spasmodic muscular motions, and then an audible breathing and visible motion of the chest. I looked at the closed eyelids, and thought I detected a quivering. Then the lids opened, shewing eyes which were grey, calm, and alive, but still unintelligent and not even curious.

In a moment of fantastic whim I whispered questions to the reddening ears; questions of other worlds of which the memory might still be present. Subsequent terror drove them from my mind, but I think the last one, which I repeated, was: "Where have you been?" I do not yet know whether I was answered or not, for no sound came from the well-shaped mouth; but I do know that at that moment I firmly thought the thin lips moved silently, forming syllables I would have vocalised as "only now" if that phrase had possessed any sense or relevancy. At that moment, as I say, I was elated with the conviction that the one great goal had been attained; and that for the first time a reanimated corpse had uttered distinct words impelled by actual reason. In the next moment there was no doubt about the triumph; no doubt that the solution had truly accomplished, at least temporarily, its full mission of restoring rational and articulate life to the dead. But in that triumph there came to me the greatest of all horrors—not horror of the thing that spoke, but of the deed that I had witnessed and of the man with whom my professional fortunes were joined.

For that very fresh body, at last writhing into full and terrifying consciousness with eyes dilated at the memory of its last scene on earth, threw out its frantic hands in a life and death struggle with the air; and suddenly collapsing into a second and final dissolution from which there could be no return, screamed out the cry that will ring eternally in my aching brain:

"Help! Keep off, you cursed little tow-head fiend—keep that damned needle away from me!"

V.

THE HORROR FROM THE SHADOWS

Many men have related hideous things, not mentioned in print, which happened on the battlefields of the Great War. Some of these things have made me faint, others have convulsed me with devastating nausea, while still others have made me tremble and look behind me in the dark; yet despite the worst of them I believe I can myself relate the most hideous thing of all—the shocking, the unnatural, the unbelievable horror from the shadows.

In 1915 I was a physician with the rank of First Lieutenant in a Canadian regiment in Flanders, one of many Americans to precede the government itself into the gigantic struggle. I had not entered the army on my own initiative, but rather as a natural result of the enlistment of the man whose indispensable assistant I was—the celebrated Boston surgical specialist Dr. Herbert West. Dr. West had been avid for a chance to serve as surgeon in a great war, and when the chance had come he carried me with him almost against my will. There were reasons why I would have been glad to let the war separate us; reasons why I found the practice of medicine and the companionship of West more and more irritating; but when he had gone to Ottawa and through a colleague's influence secured a medical commission as Major, I could not resist the imperious persuasion of one determined that I should accompany him in my usual capacity.

When I say that Dr. West was avid to serve in battle, I do not mean to imply that he was either naturally warlike or anxious for the safety of civilisation. Always an ice-cold intellectual machine; slight, blond, blue-eyed, and spectacled; I think he secretly sneered at my occasional martial enthusiasms and censures of supine neutrality. There was, however, something he wanted in embattled Flanders; and in order to secure it he had to assume a military exterior. What he wanted was not a thing which many persons want, but something connected with the peculiar branch of medical science which he had chosen quite clandestinely to follow, and in which he had achieved amazing and occasionally hideous results. It was, in fact, nothing more or less than an abundant supply of freshly killed men in every stage of dismemberment.

Herbert West needed fresh bodies because his life-work was the reanimation of the dead. This work was not known to the fashionable clientele who had so swiftly built up his fame after his arrival in Boston; but was only too well known to me, who had been his closest friend and sole assistant since the old days in Miskatonic University Medical School at Arkham. It was in those college days that he had begun his terrible experiments, first on small animals and then on human bodies shockingly obtained. There was a solution which he injected into the veins of dead things, and if they were fresh enough they responded in strange ways. He had had much trouble in discovering the proper formula, for each type of organism was found to need a stimulus especially adapted to it. Terror stalked him when he reflected on his partial failures; nameless things resulting from imperfect solutions or from bodies insufficiently fresh. A certain number of these failures had remained alive—one was in an asylum while others had vanished—and as he thought of conceivable yet virtually impossible eventualities he often shivered beneath his usual stolidity.

West had soon learned that absolute freshness was the prime requisite for useful specimens, and had accordingly resorted to frightful and unnatural expedients in body-snatching. In college, and during our early practice together in the factory town of Bolton, my attitude toward him had been largely one of fascinated admiration; but as his boldness in methods grew, I began to develop a gnawing fear. I did not like the way he looked at healthy living bodies; and then there came a nightmarish session in the cellar laboratory when I learned that a certain specimen had been a living body when he secured it. That was the first time he had ever been able to revive the quality of rational thought in a corpse; and his success, obtained at such a loathsome cost, had completely hardened him.

Of his methods in the intervening five years I dare not speak. I was held to him by sheer force of fear, and witnessed sights that no human tongue could repeat. Gradually I came to find Herbert West himself more horrible than anything he did—that was when it dawned on me that his once normal scientific zeal for prolonging life had subtly degenerated into a mere morbid and ghoulish curiosity and secret sense of charnel picturesqueness. His interest became a hellish and perverse addiction to the repellently and fiendishly abnormal; he gloated calmly over artificial monstrosities which would make most healthy men drop dead from fright and disgust; he became, behind his pallid intellectuality, a fastidious Baudelaire of physical experiment—a languid Elagabalus of the tombs.

Dangers he met unflinchingly; crimes he committed unmoved. I think the climax came when he had proved his point that rational life can be restored, and had sought new worlds to conquer by experimenting on the reanimation of detached parts of bodies. He had wild and original ideas on the independent vital properties of organic cells and nerve-tissue separated from natural physiological systems; and achieved some hideous preliminary results in the form of never-dying, artificially nourished tissue obtained from the nearly hatched eggs of an indescribable tropical reptile. Two biological points he was exceedingly anxious to settle—first, whether any amount of consciousness and rational action be possible without the brain, proceeding from the spinal cord and various nerve-centres; and second, whether any kind of ethereal, intangible relation distinct from the material cells may exist to link the surgically separated parts of what has previously been a single living organism. All this research work required a prodigious supply of freshly slaughtered human flesh—and that was why Herbert West had entered the Great War.

The phantasmal, unmentionable thing occurred one midnight late in March 1915, in a field hospital behind the lines at St. Eloi. I wonder even now if it could have been other than a daemoniac dream of delirium. West had a private laboratory in an east room of the barn-like temporary edifice, assigned him on his plea that he was devising new and radical methods for the treatment of hitherto hopeless cases of maiming. There he worked like a butcher in the midst of his gory wares—I could never get used to the levity with which he handled and classified certain things. At times he actually did perform marvels of surgery for the soldiers; but his chief delights were of a less public and philanthropic kind, requiring many explanations of sounds which seemed peculiar even amidst that babel of the damned. Among these sounds were frequent revolver-shots—surely not uncommon on a battlefield, but distinctly uncommon in an hospital. Dr. West's reanimated specimens were not meant for long existence or a large audience. Besides human tissue, West employed much of the reptile embryo tissue which he had cultivated with such singular results. It was better than human material for maintaining life in organless fragments, and that was now my friend's chief activity. In a dark corner of the laboratory, over a queer incubating burner, he kept a large covered vat full of this reptilian cell-matter; which multiplied and grew puffily and hideously.

On the night of which I speak we had a splendid new specimen—a man at once physically powerful and of such high mentality that a sensitive nervous system was assured. It was rather ironic, for he was the officer who had helped West to his commission, and who was now to have been our associate. Moreover, he had in the past secretly studied the theory of reanimation to some extent under West. Major Sir Eric Moreland Clapham-Lee, D.S.O., was the greatest surgeon in our division, and had been hastily assigned to the St. Eloi sector when news of the heavy fighting reached headquarters. He had come in an aëroplane piloted by the intrepid Lieut. Ronald Hill, only to be shot down when directly over his destination. The fall had been spectacular and awful; Hill was unrecognisable afterward, but the wreck yielded up the great surgeon in a nearly decapitated but otherwise intact condition. West had greedily seized the lifeless thing which had once been his friend and fellow-scholar; and I shuddered when he finished severing the head, placed it in his hellish vat of pulpy reptile-tissue to preserve it for future experiments, and proceeded to treat the decapitated body on the operating table. He injected new blood, joined certain veins, arteries, and nerves at the headless neck, and closed the ghastly aperture with engrafted skin from an unidentified specimen which had borne an officer's uniform. I knew what he wanted—to see if this highly organised body could exhibit, without its head, any of the signs of mental life which had distinguished Sir Eric Moreland Clapham-Lee. Once a student of reanimation, this silent trunk was now gruesomely called upon to exemplify it.

I can still see Herbert West under the sinister electric light as he injected his reanimating solution into the arm of the headless body. The scene I cannot describe—I should faint if I tried it, for there is madness in a room full of classified charnel things, with blood and lesser human debris almost ankle-deep on the slimy floor, and with hideous reptilian abnormalities sprouting, bubbling, and baking over a winking bluish-green spectre of dim flame in a far corner of black shadows.

The specimen, as West repeatedly observed, had a splendid nervous system. Much was expected of it; and as a few twitching motions began to appear, I could see the feverish interest on West's face. He was ready, I think, to see proof of his increasingly strong opinion that consciousness, reason, and personality can exist independently of the brain—that man has no central connective spirit, but is merely a machine of nervous matter, each section more or less complete in itself. In one triumphant demonstration West was about to relegate the mystery of life to the category of myth. The body now twitched more vigorously, and beneath our avid eyes commenced to heave in a frightful way.

The arms stirred disquietingly, the legs drew up, and various muscles contracted in a repulsive kind of writhing. Then the headless thing threw out its arms in a gesture which was unmistakably one of desperation—an intelligent desperation apparently sufficient to prove every theory of Herbert West. Certainly, the nerves were recalling the man's last act in life; the struggle to get free of the falling aëroplane.

What followed, I shall never positively know. It may have been wholly an hallucination from the shock caused at that instant by the sudden and complete destruction of the building in a cataclysm of German shell-fire—who can gainsay it, since West and I were the only proved survivors? West liked to think that before his recent disappearance, but there were times when he could not; for it was queer that we both had the same hallucination. The hideous occurrence itself was very simple, notable only for what it implied.

The body on the table had risen with a blind and terrible groping, and we had heard a sound. I should not call that sound a voice, for it was too awful. And yet its timbre was not the most awful thing about it. Neither was its message—it had merely screamed, "Jump, Ronald, for God's sake, jump!" The awful thing was its source.

For it had come from the large covered vat in that ghoulish corner of crawling black shadows.

VI.

THE TOMB-LEGIONS

When Dr. Herbert West disappeared a year ago, the Boston police questioned me closely. They suspected that I was holding something back, and perhaps suspected graver things; but I could not tell them the truth because they would not have believed it. They knew, indeed, that West had been connected with activities beyond the credence of ordinary men; for his hideous experiments in the reanimation of dead bodies had long been too extensive to admit of perfect secrecy; but the final soul-shattering catastrophe held elements of daemoniac phantasy which make even me doubt the reality of what I saw.

I was West's closest friend and only confidential assistant. We had met years before, in medical school, and from the first I had shared his terrible researches. He had slowly tried to perfect a solution which, injected into the veins of the newly deceased, would restore life; a labour demanding an abundance of fresh corpses and therefore involving the most unnatural actions. Still more shocking were the products of some of the experiments—grisly masses of flesh that had been dead, but that West waked to a blind, brainless, nauseous animation. These were the usual results, for in order to reawaken the mind it was necessary to have specimens so absolutely fresh that no decay could possibly affect the delicate brain-cells.

This need for very fresh corpses had been West's moral undoing. They were hard to get, and one awful day he had secured his specimen while it was still alive and vigorous. A struggle, a needle, and a powerful alkaloid had transformed it to a very fresh corpse, and the experiment had succeeded for a brief and memorable moment; but West had emerged with a soul calloused and seared, and a hardened eye which sometimes glanced with a kind of hideous and calculating appraisal at men of especially sensitive brain and especially vigorous physique. Toward the last I became acutely afraid of West, for he began to look at me that way. People did not seem to notice his glances, but they noticed my fear; and after his disappearance used that as a basis for some absurd suspicions.

West, in reality, was more afraid than I; for his abominable pursuits entailed a life of furtiveness and dread of every shadow. Partly it was the police he feared; but sometimes his nervousness was deeper and more nebulous, touching on certain indescribable things into which he had injected a morbid life, and from which he had not seen that life depart. He usually finished his experiments with a revolver, but a few times he had not been quick enough. There was that first specimen on whose rifled grave marks of clawing were later seen. There was also that Arkham professor's body which had done cannibal things before it had been captured and thrust unidentified into a madhouse cell at Sefton, where it beat the walls for sixteen years. Most of the other possibly surviving results were things less easy to speak of—for in later years West's scientific zeal had degenerated to an unhealthy and fantastic mania, and he had spent his chief skill in vitalising not entire human bodies but isolated parts of bodies, or parts joined to organic matter other than human. It had become fiendishly disgusting by the time he disappeared; many of the experiments could not even be hinted at in print. The Great War, through which both of us served as surgeons, had intensified this side of West.

In saying that West's fear of his specimens was nebulous, I have in mind particularly its complex nature. Part of it came merely from knowing of the existence of such nameless monsters, while another part arose from apprehension of the bodily harm they might under certain circumstances do him. Their disappearance added horror to the situation—of them all West knew the whereabouts of only one, the pitiful asylum thing. Then there was a more subtle fear—a very fantastic sensation resulting from a curious experiment in the Canadian army in 1915. West, in the midst of a severe battle, had reanimated Major Sir Eric Moreland Clapham-Lee, D.S.O., a fellow-physician who knew about his experiments and could have duplicated them. The head had been removed, so that the possibilities of quasi-intelligent life in the trunk might be investigated. Just as the building was wiped out by a German shell, there had been a success. The trunk had moved intelligently; and, unbelievable to relate, we were both sickeningly sure that articulate sounds had come from the detached head as it lay in a shadowy corner of the laboratory. The shell had been merciful, in a way—but West could never feel as certain as he wished, that we two were the only survivors. He used to make shuddering conjectures about the possible actions of a headless physician with the power of reanimating the dead.

West's last quarters were in a venerable house of much elegance, overlooking one of the oldest burying-grounds in Boston. He had chosen the place for purely symbolic and fantastically aesthetic reasons, since most of the interments were of the colonial period and therefore of little use to a scientist seeking very fresh bodies. The laboratory was in a sub-cellar secretly constructed by imported workmen, and contained a huge incinerator for the quiet and complete disposal of such bodies, or fragments and synthetic mockeries of bodies, as might remain from the morbid experiments and unhallowed amusements of the owner. During the excavation of this cellar the workmen had struck some exceedingly ancient masonry; undoubtedly connected with the old burying-ground, yet far too deep to correspond with any known sepulchre therein. After a number of calculations West decided that it represented some secret chamber beneath the tomb of the Averills, where the last interment had been made in 1768. I was with him when he studied the nitrous, dripping walls laid bare by the spades and mattocks of the men, and was prepared for the gruesome thrill which would attend the uncovering of centuried grave-secrets; but for the first time West's new timidity conquered his natural curiosity, and he betrayed his degenerating fibre by ordering the masonry left intact and plastered over. Thus it remained till that final hellish night; part of the walls of the secret laboratory. I speak of West's decadence, but must add that it was a purely mental and intangible thing. Outwardly he was the same to the last—calm, cold, slight, and yellow-haired, with spectacled blue eyes and a general aspect of youth which years and fears seemed never to change. He seemed calm even when he thought of that clawed grave and looked over his shoulder; even when he thought of the carnivorous thing that gnawed and pawed at Sefton bars.

The end of Herbert West began one evening in our joint study when he was dividing his curious glance between the newspaper and me. A strange headline item had struck at him from the crumpled pages, and a nameless titan claw had seemed to reach down through sixteen years. Something fearsome and incredible had happened at Sefton Asylum fifty miles away, stunning the neighbourhood and baffling the police. In the small hours of the morning a body of silent men had entered the grounds and their leader had aroused the attendants. He was a menacing military figure who talked without moving his lips and whose voice seemed almost ventriloquially connected with an immense black case he carried. His expressionless face was handsome to the point of radiant beauty, but had shocked the superintendent when the hall light fell on it—for it was a wax face with eyes of painted glass. Some nameless accident had befallen this man. A larger man guided his steps; a repellent hulk whose bluish face seemed half eaten away by some unknown malady. The speaker had asked for the custody of the cannibal monster committed from Arkham sixteen years before; and upon being refused, gave a signal which precipitated a shocking riot. The fiends had beaten, trampled, and bitten every attendant who did not flee; killing four and finally succeeding in the liberation of the monster. Those victims who could recall the event without hysteria swore that the creatures had acted less like men than like unthinkable automata guided by the wax-faced leader. By the time help could be summoned, every trace of the men and of their mad charge had vanished.

From the hour of reading this item until midnight, West sat almost paralysed. At midnight the doorbell rang, startling him fearfully. All the servants were asleep in the attic, so I answered the bell. As I have told the police, there was no wagon in the street; but only a group of strange-looking figures bearing a large square box which they deposited in the hallway after one of them had grunted in a highly unnatural voice, "Express—prepaid." They filed out of the house with a jerky tread, and as I watched them go I had an odd idea that they were turning toward the ancient cemetery on which the back of the house abutted. When I slammed the door after them West came downstairs and looked at the box. It was about two feet square, and bore West's correct name and present address. It also bore the inscription, "From Eric Moreland Clapham-Lee, St. Eloi, Flanders." Six years before, in Flanders, a shelled hospital had fallen upon the headless reanimated trunk of Dr. Clapham-Lee, and upon the detached head which—perhaps—had uttered articulate sounds.

West was not even excited now. His condition was more ghastly. Quickly he said, "It's the finish—but let's incinerate—this." We carried the thing down to the laboratory—listening. I do not remember many particulars—you can imagine my state of mind—but it is a vicious lie to say it was Herbert West's body which I put into the incinerator. We both inserted the whole unopened wooden box, closed the door, and started the electricity. Nor did any sound come from the box, after all.

It was West who first noticed the falling plaster on that part of the wall where the ancient tomb masonry had been covered up. I was going to run, but he stopped me. Then I saw a small black aperture, felt a ghoulish wind of ice, and smelled the charnel bowels of a putrescent earth. There was no sound, but just then the electric lights went out and I saw outlined against some phosphorescence of the nether world a horde of silent toiling things which only insanity—or worse—could create. Their outlines were human, semi-human, fractionally human, and not human at all—the horde was grotesquely heterogeneous. They were removing the stones quietly, one by one, from the centuried wall. And then, as the breach became large enough, they came out into the laboratory in single file; led by a stalking thing with a beautiful head made of wax. A sort of mad-eyed monstrosity behind the leader seized on Herbert West. West did not resist or utter a sound. Then they all sprang at him and tore him to pieces before my eyes, bearing the fragments away into that subterranean vault of fabulous abominations. West's head was carried off by the wax-headed leader, who wore a Canadian officer's uniform. As it disappeared I saw that the blue eyes behind the spectacles were hideously blazing with their first touch of frantic, visible emotion.

Servants found me unconscious in the morning. West was gone. The incinerator contained only unidentifiable ashes. Detectives have questioned me, but what can I say? The Sefton tragedy they will not connect with West; not that, nor the men with the box, whose existence they deny. I told them of the vault, and they pointed to the unbroken plaster wall and laughed. So I told them no more. They imply that I am a madman or a murderer—probably I am mad. But I might not be mad if those accursed tomb-legions had not been so silent.

H. P. LOVECRAFT

PICKMAN'S MODEL

YOU NEEDN'T THINK I'm crazy, Eliot—plenty of others have queerer prejudices than this. Why don't you laugh at Oliver's grandfather, who won't ride in a motor? If I don't like that damned subway, it's my own business; and we got here more quickly anyhow in the taxi. We'd have had to walk up the hill from Park Street if we'd taken the car.

I know I'm more nervous than I was when you saw me last year, but you don't need to hold a clinic over it. There's plenty of reason, God knows, and I fancy I'm lucky to be sane at all. Why the third degree? You didn't use to be so inquisitive.

Well, if you must hear it, I don't know why you shouldn't. Maybe you ought to, anyhow, for you kept writing me like a grieved parent when you heard I'd begun to cut the Art Club and keep away from Pickman. Now that he's disappeared I go round to the club once in a while, but my nerves aren't what they were.

No, I don't know what's become of Pickman, and I don't like to guess. You might have surmised I had some inside information when I dropped him—and that's why I don't want to think where he's gone. Let the police find what they can—it won't be much, judging from the fact that they don't know yet of the old North End place he hired under the name of Peters.

I'm not sure that I could find it again myself—not that I'd ever try, even in broad daylight!

Yes, I do know, or am afraid I know, why he maintained it. I'm coming to that. And I think you'll understand before I'm through why I don't tell the police. They would ask me to guide them, but I couldn't go back there even if I knew the way. There was something there—and now I can't use the subway or (and you may as well have your laugh at this, too) go down into cellars any more.

I should think you'd have known I didn't drop Pickman for the same silly reasons that fussy old women like Dr. Reid or Joe Minot or Rosworth did. Morbid art doesn't shock me, and when a man has the genius Pickman had I feel it an honour to know him, no matter what direction his work takes. Boston never had a greater painter than Richard Upton Pickman. I said it at first and I say it still, and I never swerved an inch, either, when he showed that "Ghoul Feeding." That, you remember, was when Minot cut him.

You know, it takes profound art and profound insight into Nature to turn out stuff like Pickman's. Any magazine-cover hack can splash paint around wildly and call it a nightmare or a Witches' Sabbath or a portrait of the devil, but only a great painter can make such a thing really scare or ring true. That's because only a real artist knows the actual anatomy of the terrible or the physiology of fear—the exact sort of lines and proportions that connect up with latent instincts or hereditary memories of fright, and the proper colour contrasts and lighting effects to stir the dormant sense of strangeness. I don't have to tell you why a Fuseli really brings a shiver while a cheap ghost-story frontispiece merely makes us laugh. There's something those fellows catch—beyond life—that they're able to make us catch for a second. Doré had it. Sime has it. Angarola of Chicago has it. And Pickman had it as no man ever had it before or—I hope to Heaven—ever will again.

Don't ask me what it is they see. You know, in ordinary art, there's all the difference in the world between the vital, breathing things drawn from Nature or models and the artificial truck that commercial small fry reel off in a bare studio by rule. Well, I should say that the really weird artist has a kind of vision which makes models, or summons up what amounts to actual scenes from the spectral world he lives in. Anyhow, he manages to turn out results that differ from the pretender's mince-pie dreams in just about the same way that the life painter's results differ from the concoctions of a correspondence-school cartoonist. If I had ever seen what Pickman saw—but no! Here, let's have a drink before we get any deeper. God, I wouldn't be alive if I'd ever seen what that man—if he was a man—saw!

You recall that Pickman's forte was faces. I don't believe anybody since Goya could put so much of sheer hell into a set of features or a twist of expression. And before Goya you have to go back to the mediaeval chaps who did the gargoyles and chimaeras on Notre Dame and Mont Saint-Michel. They believed all sorts of things—and maybe they saw all sorts of things, too, for the Middle Ages had some curious phases. I remember your asking Pickman yourself once, the year before you went away, wherever in thunder he got such ideas and visions. Wasn't that a nasty laugh he gave you? It was partly because of that laugh that Reid dropped him. Reid, you know, had just taken up comparative pathology, and was full of pompous "inside stuff" about the biological or evolutionary significance of this or that mental or physical

symptom. He said Pickman repelled him more and more every day, and almost frightened him towards the last—that the fellow's features and expression were slowly developing in a way he didn't like; in a way that wasn't human. He had a lot of talk about diet, and said Pickman must be abnormal and eccentric to the last degree. I suppose you told Reid, if you and he had any correspondence over it, that he'd let Pickman's paintings get on his nerves or harrow up his imagination. I know I told him that myself—then.

But keep in mind that I didn't drop Pickman for anything like this. On the contrary, my admiration for him kept growing; for that "Ghoul Feeding" was a tremendous achievement. As you know, the club wouldn't exhibit it, and the Museum of Fine Arts wouldn't accept it as a gift, and I can add that nobody would buy it, so Pickman had it right in his house till he went. Now his father has it in Salem—you know Pickman comes of old Salem stock, and had a witch ancestor hanged in 1692.

I got into the habit of calling on Pickman quite often, especially after I began making notes for a monograph on weird art. Probably it was his work which put the idea into my head, and anyhow, I found him a mine of data and suggestions when I came to develop it. He showed me all the paintings and drawings he had about; including some pen-and-ink sketches that would, I verily believe, have got him kicked out of the club if many of the members had seen them. Before long I was pretty nearly a devotee, and would listen for hours like a schoolboy to art theories and philosophic speculations wild enough to qualify him for the Danvers asylum. My hero-worship, coupled with the fact that people generally were commencing to have less and less to do with him, made him get very confidential with me; and one evening he hinted that if I were fairly close-mouthed and none too squeamish, he might show me something rather unusual—something a bit stronger than anything he had in the house.

"You know," he said, "there are things that

won't do for Newbury Street—things that are out of place here, and that can't be conceived here, anyhow. It's my business to catch the overtones of the soul, and you won't find those in a parvenu set of artificial streets on made land. Back Bay isn't Boston—it isn't anything yet, because it's had no time to pick up memories and attract local spirits. If there are any ghosts here, they're the tame ghosts of a salt marsh and a shallow cove; and I want human ghosts—the ghosts of beings highly organized enough to have looked on hell and known the meaning of what they saw.

"The place for an artist to live is the North End. If any aesthete were sincere, he'd put up with the slums for the sake of the massed traditions. God, man! Don't you realize that places like that weren't merely made, but actually grew? Generation after generation lived and felt and died there, and in days when people weren't afraid to live and die. Don't you know there was a mill on Copp's Hill in 1632, and that half the present streets were laid out by 1650? I can show you houses that have stood two centuries and a half and more; houses that have witnessed what would make a modern house crumble into powder. What do moderns know of life and the forces behind it? You call the Salem witchcraft a delusion, but I'll wager my four-times-great-grandmother could have told you things. They hanged her on Gallows Hill, with Cotton Mather looking sanctimoniously on. Mather, damn him, was afraid somebody might succeed in kicking free of this accursed cage of monotony—I wish someone had laid a spell on him or sucked his blood in the night!

"I can show you a house he lived in, and I can show you another one he was afraid to enter in spite of all his fine bold talk. He knew things he didn't dare put into that stupid *Magnalia* or that puerile *Wonders of the Invisible World*. Look here, do you know the whole North End once had a set of tunnels that kept certain people in touch with each other's houses, and the burying ground, and the sea? Let them prosecute and persecute above ground—things went on every day that they couldn't reach, and voices laughed at night that they couldn't place!

"Why, man, out of ten surviving houses built before 1700 and not moved since I'll wager that in eight I can show you something queer in the cellar. There's hardly a month that you don't read of workmen finding bricked-up arches and wells leading nowhere in this or that old place as it comes down—you could see one near Henchman Street from the elevated last year. There were witches and what their spells summoned; pirates and what they brought in from the sea; smugglers; privateers—and I tell you, people knew how to live, and how to enlarge the bounds of life, in the old time! This wasn't the only world a bold and wise man could know—faugh! And to think of today in contrast, with such pale-pink brains that even a club of supposed artists gets shudders and convulsions if a picture goes beyond the feelings of a Beacon Street teatable!

"The only saving grace of the present is that it's too damned stupid to question the past very closely. What do maps and records and guidebooks really tell of the North End? Bah! At a guess I'll guarantee to lead you to thirty or forty alleys and networks of alleys north of Prince Street that aren't suspected of ten living beings outside of the foreigners that swarm them. And what do those Dagoes know of their meaning? No, Thurber, these ancient places are dreaming gorgeously and over-flowing with wonder and terror and escapes from the commonplace, and yet there's not a living soul to understand or profit by them. Or rather, there's only one living soul—for I haven't been digging around in the past for nothing!

"See here, you're interested in this sort of thing. What if I told you that I've got another studio up there, where I can catch the night-spirit of antique horror and paint things that I couldn't even think of in Newbury Street? Naturally I don't tell those cursed old maids at the club—with Reid, damn him, whispering even as it is that I'm a sort of monster bound down the toboggan of reverse evolution. Yes, Thurber, I decided long ago that one must paint terror as well as beauty from life, so I did some exploring in places where I had reason to know terror lives.

"I've got a place that I don't believe three living Nordic men besides myself have ever seen. It isn't so very far from the elevated as distance goes, but it's centuries away as the soul goes. I took it because of the queer old brick well in the cellar—one of the sort I told you about. The shack's almost tumbling down so that nobody else would live there, and I'd hate to tell you how little I pay for it. The windows are boarded up, but I like that all the better, since I don't want daylight for what I do. I paint in the cellar, where the inspiration is thickest, but I've other rooms furnished on the ground floor. A Sicilian owns it, and I've hired it under the name of Peters.

"Now, if you're game, I'll take you there tonight. I think you'd enjoy the pictures, for, as I said, I've let myself go a bit there. It's no vast tour—I sometimes do it on foot, for I don't want to attract attention with a taxi in such a place. We can take the shuttle at the South Station for Battery Street, and after that the walk isn't much."

Well, Eliot, there wasn't much for me to do after that harangue but to keep myself from running instead of walking for the first vacant cab we could sight. We changed to the elevated at the South Station, and at about twelve o'clock had climbed down the steps at Battery Street and struck along the old waterfront past Constitution Wharf. I didn't keep track of the cross streets, and can't tell you yet which it was we turned up, but I know it wasn't Greenough Lane.

When we did turn, it was to climb through the deserted length of the oldest and dirtiest alley I ever saw in my life, with crumbling-looking gables, broken small-paned windows, and archaic chimneys that stood out half-disintegrated against the moonlit sky. I don't believe there were three houses in sight that hadn't been standing in Cotton Mather's time—certainly I glimpsed at least two with an overhang, and once I thought I saw a peaked roof-line of the almost forgotten pre-gambrel type, though antiquarians tell us there are none left in Boston.

From that alley, which had a dim light, we turned to the left into an equally silent and still narrower alley with no light at all: and in a minute made what I think was an obtuse-angled bend towards the right in the dark. Not long after this Pickman produced a flashlight and revealed an antediluvian ten-panelled door that looked damnably worm-eaten. Unlocking it, he ushered me into a barren hallway with what was once splendid dark-oak panelling—simple, of course, but thrillingly suggestive of the times of Andros and Phipps and the Witchcraft. Then he took me through a door on the left, lighted an oil lamp, and told me to make myself at home.

Now, Eliot, I'm what the man in the street would call fairly "hard-boiled," but I'll confess that what I saw on the walls of that room gave me a bad turn. They were his pictures, you know—the ones he couldn't paint or even show in Newbury Street—and he was right when he said he had "let himself go." Here—have another drink—I need one anyhow!

There's no use in my trying to tell you what they were like, because the awful, the blasphemous horror, and the unbelievable loathsomeness and moral foetor came from simple touches quite beyond the power of words to classify. There was none of the exotic technique you see in Sidney Sime, none of the trans-Saturnian landscapes and lunar fungi that Clark Ashton Smith uses to freeze the blood. The backgrounds were mostly old churchyards, deep woods, cliffs by the sea, brick tunnels, ancient panelled rooms, or simple vaults of masonry. Copp's Hill Burying Ground, which could not be many blocks away from this very house, was a favourite scene.

The madness and monstrosity lay in the figures in the foreground—for Pickman's morbid art was pre-eminently one of demoniac portraiture. These figures were seldom completely human, but often approached humanity in varying degree. Most of the bodies, while roughly bipedal, had a forward slumping, and a vaguely canine cast. The texture of the majority was a kind of unpleasant rubberiness. Ugh! I can see them now! Their occupations—well, don't ask me to be too precise. They were usually feeding—I won't say on what. They were sometimes shown in groups in cemeteries or underground passages, and often appeared to be in battle over their prey—or rather, their treasure-trove. And what damnable expressiveness Pickman sometimes gave the sightless faces of this charnel booty! Occasionally the things were shown leaping through open windows at night, or squatting on the chests of sleepers, worrying at their throats. One canvas showed a ring of them baying about a hanged witch on Gallows Hill, whose dead face held a close kinship to theirs.

But don't get the idea that it was all this hideous business of theme and setting which struck me faint. I'm not a three-year-old kid, and I'd seen much like this before. It was the faces, Eliot, those accursed faces, that leered and slavered out of the canvas with the very breath of life! By God, man, I verily believe they were alive! That nauseous wizard had waked the fires of hell in pigment, and his brush had been a nightmare-spawning wand. Give me that decanter, Eliot!

There was one thing called "The Lesson"—Heaven pity me, that I ever saw it! Listen—can you fancy a squatting circle of nameless dog-like things in a churchyard teaching a small child how to feed like themselves? The price of a changeling, I suppose—you know the old myth about how the weird people leave their spawn in cradles in exchange for the human babes they steal. Pickman was showing what happens to those stolen babes—how they grow up—and then I began to see a hideous relationship in the faces of the human and non-human figures. He was, in all his gradations of morbidity between the frankly non-human and the degradedly human, establishing a sardonic linkage and evolution. The dog-things were developed from mortals!

And no sooner had I wondered what he made of their own young as left with mankind in the form of changelings, than my eye caught a picture embodying that very thought. It was that of an ancient Puritan interior—a heavily beamed room with lattice windows, a settle, and clumsy seventeenth-century furniture, with the family sitting about while the father read from the Scriptures. Every face but one showed nobility and reverence, but that one reflected the mockery of the pit. It was that of a young man in years, and no doubt belonged to a supposed son of that pious father, but in essence it was the kin of the unclean things. It was their changeling—and in a spirit of supreme irony Pickman had given the features a very perceptible resemblance to his own.

By this time Pickman had lighted a lamp in an adjoining room and was politely holding open the door for me; asking me if I would care to see his "modern studies." I hadn't been able to give him much of my opinions—I was too speechless with fright and loathing—but I think he fully understood and felt highly complimented. And now I want to assure you again, Eliot, that I'm no mollycoddle to scream at anything which shows a bit of departure from the usual. I'm middle-aged and decently sophisticated, and I guess you saw enough of me in France to know I'm not easily knocked out. Remember, too, that I'd just about recovered my wind and gotten used to those frightful pictures which turned colonial New England into a kind of annex of hell. Well, in spite of all this, that next room forced a real scream out of me, and I had to clutch at the doorway to keep from keeling over. The other chamber had shown a pack of ghouls and witches over-running the world of our forefathers, but this one brought the horror right into our own daily life!

God, how that man could paint! There was a study called "Subway Accident," in which a flock of the vile things were clambering up from some unknown catacomb through a crack in the floor of the Boston Street subway and attacking a crowd of people on the platform. Another showed a dance on Copp's Hill among the tombs with the background of today. Then there were any number of cellar views, with monsters creeping in through holes and rifts in the masonry and grinning as they squatted behind barrels or furnaces and waited for their first victim to descend the stairs.

One disgusting canvas seemed to depict a vast cross-section of Beacon Hill, with ant-like armies of the mephitic monsters squeezing themselves through burrows that honeycombed the ground. Dances in the modern cemeteries were freely pictured, and another conception somehow shocked me more than all the rest—a scene in an unknown vault, where scores of the beasts crowded about one who had a well-known Boston guidebook and was evidently reading aloud. All were pointing to a certain passage, and every face seemed so distorted with epileptic and reverberant laughter that I almost thought I heard the fiendish echoes. The title of the picture was, "Holmes, Lowell and Longfellow Lie Buried in Mount Auburn."

As I gradually steadied myself and got readjusted to this second room of deviltry and morbidity, I began to analyse some of the points in my sickening loathing. In the first place, I said to myself, these things repelled because of the utter inhumanity and callous crudity they showed in Pickman. The fellow must be a relentless enemy of all mankind to take such glee in the torture of brain and flesh and the degradation of the mortal tenement. In the second place, they terrified because of their very greatness. Their art was the art that convinced—when we saw the pictures we saw the demons themselves and were afraid of them. And the queer part was, that Pickman got none of his power from the use of selectiveness or bizarrerie. Nothing was blurred, distorted, or conventionalized; outlines were sharp and lifelike, and details were almost painfully defined. And the faces!

It was not any mere artist's interpretation that we saw; it was pandemonium itself, crystal clear in stark objectivity. That was it, by Heaven! The man was not a fantaisiste or romanticist at all—he did not even try to give us the churning, prismatic ephemera of dreams, but coldly and sardonically reflected some stable, mechanistic, and well-established horror-world which he saw fully, brilliantly, squarely, and unfalteringly. God knows what that world can have been, or where he ever glimpsed the blasphemous shapes that loped and trotted and crawled through it; but whatever the baffling source of his images, one thing was plain. Pickman was in every sense—in conception and in execution—a thorough, painstaking, and almost scientific realist.

My host was now leading the way down the cellar to his actual studio, and I braced myself for some hellish efforts among the unfinished canvases. As we reached the bottom of the damp stairs he fumed his flash-light to a corner of the large open space at hand, revealing the circular brick curb of what was evidently a great well in the earthen floor. We walked nearer, and I saw that it must be five feet across, with walls a good foot thick and some six inches above the ground level—solid work of the seventeenth century, or I was much mistaken. That, Pickman said, was the kind of thing he had been talking about—an aperture of the network of tunnels that used to undermine the hill. I noticed idly that it did not seem to be bricked up, and that a heavy disc of wood formed the apparent cover. Thinking of the things this well must have been connected with if Pickman's wild hints had not been mere rhetoric, I shivered slightly; then turned to follow him up a step and through a narrow door into a room of fair size, provided with a wooden floor and furnished as a studio. An acetylene gas outfit gave the light necessary for work.

The unfinished pictures on easels or propped against the walls were as ghastly as the finished ones upstairs, and showed the painstaking methods of the artist. Scenes were blocked out with extreme care, and pencilled guide lines told of the minute exactitude which Pickman used in getting the right perspective and proportions. The man was great—I say it even now, knowing as much as I do. A large camera on a table excited my notice, and Pickman told me that he used it in taking scenes for backgrounds, so that he might paint them from photographs in the studio instead of carting his outfit around the town for this or that view. He thought a photograph quite as good as an actual scene or model for sustained work, and declared he employed them regularly.

There was something very disturbing about the nauseous sketches and half-finished monstrosities that leered round from every side of the room, and when Pickman suddenly unveiled a huge canvas on the side away from the light I could not for my life keep back a loud scream—the second I had emitted that night. It echoed and echoed through the dim vaultings of that ancient and nitrous cellar, and I had to choke back a flood of reaction that threatened to burst out as hysterical laughter. Merciful Creator! Eliot, but I don't know how much was real and how much was feverish fancy. It doesn't seem to me that earth can hold a dream like that!

It was a colossal and nameless blasphemy with glaring red eyes, and it held in bony claws a thing that had been a man, gnawing at the head as a child nibbles at a stick of candy. Its position was a kind of crouch, and as one looked one felt that at any moment it might drop its present prey and seek a juicier morsel! But damn it all, it wasn't even the fiendish subject that made it such an immortal fountain-head of all panic—not that, nor the dog face with its pointed ears, bloodshot eyes, flat nose, and drooling lips. It wasn't the scaly claws nor the mould-caked body nor the half-hooved feet—none of these, though any one of them might well have driven an excitable man to madness.

It was the technique, Eliot—the cursed, the impious, the unnatural technique! As I am a living being, I never elsewhere saw the actual breath of life so fused into a canvas. The monster was there—it glared and gnawed and gnawed and glared—and I knew that only a suspension of Nature's laws could ever let a man paint a thing like that without a model—without some glimpse of the nether world which no mortal unsold to the Fiend has ever had.

Pinned with a thumb-tack to a vacant part of the canvas was a piece of paper now badly curled up—probably, I thought, a photograph from which Pickman meant to paint a background as hideous as the nightmare it was to enhance. I reached out to uncurl and look at it, when suddenly I saw Pickman start as if shot. He had been listening with peculiar intensity ever since my shocked scream had waked unaccustomed echoes in the dark cellar, and now he seemed struck with a fright which, though not comparable to my own, had in it more of the physical than of the spiritual. He drew a revolver and motioned me to silence, then stepped out into the main cellar and closed the door behind him.

I think I was paralysed for an instant. Imitating Pickman's listening, I fancied I heard a faint scurrying sound somewhere, and a series of squeals or beats in a direction I couldn't determine. I thought of huge rats and shuddered. Then there came a subdued sort of clatter which somehow set me all in gooseflesh—a furtive, groping kind of clatter, though I can't attempt to convey what I mean in words. It was like heavy wood falling on stone or brick—wood on brick—what did that make me think of?

It came again, and louder. There was a vibration as if the wood had fallen farther than it had fallen before. After that followed a sharp grating noise, a shouted gibberish from Pickman, and the deafening discharge of all six chambers of a revolver, fired spectacularly as a lion tamer might fire in the air for effect. A muffled squeal or squawk, and a thud. Then more wood and brick grating, a pause, and the opening of the door—at which I'll confess I started violently. Pickman reappeared with his smoking weapon, cursing the bloated rats that infested the ancient well.

"The deuce knows what they eat, Thurber," he grinned, "for those archaic tunnels touched graveyard and witch-den and sea-coast. But whatever it is, they must have run short, for they were devilish anxious to get out. Your yelling stirred them up, I fancy. Better be cautious in these old places—our rodent friends are the one drawback, though I sometimes think they're a positive asset by way of atmosphere and colour."

Well, Eliot, that was the end of the night's adventure. Pickman had promised to show me the place, and Heaven knows he had done it. He led me out of that tangle of alleys in another direction, it seems, for when we sighted a lamp-post we were in a half-familiar street with monotonous rows of mingled tenement blocks and old houses. Charter Street, it turned out to be, but I was too flustered to notice just where we hit it. We were too late for the elevated, and walked back downtown through Hanover Street. I remember that wall. We switched from Tremont up Beacon, and Pickman left me at the corner of Joy, where I turned off. I never spoke to him again.

Why did I drop him? Don't be impatient. Wait till I ring for coffee. We've had enough of the other stuff, but I for one need something. No—it wasn't the paintings I saw in that place; though I'll swear they were enough to get him ostracised in nine-tenths of the homes and clubs of Boston, and I guess you won't wonder now why I have to steer clear of subways and cellars. It was—something I found in my coat the next morning. You know, the curled-up paper tacked to the frightful canvas in the cellar; the thing I thought was a photograph of some scene he meant to use as a background for that monster. That last scare had come while I was reaching to uncurl it, and it seems I had vacantly crumpled it into my pocket. But here's the coffee—take it black, Eliot, if you're wise.

Yes, that paper was the reason I dropped Pickman; Richard Upton Pickman, the greatest artist I have ever known—and the foulest being that ever leaped the bounds of life into the pits of myth and madness. Eliot—old Reid was right. He wasn't strictly human. Either he was born in strange shadow, or he'd found a way to unlock the forbidden gate. It's all the same now, for he's gone—back into the fabulous darkness he loved to haunt. Here, let's have the chandelier going.

Don't ask me to explain or even conjecture about what I burned. Don't ask me, either, what lay behind that mole-like scrambling Pickman was so keen to pass off as rats. There are secrets, you know, which might have come down from old Salem times, and Cotton Mather tells even stranger things. You know how damned lifelike Pickman's paintings were—how we all wondered where he got those faces.

Well—that paper wasn't a photograph of any background, after all. What it showed was simply the monstrous being he was painting on that awful canvas. It was the model he was using—and its background was merely the wall of the cellar studio in minute detail. But by God, Eliot, it was a photograph from life!

MATERNAL INSTINCT

ROBERT BLOCH

ROBERT (ALBERT) BLOCH (1917–1994) was born in Chicago and began a successful and prolific writing career at an early age. An avid reader of the most successful pulp magazine in the science fiction and horror genres, *Weird Tales,* he especially liked the work of H. P. Lovecraft and began a correspondence with him. Lovecraft encouraged Bloch's writing ambitions, resulting in Bloch selling two stories to *Weird Tales* at the age of seventeen.

Bloch went on to write hundreds of short stories and twenty novels, the most famous being *Psycho* (1959), which was memorably filmed by Alfred Hitchcock. While his early work was virtually a pastiche of Lovecraft, he went on to develop his own style. Much of his work was exceptionally dark, gory, and violent for its time, but a plethora of his short fiction has elements of humor—often relying on a pun or wordplay in the last line. A famously warm, friendly, and humorous man in real life, he defended himself against charges of being a macabre writer by saying that he wasn't that way at all. "Why, I have the heart of a small boy," he said. "It's in a jar, on my desk." He commonly created a short story by inventing a good pun for the last line, then writing a story to accompany it.

"Maternal Instinct" was first published posthumously in the anthology *Mondo Zombie,* edited by John Skipp (Baltimore: Cemetery Dance, 2006).

ROBERT BLOCH

MATERNAL INSTINCT

IT WASN'T AT all what Jill expected.

To begin with, there was no sign or inscription—nothing to identify that this was 1600 Pennsylvania Avenue.

And of course it couldn't be, technically speaking, because you had to circle around blocks away on a side street, toward what looked like the kind of abandoned warehouse the hero always goes to in a cop picture.

Only Jill wasn't a hero or a heroine or anything in between. She was just her usual self, but caught in a bind halfway between uncomfortable and unprepared. She sat silently as her driver halted the limo on the driveway before a double door and took out a beeper, some kind of subsonic item. For that matter the driver had been pretty subsonic himself; not one word out of him since he'd picked her up at the hotel. Soul of discretion, right?

But suppose he wasn't a driver? Sure, he'd flashed his papers and wore a uniform, and the limo had the look and feel of a military vehicle. But papers can be forged, uniforms faked and vehicles stolen.

Maybe she was being taken to an abandoned warehouse after all, and the bad guys were waiting in ambush behind the packing-crates or on the catwalks.

A sudden whirring sound jarred Jill's thoughts as the double door slid upward and the limo moved through the opening, headlight beams tunneling through darkness. In their periphery Jill couldn't see either crates or catwalks; the structure was an empty shell concealing the route.

Now the stretch ahead slanted down. Down into the dark, down and dirty. Thank God the limo was air conditioned. Jill wondered how this tunnel was ventilated, if at all. And why no lights? Creepy down here. *Welcome to the White House, heh-heh-heh. This is your host, Satan, broadcasting to you from the Evil Office—*

Jill tensed, uptight. Why were they stopping?

Another beam of light bobbing toward the limo from ahead, fanning the windshield and hood. She could see him now, another uniformidable figure with a flashlight. And behind him, in shadowy silhouette, a carbon copy carrying an Uzi.

Lots of gesturing. And the driver's window going down, his hand extending to exhibit some plastic. The gun-barrel dipped toward him, monitoring his movements. When the flash-beam invaded the car to flood her face she already had her plastic ready. She moved very slowly, because a sudden shot would probably damage her contact lenses and everything behind them.

Inspection completed, the driver rolled up windows and the car moved on, rounding a corner into a lighted white-walled tunnel angling upward. Another sliding door automatically activated ahead, and they wheeled past into a neon-lit underground parking area. Two clean-cut thirty-ish clones in suits with shoulder-holsters were approaching the limo as it pulled into a vacant slot. One positioned himself at the driver's door and the other walked up to hers. As he signaled she unlocked it and he nodded, smiling. When she opened the door he helped her out of the car; always the perfect gentleman, but don't forget that shoulder-holster.

"Welcome to the White House," he said. But there was no *heh-heh-heh,* and no pretense of an introduction. "Follow me, please," was all she got as he led her to an elevator on the far wall.

Her driver started up the limo and made a U-turn in the direction from which they'd come; apparently he hadn't been invited to spend the night in Lincoln's bedroom. If there really was a Lincoln's bedroom upstairs. Hey, so it wasn't a warehouse, but that didn't prove it was the White House either. Her heart began to thud: no world-class coronary, but noticeable.

Jill and her escort entered the elevator; its door closed and the car moved upward in silken silence. Then the door opened and her heart really started to pound.

Because she was in the White House. It stretched before her, beyond the opened elevator door. Now the suit stepped forward, nodding. "This way," he said.

The hall ahead seemed immense. Those high ceilings, that's what did it, dwarfing Jill and her guide as they moved down the carpeted corridor between the fancy-framed portraits and the *don't-you-dare-sit-on-it* furniture. Antiques. Antiques, priceless but impractical for use, like the high ceilings built in a time before everybody except the rich and famous became accustomed to living in cramped quarters. Under the bright lights everything here seemed spacious and gracious.

But where were the rich and famous?

The hall was deserted, side doors closed. Thick carpet muffled footsteps along an aisle empty of everything, even echoes. *Yoo-hoo, where is everybody?*

Jill tried to remember things she'd been told in childhood. About a time the alphabet had been used solely for language, not to designate an FBI, a CIA and other bureaucratic alphabet-

soup. A time when ordinary citizens visited the White House without special invitations to participate in some planned political photo-opportunities. They came because it was their desire to spend Sunday afternoon pressing the flesh of a Harding or Coolidge, but now such innocent events were history.

True, she was here by invitation herself, but not for a photo-opportunity. And there was nothing innocent about this meeting with the President.

Her heart started thumping again, just thinking about him, just as it always had since the days when she first got this thing about him. They were both juniors then—she in college, he in the U.S. Senate. After that she graduated and got the dream-job in the think-tank and he got re-elected; then there was that Clancy woman, thank God he didn't marry her, the silly little bitch would have ruined his chances for nomination for sure, she was just like all the others, those publicized, glorified one-night stands. Long ago—yes, way back in college when she'd first framed his picture from the magazine cover, Jill knew the kind of woman the President *should* marry. Somebody with looks and smarts, that was obvious, but he needed more than that. He needed someone with a real depth of devotion, who could make the White House a home; somebody fit to bear his children. And long ago, when she fitted that magazine cover photo into a frame, she knew who that woman should be. The magazine had picked him as the ideal candidate for President. Right then and there she'd nominated herself as First Lady.

Talk about silly bitches—okay, so he'd been elected, he was now halfway into his second term, and he'd never married. He wasn't gay, that's for sure, but there'd been no lasting relationships. Just as there'd been none for Jill, immersed in the deep end of the think-tank all these years because she was waiting for Mr. Right, that White Knight in the White House; someone who'd never set eyes on her in his life, let alone put her picture on the stand next to Lincoln's bed or Nixon's shredder.

Knock it off, Jill. It's not politically correct. You're thirty-two and he's forty-seven, and you're not on your way to make schoolgirl dreams come true. This is nightmare time.

No sense worrying about her biological clock; she had a job to do. Right now the *politically correct* Secret Service man was reaching out to open the door at the end of the corridor. They passed through an entryway—probably equipped with sensors and metal detectors, although the SS man's weapon didn't trigger a buzz because he halted behind her, then backed out, closing the door and leaving her alone to enter the big room beyond the entry.

At first glance it looked only vaguely office-like, furnished in a style she labeled Early Middle Management—no file cabinets or business machines, just a couch and a couple of comfortable chairs grouped around the coffee table in the corner, and a solitary desk before the window at the center of the room. The setting didn't seem very Presidential, and neither did the man behind the desk.

He was plump, balding, and as Jill observed when he rose from his chair, quite short. His eyes, captive behind thick glasses, peered out at her without expression. Jill hoped her own gaze was noncommittal, offering no hint of her surprise and disappointment. Her heart wasn't pounding now; it was sinking.

And he was coming toward her, holding out a pudgy hand, smiling an avuncular smile, saying, "Pleasure to see you, I'm Hubertus—"

"No names, Doctor."

He had entered the room from a side door at the left, and at the sound of the familiar voice she looked up and saw the familiar figure, the familiar face. His figure and face, not something lighted and made-up for the cameras as she'd feared when she first saw the man behind the desk who might have undergone such tricks of transformation in order to project a youthful image.

But the President was youthful in his own right—a *young* forty-seven with no wrinkles except those around his eyes when he smiled.

He was smiling now and taking her hand, his grip firm, warm, electric. Electric enough to set off the ringing of her biological time-clock.

Ought to ask the Doctor about that, Jill thought. *Dr. Hubertus.* She knew that name. Surgeon General of the United States. Here with her and the President.

He was gesturing toward the furniture grouping at the coffee table. "Please make yourself comfortable," he said.

Jill seated herself. "Thank you, Mr. President."

"No formalities, please." Smiling, he took the chair across from her as Dr. Hubertus moved to the couch. "We don't have time for that." He paused, smile dimming. "Or does it matter now?"

"I'm afraid it does," Jill said. "It matters very much . . ." She was conscious of something ticking, but not her biological clock. This was more like a time-bomb. A time-bomb ready to explode.

"Then let's get started. You brought the data?"

"Yes, sir."

"Forget the *sir* business." The President eyed her expectantly. "What have you got for me—is it in microchip?"

"I'm your microchip," Jill said.

Both men raised their eyebrows, but it was Jill who raised her voice, quickly. "Safer this way. Anything that can be stored can be stolen. Copied, duplicated, faked, you name it. I've had eight separate task teams on this project, each with different approaches to the problem. Five of them don't even know the others exist. And I'm the only one with total input from all eight. All the findings, all the projections, all the hard stats."

The President was staring at her. "Why you?"

"Why not? I have close to eidetic memory. And more important, nobody remembers *me* at all. I'm low-profile, even in my own field, which makes me right for the job."

"What if the wrong people got hold of you?"

"Don't worry, I'd keep my mouth shut."

"And if they tried to make you talk?"

"I'd shut my mouth harder," Jill said. "Bite down on the capsule I planted in a crown. Old-fashioned, but very effective."

The President glanced at Dr. Hubertus, who shrugged. "Suppose we get down to essentials," he said. "We can cover details later on. Right now I'd like to play questions and answers."

"Ready," Jill said.

"Cause?"

"Still unknown. Undetectable micro-organisms from an as-yet untraceable source, possibly long-latent in certain mammalian life forms but presently only observed in humans when recently energized by undetermined—"

"Skip it," said Dr. Hubertus. "We get all that mumbo jumbo from our own witch doctors. Idiots don't have a clue, probably never will. They still haven't even been able to pinpoint the source of the AIDS virus, let alone this one. Besides, its source doesn't matter now. What matters is that it's here."

"Here, there and everywhere," the President said. "That damned, elusive pimpernel." His light tone was forced, quickly disappearing as he faced Jill. "What are the current stats? Not the press-release stuff—do you have a handle on real figures?"

"Latest computation places the domestic total in the neighborhood of one-and-a-half percent." Jill leaned forward. "Which doesn't sound all that threatening until you realize this translates into almost four million people."

"*Former people.*" Dr. Hubertus nodded, eyes grim behind glass. "Dead people. Dead-alive. Who stay alive by eating the living. Who in turn become dead, and they in turn re-animate to eat more of the living who—"

"Food-chain," said the President. "That much we do know. And you don't need more than grade-school math to figure what happens once the exponential growth factor really kicks in."

"It may be worse, worldwide," Jill said. "Hard to project on a global level because we're still getting denials and censorship. But our medics team estimates domestic cases doubling in three months, doubling again a month later. In China, India, Indonesia, Latin America, the rate of increase could be much greater. If we don't come up with a solution—"

The President scowled. "How much longer have we got? I'm talking cover-up. Bottom line."

"A week."

"That's all?"

"It's cropping up all over, and there's no way of our controlling the spread. And word-of-mouth transmits faster than mouth-to-mouth. Gossip spreads an epidemic of its own."

"We've done our best," the President said. "But censorship can't contain it, even if we could jam every broadcast frequency in the world and ban checkout-counter journalism. Not with terminal patients jumping out of deathbeds and morgues running on empty. Of course cemeteries are the real problems. Empty graves are dead giveaways. So far these—these uprisings—seem to take place in rural areas where old-fashioned interments are still common. But once the cities start to go with their Forest Lawns and the kind of places you find in Long Island—" He sighed. "We've had meetings with the funeral-director people. They can't explain why these things are taking place almost at random. It isn't all that easy to break out of a modern coffin, maybe sealed and imbedded in concrete, then burrow up through six feet of earth to the surface. Even if the grave's in sandy soil—"

Jill broke in. "You've talked to undertakers. We asked seismologists. Underground temblors are common everywhere. Earth moves, rock formations shift enough to splinter cheap caskets, loosen dry soil, even if the quake never damages anything on the surface. So wherever and whenever there's enough subterranean movement, the necros may claw their way out."

The President frowned, " 'Necros?' "

Jill shrugged. "It sounds better than 'ghoul.' "

Dr. Hubertus cleared his throat. "Your people must have made some projections about this thing going public. What happens then?"

"Panic. Hysteria. Right now government control is based on military power, but gunfire won't kill the dead. And when people lose faith in government they turn to religion, but established beliefs in resurrection won't offer much comfort. The consensus here is that there'll be an explosion of crazy cults—Zombies for Jesus, the Church of the Living Dead, that kind of thing, which solves nothing."

"What does?" said the President.

"Using what we already do know about the situation."

"Such as?"

"To begin with, studies indicate we may be dealing with two kinds of necros. Type A would be those recently deceased from causes which didn't involve prolonged mental or physical malfunction. Such cases would still be driven by anthropophagism, and subject to necrosis, but at a much slower rate. We have no verified reports of any answering to this description, but the medics don't rule out the possibility, if there was no major impairment prior to death or as a result of escaping from interment."

"The big problem is Type B—victims of violence, accidents, crippling disease, or injuries escaping from their graves. They'll be most vulnerable to necrotic symptoms, and the longer they've been buried the faster they'll decay. Trouble is, it won't be fast enough. If their numbers increase at the present rate we'll be dealing with millions, tens of millions, hundreds of millions, all traumatized by their experiences but a majority simply brain-dead, driven only by a mindless hunger to feed on living flesh. You've got to take steps to prevent this situation." Jill paused, then took the plunge. "You've got to, or in a few years the earth will be blanketed with bodies—or body parts—of the living dead. The earth and the oceans. Clumps, islands, continents of wriggling corpses—"

Dr. Hubertus gestured his interruption. "Tiffany Thayer forecast it for us sixty years ago. *Doctor Arnoldi,* published by Julian Messner in 1934." He nodded. "You think-tank people

aren't the only ones who do their homework. Our own researchers have covered everything in fiction which applies to this reality. Lots of scenarios, but no solutions."

"That's why you're here," the President said. "Solutions."

Jill leaned forward once more. "We think we have one."

"What is it?"

"Cremation," Jill said.

Dr. Hubertus shook his head. "Won't work."

"Why not?"

"It'd take years to build facilities. We're facing an emergency."

"Then use emergency facilities," Jill said. "For starters, there are steel mills closed down all over the country, and industrial plants with blast furnaces. Modify present equipment and you're in business."

"That kind of business will stir up some real opposition," Hubertus told her. "We'd need a lot of secrecy—and security—for such operations. Then there's environmental pollution. Most of these installations are in large urban areas, and we can't relocate them."

"What about military bases? There are hundreds closed and idle." The President and Dr. Hubertus were listening intently now as Jill continued. "They have everything we need. Airstrips, roads, rail access already in place. Housing and accommodations for personnel. Improvise some temporary crematoriums and build permanent structures as you go along."

Jill watched the President out of the corner of her eye as she spoke. His profile was ruggedly handsome, granite-jawed. She imagined how it would look carved on Mt. Rushmore. Or, better still, lying on a pillow next to hers.

Dr. Hubertus was clearing his throat. "Sounds like a Nazi death camp."

"I know, but do we have a choice?"

The President had risen, moving to the wall beside a portrait of Washington. Jill's thought strayed. *Father of his country. Father of my child—*

"This—uh—final solution of yours," the

President said. "Did you come up with it your-self?"

"I told you there was input from each of the teams on the project. But I'm the only one with access to all of the data. What I did, you might say, was put the pieces together."

"And came up with this." The President flicked his forefinger along the side of the por-trait frame. "Just wanted to make sure the pic-ture was straight."

He glanced at Dr. Hubertus, who stood up, moving left to a point beyond the range of Jill's peripheral vision. "What do you think?" the President said.

"It could work. In which case she's right about there being no choice." Dr. Hubertus' voice sounded from behind her, and Jill started to turn, but the President was nodding, smiling to her, speaking to her.

"Well, then," he said. "Welcome aboard."

Jill felt a stinging sensation in her neck, so sharp and so swift that she never had time to bite down on her tooth.

She was dead before she hit the floor.

Actually she never hit the floor, because Hu-bertus caught her as she pitched forward. He and the President placed her on the couch and it was there that the antidote was administered—also by injection, just as the poison had been. At least that's what Dr. Hubertus told her when she started to come out of it.

"Medical miracles," he said, a hint of mock-ery in the eyes behind the lenses. "Twenty sec-onds to kill, twenty minutes to cure."

Jill blinked up at him, "I—I was actually dead?"

"Actually and clinically."

"And you brought me back to life?"

He cleared his throat. "Nobody dies now, re-member? You'd have regained consciousness on your own in a few hours, even without the injec-tion. It merely hastened the process before you suffered brain damage or any immediate inroads of physical decay."

"But why?"

"Isn't it obvious?" He shrugged. "You came up with a solution. And your solution is our problem."

"I don't—"

"If your plan went into effect it would be a thousand times worse than anything the Nazis or Soviets ever came up with in the old days. Not that it'd matter much to what you call the Type B cases, the brain-dead and fast decaying majority. Eventually some such method will be needed to dispose of their sheer mass. But your solution poses an immediate threat to those still in possession of their faculties and still physi-cally able to function. People like us."

"Us?"

"Myself." Dr. Hubertus gestured. "And the President." *No. Dear God, no.*

Jill sat up. And *he* was helping her, smiling at her. "It's true," the President said. "We're Type A." He nodded. "And now, so are you."

She stared at him. "But it can't be. I mean, nothing's changed. I don't feel any different—"

"You will," said Dr. Hubertus. "When the hunger sets in."

Hunger? That part was true. She was hun-gry, unusually so, as she'd had a full breakfast. Granted, it had been an early one, but substan-tial—juice, toast, eggs with bacon.

Jill's stomach churned. The thought of bacon nauseated her—that burned, dead meat. The real need was for something fresh, vibrant, puls-ing with life. That would truly satisfy hunger, and hunger was the sole sensation she felt now.

Dr. Hubertus confronted her with his glassed-in gaze. "Beginning to understand, are you?"

"I don't know." Jill tried to ignore the on-coming hunger pangs that were growing stron-ger, more insistent, commanding attention, demanding satisfaction.

Hubertus spoke softly. "You had to die be-cause you knew too much. There was no alterna-tive."

"Then why revive me?"

"So far Type A seems to be a rarity. We need

allies, people with your skill and intelligence, in the time ahead."

Jill frowned. "How could you be sure I'd co-operate?"

"Matter of necessity. You're one of the few fortunate to come through without physical or mental impairment, but it won't always be that way unless you get proper care and take proper precautions. We must help one another if we intend to survive."

He bent over her, speaking softly. "How long do you think we'd last if the general public knew what we were? And the only way to keep them from knowing is through constant vigilance. As you pointed out, Type A isn't immune to necrosis; all we can do is slow its ravages by cosmetic means, disguise them with deodorant and antiseptic aids. If we can buy ourselves enough time we may be able to come up with additional methods—various surgical procedures, tissue replacement techniques. Eventually we might be able to synthesize organs, or even entire bodies. But right now we must conceal our condition to remain in control."

"That's the big thing." The President's voice echoed approval. "Once we lose control of things, it's all over. For us, and the whole world."

Jill shook her head. "But whatever you do is just a holding action. Sooner or later the end will come."

"Don't be too sure." The President smiled his familiar photo-opportunity smile, grinned his campaign grin, but as she watched him now Jill realized for the first time that he was wearing makeup. Carefully, artfully and almost unnoticeably applied, but makeup, nonetheless. *Disguise the ravages.*

All right, so what was wrong with that? She wore makeup herself, and for the same purpose. Only her reasons would be greater now. Intensified, like the hunger.

Jill tried to put away the thought. Focusing on the President's face, she noticed a tiny white fleck at the corner of his lower lip. It was moving.

"There's still a chance," the President said.

"Given enough time we might find the source of this plague, and the means to halt it. But to buy that time we must be prepared to do what's necessary. Conceal our condition. Stay in power."

"But how do we protect ourselves?" Jill said. "Where do we go?"

"Nowhere." The smile on the still-handsome face was reassuring, though lightly-lipsticked. "This is the White House. I'm the President. Right now that's all the staff and employees know, and with luck we'll keep it that way. Good luck, good care, good diet—that's all we need to see us through."

Diet? Jill's twinge of revulsion gave way to the demands of a stronger instinct. *Hunger.* What was the President saying about hunger now?

"I'm beginning to think that diet is perhaps the most important factor in our survival. A Type B will feed on any form of flesh, no matter how infected or malignant. We've got an advantage here, and with the help of a few other Type A allies at the source, we'll continue to maintain a proper diet."

Jill hesitated. "Where does your food come from?"

"Bethesda." It was Dr. Hubertus who answered. "It's really a fine hospital. As Surgeon General I have certain procedures and priorities with no questions asked." He cleared his throat. "They offer quite a wide selection on their menu. And best of all, they deliver."

The President glanced at his watch. "Lunch time."

It was true, Jill discovered; Bethesda did deliver, though almost three-quarters of an hour passed before the SS man arrived with the order.

"Not to worry," Dr. Hubertus said, as the man departed. "He's one of us."

She didn't worry. And she was no longer repelled, no longer afraid of what had happened or what was to come. Let the whole world rot and wriggle; it would, in time, and she wouldn't care. All that mattered was the hunger.

Whatever virus destroyed natural existence

also perpetuated itself in this hunger, a craving that didn't succumb to decay. She wasn't really alive, it was the hunger that lived on, the hunger her companions shared. And it could live, would live forever. Unleashed and unchecked now, ready to rend and tear, ripping and splintering, chomping, chewing, feasting full.

And so it was Jill's dearest and most secret wish came true. She was having a baby with the President.

BRINGING THE FAMILY

KEVIN J. ANDERSON

THE ASTONISHINGLY PROLIFIC Kevin J.(ames) Anderson (1962–) was born in Racine, Wisconsin, began writing as a young child, and never stopped. Since selling his first novel, *Resurrection, Inc.*, at the age of twenty-five, he has produced more than a hundred books in the ensuing twenty-three years. He was a technical writer and editor for a dozen years before becoming a full-time author. He claims to have received a trophy in the "Writer with No Future" category while amassing 750 rejection slips. After he had published ten novels, Lucasfilm offered him the chance to write *Star Wars* novels, and he has gone on to write more than fifty tie-ins for the company. In addition to being prolific, Anderson is successful, with more than twenty million books in print. Among his best-known works are the ten novels coauthored with Frank Herbert's son Brian, prequels and sequels to the iconic *Dune*, all of which have been international bestsellers, as were the three books based on television's *X-Files* series. Among his frequent collaborations are works with Dean Koontz, Doug Beason, Tom Veitch, and fourteen bestselling volumes with his wife, Rebecca Moesta, in the Young Jedi Knights series. Anderson has also written comic books (for DC) and graphic novels. His numerous honors include awards or nominations for the Nebula, Bram Stoker, SFX Reader's Choice, and American Physics Society Awards, as well as having *Dune: House Harkonnen* named as a 1999 *New York Times* Notable Book.

"Bringing the Family" was first published in *The Ultimate Zombie*, edited by Byron Preiss and John Betancourt (New York: Dell, 1993).

KEVIN J. ANDERSON

BRINGING THE FAMILY

BOTH COFFINS SHIFTED as the wagon wheels hit a rut in the dirt road. Mr. Deakin, sitting beside his silent passenger, Clancy Tucker, clucked to the horses and steered them to the left.

The rhythmic creak of the wagon and the buzz of flies around the coffins were the only sounds in the muggy air. Over the past three days Mr. Deakin and Clancy had already said everything relative strangers could say to each other.

Clancy rocked back and forth to counteract the motion of the wagon. A sprawling expanse of prairie surrounded them, mile after mile of

green grassland broken only by the ribbonlike track heading north. Clancy looked up at the early afternoon sun. "Time to stop."

Mr. Deakin groaned. "We got hours of daylight left."

Clancy made his lips thin and white. "We gotta be sure we get those graves dug by dark."

"Do you realize how stupid this is, Clancy? Night after night—"

"A promise is a promise." Clancy pointed to a patch of thin grass next to a few drying puddles from the last thunderstorm. "Looks like a good place over there."

With only a grunt for an answer, Mr. Deakin

263

pulled the horses to the side and brought them to a stop. The rotten smell settled around them. Clancy Tucker had insisted on making this journey in the heat and humidity of summer; in winter and spring, he said, the ground was frozen too hard to keep reburying his ma and dad along the way.

Clancy grabbed a pickax from the wagon bed and sauntered over to the flat spot. By now they had this ritual down to a science. Mr. Deakin said nothing as he unhitched the horses, hobbled them, and began to rub them down. These horses were the only asset he had left, and he insisted on tending them before helping Clancy on his fool's errand.

Clancy swung the pickax, chopping the woven grass roots. His bright bulging eyes looked as if someone with big hands had squeezed him too tightly at the middle. He slipped one suspender off his shoulder, and a dark, damp shadow of perspiration seeped from his underarms.

As he worked, Clancy hummed an endless hymn that Mr. Deakin recognized as "Bringing in the Sheaves." The chorus went around and around without ever finding its way to the last verse. Over the hours, between the humming and the stench from the unearthed coffins, Mr. Deakin wanted to shove Clancy's head under one of the wheels.

When he finished with the horses, he pulled a shovel from between the two coffins and went over to help Clancy. To make the daily task more difficult, Clancy insisted on digging two separate graves, one for his ma and one for his dad, rather than a single large pit for both coffins.

They worked for more than an hour in the suffocating heat of afternoon, surrounded by flies and the sweat on their own bodies. Mr. Deakin had run out of snuff on the first day, and his little pocket jar held only a smear or two of the camphor ointment he kept for sore muscles, which he also used to burn the putrid smell from his nostrils.

Mr. Deakin's body ached, his hands felt flayed with blisters, and he did his best to shut off all thought. He would work like one of those escaped slaves from down south, forced to labor all day long in the cotton fields. Clancy Tucker's family had kept a freed slave to tend their home, and she had spooked Clancy badly, filling his head with strange ideas. Or maybe Clancy just had strange ideas all by himself.

A month before, Mr. Deakin would never have imagined himself stooping to such crazy tasks as digging up coffins and burying them night after night on a slow journey to Wisconsin. But an Illinois tornado had flattened his house, knocked down the barn, and left him with nothing.

Standing in the aftermath of that storm, under a sky that had cleared to a mocking blue, Mr. Deakin had wanted to shake his fist at the clouds and shout, but he only hung his head in silent despair. He had worked his whole life to compile meager possessions on a homestead and some rented cropland. It would be months before his harvest came in, and he had no way to pay the rent in the meantime; the tornado had crushed his harvesting equipment, smashed his barn. After the storm, only two horses had stood surrounded by the wreckage of their small corral, bewildered and as shocked by the disaster as Mr. Deakin.

His life ruined, Mr. Deakin had had no choice but to say yes when Clancy Tucker had made his proposition. . . .

"Make it six feet deep now!" Clancy said, throwing wet earth over his shoulder into a mound beside the grave. Fat earthworms wriggled in the clods, trying to grope their way back to darkness. Mr. Deakin felt his muscles aching as he stomped on the shovel with his boot and hefted up another load of dirt. "What difference does it make if they're six feet under or five and a half?" he muttered.

Beside him, standing waist-deep in the companion grave, Clancy looked at him strangely, as if the answer were obvious. The floppy brim of his hat cast a shadow across his face. "Why, because anything less than six feet, and *they could dig their way back up by morning*!"

Mr. Deakin felt his skin crawl and turned back to his work. Clancy Tucker either had a sick sense of humor, or just a sick mind. . . .

Only a day after the tornado had struck, when things seemed bleakest, Mr. Deakin stood alone in the ruins of his homestead. He watched Clancy Tucker walk toward him across the puddle-dotted field. "Good morning, Mr. Deakin," he had said.

"Morning," Mr. Deakin said, leaving the "good" off.

"You know my brother Jerome recently founded a town up in Wisconsin—Tucker's Grove. Can I hire you to help me bring the family up there? You look like you could use a lucky break right about now."

"How much is it worth?" Mr. Deakin asked.

Clancy folded his hands together. "I can offer you this. If you'd give us a ride on your wagon up to Wisconsin, my brother will give you your very own farm, a homestead as big as this one. And it'll be yours, not rented. Lots of land to be had up there. In the meantime, we can loan you enough hard currency to take care of your business here." Clancy held out a handful of silver coins. "We know you need the help."

Mr. Deakin could hardly believe what he heard. The Tuckers had no surviving family— Clancy and his broad-chested brother Jerome were the only sons. Who else would they be taking along?

Clancy nodded again. "It would be the Christian thing to do, Mr. Deakin. Neighbor helping neighbor."

So he had agreed to the deal. Not until they were ready to set out did he learn that Clancy wanted to haul the exhumed coffins of his recently deceased mother and father. By the time Mr. Deakin found out, Clancy had already paid some of Mr. Deakin's most important debts, binding him to his word. . . .

It was deep twilight by the time they had two graves dug and both coffins lowered into the ground with thick hemp ropes. They finished packing down the mounds of earth, leaving the rope ends aboveground for easy lifting the next

morning. Mr. Deakin built a small fire to make coffee and warm their supper.

He felt stiff and sore as he bedded down for the night, taking a blanket from the wagon bed. Now that the cool night air smelled clean around him, with no corpse odor hanging about, he wished he had saved some of that camphor for his aching muscles.

Clancy Tucker lay across the fresh earth of the two graves. Mr. Deakin grabbed another blanket and tossed it toward him, but the other man did not look up. Clancy placed his ear against the ground, as if listening for sounds of something stirring below.

ONE OF THE townspeople had used a heated iron spike to burn letters on a plank. *WELCOME TO COMPROMISE, ILLINOIS.* The population tally had been scratched out and rewritten several times, but it looked as if folk no longer kept track. The townspeople watched them approach down the dirt path.

The flat blandness of unending grassland and the corduroy of cornfields swept out to where the land met the sky. On the horizon, gray clouds began building into thunderheads.

"Don't see no church here," Clancy said, "not one with a steeple anyway."

"Town's too small probably," Mr. Deakin answered.

Clancy set his mouth. "Tucker's Grove might be small, but the very first thing Jerome's building will be his church."

Mr. Deakin saw a building attached to the side of the general store and realized that this was probably a gathering place and a saloon. Some townspeople wandered out to watch their arrival, lounging against the boardwalk rails. A gaunt man with bushy eyebrows and thinning steel-gray hair stepped out from the general store like an official emissary.

But when the storekeeper saw the coffins in back of the wagon, he wrinkled his nose. The others covered their noses and moved upwind. Without a word of greeting, the storekeeper wiped his stained white apron and said, "Who's in the coffins?"

"My beloved parents," Clancy said.

"Sorry to hear that," the storekeeper said. "Not common to see someone hauling bodies cross country in the summer heat. I reckon the first thing you'll want is some salt to fill them boxes. It'll cut down the rot."

Mr. Deakin felt his mouth go dry. He didn't want to say that they had little to pay for such an extravagant quantity of salt. But Clancy interrupted.

"Actually," he looked at the other townspeople, "we'd prefer a place to bury these coffins for the night. If you have a graveyard, perhaps? I'm sure after our long journey—" he patted the dirt-stained tops of the coffins, "they would prefer a peaceful night's rest. The ground is hallowed, ain't it?"

The storekeeper scowled. "We got a graveyard over by the stand of trees there, but no church yet. A Presbyterian circuit rider comes along every week or so, not necessarily on Sundays. He's due back anytime now, if you'd like to wait and hold some kind of service."

Mr. Deakin didn't know what to say. The entire situation seemed unreal. He tried to cut off his companion's crazy talk, but Clancy Tucker wouldn't be interrupted.

"Presbyterian? I'm a good Methodist, and my parents were good Methodists. My brother Jerome is even a Methodist minister, self-ordained."

"Clancy—" Mr. Deakin began.

Clancy sighed. "Well, it's only for the night, after all." He looked at Mr. Deakin and lowered his voice. "Hallowed ground. They won't try to come back up, so we don't need to dig so deep."

The storekeeper put his hands behind his apron. "Digging up graves after you planted the coffins? If you want to bury them in our graveyard, that's your business. But we won't be wanting you to disturb what's been reverently put to rest."

Mr. Deakin refrained from pointing out that these particular coffins had been buried and dug up a number of times already.

"You wouldn't be wanting me to break a sacred oath either, would you?" Clancy turned his bulging eyes toward the man; he didn't blink for a long time. "I swore to my parents, on their deathbeds, that I would bring them with me when I moved to Wisconsin. And I'm not leaving them here after all this way."

Seemingly from out of nowhere, Clancy produced a coin and tossed it to the storekeeper, who refused to come closer to the wagons because of the stench. "Are you trying to buy my agreement?" the storekeeper asked.

"No. It's for the horses. We'll need some oats."

THOUGH THE GRAVEYARD of Compromise was small, many wooden crosses protruded like scarecrows. The townspeople did not offer to help Mr. Deakin and Clancy dig, but a few of them watched.

Mr. Deakin pulled the wagon to an empty spot, careful not to let the horses tread on the other graves. As the two of them fell to work with their shovels, Clancy kept looking at the other grave markers. He jutted his stubbled chin toward a row of crosses, marking the graves of an entire family that had died from diphtheria, according to the scrawled words.

"My parents died from scarlet fever," Clancy said. "Jerome caught it first, and he was so sick we thought he'd never get up again. He kept rolling around, sweating, raving. He wouldn't let our Negro Maggie go near him. When the fever broke, his eyes had a whole different sparkle to them, and he talked about how God had showed him a vision of our promised land. Jerome knew he was supposed to found a town in Wisconsin.

"He kept talking about it until we got fired up by his enthusiasm. He wanted to pack up everything we had and strike off, but then Ma and Dad caught the fever themselves, probably from tending Jerome so close."

Mr. Deakin pressed his lips together and kept digging in the soft earth. He didn't want to wallow in his own loss, and he didn't want to wallow in Clancy Tucker's either.

"When they were both sweating with fever, they claimed to share Jerome's vision. They were terrified that Jerome and I would leave them behind. So I promised we would bring them along, no matter what. Oh, they wanted to come so bad. Maggie heard them and she said she could help."

Clancy didn't even pause for breath as he continued. "I could see how bothered Jerome was, because he wanted to leave right away. Our parents were getting worse and worse. They certainly couldn't stand a wagon ride, and it didn't look like they had much time left.

"One day, after Jerome had been sitting with them for a long time, he came out of their room. His face was frightful with so much grief. He said that their souls had flown off to Heaven." Clancy's eyes glowed.

"He left the day afterward, going alone to scout things out, while I took care of details until I could follow, bringing the family. Jerome is waiting for us there now."

Clancy looked up. He had a smear of mud along one cheek. His eyes looked as if they wanted to spill over with tears, but they didn't dare. "So you see why it's so important to me. Ma and Dad have to be there with us. They have their part to play, even if it's just to be the first two in our graveyard."

Mr. Deakin said nothing; Clancy didn't seem to want him to.

THE SUN BEGAN to rise in a pool of molten orange. Mr. Deakin dutifully went back to Clancy Tucker, who had slept up against a wagon wheel. Mr. Deakin's head throbbed, but he had not gotten himself so drunk in the saloon that he forgot his obligations, bizarre though they might be.

He and Clancy set to work on the dewy grass with their shovels, digging out the loosened earth they had piled into graves only the night before.

Mr. Deakin looked toward town, sensing rather than hearing the group of people moving toward them. Clancy didn't notice, but Mr. Deakin halted, propped the shovel into the dirt where it rested against the coffin lid. Clancy unearthed the top of the second coffin, and then stopped as the group approached. He went over to stand by the wagon.

The people carried sticks and farm implements, marching along with their faces screwed up and squinting as they stared into the rising sun. They swaggered as if they had just been talked into a fit of righteous anger.

At the front of the group strode a tall man dressed in a black frock coat and a stiff-brimmed black hat. Mr. Deakin realized that this must be the Presbyterian circuit rider, just in time to stir up trouble.

"We come to take action against two blasphemers!" the circuit rider said.

"Amen!" the people answered.

The preacher had a deep-throated voice, as if every word he uttered was too heavy with import to be spoken in a normal voice. He stepped close, and the sunlight shone full on his face. His weathered features were stretched over a frame of bone, as if he had seen too many cycles of abundance and famine.

The bushy-browed storekeeper stood beside him. "We ain't letting you dig up graves in our town."

"Grave robbers!" the circuit rider spat. "How dare you disturb those buried here? You'll roast in Hell."

"Amen!" the chorus said again.

Mr. Deakin made no move with his shovel, looking at the group and feeling cold. He had already lost everything he had, and he didn't care about Clancy Tucker's craziness—not enough to get lynched for it.

Clancy stood beside the wagon, holding Mr. Deakin's shotgun in his hands and pointing it

<section>

KEVIN J. ANDERSON

toward the mob. "This here gun is loaded with bird-shot. It's bound to hit most everybody with flying lead pellets. Might even *kill* someone. Whoever wants to keep me from my own parents, just take a step forward. I've got my finger right on the trigger." He paused for just a moment. "Mr. Deakin, would you kindly finish the last bit of digging?"

Mr. Deakin took the shovel and went to work, moving slowly, and watched Clancy Tucker's bulging eyes. Sweat streamed down Clancy's forehead, and his hands shook as he pointed the shotgun.

"I'm done, Clancy," Mr. Deakin said, just loud enough for the other man to hear him.

Clancy tilted the shotgun up and discharged the first barrel with a sound like a cannon. Morning birds in the outlying fields burst into the air, squawking. Clancy lowered the gun toward the mob again. "Git!"

The circuit rider looked as if he wanted to bluster some more, but the townspeople of Compromise turned to run. Not wanting to be left behind, the circuit rider turned around, his black frock coat flapping. His hat flew off as he ran, drifted in the air, then fell to the muck.

CLANCY TUCKER SHIVERED on the seat of the wagon, pulling a blanket around himself. He had cradled the empty shotgun for a long time as Mr. Deakin led the wagon around the town of Compromise, bumping over rough fields.

"I would've shot him," Clancy said. His teeth chattered together. "I really meant it. I was going to kill them! 'Thou shalt not kill!' I've never had thoughts like that before!"

Mr. Deakin made Clancy take a nap for a few hours, but the other man seemed just as disturbed after he awoke. "How am I going to live with this? I meant to kill another man! I had the gun in my hand. If I had tilted the barrel down just a bit I could have popped that circuit rider's head like a muskmelon."

"It was only bird-shot, Clancy," Mr. Deakin said, but Clancy didn't hear.

As the horses followed the dirt path, Mr. Deakin reached behind to the bed of the wagon where they kept their supplies. He rummaged under the tarpaulin and pulled out a two-gallon jug of whiskey. "Here, drink some of this. It'll smooth out your nerves."

Clancy looked at him, wide-eyed, but Mr. Deakin kept his face free of any expression. "I traded my little silver mirror for it last night in the saloon. You could use some right now, Clancy. I've never seen anybody this bad."

Clancy pulled out the cork and took a deep whiff of the contents. Startled, stinging tears came to his eyes. "I won't, Mr. Deakin! It says right in Leviticus, 'Do not drink wine nor strong drink.'"

"Oh, don't go giving me that," Mr. Deakin said, pursing his lips. "Isn't there another verse that says to give wine to those with heavy hearts so they remember their misery no more?"

Clancy blinked, as if he had never considered the idea. "That's in Proverbs, I think."

"Well, you look like you could forget some of your misery."

Clancy took out a metal cup and, with tense movements, as if someone were about to catch him at what he was doing, he poured half a cupful of the brown liquid. He screwed up his face and looked down into the cup. Mr. Deakin watched him, knowing that Clancy's lips had probably never been sullied by so much as a curse word, not to mention whiskey.

As if realizing that he had reached his point of greatest courage, Clancy lifted the cup and gulped from it. His eyes seemed to pop even farther from his head, and he bit back a loud cough. Before he could recover his voice to gasp, Mr. Deakin, hiding a smile, spoke from the corner of his mouth. "My gosh, Clancy, just pretend you're drinking hot coffee! Sip it."

Looking alarmed but determined, Clancy brought the cup back to his lips, then squeezed his eyes shut and took a smaller sip. He didn't

</section>

speak again, and Mr. Deakin ignored him. Morning shadows stretched out to the left as the wagon headed north toward Wisconsin.

Mr. Deakin made no comment when Clancy refilled the metal cup and settled back down to a regular routine of long, slow sips.

By noon the sky had begun to thicken up with thunderheads, and the air held the muggy, oppressive scent of a lumbering storm. The flies went away, but mosquitoes came out. The coffins in back of the wagon stank worse than ever.

Clancy hummed "Bringing in the Sheaves" over and over, growing louder with each verse. He turned to look at the coffins in the back of the wagon, and giggled. He spoke for the first time in hours. "Can you keep a secret, Mr. Deakin?"

Mr. Deakin wasn't sure he wanted to, and avoided answering.

"I don't think I know your Christian name, Mr. Deakin."

"How do you know I even have one?" he muttered. He had lived alone and made few friends in Illinois, working too hard to socialize much. The neighbors and townsfolk called him Mr. Deakin, and it had been a long time since he'd heard anyone refer to him as anything else. Clancy found that very funny.

"Yes, I can keep a secret," Mr. Deakin finally said.

"Promise?"

"Promise."

Clancy dropped his voice to a stage whisper. "Jerome lied!" He paused, as if this revelation were horrifying enough.

"And when did he do that?" Mr. Deakin asked, not really interested.

"When he came out of my parents' room and said that their souls had flown off to Heaven—that wasn't true at all. And he knew it! When he went into that room, after Ma and Dad were sick for so long, after he wanted to go found the new town so bad, Jerome smothered them both with their pillows!"

Mr. Deakin intentionally kept his gaze pointed straight ahead. "Clancy, you've had too much of that whiskey."

"He did Dad first, who still had some strength to struggle. But Ma didn't fight. She just laid back and closed her eyes. She knew we had promised to take them both to Tucker's Grove, and she knew we would keep our word. You always have to keep your word.

"But when Jerome said their souls had flown off to Heaven, well, that just wasn't true—because by smothering them with the pillow, he trapped their souls *inside*!"

Clancy opened his eyes. Mr. Deakin saw bloodshot lines around the irises. "What makes you say that, Clancy?" Mr. Deakin asked. He wasn't sure if he could believe any of this.

"Maggie said so." Clancy stared off into the gathering storm. "Right after they died, our Negro Maggie sacrificed one of our chickens, danced around mumbling spells. Jerome and I came back from the coffin maker's and found her inside by the bodies. He tried to whack her on the head with a shovel, then he chased her out of our house and said he'd burn her as a witch if she ever came back."

"And so Jerome left while you packed everything up and made ready to move?" Mr. Deakin asked. He had no idea what to make of killing chickens and chanting spells.

"I'm the only one who didn't see the vision. But Ma and Dad wanted to come so bad. Maggie said she was just trying to help, and it worked. That's why we have to keep burying the coffins—so the bodies stay down!" Clancy glanced at Mr. Deakin, expectant, but then his own expression changed. With a comical look of astonishment at himself, he covered his mouth with one hand, still grimy from digging out the graves at dawn.

"I promised Jerome I wouldn't tell *anybody*, and now I broke my promise. Something bad's bound to happen for sure now!" He closed his eyes and began to groan in the back of his throat.

In exasperation, Mr. Deakin reached over and yanked on the floppy brim of Clancy's hat, pulling it over his face. "Clancy, you just take another nap. Get some rest." He lowered his voice and mumbled under his breath, "And give me some peace, too."

CLANCY SLEPT MOST of the afternoon, lying in an awkward position against the backboard. Mr. Deakin urged the horses onward, racing the oncoming storm. He hadn't seen another town since Compromise, and the wild prairie sprawled as far as he could see, dotted with clumps of trees. The wagon track was only a faint impression, showing the way to go. A damp breeze licked across Mr. Deakin's face.

The first droplets of water sprinkled his cheeks, and Mr. Deakin pulled his own hat tight onto his head. As the storm picked up, the breeze and the raindrops made a rushing sound in the grasses.

Clancy grunted and woke up. He looked disoriented, saw the darkened sky, and sat up sharply. "What time is it? How long did I sleep?" He whirled to look at the coffins in the back. The patter of raindrops sounded like drumbeats against the wood.

Mr. Deakin knew what Clancy was going to say, but maintained a nonchalant expression. "Hard to tell what time it is with these clouds and the storm. Probably late afternoon . . ." He looked at Clancy. "Sunset maybe." A boom of thunder made a drawn-out, tearing sound across the sky.

"You've got to stop! We have to bury the—"

"Clancy, we'll never get them dug in time, and I'm not going to be shoveling a grave in the middle of a storm. Just cover them up with the tarp and they'll be all right."

Clancy turned to him with an expression filled with outrage and alarm. Before he could say anything, a *thump* came from the back of the wagon. Mr. Deakin looked around, wondering if he had rolled over a boulder on the path, but then the thump came again.

Out of the corner of his eye he saw one of the coffins move aside just a little.

"Oh no!" Clancy wailed. "I told you!"

An echoing thump came from the second coffin. Another burst of thunder rolled across the sky, and the horses picked up their pace, frightened by the wind and the storm.

Clancy leaned into the back of the wagon. He took a mallet from the pack of tools and, just as the first coffin bounced again, Clancy whacked the edge of the lid, striking the coffin nails to keep the top closed. The rusted and mud-specked nailheads gleamed bright with scraped metal.

Mr. Deakin had his mouth half-open, but he couldn't think of anything to say. He kept trying to convince himself that this was some kind of joke Clancy was playing, or perhaps even the townspeople of Compromise.

Just as he turned, the first coffin lid lurched, despite Clancy's hammering. The pine boards split, and the lid bent up just enough that a gnarled gray hand pushed its way out. Wet and rotting skin scraped off the edge of the wood as the claw-fingers scrabbled to find purchase and push the lid open farther. Tendons stuck out along yellowed bones. A burst of stench wafted out, and Mr. Deakin gagged but could not tear his eyes away.

The second coffin lid cracked open. He thought he saw a shadow moving inside it.

Clancy leaped into the back of the wagon and straddled one of the coffins. He banged again with the mallet, trying to keep the lid closed; but he hesitated, worried about injuring the hands and fingers groping through the cracks. "Help me, Mr. Deakin!"

A flash of lightning split across the darkness. Rain poured down, and the horses began to run. Mr. Deakin let the reins drop onto the seat and swung over the backboard into the wagon bed.

Clancy knelt beside his mother's coffin. "Please stay put! Just stay put! I'll get you there," he was saying, but his words were lost in the wind and the thunder and the rumble of wagon wheels.

One of the pine boards snapped on the father's coffin. An arm, clothed in the mildewed black of a Sunday suit, thrust out. The fingers had long, curved nails.

"Don't!" Clancy said.

Mr. Deakin was much bigger than Clancy. In the back of the wagon he planted his feet flat against the side of the first coffin. He pushed with his legs.

The single rotting arm flailed and tried to grab at his boot, but Mr. Deakin shoved. He closed his eyes and laid his head backward—and the coffin slid off the wagon bed, tottering for an instant. As the horses continued to gallop over the bumpy path, the coffin tilted over the edge onto the track.

"No!" Clancy screamed, and grabbed at him, but Mr. Deakin slapped him away. He pushed the second coffin, a lighter one this time. The lid on this coffin began to give way as well. Thin fingers crept out.

Clancy yanked at Mr. Deakin's jacket, clawing at the throat and cutting off his air, but Mr. Deakin gave a last push to knock the second coffin over the edge.

"We've got to turn around!" Clancy cried.

The second coffin crashed to the ground, tilted over, and the wooden sides splintered. Just then a sheet of lightning illuminated the sky from horizon to horizon, like an enormous concussion of flash powder used by a daguerreotype photographer.

In that instant, Mr. Deakin saw the thin, twisted body rising from the shards of the broken coffin. Lumbering behind, already free of the first coffin, stood a taller corpse, shambling toward his wife. Then all fell black again as the lightning faded.

Mr. Deakin wanted to collapse and squeeze his eyes shut, but the horses continued to gallop wildly. He scrambled back to the seat and snatched up the reins.

"This weather is going to ruin them!" Clancy moaned. "You have to go back, Mr. Deakin!"

Mr. Deakin knew full well that he was abandoning a farm of his own in Tucker's Grove; but the consequences of breaking his agreement with Clancy seemed more sane to him than staying here any longer. He snapped the reins and shouted at the horses for greater speed.

Lightning sent him another picture of the two scarecrow corpses—but they had their backs to the wagon. Walking side by side, Clancy Tucker's dead parents struck off in the other direction. Back the way they had come.

With a sudden, resigned look on his face, Clancy Tucker swung both of his legs over the side of the wagon.

"Clancy, wait!" Mr. Deakin shouted. "They're going the other way! They don't want to come after all, can't you see?"

But Clancy's voice remained determined. "It doesn't matter. I've got to take them anyway." He ducked his head down and made ready to jump. "A promise is a promise," he said.

"Sometimes breaking a promise is better than keeping it," Mr. Deakin shouted.

But Clancy let go of the wagon, tucking and rolling onto the wet grass. He clambered to his feet and ran back toward where he had last seen his parents.

Mr. Deakin did not look back, but kept the horses running into the night.

As he listened to the majestic storm overhead, as he felt the wet, fresh air with each breath he took, Mr. Deakin realized that he still had more, much more, that he did not want to lose.

RICHARD LAYMON

RICHARD (CARL) LAYMON (1947–2001) was born in Chicago, moving to California as a child. He received a B.A. in English literature from Willamette in Oregon and an M.A. in English literature from Loyola in Los Angeles. He worked as a schoolteacher, a librarian, and a report writer for a law firm before becoming a full-time novelist and short-story writer. While mainly known as a horror writer, he also wrote other fiction, notably mysteries, having stories published in *Ellery Queen's Mystery Magazine, Alfred Hitchcock's Mystery Magazine, The Second Black Lizard Anthology of Crime Fiction*, and many others.

In his primary writing genre, horror, he produced about sixty short stories and thirty novels, achieving far greater success in England and Europe than in his own country. His work has received numerous awards, including four nominations for Bram Stoker Awards from the Horror Writers Association: for *Flesh*, nominated for Best Novel in 1988; *Funland*, nominated for Best Novel in 1990; *Bad News*, nominated for Best Anthology in 2000; and *The Traveling Vampire Show*, which won as Best Novel in 2000. In addition, *Flesh* was named the Best Horror Novel of the Year by *Science Fiction Chronicle*. He also wrote several novels under the names Richard Kelly and Carl Laymon.

"Mess Hall" was originally published in *Book of the Dead*, edited by John Skipp and Craig Spector (New York: Bantam, 1989).

RICHARD LAYMON

MESS HALL

JEAN DIDN'T HEAR footsteps. She heard only the rush of the nearby stream, her own moaning, Paul's harsh gasps as he thrust into her. The first she heard of the man was his voice.

"Looks to me like fornication in a public park area."

Her heart slammed.

Oh God, no.

With her left eye, she glimpsed the man's vague shape crouching beside her in the moonlight, less than a yard away. She looked up at Paul. His eyes were wide with alarm.

This can't be happening, Jean told herself.

She felt totally helpless and exposed. Not that the guy could see anything. Just Paul's bare butt. He couldn't see that Jean's blouse was open, her bra bunched around her neck, her skirt rucked up past her waist.

"Do you know it's against the law?" the man asked.

Paul took his tongue out of Jean's mouth. He turned his head toward the man.

Jean could feel his heart drumming, his penis shrinking inside her.

"Not to mention poor taste," the man added.

"We didn't mean any harm," Paul said.

And started to get up.

Jean jammed her shoes against his buttocks, tightened her arms around his back.

"What if some *children* had wandered by?" the man asked.

"We're sorry," Jean told him, keeping her head straight up, not daring to look at the man again, instead staring at Paul. "We'll leave."

"Kiss goodbye, now."

Seemed like a weird request.

But Paul obeyed. He pressed his mouth gently against Jean's lips, and she wondered how she could manage to cover herself because it was quite obvious that, as soon as the kiss was over, Paul would have to climb off her. And there she'd be.

Later, she knew it was a shotgun.

She hadn't seen a shotgun, but she'd only given the man that single, quick glance.

Paul was giving her the goodbye kiss and she was wondering about the best way to keep the man from seeing her when suddenly it didn't matter because the world blew up. Paul's eyes exploded out of their sockets and dropped onto *her* eyes. She jerked her head sideways to get away from them. Jerked it the wrong way. Saw the clotted wetness on the moonlit trunk of a nearby tree, saw his ear cling to the bark for a moment, then fall.

Paul's head dropped heavily onto the side of her face. A torrent of blood blinded her.

She started to scream.

Paul's weight tumbled off. The man stomped her belly. He scooped her up, swung her over his shoulder, and started to run. She wheezed, trying to breathe. His foot had smashed her air out and now his shoulder kept ramming into her. She felt as if she were drowning. Only a dim corner of her mind seemed to work, and she wished it would blink out.

Better total darkness, better no awareness at all.

The man stopped running. He bent over, and Jean flopped backward. She slammed something. Beside her was a windshield plated with moonlight. She'd been dumped across the hood of a car. Her legs dangled over the car's front.

She tried to lift her head. Couldn't. So she lay there, struggling to suck in air.

The man came back.

He'd been away?

Jean felt as if she had missed a chance to save herself.

He leaned over, clutched both sides of her open blouse, and yanked her into a sitting position. He snapped a handcuff around her right wrist, passed the other bracelet beneath her knee, and cuffed her left hand. Then he lifted her off the hood. He swung her into the car's passenger seat and slammed the door.

Through the windshield, Jean saw him rush past the front of the car. She drove her knee up. It bumped her chin, but she managed to slip the handcuff chain down her calf and under the sole of her running shoe. She grabbed the door handle. She levered it up and threw her shoulder against the door and started to tumble out, but her head jerked back with searing pain as if the hair were being torn from her scalp. Her head twisted. Her cheekbone struck the steering wheel. A hand clasped the top of her head. Another clutched her chin. And he rammed the side of her face again and again on the wheel.

When she opened her eyes, her head was on the man's lap. She felt his hand kneading her breast. The car was moving fast. From the engine noise and the hiss of the tires on the pavement, she guessed they were on the interstate. The highway lights cast a faint, silvery glow on the man's face. He looked down at her and smiled.

The police artist sketch didn't have him quite right. It had the crewcut right, and the weird crazy eyes, but his nose was a little larger, his lips a lot thicker.

Jean started to lift her head.

"Lie still," he warned. "Move a muscle, I'll pound your brains out." He laughed. "How about your boyfriend's brains? Did you see how they hit that tree?"

Jean didn't answer.

He pinched her.

She gritted her teeth.

"I asked you a question."

"I saw," she said.

"Cool, huh?"

"No."

"How about his eyes? I've never seen anything like that. Just goes to show what a twelve-gauge can do to a fellow. You know, I've never killed a *guy* before. Just sweet young things like you."

Like me.

It came as no surprise, no shock. She'd seen him murder Paul, and he planned to murder her too—the same as he'd murdered the others.

Maybe he doesn't kill them all, she thought. Only one body had been found. Everyone talked as if the Reaper had killed the other six, but really they were only *missing*.

Maybe he takes them someplace and keeps them.

But he just now said he kills sweet young things. Plural. He killed them all. But maybe not. Maybe he just wants to keep me and fool with me and not kill me and I'll figure a way out.

"Where are you taking me?" she asked.

"A nice, private place in the hills where nobody will hear you scream."

The words made a chill crawl over her.

"Oooh, goosebumps. I like that." His hand glided over her skin like a cold breeze. Jean was tempted to grab his hand and bite it.

If she did that, he would hurt her again.

There'll be a world of hurt later, she thought. He plans to make me scream.

But that was later. Maybe she could get away from him before it came to that. The best thing, for now, was to give him no trouble. Don't fight him. Act docile. Then maybe he'll let his guard down.

"Do you know who I am?" he asked.

"Yes."

"Tell me."

"The Reaper."

"Very good. And I know who you are, too."

He knows me? How could he? Maybe followed me around on campus, asked someone my name.

"You're Number Eight," he said. "Just think about that. You're going to be famous. You'll be in all the newspapers, they'll talk about you on television, you'll even end up being a chapter in a book someday. Have you read any books like that? They'll have a nice little biography of you, quotes from your parents and friends. The bittersweet story of your brief but passionate relationship with that guy. What was his name?"

"Paul," she murmured.

"Paul. He'll get a good write-up, himself, since he's the first guy to die at the hands of the Reaper. Of course, they'll realize that he was incidental. You were the intended victim, Paul simply an unlucky jerk who got in the way. He got lucky, then he got unlucky. Good one, huh? Maybe I'll write the book myself. He got off and got offed. Or did he? Which came first? Did he go out with a bang?"

"Why don't you shut up?"

"Because I don't want to," he said, and raked a path up her belly with a single fingernail.

Jean cringed. Air hissed in through her teeth.

"You should be nice to me," he said. "After all, I'm the one making you famous. Of course, some of the notoriety may be a trifle embarrassing for you. That book I was telling you about, it'll have a whole lot about today. Your final hours. Who was the last person to see you alive. And of course, it won't neglect the fornication in the park. People read that, a lot of them are going to think you were asking for it. I suppose I'd have to agree with them. Didn't you know any better?"

She *had* known better. "What about the Reaper?" she'd asked when the movie let out and Paul suggested the park.

"He'll have to find his *own* gal."

"I mean it. I'm not sure it's such a great idea. Why don't we go to my place?"

"Right. So your demented roommate can listen through the wall and make noises."

"I told her not to do that anymore."

"Come on, let's go to the park. It's a neat night. We can find a place by the stream."

"I don't know." She squeezed his hand. "I'd like to, Paul, but . . ."

"Shit. Everybody's got Reaperitis. For godsake, he's in *Portland*."

"That's only a half-hour drive."

"Okay. Forget it. Shit."

They walked half a block, Paul silent and scowling, before Jean slipped a hand into the rear pocket of his pants and said, "Hey, pal, how's about a stroll in the park?"

Didn't you know any better?

His hand smacked her bare skin.

"Yes!"

"Don't you ignore me. I ask you a question, you answer. Got it?"

"Yes."

The car slowed. The Reaper's left hand eased the steering wheel over and Jean felt the car slip sideways. It tipped upward a bit, pressing her cheek against his belt buckle.

An off-ramp, she thought.

The car stopped, then made a sharp turn.

A cold tremor swept through Jean.

We're getting there, she thought. Wherever he's taking me, we're getting there. Oh, Jesus.

"You thought it couldn't happen to you," he said. "Am I right?"

"No."

"What, then? You were just too horny to care?"

"Paul would've kept on pouting." Her voice was high, shaky.

"One of those. I hate those sniveling, whiny pouters. Take me, for instance—I never pout. That's for the losers. I never lose, so I've got no reason to pout. I make *other* people lose."

He slowed the car, turned it again.

"I hate pouters, too," Jean said, trying to keep her voice steady. "They stink. They don't deserve to live."

He looked down at her. His face was a vague blur. There were no more streetlights, Jean realized. Nothing but moonlight, now.

"I bet you and I are a lot alike," she said.

"Think so, do you?"

"I've never told anyone this before, but . . . I guess it's safe to tell you. I killed a girl once."

"That so?"

He doesn't believe me!

"Yeah. It was just two years ago. I was going with this guy, Jim Smith, and . . . I really loved him. We got engaged. And then all of a sudden he started going with this bitch, Mary Jones."

"Smith and Jones, huh?" He chuckled.

"I can't help it if they had stupid names," she said, and wished she'd taken an extra second to think up names that sounded *real*, damn it. "Anyway, he spent less and less time with me, and I knew he was seeing Mary. So one night I snuck into her room in the sorority and smothered her with a pillow. Killed her. And I enjoyed it. I laughed when she died."

He patted Jean's belly. "I guess we are two of a kind. Maybe you'd like to throw in with me. I can see some advantages to an arrangement like that. You could lure the pretty young things into my car, help me subdue them. What do you think?"

She thought that she might start to cry. His offer was just what she had wanted to hear—and he knew it. He knew it, all right.

But she went along, just in case. "I think I'd like that."

"That makes it an even fifty percent," he said.

The front of the car tipped upward. Again, Jean's cheek pressed his belt buckle.

"You're the fourth to try that maneuver. Hey, forget about killing me, I'm just your type, let's be partners. Four out of eight. You're only the second to confess a prior murder, though. The other one said she pushed her kid sister out of the tree house. I sure do pick 'em. Two murderers. What are the chances of that?"

"Coincidence," Jean muttered.

"Nice try."

His right hand continued to fondle her. His left hand kept jogging the steering wheel from side to side as he maneuvered up the hill.

She could reach up and grab the wheel and maybe make them crash. But the car didn't seem to be moving very fast. At this speed, the crash might not hurt him at all.

"Let's hear the one about your rich father," he said.

"Go to hell."

He laughed. "Come on, don't ruin the score. You'll make it a hundred percent if you've got a rich father who'll pay me heaps of money to take you back to him unscathed."

She decided to try for the crash.

But the car stopped. He swung the steering wheel way over and started ahead slowly. The car bumped and rocked. Its tires crunched dirt. Leafy branches whispered and squeaked against its sides.

"We're almost there," he said.

She knew that.

"Almost time to go into your begging routine. Most of them start about now. Sometimes they hold off till we get out."

I won't beg, Jean thought. I'll run for it.

He stopped the car and turned off the engine. He didn't take the key from the ignition.

"Okay, honey. Sit up slowly and open the door. I'll be right behind you."

She sat up and turned toward the door. As she levered the handle, he clutched the collar of her blouse. He held onto it while she climbed out. Then he was standing, still gripping her collar, knuckles shoving at the back of her neck to guide her around the door. The door slammed shut. They passed the front of the car and moved toward a clearing in the forest.

The clearing was milky with moonlight. In the center, near a pale dead tree, was a ring of rocks that someone had stacked up to enclose a campfire. A pile of twigs and broken branches stood near the fire ring.

The Reaper steered Jean toward the dead tree.

She saw wood already piled inside the wall of rocks, ready for a match.

And she felt a quick glimmer of hope. *Some-one* had laid the fire.

Right. *He* probably did it. He was up here earlier, preparing.

She saw a rectangular box at the foot of the tree.

A toolbox?

She began to whimper. She tried to stop walking, but he shoved her forward.

"Oh please, please, no! Spare me! I'll do any-thing!"

"Fuck you," Jean said.

He laughed.

"I like your guts," he said. "In a little while, we may take a good look at them."

He turned her around and backed her against the tree.

"I'll have to take off one of the cuffs, now," he explained. He took a key from the pocket of his pants and held it in front of her face. "You won't try to take advantage of the moment, will you?"

Jean shook her head.

"No, I didn't think so." He shot a knee up into her belly. His forearm caught her under the chin, forcing her back as she started to double. Her legs gave out. She slid down the trunk, the barkless wood snagging her blouse and scraping her skin. A knob of root pounded her rump. She started to tumble forward, but he was there in front of her upthrust knees, blocking her fall. She slumped back against the trunk, wheezing, feeling the cuff go away from her right wrist, knowing this was it, this was the big moment she'd been waiting for, her one and only chance to make her break.

But she couldn't move. She was hurting and dazed and breathless. And even if she hadn't been disabled by the blow, her position made struggle pointless. She was folded, back tight against the tree, legs mashing her breasts, arms stretched out over her knees, toes pinned to the ground by his boots.

She knew she had lost.

Strange, though. It didn't seem to matter much.

Jean felt as if she were outside herself, ob-serving. It was someone else being grabbed un-der the armpits, someone else being lifted. She was watching a movie and the heroine was being prepared for torture. The girl's arms were being raised overhead. The loose cuff was being passed over the top of a limb. Then, it was snapped around the girl's right hand. The Reaper lifted her off her feet and carried her out away from the trunk. Then he let go. The limb was low enough so she didn't need to stand on tiptoes.

The man walked away from his captive. He crouched on the other side of the ring of rocks and struck a match. Flames climbed the tented sticks. They wrapped thick, broken branches. Pale smoke drifted up. He stood and returned to the girl.

"A little light on the subject," he said to her. His voice sounded as faint as the snapping of the fire behind him.

This is okay, she thought. It's not me. It's someone else—a stranger.

It stopped being a stranger, very fast, when she saw the knife in the Reaper's hand.

She stood rigid and stared at the dark blade. She tried to hold her breath, but couldn't stop panting. Her heart felt like a hammer trying to smash its way out of her chest.

"No," she gasped. "Please."

He smiled. "I knew you'd get around to beg-ging."

"I never did anything to you."

"But you're about to do something *for* me."

The knife moved in. She felt its cool blade on her skin, but it didn't hurt. It didn't cut. Not Jean. It cut her clothes instead—the straps of her bra, the sleeves of her blouse, the waistband of her skirt.

He took the clothes to the fire.

"No! Don't!"

He smiled and dropped them onto the flames. "You won't need them. You'll be staying right here. Here in the mess hall."

Somewhere in the distance, a coyote howled.

"That's my friend. We've got an arrange-ment. I leave a meal for him and his forest friends, and they do the cleanup for me. None of this 'shallow grave' nonsense. I just leave you here, tomorrow you'll be gone. They'll come like the good, hungry troops they are, and leave the area neat and tidy for next time. No fuss, no bother. And you, sweet thing, will be spared the embarrassment of returning to campus bare-ass."

Squatting beside the fire, he opened the toolbox. He took out pliers and a screwdriver. He set the pliers on the flat top of a rock. He picked up the screwdriver. Its shank was black even before he held it over the fire. Jean saw the flames curl around it.

"No!" she cried out. "Please!"

"No! Please!" he mimicked. Smiling, he rolled the screwdriver in his hand. "Think it's done yet?" He shook his head. "Give it a few more minutes. No need to rush. Are you savoring the anticipation?"

"You bastard!"

"Is that any way to talk?"

"HELP!" she shouted. "HELP! PLEASE, HELP ME!"

"Nobody's going to hear you but the coyotes."

"You can't do this!"

"Sure, I can. Done it plenty of times before."

"Please! I'll do anything!"

"I know just what you'll do. Scream, twitch, cry, kick, beg, drool . . . bleed. Not necessarily in that order, of course."

He stood up. Pliers in one hand, screwdriver in the other, he walked slowly toward Jean. Wisps of pale smoke rose off the shank of the screwdriver.

He stopped in front of her. "Now where oh where shall we begin? So many choice areas to choose from." He raised the screwdriver toward her left eye. Jean jerked her head aside. The tip moved closer. She shut her eye. Felt heat against its lid. But the heat faded. "No. I'll save that for later. After all, half the fun for *you* will be watching."

She shrieked and flinched rigid as something seared her belly.

The Reaper laughed.

She looked down. He had simply touched her with the nose of the pliers.

"Power of suggestion," he said. "Now, let's see how you like some *real* pain."

Slowly he moved the screwdriver toward her left breast. Jean tried to jerk away, but the handcuffs stopped her. She kicked out. He twisted away. As the edge of her shoe glanced off his hip, he stroked her thigh with the screwdriver. She squealed.

He grinned. "Don't do that again, honey, or I might get mean."

Sobbing, she watched him inch the screwdriver toward her breast again. "No. Don't. Pleeease."

A rock struck the side of the Reaper's head. It knocked his head sideways, bounced off, scraped Jean's armpit, and fell. He stood there for a moment, then dropped to his knees and slumped forward, face pressing against Jean's groin. She twisted away, and he flopped beside her.

She gazed down at him, hardly able to believe he was actually sprawled there. Maybe she'd passed out and this was no more than a wild fantasy. She was dreaming and pretty soon she would come to with a burst of pain and . . .

No, she thought. It can't be a dream. Please.

A dim corner of her mind whispered, *I knew I'd get out of this.*

She looked for the rock thrower.

And spotted a dim shape standing beside a tree on the far side of the clearing.

"You got him!" she shouted. "Thank God, you got him! Great throw!"

The shape didn't move, didn't call back to her.

It turned away.

"No!" Jean cried out. "Don't leave! He'll come to and kill me! Please! I'm cuffed here! He's got the key in his pocket. You've gotta unlock the cuffs for me. Please!"

The figure, as indistinct in the darkness as the bushes and trees near its sides, turned again and stepped forward. It limped toward the glow of the fire. From the shape, Jean guessed that her savior was a woman.

Others began to appear across the clearing.

One stepped out from behind a tree. Another rose behind a clump of bushes. Jean glimpsed movement over to the right, looked and saw a fourth woman. She heard a growl behind her, twisted around, and gasped at the sight of someone crawling toward her. Toward the Reaper, she hoped. The top of this one's head was black and hairless in the shimmering firelight. As if she'd been scalped? The flesh had been stripped from one side of her back, and Jean glimpsed pale curving ribs before she whirled away.

Now there were *five* in front of her, closing in and near enough to the fire so she could see them clearly.

She stared at them.

And disconnected again.

Came out of herself, became an observer.

The rock thrower had a black pit where her left eye should've been. The girl cuffed beneath the tree was amazed that a one-eyed girl had been able to throw a rock with such fine aim.

It was even more amazing, since she was obviously dead. Ropes of guts hung from her belly, swaying between her legs like an Indian's loincloth. Little but bone remained of her right leg below the knee—the work of the Reaper's woodland troops?

How can she walk?

That's a good one, the girl thought.

How can *any* of them walk?

One, who must've been up here *a very long time,* was managing to shamble along just fine, though both her legs were little more than bare bones. The troops had really feasted on her. One arm was missing entirely. The other arm was bone, and gone from the elbow down. Where she still had flesh, it looked black and lumpy. Some of her torso was intact, but mostly hollowed out. The right-hand side of her rib cage had been broken open. The ribs on the left were still there, and a shriveled lung was visible through the bars. Her face had no eyes, no nose, no lips. She looked as if she might be grinning.

The girl beneath the tree grinned back at her, but she didn't seem to notice.

Of course not, dope. How can she see?

How can she walk?

One of the others still had eyes. They were wide open and glazed. She had a very peculiar stare.

No eyelids, that's the trouble. The Reaper must've cut them off. Her breasts, too. Round, pulpy black disks on her chest where they should've been. Except for a huge gap in her right flank, she didn't look as if she'd been maimed by the troops. She still had most of her skin. But it looked shiny and slick with a coating of white slime.

The girl beside her didn't seem to have any skin at all. Had she been peeled? She was black all over except for the whites of her eyes and teeth—and hundreds of white things as if she had been showered with rice. But the rice moved. The rice was alive. Maggots.

The last of the five girls approaching from the front was also black. She didn't look peeled, she looked burnt. Her body was a crust of char, cracked and leaking fluids that shimmered in the firelight. She bore only a rough resemblance to a human being. She might have been shaped out of mud by a dim-witted child who gave her no fingers or toes or breasts, who couldn't manage a nose or ears, and poked fingers into the mud to make her eyes. Her crust made papery, crackling sounds as she shuffled past the fire, and pieces flaked off.

A motley crew, thought the girl cuffed to the limb.

She wondered if any of them would have enough sense to find the key and unlock the handcuffs.

She doubted it.

In fact, they didn't seem to be aware of her presence at all. They were limping and hobbling straight toward the Reaper.

Whose shriek now shattered whatever fragile force had allowed Jean to stay outside the cuffed stranger. She tried to keep her distance. Couldn't. Was sucked back inside the naked, suspended girl. Felt a sudden rush of horror and revulsion . . . and hope.

Whatever else they might be, they were the victims of the Reaper.

Payback time.

He was still shrieking, and Jean looked down at him. He was on his hands and knees. The scalped girl, also on her knees and facing him, had his head caught between her hands. She was biting the top of his head. Jean heard a wet ripping sound as the girl tore off a patch of hair and flesh.

He flopped and skidded backward, dragged by the rock thrower and the one with the slimy skin. Each had him by a foot. The scalped girl started to crawl after him, then grunted and stopped and tried to pick up the pliers. Her right hand had no fingers. She pawed at the pliers, whimpering with frustration, then sighed when she succeeded in picking up the tool using the thumb and two remaining fingers of her other hand. Quickly, she crawled along trying to catch up to her prize. She scurried past Jean. One of her buttocks was gone, eaten away to the bone.

She gained on the screaming Reaper, reached out, and clamped the pliers to the ridge of his ear and ripped out a chunk.

Halfway between Jean and the fire, the girls released his feet.

All six went at him.

He bucked and twisted and writhed, but they turned him onto his back. While some held him down, others tore at his clothes. Others tore at *him*. The scalped one took the pliers to his right eyelid and tore it off. The burnt one snatched up a hand and opened her lipless black mouth and began to chew his fingers off. While this went on, the armless girl capered like a madcap skeleton, her trapped lung bouncing inside her rib cage.

Soon the Reaper's shirt was in shreds. His pants and boxer shorts were bunched around his cowboy boots. The scalped girl had ripped his other eyelid off, and now was stretching his upper lip as he squealed. The rock thrower, kneeling beside him, clawed at his belly as if trying to get to his guts. Slime-skin bit off one of his nipples, chewed it, and swallowed. The girl who must've been skinned alive knelt beside his

head, scraping maggots off her belly and stuffing them by the handful into his mouth. No longer shrieking, he choked and wheezed.

The dancing skeleton dropped to her bare kneecaps, bent over him, and clamped her teeth on his penis. She pulled, stretching it, gnawing. He stopped choking and let out a shrill scream that felt like ice picks sliding into Jean's ears.

The scalped girl tore his lip off. She gave the pliers a snap, and watched the lip fly.

Jean watched it too. Then felt its soft plop against her thigh. It stuck to her skin like a leech. She gagged. She stomped her foot on the ground, trying to shake it off. It kept clinging.

It's just a lip, she thought.

And then she was throwing up. She leaned forward as far as she could, trying not to vomit on herself. A small part of her mind was amused. She'd been looking at hideous, mutilated corpses, such horrors as she had never seen before, not even in her nightmares. And she had watched the corpses do unspeakable things to the Reaper. With all that, she hadn't tossed her cookies.

A lip sticks to my leg, and I'm barfing my guts out.

At least she was missing herself. Most of it was hitting the ground in front of her shoes, though a little was splashing up and spraying her shins.

Finally the heaving subsided. She gasped for air and blinked tears out of her eyes.

And saw the scalped girl staring at her.

The others kept working on the Reaper. He wasn't screaming anymore, just gasping and whimpering.

The scalped girl stabbed the pliers down. They crashed through the Reaper's upper teeth. She rammed them deep into his mouth and partway down his throat, left them there, and started to crawl toward Jean.

"Get *him*," she whispered. "*He's* the one."

Then Jean thought, Maybe she wants to help me.

"Would you get the key? For the handcuffs? It's in his pants pocket."

The girl didn't seem to hear. She stopped at the puddle of vomit and lowered her face into it. Jean heard lapping sounds, and gagged. The girl raised her head, stared up at Jean, licked her dripping lips, then crawled forward.

"No. Get back."

Opened her mouth wide.

Christ!

Jean smashed her knee up into the girl's forehead. The head snapped back. The girl tumbled away.

A chill spread through Jean. Her skin prickled with goosebumps. Her heart began to slam.

It won't stop with him.

I'm next!

The scalped girl, whose torso was an empty husk, rolled over and started to push herself up.

Jean leaped.

She caught the tree limb with both hands, kicked toward the trunk but couldn't come close to reaching it. Her body swept down and backward. As she started forward again, she pumped her legs high.

She swung.

She kicked and swung, making herself a pendulum that strained higher with each sweep.

Her legs hooked over the barkless, dead limb.

She drew herself up against its underside and hugged it.

Twisting her head sideways, she saw the scalped girl crawling toward her again.

Jean had never seen her stand.

If she can't stand up, I'm okay.

But the *others* could stand.

They were still busy with the Reaper. Digging into him. Biting. Ripping off flesh with their teeth. He choked around the pliers and made high squeaky noises. As Jean watched, the charred girl crouched over the fire and put both hands into the flames. When she straightened up, she had a blazing stick trapped between the fingerless flaps of her hands. She lumbered back to the group, crouched, and set the Reaper's pants on fire.

The pants, pulled down until they were stopped by his boot tops, wrapped him just below the knees.

In seconds they were ablaze.

The Reaper started screaming again. He squirmed and kicked. Jean was surprised he had that much life left in him.

The key, she thought.

I'll have to go through the ashes.

If I live that long.

Jean began to shinny out along the limb. It scraped her thighs and arms, but she kept moving, kept inching her way along. The limb sagged slightly. It groaned. She scooted farther, farther.

Heard a faint crackling sound.

Then was stopped by a bone white branch that blocked her left arm.

"No!" she gasped.

She thrust herself forward and rammed her arm against the branch. The impact shook it just a bit. A few twigs near the far end of it clattered and fell.

The branch looked three inches thick where it joined the main limb. A little higher up, it seemed thin enough for her to break easily—but she couldn't reach that far, not with her wrists joined by the short chain of the handcuffs. The branch barred her way like the arm and hand of a skeleton pleased to keep her treed until its companions finished with the Reaper and came for her.

She clamped it between her teeth, bit down hard on the dry wood, gnashed on it. Her teeth barely seemed to dent it.

She lowered her head. Spat dirt and grit from her mouth. Turned her head.

The Reaper was no longer moving or making any sounds. Pale smoke drifted up from the black area where his pants had been burning. The charred girl who had set them ablaze now held his severed arm over the campfire. The slimy, breastless girl was pulling a boot onto one of her feet. The skinned girl, kneeling by the Reaper's head, had removed the pliers from his mouth. At first Jean thought she was pinching herself with them. That wasn't it, though. One at a time, she was squashing the maggots that squirmed on her belly. The rock thrower's head was buried in the Reaper's open torso. She reared up, coils of intestine drooping from her mouth. The rotted and armless girl lay flat between the black remains of the Reaper's legs, tearing at the cavity where his genitals used to be.

Though he was apparently dead, his victims all still seemed contented.

For now.

Straining to look down past her shoulder, Jean saw the scalped girl directly below. On her knees. Reaching up, pawing the air with the remains of her hands.

She can't get me, Jean told herself.

But the others.

Once they're done with the Reaper, they'll see that bitch down there and then they'll see me.

If *she'd* just go away!

GET OUT OF HERE!

Jean wanted to shout it, didn't dare. Could just see the others turning their heads toward the sound of her voice.

If I could just kill her!

Good luck on that one.

Gotta do something!

Jean clamped the limb hard with her hands. She gritted her teeth.

Don't try it, she thought. You won't even hurt her. You'll be down where she can get at you.

But maybe a good kick in the head'll discourage her.

Fat chance.

Jean released the limb with her legs. She felt a breeze wash over her sweaty skin as she dropped. She thrashed her feet like a drowning woman hoping to kick to the surface.

A heel of her shoe struck something. She hoped it was the bitch's face.

Then she was swinging upward and saw her. Turning on her knees and reaching high, grinning.

Jean kicked hard as she swept down.

The toe of her shoe caught the bitch in the throat, lifted her off her knees and knocked her sprawling.

Got her!

Jean dangled by her hands, swaying slowly back and forth. She bucked and tried to fling her legs up to catch the limb. Missed. Lost her hold and cried out as the steel edges of the bracelets cut into her wrists. Her feet touched the ground.

The scalped girl rolled over and crawled toward her.

Jean leaped. She grabbed the limb. She pulled herself up to it and drove her knees high but not fast enough.

The girl's arms wrapped her ankles, clutched them. She pulled at Jean, stretching her, dragging her down, reaching higher, *climbing* her. Jean twisted and squirmed but couldn't shake the girl off. Her arms strained. Her grip on the limb started to slip. She squealed as teeth ripped into her thigh.

With a *krrrack!*, the limb burst apart midway between Jean and the trunk.

She dropped straight down.

Falling, she shoved the limb sideways. It hammered her shoulder as she landed, knees first, on the girl. The weight drove Jean forward, smashed her down. Though the girl no longer hugged her legs, she felt the head beneath her thigh shake from side to side. She writhed and bucked under the limb. The teeth kept their savage bite on her.

Then *had* their chunk of flesh and lost their grip.

Clutching the limb, Jean bore it down, her shoulder a fulcrum. She felt the wood rise off her back and rump. Its splintered end pressed into the ground four or five feet in front of her head. Bracing herself on the limb, she scurried forward, knees pounding at the girl beneath her. The girl growled. Hands gripped Jean's calves. But not tightly. Not with the missing fingers. Teeth snapped at her, scraping the skin above her right knee. Jean jerked her leg back and shot it forward. The girl's teeth crashed shut. Then Jean was off her, rising on the crutch of the broken limb.

She stood up straight, hugging the upright

limb, lifting its broken end off the ground and staggering forward a few steps to get herself out of the girl's reach.

And saw the others coming. All but the rotted skeletal girl who had no arms and still lay sprawled between the Reaper's legs.

"No!" Jean shouted. "Leave me alone!"

They lurched toward her.

The charred one held the Reaper's severed arm like a club. The breastless girl with runny skin wore both his boots. Her arms were raised, already reaching for Jean though she was still a few yards away. The rock thrower had found a rock. The skinned girl aswarm with maggots picked at herself with the pliers as she shambled closer.

"NO!" Jean yelled again.

She ducked, grabbed the limb low, hugged it to her side and whirled as the branchy top of it swept down in front of her. It dropped from its height slashing sideways, its bony fingers of wood clattering and bursting into twigs as it crashed through the cadavers. Three of them were knocked off their feet. A fourth, the charred one, lurched backward to escape the blow, stepped into the Reaper's torso, and stumbled. Jean didn't see whether she went down, because the weight of the limb was hurling her around in a full circle. A branch struck the face of the scalped girl crawling toward her, popped, and flew off. Then the crawling girl was behind Jean again and the others were still down. All except the rock thrower. She'd been missed, first time around. Out of range. Now her arm was cocked back, ready to hurl a small block of stone.

Jean, spinning, released the limb.

Its barkless wood scraped her side and belly.

It flew from her like a mammoth, tined lance.

Free of its pull, Jean twirled. The rock flicked

her ear. She fell to her knees. Facing the crawler. Who scurried toward her moaning as if she already knew she had lost.

Driving both fists against the ground, Jean pushed herself up. She took two quick steps toward the crawler and kicked her in the face. Then she staggered backward. Whirled around.

The rock thrower was down, arms batting through the maze of dead branches above her.

The others were starting to get up.

Jean ran through them, cuffed hands high, twisting and dodging as they scurried for her, lurched at her, grabbed.

Then they were behind her. All but the Reaper and the armless thing sprawled between his legs, chewing on him. *Gotta get the handcuff key,* she thought.

Charging toward them, she realized the cuffs didn't matter. They couldn't stop her from driving. The car key was in the ignition.

She leaped the Reaper.

And staggered to a stop on the other side of his body.

Gasping, she bent over and lifted a rock from the ring around the fire. Though its heat scorched her hands, she raised it overhead. She turned around.

The corpses were coming, crawling and limping closer.

But they weren't that close.

"HERE'S ONE FOR NUMBER EIGHT!" she shouted, and smashed the rock down onto the remains of the Reaper's face. It struck with a wet, crunching sound. It didn't roll off. It stayed on his face as if it had made a nest for itself.

Jean stomped on it once, pounding it in farther.

Then she swung around. She leaped the fire and dashed through the clearing toward the waiting car.

SCHALKEN THE PAINTER

SHERIDAN LE FANU

GENERALLY REGARDED AS the father of the modern horror and ghost story, Joseph Sheridan Le Fanu (1814–1873) was born in Dublin to a well-to-do Huguenot family. He received a law degree but never practiced, preferring a career in journalism. He joined the staff of the *Dublin University Magazine,* which published many of his early stories, and later was the full or partial owner of several newspapers. Although active politically, he did not permit contemporary affairs to enter his fictional works. Several of his novels were among the most popular of their time, including the mysteries *Wylder's Hand* (1864) and *Uncle Silas* (1864), which was filmed as *The Inheritance* (1947), starring Jean Simmons and Derrick De Marney.

It is for his atmospheric horror stories, however, that he is most remembered today, especially "Green Tea," in which a tiny monkey drives a minister to slash his own throat; "The Familiar," in which lethal demons pursue their victims; and the classic vampire story "Carmilla," which has been filmed numerous times, including as *Vampyr* (1932), *Blood and Roses* (1960), *The Vampire Lovers* (1970), *Carmilla* (1989), and *Carmilla* (1999).

"Schalken the Painter" is regarded as Le Fanu's finest early story, and the first devoted to horror. It was originally published in the *Dublin University Magazine* in 1839; its first book publication was in the posthumous *The Purcell Papers* (London: Richard Bentley and Son, 1880), under the title "Strange Event in the Life of Schalken the Painter."

SHERIDAN LE FANU

SCHALKEN THE PAINTER

BEING A SEVENTH EXTRACT
FROM THE LEGACY OF THE
LATE FRANCIS PURCELL,
P. P. OF DRUMCOOLAGH.

YOU WILL NO doubt be surprised, my
dear friend, at the subject of the following narrative. What had I to do with Schalken, or
Schalken with me? He had returned to his native
land, and was probably dead and buried, before I
was born; I never visited Holland nor spoke with
a native of that country. So much I believe you
already know. I must, then, give you my authority, and state to you frankly the ground upon
which rests the credibility of the strange story
which I am, about to lay before you.

I was acquainted, in my early days, with a
Captain Vandael, whose father had served King
William in the Low Countries, and also in my
own unhappy land during the Irish campaigns.
I know not how it happened that I liked this
man's society, spite of his politics and religion:
but so it was; and it was by means of the free
intercourse to which our intimacy gave rise that
I became possessed of the curious tale which you
are about to hear.

I had often been struck, while visiting Vandael, by a remarkable picture, in which, though
no connoisseur myself, I could not fail to discern some very strong peculiarities, particularly
in the distribution of light and shade, as also a
certain oddity in the design itself, which interested my curiosity. It represented the interior of

what might be a chamber in some antique religious building—the foreground was occupied
by a female figure, arrayed in a species of white
robe, part of which is arranged so as to form a
veil. The dress, however, is not strictly that of
any religious order. In its hand the figure bears a
lamp, by whose light alone the form and face are
illuminated; the features are marked by an arch
smile, such as pretty women wear when engaged
in successfully practising some roguish trick; in
the background, and, excepting where the dim
red light of an expiring fire serves to define the
form, totally in the shade, stands the figure of a
man equipped in the old fashion, with doublet
and so forth, in an attitude of alarm, his hand
being placed upon the hilt of his sword, which
he appears to be in the act of drawing.

"There are some pictures," said I to my
friend, "which impress one, I know not how,
with a conviction that they represent not the
mere ideal shapes and combinations which have
floated through the imagination of the artist, but
scenes, faces, and situations which have actually
existed. When I look upon that picture, something assures me that I behold the representa-
tion of a reality."

Vandael smiled, and, fixing his eyes upon the
painting musingly, he said:

"Your fancy has not deceived you, my good
friend, for that picture is the record, and I believe a faithful one, of a remarkable and mysterious occurrence. It was painted by Schalken, and
contains, in the face of the female figure, which

occupies the most prominent place in the design, an accurate portrait of Rose Velderkaust, the niece of Gerard Douw, the first and, I believe, the only love of Godfrey Schalken. My father knew the painter well, and from Schalken himself he learned the story of the mysterious drama, one scene of which the picture has embodied. This painting, which is accounted a fine specimen of Schalken's style, was bequeathed to my father by the artist's will, and, as you have observed, is a very striking and interesting production."

I had only to request Vandael to tell the story of the painting in order to be gratified; and thus it is that I am enabled to submit to you a faithful recital of what I heard myself, leaving you to reject or to allow the evidence upon which the truth of the tradition depends, with this one assurance, that Schalken was an honest, blunt Dutchman, and, I believe, wholly incapable of committing a flight of imagination; and further, that Vandael, from whom I heard the story, appeared firmly convinced of its truth.

There are few forms upon which the mantle of mystery and romance could seem to hang more ungracefully than upon that of the uncouth and clownish Schalken—the Dutch boor—the rude and dogged, but most cunning worker in oils, whose pieces delight the initiated of the present day almost as much as his manners disgusted the refined of his own; and yet this man, so rude, so dogged, so slovenly, I had almost said so savage, in mien and manner, during his after successes, had been selected by the capricious goddess, in his early life, to figure as the hero of a romance by no means devoid of interest or of mystery.

Who can tell how meet he may have been in his young days to play the part of the lover or of the hero—who can say that in early life he had been the same harsh, unlicked, and rugged boor that, in his maturer age, he proved—or how far the neglected rudeness which afterwards marked his air, and garb, and manners, may not have been the growth of that reckless apathy not unfrequently produced by bitter misfortunes and disappointments in early life?

These questions can never now be answered.

We must content ourselves, then, with a plain statement of facts, or what have been received and transmitted as such, leaving matters of speculation to those who like them.

When Schalken studied under the immortal Gerard Douw, he was a young man; and in spite of the phlegmatic constitution and unexcitable manner which he shared, we believe, with his countrymen, he was not incapable of deep and vivid impressions, for it is an established fact that the young painter looked with considerable interest upon the beautiful niece of his wealthy master.

Rose Velderkaust was very young, having, at the period of which we speak, not yet attained her seventeenth year, and, if tradition speaks truth, possessed all the soft dimpling charms of the fair; light-haired Flemish maidens. Schalken had not studied long in the school of Gerard Douw, when he felt this interest deepening into something of a keener and intenser feeling than was quite consistent with the tranquillity of his honest Dutch heart; and at the same time he perceived, or thought he perceived, flattering symptoms of a reciprocity of liking, and this was quite sufficient to determine whatever indecision he might have heretofore experienced, and to lead him to devote exclusively to her every hope and feeling of his heart. In short, he was as much in love as a Dutchman could be. He was not long in making his passion known to the pretty maiden herself, and his declaration was followed by a corresponding confession upon her part.

Schalken, however, was a poor man, and he possessed no counterbalancing advantages of birth or position to induce the old man to consent to a union which must involve his niece and ward in the strugglings and difficulties of a young and nearly friendless artist. He was, therefore, to wait until time had furnished him with opportunity, and accident with success;

and then, if his labours were found sufficiently lucrative, it was to be hoped that his proposals might at least be listened to by her jealous guardian. Months passed away, and, cheered by the smiles of the little Rose, Schalken's labours were redoubled, and with such effect and improvement as reasonably to promise the realisation of his hopes, and no contemptible eminence in his art, before many years should have elapsed.

The even course of this cheering prosperity was, however, destined to experience a sudden and formidable interruption, and that, too, in a manner so strange and mysterious as to baffle all investigation, and throw upon the events themselves a shadow of almost supernatural horror.

Schalken had one evening remained in the master's studio considerably longer than his more volatile companions, who had gladly availed themselves of the excuse which the dusk of evening afforded, to withdraw from their several tasks, in order to finish a day of labour in the jollity and conviviality of the tavern.

But Schalken worked for improvement, or rather for love. Besides, he was now engaged merely in sketching a design, an operation which, unlike that of colouring, might be continued as long as there was light sufficient to distinguish between canvas and charcoal. He had not then, nor, indeed, until long after, discovered the peculiar powers of his pencil, and he was engaged in composing a group of extremely roguish-looking and grotesque imps and demons, who were inflicting various ingenious torments upon a perspiring and pot-bellied St. Anthony, who reclined in the midst of them, apparently in the last stage of drunkenness.

The young artist, however, though incapable of executing, or even of appreciating, anything of true sublimity, had nevertheless discernment enough to prevent his being by any means satisfied with his work; and many were the patient erasures and corrections which the limbs and features of saint and devil underwent, yet all without producing in their new arrangement anything of improvement or increased effect.

The large, old-fashioned room was silent, and, with the exception of himself, quite deserted by its usual inmates. An hour had passed—nearly two—without any improved result. Daylight had already declined, and twilight was fast giving way to the darkness of night. The patience of the young man was exhausted, and he stood before his unfinished production, absorbed in no very pleasing ruminations, one hand buried in the folds of his long dark hair, and the other holding the piece of charcoal which had so ill executed its office, and which he now rubbed, without much regard to the sable streaks which it produced, with irritable pressure upon his ample Flemish inexpressibles.

"Pshaw!" said the young man aloud, "would that picture, devils, saint, and all, were where they should be—in hell!"

A short, sudden laugh, uttered startlingly close to his ear, instantly responded to the ejaculation.

The artist turned sharply round, and now for the first time became aware that his labours had been overlooked by a stranger.

Within about a yard and a half, and rather behind him, there stood what was, or appeared to be, the figure of an elderly man: he wore a short cloak, and broad-brimmed hat with a conical crown, and in his hand, which was protected with a heavy, gauntlet-shaped glove, he carried a long ebony walking-stick, surmounted with what appeared, as it glittered dimly in the twilight, to be a massive head of gold, and upon his breast, through the folds of the cloak, there shone what appeared to be the links of a rich chain of the same metal.

The room was so obscure that nothing further of the appearance of the figure could be ascertained, and the face was altogether overshadowed by the heavy flap of the beaver which overhung it, so that not a feature could be discerned. A quantity of dark hair escaped from beneath this sombre hat, a circumstance which, connected with the firm, upright carriage of the intruder, proved that his years could not yet exceed threescore or thereabouts.

SHERIDAN LE FANU

There was an air of gravity and importance about the garb of this person, and something indescribably odd, I might say awful, in the perfect, stone-like movelessness of the figure, that effectually checked the testy comment which had at once risen to the lips of the irritated artist. He therefore, as soon as he had sufficiently recovered the surprise, asked the stranger, civilly, to be seated, and desired to know if he had any message to leave for his master.

"Tell Gerard Douw," said the unknown, without altering his attitude in the smallest degree, "that Mynher Vanderhausen of Rotterdam, desires to speak with him to-morrow evening at this hour, and, if he please, in this room, upon matters of weight—that is all. Good-night."

The stranger, having finished this message, turned abruptly, and, with a quick but silent step, quitted the room, before Schalken had time to say a word in reply.

The young man felt a curiosity to see in what direction the burgher of Rotterdam would turn on quitting the studio, and for that purpose he went directly to the window which commanded the door.

A lobby of considerable extent intervened between the inner door of the painter's room and the street entrance, so that Schalken occupied the post of observation before the old man could possibly have reached the street.

He watched in vain, however. There was no other mode of exit.

Had the old man vanished, or was he lurking about the recesses of the lobby for some bad purpose? This last suggestion filled the mind of Schalken with a vague horror, which was so unaccountably intense as to make him alike afraid to remain in the room alone and reluctant to pass through the lobby.

However, with an effort which appeared very disproportioned to the occasion, he summoned resolution to leave the room, and, having double-locked the door and thrust the key in his pocket, without looking to the right or left, he traversed the passage which had so recently, perhaps still, contained the person of his mysterious visitant, scarcely venturing to breathe till he had arrived in the open street.

"Mynher Vanderhausen," said Gerard Douw within himself, as the appointed hour approached, "Mynher Vanderhausen of Rotterdam! I never heard of the man till yesterday. What can he want of me? A portrait, perhaps, to be painted; or a younger son or a poor relation to be apprenticed; or a collection to be valued; or—pshaw! there's no one in Rotterdam to leave me a legacy. Well, whatever the business may be, we shall soon know it all."

It was now the close of day, and every easel, except that of Schalken, was deserted. Gerard Douw was pacing the apartment with the restless step of impatient expectation, every now and then humming a passage from a piece of music which he was himself composing; for, though no great proficient, he admired the art; sometimes pausing to glance over the work of one of his absent pupils, but more frequently placing himself at the window, from whence he might observe the passengers who threaded the obscure by-street in which his studio was placed.

"Said you not, Godfrey," exclaimed Douw, after a long and fruitless gaze from his post of observation, and turning to Schalken—"said you not the hour of appointment was at about seven by the clock of the Stadhouse?"

"It had just told seven when I first saw him, sir," answered the student.

"The hour is close at hand, then," said the master, consulting a horologe as large and as round as a full-grown orange. "Mynher Vanderhausen, from Rotterdam—is it not so?"

"Such was the name."

"And an elderly man, richly clad?" continued Douw.

"As well as I might see," replied his pupil; "he could not be young, nor yet very old neither, and his dress was rich and grave, as might become a citizen of wealth and consideration."

At this moment the sonorous boom of the Stadhouse clock told, stroke after stroke, the hour of seven; the eyes of both master and student were directed to the door; and it was not

288

until the last peal of the old bell had ceased to vibrate, that Douw exclaimed:

"So, so; we shall have his worship presently—that is, if he means to keep his hour; if not, thou mayst wait for him, Godfrey, if you court the acquaintance of a capricious burgomaster. As for me, I think our old Leyden contains a sufficiency of such commodities, without an importation from Rotterdam."

Schalken laughed, as in duty bound; and after a pause of some minutes, Douw suddenly exclaimed:

"What if it should all prove a jest, a piece of mummery got up by Vankarp, or some such worthy! I wish you had run all risks, and cudgelled the old burgomaster, stadholder, or whatever else he may be, soundly. I would wager a dozen of Rhenish, his worship would have pleaded old acquaintance before the third application."

"Here he comes, sir," said Schalken, in a low admonitory tone; and instantly, upon turning towards the door, Gerard Douw observed the same figure which had, on the day before, so unexpectedly greeted the vision of his pupil Schalken.

There was something in the air and mien of the figure which at once satisfied the painter that there was no mummery in the case, and that he really stood in the presence of a man of worship; and so, without hesitation, he doffed his cap, and courteously saluting the stranger, requested him to be seated.

The visitor waved his hand slightly, as, if in acknowledgment of the courtesy, but remained standing.

"I have the honour to see Mynher Vanderhausen, of Rotterdam?" said Gerard Douw.

"The same," was the laconic reply of his visitant.

"I understand your worship desires to speak with me," continued Douw, "and I am here by appointment to wait your commands."

"Is that a man of trust?" said Vanderhausen, turning towards Schalken, who stood at a little distance behind his master.

"Certainly," replied Gerard.

"Then let him take this box and get the nearest jeweller or goldsmith to value its contents, and let him return hither with a certificate of the valuation."

At the same time he placed a small case, about nine inches square, in the hands of Gerard Douw, who was as much amazed at its weight as at the strange abruptness with which it was handed to him.

In accordance with the wishes of the stranger, he delivered it into the hands of Schalken, and repeating his directions, despatched him upon the mission.

Schalken disposed his precious charge securely beneath the folds of his cloak, and rapidly traversing two or three narrow streets, he stopped at a corner house, the lower part of which was then occupied by the shop of a Jewish goldsmith.

Schalken entered the shop, and calling the little Hebrew into the obscurity of its back recesses, he proceeded to lay before him Vanderhausen's packet.

On being examined by the light of a lamp, it appeared entirely cased with lead, the outer surface of which was much scraped and soiled, and nearly white with age. This was with difficulty partially removed, and disclosed beneath a box of some dark and singularly hard wood; this, too, was forced, and after the removal of two or three folds of linen, its contents proved to be a mass of golden ingots, close packed, and, as the Jew declared, of the most perfect quality.

Every ingot underwent the scrutiny of the little Jew, who seemed to feel an epicurean delight in touching and testing these morsels of the glorious metal; and each one of them was replaced in the box with the exclamation:

"*Mein Gott,* how very perfect! not one grain of alloy—beautiful, beautiful!"

The task was at length finished, and the Jew certified under his hand the value of the ingots submitted to his examination to amount to many thousand rix-dollars.

With the desired document in his bosom, and the rich box of gold carefully pressed under his arm, and concealed by his cloak, he retraced his way, and entering the studio, found his master and the stranger in close conference.

Schalken had no sooner left the room, in order to execute the commission he had taken in charge, than Vanderhausen addressed Gerard Douw in the following terms:

"I may not tarry with you to-night more than a few minutes, and so I shall briefly tell you the matter upon which I come. You visited the town of Rotterdam some four months ago, and then I saw in the church of St. Lawrence your niece, Rose Velderkaust. I desire to marry her, and if I satisfy you as to the fact that I am very wealthy—more wealthy than any husband you could dream of for her—I expect that you will forward my views to the utmost of your authority. If you approve my proposal, you must close with it at once, for I cannot command time enough to wait for calculations and delays."

Gerard Douw was, perhaps, as much astonished as anyone could be by the very unexpected nature of Mynher Vanderhausen's communication; but he did not give vent to any unseemly expression of surprise, for besides the motives supplied by prudence and politeness, the painter experienced a kind of chill and oppressive sensation, something like that which is supposed to affect a man who is placed unconsciously in immediate contact with something to which he has a natural antipathy—an undefined horror and dread while standing in the presence of the eccentric stranger, which made him very unwilling to say anything which might reasonably prove offensive.

"I have no doubt," said Gerard, after two or three prefatory hems, "that the connection which you propose would prove alike advantageous and honourable to my niece; but you must be aware that she has a will of her own, and may not acquiesce in what we may design for her advantage."

"Do not seek to deceive me, Sir Painter," said Vanderhausen; "you are her guardian—she is your ward. She is mine if you like to make her so."

The man of Rotterdam moved forward a little as he spoke, and Gerard Douw, he scarce knew why, inwardly prayed for the speedy return of Schalken.

"I desire," said the mysterious gentleman, "to place in your hands at once an evidence of my wealth, and a security for my liberal dealing with your niece. The lad will return in a minute or two with a sum in value five times the fortune which she has a right to expect from a husband. This shall lie in your hands, together with her dowry, and you may apply the united sum as suits her interest best; it shall be all exclusively hers while she lives. Is that liberal?"

Douw assented, and inwardly thought that fortune had been extraordinarily kind to his niece. The stranger, he thought, must be both wealthy and generous, and such an offer was not to be despised, though made by a humourist, and one of no very prepossessing presence.

Rose had no very high pretensions, for she was almost without dowry; indeed, altogether so, excepting so far as the deficiency had been supplied by the generosity of her uncle. Neither had she any right to raise any scruples against the match on the score of birth, for her own origin was by no means elevated; and as to other objections, Gerard resolved, and, indeed, by the usages of the time was warranted in resolving, not to listen to them for a moment.

"Sir," said he, addressing the stranger, "your offer is most liberal, and whatever hesitation I may feel in closing with it immediately, arises solely from my not having the honour of knowing anything of your family or station. Upon these points you can, of course, satisfy me without difficulty?"

"As to my respectability," said the stranger, drily, "you must take that for granted at present; pester me with no inquiries; you can discover nothing more about me than I choose to make known. You shall have sufficient security for my respectability—my word, if you are honourable: if you are sordid, my gold."

"A testy old gentleman," thought Douw; "he must have his own way. But, all things considered, I am justified in giving my niece to him. Were she my own daughter, I would do the like by her. I will not pledge myself unnecessarily, however."

"You will not pledge yourself unnecessarily," said Vanderhausen, strangely uttering the very words which had just floated through the mind of his companion; "but you will do so if it is necessary, I presume; and I will show you that I consider it indispensable. If the gold I mean to leave in your hands satisfy you, and if you desire that my proposal shall not be at once withdrawn, you must, before I leave this room, write your name to this engagement."

Having thus spoken, he placed a paper in the hands of Gerard, the contents of which expressed an engagement entered into by Gerard Douw, to give to Wilken Vanderhausen, of Rotterdam, in marriage, Rose Velderkaust, and so forth, within one week of the date hereof.

While the painter was employed in reading this covenant, Schalken, as we have stated, entered the studio, and having delivered the box and the valuation of the Jew into the hands of the stranger, he was about to retire, when Vanderhausen called to him to wait; and, presenting the case and the certificate to Gerard Douw, he waited in silence until he had satisfied himself by an inspection of both as to the value of the pledge left in his hands. At length he said:

"Are you content?"

The painter said he would fain have another day to consider.

"Not an hour," said the suitor, coolly.

"Well, then," said Douw, "I am content; it is a bargain."

"Then sign at once," said Vanderhausen; "I am weary."

At the same time he produced a small case of writing materials, and Gerard signed the important document.

"Let this youth witness the covenant," said the old man; and Godfrey Schalken unconsciously signed the instrument which bestowed upon another that hand which he had so long regarded as the object and reward of all his labours.

The compact being thus completed, the strange visitor folded up the paper, and stowed it safely in an inner pocket.

"I will visit you to-morrow night, at nine of the clock, at your house, Gerard Douw, and will see the subject of our contract. Farewell." And so saying, Wilken Vanderhausen moved stiffly, but rapidly out of the room.

Schalken, eager to resolve his doubts, had placed himself by the window in order to watch the street entrance; but the experiment served only to support his suspicions, for the old man did not issue from the door. This was very strange, very odd, very fearful. He and his master returned together, and talked but little on the way, for each had his own subjects of reflection, of anxiety, and of hope.

Schalken, however, did not know the ruin which threatened his cherished schemes.

Gerard Douw knew nothing of the attachment which had sprung up between his pupil and his niece; and even if he had, it is doubtful whether he would have regarded its existence as any serious obstruction to the wishes of Mynher Vanderhausen.

Marriages were then and there matters of traffic and calculation; and it would have appeared as absurd in the eyes of the guardian to make a mutual attachment an essential element in a contract of marriage, as it would have been to draw up his bonds and receipts in the language of chivalrous romance.

The painter, however, did not communicate to his niece the important step which he had taken in her behalf, and his resolution arose not from any anticipation of opposition on her part, but solely from a ludicrous consciousness that if his ward were, as she very naturally might do, to ask him to describe the appearance of the bridegroom whom he destined for her, he would be forced to confess that he had not seen his face, and, if called upon, would find it impossible to identify him.

Upon the next day, Gerard Douw, having dined, called his niece to him, and having scanned her person with an air of satisfaction, he took her hand, and looking upon her pretty, innocent face with a smile of kindness, he said:

"Rose, my girl, that face of yours will make your fortune." Rose blushed and smiled. "Such faces and such tempers seldom go together, and, when they do, the compound is a love-potion which few heads or hearts can resist. Trust me, thou wilt soon be a bride, girl. But this is trifling, and I am pressed for time, so make ready the large room by eight o'clock to-night, and give directions for supper at nine. I expect a friend to-night; and observe me, child, do thou trick thyself out handsomely. I would not have him think us poor or sluttish."

With these words he left the chamber, and took his way to the room to which we have already had occasion to introduce our readers—that in which his pupils worked.

When the evening closed in, Gerard called Schalken, who was about to take his departure to his obscure and comfortless lodgings, and asked him to come home and sup with Rose and Van-derhausen.

The invitation was of course accepted, and Gerard Douw and his pupil soon found themselves in the handsome and somewhat antique-looking room which had been prepared for the reception of the stranger.

A cheerful wood-fire blazed in the capacious hearth; a little at one side an old-fashioned table, with richly-carved legs, was placed—destined, no doubt, to receive the supper, for which prep-arations were going forward; and ranged with exact regularity, stood the tall-backed chairs, whose ungracefulness was more than counter-balanced by their comfort.

The little party, consisting of Rose, her uncle, and the artist, awaited the arrival of the expected visitor with considerable impatience.

Nine o'clock at length came, and with it a summons at the street-door, which, being speedily answered, was followed by a slow and emphatic tread upon the staircase; the steps moved heavily across the lobby, the door of the room in which the party which we have de-scribed were assembled slowly opened, and there entered a figure which startled, almost ap-palled, the phlegmatic Dutchmen, and nearly made Rose scream with affright; it was the form, and arrayed in the garb, of Mynher Vanderhau-sen; the air, the gait, the height was the same, but the features had never been seen by any of the party before.

The stranger stopped at the door of the room, and displayed his form and face com-pletely. He wore a dark-coloured cloth cloak, which was short and full, not falling quite to the knees; his legs were cased in dark purple silk stockings, and his shoes were adorned with roses of the same colour. The opening of the cloak in front showed the under-suit to consist of some very dark, perhaps sable material, and his hands were enclosed in a pair of heavy leather gloves which ran up considerably above the wrist, in the manner of a gauntlet. In one hand he car-ried his walking-stick and his hat, which he had removed, and the other hung heavily by his side. A quantity of grizzled hair descended in long tresses from his head, and its folds rested upon the plaits of a stiff ruff, which effectually con-cealed his neck.

So far all was well; but the face!—all the flesh of the face was coloured with the bluish leaden hue which is sometimes produced by the opera-tion of metallic medicines administered in ex-cessive quantities; the eyes were enormous, and the white appeared both above and below the iris, which gave to them an expression of insan-ity, which was heightened by their glassy fixed-ness; the nose was well enough, but the mouth was writhed considerably to one side, where it opened in order to give egress to two long, dis-coloured fangs, which projected from the up-per jaw, far below the lower lip; the hue of the lips themselves bore the usual relation to that of the face, and was consequently nearly black. The character of the face was malignant, even Satanic, to the last degree; and, indeed, such a combination of horror could hardly be ac-counted for, except by supposing the corpse of some atrocious malefactor, which had long hung blackening upon the gibbet, to have at length become the habitation of a demon—the frightful sport of Satanic possession.

It was remarkable that the worshipful stranger suffered as little as possible of his flesh to appear, and that during his visit he did not once remove his gloves.

Having stood for some moments at the door, Gerard Douw at length found breath and collectedness to bid him welcome, and, with a mute inclination of the head, the stranger stepped forward into the room.

There was something indescribably odd, even horrible, about all his motions, something undefinable, that was unnatural, unhuman—it was as if the limbs were guided and directed by a spirit unused to the management of bodily machinery.

The stranger said hardly anything during his visit, which did not exceed half an hour; and the host himself could scarcely muster courage enough to utter the few necessary salutations and courtesies: and, indeed, such was the nervous terror which the presence of Vanderhausen inspired, that very little would have made all his entertainers fly bellowing from the room.

They had not so far lost all self-possession, however, as to fail to observe two strange peculiarities of their visitor.

During his stay he did not once suffer his eyelids to close, nor even to move in the slightest degree; and further, there was a death-like stillness in his whole person, owing to the total absence of the heaving motion of the chest, caused by the process of respiration.

These two peculiarities, though when told they may appear trifling, produced a very striking and unpleasant effect when seen and observed. Vanderhausen at length relieved the painter of Leyden of his inauspicious presence; and with no small gratification the little party heard the street-door close after him.

"Dear uncle," said Rose, "what a frightful man! I would not see him again for the wealth of the States!"

"Tush, foolish girl!" said Douw, whose sensations were anything but comfortable. "A man may be as ugly as the devil, and yet if his heart and actions are good, he is worth all the pretty-faced, perfumed puppies that walk the Mall. Rose, my girl, it is very true he has not thy pretty face, but I know him to be wealthy and liberal; and were he ten times more ugly—"

"Which is inconceivable," observed Rose.

"These two virtues would be sufficient," continued her uncle, "to counterbalance all his deformity; and if not of power sufficient actually to alter the shape of the features, at least of efficacy enough to prevent one thinking them amiss."

"Do you know, uncle," said Rose, "when I saw him standing at the door, I could not get it out of my head that I saw the old, painted, wooden figure that used to frighten me so much in the church of St. Lawrence of Rotterdam."

Gerard laughed, though he could not help inwardly acknowledging the justness of the comparison. He was resolved, however, as far as he could, to check his niece's inclination to ridicule the ugliness of her intended bridegroom, although he was not a little pleased to observe that she appeared totally exempt from that mysterious dread of the stranger which, he could not disguise it from himself, considerably affected him, as also his pupil Godfrey Schalken.

Early on the next day there arrived, from various quarters of the town, rich presents of silks, velvets, jewellery, and so forth, for Rose; and also a packet directed to Gerard Douw, which, on being opened, was found to contain a contract of marriage, formally drawn up, between Wilken Vanderhausen of the Boom-quay, in Rotterdam, and Rose Velderkaust of Leyden, niece to Gerard Douw, master in the art of painting, also of the same city; and containing engagements on the part of Vanderhausen to make settlements upon his bride, far more splendid than he had before led her guardian to believe likely, and which were to be secured to her use in the most unexceptionable manner possible—the money being placed in the hands of Gerard Douw himself.

I have no sentimental scenes to describe, no

cruelty of guardians, or magnanimity of wards, or agonies of lovers. The record I have to make is one of sordidness, levity, and interest. In less than a week after the first interview which we have just described, the contract of marriage was fulfilled, and Schalken saw the prize which he would have risked anything to secure, carried off triumphantly by his formidable rival.

For two or three days he absented himself from the school; he then returned and worked, if with less cheerfulness, with far more dogged resolution than before; the dream of love had given place to that of ambition.

Months passed away, and, contrary to his expectation, and, indeed, to the direct promise of the parties, Gerard Douw heard nothing of his niece, or her worshipful spouse. The interest of the money, which was to have been demanded in quarterly sums, lay unclaimed in his hands. He began to grow extremely uneasy.

Mynher Vanderhausen's direction in Rotterdam he was fully possessed of. After some irresolution he finally determined to journey thither—a trifling undertaking, and easily accomplished—and thus to satisfy himself of the safety and comfort of his ward, for whom he entertained an honest and strong affection.

His search was in vain, however. No one in Rotterdam had ever heard of Mynher Vanderhausen.

Gerard Douw left not a house in the Boomquay untried; but all in vain. No one could give him any information whatever touching the object of his inquiry; and he was obliged to return to Leyden, nothing wiser than when he had left it.

On his arrival he hastened to the establishment from which Vanderhausen had hired the lumbering though, considering the times, most luxurious vehicle which the bridal party had employed to convey them to Rotterdam. From the driver of this machine he learned, that having proceeded by slow stages, they had late in the evening approached Rotterdam; but that before they entered the city, and while yet nearly a mile from it, a small party of men, soberly clad,

and after the old fashion, with peaked beards and moustaches, standing in the centre of the road, obstructed the further progress of the carriage. The driver reined in his horses, much fearing, from the obscurity of the hour, and the loneliness of the road, that some mischief was intended.

His fears were, however, somewhat allayed by his observing that these strange men carried a large litter, of an antique shape, and which they immediately set down upon the pavement, whereupon the bridegroom, having opened the coach-door from within, descended, and having assisted his bride to do likewise, led her, weeping bitterly and wringing her hands, to the litter, which they both entered. It was then raised by the men who surrounded it, and speedily carried towards the city, and before it had proceeded many yards the darkness concealed it from the view of the Dutch charioteer.

In the inside of the vehicle he found a purse, whose contents more than thrice paid the hire of the carriage and man. He saw and could tell nothing more of Mynher Vanderhausen and his beautiful lady. This mystery was a source of deep anxiety and almost of grief to Gerard Douw.

There was evidently fraud in the dealing of Vanderhausen with him, though for what purpose committed he could not imagine. He greatly doubted how far it was possible for a man possessing in his countenance so strong an evidence of the presence of the most demoniac feelings, to be in reality anything but a villain; and every day that passed without his hearing from or of his niece, instead of inducing him to forget his fears, on the contrary tended more and more to exasperate them.

The loss of his niece's cheerful society tended also to depress his spirits; and in order to dispel this despondency, which often crept upon his mind after his daily employment was over, he was wont frequently to prevail upon Schalken to accompany him home, and by his presence to dispel, in some degree, the gloom of his otherwise solitary supper.

One evening, the painter and his pupil were

sitting by the fire, having accomplished a comfortable supper, and had yielded to that silent pensiveness sometimes induced by the process of digestion, when their reflections were disturbed by a loud sound at the street-door, as if occasioned by some person rushing forcibly and repeatedly against it. A domestic had run without delay to ascertain the cause of the disturbance, and they heard him twice or thrice interrogate the applicant for admission, but without producing an answer or any cessation of the sounds.

They heard him then open the hall-door, and immediately there followed a light and rapid tread upon the staircase. Schalken laid his hand on his sword, and advanced towards the door. It opened before he reached it, and Rose rushed into the room. She looked wild and haggard, and pale with exhaustion and terror; but her dress surprised them as much even as her unexpected appearance. It consisted of a kind of white woollen wrapper, made close about the neck, and descending to the very ground. It was much deranged and travel-soiled. The poor creature had hardly entered the chamber when she fell senseless on the floor. With some difficulty they succeeded in reviving her, and on recovering her senses she instantly exclaimed, in a tone of eager, terrified impatience:

"Wine, wine, quickly, or I'm lost!"

Much alarmed at the strange agitation in which the call was made, they at once administered to her wishes, and she drank some wine with a haste and eagerness which surprised them. She had hardly swallowed it, when she exclaimed, with the same urgency:

"Food, food, at once, or I perish!"

A considerable fragment of a roast joint was upon the table, and Schalken immediately proceeded to cut some, but he was anticipated; for no sooner had she become aware of its presence than she darted at it with the rapacity of a vulture, and, seizing it in her hands she tore off the flesh with her teeth and swallowed it.

When the paroxysm of hunger had been a little appeased, she appeared suddenly to become aware how strange her conduct had been, or it may have been that other more agitating thoughts recurred to her mind, for she began to weep bitterly and to wring her hands.

"Oh! send for a minister of God," said she; "I am not safe till he comes; send for him speedily."

Gerard Douw despatched a messenger instantly, and prevailed on his niece to allow him to surrender his bedchamber to her use; he also persuaded her to retire to it at once and to rest; her consent was extorted upon the condition that they would not leave her for a moment.

"Oh that the holy man were here!" she said; "he can deliver me. The dead and the living can never be one—God has forbidden it."

With these mysterious words she surrendered herself to their guidance, and they proceeded to the chamber which Gerard Douw had assigned to her use.

"Do not—do not leave me for a moment," said she. "I am lost for ever if you do."

Gerard Douw's chamber was approached through a spacious apartment, which they were now about to enter. Gerard Douw and Schalken each carried a candle, so that a sufficient degree of light was cast upon all surrounding objects. They were now entering the large chamber, which, as I have said, communicated with Douw's apartment, when Rose suddenly stopped, and, in a whisper which seemed to thrill with horror, she said:

"O God! he is here—he is here! See, see—there he goes!"

She pointed towards the door of the inner room, and Schalken thought he saw a shadowy and ill-defined form gliding into that apartment. He drew his sword, and raising the candle so as to throw its light with increased distinctness upon the objects in the room, he entered the chamber into which the shadow had glided. No figure was there—nothing but the furniture which belonged to the room, and yet he could not be deceived as to the fact that something had moved before them into the chamber.

A sickening dread came upon him, and the cold perspiration broke out in heavy drops upon his forehead; nor was he more composed when he heard the increased urgency, the agony of entreaty, with which Rose implored them not to leave her for a moment.

"I saw him," said she. "He's here! I cannot be deceived—I know him. He's by me—he's with me—he's in the room. Then, for God's sake, as you would save, do not stir from beside me!"

They at length prevailed upon her to lie down upon the bed, where she continued to urge them to stay by her. She frequently uttered incoherent sentences, repeating again and again, "The dead and the living cannot be one—God has forbidden it!" and then again, "Rest to the wakeful—sleep to the sleep-walkers."

These and such mysterious and broken sentences she continued to utter until the clergyman arrived.

Gerard Douw began to fear, naturally enough, that the poor girl, owing to terror or ill-treatment, had become deranged; and he half suspected, by the suddenness of her appearance, and the unseasonableness of the hour, and, above all, from the wildness and terror of her manner, that she had made her escape from some place of confinement for lunatics, and was in immediate fear of pursuit. He resolved to summon medical advice as soon as the mind of his niece had been in some measure set at rest by the offices of the clergyman whose attendance she had so earnestly desired; and until this object had been attained, he did not venture to put any questions to her, which might possibly, by reviving painful or horrible recollections, increase her agitation.

The clergyman soon arrived—a man of ascetic countenance and venerable age—one whom Gerard Douw respected much, forasmuch as he was a veteran polemic, though one, perhaps, more dreaded as a combatant than beloved as a Christian—of pure morality, subtle brain, and frozen heart. He entered the chamber which communicated with that in which Rose reclined, and immediately on his arrival she requested him to pray for her, as for one who lay in the hands of Satan, and who could hope for deliverance—only from heaven.

That our readers may distinctly understand all the circumstances of the event which we are about imperfectly to describe, it is necessary to state the relative position of the parties who were engaged in it. The old clergyman and Schalken were in the anteroom of which we have already spoken; Rose lay in the inner chamber, the door of which was open; and by the side of the bed, at her urgent desire, stood her guardian; a candle burned in the bedchamber, and three were lighted in the outer apartment.

The old man now cleared his voice, as if about to commence; but before he had time to begin, a sudden gust of air blew out the candle which served to illuminate the room in which the poor girl lay, and she, with hurried alarm, exclaimed:

"Godfrey, bring in another candle; the darkness is unsafe."

Gerard Douw, forgetting for the moment her repeated injunctions in the immediate impulse, stepped from the bedchamber into the other, in order to supply what she desired.

"O God do not go, dear uncle!" shrieked the unhappy girl; and at the same time she sprang from the bed and darted after him, in order, by her grasp, to detain him.

But the warning came too late, for scarcely had he passed the threshold, and hardly had his niece had time to utter the startling exclamation, when the door which divided the two rooms closed violently after him, as if swung to by a strong blast of wind.

Schalken and he both rushed to the door, but their united and desperate efforts could not avail so much as to shake it.

Shriek after shriek burst from the inner chamber, with all the piercing loudness of despairing terror. Schalken and Douw applied every energy and strained every nerve to force open the door; but all in vain.

There was no sound of struggling from within, but the screams seemed to increase in loudness, and at the same time they heard the bolts of the latticed window withdrawn, and the window itself grated upon the sill as if thrown open.

One last shriek, so long and piercing and agonised as to be scarcely human, swelled from the room, and suddenly there followed a death-like silence.

A light step was heard crossing the floor, as if from the bed to the window; and almost at the same instant the door gave way, and, yielding to the pressure of the external applicants, they were nearly precipitated into the room. It was empty. The window was open, and Schalken sprang to a chair and gazed out upon the street and canal below. He saw no form, but he beheld, or thought he beheld, the waters of the broad canal beneath settling ring after ring in heavy circular ripples, as if a moment before disturbed by the immersion of some large and heavy mass.

No trace of Rose was ever after discovered, nor was anything certain respecting her mysterious wooer detected or even suspected; no clue whereby to trace the intricacies of the labyrinth and to arrive at a distinct conclusion was to be found. But an incident occurred, which, though it will not be received by our rational readers as at all approaching to evidence upon the matter, nevertheless produced a strong and a lasting impression upon the mind of Schalken.

Many years after the events which we have detailed, Schalken, then remotely situated, received an intimation of his father's death, and of his intended burial upon a fixed day in the church of Rotterdam. It was necessary that a very considerable journey should be performed by the funeral procession, which, as it will readily be believed, was not very numerously attended. Schalken with difficulty arrived in Rotterdam late in the day upon which the funeral was appointed to take place. The procession had not then arrived. Evening closed in, and still it did not appear.

Schalken strolled down to the church—he found it open—notice of the arrival of the funeral had been given, and the vault in which the body was to be laid had been opened. The official who corresponds to our sexton, on seeing a well-dressed gentleman, whose object was to attend the expected funeral, pacing the aisle of the church, hospitably invited him to share with him the comforts of a blazing wood fire, which, as was his custom in winter time upon such occasions, he had kindled on the hearth of a chamber which communicated, by a flight of steps, with the vault below.

In this chamber Schalken and his entertainer seated themselves, and the sexton, after some fruitless attempts to engage his guest in conversation, was obliged to apply himself to his tobacco-pipe and can to solace his solitude.

In spite of his grief and cares, the fatigues of a rapid journey of nearly forty hours gradually overcame the mind and body of Godfrey Schalken, and he sank into a deep sleep, from which he was awakened by some one shaking him gently by the shoulder. He first thought that the old sexton had called him, but he was no longer in the room.

He roused himself, and as soon as he could clearly see what was around him, he perceived a female form, clothed in a kind of light robe of muslin, part of which was so disposed as to act as a veil, and in her hand she carried a lamp. She was moving rather away from him, and towards the flight of steps which conducted towards the vaults.

Schalken felt a vague alarm at the sight of this figure, and at the same time an irresistible impulse to follow its guidance. He followed it towards the vaults, but when it reached the head of the stairs, he paused; the figure paused also, and, turning gently round, displayed, by the light of the lamp it carried, the face and features of his first love, Rose Velderkaust. There was nothing horrible, or even sad, in the countenance. On the contrary, it wore the same arch smile which used to enchant the artist long before in his happy days.

A feeling of awe and of interest, too intense to be resisted, prompted him to follow the spectre, if spectre it were. She descended the stairs—he followed; and, turning to the left, through a narrow passage, she led him, to his infinite surprise, into what appeared to be an old-fashioned Dutch apartment, such as the pictures of Gerard Douw have served to immortalise.

Abundance of costly antique furniture was disposed about the room, and in one corner stood a four-post bed, with heavy black-cloth curtains around it; the figure frequently turned towards him with the same arch smile; and when she came to the side of the bed, she drew the curtains, and by the light of the lamp which she held towards its contents, she disclosed to the horror-stricken painter, sitting bolt upright in the bed, the livid and demoniac form of Vanderhausen. Schalken had hardly seen him when he fell senseless upon the floor, where he lay until discovered, on the next morning, by persons employed in closing the passages into the vaults. He was lying in a cell of considerable size, which had not been disturbed for a long time, and he had fallen beside a large coffin which was supported upon small stone pillars, a security against the attacks of vermin.

To his dying day Schalken was satisfied of the reality of the vision which he had witnessed, and he has left behind him a curious evidence of the impression which it wrought upon his fancy, in a painting executed shortly after the event we have narrated, and which is valuable as exhibiting not only the peculiarities which have made Schalken's pictures sought after, but even more so as presenting a portrait, as close and faithful as one taken from memory can be, of his early love, Rose Velderkaust, whose mysterious fate must ever remain matter of speculation.

The picture represents a chamber of antique masonry, such as might be found in most old cathedrals, and is lighted faintly by a lamp carried in the hand of a female figure, such as we have above attempted to describe; and in the background, and to the left of him who examines the painting, there stands the form of a man apparently aroused from sleep, and by his attitude, his hand being laid upon his sword, exhibiting considerable alarm: this last figure is illuminated only by the expiring glare of a wood or charcoal fire.

The whole production exhibits a beautiful specimen of that artful and singular distribution of light and shade which has rendered the name of Schalken immortal among the artists of his country. This tale is traditionary, and the reader will easily perceive, by our studiously omitting to heighten many points of the narrative, when a little additional colouring might have added effect to the recital, that we have desired to lay before him, not a figment of the brain, but a curious tradition connected with, and belonging to, the biography of a famous artist.

WHILE ZOMBIES WALKED

THORP McCLUSKY

THORP McCLUSKY (1906–1975) studied music at Syracuse University but spent most of his life as a freelance writer in New Jersey. As is true for most journalists and fiction authors who don't enjoy great success in a single literary genre or special field of expertise, McClusky wrote both fiction and nonfiction in wildly disparate areas. He enjoys a modest reputation as the author of about forty short stories for the pulps, mostly in the horror category, occasionally for the prestigious *Weird Tales*, though he also wrote Westerns and mysteries. Among his best-known works are the serial *Loot of the Vampire,* published in book form in 1975, and the frequently reprinted "The Crawling Horror." He used a variety of pseudonyms, including L. MacKay Phelps, Thorp McClosky, Otis Cameron, and Larry Freud.

Among his juveniles are *Chuck Malloy Railroad Detective on the Streamliner* (Big Little Book, 1938) and *Calling W-1-X-Y-Z Jimmy Kean and the Radio Spies* (Better Little Books, 1939). Most of his pulp fiction was published in the 1930s and 1940s, after which he mainly produced journalism for *The Saturday Evening Post, Man's Magazine,* and others. His single nonfiction book was *Your Health and Chiropractic* (1962). He also served as the editor of *Motor* magazine.

"While Zombies Walked" was the uncredited inspiration for the B movie *Revenge of the Zombies,* produced by Monogram in 1943. Directed by Steve Sekely, with an "original" screenplay by Van Norcross and Ed Kelso, it starred John Carradine, Robert Lowery, Gale Storm, and Mantan Moreland. The story was first published in the September 1939 issue of *Weird Tales*.

THORP McCLUSKY

WHILE ZOMBIES WALKED

THE PACKARD ROADSTER had left the lowland and was climbing into the hills. It was rough going; this back road was hardly more than two deep, grass-grown ruts—the car barely crawled. Overhead the vivid greenery of the trees nearly met, shrouding, intensifying the heat.

Eileen's letter had brought Anthony Kent down the Atlantic seaboard, his heart leaden, his thoughts troubled. There had been a strangeness in Eileen's brusque dismissal.

"Tony," the letter had read, "you must not come to see me this summer. You must not write to me any more. I do not want to see you or hear from you again!"

It had not been like Eileen—that letter; Eileen would at least have been gentle. It was as though that letter had been dictated by a stranger, as though Eileen had been but a puppet, writing words which were not her own. . . .

"Back in the hills aways," an emaciated, filthy white man, sitting on the steps of a dilapidated shack just off the through highway, had said sourly, in answer to Tony's inquiry. But Tony, glancing at his speedometer, saw that he had already come three and seven-tenths miles. Had the man deliberately misdirected him? After that first startled glance there had been a curious flat opacity in the man's eyes. . . .

Abruptly, rounding a sharp bend in the narrow road, the car came upon a small clearing, in the heart of which nestled a tiny cabin. But at a glance Tony saw that the cabin was deserted. No smoke curled from the rusty iron stovepipe, no dog lay panting in the deep shade, the windows stared bleakly down the road.

Yet a planting of cotton still struggled feebly against the lush weeds! This was the third successive shack on that miserable road that had been, for some strange reason, suddenly abandoned. The peculiarity of this circumstance escaped Tony. His thoughts, leaden, bewildered, full of the dread that Eileen no longer loved him, were turned too deeply inward upon themselves.

It had been absurd of Eileen—throwing up her job with the Lacey-Kent people to rush off down here the instant she heard of her great-uncle's stroke. Absurd, because she could have done more for the old fellow by remaining in New York.

And yet old Robert Perry had raised his dissolute nephew's little girl almost from babyhood, had put her through Brenau College;

Tony realised that Eileen's gesture had been the only one compatible with her nature.

But why had she jilted him?

The woebegone shack had merged into the forest. The road, if anything, was growing worse; the car was climbing a gentle grade. Now, as it topped the rise, Tony saw outspread before his eyes a small valley, hemmed in by wooded hills. A rambling, pillared house, half hidden by mimosa and magnolias, flanked by barns, out-buildings, and a tobacco shed, squatted amid broad, level acres lush with cotton.

At first glance the place seemed peculiarly void of life. No person moved in the wide yard surrounding the house; no smoke curled from the field-stone chimney. But as Tony's gaze swept the broad, undulating fields he saw men working, men who were clad in grimy, dirt-greyed garments that were an almost perfect camouflage. Only a hundred feet down the road a man moved slowly through the cotton.

Tony stopped the car opposite the man.

"Is this the Perry place?" he called, his voice sharp and distinct through the afternoon's heat and stillness.

But the grey-clad toiler never lifted his gaze from the cotton beneath his eyes, never so much as turned his head or paused in his work to sig-nify that he had heard.

Tony felt anger rising in him. His nerves were taut with worry, and he had driven many miles without rest. At least the fellow could leave off long enough to give him a civil answer!

But then, the man might be a little deaf. Tony shrugged, jumped from the car and ploughed through the cotton.

"Is this the Perry place?" he bawled.

The man was not more than six feet from Tony, working toward him, with lowered head and shadowed face. But if he heard, he gave no sign.

Sudden, blind rage swept Tony. Had his nerves not been almost at snapping-point he would never have done what he did; he would have let the man's amazing boorishness pass without a word, would have turned back to his car in disgust. But Tony, that day, was not him-self.

"Why you—" he choked. He took a sudden step forward and jerked the man roughly erect.

For an instant Tony glimpsed the man's eyes, grey, sunken, filmed, expressionless as though the man were either blind or an idiot. And then the man, as if nothing had occurred, was once more slumping over the cotton!

"God Almighty!" Tony breathed. And sud-denly a chill like ice pressing against his spine swept him, sent his mind swirling and his knees weakly buckling.

The man wore a shapeless, broad-brimmed hat, fastened on his head by a band of elastic be-neath his chin. But the savage shaking Tony had given him had jolted it awry.

Above the man's left temple, amid the grey-flecked hair, jagged splinters of bone gleamed through torn and discoloured flesh! And a grey-ish ribbon of brain-stuff hung down beside the man's left ear!

The man was working in the cotton—with a fractured skull!

TONY'S THOUGHTS WERE reeling, his mind dazed. How that man could continue to work with his brains seeping through a hole in his head was a question so unanswerable he did not even consider it. And yet, dimly, he re-membered the almost miraculous stories that had come out of the war, stories of men who had lived with bullet-holes through their heads and with shell fragments imbedded inches deep within their brain-cases. Something like that must have happened to this man. Some horrible accident must have numbed or destroyed every spark of intelligence in him, must have bizarrely left him with only the mechanical impulse to work.

He must be taken to the house at once, Tony knew. Gently Tony grasped his shoulders. And in the mid-afternoon's heat his nerves crawled.

The stooping body beneath the frayed cotton shirt was snake-cold!

"Lord—he's dying—standing on his feet!" Tony mumbled.

The man resisted Tony's efforts to direct him toward the car. As Tony pushed him gently, he resisted as gently, turning back toward the cotton. As Tony, gritting his teeth, grasped those cold shoulders and tugged with all his strength, the man hung back with a strange, weird tenaciousness.

Suddenly Tony released his grip. He was afraid to risk stunning the man with a blow, for a blow might mean death. Yet, strong as he was, he could not budge the man from the path he was chopping along the cotton.

There was only one thing to do. He must go to the house and get help.

Stumbling, his mind vague with horror, Tony made his way to the car, and sent it hurtling the last half-mile down the narrow road to the house.

Only subconsciously, as he plunged up the uneven walk between fragrant, flowering shrubs, did he notice the strange discrepancy between the well-kept appearance of the fields and the dilapidation of the house. His mind was too full of the plodding horror he had seen. But the windows of the house were almost opaque with dirt, and at some of them dusty curtains hung limply while others stared nakedly blank. The screens on the long low porch were torn and rusted as though they had received no attention since spring; the lawn and the shrubbery were unkempt.

Three or four dust-grey wicker chairs stood along the porch. In one of those chairs sat a man.

He was old, and sparsely built. Had he been standing erect he would have measured well over six feet, but he lay back in his chair with his legs extending supinely before him. Tony knew instantly that this was Eileen's great-uncle, Robert Perry.

As he plunged up the dirt-encrusted steps Tony exclaimed hoarsely, "Mr. Perry? I'm Tony Kent. There's a man—"

The old man was leaning slightly forward in his chair. His blue eyes in his deeply lined face suddenly flamed.

"Have you got a gun?" The words were taut and low.

"No." Tony shook his head impatiently. His mind was full of the horror he had seen working back there in the field. A gun! What did he want with a gun? Did old Robert Perry think he would be dangerous—the story-book rejected-lover type, perhaps? Nonsense. Urgent, staccato words tumbled from his lips as he ignored the question.

"Mr. Perry—there's a man back there with the whole top of his head split open. He's stark mad; he wouldn't speak to me or come with me. But—he'll die if he's left where he is! It's a wonder he isn't dead already."

There was a long silence before the old man answered. "Where did you see this man?"

"Back there—back in the cotton."

Old Robert Perry shook his head, spoke in a muttered whisper, as if to himself, "Die? He can't—die!"

Abruptly he paused. The screen door leading into the house had opened. Two Negroes and a white man had come out on the porch.

The two Negroes were nondescript enough—mere plantation blacks. But the white man!

He was tall and wide as a door. He was so huge that any person attempting to guess his weight would have considered himself lucky if he got the figure within a score of pounds of the truth; he was bigger than any man Tony had ever seen outside a sideshow. And he was not a glandular freak; he was muscled like a jungle beast; his whole posture, his whole carriage silently shrieked super-human vitality. His gargantuan face, beneath the broad-brimmed, rusty black hat he wore, was pale as the belly of a dead fish, pale with the pallor of one who shuns the sunlight. His eyes were wide-set, coal-black, and staring; Tony had glimpsed that same intensity of gaze before in the eyes of religious and sociological fanatics. His nose was fleshy and well-muscled at the tip; his lips were thin and straight and tightly compressed. Garbed as he was in a knee-length, clerical coat of greenish, faded black, still wearing a frayed, filthy-white episcopal collar, he looked what he must have been, a pastor without honour, a renegade man of God.

He stood silently there on the porch and looked disapprovingly at Tony. His thin, weak, reformer's lips beneath that powerful, sensual nose tightened. Then, quietly, he spoke, not to Tony but to the paralytic old man:

"Who is this—person, Mr. Perry?"

Tony's fists clenched at the man's insolence. His anger turned to astonishment as he heard the old man answer almost cringingly: "This is Anthony Kent, Reverend Barnes—Anthony Kent, from New York City. Anthony—the Reverend Warren Barnes, who is stopping with us for a while. He has been very kind to us during my—illness."

Tony nodded coldly. The funereal-clad colossus stared for a long moment at this unexpected guest, and Tony could feel the menace smouldering in him like banked fires. But when he spoke for the second time his words were innocuous enough.

"I'm temporarily in charge here." His voice was vibrant as a great hollow drum. "Mr. Perry's mind, since he suffered his most unfortunate stroke, has not always been entirely clear, and Miss Eileen too. I am temporarily without a pastorate, and I am glad to help in any way that I can. You understand, I'm sure?" He smiled, the sickeningly pious smile of the chronic hypocrite, and ostentatiously clasped his hands.

Again Tony nodded. "Yes, I understand, Reverend," he said quickly, although some obscure sixth sense had already warned him that this man was as slimy and dangerous as a water-moccasin—and as treacherous. But—that man in the field, working in the cotton with the brain-stuff hanging down behind his ear! Hurriedly, Tony went on, "I spoke to Mr. Perry when I came up the steps—something must be done at once—there's a man working out there

in the field beside the road with something seriously wrong with his head. My God, I looked at him, and it looked to me as though his skull was fractured!"

With surprising swiftness the colossus turned upon Tony. "What's that you say? It looked as though *what?*"

Tony rasped, "A man working in the field with a fractured skull, Reverend! His head looks staved in—bashed open—God knows how he can still work. He's got to be brought to the house."

The giant's too brilliant, too intense black eyes were suddenly crafty. He laughed, patronisingly, as though humouring a child or a drunkard. "Oh, come, come, Mr. Kent; such things are impossible, you know. A trick of the light, or perhaps your weariness; you've driven a long distance, haven't you? One's eyes play strange tricks upon one."

He peered at Tony, and suddenly the expression on his face changed. "But if you're worried, we'll convince you, put your mind at ease. You go and get Cullen, Mose and Job. Jump smart, niggers!" He pointed up the road. "Jump smart; bring Cullen back here; Mr. Kent's got to be shown." His thin lips curled scornfully.

The two Negroes "jumped smart." The Reverend Warren Barnes calmly seated himself in one of the wicker chairs near paralytic old Robert Perry and waved carelessly toward a vacant chair. Tony sat down—glanced inquiringly at Eileen's uncle. But the aged man remained silent, apathetic, indifferent. Obviously, Tony thought, his mind *was* enfeebled; in that, at least, the Reverend Barnes had been truthful.

Almost diffidently, Tony addressed the white-haired old paralytic.

"I've come here to speak with Eileen, Mr. Perry. I can't believe that she meant—what she wrote in her last letter. Regardless of whether or not her feelings toward me have changed, I must speak to her. Where is she?"

When the old man spoke his voice was flat and hard. "Eileen has written to tell you that she wished to terminate whatever had been between you. Perhaps she has decided that she would prefer not to become too deeply involved with a Northerner. Perhaps she has other reasons. But in any case, Mr. Kent, you are not acting the gentleman in coming here and attempting to renew an acquaintanceship that has been quite definitely broken off."

The words were brutal, and not at all the sort of speech Tony would have expected, a moment ago, from a man whose mind had dimmed through age and shock. A sharp, involuntary retort surged to Tony's lips. Suddenly, then, the Reverend Barnes guffawed loudly.

"There, Mr. Kent!" he chuckled. It was a sound utterly unministerial, utterly coarse, sardonic and evil. "There—coming down the road. Is that the man you saw working in the cotton— with the fractured skull?"

Walking into the yard between the two Negroes was the white man Tony had encountered earlier. He was plodding along steadily, almost rapidly, with no assistance from his coloured companions. The straw hat was set tightly down upon his head, shading his face and covering his temples. There was no bit of greyish stuff hanging down beside his left ear.

The three men halted before the porch. The Reverend Barnes, grinning broadly, showing great, yellowed, decaying teeth, stood up and put his hands on the porch rail. Abruptly he spoke to Tony.

"Is this the man, Mr. Kent?"

Tony, his mind numb with amazement, answered, "It's the man, all right."

The Reverend Barnes's grin deepened. "Are you all right, Cullen? Do you feel quite able to work? Not ill, or anything?"

There was a long, long pause before the man answered. And when at last he spoke, his voice was curiously cadenceless, as though speech were an art he seldom practised. But there was no doubt about what he said.

"Ahm all right, Reverend Barnes. Ah feels good."

The big man chuckled, as though in appreciation of some ghastly joke.

"You haven't any headache?" he persisted. "No dizziness from the sun, perhaps? You don't want to knock off for the rest of the day?"

After a moment the reply came.

"Ah ain' got no haidache. Ah kin work."

The Reverend Barnes smiled pontifically. "Very well, then, Cullen. You may go back to work."

"Wait!" Tony exclaimed. "Tell him to take off his hat."

The big man wheeled slowly; slowly his right hand lifted, like that of some mighty patriarch about to pronounce a benediction—or a damning curse. For an instant Tony glimpsed murder in his eyes. Then his hand fell, and he spoke smoothly, quietly, to Cullen.

"Take off your hat, Cullen."

With maddening, mechanical slowness the man lifted his hat, and Tony saw a mat of iron-grey hair, caked with dirt.

"Put your hat back on, Cullen. You may go back to work."

The man turned, was plodding slowly from the yard. And in that instant, striking vaguely against his dazed consciousness, the realisation came to Tony that only the hair on the left side of the man's skull was matted with ground-in dust—the hair above his right ear was relatively clean! He opened his lips to speak. But the Reverend Barnes, as if anticipating him, was saying with amused, contemptuous finality:

"He's gone back to work. Dirty fellows, aren't they—these poor white trash?"

And Tony, wondering if his own reason were tottering, let the man go. . . .

The big man settled comfortably back in his chair.

"You thought you saw something you didn't," he said. His voice was soft now, soft and tolerant as silk. "Eye-strain, nervousness that's very close to hysteria. You must look after yourself."

For an instant Tony cradled his face in his

hands. Yes, he must get hold of himself; his mind was overwrought. He raised his head and looked at the old man. "Eileen," he said doggedly. "I must see her."

Old Robert Perry opened his lips to speak. And suddenly the big man turned in his chair to stare deeply into the aged paralytic's eyes.

"You would like to see Miss Eileen?" he asked Tony, then, with grave courtesy, "But certainly, Mr. Perry. He's come such a distance; it would be a pity—"

"Whatever you say."

The Reverend Barnes rose from his chair, smiled sorrowfully and pityingly toward Tony.

"Job, Mose," he said to the two Negroes, "stay here on the porch, in case Mr. Perry has one of his spells." He nodded significantly to Tony. "I'll call Miss Eileen. Such a lovely, sweet girl!"

Leisurely, moving on the balls of his feet like some magnificent jungle beast, he rose and stalked across the porch, opened the rusty screen door and disappeared within the house.

Mr. Perry did not speak; neither did Tony. There was something in the air that eluded him, Tony knew—some mystery that even Mr. Perry himself concealed, some mystery that seemed as elusive as the breeze stirring the magnolias.

FOOTSTEPS WITHIN THE house, and Eileen Perry, small, slender, with the wistful beauty of a spring flower, came onto the porch. Behind her, as if carelessly, his face overspread with a pious smirk, lounged Reverend Barnes.

Tony started up eagerly.

"Eileen!"

For a moment she did not speak. Only her splendid eyes looked at him hungrily, with ill-concealed terror rising in their depths.

"You shouldn't have come, Tony," she said then, simply.

The words were a rebuff. Yet Tony fancied that he had seen her hands lift toward him. He took a single step forward. But, as if to elude him, she stepped swiftly to the rail, stood with her back toward him.

"I *had* to come, Eileen," Tony said. His voice sounded oddly choked. "I love you. I had to know if you meant—those words you wrote, or if it was some strange madness—"

"Madness?" She laughed, and there was sudden hysteria in her low contralto voice. "Madness? No. I've changed, Tony. You may think what you please about me; you may think that I'm fickle, or that I'm insane—whatever you will. But—above everything else in the world I did not want you to come here. Is that plain enough for you? I thought I tried to tell you that in my letter. And now—I wish that you would go."

As a man who dreams a nightmare, Tony heard his own voice, muttering, "But don't you *love me*, Eileen?"

For a moment he believed that she would speak, but she did not. She turned, and, without a backward look, walked into the house.

The giant, Reverend Barnes, was rubbing his hands together—an incongruous, absurd gesture in a man of his physique. And then, after a moment, he laughed, a hoarse, obscene guffaw. But Tony, heartbroken, heard the insulting sound as no more than a disquieting rumble that had no meaning. His lips quivering, his eyes misty with the sudden tears he could not restrain, he walked slowly across the porch.

Then, as though the longing in them could bring her back to him, his tear-dimmed eyes gazed into the emptiness where Eileen had stood, looked unseeingly across the flowering mimosa, stared downward for a second at the porch rail.

A single word had been written on that rail, written in dust with a fingertip. Tony's mind did not register the significance of that word; it was transmitted only to his subconscious. But, as if mechanically, his lax lips moved.

The sombrely clad giant suddenly tensed, took a step forward.

"What was that you said, Mr. Kent?"

Mechanically Tony repeated the word.

The big man's eyes swept the rail. The grin had abruptly gone from his face; his muscles knotted beneath his rusty black coat.

And then he leaped. And simultaneously leaped the two Negroes who had lingered, diffidently, down the porch.

Monstrous, spatulate, pasty-white hands clenched into Tony's throat. Abruptly fighting, not with his numbed brain, but with a primitive, involuntary instinct of the flesh for self-preservation, Tony sent his fists lashing into the pair of black faces before him. But the giant renegade minister was on his shoulders like an albino shrouded leopard; the Negroes were tearing at his arms. His knees were buckling.

Like a slender tree stricken by the woodsman's axe, he wavered and plunged headlong. There was a cascade of darting light as his head crashed against the dusty pine boards. Then came oblivion.

ANTHONY KENT AWOKE to swirling, throbbing pain. His skull beat and hammered; the dim walls of a small room, barren save for the straw-mattressed cot on which he lay, swooped and gyrated before his eyes.

Slowly he recalled what had occurred. The Reverend Barnes, that magnificent jackal, had struck him down as he stood on the porch. He was in some long-disused room, presumably a servant's bedchamber, within the old Perry house.

A word was struggling upward from deep within his brain. What was that word? Almost he remembered it. It was the word Eileen had written in dust on the porch rail, a word repulsive and hideous.

Eileen had been trying to tell him something, trying to convey some message to him. Eileen, then, loved him!

What was the word?

There was a small, square window in the room, through which a feeble, yellowish light struck high up on the opposite wall. The sun was setting, then; he had been unconscious for hours. But it was not at the window that Tony glanced despairingly. It was at the two-by-six pine beams nailed closely together across that small square space!

Tony stumbled to his feet, reeled to the window and shook those wooden bars with all his strength. But they were solid white pine, and they had been spiked to the house with twenty-penny nails.

Through the narrow apertures between the beams Tony could see the broad, level fields, and the road, sloping gently upward to disappear within the encircling forest.

People were coming down that road now, grey, dusty people who plodded toward the house. They appeared almost doll-like, for the room in which Tony was imprisoned was on the side of the house, and long before the road swung in toward the yard they passed beyond his vision. But as Tony watched them his nerves crawled.

They walked so slowly, so listlessly, with dragging footsteps! And they stumbled frequently against one another, and against the stones in the road, as though they were almost blind. Almost they walked like soldiers suffering from shell-shock, but recently discharged from some hospital in hell.

For many were maimed. One walked with a deep, broken stoop, as though his chest had been crushed against his backbone. Another's leg was off below the knee, and in place of an artificial limb he wore a stick tied against the leg with rope, a stick that reached from twelve inches beyond the stump to the hip. A third had only one arm; a fourth was skeleton-thin.

In the Name of God whence had these maimed toilers come?

And then a soundless scream rattled in Tony's throat; for, coming down the road alone, walking with the same dragging lifelessness as did the others, was another of the grey toilers. And, as the man turned the wide sweep in the road that would lead him to the house and beyond Tony's vision, Tony glimpsed, in the last yellow rays of the setting sun, the horror that had once been his face!

Had once been his face! For, from beneath the ridge of his nose downward, *the man had no face!* The vertebrate whiteness of his spine, naked save for ragged strings of dessicated flesh, extended with horrid starkness from the throat of his shirt to merge with the shattered base of a bony skull!

HIDEOUS MINUTES PASSED, minutes through which Tony fought to retain some semblance of sanity. At last he staggered weakly to the door, only one thought in his mind—to escape that mad place and take Eileen with him.

But the door, like the bars across the window, was made of heavy pine. From its resistance to his assault Tony knew that it was secured by bars slotted through iron sockets. It was impregnable.

Darkness was within that room now. Night had come quickly with the setting of the sun, velvety, semi-tropical night. The window was a purplish square through which a star gleamed brilliantly; the pine bars were invisible in the gloom. Tony was engulfed in blackness.

Yet, in a corner near the floor, there was a lessening of the darkness. Tony, crouching there, saw that the light came through a quarter-inch crack between the planks. Throwing himself down, he glued his eyes to that crack.

He could see only a small portion of the room beneath him, a rectangle roughly three feet by twelve, yet that was enough to tell him that the room was the dining-room of the old house. The middle of an oaken table, littered with dishes and scraps of food, bisected his field of vision.

At that table, his back toward Tony, sat the apostate Reverend Barnes. A little way down the table a black hand and arm appeared and disappeared with irregular frequency. The rumble of voices floated upward through the narrow slit.

"God!" Tony thought. "If only I had a gun!"

He remembered, then, that the old paralytic had asked him if he had a gun.

From the mutter of voices Tony guessed that there were three men seated about that table; the two Negroes were talking volubly yet with a low, curious tenseness; the Reverend Barnes interrupting only infrequently with monosyllabic grunts. All three seemed to be waiting.

Beside the big man's pallid white hand, on the naked oaken table, sprawling disjointedly amid soggy bits of bread and splotches of grease and chicken bones, lay an incongruous object, a little doll that had been wretchedly sewn together from various bits of cotton cloth. It possessed a face, crudely drawn with black grease or charcoal, and a tuft of kinky hair surmounted the shapeless little bag that represented its head. Obviously it caricatured a Negro.

From time to time, hunching over the table like a great gross idol, his shiny, worn clerical coat taut across his massive shoulders, the renegade minister would pick up the little rag doll, flop its lax arms and legs about, and put it down again.

Suddenly, then, a door, invisible to Tony, opened and closed. The conversation of the two Negroes abruptly ceased. Two black men shuffled slowly across the dining-room floor, came close to the table, opposite the colossus. Tony could see them both.

The face of one was rigid and grim, and he held his companion firmly by the arm. The second Negro was swaying drunkenly. His lips were loose and his eyes bleared. Yet there was terror in him.

The Reverend Barnes hunched lower over the table. Tony could see the big muscles in his back ribbing beneath his rusty coat, and the big brass collar-button at the back of his pillar-like neck. "You're here at last, nigger?" he asked softly. "You're late. What delayed you? They came from the cotton a long time ago, we have already eaten supper."

The drunken man mouthed some reply that was unintelligible, terror-ridden.

The giant's shoulders seemed to tighten into a ball of muscle. "You're drunk, nigger," he said, and his voice trembled with contemptuous loathing. "I smell corn liquor on your breath.

It stifles me; how any man can so degrade him-self—'Look not upon the wine when it is red.' "
He paused. "You fool; I told you not to drink. How can you stay down the road and watch for strangers if you're drunk? You can't be trusted to wave the sheet when you're drunk. You failed today. What have you to say for yourself?"

Words tumbled from the man's slobbering mouth. "Ahm not drunk. Ah tuk de cawn foh toofache—"

The giant shrugged. "A stranger came up the road today before we could hide them in the cot-ton. You're drunk, nigger. I have forgiven you twice. But this is the third time."

He picked up the little doll.

"This is you, nigger. This is made with your sweat and your hair—"

A scream burst from the man's throat. He had begun to shake horribly.

"Hold him, niggers," the giant said imper-turbably. "I want to study this; I want to watch it work."

Black hands grasped the writhing, shudder-ing man.

The Reverend Barnes picked up a fork. He was holding the little doll in his left hand, looking at it speculatively. And it seemed to Tony—although it may have been a trick of the light—that the lifeless doll writhed and moved of itself, in ghastly synchronisation with the trembling and shuddering of the terror-maddened human it caricatured.

Carefully, the Reverend Barnes stuck a prong of the fork through a leg of the doll. There was a slight rending of cotton.

The shuddering wretch screamed—horribly! And the colossus nodded his head as if in satis-faction.

Again the fork probed into the doll. But this time the big man jabbed all four tines through the little doll's middle. And this time no scream, but only a gasping, rending moan came from the Negro so firmly held by the strong hands of his kind. And suddenly he was hanging limply there, like a slaughtered thing. . . .

The Reverend Barnes pulled the fork from the doll, tossed the torn doll carelessly on the floor.

"He's dead, niggers," he said then, callously. "He's stone dead."

As Tony lay sprawled on that rough pine flooring, peering down with horrified fascina-tion into the room below, the incredible realisa-tion grew and grew in him that he had witnessed the exercise of powers so primitive, so elemen-tal, so barbaric that descendants of the so-called higher civilisations utterly disbelieve them.

God! Was this voodoo? Perhaps, but the Rev-erend Barnes was a white man; how had he be-come an adept? Was it something akin to voodoo but deeper, darker? Had that wretched Negro died through fright, or had there really been some horrible affinity between his living body and the lifeless doll?

What of the thing without a face, walking down the road?

The word that Eileen had written in the dust on the porch rail was hammering at Tony's con-sciousness. Almost he grasped it, yet it eluded him. An unfamiliar word, reeking of evil. . . .

For a long time there was only silence from the room below—silence, and a thickening haze of bluish smoke. The Negroes, Tony guessed, were smoking, although the big man almost di-rectly beneath his eyes was not. Abruptly, then, the Reverend Barnes rose to his feet. Tony heard him walk across the floor; there was the sound of a door opening, and then a deep, throaty chuckle.

"No need for you to do the dishes tonight, Miss Eileen. Just leave them where they are; we don't need them any more. Come with me; I'm going to take you back to your room."

Tony heard the man padding heavily yet softly across the floor, and Eileen's reluctant, lighter footsteps. The dining-room door opened and closed.

Tony stumbled to his feet, then shook the door with a despair that was almost madness. Exhausted at last, he clung limply to the iron latch, panting.

Minutes passed—minutes that seemed hours.

Suddenly, from close to his ears, Tony heard muffled sounds of sobbing. Eileen, crying as though her heart was broken, was imprisoned in the next room!

"Eileen!"

Abruptly the sobbing ceased.

"Tony!" The girl's voice came almost clearly into the room, as though she had moved close to the wall. "You didn't—escape them, Tony?"

"They ganged me," Tony said grimly. "I think they were going to let me go, but that big two-faced rattlesnake saw what you wrote on the porch rail, and then they jumped me."

There was a gasp from beyond the wall and then a long silence. At last Eileen said, softly and penitently, "I'm sorry, Tony. I thought that you would read it and—understand—and come back later with help. I'm sorry that I got you into this, Tony. I tried to keep you out. But when you came here I—I loved you so, and I wanted so terribly to escape. I had a wild hope that when you got safe away, even though you didn't understand, you would ask someone who knew and could tell you what zombies meant—"

Zombies! That was the word she had written in dust on the porch rail! And instantly, with kaleidoscopic clarity, there flashed across Tony's brain a confusion of mental images he had acquired through the years—an illustration from a book on jungle rites—a paragraph from a voodoo thriller—scenes from one or two fantastic motion pictures he had witnessed. . . .

Zombies! Corpses kept alive by hideous sorcery to work and toil without food or water or pay—mindless, dead things that outraged Nature with every step they took! These were zombies, the books glibly said, grim products of Afro-Haitian superstition. . . .

The men who wrote those books had never suggested that zombies might be real—that the powers which controlled them might be an heritage of the blacks exactly as self-hypnotism is a highly developed faculty among the Hindus. No, the books had been patronisingly written, with more than a hint of amused superiority evident in them; their authors had incredibly failed to understand that even savages could not practise elaborate rites unless there was efficacy in them. . . .

"Zombies!" Tony muttered dazedly. And then, eagerly, "But—you love me, Eileen, I knew it; I knew you couldn't mean those things you wrote—"

"He made me write them," Eileen whispered. "He—came here in the spring, Tony. Uncle thinks that they ran him away—from wherever he was—before. He brought four Negroes with him.

"Uncle was old, Tony, and he didn't keep much help here—only six or seven coloured men. The place was run down, Tony; after Uncle had put me through college he didn't have much incentive for keeping it up; he's always told me that I could have it for a sort of country home—after he died.

"But then—this man who said he had been a minister came, and saw all these unworked acres and how isolated the place was.

"He went to Uncle, and told Uncle that he would furnish extra help if Uncle would give him half the crop.

"It was after the—help came that Uncle's Negroes left. Some of them even moved out of their shacks—out of the county. And this man—this Reverend Barnes, had already made a little doll and told Uncle that it was supposed to represent him. He tied the little doll's legs together with Uncle's hair and told Uncle that with stiff legs Uncle wouldn't be able to run away and get help. He told Uncle that any time he wanted to, he could stick a pin through the little doll and Uncle would die.

"And—Uncle can't move his legs! It's true, Tony, every word he said. That man, that—devil, can do anything he says.

"He read all my letters to Uncle, and all of Uncle's letters to me, too, before he sent them down to the post office. He tried to keep me from coming here.

"And when I did come he made another doll, Tony, to represent me. It's stuffed with my hair, Tony; they held me while he cut my hair. He's got little dolls that represent everyone here; he keeps them in a bag inside his shirt.

"He can kill us all, Tony, whenever he pleases!"

Hysteria had begun to creep into her voice. She paused for a moment. When she went on, her voice was calmer.

"He keeps one of his coloured men as a lookout in a tree at the top of the hill. The man can see way down to the main road. When he sees anyone turn up this way he opens out a big sheet and they hide the—*helpers*—"

Tony chuckled grimly.

"He didn't open out the sheet today," he muttered. "He was drunk." He tried to make his voice sound confident. "Eileen, sweetheart—we'll have to get out of this. It shouldn't be impossible, if we can only keep calm and try and think."

There was a silence. Then Eileen's words came back with quiet, hopeless finality.

"We can't break out of these rooms, Tony. The house is too strongly built. And—I think that tonight he's going to do something dreadful to us. I think that he's afraid to stay here any longer. But before he leaves this place he's going to—Tony, I know that man! He's ruthless, and he's—mad. Sometimes I think that he was really a minister. But not now, not now. He's pure devil now!"

HOW LONG TONY and Eileen, with the terrible earnestness of despair, talked to each other through the wall that night, neither ever knew. But it must have been for hours, for they talked of many things, yet never of the horror that menaced them. And they spoke calmly, quietly, with gentle tenderness. . . .

Why should the doomed speak of that which they cannot evade?

Both knew that they were utterly in the giant madman's hands, to do with, save for a miracle, as he pleased. Both knew that the apostate minister was merciless. . . .

There was no moon. But it must have been close to midnight when Tony heard the footsteps

of several men on the stairs, the grating of the locks on Eileen's door, the sound of a brief, futile struggle, and then Eileen's despairing cry, "Good-bye, Tony, sweet—"

Frothing like a rabid beast, he hurled himself at the door, at the barred window, at the walls, beating at them with his naked fists until his knuckles were raw and numb and sweat poured in rivulets from his body.

Grim minutes passed. And then the footsteps returned. There was the sound of pine bars being withdrawn. Tony waited, crouching.

When they entered he leaped. But there was no strength in him—only a terrible, hopeless fury. Quickly they seized his arms, bound his hands firmly behind him with rope, dragged him, struggling impotently, down a steep flight of stairs, through the ground floor hall, and down a second flight of stairs, musty and noisome.

Here they paused for a moment while they fumbled with the latch of a door. At last the door swung open, and they dragged Tony forward into an immense, dimly lit chamber. The door swung shut; the old-fashioned iron latch clicked.

This was the cellar of the plantation house, an enormous, cavernous place, extending beneath the whole rambling structure. Once designed for the storage of everything necessary to the subsistence of the householders living on the floors above, its vast spaces were broken by immense, mouldy bins. An eight-foot cistern loomed gigantically in a dark corner; wine shelves extended along one entire wall. The whole monstrous place had been dug half from the clayey soil and half from the solid rock; the floor underfoot, rough and uneven, was seamed and stratified rock.

Two oil lanterns, hanging from beams in the cobwebby ceiling, lighted no more than the merest fraction of that great vault; the farther recesses were shrouded in blackness.

The three Negroes—Mose, Job, and the man who had brought in the drunken lookout—waited expectantly, their black hands strong on Tony's arms. And suddenly Tony was a raging fury, tearing madly at those restraining hands. . . .

There in the centre of the old cellar, kneeling over a small, fragile form lying still and motionless on the mouldy rock, was the gigantic, black-clad Reverend Barnes!

That still, fragile form was Eileen!

At the sound of Tony's struggles the giant looked up, stood erect. Great beads of perspiration bedewed his unnaturally pallid forehead—yet there was a pursy, significant grin on his face.

"Hard work, this, Mr. Kent," he said genially. "Much harder work than you would think."

"What are you doing to her!"

There was exultant triumph in the booming reply.

"I am binding her with a spell, so that she will always do what I say. This is powerful obeah, Mr. Kent. I never dreamed—" He paused, while a swift dark shadow overspread his huge face, so strong and yet so weak. But the shadow passed as swiftly as it had come, and once again his eyes blazed with evil. "Within a few moments I shall put the same spell on you, also, so that you too will always do what I say."

Chuckling, he spoke to Tony's guards.

"Tie his feet securely and pitch him there by the wine-bin. I'll not want him until later."

With both his hands and feet tightly bound, the three Negroes dumped Tony down on the jagged rock beside the wine-bin. Tony's face was turned toward where the fallen minister squatted beneath the lanterns, a monstrous, Luciferian image.

"Sit down on the floor, niggers," he said slowly. "Relax and rest; there's no need to stand." The deep, resonant voice throbbed with kindliness. "I must think."

Obediently, the three squatted in a row on their haunches and sat looking with silent expectation at this white conjure-man who was their master.

The frock-coated figure shook its head slowly, as though its brain were cobwebby. Then, slowly, it opened the front of its filthy linen shirt, baring the grey-white of its chest—the chest of a powerful and sedentary man, who yet had always shunned the healthful sunlight—the chest of a physical animal whose warped brain had, perhaps through most of its years, abhorred the physical as immoral and unclean. A bag hung there at the figure's chest, suspended by a cord around its neck. Two big hands dipped into that gaping pouch. . . .

Tony was struggling, struggling, rolling his body back and forth in straining jerks, trying to loosen the ropes that bound his feet and hands.

That bag of cotton dolls! One of those dolls represented Eileen.

Tony's shoulder crashed against the beams beneath the wine-bins, leaped with pain as an exposed nail tore the flesh. But the ropes held. . . .

The big man's forearms, beneath the shiny black coat, were suddenly bulging—and in that instant the three Negroes who had been squatting on their haunches were rolling and writhing on the floor, their hands clawing at their throats, their bodies jerking and twisting, their faces purpling, their eyes bulging!

Slow minutes passed. And still the giant, renegade minister crouched there, motionless, his big forearms knotted, his face drawn into a sardonic grimace.

The struggles of the three were becoming feebler. Their arms and legs were beating spasmodically, as though consciousness had gone from them. And at last even that spasmodic twitching ceased and they lay still.

Yet the Reverend Barnes did not stir.

But then, after it seemed to Tony that an eternity had passed, he withdrew his hands from the bag. In his left hand he held by the throat two little cotton dolls, in his right hand, one. With a careless gesture he tossed them to the floor, rose to his feet, and stood slowly flexing and unflexing his fingers. At last he stooped over the three motionless Negroes and grunted with satisfaction.

"Fools, to think that I would ever keep you after your work was done!" He was swaying slightly. Seemingly he had forgotten Tony.

But Tony was stealthily, warily sawing his bound hands back and forth, back and forth across the bit of nail that jutted from the base of the wine-bin. Strand by strand he was breaking the half-inch hemp.

The Reverend Barnes had returned to his position beside Eileen, was once more squatting beside her. She had not moved. But she lay unbound; the colossus was very sure of his sorcery!

For long minutes he sat motionless, his shoulders drooped, his muscles flaccid. At last, with a deep sigh, he raised his head and looked at Eileen.

"Beautiful, beautiful womanhood!" he whispered softly. "All my life I've wanted a woman like you—"

He reached out a big, splayed and unhealthily colourless hand, touched Eileen's body. Beneath his gentle touch she stirred and moaned.

And suddenly Tony was cursing him wildly.

"Damn you; you hound of hell in priest's clothing!"

The Reverend Barnes's huge hand paused in its caressing.

"You feel jealousy, Mr. Kent?"

Tony could not see the expression on the man's face; he was a black-robed bulk against the lantern light. But there was a terrible gentleness in his voice.

"You filthy—" Tony choked. Words would no longer come to him; his rage was beyond words.

"Mr. Kent," the big man said softly, and Tony sensed that a slow, utterly evil smile was stealing across his face, "in a little while—such a little while—you'll no longer care what I do with her. You'll be beyond caring."

He swung about to face Tony.

"But—before I—dispose of you," he continued, with startling unexpectedness, "I'm going to tell you the—truth about myself. Why? Perhaps because I want to explain myself, to justify myself to myself. I don't know. Perhaps, in this moment, I have a sudden clear premonition of God's inevitable vengeance—for I am damned, Kent; I know full well that I am damned.

"I have been a preacher for twenty years, Kent. Not the soft-spoken, politically minded type that ultimately lands the rich city churches; sin was too real to me for that; I fought the Devil tooth and claw.

"Perhaps that was the trouble. My ecclesiastical superiors were never certain of me. They thought of me as a sort of volcano that might explode at any time; I was unpredictable. And they suspected, too, I think, the devil in me— the physical lustiness and the desire for material things I fought so hard to stifle. They gave me only the poorest, backcountry churches, they starved me; I was hungry for a mate and I could not even afford a wife. I think they hoped that I would fall into sin, so that they might thus be circumspectly rid of me.

"My last church was a pine shack twenty miles deep in a swamp. My parishioners were almost all Negroes—Negroes and a few whites so poverty-stricken that not one had ever seen a railway train or worn factory-made shoes. And inbreeding, in that disease-ridden country, was the rule, not the exception; you have no idea. . . .

"I worked, there in that earthly hell, like a madman. There was something there, something tangible, for me to fight—and I have always been a literal man. It was a shaman—what you would call a medicine-man or witch doctor. He was, of course, a coloured man.

"It may sound incredible, but I *competed* against that man for almost a year. We were exactly like rival salesmen. I sold faith, and enforced my sales with threats of hell-fire and damnation; he manufactured charms and love-potions, prophesied the future and healed the sick.

"Of course I went after him hammer and tongs. I blasted him in church; I ridiculed him; I told those poor ignorant people that his salves and his potions and his prophecies were no good. Eight months after I arrived there I began to feel that I was winning. . . .

"After about a year had passed he came to see me. We knew each other, of course; I will describe him—a very gentle old man, very tall, very thin and grey. He told me that he wanted me to go away. I think that he knew my weakness, the bitterness in me, better than I knew it myself.

"He raised no religious arguments; in fact, I don't think there were ever any really fundamental differences between us. You know that Holy Writ speaks of witches and warlocks and demons, and my chief objection to this man lay in my private conviction that he was a faker, a mumbo-jumbo expert pulling the wool over the eyes of fools. And, even though I am a fundamentalist, still, this is the twentieth century. The upshot of it was that I laughed at him and listened.

"He merely told me that if I would go away he would teach me his power. What power? I said. I should have known that he was trying to trap me—to strike a bargain. He looked at me. 'Among other things, to raise the dead, that they may do your bidding,' he said, very slowly and seriously, 'although I have never myself done this obeah, because there has never been the need.'

"I laughed at him very loudly then, and for a long time.

" 'Well,' I told him, after I got my breath back, 'I am a pretty poor preacher—if the calibre of my parish offers any criterion whatever. Perhaps I am not destined for the life of a minister, after all. Certainly my superiors don't think so. Therefore, if you will teach me these things of which you speak, and if they work, I will never preach another word as long as I live. But, if they do not work, you will come to church on Sunday, and proclaim yourself a faker before the entire congregation.'

"I felt very sure of myself, then, and I expected him to attempt to avoid the showdown. But he only answered me, quietly and gravely, 'I am the seventh son of a seventh son. I will teach you the obeah my father taught me, and if it works you will go away.'

"So—and I will tell you that I kept my tongue in my cheek all the while—I learned the rituals he taught me, learned them word for word, and wrote them down, phonetically, on paper to his dictation.

"But—he had not lied!"

The black-clad giant paused, and Tony saw that he was trembling. Presently the trembling passed, and, in a quiet, colourless monotone, the apostate minister added, "I knew, then, that I was eternally damned."

Tony shook his head. "No. Give up this—madness. No man has ever had the power to—condemn his own soul!"

The colossus shook its head; Tony could see a sneer hardening on its lips.

"I'll—pay! Because I have, now, what I have always wanted—power! Power over other men—and women! Shall I tell you what I am presently going to do with you? I'm going to make you so that you will forget everything; you will walk and talk only when I tell you to; you will do only what I say. You have money; I will make you take your car, and drive Miss Eileen and me to New York. There you will go to the bank, or wherever it is you keep your money, and draw everything out for me. Then, once again, you will get in your car and drive, but this time you will be alone, and while you are driving I will stick a pin into a little doll. 'Heart failure,' the doctors will say."

For a moment Tony did not speak. Then with a strange steadiness, he asked: "But—Eileen?"

The big man chuckled. "You ask that question of a man who has denied himself women through all his life? Eileen will belong to me."

Abruptly, ignoring the bound, suddenly raging man on the floor beside the wine-bin, he turned away. But now, when again he squatted close to Eileen, he did not remain motionless. From somewhere about his clothing he produced a needle and thread, and bits of cloth, and he was sewing. And as he sewed he muttered strange words to himself, in a tongue Tony had never heard before, muttered those words in a cadenceless monotone, as though he himself did not understand them, but was repeating them by rote, as perhaps, they had been taught to him by some aged coloured wizard. . . .

Tony's bound wrists rubbed back and forth, back and forth across the nail. Suddenly the strands binding his hands loosed.

Slowly, inch by inch, Tony hunched along the wine-bin, drawing up his feet. Warily he watched the big, crouching man; at any moment the Reverend Barnes might notice. . . .

But seemingly, the colossus was too preoccupied.

In furtive, small strokes, Tony's ankles sawed across the nail.

Suddenly the apostate minister stood up. He was looking at his handiwork, a grotesque little thing of odds and ends, crudely sewn yet unmistakably, with its limp, flopping appendages, a doll. And then he grunted approvingly, came toward Tony with the doll in his left hand.

"I'll have to take a few strands of your hair," he said grimly. His right hand reached downward toward Tony's scalp.

And then Tony's hands lashed from behind his back, clutched the pillar-like legs, strained. Abruptly the colossus sprawled his length on the uneven rock, his hands outsplayed. The little doll slid unheeded across the cold stone.

Jack-knifing his bound feet beneath him, Tony hurled himself across the floor. And with that tremendous effort the frayed ropes about his ankles ripped away.

Instantly he was atop the big man, his fingers sunk deep into the pasty white throat, his legs locked about giant hips.

But his antagonist's strength seemed superhuman. Only a half hour before those spatulate hands, as surely as though they had been about black throats, had simultaneously strangled three men. Rope-like torso muscles tautened; powerful hands tore at Tony's forearms.

The powerful hands lifted, tightened about Tony's throat. And as those huge talons flexed, a roaring began in Tony's ears, red spots danced madly before his eyes, the dim cellar swirled and heaved.

The colossus, hands still locked about Tony's throat, surged slowly to his feet. Contemptuously he looked into Tony's bloodshot, staring eyes, hurled him reeling across the rock-gouged vault.

And in that instant something hard and sharp split the base of his skull like an intolerable lightning. Bright sparks spun crazily before his eyes—flickered out in utter blackness. He felt himself falling, falling into eternity. . . .

Old Robert Perry, his eyes blazing with inhuman hate, stood above the Reverend Barnes's sprawling corpse, watching the red blood dim the lustre of the axe-blade he had sunk inches deep into the giant's skull!

"That hellish paralysis!" he was babbling, inanely. "That hellish paralysis—gone just in time!"

Old Robert Perry wheeled. In the feeble yellow light beneath the lantern he saw Eileen, awake now, huddled on the floor, pointing—her eyes pools of horror. And, following with his gaze her outstretched hand, he saw them, coming from the dark bins, the dead things the fallen minister had torn from their graves to toil in the cotton! They came pouring from those great bins with dreadful haste, their faces no longer stony and still, but writhing and tortured. And from the mouths of those that yet possessed mouths poured wild wailings.

Old Robert Perry was trembling—trembling.

"God!" he mumbled. "Their master's dead, and now they seek their graves!"

Dimly, as one who dreams in fever, he saw them passing him, no longer with stumbling, hopeless footsteps, but hurriedly, eagerly, crowding one another aside in their haste to escape into the night and return to their graves. And the flesh on his back crawled, and loosed, and crawled again. . . .

The zombies, dead things no longer beneath the fallen giant's unholy spell, twisted, broken, rotted by the diseases that had killed them, seeking the graves from which they had been torn!

"God!"

And then they were gone, gone in the night, and the sound of their wailing was a diminishing, scattering thinness in the distance. . . .

Old Robert Perry stared dazedly about, at Eileen, huddled on the floor, sobbing with little, half-mad cries that wrung his heart—at Tony, staggering drunkenly to his feet, stumbling blindly toward his beloved.

"Eileen!"

The name reached out from Tony's heart like the caress of strong arms. Reeling, he followed that cry across the floor to her, dropped to the rock beside her, gathered her in his arms.

DAWN WAS NEAR when at last old Robert Perry and young Anthony Kent trudged wearily through the purple night toward the plantation house.

The belated moon, preceding the sun by only a few hours, glimmered in the east, a golden, enchanted shield; the woods were still.

The two men did not speak. Their thoughts were full of the horror that had been, of the great pit they had dug in the night and filled with the bodies of the giant renegade and his followers.

Yet, as they drew closer and closer to the rambling old house that nestled, moonbathed and serene, in the valley beneath them, words came at last.

"Anthony Kent," the old planter said earnestly, "I have lived on this land through near four generations. I have heard the Negroes talk—of things like this. But I would never have believed—unless the truth had been thrust in my face."

Tony Kent shifted his spade to his left shoulder before he replied.

"Perhaps it's better," he said slowly, "that men are inclined to scepticism. Perhaps, as time goes on, these evil, black arts will die out. It may all be part of some divine plan."

Their footsteps made little crunching sounds in the road.

"Thank God that the fiend and his niggers were strangers hereabouts!" the old man said fervently. "They won't be missed. Nobody, of course, would ever believe—what really happened."

"No," Tony said. "But it's all over, now. Those dead things have gone—back to their graves."

They were close to the house. On the long walk, before the low screened porch, a small white-clad figure waited. And then it was running swiftly, eagerly toward them.

"Eileen!"

The name was a pulsing song. And then she was locked in Tony's arms, and he was kissing her upturned, tremulous lips.

APRIL FLOWERS, NOVEMBER HARVEST

MARY A. TURZILLO

A PROFESSOR OF English at Kent State University, Dr. Mary A. Turzillo has written critical articles and scholarly works, mainly on science fiction subjects and themes. Under the pseudonym Mary T. Brizzi, she wrote *Starmont Reader's Guide to Philip José Farmer* (1981) and *Starmont Reader's Guide to Anne McCaffrey* (1985). She has also written under the bylines Mary Turzillo and M. A. Turzillo.

An award-winning poet, she has been published in numerous journals nationally, as well as producing two collections of verse, *Your Cat & Other Space Aliens* (2007) and *Dragon Soup* (2008), a collaboration with artist and poet Marge Simon.

A longtime member of the Science Fiction Writers of America, she was given the Nebula Award by that organization for Best Novelette for *Mars Is No Place for Children*, originally published in *Science Fiction Age* (2000); her story "Pride" was nominated for a Nebula for Best Short Story of 2007; it was first published in *Fast Forward I*. Her only novel to date, *An Old-Fashioned Martian Girl*, was serialized in *Analog* magazine (July–November, 2004).

Professor Turzillo is married to the science fiction and horror writer Geoffrey A. Landis; they live in Ohio.

"April Flowers, November Harvest" was originally published in the May 1993 issue of *Midnight Zoo*.

MARY A. TURZILLO

APRIL FLOWERS, NOVEMBER HARVEST

THE SHALLOW GRAVE lay quiet for over a year; then violets sprouted from the black dirt on Maggie's eyes, and bloodroot from the clods in her hands.

Six months later, she arose.

The world was enervatingly warm even in the early November snow of Ohio, but she had to find something warmer still. Not the live thing that had been in her abdomen; that was dead. Something hot and furious, like a rat scrabbling at the edge of the woods.

THE SNOW WASN'T laying yet, but flakes drifted down and melted on Dwayne's young, strong hands, on the chain saw, and on the bark of the slabs he was cutting. He loved the harsh scream of the saw; it insulated him in a cloud of noise, like cotton batting, inside which he could savor the cold sharp smell of wood mulch and the piney sawdust. His arms ached with the weight of the chain saw, and he saw he had cut nearly all of the wood. He turned off the saw, and the silence welled up like water.

The neighbors were complaining, Sheila claimed. Said the house looked like a shanty. The unfinished back porch, and all that stacked wood, the tools, gas cans, odd lengths of lumber on the gravel path and among the thick leaves behind the house. But Sheila's brother worked at the yard and got the slabs for the cost of hauling them away. The slabs would help them through the winter without worrying about the growing burden of bills. And the new baby, their first child, would need a warm house. Caterpil-

lars had broad black stripes in their rusty wool, forecasting a bad winter.

She fretted at Dwayne, Sheila did. The baby was damn near due, and he got jumpy from the way she was always wanting things and complaining. The last days of the pregnancy made her that way, he figured, that and being laid off from Excelsior Lamp Plant.

Sheila stood framed in the back door, holding the screen door open. Her huge stomach wasn't cute anymore; it made her monstrous. She thrust one hip out in impatience.

"Didn't know you were calling," he said in his low, slow voice.

"Telephone. They hung up, though." She focused her close-set eyes on him. Her face was still gaunt, though puffy around her eyes.

"Maybe they'll call back."

"Don't know." She shifted her weight off the doorframe and stepped awkwardly back into the house. "You ready for something to eat?"

"Reckon. Got to put the saw away, though. Bound to be too dark to cut any more after supper." He reached out to pat her abdomen, a familiar gesture. But she stepped heavily out of his way and went back to the kitchen.

Supper was hamburgers, served in the frying pan on a hot pad, with canned peas and carrots. Dwayne placed a hamburger on a slice of white bread, smeared it with mustard, and covered it with another slice. Virtuously, he ate the vegetables before the sandwich. They tasted good, watery and bland. The mustard cut through the rich grease of the hamburger. He chewed deliberately, swallowed with relish.

Sheila ate steadily, mostly hamburger. She spooned grease over a slice of bread, salted and ate it with knife and fork. Neither spoke.

The phone rang, and Sheila heaved herself out of the chair, throwing her bulk in front of Dwayne to get to it first.

"They hung up," she accused.

"Let it go. They'll call back."

Sheila dropped back into the chair. "It was that friend of yours."

"What friend?"

"That woman friend of yours. Called herself Maggie."

Dwayne took another slice of bread. "I have reason to believe Maggie is no longer around this town."

"That call before. It was a woman. Sounded like Maggie. It did."

Dwayne laid his fork down. "That what's eating you?"

Sheila nodded once, staring into her plate, mouth drawn in a bitter bow.

He took another hamburger steak to make up a sandwich. "I believe Maggie is living in Denver."

Sheila darted a sharp look at him. "Denver? Where did you get that?"

"A feeling. She went away. Her sister said she had a man friend, old guy in Denver."

"You been to talk to her sister?"

"No. This was a while back. Before you and me got married."

Sheila chewed, swallowed, laid her silverware on the Formica tabletop. "That whore," she muttered.

Dwayne felt his ire rising, but said nothing.

"I said, she's a whore!"

"Well, she's no business of yours, because she ain't around here anymore."

"Then who was that on the telephone?"

Dwayne threw his sandwich on the plate and reared back on the chair, scraping against the new vinyl tile floor. "You tell me. Probably some yo-yo out of your past."

She picked up the plastic dishes and clattered them angrily into the sink. "It was a woman."

"Thought you said she hung up."

"Before. The one that called while you was cutting slabs."

The thought of the chain saw brought bloody images to Dwayne's mind, and he judged he'd best go back outside till this whole thing blew over. When he came back in, Sheila was asleep with an issue of *Cosmopolitan* on her huge stomach.

MAGGIE HAD TO warm her cold hands and breasts. She had to transfer some of the energy from this world, the world of the clearing, the town world, back into the forest mulch. That way the rich soil would yield an abundance of mayapple, adder's tongue, and

blue cohosh come spring. Otherwise her coldness, and that of the withered life in her womb,
would blast the forest floor. So she reasoned.
So she explained her journey into the suburban
development.

Most of the houses had no landscape plant-
ings, or where they did, they were still spindly
shrubs, set next to a painted rock at the end of
the drive, or maple saplings in a bed of pebbles,
attended by a plaster fawn. It wasn't hard to find
Dwayne and Sheila's house.

"DWAYNE. DWAYNE!"

At first Dwayne thought he was on midnight
turn again and had overslept. But he squinted at
the red glowworms that spelled the time, and it
was 3:27, not time to get up for any shift. Sheila
turned on the light.

"Dwayne, there's something wrong. It
hurts."

Dwayne rolled over and discovered the bed
soggy and warm. He at first thought Sheila had
added bed-peeing to the idiosyncrasies of her
pregnancy, then remembered what else a wet
bed could mean.

"Dwayne, I'm scared!"

Dwayne rolled to a sitting position and
scrubbed his bristly face with his knuckles. "For
God's sake, Sheila. You're in labor."

This day will see the birth of my son, thought
Dwayne. Or maybe my daughter. Without panic,
he bundled Sheila into the pickup and drove her
to Clay River Memorial Hospital. She began
screaming before they got her through Admis-
sions.

MAGGIE BATHED IN a stream and put
the filthy clothing back on. The stream didn't
seem cold, though she had to break the ice. It
was hard to wash her hair, which was matted
with twigs and black woods soil. *I am now the
wood sprite,* she hummed. *Herbs and flowers spring
from my body.* The wind whipped her wet hair,

freezing locks to her cheeks, but it would dry,
even in this weather. Her lacy stretch top and
purple jeans were dirty and torn. She headed for
her sister Kathy's house. A pretty spring dress
would be nice.

KATHY WRAPPED THE afghan around
her. She wasn't used to the cold yet this year.
Hadn't it been around this date—? She put the
thought of her missing sister out of her mind and
flicked the remote control to another channel.
She watched, fascinated, for a while. The program was about runaways, kids that became junk-
ies and prostitutes in big cities. Her sister—her
feelings caved in on her. She wished Ken and the
boys were home, to distract her from thoughts of
where poor Maggie might be. Angrily, she swallowed tears and flicked to another channel. This
one was better, a sitcom about morticians.

Darn, the house seemed drafty. She huddled
the afghan around her and went to check the
thermostat.

On her way, she noticed the back door was
standing open.

DWAYNE GOT HOME around four p.m.
The nurses had encouraged him to be in the delivery room when the baby was being born, and he
was elated that he had been. It was bloody and violent, as he expected, but it moved very fast for a
first birth. Sheila had done a lot of yelling, maybe
more because he was there to hear it, and toward
the end she cursed like a shop foreman. But that
was all irrelevant. They had a daughter. The kid
looked just as bad as the nurse had warned them
she would, with her tiny dried-fruit face and head
lopsided like a bruised grapefruit, and he decided
she was going to take after Dwayne's mother, instead of Sheila, and be a beauty.

Stripping off his sweatshirt, he noticed that
the weather was gray and threatening. That
seemed wrong for the occasion, so he made himself a sandwich with the bologna in the fridge,

MARY A. TURZILLO

drained a can of lite beer, changed the sheets, and went to bed.

SOMETHING WOKE HIM.

A shape stood quietly between him and the cold light leaking through the drapes from the neighbor's security lamp. A human form. He examined it, frozen with alarm. The Smith & Wesson was in a cardboard box under the bed. He told Sheila they'd have to come up with a better place for it once the kid got old enough to crawl. And when the kid, his daughter, got a little older, maybe nine or so, he'd teach her to use it.

The shape had a cloud of unkempt hair, dark in the twilight of the bedroom. Whoever it was, it was watching him.

"Dwayne." The voice was low, full of painful music.

"My God," he whispered finally, "Maggie."

The figure stirred, but didn't answer.

IN THE GREENISH light of the door to the hospital corridor, Sheila saw what had wakened her: a nurse, carrying something. The something was her baby, and the baby was crying feebly, like a kitten. "Feeding time," said the nurse.

"MAGGIE," DWAYNE WHISPERED, full of muted glad awe. "I thought you was living in Denver. You ran off."

Maggie shrugged. "You expected me to stay, after all you said?"

Dwayne pulled the covers around him, not against the cold, but out of sudden shame. "I couldn't be sure. You weren't sure yourself, even."

She shrugged. "Are you sure with this one?"

"Yes. Mostly. Anyway, she'll have my name. She's legitimate. Where did you hear?"

"News travels fast."

"I guess I should say I'm sorry. I loved you, then afterward I loved Sheila. Now I guess it don't matter." He felt pangs of remembered

tenderness. "God, Maggie, it's good to see you."

"How was the birth?"

"Hell, I could have delivered the kid myself."

She laughed, out of season with the time and place. "Always the farm boy. Close to the earth, huh?"

Dwayne laughed, reluctant, not understanding the joke. "But where have you been? Where did you run to? Your sister thought you went west, to that guy in Denver, but she never heard."

Maggie was silent. He saw only her silhouette, lovely and vulnerable against the faint light from the window. Then her lips curved, parted. "Can I use your shower? I'm cold, and I haven't had a decent bath in a while."

THE HOT WATER gradually warmed her night-cold flesh, until her heart began to beat, slowly, then quicker. She washed her hair again, lathering twice with shampoo that smelled like strawberries. The water's heat oppressed her, yet she knew she needed it.

She left the spring dress hanging on the back of the door and wrapped herself in a big pink towel. For a moment, she flicked on the light, wiped steam from the mirror. Even the hot water had not brought color to her face, so she smoothed on blush and powder from the vanity. Sheila's cosmetics. Dwayne's wife's stuff.

Dwayne was sitting on the bed, his back to her, face buried in his hands. She slipped up to him and brushed his warm neck with the back of her cool hand.

"Maggie, Maggie," he sighed. "What do you want with me?"

She had prayed for this reprieve, this moment, in the last moments before the pills had washed the world away. It hadn't been Dwayne who had buried her, then. It must have been the biker and his friends.

AFTER SHE WAS gone, Dwayne knew she had not really given her body or her love, but

320

taken something away from him. He made instant coffee and drank it, scalding. Maybe, long ago, he had made the wrong choice, but something told him that now it was way too late.

Then he remembered that he hadn't found out where she had been those two years. He had forgotten even to ask her if she had gotten the abortion.

THERE WAS A cold place in the rafters of the garage. Maggie propped a ladder against the wall and lugged a tarp up to the place where the hundred-watt bulb would not cast too much light should Dwayne look into the garage during her brief stay. The position of the ladder itself Dwayne would lay to absentmindedness or a neighbor's borrowing and returning it without asking. She pulled two one-by-eights together across the rafters and sank down on them, wrapping the tarp around her, not for warmth, but for concealment. The false heat leaked slowly from her body.

SHEILA AND DWAYNE named the baby Melissa. It wasn't really a family name, but Sheila liked it. Melissa was an early rising baby, and Dwayne wasn't surprised that Sheila gave up breast-feeding shortly after they brought the kid home. They took turns with Melissa's night feeding. At first, they tried to get her to sleep later in the morning by giving her a three a.m. bottle, but Sheila had a tendency to sleep through the clock radio. Melissa's increasingly healthy wails in the early morning were harder to sleep through.

Sheila had a cold. Both she and Dwayne were exhausted. It wasn't Dwayne's night to feed the baby, but Sheila had taken a double dose of cold medicine and stirred only slightly when the baby cried.

Dwayne groaned. It was only one thirty; maybe if he lay still a little longer, the baby would go back to sleep for a while.

He dozed. The baby whimpered. Maybe she had a touch of her mother's cold, too. He told himself he ought to feel pity for the wet little bundle of warmth and discomfort, but so far she seemed barely human to him. More like a calf or a baby bird than another person. In theory, she would grow into a human, his daughter, somebody he would teach things to, somebody to take to school and ball games. But now, she seemed no more human than the clock radio. Or the time clock at the plant.

Sounds, stirring, from the hall, then from the baby's room. The creak of the crib rail being lowered. The baby wailed louder, then stopped, as if suddenly attached to a nipple.

MAGGIE HAD SOUGHT this moment since waking in the woods. Soon, she could go back, fulfilled. The baby nuzzled her and she opened the buttons of the spring dress. The baby's mouth was hot and eager against her breast, groping, finding.

Together, their hearts slowed. At length, she laid the baby back in the crib.

DWAYNE WOKE, SHIVERING, after what seemed only moments. It was late, almost nine, and no sound came from Melissa's room. "Sheila?" Sheila stirred, snuffling and groaning. "Did you open a window when you got up to feed the baby?"

Sheila rubbed her face into the pillow and looked at him blearily. "Feed Melissa? When?"

THE OLD MAN AND THE DEAD

MORT CASTLE

MORT(ON) CASTLE (1946–) published his first novel in 1967 and has always worked at two primary jobs: writing and teaching, with forays into being a musician (banjo, guitar, mandolin, fiddle, and dobro), stand-up comedian, stage hypnotist, writer of advertising copy, and editor of magazines (fiction editor for *Doorways* magazine) and comic books (executive editor of Thorby Comics). In addition to eleven years as a high school teacher, Castle teaches at Columbia College in Chicago and conducts an annual writing workshop at the World Horror Convention; he claims that more than two thousand of his students have seen their work in print. He has written and edited *Writing Horror: A Handbook by the Horror Writers of America* (1997), revised as *On Writing Horror* (2006). His experience as a stand-up comic has made him a desirable keynote speaker at conventions, where he has made more than eight hundred presentations.

Castle's more than three hundred and fifty short stories and seven novels have been nominated for numerous prizes and awards, including six Bram Stoker Awards. His literary fiction has been nominated for four Pushcart Prizes. Among his novels are *Cursed Be the Child* (1990), *The Deadly Election* (1976), and *The Strangers* (1984), which has been optioned for a motion picture by Whitewater Films.

"The Old Man and the Dead," an homage of sorts to Ernest Hemingway, was first published in *Book of the Dead 2: Still Dead,* edited by John Skipp and Craig Spector (New York: Bantam, 1992).

MORT CASTLE

THE OLD MAN AND THE DEAD

I

IN OUR TIME there was a man who wrote as well and truly as anyone ever did. He wrote about courage and endurance and sadness and war and bullfighting and boxing and men in love and men without women. He wrote about scars and wounds that never heal.

Often, he wrote about death. He had seen much death. He had killed. Often, he wrote well and truly about death. Sometimes. Not always.

Sometimes he could not.

II

MAY 1961
MAYO CLINIC
ROCHESTER, MINNESOTA

"Are you a Stein? Are you a Berg?" he asked.

"Are you an anti-Semite?" the psychiatrist asked.

"No." He thought. "Maybe. I don't know. I used to be, I think. It was in fashion. It was all right until that son of a bitch Hitler."

"Why did you ask that?" the psychiatrist asked.

The old man took off his glasses. He was not really an old man, only 61, but often he thought of himself as an old man and truly, he looked like an old man, although his blood pressure was in control and his diabetes remained borderline. His face had scars. His eyes were sad. He looked like an old man who had been in wars.

He pinched his nose above the bridge. He wondered if he was doing it to look tired and worn. It was hard to know now when he was being himself and when he was being what the world expected him to be. That was how it was when all the world knew you and all the world knows you if you have been in *Life* and *Esquire*.

"It's I don't think a Jew would understand. Maybe a Jew couldn't."

The old man laughed then but it had nothing funny to it. He sounded like he had been socked a good one. "*Nu?* Is that what a Jew would say? *Nu?* No, not a Jew. Not a communist. Nor an empiricist. I'll tell you who else. The existentialists. Those wise guys sons of bitches. Oh, they get ink these days, don't they? Sit in the cafés and drink the good wine and the good dark coffee and smoke the bad cigarettes and think they've discovered it all. Nothingness. That is what they think they've discovered it all. Nothingness. That is what they think they've discovered. How do you like it now, Gentlemen?

"They are wrong. Yes. They are wrong."

"How so?"

"There is something. It's not pretty. It's not nice. You have to be drunk to talk about it, drunk or shell-shocked, and then you usually can't talk about it. But there is something."

323

III

The poet Bill Wantling wrote of him: "He explored the *pues y nada* and the *pues y nada*." So then so. What do you know of it Mr. Poet Wantling? What do you know of it?

F—— you all. I obscenity in the face of the collective wisdom. I obscenity in the face of the collective wisdoms. I obscenity in the mother's milk that suckled the collective wisdoms. I obscenity in the too easy mythos of all the collective wisdoms and in the face of my young, ignorant, unknowing self that led me to proclaim my personal mantra of ignorance, the *pues y nada y pues y nada y pues y nada pues y nada*. . . . In the face of Buddha. In the face of Mohammed. In the face of the God of Abraham, Issac, and Jacob.

In the face of that poor skinny dreamer who died on the cross. Really, when it came down to it, he had some good moves in there. He didn't go out bad. He was tough. Give him that. Tough like Stan Ketchel, but he had no counter-moves. Just this sweet, simple, sad ass faith. Sad ass because, what little he understood, no, from what I have seen, he had it bass-ackwards.

How do you like it now, Gentlemen? How do you like it now? Is it time for a prayer? Very well then, Gentlemen.

Let us pray.

Baa-baa-baa, listen to the lambs bleat,

Baa-baa-baa, listen to the lambs bleat.

Truly, world without end.

Truly.

Not Amen.

I can not will not just cannot no cannot bless nor sanctify nor affirm the obscenity the horror.

Can you, Mr. Poet Bill Wantling? Can you, Gentlemen?

How do you like it now?

In Hell and in a time of hell, a man's got no bloody chance, F—— you as we have been F——ed. All of us. All of us.

There is your prayer.

Amen.

IV

"Ern—"

"No. Don't call me that. That's not who I want to be."

"That is your name."

"Goddamn it. F—— you. F—— you twice. I've won the big one. The goddamn Nobel. I'm the one. The heavyweight champ, no middleweight. I *can* be *who* I want to be. I've earned that."

"Who is it you want to be?"

"*Mr. Papa.* I'm damned good for that. Mr. Papa. That is how I call myself. That is how Mary calls me. They call me 'Mr. Papa' in Idaho and Cuba and *Paris Review.* The little girls whose tight dancer bottoms I pinch, the little girls I call 'daughter,' the lovely little girls, and A. E. and Carlos and Coop and Marlene, Papa or Mr. Papa, that's how they call me.

"Even Fidel. I'm Mr. Papa to Fidel. I call him Señor Beisbol. Do you know, he's got a hell of a slider, Fidel. How do you like it now, Mr. Doctor? *Mr.* Papa."

"*Mr. Papa?* No, I don't like it. I don't like the word games you play with me, nor do I think your 'Mr. Papa' role belongs in this office. You're here so we can *help* you."

"Help me? That is nice. That is just so goddamn pretty."

"We need the truth."

"That's all Pilate wanted. Not so much. And wasn't he one swell guy?"

"Who are you?" persisted the psychiatrist.

"Who's on first?"

"What?"

"*What's* on second! Who's on first. I like them, you know. Abbott and Costello. They could teach that sissy Capote a thing or two about word dance. Who's on first? How do you like it now, Gentlemen? Oh, yes, they could teach Mr. James Jones a little. Thinks he's Captain Steel Balls now. Thinks he's ready to go against the champ. Mailer, the loud mouth Hebe. Uris, even *Uris,* for God's sake, the original Hollywood piss-ant. Before they take me on, any of them, let them do a prelim with Abbott and Costello. Who's on first? That is good."

"What's not good is that you're avoiding. Simple question." The psychiatrist was silent, then he said, sternly, "Who are you?"

The old man said nothing. His mouth worked. He looked frail then. Finally he said, "Who am I truly?"

"Truly."

"*Verdad?*"

"*Sí. Verdad.*"

"Call me *Adam . . .*"

"*Adam?* Oh, *Mr. Papa, Mr. Nobel Prize,* that is just too pretty. How do *you* like it now, thrown right back at you? You see, I can talk your talk. Let us have a pretension contest. Call me 'Ishmael.' Now do we wait for God to call you his beloved son in whom he is well pleased?"

The old man sighed. He looked very sad, as though he wanted to kill himself. He had put himself on his honor to his personal physician and his wife that he would not kill himself, and honor was very important to him, but he looked like he wanted to kill himself.

The old man said, "No. Adam. Adam Nichols. That was the one who was truly me in the stories."

"I thought it was Nick Adams in—"

"*Those* were the stories I let them publish. There were other stories I wrote about me when I used to be Adam Nichols. Some of those stories no one would have published. Believe me. Maybe *Weird Tales.* Some magazine for boys who don't yet know about f———ing.

"Those stories, they were the real stories."

V

A DANCE WITH A NUN

Adam Nichols had the bed next to his friend Rinelli in the attic of the villa that had been taken over for a hospital and with the war so far off they usually could not even hear it it was not too bad. It was a small room, the only one for pa-tients all the way up there, and so just the two of them had the room. When you opened the window, there was usually a pleasant breeze that cleared away the smell of dead flesh.

Adam would have been hurting plenty but every time the pain came they gave him morphine and so it wasn't so bad. He had been shot in the calf and the hip and near to the spine and the doctor had to do a lot of cutting. The doctor told him he would be fine. Maybe he wouldn't be able to telemark when he skied, but he would be all right, without even a limp.

The doctor told him about a concert violinist who'd lost his left hand. He told him about a gallery painter who'd been blinded in both eyes. He told him about an ordinary fellow who'd lost both testicles. The doctor said Adam had reason to count his blessings. He was trying to cheer Adam up. Hell, the doctor said, trying to show he was a regular guy who would swear, there were lots had it worse, plenty worse.

Rinelli had it worse. You didn't have to be a doctor to know that. A machine gun got Rinelli in the stomach and in the legs and in between. The machine gun really hemstitched him. They changed his bandages every hour or so but there was always a thick wetness coming right through the blanket.

Adam Nichols thought Rinelli was going to die because Rinelli said he didn't feel badly at all and they weren't giving him morphine or anything much else really. Another thing was Rinelli laughed and joked a great deal. Frequently, Rinelli said he was feeling "swell"; that was an American word Adam had taught him and Rinelli liked it a lot.

Rinelli joked plenty with Sister Katherine, one of the nurses. He teased hell out of her. She was an American nun and very young and very pretty with sweet blue eyes that made Adam think of the girls with Dutch bobs and round collars who wore silly hats who you saw in the Coca-Cola advertisements. When he first saw her, Rinelli said to Adam Nichols in Italian, "What a waste. What a shame. Isn't she a great girl? Just swell."

There was also a much older nun there called Sister Anne. She was a chief nurse and this was not her first war. Nobody joked with her even if he was going to die. What Rinelli said about her was that when she was a child she decided to be a bitch and because she wasn't British, the only thing left was for her to be a nun. Sister Anne had a profile as flat as the blade of a shovel. Adam told Rinelli he'd put his money on Sister Anne in a twenty-rounder with Jack Johnson. She had to have a harder coconut than any nigger.

Frequently, it was Sister Katherine who gave Adam his morphine shot. With her help, he had to roll onto his side so she could jab the hypodermic into his buttock. That was usually when Rinelli would start teasing.

"Sister Katherine," Rinelli might say, "when you are finished looking at Corporal Nichols's backside, would you be interested in seeing mine?"

"No, no thank you," Sister Katherine would say.

"It needs your attention, Sister. It is broken, I am afraid. It is cracked right down the middle."

"Please, Sergeant Rinelli—"

"Then if you don't want to see my backside, could I perhaps interest you in my front side?"

Sister Katherine would blush very nicely then and do something so young and sweet with her mouth that it was all you could do not to just squeeze her. But then Rinelli would get to laughing and you'd see the bubbles in the puddle on the blanket over his belly, and that wasn't any too nice.

One afternoon, Rinelli casually asked Sister Katherine, "Am I going to live?" Adam Nichols knew Rinelli was not joking then.

Sister Katherine nodded. "Yes," she said. "You are going to get well and then you will go back home."

"No," Rinelli said, still sounding casual, "Pardon me, I really don't want to contradict, but no, I do not think so."

Adam Nichols did not think so, either, and he had been watching Sister Katherine's face so he thought she did not think so as well.

Sister Katherine said rather loudly, "Oh, yes, Sergeant Rinelli. I have talked with the doctors. Yes, I have. Soon you will begin to be better. It will be a gradual thing, you will see. Your strength will come back. Then you can be invalided home."

With his head turned, Adam Nichols saw Rinelli smile.

"Good," Rinelli said. "That is very fine. So, Sister Katherine, as soon as I am better and my strength comes back to me, but before I am sent home, I have a favor to ask of you."

"What is that, Sergeant Rinelli?"

"I want you to dance with me."

Sister Katherine looked youngest when she was trying to be deeply serious. "No, no," she said, emphatically. "No, it is not permitted. Nuns cannot dance."

"It will be a secret dance. I will not tell Sister Anne, have no fear. But I do so want to dance with you."

"Rest now, Sergeant Rinelli. Rest, Corporal Nichols. Soon everything will be fine."

"Oh, yes," Rinelli said, "soon everything will be just swell."

WHAT ADAM NICHOLS liked about morphine was that it was better than getting drunk because you could slip from what was real to what was not real and not know and not care one way or the other. Right now in his mind, he was up in Michigan. He was walking through the woods, following the trail. Ahead, it came into sight, the trout pool, and his eyes took it all in, and he was seeking the words so he could write this moment truly.

Beyond this trail
a stream lies
faintly marked by rising mist.

Twisting and tumbling
around barriers,
it flows
into a shimmering pool,

black with beauty
and
full of fighting trout.

Adam Nichols had not told many people about this writing thing, how he believed he would discover a way to make words present reality so it was not just reality but more real than reality. He wanted writing to jump into what he called the fifth dimension. But until he learned to do it, and for now, writing was a secret for him.

The war was over. Sometimes he tried to write about it but he usually could not. Too often when he would try to write about it, he would find himself writing about what other men had seen and done and not what he himself had seen and done and had to give it up as a bad job.

Adam Nichols put down his tackle and rod and sat down by the pool and lit a cigarette. It tasted good. There is a clean, clear and sharp smell when you light a cigarette outdoors. He was not surprised to find Rinelli sitting alongside him even though Rinelli was dead. Rinelli was smoking, too.

"Isn't this fine? Isn't this everything I said it would be?" Adam Nichols asked.

"It's grand, it sure is. It's just swell," Rinelli answered.

"Tonight, we'll drink some whiskey with really cold water. And we'll have one hell of a meal," Adam Nichols said. "Trout. I've got my old man's recipe." He drew reflectively on his cigarette. "My old man, he was the one who taught me to hunt and fish. He was the one taught me to cook outdoors."

"You haven't introduced me to your father," Rinelli said.

"Well, he's dead, you see. He was a doctor and he killed himself. He put his gun to his head and he killed himself."

"What do you figure, then? Figure he's in hell now?"

"I don't know. Tell you, Rinelli, I don't really think there's anything like that. Hell. Not really."

Rinelli looked sad and that's when Adam Nichols saw how dead Rinelli's eyes were and remembered all over again that Rinelli was dead.

"Well, Adam, you know me, I don't like to argue, but I tell you, there is, too, a hell. And I sure as hell wish I were there right now."

Rinelli snapped the last half inch of his cigarette into the trout pool. A small fish bubbled at it as the trout pool turned into blood.

A FEW DAYS later Rinelli was pretty bad off. Sometimes he tried to joke with Adam but he didn't make any sense and sometimes he talked in Italian to people who weren't there. He looked gray, like a dirty sheet. When he fell asleep, there was a heavy, wet rattle in his throat and his mouth stayed open.

Adam Nichols wasn't feeling any too swell himself. It was funny, how when you were getting better, you hurt lots worse. Sister Katherine jabbed a lot of morphine into him. It helped, but he still hurt and he knew he wasn't always thinking straight.

There were times he thought he was probably crazy because of the pain and the morphine. That didn't bother him really. It was just that he couldn't trust anything he saw.

At dusk, Adam Nichols opened his eyes. He saw Sister Katherine by Rinelli's bed. She had her crucifix and she was praying hard and quiet with her lips moving prettily and her eyes almost closed.

"That's good," Rinelli said. "Thank you. That is real nice." His voice sounded strong and casual and vaguely bored.

Sister Katherine kept on praying.

"That's just swell," Rinelli said. He coughed and he died.

Sister Katherine pulled the sheets up over Rinelli's face. She went to Adam. "He's gone."

"Well, I guess so."

"We will not be able to move him for a while. We do not have enough people, and there's no room. . . ." Sister Katherine looked like she had something unpleasant in her mouth. "There is no room in the room we're using for the morgue."

"That's okay," Adam Nichols said. "He can stay here. He's not bothering me."

"All right then," Sister Katherine said. "All right. Do you need another shot of morphine?"

"Yes," Adam said, "I think so. I think I do."

Sister Katherine gave him the injection, and later there was another, and then, he thought, perhaps another one or even two. He knew he had had a lot of morphine because what he saw later was really crazy and couldn't have actually happened.

It was dark and Sister Katherine came in with her little light. Rinelli sat up in bed then. That had to be the morphine, Adam Nichols told himself. Rinelli was dead as a post. But there he was, sitting up in bed, with dead eyes, and he was stretching out his arms and then it all happened quick just like in a dream but Rinelli was out of bed and he was hugging Sister Katherine like he was drunk and silly.

He's dancing with her, that's what he's doing, Adam Nichols thought, and he figured he was thinking that because of all the morphine. Sure, he said he was going to dance with Sister Katherine before he went home. "Hey, Rinelli," Adam Nichols said. "Quit fooling around, why don't you?"

Sister Katherine was yelling pretty loud and then she wasn't yelling all that loud because it looked like Rinelli was kissing her, but then you saw that wasn't it. Rinelli was biting her nose real hard, not like kidding around, and she was bleeding pretty much and she twisted and pushed real hard on Rinelli.

Rinelli staggered back. With blood on his dead lips. With something white and red and pulpy getting chewed by his white teeth. With a thin bit of pink gristle by the corner of his mouth.

Sister Katherine was up against the wall. The middle of her face was a black and red gushing hole. Her eyes were real big and popping. She was yelling without making a sound. She kind of looked like a comic strip.

It was a bad dream and the morphine, Adam Nichols thought, a real bad dream, and he wished he'd wake up.

Then Sister Anne came running in. Then she ran out. Then she ran back in. Now she had a Colt .45. She knocked back the slide like she really meant business. Rinelli went for her. She held her arm straight out. The gun was just a few inches from Rinelli's forehead when Sister Anne let him have it. Rinelli's head blew up wetly in a lot of noise. A lot of the noise was shattering bone. It went all over the place.

That was all Adam Nichols could remember the next morning. It wasn't like something real you remember. It was a lot more like a dream. He told himself it had to be the morphine. He told himself that a number of times. The windows were open and the breeze was nice but the small room smelled of strong disinfectant. There was no one in the other bed.

When Sister Anne came in to bring his breakfast and give him morphine, Adam Nichols asked about Rinelli.

"Well, he's dead," Sister Anne said. "I thought you knew."

Adam Nichols asked about Sister Katherine.

"She's no longer here," the old nun said, tersely.

"I thought something happened last night. I thought I saw something awful."

"It's better you don't think about it," Sister Anne said. "It's war and everybody sees a lot of awful things. Just don't think about it."

VI

"Let's talk about your suicidal feelings."

"There are times I want to kill myself. How's that?"

"You know what I mean."

"Who's on first?"

"You pride yourself on being a brave man."

"I am. Buck Lanham called me the bravest man he's ever known."

"Hooray. I'll see you get a medal."

"Maybe I deserve a medal. I've pissed in the face of death." The old man winked then. That and what he had just said made him look ridiculous. It made him look ancient and crazy. "I have killed, after all."

"I know. You are a very famous killer. You have antlers and tusks and rhino horns. You've shot cape buffalo and geese and bears and wild goats. That makes you extremely brave. You deserve medals."

"Who are you to deride me?" The old man was furious. He looked threatening and silly. "Who are you to hold me in contempt? I have killed men!"

VII

The time is a drunken blur in his memory. It is the "rat race" summer and fall of 1944, and he is intensely alive. A "war correspondent," that is what he is supposed to be, but that is not all he can allow himself to be.

He has to go up against Death every time. With what he knows, oh, yes, he has to meet the flat gaze of Mr. Death, has to breathe Mr. Death's hyena breath, he has to.

That is part of it.

He calls himself a soldier. He wouldn't have it any other way. This is a war. He appoints himself an intelligence officer. He carries a weapon, a .32 caliber Colt revolver.

And don't the kids love him, though? God, he sure loves them. They are just so goddamned beautiful, the doomed ones and the fortunate, the reluctant warriors and those who've come to know they love it. They are beautiful men as only men can be beautiful.

You see, women, well, women are women, and it is the biological thing, the trap by which we are snared, the old peg and awl, the old belly-rub and sigh and there you have it, and so a real man does need a woman, must have a woman so he does not do heinous things, but it is in the company of men that men find themselves and each other.

These kid warriors, these glorious snot-noses

like he used to be, they know he is tough. He is the legit goods. He can outshoot them, rifle or pistol, even the Two-Gun Pecos Pete from Arizona. Want to play cards, he'll stay up the night, drinking and joking. He puts on the gloves and boxes with them. He'll take one to give one and he always gives as good as he gets.

He has a wind-up phonograph and good records: Harry James and the Boswells and Hot Lips Paige. He has Fletcher Henderson and Basie and Ellington. The Andrews Sisters, they can swing it, and Russ Colombo. Sinatra, he'll be fine once they let him stop doing the sappy stuff. There are nights of music and drinking and in the following days there are the moments burned into his mind, the moments that become the stories. Old man?

Well, he can drink the kids blind-eyed and to hell and gone. He stays with them, drink for drink. The hell with most of the kiss-ass officers. They don't know how foolish they are. They don't know they are clichés. The enlisted men, John Q. Public, Mr. O. K. Joe American, Johnny Gone for a Soldier, it's the enlisted man who's going to save the world from that Nazi bastard. It's the enlisted men he honest to God loves.

The enlisted men call him "Papa."

How do you like it now, Gentlemen?

The kraut prisoner was no enlisted man. He was an officer. Stiff-necked son of a bitch. *Deutschland über alles.* Arrogant pup. *Übermensch.*

No, the German will not reveal anything. He will answer none of their questions. They can all go to hell. That's what the German officer says. They can all get f——.

Papa shakes a fist in the kraut's face. Papa says, "You're going to talk and tell us every damned thing we want to know or I'll kill you, you Nazi son of a bitch."

The German officer does not change expression. He looks bored. What he says is: "You are not going to kill me, old man. You do not have the courage. You are hindered by a decadent morality and ethical code. You come from a race of mongrelized degenerates and cowards. You abide by the foolishness of the Geneva Convention. I am an unarmed prisoner of war. You will do nothing to me."

Later, he would boastfully write about this incident to the soft-spoken, courtly gentlemen who published his books. He said to the German officer, "What a mistake you made, brother."

And then I shot that smug prick. I just shot him before anyone could tell me I shouldn't. I let him have three in the belly, just like that, real quick, from maybe a foot away. Say what you want, maybe they were no supermen, but they weren't any panty-waists, either. Three in the belly, Pow-Pow-Pow, *and he's still standing there, and damned if he isn't dead but doesn't know it, but he is pretty surprised and serves him right, too.*

Then everyone else, all the Americans and a Brit or two are yelling and pissing around like they don't know whether to shit, go blind, or order breakfast, and here's this dead kraut swaying on his feet, and maybe I'm even thinking I'm in a kettle of bad soup, but the hell with it. But have to do it right, you know, arrogant krautkopf or not. So I put the gun to his head and I let him have it, bang! *and his brains come squirting right out his nose, gray and pink, and, you know, it looks pretty funny, so someone yells, "Gesundheit!" and that's it, brother. That's all she wrote and we've got us one guaranteed dead Nazi.*

VIII

A rose is a rose is a rose
The dead are the dead are the dead
*   except when*
they aren't and how do you like it
let's talk and
Who is on first
I know what I know and I am afraid
*   and I am*
afraid

IX

HOMAGE TO SPAIN

1. An Old Man's Luck

The dusty old man sat on the river bank. He wore steel rimmed spectacles. He had already traveled 12 kilometers and he was very tired. He thought it would be a while before he could go on.

That is what he told Adam Nichols.

Adam Nichols told him he had to cross the pontoon bridge. He really must and soon. When the shelling came, this would not be a good place to stay. The old man in the steel rimmed spectacles thanked Adam Nichols for his concern. He was a very polite old man. The reason he had stayed behind was to take care of the animals in his village. He smiled because saying "his village" made him feel good. There were three goats, two cats, and six doves. When he had no other choice and really had to leave, he opened the door to the doves' cage and let them fly. He was not too worried about the cats, really, the old man told Adam Nichols; cats are always all right. Cats had luck. Goats were another thing. Goats were a little stupid and sweet and so they had not much luck.

It was just too bad about the goats, the old man said. It was a sad thing.

Adam agreed. But the old man had to move along. He really should.

The old man said thank you. He was grateful for the concern. But he did not think he could go on just yet. He was very tired and he was 76 years old.

He asked a question. Did Adam truly think the cats would be all right?

Yes, Adam said, we both know cats have luck.

Adam thought they had a lot more luck than sweet and stupid goats and 76-year-old men who can go no farther than 12 kilometers when there is going to be shelling.

2. Hunters in the Morning Fog

Miguel woke him. They used to call him Miguelito but the older Miguel had been shot right through the heart, a very clean shot, and so now this one was Miguel. The sun had just come up and there was fog with cold puff-like clouds near to the ground. "Your rifle," Miguel said. "We are going hunting."

"Hey," Adam Nichols said, "what the hell?" He wanted coffee or to go back to sleep.

"Just come," Miguel said.

There were five of them, Pilar, who was as tough as any man, and Antonio, and Jordan, the American college professor, and Miguel, who used to be Miguelito, and Adam Nichols. They went out to the field. Yesterday it was a battlefield. The day before that it had just been a green, flat field. Some of the dead lay here and there. Not all of the dead were still. Some were already up and some were now rising, though most lay properly still and dead. Those who were up mostly staggered about like drunks. Some had their arms out in front of them like Boris Karloff in the *Frankenstein* movie. They did not look frightening. They looked stupid. But they were frightening even if they did not look frightening because they were supposed to be dead.

"Say, what the hell?" Adam Nichols asked. His mouth was dry.

"It happens sometimes," Pilar said. "That is what I have heard. It appears to be so, though this is the first time I personally have seen it."

Pilar shrugged. "The dead do not always stay dead. They come back sometimes. What they do then is quite sickening. It is revolting and disgusting. When come back, they are cannibals. They wish to eat living people. And if they bite you, they cause a sickness, and then you die, and then after that, you become like them and you wish to eat living people. We have to shoot them. A bullet in the head, that is what stops them. It's not so bad, you know. It's not like they are really alive."

"I don't go for this," Adam said.

"Don't talk so much," Pilar said. "I like you very much, *Americano,* but don't talk so much."

She put her rifle to her shoulder. It was an old '03 Springfield. It had plenty of stopping power. Pilar was a good shot. She fired and one of the living dead went down with the middle of his face punched in.

"Come on," Pilar said, commanding. "We stay together. We don't let any of these things get too close. That is what they are. Things. They aren't strong, but if there are too many, then it can be trouble."

"I don't think I like this," Adam Nichols said. "I don't think I like it at all."

"I am sorry, but what you like and what you dislike is not all that important, if you will forgive my saying so," Miguel said. "What does matter is that you are a good shot. You are one of our best shots. So, if you please, shoot some of these unfortunate dead people."

Antonio and Pilar and Jordan and Miguel and Adam Nichols shot the living dead as the hunting party walked through the puffy clouds of fog that lay on the field. Adam felt like his brain was the flywheel in a clock about to go out of control. He remembered shooting black squirrels when he was a boy. Sometimes you shot a black squirrel and it fell down and then when you went to pick it up it tried to bite you and you had to shoot it again or smash its head with a rock or the stock of your rifle. He tried to make himself think this was just like shooting black squirrels. He tried to make himself think it was even easier, really, because dead people moved a lot slower than black squirrels. It was hard to shoot a squirrel skittering up a tree. It was not so hard to shoot a dead man walking like a tired drunk toward you.

Then Adam saw the old man who had sat by the pontoon bridge the other day. The old man's steel rimmed spectacles hung from one ear. They were unshattered. He looked quite silly, like something in a Chaplin film. Much of his chest had been torn open and bones stuck out at crazy angles. There were wettish tubular-like things wrapped about the protruding bones of his chest.

He was coming at Adam Nichols like a trusting drunk who finds a friend and knows the friend will see him home.

"Get that one," said Jordan, the American college professor. "That one is yours."

Yes, Adam Nichols thought, the old man is mine. We have talked about goats and cats and doves.

Adam Nichols sighted. He took in a breath and held it. He waited.

The old man stumbled toward him.

Come, old man, Adam Nichols thought. *Come with your chest burst apart and your terrible appetite. Come with the mindless brute insistence that makes you continue. Come to the bullet that will give you at least the lie of a dignified ending. Come unto me, old man. Come unto me.*

"You let him draw too close," Miguel said. "Shoot him now."

Come, old man, Adam Nichols thought. *Come, because I am your luck. Come because I am all the luck you are ever going to have.*

Adam pulled the trigger. It was a fine shot. It took off the top of the old man's head. His glasses flew up and he flew back and lay on the fog-heavy ground.

"Good shot," Jordan said.

"No," Adam said, "just good luck."

3. In a Hole in the Mountain

It is not true that every man in Spain is named Paco, but it is true that if you call "Paco!" on the street of any city in Spain, you will have many more than one *"Qué?"* in response.

It was with a Paco that Adam Nichols found himself hiding from the fascist patrols. Paco's advanced age and formidable mustache made him look *Gitano.* Paco was a good fighter, and a good Spaniard, but not such a good communist. He said he was too old to have politics, but not too old to kill fascists.

Adam Nichols was now a communist because of some papers he had signed. Now he blew up things. For three months, he had been to a special school in Russia to learn demolitions. Adam Nichols was old enough now to know his talents. He was good at teaching young people to speak Spanish, and so for a while he had been a bored

and boring high school teacher of Spanish in Oak Park, Illinois. Blowing up things and killing fascists was much more interesting, so he had gone to Spain.

There were other reasons, too. He seldom let himself ponder these.

The previous day, Adam Nichols had blown up a railroad trestle that certain military leaders had agreed was important, and, except for old Paco, the comrades who had made possible this act of demolition were all dead. The fascists were seeking the man who had destroyed the trestle. But Paco knew how to hide.

Where Paco and Adam were hiding was too small to be a cave. It was just a hole in a mountain side. It was hard to spot unless you knew just what you were looking for.

It was dark in the hole. Paco and Adam could not build a fire. But it was safe to talk if you talked in the same low embarrassed way you did in the confessional. Because they were so close, there were times when Adam could almost feel that Paco was breathing for him and that he was breathing for Paco. A moment came to Adam Nichols that made him think, *This is very much like being lovers,* but then he decided it was not so. He would never be as close with a lover as he was now with Paco.

After many hours of being with Paco in the close dark, Adam said, "Paco, there is something I wish to ask thee." Adam Nichols spoke in the most formal Spanish. It was what was needed.

Gravely, though he was not a serious man, Paco said, "Then ask, but remember, Comrade, I am an aged man, and do not mistake age for wisdom." Paco chuckled. He was pleased he had remembered to say "comrade." Sometimes he forgot. It was hard to be a good communist.

"I need to speak of what I have seen. Of abomination. Of horror. Of impossibility."

"Art thou speaking of war?"

"*Sí.*"

"Then, dost thou speak of courage, too?" Paco asked. "Of decency? Or self-sacrifice?"

"No, *Viejo,*" Adam Nichols said. "Of these

things, much has been said and much written. Courage, decency, self-sacrifice are to be found in peace or war. Stupidity, greed, arrogance are to be found in peace or war. But I wish to speak with thee of that which I have seen only during time of war. It is madness. It is what cannot be."

Paco said, "What wouldst thou ask of me?"

"Paco," Adam Nichols said, "do the dead walk?"

"Hast thou seen this?"

"*Verdad.* I have seen this. No. I think I have seen this. Years ago, a long time back, in that which was my first war, I thought I saw it. It was in that war, Paco *Viejo,* that I think I became a little crazy. And now I think I have seen it in this war. There were others with me when we went to kill the dead. They would not talk of it, after. After, we all got drunk and made loud toasts which were vows of silence." Adam Nichols was silent for a time. Then he said again, "Do the dead walk?"

"Thou hast good eyes, Comrade Adam. Thou shootest well. Together we have been in battle. Thou dost not become crazy. What thou hast seen, thou hast seen truly."

Adam Nichols was quiet. He remembered when he was a young man and his heart was broken by a love gone wrong and the loss of well-holding arms and a smile that was for no one else but him. He felt worse now, filled with sorrow and fear both, and with his realizing the world was such a serious place. He said, "It is a horrible thing when the dead walk."

"*Verdad.*"

"Dost thou understand what happens?"

"Perhaps."

"Then perhaps you can tell me."

"Perhaps." Paco sighed. His sigh seemed to move the darkness in waves. "Years ago, I knew a priest. He was not a fascist priest. He was a nice man. The money in his plate did not go to buy candlesticks. He built a motion picture theater for his village. He knew that you need to laugh on Saturdays more than you need stained glass windows. The movies he showed were very

good movies. Buster Keaton. Harold Lloyd. Joe Bonomo. John Gilbert. KoKo the Klown and Betty Boop cartoons. This priest did not give a damn for politics, he told me. He gave a damn about people. And that is the reason, I believe, that he stopped being a priest. He had some money. He had three women who loved him and were content to share him. I think he was all right, this priest.

"It was he who told me of the living dead."

"And canst thou tell me?"

"Well, yes, I believe I can. There is no reason not to. I have sworn no oaths."

"What is it, then? Why do the dead rise? Why do they seek the flesh of the living?"

"This man who had been a priest was not certain about Heaven, but he was most definite about Hell. Yes, Hell was the Truth. Hell was for the dead.

"But when we turn this Earth of ours into Hell, there is no need for the dead to go below.

"Why should they bother?

"And canst thou doubt that much of this ball of mud upon which we dwell is today hell, Comrade? With each new war and each new and better way of making war, there is more and more hell and so we have more and more inhabitants of hell with us.

"And of course, no surprise, they have their hungers. They are demons. At least that is what some might call them, though I myself seldom think to call them anything. And the food of demons is human flesh. It is a simple thing, really."

"Paco . . ."

"*Sí?*"

"This is not rational."

"And art thou a rational man?"

"Yes. No."

"So?"

"'The Living Dead,' maybe that's what somebody would call them. Well, hell, don't you think that would make some newspaperman just ecstatic? It would be bigger than 'Lindy in Paris'! Bigger than—"

"And thou dost believe such a newspaper

story could be printed? And perhaps the *Book of the Living Dead* could be written? And perhaps a motion picture of the Living Dead as well, with Buster Keaton, perhaps? Comrade Adam, such revelation would topple the world order.

"Perhaps someday the world will be ready for such awful knowledge, Comrade Adam.

"For now, it is more than enough that those of us who know of it must know of it, thank you very kindly.

"And with drink and with women and with war and with whatever gives us comfort, we must try not to think over much about what it is we know."

"Paco," Adam Nichols said in the dark, "I think I want to scream. I think I want to scream now."

"No, Comrade. Be quiet now. Breathe deep. Breathe with me and deep. Let me breathe for you. Be quiet."

"All right," Adam said after a time. "It is all right now."

A day later, Paco thought it would be safe to leave the hole in the side of the mountain. They were spotted by an armored car full of fascists. A bullet passed through Paco's lung. It was a mortal shot.

"Bad luck, Paco," Adam Nichols said. He put a bullet into the old man's brain and went on alone.

X

"You're really not helping me. You know that."

"Bad on me. I thought I was here for you to help me. My foolishness. Damn the luck."

"I've decided, then, we'll go the way we did before, with electro-convulsive therapy. We'll—"

I am for god's sake 61 years old and I am going to die because of occluded arteries or because of a cirrhotic liver or because of an aneurysm in brain or belly waiting to go pop, or because of some damn thing—and when I die I wish to be dead to be dead and that is all.

"—a series of 12. We've often had good results—"

and, believe me, I am not asking for Jesus to make me a sunbeam, I am not asking for heaven in any way, shape, or form. Gentlemen, when I die I wish to be dead.

"—particularly with depression. There are several factors, of course—"

I'm looking for dead, that's D-E-A-D, and I don't want to be a goddamn carnival freak show act and man is just a little lower than the angels and pues y nada and you get older and you get confused and you become afraid.

"We'll begin tomorrow—"

no bloody chance because now the world is hell and if you doubt it, then you don't know the facts, Gentlemen. No bloody chance. We ended the war by dropping hell on Nagasaki and on Hiroshima, and we opened up Germany and discovered all those hells, and during the siege of Stalingrad, the living ate the dead, and ta-ta, Gentlemen, turnabout is fair play, and we're just starting to know the hells that good old Papa Joe put together no bloody chance and we're not blameless, oh, no, ask that poor nigger hanging burning from the tree, ask the Rosenbergs who got cooked up nice and brown, ask—welcome to hell, and how do you like it now, Gentlemen?

When the world is hell, the dead walk.

XI

When they returned to Ketchum, Idaho, on June 30, the old man was happy. Anyone who saw him will tell you. He was not supposed to drink because of his anti-depressant medication, but he did drink. It did not affect him badly. He sang several songs. One was *"La Quince Brigada,"* from the Spanish Civil War. He sang loudly and off-key; he made a joyful racket. He said one of the great regrets of his life was that he had never learned to play the banjo.

Later, he had his wife, Mary, put on a Burl Ives record on the Webcor phonograph. It was a 78, "The Riddle Song." He listened to it several times.

> *How can there be a cherry*
> *that has no stone?*
>
> *How can there be a chicken*
> *that has no bone?*
>
> *How can there be a baby*
> *with no crying?*

Mary asked if the record made him sad.

No, he said, he was not sad at all. The record was beautiful. If there are riddles, there are also answers to riddles.

So, so then, I have not done badly. Some good stories, some good books. I have written well and truly. I have sometimes failed, but I have tried. I have sometimes been a foolish man, and even a small-minded or mean-spirited one, but I have always been a man, and I will end as a man.

It was early and he was the only one up. The morning of Sunday, July 2, was beautiful. There were no clouds. There was sunshine.

He went to the front foyer. He liked the way the light struck the oak-paneled walls and the floor. It was like being in a museum or in a church. It was a well-lighted place and it felt clean and airy.

Carefully, he lowered the butt of the Boss shotgun to the floor. He leaned forward. The twin barrels were cold circles in the scarred tissue just above his eyebrows.

He tripped both triggers.

JUMBEE

HENRY S. WHITEHEAD

IT WOULD BE difficult to imagine a more unlikely contributor to the strange and violent pulp magazines than the Reverend Henry St. Clair Whitehead (1882–1932). Born in Elizabeth, New Jersey, he graduated from Harvard University, where he played football and studied with the poet and philosopher George Santayana, earning a doctorate in philosophy in 1904. He became a newspaper editor and served as the commissioner of the Amateur Athletic Union, then went to the Berkeley Divinity School in Middletown, Connecticut. He was ordained a deacon in the Episcopal Church in 1912, serving in a series of increasingly important and responsible positions, progressing from rector and children's pastor to the post of archdeacon to the Virgin Islands in the West Indies from 1921 to 1929. He wrote frequently of ecclesiastical matters and, while living on St. Croix, gathered ideas and background material on voodoo and native legends and superstitions for the fiction he was to write for such pulp magazines as *Adventure, Weird Tales,* and *Strange Tales.*

His first published story was "The Intarsia Box," which appeared in *Adventure* in 1923, and he began a lifelong connection to *Weird Tales* with the publication of "Tea Leaves" the following year. He developed a steady correspondence and friendship with H. P. Lovecraft, with whom he collaborated on a story, "The Trap," in 1931. In his relatively brief career of less than a decade, he published more than forty pulp stories, twenty-five for *Weird Tales.* Two collections of his stories were published posthumously, *Jumbee and Other Uncanny Tales* (1944) and *West India Lights* (1946).

"Jumbee" was originally published in the September 1926 issue of *Weird Tales;* it was first collected in *Jumbee and Other Uncanny Tales* (Sauk City, WI: Arkham House, 1944).

HENRY S. WHITEHEAD

JUMBEE

MR. GRANVILLE LEE, a Virginian of Virginians, coming out of the World War with a lung wasted and scorched by mustard gas, was recommended by his physician to spend a winter in the spice-and-balm climate of the Lesser Antilles—the lower islands of the West Indian archipelago. He chose one of the American islands, St. Croix, the old Santa Cruz—Island of the Holy Cross—named by Columbus himself on his second voyage; once famous for its rum.

It was to Jaffray Da Silva that Mr. Lee at last turned for definite information about the local magic; information which, after a two months' residence, accompanied with marked improvement in his general health, he had come to regard as imperative, from the whetting glimpses he had received of its persistence on the island.

Contact with local customs, too, had sufficiently blunted his inherited sensibilities, to make him almost comfortable, as he sat with Mr. Da Silva on the cool gallery of that gentleman's beautiful house, in the shade of forty years' growth of bougainvillea, on a certain afternoon. It was the restful gossipy period between five o'clock and dinnertime. A glass jug of foaming rum-swizzel stood on the table between them.

"But, tell me, Mr. Da Silva," he urged, as he absorbed his second glass of the cooling, mild drink, "have you ever, actually, been confronted with a '*Jumbee*'?—ever really seen one? You say, quite frankly, that you believe in them!"

This was not the first question about *Jumbees* that Mr. Lee had asked. He had consulted planters; he had spoken of the matter of *Jumbees* with courteous, intelligent, coloured storekeepers about the town, and even in Christiansted, St. Croix's other and larger town on the north side

of the island. He had even mentioned the matter to one or two coal-black sugar-field labourers; for he had been on the island just long enough to begin to understand—a little—the weird jargon of speech which Lafcadio Hearn, when he visited St. Croix many years before, had not recognised as "English."

There had been marked differences in what he had been told. The planters and storekeepers had smiled, though with varying degrees of intensity, and had replied that the Danes had invented *Jumbees*, to keep their estate-labourers indoors after nightfall, thus ensuring a proper night's sleep for them, and minimising the depredations upon growing crops. The labourers whom he had asked, had rolled their eyes somewhat, but, it being broad daylight at the time of the enquiries, they had broken their impassive gravity with smiles, and sought to impress Mr. Lee with their lofty contempt for the beliefs of their fellow blacks, and with queerly-phrased assurances that Jumbee is a figment of the imagination.

Nevertheless, Mr. Lee was not satisfied. There was something here that he seemed to be missing—something extremely interesting, too, it appeared to him; something very different from "Bre'r Rabbit" and similar tales of his own remembered childhood in Virginia.

Once, too, he had been reading a book about Martinique and Guadeloupe, those ancient jewels of France's crown, and he had not read far before he met the word "Zombi." After that, he knew, at least, that the Danes had not "invented" the Jumbee. He heard, though vaguely, of the labourer's belief that Sven Garik, who had long ago gone back to his home in Sweden, and Garrity, one of the smaller planters now on the island, were "wolves"! Lycanthropy, animal-metamorphosis, it appeared, formed part of this strange texture of local belief.

Mr. Jaffray Da Silva was one-eighth African. He was, therefore, by island usage, "coloured," which is as different from being "black" in the West Indies as anything that can be imagined. Mr. Da Silva had been educated in the continental European manner. In his every word and action, he reflected the faultless courtesy of his European forbears. By every right and custom of West Indian society, Mr. Da Silva was a coloured gentleman, whose social status was as clear-cut and definite as a cameo.

These islands are largely populated by persons like Mr. Da Silva. Despite the difference in their status from what it would be in North America, in the islands it has its advantages—among them that of logic. To the West Indian mind, a man whose heredity is seven-eighths derived from gentry, as like as not with an authentic coats-of-arms, is entitled to be treated accordingly. That is why Mr. Da Silva's many clerks, and everybody else who knew him, treated him with deference, addressed him as "sir," and doffed their hats in continental fashion when meeting; salutes which, of course, Mr. Da Silva invariably returned, even to the humblest, which is one of the marks of a gentleman anywhere.

Jaffray Da Silva shifted one thin leg, draped in spotless white drill, over the other, and lit a fresh cigarette.

"Even my friends smile at me, Mr. Lee," he replied, with a tolerant smile, which lightened for an instant his melancholy, ivory-white countenance. "They laugh at me more or less because I admit I believe in Jumbees. It is possible that everybody with even a small amount of African blood possesses that streak of belief in magic and the like. I seem, though, to have a peculiar aptitude for it! It is a matter of experience, with me, sir, and my friends are free to smile at me if they wish. Most of them—well, they do not admit their beliefs as freely as I, perhaps!"

Mr. Lee took another sip of the cold swizzel. He had heard how difficult it was to get Jaffray Da Silva to speak of his "experiences," and he suspected that under his host's even courtesy lay that austere pride which resents anything like ridicule, despite that tolerant smile.

"Please proceed, sir," urged Mr. Lee, and was quite unconscious that he had just used a word which, in his native South, is reserved for gentlemen of pure Caucasian blood.

"When I was a young man," began Mr. Da Silva, "about 1894, there was a friend of mine named Hilmar Iversen, a Dane, who lived here in the town, up near the Moravian Church on what the people call 'Foun'-Out Hill.' Iversen had a position under the government, a clerk's job, and his office was in the Fort. On his way home he used to stop here almost every afternoon for a swizzel and a chat. We were great friends, close friends. He was then a man a little past fifty, a butter tub of a fellow, very stout, and, like many of that build, he suffered from heart attacks.

"One night a boy came here for me. It was eleven o'clock, and I was just arranging the mosquito-net on my bed, ready to turn in. The servants had all gone home, so I went to the door myself, in shirt and trousers, and carrying a lamp, to see what was wanted—or, rather, I knew perfectly well what it was—a messenger to tell me Iversen was dead!"

Mr. Lee suddenly sat bolt-upright.

"How could you know that?" he enquired, his eyes wide.

Mr. Da Silva threw away the remains of his cigarette.

"I sometimes know things like that," he answered, slowly. "In this case, Iversen and I had been close friends for years. He and I had talked about magic and that sort of thing a great deal, occult powers, manifestations—that sort of thing. It is a very general topic here, as you may have seen. You would hear more of it if you continued to live here and settled into the ways of the island. In fact, Mr. Lee, Iversen and I had made a compact together. The one of us who 'went out' first, was to try to warn the other of it. You see, Mr. Lee, I had received Iversen's warning less than an hour before.

"I had been sitting out here on the gallery until ten o'clock or so. I was in that very chair you are occupying. Iversen had been having a heart attack. I had been to see him that afternoon. He looked just as he always did when he was recovering from an attack. In fact he intended to return to his office the following morning. Neither of us, I am sure, had given a thought to the possibility of a sudden sinking spell. We had not even referred to our agreement.

"Well, it was about ten, as I've said, when all of a sudden I heard Iversen coming along through the yard below there toward the house along that gravel path. He had, apparently, come through the gate from the Kongensgade—the King Street, as they call it nowadays—and I could hear his heavy step on the gravel very plainly. He had a slight limp. 'Heavy crunch-light-crunch; plod-plod—plod-plod'; old Iversen to the life, there was no mistaking his step. There was no moon that night. The half of a waning moon was due to show itself an hour and a half later, but just then it was virtually pitch-black down there in the garden.

"I got up out of my chair and walked over to the top of the steps. To tell you the truth, Mr. Lee, I rather suspected—I have a kind of aptitude for that sort of thing—that it was not Iversen himself; how shall I express it? I had the idea from somewhere inside me, that it was Iversen trying to keep our agreement. My instinct assured me that he had just died. I can not tell you how I knew it, but such was the case, Mr. Lee.

"So I waited, over there just behind you, at the top of the steps. The footfalls came along steadily. At the foot of the steps, out of the shadow of the hibiscus bushes, it was a trifle less black than farther down the patch. There was a faint illumination, too, from a lamp inside the house. I knew that if it were Iversen, himself, I should be able to see him when the footsteps passed out of the deep shadow of the bushes. I did not speak.

"The footfalls came along toward that point, and passed it. I strained my eyes through the gloom, and I could see nothing. Then I knew, Mr. Lee, that Iversen had died, and that he was keeping his agreement.

"I came back here and sat down in my chair, and waited. The footfalls began to come up the steps. They came along the floor of the gallery, straight toward me. They stopped here, Mr. Lee, just beside me. I could *feel* Iversen standing here, Mr. Lee." Mr. Da Silva pointed to the floor with his slim, rather elegant hand.

"Suddenly, in the dead quiet, I could feel my hair stand up all over my scalp, straight and stiff. The chills started to run down my back, and up again, Mr. Lee. I shook like a man with the ague, sitting here in my chair.

"I said: 'Iversen, I understand! Iversen, I'm afraid!' My teeth were chattering like castanets, Mr. Lee. I said: 'Iversen, please go! You have kept the agreement. I am sorry I am afraid, Iversen. The flesh is weak! I am not afraid of *you*, Iversen, old friend. But you will understand, man! It's not ordinary fear. My intellect is all right, Iversen, but I'm badly panic-stricken, so please go, my friend.'

"There had been silence, Mr. Lee, as I said, before I began to speak to Iversen, for the footsteps had stopped here beside me. But when I said that, and asked my friend to go, I could *feel* that he went at once, and I knew that he had understood how I meant it! It was, suddenly, Mr. Lee, as though there had never been any footsteps, if you see what I mean. It is hard to put into words. I daresay, if I had been one of the labourers, I should have been halfway to Christiansted through the estates, Mr. Lee, but I was not so frightened that I could not stand my ground.

"After I had recovered myself a little, and my scalp had ceased its prickling, and the chills were no longer running up and down my spine, I rose, and I felt extremely weary, Mr. Lee. It had been exhausting. I came into the house and drank a large tot of French brandy, and then I felt better, more like myself. I took my hurricane-lantern and lighted it, and stepped down the path toward the gate leading to the Kongens-gade. There was one thing I wished to see down there at the end of the garden. I wanted to see if the gate was fastened, Mr. Lee. It was. That huge iron staple, that you noticed, was in place. It has been used to fasten that old gate since some time in the eighteenth century, I imagine. I had not supposed anyone had opened the gate, Mr. Lee, but now I knew. There were no footprints in the gravel, Mr. Lee. I looked carefully. The marks of the bush-broom where the house-boy had swept the path on his way back from closing the gate were undisturbed, Mr. Lee.

"I was satisfied, and no longer even a little frightened. I came back here and sat down, and thought about my long friendship with old Iversen. I felt very sad to know that I should not see him again alive. He would never stop here again afternoons for a swizzel and a chat. About eleven o'clock I went inside the house and was preparing for bed when the rapping came at the front door. You see, Mr. Lee, I knew at once what it would mean.

"I went to the door, in shirt and trousers and stocking feet, carrying a lamp. We did not have electric light in those days. At the door stood Iversen's house-boy, a young fellow about eighteen. He was half-asleep, and very much upset. He 'cut his eyes' at me, and said nothing.

" 'What is it, mon?' I asked the boy.

" 'Mistress Iversen send ax yo' sir, please come to de house. Mr. Iversen die, sir.'

" 'What time Mr. Iversen die, mon—you hear?'

" 'I ain' able to say what o'clock, sir. Mistress Iversen come wake me where I sleep in a room in the yard sir, an' sen' me please call you—I t'ink he die about an hour ago, sir.'

"I put on my shoes again, and the rest of my clothes, and picked up a St. Kitts supplejack— I'll get you one; it's one of those limber, grape-vine walking sticks, a handy thing on a dark night—and started with the boy for Iversen's house.

"When we had arrived almost at the Moravian Church, I saw something ahead, near the roadside. It was then about eleven-fifteen, and the streets were deserted. What I saw made me curious to test something. I paused, and told the boy to run on ahead and tell Mrs. Iversen I would be there shortly. The boy started to trot ahead. He was pure black, Mr. Lee, but he went past what I saw without noticing it. He swerved a little away from it, and I think, perhaps, he slightly quickened his pace just at that point, but that was all."

"What did you see?" asked Mr. Lee, interrupting. He spoke a trifle breathlessly. His left lung was, as yet, far from being healed.

"The Hanging Jumbee," replied Mr. Da Silva, in his usual tones.

"Yes! There at the side of the road were three Jumbees. There's a reference to that in *The History of Stewart McCann*. Perhaps you've run across that, eh?"

Mr. Lee nodded, and Mr. Da Silva quoted:

" 'There they hung, though no ladder's rung

" 'Supported their dangling feet.'

"And there's another line in *The History*," he continued, smiling, "which describes a typical group of Hanging Jumbee:

" 'Maiden, man-child, and shrew.'

"Well, there were the usual three Jumbees, apparently hanging in the air. It wasn't very light, but I could make out a boy of about twelve, a young girl, and a shrivelled old woman—what the author of *The History of Stewart McCann* meant by the word 'shrew.' He told me himself, by the way, Mr. Lee, that he had put feet on his Jumbees mostly for the sake of a convenient rhyme—poetic license! The Hanging Jumbee have no feet. It is one of their peculiarities. Their legs stop at the ankles. They have abnormally long, thin African legs. They are always black, you know. Their feet—if they have them—are always hidden in a kind of mist that lies along the ground wherever one sees them. They shift and 'weave,' as a full-blooded African does—standing on one foot and resting the other—you've noticed that, of course—or scratching the supporting ankle with the toes of the other foot. They do not swing in the sense that they seem to be swung on a rope—that is not what it means; they do not twirl about. But they do—always—face the oncomer. . . .

"I walked on, slowly, and passed them; and they kept their faces to me as they always do. I'm used to that. . . .

"I went up the steps of the house to the front gallery, and found Mrs. Iversen waiting for me. Her sister was with her, too. I remained sitting with them for the best part of an hour. Then two old black women who had been sent for, into the country, arrived. These were two old women who were accustomed to prepare the dead for burial. Then I persuaded the ladies to retire, and started to come home myself.

"It was a little past midnight, perhaps twelve-fifteen. I picked out my own hat from two or three of poor old Iversen's that were hanging on

the rack, took my supplejack, and stepped out of the door onto the little stone gallery at the head of the steps.

"There are about twelve or thirteen steps from the gallery down to the street. As I started down them I noticed a third old black woman sitting, all huddled together, on the bottom step, with her back to me. I thought at once that this must be some old crone who lived with the other two—the preparers of the dead. I imagined that she had been afraid to remain alone in their cabin, and so had accompanied them into the town—they are like children, you know, in some ways—and that, feeling too humble to come into the house, she had sat down to wait on the step and had fallen asleep. You've heard their proverbs, have you not? There's one that exactly fits this situation that I had imagined: 'Cockroach no wear crockin' boot when he creep in fowl-house!' It means: 'Be very reserved when in the presence of your betters!' Quaint, rather! The poor souls!

"I started to walk down the steps toward the old woman. That scant halfmoon had come up into the sky while I had been sitting with the ladies, and by its light everything was fairly sharply defined. I could see that old woman as plainly as I can see you now, Mr. Lee. In fact, I was looking directly at the poor creature as I came down the steps, and fumbling in my pocket for a few coppers for her—for tobacco and sugar, as they say! I was wondering, indeed, why she was not by this time on her feet and making one of their queer little bobbing bows—'cockroach bow to fowl,' as they might say! It seemed this old woman must have fallen into a very deep sleep, for she had not moved at all, although ordinarily she would have heard me, for the night was deathly still, and their hearing is extraordinarily acute, like a cat's, or a dog's. I remember that the fragrance from Mrs. Iversen's tuberoses in pots on the gallery railing, was pouring out in a stream that night, 'making a greeting for the moon!' It was almost overpowering.

"Just as I was putting my foot on the fifth

step, there came a tiny little puff of fresh breeze from somewhere in the hills behind Iversen's house. It rustled the dry fronds of a palm-tree that was growing beside the steps. I turned my head in that direction for an instant.

"Mr. Lee, when I looked back, down the steps, after what must have been a fifth of a second's inattention, that little old black woman who had been huddled up there on the lowest step, apparently sound asleep, was gone. She had vanished utterly—and, Mr. Lee, a little white dog, about the size of a French poodle, was bounding up the steps toward me. With every bound, a step at a leap, the dog increased in size. It seemed to swell out there before my very eyes.

"Then I was really frightened—thoroughly, utterly frightened. I knew if that animal so much as touched me, it meant death, Mr. Lee—absolute, certain death. The little old woman was a 'sheen'—*chien*, of course. You know of lycanthropy—wolf-change—of course. Well, this was one of our varieties of it. I do not know what it would be called, I'm sure. 'Canicanthropy,' perhaps. I don't know, but something—something, first-cousin-once-removed from lycanthropy, and on the downward scale, Mr. Lee. The old woman was a were-dog!

"Of course, I had no time to think, only to use my instinct. I swung my supplejack with all my might and brought it down squarely on that beast's head. It was only a step below me then, and I could see the faint moonlight sparkle on the slaver about its mouth. It was then, it seemed to me, about the size of a medium-sized dog—nearly wolf-size, Mr. Lee, and a kind of deathly white. I was desperate, and the force with which I struck caused me to lose my balance. I did not fall, but it required a moment or two for me to regain my equilibrium. When I felt my feet firm under me again, I looked about, frantically, on all sides, for the 'dog.' But it, too, Mr. Lee, like the old woman, had quite disappeared. I looked all about, you may well imagine, after that experience, in the clear, thin moonlight. For yards about the foot of the steps, there was no place—not even a small nook—where either the 'dog' or

the old woman could have been concealed. Neither was on the gallery, which was only a few feet square, a mere landing.

"But there came to my ears, sharpened by that night's experiences, from far out among the plantations at the rear of Iversen's house, the pad-pad of naked feet. Someone—something—was running, desperately, off in the direction of the centre of the island, back into the hills, into the deep 'bush.'

"Then, behind me, out of the house onto the gallery rushed the two old women who had been preparing Iversen's body for its burial. They were enormously excited, and they shouted at me unintelligibly. I will have to render their words for you.

" 'O, de Good Gahd protec' you, Marster Jaffray, sir—de Joombie, de Joombie! De "Sheen," Marster Jaffray! He go, sir?'

"I reassured the poor old souls, and went back home." Mr. Da Silva fell abruptly silent. He slowly shifted his position in his chair, and reached for, and lighted, a fresh cigarette. Mr. Lee was absolutely silent. He did not move. Mr. Da Silva resumed, deliberately, after obtaining a light.

"You see, Mr. Lee, the West Indies are different from any other place in the world, I verily believe, sir. I've said so, anyhow, many a time, although I have never been out of the islands except when I was a young man, to Copenhagen. I've told you exactly what happened that particular night."

Mr. Lee heaved a sigh.

"Thank you, Mr. Da Silva, very much indeed, sir," said he, thoughtfully, and made as though to rise. His service wristwatch indicated six o'clock.

"Let us have a fresh swizzel, at least, before you go," suggested Mr. Da Silva. "We have a saying here in the island, that a man can't travel on one leg! Perhaps you've heard it already."

"I have," said Mr. Lee.

"Knud, Knud! You hear, mon? Knud—tell Charlotte to mash up another bal' of ice—you hear? Quickly now," commanded Mr. Da Silva.

MARBH BHEO

PETER TREMAYNE

PETER BERRESFORD ELLIS (1943–) was born in Coventry, Warwickshire, the son a Cork-born journalist whose family can be traced back in the area to 1288. Ellis, most of whose fiction has been published under the Peter Tremayne pseudonym, took his B.A. and master's degrees in Celtic studies, then followed his father's footsteps to become a journalist. His first book, *Wales: A Nation Again* (1968), was a history of the Welsh struggle for independence, followed by popular titles in Celtic studies. He has served as international chairman of the Celtic League (1988–1990) and is the honorary life president of the Scottish 1820 Society and honorary life member of the Irish Literary Society.

He has produced eighty-eight full-length books, a similar number of short stories, and numerous scholarly pamphlets. As Tremayne, he has written eighteen worldwide bestselling novels about the seventh-century Irish nun-detective, Sister Fidelma, which has more than three million copies in print. As Peter MacAlan, he produced eight thrillers (1983–1993). In the horror field, he has written more than two dozen novels, mostly inspired by Celtic myths and legends, including *Dracula Unborn* (1977), *The Revenge of Dracula* (1978), and *Dracula, My Love* (1980).

"Marbh Bheo" was originally published in the anthology *The Mammoth Book of Zombies*, edited by Stephen Jones (London: Robinson Publishing, 1993).

343

PETER TREMAYNE

MARBH BHEO

IT WAS DARK when I reached the old cottage. The journey had been far from easy. I suppose a city-bred person such as myself would find most rural journeys difficult. I had certainly assumed too much. As the crow flies, I had been told that the cottage was only some twenty-one miles from the centre of Cork City. But in Ireland the miles are deceptive. I know there is a standard joke about "the Irish mile" but there is a grain of truth in it. For the Boggeragh Mountains, in whose shadows the cottage lay, are a brooding, windswept area where nothing grows but bleak heather, a dirty stubble which clings tenaciously to the grey granite thrusts of the hills, where the wind whistles and sings over a moonscape of rocks pricking upwards to the heavens. To walk a mile in such terrain, among the heights and terrible grandeur of the wild, rocky slopes and gorse you have to allow two hours. A mile on a well-kept road is not like a mile on a forgotten track amidst these sullen peaks.

What was I doing in such an inhospitable area in the first place? That is the question which you will undoubtedly ask.

Well, it was not through any desire on my part. But one must live and my livelihood depended on my job with RTÉ. I am a researcher with Telefís Éireann, the Irish state television. Initially it was the idea of some bright producer that we make a programme on Irish folk customs. So that was the initial impetus which found me searching among dusty tomes in an old occult bookstore, in a little alley off Sheares Street on the nameless island in the River Lee which constitutes the centre of the city of Cork. The area is often mentioned in the literature of Cork as the place where once the fashionable world came to see and be seen. That era of glory has departed and now small artisans' houses and shops crowd upon it claustrophobically.

I had been told to research the superstitions connected with the dead and I was browsing through some volumes when I became aware of an old woman standing next to me. She was peering at the book that I was examining with more than a degree of interest.

"So you are interested in the Irish customs and superstitions relating to the dead, young man?" she observed in an imperious tone, her voice slightly shrill and sharp.

I looked at her. She was of small stature, the shoulders bent, but she wore a long black dress, with matching large hat and veil, almost like a figure out of a Victorian drama. From such a guise it was hard to see her features but she gave the air of a world long gone, of a time almost forgotten.

"I am," I replied courteously.

"An interesting subject. There are many stories of the dead who come to life again in West Cork. If you travel round the rural communities you will hear some quite incredible stories."

"Really?" I inquired politely. "You mean zombies?"

She sniffed disparagingly.

"Zombies! That is a voodoo superstition originating in Africa. You are in Ireland, young man. No, I mean the *marbh bheo*."

She pronounced this as "ma'rof vo."

"What's that?" I demanded.

"A corpse that lives," she replied. "You will find many a tale about the *marbh bheo* in rural Ireland."

She sniffed again. It seemed a habit.

"Yes, really, young man. There are many stories that will make your hair curl. Stories that are fantastic and terrible. Tales of being buried alive. The tale of Tadhg Ó Catháin who, in punishment for his wicked life, was condemned to be ridden every night by a hideous living corpse, a *marbh bheo*, who demanded burial and drove him from churchyard to churchyard as the dead rose up in each one to refuse the corpse burial. There are the corpses who wait in haunted lakes to devour the drowned ones, and the unholy undead creatures who haunt the raths. Oh yes, young man, there are many fantastic tales to be heard and some not a mile or so from this very spot."

An idea crossed my mind as she spoke.

"Do you know any local people who are experts in such tales?" I inquired. "You see, I am working on a television programme and want to speak to someone . . ."

She sniffed yet again.

"You wish to speak to someone who has knowledge about the *marbh bheo?*"

I smiled. She made it sound so natural as if I were merely asking to speak to someone who could advise me on bee-keeping. I nodded eagerly.

"Go to Musheramore Mountain and ask for 'Teach Droch-Chlú.' At 'Teach Droch-Chlú' you will find Father Nessan Doheny. He will speak with you."

I put down the book that I had been examining, turned to reach for my attaché case and took out my notebook. I turned back to the old lady but much to my amazement she had gone. I looked round the bookstore. The owner was upstairs and I asked him if he had seen or knew her but he had not. With a shrug, I jotted down the names that she had given me. After all, in an occult bookstore you are apt to meet the weirdest people. But I was pleased with the meeting. Here was a more interesting lead than spending days browsing through books. A good television programme relies on personalities, raconteurs, and not the recitation of dry and dusty facts by a narrator.

Musheramore is the largest peak in the Boggeragh Mountains, not far from Cork. I checked the phone book and found no listing for Father Nessan Doheny nor for "Teach Droch-Chlú." But the place was so near, and city dweller that I am, I thought I would be able to ride the twenty-one miles to Musheramore and back in one evening. I should explain that I am the proud possessor of a vintage Triumph motorcycle. Motorbikes are a hobby of mine. I thought that I could have a chat with the priest and then be back in Cork long before midnight.

I rode out of Cork on the Macroom road, which is a good straight and wide highway, and then turned north on a small track towards the village of Ballynagree with Musheramore a black dominating peak in the distance. That was easy. I stopped at a local garage, just north of Ballynagree, filled up with petrol and asked the way to "Teach Droch-Chlú." The garage man, whose name-badge on his overalls pronounced him to be "Manus," gave me an old fashioned glance, as though I had said something which secretly amused him. His face assumed a sort of knowing grin as he gave me some directions.

That was when the real journey began.

It took me an hour to negotiate the directions and reach the place. Though it shames me to say it, my Irish is not particularly good. In a country which is reputedly bilingual, but where English is more widely spoken than Irish, one can get by with little use of the language. Therefore, while I knew that "Teach" meant a house, I had no idea of the full meaning of the name. And the cottage, for such it proved to be, was harder to find than I would ever have thought.

It lay in a scooped out hollow of the mountain, surrounded by dark trees and shrubs which formed a hedgerow. It looked old, dank and depressing. And when I eventually found the place, darkness had spread its enveloping cloak all around.

I parked my motorbike and walked along a winding path, with the sharp barbs of pyracantha bushes scratching my hands and snagging my jacket. I finally reached the low lintelled door.

When I knocked on its paint-peeling panels, a reedy voice bade me enter.

Father Nessan Doheny, or so I presumed the gaunt figure to be, sat in a high-backed chair by a smouldering turf fire; his hair was white, the eyes colourless and pale, seeming without animation, and his skin was like yellow parchment. His thin, claw-like hands were folded on his lap. I would have placed his age more towards ninety than younger. He was clad in a dark, shining suit with only his white Roman collar to throw it into relief. There was a chilly atmosphere in the room in spite of the smouldering fire.

"The dead?" he piped shrilly, after I had explained my purpose. His thin bloodless lips cracked upwards. It might have been a smile. "Have the living so little to interest them that they need to know of the dead?"

"It's for a television programme on folklore, Father," I humoured him.

"Folklore, is it?" he cackled. "Now the dead are reduced to folklore."

He fell silent for such a long while that I thought maybe the ancient priest had grown senile in his ageing and had fallen asleep, but he eventually raised his face to mine and shook his head.

"I could tell you many tales about the dead. They are as real as the living. Why, not far from here is a farmstead. It is the custom in these parts that when throwing away water at night, for you will find many a house that has still to draw its water from wells, that the person casting out the water should cry: '*Tóg ort as uisce!*' Meaning—away with yourself from the water."

I knew this to be a rural expression better rendered into English as "look out for the water."

"Why would they say this, Father?"

"Because the belief is that water falling on a corpse burns it, for water is purity. Well, there came a night when a woman of a farm not far from here, threw out a jug of water and forgot the warning cry. Instantly, she heard a shriek of a person in pain. No one was seen in the darkness. Around midnight, the door came open and a black lamb entered the house, having its back scalded. It lay down moaning by the hearth and died before the farmer and his wife knew what to do.

"The farmer buried the lamb the next morning. At midnight that night the door came open again and the lamb entered. Its back was scalded as before. It lay down and died. The farmer buried it again. When this happened a third time, the farmer sent for me. I was then a young priest but I knew what had happened immediately and laid the dead spirit to rest by the solemnity of exorcism. The black lamb appeared no more."

I was hastily scribbling notes. I had to put down one of my notebooks on a side table as I bent to my task.

"Absolutely great, Father. That will make a nice tale. First class."

He gazed at me sourly.

"It is no game we are talking about. The dead have equal powers to the living and you should be warned not to mock them, young man."

I smiled indulgently.

"Don't worry, Father. I'll not mock them. I just want to get this programme together . . ."

Father Doheny winced as if in pain but I prattled on obliviously.

"Are there such things as zombies in Ireland?"

He sniffed. It suddenly reminded me of the old woman and the answer she had given me.

"You mean a corpse reanimated by sorcery?"

"Yes. Don't we have any stories about the walking dead in Ireland? I mean, what do you call it, a *marbh bheo?*"

His pale eyes seemed to gaze right through me.

"Of course the dead walk. There is only the

faintest veil between this land of the living and the land of the dead. At the right time and with the right stimulus the dead can enter into our world with the same ease as we can enter into their world."

I could not help smirking.

"That's hardly the official Church line from Rome."

His thin lips compressed in annoyance.

"The ancients knew these things long before the coming of Christianity. It would be better not to take them lightly."

Father Nessan Doheny was a delight. I was scribbling away as fast as I could, imagining a whole series of programmes devoted to the ageing priest sitting recounting his bizarre tales.

"Go on, Father," I prompted. "How easy is it to cross through this veil, you speak of, into the land of the dead?"

"Easy enough, boy. Over at Caherbarnagh, when I was a young priest, there was living a woman. One day she was returning to her cottage when she stopped to drink by a small stream. As she rose to her feet she suddenly heard the sound of low music. A group of people were coming down the path, singing a strange, soothing song. It puzzled her and she felt a shiver of apprehension. Then she realised that close by her a tall, young man was standing watching her, his face strange and pale, the eyes wide and blank.

"She demanded to know who he was. He shook his head and warned her that she was in great danger and unless she fled with him, evil would befall her. She began to trot off with him and the people coming down the path with their music cried out: 'Come back!' Yet fear lent her wings and she ran and ran with the young man until they reached the edge of a small wood. The young man halted and pronounced them safe. Then he asked her to look upon his face.

"When she did so, she recognised him as her elder brother who had been drowned the year before. He was drowned while swimming in the dark waters of Loch Dalua and his body had never been recovered. What was she to do? She felt

evil near and ran home to send for me, the local priest, confessing all. There was fear and trembling on her when she told me her tale and after she had made that final confession, she died."

"That's a terrific tale," I said, entering it enthusiastically in my notebook.

"There are tales of the dead in every corner of the land," nodded the old priest.

I became aware of an old clock chiming in the corner. I could not believe it. It was ten o'clock already. I sighed. Well, I was getting so much good material that it was a shame to break off now to make sure I was back in Cork at a reasonable hour.

"But what about this *marbh bheo*, Father," I asked. "These stories you have told me are more of ghosts than the walking dead. Are there stories of reanimated corpses?"

The priest's expression did not change.

"Ghosts, walking dead, the dead are dead in whatever form they come."

"But reanimated corpses?" I pressed. "What of them?"

"If I must speak, then I must," the old priest said almost half to himself, half as if speaking to some third party. "Must I speak?"

Naturally, I thought the question was addressed to me and answered in the affirmative.

"I will speak then. I will tell you a tale; a tale of a great English lord who used to own these mountains in the days before Ireland won her independence from England."

I glanced at the clock and said: "Is it a tale about the walking dead, the *marbh bheo*?"

The priest ignored me.

"The lord was called the Earl of Musheramore, Baron of Lyre and Lisnaraha. He had a great castle and estate which covered most of the Boggeragh Mountains. He and his family before him since the days of the English conquests and the flight of our noble families to Europe. The estate was a prosperous one and the Earl of Musheramore was rich and powerful."

His voice assumed a droning tone, hypnotic and soporific.

The real point of his story had taken place

in the days of the "Great Hunger." During the mid nineteenth century, the potato crops failed. Because the peasants of Ireland had been so reduced in poverty by the absentee English landlords, the potato had become the staple diet, mixed with a little poaching on the estate, game from the land and fish from the rivers and lochs. The lords of the land severely punished any people caught taking the game or the fish. One young man who had dared to poach a couple of rabbits from Lord Musheramore, to help feed his large family, was transported to Van Diemen's Land in Australia for seven years. That was the type of fate that awaited any peasant who poached on their lord's land. The law was vigorously imposed by landlords' agents, usually impoverished former officers of the British army, who were employed to run things in the absence of the owners.

So, of course, when the potato crop failed, the people began to starve. In a space of three years the population of the country had been reduced by two and a half million. Yet the landlords and their agents still demanded the rent on the tiny peasant hovels, evicted people into the winter snows and frosts; men, women, children and babes in arms, if they could not pay, were evicted, their cabins torn down to prevent reoccupation. Under such straits they perished from exposure, malnutrition and other attendant diseases. Cholera struck everywhere.

Yet the landlords prospered. Great shiploads of the landlords' produce—grain, wheat, flax, cattle, sheep, poultry—were being loaded aboard the ships in Irish harbours and sent to England for sale. For every charity relief ship, raised by the Irish communities abroad, sailing into an Irish port, six ships loaded with grain and livestock were sailing out of the ports to England.

A great bitterness spread over the land. An attempt to rise up against the rulers was severely crushed by the military.

On the estate of Lord Musheramore, the peasants gathered in a body, kneeling on the well-kept green lawns outside Musheramore Castle, holding up their hands in supplication to his lordship, pleading for his help to keep them alive for the forthcoming winter, a winter that many were already doomed not to see, so wracked by malnutrition had they become.

Lord Musheramore was a vain young man. He was about thirty years old, with a dark, aquiline face and sneering mouth. Since his inheritance he had only visited his estate once. He preferred to live in a house in London where he could visit the playhouses, taverns, and the gaming houses where he loved to win or lose moderate fortunes on the throw of the dice or the fall of cards. But he had come to visit during that summer to ensure that the produce of his estate was not being squandered on any "famine relief."

He was somewhat alarmed at the concourse of people that gathered on the castle lawns. There were hundreds of people from the cottages and the villages which his estate encompassed. He sent his overseer straightaway to the military at Mallow and three companies of English hussars soon arrived and surrounded the castle to protect it from attack. The captain in charge, acting on Lord Musheramore's orders, told the people to disperse. When they hesitated, he charged his troops into them. The hussars went berserk, swinging their sabres and shouting like banshees. The result was that many died, including the local priest who had come to add his authority to the pleas of the peasants.

Now among the people gathered that day was an old woman named Bríd Cappeen. She had been shunned by the people in better days for she had the reputation of being something of a witch. She was, indeed, a wise woman. She had escaped the soldiers with no more than a sabre's cut across her thin, angular face. But the scar on her heart was deeper than that. Old Bríd Cappeen knew the ways of the ancients, the old ways that were practised from time immemorial, whose origins were forgotten even by the time of the coming of Christianity. She could search the entrails of a dead chicken and find the answer to the future in its bloodied remains.

Bríd Cappeen had fled to the gorse covered

mountainside when the soldiers attacked and had hidden all day there. That night she crept down the mountain to the lawn where the corpses of the peasants had been laid out ready for disposal. She searched the pile of corpses, wild and demented, until she found the one she wanted. The body of a man whose wounds had not caused any limbs to be severed. Then with the strength derived from God alone knows where, or maybe from the Devil, Bríd Cappeen hauled that corpse away into the night. She hauled it up to her lonely cave in the mountain.

There, in the cave, she practised the old rituals, conjuring words that no scholar of the ancient Gaelic tongue would recognize. She sought and found herbs and threw them into a steam kettle on a small fire and bathed the body of the man and, finally, as the moon reached the point in the night sky which signified the hour of midnight, the limbs of the man began to tremble, to pulsate and the eyes came open.

Old Bríd Cappeen let out a growl of satisfaction.

She had created the *marbh bheo;* she had conjured the "living corpse" to her bidding.

In the ancient times it was told that vengeance could be visited on a wrongdoer by a druid or druidess who could reanimate the body of a person wrongly slain. Old Bríd Cappeen began to enact that vengeance.

She sent out the reanimated body of the corpse on its dreadful quest. Lord Musheramore, Baron of Lyre and Lisnaraha, was about to board the ship for England in Cork harbour one evening when he was attacked and literally torn apart by a man whom no one could identify. The police and soldiers swore that they opened fire and hit the attacker several times. The local magistrate took this with cynical humour, for the attacker escaped clean away and there was no blood on the cobbles of the quay except the aristocratic blood of Lord Musheramore.

The captain of the hussars was attacked next in his own quarters, safe in the barracks at Mallow. He, too, was torn apart. The attacker was evidently a man of amazing strength and iron purpose for he had broken through the stone and iron walls of the barracks to get into the captain's quarters. When they found what was left of the captain, many soldiers, veterans who had served in campaigns in India and Africa, were sick and broke down in terror.

Then, Major Farran, the overseer of Lord Musheramore's estate, was set on one evening while out with his two great hounds. Farran was a stocky man, afraid of nothing in this world nor the next, or so he boasted. He carried two hand pistols and the hounds that bounded at his side were not just for company. They had been known to tear a person to pieces at his command. Major Farran was hated amongst Musheramore's peasants. He knew it and, curious man that he was, thrived on it. He liked the aura of fear that he was able to spread around him. But he was wise enough to take precautions against any attack those who hated him might make.

But pistols and hounds did not protect him that evening.

It was three full days before all his remains were found along the bloodstrewn pathway. And the doctor confessed that he had no way of knowing the flesh of Major Farran from the flesh of the mutilated hounds.

And all the while Bríd Cappeen crooned away in her cave on the slopes of the mountain.

She was not satisfied with immediate vengeance on those who had wronged the people of Musheramore's estate. She became determined to make all who were connected with the Musheramore family pay for the deaths of her relatives and fellow villagers. Vengeance became her creed, her passion, her overwhelming desire. And the *marbh bheo* was the instrument of her vengeance.

For years, thereafter, there were reports of the demented Bríd Cappeen scouring the night shrouded country of the Boggeragh Mountains in search of vengeance with her living corpse at her side.

Father Doheny stopped talking abruptly, leaving me forward, open mouthed, on the edge of the seat.

"That's a fantastic tale, Father," I stammered at last, realising that he had come to an end of it. "Was there really such a person as Lord Musheramore?"

He made no reply, sitting gazing down at the smouldering turf.

I shivered slightly for the turf was not sending out any warmth into the tiny cottage room.

"Would you be prepared to come to our studios in Cork and talk on the programme about the *marbh bheo?* We could pay you something, of course."

I suddenly felt a draught on the back of my neck.

I turned and saw the cottage door had opened. To my surprise, because of the lateness of the hour, I saw the old woman I had met in the occult bookstore. Her black shrouded figure was framed in the gloom of its opening. Her Victorian dress seemed to be flapping around her in the wind that had risen across the mountains; flapping like the wings of a dark raven.

"Your business here is finished," she said imperiously, in a voice that cracked with age.

"I am here to see Father Doheny." I smarted at her lack of manners and turned to the old priest seeking support. "At your suggestion, too," I added, perhaps defensively.

The old man seemed to have nodded off in his high-backed wooden chair, for his jaw was lowered to his chest and his eyes were closed.

"Well, you have seen him. He has spoken to you. Begone now!"

I stared incredulously at the effrontery of the old woman.

"I rather think that it is none of your business to instruct me in another's house, madam," I said sternly.

Behind the blackness of her veil, she opened her mouth and an hysterical cackle caused the hairs on the nape of my neck to prickle with apprehension.

"I am in charge here," she wheezed, once she had recovered from her mirth, if that horrific sound was mirth.

"You mean, you are Father Doheny's housekeeper?" I could hardly keep the astonishment from my voice for the old woman looked incapable of carrying a teapot from the hearth to the table, let alone performing any of the chores expected of a housekeeper.

She cackled again.

"It is late, boy," she finally replied. "I would be about your business. There is an evil across this mountain at night. I would have a care of it."

She threw out a gnarled claw in a dismissive gesture.

I glanced again at Father Doheny but he showed no sign of stirring and so I gathered my notes, rose and put on my coat with all the dignity I could muster.

She ignored me as I bade her a "goodnight" but simply stood aside from the door.

Outside the cottage the moon was up in a sky across which fretful clouds moved hurriedly as the wind blew and wailed over the crevices of rocks. A frost lay forming its white veins over the ground. The temperature must have dropped considerably since I had arrived. In the distance I could hear the howling of dogs. The sound seemed ethereal and unreal in the night air.

I went to my motorcycle and, trusting that I was not disturbing the old priest's slumber, I kicked the starter. It took a while to get the Triumph's engine warmed and ready enough for me to begin to wind my way down the mountain track.

I had not gone more than a mile when I realised that I had left one of my notebooks on the small table in Father Doheny's cottage. With a sigh I halted and turned the Triumph gently on the muddy track and pushed back towards "Teach Droch-Chlú."

I halted my bike and made my way along the track to the dark outline of the cottage.

Something caused me not to knock but to halt outside.

A shrill chanting came to my ears.

It was the voice of the old woman. It was

some time before I could actually make out the sound of the words and then they meant little to me for they were in an ancient form of Irish.

Something prompted me to peer in through the small panes of the window.

I could make out the old priest, now standing still in the middle of the room. The old woman was before him, huddled with bent shoulders, crooning away. I was surprised to see that in her hands she held one of those old fashioned cavalry sabres, with a curved blade. There was something peculiarly disturbing about the way she was carrying on, chanting and crooning in that shrill voice.

Abruptly she stopped.

"Remember, Doheny," she commanded.

The old priest stood stiff and upright, his colourless eyes staring straight above her.

"You must remember. This is what they did."

Before I could cry out a warning, the old woman had raised the sabre and, with the full force of her seemingly frail frame, she thrust the point of the weapon through the old priest just about the level of his heart. I saw the end of the blade emerge through the back of his jacket. Yet he had not even staggered under the impact of the blow.

My jaw hung open. There are no words to express the shock and terror that scene gave me.

Worse was to come.

The old woman let go of the sabre and stepped away from him.

"Remember, Doheny!"

The old priest's claw-like hands came to the handle of the sabre and then, with a mighty tug, he pulled the great blade out of his body with a slow, deliberate motion. It was bright and shining and without a speck of blood upon its blade.

I stood at the small window transfixed with terror.

I could not believe what I had seen. It was impossible. She had thrust a sharp sword through a frail old priest and the priest had not batted an eye. He had merely withdrawn it. And it had made no wound!

"Remember, Doheny!"

I suppressed a cry of fear, turned and ran back to my bike. Panic seemed to impede my every move. I tried to start the motor but everything I did seemed wrong. I heard a cry from the old woman, became aware of a shadow on the path. I could feel fetid breath on my neck. Then the bike started with a roar and I was speeding away.

The track was twisting, the mud on the road slowed the machine. I felt as if I was in some cross-country bike race, swerving, twisting, leaping down the mountain pathway in the direction of the nearest village which was Ballynagree. I had never ridden so hard in all my life, ridden as if a thousand devils from hell were at my heels.

Just as I was beginning to relax, I saw a small hump-back bridge over a winding mountain torrent. I knew it to be an old granite stone bridge which was scarcely the width of three people walking. I eased back the throttle on my machine to negotiate it in safety and then . . .

Then, by the light of my front lamp, I saw the pale figure of the priest standing in the centre of the bridge; standing waiting for me.

In fright, I tugged at the handlebars of my machine, wrenching them, as I made a silly and futile attempt to ride through the gushing stream rather than run over the bridge.

My front wheel hit a stone and the next thing I knew was that I was cartwheeling over and over in the air before smashing down on a soft muddy surface of the bank. The impact still drove the breath out of my body and I lost consciousness.

It was only a momentary loss. I remember coming to with a swimming, nauseous sensation. I blinked.

A foot away from my face were the pale, parchment features of the priest. The colourless eyes seemed to be staring through me. His breath was stale, fetid and there was a terrible stench of death on him. I felt his hands at my throat. Large, powerful claws, squeezing.

"Stop, Doheny!"

It was the old woman's shrill tones. Beyond the priest's shoulder I caught a glimpse of her, the veil thrown back, while the skull-like face was staring in triumph with a livid weal of a scar showing diagonally from forehead to cheek.

The pressure eased a little.

"He is not one of them, Doheny. Leave him be. He is to be witness to what we have done. Leave him be. What we have done will live in him and he will pass it on so that it will be known. Leave him be."

The old priest, with incredible strength, shook me as if I were no more than a rag doll.

"Leave him be," commanded the old woman again.

And then I must have fainted.

When I came to, there was no one about. I pressed my hand against my throbbing temples and rose unsteadily to my feet. For a moment or two I could not remember how I had wound up in the mud of the mountain stream. Then I did remember. I gave a startled glance about me but could see no sign of the old priest and woman. The mountainside was in darkness. The only movement was that of the trees whispering, swaying and rustling in the winds that moaned softly over the mountain.

I stood a moment or two attempting to get my bearings. Then I saw the black heap of my Triumph motorbike lying in the shallows of the stream. I tried to move it out of the water but saw immediately, by the buckled wheel and splintered spokes, that even if I could start the machine it would be useless. Nevertheless, I attempted to start it. The starter gave a weak "phutt" and remained lifeless. It was obviously waterlogged.

I manoeuvred it to the bank of the stream and then waded up to the humpback bridge. There was nothing for it but to start walking down the mountain to Ballynagree. My head was throbbing and my mind was a whirl of conflicting thoughts. Was someone playing some terrible joke, a joke which was in bad taste? But no one would go to that extreme? Surely?

It took three hours of trekking down the muddy pathway before I saw the first signs of habitation.

I finally saw the dark outline of the garage where I had stopped for petrol. I stumbled towards it numb and frozen and hammered on the door. It was a while before I heard a window go up in the room above the garage front. A light shone down and a voice cried: "Who's there?"

"My motorbike has broken down and I'm stranded," I yelled. "Can I get a taxi from here or stay the rest of the night?"

"Man, do you realize that it is three o'clock in the morning?" came the stern reply.

"I was stranded on the mountain, on Musheramore Mountain," I replied.

A woman's voice came softly to my ears although I could not hear what was said.

The window came down with an abrupt bang. I waited hopefully. A light eventually shone in the downstairs window. Then the door was opened.

"Come away in," said the male voice.

I entered, feeling ice cold and drained from my experience.

As the light fell on me, the garage man recognized me.

"You're the young man who asked me the way to 'Teach Droch-Chlú' earlier this evening, aren't you?"

I nodded. It was the man whose overalls had proclaimed his name to be "Manus."

"That's right. My motorbike has broken down. I need a cab."

The man shook his head, nonplussed.

"You look all in." He turned and drew up a bottle of Jameson from a cupboard and a glass. "This will warm you up," he said, pouring the whiskey and pushing the glass into my hands.

"What were you doing up at 'Teach Droch-Chlú' at this time of night? Are you a ghost hunter? Is that it?" And without waiting for a reply he continued: "I can telephone Macroom for a car to collect you, if you like. Where do you want to get to?"

"To Cork City."

"And where did your bike break down?"

"Up the mountain track somewhere, near a river crossing. By a humpbacked bridge."

"Ah, the spot is known to me. I'll go and pick your bike up tomorrow. Give me a number where I can contact you and I'll let you know what repairs need to be done."

I nodded, frowning at him as I sipped my whiskey.

"Why did you ask if I was a ghost hunter?"

"You asked for 'Teach Droch-Chlú.' That's what the locals call it hereabouts, the house of evil reputation. We call it that on account that it has a reputation of being haunted. You know, it is one of the old 'famine' cottages which have survived in these parts."

I gave a diffident shake of the head and pressed the whiskey to my lips, enjoying its fiery warmth through my chill body.

"I was looking for Father Nessan Doheny," I explained.

The burly man stared at me a moment as if in surprise and then gave a low chuckle.

"So I *was* right then? Well now, I hope that you didn't find him."

I stopped rubbing my hands together and gazed at him in astonishment.

"Why do you say that?"

"Because Father Nessan Doheny has been dead these last one hundred and sixty years."

A chill, like ice, shot down my spine.

"Dead one hundred and sixty years?"

"Surely. Didn't you know the story? He led his flock to Musheramore Castle during the time of the 'Great Hunger' to plead with Lord Musheramore to help the surviving peasants and stop the evictions. The soldiers were called in from Mallow and given orders to charge the people who were kneeling on the lawn of the castle in prayer. Father Nessan Doheny was sabred to death with many of his flock."

I swallowed hard.

"And . . . and what happened to Bríd Cappeen?"

He roared with laughter.

"Then you *do* know the old legend! Of course you did. It is local knowledge that 'Teach Droch-Chlú' was her old cabin. All part of the old legend. Well frankly, I think it is simply that. No more than a legend. Poor Father Doheny and the demented Bríd Cappeen are long since dead. To think on it, the idea of an old woman reanimating the corpse of a priest to enact vengeance on Lord Musheramore and his ilk! God save us!" He genuflected piously. "It is a legend and nothing else."

THE HOLLOW MAN

THOMAS BURKE

(SYDNEY) THOMAS BURKE (1886–1945) was born in the London suburb of Clapham, but when he was only a few months old his father died and he was sent to the East End to live with his uncle until the age of ten, when he was put into a home for respectable middle-class children without means. He sold his first story, "The Bellamy Diamonds," when he was fifteen. His first book, *Nights in Town: A London Autobiography,* was published in 1915, soon followed by the landmark volume *Limehouse Nights* (1916), a collection of stories that had originally been published in the magazines *The English Review, Colour,* and *The New Witness.* This volume of romantic but violent stories of the Chinese district of London was enormously popular and, though largely praised by critics, there were objections to the depictions of interracial relationships, opium use, and other "depravities." Several of the stories in *Limehouse Nights* served as the basis for films, most notably D. W. Griffith's *Broken Blossoms* (1919), based on "The Chink and the Child." It starred one of America's most beloved actresses, Lillian Gish, as the daughter of a sadistic prizefighter, and Richard Barthelmess as a kind Chinese youth. Charlie Chaplin based his silent movie *A Dog's Life* (1918) on material from the book. Sequels to this volume include *Whispering Windows* (published in the United States as *More Limehouse Nights,* 1921) and *The Pleasantries of Old Quong* (*A Tea-Shop in Limehouse* in the United States, 1931), which contains the short story "The Hands of Mr. Ottermole"; based on the Jack the Ripper murders, it was voted the best detective short story of all time in 1949 by Ellery Queen and eleven other mystery writers.

"The Hollow Man" was first published in the author's collection *Night-Pieces* (London: Constable, 1935).

THOMAS BURKE

THE HOLLOW MAN

HE CAME UP one of the narrow streets which lead from the docks, and turned into a road whose farther end was gay with the lights of London. At the end of this road he went deep into the lights of London, and sometimes into its shadows. Farther and farther he went from the river, and did not pause until he had reached a poor quarter near the centre.

He made a tall, spare figure, clothed in a black mackintosh. Below this could be seen brown dungaree trousers. A peaked cap hid most of his face; the little that was exposed was white and sharp. In the autumn mist that filled the lighted streets as well as the dark he seemed a wraith, and some of those who passed him looked again, not sure whether they had indeed seen a living man. One or two of them moved their shoulders, as though shrinking from something.

His legs were long, but he walked with the short, deliberate steps of a blind man, though he was not blind. His eyes were open, and he stared straight ahead; but he seemed to see nothing and hear nothing. Neither the mournful hooting of sirens across the black water of the river, nor the genial windows of the shops in the big streets near the centre drew his head to right or left. He walked as though he had no destination in mind, yet constantly, at this corner or that, he turned. It seemed that an unseen hand was guiding him to a given point of whose location he was himself ignorant.

He was searching for a friend of fifteen years ago, and the unseen hand, or some dog-instinct, had led him from Africa to London, and was now leading him, along the last mile of his search, to a certain little eating-house. He did not know that he was going to the eating-house of his friend Nameless, but he did know, from the time he left Africa, that he was journeying towards Nameless, and he now knew that he was very near to Nameless.

Nameless didn't know that his old friend was anywhere near *him*, though, had he observed conditions that evening, he might have wondered why he was sitting up an hour later than usual. He was seated in one of the pews of his prosperous Workmen's Dining-Rooms—a little gold-mine his wife's relations called it—and he was smoking and looking at nothing. He had added up the till and written the copies of the bill of fare for next day, and there was nothing to keep him out of bed after his fifteen hours' attention to business. Had he been asked why he was sitting up later than usual, he would first have answered that he didn't know that he was, and would then have explained, in default of any other explanation, that it was for the purpose of having a last pipe. He was quite unaware that he was sitting up and keeping the door unlatched because a long-parted friend from Africa was seeking him and slowly approaching him, and needed his services. He was quite unaware that he had left the door unlatched at that late hour—half-past eleven—to admit pain and woe.

But even as many bells sent dolefully across the night from their steeples their disagreement as to the point of half-past eleven, pain and woe were but two streets away from him. The mackintosh and dungarees and the sharp white face were coming nearer every moment.

There was silence in the house and in the streets; a heavy silence, broken, or sometimes stressed, by the occasional night-noises—motor horns, back-firing of lorries, shunting at a distant terminus. That silence seemed to envelop the house, but he did not notice it. He did not notice the bells, and he did not even notice the lagging step that approached his shop, and passed—and returned—and passed again—and halted. He was aware of nothing save that he was smoking a last pipe, and he was sitting in somnolence, deaf and blind to anything not in his immediate neighbourhood.

But when a hand was laid on the latch, and the latch was lifted, he did hear that, and he looked up. And he saw the door open, and got up and went to it. And there, just within the door, he came face to face with the thin figure of pain and woe.

TO KILL A fellow-creature is a frightful thing. At the time the act is committed the murderer may have sound and convincing reasons (to him) for his act. But time and reflection may bring regret; even remorse; and this may live with him for many years. Examined in wakeful hours of the night or early morning, the reasons for the act may shed their cold logic, and may cease to be reasons and become mere excuses. And these naked excuses may strip the murderer and show him to himself as he is. They may begin to hunt his soul, and to run into every little corner of his mind and every little nerve, in search of it.

And if to kill a fellow-creature and to suffer recurrent regret for an act of heated blood is a frightful thing, it is still more frightful to kill a fellow-creature and bury his body deep in an African jungle, and then, fifteen years later, at about midnight, to see the latch of your door lifted by the hand you had stilled and to see the man, looking much as he did fifteen years ago, walk into your home and claim your hospitality.

WHEN THE MAN in mackintosh and dungarees walked into the dining-rooms Nameless stood still; stared; staggered against a table; supported himself by a hand, and said, "Oh."

The other man said, "Nameless."

Then they looked at each other; Nameless with head thrust forward, mouth dropped, eyes wide; the visitor with a dull, glazed expression. If Nameless had not been the man he was—thick, bovine, and costive—he would have flung up his arms and screamed. At that moment he felt the need of some such outlet, but did not know how to find it. The only dramatic expression he gave to the situation was to whisper instead of speak.

Twenty emotions came to life in his head and spine, and wrestled there. But they showed themselves only in his staring eyes and his whisper. His first thought, or rather, spasm, was Ghosts-Indigestion-Nervous-Breakdown. His second, when he saw that the figure was substantial and real, was Impersonation. But a slight movement on the part of the visitor dismissed that.

It was a little habitual movement which belonged only to that man; an unconscious twitching of the third finger of the left hand. He knew then that it was Gopak. Gopak, a little changed, but still, miraculously, thirty-two. Gopak, alive, breathing, and real. No ghost. No phantom of the stomach. He was as certain of that as he was that fifteen years ago he had killed Gopak stone-dead and buried him.

The blackness of the moment was lightened by Gopak. In thin, flat tones he asked, "May I sit down? I'm tired." He sat down, and said: "So tired."

Nameless still held the table. He whispered: "Gopak . . . Gopak . . . But I—I *killed* you. I killed you in the jungle. You were dead. I know you were."

Gopak passed his hand across his face. He seemed about to cry. "I know you did. I know. That's all I can remember—about this earth. You killed me." The voice became thinner and flatter. "And then they came and—disturbed me. They woke me up. And brought me back." He sat with shoulders sagged, arms drooping, hands hanging between knees. After the first recognition he did not look at Nameless; he looked at the floor.

"Came and disturbed you?" Nameless leaned forward and whispered the words. "Woke you up? Who?"

"The Leopard Men."

"The what?"

"The Leopard Men." The watery voice said it as casually as if it were saying "the night watchman."

"The Leopard Men?" Nameless stared, and his fat face crinkled in an effort to take in the situation of a midnight visitation from a dead man, and the dead man talking nonsense. He felt his blood moving out of its course. He looked at his own hand to see if it was his own hand. He looked at the table to see if it was his table. The hand and the table were facts, and if the dead man was a fact—and he was—his story might be a fact. It seemed anyway as sensible as the dead man's presence. He gave a heavy sigh from the stomach. "A-ah . . . The Leopard Men . . . Yes, I heard about them out there. Tales."

Gopak slowly wagged his head. "Not tales. They're real. If they weren't real—I wouldn't be here. Would I?"

Nameless had to admit this. He had heard many tales "out there" about the Leopard Men, and had dismissed them as jungle yarns. But now, it seemed, jungle yarns had become commonplace fact in a little London shop. The watery voice went on. "They do it. I saw them. I came back in the middle of a circle of them. They killed a nigger to put his life into me. They wanted a white man—for their farm. So they brought me back. You may not believe it. You wouldn't *want* to believe it. You wouldn't want to—see or know anything like them. And I wouldn't want any man to. But it's true. That's how I'm here."

"But I left you absolutely dead. I made every test. It was three days before I buried you. And I buried you deep."

"I know. But that wouldn't make any difference to them. It was a long time after when they came and brought me back. And I'm still dead, you know. It's only my body they brought back." The voice trailed into a thread. "And I'm so tired."

Sitting in his prosperous eating-house Nameless was in the presence of an achieved miracle, but the everyday, solid appointments of the eating-house wouldn't let him fully comprehend it. Foolishly, as he realised when he had spoken, he asked Gopak to explain what had happened. Asked a man who couldn't really be alive to explain how he came to be alive. It was like asking Nothing to explain Everything.

Constantly, as he talked, he felt his grasp on his own mind slipping. The surprise of a sudden visitor at a late hour; the shock of the arrival of a long-dead man, and the realisation that this long-dead man was not a wraith, were too much for him.

During the next half-hour he found himself talking to Gopak as to the Gopak he had known seventeen years ago when they were partners. Then he would be halted by the freezing knowledge that he was talking to a dead man, and that a dead man was faintly answering him. He felt that the thing couldn't really have happened, but in the interchange of talk he kept forgetting the improbable side of it, and accepting it. With each recollection of the truth, his mind would clear and settle in one thought—"I've got to get rid of him. How am I going to get rid of him?"

"But how did you get here?"

"I escaped." The words came slowly and thinly, and out of the body rather than the mouth.

"How?"

"I don't—know. I don't remember anything—except our quarrel. And being at rest."

"But why come all the way here? Why didn't you stay on the coast?"

"I don't—know. But you're the only man I know. The only man I can remember."

"But how did you find me?"

"I don't know. But I had to—find you. You're the only man—who can help me."

"But how can I help you?"

The head turned weakly from side to side. "I don't—know. But nobody else—can."

Nameless stared through the window, looking on to the lamplit street and seeing nothing of it. The everyday being which had been his half an hour ago had been annihilated; the everyday beliefs and disbeliefs shattered and mixed together. But some shred of his old sense and his old standards remained. He must handle this situation. "Well—what you want to do? What you going to do? I don't see how I can help you. And you can't stay here, obviously." A demon of perversity sent a facetious notion into his head—introducing Gopak to his wife—"This is my dead friend."

But on his last spoken remark Gopak made the effort of raising his head and staring with the glazed eyes at Nameless. "But I *must* stay here. There's nowhere else I can stay. I *must* stay here. That's why I came. You got to help me."

"But you can't stay here. I got no room. All occupied. Nowhere for you to sleep."

The wan voice said: "That doesn't matter. I *don't* sleep."

"Eh?"

"I *don't* sleep. I haven't slept since they brought me back. I can sit here—till you can think of some way of helping me."

"But how *can* I?" He again forgot the background of the situation, and began to get angry at the vision of a dead man sitting about the place waiting for him to think of something. "How *can* I if you don't tell me how?"

"I don't—know. But you got to. You killed me. And I was dead—and comfortable. As it all came from you—killing me—you're responsible for me being—like this. So you got to—help me. That's why I—came to you."

"But what do you want me to do?"

"I don't—know. I can't—think. But nobody but you can help me. I had to come to you. Something brought me—straight to you. That means that you're the one—that can help me. Now I'm with you, something will—happen to help me. I feel it will. In time you'll—think of something."

Nameless found his legs suddenly weak. He sat down and stared with a sick scowl at the hideous and the incomprehensible. Here was a dead man in his house—a man he had murdered in a moment of black temper—and he knew in his heart that he couldn't turn the man out. For one thing, he would have been afraid to touch him; he couldn't see himself touching him. For another, faced with the miracle of the presence of a fifteen-years-dead man, he doubted whether physical force or any material agency would be effectual in moving the man.

His soul shivered, as all men's souls shiver at the demonstration of forces outside their mental or spiritual horizon. He had murdered this man, and often, in fifteen years, he had repented the act. If the man's appalling story were true, then he had some sort of right to turn to Nameless. Nameless recognised that, and knew that whatever happened he couldn't turn him out. His hot-tempered sin had literally come home to him.

The wan voice broke into his nightmare.

"You go to rest, Nameless. I'll sit here. You go to rest." He put his face down to his hands and uttered a little moan. "Oh, why can't I rest?"

NAMELESS CAME DOWN early next morning with a half-hope that Gopak would not be there. But he was there, seated where Nameless had left him last night. Nameless made some tea, and showed him where he might wash. He washed listlessly, and crawled back to his seat, and listlessly drank the tea which Nameless brought to him.

To his wife and the kitchen helpers Nameless mentioned him as an old friend who had had a bit of a shock. "Shipwrecked and knocked on the head. But quite harmless, and he won't be staying long. He's waiting for admission to a home. A good pal to me in the past, and it's the least I can do to let him stay here a few days. Suffers from sleeplessness and prefers to sit up at night. Quite harmless."

But Gopak stayed more than a few days. He outstayed everybody. Even when the customers had gone Gopak was still there.

On the first morning of his visit when the regular customers came in at mid-day, they looked at the odd, white figure sitting vacantly in the first pew, then stared, then moved away. All avoided the pew in which he sat. Nameless explained him to them, but his explanation did not seem to relieve the slight tension which settled on the dining-room. The atmosphere was not so brisk and chatty as usual. Even those who had their backs to the stranger seemed to be affected by his presence.

At the end of the first day Nameless, noticing this, told him that he had arranged a nice corner of the front-room upstairs, where he could sit by the window, and took his arm to take him upstairs. But Gopak feebly shook the hand away, and sat where he was. "No. I don't want to go. I'll stay here. I'll stay here. I don't want to move."

And he wouldn't move. After a few more pleadings Nameless realised with dismay that his refusal was definite; that it would be futile to press him or force him; that he was going to sit in that dining-room for ever. He was as weak as a child and as firm as a rock. He continued to sit in that first pew, and the customers continued to avoid it, and to give queer glances at it. It seemed that they half-recognised that he was something more than a fellow who had had a shock.

During the second week of his stay three of the regular customers were missing, and more than one of those that remained made acidly facetious suggestions to Nameless that he park his lively friend somewhere else. He made things too exciting for them; all that whoopee took them off their work, and interfered with digestion. Nameless told them he would be staying only a day or so longer, but they found that this was untrue, and at the end of the second week eight of the regulars had found another place.

Each day, when the dinner-hour came, Nameless tried to get him to take a little walk, but always he refused. He would go out only at night, and then never more than two hundred yards from the shop. For the rest, he sat in his pew, sometimes dozing in the afternoon, at other times staring at the floor. He took his food abstractedly, and never knew whether he had had food or not. He spoke only when questioned, and the burden of his talk was "I'm so tired."

One thing only seemed to arouse any light of interest in him; one thing only drew his eyes from the floor. That was the seventeen-year-old daughter of his host, who was known as Bubbles, and who helped with the waiting. And Bubbles seemed to be the only member of the shop and its customers who did not shrink from him.

She knew nothing of the truth about him, but she seemed to understand him, and the only response he ever gave to anything was to her childish sympathy. She sat and chatted foolish chatter to him—"bringing him out of himself," she called it—and sometimes he would be brought out to the extent of a watery smile. He came to recognise her step, and would look up before she entered the room. Once or twice in the evening, when the shop was empty, and Nameless was sitting miserably with him, he would ask, without lifting his eyes, "Where's Bubbles?" and would be told that Bubbles had gone to the pictures or was out at a dance, and would relapse into deeper vacancy.

Nameless didn't like this. He was already visited by a curse which, in four weeks, had destroyed most of his business. Regular customers had dropped off two by two, and no new customers came to take their place. Strangers who dropped in once for a meal did not come again; they could not keep their eyes or their minds off the forbidding, white-faced figure sitting motionless in the first pew. At mid-day, when the place had been crowded and latecomers had to wait for a seat, it was now two-thirds empty; only a few of the most thick-skinned remained faithful.

And on top of this there was the interest of the dead man in his daughter, an interest which seemed to be having an unpleasant effect. Nameless hadn't noticed it, but his wife had. "Bubbles don't seem as bright and lively as she was. You noticed it lately? She's getting quiet—and a bit slack. Sits about a lot. Paler than she used to be."

"Her age, perhaps."

"No. She's not one of these thin dark sort. No—it's something else. Just the last week or two I've noticed it. Off her food. Sits about doing nothing. No interest. May be nothing—just out of sorts, perhaps . . . How much longer's that horrible friend of yours going to stay?"

THE HORRIBLE FRIEND stayed some weeks longer—ten weeks in all—while Nameless watched his business drop to nothing and his daughter get pale and peevish. He knew the cause of it. There was no home in all England like his: no home that had a dead man sitting in it for ten weeks. A dead man brought, after a long time, from the grave, to sit and disturb his

customers and take the vitality from his daughter. He couldn't tell this to anybody. Nobody would believe such nonsense. But he *knew* that he was entertaining a dead man, and, knowing that a long-dead man was walking the earth, he could believe in any result of that fact. He could believe almost anything that he would have derided ten weeks ago. His customers had abandoned his shop, not because of the presence of a silent, white-faced man, but because of the presence of a dead-living man. Their minds might not know it, but their blood knew it. And, as his business had been destroyed, so, he believed, would his daughter be destroyed. Her blood was not warning her; her blood told her only that this was a long-ago friend of her father's, and she was drawn to him.

It was at this point that Nameless, having no work to do, began to drink. And it was well that he did so. For out of the drink came an idea, and with that idea he freed himself from the curse upon him and his house.

The shop now served scarcely half a dozen customers at mid-day. It had become ill-kempt and dusty, and the service and the food were bad. Nameless took no trouble to be civil to his few customers. Often, when he was notably under drink, he went to the trouble of being very rude to them. They talked about this. They talked about the decline of his business and the dustiness of the shop and the bad food. They talked about his drinking, and, of course, exaggerated it.

And they talked about the queer fellow who sat there day after day and gave everybody the creeps. A few outsiders, hearing the gossip, came to the dining-rooms to see the queer fellow and the always-tight proprietor; but they did not come again, and there were not enough of the curious to keep the place busy. It went down until it served scarcely two customers a day. And Nameless went down with it into drink.

Then, one evening, out of the drink he fished an inspiration.

He took it downstairs to Gopak, who was sitting in his usual seat, hands hanging, eyes on the floor. "Gopak—listen. You came here because I was the only man who could help you in your trouble. You listening?"

A faint "Yes" was his answer.

"Well, now. You told me I'd got to think of something. I've thought of something. . . . Listen. You say I'm responsible for your condition and got to get you out of it, because I killed you. I did. We had a row. You made me wild. You dared me. And what with that sun and the jungle and the insects, I wasn't meself. I killed you. The moment it was done I could 'a cut me right hand off. Because you and me were pals. I could 'a cut me right hand off."

"I know. I felt that directly it was over. I knew you were suffering."

"Ah! . . . I have suffered. And I'm suffering now. Well, this is what I've thought. All your present trouble comes from me killing you in that jungle and burying you. An idea came to me. Do you think it would help you—I—if I—if I—killed you again?"

For some seconds Gopak continued to stare at the floor. Then his shoulders moved. Then, while Nameless watched every little response to his idea, the watery voice began. "Yes. Yes. That's it. That's what I was waiting for. That's why I came here. I can see now. That's why I had to get here. Nobody else could kill me. Only you. I've got to be killed again. Yes, I see. But nobody else—would be able—to kill me. Only the man who first killed me . . . Yes, you've found—what we're both—waiting for. Anybody else could shoot me—stab me—hang me—but they couldn't kill me. Only you. That's why I managed to get here and find you." The watery voice rose to a thin strength. "That's it. And you must do it. Do it now. You don't want to, I know. But you must. You *must*."

His head drooped and he stared at the floor. Nameless, too, stared at the floor. He was seeing things. He had murdered a man and had escaped all punishment save that of his own mind, which had been terrible enough. But now he was going to murder him again—not in a jungle but in a city; and he saw the slow points of the result.

He saw the arrest. He saw the first hearing. He saw the trial. He saw the cell. He saw the rope. He shuddered.

Then he saw the alternative—the breakdown of his life—a ruined business, poverty, the poor-house, a daughter robbed of her health and perhaps dying, and always the curse of the dead-living man, who might follow him to the poor-house. Better to end it all, he thought. Rid himself of the curse which Gopak had brought upon him and his family, and then rid his family of himself with a revolver. Better to follow up his idea.

He got stiffly to his feet. The hour was late evening—half-past ten—and the streets were quiet. He had pulled down the shop-blinds and locked the door. The room was lit by one light at the farther end. He moved about uncertainly and looked at Gopak. "Er—how would you—how shall I—"

Gopak said, "You did it with a knife. Just under the heart. You must do it that way again."

Nameless stood and looked at him for some seconds. Then, with an air of resolve, he shook himself. He walked quickly to the kitchen.

Three minutes later his wife and daughter heard a crash, as though a table had been overturned. They called but got no answer. When they came down they found him sitting in one of the pews, wiping sweat from his forehead. He was white and shaking, and appeared to be recovering from a faint.

"Whatever's the matter? You all right?"

He waved them away. "Yes, I'm all right. Touch of giddiness. Smoking too much, I think."

"Mmmm. Or drinking . . . Where's your friend? Out for a walk?"

"No. He's gone off. Said he wouldn't impose any longer, and 'd go and find an infirmary." He spoke weakly and found trouble in picking words. "Didn't you hear that bang—when he shut the door?"

"I thought that was you fell down."

"No. It was him when he went. I couldn't stop him."

"Mmmm. Just as well, I think." She looked about her. "Things seem to 'a gone all wrong since he's been here."

There was a general air of dustiness about the place. The tablecloths were dirty, not from use but from disuse. The windows were dim. A long knife, very dusty, was lying on the table under the window. In a corner by the door leading to the kitchen, unseen by her, lay a dusty mackintosh and dungaree, which appeared to have been tossed there. But it was over by the main door, near the first pew, that the dust was thickest—a long trail of it—greyish-white dust.

"Really, this place gets more and more slap-dash. Just *look* at that dust by the door. Looks as though somebody's been spilling ashes all over the place."

Nameless looked at it, and his hands shook a little. But he answered, more firmly than before: "Yes, I know. I'll have a proper clean-up tomorrow."

For the first time in ten weeks he smiled at them; a thin, haggard smile, but a smile.

THEY BITE

ANTHONY BOUCHER

ANTHONY BOUCHER, THE pseudonym of William Anthony Parker White (1911–1968), established successful careers as a writer of mystery and science fiction, critic, translator, editor, and anthologist. Born in Oakland, California, he received a B.A. from the University of Southern California and an M.A. in German from the University of California (Berkeley). He later became sufficiently proficient in French, Spanish, and Portuguese to translate mystery stories into English, becoming the first to translate Jorge Luis Borges into English. Under the Boucher pseudonym he wrote well-regarded fair-play detective novels, beginning with *The Case of the Seven of Calvary* (1937), followed by *Nine Times Nine* (1940), which, improbably, was voted the ninth best locked-room mystery of all time in a poll of fellow writers and critics; it was written under the pseudonym H. H. Holmes, an infamous nineteenth-century serial killer. He wrote prolifically in the 1940s, producing at least three scripts a week for such popular radio programs as *Sherlock Holmes, The Adventures of Ellery Queen*, and *The Casebook of Gregory Hood*. He also wrote numerous science fiction and fantasy stories, reviewed books in those genres as H. H. Holmes for the *San Francisco Chronicle* and *Chicago Sun-Times*, and produced notable anthologies in the science fiction, fantasy, and mystery genres. He served as the longtime mystery reviewer of the *New York Times* (1951–1968) and *Ellery Queen's Mystery Magazine* (1957–1968). He was one of the founders of the Mystery Writers of America in 1946. The annual World Mystery Convention is familiarly known as the Bouchercon in his honor, and the Anthony Awards are also named for him.

"They Bite" was originally published in the June 1942 issue of *Unknown Worlds;* it was first collected in *The Compleat Werewolf* (New York: Simon & Schuster, 1969).

ANTHONY BOUCHER

THEY BITE

THERE WAS NO path, only the almost vertical ascent. Crumbled rock for a few yards, with the roots of sage finding their scanty life in the dry soil. Then jagged outcroppings of crude crags, sometimes with accidental footholds, sometimes with overhanging and untrustworthy branches of greasewood, sometimes with no aid to climbing but the leverage of your muscles and the ingenuity of your balance.

The sage was as drably green as the rock was drably brown. The only color was the occasional rosy spikes of a barrel cactus.

Hugh Tallant swung himself up onto the last pinnacle. It had a deliberate, shaped look about it—a petrified fortress of Lilliputians, a Gibraltar of pygmies. Tallant perched on its battlements and unslung his field glasses.

The desert valley spread below him. The tiny cluster of buildings that was Oasis, the exiguous cluster of palms that gave name to the town and shelter to his own tent and to the shack he was building, the dead-ended highway leading straightforwardly to nothing, the oiled roads diagraming the vacant blocks of an optimistic subdivision.

Tallant saw none of these. His glasses were fixed beyond the oasis and the town of Oasis on the dry lake. The gliders were clear and vivid to him, and the uniformed men busy with them were as sharply and minutely visible as a nest of ants under glass. The training school was more than usually active. One glider in particular, strange to Tallant, seemed the focus of attention.

Men would come and examine it and glance back at the older models in comparison.

Only the corner of Tallant's left eye was not preoccupied with the new glider. In that corner something moved, something little and thin and brown as the earth. Too large for a rabbit, much too small for a man. It darted across that corner of vision, and Tallant found gliders oddly hard to concentrate on.

He set down the bifocals and deliberately looked about him. His pinnacle surveyed the narrow, flat area of the crest. Nothing stirred. Nothing stood out against the sage and rock but one barrel of rosy spikes. He took up the glasses again and resumed his observations. When he was done, he methodically entered the results in the little black notebook.

His hand was still white. The desert is cold and often sunless in winter. But it was a firm hand, and as well trained as his eyes, fully capable of recording faithfully the designs and dimensions which they had registered so accurately.

Once his hand slipped, and he had to erase and redraw, leaving a smudge that displeased him. The lean, brown thing had slipped across the edge of his vision again. Going toward the east edge, he would swear, where that set of rocks jutted like the spines on the back of a stegosaur.

Only when his notes were completed did he yield to curiosity, and even then with cynical self-reproach. He was physically tired, for him an unusual state, from this daily climbing and from clearing the ground for his shack-to-be. The eye muscles play odd nervous tricks. There could be nothing behind the stegosaur's armor.

There was nothing. Nothing alive and moving. Only the torn and half-plucked carcass of a bird, which looked as though it had been gnawed by some small animal.

IT WAS HALFWAY down the hill—hill in Western terminology, though anywhere east of the Rockies it would have been considered a sizable mountain—that Tallant again had a glimpse of a moving figure.

But this was no trick of a nervous eye. It was not little nor thin nor brown. It was tall and broad and wore a loud red-and-black lumberjacket. It bellowed, "Tallant!" in a cheerful and lusty voice.

Tallant drew near the man and said, "Hello." He paused and added, "Your advantage, I think."

The man grinned broadly. "Don't know me? Well, I daresay ten years is a long time, and the California desert ain't exactly the Chinese rice fields. How's stuff? Still loaded down with Secrets for Sale?"

Tallant tried desperately not to react to that shot, but he stiffened a little. "Sorry. The prospector getup had me fooled. Good to see you again, Morgan."

The man's eyes had narrowed. "Just having my little joke," he smiled. "Of course you wouldn't have no serious reason for mountain climbing around a glider school, now, would you? And you'd kind of need field glasses to keep an eye on the pretty birdies."

"I'm out here for my health." Tallant's voice sounded unnatural even to himself.

"Sure, sure. You were always in it for your health. And come to think of it, my own health ain't been none too good lately. I've got me a little cabin way to hell-and-gone around here, and I do me a little prospecting now and then. And somehow it just strikes me, Tallant, like maybe I hit a pretty good lode today."

"Nonsense, old man. You can see—"

"I'd sure hate to tell any of them Army men out at the field some of the stories I know about China and the kind of men I used to know out there. Wouldn't cotton to them stories a bit, the Army wouldn't. But if I was to have a drink too many and get talkative-like—"

"Tell you what," Tallant suggested brusquely. "It's getting near sunset now, and my tent's chilly for evening visits. But drop around in the morning and we'll talk over old times. Is rum still your tipple?"

"Sure is. Kind of expensive now, you understand—"

"I'll lay some in. You can find the place easily—over by the oasis. And we . . . we might be able to talk about your prospecting, too."

Tallant's thin lips were set firm as he walked away.

THE BARTENDER OPENED a bottle of beer and plunked it on the damp-circled counter. "That'll be twenty cents," he said, then added as an afterthought, "Want a glass? Sometimes tourists do."

Tallant looked at the others sitting at the counter—the red-eyed and unshaven old man, the flight sergeant unhappily drinking a Coke—it was after Army hours for beer—the young man with the long, dirty trench coat and the pipe and the new-looking brown beard—and saw no glasses. "I guess I won't be a tourist," he decided.

This was the first time Tallant had had a chance to visit the Desert Sport Spot. It was as well to be seen around in a community. Otherwise people begin to wonder and say, "Who is that man out by the oasis? Why don't you ever see him anyplace?"

The Sport Spot was quiet that night. The four of them at the counter, two Army boys shooting pool, and a half-dozen of the local men gathered about a round poker table, soberly and wordlessly cleaning a construction worker whose mind seemed more on his beer than on his cards.

"You just passing through?" the bartender asked sociably.

Tallant shook his head. "I'm moving in. When the Army turned me down for my lungs, I decided I better do something about it. Heard so much about your climate here I thought I might as well try it."

"Sure thing," the bartender nodded. "You take up until they started this glider school, just about every other guy you meet in the desert is here for his health. Me, I had sinus, and look at me now. It's the air."

Tallant breathed the atmosphere of smoke and beer suds, but did not smile. "I'm looking forward to miracles."

"You'll get 'em. Whereabouts you staying?"

"Over that way a bit. The agent called it 'the old Carker place.'"

Tallant felt the curious listening silence and frowned. The bartender had started to speak and then thought better of it. The young man with the beard looked at him oddly. The old man fixed him with red and watery eyes that had a faded glint of pity in them. For a moment, Tallant felt a chill that had nothing to do with the night air of the desert.

The old man drank his beer in quick gulps and frowned as though trying to formulate a sentence. At last he wiped beer from his bristly lips and said, "You wasn't aiming to stay in the adobe, was you?"

"No. It's pretty much gone to pieces. Easier to rig me up a little shack than try to make the adobe livable. Meanwhile, I've got a tent."

"That's all right, then, mebbe. But mind you don't go poking around that there adobe."

"I don't think I'm apt to. But why not? Want another beer?"

The old man shook his head reluctantly and slid from his stool to the ground. "No thanks. I don't rightly know as I—"

"Yes?"

"Nothing. Thanks all the same." He turned and shuffled to the door.

Tallant smiled. "But why should I stay clear of the adobe?" he called after him.

The old man mumbled.

"What?"

"They bite," said the old man, and went out shivering into the night.

THE BARTENDER WAS back at his post. "I'm glad he didn't take that beer you offered him," he said. "Along about this time in the evening I have to stop serving him. For once he had the sense to quit."

Tallant pushed his own empty bottle forward. "I hope I didn't frighten him away."

"Frighten? Well, mister, I think maybe that's just what you did do. He didn't want beer that sort of came, like you might say, from the old Carker place. Some of the old-timers here, they're funny that way."

Tallant grinned. "Is it haunted?"

"Not what you'd call haunted, no. No ghosts there that I ever heard of." He wiped the counter with a cloth and seemed to wipe the subject away with it.

The flight sergeant pushed his Coke bottle away, hunted in his pocket for nickels, and went over to the pinball machine. The young man with the beard slid onto his vacant stool. "Hope old Jake didn't worry you," he said.

Tallant laughed. "I suppose every town has its deserted homestead with a grisly tradition. But this sounds a little different. No ghosts, and they bite. Do you know anything about it?"

"A little," the young man said seriously. "A little. Just enough to—"

Tallant was curious. "Have one on me and tell me about it."

The flight sergeant swore bitterly at the machine.

Beer gurgled through the beard. "You see," the young man began, "the desert's so big you can't be alone in it. Ever notice that? It's all empty and there's nothing in sight, but there's always something moving over there where you can't quite see it. It's something very dry and thin and brown, only when you look around it isn't there. Ever see it?"

"Optical fatigue—" Tallant began.

"Sure. I know. Every man to his own legend. There isn't a tribe of Indians hasn't got some way of accounting for it. You've heard of the Watchers? And the twentieth-century white man comes along, and it's optical fatigue. Only in the nineteenth century things weren't quite the same, and there were the Carkers."

"You've got a special localized legend?"

"Call it that. You glimpse things out of the corner of your mind, same like you glimpse lean, dry things out of the corner of your eye. You encase 'em in solid circumstance and they're not so bad. That is known as the Growth of Legend. The Folk Mind in Action. You take the Carkers and the things you don't quite see and you put 'em together. And they bite."

Tallant wondered how long that beard had been absorbing beer. "And what were the Carkers?" he prompted politely.

"Ever hear of Sawney Bean? Scotland—reign of James First, or maybe the Sixth, though I think Roughead's wrong on that for once. Or let's be more modern—ever hear of the Benders? Kansas in the 1870s? No? Ever hear of Procrustes? Or Polyphemus? Or Fee-fi-fo-fum?

"There are ogres, you know. They're no legend. They're fact, they are. The inn where nine guests left for every ten that arrived, the mountain cabin that sheltered travelers from the snow, sheltered them all winter till the melting spring uncovered their bones, the lonely stretches of road that so many passengers traveled halfway—you'll find 'em everywhere. All over Europe and pretty much in this country too before communications became what they are. Profitable business. And it wasn't just the profit. The Benders made money, sure; but that wasn't why they killed all their victims as carefully as a kosher butcher. Sawney Bean got so he didn't give a damn about the profit; he just needed to lay in more meat for the winter.

"And think of the chances you'd have at an oasis."

"So these Carkers of yours were, as you call them, ogres?"

"Carkers, ogres—maybe they were Benders. The Benders were never seen alive, you know, after the townspeople found those curiously butchered bodies. There's a rumor they got this far west. And the time checks pretty well. There wasn't any town here in the eighties. Just a couple of Indian families, last of a dying tribe living on at the oasis. They vanished after the Carkers moved in. That's not so surprising. The white race is a sort of super-ogre, anyway. Nobody worried about them. But they used to worry about why so many travelers never got across this stretch of desert. The travelers used to stop over at the Carkers', you see, and somehow they often never got any farther. Their wagons'd be found maybe fifteen miles beyond in the desert. Sometimes they found the bones, too, parched and white. Gnawed-looking, they said sometimes."

"And nobody ever did anything about these Carkers?"

"Oh, sure. We didn't have King James Sixth—only I still think it was First—to ride up on a great white horse for a gesture, but twice Army detachments came here and wiped them all out."

"Twice? One wiping-out would do for most families." Tallant smiled.

"Uh-uh. That was no slip. They wiped out the Carkers twice because, you see, once didn't do any good. They wiped 'em out and still travelers vanished and still there were gnawed bones. So they wiped 'em out again. After that they gave up, and people detoured the oasis. It made a longer, harder trip, but after all—"

Tallant laughed. "You mean to say these Carkers were immortal?"

"I don't know about immortal. They somehow just didn't die very easy. Maybe, if they were the Benders—and I sort of like to think they were—they learned a little more about what they were doing out here on the desert. Maybe they put together what the Indians knew and what they knew, and it worked. Maybe Whatever they made their sacrifices to understood them better out here than in Kansas."

"And what's become of them—aside from seeing them out of the corner of the eye?"

"There's forty years between the last of the Carker history and this new settlement at the oasis. And people won't talk much about what they learned here in the first year or so. Only that they stay away from that old Carker adobe. They tell some stories— The priest says he was sitting in the confessional one hot Saturday afternoon and thought he heard a penitent come in. He waited a long time and finally lifted the gauze to see was anybody there. Something was there, and it bit. He's got three fingers on his right hand now, which looks funny as hell when he gives a benediction."

Tallant pushed their two bottles toward the bartender. "That yarn, my young friend, has earned another beer. How about it, bartender? Is he always cheerful like this, or is this just something he's improvised for my benefit?"

The bartender set out the fresh bottles with great solemnity. "Me, I wouldn't've told you all that myself, but then, he's a stranger too and maybe don't feel the same way we do here. For him it's just a story."

"It's more comfortable that way," said the young man with the beard, and he took a firm hold on his beer bottle.

"But as long as you've heard that much," said the bartender, "you might as well— It was last winter, when we had that cold spell. You heard funny stories that winter. Wolves coming into prospectors' cabins just to warm up. Well, business wasn't so good. We don't have a license for hard liquor, and the boys don't drink much beer when it's that cold. But they used to come in anyway because we've got that big oil burner.

"So one night there's a bunch of 'em in here—old Jake was here, that you was talking to, and his dog Jigger—and I think I hear somebody else come in. The door creaks a little. But I don't see nobody, and the poker game's going, and we're talking just like we're talking now, and all of a sudden I hear a kind of a noise like *crack!* over there in that corner behind the jukebox near the burner.

"I go over to see what goes and it gets away before I can see it very good. But it was little and thin and it didn't have no clothes on. It must've been damned cold that winter."

"And what was the cracking noise?" Tallant asked dutifully.

"That? That was a bone. It must've strangled Jigger without any noise. He was a little dog. It ate most of the flesh, and if it hadn't cracked the bone for the marrow it could've finished. You can still see the spots over there. The blood never did come out."

There had been silence all through the story. Now suddenly all hell broke loose. The flight sergeant let out a splendid yell and began pointing excitedly at the pinball machine and yelling for his payoff. The construction worker dramatically deserted the poker game, knocking his chair over in the process, and announced lugubriously that these guys here had their own rules, see?

Any atmosphere of Carker-inspired horror was dissipated. Tallant whistled as he walked over to put a nickel in the jukebox. He glanced casually at the floor. Yes, there was a stain, for what that was worth.

He smiled cheerfully and felt rather grateful to the Carkers. They were going to solve his blackmail problem very neatly.

TALLANT DREAMED OF power that night. It was a common dream with him. He was a ruler of the new American Corporate State that would follow the war; and he said to this man, "Come!" and he came, and to that man, "Go!" and he went, and to his servants, "Do this!" and they did it.

Then the young man with the beard was standing before him, and the dirty trench coat was like the robes of an ancient prophet. And the young man said, "You see yourself riding high, don't you? Riding the crest of the wave— the Wave of the Future, you call it. But there's a deep, dark undertow that you don't see, and that's a part of the Past. And the Present and even your Future. There is evil in mankind that is blacker even than your evil, and infinitely more ancient."

And there was something in the shadows behind the young man, something little and lean and brown.

TALLANT'S DREAM DID not disturb him the following morning. Nor did the thought of the approaching interview with Morgan. He fried his bacon and eggs and devoured them cheerfully. The wind had died down for a change, and the sun was warm enough so that he could strip to the waist while he cleared land for his shack. His machete glinted brilliantly as it swung through the air and struck at the roots of the brush.

When Morgan arrived his full face was red and sweating.

"It's cool over there in the shade of the adobe," Tallant suggested. "We'll be more comfortable." And in the comfortable shade of the adobe he swung the machete once and clove Morgan's full, red, sweating face in two.

It was so simple. It took less effort than uprooting a clump of sage. And it was so safe. Morgan lived in a cabin way to hell-and-gone and was often away on prospecting trips. No one would notice his absence for months, if then. No one had any reason to connect him with Tallant. And no one in Oasis would hunt for him in the Carker-haunted adobe.

The body was heavy, and the blood dripped warm on Tallant's bare skin. With relief he dumped what had been Morgan on the floor of the adobe. There were no boards, no flooring. Just the earth. Hard, but not too hard to dig a grave in. And no one was likely to come poking around in this taboo territory to notice the grave. Let a year or so go by, and the grave and the bones it contained would be attributed to the Carkers.

The corner of Tallant's eye bothered him again. Deliberately he looked about the interior of the adobe.

The little furniture was crude and heavy, with no attempt to smooth down the strokes of the ax. It was held together with wooden pegs or half-rotted thongs. There were age-old cinders in the fireplace, and the dusty shards of a cooking jar among them.

And there was a deeply hollowed stone, covered with stains that might have been rust, if stone rusted. Behind it was a tiny figure, clumsily fashioned of clay and sticks. It was something like a man and something like a lizard, and something like the things that flit across the corner of the eye.

Curious now, Tallant peered about further. He penetrated to the corner that the one unglassed window lighted but dimly. And there he let out a little choking gasp. For a moment he was rigid with horror. Then he smiled and all but laughed aloud.

This explained everything. Some curious individual had seen this, and from his accounts had burgeoned the whole legend. The Carkers had indeed learned something from the Indians, but that secret was the art of embalming.

It was a perfect mummy. Either the Indian art had shrunk bodies, or this was that of a ten-year-old boy. There was no flesh. Only skin and bone and taut, dry stretches of tendon between. The eyelids were closed; the sockets looked hollow under them. The nose was sunken and almost lost. The scant lips were tightly curled back from the long and very white teeth, which stood forth all the more brilliantly against the deep-brown skin.

It was a curious little trove, this mummy. Tallant was already calculating the chances for raising a decent sum of money from an interested anthropologist—murder can produce such delightfully profitable chance by-products—when he noticed the infinitesimal rise and fall of the chest.

The Carker was not dead. It was sleeping.

Tallant did not dare stop to think beyond the instant. This was no time to pause to consider if such things were possible in a well-ordered world. It was no time to reflect on the disposal of the body of Morgan. It was a time to snatch up your machete and get out of there.

But in the doorway he halted. There, coming across the desert, heading for the adobe, clearly seen this time, was another—a female.

He made an involuntary gesture of indecision. The blade of the machete clanged ringingly against the adobe wall. He heard the dry shuffling of a roused sleeper behind him.

He turned fully now, the machete raised. Dispose of this nearer one first, then face the female. There was no room even for terror in his thoughts, only for action.

The lean brown shape darted at him avidly. He moved lightly away and stood poised for its second charge. It shot forward again. He took one step back, machete arm raised, and fell headlong over the corpse of Morgan. Before he could rise, the thin thing was upon him. Its sharp teeth had met through the palm of his left hand.

The machete moved swiftly. The thin dry body fell headless to the floor. There was no blood.

The grip of the teeth did not relax. Pain coursed up Tallant's left arm—a sharper, more bitter pain than you would expect from the bite. Almost as though venom—

He dropped the machete, and his strong white hand plucked and twisted at the dry brown lips. The teeth stayed clenched, unrelaxing. He sat bracing his back against the wall and gripped the head between his knees. He pulled. His flesh ripped, and blood formed dusty clots on the dirt floor. But the bite was firm.

His world had become reduced now to that hand and that head. Nothing outside mattered. He must free himself. He raised his aching arm to his face, and with his own teeth he tore at that unrelenting grip. The dry flesh crumbled away in desert dust, but the teeth were locked fast. He tore his lip against their white keenness, and tasted in his mouth the sweetness of blood and something else.

He staggered to his feet again. He knew what he must do. Later he could use cautery, a tourniquet, see a doctor with a story about a Gila monster—their heads grip too, don't they?— but he knew what he must do now.

He raised the machete and struck again.

His white hand lay on the brown floor, gripped by the white teeth in the brown face. He propped himself against the adobe wall, momentarily unable to move. His open wrist hung over the deeply hollowed stone. His blood and his strength and his life poured out before the little figure of sticks and clay.

The female stood in the doorway now, the sun bright on her thin brownness. She did not move. He knew that she was waiting for the hollow stone to fill.

COME ONE, COME ALL

GAHAN WILSON

GAHAN WILSON (1930–) was born in Evanston, Illinois. A self-described loner and weird kid, he was a fan of science fiction and fantasy, but was especially taken with the horror stories in *Weird Tales*. Influenced by the fiction of H. P. Lovecraft and the cartoons of Charles Addams, he made his earliest sales of bizarre cartoons to *Weird Tales*, followed by sales to *Collier's, Look*, and eventually *National Lampoon, The New Yorker*, and *Playboy*, the latter two still publishing his original, hilarious cartoons of gigantic and grotesque monsters and other macabre visitations.

In addition to his work as a cartoonist, Wilson has shown himself to be a gifted writer, producing such humorous novels as *Eddy Deco's Last Caper* (1987) and *Everybody's Favorite Duck* (1988); children's fantasy novels, including *Harry, the Fat Bear Spy* (1973), *Harry and the Sea Serpent* (1976), and *Harry and the Snow Melting Ray* (1978); more than fifteen collections of his cartoons; and highly popular stories for Harlan Ellison's famous anthology *Again, Dangerous Visions* (1972), *Playboy, The Magazine of Fantasy & Science Fiction*, and others. He also created a computer game titled *Gahan Wilson's The Ultimate Haunted House*. He received the World Fantasy Convention Award in 1981 and the National Cartoonist Society's Milton Caniff Lifetime Achievement Award in 2005.

"Come One, Come All" was first published in the anthology *Book of the Dead 2: Still Dead*, edited by John Skipp and Craig Spector (New York: Bantam, 1992).

GAHAN WILSON

COME ONE, COME ALL

PROFESSOR MARVELLO TIGHTENED two guy ropes with an expert twist of his strong, pudgy little hands in order to make the poles holding the big canvas sign spread out above the platform stand a little taller, then he squinted upwards at it with a slightly grim, lopsided smile of satisfaction.

The sign read

  * MARVELLO'S * MIRACULOUS * MIDWAY *

in ornate, gold-encrusted letters four and a half feet high—exactly the height of Professor Marvello himself, by his personal instructions—and a multitude of spotlights helped each letter glitter proudly out at the silent, surrounding darkness.

Marvello regarded the effect with satisfaction as he carefully and neatly made the ropes' ends fast around their shared cleat, then he meticulously brushed a speck of Kansas dust off the lapel of his red and white checkered coat and adjusted the bright yellow plastic carnation in its button hole.

"A nice night," he murmured to himself softly, sweeping the horizon with a benign if slightly wary gaze, and taking a long, fond sniff of the warm, wheat-smelling night air blowing in from the dark fields all around. Professor Marvello had been plain Homer Muggins of Missouri in his youth and he still admired simple, farmy scents. "A hellavuh nice night."

Then, adjusting his straw boater, he turned to business, flicking his bright little blue eyes down to see if the light was glowing on the solar battery like it ought to be, jabbing back a switch to start the circus music whooping, and plucking the microphone from its metal perch on the banner-bedecked rostrum. That done, Marvello squared his small but sturdy shoulders, softly cleared his throat, and spoke.

"Ladies and gentle—"

Too loud. You didn't need it that loud because there was no competition. No competition at all. He stooped with a slight grunt, bending to turn the knob down on the speaker system, then straightened his rotund little body so that it stood proudly erect as before and spoke again.

"Ladies and gentlemen, boys and girls," he said, and the nasal drone of his voice swirled out from a baker's dozen of speakers and rolled over the midnight landscape of flat, dimly-furrowed earth, sparse trees and long-deserted farmhouses. "Come on, come on, come on. Welcome to the fabulous, most wonderful, undeniably and by far greatest show left in the world. Come and see and be astounded by the one, the only Marvello's Miraculous Midway—the sole remaining sideshow in the world."

He paused, hacked, and spat over the edge of the platform onto the dusty ground. He gazed at the dust, at its dryness, half-reached for the flask of whiskey in his hip pocket, but then decided against it. Not yet. Later.

Did he hear a shuffle? His eyes guardedly darted this way and that. Not sure. Sometimes they stayed hidden just out of sight, watching you put up the show, standing on one foot and then the other, no idea what to do with their hands, hardly able to wait. Like kids, he thought, like kids.

"Don't miss it, don't miss it, don't miss it," he intoned. "Come one, come all, and bring your friends and loved ones so that everyone in this lovely area, in this beautiful county of this remarkable state, can be fortunate enough to experience the entertainment thrill of their lifetime, so to speak. So to speak."

Yes, yes indeed, there was a shuffle. He avoided looking in its direction, plucked a large polka-dotted handkerchief from his other hip pocket, the one not containing the flask, and wiped his brow in order to conceal his covert peering.

There it was, just by the popcorn stand. Raggedy, forlorn, and skeletal. It was dressed in torn blue denim overalls and the tattered remains of a wide-brimmed straw hat. There was no shirt, there were no shoes. It stared at him, mouth agape, and he could just make out the dull last remnant of a glint in its eyes and a vague glistening in its mouth.

"Good evening, sir," Professor Marvello said, giving it a formal little bow, an encouragingly toothy grin. "I observe you possess the percipiency to have been attracted by the sounds and sights of our outstanding exhibition. May I be so bold as to congratulate you on your good taste and encourage you to step a little closer?"

It swayed, obviously undecided. Professor

Marvello increased the wattage of his grin and, producing a bamboo cane from inside the rostrum, employed it to point at an enormous depiction of a huge-breasted Hawaiian hula dancer painted in classic circus poster style on a bellying rectangle of canvas.

"Miss La Frenza Hoo Pah Loo Hah," he announced proudly, and leaning forward towards the wary watcher, winked confidentially and continued in a lower tone as one man of the world speaking to another, his S-shaped smile taking on a new chumminess and his voice growing increasingly husky and intimate.

"I am sure, my dear sir, that a man of your obvious sophistication and, if I may say it, *je ne sais quoi,* is well aware of the extraordinary sensual jollies which may be produced by the skilled locomotion of swaying hips and other anatomical accessories on the part of a well-trained and imaginative practitioner of the art of hula dancing. Permit me to assure you that the lovely Miss Hoo Pah Loo Hah is *extremely* knowledgeable in these matters and will not fail to delight the sensibilities of a bon vivant such as yourself. Come a little closer, there, my good man, don't be shy."

The figure swayed, its dark green, stiff arms lolling, and then one large, bony foot pushed forward, stirring up a little puff of dust.

"That's the way, that's the way," said Marvello in an encouraging tone. "There's the brave fellow. Excellent. You're doing just fine. I trust, in passing, you've observed how plump the lovely Miss La Frenza Hoo Pah Loo Hah is, my dear fellow: how fat her hips, how round and fulsome her breasts, how meaty she is in all respects. I trust you've not let those aspects of our lovely dancer get by you, my good sir."

The overalled figure paused as if to study the poster with increased intensity, or perhaps it was only getting its balance. There was a kind of gathering, a moment of staggering confusion, then it lurched itself forward with a series of crablike waddles until it had worked its way well into the brightly lit area before Professor Marvello's platform. This one had semi-mummified, its skin had dried more than rotted, and the dark green-brown of its bony, beaky head and face bore more than a slight resemblance to an Egyptian pharaoh's.

"Over here, over here, my wizened chum," said Professor Marvello with encouraging enthusiasm, indicating the tent's entrance with a wave of his bamboo cane. "Keep heading towards that welcoming aperture before you, spur yourself on with rapt contemplation of the sexual gyrative wonders the lovely Hoo Pah Loo Hah will perform before you as envisioned in your most private dreams, and of course never forget nor neglect the generous pulchritude of her charms, which is to say the amazingly large amount of tender flesh which bedecks her frame."

When the mummy farmer paused at the entrance, Professor Marvello raised the tent flap invitingly with the tip of his cane.

"No need to pay, my good man," he intoned, though the thing had not made the slightest attempt to reach into its pockets. "The Marvello Miraculous Midway is a rare phenomenon indeed in this hard world, my dear sir, being gratis, entirely free of charge. A generous, altruistic effort to brighten the, ah, lives of such unfortunates as yourself. Go right on in, do go right on in."

A few prompting prods from the tip of Marvello's cane between the separating vertebrae of its narrow, bony back, and the overalled entity finally committed itself and lurched on into the tent to be greeted by the soft throbbings of Hawaiian music, the heady scents of tropic flowers.

"Almost looked happy for a moment there," murmured Professor Marvello thoughtfully, nudging the tent flap so that it fell softly back into place as the music and the scent of flowers ceased abruptly.

Nearly at once there was another timid shuffling, this from the far left, hard by the ring toss stand, and two figures edged sidewise into view. What was left of a mother and daughter.

They were dressed in faded, flowered frocks which were frayed and torn and flecked with a multitude of dark, dry stains. The girl was missing her scalp on one side of her head, but a glistening gold braid with a large pink bow on its end grew from the other. Her mother held her hand tightly but mechanically, a habit that had somehow survived the loss of everything else.

"Fun for the entire family," Professor Marvello cooed into his microphone, essaying a fatherly wink which somehow slipped over into the lewd. "Let me assure you, Madame, and your precious little princess standing so trustingly by your side, that the Marvello Miraculous Midway fully satisfies both young and old. Both of you may positively and without reservation enjoy it to the full, as we unhesitatingly guarantee to completely and entirely please folks from eight to eighty. Do come up, do come up."

He turned and waved his cane at the flapping portrait of a man whose mighty body bulged everywhere with layer upon layer of huge, rippling muscles, but whose calm, heroically mustachioed face radiated an almost saintly kindliness. With serene calm the man was carefully lifting a school bus packed full of laughing children high above a torrent of swirling water.

"Observe a true wonder of the world—Hugo, the Gentle Giant. He has the strength of a lion, but within his huge chest softly beats the heart of a doting lambkin. Here we are privileged to witness him depicted performing his daring, legendary rescue of a group of innocent children from the raging waters of the Jamestown flood. That's right, dears, come a little closer. That's right. My, what a sweet little girl. You must be very proud, Mother."

They swayed closer and Marvello noticed the girl's sharp, tiny teeth were constantly snapping, chewing on the air she walked through. He gave her an especially intimate grin.

"I'll wager Hugo has a lollipop or some other sweet edible possibly more to your taste, little missy," he confided. "Something chewy, something wet, something juicy, something nice! The gentle giant has never been able to resist the tender implorements of hungry little children, dear."

The child's eyes lost some of their glaze as

she neared, tugging at her mother now. Marvello could hear her teeth clacking dryly. He reflected that it was a remarkably nasty little sound and gently prodded the tent flap up invitingly as he touched a hidden button which caused a deep, kindly voice to boom out from inside the tent amidst the excited chirpings of happy children.

"It sounds like everyone's having a fine old time," Marvello observed, leaning over his rostrum and smiling gently down. "A fine old time. Why don't you go join them, darlings?"

He paused, furtively turned a dial, and then appeared to listen in happy surprise as the children's voices coming from inside the tent were suddenly amplified in a burst of avid glee and enthusiastic crunchings and slobberings and gulpings became increasingly audible.

"Harken," hissed Marvello excitedly, holding his hand cupped dramatically behind an ear. "Harken at that, will you? It's my guess dear old Hugo has just now given his little chums inside some particularly tasty morsels—he has a whole tub full of them, you know—something ripe and gooey, something positively *dripping,* just the way I know you sweet things like 'em, eh? *Eh?*"

He leaned lower over his rostrum and leered openly at the two of them.

"Take a friendly tip from me, from your dear old uncle Professor Marvello," he whispered, *"and hurry on in before it's all et up!"*

The girl's feverish pulling increased into a desperate frenzy of haulings and jerkings, and the two of them were halfway into the tent when the mother balked stubbornly, her filmy eyes bulging up at Professor Marvello with slowly increasing interest, staring up at the smooth pink skin of his neat little double chin in particular.

"No, Mother, no," said the professor with a dry, friendly chuckle, firmly pointing at the entrance with his bamboo cane. "No, *non, nyet, nein* . . . the food's in there, sweetness. Inside the tent with dear old Hugo."

The mother's cracked lips writhed back, the lower one splitting slightly with the effort, and this brought her teeth entirely into view for the first time. They had been longer than the ordinary run of teeth in life to the point of deformity, but now, because of the shrinkage of her gums, they were of an appalling size and curvature. When she fully opened her mouth wide in Marvello's direction, it looked like a mantrap fitted out with yellowed boar's tusks. Quietly, without fuss, he placed the tip of his cane on the side of her shoulder, on the meatiest part so it would get a good purchase, then he shoved it with an efficient and expert brutality, timing his nudge with the haulings of her still-tugging daughter, and sent the two of them tumbling clumsily into the tent's opening.

"Get inside there, inside with you, you grinning, rotting cunt," Marvello drawled softly, nudging the flap so that it rolled down smartly and pushing another button which caused the sounds of Hugo and the happy children to cease forthwith.

There was a faint sparking noise from within the tent and a wisp of acrid burning wafted outwards. Marvello frowned slightly at this and consulted a series of dials set into the rear of the rostrum just to make sure all the readings were correct. It would never do to have a mechanical failure during a performance. It would never do at all.

He paused to give his face another wipe with his polka-dot hanky and to reponder the advisability of a sip from the flask. It was dry work; neither man nor beast could deny that it was dry work. He had allowed himself to pull the flask a third of the way out of his pocket when he froze at the sound of a persistent and complicated growling coming from the darkness to his left. He let the flask slip back into its hiding place and peered carefully in the direction of the growling, his hand screening his eyes from the spotlights overhead.

At first he saw nothing, but then he became aware of activity in the darkness outside the midway, an ominous black milling highlit with small metallic gleams. It stirred closer, then suddenly boiled out into the lighted area to reveal itself as a group of fifteen to twenty very large ones moving together as a unit.

They were a shaggy, snarling army of the night. Huge, all of them, built like bears and almost as hairy, and they all favored black leather outfits with bones and flames painted on them and lots of stainless steel rivets pounded in along the hems. Some wore visored caps, others Nazi helmets, the rest went bareheaded to show off bizarre shavings and haircuts, and a few had lost their scalps entirely. One of these last had a crude swastika hacked crudely into the top of his skull.

They were a group of bikers who had somehow, almost touchingly, managed to stay together after death. The gaudily terrifying tattoos on their skin may have faded or dimmed with mildew when they had not sloughed off altogether, and some of their bulging muscles and beer bellies might be lying exposed and rotting in swaying hammocks of flesh gone to leather, but their sense of being a group had survived into their new condition beyond a doubt. They all still glared balefully out at the world from a common center.

"Come this way, my dear gentlemen, do, for your pleasure's sake, come this way," Marvello intoned into the mike, upping the bass dial slightly to give his voice a little more authority. "I perceive without difficulty that you have wandered long and far—both in life and in your present status, from the looks of you—and it is my considered professional opinion that you all are tired, very tired, very, *very* tired, yes, every one of you without exception, yes, and that you could all do with a little relaxation. Relaxation."

First they gaped vaguely around at the show in general, staring at the bright lights and flapping pictures and glittering words, but one by one their eyes began shifting in the same direction during Marvello's spiel until they had all zeroed in on the professor himself, the only living human in sight. Their stomachs began to rumble audibly and then they started to whine and bark, first one by one and then in a pack, like wandering wolves instinctively organizing at the sight of a lost and lonely child.

"Relaxation . . ." Marvello murmured the word thoughtfully once more, seeming to be blissfully unaware that any harm might befall him from his visitors. "And you have come to the right place for it, gentlemen, you couldn't have come to a better, because we have here on the premises of Marvello's Miraculous Midway one of the all-time expert practitioners of producing that enviable condition."

He turned and pointed with his bamboo cane at a large canvas rectangle bearing the painting of a thin, brown man wearing a turban and a loin cloth, staring intensely with his large, dark eyes, and holding his hands poised weirdly out before him with all his fingertips pointed directly at the viewer.

"Allow me to direct your attention to this depiction of one of my most valued and trusted associates, the Swami Pootcha Ahsleep," intoned Marvello, beaming down at his guests in a friendly fashion, a man anxious to share a boon. "Pootcha Ahsleep."

The bikers steadily continued their sinister, shuffling approach and Marvello noticed that their odors preceded them and was interested to smell that the peculiar stench of tanned leather gone mouldy had at last managed to completely dominate their other mingled stenches of decay.

"The Swami and myself," he continued, "both studied the occult arts at the very same Tibetan monastery during our childhood, but I am not ashamed to freely admit that Ahsleep, my old-time pal and fellow scholar, far exceeded me in a number of the difficult arts there imparted, particularly outshining me in the little-understood and seldom-mastered skills of *hypnotism!*"

As he uttered this last word with great emphasis, his hand moved smoothly under his rostrum and the Swami's eyes painted on the poster suddenly began to lighten and darken in a slow, even pulsing as the sound of a snake charmer's horn began to wail eerily from the tent's interior. For the first time the bikers paused in their meaningful progress toward the professor and shifted their large, jackbooted feet with the beginnings of indecision as they stared up with steadily-increasing interest at the poster's throbbing eyes.

"I see you have noticed the irresistible fascination which the Swami's eyes inevitably hold for any intelligent observer," pointed out Marvello, lowering the bass even further and emphasizing the singsong quality which he had allowed to creep into his voice, allowing it to move in and out of the melody of the Hindu flute. "It is very hard to take one's eyes from their deep, hypnotic gaze, very hard. I'm willing to hazard you gentlemen even now are finding it increasingly difficult to look away even as I speak to you, that you are starting to discover that it is, in fact, impossible. Impossible. That you cannot look away. You cannot look away."

One particularly huge biker at the rear had rather worried Marvello from the start, since for most of his hulking approach his head had been held at an odd, low angle and the professor had been unable to determine if the man actually had any eyes left with which to see the Swami's flashing gaze, but now, at the professor's last words, the biker's head had lifted with a painful-looking, sudden twist of his inflated, purple neck, and Marvello was greatly relieved to observe that it seemed he did have one eye left, after all. Not much of it, true, but enough for the purpose.

Gently, making as little fuss about it as possible, Marvello teased the tent flap open. The snake charmer music subtly increased in volume, grew more complicated, and the professor timed his commands to match its cadence.

"Walk into the tent, gentlemen," he intoned softly, intimately, close to the microphone. "Walk into the tent for peace at last, lovely, soothing peace. It's waiting in the tent, my wandering friends, my little lost sheep. All you need to do is stumble in any which way you can and take it for your own. Walk into the tent for peace. For peace."

With their various shuffles, staggers and lurches in almost perfect rhythm, they began moving toward the opening with their gaze fixed dutifully on the throbbing eyes of Pootcha Ahsleep. They had almost gotten there when the large biker Marvello had noticed in particular, the cyclops with the faulty eye, hesitated and then halted entirely. He twisted his head this way and that in a mounting panic, and then he began to howl monotonously, to push and flail at his companions desperately in a sort of clumsy fit.

"Damn," murmured Marvello under his breath, for he saw that the fellow's piss yellow, distended staring eye had chosen this unfortunate moment to explode altogether and that its slimy juices were even now slithering smoothly down from his freshly-emptied socket, down along the rough stubble of his cheek.

Now that he was totally blind he could no longer see Pootcha Ahsleep's hypnotic gaze, and since his retention span was almost nonexistent if not entirely so, he had forgotten that gaze completely and was no longer under the Swami's spell. As his pointless, panicky struggles and flailings increased, he began to seriously impede the steady, tentward drift of his companions.

"*All* of you must go into the tent, dear fellows," Marvello commanded, rising to the challenge. "*Every one* of you, with no exceptions, that's what the Swami wants. Recall that you are an organization of sorts, and press together proudly as you did when you thundered down the highway on your mighty machines, your fine black hogs. Keep the herd entire, keep the pack complete. That's the way, boys, that's the way."

The others had now crowded firmly around their blind companion, heaving a surrounding wall of hairy flesh up against him until they had actually lifted him, so that the black toes of his boots scuffed the ground uselessly and he was as helpless as a small child hauled through a mall by its mother.

"Good lads," drawled Marvello, watching the bikers shuffle into the tent, carrying the struggling rebel along in the center of the group with the pressure of their rotting shoulders and bellies. "Good lads."

He lifted his cane, holding it at the ready, and

when the last of the bikers had finally stumbled into the tent, he darted its tip at the flap with the speed and accuracy of a striking cobra, closing the opening instantly.

"That had a distinct and genuine potential of becoming downright unpleasant," he mused into the darkness, turning off the Hindu music abruptly.

Without bothering to enter into any further debate with himself, he plucked the flask from his hip pocket, unscrewed its cap with dispatch, and gratefully swallowed a good full inch of its contents. Perhaps he should altogether abandon this little hobby he'd developed of buck and winging the first stages of the scooping. Those damn bikers could have done him in. He replaced the cap on the flask and slid the flask back into his pocket, then took up the microphone.

"I believe," he said, smiling benignly around at the empty midway, "I believe the time has come for the Grand Finale."

What had happened up to now was, as Marvello would have freely admitted, a mere frivolity, a bit of harmless self-indulgence, a catering to his sense of whimsy. Now the evening was wearing on and he had his quota to meet and it was time for sterner stuff, it was time to really crank the Midway up full blast, it was time to let her rip.

He bent to his rostrum with a faint sigh of resignation and began a major readjustment of the control board built into its rear, and as he pushed its buttons and turned its knobs and slid its levers along their slots, a vast alteration began taking place along the abbreviated midway.

First the lights dimmed almost to darkness, so that the towering silhouettes of the signs and tent peaks seemed a sort of Stonehenge; then, after a significant pause, the lights began to glow again, but changed from their former bright, bodacious white to sinister variations on the color red, ranging from burning crimsons to ominous scarlets, which were all of them so splashed and spattered with bright gouts of orange and rust that the whole place seemed to be suddenly soaked in gore.

Following that, the crudely painted, innocent carny posters of freaks and fire-eaters and rounded women in spangled tights rolled out of sight while their places were smoothly taken by huge blank screens which rolled smoothly into view in order to receive the projections of three-dimensional, violently colored, moving pictures showing freshly ripped-out bowels quivering in random loops, still-beating hearts exposed in chests newly torn open, and many such other anatomical wonders.

At the same time the entire area was suddenly infused with the overpowering odor of fresh-spilled blood and the air was rent with a ghastly din of screams and shrieks mixed with the sounds of flesh being hacked and sawed amid the gurglings and splashes of spouting arteries and spilling guts.

"Very well, very well," murmured Professor Marvello softly, giving the ghastly effect his labors had created a steady, professional appraisal, carefully and critically observing all its grisly nuances.

"Not bad, not bad at all," he finally opined. "Perhaps a few more sobbing women, a little upping of the stench of newly-opened innards."

He bent to turn a dial, then brightened and smiled as awful feminine gaspings and groanings joined the cacophony sounding about him and a new, tangy reek invaded his nostrils.

"Just the needed touch," he said to himself, adjusting his boater and bow tie contentedly.

He took up his microphone and spoke into it loudly and clearly so that his voice rang out resoundingly through the sea of darkness all around.

"Ladies and gentlemen, boys and girls. This is it, this is it. What you've been shambling around trying to find out there in those used-up fields and little bitty no-account towns, what you've been yearning for, hungering for, and likely starting to doubt to believe could possibly exist."

He pulled a lever and a thick, vomitous, charnel stench blew enthusiastically out of the four outlets of a tall pipe overhead, gouting forth its ripe, rich odors into each cardinal direction simultaneously.

"It's here, it's here, in Marvello's Miraculous Midway, my good friends, right here on this very spot where you hear the sound of my voice inviting you one and all. Inviting you all. Forget those friends and loved ones you've sucked dry so long ago, dear hearts, leave off trying to content yourselves with the wandering, shriveled cows and dogs and cats you run across less and less these days, and come on in, come on in!"

Marvello heard a faint, choking meep and turned to see a tiny shape crawling into the gory light of the Midway. It was the corpse of a baby dressed in a long lacy dress that trailed along behind it as it hauled itself determinedly through the Kansas dust with what was left of its tiny, rotting fingers.

"Not much, but you're a start," said Marvello, observing the little creature with interest as it struggled toward the entrance. "If I'd have known the likes of you was out there, I'd have lured you in during the preamble with Wally Mysto and his Edible Animal Puppets. Land's sake, I do declare this little nipper must have drowned in its baptismal font. Yes, I'd have sworn the likes of you would have shown up for one of the earlier shows, sweetness, yes I would, but there's no accounting for taste."

He made no move to close the flap as the baby cleared the entrance and entered the tent. He'd only done it with his earlier visitors because he liked the effect, the truth be told. A vague electrical sputtering, a curl of smoke, and perhaps the faintest hint of a tiny, cut-off wail were ignored completely by Marvello because a surrounding murmur of activity had taken his full attention. He straightened and stared into the surrounding darkness.

There were so many of them, but then there were always so many of them. The first few rows now emerging into the ruddy light were distinct, you could read their separate forms, see their individual bodies, observe that one was little more than bones and shreds of leather, another was so ballooned with gas it could not bend its limbs

but only totter, and that a third had the steel sutures the surgeons had clipped onto its arteries still dangling from its opened chest, but once you got past the first few rows of them, they all started to merge into one heaving thing moving at you. Steadily. Hungrily. Endlessly.

"Come one, come all," said Marvello softly, staring out at them. "Come one, come all."

He took a pull at the flask, replaced it, and leaned into the microphone, standing firmly on the balls of his little feet.

"Juicy, juicy, juicy," he crooned, watching the front curve of them filling in the midway. "Lots of blood, lots of blood, lots of blood. Lots of fresh, chewy flesh, too, friends, lots of it. Sweet, sweet flesh like you haven't had between your teeth since God alone knows how long. Yummy, yummy, yummy."

He reached down to push a button and a soft red coiling of light began making its way 'round and 'round the opening of the tent, pulsing like a newly opened, still bleeding wound. They saw it, of course, they always saw it, and they headed for it just like flies heading for shit, as they were meant to.

He'd often noticed those among them that reminded him of people he'd known and he'd wonder *was* that old Charlie Carter he just saw stumble in there? *Was* that whatsisname who used to sell papers at that newsstand on the corner of Dearborn and Washington? Was that *Clara?* She had a great laugh, did Clara. He could remember just how it felt when he held her shoulders. He'd sure as hell hoped that thing hadn't been Clara.

They started cramming themselves into the entrance. Somehow or other they always managed it. There were snarls and struggles and so on, but in the end they always somehow managed it.

"That's right, dear hearts," he said, smiling down at them, but he knew there weren't any of them listening to him now, not after he'd turned on the doorway lights. "Have a fine old time, enjoy yourselves to the fullest."

At this stage of the game he could sing old

sweet songs if it struck his fancy, and he sometimes did, just for the hell of it, or because he was feeling mellow. From here on in the Midway did all the work. From here on in it was purely automatic. But the old habits die hard.

"Let that one-legged gentleman through, folks," he said after he'd observed a hopping fragment get pushed aside by the eager multitude for the fourth or fifth time. "There may not be all that much left of him, but I absolutely guarantee that what there is is just as hungry as the most complete among you. I absolutely guarantee it."

He smiled quietly and took another pull from his flask. What the hell, he thought, what the hell, the night's work was drawing softly and successfully to its close, so what the hell.

The damndest thing was that once he actually *had* seen someone he knew go into the tent, really and truly had, no doubt about it, but the whole thing had given him a real hoot, a genuine kick in the ass, praise be, because it'd been a man he'd truly hated, Mr. Homer Garner, onetime proprietor of the Garner Hardware Company of Joplin, a real revolving son of a bitch who'd done him dirty back when he was just a kid and really needed the money, didn't know any better way to get hold of it. It had given Marvello undiluted joy to observe the even-uglier-than-usual, pus-leaking remnants of Mr. Homer Garner shamble helplessly into the tent.

He was glad, you might even say genuinely grateful, that he'd never seen anybody he liked go in there, since he was certain sure he would not have enjoyed that in the least. Of course the danger of such a thing happening had diminished considerably through the years. He didn't suppose there were all that many left in either category, those he'd hated or those he'd liked, when you came right down to it. He supposed most of them were dead by now, *really* dead, not just shuffling-around dead. Dead and buried dead, the good, old fashioned way.

Marvello leaned over the rostrum, propping himself on spread fingertips, and sized up the Midway. The crowd was down to the final strag-

glers now, the really timid ones, wandering in at last from wherever they'd been shyly hiding their bones. It wouldn't be long at all now. The show was almost over.

He glanced down at the glowing readout, watching how the number was growing at a slower and slower pace now that the big rush was over. They kind of relaxed when there weren't so many of them around. They almost sort of strolled in when you got down to the last little trickle.

The readout showed a good score, of course. It was always a good score.

"You don't want to miss it," he called out softly to the final, staggering arrivals, then he took another pull, washing the booze around his teeth before he swallowed it. "Nossir, you don't want to miss it."

One left, now, just one. Standing out there in a cockeyed stance, swaying, looking around with its dim eyes, pawing the air with its shriveled little hands. A tough one to turn, this baby. A real hard sell.

"All your friends and loved ones are in there, my handsome fellow," he said, smiling out at the solitary figure.

On an impulse, he turned off the lights moving around the doorway, the lights that pulled them in no matter what. He felt like bringing this one in himself.

"Why be lonely?" he called out, cooing, first waving his cane in the air to get the thing's attention, and then, when he'd caught its eye, pointing it at the entrance and giving its tip a tiny, emphasizing twirl. "Come, come, your solitude serves no purpose, and it's self-inflicted to boot. Cut it short, old chum, cut it short. All those near and dear are but a few short steps away, a mere totter or two. They are all eagerly awaiting your august presence inside. They're all inside."

It looked up at Marvello, aware of him for the first time. Rags of skin swung from its forearms, blowing slightly in the night breeze. It took a step or two forward. It lifted its head and sucked the odors coming from the tent through its nose hole.

"Smells even better *in* the tent, friend,"

he said. "Say, don't be a spoil sport, don't be a party pooper. You only lived once."

It wavered idiotically for another half minute and then, its jaws starting to work, starting to wetten, it began to shuffle steadily ahead. Marvello nodded down at it, finishing off his flask as it passed by him and stepped into the darkness of the entrance. There was a final electrical crackling, a last wisp of smoke.

Marvello carefully slipped the flask back into its pocket, threw a series of switches, then hopped gracefully off the platform just a moment before it began to pull itself smoothly back into a slot which had opened at the bottom of the tent.

The showman stood on the hot, dry, dusty ground, his hands in his pockets, and watched, interested as always, while the entire Midway slowly started to fold in on itself. Marvello never failed to enjoy this moment. Sometimes he felt it was, in a way, the best part of the whole show.

First the poles shortened, smoothly telescoping, then the wires and ropes rolled back in perfect synchronization onto hidden spools as the fabric of the main and smaller tents sucked inward, beginning with large tucks, then working down to smaller and smaller ones, all of them tidy, all of them precise, and soon the whole thing had reduced itself to a neat rectangular block which confined and sculpted itself still further, until, when it had neatly resolved itself unmistakably into the shape of a huge truck, highly polished panels rose from all around its base to form the truck's sides and top and wheel guards, and shiny bits of chrome and glass rotated into view to make up its grille and headlights and trim.

There on the side of the truck, in proud, tall letters of glistening gold, a bold sign read:

* MARVELLO'S * MIRACULOUS *
MEATPIES *

Marvello regarded the truck with satisfaction for a long moment before he walked to its side, opened its door, and made himself comfortable in the driver's seat. He turned the waiting ignition key, and when the engine instantly began a strong, steady purring, he reached forward to the glove compartment, extracted the full bottle of whiskey waiting there, pulled its cork, and took two long, slow, deeply satisfactory swallows.

He rolled down the window, looked out in a friendly fashion at the empty space which had been the Midway just a little while before, and gave it a friendly wave. He drove smoothly across the soft bumpiness of the field until he reached the straight, flat Kansas highway, and there he turned northward, following the beams of his headlights onto his next gig.

IT HELPS IF YOU SING

RAMSEY CAMPBELL

OFTEN DESCRIBED BY critics and fellow writers as the greatest stylist of the contemporary horror genre, (John) Ramsey Campbell (1946–) was born in Liverpool and set many of his novels and stories there and in the fictional city of Brichester in the same region. Heavily influenced by the work of H. P. Lovecraft, he published three short-story collections in a similar style before producing his first novel, *The Doll Who Ate His Mother* (1976; revised edition 1985). The following year, 1977, he wrote the novelizations of three films as Carl Dreadstone (a house name under which three additional novels were written by others), successfully bringing a pulpy style that evoked the classic films (*The Bride of Frankenstein, Dracula's Daughter,* and *The Wolfman*). Among the best of his later novels are *The Face That Must Die* (1979), *Incarnate* (1983), *Ancient Images* (1989), *Midnight Sun* (1991), and *The Grin of the Dark* (2008). Among the many awards Campbell has received are five World Fantasy nominations (three winners), sixteen British Fantasy Society nominations (ten winners), and two Bram Stoker Award nominations (both winners). He has been named the lifetime president of the British Fantasy Society.

While much of his work is explicitly violent, Campbell's use of metaphor, symbolism, and imagery allows a poetic tone to suffuse his prose, suggesting horrors that remain in the memory long after the initial shock of a starkly brutal occurrence has passed.

"It Helps If You Sing" was first published in *Book of the Dead,* edited by John Skipp and Craig Spector (New York: Bantam, 1989).

RAMSEY CAMPBELL

IT HELPS IF YOU SING

THEY COULD BE on their summer holidays. If they were better able to afford one than he was, Bright wished them luck. Now that it was daylight, he could see into all the lowest rooms of the high rise opposite, but there was no sign of life on the first two floors. Perhaps all the tenants were singing the hymns he could hear somewhere in the suburb. He took his time about making himself presentable, and then he went downstairs.

The lifts were out of order. Presumably it was a repairman who peered at him through the smeary window of one scrawled metal door on the landing below his. The blurred face startled him so much that he was glad to see people on the third floor. Weren't they from the building opposite, from one of the apartments that had stayed unlit last night? The woman they had come to visit was losing a smiling contest with them. She stepped back grudgingly, and Bright heard the bolt and chain slide home as he reached the stairs.

The public library was on the ground floor. First he strolled to the job center among the locked and armored shops. There was nothing for a printer on the cards, and cards that offered training in a new career were meant for people thirty years younger. They needed the work more than he did, even if they had no families to provide for. He ambled back to the library, whistling a wartime song.

The young job-hunters had finished with the newspapers. Bright started with the tabloids, saving the serious papers for the afternoon, though even those suggested that the world over the horizon was seething with disease and crime and promiscuity and wars.

Good news wasn't news, he told himself, but the last girl he'd ever courted before he'd grown too set in his ways was out there somewhere, and the world must be better for her. Still, it was no wonder that most readers came to the library for fiction rather than for the news. He supposed the smiling couple who were filling cartons with books would take them to the housebound, although some of the titles he glimpsed seemed unsuitable for the easily offended. He watched the couple stalk away with the cartons, until the smoke of a distant bonfire obscured them.

The library closed at nine. Usually Bright would have been home for hours and listening to his radio cassette player, to Elgar or Vera Lynn or the dance bands his father used to play on the wind-up record player, but something about the day had made him reluctant to be alone. He read about evolution until the librarian began to harrumph loudly and smite books on the shelves.

Perhaps Bright should have gone up sooner. When he hurried round the outside of the building to the lobby, he had never seen the suburb so lifeless. Identical gray terraces multiplied to the horizon under a charred sky; a pair of trampled books lay amid the breathless litter on the anonymous concrete walks. He thought he heard a cry, but it might have been the start of the hymn that immediately was all he could hear, wherever it was.

The lifts still weren't working; both sets of doors that gave onto the scribbled lobby were open, displaying thick cables encrusted with darkness. By the time he reached the second floor he was slowing, grasping any banisters that hadn't been prised out of the concrete. The few lights that were working had been spray-painted until they resembled dying coals. Gangs of shadows flattened themselves against the walls, waiting to mug him. As he climbed, a muffled sound of hymns made him feel even more isolated. They must be on television, he could hear them in so many apartments.

One pair of lift doors on the fifth floor had jammed open. Unless Bright's eyes were the worse for his climb, the cable was shaking. He labored upstairs to his landing, where the corresponding doors were open too. Once his head stopped swimming, he ventured to the edge of the unlit shaft. There was no movement, and nothing on the cable except the underside of the lift on the top floor. He turned toward his apartment. Two men were waiting for him.

Apparently they'd rung his bell. They were staring at his door and rubbing their hands stiffly. They wore black T-shirts and voluminous black overalls, and sandals on their otherwise bare feet. "What can I do for you?" Bright called.

They turned together, holding out their hands as if to show him how gray their palms looked under the stained lamp. Their narrow bland faces were already smiling. "Ask rather what we can do for you," one said.

Bright couldn't tell which of them had spoken, for neither smile gave an inch. They might be two men or even two women, despite their close-cropped hair. "You could let me at my front door," Bright said.

They gazed at him as if nothing he might say would stop them smiling, their eyes wide as old pennies stuck under the lids. When he pulled out his key and marched forward, they stepped aside, but only just. As he slipped the key into the lock, he sensed them close behind him, though he couldn't hear them. He pushed the door open, no wider than he needed to let himself in. They followed him.

"Whoa, whoa." He swung round in the stubby vestibule and made a grab at the door, too late. His visitors came plodding in, bumping the door against the wall. Their expressions seemed more generalized than ever. "What the devil do you think you're doing?" Bright cried.

That brought their smiles momentarily alive, as though it were a line they'd heard before. "We haven't anything to do with him," their high flat voices said, one louder than the other.

"And we hope you won't have," one added while his companion mouthed. They seemed no surer who should talk than who should close the door behind them. The one by the hinges elbowed it shut, almost trapping the other before he was in, until the other blundered through and squashed his companion behind the door. They might be fun, Bright supposed, and he could do with some of that. They seemed harmless enough, so long as they didn't stumble against anything breakable. "I can't give you much time," he warned them.

They tried to lumber into the main room together. One barged through the doorway and the other stumped after him, and they stared about the room. Presumably the blankness of their eyes meant they found it wanting, the sofa piled with Bright's clothes awaiting ironing, the snaps he'd taken on his walks in France and Germany and Greece, the portrait of herself his last girl-friend had given him, the framed copy of the article he'd printed for the newspaper shortly before he'd been made redundant, about how life should be a hundred years from now, advances in technology giving people more control over their own lives. He resented the disapproval, but he was more disconcerted by how his visitors looked in the light of his apartment: gray from heads to toes, as if they needed dusting. "Who are you?" he demanded. "Where are you from?"

"We don't matter."

"Atter," the other agreed, and they said almost in unison: "We're just vessels of the Word."

"Better give it to me, then," Bright said, staying on his feet so as to deter them from sitting: God only knew how long it would take them to stand up. "I've a lot to do before I can lie down."

They turned to him as if they had to move their whole bodies to look. Whichever responded, the voice through the fixed smile sounded more pinched than ever. "What do you call your life?"

They had no reason to feel superior to him. The gray ingrained in their flesh suggested disuse rather than hard work, and disused was how they smelled in the small room. "I've had a fair life, and it's only right I should make way for someone who can work the new machines. I've had enough of a life to help me cope with the dole."

His visitors stared as if they meant to dull him into accepting whatever they were offering. The sight of their faces stretched tight by their smiles was so disagreeably fascinating that he jumped, having lost his sense of time passing, when one spoke. "Your life is empty until you let him in."

"Isn't two of you enough? Who's that, now?"

The figure on his left reached in a pocket, and the overalls pulled flat at the crotch. The jerky hand produced a videocassette that bore a picture of a priest. "I can't play that," Bright said.

His visitors pivoted sluggishly to survey the room. Their smiles turned away from him, turned back unchanged. They must have seen that his radio could play cassettes, for now the righthand visitor was holding one. "Listen before it's too late," they urged in unison.

"As soon as I've time." Bright would have promised more just then to rid himself of their locked smiles and their stale sweetish odor. He held open the door to the vestibule and shrank back as one floundered in the doorway while the other fumbled at the outer door. He held his breath as the second set of footsteps plodded through the vestibule, and let out a gasp of relief as the outer door slammed.

Perhaps deodorants were contrary to their faith. He opened the window and leaned into the night to breathe. More of the building opposite was unlit, as if a flood of darkness were rising through the floors, and he would have expected to see more houses lit by now. He could hear more than one muffled hymn, or perhaps the same one at different stages of its development. He was wondering where he'd seen the face of the priest on the videocassette.

When the smoke of a bonfire began to scrape his throat, he closed the window. He set up the ironing board and switched on the electric iron. It took him half an hour to press his clothes, and he still couldn't remember what he'd read about the priest. Perhaps he could remind himself. He carried the radio to his chair by the window.

As he lifted the cassette out of its plastic box,

he winced. A sharp corner of the cassette had pricked him. He sucked his thumb and gnawed it to dislodge the sliver of plastic that had penetrated his skin. He dropped the cassette into the player and snapped the aperture shut, then he switched on, trying to ignore the ache in his thumb. He heard a hiss, the click of a microphone, a voice. "I am Father Lazarus. I'm going to tell you the whole truth," it said.

It was light as a disc jockey's voice, and virtually sexless. Bright knew the name; perhaps he would be able to place it now that the ache was fading. "If you knew the truth," the voice said, "wouldn't you want to help your fellow man by telling him?"

"Depends," Bright growled, blaming the voice for the injury to his thumb.

"And if you've just said no, don't you see that proves you don't know the truth?"

"Ho ho, very clever," Bright scoffed. The absence of the pain was unexpectedly comforting: it felt like a calm in which he need do nothing except let the voice reach him. "Get on with it," he muttered.

"Christ was the truth. He was the word that couldn't deny itself although they made him suffer all the torments of the damned. Why would they have treated him like that if they hadn't been afraid of the truth? He was the truth made flesh, born without the preamble of lust and never indulging in it himself, and we have only to become vessels of the truth to welcome him back before it's too late."

Not too late to recall where he'd seen the priest's face, Bright thought, if he didn't nod off first, he felt so numbed. "Look around you," the voice was saying, "and see how late it is. Look and see the world ending in corruption and lust and man's indifference."

The suggestion seemed knowing. If you looked out at the suburb, you would see the littered walkways where nobody walked at night except addicts and muggers and drunks. There was better elsewhere, Bright told himself, and managed to turn his head on its stiff neck toward the portrait photograph. "Can you want the

world to end this way?" the priest demanded. "Isn't it true that you wish you could change it but feel helpless? Believe me, you can. Christ says you can. He had to suffer agonies for the truth, but we offer you the end of pain and the beginning of eternal life. The resurrection of the body has begun."

Not this body, Bright thought feebly. His injured hand alone felt as heavy as himself. Even when he realized that he'd left the iron switched on, it seemed insufficient reason for him to move. "Neither men nor women shall we be in the world to come," the voice was intoning. "The flesh shall be freed of the lusts that have blinded us to the truth."

He blamed sex for everything, Bright mused, and instantly he remembered. EVANGELIST IS VOODOO WIDOWER, the headline inside a tabloid had said, months ago. The priest had gone to Haiti to save his wife's people, only for her to return to her old faith and refuse to go home with him. Hadn't he been quoted in the paper as vowing to use his enemies' methods to defeat them? Certainly he'd announced that he was renaming himself Lazarus. His voice seemed to be growing louder, so loud that the speaker ought to be vibrating. "The Word of God will fill your emptiness. You will go forth to save your fellow man and be rewarded on the day of judgment. Man was made to praise God, and so he did until woman tempted him in the garden. When the sound of our praise is so great that it reaches heaven, our savior shall return."

Bright did feel emptied, hardly there at all. If giving in to the voice gave him back his strength, wouldn't that prove it was telling the truth? But he felt as if it wanted to take the place of his entire life. He gazed at the photograph, remembering the good-byes at the bus station, the last kiss and the pressure of her hands on his, the glow of the bus turning the buds on a tree into green fairy lights as the vehicle vanished over the crest of a hill, and then he realized that the priest's voice had stopped.

He felt as if he'd outwitted the tape until a choir began the hymn he had been hearing all day. The emptiness within him was urging him to join in, but he wouldn't while he had any strength. He managed to suck his bottom lip between his teeth and gnaw it, though he wasn't sure if he could feel even a distant ache. Voodoo widower, he chanted to himself to break up the oppressive repetition of the hymn, voodoo widower. He was fending off the hymn, though it seemed impossibly loud in his head, when he heard another sound. The outer door was opening.

He couldn't move, he couldn't even call out. The numbness that had spread from his thumb through his body had sculpted him to the chair. He heard the outer door slam as bodies blundered voicelessly about the vestibule. The door to the room inched open, then jerked wide, and the two overalled figures struggled into the room.

He'd known who they were as soon as he'd heard the outer door. The hymn on the tape must have been a signal that he was finished— that he was like them. They'd tampered with the latch on their way out, he realized dully. He seemed incapable of feeling or reacting, even when the larger of the figures leaned down to gaze into his eyes, presumably to check that they were blank, and Bright saw how the gray, stretched lips were fraying at the corners. For a moment Bright thought the man's eyes were going to pop out of their seedy sockets at him, yet he felt no inclination to flinch. Perhaps he was recognizing himself as he would be—yet didn't that mean he wasn't finished after all?

The man stood back from scrutinizing him and turned up the volume of the hymn. Bright thought the words were meant to fill his head, but he could still choose what to think. He wasn't that empty, he'd done his bit of good for the world, he'd stood aside to give someone else a chance. Whatever the priest had brought back from Haiti might have deadened Bright's body, but it hadn't quite deadened his mind. He fixed his gaze on the photograph and thought of the day he'd walked on a mountain with her. He was beginning to fight back toward his feelings when the other man came out of the kitchen, bearing the sharpest knife in the place.

They weren't supposed to make Bright suffer, the tape had said so. He could see no injuries on them. Suppose there were mutilations that weren't visible? "Neither men nor women shall we be in the world to come." At last Bright understood why his visitors seemed sexless. He tried to shrink back as the man who had turned up the hymn took hold of the electric iron.

The man grasped it by the point before he found the handle. Bright saw the gray skin of his fingers curl up like charred paper, but the man didn't react at all. He closed his free hand around the handle and waited while his companion plodded toward Bright, the edge of the knife blade glinting like a razor. "It helps if you sing," said the man with the knife. Though Bright had never been particularly religious, nobody could have prayed harder than he started to pray then. He was praying that by the time the first of them reached him, he would feel as little as they did.

THE GHOULS
R. CHETWYND-HAYES

R(ONALD HENRY GLYNN) CHETWYND-HAYES (1919–2001) was born in Isleworth, West London. He left school at the age of fourteen, worked in a variety of menial jobs, including as an extra in crowd scenes in British war films, then served in the army in World War II.

Known in the United Kingdom as "Britain's Prince of Chill," he began his writing career with a science fiction novel, *The Man from the Bomb* (1959), then sold a supernatural romance, *The Dark Man* (1964), which has had several film options. He sold his first horror story, "The Thing," to Herbert van Thal for *The Seventh Pan Book of Horror Stories* (1966). Having noticed a great number of horror titles on the shelves of a bookseller, he wrote his own collection of horror stories and submitted it to two publishers simultaneously, embarrassing himself when they both accepted it. Becoming a highly prolific writer of short stories in the genre, he was given the Lifetime Achievement Award by both the Horror Writers of America and the British Fantasy Society in 1989. His stories were adapted for the films *From Beyond the Grave* (1973) and *The Monster Club* (1980). His story "Housebound" was the basis for an episode of *Rod Serling's Night Gallery* titled "Something in the Woodwork" (1973).

"The Ghouls" was first published in the author's short story collection, *The Night Ghouls* (London: Fontana, 1975).

R. CHETWYND-HAYES

THE GHOULS

THE DOORBELL RANG. A nasty long shrill ring that suggested an impatient caller or a faulty bell-button. Mr. Goldsmith did not receive many visitors. He muttered angrily, removed the saucepan of baked beans from the gas ring, then trudged slowly from the tiny kitchen across the even smaller hall and opened the front door. The bell continued to ring.

A tall, lean man faced him. One rigid finger seemed glued to the bell-button. The gaunt face had an unwholesome greenish tinge. The black, strangely dull eyes stared into Mr. Goldsmith's own and the mouth opened.

"Oosed o love hore . . ."

The shrill clatter of the doorbell mingled with the hoarse gibberish and Mr. Goldsmith experienced a blend of fear and anger. He shouted at the unwelcome intruder.

"Stop ringing the bell."

"Oosed o love hore . . ." the stranger repeated.

"Stop ringing the bloody bell." Mr. Goldsmith reached round the door frame and pulled the dirt-grimed hand away. It fell limply down to its owner's side, where it swung slowly back and forth, four fingers clenched, the fifth—the index finger—rigid, as though still seeking a bell-button to push. In the silence that followed, Mr. Goldsmith cleared his throat.

"Now, what is it you want?"

"Oosed o love hore." The stranger said again unintelligibly, then pushed by Mr. Goldsmith and entered the flat.

"Look here . . ." The little man ran after the intruder and tried to get in front of him, but the tall, lean figure advanced remorselessly towards the living-room, where it flopped down in Mr. Goldsmith's favourite armchair and sat looking blankly at a cheap Gauguin print that hung over the fireplace.

"I don't know what your little game is," Mr. Goldsmith was trying hard not to appear afraid, "but if you're not out of here in two minutes flat, I'll have the law around. Do you hear me?"

The stranger had forgotten to close his mouth. The lower jaw hung down like a lid with a broken hinge. His threadbare, black overcoat was held in place by a solitary, chipped button. A frayed, filthy red scarf was wound tightly round his scrawny neck. He presented a horrible, loathsome appearance. He also smelt.

The head came round slowly and Mr. Goldsmith saw the eyes were now watery, almost as if they were about to spill over the puffy lids and go streaming down the green-tinted cheeks.

"Oosed o love hore."

The voice was a gurgle that began somewhere deep down in the constricted throat and the words seemed to bubble like stew seething in a saucepan.

"What? What are you talking about?"

The head twisted from side to side. The loose skin round the neck concertinaed and the hands beat a tattoo on the chair arms.

"O-o-sed t-o-o l-o-v-e h-o-r-e."

"Used to live here!" A blast of understanding lit Mr. Goldsmith's brain and he felt quite pleased with his interpretative powers. "Well, you don't live here now, so you'll oblige me by getting out."

The stranger stirred. The legs, clad in a pair of decrepit corduroy trousers, moved back. The hands pressed down on the chair arms, and the tall form rose. He shuffled towards Mr. Goldsmith and the stomach-heaving stench came with him. Mr. Goldsmith was too petrified to move and could only stare at the approaching horror with fear-glazed eyes.

"Keep away," he whispered. "Touch me and . . . I'll shout . . ."

The face was only a few inches from his own. The hands came up and gripped the lapels of his jacket and with surprising strength, he was gently rocked back and forth. He heard the gurgling rumble; it gradually emerged into speech.

"Oi . . . um . . . dud . . . Oi . . . um . . . dud . . ."

Mr. Goldsmith stared into the watery eyes and had there been a third person present he might have supposed they were exchanging some mutual confidence.

"You're . . . what?"

The bubbling words came again.

"Oi . . . um . . . dud."

"You're bloody mad," Mr. Goldsmith whispered.

"Oi . . . um . . . dud."

Mr. Goldsmith yelped like a startled puppy and pulling himself free, ran for the front door. He leapt down the stairs, his legs operating by reflex, for there was no room for thought in his fear-misted brain.

Shop fronts slid by; paving stones loomed up, their rectangular shapes painted yellow by lamplight; startled faces drifted into his blurred vision, then disappeared and all the while the bubbling, ill-formed words echoed along the dark corridors of his brain.

"Oi . . . um . . . dud."

"Just a moment, sir."

A powerful hand gripped his arm and he swung round as the impetus of his flight was checked. A burly policeman stared down at him, suspicion peeping out of the small, blue eyes.

"Now, what's all this, sir. You'll do yourself an injury, running like that."

Mr. Goldsmith fought to regain his breath, eager to impart the vital knowledge. To share the burden.

"He's . . . he's dead."

The grip on his arm tightened.

"Now, calm yourself. Start from the beginning. Who's dead?"

"He . . ." Mr. Goldsmith gasped . . . "he rang the bell, wouldn't take his finger off the button . . . used to live there . . . then he sat in my chair . . . then got up . . . and told me . . . he was dead . . ."

A heavy silence followed, broken only by the purr of a passing car. The driver cast an interested glance at the spectacle of a little man being held firmly by a large policeman. The arm of the law finally gave utterance.

"He told you he was dead?"

"Yes." Mr. Goldsmith nodded, relieved to have shared his terrible information with an agent of authority. "He pronounced it *dud*."

"A northern corpse, no doubt," the policeman remarked with heavy irony.

"I don't think so," Mr. Goldsmith shook his head. "No, I think his vocal cords are decomposing. He sort of bubbles his words. They . . . well, ooze out."

"Ooze out," the constable repeated drily.

"Yes." Mr. Goldsmith remembered another important point. "And he smells."

"Booze?" enquired the policeman.

"No, a sort of sweet, sour smell. Rather like bad milk and dead roses."

The second silence lasted a little longer than the first, then the constable sighed deeply.

"I guess we'd better go along to your place of residence and investigate."

"Must we?" Mr. Goldsmith shuddered and the officer nodded.

"Yes, we must."

• • •

THE FRONT DOOR was still open. The hall light dared Mr. Goldsmith to enter and fear lurked in dark corners.

"Would you," Mr. Goldsmith hesitated, for no coward likes to bare his face, "would you go in first?"

"Right." The constable nodded, squared his shoulders, and entered the flat. Mr. Goldsmith found enough courage to advance as far as the doormat.

"In the living-room," he called out. "I left him in the living-room. The door on the left."

The police officer walked ponderously into the room indicated and after a few minutes came out again.

"No one there," he stated simply.

"The bedroom." Mr. Goldsmith pointed to another door. "He must have gone in there."

The policeman dutifully inspected the bedroom, the kitchen, then the bathroom before returning to the hall.

"I think it's quite safe for you to come in," he remarked caustically. "There's no one here—living or dead."

Mr. Goldsmith reoccupied his domain, much like an exiled king remounting his shaky throne.

"Now," the policeman produced a notebook and ball-point pen, "let's have a description."

"Pardon?"

"What did the fellow look like?" the officer asked with heavy patience.

"Oh. Tall, thin—very thin, his eyes were sort of runny, looked as if they might melt at any time, his hair was black and matted and he was dressed in an overcoat with one button . . ."

"Hold on," the officer admonished. "You're going too fast. Button . . ."

"It was chipped," Mr. Goldsmith added importantly. "And he wore an awful pair of corduroy trousers. And he looked dead. Now I come to think of it, I can't remember him breathing. Yes, I'm certain, he didn't breathe."

The constable put his notebook away, and took up a stance on the hearthrug.

"Now, look, Mr . . ."

"Goldsmith. Edward. J. Goldsmith."

"Well, Mr. Goldsmith . . ."

"The J is for Jeremiah but I never use it."

"As I was about to say, Mr. Goldsmith," the constable wore the expression of a man who was labouring under great strain, "I've seen a fair number of stiffs—I should say, dead bodies—in my time, and not one of them has ever talked. In fact, I'd say you can almost bank on it. They can burp, jerk, sit up, flop, bare their teeth, glare, even clutch when rigor mortis sets in, but never talk."

"But he said he was." Mr. Goldsmith was distressed that this nice, helpful policeman seemed unable to grasp the essential fact. "He said he was dud, and he looked and smelt dead."

"Ah, well now, that's another matter entirely." The constable looked like Sherlock Holmes, about to astound a dim-witted Watson. "This character you've described sounds to me like old Charlie. A proper old lay-about, sleeps rough and cadges what he can get from hotel kitchens and suchlike. A meths drinker no doubt and long ago lost whatever wits he ever had. I think he came up here for a hand-out. Probably stewed to the gills and lumbered by you when the door was open, intending to doss down in your living-room. I'll report this to the station sergeant and we'll get him picked up. No visible means of subsistence, you understand."

"Thank you." Mr. Goldsmith tried to feel relieved. "But . . ."

"Don't you worry anymore." The constable moved towards the door. "He won't bother you again. If you are all that worried, I'd have a chain put on your front door, then you can see who's there before you let them in."

Mr. Goldsmith said, "Yes," and it was with a somewhat lighter heart that he accompanied the policeman to the front door and politely handed him his helmet.

"A talking dead man!" The constable shook his head and let out a series of explosive chuckles. "Strewth!"

Mr. Goldsmith shut the door with a little

bang and stood with his back leaning against its mauve panels. By a very small circle of friends he was considered to be wildly artistic.

"He was." He spoke aloud. "He was dead. I know it."

HE REHEATED THE baked beans, prepared toast under the grill and opened a tin of mushrooms, then dined in the kitchen.

The evening passed. The television glared and told him things he did not wish to know; the newspaper shocked him and the gas fire went out. There were no more fivepenny pieces so he had no option but to go to bed.

The bed was warm; it was safe, it was soft. If anything dreadful happened he could always hide under the sheets. His book was comforting. It told a story of a beautiful young girl who could have been a famous film star if only she would sleep with a nasty, fat producer, but instead she cut the aspiring mogul down to size, and married her childhood sweetheart who earned twenty pounds a week in the local bank. Mr. Goldsmith derived much satisfaction from this happy state of affairs and, placing the book under his pillow, turned out the light and prepared to enter the land of dreams.

He almost got there.

His heart slowed down its beat. His brain flashed messages along the intricate network of nerves and contented itself all was well, although the stomach put in a formal complaint regarding the baked beans. It then began to shut off his five senses, before opening the strong-room where the fantasy treasures were stored. Then his ears detected a sound and his brain instantly ordered all senses on the alert.

Mr. Goldsmith sat up and vainly fumbled for the light switch, while a series of futile denials tripped off his tongue.

"No . . . no . . . no . . ."

The wardrobe doors were opening. It was a nice, big wardrobe, fitted with two mirror doors and Mr. Goldsmith watched the gleaming surfaces flash as they parted. A dark shape emerged from the bowels of the wardrobe; a tall, lean, slow-moving figure. Mr. Goldsmith would have screamed, had such a vocal action been possible, but his throat was dry and constricted and he could only manage a few croaking sounds. The dark figure shuffled towards the bed, poised for a moment like a tree about to fall, then twisted round and sat down. Mr. Goldsmith's afflicted throat permitted a whimpering sound as the long shape swung its legs up and lay down beside him. He could not see very well but he could smell and he could also hear. The strangled words bubbled up through the gloom.

"Oo . . . broot . . . cupper . . . Oi . . . hote . . . cuppers . . ."

They lay side by side for a little while, Mr. Goldsmith's whimpers merging with the bubbling lament.

"Oo . . . broot   cupper . . . Oi . . . um . . . dud . . . hote . . . cuppers . . . oll . . . cuppers . . . stunk . . ."

Mr. Goldsmith dared to toy with the idea of movement. He longed to put distance between himself and whatever lay bubbling on the bed. His hand moved prior to pulling back the bedclothes. Instantly cold fingers gripped his wrist, then slid down to his palm to grasp his hand.

"Oi . . . um . . . dud . . ."

"Not again," Mr. Goldsmith pleaded. "Not again."

Minutes passed. Mr. Goldsmith tried to disengage his hand from the moist, cold grip, but it only tightened. Eventually, the form stirred and to Mr. Goldsmith's horror, sat up and began to grope around with its free hand. The light shattered the gloom, chasing the shadows into obscure corners and Mr. Goldsmith found himself looking at that which he did not wish to see.

The face had taken on a deeper tinge of green; the eyes were possibly more watery and seemed on the point of dribbling down the cheeks. The mouth was a gaping hole where the black tongue writhed like a flattened worm. The bubbling sound cascaded up the windpipe with the threatening roar of a worn out geyser.

"G-oot dr-oosed . . ."

The figure swung its legs off the bed and began to move towards the fireplace, still retaining its icy grip on Mr. Goldsmith's hand, and forcing him to wriggle through the bedclothes and go stumbling after it. Over the mantelpiece was an old brass-handled naval cutlass, picked up for thirty shillings, back in the days when Mr. Goldsmith had first read *The Three Musketeers*. This, the creature laboriously removed from its hooks and turning slowly, raised it high above the terrified little man's head. The bubbling sound built up and repeated the earlier order.

"G-oot dr-oosed . . ."

Mr. Goldsmith got dressed.

THEY WALKED DOWN the empty street, hand-in-hand, looking at times like a father dragging his reluctant son to school. Mr. Goldsmith hungered for the merest glimpse of his friend the policeman, but the creature seemed to know all the back streets and alleys, pulling its victim through gaping holes in fences, taking advantage of every shadow, every dark corner. This, Mr. Goldsmith told himself in the brief periods when he was capable of coherent thought, was the instinct of an alley cat, the automatic reflexes of a fox. The creature was making for its hole and taking its prey with it.

They were in the dock area. Black, soot-grimed buildings reached up to a murky sky. Cobbled alleys ran under railway arches, skirted grim-faced warehouses, and terminated in litter-ridden wastelands cleared by Hitler's bombs, thirty years before. Mr. Goldsmith stumbled over uneven mounds crowned with sparse, rusty grass. He even fell down a hole, only to be promptly dragged out as the creature advanced with the ponderous, irresistible momentum of a Sherman tank.

The ground sloped towards a passage running between the remnants of brick walls. Presently there was a ceiling to which morsels of plaster still clung. Then the smell of burning wood—and a strange new stench of corruption.

They were in what had once been the cellar of a large warehouse. The main buildings had been gutted and their skeletons removed, but the roots, too far down to be affected by flame or bomb, still remained. The walls wept rivulets of moisture, the ceiling sagged, the floor was an uneven carpet of cracked cement, but to all intents, the cellar existed. An ancient bath stood on two spaced rows of bricks. Holes had been pierced in its rusty flanks, and it now held a pile of burning wood. Flame-tinted smoke made the place look like some forgotten inferno; it drifted up to the ceiling and coiled lazily round the black beams like torpid snakes looking for darkness. A number of hurricane lamps hung from beams and walls, so that once again Mr. Goldsmith was forced to look at that which he would rather have not seen.

They were crouched in a large circle round the fire, dressed in an assortment of old clothes, with green-tinted faces and watery eyes, gaping mouths and rigid fingers. Mr. Goldsmith's companion quelled any lingering doubts he might have had with the simplicity of a sledgehammer cracking a walnut.

"Oll . . . dud . . . oll . . . dud . . ."

"What's all this then?"

Two men stood behind Mr. Goldsmith and his companion. One was a tall, hulking fellow and the other a little runt of a man with the face of a crafty weasel. It was he who had spoken. He surveyed Mr. Goldsmith with a look of profound astonishment, then glared at the creature.

"Where the hell did you find him?"

The bubbling voice tried to explain.

"Ooosed o love thore . . ."

"You bloody stupid git." The little man began to pummel the creature about the stomach and chest and it retreated, the bubbling voice rising to a scream, like a steam kettle under full pressure.

"Oosed o love thore . . . broot cupper . . ."

The little man ceased his punitive operations and turned an anxious face towards his companion.

"'Ere what's all this, then? Did 'e say copper? His Nibs won't like that. Don't get the law worked up, 'e said."

The big man spoke slowly, his sole concern to calm his friend.

"Don't carry on, Maurice. Old Charlie's about 'ad it, ain't 'e? 'E'll be dropping apart soon if they don't get 'im mended and varnished up. The old brainbox must be in an 'ell of a state."

But Maurice would not be comforted. He turned to Mr. Goldsmith and gripped his coat front.

"Did you bring the law in? You call a copper?"

"I certainly summoned a police officer, when this," Mr. Goldsmith hesitated, "when this . . . person, refused to leave my flat."

"Cor strike a light." Maurice raised his eyes ceilingward. "'E calls a copper a police officer! Respectable as Sunday dinner. Probably got a trouble and strife who'll scream to 'igh 'eavens when 'er little wandering boy don't come 'ome for his milk and bickies."

"You married?" the big man asked, and Mr. Goldsmith, inspired by the wish to pacify his captors, shook his head.

"Live alone, aye?" The big man chuckled. "Thought so. Recognize the type. Keep yer 'air on, Maurice, he'll be just another missing person. The DPs will handle it."

"Yeah, Harry." Maurice nodded and released Mr. Goldsmith. "You're right. We'd better tie 'im up somewhere until His Nibs gets 'ere. He'll decide what to do with 'im."

Harry produced a length of rope and Mr. Goldsmith meekly allowed himself to be tied up, while "Charlie," for such it appeared was the creature's name, kept nudging Maurice's arm.

"Um . . . woont . . . meethy . . ."

"You don't deserve any methy." Maurice pushed the terrible figure to one side. "Making a bugger-up like this."

"Meethy . . ." Charlie repeated, "um . . . woont . . . meethy . . ."

"Bit of a waste of the blue stuff," Maurice

remarked drily. "'E's coming apart at the seams. Let me bash 'is 'ead in."

"Naw." Maurice shook his head. "'Is Nibs don't like us taking liberties with units. Besides the new repairing and varnishing machine can do wonders with 'em. 'E'd better have 'is ration with the rest."

Mr. Goldsmith, suitably bound, was dumped into a corner where he soon witnessed a scene that surpassed all the horror that had ridden on his shoulders since Charlie had rung his doorbell.

Harry came out of a cubby hole bearing a large saucepan with no handle. Maurice followed with a chipped mug. At once there was a grotesque stirring round the nightmare circle; legs moved, arms waved, mouths opened in the familiar bubbling speech and raucous cries. Placing the saucepan on a rickety table, Maurice began to call out in a high pitched voice.

"Methy . . . come on then . . . methy, methy, methy . . ."

There was a scrambling and scuffling, a united, bubbling, gurgling, raucous scream, and the entire pack came lumbering forward, pushing the feeble to one side, clawing in their determination to reach the enamel saucepan and the chipped mug. One scarecrow figure, clad in the remnants of an old army overcoat, fell or was pushed and landed with a resounding crash a few yards from Mr. Goldsmith. When he tried to rise, his left leg crumbled under him and the horrified spectator saw the jagged end of a thigh bone jutting out from a tear in threadbare trousers. There was no expression of pain on the green-tinted face but whatever spark of intelligence that still flickered in the brain finally prompted the creature to crawl over the uneven ground until it reached the table. Maurice looked down and kicked the writhing figure over on to its back. It lay howling in protest, like an upturned beetle, legs and arms flailing helplessly.

The chipped mug was dipped into the saucepan, a quarter filled with some blue liquid, then presented to the nearest gaping mouth. A green-tinted, wrinkled neck convulsed, then the mug was snatched away to be filled for the next consumer. Harry pulled the "fed one" to one side, then gave it a shove that sent the bundle of skin-wrapped bones lurching across the floor. Whatever the liquid was that came out of the saucepan, its effect on the receiver was little short of miraculous. All straightened up; some danced in a revolting, flopping, jumping movement. One creature did six knee-bends before its right knee made an ominous cracking sound. Another began clapping its hands and Maurice called out, "Cut that out," but his warning came too late. One hand fell off and landed on the floor with a nasty, soft thud. Mr. Goldsmith's stomach was considering violent action when Harry sauntered over and pointed to the offending item.

"Pick that up," he ordered.

The creature, still trying to clap with one hand, gazed at the big man with blank, watery eyes.

"Glop . . . glop," it bubbled.

"Never mind the glop-glop business. Pick the bloody thing up. I'm not 'aving you leave yer bits and pieces about. I'm telling yer for the last time—pick it up."

He raised a clenched fist and the creature bent down and took hold of its late appendage.

"Now put it in the bin," Harry instructed, pointing to an empty oil drum by the far wall. "You lot might be bone idle, but yer not going to be dead lazy."

Harry then turned to Maurice, who was completing his culinary duties.

"This lot's dead useless, Maurice. They're falling to bits. If this goes on, all we'll 'ave is a load of wriggling torsos. You've put too much EH471 in that stuff."

"Balls." Maurice cuffed a too eager consumer, who promptly retreated with one ear suspended by a strand of skin. "We can do some running repairs, can't we? A bit of tape, a few slats of wood, a few brooms. You carry on like a nun in a brothel."

"Well, so long as you explain the breakages to 'Is Nibs, it's all right with me," Harry stated, kicking a wizened little horror that was trying to turn a somersault on one hand and half an arm. "What's 'e hope to do with this lot?"

"Search me," Maurice shrugged. "Probably carve 'em up. 'E could take a leg from one, an arm from another, swop a few spare parts, and get 'imself a few working models."

Mr. Goldsmith had for some time been aware that some of the more antiquated models were displaying an unhealthy interest in his person. One, who appeared to have a faulty leg, shuffled over and examined the little man's lower members with a certain air of deliberation. A rigid forefinger poked his trouser leg, then the creature whose vocal cords seemed to be in better working order than Charlie's croaked: "Good . . . good."

"Go away," Mr. Goldsmith ordered, wriggling his legs frantically. "Shush, push off."

The creature pulled his trouser leg up and stared at the plump white flesh, like a cannibal viewing the week-end joint. He dribbled.

"Maurice—Harry." A sharp voice rang out. "What is the meaning of this? Get the units lined up at once."

It could have been the voice of a sergeant-major admonishing two slack NCOs; or a managing-director who has walked in on an office love-in. Maurice and Harry began to shout, pulling their charges into a rough file, pushing, swearing, punching, occasionally kicking the fragile units. His own particular tormentor was seized by the scruff of the neck and sent hurling towards the ragged line, that drooped, reeled, gurgled and bubbled in turn.

"Careful, man," the voice barked, "units cost money. Repairs take time."

"Sir." Maurice froze to a momentary attitude of attention, then went on with his marshalling activity with renewed, if somewhat subdued energy.

"Get into line, you dozy lot. Chests out, chins in, those who 'ave 'ands, down to yer flipping sides. Harry, a couple of brooms for that basket, three from the end. If 'e falls down, 'is bleeding 'ead will come off."

For the first time Mr. Goldsmith had the opportunity to examine the newcomer. He saw a mild-looking, middle-aged man, in a black jacket and pin-striped trousers. Glossy bowler hat, horn-rimmed spectacles and a brief case, completed the cartoonist conception of a civil servant. Maurice marched up to this personage and swung up a rather ragged salute.

"Units lined up and ready for your inspection, sir."

"Very well." His Nibs, for such Mr. Goldsmith assumed him to be, handed his brief case to Harry, then began to walk slowly along the file, scrutinizing each unit in turn.

"Maurice, why has this man got a hand missing?"

"Clapping, sir. The bleeder . . . beg pardon, the unit got carried away after methy, sir. Sort of came off in his 'and, sir."

His Nibs frowned.

"This is rank carelessness, Maurice. I have stressed time and time again, special attention must be paid to component parts at all times. Spare hands are hard to come by and it may become necessary to scrap this unit altogether. Don't let me have to mention this matter again."

"Sir."

His Nibs passed a few more units without comment, then stopped at the man whose ear still dangled by a single thread. He made a tut-tutting sound.

"Look at this, Maurice. This unit is a disgrace. For heaven's sake get him patched up. What HQ would say if they saw this sort of thing, I dare not think."

"Sir." Maurice turned his head and barked at Harry over one shoulder. "Take this unit and put his lughole back on with a strip of tape."

When His Nibs reached the unit propped up on two brooms, he fairly exploded.

"This is outrageous. Really, Maurice, words fail me. How you could allow a unit to come on parade in this condition, is beyond my comprehension."

"Beg pardon, sir, it fell over, sir."

"Look at it," His Nibs went on, ignoring the interruption. "The neck's broken." He touched the head and it wobbled most alarmingly. "The eyeballs are a disgrace, half an arm is missing, one leg is as about as useful as a woollen vest at a nudist picnic, and one foot is back to front."

Maurice glared at the unfortunate unit who was doing his best to bubble-talk. His Nibs sighed deeply.

"There is little point in berating the unit now, Maurice. The damage is done. We'll have to salvage what we can and the rest had better go into the scrap-bin."

Having completed his inspection, His Nibs turned and almost by chance his gaze alighted on Mr. Goldsmith.

"Maurice, what is this unit doing tied up?"

"Beg pardon, sir, but this ain't no unit, sir. It's a consumer that Charlie Unit brought in by error, sir."

His Nibs took off his spectacles, wiped them carefully on a black edged handkerchief, then replaced them.

"Let me get this clear, Maurice. Am I to understand that this is a live consumer? An actual, Mark one, flesh and blood citizen? In fact, not to mince words—a voter?"

"Yes, sir. A proper old Sunday-dinner-eater, go-to-Churcher, and take-a-bath-every-dayer, sir."

"And how, may I ask, did this unfortunate mistake occur?"

"Sent Charlie Unit out with a resurrection party, sir. Wandered off on his own; sort of remembered a place where 'e used to live, found this geezer—beg pardon, sir—this consumer, and brought 'im back 'ere, sir."

"Amazing!" His Nibs examined Mr. Goldsmith with great care. "A bit of luck, really. I mean, he'll need no repairs and with care he'll be ready for a Mark IV MB in no time at all."

"That's what I thought, sir." Maurice smirked and looked at Mr. Goldsmith with great satisfaction. "Might start a new line, sir. Bring 'em back alive."

"That's the next stage." His Nibs took his brief case from Harry. "In the meanwhile you had better untie him and I'll take him down to the office."

THE OFFICE WAS situated through the cubby hole and down twelve steps. It was surprisingly comfortable. A thick carpet covered the floor, orange wallpaper hid the walls and His Nibs seated himself behind a large, mahogany desk.

"Take a seat, my dear fellow," he invited, "I expect you'd like a cup of tea after your ordeal."

Mr. Goldsmith collapsed into a chair and nodded. The power of speech would return later, of that he felt certain. His Nibs picked up a telephone receiver.

"Tea for two," he ordered, "and not too strong. Yes, and some digestive biscuits. You'll find them filed under pending."

He replaced the receiver and beamed at Mr. Goldsmith.

"Now, I expect you're wondering what this is all about. Probably got ideas that something nasty is taking place, eh?"

Mr. Goldsmith could only nod.

"Then I am delighted to put your mind at rest. Nothing illegal is taking place here. This, my dear chap, is a government department."

Mr. Goldsmith gurgled.

"Yes," His Nibs went on, "a properly constituted government department, sired by the Ministry of Health, and complete with staff, filing cabinets and teacups. When I tell you this project sprang from the brain of a certain occupier of a certain house, situated in a certain street, not far from the gasworks at Westminster, I am certain that whatever doubts you may have entertained will be instantly dispelled."

Mr. Goldsmith made a sound that resembled an expiring bicycle tyre.

"I expect," His Nibs enquired, "you are asking yourself—why?"

Mr. Goldsmith groaned.

"The answer to your intelligent question can

be summed up in two words. Industrial strife. Until recently there was a dire labour shortage, and the great man to whom I referred was bedevilled by wage claims, strikes and rude men in cloth caps who would never take no for an answer. Then one night over his bedtime cup of cocoa, the idea came to him. The idea! Nay, the mental earthquake."

The door opened and a blond vision came in, carrying a tea tray. The vision had long blond hair and wore a neat tailored suit with brass buttons. Mr. Goldsmith said: "Cor."

"Ah, Myna and the cup that cheers," announced His Nibs with heavy joviality. "Put it down on the desk, my dear. Did you warm the pot?"

"Yes, sir." Myna smiled and put her tray down.

"Have the national intake figures come through yet?" His Nibs enquired.

"Yes, sir."

"And?"

"Three thousand, nine hundred and thirty-four."

"Capital, capital." His Nibs rubbed his hands together in satisfaction, then aimed a slap at Myna's bottom which happened to be conveniently to hand. The after effect was alarming.

Myna jerked, stiffened her fingers, opened her mouth and bubbled three words.

"Oi . . . um . . . dud . . ."

"Excuse me," His Nibs apologized to Mr. Goldsmith, "merely a technical hitch."

Rising quickly, he hurried round to Myna's front and twisted two brass buttons. The fingers relaxed, the eyes lit up and the mouth closed.

"Anything else, sir?" she enquired.

"No thank you, my dear," His Nibs smiled genially, "not for the time being."

Myna went out and His Nibs returned to his desk.

"Latest stream-lined model," he confided, "fitted with the Mark IV computer brain, but one has to be jolly careful. Slightest pat in the wrong place and puff—the damn thing goes

haywire. Now where was I? Oh, yes. The great idea."

He leant forward and pointed a finger at Mr. Goldsmith.

"Do you know how many living people there are in Britain today?"

"Ah—ah . . ." Mr. Goldsmith began.

"Precisely." His Nibs sat back. "Sixty-two million, take or lose a million. Sixty-two million actual or potential voters. Sixty-two million consumers, government destroyers and trade unionists. Now, what about the others?"

"Others," echoed Mr. Goldsmith.

"Ah, you've got the point. The dead. The wastage, the unused. One person in two thousand dies every twenty-four hours. That makes 30,000 bucket-kickers a day, 3,000,000 a year. One man, and one man only, saw the potential. Sitting there in his terrace house, drinking his cocoa and watching television, it came to him in a flash. Why not use the dead?"

"Use the dead," Mr. Goldsmith agreed.

"Taking up valuable building space." His Nibs was becoming quite heated. "Rotting away at the state's expense, using up marble and stonemason's time, and not paying a penny in taxes. He knew what had to be done. How to get down to the 'bones' of the matter."

For a while His Nibs appeared to be lost in thought. Mr. Goldsmith stared at a slogan that had been painted in black letters on the opposite wall

WASTE NOT—WANT NOT

Presently the precise voice went on.

"First we imported a few voodoo experts from the West Indies. After all, they had been turning out zombies for centuries. But we had to improve on their technique of course. I mean to say, we couldn't have them dancing round a fire, dressed up in loincloths and slitting cockerels' throats. So our chaps finally came up with METHY. *Ministry Everlasting Topside Hardened Youth.* No one knows what it means of course, but that is all to the good. If some of Them from the other side got hold of the formula, I shudder to think what might happen. The basis is methylated spirit—we found that pickled fairly well—then there's R245 and a small amount of E294 and, most important, 25 percent EH471 with 20 percent HW741 to cancel it out. You do follow me?"

Mr. Goldsmith shook his head, then fearful of giving offence, nodded violently.

"You have keen perception," His Nibs smiled. "It makes a nice change to talk to a consumer of the lower-middle class who does not confuse the issue by asking embarrassing questions. The latest stage is the Mark IV Mechanical Brain. After the unit has been repaired, decoked, and sealed with our all-purpose invisible varnish the nasty old, meddling brain is removed and Dr. You-Know-Who inserts his M. IV M.B., which does what it's told and no nonsense. No trade unions, no wage claims—no wages, in fact—no holidays, no food. Give 'em a couple of cups of METHY a day and they're good for years. Get the idea?"

Mr. Goldsmith found his voice.

"Who employs them?"

"Who doesn't?" His Nibs chuckled, then lowered his voice to a confidential whisper.

"Keep this under your hat, but you may remember a certain very large house situated at the end of the Mall, which had rather a lot of problems over the housekeeping bills."

Mr. Goldsmith turned pale.

"Not any more. All the lower servants were elevated from the churchyard, and some of the senior go out through one door and come back in through another, if you get my meaning. In fact there has been a suggestion . . . Well, never mind, that is still but a thought running round in a cabinet.

"Now, what are we going to do about you?"

Mr. Goldsmith stared hopefully at his questioner. He dared to put forward a suggestion.

"I could go home."

His Nibs smilingly shook his head.

"I fear not. You've seen too much and thanks to my flapping tongue, heard too much. No, I think we'd better give you the treatment. A nice little street accident should fill the bill. You wouldn't fancy walking under a moving bus, I suppose?"

Mr. Goldsmith displayed all the symptoms of extreme reluctance.

"You're sure? Pity. Never mind, Harry can simulate these things rather well. A broken neck, compound fracture of both legs; nothing we can't fix later on, then a tip-top funeral at government expense and the certainty of life after death. How's that sound?"

Mr. Goldsmith gulped and started a passionate love affair with the door.

"I can see you are moved," His Nibs chuckled. "You've gone quite pale with joy. I envy you, you know. It's not all of us who can serve our country. Remember: 'They also serve who only lie and rotticate.' Ha . . . ha . . . ha . . ."

His Nibs roared with uncontrollable merriment and lifted the receiver of his desk telephone.

"Myna, be a good girl and get Harry on the intercom. What! Teabreak! We'll have none of that nonsense here. Tell him to get down here in two minutes flat, or I'll have him fitted with an M. IV MB before he can put water to tea-bag."

He slammed the receiver down and glared at Mr. Goldsmith.

"Teabreak! I promise you, in five years' time there'll be no more teabreaks or dinner breaks, or three weeks' holiday with pay. We'll teach 'em."

The door opened and Harry all but ran into the office. He stamped his feet, stood rigidly to attention and swung up a salute.

"Resurrection Operator Harry Briggs reporting, sir."

His Nibs calmed down, wiped his brow on the black-edged handkerchief and reverted to his normal, precise manner of speech.

"Right, Harry, stand easy. This consumer is to be converted into a unit. I thought something in the line of a nice, tidy street accident. He won't be a missing person then, see. What are your suggestions?"

"Permission to examine the consumer, sir?"

His Nibs waved a languid hand.

"Help yourself, Harry."

Harry came over to Mr. Goldsmith and tilted his head forward so that his neck was bared.

"A couple of nifty chops should break his neck, sir, and I could rough his face up a bit—bash it against the wall. Then, with your permission, sir, run a ten-ton truck over his stomach—won't do 'is guts much good but 'e won't be needing 'em."

"Methy," His Nibs explained to Mr. Goldsmith, "works through the nervous system. The stomach is surplus to requirements."

"Then I thought a couple of swipes with an iron bar about 'ere." Harry pointed to Mr. Goldsmith's trembling thighs. "And 'ere." He indicated a spot above the ankles. "Won't do to touch the knee caps, seeing as 'ow they're 'ard to replace."

"You'll have no trouble with repairs afterwards?" His Nibs enquired.

"Gawd bless us, no, sir. A couple of rivets in the neck, a bit of patching up here and there. We'll have to replace the eyes. They gets a bit runny after a bit. Otherwise, 'e'll make a first-class unit, such as you can be proud of, sir."

"Very creditable." His Nibs beamed his approval. "You'd better fill in an LD142 and lay on transport to transfer the, eh . . . unit to the accident point. Let me see . . ." He consulted a desk diary. "Today's Wednesday—coroner's inquest on Friday—yes, we can fit the funeral in next Tuesday."

"Tuesday, sir," Harry nodded.

"Then your resurrection units can get cracking Tuesday night. No point in letting things rot, eh?"

His Nibs roared again and Harry permitted himself a respectful titter.

"Well, my dear chap," His Nibs said to Mr. Goldsmith. "This time next week you should be doing something useful."

"Where were you thinking of fitting 'im in, sir?" Harry enquired.

"We'll start him off as a porter at Waterloo Station. The railway union have a wage claim in the pipeline and one more non-industrial action vote will do no harm. Right, Harry, take him away."

Fear may make cowards; it can also transform a coward into a man of action. The sight of Harry's large hand descending on to his neck triggered off a series of reflexes in Mr. Goldsmith which culminated in him leaping from his chair and racing for the door. His behaviour up to that moment had been co-operative, so both His Nibs and Harry were taken by surprise and for three precious moments could only stare after him with speechless astonishment. Meanwhile, Mr. Goldsmith was through the door and passing Myna, who presumably had not been programmed for such an emergency, for she sat behind her desk, typing away serenely, ignoring Harry's bellows of rage. But they spurred the little man to greater efforts and he mounted the stairs with the determination of an Olympic hurdler chasing a gold medal. He burst into the cellar, by-passing the recumbent units and was on his way to the exit before a startled Maurice had been galvanized into action.

He was like a rabbit chased by two blood-thirsty hounds, when he pounded up the ramp and came to the waste ground. A sickly moon played hide and seek from behind scudding clouds and a black cat screamed its fear and rage, as he went stumbling over mounds and potholes, discarded tins clattering before his blundering feet. They were about twenty feet behind, silent now, for the unmentionable was heading for the domain of the commonplace and their business must be done in shadows without sound or word.

Mr. Goldsmith crossed a cobbled road, galloped under a railway arch and stumbled into a narrow alley. A convenient hole in a fence presented itself; he squeezed through just before running footsteps rounded the nearest corner.

They came to a halt only a few paces from his hiding place. Maurice's voice was that of a weasel deprived of a supper.

"The little bleeder's got away."

"Won't get far," Harry comforted.

"Better get back," Maurice admitted reluctantly. "His Nibs will have to notify a DPC."

The footsteps shuffled, then retreated and Mr. Goldsmith dared to breathe again. He emerged from his hole and began to trudge wearily down the alley. He wandered for a long time, completely lost, shying from shadows, running before a barking dog, adrift in a nightmare. He came out into a small square and there on the far side, its steeple reaching up towards the moon, was a church. The doors were tight shut, but the building evoked childhood memories, and he knelt on the steps, crying softly, like a child locked out by thoughtless parents.

Heavy footsteps made him start and he rose quickly, before casting a terrified glance along the moonlit pavement. A tall, burly figure was moving towards him with all the majesty of a frigate under full sail. His silver buttons gleamed like stars in a velvet sky. His badge shone like a beacon of hope. Mr. Goldsmith gave a cry of joy and ran towards his protector. He gripped the great, coarse hands; he thrust his face against the blue tunic and sobbed with pure relief.

"Now, what's all this?" the officer enquired. "Not more dead men that talk?"

"Hundreds of them." Mr. Goldsmith stammered in his effort to be believed. "They are emptying the churchyards. You've got to stop them."

"There, there. You leave it all to me, sir. Just come along to the station and we'll get it all down in a statement."

"Yes . . . yes." Mr. Goldsmith perceived the sanity in such an arrangement. "Yes, I . . . I will make a statement. Then you'll lock me up, won't you? So they can't reach me?"

"Anything you say," the constable agreed. "We'll lock you up so well, no one will ever be able to reach you again. Come along now."

They moved away from the locked church with Mr. Goldsmith pouring out a torrent of words. The policeman was a good listener and encouraged him with an occasional: "Beyond belief, sir . . . You don't say so, sir . . . It only goes to show . . . Truth is stranger than fiction."

Mr. Goldsmith agreed that it was, but a disturbing factor had caused a cold shiver to mar his newly acquired sense of well-being.

"Why are we going down this alley?"

"A short cut, sir," the constable replied. "No sense in tiring ourselves with a long walk."

"Oh." Mr. Goldsmith snatched at this piece of logic like a condemned man at the rope which is to hang him. "Is the station far?"

"A mere stone's throw, sir. A last, few steps, you might say."

They progressed the length of the passage, then turned a corner. The officer trod on an upturned dustbin lid and promptly swore. "Damned careless of someone. You might have broken your neck, sir."

"This is the way I came," Mr. Goldsmith stated and the policeman's grip tightened.

"Is it now, sir? Sort of retracing your footsteps."

Hope was sliding down a steep ramp as Mr. Goldsmith started to struggle. "You . . ." But the grip on his arm was a band of steel. He clawed at the blue tunic and twisted a silver button. The bubbling words came from a long way off.

"Oi . . . um . . . dud . . ."

The moon peeped coyly from behind a cloud and watched a burly, but dead policeman drag a struggling little man towards eternity.

THE CORPSE-MASTER

SEABURY QUINN

NO CHARACTER APPEARED in the pages of the prestigious pulp
magazine *Weird Tales* with greater regularity than Jules de Grandin, the occult
detective created by Seabury (Grandin) Quinn (1889–1969). The first de Grandin story, "The Horror on the Links," appeared in the October 1925 issue, and
he battled vampires, zombies, werewolves, mummies, ghosts, and other supernatural foes in ninety-three stories over the next thirty years.

Quinn was born in Washington, D.C., graduated from the law school of the
National University and practiced until serving in World War I, was a lawyer
for the government during World War II, and returned to the legal profession
later in life. In between, he was a prolific pulp writer and edited several trade
publications of the funeral business. Under the pseudonym Jerome Burke, he
wrote fictionalized human-interest stories that had been told to him as reminis-
cences of funeral directors. He was instrumental in founding the Washington
Science Fiction Association. His first published story, "The Stone Image," appeared in the May 1, 1919, issue of *The Thrill Book*. The first of his 154 stories
for *Weird Tales* was "The Phantom Farmhouse" in the October 1923 issue. He
wrote about five hundred stories in all.

Jules de Grandin, a noted French surgeon and intelligence agent who moves
to America, settles in the town of Harrisonville, New Jersey, with his friend Dr.
Trowbridge, who chronicles the cases of apparently supernatural and occult
crimes, most of which turn out to be rationally explained, merely the result of
human ingenuity and, frequently, depravity.

"The Corpse-Maker" was originally published in the July 1929 issue of *Weird
Tales;* it was first collected in book form in *The Phantom Fighter* (Sauk City, WI:
Mycroft & Moran, 1966).

SEABURY QUINN

THE CORPSE-MASTER

THE AMBULANCE-GONG INSISTENCE of my night bell brought me up standing from a stuporlike sleep, and as I switched the vestibule light on and unbarred the door, "Are you the doctor?" asked a breathless voice. A disheveled youth half fell through the doorway and clawed my sleeve desperately. "Quick—quick, Doctor! It's my uncle, Colonel Evans. He's dying. I think he tried to kill himself—"

"All right," I agreed, turning to sprint up-

stairs. "What sort of wound has he?—or was it poison?"

"It's his throat, sir. He tried to cut it. Please, hurry, Doctor!"

I took the last four steps at a bound, snatched some clothes from the bedside chair and charged down again, pulling on my garments like a fireman answering a night alarm. "Now, which way—" I began, but:

"*Tiens,*" a querulous voice broke in as Jules

de Grandin came downstairs, seeming to miss half treads in his haste. "Let him tell us where to go as we go there, my old one! It is that we should make the haste. A cut throat does not wait patiently."

"This is Dr. de Grandin," I told the young man. "He will be of great assistance—"

"*Mais oui*," the little Frenchman agreed, "and the Trump of Judgment will serve excellently as an alarm clock if we delay our going long enough. Make haste, my friend!"

"Down two blocks and over one," our caller directed as we got under way, "376 Albion Road. My uncle went to bed about ten o'clock, according to the servants, and none of them heard him moving about since. I got home just a few minutes ago, and found him lying in the bathroom when I went to wash my teeth. He lay beside the tub with a razor in his hand, and blood was all over the place. It was awful!"

"Undoubtlessly," de Grandin murmured from his place on the rear seat. "What did you do then, young Monsieur?"

"Snatched a roll of gauze from the medicine cabinet and staunched the wound as well as I could, then called Dockery the gardener to hold it in place while I raced round to see you. I remembered seeing your sign sometime before."

We drew up to the Evans house as he concluded his recital, and rushed through the door and up the stairs together. "In there," our companion directed, pointing to a door from which there gushed a stream of light into the darkened hall.

A man in bathrobe and slippers knelt above a recumbent form stretched full-length on the white tiles of the bathroom. One glance at the supine figure and both de Grandin and I turned away, I with a deprecating shake of my head, the Frenchman with a fatalistic shrug.

"He has no need of us, that poor one," he informed the young man. "Ten minutes ago, perhaps yes; now"—another shrug—"the undertaker and the clergyman, perhaps the police—"

"The police? Surely, Doctor, this is suicide—"

"Do you say so?" de Grandin interrupted

sharply. "Trowbridge, my friend, consider this, if you please." Deftly he raised the dead man's thin white beard and pointed to the deeply incised slash across the throat. "Does that mean nothing?"

"Why—er—"

"Perfectly. Wipe your pince-nez before you look a second time, and tell me that you see the cut runs diagonally from right to left."

"Why, so it does, but—"

"But Monsieur the deceased was right-handed—look how the razor lies beneath his right hand. Now, if you will raise your hand to your own throat and draw the index finger across it as if it were a knife, you will note the course is slightly out of horizontal—somewhat diagonal—slanting downward from left to right. It is not so?"

I nodded as I completed the gesture.

"*Très bien.* When one is bent on suicide he screws his courage to the sticking point, then, if he has chosen a cut throat as means of exit, he usually stands before a mirror, cuts deeply and quickly with his knife, and makes a downward-slanting slash. But as he sees the blood and feels the pain his resolution weakens, and the gash becomes more and more shallow. At the end it trails away to little more than a skin-scratch. It is not so in this case; at its end the wound is deeper than at the beginning.

"Again, this poor one would almost certainly have stood before the mirror to do away with himself. Had he done so he would have fallen crosswise of the room, perhaps; more likely not. One with a severed throat does not die quickly. He thrashes about like a fowl recently decapitated, and writes the story of his struggle plainly on his surroundings. What have we here? Do you—does anyone—think it likely that a man would slit his gullet, then lie down peacefully to bleed his life away, as this one appears to have done? *Non, non;* it is not *en caractère!*

"Consider further"—he pointed with dramatic suddenness to the dead man's bald head—"if we desire further proof, observe him!"

Plainly marked there was a welt of bruised

flesh on the hairless scalp, the mark of some blunt instrument.

"He might have struck his head as he fell," I hazarded, and he grinned in derision.

"*Ah bah*, I tell you he was stunned unconscious by some miscreant, then dragged or carried to this room and slaughtered like a poleaxed beef. Without the telltale mark of the butcher's bludgeon there is ground for suspicion in the quietude of his position, in the neat manner the razor lies beneath his hand instead of being firmly grasped or flung away, but with this bruise before us there is but one answer. He has been done to death; he has been butchered; he was murdered."

"WILL YE BE seein' Sergeant Costello?" Nora McGinnis appeared like a phantom at the drawing room door as de Grandin and I were having coffee next evening after dinner. "He says—"

"Invite him to come in and say it for himself, *ma petite*," Jules de Grandin answered with a smile of welcome at the big red-headed man who loomed behind the trim figure of my household factotum. "Is it about the Evans killing you would talk with us?" he added as the detective accepted a cigar and demi-tasse.

"There's two of 'em, now, sir," Costello answered gloomily. "Mulligan, who pounds a beat in th' Eighth Ward, just 'phoned in there's a murder dressed up like a suicide at th' Rangers' Club in Frémont Street."

"*Pardieu*, another?" asked de Grandin. "How do you know the latest one is not true suicide?"

"Well, sir, heres' th' pitch. When th' feller from th' club comes runnin' out to say that Mr. Wolkof's shot himself, Mulligan goes in and takes a look around. He finds him layin' on his back with a little hole in his forehead an' th' back blown out o' his head, an', bein' th' wise lad, he adds up two an' two and makes it come out four. He'd used a Colt .45, this Wolkof feller, an' it was layin' halfway in his hand, restin' on his half-closed fingers, ye might say. That didn't

look too kosher. A feller who's been shot through the forehead is more likely to freeze tight to th' gun than otherwise. Certain'y he don't just hold it easy-like. Besides, it was an old-fashioned black-powder gun, sir, what they call a low-velocity weapon, and if it had been fired close against the dead man's forehead it should 'a' left a good-sized smudge o' powder-stain. There wasn't any."

"One commends the excellent Mulligan for his reasoning," de Grandin commented. "He found this Monsieur Wolkof lying on his back with a hole drilled through his head, no powder-brand upon his brow where the projectile entered, and the presumably suicidal weapon lying loosely in his hand. One thing more: it may not be conclusive, but it would be helpful to know if there were any powder-stains upon the dead man's pistol-hand."

"As far's I know there weren't, sir," answered Costello. "Mulligan said he took partic'lar notice of his hands, too. But ye're yet to hear th' cream o' th' joke. Th' pistol was in Mr. Wolkof's open right hand, an' all th' club attendants swear he was left-handed—writin', feedin' himself an' shavin' with his left hand exclusively. Now, I ask ye, Dr. de Grandin, would a man all steamed up to blow his brains out be takin' th' trouble to break a lifetime habit of left-handedness when he's so much more important things to think about? It seems to me that—"

"Ye're wanted on th' 'phone, Sergeant," announced Nora from the doorway. "Will ye be takin' it in here, or usin' th' hall instrument?"

"Hullo? Costello speakin'," he challenged. "If it's about th' Wolkof case, I'm goin' right over—glory be to God! No! Och, th' murderin' blackguard!

"Gentlemen," he faced us, fury in his ruddy face and blazing blue eyes, "it's another one. A little girl, this time. They've kilt a tiny, wee baby while we sat here like three damn' fools and talked! They've took her body to th' morgue—"

"Then, *nom d'un chameau*, why are we remaining here?" de Grandin interrupted. "Come, *mes amis*, it is to hasten. Let us go all quickly!"

• • •

WITH MY HORN tooting almost continuously, and Costello waving aside crossing policemen, we rushed to the city mortuary. Parnell, the coroner's physician, fussed over a tray of instruments, Coroner Martin bustled about in a perfect fever of eagerness to begin his official duties; two plainclothes men conferred in muted whispers in the outer office.

Death in the raw is never pretty, as doctors, soldiers and embalmers know only too well. When it is accompanied by violence it wears a still less lovely aspect, and when the victim is a child the sight is almost heart-breaking. Bruised and battered almost beyond human semblance, her baby-fine hair matted with mixed blood and cerebral matter, little Hazel Clark lay before us, the queer, unnatural angle of her right wrist denoting a Colles' fracture; a subclavicular dislocation of the left shoulder was apparent by the projection of the bone beneath the clavicle, and the vault of her small skull had been literally beaten in. She was completely "broken" as ever a medieval malefactor was when bound upon the wheel of torture for the ministrations of the executioner.

For a moment de Grandin bent above the battered little corpse, viewing it intently with the skilled, knowing eye of a pathologist, then, so lightly that they scarcely displaced a hair of her head, his fingers moved quickly over her, pausing now and again to prod gently, then sweeping onward in their investigative course. "*Tiens*, he was a gorilla for strength, that one," he announced, "and a veritable gorilla for savagery, as well. What is there to tell me of the case, *mes amis*?" he called to the plainclothes men.

Such meager data as they had they gave him quickly. She was three and a half years old, the idol of her lately widowed father, and had neither brothers nor sisters. That afternoon her father had given her a quarter as reward for having gone a whole week without meriting a scolding, and shortly after dinner she had set out for the corner drug store to purchase an ice cream cone

with part of her righteously acquired wealth. Attendants at the pharmacy remembered she had left the place immediately and set out for home; a neighbor had seen her proceeding up the street, the cone grasped tightly in her hand as she sampled it with ecstatic little licks. Two minutes later, from a spot where the privet hedge of a vacant house shadowed the pavement, residents of the block had heard a scream, but squealing children were no novelty in the neighborhood, and the cry was not repeated. It was not till her father came looking for her that they recalled it.

From the drug store Mr. Clark traced Hazel's homeward course, and was passing the deserted house when he noticed a stain on the sidewalk. A lighted match showed the discoloration was a spot of blood some four inches across, and with panic premonition tearing at his heart he pushed through the hedge to the unmowed lawn of the vacant residence. Match after match he struck while he called "Hazel! Hazel!" but there was no response, and he saw nothing till he was about to return to the street. Then, in a weed-choked rose bed, almost hidden by the foliage, he saw the gleam of her pink pinafore. His cries aroused the neighborhood, and the police were notified.

House-to-house inquiry by detectives finally elicited the information that a "short, stoop-shouldered man" had been seen walking hurriedly away a moment after the child's scream was heard. Further description of the suspect was unavailable.

"*Pardieu,*" de Grandin stroked his small mustache thoughtfully as the plainclothes men concluded, "it seems we have to search the haystack for an almost microscopic needle, *n'est-ce pas?* There are considerable numbers of small men with stooping shoulders. The task will be a hard one."

"Hard, hell!" one of the detectives rejoined in disgust. "We got no more chance o' findin' that bird than a pig has o' wearin' vest-pockets."

"Do you say so?" the Frenchman demanded, fixing an uncompromising cat-stare on the speaker. "*Alors*, my friend, prepare to meet a fully tailored porker before you are greatly older.

Have you forgotten in the excitement that I am in the case?"

"Sergeant, sir," a uniformed patrolman hurried into the mortuary, "they found th' weapon used on th' Clark girl. It's a winder-sash weight. They're testin' it for fingerprints at headquarters now."

"Humph," Costello commented. "Anything on it?"

"Yes, *sir.* Th' killer must 'a' handled it after he dragged her body into th' bushes, for there's marks o' bloody fingers on it plain as day."

"O.K., I'll be right up," Costello replied. "Take over, Jacobs," he ordered one of the plainclothes men. "I'll call ye if they find out anything, Dr. de Grandin. So long!"

The Sergeant delayed his report, and next morning after dinner the Frenchman suggested, "Would it not be well to interview the girl's father? I should appreciate it if you will accompany and introduce me."

"He's in the drawing room," the maid told us as we knocked gently on the Clark door. "He's been there ever since they brought her home, sir. Just sitting beside her and—" she broke off as her throat filled with sobs. "If you could take his mind off of his trouble it would be a Godsend. If he'd only cry, or sumpin—"

"Grief is a hot, consuming fire, Madame," the little Frenchman whispered, "and only tears can quell it. The dry-eyed mourner is the one most likely to collapse."

Coroner Martin had done his work as a mortician with consummate artistry. Under his deft hands all signs of the brutality that struck the child down had been effaced. Clothed in a short light-pink dress she lay peacefully in her casket, one soft pink cheek against the tufted silken pillow sewn with artificial forget-me-nots, a little bisque doll, dressed in a frock the exact duplicate of her own, resting in the crook of her left elbow. Beside the casket, a smile sadder than any grimace of woe on his thin, ascetic features, sat Mortimer Clark.

As we tiptoed into the darkened room we heard him murmur, "Time for shut-eye town,

daughter. Daddy'll tell you a story." For a moment he looked expectantly into the still childish face on the pillow before him, as if waiting for an answer. The little gilt clock on the mantel ticked with a sort of whispering haste; far down the block a neighbor's dog howled dismally; a light breeze bustled through the opened windows, fluttering the white-scrim curtains and setting the orange flames of the tall candles at the casket's head and foot to flickering.

It was weird, this stricken man's vigil beside his dead, it was ghastly to hear him addressing her as if she could hear and reply. As the story of the old woman and her pig progressed I felt a kind of terrified tension about my heart. ". . . the cat began to kill the rat, the rat began to gnaw the rope, the rope began to hang the butcher—"

"*Grand Dieu,*" de Grandin whispered as he plucked me by the elbow, "let us not look at it, Friend Trowbridge. It is a profanation for our eyes to see, our ears to hear what goes on here. *Sang de Saint Pierre,* I, Jules de Grandin, swear that I shall find the one who caused this thing to be, and when I find him, though he take refuge beneath the very throne of God, I'll drag him forth and cast him screaming into hell. God do so to me, and more also, if I do not!" Tears were coursing down his cheeks, and he let them flow unabashed.

"You don't want to talk to him, then?" I whispered as we neared the front door.

"I do not, neither do I wish to tell indecent stories to the priest as he elevates the Host. The one would be no greater sacrilege than the other, but—*ah*?" he broke off, staring at a small framed parchment hanging on the wall. "Tell me, my friend," he demanded, "what is it that you see there?"

"Why, it's a certificate of membership in the Rangers' Club. Clark was in the Army Air Force, and—"

"*Très bien,*" he broke in. "Thank you. Our ideas sometimes lead us to see what we wish when in reality it is not there; that is why I sought the testimony of disinterested eyes."

"What in the world has Clark's membership in the Rangers got to do with—"

"*Zut!*" he waved me to silence. "I think, I cogitate, I concentrate, my old one. Monsieur Evens—Monsieur Wolkof, now Monsieur Clark—all are members of that club. *C'est très étrange.* Me, I shall interview the steward of that club, my friend. Perhaps his words may throw more light on these so despicable doings than all the clumsy, well-meant investigations of our friend Costello. Come, let us go away. Tomorrow will do as well as today, for the miscreant who fancies himself secure is in no hurry to decamp, despite the nonsense talked of the guilty who flee when no man pursueth."

WE FOUND COSTELLO waiting for us when we reached home. A very worried-looking Costello he was, too. "We've checked th' finger-prints on th' sash-weight, sir," he announced almost truculently.

"*Bon,*" the Frenchman replied carelessly. "Is it that they are of someone you can identify?"

"I'll say they are," the sergeant returned shortly. "They're Gyp Carson's—th' meanest killer th' force ever had to deal with."

"Ah," de Grandin shook off his air of preoccupation with visible effort, "it is for you to find this Monsieur Gyp, my friend. You have perhaps some inkling of his present whereabouts?"

The sergeant's laugh was almost an hysterical cackle. "That we have, sir, that we have! They burnt—you know, electrocuted—him last month in Trenton for th' murder of a milk-wagon driver durin' a hold-up. By rights he should be in Mount Olivet Cemetery this minute, an' by th' same token he should 'a' been there when the little Clark girl was kilt last night."

"A-a-ah?" de Grandin twisted his wheat-blond mustache furiously. "It seems this case contains the possibilities, my friend. Tomorrow morning, if you please, we shall go to the cemetery and investigate the grave of Monsieur Gyp. Perhaps we shall find something there. If we find

nothing we shall have found the most valuable information we can have."

"If we find nothin'—" The big Irishman looked at him in bewilderment. "All right, sir. I've seen some funny things since I been runnin' round with you, but if you're tellin' me—"

"*Tenez,* my friend, I tell you nothing; nothing at all. I too seek information. Let us wait until the morning, then see what testimony pick and shovel will give."

A SUPERINTENDENT AND two workmen waited for us at the grave when we arrived at the cemetery next morning. The grave lay in the newer, less expensive portion of the burying ground where perpetual care was not so conscientiously maintained as in the better sections. Scrub grass fought for a foothold in the clayey soil, and the mound had already begun to fall in. Incongruously, a monument bearing the effigy of a weeping angel leaned over the grave-head, while a footstone with the inscription OUR DARLING guarded its lower end.

The superintendent glanced over Costello's papers, stowed them in an inner pocket and nodded to the Polish laborers. "Git goin'," he ordered tersely, "an' make it snappy."

The diggers' picks and spades bored deep and deeper in the hard-packed, sun-baked earth. At last the hollow sound of steel on wood warned us their quest was drawing to a close. A pair of strong web straps was let down and made fast to the rough chestnut box in which the casket rested, and the men strained at the thongs to bring their weird freight to the surface. Two pick-handles were laid across the violated grave and on them the box rested. With a wrench the superintendent undid the screws that held the clay-stained lid in place and laid it aside. Within we saw the casket, a cheap, square-ended affair covered with shoddy gray broadcloth, the tinny imitation-silver name plate and crucifix on its lid already showing a dull brown-blue discoloration.

"*Maintenant!*" murmured de Grandin breathlessly as the superintendent began unlatching the fastenings that held the upper portion of the casket lid. Then, as the last catch snapped back and the cover came away:

"Feu noir de l'enfer!"

"Good heavens!" I exclaimed.

"For th' love o' God!" Costello's amazed antiphon sounded at my elbow.

The cheap sateen pillow of the casket showed a depression like the pillow of a bed recently vacated, and the poorly made upholstery of its bottom displayed a wide furrow, as though flattened by some weight imposed on it for a considerable time, but sign or trace of human body there was none. The case was empty as it left the factory.

"Glory be to God!" Costello muttered hoarsely, staring at the empty casket as though loath to believe his own eyes. "An' this is broad daylight," he added in a kind of wondering afterthought.

"Précisément," de Grandin's acid answer came back like a whipcrack. "This is diagnostic, my friend. Had we found something here it might have meant one thing or another. Here we find nothing; nothing at all. What does it mean?"

"I know what it means!" The look of superstitious fear on Costello's broad red face gave way to one of furious anger. "It means there's been some monkey-business goin' on—who had this buryin'?" he turned savagely on the superintendent.

"Donally," the other returned, "but don't blame me for it. I just work here."

"Huh, Donally, eh? We'll see what Mr. Donally has to say about this, an' he'd better have plenty to say, too, if he don't want to collect himself from th' corners o' a four-acre lot."

Donally's Funeral Parlors were new but by no means prosperous-looking. Situated in a small side street in the poor section of town, their only pretention to elegance was the brightly-gleaming gold sign on their window:

JOSEPH DONALLY
FUNERAL DIRECTOR & EMBALMER
SEXTON ST. ROSE'S R.C. CHURCH

"See here, young feller me lad," Costello began without preliminary as he stamped unceremoniously into the small, dark room that constituted Mr. Donally's office and reception foyer, "come clean, an' come clean in a hurry. Was Gyp Carson dead when you had his funeral?"

"If he wasn't we sure played one awful dirty trick on him," the mortician replied. "What'd ye think would happen to you if they set you in that piece o' furniture down at Trenton an' turned the juice on? What d'ye mean, 'was he dead'?"

"I mean just what I say, wise guy. I've just come from Mount Olivet an' looked into his coffin, an' if there's hide or hair of a corpse in it I'll eat it, so I will!"

"What's that? You say th' casket was empty?"

"As your head."

"Well, I'll be—" Mr. Donally began, but Costello forestalled him:

"You sure will, an' all beat up, too, if you don't spill th' low-down. Come clean, now, or do I have to sock ye in th' jaw an' lock ye up in th' bargain?"

"Whatcher tryin' to put over?" Mr. Donally demanded. "Think I faked up a stall funeral? Lookit here, if you don't believe me." From a pigeon hole of his desk he produced a sheaf of papers, thumbed through them, and handed Costello a packet fastened with a rubber band.

Everything was in order. The death certificate, signed by the prison physician, showed the cause of death as cardiac arrest by fibrillary contraction induced by three shocks of an alternating current of electricity of $7\frac{1}{2}$ amperes at a pressure of 2,000 volts.

"I didn't have much time," Donally volunteered. "The prison doctors had made a full post, an' his old woman was one o' them old-fashioned folks that don't believe in embalmin', so there was nothin' to do but rush him to th' graveyard an' plant him. Not so bad for me, though, at that. I sold 'em a casket an' burial suit an' twenty-five limousines for th' funeral, an' got a cut on th' monument, too."

De Grandin eyed him speculatively. "Have

you any reason to believe attempts at resuscitation were made?" he asked.

"Huh? Resuscitate *that?* Didn't I just tell you they'd made a full autopsy on him at the prison? Didn't miss a damn thing either. You might as well try resuscitatin' a lump o' hamburger as bring back a feller which had had that done to him."

"Quite so," de Grandin nodded. "I did but ask. Now—"

"Now we don't know no more than we did an hour ago," the sergeant supplied. "I might 'a' thought this guy was in cahoots with Gyp's folks, but th' prison records show he was dead, an' th' doctors down at Trenton don't certify nobody's dead if there's a flicker o' eyelash left in him. Looks as if we've got to find some gink with a fad for grave-robbin', don't it, Dr. de Grandin?

"But say"—a sudden gleam of inspiration overspread his face—"suppose someone had dug him up an' taken an impression of his fingerprints, then had rubber gloves made with th' prints on th' outside o' th' fingers? Wouldn't it be a horse on th' force for him to go around murderin' people, an' leave his weapons lyin' round promiscuous-like, so's we'd be sure to find what we thought was his prints, only to discover they'd been made by a gunman who'd been burnt a month or more before?"

"*Tiens*, my friend, your supposition has at least the foundation of reason beneath it," de Grandin conceded. "Do you make search for one who might have done the thing you suspect. Me, I have certain searching of my own to do. Anon we shall confer, and together we shall surely lay this so vile miscreant by the heels."

"AH, BUT IT has been a lovely day," he assured me with twinkling eyes as he contemplated the glowing end of his cigar that evening after dinner. "Yes, *pardieu*, an exceedingly lovely day! This morning when I went from that Monsieur Donally's shop my head whirled like that of an unaccustomed voyager stricken by sea-

sickness. Only miserable uncertainty confronted me on every side. Now"—he blew a cone of fragrant smoke from his lips and watched it spiral slowly toward the ceiling—"now I know much, and that I do not actually know I damn surmise. I think I see the end of this so tortuous trail, Friend Trowbridge."

"How's that?" I encouraged, watching him from the corners of my eyes.

"How? *Cordieu*, I shall tell you! When Friend Costello told us of the murder of Monsieur Wolkof—that second murder which was made to appear suicide—and mentioned he met death at the Rangers' Club, I suddenly recalled that Colonel Evans, whose death we had so recently deplored, was also a member of that club. It struck me at the time there might be something more than mere coincidence in it; but when that pitiful Monsieur Clark also proved to be a member, *nom d'un asperge*, coincidence ceased to be coincidence and became moral certainty.

" 'Now,' I ask me, 'what lies behind this business of the monkey? Is it not strange two members of the Rangers' Club should have been slain so near together, and in such similar circumstances, and a third should have been visited with a calamity worse than death?'

" 'You have said it, *mon garçon*,' I tell me. 'It is indubitably as you say. Come, let us interview the steward of that club, and see what he shall say.'

"*Nom d'un pipe*, what did he not tell? From him I learn much more than he said. I learn, by example, that Messieurs Evans, Wolkof and Clark had long been friends; that they had all been members of the club's grievance committee; that they were called on some five years ago to recommend expulsion of a Monsieur Wallagin—*mon Dieu*, what a name!

" 'So far, so fine,' I tell me. 'But what of this Monsieur-with-the-Funny-Name? Who and what is he, and what has he done to be flung out of the club?'

"I made careful inquiry and found much. He has been an explorer of considerable note and has written some monographs which showed he understood the use of his eyes. *Hélas*, he knew also how to use wits, as many of his fellow members learned to their sorrow when they played cards with him. Furthermore, he had a most unpleasant stock of stories which he gloried to tell—stories of his doings in the far places which did not recommend him to the company of self-respecting gentlemen. And so he was removed from the club's rolls, and vowed he would get level with Messieurs Evans, Clark and Wolkof if it took him fifty years to do so.

"Five years have passed since then, and Monsieur Wallagin seems to have prospered exceedingly. He has a large house in the suburbs where no one but himself and one servant—always a Chinese—lives, but the neighbors tell strange stories of the parties he holds, parties at which pretty ladies in strange attire appear, and once or twice strange-looking men as well.

"*Eh bien*, why should this rouse my suspicions? I do not know, unless it be that my nose scents the odor of the rodent farther than the average. At any rate, out to the house of Monsieur Wallagin I go, and at its gate I wait like a tramp in the hope of charity.

"My vigil is not unrewarded. But no. Before I have stood there an hour I behold one forcibly ejected from the house by a gross person who reminds me most unpleasantly of a pig. It is a small and elderly Chinese man, and he has suffered greatly in his *amour propre.* I join him in his walk to town, and sympathize with him in his misfortune.

"My friend"—his earnestness seemed out of all proportion to the simple statement—"he had been forcibly dismissed for putting salt in the food which he cooked for Monsieur Wallagin's guests."

"For salting their food?" I asked. "Why—"

"One wonders why, indeed, Friend Trowbridge. Consider, if you please. Monsieur Wallagin has several guests, and feeds them thin gruel made of wheat or barley, and bread in which no salt is used. Nothing more. He personally tastes of it before it is presented to them, that he may make sure it is unsalted."

"Perhaps they're on some sort of special diet," I hazarded as he waited for my comment. "They're not obliged to stay and eat unseasoned food, are they?"

"I do not know," he answered soberly. "I greatly fear they are, but we shall know before so very long. If what I damn suspect is true we shall see devilment beside which the worst produced by ancient Rome was mild. If I am wrong— *alors,* it is that I am wrong. I think I hear the good Costello coming; let us go with him."

Evening had brought little surcease from the heat, and perspiration streamed down Costello's face and mine as we drove toward Morrisdale, but de Grandin seemed in a chill of excitement, his little round blue eyes were alight with dancing elf-fires, his small white teeth fairly chattering with nervous excitation as he leant across the back of the seat, urging me to greater speed.

The house near which we parked was a massive stone affair, standing back from the road in a jungle of greenery, and seemed to me principally remarkable for the fact that it had neither front nor rear porches, but rose sheer-walled as a prison from its foundations.

Led by the Frenchman we made cautious way to the house, creeping to the only window showing a gleam of light and fastening our eyes to the narrow crack beneath its not-quite-drawn blind.

"Monsieur Wallagin acquired a new cook this afternoon," de Grandin whispered. "I made it my especial business to see him and bribe him heavily to smuggle a tiny bit of beef into the soup he prepares for tonight. If he has been faithful in his treachery we may see something, if not— *pah*, my friends, what is it we have here?"

We looked into a room which must have been several degrees hotter than the stoke-hole of a steamer, for the window was shut tightly and a great log fire blazed on the wide hearth of the fireplace almost opposite our point of vantage. Its walls were smooth-dressed stone, the floor was paved with tile. Lolling on a sort of divan made of heaped-up cushions sat the master of the house, a monstrous bulk of a man with enormous paunch, great fat-upholstered shoulders between which perched a hairless head like an owl's in its feathers, and eyes as cold and gray as twin inlays of burnished agate.

About his shoulders draped a robe of Paisley pattern, belted at the loins but open to the waist, displaying his obese abdomen as he squatted like an evil parody of Mi-lei-Fo, China's Laughing Buddha.

As we fixed our eyes to the gap under the curtain he beat his hands together, and as at a signal the door at the room's farther end swung open to admit a file of women. All three were young and comely, and each a perfect foil for the others. First came a tall and statuesque brunette with flowing unbound black hair, sharp-hewn patrician features and a majesty of carriage like a youthful queen's. The second was a petite blonde, fairylike in form and elfin in face, and behind her was a red-haired girl, plumply rounded as a little pullet. Last of all there came an undersized, stoop-shouldered man who bore what seemed an earthern vessel like a New England bean-pot and two short lengths of willow sticks.

"Jeeze!" breathed Costello. "Lookit him, Dr. de Grandin; 'tis Gyp Carson himself!"

"Silence!" the Frenchman whispered fiercely. "Observe, my friends; did I not say we should see something? *Regardez-vous!*"

At a signal from the seated man the women ranged themselves before him, arms uplifted, heads bent submissively, and the undersized man dropped down tailor-fashion in a corner of the room, nursing the clay pot between his crossed knees and poising his sticks over it.

The obese master of the revels struck his hands together again, and at their impact the man on the floor began to beat a rataplan upon his crock.

The women started a slow rigadoon, sliding their bare feet sidewise, stopping to stamp out a grotesque rhythm, then pirouetting languidly and taking up the sliding, sidling step again. Their arms were stretched straight out, as if they had been crucified against the air, and as they danced they shook and twitched their shoulders with a motion reminiscent of the shimmy of the

early 1920s. Each wore a shift of silken netlike fabric that covered her from shoulder to instep, sleeveless and unbelted, and as they danced the garments clung in rippling, half-revealing, half-concealing folds about them.

They moved with a peculiar lack of verve, like marionettes actuated by unseen strings, sleep-walkers, or persons in hypnosis; only the drummer seemed to take an interest in his task. His hands shook as he plied his drumsticks, his shoulders jerked and twitched and writhed hysterically, and though his eyes were closed and his face masklike, it seemed instinct with avid longing, with prurient expectancy.

"*Les aisselles*—their axillae, Friend Trowbridge, observe them with care, if you please!" de Grandin breathed in my ear.

Sudden recognition came to me. With the raising of their hands in the performance of the dance the women exposed their armpits, and under each left arm I saw the mark of a deep wound, bloodless despite its depth, and closed with the familiar "baseball stitch."

No surgeon leaves a wound like that, it was the mark of the embalmer's bistoury made in cutting through the superficial tissue to raise the axillary artery for his injection.

"Good God!" I choked. The languidness of their movements . . . their pallor . . . their closed eyes . . . their fixed, unsmiling faces . . . now the unmistakable stigmata of embalmment! These were no living women, they were—

De Grandin's fingers clutched my elbow fiercely. "Observe, my friend," he ordered softly. "Now we shall see if my plan carried or miscarried."

Shuffling into the room, as unconcerned as if he served coffee after a formal meal, came a Chinese bearing a tray on which were four small soup bowls and a plate of dry bread. He set the tray on the floor before the fat man and turned away, paying no attention to the dancing figures and the drummer squatting in the corner.

An indolent motion of the master's hand and the slaves fell on their provender like famished beasts at feeding time, drinking greedily from the coarse china bowls, wolfing the unbuttered bread almost unchewed.

Such a look of dawning realization as spread over the four countenances as they drained the broth I have seen sometimes when half-conscious patients were revived with powerful restoratives. The man was first to show it, surging from his crouching position and turning his closed eyes this way and that, like a caged thing seeking escape from its prison. But before he could do more than wheel drunkenly in his tracks realization seemed to strike the women, too. There was a swirl of fluttering draperies, the soft thud of soft feet on the tiled floor of the room, and all rushed pellmell to the door.

The sharp clutch of de Grandin's hand roused me. "Quick, Friend Trowbridge," he commanded. "To the cemetery; to the cemetery with all haste! *Nom d'un sale chameau,* we have yet to see the end of this!"

"Which cemetery?" I asked as we stumbled toward my parked car.

"*N'importe,*" he returned. "At Shadow Lawn or Mount Olivet we shall see that which will make us call ourselves three shameless liars!"

Mount Olivet was nearest of the three municipalities of the dead adjacent to Harrisonville, and toward it we made top speed. The driveway gates had closed at sunset, but the small gates each side the main entrance were still unlatched, and we raced through them and to the humble tomb we had seen violated that morning.

"Say, Dr. de Grandin," panted Costello as he strove to keep pace with the agile little Frenchman, "just what's th' big idea? I know ye've some good reason, but—"

"Take cover!" interrupted the other. "Behold, my friends, he comes!"

Shuffling drunkenly, stumbling over mounded tops of sodded graves, a slouching figure came careening toward us, veered off as it neared the Carson grave and dropped to its knees beside it. A moment later it was scrabbling at the clay and gravel which had been disturbed by the grave-diggers that morning, seeking desperately to burrow its way into the sepulcher.

"Me God!" Costello breathed as he rose unsteadily. I could see the tiny globules of fear-sweat standing on his forehead, but his inbred sense of duty overmastered his fright. "Gyp Carson, I arrest you—" he laid a hand on the burrowing creature's shoulder, and it was as if he touched a soap bubble. There was a frightened mouselike squeak, then a despairing groan, and the figure under his hand collapsed in a crumpled heap. When de Grandin and I reached them the pale, drawn face of a corpse grinned at us sardonically in the beam of Costello's flashlight.

"Dr.—de—Grandin, Dr.—Trowbridge—for th' love o' God give me a drink o' sumpin!" begged the big Irishman, clutching the diminutive Frenchman's shoulder as a frightened child might clutch its mother's skirts.

"Courage, my old one," de Grandin patted the detective's hand, "we have work before us tonight, remember. Tomorrow they will bury this poor one. The law has had its will of him; now let his body rest in peace. Tonight—*sacré nom,* the dead must tend the dead; it is with the living we have business. *En avant;* to Wallagin's, Friend Trowbridge!"

"Your solution of the case was sane," he told Costello as we set out for the house we'd left a little while before, "but there are times when very sanity proves the falseness of a conclusion. That someone had unearthed the body of Gyp Carson to copy his fingerprints seemed most reasonable, but today I obtained information which led me up another road. A most unpleasant road, *parbleu!* I have already told you something of the history of the Wallagin person; how he was dismissed from the Rangers' Club, and how he vowed a horrid vengeance on those voting his expulsion. That was of interest. I sought still further. I found that he resided long in Haiti, and that there he mingled with the *Culte de Morts.* We laugh at such things here, but in Haiti, that dark stepdaughter of mysterious Africa's dark mysteries, they are no laughing matter. No. In Port-au-Prince and in the backlands of the jungle they will tell you of the *zombie—*

who is neither ghost nor yet a living person resurrected, but only the spiritless corpse ravished from its grave, endowed with pseudo-life by black magic and made to serve the whim of the magician who has animated it. Sometimes wicked persons steal a corpse to make it commit crime while they stay far from the scene, thus furnishing themselves unbreakable alibis. More often they rob graves to secure slaves who labor ceaselessly for them at no wages at all. Yes, it is so; with my own eyes I have seen it.

"But there are certain limits which no sorcery can transcend. The poor dead *zombie* must be fed, for if he is not he cannot serve his so execrable master. But he must be fed only certain things. If he taste salt or meat, though but the tiniest *soupçon* of either be concealed in a great quantity of food, he at once realizes he is dead, and goes back to his grave, nor can the strongest magic of his owner stay him from returning for one little second. Furthermore, when he goes back he is dead forever after. He cannot be raised from the grave a second time, for Death which has been cheated for so long asserts itself, and the putrefaction which was stayed during the *zombie*'s period of servitude takes place all quickly, so the *zombie* dead six months, if it returns to its grave and so much as touches its hand to the earth, becomes at once like any other six-months-dead corpse—a mass of putrescence pleasant neither to the eye nor nose, but preferable to the dead-alive thing it was a moment before.

"Consider then: the steward of the Rangers' Club related dreadful tales this Monsieur Wallagin had told all boastfully—how he had learned to be a *zombie*-maker, a corpse-master, in Haiti; how the mysteries of *Papa Nebo, Gouédé Mazacca* and *Gouédé Oussou,* those dread oracles of the dead, were opened books to him.

" 'Ah-ha, Monsieur Wallagin,' I say, 'I damn suspect you have been up to business of the monkey here in this so pleasant State of New Jersey. You have, it seems, brought here the mysteries of Haiti, and with them you wreak vengeance on those you hate, *n'est-ce pas?*'

"Thereafter I go to his house, meet the little, discharged Chinese man, and talk with him. For why was he discharged with violence? Because, by blue, *he had put salt in the soup of the guests whom Monsieur Wallagin entertains.*

" 'Four guests he has, you say?' I remark. 'I had not heard he had so many.'

" '*Nom d'un nom,* yes,' the excellent *Chinois* tells me. 'There are one man and three so lovely women in that house, and all seem walking in their sleep. At night he has the women dance while the man makes music with the drum. Sometimes he sends the man out, but what to do I do not know. At night, also, he feeds them bread and soup with neither salt nor meat, food not fit for a mangy dog to lap.'

" 'Oh, excellent old man of China, oh, paragon of all Celestials,' I reply, 'behold, I give you money. Now, come with me and we shall hire another cook for your late master, and we shall bribe him well to smuggle meat into the soup he makes for those strange guests. Salt the monster might detect when he tastes the soup before it are served, but a little, tiny bit of beef-meat, *non.* Nevertheless, it will serve excellently for my purposes.'

"*Voila,* my friends, there is the explanation of tonight's so dreadful scenes."

"But what are we to do?" I asked. "You can't arrest this Wallagin. No court on earth would try him on such charges as you make."

"Do *you* believe it, Friend Costello?" de Grandin asked the detective.

"Sure, I do, sir. Ain't I seen it with me own two eyes?"

"And what should be this one's punishment?"

"Och, Dr. de Grandin, are you kiddin'? What would we do if we saw a poison snake on th' sidewalk, an' us with a jolly bit o' blackthorn in our hands?"

"*Précisément,* I think we understand each other perfectly, *mon vieux.*" He thrust his slender, womanishly small hand out and lost it in the depths of the detective's great fist.

"Would you be good enough to wait us here,

Friend Trowbridge?" he asked as we came to a halt before the house. "There is a trifle of unfinished business to attend to and—the night is fine, the view exquisite. I think that you would greatly enjoy it for a little while, my old and rare."

IT MIGHT HAVE been a quarter-hour later when they rejoined me. "What—" I began, but the perfectly expressionless expression on de Grandin's face arrested my question.

"*Hélas*, my friend, it was unfortunate," he told me. "The good Costello was about to arrest him, and he turned to flee. Straight up the long, steep stairs he fled, and at the topmost one, *parbleu*, he missed his footing and came tumbling down! I greatly fear—indeed, I know—his neck was broken in the fall. It is not so, *mon sergent?*" he turned to Costello for confirmation. "Did he not fall downstairs?"

"That he did, sir. Twice. Th' first time didn't quite finish him."

THE UPPER BERTH

F. MARION CRAWFORD

ALTHOUGH HE DESCRIBED himself as American and referred to America as home, F.(rancis) Marion Crawford (1854–1909) was born in Bagni di Lucca, Italy, and was mainly educated at Cambridge University (England), the University of Heidelberg (Germany), and the University of Rome (Italy). He spent two years in India, studying Sanskrit. In 1881, he moved to Italy, where he lived permanently, though he spent many winters in New York.

His books were very successful from the beginning, though a rather sumptuous lifestyle and enormous generosity forced him to work at a ferocious pace, producing about five thousand words a day and two or more novels a year almost until the day he died. He was primarily a romanticist and was often accused of writing too quickly and too prolifically to allow the full expression of his talent. His villains were absolutely black, his heroes were unrealistically virtuous, and his women characters of unsurpassed perfection, which, a cousin of his noted, was the way he saw people in the real world.

His vivid, picturesque novels, for all the impressive sales and popularity during his lifetime, have not stood the test of time and few modern readers are likely to know, much less be tempted to dip into, what are regarded as his finest works: *Saracinesca* (1887), *Sant' Ilario* (1888), or *Don Orsino* (1891). The same is not true of "The Upper Berth," his most famous and frequently anthologized tale, which H. P. Lovecraft described as "one of the most tremendous horror stories in all literature" in his critical history, *Supernatural Horror in Literature*.

"The Upper Berth" was first collected in a very rare book, *The Broken Shaft* (New York: Putnam, 1886), and then, because of its reputation as a small masterpiece, it was published in the collection *The Upper Berth* (London: T. Fisher Unwin, 1894).

F. MARION CRAWFORD

THE UPPER BERTH

SOMEBODY ASKED FOR the cigars. We had talked long, and the conversation was beginning to languish; the tobacco smoke had got into the heavy curtains, the wine had got into those brains which were liable to become heavy, and it was already perfectly evident that, unless somebody did something to rouse our oppressed spirits, the meeting would soon come to its natural conclusion, and we, the guests, would speedily go home to bed, and most certainly to sleep. No one had said anything very remarkable; it may be that no one had anything very remarkable to say. Jones had given us every particular of his last hunting adventure in Yorkshire. Mr. Tompkins, of Boston, had explained at elaborate length those working principles, by the due and careful maintenance of which the Atchison, Topeka, and Santa Fé Railroad not only extended its territory, increased its departmental influence, and transported live stock without starving them to death before the day of actual delivery, but, also, had for years succeeded in deceiving those passengers who bought its tickets into the fallacious belief that the corporation aforesaid was really able to transport human life without destroying it. Signor Tombola had endeavoured to persuade us, by arguments which we took no trouble to oppose, that the unity of his country in no way resembled the average modern torpedo, carefully planned, constructed with all the skill of the greatest European arsenals, but, when constructed, destined to be directed by feeble hands into a region where it must undoubtedly explode, unseen, unfeared, and unheard, into the illimitable wastes of political chaos.

It is unnecessary to go into further details. The conversation had assumed proportions which would have bored Prometheus on his rock, which would have driven Tantalus to distraction, and which would have impelled Ixion to seek relaxation in the simple but instructive dialogues of Herr Ollendorff, rather than submit to the greater evil of listening to our talk. We had sat at table for hours; we were bored, we were tired, and nobody showed signs of moving.

Somebody called for cigars. We all instinctively looked towards the speaker. Brisbane was a man of five-and-thirty years of age, and remarkable for those gifts which chiefly attract the attention of men. He was a strong man. The external proportions of his figure presented nothing extraordinary to the common eye, though his size was above the average. He was a little over six feet in height, and moderately broad in the shoulder; he did not appear to be stout, but, on the other hand, he was certainly not thin; his small head was supported by a strong and sinewy neck; his broad muscular hands appeared to possess a peculiar skill in breaking walnuts without the assistance of the ordinary cracker, and, seeing him in profile, one could not help remarking the extraordinary breadth of his sleeves, and the unusual thickness of his chest. He was one of those men who are commonly spoken of among men as deceptive; that is to say, that though he looked exceedingly strong he was in reality very much stronger than he looked. Of his features I need say little. His head is small, his hair is thin, his eyes are blue, his nose is large, he has a small moustache, and a square jaw. Everybody knows Brisbane, and when he asked for a cigar everybody looked at him.

"It is a very singular thing," said Brisbane.

Everybody stopped talking. Brisbane's voice was not loud, but possessed a peculiar quality of penetrating general conversation, and cutting it like a knife. Everybody listened. Brisbane, perceiving that he had attracted their general attention, lit his cigar with great equanimity.

"It is very singular," he continued, "that thing about ghosts. People are always asking whether anybody has seen a ghost. I have."

"Bosh! What, you? You don't mean to say so, Brisbane? Well, for a man of his intelligence!"

A chorus of exclamations greeted Brisbane's remarkable statement. Everybody called for cigars, and Stubbs the butler suddenly appeared from the depths of nowhere with a fresh bottle of dry champagne. The situation was saved; Brisbane was going to tell a story.

I am an old sailor, said Brisbane, and as I have to cross the Atlantic pretty often, I have my favourites. Most men have their favourites. I have seen a man wait in a Broadway bar for three-quarters of an hour for a particular car which he liked. I believe the bar-keeper made at least one-third of his living by that man's preference. I have a habit of waiting for certain ships when I am obliged to cross that duck-pond. It may be a prejudice, but I was never cheated out of a good passage but once in my life. I remember it very well; it was a warm morning in June, and the Custom House officials, who were hanging about waiting for a steamer already on her way up from the Quarantine, presented a peculiarly hazy and thoughtful appearance. I had not much luggage—I never have. I mingled with the crowd of passengers, porters, and officious individuals in blue coats and brass buttons, who seemed to spring up like mushrooms from the deck of a moored steamer to obtrude their unnecessary services upon the independent passenger. I have

often noticed with a certain interest the spontaneous evolution of these fellows. They are not there when you arrive; five minutes after the pilot has called "Go ahead!" they, or at least their blue coats and brass buttons, have disappeared from deck and gangway as completely as though they had been consigned to that locker which tradition unanimously ascribes to Davy Jones. But, at the moment of starting, they are there, clean-shaved, blue-coated, and ravenous for fees. I hastened on board. The Kamtschatka was one of my favourite ships. I say was, because she emphatically no longer is. I cannot conceive of any inducement which could entice me to make another voyage in her. Yes, I know what you are going to say. She is uncommonly clean in the run aft, she has enough bluffing off in the bows to keep her dry, and the lower berths are most of them double. She has a lot of advantages, but I won't cross in her again. Excuse the digression. I got on board. I hailed a steward, whose red nose and redder whiskers were equally familiar to me.

"One hundred and five, lower berth," said I, in the businesslike tone peculiar to men who think no more of crossing the Atlantic than taking a whisky cocktail at downtown Delmonico's.

The steward took my portmanteau, great coat, and rug. I shall never forget the expression of his face. Not that he turned pale. It is maintained by the most eminent divines that even miracles cannot change the course of nature. I have no hesitation in saying that he did not turn pale; but, from his expression, I judged that he was either about to shed tears, to sneeze, or to drop my portmanteau. As the latter contained two bottles of particularly fine old sherry presented to me for my voyage by my old friend Snigginson van Pickyns, I felt extremely nervous. But the steward did none of these things.

"Well, I'm d——d!" said he in a low voice, and led the way.

I supposed my Hermes, as he led me to the lower regions, had had a little grog, but I said nothing, and followed him. One hundred and five was on the port side, well aft. There was nothing remarkable about the state-room. The lower berth, like most of those upon the Kamtschatka, was double. There was plenty of room; there was the usual washing apparatus, calculated to convey an idea of luxury to the mind of a North-American Indian; there were the usual inefficient racks of brown wood, in which it is more easy to hang a large-sized umbrella than the common tooth-brush of commerce. Upon the uninviting mattresses were carefully folded together those blankets which a great modern humorist has aptly compared to cold buckwheat cakes. The question of towels was left entirely to the imagination. The glass decanters were filled with a transparent liquid faintly tinged with brown, but from which an odor less faint, but not more pleasing, ascended to the nostrils, like a far-off sea-sick reminiscence of oily machinery. Sad-coloured curtains half-closed the upper berth. The hazy June daylight shed a faint illumination upon the desolate little scene. Ugh! how I hate that state-room!

The steward deposited my traps and looked at me, as though he wanted to get away—probably in search of more passengers and more fees. It is always a good plan to start in favour with those functionaries, and I accordingly gave him certain coins there and then.

"I'll try and make yer comfortable all I can," he remarked, as he put the coins in his pocket. Nevertheless, there was a doubtful intonation in his voice which surprised me. Possibly his scale of fees had gone up, and he was not satisfied; but on the whole I was inclined to think that, as he himself would have expressed it, he was "the better for a glass." I was wrong, however, and did the man injustice.

II.

Nothing especially worthy of mention occurred during that day. We left the pier punctually, and it was very pleasant to be fairly under way, for the weather was warm and sultry, and the motion of the steamer produced a refreshing breeze. Everybody knows what the first day at sea is like. People pace the decks and stare at each other, and occasionally meet acquaintances whom they did not know to be on board. There is the usual uncertainty as to whether the food will be good, bad, or indifferent, until the first two meals have put the matter beyond a doubt; there is the usual uncertainty about the weather, until the ship is fairly off Fire Island. The tables are crowded at first, and then suddenly thinned. Pale-faced people spring from their seats and precipitate themselves towards the door, and each old sailor breathes more freely as his sea-sick neighbour rushes from his side, leaving him plenty of elbow room and an unlimited command over the mustard.

One passage across the Atlantic is very much like another, and we who cross very often do not make the voyage for the sake of novelty. Whales and icebergs are indeed always objects of interest, but, after all, one whale is very much like another whale, and one rarely sees an iceberg at close quarters. To the majority of us the most delightful moment of the day on board an ocean steamer is when we have taken our last turn on deck, have smoked our last cigar, and having succeeded in tiring ourselves, feel at liberty to turn in with a clear conscience. On that first night of the voyage I felt particularly lazy, and went to bed in one hundred and five rather earlier than I usually do. As I turned in, I was amazed to see that I was to have a companion. A portmanteau, very like my own, lay in the opposite corner, and in the upper berth had been deposited a neatly folded rug with a stick and umbrella. I had hoped to be alone, and I was disappointed; but I wondered who my room-mate was to be, and I determined to have a look at him.

Before I had been long in bed he entered. He was, as far as I could see, a very tall man, very thin, very pale, with sandy hair and whiskers and colourless grey eyes. He had about him, I thought, an air of rather dubious fashion; the sort of man you might see in Wall Street, without being able precisely to say what he was doing there—the sort of man who frequents the

Café Anglais, who always seems to be alone and who drinks champagne; you might meet him on a race-course, but he would never appear to be doing anything there either. A little over-dressed—a little odd. There are three or four of his kind on every ocean steamer. I made up my mind that I did not care to make his acquaintance, and I went to sleep saying to myself that I would study his habits in order to avoid him. If he rose early, I would rise late; if he went to bed late, I would go to bed early. I did not care to know him. If you once know people of that kind they are always turning up. Poor fellow! I need not have taken the trouble to come to so many decisions about him, for I never saw him again after that first night in one hundred and five.

I was sleeping soundly when I was suddenly waked by a loud noise. To judge from the sound, my room-mate must have sprung with a single leap from the upper berth to the floor. I heard him fumbling with the latch and bolt of the door, which opened almost immediately, and then I heard his footsteps as he ran at full speed down the passage, leaving the door open behind him. The ship was rolling a little, and I expected to hear him stumble or fall, but he ran as though he were running for his life. The door swung on its hinges with the motion of the vessel, and the sound annoyed me. I got up and shut it, and groped my way back to my berth in the darkness. I went to sleep again; but I have no idea how long I slept.

When I awoke it was still quite dark, but I felt a disagreeable sensation of cold, and it seemed to me that the air was damp. You know the peculiar smell of a cabin which has been wet with sea-water. I covered myself up as well as I could and dozed off again, framing complaints to be made the next day, and selecting the most powerful epithets in the language. I could hear my room-mate turn over in the upper berth. He had probably returned while I was asleep. Once I thought I heard him groan, and I argued that he was sea-sick. That is particularly unpleasant when one is below. Nevertheless I dozed off and slept till early daylight.

The ship was rolling heavily, much more than on the previous evening, and the grey light which came in through the porthole changed in tint with every movement according as the angle of the vessel's side turned the glass seawards or skywards. It was very cold—unaccountably so for the month of June. I turned my head and looked at the porthole, and saw to my surprise that it was wide open and hooked back. I believe I swore audibly. Then I got up and shut it. As I turned back I glanced at the upper berth. The curtains were drawn close together; my companion had probably felt cold as well as I. It struck me that I had slept enough. The state-room was uncomfortable, though, strange to say, I could not smell the dampness which had annoyed me in the night. My room-mate was still asleep—excellent opportunity for avoiding him, so I dressed at once and went on deck. The day was warm and cloudy, with an oily smell on the water. It was seven o'clock as I came out—much later than I had imagined. I came across the doctor, who was taking his first sniff of the morning air. He was a young man from the West of Ireland—a tremendous fellow, with black hair and blue eyes, already inclined to be stout; he had a happy-go-lucky, healthy look about him which was rather attractive.

"Fine morning," I remarked, by way of introduction.

"Well," said he, eying me with an air of ready interest, "it's a fine morning and it's not a fine morning. I don't think it's much of a morning."

"Well, no—it is not so very fine," said I.

"It's just what I call fuggly weather," replied the doctor.

"It was very cold last night, I thought," I remarked. "However, when I looked about, I found that the porthole was wide open. I had not noticed it when I went to bed. And the state-room was damp, too."

"Damp!" said he. "Whereabouts are you?"

"One hundred and five—"

To my surprise the doctor started visibly, and stared at me.

"What is the matter?" I asked.

"Oh—nothing," he answered; "only everybody has complained of that state-room for the last three trips."

"I shall complain too," I said. "It has certainly not been properly aired. It is a shame!"

"I don't believe it can be helped," answered the doctor. "I believe there is something—well, it is not my business to frighten passengers."

"You need not be afraid of frightening me," I replied. "I can stand any amount of damp. If I should get a bad cold I will come to you."

I offered the doctor a cigar, which he took and examined very critically.

"It is not so much the damp," he remarked. "However, I dare say you will get on very well. Have you a room-mate?"

"Yes; a deuce of a fellow, who bolts out in the middle of the night and leaves the door open."

Again the doctor glanced curiously at me. Then he lit the cigar and looked grave.

"Did he come back?" he asked presently.

"Yes. I was asleep, but I waked up and heard him moving. Then I felt cold and went to sleep again. This morning I found the porthole open."

"Look here," said the doctor, quietly, "I don't care much for this ship. I don't care a rap for her reputation. I tell you what I will do. I have a good-sized place up here. I will share it with you, though I don't know you from Adam."

I was very much surprised at the proposition. I could not imagine why he should take such a sudden interest in my welfare. However, his manner as he spoke of the ship was peculiar.

"You are very good, doctor," I said. "But really, I believe even now the cabin could be aired, or cleaned out, or something. Why do you not care for the ship?"

"We are not superstitious in our profession, sir," replied the doctor. "But the sea makes people so. I don't want to prejudice you, and I don't want to frighten you, but if you will take my advice you will move in here. I would as soon see you overboard," he added, "as know that you or any other man was to sleep in one hundred and five."

"Good gracious! Why?" I asked.

"Just because on the last three trips the people who have slept there actually have gone overboard," he answered, gravely.

The intelligence was startling and exceedingly unpleasant, I confess. I looked hard at the doctor to see whether he was making game of me, but he looked perfectly serious. I thanked him warmly for his offer, but told him I intended to be the exception to the rule by which every one who slept in that particular state-room went overboard. He did not say much, but looked as grave as ever, and hinted that before we got across I should probably reconsider his proposal. In the course of time we went to breakfast, at which only an inconsiderable number of passengers assembled. I noticed that one or two of the officers who breakfasted with us looked grave. After breakfast I went into my state-room in order to get a book. The curtains of the upper berth were still closely drawn. Not a word was to be heard. My room-mate was probably still asleep.

As I came out I met the steward whose business it was to look after me. He whispered that the captain wanted to see me, and then scuttled away down the passage as if very anxious to avoid any questions. I went toward the captain's cabin, and found him waiting for me.

"Sir," said he, "I want to ask a favour of you."

I answered that I would do anything to oblige him.

"Your room-mate has disappeared," he said. "He is known to have turned in early last night. Did you notice anything extraordinary in his manner?"

The question coming, as it did, in exact confirmation of the fears the doctor had expressed half an hour earlier, staggered me.

"You don't mean to say he has gone overboard?" I asked.

"I fear he has," answered the captain.

"This is the most extraordinary thing—" I began.

"Why?" he asked.

"He is the fourth, then?" I explained. In answer to another question from the captain, I explained, without mentioning the doctor, that I had heard the story concerning one hundred and five. He seemed very much annoyed at hearing that I knew of it. I told him what had occurred in the night.

"What you say," he replied, "coincides almost exactly with what was told me by the room-mates of two of the other three. They bolt out of bed and run down the passage. Two of them were seen to go overboard by the watch; we stopped and lowered boats, but they were not found. Nobody, however, saw or heard the man who was lost last night—if he is really lost. The steward, who is a superstitious fellow, perhaps, and expected something to go wrong, went to look for him this morning, and found his berth empty, but his clothes lying about, just as he had left them. The steward was the only man on board who knew him by sight, and he has been searching everywhere for him. He has disappeared! Now, sir, I want to beg you not to mention the circumstance to any of the passengers; I don't want the ship to get a bad name, and nothing hangs about an ocean-goer like stories of suicides. You shall have your choice of any one of the officers' cabins you like, including my own, for the rest of the passage. Is that a fair bargain?"

"Very," said I; "and I am much obliged to you. But since I am alone, and have the state-room to myself, I would rather not move. If the steward will take out that unfortunate man's things, I would as leave stay where I am. I will not say anything about the matter, and I think I can promise you that I will not follow my room-mate."

The captain tried to dissuade me from my intention, but I preferred having a state-room alone to being the chum of any officer on board. I do not know whether I acted foolishly, but if I had taken his advice I should have had nothing more to tell. There would have remained the disagreeable coincidence of several suicides occurring among men who had slept in the same cabin, but that would have been all.

That was not the end of the matter, however, by any means. I obstinately made up my mind

that I would not be disturbed by such tales, and I even went so far as to argue the question with the captain. There was something wrong about the state-room, I said. It was rather damp. The porthole had been left open last night. My room-mate might have been ill when he came on board, and he might have become delirious after he went to bed. He might even now be hiding somewhere on board, and might be found later. The place ought to be aired and the fastening of the port looked to. If the captain would give me leave, I would see that what I thought necessary were done immediately.

"Of course you have a right to stay where you are if you please," he replied, rather petulantly; "but I wish you would turn out and let me lock the place up, and be done with it."

I did not see it in the same light, and left the captain, after promising to be silent concerning the disappearance of my companion. The latter had had no acquaintances on board, and was not missed in the course of the day. Towards evening I met the doctor again, and he asked me whether I had changed my mind. I told him I had not.

"Then you will before long," he said, very gravely.

III.

We played whist in the evening, and I went to bed late. I will confess now that I felt a disagreeable sensation when I entered my state-room. I could not help thinking of the tall man I had seen on the previous night, who was now dead, drowned, tossing about in the long swell, two or three hundred miles astern. His face rose very distinctly before me as I undressed, and I even went so far as to draw back the curtains of the upper berth, as though to persuade myself that he was actually gone. I also bolted the door of the state-room. Suddenly I became aware that the porthole was open, and fastened back. This was more than I could stand. I hastily threw on my dressing-gown and went in search of Robert, the steward of my passage. I was very angry, I remember, and when I found him I dragged him roughly to the door of one hundred and five, and pushed him towards the open porthole.

"What the deuce do you mean, you scoundrel, by leaving that port open every night? Don't you know it is against the regulations? Don't you know that if the ship heeled and the water began to come in, ten men could not shut it? I will report you to the captain, you blackguard, for endangering the ship!"

I was exceedingly wroth. The man trembled and turned pale, and then began to shut the round glass plate with the heavy brass fittings.

"Why don't you answer me?" I said, roughly.

"If you please, sir," faltered Robert, "there's nobody on board as can keep this 'ere port shut at night. You can try it yourself, sir. I ain't a-going to stop hany longer on board o' this vessel, sir; I ain't, indeed. But if I was you, sir, I'd just clear out and go and sleep with the surgeon, or something, I would. Look 'ere, sir, is that fastened what you may call securely, or not, sir? Try it, sir, see if it will move a hinch."

I tried the port, and found it perfectly tight.

"Well, sir," continued Robert, triumphantly, "I wager my reputation as a A1 steward, that in 'arf an hour it will be open again; fastened back, too, sir, that's the horful thing—fastened back!"

I examined the great screw and the looped nut that ran on it.

"If I find it open in the night, Robert, I will give you a sovereign. It is not possible. You may go."

"Soverin' did you say, sir? Very good, sir. Thank ye, sir. Good night, sir. Pleasant reepose, sir, and all manner of hinchantin' dreams, sir."

Robert scuttled away, delighted at being released. Of course, I thought he was trying to account for his negligence by a silly story, intended to frighten me, and I disbelieved him. The consequence was that he got his sovereign, and I spent a very peculiarly unpleasant night.

I went to bed, and five minutes after I had rolled myself up in my blankets the inexorable Robert extinguished the light that burned steadily behind the ground-glass pane near the door. I lay quite still in the dark trying to go to sleep, but I soon found that impossible. It had been some satisfaction to be angry with the steward, and the diversion had banished that unpleasant sensation I had at first experienced when I thought of the drowned man who had been my chum; but I was no longer sleepy, and I lay awake for some time, occasionally glancing at the porthole, which I could just see from where I lay, and which, in the darkness, looked like a faintly-luminous soup-plate suspended in blackness. I believe I must have lain there for an hour, and, as I remember, I was just dozing into sleep when I was roused by a draught of cold air and by distinctly feeling the spray of the sea blown upon my face. I started to my feet, and not having allowed in the dark for the motion of the ship, I was instantly thrown violently across the state-room upon the couch which was placed beneath the porthole. I recovered myself immediately, however, and climbed upon my knees. The porthole was again wide open and fastened back!

Now these things are facts. I was wide awake when I got up, and I should certainly have been waked by the fall had I still been dozing. Moreover, I bruised my elbows and knees badly, and the bruises were there on the following morning to testify to the fact, if I myself had doubted it. The porthole was wide open and fastened back—a thing so unaccountable that I remember very well feeling astonishment rather than fear when I discovered it. I at once closed the plate again and screwed down the loop-nut with all my strength. It was very dark in the state-room. I reflected that the port had certainly been opened within an hour after Robert had at first shut it in my presence, and I determined to watch it and see whether it would open again. Those brass fittings are very heavy and by no means easy to move; I could not believe that the clump had been turned by the shaking of the screw. I stood peering out through the thick glass at the alternate white and grey streaks of the sea that foamed beneath the ship's side. I must have remained there a quarter of an hour.

Suddenly, as I stood, I distinctly heard something moving behind me in one of the berths, and a moment afterwards, just as I turned instinctively to look—though I could, of course, see nothing in the darkness—I heard a very faint groan. I sprang across the state-room, and tore the curtains of the upper berth aside, thrusting in my hands to discover if there were any one there. There was some one.

I remember that the sensation as I put my hands forward was as though I were plunging them into the air of a damp cellar, and from behind the curtain came a gust of wind that smelled horribly of stagnant sea-water. I laid hold of something that had the shape of a man's arm, but was smooth, and wet, and icy cold. But suddenly, as I pulled, the creature sprang violently forward against me, a clammy, oozy mass, as it seemed to me, heavy and wet, yet endowed with a sort of supernatural strength. I reeled across the state-room, and in an instant the door opened and the thing rushed out. I had not had time to be frightened, and quickly recovering myself, I sprang through the door and gave chase at the top of my speed, but I was too late. Ten yards before me I could see—I am sure I saw it—a dark shadow moving in the dimly lighted passage, quickly as the shadow of a fast horse thrown before a dog-cart by the lamp on a dark night. But in a moment it had disappeared, and I found myself holding on to the polished rail that ran along the bulkhead where the passage turned towards the companion. My hair stood on end, and the cold perspiration rolled down my face. I am not ashamed of it in the least: I was very badly frightened.

Still I doubted my senses, and pulled myself together. It was absurd, I thought. The Welsh rare-bit I had eaten had disagreed with me. I had been in a nightmare. I made my way back to my state-room, and entered it with an effort. The whole place smelled of stagnant sea-water, as it had when I had waked on the previous evening. It required my utmost strength to go in and grope among my things for a box of wax lights. As I lighted a railway reading-lantern which I al-ways carry in case I want to read after the lamps are out, I perceived that the porthole was again open, and a sort of creeping horror began to take possession of me which I never felt before, nor wish to feel again. But I got a light and proceeded to examine the upper berth, expecting to find it drenched with sea-water.

But I was disappointed. The bed had been slept in, and the smell of the sea was strong; but the bedding was as dry as a bone. I fancied that Robert had not had the courage to make the bed after the accident of the previous night—it had all been a hideous dream. I drew the curtains back as far as I could and examined the place very carefully. It was perfectly dry. But the porthole was open again. With a sort of dull bewilderment of horror, I closed it and screwed it down, and thrusting my heavy stick through the brass loop, wrenched it with all my might, till the thick metal began to bend under the pressure. Then I hooked my reading-lantern into the red velvet at the head of the couch, and sat down to recover my senses if I could. I sat there all night, unable to think of rest—hardly able to think at all. But the porthole remained closed, and I did not believe it would now open again without the application of a considerable force.

The morning dawned at last, and I dressed myself slowly, thinking over all that had happened in the night. It was a beautiful day and I went on deck, glad to get out in the early, pure sunshine, and to smell the breeze from the blue water, so different from the noisome, stagnant odour from my state-room. Instinctively I turned aft, towards the surgeon's cabin. There he stood, with a pipe in his mouth, taking his morning airing precisely as on the preceding day.

"Good-morning," said he, quietly, but looking at me with evident curiosity.

"Doctor, you were quite right," said I. "There is something wrong about that place."

"I thought you would change your mind," he answered, rather triumphantly. "You have had a bad night, eh? Shall I make you a pick-me-up? I have a capital recipe."

"No, thanks," I cried. "But I would like to tell you what happened."

I then tried to explain as clearly as possible precisely what had occurred, not omitting to state that I had been scared as I had never been scared in my whole life before. I dwelt particularly on the phenomenon of the porthole, which was a fact to which I could testify, even if the rest had been an illusion. I had closed it twice in the night, and the second time I had actually bent the brass in wrenching it with my stick. I believe I insisted a good deal on this point.

"You seem to think I am likely to doubt the story," said the doctor, smiling at the detailed account of the state of the porthole. "I do not doubt it in the least. I renew my invitation to you. Bring your traps here, and take half my cabin."

"Come and take half of mine for one night," I said. "Help me to get at the bottom of this thing."

"You will get to the bottom of something else if you try," answered the doctor.

"What?" I asked.

"The bottom of the sea. I am going to leave the ship. It is not canny."

"Then you will not help me to find out—"

"Not I," said the doctor, quickly. "It is my business to keep my wits about me—not to go fiddling about with ghosts and things."

"Do you really believe it is a ghost?" I inquired, rather contemptuously. But as I spoke I remembered very well the horrible sensation of the supernatural which had got possession of me during the night. The doctor turned sharply on me—

"Have you any reasonable explanation of these things to offer?" he asked. "No; you have not. Well, you say you will find an explanation. I say that you won't, sir, simply because there is not any."

"But, my dear sir," I retorted, "do you, a man of science, mean to tell me that such things cannot be explained?"

"I do," he answered, stoutly. "And, if they could, I would not be concerned in the explanation."

I did not care to spend another night alone in the state-room, and yet I was obstinately determined to get at the root of the disturbances. I do not believe there are many men who would have slept there alone, after passing two such nights. But I made up my mind to try it, if I could not get any one to share a watch with me. The doctor was evidently not inclined for such an experiment. He said he was a surgeon, and that in case any accident occurred on board he must always be in readiness. He could not afford to have his nerves unsettled. Perhaps he was quite right, but I am inclined to think that his precaution was prompted by his inclination. On inquiry, he informed me that there was no one on board who would be likely to join me in my investigations, and after a little more conversation I left him. A little later I met the captain, and told him my story. I said that if no one would spend the night with me I would ask leave to have the light burning all night, and would try it alone.

"Look here," said he, "I will tell you what I will do. I will share your watch myself, and we will see what happens. It is my belief that we can find out between us. There may be some fellow skulking on board, who steals a passage by frightening the passengers. It is just possible that there may be something queer in the carpentering of that berth."

I suggested taking the ship's carpenter below and examining the place; but I was overjoyed at the captain's offer to spend the night with me. He accordingly sent for the workman and ordered him to do anything I required. We went below at once. I had all the bedding cleared out of the upper berth, and we examined the place thoroughly to see if there was a board loose anywhere, or a panel which could be opened or pushed aside. We tried the planks everywhere, tapped the flooring, unscrewed the fittings of the lower berth and took it to pieces—in short, there was not a square inch of the state-room which was not searched and tested. Everything was in perfect order, and we put everything back in its place. As we were finishing our work, Robert came to the door and looked in.

"Well, sir—find anything, sir?" he asked with a ghastly grin.

"You were right about the porthole, Robert," I said, and I gave him the promised sovereign. The carpenter did his work silently and skilfully, following my directions. When he had done he spoke.

"I'm a plain man, sir," he said. "But it's my belief you had better just turn out your things and let me run half a dozen four-inch screws through the door of this cabin. There's no good never came o' this cabin yet, sir, and that's all about it. There's been four lives lost out o' here to my own remembrance, and that in four trips. Better give it up, sir—better give it up!"

"I will try it for one night more," I said.

"Better give it up, sir—better give it up! It's a precious bad job," repeated the workman, putting his tools in his bag and leaving the cabin.

But my spirits had risen considerably at the prospect of having the captain's company, and I made up my mind not to be prevented from going to the end of the strange business. I abstained from Welsh rare-bits and grog that evening, and did not even join in the customary game of whist. I wanted to be quite sure of my nerves, and my vanity made me anxious to make a good figure in the captain's eyes.

IV.

The captain was one of those splendidly tough and cheerful specimens of seafaring humanity whose combined courage, hardihood, and calmness in difficulty leads them naturally into high positions of trust. He was not the man to be led away by an idle tale, and the mere fact that he was willing to join me in the investigation was proof that he thought there was something seriously wrong, which could not be accounted for on ordinary theories, nor laughed down as a common superstition. To some extent, too, his reputation was at stake, as well as the reputation of the ship. It is no light thing to lose passengers overboard, and he knew it.

About ten o'clock that evening, as I was smoking a last cigar, he came up to me and drew me aside from the beat of the other passengers who were patrolling the deck in the warm darkness.

"This is a serious matter, Mr. Brisbane," he said. "We must make up our minds either way—to be disappointed or to have a pretty rough time of it. You see, I cannot afford to laugh at the affair, and I will ask you to sign your name to a statement of whatever occurs. If nothing happens to-night we will try it again to-morrow and next day. Are you ready?"

So we went below, and entered the stateroom. As we went in I could see Robert the steward, who stood a little further down the passage, watching us, with his usual grin, as though certain that something dreadful was about to happen. The captain closed the door behind us and bolted it.

"Supposing we put your portmanteau before the door," he suggested. "One of us can sit on it. Nothing can get out then. Is the port screwed down?"

I found it as I had left it in the morning. Indeed, without using a lever, as I had done, no one could have opened it. I drew back the curtains of the upper berth so that I could see well into it. By the captain's advice I lighted my reading-lantern, and placed it so that it shone upon the white sheets above. He insisted upon sitting on the portmanteau, declaring that he wished to be able to swear that he had sat before the door.

Then he requested me to search the stateroom thoroughly, an operation very soon accomplished, as it consisted merely in looking beneath the lower berth and under the couch below the porthole. The spaces were quite empty.

"It is impossible for any human being to get in," I said, "or for any human being to open the port."

"Very good," said the captain, calmly. "If we see anything now, it must be either imagination or something supernatural."

I sat down on the edge of the lower berth.

"The first time it happened," said the captain, crossing his legs and leaning back against the door, "was in March. The passenger who slept here, in the upper berth, turned out to have been a lunatic—at all events, he was known to have been a little touched, and he had taken his passage without the knowledge of his friends. He rushed out in the middle of the night, and threw himself overboard, before the officer who had the watch could stop him. We stopped and lowered a boat; it was a quiet night, just before that heavy weather came on; but we could not find him. Of course his suicide was afterwards accounted for on the ground of his insanity."

"I suppose that often happens?" I remarked, rather absently.

"Not often—no," said the captain; "never before in my experience, though I have heard of it happening on board of other ships. Well, as I was saying, that occurred in March. On the very next trip—What are you looking at?" he asked, stopping suddenly in his narration.

I believe I gave no answer. My eyes were riveted upon the porthole. It seemed to me that the brass loop-nut was beginning to turn very slowly upon the screw—so slowly, however, that I was not sure it moved at all. I watched it intently, fixing its position in my mind, and trying to ascertain whether it changed. Seeing where I was looking, the captain looked too.

"It moves!" he exclaimed, in a tone of conviction. "No, it does not," he added, after a minute.

"If it were the jarring of the screw," said I, "it would have opened during the day; but I found it this evening jammed tight as I left it this morning."

I rose and tried the nut. It was certainly loosened, for by an effort I could move it with my hands.

"The queer thing," said the captain, "is that the second man who was lost is supposed to have got through that very port. We had a terrible time over it. It was in the middle of the night, and the weather was very heavy; there was an alarm that one of the ports was open and the sea running in. I came below and found everything flooded, the water pouring in every time she rolled, and the whole port swinging from the top bolts—not the porthole in the middle. Well, we managed to shut it, but the water did some damage. Ever since that the place smells of sea-water from time to time. We supposed the passenger had thrown himself out, though the Lord only knows how he did it. The steward kept telling me that he could not keep anything shut here. Upon my word—I can smell it now, cannot you?" he inquired, sniffing the air suspiciously.

"Yes—distinctly," I said, and I shuddered as that same odour of stagnant sea-water grew stronger in the cabin. "Now, to smell like this, the place must be damp," I continued, "and yet when I examined it with the carpenter this morning everything was perfectly dry. It is most extraordinary—hallo!"

My reading-lantern, which had been placed in the upper berth, was suddenly extinguished. There was still a good deal of light from the pane of ground glass near the door, behind which loomed the regulation lamp. The ship rolled heavily, and the curtain of the upper berth swung far out into the state-room and back again. I rose quickly from my seat on the edge of the bed, and the captain at the same moment started to his feet with a loud cry of surprise. I had turned with the intention of taking down the lantern to examine it, when I heard his exclamation, and immediately afterwards his call for help. I sprang towards him. He was wrestling with all his might, with the brass loop of the port. It seemed to turn against his hands in spite of all his efforts. I caught up my cane, a heavy oak stick I always used to carry, and thrust it through the ring and bore on it with all my strength. But the strong wood snapped suddenly, and I fell upon the couch. When I rose again the port was wide open, and the captain was standing with his back against the door, pale to the lips.

"There is something in that berth!" he cried, in a strange voice, his eyes almost starting from his head. "Hold the door, while I look—it shall not escape us, whatever it is!"

But instead of taking his place, I sprang upon the lower bed, and seized something which lay in the upper berth.

It was something ghostly, horrible beyond words, and it moved in my grip. It was like the body of a man long drowned, and yet it moved, and had the strength of ten men living; but I gripped it with all my might—the slippery, oozy, horrible thing. The dead white eyes seemed to stare at me out of the dusk; the putrid odour of rank sea-water was about it, and its shiny hair hung in foul wet curls over its dead face. I wrestled with the dead thing; it thrust itself upon me and forced me back and nearly broke my arms; it wound its corpse's arms about my neck, the living death, and overpowered me, so that I, at last, cried aloud and fell, and left my hold.

As I fell the thing sprang across me, and seemed to throw itself upon the captain. When I last saw him on his feet his face was white and his lips set. It seemed to me that he struck a violent blow at the dead being, and then he, too, fell forward upon his face, with an inarticulate cry of horror.

The thing paused an instant, seeming to hover over his prostrate body, and I could have screamed again for very fright, but I had no voice left. The thing vanished suddenly, and it seemed to my disturbed senses that it made its exit through the open port, though how that was possible, considering the smallness of the aper-

ture, is more than any one can tell. I lay a long time upon the floor, and the captain lay beside me. At last I partially recovered my senses and moved, and I instantly knew that my arm was broken—the small bone of the left forearm near the wrist.

I got upon my feet somehow, and with my remaining hand I tried to raise the captain. He groaned and moved, and at last came to himself. He was not hurt, but he seemed badly stunned.

WELL, DO YOU want to hear any more? There is nothing more. That is the end of my story. The carpenter carried out his scheme of running half a dozen four-inch screws through the door of one hundred and five; and if ever you take a passage in the Kamtschatka, you may ask for a berth in that state-room. You will be told that it is engaged—yes—it is engaged by that dead thing.

I finished the trip in the surgeon's cabin. He doctored my broken arm, and advised me not to "fiddle about with ghosts and things" any more. The captain was very silent, and never sailed again in that ship, though it is still running. And I will not sail in her either. It was a very disagreeable experience, and I was very badly frightened, which is a thing I do not like. That is all. That is how I saw a ghost—if it was a ghost. It was dead, anyhow.

VENGEANCE OF THE LIVING DEAD

RALSTON SHIELDS

LITTLE IS KNOWN of the obscure pulp writer John R. Baxter, who produced only about a dozen stories using the pseudonym Ralston Shields. He seems to have written only for the lower-end weird menace pulp magazines owned by Popular Publications. These periodicals, also known as shudder pulps, were noted for their high levels of sex and sadism, pushing the boundaries of acceptability so far that they were finally forced out of business during World War II. Among his works of fiction, mostly novellas of between eight and twelve thousand words, were such understated horror tales as "The Blood Kiss" (*Dime Mystery Magazine*, May 1937), "Daughter of the Devil" (*Horror Stories*, October/November 1937), "Priestess of Pestilence" (*Terror Tales*, May/June 1939), "Food for the Fungus Lady" (*Horror Stories*, December 1939/January 1940), "The Dictator and the Zombie" (*Terror Tales*, January/February 1940), "Mistress of the Blood-Drinkers" (*Horror Stories*, March 1940), and "Tropic Voodoo" (*Thrilling Adventure*, May 1942). Although Shields is known only to pulp experts and aficionados today, a collection of his stories, which were noted for their superior literary quality and relatively subtle atmospheric power, is planned for the near future.

"Vengeance of the Living Dead" was originally published in the September 1940 issue of *Terror Tales*.

RALSTON SHIELDS

VENGEANCE OF THE LIVING DEAD

DINNER WAS FINISHED, the blinds were drawn, and a pleasant fire crackled in the hearth of Dr. Beswick's informal but charming library. The Director of the Pardee-Fleischer Foundation for Scientific Research was seated at his large teakwood desk; he had summoned Kandru, his Negro servant, and was giving the man certain instructions. These instructions were unusual, to say the least; but the wrinkled ape-like face of the wizened little black showed no more astonishment than might have been expected if his master had been suggesting a menu for tomorrow's dinner. Years ago, in the African bush, Dr. Beswick had saved Kandru from almost certain death; and from that time on, the little Negro had considered himself the personal property of the white man. By some strange quirk of primitive psychology, he had simply ceased to function as a separate individual; he had attached himself to Dr. Beswick's personality as a kind of auxiliary intelligence, to be used as his master saw fit. The doctor's own right hand would no more have failed to obey the dictates of his will, than his servant Kandru.

"Twenty years ago," Beswick was saying, "when we first met in your native land, Kandru, you were the most skillful of your whole tribe in the use of a blow-gun. I fancy you must have fallen off a little since then, for lack of practise; but this room is not large. Suppose you were hidden with your tube behind the draperies of the window-recess yonder—do you think you

could be dead sure, absolutely positive, of hitting a man inside this library with your first dart? There must be no mistake; Stuart is a powerful devil, strong as an ox; if the first dart misses, there may be no chance to send another. . . ."

Kandru regarded his master solemnly with tiny, deep-set, ape-like eyes. "Me hit um," he grunted. During the twenty years he had spent in the United States, the man had learned to use only the most elementary English. And yet, although Dr. Beswick in addressing him never attempted to simplify his speech in the least, Kandru was never at a loss to understand; it almost seemed that he grasped Beswick's intent by a kind of thought-transference.

"Very good." In the doctor's cold gray eyes, made all the more penetrating by the heavy lenses he wore, there flickered a glint of approval; after an instant, however, this was gone. Beswick's every feature and physical characteristic seemed to indicate a nature that was chilly, uncommunicative, and implacable. He was a gaunt, slightly stooped man of about fifty, with iron-gray hair, narrow countenance and the clammy, unnaturally pallid complexion that often is associated with years of work in the unwholesome fumes and vapors of the scientific laboratory. Only one feature of the man's physiognomy belied the impression that he was utterly a creature of the intellect, emotionless as an image of stone: his mouth—his moist, loose-lipped and full-blooded mouth. Here was a clue to an aspect of his character deeply buried under his external coldness: a hint that somewhere in the shadows of his soul lurked all the passions, hatreds and terrors of which human-kind is capable. Dr. Beswick's appearance, his manner, even his choice of words in speaking, might be those of an austere and lofty-minded scientist, a paragon of the type whom the Twentieth Century claims for its highest human product; but his wet red lips could well have belonged to one of the abominable emperors of the Roman decadence—a Negro, a Tiberius, a Caligula. . . .

"Very good, Kandru, very good indeed . . . But I don't want you to use one of your own African darts—do you understand that? The poison on such a dart would kill him in a few minutes; and I have other plans. Here—this afternoon, I made these, copying them exactly from your own. . . ." He handed the Negro four or five little wooden slivers, tipped at one end with sharp metal points, and tufted with lamb's wool at the other.

"They should fit your blow-gun perfectly. The only difference between my darts and yours is in the poison smeared on the tips. Instead of dying, a man pricked by one of these will merely be paralyzed; after a few minutes, he will completely recover. However, it won't take long for the two of us to tie up Dr. Stuart so he will be altogether helpless; and after that, I shall prefer that he regain complete possession of his faculties. . . .

"Now, let's go over the whole thing, to be sure you understand what to do. Any time now, Dr. Stuart should arrive. When the bell rings, you must take these darts, and your tube, and stand in the window-recess, hidden by the curtain. I'll let Stuart in myself. Probably he and I will talk for a while. Then I will go get my wife, and bring her into the room. When Stuart sees the B'wani Wanda, and realizes how she has—altered—since he left four months ago for Tibet, he will be very angry. There will be loud words. You must watch very closely then; you must have your blow-gun ready, lifted to your

lips. Presently, I will take off my glasses; that will be your signal. You must send your dart; and you must not miss. Now is that all plain? Do you understand everything?"

Kandru nodded like an effigy of stained wood and wrinkled leather. "All plain," he assented. "Kandru un'nerstand; him not miss. . . ."

Dr. Beswick continued for a long moment to hold his servant's eyes with his own gaze; at the same time, he slowly ran his tongue over his lips, moistening them. "That will be all, Kandru," he said, finally. "There is nothing more to do but wait for the door-bell to ring."

He took up a pencil, and began to write on some clean sheets of paper which lay on the desk before him. As for the Negro, now that his master had finished speaking, he sank down silently before the hearth, and sat there gazing patiently into the heart of the leaping flames.

For perhaps twenty-five minutes they remained as they were, the doctor writing calmly at his desk, and Kandru squatting immovable and expressionless on his heels in the firelight. When the door-bell jangled at last, neither of them started, or betrayed the least nervous reaction. Kandru rose silently to his feet, and with his blow-gun and the darts which the doctor had given him, took his place behind the velvet curtains of the window-recess. Dr. Beswick only ran his tongue over his lips once more, and after a moment laid down his pencil. Presently he left his chair, and passed out of the library into the adjoining entrance hall.

Two minutes later, he returned to the pleasantly fire-lit room, ushering before him a huge man, powerfully built, tall and broad at the same time—really a splendid figure, his bearded face handsome after a bluff fashion, his deep-set and extremely blue eyes eloquent of a frank and forthright personality. Despite his full black beard, and a certain air of having experienced many things at the hands of life and fate, there was something youthful about him, a spring and zest in his movements which implied that he had yet to see his fortieth birthday.

"How very good to see you, my dear Stuart," Dr. Beswick was saying; he had assumed a manner, which, for a man of his dour habits, was almost effusive. "Believe me, I've counted the days while you were gone; I can hardly wait to hear everything from your own lips. When I recommended to our Foundation that you be given the post as leader of the Tibetan expedition, I knew you'd make a success of the undertaking. I need scarcely say that the reports that have reached us of your discoveries have more than vindicated my judgement. But you can't blame me for being eager to hear about your own personal adventures; I'm certain you have a great deal to tell. One doesn't spend two months in Nepal and Tibet without a few hair's breadth escapes. . . .

"But do sit down, my dear fellow, and make yourself comfortable. Here, this chair by the fire! And what will you have to drink? The regular thing for you, if I recall, is Scotch and plain water—do I have it right? And—oh, yes—before you begin, perhaps I'd better call Wanda; doubtless you'll want her to be in on this. She always took such an—interest in your doings, old chap, before you left for the Orient. . . ."

TOM STUART SEATED himself in the chair indicated by his host; also he accepted the glass that was proffered him. However, before bringing the liquor to his lips, he spoke. "If you don't mind, Beswick, I'd rather you didn't call Wanda just yet. I—there are a few things I'd like to tell you, before she comes."

BESWICK RAISED HIS eyebrows as if in mild surprise. "You mean—you saw things which go against our Western standards of good taste, and you feel it would be embarrassing to Wanda if you spoke of them in her presence? Is that it?"

But Stuart shook his head; he was silent for a moment before answering. His honest blue eyes were troubled, as if he were turning over in his mind something he did not want to say, and yet knew he could not avoid saying. At last, however, the words came from his lips, spoken as if by another volition than his own.

"Wanda's hardly a prude or a puritan, Beswick. It isn't likely that she'd be shocked by anything I have to relate. No, it's another matter that I want to speak to you about—something personal—something that should have been settled before I ever left on the Pardee-Fleischer expedition.

"You know, I learned a good many things above and beyond the scientific data I was sent for, during these past months in the mountains of Asia. Even though I was able to classify a number of plants and animals entirely new to science, and to confirm at least one important anthropological hypothesis, I don't regard those discoveries as the most important fruit of the journey.

"You know, Beswick, there are men living in the monasteries of Nepal and Tibet, who understand thoroughly certain aspects of Nature and the very existence of which is only beginning to be recognized by our Western science. I was able to win the confidence of one of these High Lamas, and he consented to teach me as much of his occult knowledge as my undeveloped intellect could absorb. At first, the things he told me struck me as so much superstitious gibberish, sheer fantasy and nothing more. . . .

"But this old lama was a man who dealt not only in words, but in deeds likewise. Through the aid of his powers, I was able to see things, and to experience things, which are entirely beyond my skill to describe. I can only say this much: I now possess an understanding of the nature of man, spiritual and physical, which transcends anything I had dreamed of before my visit to Tibet.

"To me, it is positive knowledge, more certain than any mere theory or hypothesis, that the human animal possesses a soul; that this intelligence, this real self, whatever you want to name it, is a separate spiritual entity which merely uses the body as a tool; and that this essence of personality survives the death of the body, untarnished and unchanged to the end of eternity. . . ."

As he spoke the explorer's enthusiasm grew as if in spite of himself; he seemed to be carried away by his own words. But then he caught the glance of Dr. Beswick, which remained cold as ice, notwithstanding the warm cloak of cordiality he had chosen to draw over himself. Stuart checked himself almost abruptly.

"Sorry," he apologized. "I keep forgetting that some realities are purely personal. We have no business to ask others to take them seriously, on the mere face value of our words. What I'm really driving at is this, Beswick: the things I learned in Tibet have altered my whole scale of values, moral and ethical as well as intellectual. Whatever you may think of my reasons for this change in viewpoint, I must ask you to believe that the change itself is very real to me, very genuine. For example, it is no longer possible for me to practise a deception or a dishonesty of any sort. To a man who has looked deeply into the wonderful workings of the universe, as I have, integrity of mind and action is no longer a convenience—it somehow becomes a profound necessity."

Beswick continued to regard his guest with an expression that revealed no more than a definite but altogether polite surprise. "But my dear fellow," he remarked, "I still don't understand. I wasn't aware that you were inclined to dishonesty of any sort, even before your visit to the Himalayas."

The troubled expression which had shown itself earlier on Stuart's bluff features appeared again now, somewhat deepened if anything.

"But I *have* been dishonest, Beswick," he said, slowly. "Dishonest in a matter which involves you as well as myself. That's what I wanted to mention before Wanda comes into the room; I thought it would be—easier.

"I love her, you see; I'm in love with your wife. And I believe that she loves me. Wanda and I belong to each other, Beswick, inevitably and absolutely. It's one of those things that can't be

mistaken; we shall belong to each other until the end of time. . . ."

CHAPTER TWO

THE STING OF FATE

Anxiously, Tom Stuart regarded the older man, as if trying to gauge the effect of this revelation. Beswick said nothing, however; he continued to sit there as if his visitor had just made some utterly casual remark about the weather. Stuart had no choice but to continue, amplifying and explaining his statement.

"There's no use going into the beginnings of the matter," he said, still choosing his words carefully and slowly. "When I accepted my post with the Foundation three years ago, it was inevitable that I should see Wanda from time to time, since she was your wife. Neither of us planned it deliberately; it simply happened, and there came a day when we had to face the facts. The development of the situation was not unusual; it was the old shabby story of firm resolves to make a clean breast of things, followed by one postponement after another.

"Not that our love was something to be ashamed of; I didn't think so then, and I still don't think so. As I said to begin with, such things are inevitable, and it is foolish to deny them. The sordid part of it was our cowardice in attempting concealment, because it was easier to avoid issues than to face them.

"Do you remember the night, four months ago, when you invited me here to dinner? Wanda and I had resolved that we would hide our love no longer; we'd tell you that evening for sure, and ask you to consent to a divorce—trusting that you would understand and forgive. But then you told me that I had been selected to lead the expedition to Tibet; and somehow—that changed everything. . . ."

At this point in his confession, Stuart's bronzed cheeks flushed dull brick red. He cast down his eyes. "It's not a very pretty thing to admit, Beswick—that sudden change in our resolution. It sounds almost as if—as if Wanda and I had feared that you would change your mind about giving me the leadership of the Tibetan party—as if we thought you small enough to allow personal affairs to influence you in such a matter. I'm afraid there isn't much I can say to defend our conduct, Beswick."

Once more, Tom Stuart lifted his eyes to meet the even gaze of the scientist. Into the huge bearded man's expression had suddenly come something almost boyish—that rare and irresistible quality of frankness and regret mingled with sheer childlike trust, which makes no extenuation of deeds committed, but appeals entirely to the understanding and kindness and forgiveness of the injured party.

He concluded: "And there it is; the whole truth as straight as I can give it to you. I—I hope it isn't too much of a shock, old man. Believe me, I'd sooner have cut off my left hand than tell you this; but there wasn't any choice. . . ."

For a long time, Beswick sat there without saying anything, or making any sign. And when, finally, he broke his silence, the tones of his voice were entirely casual.

"Youth and youth," he murmured. "Both young, you and my wife; and I have gray hair. Who can annul the laws of Nature? But I'd better get Wanda, perhaps, Stuart, before I say any more." He rose to his feet. "You don't object, now that you've made everything plain?"

"Call her by all means." As Stuart rose likewise from his armchair, his honest countenance cleared; he was openly relieved to see that the other had taken his bombshell so calmly. "Then we can discuss the situation from every angle, and decide what is to be done. It was only—only while I was breaking the news to you, old chap, that I somehow felt—it would be easier, without her. . . ."

AS HE LEFT the room, Dr. Beswick actually smiled. It was a rather horrible smile that hovered on his incongruously red lips; a smile full of craft and cruelty and malice; but Stuart, caught up in his own thoughts, did not notice. The huge man felt his heart pounding in his chest; in one moment more, he would see *her*—the dearest thing in the world to him, the treasure of his dreams, Wanda. . . . And at the same time, he cautioned himself that he must consider Beswick's feelings; after all, in the man's own house—even if everything *did* seem to be straightened out now. . . . Somehow, he must restrain himself from taking her in his arms; he must be content with holding her cool hand in his own, and letting his love speak only from his eyes. Later—somehow, in some way—things would be worked out so that they could be together without restraint; but for the present, he must hold himself in check.

And then, presently, Wanda Beswick entered the library; she stood there, tall and slender and heart-breakingly lovely. She was one of those waxen-white women with skin textured like flower-petals unfolded in some distant tropical rainforest. A coil of gleaming black hair rested on the nape of her slender neck; this, and her perfectly-formed scarlet lips contrasted strikingly with her pallid complexion. She was gowned in a sheath of dull silver brocade, designed to enhance the grace of her lithe body, at once fully rounded and delicately slender.

For Tom Stuart, when Wanda came into his field of vision, every resolve, every admonition he had given himself, was swept away in a flood of emotion. For four long months, this woman's loveliness had been burning in his thoughts; and now that he was face to face with her, he was like one suddenly intoxicated by a potent and irresistible drug. Dr. Beswick, whose feelings Stuart had intended to respect, had come into the room with his wife; but the tall, bearded man was suddenly oblivious of his presence; there was room for only one thought in his brain. . . .

He strode past Beswick to Wanda's side; he gathered her in his arms, and held her close to him. For a long time, he stood thus motionless, breathing the perfume of her wonderful hair. But then he slowly held her away from him at arm's length, as if to feast his eyes on her love-liness. "My darling," he whispered. "How I have dreamed of you! It seems so long! Tell me, did you get my letters? I had several chances to write, you know; I sent you long letters."

She did not answer his question; but Stuart at first supposed that she was so overcome with emotion that she was unable to speak. It was only after a moment that he realized that some-thing was wrong. The look in her eyes was the thing which first made a little chill of nameless fear quiver along his spine. Somehow, her eyes were different; there was no physical change, they were dark and liquid as always, fringed with long delicate lashes: but they no longer reflected anything—they no longer spoke to him. . . .

Wanda's eyes were *empty:* that was it; they were vacant as the eyes of an idiot, from whose living body the soul has fled—or a small baby, in whom the soul has not yet been awakened.

Very quietly and gently, Stuart repeated his question. "Wanda; my letters . . . did any of them reach you?"

She did not reply; only her lips slackened a little; from one corner of her exquisite mouth trickled a glistening rivulet of saliva. It was hardly noticeable; and yet there was something infinitely horrible about the sight: a perfectly gowned and lovely woman, in the very flower of maturity, *drooling*—actually slobbering like a small, helpless infant. . . .

SUDDENLY, A SPASM of frantic energy coursed through Stuart's giant frame. He shook Wanda violently, as if to stir up in her awareness something that escaped him; at the same time, he fairly roared, "Wanda! Answer me, I tell you! Speak, Wanda—for God's sake, speak to me!"

Now, at last, enough impression seemed to be made on Wanda's brain to elicit a response from her; but her reaction was almost more shocking than a continuation of her apathy would have been.

Whimpering, she pulled away from Stuart. "No," she whined, in the voice of a resentful little girl. "*Don't* shake Wanda! Nasty man with black beard leave Wanda alone. Wanda won't play. . . ."

Slowly, Stuart's arms sank down, and hung limply at his sides. His brief outburst had sub-sided utterly; now he was a man stunned, utterly nonplussed; the only emotion in his eyes was pain, mingled with complete bewilderment.

"Wanda," he muttered. "What's wrong? What's happened to you?"

Slowly, he turned his massive head in the di-rection of Beswick, who stood by, peering with a dreadful bird-like intentness through his heavy glasses. Stuart's bewildered eyes focused as if with an effort on the older man; when he spoke, it was still almost plaintively, in the voice of a man confronted with something beyond his un-derstanding.

"Is something wrong with her, Beswick?" he asked. "Something's happened—while I was gone?"

Beswick slowly nodded. "Quite correct, Stuart. Something has happened. And there's something very decidedly wrong with her—at least from your point of view." He spoke delib-erately, as if each word were a morsel of food, to be savored by his tongue and his moist red lips, tasted and relished with all the voluptuous en-joyment of the *gourmet.*

But then, suddenly, his manner changed. "You fool," he rasped, his speech acrid now as if tinctured by an inexhaustible well of bitterness in his soul. "What did you take me for, during the past year, when you were making love to my wife? Did you suppose I was a blindman, or an utter imbecile? Did you imagine I wasn't aware of what was going on between you and Wanda? It wasn't difficult, you know, once I'd noticed you mooning at each other with love-sick eyes, to arrange things so you'd suppose you were alone together—while I watched from a place of concealment.

"And just now, when you decided at last to flaunt your deception in my face, you did so in the expectation that I would meekly bow to the inevitable, and step out of the picture—a quiet little divorce—you and Wanda would set up housekeeping together—and you'd even invite me to dinner once in a while, just to prove that we were all civilized, and no hard feelings. . . . I know all your arguments, Stuart, all the arguments you and Wanda accepted as self-evident, along with the rest of your sophisticated, enlightened generation. She married me when she was a mere girl, too young to know her own mind, dazzled by my wealth and position; but then True Love comes along, and of course she can't be expected to go on living with a man old enough to be her father. . . . Oh, I know the whole rationalization as well as you do yourself. But the point is, it doesn't impress me!

"Why should I be cast aside like an old and worn-out garment that has outlived its usefulness? I can assure you I'm not so old that I fail to appreciate Wanda's loveliness. And I refuse to be cheated out of a thing that belongs to me, for all the notions you and your kind take so readily for granted—self-sacrifice, and unselfishness, and doing the decent thing, and all the rest of it.

"No, no, my friend; you don't get rid of me so easily. I made up my mind to that, the very same night I confirmed my suspicions about you and Wanda; and it didn't take me long to decide on a plan of action."

"YOU MIGHT BE interested to learn that the idea of the Pardee-Fleischer Tibetan expedition originated with me. It took a little time to convince our directors that such a thing should be undertaken; but once I had done that, it was very simple to obtain the leadership of the venture for you. Tibet is a long way from the United States; and I wanted to feel that you were safely disposed of for a certain length of time.

"That gave me an opportunity, you see, to deal with the case of my lovely but slightly tarnished partner in marriage. The—treatments I had decided upon as appropriate in her case necessitated a definite period of weeks; and I did not want to be disturbed by any embarrassing inquiries, such as you would have made, concerning her whereabouts."

While Beswick was speaking, Tom Stuart's expression reflected a strange gamut of emotion; pained bewilderment gave place to sheer horror, until he stared at the older man as if he were confronted by a loathsome and venomous reptile, an adder, a cobra, instead of a human being.

"You?" he said thickly, speaking as if his throat were half-paralyzed. "You—did this—to Wanda . . . ?"

Deliberately Beswick went through his horrible mannerism of moistening his lips with his tongue; even the bitterness he had for a time been unable to conceal was replaced now by a dreadful complacency at the thought of his own cleverness. "It was a most interesting experiment," he purred. "To transform an alert and intelligent adult woman into a mental defective, somewhat between a high-grade idiot and a very retarded imbecile. Certain drugs, mescal and cocaine derivatives, administered secretly in her food, made it easier; but the real work was done by radiations of extremely short frequency, which I focused upon her while she slept. The rays leave no external trace; Wanda's friends are greatly shocked to learn that she is suffering from a mental derangement; but no one is suspicious of foul play—these psychotic states are so little understood, you know; it might be hereditary as well as not.

"I was under the impression that my treatments had actually destroyed Wanda's intelligence, once and for all; but it may be, Stuart, that your interesting discoveries, which you brought back from the High Lama in Tibet, indicate another hypothesis." Beswick's tone, at this point, sharpened itself with an odious edge of sarcasm. "Perhaps Wanda's soul, to use your romantic term, was not destroyed at all by my radiations, but merely driven out of her body, leaving her with only the reflexive powers of speech and action that reside in the lower centers of the brain. That possibility worries me very little, however; I'm not interested in her soul; it can float about in the spaces of the universe till doomsday, for all I care.

"No, my friend, the condition and location of Wanda's soul does not interest me, to be utterly frank with you. As she is now, Wanda needs very little care; she's like a small child, quite happy so long as she is given something to play with, something she can do with her hands, like cutting out paper dolls or digging in a sand pile. And her beauty, as you notice, remains quite unimpaired. An ideal arrangement, my dear Stuart—I flatter myself that I was very clever to think of it."

While he had listened to these taunts, Stuart's face had gone first dull red, and then it had paled to a startling blank whiteness. His shoulders raised themselves slightly; he clenched fists like two powerful hammers, at the same time thrusting his massive bearded head forward. He took a step toward Beswick. "You unspeakable swine! Do you think you can get away with this—and live? By God, I'll . . . I'll tear you apart with my bare hands. . . ."

The menacing advance of the huge bearded man was in truth something to quail at; a wild animal, enraged to the point of madness, a gorilla or a tiger, would scarcely have been more ominous.

The gaunt, stooped, gray-haired scientist, however, remained perfectly calm. He casually removed his strong eye-glasses, as if to rest his eyes for a moment. . . .

CHAPTER THREE

THE MURDER MACHINE

Instantly, a small tufted missile sped across the room from the closed draperies of the window opposite the fireplace. It was true to its mark: its sharp needle-point pricked the flesh of Tom Stuart's neck, just between his collar and the line of his hair. Kandru had carried out his instructions with precision. . . .

Stuart was not even aware of the slight prick made by the tiny dart in his neck, so intent was he upon the fulfillment of his towering anger. The first intimation that came to him was a curious feeling of stiffness. He wanted to lunge forward, to seize Beswick with his hooked fingers, to throttle the life from him. But, somehow, his limbs would not obey his will; he felt an involuntary tension of the muscles over his whole body.

And then, as the drug Dr. Beswick had smeared on the dart took full effect, Stuart was no longer even able to stand erect. He remained fully conscious; but he pitched helplessly forward, like a stone effigy off balance. He began to make an outcry; but his very organs of speech were paralyzed; nothing came from his lips but a horrible dry croaking, inarticulate and meaningless.

And then, for all the world like some dark and evil spider that has remained in concealment until a strategic moment, the Negro servant, Kandru, scuttled forth from the red velvet curtains across the room. He joined Dr. Beswick, who was already kneeling beside the helpless form of Stuart with a coil of rope which he had taken from his desk. Together, master and servant bound the drugged man, with knots and loops that were cruelly tight; even Stuart's immense strength, when he regained consciousness, would avail him nothing against these bonds. While they made him captive, he continued to watch with open eyes—eyes that were like uncovered pits through which could be seen a hell of horror, baffled rage and sickening apprehension.

As all this took place, Wanda continued to stand there; but she had lost all interest in the man whom once she had loved. She was playing a childish game with her fingers, twining and intertwining them with a certain clumsy solemnity. However, when Kandru and Beswick began to move the helpless giant from the room, Wanda followed behind them.

Down a long corridor went that strange procession; then they shoved and pulled Stuart into a large, white-tiled room, equipped with the gleaming apparatus of a scientific laboratory. With great effort, they heaved him on a white-enamelled stand supported on rubber wheels— a piece of furniture similar to an operating table such as might be found in a hospital. The table was equipped with metal clamps; Dr. Beswick proceeded to fasten these about Stuart's massive body, so that he was held immovably in place.

While Kandru watched with the inscrutable visage of a man scarcely removed from a jungle savage, and Wanda with her habitual imbecile fixity of feature, Dr. Beswick proceeded with his design. He wheeled the enamelled stand across the room, and adjusted it in place beneath a curious mechanism—a tall iron frame shaped like an inverted U. From the cross-bar at the top of the uprights, dangled a long, glittering and very heavy blade of steel, its needle-point directly above the heart of the huge man who lay helpless on the operating table. This grim sword was attached to a trigger device, evidently intended to let it fall at a jerk upon a cord which depended from a ceiling pulley, a few feet to one side. In effect, Dr. Beswick's mechanism was a slight variant of the classic instrument of execution as used in France since the days of the Terror—a guillotine, which differed from the original only in that its victim would be skewered through the heart, instead of decapitated. . . .

IT BECAME EVIDENT, now, that the doctor's precaution in shackling and binding his victim had been far from groundless. Though he could still not speak, the effect of the paralyzing drug was beginning to wear away from Stuart's body. His tremendous muscles swelled and strained, and his great body heaved with fierce effort.

However, it was of no avail; he could scarcely stir.

Deliberately, his red lips curved in a cruel smile, Dr. Beswick toyed with the trigger-cord of his abominable machine.

"Can you hear me, old chap?" he murmured to Stuart. "I think you can—my drug contained nothing to impair the hearing. I'd like you to understand the full beauty of the vengeance I'm about to take upon you, before it is consummated.

"I, at least, have the virtue of frankness, you observe. I don't pretend to be any better than I am. I know that the emotion of revenge is not a very laudable one; but it so happens that I feel vindictive, and I intend to indulge myself. Frankly, I hate you, Stuart. I envy you for your youth, and your strength, and your virile good looks. And I loathe and detest you because my wife preferred you to myself. For a whole lifetime, I have conducted myself as a reputable and constructive member of society. I have contributed to scientific progress; I have earned the respect, and even the admiration, of the whole world. But now, at last, I intend to enjoy myself. I shall satisfy every murderous impulse that civilization tends to suppress in us. I shall be cruel and merciless, not only with considerable enthusiasm—but with all the finesse of a subtle mind.

"Let me remove even the slight satisfaction you may feel, in supposing that I will be detected and be punished for that which is about to happen to you. Obviously, neither Kandru nor Wanda will give me away. And even in the event that someone knew you were coming to my house this evening, Stuart, even in the unlikely event that suspicion should be awakened against me—it will be impossible for anything whatever to be proved against me. I have the means, in this laboratory, of chemically destroying every trace of your body and clothing; and you may be sure that I shall perform the process completely and carefully.

"But I begin to share the suspense you must be feeling, my dear fellow. Let us, as the vernacular saying has it, get down to brass tacks!" Smiling in hideous enjoyment of his own miserable joke, Beswick indicated the blade suspended over Stuart's heart. "I have no literal brass tacks to stick in your flesh, to be sure; but perhaps this little device of mine will substitute.

"No, no—don't cringe and turn pale, just yet, Stuart. You must save a little emotion; because you don't quite yet know the full extent of my subtlety. I had intended to do the obvious thing, I will admit; to kill you simply and directly with my own hands. But then I had the inspiration which led me to construct all this elaborate equipment.

"I shall not kill you myself; instead, Wanda shall do the deed. It will not be difficult to persuade her to pull the cord, and release the suspended knife. Her mentality is hardly suggestible, I will admit; but she happens to find bright objects irresistibly attractive. This is a common tendency for idiots and small children, as you doubtless know. My watch, for example . . ." He removed his large, sparkling silver watch from his pocket, and dangled it on its chain before Wanda's gaze. Instantly, her features were animated with a kind of childish desire; she reached out eagerly to take the shining object in her fingers.

BUT DR. BESWICK lifted it high, keeping it just beyond her reach, and yet still in plain view, so that she continued to regard it with simple-minded interest. "You see, Stuart," he continued, "how easy it will be to make Wanda play the role of your executioner. I have only to tie my watch-chain to the trigger-cord of my little apparatus; and she will grab the watch in a twinkling. The sword will drop, and you will be skewered like an insect in a collector's frame. . . . Now, frankly, my friend, looking at the situation quite impersonally, doesn't my scheme have a charming irony? You injure me by attempting to steal my wife; and I get my revenge by watching her slaughter you with her own lovely hands. . . . I flatter myself for the idea; I really do."

Very gently, Dr. Beswick restrained Wanda, while he fastened his watch to the dangling trip-cord. "Be patient, my dear," he murmured.

"You may play with the pretty watch in a moment; you may play with it to your heart's content . . . !"

While Beswick was occupied, Tom Stuart at last began to regain the use of his vocal cords. Speaking in a voice that came with difficulty, yet still managed to convey sheer desperation, he addressed himself neither to Wanda nor Beswick—but rather to the Negro servant, who still remained in the room.

"Kandru," he whispered. "Kandru—you must prevent this, do you understand? He's mad—your master is mad, crazy, out of his mind. Get help; call the police; do something, for God's sake. You—can't let this—happen. . . ."

Kandru might have been a sinister wooden sculpture, for all the response he showed to this plea; it was obvious that no hope lay in that direction. While his master continued to live, he would have ears for the voice of none other. Unless commanded by Beswick, he would take no part in the grisly drama, but neither would he dream of hindering or questioning his will.

Beswick himself, however, chose to notice Stuart's desperate supplication. "You consider me insane—a madman, a lunatic? Quite the contrary, my dear fellow; I assure you that I'm fully responsible for my actions. If I believed in your theories about the survival of the soul, it might even deter me from my course—because I'm quite convinced that I should be condemned to everlasting punishment. Certainly I should deserve it. But I fear I must remain a confirmed materialist, until I'm presented with some tangible proof of the reality of supernatural values; and so I mean to proceed without further interruption. . . .

"Now, Wanda, you can reach for the pretty watch, if you like. See—it's swinging back and forth on the long string. Isn't it lovely and shiny? Do you think you can grab it with your fingers, Wanda?"

As she saw the watch dangling on the trigger-cord, Wanda's expression of interest brightened. Tentatively, she stretched forth her lovely arm to seize it. With diabolical cunning, Beswick had tied it at such a height that she could barely touch it, while standing on tip-toe. She tried, but she could not quite grasp it.

SHE WOULD HAVE continued her efforts; but Stuart, in his extremity, managed to regain full use of his vocal organs. He suddenly shrieked at her, "Wanda! No, for God's sake! Don't let him make you do this, Wanda! It's Tom, Wanda, Tom Stuart; Tom, who loves you!"

Stuart's voice was fraught with desperation, not so much from physical fear as from the pure horror of watching the woman he loved about to commit this senseless and grisly butchery—but when Wanda recoiled from the watch at his words, it was only the sheer harsh volume of the outcry that caused her reaction. Plainly, she was utterly insensible to the pleading of the man she had once adored; she was nothing more than a small child shrinking away from a loud noise which it does not understand.

A shade of annoyance crossed Beswick's pallid countenance. "You've frightened her," he snapped. "Well, there's a way to prevent that. . . ." And he busied himself for a moment to find a strip of cloth in a nearby cabinet. With this, he approached Stuart, intending to gag him, and prevent any further outcry.

However, as he bent over his victim, Stuart's blue eyes caught his own with a glance that made him pause in spite of himself. And when the huge man began to speak once more, Beswick could not avoid attending to his words. They were uttered in a low, even tone, free now from any trace of the wild hysteria which a moment past had frightened Wanda. It seemed that Stuart, by a huge and abrupt effort of the will, had in the space of a few seconds conquered all fear, and had resigned himself to his fate.

"Beswick," he said, "you've won this round of the game. There's nothing on earth I can do to prevent you from committing this murder. You can torment and mutilate my body; but the real me won't be changed—any more than you

could change or injure the real self of Wanda, with your abominable drugs and radiations. You drove her soul out of the shell of her body, as you will presently drive out mine; that her flesh continues to live, as a mere automaton, whereas mine will be killed outright, makes no difference at all. Presently our two souls will be joined in the consummation they were never able to find in this world. I shall find Wanda, and we shall be as one for all eternity, in the world of spirits. I shall have only one duty, Beswick—one duty which I must fulfill, when I am released from my body, before I can fly to my soul's desire. . . .

"According to the laws of Karma, which regulate the course of every atom and every spirit in the universe, I must punish you for your misdeeds. I must follow you down the endless corridors of eternity, until at last you are trapped and helpless. I who am your victim now, must in the end play the role of executioner. There is no escape for you, Beswick; no hope—in all the shadows of eternal night, no hope. No hope . . ."

CHAPTER FOUR

THE FULFILLMENT OF KARMA

Now, for the first time, the ghoulish ecstasy of hate in the heart of the scientist was shot through with a tremor of fear. Somehow, these calm words of the man he was about to murder carried such a note of conviction, of utter and fatal certainty, that even Beswick's ingrained materialism was shaken. He could not repress an outward reaction to this qualm that disturbed his inward orgy of malice; and this reaction, strangely enough, was a flare of sudden and violent rage.

An ugly snarl contorting his full lips, Dr. Beswick gagged his helpless victim cruelly, so he could not utter a further sound. And not content with this violence, he struck the face of the huge man savagely with his hand.

"Liar," he hissed. "Liar, and fool! Suppose you did *live* on as a ghost or a spirit—why should I be afraid of a mere puff of wind, conscious or not? You wouldn't have any body; what could you do to injure me?

"But even that is impossible. There's nothing on the other side of death. *Nothing, do you hear?* Blackness, oblivion, nothingness! You're going out like a light; your body will rot in a tank of acid; and that will be your finish, for ever and ever! Do you hear that, Stuart! For ever and ever . . ."

Beswick was so absorbed in his own words, as he hurled these taunts at Stuart, that he failed to notice the actions of Wanda. She had forgotten her fright of a few moments past, and was renewing her interest in the bright dangling watch. Standing on tip-toe, she made a supreme effort to reach the shiny object which so fascinated her crude remnants of intelligence. At last she was able to clasp it between the very tips of her slender fingers; and with a little sigh of satisfaction, she pulled it down towards her.

There was a click of the trigger mechanism, and the heavy sword hurtled downward. Beswick was leaning close to Stuart as he spoke, and the evil weapon barely missed his head as it buried itself in the huge man's chest. As it was, a leaping fountain of warm blood spattered the face and clothes of the scientist, before he could draw away. . . .

After he had recovered from his shock of surprise, Beswick's main feeling was one of angry disappointment, which only increased the black rage already aroused in him by Stuart's threatening words. In a sense, he had fulfilled his long-cherished plan of revenge; things had gone exactly as he had intended; Wanda, with her own hand, had killed her former lover. And yet Beswick was not satisfied. There had been no time to gloat over the agony of the man he hated—indeed, Stuart's expression in death, as he lay there transfixed and bleeding, showed no agony at all, but rather a profound and entire peace. Somehow, the gaunt, gray-haired scientist had pictured the consummation of his plot in different colors; he felt cheated.

However, seeing that Tom Stuart was at last beyond his power, he wasted no time in carrying his scheme through to the end. With Kandru's help, he prepared a great vat of corrosive chemicals; and then he began to dismember the inert and mutilated body on the operating table. One grisly chunk of flesh after another he dropped into the fuming, seething hell-broth.

Finally, after he had removed every trace of blood on the laboratory floor and furniture, he turned to his Negro servant. "All right, Kandru. You can go to your quarters now. I shan't need you any more tonight. We'll empty the tank of acid in the morning. . . ."

WHEN KANDRU HAD passed silently to his quarters in an adjoining room, Beswick took Wanda by the hand, and led her out of the ghastly laboratory by another door.

"The fool," Beswick muttered. "Did he think I would ever let him take you from me, Wanda? You're mine, my white lovely Wanda; you belong to me alone, and nothing will ever make me let you go. . . ."

He led her into the adjoining bedroom, and made her lie down on the brocade covers of the wide bed. She followed quite docile and willing; plainly she was tired and sleepy, after all the excitement of the evening, and was only too glad to be put to bed. Beswick watched her long lashes close over her liquid dark eyes; her breathing grew deep and slow; soon she was lost in sweet and innocent slumber.

He told himself that, everything considered, it had been a most satisfactory evening—at least it seemed so now, in retrospect. Quickly he had commenced to scrub away some bloodstains that remained under his finger-nails—when he caught a sound that made him pause and wheel abruptly away from the wash-stand. The dry little tune choked to silence in his throat. He could have sworn that he was not mistaken: a voice, a man's voice, had spoken his name. It had sounded from behind him, from the bedroom—not loud, but clear and distinct.

With a single stride, Beswick was at the door, peering into the softly lighted chamber. It was quite empty; there was no one present except Wanda, who still lay quietly on the bed. There was no possible place of concealment for anyone else; he *had* been mistaken then, after all. . . .

Almost angrily, as he returned to the wash-basin, Beswick told himself not to be a fool. There was nothing to get jumpy and nervous about; it was absurd to imagine things like that voice, sounding from nowhere. At this rate, he would soon be as bad as that fool Stuart, with his talk of Oriental mysteries, of ghosts and spirits floating around without any bodies. . . . Nevertheless, Dr. Beswick did not resume his humming, as he went on with the task of cleaning his hands.

He had removed the last trace of blood, and was wiping his fingers on a towel, when he heard his name spoken once again.

"Beswick!" It sounded, distinctly and evenly, in deep-throated masculine accents; and this time, he knew there could be no possible error. It was very close, too; as if the speaker stood framed in the door between the bathroom and the bedroom.

On the previous occasion, Beswick had whirled in sudden alarm; but now he felt a chill of fear that almost paralyzed him. Slowly, slowly, he forced himself to turn in the direction of the voice, hardly daring to guess what he would find confronting him in the doorway.

WHEN HE SAW that it was only Wanda, his relief was almost overwhelming in its intensity. It was so great, indeed, that he forgot for an instant to wonder how his wife had been able to leave the bed and approach him so silently behind his back; and also he forgot the fact that his name had been spoken in a man's voice, rather than a woman's.

But Beswick's respite from terror was only momentary. As Wanda stood there before him, superbly beautiful in her long white silken robe, he realized that in some subtle and indefinable

way, she had changed. She kept her right hand behind her back, as though it held something she wished to conceal. And in her eyes, the vacant look had given place to an expression of insight, of sheer intelligence, that was almost more than human.

Beswick checked himself from almost automatically ordering his wife back to bed, as if she were a disobedient child; the strong sense that she had undergone some weird psychic metamorphosis, kindled again the embers of his fear until the flames of panic leaped dangerously. He could not have told why; but he felt a strange impulse to flee, to escape at all costs from the level gaze of those dark eyes; and almost without conscious volition, he began to sidle toward the other door of the bathroom—the one that led to the gleaming scientific laboratory.

But then, Wanda's lips parted; and the sound of spoken words came from her throat. "It's no use, Beswick. You can't escape. It won't do you any good to run away. . . ."

As he heard these syllables, Beswick's heart seemed transformed to cold stone in his body; the paralysis of his terror became complete, and he was rooted to the spot where he stood. It was not so much the meaning he got from the grim phrases that terrified him, as the actual tones that pronounced them.

There was no doubt whatever that the voice he heard, issued from Wanda's soft, feminine lips; and yet it was most certainly not a woman's voice. It was the unmistakable utterance of a man, a powerful man, virile, deep-chested and forceful. . . .

The increasing realization that froze Dr. Beswick's soul prevented him, for the time being, from moving a limb; but he did manage to speak a few syllables in a dry, croaking and almost toneless voice.

"Stuart . . . You told—the truth. *You* have *come back—from the dead.* . . ."

"Correct, at the very first guess, Beswick." The effect of that stern baritone coming from Wanda's body might conceivably have been ridiculous under other circumstances. As things were, the very grotesqueness of the phenomenon, its shocking and profoundly unnatural quality, added the final touch of horror to a situation already fraught with soul-shaking implications.

TOM STUART'S VOICE continued:

"Already you are reaping the harvest sown by your abominable deeds. . . . Do you remember your taunt, that you made only a short time ago, Beswick? While you spoke, I was already separating my consciousness from the body you were about to destroy—an ability I acquired in the remote mountains of Tibet. But I heard you distinctly, nevertheless. These were your words: *'Suppose you did live on, as a ghost or a spirit—why should I be afraid of a mere puff of wind, conscious or not? You wouldn't have any body; what could you do to injure me . . . ?'*

"You were quite correct, Beswick, in a certain limited sense; my disembodied spirit could not affect you in any way, so long as you remained in the flesh. But you failed to realize one thing, in your conceited scientific ignorance. There, at hand, ready and waiting, was a sound physical body; the flesh and blood which once belonged to Wanda; the earthly vehicle through which I am speaking and acting at the present moment. You are a connoisseur of ironies, Beswick, so permit me to point out this one for your delectation.

"It was your own abominable treatment with drugs and electric rays that drove Wanda's soul out of her body, leaving it a mere empty shell without a guiding intelligence. I had only to wait until the right moment to take possession of its untenanted brain and nervous system. For the time being it is my body, the body of Tom Stuart, to be used in obedience to my will. And now, James Beswick, it becomes my duty, in fulfillment of the inscrutable laws of Karma, to punish you for your ghastly and deliberate crimes. . . ."

Slowly, as Tom Stuart's voice spoke those grim words, Wanda Beswick's slender arm came into view, the hand grasping an object that un-til now had remained in concealment behind her back. It was a heavy silver candlestick, one of a pair that graced the dressing table in the bedroom: a formidable bludgeon, with its long shank and leaded base.

"It becomes my duty," the voice of Stuart intoned, "to shatter and destroy the house of flesh in which lurks your miserable soul. Your unclean spirit shall be driven forth from its earthly refuge, to be seized as it deserves by the owl-eyed demons of the Nether World. . . ."

The sight of the heavy candlestick, raised slowly and menacingly before his eyes, had the effect of breaking at least partially the paralysis of terror which had gripped Beswick. Whining in a perfectly inarticulate excess of fear, slobbering and wheezing, he began to inch backward, through the open door that gave entrance to the laboratory.

Inexorably, Wanda's beautiful white-robed body, animated by the spirit of Tom Stuart, advanced upon him; slow and deliberate as the movement of Fate itself, and equally relentless.

AND SO, INCH by inch, foot by foot, James Beswick was forced backward into his laboratory. Half-across the room he retreated, unable to do more than shuffle spasmodically, as if he were struggling against some horrible unseen magnetism that controlled him against his will.

At last, however, gathering all his resources of energy into a single titanic effort, he managed to break the spell; his semi-paralyzed muscles were abruptly galvanized into action, and he wheeled in his tracks as if to burst from the room in a mad dash for freedom.

He did not see the great porcelain vat of acid directly behind him—the devil's cauldron in which he had earlier dissolved the tormented body of Stuart, piece by piece. The rim of the tank caught him directly at the back of the knee-joint; and he lost his balance. Perceiving in a flash what had happened, he tried frantically to save himself; but the impetus of his panic was too great. . . .

As he toppled into the vat, he screamed once—a dreadful, rasping, piercing wail—the utterance of a soul already trapped in the murky pit of eternal damnation and agony.

The seething chemical splashed and closed over his writhing body. Once, for a brief moment, he stretched forth a hand, the fingers already blackened and charred as if by searing flames. But then the frantically gesturing limb was gone again; and no trace remained of James Montague Beswick save an oily scum which gathered slowly on the bubbling surface of the acid. . . .

A few moments later, the Negro servant, Kandru, burst through the door. He had heard the dying scream of his master, and had rushed from his room to see what was wrong. The sight which confronted him, in the mercilessly clear light that flooded the white-walled, glittering laboratory, was sufficiently awesome to strike even his primitive, insensate intelligence with wonder and terror.

Slender, gardenia-pale, flawlessly beautiful, Wanda Beswick was deliberately stepping into the fuming tank of acid in the middle of the floor, as if it were nothing more than a pool of clear water.

Where her flesh came in contact with the chemical, it was visibly seared and disintegrated; and yet she showed no sign of pain whatever. Her eyes caught the murky eyes of the Negro, even as she sank slowly into the corrosive liquid. And then Kandru heard the solemn tones of a man's voice, which strangely seemed to come from the slender body of the disappearing woman.

"A judgement has been performed," the voice said, "and a tragedy concerning three human souls has ended. When this outworn shell of flesh is consumed and disintegrated, two of those souls will find each other, and they will be joined together for all eternity in the bliss and utter fulfillment of love. The third has already found the reward which he earned for himself by his actions.

"As for you, Black Man, you have sinned; and yet you are not entirely to blame; you are dominated by an intelligence more subtle than your own. Before you lies the remainder of this life, and all the eternity of mortal re-births, recurring until you reach the stage of full responsibility for your own actions. Let the fate of your master, who has been swallowed up by the darkness without dawn, be your warning, that you may profit by the lessons of experience. Heed these words, Black Man—the words of one who has passed through the flames of human suffering and already beholds the cool radiance of truth. . . ."

As he heard this solemn pronouncement—even though the literal meaning of the syllables was beyond his comprehension—Kandru felt a strange emotion of wonder and the profoundest awe. Many years ago, as a small child, he had strayed into the gloomy and eternal shadows of the rainforest in his native Africa, and he had felt something of this same soul-stirring intimation: a sense of dark mystery, of unseen eyes regarding him from the fathomless shadows—a sense, above all, of his own weakness and insignificance and lack of understanding.

His reaction now, as it had been then, was almost automatic; the response of his race for untold generations to the presence of the Unknown. Uttering something between a wail and a ritual chant, Kandru sank to his knees, and grovelled forward on the tiled floor. His arms outstretched, fingers groping and tense, he bowed down again and again before the Universal Mystery.

THE SONG THE ZOMBIE SANG

HARLAN ELLISON AND
ROBERT SILVERBERG

HARLAN (JAY) ELLISON (1934–) was born in Cleveland, Ohio. After jobs in widely diverse fields, he became a prolific short-story writer, essayist, critic, novelist, screen- and teleplay writer, becoming perhaps the most honored author of speculative fiction who ever lived. He has won ten Hugo Awards (for best science fiction or fantasy work), four Nebula Awards, including the Grand Master for lifetime achievement (presented by the Science Fiction and Fantasy Writers of America), five Bram Stoker Awards, including one for lifetime achievement (given by the Horror Writers Association), eighteen *Locus* poll awards (presented by the preeminent fan magazine in the speculative fiction field), two Edgar Allan Poe Awards from the Mystery Writers of America, and is the only writer ever to win the Writers Guild of America award for Most Outstanding Teleplay four times.

Robert Silverberg (1935–) was born in Brooklyn, New York, and received his B.A. from Columbia University in 1956. Introverted and alienated, he began to write science fiction stories while still in school, winning a Hugo Award in 1956 as Best New Writer. He was enormously prolific, turning out more than a million words a year, by his own account, under numerous pseudonyms, and in collaboration with many of America's greatest writers of speculative fiction, including Isaac Asimov, Randall Garrett, Harlan Ellison, and Arthur C. Clarke. Among his numerous awards, and even more nominations, are three Hugos, five Nebulas, and a Grand Master award from the Science Fiction and Fantasy Writers of America.

"The Song the Zombie Sang" was first published in the December 1970 issue of *Cosmopolitan*.

HARLAN ELLISON AND ROBERT SILVERBERG

THE SONG THE ZOMBIE SANG

FROM THE FOURTH balcony of the Los Angeles Music Center the stage was little more than a brilliant blur of constantly changing chromatics—stabs of bright green, looping whorls of crimson. But Rhoda preferred to sit up there. She had no use for the Golden Horseshoe seats, buoyed on their grab-grav plates, bobbling loosely just beyond the fluted lip of the stage. Down there the sound flew off, flew up and away, carried by the remarkable acoustics of the Center's Takamuri dome. The colors were important, but it was the sound that really mattered, the patterns of resonance bursting from the hundred quivering outputs of the ultracembalo.

And if you sat below, you had the vibrations of the people down there—

She was hardly naive enough to think that the poverty that sent students up to the top was more ennobling than the wealth that permitted access to a Horseshoe; yet even though she had never actually sat through an entire concert down there, she could not deny that music heard from the fourth balcony was purer, more affecting, lasted longer in the memory. Perhaps it *was* the vibrations of the rich.

Arms folded on the railing of the balcony, she stared down at the rippling play of colors that washed the sprawling proscenium. Dimly she was aware that the man at her side was saying something. Somehow responding didn't seem important. Finally he nudged her, and she turned to him. A faint, mechanical smile crossed her face. "What is it, Laddy?"

Ladislas Jirasek mournfully extended a chocolate bar. Its end was ragged from having been nibbled. "Man cannot live by Bekh alone," he said.

"No, thanks, Laddy." She touched his hand lightly.

"What do you see down there?"

"Colors. That's all."

"No music of the spheres? No insight into the truths of your art?"

"You promised not to make fun of me."

He slumped back in his seat. "I'm sorry. I forget sometimes."

"Please, Laddy. If it's the liaison thing that's bothering you, I—"

"I didn't say a word about liaison, did I?"

"It was in your tone. You were starting to feel sorry for yourself. Please don't. You know I hate it when you start dumping guilt on me."

He had sought an official liaison with her for months, almost since the day they had met in Contrapuntal 301. He had been fascinated by her, amused by her, and finally had fallen quite hopelessly in love with her. Still she kept just beyond his reach. He had had her, but had never possessed her. Because he did feel sorry for himself, and she knew it, and the knowledge put him, for her, forever in the category of men who were simply not for long-term liaison.

She stared down past the railing. Waiting. Taut. A slim girl, honey-colored hair, eyes the lightest gray, almost the shade of aluminum. Her fingers lightly curved as if about to pounce

446

on a keyboard. Music uncoiling eternally in her head.

"They say Bekh was brilliant in Stuttgart last week," Jirasek said hopefully.

"He did the Kreutzer?"

"And Timijian's Sixth and *The Knife* and some Scarlatti."

"Which?"

"I don't know. I don't remember what they said. But he got a ten-minute standing ovation, and *Der Musikant* said they hadn't heard such precise ornamentation since—"

The houselights dimmed.

"He's coming," Rhoda said, leaning forward. Jirasek slumped back and gnawed the chocolate bar down to its wrapper.

COMING OUT OF it was always gray. The color of aluminum. He knew the charging was over, knew he'd been unpacked, knew when he opened his eyes that he would be at stage right, and there would be a grip ready to roll the ultracembalo's input console onstage, and the filament gloves would be in his right-hand jacket pocket. And the taste of sand on his tongue, and the gray fog of resurrection in his mind.

Nils Bekh put off opening his eyes.

Stuttgart had been a disaster. Only he knew how much of a disaster. *Timi would have known,* he thought. *He would have come up out of the audience during the scherzo, and he would have ripped the gloves off my hands, and he would have cursed me for killing his vision.* And later they would have gone to drink the dark, nutty beer together. But Timijian was dead. *Died in '20,* Bekh told himself. *Five years before me.*

I'll keep my eyes closed, I'll dampen the breathing. Will the lungs to suck more shallowly, the bellows to vibrate rather than howl with winds. And they'll think I'm malfunctioning, that the zombianic response wasn't triggered this time. That I'm still dead, really dead, not—

"Mr. Bekh."

He opened his eyes.

The stage manager was a thug. He recognized the type. Stippling of unshaved beard. Crumpled cuffs. Latent homosexuality. Tyrant to everyone backstage except, perhaps, the chorus boys in the revivals of Romberg and Friml confections.

"I've known men to develop diabetes just catching a matinee," Bekh said.

"What's that? I don't understand."

Bekh waved it away. "Nothing. Forget it. How's the house?"

"Very nice, Mr. Bekh. The houselights are down. We're ready."

Bekh reached into his right-hand jacket pocket and removed the thin electronic gloves, sparkling with their rows of minisensors and pressors. He pulled the right glove tight, smoothing all wrinkles. The material clung like a second skin. "If you please," he said. The grip rolled the console onstage, positioned it, locked it down with the dogging pedals, and hurried offstage left through the curtains.

Now Bekh strolled out slowly. Moving with great care: tubes of glittering fluids ran through his calves and thighs, and if he walked too fast the hydrostatic balance was disturbed and the nutrients didn't get to his brain. The fragility of the perambulating dead was a nuisance, one among many. When he reached the grab-grav plate he signalled the stage manager. The thug gave the sign to the panel-man, who passed his fingers over the color-coded keys, and the grab-grav plate rose slowly, majestically. Up through the floor of the stage went Nils Bekh. As he emerged, the chromatics keyed sympathetic vibrations in the audience, and they began to applaud.

He stood silently, head slightly bowed, accepting their greeting. A bubble of gas ran painfully through his back and burst near his spine. His lower lip twitched slightly. He suppressed the movement. Then he stepped off the plate, walked to the console, and began pulling on the other glove.

He was a tall, elegant man, very pale, with harsh brooding cheekbones and a craggy, massive nose that dominated the flower-gentle eyes, the thin mouth. He looked properly romantic. An important artistic asset, they told him when he was starting out, a million years ago.

As he pulled and smoothed the other glove, he heard the whispering. When one has died, one's hearing becomes terribly acute. It made listening to one's own performances that much more painful. But he knew what the whispers were all about. Out there someone was saying to his wife:

"Of course he doesn't *look* like a zombie. They kept him in cold till they had the techniques. *Then* they wired him and juiced him and brought him back."

And the wife would say, "How does it work, how does he keep coming back to life, what is it?"

And the husband would lean far over on the arm of his chair, resting his elbow, placing the palm of his hand in front of his mouth and looking warily around to be certain that no one would overhear the blurred inaccuracies he was about to utter. And he would try to tell his wife about the residual electric charge of the brain cells, the persistence of the motor responses after death, the lingering mechanical vitality on which they had seized. In vague and rambling terms he would speak of the built-in life-support system that keeps the brain flushed with necessary fluids. The surrogate hormones, the chemicals that take the place of blood. "You know how they stick an electric wire up a frog's leg, when they cut it off. Okay. Well, when the leg jerks, they call that a galvanic response. Now if you can get a whole *man* to jerk when you put a current through him—not really jerking, I mean that he walks around, he can play his instrument—"

"Can he think too?"

"I suppose. I don't know. The brain's intact. They don't let it decay. What they do, they use every part of the body for its mechanical function—the heart's a pump, the lungs are bellows—and they wire in a bunch of contacts and leads, and then there's a kind of twitch, an artificial burst of life—of course, they can keep it going only five, six hours, then the fatigue-

poisons start to pile up and clog the lines—but that's long enough for a concert, anyway—"

"So what they're really doing is they take a man's brain, and they keep it alive by using his own body as the life-support machine," the wife says brightly. "Is that it? Instead of putting him into some kind of box, they keep him in his own skull, and do all the machinery inside his body—"

"That's it. That's it exactly, more or less. More or less."

Bekh ignored the whispers. He had heard them all hundreds of times before. In New York and Beirut, in Hanoi and Knossos, in Kenyatta and Paris. How fascinated they were. Did they come for the music, or to see the dead man walk around?

He sat down on the player's ledge in front of the console, and laid his hands along the metal fibers. A deep breath: old habit, superfluous, inescapable. The fingers already twitching. The pressors seeking the keys. Under the close-cropped gray hair, the synapses clicking like relays. Here, now. Timijian's Ninth Sonata. Let it soar. Bekh closed his eyes and put his shoulders into his work, and from the ring of outputs overhead came the proper roaring tones. There. It has begun. Easily, lightly, Bekh rang in the harmonics, got the sympathetic pipes vibrating, built up the texture of sound. He had not played the Ninth for two years. Vienna. How long is two years? It seemed hours ago. He still heard the reverberations. And duplicated them exactly; this performance differed from the last one no more than one playing of a recording differs from another. An image sprang into his mind: a glistening sonic cube sitting at the console in place of a man. Why do they need me, when they could put a cube in the slot and have the same thing at less expense? And I could rest. And I could rest. There. Keying in the subsonics. This wonderful instrument! What if Bach had known it? Beethoven? To hold a whole world in your fingertips. The entire spectrum of sound, and the colors, too, and more: hitting the audience in a dozen senses at once. Of course, the music is what matters. The frozen, unchanging music. The pattern of sounds emerging now as always, now as he had played it at the premiere in '19. Timijian's last work. Decibel by decibel, a reconstruction of my own performance. And look at them out there. Awed. Loving. Bekh felt tremors in his elbows; too tense, the nerves betraying him. He made the necessary compensations. Hearing the thunder reverberating from the fourth balcony. What is this music all about? Do I in fact understand any of it? Does the sonic cube comprehend the B Minor Mass that is recorded within itself? Does the amplifier understand the symphony it amplifies? Bekh smiled. Closed his eyes. The shoulders surging, the wrists supple. Two hours to go. Then they let me sleep again. Is it fifteen years, now? Awaken, perform, sleep. And the adoring public cooing at me. The women who would love to give themselves to me. Necrophiliacs? How could they even want to touch me? The dryness of the tomb on my skin. Once there were women, yes, Lord, yes! Once. Once there was life, too. Bekh leaned back and swept forward. The old virtuoso swoop; brings down the house. The chill in their spines. Now the sound builds toward the end of the first movement. Yes, yes, so. Bekh opened the topmost bank of outputs and heard the audience respond, everyone sitting up suddenly as the new smash of sound cracked across the air. Good old Timi: a wonderful sense of the theatrical. Up. Up. Knock them back in their seats. He smiled with satisfaction at his own effects. And then the sense of emptiness. Sound for its own sake. Is this what music means? Is this a masterpiece? I know nothing any more. How tired I am of playing for them. Will they applaud? Yes, and stamp their feet and congratulate one another on having been lucky enough to hear me tonight. And what do they know? What do I know. I am dead. I am nothing. I am nothing. With a demonic two-handed plunge he hammered out the final fugal screams of the first movement.

Weatherex had programmed mist, and somehow it fit Rhoda's mood. They stood on the glass landscape that swept down from the Music Cen-

ter, and Jirasek offered her the pipe. She shook her head absently, thinking of other things. "I have a pastille," she said.

"What do you say we look up Inez and Treat, see if they want to get something to eat?"

She didn't answer.

"Rhoda?"

"Will you excuse me, Laddy? I think I want to be all by myself for a while."

He slipped the pipe into his pocket and turned to her. She was looking through him as if he were no less glass than the scene surrounding them. Taking her hands in his own, he said, "Rhoda, I just don't understand. You won't even give me time to find the words."

"Laddy—"

"No. This time I'll have my say. Don't pull away. Don't retreat into that little world of yours, with your half-smiles and your faraway looks."

"I want to think about the music."

"There's more to life than music, Rhoda. There has to be. I've spent as many years as you working inside my head, working to create something. You're better than I am, you're maybe better than anyone I've ever heard, maybe even better than Bekh some day. Fine: you're a great artist. But is that all? There's something more. It's idiocy to make your art your religion, your whole existence."

"Why are you doing this to me?"

"Because I love you."

"That's an explanation, not an excuse. Let me go, Laddy. Please."

"Rhoda, art doesn't mean a damn thing if it's just craft, if it's just rote and technique and formulas. It doesn't mean anything if there isn't love behind it, and caring, and commitment to life. You deny all that. You split yourself and smother the part that fires the art . . ."

He stopped abruptly. It was not the sort of speech a man could deliver without realizing, quickly, crushingly, how sententious and treacly it sounded. He dropped her hands. "I'll be at Treat's, if you want to see me later." He turned and walked away into the shivering reflective night.

Rhoda watched him go. She suspected there were things she should have said. But she hadn't said them. He disappeared. Turning, she stared up at the overwhelming bulk of the Music Center, and began slowly to walk toward it.

"MAESTRO, YOU WERE exquisite tonight," the Pekinese woman said in the Green Room. "Golden," added the bullfrog sycophant. "A joy. I cried, really cried," trilled the birds. Nutrients bubbled in his chest. He could feel valves flapping. He dipped his head, moved his hands, whispered thankyous. Staleness settled grittily behind his forehead. "Superb." "Unforgettable." "Incredible." Then they went away and he was left, as always, with the keepers. The man from the corporation that owned him, the stage manager, the packers, the electrician. "Perhaps it's time," said the corporation man, smoothing his mustache lightly. He had learned to be delicate with the zombie.

Bekh sighed and nodded. They turned him off.

"WANT TO GET something to eat first?" the electrician said. He yawned. It had been a long tour, late nights, meals in jetports, steep angles of ascent and rapid reentries.

The corporation man nodded. "All right. We can leave him here for a while. I'll put him on standby." He touched a switch.

The lights went off in banks, one by one. Only the nightlights remained for the corporation man and the electrician, for their return, for their final packing.

The Music Center shut down.

In the bowels of the self-contained system the dust-eaters and a dozen other species of cleanup machines began stirring, humming softly.

In the fourth balcony, a shadow moved. Rhoda worked her way toward the downslide, emerging in the center aisle of the orchestra, into the Horseshoe, around the pit, and onto the stage. She went to the console and let her hands rest an inch above the keys. Closing her eyes, catching her breath. I will begin my concert with the Timijian Ninth Sonata for Unaccompanied Ultracembalo. A light patter of applause, gathering force, now tempestuous. Waiting. The fingers descending. The world alive with her music. Fire and tears, joy, radiance. All of them caught in the spell. How miraculous. How wonderfully she plays. Looking out into the darkness, hearing in her tingling mind the terrible echoes of the silence. Thank you. Thank you all so much. Her eyes moist. Moving away from the console. The flow of fantasy ebbing.

She went on into the dressing room and stood just within the doorway, staring across the room at the corpse of Nils Bekh in the sustaining chamber, his eyes closed, his chest still, his hands relaxed at his sides. She could see the faintest bulge in his right jacket pocket where the thin gloves lay, fingers folded together.

Then she moved close to him, looked down into his face, and touched his cheek. His beard never grew. His skin was cool and satiny, a peculiarly feminine texture. Strangely, through the silence, she remembered the sinuous melody of the *Liebestod,* that greatest of all laments, and rather than the great sadness the passage always brought to her, she felt herself taken by anger. Gripped by frustration and disappointment, choked by betrayal, caught in a seizure of violence. She wanted to rake the pudding-smooth skin of his face with her nails. She wanted to pummel him. Deafen him with screams. Destroy him. For the lie. For the lies, the many lies, the unending flow of lying notes, the lies of his life after death.

Her trembling hand hovered by the side of the chamber. Is this the switch?

She turned him on.

He came out of it. Eyes closed. Rising through a universe the color of aluminum. Again, then. Again. He thought he would stand there a moment with eyes closed, collecting himself, before going onstage. It got harder and harder. The last time had been so bad. In Los Angeles, in that vast building, balcony upon balcony, thousands of blank faces, the ultracembalo such a master-piece of construction. He had opened the concert with Timi's Ninth. So dreadful. A sluggish performance, note-perfect, the tempi flawless, and yet sluggish, empty, shallow. And tonight it would happen again. Shamble out on stage, don the gloves, go through the dreary routine of re-creating the greatness of Nils Bekh.

His audience, his adoring followers. How he hated them! How he longed to turn on them and denounce them for what they had done to him. Schnabel rested. Horowitz rested. Joachim rested. But for Bekh there was no rest. They had not allowed him to go. Oh, he could have refused to let them sustain him. But he had never been that strong. He had had strength for the loveless, lightless years of living with his music, yes. For that there had never been enough time. Strong was what he had had to be. To come from where he had been, to learn what had to be learned, to keep his skills once they were his. Yes. But in dealing with people, in speaking out, in assert-ing himself . . . in short, having courage . . . no, there had been very little of that. He had lost Dorothea, he had acceded to Wizmer's plans, he had borne the insults Lisbeth and Neil and Cosh—ah, gee, Cosh, was he still alive?—the in-sults they had used to keep him tied to them, for better or worse, always worse. So he had gone with them, done their bidding, never availed himself of his strength—if in fact there was strength of that sort buried somewhere in him—and in the end even Sharon had despised him.

So how could he go to the edge of the stage, stand there in the full glare of the lights and tell them what they were? Ghouls. Selfish ghouls. As dead as he was, but in a different way. Unfeeling, hollow.

But if he could! If he could just once outwit the corporation man, he would throw himself forward and he would shout—

Pain. A stinging pain in his cheek. His head jolted back; the tiny pipes in his neck pro-tested. The sound of flesh on flesh echoed in his mind. Startled, he opened his eyes. A girl before him. The color of aluminum, her eyes. A young

face. Fierce. Thin lips tightly clamped. Nostrils flaring. Why is she so angry? She was raising her hand to slap him again. He threw his hands up, wrists crossed, palms forward, to protect his eyes. The second blow landed more heavily than the first. Were delicate things shattering within his reconstructed body?

The look on her face! She hated him.

She slapped him a third time. He peered out between his fingers, astonished by the vehe-mence of her eyes. And felt the flooding pain, and felt the hate, and felt a terribly wonderful sense of life for just that one moment. Then he remembered too much, and he stopped her.

He could see as he grabbed her swinging hand that she found his strength improbable. Fifteen years a zombie, moving and living for only seven hundred four days of that time. Still, he was fully operable, fully conditioned, fully muscled.

The girl winced. He released her and shoved her away. She was rubbing her wrist and staring at him silently, sullenly.

"If you don't like me," he asked, "why did you turn me on?"

"So I could tell you I know what a fraud you are. These others, the ones who applaud and grovel and suck up to you, they don't know, they have no idea, but *I* know. How can you do it? How can you have made such a disgusting spectacle of yourself?" She was shaking. "I heard you when I was a child," she said. "You changed my whole life. I'll never forget it. But I've heard you lately. Slick formulas, no real in-sight. Like a machine sitting at the console. A player piano. You know what player pianos were, Bekh. That's what you are."

He shrugged. Walking past her, he sat down and glanced in the dressing-room mirror. He looked old and weary, the changeless face changing now. There was a flatness to his eyes. They were without sheen, without depths. An empty sky.

"Who are you?" he asked quietly. "How did you get in here?"

"Report me, go ahead. I don't care if I'm arrested. Someone had to say it. You're shameful! Walking around, pretending to make music— don't you see how awful it is? A performer is an interpretative artist, not just a machine for playing the notes. I shouldn't have to tell you that. An interpretative artist. Artist. Where's your art now? Do you see beyond the score? Do you grow from performance to performance?"

Suddenly he liked her very much. Despite her plainness, despite her hatred, despite himself. "You're a musician."

She let that pass.

"What do you play?" Then he smiled. "The ultracembalo, of course. And you must be very good."

"Better than you. Clearer, cleaner, deeper. Oh, God, what am I doing here? You *disgust* me."

"How can I keep on growing?" Bekh asked gently. "The dead don't grow."

Her tirade swept on, as if she hadn't heard. Telling him over and over how despicable he was, what a counterfeit of greatness. And then she halted in midsentence. Blinking, reddening, putting hands to lips. "Oh," she murmured, abashed, starting to weep. "Oh. *Oh!*"

She went silent.

It lasted a long time. She looked away, studied the walls, the mirror, her hands, her shoes. He watched her. Then, finally, she said, "What an arrogant little snot I am. What a cruel foolish bitch. I never stopped to think that you— that maybe—I just didn't think—" He thought she would run from him. "And you won't forgive me, will you? Why should you? I break in, I turn you on, I scream a lot of cruel nonsense at you—"

"It wasn't nonsense. It was all quite true, you know. Absolutely true." Then, softly, he said, "Break the machinery."

"Don't worry. I won't cause any more trouble for you. I'll go, now. I can't tell you how foolish I feel, haranguing you like that. A dumb little puritan puffed up with pride in her own art. Telling *you* that you don't measure up to my ideals. When I—"

"You didn't hear me. I asked you to break the machinery."

She looked at him in a new way, slightly out of focus. "What are you talking about?"

"To stop me. I want to be gone. Is that so hard to understand? You, of all people, should understand that. What you say is true, very very true. Can you put yourself where I am? A thing, not alive, not dead, just a thing, a tool, an implement that unfortunately thinks and remembers and wishes for release. Yes, a player piano. My life stopped and my art stopped, and I have nothing to belong to now, not even the art. For it's always the same. Always the same tones, the same reaches, the same heights. Pretending to make music, as you say. Pretending."

"But I can't—"

"Of course you can. Come, sit down, we'll discuss it. And you'll play for me."

"Play for you?"

He reached out his hand and she started to take it, then drew her hand back. "You'll have to play for me," he said quietly. "I can't let just anyone end me. That's a big, important thing, you see. Not just anyone. So you'll play for me." He got heavily to his feet. Thinking of Lisbeth, Sharon, Dorothea. Gone, all gone now. Only he, Bekh, left behind, some of him left behind, old bones, dried meat. Breath as stale as Egypt, blood the color of pumice. Sounds devoid of tears and laughter. Just sounds.

He led the way, and she followed him, out onto the stage, where the console still stood uncrated. He gave her his gloves, saying, "I know they aren't yours. I'll take that into account. Do the best you can." She drew them on slowly, smoothing them.

She sat down at the console. He saw the fear in her face, and the ecstasy, also. Her fingers hovering over the keys. Pouncing. God, Timi's Ninth! The tones swelling and rising, and the fear going from her face. Yes. Yes. He would not have played it that way, but yes, just so. Timi's notes filtered through *her* soul. A striking interpretation. Perhaps she falters a little, but why not?

The wrong gloves, no preparation, strange circumstances. And how beautifully she plays. The hall fills with sound. He ceases to listen as a critic might: he becomes part of the music. His own fingers moving, his muscles quivering, reaching for pedals and stops, activating the pressors. As if he plays through her. She goes on, soaring higher, losing the last of her nervousness. In full command. Not yet a finished artist, but so good, so wonderfully good! Making the mighty instrument sing. Draining its full resources. Underscoring this, making that more lean. Oh, yes! He is in the music. It engulfs him. Can he cry? Do the tearducts still function? He can hardly bear it, it is so beautiful. He has forgotten, in all these years. He has not heard anyone else play for so long. Seven hundred four days. Out of the tomb. Bound up in his own meaningless performances. And now this. The rebirth of music. It was once like this all the time, the union of composer and instrument and performer, soul-wrenching, all-encompassing. For him. No longer. Eyes closed, he plays the movement through to its close by way of her body, her hands, her soul. When the sound dies away, he feels the good exhaustion that comes from total submission to the art.

"That's fine," he said, when the last silence was gone. "That was very lovely." A catch in his voice. His hands were still trembling; he was afraid to applaud.

He reached for her, and this time she took his hand. For a moment he held her cool fingers. Then he tugged gently, and she followed him back into the dressing room, and he lay down on the sofa, and he told her which mechanisms to break, after she turned him off, so he would feel no pain. Then he closed his eyes and waited.

"You'll just—go?" she asked.

"Quickly. Peacefully."

"I'm afraid. It's like murder."

"I'm dead," he said. "But not dead enough. You won't be killing anything. Do you remember how my playing sounded to you? Do you remember why I came here? Is there life in me?"

"I'm still afraid."

"I've earned my rest," he said. He opened his eyes and smiled. "It's all right. I like you." And, as she moved toward him, he said, "Thank you."

Then he closed his eyes again.

She turned him off.

THEN SHE DID as he had instructed her.

Picking her way past the wreckage of the sustaining chamber, she left the dressing room. She found her way out of the Music Center—out onto the glass landscape, under the singing stars, and she was crying for him.

Laddy. She wanted very much to find Laddy now. To talk to him. To tell him he was almost right about what he'd told her. Not entirely, but more than she had believed . . . before. She went away from there. Smoothly, with songs yet to be sung.

And behind her, a great peace had settled. Unfinished, at last the symphony had wrung its last measure of strength and sorrow.

It did not matter what Weatherex said was the proper time for mist or rain or fog. Night, the stars, the songs were forever.

MEN WITHOUT BLOOD

JOHN H. KNOX

ALTHOUGH JOHN H. KNOX (1905–1983) was known as a pulp writer, the son of a pastor in Abilene, Texas, grew up loving Shakespeare, poetry, and the world's greatest literature; among his favorites were such serious and inaccessible authors as Thomas Mann, Knut Hamsun, and Marcel Proust. During the Great Depression, he spent two years working at odd jobs while living the life of a hobo, riding railcars, before returning to Texas to devote his free time to writing. While his first sale was a poem, he saw a large pulp magazine market and aimed his prose style in that direction with nearly immediate success. He sold a story to the new and prestigious *Dime Detective* magazine, "Frozen Energy," which ran in its December 1933 issue, and he was able to sell a story virtually every month for the next seven years, either under his own name or a pseudonym, producing more than a million words in all. Most of the tales were in the horror and weird menace category, seldom relying on supernatural elements but featuring graphic scenes of violence and harrowing descriptions of torture. When socially conscious groups and politicians effectively forced the pulps to eliminate these lurid stories from their pages, Knox took jobs as a steelworker, farmer, and real estate agent. He sold a few more stories to *Dime Detective* and *Black Mask* after World War II, but the pulp era was over, and so was Knox's writing career when a long novel on which he had worked for years was lost in a fire.

"Men without Blood" was first published in the January 1935 issue of *Horror Stories*.

JOHN H. KNOX

MEN WITHOUT BLOOD

FOG, LIKE A blind amorphous monster, imposed its tenuous bulk upon the city. A great grey-bellied beast, it brooded above the skyline, pushed down its clammy filaments into the canyon of the street, strangling the bleary street lamps, puffing convulsed wraiths into the dank, black alleys of the slums.

The man who sat in the sickly light from the globe above the flop-house door spoke in an alcoholic wheeze. Fear, like the imponderable pressure of the fog, had settled over this mean and evil district, and this man, for the moment, was its spokesman.

He said, sniffing as he knuckled his bulbous nose, "The p'lice don't know nothin' that goes on here, and people don't give explanations that wouldn't be believed. P'lice couldn't do nothin' anyhow; fightin' things that ain't really men, things that got no blood in their veins."

"That's a rather wild statement," Dwight commented.

"You ain't seen one of them things," the man muttered. "I have—two of 'em. There's more. Lame Lena that sells papers on the corner seen one last night. Knock sounds at her door. She opens it. This thing is standin' there, ugly as a dead monkey. 'What you want?' Lena asks, bitin' her gums. 'Blood,' the thing says. Lena slams the door and bolts it."

"Lena may have gone a little too heavy on the sheep-dip," Dwight suggested.

The man sucked at his greasy stub of a pipe; his rheum-clogged eyes rolled furtively over the gaseous billows of mist that choked the street. "But that ain't all," he said. "Curley Lennox seen one bite a dog's throat in an alley one mornin' 'bout sunup. The mutt howled and fought, but the Thing didn't seem to mind. It run off though, when Curley come up. The dog was dead."

"That's news," Dwight said, "when a man bites a dog."

The jest went unapplauded. In spite of himself it gave Dwight a queer feeling. You couldn't laugh about these matters, apparently.

"Another one bust into an opium dive," the man went on. "I won't say where. But the Chink had a corpse to get rid of later. The rest of 'em run off and left this feller—after they seen the Thing wouldn't bleed no matter how much they cut him."

"Good God!" Dwight exclaimed. "You mean, seriously . . . ?"

"Didn't I tell you?" the man growled irately. "Didn't I say there ain't no blood in 'em?"

"A figure of speech, I supposed . . . ?"

"Figger of speech, hell! Listen, I seen that fight in Hongkong Charlie's place my-self."

"Let's hear about that."

The man rocked forward in his chair which leaned against the fog-sweaty building, and knocked the dottle from his pipe. "Three nights ago, it was," he rumbled. "I'd dropped in fer a spread of chowmein and a little snifter. I sees this Thing with the dead-pan sittin' there an' it gives me the creeps to look at him. But I goes on eatin'.

"Next thing I know there's a howl, an' this Thing has grabbed a Chink kid an' started to run out with him. Up jumps Emilio the Spick, who's sittin' by the door, and out comes Emilio's knife. As slick a knife-fighter as ever cut a Gringo's guts, that Mex. But does it do him any good? The Thing drops the kid, and they fight. The Thing's got no weapon, so it fights with its hands clawed. Emilio cuts him to ribbons, so to speak. Face, arms, throat slashed.

"Then of a sudden Emilio jumps back, goes white, crosses himself and begins to gibber in Mexican. That was when he seen the Thing wouldn't bleed. I seen it, too. There was a gash you could see the raw edges of—like a piece of bled beef."

"And no blood?"

"No blood. And, mister, that Thing went out, and nobody follered it, neither. . . ."

His words trailed off. Light footsteps sounded on the clammy pavement.

DWIGHT TURNED IN the direction of the man's bleary glance. The slender figure of a girl was materializing from the mist. She walked with lowered head and face half hidden by the collar of her smartly tailored coat, but Dwight caught a brief glimpse of black, mysterious eyes, that sent a curious glow tingling in his veins, and he noticed how the wan light from the smoky globe lay softly on the perfect texture of her skin. No harpy of the pavements, that girl!

He was wondering what could bring her into this evil district, when, to his surprise, the girl with a sort of furtive duck turned in at the flop-house doorway and mounted the stairs. He saw her trim ankles vanish in the sickly light, heard the click of her heels in the hallway above and turned back bewildered.

The man grinned. His puffy, stubble-rough jowls spread in fat folds over the frayed collar of his coat. "Surprises you, eh—to see a doll like that in here?"

"Rather," Dwight said. "Who is she?"

The sagging shoulders shrugged.

"You're askin' me. Took me by surprise, too, when she come in this evening and paid fer a room. But should I ask questions? She paid; I reckon she knows her business."

"Yes," Dwight said abstractedly. "Still, with all due respect for your establishment . . . But look here, what's your opinion about these monsters?"

The man screwed his flabby face into a grimace and spat. "Ugh! I don't know. Only they ain't human."

"Why do you say that?"

"Somethin'—a look about 'em. Faces with a greenish gleam on the skin, like you might see on a Chinese vase, eyes so cold and empty it makes you shiver, like when you look over a high cliff . . ." He paused, his brow creased intently. "I tell you they look like them figures of dead murderers from Paley's Waxworks come to life!"

Dwight looked sharply at him, but did not pursue his inquiries in that direction. "I'd give something to see one of your monsters," he said.

The man looked at him narrowly; sudden suspicion gleamed in his rheumy eyes. "You ain't a reporter?"

"No," Dwight said, "I'm a capitalist."

The man laughed. Dwight, too, smiled. Queerly, it happened to be the truth. He didn't add that conducting a private detective agency was his way of escaping the boredom of an idle existence.

"You'd really like to see one of them buzzards?"

"Five dollars' worth," Dwight said.

Greed gleamed rawly in the man's face. "All right," he agreed. "But just a peek. I don't want no disturbance—from him."

"You've got one—in here?"

The man nodded, dragged his shapeless bulk upright. "Came in this afternoon. Face all muffled. But I seen the eyes—the skin. I reckon he's sleepin' now, if they sleep. You can take a peek at him."

Dwight slapped a bill into the grimy palm and followed the scrape of the ragged shoes up the stairway. A dim, fly-specked bulb lighted the upper hall. It was bare of carpet and oily grime stained the floor and cracked plaster walls. The smell was the immemorial reek of such a place. Dwight stared about warily. It might be a trap; you never knew in a dive like this.

The slithering shoes paused. The landlord gripped his arm, shoved his head so close that the smell of sour alcohol was sickening. "He's in Twenty-two," he hissed. "We'll go easy, mister."

He slunk softly to the door and Dwight crept behind him. The transom was dark; there was no sound from within. The man's warty hand was on the knob; he gave the door a little push.

"H'mm!" This time aloud. He shoved the door wide. "Empty!"

"What's this," Dwight growled, "a game?"

The squat man's face was puckered with real surprise.

"So help me . . ." he began, "he ain't come down the stairs."

"Since he's not human," Dwight muttered sourly, "I suppose—"

"Don't laugh!" the man said grimly. "He's here—somewhere."

Then it dawned on Dwight what was in the man's mind.

"Damn!" he swore. "That girl! Where's her room?"

"Twenty-six," the man sputtered, and started forward.

Dwight followed, taking long strides on tiptoe. But they didn't reach the door. It was Dwight who grabbed the other's arm and drew him suddenly back. He had stopped at the closed door of Twenty-five. Feeling the iron grip on his arm, the landlord sputtered, rolled his eyes.

"Jeez! What is it?"

Dwight's features had clouded: the grip of his lean fingers tightened on the pudgy arm, "Look!" he said between gritted teeth.

"What . . . where?" The man raised his frightened eyes, stared.

The transom hung ajar, forming a dark and hazy mirror, and in the moist, distorted depths something was swimming, something like a human body which seemed to move gently with a curious volition not its own.

The man looked helplessly at Dwight; his jaw dropped, but instead of speech a flood of saliva ran out of his mouth and drooled from his pendulous under-lip. Dwight's face was a corded brown mask; the brows dipped severely over eyes gone black and hard as lumps of basalt. A revolver had appeared in one hand; with the other he was pushing the door slowly open. Then he stopped. He felt the shaking body of the landlord, now pressed against him, stiffen with a jerk. The hair on Dwight's neck bristled as he stared.

Between him and the open window, past which the grey and ghostly fog was boiling, the body of a man was hanging in mid-air. Headless and half naked, it dangled by its feet from a rusty iron chandelier, swaying with the gentle momentum of a dying pendulum. Directly beneath the bloody stub of a neck was a white wash-basin, and with each grotesque motion of the swinging corpse, fresh drops of the viscous, ruddy fluid were shaken down into the half-filled bowl.

There was no one else in the room.

Dwight turned. His companion, who had been gaping in speechless vertigo, now began to blubber his innocence in a terrified whimper.

"Shut up!" Dwight ordered hoarsely, and pushed past into the hall. Three long strides brought him to the door of Twenty-six. He twisted the knob. Locked. He rattled it, yelled, "Open it up!"

The hurried scrape of feet and a low muttering reached his ears. He backed away to the opposite wall, braced his thick shoulders and lunged. With a crack the flimsy lock gave, and Dwight's body hurtled like a projectile into the room. His shins struck a chair. He sprawled, cursing his luck, snatching for the revolver which had been jarred from his hand.

Then he froze, his hand poised in mid-reach, staring. In the embrasure of the open window three heads were visible. One of them was the head of the dark-eyed girl who now held in one tense hand a black automatic. Beside, and slightly behind her, wreathed like a goblin in the swirling fog, was something which might have been a man, something which wore human garments, but whose gaping mouth was literally split from jaw to jaw, so that a purplish tongue lolled between tiers of yellow teeth dropped wide apart. And in this creature's hand was the third head—a gory, nauseous thing, with bugging eyes and coarse red hair now twisted between the fiend's wax-yellow fingers.

For a moment, a curious sort of horror, detached and impersonal, swallowed up all physical fear in Dwight's mind. Then his hand moved toward the revolver a few inches away. But almost touching it, he jerked stiff again.

"Do you think I won't shoot?" the girl asked.

Dwight thought she would. He saw the barely perceptible tightening of her finger on the trigger, and froze into immobility.

"Back to the door!" the girl ordered. "Then face about!"

Dwight obeyed. The gun crashed behind him; the light globe shattered and fell in fragments as darkness swallowed the room.

Dwight ducked, ran to the window. It opened on a fire-escape landing, and below he could make out dimly two figures descending the iron ladder into the alley. He whirled about, retrieved his revolver and climbed out. But already a car with wet top glistening through the fog was slinking out into the street.

He climbed back into the room, swung out into the hall and almost collided with the craven landlord who was creeping toward the door.

"God!" the latter swore hoarsely. "God! Wot'll I do?"

"Call the police, you fool!" Dwight growled and shoved him aside.

A moment later he was in the mist dreary street, legging it with swift strides toward his office, a definite plan in his mind.

SELF-SCHOOLED IN A dangerous calling, Stanley Dwight had two antidotes for nerves—action and more action. He also had a system of mental discipline which served him well in circumstances like the present. And as he strode, like a tall determined phantom, through the frothing billows of fog, he brushed from his mind the morbid, disconcerting horror which clung like a foul miasma about the night's events, and attacked the problem in a cold and analytical fashion. So by the time he had climbed the stairs, navigated the hall and swung open the door of his office he had already made up his mind as to his next move. Then he picked up the note on the desk marked "Urgent," and frowned. It was from his office boy and sales assistant, and it read:

Old Prof. Collins has kept the phone jangling all afternoon. Is he high behind? He says are you going to let them cut his throat or aren't you? If he's not already croaked, you better call him.

Jimmy.

Dwight tossed the note back and swore. "Croak him!" he fumed. "What that old egotist needs is a blind bridle to keep him from breaking his neck every time a paper blows across his path!"

He turned away toward an inner door with the firm intention of going on with his other plans. "But no," he said reflectively, and stopped. "No, he may scare himself to death. But I won't waste much time on him!"

He went out, closed the door, clumped back into the street and hailed a taxi. The car ploughed through the sodden murk of the streets and came to a halt before a cottage on the fringes of the university campus. Dwight told the driver to wait.

Professor Collins, wearing a dressing-gown and carrying a revolver in one slightly tremulous hand, answered the door. He was a small, dumpy man, with scraggly hair fringing a pate as white and ponderous as a roc's egg. His pink face was clean shaven and its cherubic cast belied the erratic temper and the intellect for which the eccentric scientist was noted. Dwight saw at once that the professor was at present as swollen as a toad with indignation and uneasiness. He followed the professor into his bachelor study, prepared for the outburst.

There the dumpy scientist squared off and faced him. And the outburst came.

"Well!" he exploded. "My well-being, I suppose, is a matter of small moment to the world. Still, since I have employed you to protect—"

"So they've written again?" Dwight inquired laconically. "Let's see the note."

He watched the professor as he fumbled among his papers. Pompous and egotistical! Ignorant people often took him for an ass. Better-informed people, of course, knew that the man who had startled the scientific world with his discoveries in the fields of biology and organic chemistry could scarcely be that. Dwight had been in one of his classes and was accustomed to the professor's tantrums.

"It's signed this time," Professor Collins said indignantly as he thrust the sheet toward Dwight.

Dwight took it, glanced at it abstractedly, then stiffened abruptly with interest and alarm. It wasn't the substance of the note that excited him. The order to leave his laboratory unlocked was natural enough in view of the fact that valuable supplies had already been stolen. It was the signature that caught Dwight's eye.

The note read:

Last warning. Vacate your house for the night and leave your laboratory unlocked. What we need we will get. Disregard this order and a fate worse than death will be yours.

The Six without Blood.

Dwight looked up sharply. It had been his intention to minimize the seriousness of the thing. His real opinion had been that mischievous students had taken advantage of the professor's nervousness since the recent robbery to play a joke on him. Now, matters had assumed a different aspect. Was it possible—this grotesquely horrible conjecture which had dawned, nebulous and half-formed, in his mind?

"Look here," he said bluntly, "you haven't come entirely clean with me in this business. What were the chemicals which were stolen?"

The professor paled, moistened dry lips nervously. "Why do you ask that?" His manner now was considerably subdued. "Maybe you know," Dwight countered. The professor fidgeted; then, as with an effort, he brought his eyes level with the detective's. "I see I'll have to tell you," he said. "I had two reasons for holding that back. First, the habit of a lifetime of guarding my incomplete experiments from a prying world. And second—" Here he paused, and a grim look hardened his mobile features—"and second, the possible consequences to society of a discovery of the properties of that compound."

Dwight leaned forward, the muscles of his face tensing. "Be plainer," he said curtly. "Just what do you mean?"

"I mean," said Collins, "that if the properties of those drugs were discovered by evil minds, the very fabric of civilization would be unsafe!"

Dwight sprang to his feet scowling. "Then your damned secrecy," he growled, "may cost a ghastly price! I don't know what your stuff was, but I begin to suspect a connection between it and an unspeakable horror. Did it have something to do with blood?"

Professor Collins paled; his mouth popped open in astonishment. "It does indeed," he stammered, "but how could you have known?"

"I don't," Dwight said, "but I imagine there are others who do. Tell me quickly what effect the stuff has."

Professor Collins nodded, swallowed with difficulty, got up. "Great God!" he breathed. "What have I done? I knew that there were graves that should never be opened!" His words trailed off in a sort of sob. Then he straightened, clenched his hands, blinked at Dwight. "But perhaps it isn't too late! You shall know all, the whole incredible secret. I have it all written down—a paper I was preparing. I'll bring it." He trotted toward a half-open door which gave on his laboratory.

The door closed behind him. Dwight took a deep breath. His head was throbbing. Thank God he had come here after all! Now he would know. Certainly Providence must have brought him here, brought him to the only man perhaps with the power to devise an antidote for the horror he had unwittingly unleashed.

What did it all mean? *Blood . . . graves opened . . .* Dwight could only guess, and his brain whirled with the chaotic vision of monsters reanimated, monsters with some frightful hell-brew in their veins, monsters more hideous and appalling than beasts, soulless, pitiless, conscienceless! He saw them in a multiplying horde boil up from the dank dens and alleys, swarm through the fetid gutters, gibbering insanely, shrieking like the damned, driven perhaps by a loathsome thirst for what their bodies lacked, howling for blood, blood, blood. . . .

The vision swirled and vanished; reality thundered back as a sound from the laboratory sent an electric current rippling through Dwight's veins. A crash, a muttered oath, and then the scream—a shrill ululation of fear and agony which rose until the walls seemed to shiver before its impact—then died in a convulsed, blubbering sob snapped sharply off!

CHAPTER TWO

WHERE CORPSES WALKED

Dwight hurled his body toward the door. He tried the knob, beat on it with his fists. It was locked—an automatic spring lock on the inside, he supposed. Damn the man's absent-mindedness!

"Professor! Professor!"

There was no reply. More than fear, Dwight realized now, had been in that wail. He threw his weight against the door, battered it until the bones of his shoulders ached. But it would not yield.

He crouched, applied his eye to the keyhole. His knee-joints went watery at what he saw.

Horror like a slimy thing crawled into his throat and choked him.

In the small area of visibility which the keyhole afforded, two figures could be seen. One was the headless body of Professor Collins, sprawled hideously in a welter of blood upon the floor! The other was the grisly Thing lifting its lean, cadaverous body over the sill of the window. In one harpy-like claw, it carried a flagon of some dark liquid, in the other a sheaf of papers.

For an instant the Thing turned its head. Dwight would never forget that brief glimpse of its face. For it was the face of a revenant, a ghoul, a *thing without blood!*

The stunned paralysis which held Dwight lasted for only a moment. He sprang to a side door, gun in hand, and dived out into the black and vaporous night. Groping his way through the sodden murk, he reached the open laboratory window. But the specter had vanished, swallowed up by the humid, incorporeal fog which seemed its proper element. Except for the ghastly, decapitated body, the laboratory was empty.

Then, in the alley behind the place, an automobile motor roared its hoarse vibrations through the smoking mist. Dwight stumbled toward the front of the house, saw that his taxi was still there.

"Get started!" he yelled. "Follow the car that leaves the alley!"

The driver nodded. As the car shot forth, he swung swiftly in pursuit.

But it was hopeless. The fog, that clammy monster who fights for crime, spread the shadow of his tenuous wings about the ghostly fugitives. Somewhere, soon, they made a quick turn and were lost in the greyness.

Dwight saw then that it was useless to attempt to pick them up again. He had seen the car but dimly. He settled back and gave the driver his downtown address. No use in going back to the place. Professor Collins was beyond all help now, and the papers had been stolen. He would phone a report of the murder to the police and then follow the faint and bloody trail alone.

He got out at his office and hurried in. And the first thing he did was to take a stiff drink of whiskey, a very stiff one. . . .

THIRTY MINUTES LATER, Stanley Dwight, unrecognizable in his shabby topcoat and flop-brimmed hat, and with his face considerably the worse for a little deftly applied make-up, shuffled his sagging shoes along a fog-muggy street of pawnshops, penny arcades and cheap clothing stores. Ahead of him, in the middle of the block, a spot of light stood out under the grey nimbus of the fog. Colored globes, which winked like evil eyes, formed an arc over the foyer of an old theater and lit up the cracking sign: *Paley's Wax Museum*, past which the fog in pink and green wraiths was drifting.

A thinning crowd of grey, nondescript figures stood hunched and half interested before the painted box where a gold-toothed spieler with a scenic necktie was talking hoarsely and gesturing with a cane toward the sample exhibits.

"There he is, ladies and gentlemen," said the spieler, pointing toward the waxen image of a burly young giant who stood on a pine plank gallows surrounded by a wide assortment of lethal weapons. "There he is—a man who loved his feller man! Yes sir, why he loved his feller man so much that he ate him!"

Even the unresponsive crowd stirred a little at this ghastly pronouncement. A murmur like a challenge rose from the seedy ranks.

"You don't believe it? It's a matter of police records. And the man boasted of it himself. He ate his pal when the two of 'em was starvin', hemmed up by the law in a Florida swamp. Bysshe Guttman was his name—the only authenticated modern American cannibal! He saved a million bucks from his crimes, hid it away. But the law finally got him. He was drowned a month ago while trying to escape from Alcatraz Island. His body was never recovered from the swift current. So the fishes ate the great lover of humanity!"

He cleared his throat, spat discreetly within his box and turned to another figure. This was of a small man, incredibly hairy, with a thick black beard muffling his features, and smoked glasses over his eyes. He wore an Inverness cape and there was something monstrous and evil about the soft, almost dainty hands which were outstretched as if for inspection.

"See them hands, ladies and gentlemen?" the spieler barked. "The hands of a sorcerer! Dr. Magwood was this soft-speakin' little feller's name—a skilled surgeon, a madman, a pleasure-killer. In the dark of night he done his bloody deeds for pleasure, curtin' his victims in pieces an' arrangin' them in neat piles. Foxy as a devil, he claimed he could do magic, even raise the dead. He was supposed to have been killed by a mob, but it ain't certain. Now, ladies and gentlemen, inside you will see . . ."

Dwight heard no more. He shuffled to the curtained entrance, asked to see the manager and was directed to a narrow flight of steps that led him up to a cubbyhole office. The man behind the battered desk lifted a thin, crafty face to regard his visitor.

"You're the manager?"

"Yes."

"I want to collect that ten dollars you offer to anyone who'll spend the night in your Gallery of Ghosts."

The manager studied him shrewdly, rolled a smoking cigar between thin fingers. "We've had a little trouble with that stunt," he said. "Several men got so scared they ran out in the middle of the night."

"I don't care. I need the ten bucks. I'm broke, out of a job. It's good publicity. . . ."

"Sure, it's good publicity." A pause. "Got a family?"

"No. What difference does that make?"

"We got to know these things. How's your health—nerves good?"

"Nothing wrong with me. Just not eatin' enough."

"Well, I suppose—if you want to try . . ."

"Thanks," Dwight said. "When do I start?"

"It's about closin' time now," the manager said. "I'll have 'em put a cot in there for you."

Fifteen minutes later Stanley Dwight sat alone on a narrow balcony which overlooked a huge and dimly lighted room. Around and below him, like a vast congregation of the unhallowed dead which the very grave had rejected, the pallid effigies of evil were grouped. Dwight was watching the door which had just closed. The man who had brought him here might still be spying, so for a time he sat perfectly still on his cot.

Three colored ceiling lights threw out a faint and greenish luminescence of a brightness about the equivalent of moonlight. Under this weird unearthly glow, the silent and ghostly place took on the look and atmosphere of a morgue—but a morgue in which no veil or covering softened the icy contours of death's horror, a morgue in which the unhallowed dead had risen with stiff, corroded limbs to mock in a motionless pantomime whatever black and bestial deed had won them this posthumous infamy.

Reaching into his pocket, Dwight took out a folded piece of paper which he had been carrying about for several days. It was one of those anonymous tips, some worthless, some valuable, which drift to the office of every detective. It had come to him unsigned through the mail. It read:

Have a look in on Paleys Waxworks. The police are too dumb. Men go in there and dont come out. Somebody dressed like them runs out yellin to fool people. Tramps and drifters are all theyll take, so nobody wont know the difference. A strate tip.

Dwight pondered the queer message.

Until tonight he had given it little thought. Now, with only a blank void like the fog confronting him, it seemed a clue worth following. It was little enough, but it was something. The flop-house keeper's mention of the resemblance between the monsters and the wax-effigies had brought the note back into his mind. Then too,

this place was located in the very heart of the district which the execrable creatures seemed to have chosen for their hunting ground.

Added to this were the words of Professor Collins which, together with his ghastly end, had engendered that appalling hypothesis in Dwight's mind—and now he seemed to see a possible connection between the scattered pieces of the jigsaw puzzle. He meant to wait now, see if anything happened. If not, he would make a thorough search of the place. He wanted particularly to examine some of the effigies, to see if, as rumor had it, there were real corpses among them.

Dwight put the note away, stood up and looked about him. "The Six without Blood!" Here at least were men without blood. Their frozen attitudes, their gruesome postures, their staring lifeless eyes seemed to mock his thoughts, jeer at him horribly. The figure nearest to him, that of a sallow young man who had murdered his father-in-law by thrusting his head into a gas stove, was seated beside the replica of his fiendishness, staring at it with an expression almost of pride.

Feeling that by now he should be safe from the manager's eyes, Dwight stepped to the figure. He stripped the baggy clothes from the stiff frame, wrapped his own topcoat about it and threw it on its side upon the cot. He laid his hat over the thing's eyes. At a little distance it might have been his own body, peacefully asleep.

He then took up his position in the chair by the stove. He adjusted his limbs in the very attitude of the effigy, and sat very still with his revolver on the edge of the chair beside him.

Silence and forced inaction are the immemorial allies of fear. Dwight, who prided himself on the steadiness of his own nerves, thought of how an ordinary man might feel in this place alone. He thought of it with a certain amusement but also with a certain vague flutter of uneasiness. The imagination is a powerful and terrible instrument. For instance, with very little encouragement from excited nerves, Dwight could imagine that he had seen a figure—the figure of a murderess in a group below—move slightly as if tired of the posture. Well, that was patently absurd. He expected something to happen, but no such fantastic business as that. He laughed it aside and waited.

The place was deathly still. A jittery man might positively lose his mind staring too long at the horrible, frozen immobility of these grisly figures. With the thin green light over it, it was like some ghastly tableau frozen in ice. It was like something a man might see if he came upon some village where a sudden catastrophe had left the whole population frozen in its tracks, standing hideously in their familiar attitudes with a frightful, timeless patience, as if for ages unnumbered they had stood thus, and for other ages would so stand. He imagined how such a man might wander for days among staring dead faces, until his mind cracked and he shrieked for them to move or speak.

A totally unexpected throb of cold shot through Dwight's veins. At first he thought that it was the idea itself which had excited it—then he realized that in reality it had been an impression that the wax figure slightly behind him had moved. But he did not turn. If anyone were watching now it would be fatal to betray the fact that he had substituted the wax figure for his own upon the bed. As for that wax likeness of a dead murderer, well . . .

His thoughts scattered like leaves before a puff of cold wind. He did not move or start, but now his eyes narrowed in earnest. It was the slight figure of the hirsute Dr. Magwood which had been brought inside at closing time and which now stood here on the balcony just under the dangling noose of the portable gallows. It had seemed to him that this figure had bent slightly as if to peer at the thing that lay upon his cot.

Now, without making a movement, Dwight studied the figure's face. Something like a gleam of life showed in the eyes behind the smoked spectacles. He hadn't noticed it before. The figure was perfectly still now. Why did it give such a curious impression of life and intelligence? It was looking at the cot, looking with a sort of rapt gloating, like an obscene fat spider leering at a captured fly.

Dwight stiffened, stiffened into a cold rigidity that rivaled the frightful statues themselves. For from somewhere in the room below, the rusty mechanism of a clock began to purr and chime. The sound was somehow ghastly in that tomblike chamber.

Then, on the stroke of twelve, the short figure of the evil Dr. Magwood bent forward with a movement slow and mechanical! While Dwight watched with a strange breathlessness and a slow, clammy crawling of his skin, the bearded ogre reached up, caught the noose of the gallows rope and began to draw it slowly down!

Dwight fought to keep his muscles steady. An hallucination had been his first thought. Now, as a flash of reason told him that the thing was really taking place, the horror of that creeping, ghostly pantomime held him with a dreadful fascination. For the feet of the bearded doctor made no sound, yet they were moving nearer and nearer to the cot. And the fiend's grisly lips, which showed like bloodless slabs of flesh between the beard, were parted in a smile of insane gloating!

Dwight held himself ready to spring up, gun in hand. He now understood what sort of hellishness had been going on in here! And at the thought of the unsuspecting men who had awakened at midnight to find this creeping demon with his noose bending above them, his blood ran cold. For the squat figure in the cape was now bending above the cot, was reaching out his pudgy, obscene hands with a sort of hideous gentleness to place the noose over his victim's head.

Now! Now was the moment! And while the hair bristled on his scalp, Dwight slid one hand across his lap to seize the revolver at his side.

Then abruptly cold horror like strangling fingers of ice closed on his throat. For where the pistol had been, the fingers of his groping hand encountered something as repulsive as the touch of rotting flesh. At the same moment he lunged away. Lunged but could not move—for fingers like the jaws of a vise were on his shoulders, dragging him back!

He struggled to his feet, still unable to turn and face the nameless horror which had fastened itself upon his back, for the strength of the thing which held him was like that of a boa constrictor. A cold and hairy arm had encircled his throat in a deadly strangle-hold which held the air in his bursting lungs and seemed to be forcing his eyes from their sockets with the torturous pressure.

Still he fought with his waning strength, for the horrid little monster of a doctor was moving toward him now, a low chuckle quivering in his throat.

A choked cry of fear and defiance rattled from Dwight's lungs and he made a desperate lunge at the fiend. Something stung his arm, something like the jab of a hypodermic. His senses began to swim. Giddily he reeled, felt himself released to stagger forward blindly.

Blackness passed for a moment over Stanley Dwight's mind, blackness which he felt, in that awful moment of awakening consciousness, had been something sweet and merciful. For now his hands were bound to his sides, the noose was about his neck, and he was being dragged up, up from the floor. He saw the green lights spinning; he saw the bearded face of the doctor, floating hazily like the head of a demon. Then the dark flowed back, gratefully swallowing mind and senses.

CHAPTER THREE

HOSTAGE OF THE DEAD

Dwight opened his eyes. For a long time, it seemed, he had lain there in a semi-conscious stupor. Now his nerves jerked thoroughly alive. Instinct warned him of the nearness of some living presence.

He blinked into the eerie twilight of the tunnel-like passage in which he lay, realized that he was lying upon a clammy floor of stone, his hands and arms still bound. He flung his body over. Pain shot through him at the first movement of his wrenched and swollen neck. But in the shock which now smote his cringing nerves, the pain was forgotten.

A silent figure was bending above him. It was a woman. Pink tights ruffled at the waist—the outmoded chorus-girl costume of the murderess he had seen move in the waxworks! Next his eye fell on the point of light that gleamed dully on the blade of the knife she held, striking the weird attitude of some sacrificial priestess.

Then he saw the face, and a queer sob of mingled incredulity and despair forced itself between his gritted teeth. For it was the face of the girl with the dark eyes and hair whom he had seen in the flop-house! The black eyes bored into his now with a strange fanatical gleam that gave to her face a mingled beauty and horror. The knife seemed on the point of descending. . . . Dwight's jaw set; he steeled himself for the blow.

And then the frozen look on the girl's face changed. Human feeling betrayed itself, a sort of startled anxiety, "Oh!" she sobbed. Then in a suppressed whisper, "I almost killed you— I thought you were one of *them!*"

"The first break I've had," Dwight grunted. "Cut these ropes quick! Who are you!"

"My name doesn't matter," she said. With quick fingers she slit the ropes and released him. "I came here to kill. You're going to help me."

Dwight got to his feet. "I'm going to get out!" he said.

"But you can't!" the girl whispered. "We're prisoners. The trap-door that leads into the waxworks is guarded, and it's the only exit. They caught me hiding in there, just as they did you. But they didn't search me; I had the knife hidden under my sash. I pretended to be unconscious and they left me in this passage. Now I'm going on. I'm going to kill *him* anyhow!"

"*Him?* Who do you mean?"

"Dr. Magwood."

"Then," Dwight stammered, "it *is* Magwood—here, alive?"

She nodded.

"And what's that got to do with you?"

"You remember," she said, "that man with me there in the rooming-house—the poor creature with the mutilated face? He's Fred, my brother. He *was* Fred, I mean. Now he's a maniac with a broken mind, one of this fiendish doctor's victims."

"Tell me about him—Magwood," Dwight said. "What's he doing?"

"Bringing dead murderers back to life!" she sobbed. "He's stolen the formula for some sort of synthetic blood to revive them. But he has to have fresh human blood for his work. He traps his victims in the waxworks, just as Fred was trapped. He drains the blood from these victims, then revives them with his chemicals and they become monsters.

"Those he can't revive are embalmed and put in this museum. Fred and two others managed to escape. But they couldn't become men again. The stuff in their veins made them thirst for blood. You saw—there—there in that room. It was dreadful. I had searched for Fred, found him there. But he had killed a man, was trying to drink—God! I can't say it.

"You see, that's why I couldn't go to the police. I managed to get him away, take him home, lock him up. He swore he would get the two other victims and come here, kill them all. But—" she sobbed fiercely, "that's what I'm going to do!"

"Rot!" Dwight snapped. "With a knife? We'll go back, fight our way out, then come back with the police—"

Dwight broke off to follow the girl's tense gaze. She was staring toward a ruffled ribbon of light which showed beneath a curtain at the end of the passage. Sounds came from beyond that curtain—a murmur of voices, a rhythmic creak, creak, like the noise of a rusty pendulum. A medley of strange chemical smells drifted to their nostrils, and a persistent reek like the sickening, bloody smell of a slaughterhouse.

A voice rose above the murmur: "A little more blood, Brutus, a little more blood."

Dwight seized the girl's arm. "Come!" he whispered.

She pulled away. "No!" she said. "I'm going in!" And she ran stumbling toward the curtain, the knife in her hand.

With an oath, Dwight raced after her. But he was too late. She flung the curtain aside and went staggering into the room. Dwight followed—and as the thick velvet curtains rippled past his body, talon-like hands clawed at him from either side, gripping his arms and shoulders. He fought, but his body was dragged back, held as in a straitjacket.

Further struggle was useless. The two powerful creatures, with the bloodless, dead faces and cold, empty eyes, pressed their loathsome bodies against him, pinioned his arms securely. Another of the beasts was holding the sobbing girl.

The blood throbbed hotly in Dwight's temples. His throat seemed dry, scaly. He stared helplessly about the strange long room—something between a laboratory and an abattoir. Long tables held test-tubes and retorts and all the gleaming apparatus of the chemist. There were shelves of chemicals and curious-looking machines.

In one corner a weird contrivance caught Dwight's wildly gazing eyes. It was something like a child's seesaw, mounted on a frame of gleaming steel. Strapped to it was the naked body of a man, and at each end one of the grisly, grey man-monsters was keeping the contraption in motion, bending and straightening his gaunt, repulsive body with the stiff and rigid movements of an automaton. This accounted for the creaking sound which Dwight had heard in the passage.

His captors had made no move; they seemed to be awaiting orders. Here and there about the walls of the room, numbers of the repellent creatures were squatting on their haunches like apes, their lean, hairy arms dangling, their bloodless faces stamped with a listless and dismal despair. And worse—hunger, stark hunger was in their insane eyes as they watched him through the red, uncanny mist of light which fell from globes in the ceiling. Dwight shuddered.

"Prepare the girl!" The words came from somewhere behind, in a lisping voice that was somehow vile and unnatural.

Dwight jerked his head about. Beyond a nearby laboratory table, the shaggy head of Dr. Magwood was visible, thrusting up from the hunched shoulders, caped in black like the body of some loathsome bat. He was moving about briskly with tubes and phials.

The fiend who held the girl moved away with her. Dwight held himself in check, trying to formulate some plan. With a morbid fascination he watched the frightful doctor's hands, thought of the man's unspeakable practices. Those were the hands that cut human beings to pieces—for pleasure! God! It would be better if he and the girl were dead and in decent graves!

Magwood was holding a test-tube in each hand. He poured liquid from one to the other. *Pfff!* A small explosion shattered the tube and sent billows of acrid smoke into the air. The doctor sprang back, neither injured nor alarmed, and began wiping his hands on a towel. Now he looked at Dwight, fingering him with his eyes as a butcher might a calf brought in for slaughtering.

"Strip him and bind him," Magwood lisped, "and take him to the meat room."

The meat room! Dwight fought again, straining and snarling like a trapped animal. But other monsters sprang to the assistance of those who held him. Their rasplike hands tied him and lifted him and carried him, still struggling, to that place of unspeakable dread.

THEY WENT THROUGH a narrow doorway, and Dwight was flung without ceremony upon the floor. He heard the door close; he lifted his eyes, and an almost intolerable impulse to retch and vomit seized him. The reek of the place was frightful, and what he saw was indescribably worse. For from the walls of this small abattoir, there hung by meat hooks, like so much beef in a market, four hideous bodies, headless, naked, with small glass bowls beneath each gory neck to catch the dripping blood!

There was a small, round hole in the door at about eye level, a peek-hole apparently, where the captors could stare in at their victims. Dwight staggered to his feet, inched his way to the door and stared out.

He gasped, grinding his teeth together and digging the nails of his fingers into his palms. For two of the nauseous revenants were carrying the body of the girl toward the seesaw contraption. Limp and inert, her slender body lay in their clutches like a wilted flower, her dark hair trailing back from the pallid face.

Horror and a sickened fascination glued Dwight's eyes to the scene. He saw the ghouls halt the motion of the seesaw, narrowed his eyes to stare at the great muscular body that lay upon it. Panic swept over him as he recognized in the square, brutal features the face of the murderer, Bysshe Guttman, the man who had been drowned a month before in the swift currents off Alcatraz!

Disgust, loathing and a vertigo of incredulous terror gripped him then, held him in its frozen talons as he watched the inert body of the girl being placed upon the machine, saw her strapped there at the side of the dead cannibal, while a strange contrivance of tubes with a dial and siphon was fastened to her numb wrists. He went berserk then, writhing at his bonds, beating his helpless body against the door which would not yield.

Gradually he sobered, took a desperate grip on his throbbing nerves and tried to think. The opening of a door behind him caused him to swing his body clumsily about. A man had come into the room and stood confronting him, and for a wild instant Dwight thought that his reason had cracked. For the man who stood in the doorway was Professor Collins!

After a moment the professor spoke. "It seems," he said calmly, "that we are in the same boat."

Dwight found his voice. "Good God! What—? I thought—"

"It might have occurred to you," said the professor, "that I would be more valuable to them alive than dead. That headless wax figure on the floor in a pool of blood was a thing easily contrived. It served to establish my death and they stole it out of there later."

"Good God!" Dwight burst out. "They'll use you in this business too, then?"

"Perhaps . . ." Collins seemed resigned now, all trace of his erratic temper vanished. "And you too—if you'll permit a rather grisly jest."

"What do they intend to do with us—the girl and me?"

"The girl is being used now," Professor Collins said, "in the process of resurrecting Guttman."

"Then Guttman is . . . ?"

"Technically alive now. Magwood tells me that he had planned the thing before Guttman's escape. Guttman expected to be drowned, but Magwood had promised to revive him, and he thought it worth the chance. For almost thirty days the man's heart has been beating. There are moments, he says, when a flicker of consciousness is evident. In the end, I have no doubt, he will live."

"With your chemicals in his veins—like these others?"

Collins shook his head; there was the hint of a smile on his lips now.

"I'm afraid I exaggerated a bit in my excitement," he said. "Frankly, there is no magical chemical, as you believe—only a system. I have used it with considerable success on animals and it consists in the use of artificial respiration, artificial heating of the body, injections of defibrinated blood, physiological salts and *epinephrine*, or adrenaline. Even my seesaw plan, which you

see them using, has been experimented with before. It forces the blood to circulate by constantly shifting the center of gravity."

"But these monsters," Dwight protested. "What is it that flows in their veins—surely not blood? They won't bleed."

"Not after Magwood has dosed them with a newly developed hemostatic, the work of a Canadian doctor who perfected it to the extent that it will instantly stop bleeding from even a major blood vessel.

"These creatures you see are not reanimated corpses. They did not die. When they were weakened by pain and fear and loss of blood, which Magwood extracted for his use, they were dosed with the hemostatic and told that they were no longer human. Magwood's hypnotic suggestion and the fact that they would not bleed has convinced them that they are nothing but walking cadavers. It also awakened an insane craving for blood. He feeds them small doses and keeps them in a state of docile slavery."

"And these?" Dwight jerked his head toward the banging bodies.

"They were too unruly, Magwood informs me. He finds other uses for them."

Dwight's face twisted into a sickened scowl; a crawling nausea turned and twisted in the pit of his stomach. The tense silence of the place was punctuated by the creaking of the machine on which the body of the girl was strapped like a human sacrifice, while the blood in her veins was being sapped by the loathsome thing beside her. In the end she would be another of these repulsive ghouls!

Some emotion deeper than fear stirred in Dwight then, something primeval, inherent in his blood. His black eyes blazed with a new fire as he lifted them now to Professor Collins' face.

"Look here," he said, "you're not in the same fix as we are. He won't kill you; he needs you. But with your help, I'll destroy this monster, even if it costs my life, which it probably will. It'll likely cost yours too. But you won't stand back on that account, will you, Professor?"

Collins did not answer at once. As Dwight stared at him, he felt the blood draining from his own cheeks, felt a more appalling horror than any which had gripped him. For Collins had looked away, was staring abstractedly at the wall.

"Speak, man!" Dwight half screamed. "Are you a fiend too, or just a coward?"

Collins' glance swung back; the eyes were cold, emotionless. "You cannot understand, perhaps," he said, "but neither life nor death nor any human value means anything to me—nothing but science. Science is my life, my god!"

"You're a coward!" Dwight snarled. "You're yellow to the quivering marrow of your bones!"

He stopped, biting off his words sharply. A queer alarming light had sprung into the professor's eyes. It was the lurid glimmer of monomania, the flame that hides in darkness, unseen by normal eyes except when betrayed by a moment's passion!

"My God!" The words forced themselves in a half groan from Dwight's throat. "My God! I see it now. There is no Magwood; there is only Collins!"

No flicker of emotion showed in the professor's face, but strange yellow lights were crawling in his eyeballs. "Have it your way," he said quietly. "What of it? Society has dogged me with its taboos, refused me living men for my experiments. But science will not be thwarted. I wondered how long the wig and whiskers and cape would fool you. It doesn't matter. In a few hours you will be hanging on the wall here like any other dog." A look of deep-rooted cruelty betrayed itself in the immobile features as he added, "But first I'll let you see the girl, let you see what we do to her!"

That was the last straw. Dwight's nerves cracked. Reason was swamped; only the blind and driving impetus of outraged instincts remained as he threw his shackled body toward the fiend.

Heels against the wall, he thrust out his lowered head like a battering ram, drove with all his power. It caught the professor in the belly, jarred him back against the opposite wall.

Dwight toppled to the floor, writhing and kicking like a tied cat.

Rage, suddenly unleashed, burned like an angry fire in the professor's face. A knife leaped into his hand and he sprang like an insane, gibbering monkey upon the helpless body of his victim. Dwight kicked, butted with his head, rolled over and over, threshing his bound body from right to left, while the little monster clung to him like a catamount. He seemed determined to cut Dwight's throat without injuring the rest of the body. And it was this intent which gave Dwight his few minutes' respite from death.

But Dwight was weakening. At last, with burning lungs racked by the unequal struggle, he found himself flat on his back, saw the blade of the knife inexorably descending toward his jugular vein.

The knife stopped in mid-air. From the main room had come the staccato sound of gunfire! Pandemonium seemed to break loose then. There were cries and curses, the crash of objects thrown and broken, the slap of running feet!

Collins sprang to his feet, dropped the knife, dived through the door.

Flinging his body about, Dwight seized the knife with savage eagerness. While out there the sounds of battle heightened, he struggled with his bonds. He managed at last to free his wrists and ankles. Then he peered out the door. His mouth widened in amazement.

Already the place was a shambles of corpses and milling bodies. The grey-faced monsters were fighting in a pack, like wolves. Urging them on was Collins, with an automatic in each hand, firing at the three men in the curtained entrance.

Those three, automatics in their hands, were spraying the room with a murderous fire! Shoulder to shoulder they stood, shouting cries and jeers at the cornered ghouls, and their faces were like the faces of their foes. They were, Dwight realized now, the three who had sworn to come back and wipe out this place of torment. One of them he recognized, by his split mouth and hanging lower jaw, as the brother of the dark-haired girl. They had arrived just in time.

But the relief which had flared in Dwight's breast was smothered a moment later by mounting despair. He had turned toward the now motionless seesaw. Bullets were whistling through the air, spattering the plastered wall behind it. The half-alive murderer and the living girl were equally exposed to that annihilating gunfire—and it was evident, as men tumbled from the grey and howling ranks of the ghouls, that the crazed gunmen had failed to see or recognize the girl, and would not stop until all life was wiped out of the place.

Dwight measured the distance between him and the girl. He might reach and free her—but they could never escape. They would never survive that fire.

Then inspiration dawned upon his brain with a wild surge of joy. It was a single picture, flashed from his memory—the doctor, the two chemicals which when mixed had caused the small explosion!

Dwight dropped to his hands and knees. He darted out the door and scuttled like a rabbit for the shelter of the nearby laboratory table. One of the ghouls loomed up before him, with up-raised knife. He tackled the hideous shape by the legs. It fell heavily to the floor and he raced on. Bullets sang past him; a slug tore a bite from his heel but he did not stop.

A moment later the two bottles were in his trembling hands. He placed one of them against the wall, then darted back a few yards and hurled the other at it.

A dull concussion thundered in the air. A sheet of fire leaped out like a spreading stain across the room. Abruptly the atmosphere was choked by a thick and soggy smoke, acrid and stifling, that rolled and boiled its blinding vapor over the scene of carnage.

The cries redoubled. For a moment bullets ceased to fly.

Knife in hand, Dwight plunged through the smoke, fought his way through the struggling, blinded ghouls to the girl. He found her struggling weakly into consciousness, slashed the bonds that held her, threw her across his shoulder. Then, following the wall, he groped toward the entrance. Now the maniacs had come to grips in the blinding fog of smoke with knife and tooth and claw. Heaving bodies were all about him; a knife slashed his shoulder. But he fought his way to the entrance, plunged down the now deserted passage. He climbed painfully through the trap-door that opened in the floor of the waxworks. There he laid the girl aside and heaped a pile of heavy furniture over the basement's only exit, locking the battling fiends in their smoky hell.

Then he called the police.

AN HOUR LATER Dwight, with the weak but otherwise uninjured girl, sat cozily in the back seat of a police car which was whisking them to their respective homes.

Still a little dazed, the girl had listened to his explanation in silence. Now she asked: "But why did he do it? Why would a respected scientist stoop to such a thing?"

"As he boasted," Dwight said, "science was his god. Anything, even the use of humans in his experiments, was justified in his mind. Society, of course, would not permit it, and that irked him. He wanted to raise the dead, to be a sort of god himself.

"Then the idea of getting Guttman to escape and take a chance on a revival after he was drowned must have occurred to him. He had a special reason for that. Guttman was reputed to have a million dollars hidden, and with that money Collins could have financed his dangerous experiments to the end of his days. And that was what he desired most in life.

"The reason he brought me into it is obvious. He wanted a reliable report of his death to be circulated. That would leave him to work unhindered in his secret slaughterhouse, and it would also leave his reputation unstained."

"It's horrible, horrible," the girl muttered. "I—I'm glad, now, that my poor brother was killed. It—it's better for him. But I can't forget the horror of it all."

"You can try," Dwight said. "And if you'll let me, I'll try to help you. I think I can. There are so many things I want to talk to you about. You might begin by telling me your name."

Smiling wanly, she told him. They nestled a little closer together on the seat. Outside the window of the car the fog swirled and billowed, but it was no longer sinister. It seemed soft and somehow comforting, like a pleasant veil that shut out all fearful memories, and walled them in an intimate world of their own.

THE BROKEN FANG

UEL KEY

SAMUEL WHITTELL KEY (1874–1948), who wrote under the pseudonym Uel Key, was born in York, England, and was educated at Westminster and St. Mary's College, Cambridge University. The Reverend Key served as a clerk in holy orders for most of his life. Among his works were *The Material in Support of the Spiritual* (1916) and *The Solace of the Soul* (1918). He wrote short stories for such publications as *London Magazine* and *Pictorial Magazine*.

In 1917, he began a series of virulently anti-German stories for *Pearson's Magazine* featuring his series protagonist, Professor Arnold Rhymer, an English medical doctor and lecturer who works closely with Scotland Yard to solve weird and seemingly occult mysteries. Although the stories are described as tales of psychic investigation, they mainly deal with cases the professor believes to be of German psychic espionage. Much like Sherlock Holmes, with whom Key's publisher attempted to compare the detective, he is tall, slender, and given to keen observations and deductions. Rhymer appeared in two books: *The Broken Fang and Other Experiences of a Specialist in Spooks* (London: Hodder & Stoughton, 1920), which contained five stories ("The Broken Fang," "The Shrouded Dome," "A Post-Mortem Reversal," "A Prehistoric Vendetta," and "A Sprig of Sweet Briar"), and *The Yellow Death (A Tale of Occult Mysteries): Recording a Further Experience of Professor Rhymer the "Spook" Specialist* (London: Books Ltd.,1921).

"The Broken Fang" was originally published in 1917 in *Pearson's Magazine*.

UEL KEY

THE BROKEN FANG

"SORRY TO TROUBLE you, sir, but can you help to clear up a mystery which, I'm bound to own, is baffling us?"

The individual thus addressing Professor Arnold Rhymer, M.D.—the young and distinguished *savant* in psychical phenomena—was a big, finely-built man. He placed his hat and stick on the table and deposited his frame in an easy chair, to which the professor motioned him.

"My name is Brown," he explained, "Detective-Inspector Brown of the C.I.D.,

Scotland Yard. My chief has put me on to a case which doesn't seem quite—well—normal, you know. These sort of problems are in your line, I believe; or else I shouldn't have bothered you."

"What's the nature of your case?"

"The Blankborough murders. Surely you've read about these mysterious crimes committed near the country town of Blankborough?"

"Yes," Rhymer admitted, "but the papers don't give much detail."

"I know, for we've suppressed details to disarm the criminal, until we've got hold of some sort of clue towards identification. That'll be no easy matter, though, I dare bet. Will you help us, sir?"

"I'll give you what assistance I can," he replied, "but I shall want some details first, for I know nothing more than the newspapers have outlined, and, as you admit, that amounts to very little."

"I'll be frank with you," the detective affirmed; "but what I've to tell you is confidential."

"I shan't say a word."

"The police-surgeon," Brown continued, "laid emphasis upon two points of deduction. The first was that he did not believe—judging from the appearance of the corpses—that the victims had succumbed as a direct result of the mutilated condition of the bodies."

"That was certainly the impression I gathered from the reports," Rhymer volunteered. "Three healthy young men murdered in one week, in the same locality—close to a peaceful country town, and their bodies mutilated with some sharp instrument."

"Just so," Brown acquiesced, "only the surgeon held a different opinion, since he discovered two punctures in the neck of each victim, and he was convinced that death was primarily due to a loss of blood from these incisions. His second deduction was that these wounds were inflicted with something sharp and wedge-shaped, and that the identically same thing was not used in wounding the third victim—or possibly the first—since the end was found broken off and embedded in the neck of the second victim."

Rhymer seemed puzzled as he mentally absorbed these details.

"Were the wounds in the necks small?" he queried.

"Quite."

"Merely incisions, not gashes?"

"Yes."

"Then it seems improbable that the victims rapidly bled to death from these wounds alone?"

"That's what struck me at the time; but I've

yet to add that the surgeon's opinion was that death supervened in each case from haemorrhage, probably due to suction, as though a small vacuum pump had been applied to the incisions."

"Or the mouth of some living creature?" Rhymer hazarded with a significant glance.

"Good heavens! that never occurred to me," the detective cried.

Rhymer pursed his lips and his brow contracted as he asked:

"What was the broken piece like, found in the wound of victim number two?"

For reply, Brown searched his waistcoat pockets and produced a small metal box. This he opened and handed to Rhymer.

The latter took it and, glancing within, suddenly stifled an exclamation, for that which he beheld, revealed a supposition more horrible than he had previously contemplated.

"Don't mislay that piece of evidence, whatever you do," he enjoined, handing the box back to the detective. "This is going to prove a complicated case," he added, "but it'll furnish us with interest and excitement as well, I'll be bound."

"I guessed it would be in your line, sir, for I've heard tell that you're O.K. on abnormal problems, and this one's creepy enough for anything."

LATER ON IN the day Professor Rhymer left his flat in Whitehall Court and, meeting Inspector Brown, by arrangement, at Charing Cross station, they boarded an evening train for Blankborough, arriving there an hour later. They at once proceeded to the best of the several inns which the little town afforded. This house—quite a superior hostelry of its kind—was known as the King's Arms Hotel. Brown had previously taken up his quarters there when recently visiting the scene of the murders. After a frugal war-meal, Rhymer proposed a quiet stroll, where they might be free from interruption or chance eavesdroppers. Accordingly they sauntered out into the old-fashioned town—the detective leading his companion along several back streets and alleys, which eventually brought them into a lonely country lane.

"Now we are free to talk without much fear of being overheard," Rhymer remarked, "and there are several things I want to ask you."

"Fire away, then, sir."

"I take it you've viewed the bodies of the victims."

"Yes," replied Brown, "I saw them yesterday."

"Did you happen to notice if each body was mutilated in a similar manner?"

"I noticed that the mutilations were alike in this respect—the bodies appeared to have been ruthlessly hacked about with a keen-bladed weapon of sorts. It resembled the work of a fanatic more than a responsible person."

"So the police-surgeon thought these poor fellows weren't killed by violence as their remains seemed to suggest?"

"He intimated as much."

"Then how on earth did he account for their mangled condition?"

"Oh, he put that down to the assassin's endeavour to create a false impression, that its victims had been killed in that way; or possibly to lessen the chance of identification. He was, however, inclined to favour the former theory, since the corpses were not so badly disfigured as to cause any difficulty in the latter direction."

"Were the victims robbed?"

"No; they were all respectable young fellows, of the artisan type, who don't usually carry valuables about; but their pockets, containing some treasury notes and loose silver—being pay day—were intact. A solid gold watch was discovered on one of the bodies—evidently a presentation, from the inscription it contained. So robbery is entirely out of the question."

"One thing's very evident," Rhymer remarked, "these murders were not committed by an ordinary individual. They're not a bit like common crimes done for revenge or robbery;

there's evidently a far deeper motive than external appearances present."

"Not unlike the old 'Jack-the-Ripper' tragedies," Brown remarked.

"Yes, there is some similarity, only his victims were women," Rhymer observed, "but in this case they are men, and it's significant to note that they were young and active as well."

"Which looks as though the murderer possessed considerable muscular strength, and audacity into the bargain—"

"Hulloa! What's this?" Rhymer suddenly interrupted, coming to a standstill and gazing straight in front of him.

Brown hurriedly glanced in the same direction, where he beheld a blurred figure rapidly approaching them along the narrow lane. It was about fifty yards ahead. The midsummer twilight was rapidly fading, so it was difficult to see clearly at that distance. Its general aspect, however, was so forbidding, that Rhymer grasped the detective sharply by the arm and dragged him into a gap in the hedge, at the same time motioning him to silence.

They were only just in time, for a moment or two later the object was alongside their hiding-place, thus enabling them to obtain a clearer vision of it without being observed themselves.

This transitory view, as the figure shot past them, was far from reassuring. As they crouched there, an accountable sense of chilliness was prevalent. Brown afterwards owned up to an uncontrollable feeling of nausea as he beheld the figure. The unearthly face conveyed features devilish in their cold and pitiless cruelty, lifeless in their immobility, vacant in their utter lack of human expression—lifeless, yet living. The eyes were lack-lustre, yet wide open and round. The figure resembled that of a male, judging by its height and build. It was hatless and enveloped in a long cloak, from the folds of which an emaciated hand protruded—grasping a long, gleaming knife.

As the Creature swept past, a fetid, pungent smell was evident—horribly nauseous and corrupt.

Almost directly after the Thing had passed their place of concealment, Rhymer sprang into the lane.

"Come along," he urged in a loud whisper, "as quietly as you can. We mustn't lose sight of it." Then, setting off after the retreating figure, beckoned Brown to follow.

The detective was middle-aged, stout and out of training, whereas Rhymer was lean and agile. As a consequence, he soon outdistanced the former, resulting in him and the object of his chase shortly being hidden from the detective by a sharp bend in the lane.

A few moments later, Brown was alarmed by the sudden report of a shot, followed by a hoarse cry for help. Redoubling his efforts he was soon round the aforementioned bend, and there, a few yards in front, he beheld two figures sprawling in the middle of the lane.

As he hastened to the spot where they were struggling, his ears were assailed by a sound like that of a ferocious animal when worrying its prey. Then the figure that was uppermost in the scrimmage suddenly sprang up, and turning upon the detective a ghastly face, distorted with the fierce passion of blood-lust, revealed the repulsive features of the Creature they were pursuing. With an indescribable, sickening, voiceless wail—which, somehow, seemed to give expression to anguish born of ungratified desire—it sprang, with one frenzied leap, over the hedge and disappeared.

Quickly approaching the other figure, which lay in a motionless heap upon the road, Brown beheld the limp form of the professor. Gently raising him, he was infinitely relieved to see him open his eyes.

He sighed audibly, and then stared with a dazed expression. In less than a moment, however, full consciousness returned. A flashing light of comprehension shone in his eyes as he regarded his rescuer.

"Have you collared it?" he cried.

"If you mean the thing that's just attacked you, I haven't."

"You don't mean to say that devil's given us the slip?"

"I'm sorry, sir, but the brute was one too many for both of us; it jumped clean over the hedge before one could say 'Jack Robinson'; but I hope you're not seriously hurt?"

"I shall be all right in a few minutes; but it's a confounded nuisance that 'freak's' got away," said he, looking far more annoyed than injured. Raising his hand he placed the tips of his fingers upon his neck for a moment, and as he withdrew them Brown observed they were smeared with blood. Glancing with a thrill of apprehension at Rhymer's neck, he observed two small incisions from which a slight stream of blood was slowly oozing.

"Good heavens!" he exclaimed, "your injury's similar to those of the three Blankborough victims; only, thank goodness, you've escaped with your life and any, more serious, wounds."

"Your arrival, undoubtedly, saved me from a loathsome death, and butchery as well," he replied as he took a white silk handkerchief from his pocket and deftly bound it round his neck, adding, "Then you didn't come to grips with that fiend?"

"No, for the beggar bolted directly it saw me, before I had a chance even of attempting to seize it. What was the shot I heard?" he added.

"The report of my automatic pistol, and the strange thing is, I plugged the beggar at close quarters, clean through the body—impossible to have missed at such a close range—just as it tackled me—the moment I rounded the bend in the lane, where it had apparently halted."

"Didn't attempt to stab you with that knife it carried?"

"That's the remarkable thing about it," he replied. "The Creature—who possessed abnormal strength—made one spring and floored me, at the same time dropping the knife, which fell with a clatter upon the road. Then it pinned me firmly down with its hands and knees, and bent its face close to mine. I was quite helpless in its grasp. It bared its fangs with a snarl, and deliberately bit me in the neck. I was speechless for the moment with horror, but by a supreme effort I succeeded in raising a cry for help, though the exertion proved too much and I lost consciousness."

"It's evident you've narrowly escaped the fate of those other poor fellows. Great Scot, it was a near shave! Here, take a pull at this," he added, producing a flask from his pocket.

The stimulant rapidly revived Rhymer.

"Thanks," he exclaimed, returning the flask. "That's better. Now we must be getting on, for there's no time to be lost if we are to follow up this clue."

"Anyhow, we've had a glimpse of the criminal we're after, that's very evident," Brown asserted, "and we shall both be able to swear to its identity, since I, for one, shall never forget the features of that monstrosity, if I live to be a hundred. Besides, since you say you've lodged a bullet in its carcase, it's not likely to travel far. We had better search over the hedge yonder."

"You're free to search to your heart's content, but I'm going straight back to the hotel to cauterise and dress this bite in my neck."

Brown looked askance at this remark, which was uttered with a trace of petulance.

"This thing cannot be dealt with by the customary C.I.D. methods," Rhymer went on to explain, "for I'm convinced that neither powder and shot nor even cold steel will have any effect in the ultimate capture of this Living-death, which you vainly hope to find over that hedge. Neither would your steel bracelets have any purchase upon its wrists. We're up against something abnormal here, and we must cut our coat according to our cloth."

Brown at first appeared a trifle crestfallen, after listening to these disparaging comments upon his latest suggestion. The extraordinary circumstances sorely puzzled him, but he had the intuition to realise that some influence outside the usual rut of criminal investigation was facing them, and being previously assured of Rhymer's experience in such matters, was content to be guided by him, at any rate for the present.

"I'm blessed if I can follow the hang of the thing," Brown grumbled, "for I had labelled your assailant as a dangerous lunatic at large. Your last remark, however, puts quite another complexion on the matter."

"You detectives are such a hidebound crowd," Rhymer remarked with an indulgent smile, "you try to handcuff clues as well as criminals. Give me plenty of scope when hot upon a clue, then I can forge ahead unencumbered."

"Have you any definite clue, sir, to follow?"

"Yes, Brown, I've three. First, there are the incisions in my neck; secondly, there is this," and displaying the palm of his right hand, he exhibited a fragment of dark cloth, which, from its frayed appearance, had evidently been torn from some garment in the recent struggle. "And here is the third," he added, betraying a note of triumph, as, taking a few steps, he stooped and picked up an object lying at the side of the road.

"Ah! the assassin's knife," Brown exclaimed.

"Precisely, and it's probably the identical weapon with which those poor chaps' bodies were so hacked about, so it's an important link in our chain of evidence."

"And a deucedly significant one, too," Brown added.

There was the twinkle of a smile in Rhymer's eyes as he inquired:

"Are you still inclined to search for your escaped lunatic over the hedge, or shall we return to our quarters?"

The detective stiffened as he replied:

"It's my duty as an officer of the law to let no chance slip by, my professional credit's at stake, remember; but I am quite willing to be guided by you—especially as I asked for your assistance."

"And you are welcome to it, Brown, as well as all the official credit, if success crowns our efforts. But I must ask you to act upon the lines that I point out. Is that agreed?"

"Quite, sir, and with your acumen you will be certain to find out something further that will help us to bottom this mystery after all."

"Hope I may, Brown, I'm sure; so let's turn in for the night. I'm feeling a bit fagged after my wrestling-bout with that anaemic-looking blighter."

"HOPE YOU'RE FEELING no worse, sir, after last night's experiences," the detective inquired the following morning when he and Rhymer met at breakfast.

"I'm as fit as a fiddle, thanks," said he; "a good night's rest works wonders. It takes a lot to keep me awake long, when once I'm between the sheets."

"How's your neck?" the detective added, glancing at a neat strip of sticking-plaster covering the injured part.

"Oh, just a trifle sore, that's all. The incisions weren't deep. I cauterised them last night, so don't contemplate any trouble in that direction."

After breakfast they adjourned to the privacy of Rhymer's bedroom in order to map out future plans. During their discussion he produced the incriminating knife, and, handing it to Brown, remarked:

"Quite an antique, eh?"

The latter examined it with keen interest.

"Evidently," said he, "but its age doesn't lessen the cut-throat appearance of the engraven blade, set in its massive handle. A remarkable tool, I must admit, resembling, more than anything I've ever seen, a Kukri, the Gurka fighting weapon. One thing's evident, though—"

"What's that?" Rhymer interrupted.

"Why, that it belongs to the ugly brute we fell foul of last night."

"Sorry to disagree with you," said Rhymer, "but we have yet to discover the real owner of this piece of cutlery, and until that's accomplished we're a long way off a solution of the mystery."

Brown, unconvinced, shook his head.

"Well, it's beyond me even to guess what you're driving at. Anyhow, the weapon was owned by that individual temporarily—we can both swear to that—and possession is nine points of the law."

"I shouldn't try and guess, if I were you," Rhymer advised. "Guessing is always destructive to logic. Far better observe small facts upon which large impressions may depend."

"Then *you* haven't any idea as to whom else this knife may belong?"

"Not the vaguest."

"And yet you refuse to believe it belongs to the creature who dropped it?"

"That's my opinion."

"It's all an insoluble mystery to me," said Brown, "it gets thicker instead of clearer."

"On the contrary," Rhymer contradicted, "it clears every instant."

"Then, hang it all, sir, can't you help me out of the fog?"

"That's what I'm trying to do."

"How?"

"By taking steps to discover the owner of the knife, of course. I wonder if our landlord has an up-to-date copy of the local directory? I'll go and find out."

Subsequent inquiry produced a recent edition of this book, and for the next few minutes they were poring over its pages.

It contained the customary list of private and commercial residents. Among the former, one name attracted Rhymer's attention:

"Ludwig Holtsner. The Gables."

"An enemy in our midst," he exclaimed, pointing it out to Brown. "That fellow ought to have been interned."

"He's bound to be naturalised," the detective replied.

"All the more suspicious and dangerous. If I had my way, all Boche-born individuals residing in this country—notwithstanding their naturalisation—should be interned. Boches will be Boches, and a mere scrap of paper, identifying them as naturalised British subjects, won't wipe out the inherited taint of Kultur. I don't trust the breed, and when I come across a male or female Boche my suspicions are instantly aroused."

"We keep a sharp enough eye upon any suspicious characters of that sort," Brown affirmed a trifle aggressively—so Rhymer thought.

"I'm not casting any slur upon the efficacy of the police in their dealings with aliens, but even they have been gulled by the Hun, over here, more than once."

"I didn't suggest you were, sir, but we often get blame we don't deserve, so we are bound to drop an occasional word of protest."

"I'm not contesting your rights in that direction, Brown."

"All right, sir, but I like to justify my assertions, so I'll just slip round to the police station and hear what the local superintendent has to say about this Ludwig Holtsner. He won't have failed to make full inquiries, I know."

"An excellent idea, Brown, only take care not to say a word about our adventure last night, since secrecy regarding our actions—for the present—will best promote our chance of ultimate success."

"Very good, sir."

Half an hour later Brown returned, having achieved his visit to the police station.

"Well, obtained any useful information?" Rhymer inquired.

"Not much in support of your suspicion, anyhow, regarding this Mr. Holtsner," he replied. "The superintendent told me that he took out naturalisation papers many years ago, and is quite all right. A man of local influence—he hastened to assure me—a wealthy bachelor and occupying a large house which he purchased."

"Any other particulars?"

"Nothing of much importance, I imagine."

"Did the superintendent say how Holtsner occupied his time?"

"Oh yes, he studied science a lot and was quite a keen Egyptologist."

Rhymer's eyes sparkled as he heard this last piece of information. Instantly his faculties were on the alert.

"They are all quite all-right until they're caught red-handed. And then—well—there's the very devil to pay. But, at all events, you've brought back one valuable piece of evidence in support of a theory I've already broached."

"Oh! What's that?"

"My dear Inspector, do try a little analysis yourself," he enjoined with a touch of impatience. "I've already given you some broad hints as to my methods. Now it's up to you to apply them."

Brown looked distinctly piqued.

"Very well, sir, as you choose to put it in that fashion. I've nothing more to say—"

"Which will afford you a better opportunity for mental analysis," Rhymer chipped in with an apologetic smile. "And may I give you a golden rule which I was taught by a famous detective?" He paused for a reply.

"Get on with it, then."

"Well, when you have worn out the possible, whatever is left, however impossible, comes mighty near the truth."

NO PLACE CAN be more productive of local information than the bar-parlour of a country town hotel. Brown was keenly alive to this fact, and that was why he got Rhymer to join him in the bar of the King's Arms later on in the day.

"We may pick up some useful information here, sir, if we keep our eyes and ears open."

"A suggestion full of possibilities, Brown, so let's pledge our success in a drop of dry ginger. Can't make it anything stronger, if I'm to stand treat. It's forbidden by D.O.R.A.—and you are one of her guardians."

They had been silently smoking for some little time, when two men entered the room, which was fairly full. They sat down at a vacant table next to that at which Rhymer and Brown were seated.

Having called for some liquid refreshment, they opened a brisk conversation. Their general appearance plainly identified them as menservants, who had dropped in at their favourite house of call for a friendly chat over the cup that cheers and loosens the tongue.

"Well, Alf," the taller of the two was heard by their neighbours to remark, "how's your governor been treating you of late?"

"Not 'alf, Jim," was the reply. "'E's balmy, 'e is. I tell yer it's fair getting on my nerves."

"Why, wot's 'e been a-doing of now, Alf—anything fresh?"

"Fresh!" he reiterated disdainfully. "Not much—same old row, blaming me for things I ain't done. That's all."

"Wot 'aven't yer done?"

"Nothing. It's 'im 'as done it. Gone and lost a bloomin' old knife that belonged to some 'eathen wot lived 'undreds of years ago—says it's worth pots of money, and because 'e can't find it, swears I've pinched it. I like 'is cheek."

At this point their conversation was interrupted by the arrival of a third man who joined them, and a few moments later, after draining their glasses, they left the bar together.

Rhymer casually arose and, strolling across to the counter, addressed the barmaid behind:

"Can you tell me, miss, who those two men were, sitting at the table next to ours? They've just left with a friend."

"Yes, sir," she replied with a glance of slight inquiry, "the short one was James Smith, a footman at Sir William Doone's, and the other Alfred Ball, valet to Mr. Holtsner."

"Thanks," said he, "then I'm mistaken. One of them reminded me of a servant that left me some years ago," he mendaciously added, to ease her mind of any faint suspicion he might have aroused as to the real reason of his inquiry.

A few minutes later, Rhymer and Brown were again closeted in the former's bedroom.

"We're progressing like a house on fire," the former affirmed, rubbing his hands. "You overheard what that fellow said about the knife? Well, the barmaid confirmed my suspicion that he was a servant of Holtsner's, so now it's pretty evident to whom the knife belongs."

"Quite clear," said Brown, "and you were right after all. We may also take it that the knife was stolen from the Gables by that blooming chump we met in the lane, and without Holtsner's knowledge, too."

"That's more than probable, and I'll go a step further in suggesting that Holtsner's not en-tirely ignorant of this Creature's presence in the locality, although he may not be actually aware it was the thief, since then he would scarcely have blamed Alfred Ball for his loss. Still, it must be remembered that a man, being acquainted with anything abnormal haunting his premises, usually wants to hush it up, since it gives the place a bad name."

"Quite so," said Brown. "Yet there's something more beneath than meets the eye; although I admit the fog's clearing a bit."

"Suspicions are becoming certainties, you mean," Rhymer added. "But, look here, we mustn't lose another minute. It's now six-thirty," consulting his watch, "and we've got to visit this German fellow as soon as possible, under cover of some pretext or other. Our episode in finding the knife is a good enough excuse for calling, even at this hour, in order to restore it to him."

"That will also place him under an obligation," said Brown, "which may help matters forward a bit."

"That's quite probable."

"Do you know whereabouts his house is?" Brown inquired after a pause.

"Yes, I asked the landlord when returning the directory. It's not more than a quarter of an hour's walk, so let's get off."

"We shall need extra caution at this stage," Rhymer remarked, as they were hurrying along the lane which they had traversed the previous night. "I'm positive it would be wiser for me to call on Holtsner alone, until I discover how the land lies; so I hope you won't mind waiting for me outside. We must avoid exciting this man's suspicion, and if we both arrive together he might suspect the real object of our visit."

He spoke with a seriousness which gave authority to his words.

At first Brown seemed inclined to protest, but after a little consideration, fell in with the proposition.

"I'm sure I am advising you for the best," Rhymer remarked as he halted opposite a pair of massive, iron gates guarding a long and tortuous drive. "This is the Gables, I expect," he added. "If I should fail to return within—say—half an hour, you'd better call for me."

With this parting injunction he entered the drive and soon disappeared round a curve in the shrub-lined avenue.

Arriving at the house, he was admitted by a man-servant whom he recognised as Alfred Ball.

"I've called to see Mr. Holtsner," said he, presenting his card, "kindly inform him it's a matter of business."

"I'm not sure if the master's at home, sir," was the non-committal reply, "but I'll inquire if you'll please step inside."

He then conducted him to a small room at the further end of the hall.

A few minutes later the door opened, and a tall, middle-aged man entered, of fair complexion with closely-cropped hair and a bristly moustache.

He was inclined to obesity and wore a pair of gold-rimmed spectacles fitted with powerful lenses, which accentuated the prominency of his protruding eyes.

He bowed to his visitor, exclaiming in a deep, guttural voice—as he glanced at the visiting card held between his podgy thumb and forefinger:

"Professor Rhymer, I presume?"

"That is my name, Mr. Holtsner," he replied as he mentally sized up the fat German. "I must apologise for this late call, but I've found an article which I believe you've had stolen," handing him a brown-paper parcel.

Holtsner took it with a look of blank inquiry, and proceeded to remove the paper, exclaiming:

"Something I've had stolen—what can it be—er—where did you find it?"

"In the lane outside your drive."

"In the lane—" Holtsner reiterated, pausing all of a sudden—arrested by the discovery of the knife which the parcel now disclosed.

"Well—how on earth—" he continued with an apparent effort, but the remainder of his speech died away upon his lips as he glanced suspiciously at the professor.

Rhymer met his look squarely with a well-feigned expression of innocent surprise, as though at a loss to account for his hesitation.

"You were going to say, Mr. Holtsner, 'How on earth did I guess that this interesting antique belonged to you?'" he suggested with a frank smile. "Well, I can soon satisfy you upon that score, for I chanced to overhear some one casually remark that you had lost a valuable knife, and as I had previously happened to stumble across one in the lane, whilst enjoying a stroll, I thought I'd call and inquire if it was yours. If it's not, then I'd better leave it at the police station."

This assumption of candour seemed to reassure Holtsner.

"Yes, this belongs to me; it was stolen from my museum," he acknowledged somewhat reluctantly; "but who did you overhear say I'd lost it?"

"Excuse me, sir, but it would hardly be fair for me to say, since the information was not intended for my ears. I only overheard it by chance."

Holtsner was on the verge of resenting Rhymer's refusal to satisfy his inquiry, but he evidently thought better of it, apologetically exclaiming:

"Quite so, I oughtn't to have asked. I'm a keen collector of antiques, and was put out at losing this valuable relic of a lost Egyptian art. Its sudden recovery flustered me, so pray accept my apologies and thanks as well, for what you've done. By the way," he added with assumed unconcern, "you don't happen to have mentioned the matter to the police?"

"No," said Rhymer.

"Ah! it's just as well you didn't," said he, with an involuntary sigh of relief. "You see, I suspect one of my servants of the theft, and I've no wish to prosecute. The police are so officious in these matters—I'm sure you'll understand?"

"Perfectly," was the response.

It was evident to Rhymer's keen sense of observation that Holtsner's apparent agitation was not solely due to the cause he so lamely advanced. There was something he was anxious to hide. The man might be a collector, in fact, the local superintendent of police had informed Brown that such was the case; but the loss of a valuable antique and its subsequent restoration by a stranger, who had simply picked it up upon the road, would hardly account for its owner appearing as disturbed as Holtsner seemed to be.

His very attitude invited suspicion, but Rhymer was cute enough to conceal any trace of his conviction that Holtsner was playing a deep game; so, assuming an attitude of nonchalance, he said:

"I'm awfully glad I've found your knife, since it's afforded me the privilege of making your acquaintance, and being a scientist and collector myself, it's a pleasure to meet others with similar tastes."

Rhymer's diplomatic reply seemed to set the German's suspicions at rest, for he inquired:

"Are you staying long in the neighbourhood?"

"Only a few days. I've run down with a friend from town to make a geological survey."

Rhymer invented this excuse on the spur of the moment, since he judged it would avert further suspicion that might arise in Holtsner's mind, should he come across him and Brown roaming about the vicinity.

"An attractive branch of science," said Holtsner, "and it may interest you to know that I have some geological specimens found in the neighbourhood, which I'd like to show you in my museum."

That was just what Rhymer desired. He didn't care a rap about the specimens, but he did want to get into the museum. So, without displaying any sign of the satisfaction he felt, replied:

"Thanks, I *should* like to see these specimens; but I fear I can't stop now. I'm overdue to join my friend at our hotel, but as he is also keen on geology, may I bring him along as well? Shall we say to-morrow?"

"By all means. How would the morning suit you? I'm a man of leisure, so my time's at your convenience."

"That'll do admirably," he replied, and, bid-

ding his host good-bye, took his departure, rejoining Brown a few minutes later in the lane.

"Thought you were never coming," was the detective's greeting. "I was going to call for you in another minute. You've exceeded your time-limit and I was beginning to get anxious."

"It's fortunate you didn't; as it was, I had some difficulty in getting away when I did, and if you had suddenly turned up we should have been in the deuce of a mess. So far I've fixed things up all right. The man acknowledges he's the owner of the knife, and though he seemed suspicious at first, I think I succeeded in blinding him as to the purpose of my visit. Told him I was down here with a friend to make a geological survey. He seemed to swallow the fable readily enough, and invited me to look at a museum he has on the premises. I'd have liked to go, there and then, but the event of your sudden appearance upon the scene—as requested—precluded my doing so. I got him, however, to ask the two of us to see the museum to-morrow morning."

Brown pondered a few moments.

"That's top hole," he at length exclaimed, "for now we may be able to pick up some evidence in that place."

"Exactly what I hope to do, for he let out that the knife was stolen from it."

"Then in all probability the assassin will have left some traces there—finger marks or similar clues," Brown hazarded.

"I hope to find something more tangible than that."

"Hang it all, sir, what more could you find without you knocked up against the actual criminal?"

"Nothing whatever."

Brown stared at his collaborator, and was on the point of making some further remark when he suddenly remembered the professor's former tip—"Try and do a little analysis yourself"—so he tried and relapsed into silence.

"By the way," Rhymer presently inquired, "do you know anything about geology?"

"Well—yes—a trifle. I studied it a little in my

school days; but I've only a very hazy recollection of the subject now."

"No matter, all I want you to do is to make out you're keen on the thing when we visit Holtsner to-morrow morning."

IN DUE COURSE Rhymer and Brown turned up at the Gables, and were courteously received by Holtsner. Without wasting any time, their host led them into the museum—a large and lofty apartment built off from the house, though connected by a short passage with a door at either end.

Brown no sooner entered this apartment than he experienced a sensation of vague, unaccountable horror. A conviction of some eerie presence gripped tight hold of him. He advanced into the centre of the room, still oppressed with this novel sensation, which increased rather than diminished. He was no coward, neither was he superstitious, so the horror which obsessed him was all the more apprehensive.

Suddenly his gaze was attracted by a row of mummy cases which stood on end in a long showcase—fitted with glass doors—extending the full length of one end of the building.

He stared, awe-inspired, at the row of garishly-painted wooden boxes, containing their human relics of a bygone age. The lid of one was open, disclosing a swathed and bandaged form. Its lofty cheek bones, massive jaw, and aquiline nose depicted power and diffused a subtle influence—a latent force which was indefinable.

"My Egyptian mummies seem to interest you, sir," Holtsner exclaimed, mistaking the keen attention Brown bestowed upon these curiosities as indicating admiration rather than horror.

"They're apt to give one the creeps," he replied with an effort to hide his uneasiness, "but that object in the open box seems to be in good condition—"

"What on earth do you know, Brown, about the condition of mummies?" Rhymer suddenly interrupted, giving the detective a warning look, unobserved by Holtsner. "Geology is more in your line, so, for goodness sake, stick to it and don't air your views upon matters you know nothing about."

"What do you know about mummies?" Brown retorted.

"Not much," said Rhymer, flashing him another significant glance, "but sufficient to convince me the Egyptian lady or gentleman in that box is as old as Adam and not any better preserved than the majority of its class."

"Professor Rhymer is quite right," Holtsner was quick to assert, with what appeared to Rhymer undue emphasis; "all these mummies date back to a remote Egyptian dynasty; but," he added with precipitancy, "as you and your friend are keen on geological specimens, if you'll look at this case over here, you'll find some fossils of local interest."

"Ah, that's more in our line, Brown, isn't it?" said Rhymer as he moved towards his host, followed by the detective.

The specimens indicated were mainly echinoderms, lamellibranchs, and gasteropods, which were neatly labelled and displayed in glass cases. While they were inspecting these, Holtsner moved away in another direction in order to pick up some object off a table, apart from where they had all been standing.

Rhymer seized this opportunity to whisper into the detective's ear:

"For heaven's sake, man, don't allude again to those mummies, but do try and feign some sort of enthusiasm over these blessed fossils." Then, raising his voice for Holtsner's benefit, exclaimed:

"What a topping specimen of the *Tritonium corrugatum!* Observe the fusiform shell—the elongated spire and the slightly curved anterior canal. The gasteropods are very beautiful. Well, I fear we must be making a move if we are to get to town in time for that lecture to-night, and I don't want to miss it. I've some letters to get off, too, before we leave by the afternoon train."

Holtsner overheard these remarks, as Rhymer intended he should, and as he again approached his guests, a look of satisfaction overspread his features.

"Jolly fine collection of yours, Mr. Holtsner," Rhymer enthusiastically observed, "sorry we must be going—awfully obliged to you for showing us round.—Quite envy you the possession of such a museum."

"Pray don't mention it, sir; only too delighted, I'm sure. It's a pleasure to show one's things to those who can appreciate them. Hope you and your friend will drop in again, when you've more time at your disposal."

"I can promise you that much," was Rhymer's unspoken comment, "only the visit will be a strictly private one as far as your knowledge is concerned." Then aloud he exclaimed:

"Many thanks, some day we may, I hope, have another look round."

As soon as Rhymer and the detective had left the Gables, the former exclaimed:

"By Jove! But you made an unfortunate remark about that mummy, and, unwittingly—I presume—stumbled nearer the truth than you had any idea of. Holtsner, too, pricked up his ears. You kind of 'put the wind up him,' as the 'Tommies' say. However, I doubt if any real harm's done, since he appeared somewhat reassured after I'd chipped in with my contradictory remark."

"Whatever are you driving at?" Brown exclaimed, apparently nettled.

"Wait till you and I have got into that museum alone—which we must do to-night by hook or by crook—and then you'll know. We've got to fix up a private view of those mummies. I've made it pretty clear to the Boche, our professed intention of going to London this afternoon, and though he's still inclined to suspicion, I think we've managed fairly to mislead him with regard to our interest in his mummies. Anyhow, he won't be expecting us back in Blankborough until to-morrow, and that's a feather in the cap of our plan."

AFTER LUNCH RHYMER and Brown left the hotel for the station, with a handbag apiece, in order to convey the impression they were off for the night. Upon their arrival at the booking-office, Rhymer loudly demanded two tickets for Charing Cross. Having entered a first-class smoker and finding themselves alone, Brown remarked:

"You seemed anxious to let everybody know where we were going, sir, by the way you yelled out for the tickets."

"Not every one, Brown—only Ball, Holtsner's servant, whom I spotted spying upon us—as he imagined unobserved—from behind a barrow piled up with luggage. I warned you that the Boche was still suspicious. Now he'll soon be posted up with the information that we have cleared out, with our kit, for a night in town."

As the train approached the next station—three miles from Blankborough—Rhymer abruptly signified that it was to be their destination. A few minutes later they were out on the platform. Then, without any further word of explanation, Rhymer set off at a leisurely pace along the road, in the direction from which they had just come, with Brown—looking annoyed and puzzled—following in his wake.

The former volunteered no explanation until they arrived opposite a stile, where he suddenly halted.

"We'll take it easy for a bit here. Hope you've brought your pipe, Brown?—Then let's light up, for on no account must we turn up at Blankborough again before dusk."

THE MUSEUM ATTACHED to the Gables had two entrances. One leading from the house, through which Holtsner had conducted his visitors that morning, the other giving access from the garden.

Outside the latter entrance—in the evening—Rhymer and Brown, concealed behind a thick bush, were watching the door, which was slightly ajar.

Suddenly the former slipped from his hiding-place—motioning the detective to remain where he was—and advanced on tiptoe towards the entrance.

Upon arriving there, he glued his eye to the chink between the hinges, intently observing something within. His inspection appeared to afford him satisfaction, judging by his expression when he subsequently returned to the seclusion of the bush.

"Sure enough, we're on the right track," he whispered. "Pay careful attention to what I'm going to say now."

"I'm listening, sir."

"At any moment a figure may slip out of that door, closely resembling the freak we saw the night before last. Follow it, only keep at a safe distance, to avoid being seen if possible."

Brown stifled an exclamation, and as a ray of moonlight struck his face, forcing its way through an aperture in the bush, Rhymer detected an expression akin to fear. Then with a challenging glance the former asserted:

"I'm no coward, sir, and I've yet to meet the crook I wouldn't tackle—provided it's human—but to stand up against a fiend like the one that went for you the other night—well—it's a bit more than I bargained for."

"Don't blame you either, but so far my investigations give me confidence in assuming that as long as you don't directly impede this Creature's progress, it won't attack you. Follow at a safe distance and watch, that's all I ask you to do. I don't think *I* should have been mauled the other night had I not mentally registered a determination to go for the brute. My intentions were apparently conveyed by telepathy to the Creature's system of comprehension, hence the 'scrap,' which proved a 'knock-out' for me."

A creaking sound in the direction of the museum caused both men to turn round sharply, and there, illuminated by a ray of light from the now wide-opened door, a figure glided into the moonlight without.

"Quick!" Rhymer exclaimed with bated breath, "don't lose sight of it."

With a sharp intaking of breath, Brown started in pursuit, keeping his distance as directed, while Rhymer, with one rapid glance around, slipped through the open door of the museum.

Within the threshold he halted, as his eyes fell upon a recumbent figure stretched on a couch, over which a shaded electric lamp was burning, suspended from the vaulted ceiling.

Approaching on tiptoe, he recognised Holtsner. The German appeared to be in a deep sleep. A closer examination, however, revealed the man to be in a sort of trance, for his breathing was imperceptible. But for the faint trace of colour in his face, he might have been dead.

Rhymer then produced a small pocket mirror, and, placing it close to the man's nostrils, observed a slight blur on the surface. With a nod of satisfaction he replaced the glass in his pocket and was about to make a further inspection of the apartment, when his attention was suddenly arrested by the sound of stealthy footsteps in the passage that connected the museum with the house.

In a flash he surveyed his surroundings, and, spotting a curtained recess in the wall nearest him, slipped within. He had barely covered his retreat when the door slowly opened and some one entered whom he recognised—through a small rent in the curtain—as Alfred Ball.

The latter carefully closed the door behind him and locked it..Next he cautiously approached the couch upon which his master lay, as if anxious to avoid disturbing him. Bestowing a cursory glance at the sleeper, he fetched a small table from another part of the room, placing it by the couch. Going to a cabinet he produced two stoppered bottles and a graduated glass measure, which he laid on the table by Holtsner's side. Then he crossed to another cupboard from which he took a coil of stout cord. Retaining this, he placed a chair close to the outer door—which was still slightly ajar—and sat down, with his head thrown forward, in an attitude of alertness.

About ten minutes later, without any warning, the door was violently flung back, and in rushed a figure which Rhymer recognised to be the one he and Brown had previously seen leaving the museum.

Its eyes were lit up with a fierce passion. The

lips and chin daubed with blood—fresh blood—hardly yet dry. It made straight for the couch upon which Holtsner was lying, and, in another moment, would have reached him, had not Ball sprung up and whisked the cord—which was fitted with a running noose—neatly over the Creature's head, fetching it, with a smart jerk, sprawling on the floor.

Simultaneously with the crash occasioned by the falling body, Holtsner languidly raised himself, stretching his arms; and, as he moved, the monster—struggling violently on the floor, hampered by the coils of the lasso—became motionless—a horrid, inert mass of bone and sinew.

Holtsner wearily dragged himself into a sitting posture and, leaning towards the table, poured out a few drops of liquid from each of the two bottles into the glass measure, and, with a trembling hand, tossed the stuff down his throat.

"That's better, Otto," he gasped. "These frequent trances are beginning to take it out of me."

"Number two has strafed another enemy of the Fatherland," the servant vehemently asserted, his features fairly distorted with "hate." "Look! there's the blood of some pig-swine on its lips."

The two wretches were conversing in German, a language with which Rhymer was well acquainted. He was not a little surprised to discover that Ball was a Boche, for his cockney accent and speech, when recently in the King's Arms, was so perfectly assumed. But, when he gathered, from their recent remarks, that another murder had undoubtedly been committed, he became intensely anxious about Brown; and keen though he was to see what else Holtsner and his accomplice were up to, he inwardly raved to get away and find out where the inspector might be.

"Must stick where I am for the present," he soliloquised, "until those two devils clear out. Confound it all!—I do hope poor Brown's all right."

Meanwhile, Holtsner and Otto (to give the latter his correct name) set about a very revolting performance. A basin of water and a sponge were first produced, with which Otto, kneeling on the floor, carefully removed the bloodstains from the jaws of the motionless Thing lying there.

He then approached the large case with the glass doors—in which the mummies were stored—and, lifting out one of the tawdry Egyptian death-boxes, which was empty, laid it, with Holtsner's assistance, upon the floor. Opening the lid, they proceeded to place the inanimate Creature within, having first removed the lasso. Shutting down the hinged lid, they locked it, and, lifting the case between them, deposited it in its former place. Crossing the apartment to a small steel safe let into the wall, Holtsner unlocked the door, taking from within a leather notebook. Opening it he made an entry with a fountain pen.

He then put it back in the safe and began a rapid conversation with Otto, but their voices were so low that Rhymer was unable to hear what they said.

However, he was not kept much longer in suspense, for after stowing away the several articles they had been using, and carefully scrutinising the apartment to make sure nothing incriminating was left about, they left the museum by the door communicating with the house, having first switched off the electric light.

Rhymer lost no time in quitting his cramped quarters. Noiselessly crossing the floor, he slipped back the latch of the garden door, opened it, and, as he bolted out, suddenly found himself confronted by a figure.

"Great Scot! How you startled me, Brown," he exclaimed, upon discovering he had barged into the burly figure of the detective, "how long have you been here?"

"For some little while, and I've seen what's been going on inside there, through a chink in the door. But where on earth have you been? I didn't see you in the place."

"I was there right enough, concealed behind a curtain, where, like you, I could see without being seen. I'm glad you saw this sickening spectacle, since a witness will be useful. Why didn't you follow up the Thing as I asked?"

"I did my best, but It was too much for me. I couldn't keep up the pace. Lor'! how the Thing did scoot. Lost sight of it at the high boundary wall—topped with broken glass—which encloses the grounds. It scaled this with perfect ease, though it was too high for me to attempt. There I remained on the look-out for about a quarter of an hour, when I suddenly spotted it again doubling back on its original tracks. So, quickly hiding behind the trunk of a tree until it had passed, I followed it back here again. Had it not been for the bright moonlight, I couldn't have done as much as I did—but preserve me from ever seeing a sight like that in the museum again."

"Quite Teutonic, wasn't it?"

"Teutonic?—Why, I call it diabolical."

"The same thing," Rhymer observed. "Anyhow you did your best, but I fear we shall shortly hear of another of these wretched murders as a result of to-night's work. You've got your electric torch and some skeleton keys, haven't you?"

"Yes, I have."

"Good, then we'll proceed without delay. There's some more evidence I'm anxious to secure in there," he added, nodding in the direction of the museum. "I daren't switch on the light, as they might see the reflection from the house. There's a safe inside we must investigate. Quite an ordinary affair, I imagine, so one of your skeleton keys should fix up the job."

It transpired as Rhymer had predicted. The safe was soon opened and the notebook produced. With the aid of Brown's torch they examined the contents. It proved to be a ruled manuscript, only just commenced. Some brief instructions, written in a German fist, occupied the first two or three pages.

Brown didn't know any German, but Rhymer was able to read the contents. It only took him a few minutes, and as he proceeded, first bewilderment and then horror gripped him. Turning, at length, to Brown, he exclaimed:

"It's almost incredible! However, we've no time now to go into details. We must get away as quickly and quietly as possible. Every moment increases the risk of discovery."

He then replaced the incriminating document in the safe and locked it.

Silently the two men left the chamber of mystery by the garden door, closing it carefully behind them. As they were walking to the inn, Rhymer suddenly exclaimed:

"It's amazing to think what fiends these Boches are. They'll stick at nothing. That book in the safe yonder contains some documentary evidence revealing one of the most revolting plots that could foul the imagination. Nothing short of Kultur—with a capital K—could hit upon such a conspiracy. Thank goodness, it's been our good luck to knock up against the thing in time, before these murders became wholesale, which, judging from the evidence, might shortly have been the case."

"Good heavens! Do you mean to say that these Blankborough murders are part and parcel of a Boche conspiracy?"

"Undoubtedly that's the bald state of affairs, due, of course, to the tolerance of a naturalised enemy in our midst. And if we are to nip in the bud a scheme devised by demons in human form, we must lose no time in acquainting the authorities with our discovery. Yours is a name to conjure with at the 'Yard': could you possibly get me a personal interview with your chief first thing to-morrow morning?"

"Then you believe Holtsner to be responsible for these murders?" Brown asked, evading the other question.

"Undoubtedly so; and for a good deal more besides."

"Then he must be, somehow, employing demoniacal agencies?"

"That's more than probable, after what we've both witnessed."

"Well, I'm jiggered! Can't understand it even now, but I can believe anything of the Boche, and though you've not yet told me all the details of the plot revealed in that book, I'm willing to 'phone to my chief and ask him to receive you as early as possible to-morrow morning."

"Thanks," was Rhymer's brief, but grateful response.

BROWN'S CHIEF DIDN'T appear very favourably disposed towards Rhymer as the latter was ushered at eight A.M. the following morning into his sanctum at the "Yard."

"This is an extraordinarily early hour to fix for an interview, sir," he curtly announced, as he motioned Rhymer to a chair. "Your business must be correspondingly urgent, I presume."

"Couldn't be more so."

"Humph! Then I hope you'll waste no time in getting through with it. I'm up to my ears in work, and had it not been for Inspector Brown's urgent call upon the 'phone, I shouldn't have been here to meet you. I'm for ever being rung up to listen to matters of so-called 'national importance' from unofficial quarters, which usually result in the discovery of a mare's nest."

"I don't think you'll find my communication to be one of that sort, I only wish you might; besides, Inspector Brown can corroborate it."

"So I understand. Please proceed, Professor Rhymer."

Without further preamble he began to relate all that had occurred at Blankborough since his arrival there in Brown's company, including the evidence he had obtained from the notebook in Holtsner's safe.

The official listened attentively as Rhymer continued his narrative. He never once interrupted until the report was completed.

Then abruptly turning towards the professor, exclaimed:

"This is indeed a serious matter, if you are correct in your allegations, but I can hardly believe it."

"Surely, sir, nothing the Boche might do is beyond your powers of credibility?"

"Under the circumstances, I admit you have

acted judiciously in reporting the matter so promptly," said he, ignoring Rhymer's last remark, "but it's scarcely comprehensible."

"Anyhow, I've clearly stated the facts, sir."

"I know, and I'm quite aware there's something out of the ordinary rut in these Blankborough crimes, and though I'm not predisposed to place much faith in psychological phenomena, you have certainly impressed me with your view of the matter."

Just then the telephone on the chief's desk rang up. He picked up the receiver and held it to his ear, thoughtfully replacing it a few moments later.

"These crimes are decidedly getting ahead of us. I've just received intimation of another murder last night at Blankborough, so your inference, sir, has been corroborated."

Rhymer exhibited no surprise at this statement.

"It's only what I expected," said he, "and it supplements my plea for immediate and drastic measures."

The official regarded him meditatively.

"May I make a suggestion?" Rhymer ventured.

"By all means."

"Then, for goodness sake, sir, do use your influence to set the machinery in motion. Issue a confidential communication to every police centre throughout the British Isles, with instructions to furnish fresh reports relating to any naturalised Boches residing in each locality; especially ear-marking those engaged in scientific pursuits, and noting whether they are in possession of any Egyptian mummies. It would be well to insist upon all cargoes, shipped through neutral ports, being searched, and if any of these embalmed specimens are found on board, have them instantly confiscated as contraband. That would effectually put a stop to these atrocities."

"I can see no difficulty in adopting the first part of your suggestion, but the latter might meet with serious obstacles."

"Well, all I can say is that the safety of hundreds of human lives depends upon it."

The chief fell to brooding again.

"Upon my word," said he, "I believe you're right, and I'm half inclined to try it—as far as it lies in my power; but others in authority will have to be consulted first."

"I realised that from the commencement, but surely no responsible person in his right senses would hesitate to take prompt measures to quell a serious menace like this, for, should the German Intelligence Department get an inkling that we are on their tracks, all evidence would quickly be effaced by them."

"That's very evident, but we must arrest this Holtsner fellow first."

"Exactly: and if you'll give me a free hand, I'll undertake to catch him red-handed. Then you can more easily effect a wholesale arrest of naturalised Boches throughout the country on a charge of conspiracy, once their leader is safely under lock and key."

"I'm relying a lot upon your assurances, Professor, and if you have made a blunder, then there'll be the deuce of a row."

"I assure you I've made no mistake."

"Well, I'll risk it."

"And you'll let me have Brown's services for a little while longer at Blankborough?"

The chief pondered, and then with a look of resignation, said:

"Quite irregular, you know, since this case is officially in Brown's hands. It'll be creating a precedent, too. But the circumstances are exceptional, so I suppose I must agree."

"Then Brown may return with me to Blankborough with a warrant for Holtsner's and Ball's arrest, and act under my directions?"

"Since you urge it, yes," he reluctantly replied.

He pressed an electric push at the side of his desk, a plain-clothes officer shortly making his appearance.

"Tell Detective-Inspector Brown I want to see him."

In a few moments the latter arrived.

"Professor Rhymer's officially assisting in the Blankborough murder case. You will return with him and work together until further notice."

AFTER LEAVING SCOTLAND Yard, Rhymer and the detective entered the first small restaurant they came across.

"We can discuss some breakfast here, and our future plans into the bargain, for we appear to be the sole occupants," Rhymer remarked as he sat down at a small table.

"Not a bad idea either, sir, a journey before breakfast gives one an appetite."

"Our case is almost complete," Rhymer affirmed after the waitress had departed with their order, "but even now we mustn't err on the side of over-confidence."

"I'm quite alive to that fact, sir."

"I don't propose returning to Blankborough till later in the day. Then we'll hire a car and arrange to be dropped within easy walking distance of the Gables. After breakfast I want you to 'phone to the local superintendent at Blankborough, and get him to send two plain-clothes men to meet us at some convenient spot, which I'll leave you to fix up."

"Very good, sir."

"Be sure you warn the superintendent to make all arrangements strictly on the Q.T."

"I'll take care of that."

"Well, now—I think—we've fairly staged the scene for Holtsner's final appearance, so it only remains for you to ring up the Blankborough superintendent—the curtain must wait till tonight—while I go and secure a car."

"What time do you propose starting from town?"

"We don't want to reach our destination before dusk, so if we leave about seven-thirty, that will get us to our rendezvous by nine o'clock."

"Then I had better mention that to the superintendent when 'phoning?"

"Of course. Tell him nine or thereabouts; better make it rather before than after."

"Where shall we meet, sir?"

"Oh, at my flat in Whitehall Court—you know the number. Come early and we'll have a bite of something before starting."

"Thanks, I'm much obliged."

"So long then, Brown—don't forget your warrant for arrest."

SHORTLY AFTER DUSK four men silently approached the garden door of Holtsner's museum: Rhymer, Brown, and two stalwart fellows from the local police force; the latter having met the car, containing the former, at a prearranged spot on the outskirts of the town.

"Conceal yourself with the two men behind that bush, Brown, while I manoeuvre the enemy's camp," Rhymer enjoined as he crept up to the door. He found it shut. Bending down he peered through the keyhole. The inspection appeared to satisfy him, for he turned and beckoned to the others. They all three approached, led by Brown, and assembled in a group at the threshold. Rhymer then inserted a skeleton key in the latch. Cautiously opening the door he peeped within, and, pointing to the curtained recess, said:

"Inspector Brown and I will hide in there, and you two will return to your former place of concealment. Take this," he added, giving the foremost of the two the skeleton key, "but don't attempt to use it under any circumstances, unless you hear two loud blasts of a whistle. Then enter sharp—understand?"

"Yes, sir."

"Remember not to stir before the given signal."

The two men saluted and returned to their allotted post, whereupon Rhymer immediately entered the museum with the detective, noiselessly latching the door behind them.

"Now then, quick!" he exclaimed, slipping across the apartment and raising the curtain which covered the recess. A moment later they were both hidden behind its folds.

They were only there about ten minutes—which seemed to them as many hours—when the door communicating with the house suddenly opened. Glancing through a couple of slits in the curtain, they distinguished, in the dim light, Holtsner and his servant Ball entering the room. The former switched on the light, and together they approached the large case with the glass doors. Opening this they lifted out one of the mummy cases, which Rhymer observed was not the same as that they had replaced the night before.

"It's number three's turn now," Ball remarked with a malicious grin.

Holtsner grunted some unintelligible reply. Then they propped up the box on end against the wall. Holtsner produced a key and, unlocking the receptacle of death, threw back the lid, exposing the effigy within.

A gaunt, shrivelled, parchment-like freak was exhibited. The emaciated neck and head surmounted by a shock of tousled hair. The bulbous, moist-lipped mouth leering with vapid expression. Then Holtsner, with a deep sigh, stretched himself upon the couch, while Ball, crouching over him, passed his hands backwards and forwards across the recumbent man's face.

He had not made more than a dozen "passes" before his body became perfectly rigid, and at the same moment Rhymer observed a distinct tremor passing through the mummified figure occupying the open case.

The Thing appeared to be suscipient to some mysterious endowment of life and motion. Brown evidently observed this manifestation as well, for he laid a trembling hand upon Rhymer's arm, as if to draw his attention to the abnormal change. The Creature's lips were now puckered with a sucking motion, relaxing into a diabolical grin. Then the nostrils dilated, as though about to renew their former function of breathing—and—then—two shrill screams pierced the horrible silence. Rhymer could stand it no longer. He had seen enough.

"Brown," he cried as he replaced the police whistle in his pocket, "get your pistol ready," and smartly drawing back the curtain, the rings rattling along the rod supporting it, discovered himself and his companion to the other occupants of the room.

The effect of this dramatic stroke was instantaneous, for Holtsner immediately awoke, and leapt off the couch. Simultaneously the flicker of returning animation left the mummified corpse, while Ball and Holtsner—their features distorted with uncontrollable fury—sprang, with one accord, towards the intruders.

Their action, however, was abruptly checked by the gleaming barrels of their adversaries' pistols. Then the sound of a key grating in the latch of the garden door caused the two Boches to wheel round in that direction, only to find their retreat cut off by the entry of two more men similarly armed.

"Hands up! Herr Graf Friedrich von Verheim and Otto Krupp of the German Secret Service," cried Rhymer, "attempt any resistance and you'll be shot at sight as dangerous spies. The game's up, let me tell you."

The two men instantly obeyed, unadulterated "hate" written broadcast on their faces. Turning to Brown, Rhymer added:

"Search these men for any weapons they may have concealed."

The subsequent examination only produced a sheathed knife, found on the pseudo Alfred Ball.

"What's the meaning of this unwarrantable outrage?" von Verheim blustered with a forced expression of outraged innocence. "Himmel! but I'll have the law upon you for forcing your way into my house."

"It's no use, von Verheim, we've nabbed you red-handed, and Detective-Inspector Brown, here, from Scotland Yard, has a warrant for your arrest, so you'd better come quietly."

"Bah! What evidence have you?" he sneered with a cunning look of effrontery.

"Sufficient to have you both convicted and hanged for conniving in the act of wilful and premeditated murder."

At this retort a vague look of relief illuminated the crafty face of the Boche.

"So!" he hissed with unbridled derision, "you think, then, you clever pig of an Englishman, that one of your juries will convict me and my comrade of murder, committed by some madman running riot about the country, and whom your clever policemen are incapable of arresting."

"No, von Verheim, it won't be necessary for a jury to convict on that score, for we've a far graver charge to bring against you and your accomplices than murder—in the ordinary sense of the word."

Von Verheim arrogantly raised his eyebrows.

"The contents of a notebook in your safe over there—"

"*Mein Gott!*" he gasped, interrupting Rhymer as the latter produced this trump card. His face underwent an appalling change. From a semblance of arrogance and bravado, it assumed a deathly pallor. "*Ach Himmel!*" he spluttered. "So! you've been to that safe—Otto, what did I tell you? I suspected these English pigs were thieves.—*Donner und blitzen!* What will the All Highest say?"

Then, in a burst of frenzy, turning his twitching face towards his confederate, he cried:

"The elixir—quick, Otto—I'm faint—the bottle—it's in the drawer there!"

The servant made a move in obedience to von Verheim's demand, but was quickly arrested in the act by a sharp command from Rhymer:

"Move another step," he cried, "and you're a dead man. I'll get the bottle." And, motioning Brown to keep an extra watchful eye on Otto Krupp, he quickly approached the table indicated by von Verheim. The latter made a sly movement as though to intercept him, but was promptly pulled up by the detective.

"Remember you're covered by the police officers behind you," he barked, "and they've instructions to shoot."

The threat was effectual, and Rhymer reached the table without further interruption. Opening the drawer, he produced a small though businesslike bomb, quite big enough to have blown the whole place to atoms.

"So this is your bottle of elixir, von Verheim?" he queried with sarcasm, regarding the Boche with a gleam of triumph in his eyes. "An effective dose, too, for strafing the safe and its contents, ourselves into the bargain. I suppose that wouldn't have been of any account, provided you were able to obliterate all evidence of your Hunnish plot."

Without giving von Verheim the opportunity of replying to this indictment, Rhymer nodded to the officers behind, who promptly seized both the Boches and handcuffed them.

So expeditiously was this accomplished that the prisoners were afforded little, if any, opportunity of resistance.

"Now," he exclaimed, "Inspector Brown will read the warrant."

While this formality was being discharged, von Verheim and his accomplice maintained a forced attitude of indifference, and not until the two officers began to lead them away, did either of them evince any further sign of protest. Then, with a look of malignant "hate," von Verheim, turning towards Rhymer, shouted:

"I hate your country! I loathe your government! Let them murder me and my comrade. What do we care?—Bah!—We defy you, even now.—Kill the body—yes—and you release the spirit to live and effect a greater vengeance—inflamed by the unquenchable fire of eternal 'hate.' "

A casual observer might have construed this furious tirade as nothing more or less than an outburst of rage proceeding from a man baffled in the pursuit of a long-prepared scheme of revenge. But to Rhymer it conveyed an extremely subtle threat, beneath which lurked an element of significance, far deeper than anger alone could account for. However, he made no comment, beyond a significant motion of his head directing the instant removal of the prisoners, which was promptly effected through the garden door.

Then turning to Brown he abruptly exclaimed:

"We mustn't lose a minute, for there's no knowing who may be lurking about this place, though I believe we have taken these spies com-

pletely by surprise. Lock both doors, please, and be ready for any emergency."

Brown did as he was requested, after which Rhymer opened the safe again with his skeleton key, and securing the notebook, placed it in his pocket.

"Now," said he, "as soon as we get back to our hotel, I'll acquaint you with all the facts I've collected during the last few days. But, before we leave this unhallowed spot, I want to search for another piece of evidence."

He approached the open mummy case, where it stood propped up against the wall, closely examining the gaping mouth with its row of discoloured teeth. A few seconds later he turned to the inspector, his eyes sparkling with satisfaction.

"Have you got that little box," he cried, "you showed me at our first meeting?"

"Yes."

"Let me have it, then—quick!"

He almost snatched the box from Brown's hand as he produced it from his pocket, and opening the lid took out a tiny piece of some discoloured-looking substance, pointed at one end, carefully placing it between the leering lips of the mummy.

"The exact counterpart!" he cried, a moment later, in a tone of triumph. "Look, Brown, don't you see what it is?"

"Well, I thought it was a piece of bone," he ventured with indecision, "which the surgeon took from one of the victims' necks."

"Of course it's a piece of bone, or rather ivory, and what's of more consequence still—a piece of one of the *canine* or eye-teeth of this preserved corpse. Don't you see it fits the broken stump, and must have previously been snapped off? It's a BROKEN FANG!—doesn't that suggest a clue?"

"Great Scot, sir! Why, the brute must have bitten that poor fellow, and broken off one of its teeth in the effort! Good heavens! Surely the Thing's not a vampire?"

"That's what I've suspected it to be all along."

"But I always regarded vampires to be purely mythical," said Brown.

"When you become acquainted with the contents of this book," patting the incriminating article in his breast-pocket, "you'll alter your opinion. However, let me point out something else relating to this Thing here. Look at the skull. Do you see those two small holes?"

Brown signified assent.

"Well, you can't deny that they are bullet holes; therefore the natural inference is that this nondescript Creature met its death, originally, by shooting, which summarily rejects von Verheim's assertion that it is the corpse of an ancient Egyptian. Firearms weren't used in those remote times."

"But don't you remember," Brown hazarded, "shooting at the Creature in the lane—mightn't that account for the bullet holes in the skull?"

Rhymer regarded the detective for a moment with a half-suppressed look of amusement.

"By Jove, Brown," he cried, "you're waking up at last to the psychological probabilities of the case," and slapping him on the shoulder, added:

"So now you begin to realise that this corpse, like the other we saw, is not quite so defunct as normal conditions would infer. But don't be too cock-sure yet. You've fallen into one error, for I told you I shot that other 'freak' *through the body,* and there is no corresponding bullet mark in the abdominal region of this corpse."

Brown scratched his head in evident perplexity, then, with a bantering smile, observed:

"When I passed a remark in front of von Verheim, the other morning, upon the apparently well-preserved condition of these mummies, you promptly shut me up."

"I admit the charge," Rhymer responded, "but I had a good reason for doing so, as you will soon realise. But come," he continued, "let's examine a few more of these grotesque coffins before we make tracks."

Two or three were accordingly wrenched open (they were all fitted with modern locks) and their occupants exposed. An exceptionally hideous specimen was eventually uncovered, which, upon closer inspection, revealed a small hole in the abdomen, with a corresponding bullet flattened firmly against the spinal column behind.

"Now, Brown, what do you think of that? Seems as though more than one agent was employed in these crimes, eh?"

"Looks uncommonly like it."

"Holloa! What's that?" Rhymer suddenly exclaimed, as his keen glance happened to fall upon a long, dark cloak suspended from a peg in the corner. With a few strides he reached it, and taking it down examined the garment. A moment later his hand was in his pocket, and out came a letter-case, from which he produced a small piece of cloth, and comparing it with the cloak, exclaimed:

"Here you are, Brown, another piece of evidence."

"What's that?" the inspector inquired as he crossed over to where Rhymer was standing.

The latter, by way of reply, spread out the cloak, exhibiting a gap in the hem from which a piece of the material had been torn.

"See that?" he inquired.

"By Jove!—yes, and you've got the missing fragment?"

Rhymer triumphantly waved aloft a small piece of frayed cloth, exclaiming:

"This is the identical piece I found in my hand after my 'scrap' the other night with the vampire."

"And it matches the ulster."

"Perfectly."

"Well, I'm—"

"No, you're not yet," Rhymer hastily interrupted, "but let's get out of this, or there's no saying what might happen. It's a confoundedly rum spot," and buttoning up his coat, he switched off the light, and, followed by the inspector, made his exit through the garden door.

"IT IS QUITE evident," said Rhymer in the course of a conversation with the detective later the same night, "that any one who investigates the phenomena of psychology, will, at some time or other, come across complicated influences devoid of explanation by common or garden theories. Now the case we have in hand seems to be one of these. Of course you've heard of the widespread and ancient belief in vampires—bodies which the earth has rejected, and, therefore, do not properly decay?"

"Yes, but as I recently remarked, I only regarded them as fairy tales."

"Well, as I said before, I think you'll alter your opinion, if you haven't done so already, when you've heard all I have to tell you. To begin with, vampires are accredited with sucking the life-blood from their victims, and, as you have already told me, the police-surgeon attributed the death of the Blankborough victims as primarily due to some blood-sucking process—"

"Yes, by Jove! But you'd never get a judge and jury to accept such a theory, let alone convict on it."

"I've no intention of asking for a conviction on that count; but do let me get on with what I have to say. This manuscript contains sufficient evidence to convict both our prisoners as dangerous spies, without introducing these murders or any psychical proof at all. Von Verheim is a distinguished German scientist and psychologist, so I fished out when in London, whose decease was falsely reported many years ago, and who has been residing in this country all the time, unsuspected."

"Then he was naturalised under the name of Holtsner."

"Naturally, and being employed by the German Secret Service, was supported by them in his deception."

"That shows the war has long been contemplated by the Huns," said Brown.

"There's no doubt about that.—But, confound it all, what a chap you are to interrupt.—Well, so much for von Verheim, and now we come to Otto Krupp. He was an old pupil of the former, and a qualified chemist. A shrewd fellow, too, who has obtained a complete mastery of the English language—"

"That's very evident," said Brown, "for he took us both in, pretty neatly, at the King's Arms the other evening, with his cockney speech and accent."

Rhymer, ignoring the interruption, continued:

"There is a very brief but sufficiently clear record in von Verheim's notebook, of a monstrous scheme for the importation over here of the corpses of German soldiers killed in battle: these bodies having previously been immersed in some special preparation—discovered by him—for definitely arresting decomposition—"

"Now I see why you wanted the chief to have all cargoes examined, coming through neutral ports."

"Exactly, for these bodies were to be sent over, camouflaged as Egyptian mummies, and delivered at the private residences of various naturalised Germans. These wretched aliens are described by von Verheim as 'mediumistic' and capable of freeing, at will, the spirits from their bodies, and then, by 'possessing' these preserved corpses, convert them into vampires, 'controlling' them to commit any atrocities their Teutonic imaginations might devise."

"Then that's what von Verheim was up to in the museum when we interrupted him."

"Undoubtedly, and by means of this demoniacal agency, they hoped to commit wholesale murders with little chance of discovery."

"What on earth did they hope to achieve by such a course?"

"An expansion of the Boche mania for 'frightfulness,' I imagine; although the written evidence reveals that only fit men of military age were to be attacked by these vampires. This looks as though they were plotting to diminish the strength of our fighting units as well."

"Then the mutilating business was evidently a cunning attempt to conceal the vampire element?"

"Exactly."

"The whole thing seems too horrible," Brown exclaimed, aghast, "it's barely credible."

"I repeat, nothing is incredible where the

Boche is concerned; we've already had sufficient proof of that."

"I wonder why Krupp made that convicting admission about the missing knife at the King's Arms the other night?"

"Presumably with the hope that some one might have chanced to pick it up, and overhearing to whom it belonged, would promptly return it to him or his master."

"He little thought that it would lead to their ultimate detection."

"No; but they were on the alert. The figure you followed last night hadn't a knife, so they evidently abandoned the mutilating 'stunt' as too risky. I've also ascertained that the fourth victim, murdered last night, was not mutilated."

"But do you believe this scheme could have been extensively worked?"

"Most decidedly. The assassinations would have spread broadcast, and these vampires, whose strength—when possessed with temporary life—is prodigious, would have played the very deuce, if once the evil had got a firm hold. For though the Boche has yet to be born whom any average Britisher would fear to tackle, and knock out into the bargain, still, there is a limit to all human endurance: and even the bravest amongst us would look askance when faced with a supernatural menace like this."

"That I readily admit."

"Exactly. Well, vampires are invulnerable, and unless unearthed and literally dismembered or burnt, when in a condition of inactivity, they cannot be suppressed. So the only effective remedy for the evil is that which we are adopting, in discovering the whereabouts of the living fiends who are 'possessing' these vampire bodies, and forcibly removing them out of harm's way."

"It'll be a difficult job to find the others," said Brown.

"I think not, for von Verheim was the head and moving spirit in the entire scheme, and by now he and his accomplice will be safely under lock and key. The notebook, remember, contains a list of those aliens over here concerned in the conspiracy, as well as an entry of the four Blankborough victims—we saw von Verheim enter the last—which I shall send to your chief. In addition, documentary evidence here proves that von Verheim and Krupp have been involved in conveying important information to the enemy, which has been puzzling the authorities for some time past. This evidence, alone, is sufficient to convict them. However, unless I'm much mistaken in your chief, the remainder of the gang will soon be interned or even more efficiently disposed of."

"It's a good job I sought your assistance when I did, sir," Brown exclaimed with an expressive nod of his head, "for though we shan't be able to satisfy the public as to who the perpetrators of these atrocities are, we have, undoubtedly, knocked on the head a very grave menace to the country. A great pity the B.P. won't know this, since they'll be sure to blame us police for apparently failing to bring home these crimes to the real culprits."

"Never mind," said Rhymer, "console your official mind with the knowledge that you, your chief, and I have learned the truth, and we shall shortly get our own back in the satisfaction of knowing that von Verheim and his gang have got their deserts."

"After all, that's some recompense," Brown admitted—still hankering after public recognition.

"Some?—A great deal, I call it, since a widespread catastrophe has narrowly been averted. And our job, after all, is to serve King and Country, and if we've done that to the best of our ability, 'then,' say I, 'hang public opinion.' "

THEODORE STURGEON

BORN EDWARD HAMILTON WALDO (1918–1985) in Staten Island, New York, the author's name was legally changed at the age of eleven when his mother remarried. He had a variety of jobs before becoming a full-time writer, including circus performer, sailor in the merchant marine, hotel manager in the West Indies, construction worker in Puerto Rico and elsewhere, advertising copywriter, and literary agent. He sold several nongenre stories before making his important first sale to *Astounding Science Fiction,* "The Ether Breather," in 1939, becoming a regular contributor to it and its sister publication, *Unknown,* as well as other pulp magazines and, later, the digest-size science fiction magazines that replaced them.

Sturgeon had serious literary talent and was admired by, and was an influence on, his peers far disproportionate to his success with readers. Among the writers who acknowledged his influence on their work are Harlan Ellison, Samuel R. Delany, Ray Bradbury, and Kurt Vonnegut, who based his character Kilgore Trout on Sturgeon. He wrote only about a half dozen novels, not counting hackwork novelizations of motion pictures, such as *The King and Four Queens* (1956) and *Voyage to the Bottom of the Sea* (1961), and the hoax *I, Libertine,* under the pseudonym Frederick R. Ewing, which had been promoted by a radio talk show host as a modern erotic classic and, as demand for nonexistent copies built up, Sturgeon was hired to write it; most important, he wrote *More Than Human* (1953) and *Some of Your Blood* (1961), a neglected masterpiece of vampire literature. He frequently wrote for such television series as *Star Trek* (inventing the shibboleth "Live long and prosper") and *Land of the Lost.*

He gave his name to what is now known as "Sturgeon's Law" when he first uttered the truism, "Ninety percent of science fiction is crud, but, then, ninety percent of *everything* is crud."

"It" was first published in the August 1940 issue of *Unknown.*

THEODORE STURGEON

IT

IT WALKED IN the woods.

It was never born. It existed. Under the pine needles the fires burn, deep and smokeless in the mold. In heat and in darkness and decay there is growth. There is life and there is growth. It grew, but it was not alive. It walked unbreathing through the woods, and thought and saw and was hideous and strong, and it was not born and it did not live. It grew and moved about without living.

It crawled out of the darkness and hot damp mold into the cool of a morning. It was huge. It was lumped and crusted with its own hateful substances, and pieces of it dropped off as it went its way, dropped off and lay writhing, and stilled, and sank putrescent into the forest loam.

It had no mercy, no laughter, no beauty. It had strength and great intelligence. And—perhaps it could not be destroyed. It crawled out of its mound in the wood and lay pulsing in the sunlight for a long moment. Patches of it shone wetly in the golden glow, parts of it were nubbled and flaked. And whose dead bones had given it the form of a man?

It scrabbled painfully with its half-formed hands, beating the ground and the bole of a tree. It rolled and lifted itself up on its crumbling elbows, and it tore up a great handful of herbs and shredded them against its chest, and it paused and gazed at the gray-green juices with intelligent calm. It wavered to its feet, and seized a young sapling and destroyed it, folding the slender trunk back on itself again and again, watching attentively the useless, fibered splinters. And it squealed, snatching up a fear-frozen field-creature, crushing it slowly, letting blood and pulpy flesh and fur ooze from between its fingers, run down and rot on the forearms.

It began searching.

KIMBO DRIFTED THROUGH the tall grasses like a puff of dust, his bushy tail curled tightly over his back and his long jaws agape. He ran with an easy lope, loving his freedom and the power of his flanks and furry shoulders. His tongue lolled listlessly over his lips. His lips were black and serrated, and each tiny pointed liplet swayed with his doggy gallop. Kimbo was all dog, all healthy animal.

He leaped high over a boulder and landed with a startled yelp as a long-eared cony shot from its hiding place under the rock. Kimbo hurtled after it, grunting with each great thrust of his legs. The rabbit bounced just ahead of him, keeping its distance, its ears flattened on its curving back and its little legs nibbling away at a distance hungrily. It stopped, and Kimbo pounced, and the rabbit shot away at a tangent and popped into a hollow log. Kimbo yelped again and rushed snuffling at the log, and knowing his failure, curvetted but once around the stump and ran on into the forest. The thing that watched from the wood raised its crusted arms and waited for Kimbo.

Kimbo sensed it there, standing dead-still by

496

the path. To him it was a bulk which smelled of carrion not fit to roll in, and he snuffled distastefully and ran to pass it.

The thing let him come abreast and dropped a heavy twisted fist on him. Kimbo saw it coming and curled up tight as he ran, and the hand clipped stunningly on his rump, sending him rolling and yipping down the slope. Kimbo straddled to his feet, shook his head, shook his body with a deep growl, came back to the silent thing with green murder in his eyes. He walked stiffly, straight-legged, his tail as low as his lowered head and a ruff of fury round his neck. The thing raised its arms again, waited.

Kimbo slowed, then flipped himself through the air at the monster's throat. His jaws closed on it; his teeth clicked together through a mass of filth, and he fell choking and snarling at its feet. The thing leaned down and struck twice, and after the dog's back was broken, it sat beside him and began to tear him apart.

"BE BACK IN an hour or so," said Alton Drew, picking up his rifle from the corner behind the wood box. His brother laughed.

"Old Kimbo 'bout runs your life, Alton," he said.

"Ah, I know the ol' devil," said Alton. "When I whistle for him for half an hour and he don't show up, he's in a jam or he's treed something wuth shootin' at. The ol' son of a gun calls me by not answerin'."

Cory Drew shoved a full glass of milk over to his nine-year-old daughter and smiled. "You think as much o' that houn'dog o' yours as I do of Babe here."

Babe slid off her chair and ran to her uncle. "Gonna catch me the bad fella, Uncle Alton?" she shrilled. The "bad fella" was Cory's invention—the one who lurked in corners ready to pounce on little girls who chased the chickens and played around mowing machines and hurled green apples with a powerful young arm at the sides of the hogs, to hear the synchronized thud and grunt; little girls who swore with an Aus-

trian accent like an ex-hired man they had had; who dug caves in haystacks till they tipped over, and kept pet crawfish in tomorrow's milk cans, and rode work horses to a lather in the night pasture.

"Get back here and keep away from Uncle Alton's gun!" said Cory. "If you see the bad fella, Alton, chase him back here. He has a date with Babe here for that stunt of hers last night." The preceding evening, Babe had kind-heartedly poured pepper on the cows' salt block.

"Don't worry, kiddo," grinned her uncle, "I'll bring you the bad fella's hide if he don't get me first."

Alton Drew walked up the path toward the wood, thinking about Babe. She was a phenomenon—a pampered farm child. Ah well—she had to be. They'd both loved Clissa Drew, and she'd married Cory, and they had to love Clissa's child. Funny thing, love. Alton was a man's man, and thought things out that way; and his reaction to love was a strong and frightened one. He knew what love was because he felt it still for his brother's wife and would feel it as long as he lived for Babe. It led him through his life, and yet he embarrassed himself by thinking of it. Loving a dog was an easy thing, because you and the old devil could love one another completely without talking about it. The smell of gun smoke and the smell of wet fur in the rain were perfume enough for Alton Drew, a grunt of satisfaction and the scream of something hunted and hit were poetry enough. They weren't like love for a human, that choked his throat so he could not say words he could not have thought of anyway. So Alton loved his dog Kimbo and his Winchester for all to see, and let his love for his brother's women, Clissa and Babe, eat at him quietly and unmentioned.

His quick eyes saw the fresh indentations in the soft earth behind the boulder, which showed where Kimbo had turned and leaped with a single surge, chasing the rabbit. Ignoring the tracks, he looked for the nearest place where a rabbit might hide, and strolled over to the stump. Kimbo had been there, he saw, and had been there too late. "You're an ol' fool," muttered Alton. "Y' can't catch a cony by chasin' it. You want to cross him up some way." He gave a peculiar trilling whistle, sure that Kimbo was digging frantically under some nearby stump for a rabbit that was three counties away by now. No answer. A little puzzled, Alton went back to the path. "He never done this before," he said softly. There was something about this he didn't like.

He cocked his .32-40 and cradled it. At the county fair someone had once said of Alton Drew that he could shoot at a handful of salt and pepper thrown in the air and hit only the pepper. Once he split a bullet on the blade of a knife and put two candles out. He had no need to fear anything that could be shot at. That's what he believed.

THE THING IN the woods looked curiously down at what it had done to Kimbo, and moaned the way Kimbo had before he died. It stood a minute storing away facts in its foul, unemotional mind. Blood was warm. The sunlight was warm. Things that moved and bore fur had a muscle to force the thick liquid through tiny tubes in their bodies. The liquid coagulated after a time. The liquid on rooted green things was thinner and the loss of a limb did not mean loss of life. It was very interesting, but the thing, the mold with a mind, was not pleased. Neither was it displeased. Its accidental urge was a thirst for knowledge, and it was only—interested.

It was growing late, and the sun reddened and rested awhile on the hilly horizon, teaching the clouds to be inverted flames. The thing threw up its head suddenly, noticing the dusk. Night was ever a strange thing, even for those of us who have known it in life. It would have been frightening for the monster had it been capable of fright, but it could only be curious; it could only reason from what it had observed.

What was happening? It was getting harder to see. Why? It threw its shapeless head from side to side. It was true—things were dim, and growing dimmer. Things were changing shape, taking on a new and darker color. What did the creatures it had crushed and torn apart see? How did they see? The larger one, the one that had attacked, had used two organs in its head. That must have been it, because after the thing had torn off two of the dog's legs it had struck at the hairy muzzle; and the dog, seeing the blow coming, had dropped folds of skin over the organs—closed its eyes. Ergo, the dog saw with its eyes. But then after the dog was dead, and its body still, repeated blows had had no effect on the eyes. They remained open and staring. The logical conclusion was, then, that a being that had ceased to live and breathe and move about lost the use of its eyes. It must be that to lose sight was, conversely, to die. Dead things did not walk about. They lay down and did not move. Therefore the thing in the wood concluded that it must be dead, and so it lay down by the path, not far away from Kimbo's scattered body, lay down and believed itself dead.

ALTON DREW CAME up through the dusk to the wood. He was frankly worried. He whistled again, and then called, and there was still no response, and he said again, "The ol' fleabus never done this before," and shook his heavy head. It was past milking time, and Cory would need him. "Kimbo!" he roared. The cry echoed through the shadows, and Alton flipped on the safety catch of his rifle and put the butt on the ground beside the path. Leaning on it, he took off his cap and scratched the back of his head, wondering. The rifle butt sank into what he thought was soft earth; he staggered and stepped into the chest of the thing that lay beside the path. His foot went up to the ankle in its yielding rottenness, and he swore and jumped back.

"*Whew!* Sompn sure dead as hell there! Ugh!" He swabbed at his boot with a handful of leaves while the monster lay in the growing blackness with the edges of the deep footprint in its chest sliding into it, filling it up. It lay there regarding him dimly out of its muddy eyes, thinking it was dead because of the darkness, watching the articulation of Alton Drew's joints, wondering at this new uncautious creature.

Alton cleaned the butt of his gun with more leaves and went on up the path, whistling anxiously for Kimbo.

CLISSA DREW STOOD in the door of the milk shed, very lovely in red-checked gingham and a blue apron. Her hair was clean yellow, parted in the middle and stretched tautly back to a heavy braided knot. "Cory! Alton!" she called a little sharply.

"Well?" Cory responded gruffly from the barn, where he was stripping off the Ayrshire. The dwindling streams of milk plopped pleasantly into the froth of a full pail.

"I've called and called," said Clissa. "Supper's cold, and Babe won't eat until you come. Why—where's Alton?"

Cory grunted, heaved the stool out of the way, threw over the stanchion lock and slapped the Ayrshire on the rump. The cow backed and filled like a towboat, clattered down the line and out into the barnyard. "Ain't back yet."

"Not back?" Clissa came in and stood beside him as he sat by the next cow, put his forehead against the warm flank. "But, Cory, he said he'd—"

"Yeh, yeh, I know. He said he'd be back fer the milkin'. I heard him. Well, he ain't."

"And you have to— Oh, Cory, I'll help you finish up. Alton would be back if he could. Maybe he's—"

"Maybe he's treed a blue jay," snapped her husband. "Him an' that damn dog." He gestured hugely with one hand while the other went on milking. "I got twenty-six head o' cows to milk. I got pigs to feed an' chickens to put to bed. I got to toss hay for the mare and turn the team out. I got harness to mend and a wire down in the night pasture. I got wood to split an' carry." He milked for a moment in silence, chewing on his lip. Clissa stood twisting her hands together, trying to think of something to stem the tide. It wasn't the first time Alton's hunting had interfered with the chores. "So I got to go ahead with it. I can't interfere with Alton's spoorin'. Every damn time that hound o' his smells out a squirrel I go without my supper. I'm gettin' sick an'—"

"Oh, I'll help you!" said Clissa. She was thinking of the spring, when Kimbo had held four hundred pounds of raging black bear at bay until Alton could put a bullet in its brain, the time Babe had found a bearcub and started to carry it home, and had fallen into a freshet, cutting her head. You can't hate a dog that has saved your child for you, she thought.

"You'll do nothin' of the kind!" Cory growled. "Get back to the house. You'll find work enough there. I'll be along when I can. Dammit, Clissa, don't cry! I didn't mean to— Oh, shucks!" He got up and put his arms around her. "I'm wrought up," he said. "Go on now. I'd no call to speak that way to you. I'm sorry. Go back to Babe. I'll put a stop to this for good tonight. I've had enough. There's work here for four farmers an' all we've got is me an' that . . . that huntsman. Go on now, Clissa."

"All right," she said into his shoulder. "But, Cory, hear him out first when he comes back. He might be unable to come back this time. Maybe he . . . he—"

"Ain't nothin' kin hurt my brother that a bullet will hit. He can take care of himself. He's got no excuse good enough this time. Go on, now. Make the kid eat."

Clissa went back to the house, her young face furrowed. If Cory quarreled with Alton now and drove him away, what with the drought and the creamery about to close and all, they just couldn't manage. Hiring a man was out of the question. Cory'd have to work himself to death, and he just wouldn't be able to make it. No one man could. She sighed and went into the house.

It was seven o'clock, and the milking not done yet. Oh, why did Alton have to—

Babe was in bed at nine when Clissa heard Cory in the shed, slinging the wire cutters into a corner. "Alton back yet?" they both said at once as Cory stepped into the kitchen; and as she shook her head he clumped over to the stove, and lifting a lid, spat into the coals. "Come to bed," he said.

She lay down her stitching and looked at his broad back. He was twenty-eight, and he walked and acted like a man ten years older, and looked like a man five years younger. "I'll be up in a while," Clissa said.

Cory glanced at the corner behind the wood box where Alton's rifle usually stood, then made an unspellable, disgusted sound and sat down to take off his heavy muddy shoes.

"It's after nine," Clissa volunteered timidly.

Cory said nothing, reaching for house slippers.

"Cory, you're not going to—"

"Not going to what?"

"Oh, nothing. I just thought that maybe Alton—"

"Alton!" Cory flared. "The dog goes hunting field mice. Alton goes hunting the dog. Now you want me to go hunting Alton. That's what you want?"

"I just— He was never this late before."

"I won't do it! Go out lookin' for him at nine o'clock in the night? I'll be damned! He has no call to use us so, Clissa."

Clissa said nothing. She went to the stove, peered into the wash boiler, set it aside at the back of the range. When she turned around, Cory had his shoes and coat on again.

"I knew you'd go," she said. Her voice smiled though she did not.

"I'll be back durned soon," said Cory. "I don't reckon he's strayed far. It is late. I ain't feared for him, but—" He broke his 12-gauge shotgun, looked through the barrels, slipped two shells in the breech and a box of them into his pocket. "Don't wait up," he said over his shoulder as he went out.

"I won't," Clissa replied to the closed door, and went back to her stitching by the lamp.

The path up the slope to the wood was very dark when Cory went up it, peering and calling. The air was chill and quiet, and a fetid odor of mold hung in it. Cory blew the taste of it out through impatient nostrils, drew it in again with the next breath, and swore. "Nonsense," he muttered. "Houn'dog. Huntin', at ten in th' night, too. Alton!" he bellowed. "Alton Drew!" Echoes answered him, and he entered the wood. The huddled thing he passed in the dark heard him and felt the vibrations of his footsteps and did not move because it thought it was dead.

Cory strode on, looking around and ahead and not down since his feet knew the path.

"Alton!"

"That you, Cory?"

Cory Drew froze. That corner of the wood was thickly set and as dark as a burial vault. The voice he heard was choked, quiet, penetrating.

"Alton?"

"I found Kimbo, Cory."

"Where the hell have you been?" shouted Cory furiously. He disliked this pitch-blackness; he was afraid at the tense hopelessness of Alton's voice, and he mistrusted his ability to stay angry at his brother.

"I called him, Cory. I whistled at him, an' the ol' devil didn't answer."

"I can say the same for you, you . . . you louse. Why weren't you to milkin'? Where are you? You caught in a trap?"

"The houn' never missed answerin' me before, you know," said the tight, monotonous voice from the darkness.

"Alton! What the devil's the matter with you? What do I care if your mutt didn't answer? Where—"

"I guess because he ain't never died before," said Alton, refusing to be interrupted.

"You *what?*" Cory clicked his lips together twice and then said, "Alton, you turned crazy? What's that you say?"

"Kimbo's dead."

"Kim . . . oh! Oh!" Cory was seeing that picture again in his mind—Babe sprawled unconscious in the freshet, and Kimbo raging and snapping against a monster bear, holding her back until Alton could get there. "What happened, Alton?" he asked more quietly.

"I aim to find out. Someone tore him up."

"Tore him up?"

"There ain't a bit of him left tacked together, Cory. Every damn joint in his body tore apart. Guts out of him."

"Good God! Bear, you reckon?"

"No bear, nor nothin' on four legs. He's all here. None of him's been et. Whoever done it just killed him an'—tore him up."

"Good God!" Cory said again. "Who could've—" There was a long silence, then. "Come 'long home," he said almost gently. "There's no call for you to set up by him all night."

"I'll set. I aim to be here at sunup, an' I'm goin' to start trackin', an' I'm goin' to keep trackin' till I find the one done this job on Kimbo."

"You're drunk or crazy, Alton."

"I ain't drunk. You can think what you like about the rest of it. I'm stickin' here."

"We got a farm back yonder. Remember? I ain't going to milk twenty-six head o' cows again in the mornin' like I did jest now, Alton."

"Somebody's got to. I can't be there. I guess you'll just have to, Cory."

"You dirty scum!" Cory screamed. "You'll come back with me now or I'll know why!"

Alton's voice was still tight, half-sleepy. "Don't you come no nearer, Bud."

Cory kept moving toward Alton's voice.

"I said"—the voice was very quiet now—*"stop where you are."* Cory kept coming. A sharp click told of the release of the .32-40's safety. Cory stopped.

"You got your gun on me, Alton?" Cory whispered.

"That's right, Bud. You ain't a-trompin' up these tracks for me. I need 'em at sunup."

A full minute passed, and the only sound in the blackness was that of Cory's pained breathing. Finally:

"I got my gun, too, Alton. Come home."

"You can't see to shoot me."

"We're even on that."

"We ain't. I know just where you stand, Cory. I been here four hours."

"My gun scatters."

"My gun kills."

Without another word Cory Drew turned on his heel and stamped back to the farm.

BLACK AND LIQUESCENT it lay in the blackness, not alive, not understanding death, believing itself dead. Things that were alive saw and moved about. Things that were not alive could do neither. It rested its muddy gaze on the line of trees at the crest of the rise, and deep within it thoughts trickled wetly. It lay huddled, dividing its new-found facts, dissecting them as it had dissected live things when there was light, comparing, concluding, pigeonholing.

The trees at the top of the slope could just be seen, as their trunks were a fraction of a shade lighter than the dark sky behind them. At length they, too, disappeared, and for a moment sky and trees were a monotone. The thing knew it was dead now, and like many a being before it, it wondered how long it must stay like this. And then the sky beyond the trees grew a little lighter. That was a manifestly impossible occurrence, thought the thing, but it could see it and it must be so. Did dead things live again? That was curious. What about dismembered dead things? It would wait and see.

The sun came hand over hand up a beam of light. A bird somewhere made a high yawning peep, and as an owl killed a shrew, a skunk pounced on another, so that the night-shift deaths and those of day could go on without cessation. Two flowers nodded archly to each other, comparing their pretty clothes. A dragonfly nymph decided it was tired of looking serious and cracked its back open, to crawl out and dry gauzily. The first golden ray sheared down between the trees, through the grasses, passed over the mass in the shadowed bushes. "I am alive again," thought the thing that could not possibly live. "I am alive, for I see clearly." It stood up on its thick legs, up into the golden glow. In a little while the wet flakes that had grown during the night dried in the sun, and when it took its first steps, they cracked off and a little shower of them fell away. It walked up the slope to find Kimbo, to see if he, too, were alive again.

BABE LET THE sun come into her room by opening her eyes. Uncle Alton was gone—that was the first thing that ran through her head. Dad had come home last night and had shouted at mother for an hour. Alton was plumb crazy. He'd turned a gun on his own brother. If Alton ever came ten feet into Cory's land, Cory would fill him so full of holes he'd look like a tumbleweed. Alton was lazy, shiftless, selfish, and one or two other things of questionable taste but undoubted vividness. Babe knew her father. Uncle Alton would never be safe in this county.

She bounced out of bed in the enviable way of the very young, and ran to the window. Cory was trudging down to the night pasture with two bridles over his arm, to get the team. There were kitchen noises from downstairs.

Babe ducked her head in the washbowl and shook off the water like a terrier before she toweled. Trailing clean shirt and dungarees, she went to the head of the stairs, slid into the shirt, and began her morning ritual with the trousers. One step down was a step through the right leg. One more, and she was into the left. Then, bouncing step by step on both feet, buttoning one button per step, she reached the bottom fully dressed and ran into the kitchen.

"Didn't Uncle Alton come back a-tall, Mum?"

"Morning, Babe. No, dear." Clissa was too

quiet, smiling too much, Babe thought shrewdly. Wasn't happy.

"Where'd he go, Mum?"

"We don't know, Babe. Sit down and eat your breakfast."

"What's a misbegotten, Mum?" Babe asked suddenly. Her mother nearly dropped the dish she was drying. "Babe! You must never say that again!"

"Oh. Well, why is Uncle Alton, then?"

"Why is he what?"

Babe's mouth muscled around an outsize spoonful of oatmeal. "A misbe—"

"Babe!"

"All right, Mum," said Babe with her mouth full. "Well, why?"

"I told Cory not to shout last night," Clissa said half to herself.

"Well, whatever it means, he isn't," said Babe with finality. "Did he go hunting again?"

"He went to look for Kimbo, darling."

"Kimbo? Oh Mummy, is Kimbo gone, too? Didn't he come back either?"

"No, dear. Oh, please, Babe, stop asking questions!"

"All right. Where do you think they went?"

"Into the north woods. Be quiet."

Babe gulped away at her breakfast. An idea struck her; and as she thought of it she ate slower and slower, and cast more and more glances at her mother from under the lashes of her tilted eyes. It would be awful if Daddy did anything to Uncle Alton. Someone ought to warn him.

Babe was halfway to the woods when Alton's .32-40 sent echoes giggling up and down the valley.

CORY WAS IN the south thirty, riding a cultivator and cussing at the team of grays when he heard the gun. "Hoa," he called to the horses, and sat a moment to listen to the sound. "One-two-three. Four," he counted. "Saw someone, blasted away at him. Had a chance to take aim and give him another, careful. My God!"

He threw up the cultivator points and steered the team into the shade of three oaks. He hobbled the gelding with swift tosses of a spare strap, and headed for the woods. "Alton a killer," he murmured, and doubled back to the house for his gun. Clissa was standing just outside the door.

"Get shells!" he snapped and flung into the house. Clissa followed him. He was strapping his hunting knife on before she could get a box off the shelf. "Cory——"

"Hear that gun, did you? Alton's off his nut. He don't waste lead. He shot at someone just then, and he wasn't fixin' to shoot pa'tridges when I saw him last. He was out to get a man. Gimme my gun."

"Cory, Babe——"

"You keep her here. Oh, God, this is a helluva mess! I can't stand much more." Cory ran out the door.

Clissa caught his arm. "Cory, I'm trying to tell you. Babe isn't here. I've called, and she isn't here."

Cory's heavy, young-old face tautened. "Babe— Where did you last see her?"

"Breakfast." Clissa was crying now.

"She say where she was going?"

"No. She asked a lot of questions about Alton and where he'd gone."

"Did you say?"

Clissa's eyes widened, and she nodded, biting the back of her hand.

"You shouldn't ha' done that, Clissa," he gritted, and ran toward the woods. Clissa looked after him, and in that moment she could have killed herself.

Cory ran with his head up, straining with his legs and lungs and eyes at the long path. He puffed up the slope to the woods, agonized for breath after the forty-five minutes' heavy going. He couldn't even notice the damp smell of mold in the air.

He caught a movement in a thicket to his right, and dropped. Struggling to keep his breath, he crept forward until he could see

clearly. There was something in there, all right. Something black, keeping still. Cory relaxed his legs and torso completely to make it easier for his heart to pump some strength back into them, and slowly raised the 12-gauge until it bore on the thing hidden in the thicket.

"Come out!" Cory said when he could speak. Nothing happened.

"Come out or by God I'll shoot!" rasped Cory.

There was a long moment of silence, and his finger tightened on the trigger.

"You asked for it," he said, and as he fired the thing leaped sideways into the open, screaming.

It was a thin little man dressed in sepulchral black, and bearing the rosiest little baby-face Cory had ever seen. The face was twisted with fright and pain. The little man scrambled to his feet and hopped up and down saying over and over, "Oh, my hand! Don't shoot again! Oh, my hand! Don't shoot again!" He stopped after a bit, when Cory had climbed to his feet, and he regarded the farmer out of sad china-blue eyes. "You shot me," he said reproachfully, holding up a little bloody hand. "Oh, my goodness!"

Cory said, "Now, who the hell are you?"

The man immediately became hysterical, mouthing such a flood of broken sentences that Cory stepped back a pace and half-raised his gun in self-defense. It seemed to consist mostly of "I lost my papers," and "I didn't do it," and "It was horrible. Horrible. Horrible," and "The dead man," and "Oh, don't shoot again!"

Cory tried twice to ask him a question, and then he stepped over and knocked the man down. He lay on the ground writhing and moaning and blubbering and putting his bloody hand to his mouth where Cory had hit him.

The man rolled over and sat up. "I didn't do it!" he sobbed. "I didn't! I was walking along and I heard the gun and I heard some swearing and an awful scream and I went over there and peeped and I saw the dead man and I ran away and you came and I hid and you shot me and——"

"*Shut up!*" The man did, as if a switch had

been thrown. "Now," said Cory, pointing along the path, "you say there's a dead man up there?"

The man nodded and began crying in earnest. Cory helped him up. "Follow this path back to my farmhouse," he said. "Tell my wife to fix up your hand. *Don't* tell her anything else. And wait there until I come. Hear?"

"Yes. Thank you. Oh, thank you. *Snff.*"

"Go on now." Cory gave him a gentle shove in the right direction and went alone, in cold fear, up the path to the spot where he had found Alton the night before.

He found him here now, too, and Kimbo. Kimbo and Alton had spent several years together in the deepest friendship; they had hunted and fought and slept together, and the lives they owed each other were finished now. They were dead together.

It was terrible that they died the same way. Cory Drew was a strong man, but he gasped and fainted dead away when he saw what the thing of the mold had done to his brother and his brother's dog.

THE LITTLE MAN in black hurried down the path, whimpering and holding his injured hand as if he rather wished he could limp with it. After a while the whimper faded away, and the hurried stride changed to a walk as the gibbering terror of the last hour receded. He drew two deep breaths, said: "My goodness!" and felt almost normal. He bound a linen handkerchief around his wrist, but the hand kept bleeding. He tried the elbow, and that made it hurt. So he stuffed the handkerchief back in his pocket and simply waved the hand stupidly in the air until the blood clotted.

It wasn't much of a wound. Two of the balls of shot had struck him, one passing through the fleshy part of his thumb and the other scoring the side. As he thought of it, he became a little proud that he had borne a gunshot wound. He strolled along in the midmorning sunlight, feeling a dreamy communion with the boys at the front. "The whine of shot and shell—" Where had he

read that? Ah, what a story this would make! "And there beside the"—what was the line?—"the embattled farmer stood." Didn't the awfulest things happen in the nicest places? This was a nice forest. No screeches and snakes and deep dark menaces. Not a story-book wood at all. Shot by a gun. How exciting! He was now—he strutted—a gentleman adventurer. He did not see the great moist horror that clumped along behind him, though his nostrils crinkled a little with its foulness.

The monster had three little holes close together on its chest, and one little hole in the middle of its slimy forehead. It had three close-set pits in its back and one on the back of its head. These marks were where Alton Drew's bullets had struck and passed through. Half of the monster's shapeless face was sloughed away, and there was a deep indentation on its shoulder. This was what Alton Drew's gun butt had done after he clubbed it and struck at the thing that would not lie down after he put his four bullets through it. When these things happened the monster was not hurt or angry. It only wondered why Alton Drew acted that way. Now it followed the little man without hurrying at all, matching his stride step by step and dropping little particles of muck behind it.

The little man went on out of the wood and stood with his back against a big tree at the forest's edge, and he thought. Enough had happened to him here. What good would it do to stay and face a horrible murder inquest, just to continue this silly, vague quest? There was supposed to be the ruin of an old, old hunting lodge deep in this wood somewhere, and perhaps it would hold the evidence he wanted. But it was a vague report—vague enough to be forgotten without regret. It would be the height of foolishness to stay for all the hick-town red tape that would follow that ghastly affair back in the wood. Ergo, it would be ridiculous to follow that farmer's advice, to go to his house and wait for him. He would go back to town.

The monster was leaning against the other side of the big tree.

The little man snuffled disgustedly at a sudden overpowering odor of rot. He reached for his handkerchief, fumbled and dropped it. As he bent to pick it up, the monster's arm *whuffed* heavily in the air where his head had been—a blow that would certainly have removed that baby-faced protuberance. The man stood up and would have put the handkerchief to his nose had it not been so bloody. The creature behind the tree lifted its arms again just as the little man tossed the handkerchief away and stepped out into the field, heading across country to the distant highway that would take him back to town. The monster pounced on the handkerchief, picked it up, studied it, tore it across several times and inspected the tattered edges. Then it gazed vacantly at the disappearing figure of the little man, and finding him no longer interesting, turned back into the woods.

BABE BROKE INTO a trot at the sound of the shots. It was important to warn Uncle Alton about what her father had said, but it was more interesting to find out what he had bagged. Oh, he'd bagged it, all right. Uncle Alton never fired without killing. This was about the first time she had ever heard him blast away like that. Must be a bear, she thought excitedly, tripping over a root, sprawling, rolling to her feet again, without noticing the tumble. She'd love to have another bearskin in her room. Where would she put it? Maybe they could line it and she could have it for a blanket. Uncle Alton could sit on it and read to her in the evening— Oh, no. No. Not with this trouble between him and Dad. Oh, if she could only do something! She tried to run faster, worried and anticipating, but she was out of breath and went more slowly instead.

At the top of the rise by the edge of the woods she stopped and looked back. Far down in the valley lay the south thirty. She scanned it carefully, looking for her father. The new furrows and the old were sharply defined, and her keen eyes saw immediately that Cory had left the line with the cultivator and had angled the team over to the shade trees without finishing his row. That wasn't like him. She could see the team now, and Cory's pale-blue denim was not in sight.

A little nearer was the house; and as her gaze fell on it she moved out of the cleared pathway. Her father was coming; she had seen his shotgun and he was running. He could really cover ground when he wanted to. He must be chasing her, she thought immediately. He'd guessed that she would run toward the sound of the shots, and he was going to follow her tracks to Uncle Alton and shoot him. She knew that he was as good a woodsman as Alton; he would most certainly see her tracks. Well, she'd fix him.

She ran along the edge of the wood, being careful to dig her heels deeply into the loam. A hundred yards of this, and she angled into the forest and ran until she reached a particularly thick grove of trees. Shinnying up like a squirrel, she squirmed from one close-set tree to another until she could go no farther back toward the path, then dropped lightly to the ground and crept on her way, now stepping very gently. It would take him an hour to beat around for her trail, she thought proudly, and by that time she could easily get to Uncle Alton. She giggled to herself as she thought of the way she had fooled her father. And the little sound of laughter drowned out, for her, the sound of Alton's hoarse dying scream.

She reached and crossed the path and slid through the brush beside it. The shots came from up around here somewhere. She stopped and listened several times, and then suddenly heard something coming toward her, fast. She ducked under cover, terrified, and a little baby-faced man in black, his blue eyes wide with horror, crashed blindly past her, the leather case he carried catching on the branches. It spun a moment and then fell right in front of her. The man never missed it.

Babe lay there for a long moment and then picked up the case and faded into the woods. Things were happening too fast for her. She wanted Uncle Alton, but she dared not call. She stopped again and strained her ears. Back toward the edge of the wood she heard her father's voice, and another's—probably the man who had dropped the brief case. She dared not go over there. Filled with enjoyable terror, she thought hard, then snapped her fingers in triumph. She and Alton had played Injun many times up here; they had a whole repertoire of secret signals. She had practiced birdcalls until she knew them better than the birds themselves. What would it be? Ah—blue jay. She threw back her head and by some youthful alchemy produced a nerve-shattering screech that would have done justice to any jay that ever flew. She repeated it, and then twice more.

The response was immediate—the call of a blue jay, four times, spaced two and two. Babe nodded to herself happily. That was the signal that they were to meet immediately at the Place. The Place was a hide-out that he had discovered and shared with her, and not another soul knew of it; an angle of rock beside a stream not far away. It wasn't exactly a cave, but almost. Enough so to be entrancing. Babe trotted happily away toward the brook. She had just known that Uncle Alton would remember the call of the blue jay, and what it meant.

In the tree that arched over Alton's scattered body perched a large jay bird, preening itself and shining in the sun. Quite unconscious of the presence of death, hardly noticing the Babe's realistic cry, it screamed again four times, two and two.

IT TOOK CORY more than a moment to recover himself from what he had seen. He turned away from it and leaned weakly against a pine, panting. Alton. That was Alton lying there, in—parts.

"God! God, God, God—"

Gradually his strength returned, and he forced himself to turn again. Stepping carefully, he bent and picked up the .32-40. Its barrel was bright and clean, but the butt and stock were smeared with some kind of stinking rottenness. Where had he seen the stuff before? Some-where—no matter. He cleaned it off absently, throwing the befouled bandanna away afterward. Through his mind ran Alton's words—was that only last night?—"*I'm goin' to start trackin'. An' I'm goin' to keep trackin' till I find the one done this job on Kimbo.*"

Cory searched shrinkingly until he found Alton's box of shells. The box was wet and sticky. That made it—better, somehow. A bullet wet with Alton's blood was the right thing to use. He went away a short distance, circled around till he found heavy footprints, then came back.

"I'm a-trackin' for you, Bud," he whispered thickly, and began. Through the brush he followed its wavering spoor, amazed at the amount of filthy mold about, gradually associating it with the thing that had killed his brother. There was nothing in the world for him any more but hate and doggedness. Cursing himself for not getting Alton home last night, he followed the tracks to the edge of the woods. They led him to a big tree there, and there he saw something else—the footprints of the little city man. Nearby lay some tattered scraps of linen, and—what was that?

Another set of prints—small ones. Small, stub-toed ones. Babe's.

"Babe!" Cory screamed. "Babe!"

No answer. The wind sighed. Somewhere a blue jay called.

Babe stopped and turned when she heard her father's voice, faint with distance, piercing.

"Listen at him holler," she crooned delightedly. "Gee, he sounds mad." She sent a jay bird's call disrespectfully back to him and hurried to the Place.

It consisted of a mammoth boulder beside the brook. Some upheaval in the glacial age had cleft it, cutting out a huge V-shaped chunk. The widest part of the cleft was at the water's edge, and the narrowest was hidden by bushes. It made a little ceilingless room, rough and uneven and full of pot-holes and cavelets inside, and yet with quite a level floor. The open end was at the water's edge.

Babe parted the bushes and peered down the cleft.

"Uncle Alton!" she called softly. There was no answer. Oh, well, he'd be along. She scrambled in and slid down to the floor.

She loved it here. It was shaded and cool, and the chattering little stream filled it with shifting golden lights and laughing gurgles. She called again, on principle, and then perched on an outcropping to wait. It was only then she realized that she still carried the little man's brief case.

She turned it over a couple of times and then opened it. It was divided in the middle by a leather wall. On one side were a few papers in a large yellow envelope, and on the other some sandwiches, a candy bar, and an apple. With a youngster's complacent acceptance of manna from heaven, Babe fell to. She saved one sandwich for Alton, mainly because she didn't like its highly spiced bologna. The rest made quite a feast.

She was a little worried when Alton hadn't arrived, even after she had consumed the apple core. She got up and tried to skim some flat pebbles across the roiling brook, and she stood on her hands, and she tried to think of a story to tell herself, and she tried just waiting. Finally, in desperation, she turned again to the brief case, took out the papers, curled up by the rocky wall and began to read them. It was something to do, anyway.

There was an old newspaper clipping that told about strange wills that people had left. An old lady had once left a lot of money to whoever would make the trip from the Earth to the Moon and back. Another had financed a home for cats whose masters and mistresses had died. A man left thousands of dollars to the first man who could solve a certain mathematical problem and prove his solution. But one item was blue-penciled. It was:

One of the strangest of wills still in force is that of Thaddeus M. Kirk, who died in 1920. It appears that he built an elaborate mausoleum with burial vaults for all the remains of his family. He collected and removed caskets from all over the country to fill the designated niches. Kirk was the last of his line; there were no relatives when he died. His will stated that the mausoleum was to be kept in repair permanently, and that a certain sum was to be set aside as a reward for whoever could produce the body of his grandfather, Roger Kirk, whose niche is still empty. Anyone finding this body is eligible to receive a substantial fortune.

Babe yawned vaguely over this, but kept on reading because there was nothing else to do. Next was a thick sheet of business correspondence, bearing the letterhead of a firm of lawyers. The body of it ran:

In regard to your query regarding the will of Thaddeus Kirk, we are authorized to state that his grandfather was a man about five feet, five inches, whose left arm had been broken and who had a triangular silver plate set into his skull. There is no information as to the whereabouts of his death. He disappeared and was declared legally dead after the lapse of fourteen years.

The amount of the reward as stated in the will, plus accrued interest, now amounts to a fraction over sixty-two thousand dollars. This will be paid to anyone who produces the remains, providing that said remains answer descriptions kept in our private files.

There was more, but Babe was bored. She went on to the little black notebook. There was nothing in it but penciled and highly abbreviated records of visits to libraries; quotations from books with titles like *History of Angelina and Tyler Counties* and *Kirk Family History*. Babe threw that aside, too. Where could Uncle Alton be?

She began to sing tunelessly, "Tumalumalum tum, ta ta ta," pretending to dance a minuet with flowing skirts like a girl she had seen in the movies. A rustle of the bushes at the entrance to the Place stopped her. She peeped upward, saw them being thrust aside. Quickly she ran to a tiny cul-de-sac in the rock wall, just big enough for her to hide in. She giggled at the thought of how surprised Uncle Alton would be when she jumped out at him.

She heard the newcomer come shuffling down the steep slope of the crevice and land heavily on the floor. There was something about the sound—what was it? It occurred to her that though it was a hard job for a big man like Uncle Alton to get through the little opening in the bushes, she could hear no heavy breathing. She heard no breathing at all!

Babe peeped out into the main cave and squealed in utmost horror. Standing there was, not Uncle Alton, but a massive caricature of a man: a huge thing like an irregular mud doll, clumsily made. It quivered and parts of it glistened and parts of it were dried and crumbly. Half of the lower left part of its face was gone, giving it a lopsided look. It had no perceptible mouth or nose, and its eyes were crooked, one higher than the other, both a dingy brown with no whites at all. It stood quite still looking at her, its only movement a steady unalive quivering of its body.

It wondered about the queer little noise Babe had made.

Babe crept far back against a little pocket of stone, her brain running round and round in tiny circles of agony. She opened her mouth to cry out, and could not. Her eyes bulged and her face flamed with the strangling effort, and the two golden ropes of her braided hair twitched and twitched as she hunted hopelessly for a way out. If only she were out in the open—or in the wedge-shaped half-cave where the thing was— or home in bed!

The thing clumped toward her, expressionless, moving with a slow inevitability that was the sheer crux of horror. Babe lay wide-eyed and frozen, mounting pressure of terror stilling her lungs, making her heart shake the whole world. The monster came to the mouth of the little pocket, tried to walk to her and was stopped by the sides. It was such a narrow little fissure;

and it was all Babe could do to get in. The thing from the wood stood straining against the rock at its shoulders, pressing harder and harder to get to Babe. She sat up slowly, so near to the thing that its odor was almost thick enough to see, and a wild hope burst through her voiceless fear. It couldn't get in! It couldn't get in because it was too big!

The substance of its feet spread slowly under the tremendous strain, and at its shoulder appeared a slight crack. It widened as the monster unfeelingly crushed itself against the rock, and suddenly a large piece of the shoulder came away and the being twisted slushily three feet farther in. It lay quietly with its muddy eyes fixed on her, and then brought one thick arm up over its head and reached.

Babe scrambled in the inch farther she had believed impossible, and the filthy clubbed hand stroked down her back, leaving a trail of muck on the blue denim of the shirt she wore. The monster surged suddenly and, lying full length now, gained the last precious inch. A black hand seized one of her braids, and for Babe the lights went out.

When she came to, she was dangling by her hair from that same crusted paw. The thing held her high, so that her face and its featureless head were not more than a foot apart. It gazed at her with a mild curiosity in its eyes, and it swung her slowly back and forth. The agony of her pulled hair did what fear could not do—gave her a voice. She screamed. She opened her mouth and puffed up her powerful young lungs, and she sounded off. She held her throat in the position of the first scream, and her chest labored and pumped more air through the frozen throat. Shrill and monotonous and infinitely piercing, her screams.

The thing did not mind. It held her as she was, and watched. When it had learned all it could from this phenomenon, it dropped her jarringly, and looked around the half-cave, ignoring the stunned and huddled Babe. It reached over and picked up the leather brief case and tore it twice across as if it were tissue.

It saw the sandwich Babe had left, picked it up, crushed it, dropped it.

Babe opened her eyes, saw that she was free, and just as the thing turned back to her she dove between its legs and out into the shallow pool in front of the rock, paddled across and hit the other bank screaming. A vicious little light of fury burned in her; she picked up a grapefruit-sized stone and hurled it with all her frenzied might. It flew low and fast, and struck squash-ily on the monster's ankle. The thing was just taking a step toward the water; the stone caught it off balance, and its unpracticed equilibrium could not save it. It tottered for a long, silent moment at the edge and then splashed into the stream. Without a second look Babe ran shriek-ing away.

Cory Drew was following the little gobs of mold that somehow indicated the path of the murderer, and he was nearby when he first heard her scream. He broke into a run, dropping his shotgun and holding the .32-40 ready to fire. He ran with such deadly panic in his heart that he ran right past the huge cleft rock and was a hun-dred yards past it before she burst out through the pool and ran up the bank. He had to run hard and fast to catch her, because anything behind her was that faceless horror in the cave, and she was living for the one idea of getting away from there. He caught her in his arms and swung her to him, and she screamed on and on and on.

Babe didn't see Cory at all, even when he held her and quieted her.

THE MONSTER LAY in the water. It neither liked nor disliked the new element. It rested on the bottom, its massive head a foot beneath the surface, and it curiously considered the facts that it had garnered. There was the little humming noise of Babe's voice that sent the monster questing into the cave. There was the black material of the brief case that resisted so much more than green things when he tore it. There was the little two-legged one who sang and brought him near, and who screamed when he came. There was this new cold moving thing he had fallen into. It was washing his body away. That had never happened before. That was in-teresting. The monster decided to stay and ob-serve this new thing. It felt no urge to save itself; it could only be curious.

The brook came laughing down out of its spring, ran down from its source beckoning to the sunbeams and embracing freshets and help-ful brooklets. It shouted and played with stream-ing little roots, and nudged the minnows and pollywogs about in its tiny backwaters. It was a happy brook. When it came to the pool by the cloven rock it found the monster there, and plucked at it. It soaked the foul substances and smoothed and melted the molds, and the waters below the thing eddied darkly with its diluted matter. It was a thorough brook. It washed all it touched, persistently. Where it found filth, it removed filth; and if there were layer on layer of foulness, then layer by foul layer it was removed. It was a good brook. It did not mind the poison of the monster, but took it up and thinned it and spread it in little rings around rocks down-stream, and let it drift to the rootlets of water plants, that they might grow greener and love-lier. And the monster melted.

"I am smaller," the thing thought. "That is interesting. I could not move now. And now this part of me which thinks is going, too. It will stop in just a moment, and drift away with the rest of the body. It will stop thinking and I will stop being, and that, too, is a very interesting thing."

So the monster melted and dirtied the wa-ter, and the water was clean again, washing and washing the skeleton that the monster had left. It was not very big, and there was a badly healed knot on the left arm. The sunlight flickered on the triangular silver plate set into the pale skull, and the skeleton was very clean now. The brook laughed about it for an age.

THEY FOUND THE skeleton, six grim-lipped men who came to find a killer. No one had believed Babe, when she told her story days later. It had to be days later because Babe had screamed for seven hours without stopping, and had lain like a dead child for a day. No one believed her at all, because her story was all about the bad fella, and they knew that the bad fella was simply a thing that her father had made up to frighten her with. But it was through her that the skeleton was found, and so the men at the bank sent a check to the Drews for more money than they had ever dreamed about. It was old Roger Kirk, sure enough, that skeleton, though it was found five miles from where he had died and sank into the forest floor where the hot molds built around his skeleton and emerged—a monster.

So the Drews had a new barn and fine new livestock and they hired four men. But they didn't have Alton. And they didn't have Kimbo. And Babe screams at night and has grown very thin.

LEAGUE OF THE GRATEFUL DEAD

DAY KEENE

DAY KEENE, THE pseudonym of Gunnard Hjerstedt (1904–1969), was born on the south side of Chicago. As a young man he became active as an actor and playwright in repertory theater with such friends as Melvyn Douglas and Barton MacLane. When they decided to go to Hollywood, Keene instead opted to become a full-time writer, mainly for radio soap operas. He became the head writer for the wildly successful *Little Orphan Annie,* which premiered on NBC's Blue Network on April 6, 1931, and ran for nearly thirteen years, as well as the mystery series *Kitty Keene, Inc.,* about a beautiful female private eye with a showgirl past; it began on the NBC Red Network on September 13, 1937, and ran for four years. Keene then abandoned radio to write mostly crime and mystery stories for the pulps, then for the newly popular world of paperback original novels, for which his dark, violent, and relentlessly fast-paced stories were perfectly suited, producing nearly fifty mysteries between 1949 and 1965. Among his best and most successful novels were his first, *Framed in Guilt* (1949), the recently reissued classic noir *Home Is the Sailor* (1952), *Joy House* (1954, filmed by MGM in 1964 and also released as *The Love Cage,* with Alain Delon, Jane Fonda, and Lola Albright), and *Chautauqua* (1960, written with Dwight Vincent, the pseudonym of mystery writer Dwight Babcock; it was filmed by MGM in 1969 and also released as *The Trouble with Girls,* starring Elvis Presley and Marlyn Mason).

"League of the Grateful Dead" was first published in the February 1941 issue of *Dime Detective.*

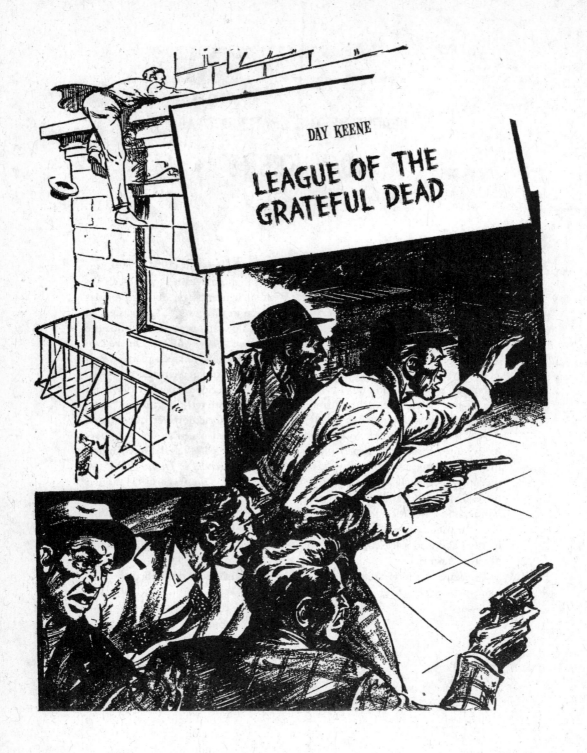

DAY KEENE

LEAGUE OF THE GRATEFUL DEAD

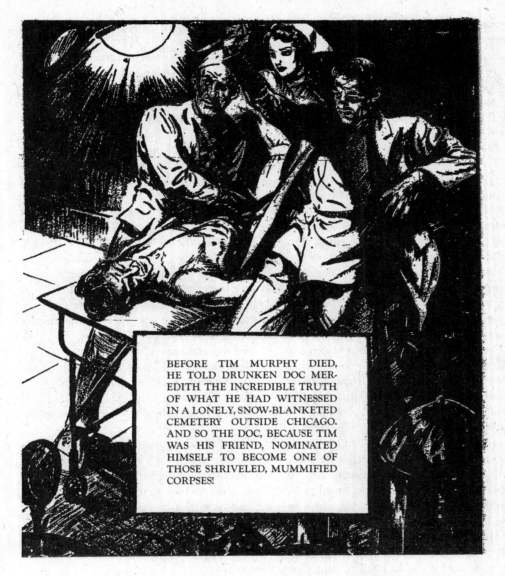

BEFORE TIM MURPHY DIED, HE TOLD DRUNKEN DOC MEREDITH THE INCREDIBLE TRUTH OF WHAT HE HAD WITNESSED IN A LONELY, SNOW-BLANKETED CEMETERY OUTSIDE CHICAGO. AND SO THE DOC, BECAUSE TIM WAS HIS FRIEND, NOMINATED HIMSELF TO BECOME ONE OF THOSE SHRIVELED, MUMMIFIED CORPSES!

CHAPTER ONE

WANTED—CORPSES

IT HAPPENED IN Chicago. The first of the mummified corpses, its tight, parchment skin stretched across its bony features, and a lighted cigarette still burning in one corner of its shriveled lips, was found sitting on a Help-Keep-the-City-Clean box leering through its hollow sockets at the busy traffic on the corners of La Salle Street and Monroe.

The second corpse was found huddled in the doorway of the West North Avenue Station by desk sergeant Phil Regan of the 30th District Police when he went off duty in the morning.

One man had been a multi-millionaire. The other had been on W.P.A. They had only one thing in common. Despite the fact that reputable witnesses swore that both had been alive and seemingly in the best of health five minutes before their mummified bodies were found, both men were listed on the records of the Department of Health as "dead" and should have been rotting in their graves for weeks.

The third mummified corpse was a woman of the streets. But she wasn't found. Tim Murphy of the *Morning Reformer* and a bartender named Thompson watched her die. She mummified right before their eyes as she sat on a high legged stool in a dingy North Clark Street bar. One minute she had been a red-lipped, hard-eyed wanton, smoke curling from a cigarette clenched between white teeth as she talked with crisp, staccato bitterness. Within the next five minutes she was dead. Her soft, white flesh had shrunk upon her bones to leave her a withered mummy whose dried brown skin stretched tight across her straining skull and whose empty eye sockets stared down vacantly at the thin brown sticks that had been her legs, and on which her sheer hose hung in folds.

At least so Thompson, the bartender, testified before they led him away, a shrieking maniac, to an asylum.

Tim Murphy couldn't testify. His was the fourth of the mummified corpses to be found. But before he died he told the incredible truth of what, acting on the dead woman's tip, he had witnessed in a lonely, snow-blanketed cemetery on the outskirts of Chicago. He told it to drunken Doc Meredith, who in turn used the ladder of eerie tragedy and fantastic horror to climb back to the personal and professional heights from which he had fallen. But that comes later in our story—much later.

NIGHT, COLD WINTER night, had begun to creep up Clark Street from the tall spires of the Loop in swirls of icy pellets that battered against the frosted, lighted window of the bar like so many frozen fingertips that were anxious to be warm. From where he sat on the high, leather-cushioned bar stool, a paper spread on the bar before him, Tim Murphy raised his eyes to the window. Ghost-like figures flitted past it, eager to be home—those who had homes. The reporter poured himself another drink from the bottle at his elbow, sighed deeply.

"Tough on a guy who hasn't got some place to crawl into on a night like this, eh?"

But for himself and the bartender, the bar was deserted. The bartender paused in his toweling to fleck a bit of lint from a brandy glass with his thumb.

"It sure must be," he agreed. He nodded at the headline of the paper on the bar. It read: FIND SECOND MUMMIFIED CORPSE.

"But them guys," he continued after a moment, "won't worry about where they're going to sleep tonight. Were you in on that, Tim?"

"I saw both corpses," Murphy admitted.

"What did they look like?" the bartender wanted to know.

The reporter shrugged.

"Just like the mummies you see over in the Field Museum. Only"— he hesitated for a word—"well, fresher."

"How do you explain it, Tim?" the bartender asked.

"I don't," Murphy told him. "The thing is impossible. Somebody's screwy. Witnesses have testified that they saw both guys alive five or ten minutes before they were found. And down on the records at the City Hall, both guys are listed as dead. One died four weeks ago. And the other, that broker, died two months ago."

The bartender eyed the brandy glass with a critical eye.

"Then supposin' the witnesses are mistaken, could guys turn into mummies in that time?"

Murphy sipped his drink, glanced up at the clock on the back bar.

"Don't ask me. That's why I'm waiting for Doc. I thought perhaps he'd know."

The bartender opened a cigar box on the back bar and took out a small, clipped bundle of tabs.

"Four-twenty you owe me for his tabs," he

told Murphy. "He was in here last night until I closed."

The reporter laid a five-dollar bill on the bar and tore the tabs into pieces.

"Yeah. I know. He came back to the apartment last night as stiff as an owl."

"Why be a sucker for that rum hound, Murphy? What if he was a big shot doctor once? Why I'll bet he wouldn't even have talked to you when he was a big shot."

"So what?" Murphy bristled. "When he was a big shot he didn't need a friend. But now that he's down on his luck, he does. Why? You want to make something of it?"

"Certainly not, certainly not," the bartender soothed. "Just keep your shirt on, Murph. So you want to support him, that's your business. But you don't have to keep him lushed up, do you?"

The reporter toyed with his glass.

"Booze is about the only thing that he's got left. It keeps him from remembering. But I've got faith in that guy. Doc'll make a comeback some day. Besides, I like him."

In that one last statement Tim Murphy summed up his philosophy of life. If he liked a man, he'd go to hell for him. If he didn't, the man could go to hell, and the back of his hand from Tim Murphy.

THE DOOR TO the street banged open and shut. Both men looked up instinctively. Neither of them recognized the girl who stood in the doorway shaking the snow and sleet from a cheap, white fur jacket. Her hair was a bleached and frowsy yellow. Her profession was obvious.

"Sorry, sister," the bartender waved her out.

The girl's smile faded. She glowered at him with cat green eyes. Her lips were two crimson slashes across a dead white face that had once been pretty.

"Who's talking to you?" she demanded. She walked slowly down the bar to where Murphy sat and climbed up on the stool beside him.

"You're Tim Murphy, the hot-shot reporter of the *Morning Reformer*, aren't you?" she accused.

"My name is Murphy," he admitted.

She smiled at the bartender.

"A double brandy, please. The gentleman is paying."

He looked at Murphy.

"Give her a drink," the reporter told him.

The girl sipped at her drink in silence, then turned back to Murphy.

"You're a good guy, Murphy. Everybody says so. That's why I've come to you. They told me in the restaurant next door that I'd probably find you in here."

"Yes?" Murphy said. His tone was noncommittal. The girl, he decided, for all her attempt at nonchalance, was on the verge of panic. Her lips were quivering and the muscles of her neck stood out like cords. "Yes—?" he asked once again.

Fear fought with avarice in the girl's green eyes.

"How much will your paper pay for the biggest story that it ever printed, Murphy?"

Murphy lit a cigarette. "Concerning what?" he asked.

The girl tapped the headline of the paper on the bar.

"Concerning the devil," she told him. "I don't know how he did it, but I know who killed those fellows."

"A cigarette?" Murphy offered.

"No, thanks. I've some of my own," she refused. She opened a shoddy handbag, extracted a package of cigarettes, lit one from the match he held, then fished in her bag again. She found what she was looking for and laid it on the bar. It was a small red card printed in flamboyant gold. "You seen one of these yet, Murphy?"

Murphy picked up the card, sat looking at it.

"Yes. I have," he told her.

There was small doubt the man was a charlatan, but his advertisement was tempting. Too strong for any of the daily papers, it was printed in gold on scarlet cards and passed out discreetly on the corners. It was simple and to the point. It read—

WANTED—CORPSES: *Have you a loved one who has died? Would you like to bring them back to life, know again the thrill of their caresses? You can. Would you like to assure yourself of ever-lasting life, know youth again and all the plea-sures it once held? You can. See Satan—Suite 21A, Braddock Building.*

They had flocked, still flocked to Suite 21A by the dozens: the rich, the poor, the young, the old, the halt, the maimed. And they went away seemingly satisfied. But what Satan promised, or what Satan did, the general public didn't know. For Satan wouldn't talk to anyone but a legiti-mate applicant—and his consultants wouldn't talk at all.

THE HANDS OF the police were tied, had been tied for six months. That it was a racket, they knew. But until someone filed a complaint they were helpless.

So were the papers. Murphy, with every other leg man in town, had tried to crack the story since the printed cards had first appeared. But they couldn't. Satan could smell printer's ink through the closed inner door of his expensively furnished suite of offices. All that any reporter or sob sister had ever gotten was a bland smile from Satan's smug-faced Oriental secretary and a courteous, "So sorry. Satan no can see." There were even a dozen descriptions of what the man himself looked like.

Murphy laid the card down on the headline of the paper.

"You mean the two are connected?"

The girl nodded. Her face seemed suddenly lined and haggard. She had difficulty in breath-ing.

"That's right." She turned to the bartender, smiled. "Give me a glass of water, will you, Jack? I guess I'm scared," she admitted. "I feel like I'm burning up."

She gulped the water greedily, sucked deeply at her cigarette and spoke through a wreath of smoke as she tapped the card on the bar with a too long, crimson fingernail.

"I went to him two months ago. He told me he could bring Bill back to life." She paused, added bitterly. "But he never. That's why I'm talking."

Murphy studied the girl's face, puzzled. In the indirect, fluorescent lighting of the barroom she seemed much older than he first had judged her to be.

"You aren't sick, are you, sister?"

"No," she shook her head. "Just a little scared, that's all." She glanced at the clock on the back bar. The hands stood at three minutes to eight. She laughed, nervously defiant. "He told me I'd die by eight o'clock. But I'm still alive, aren't I?"

"Who told you that you'd die?" Murphy asked.

She tapped the card on the bar impatiently.

"He did. The devil. He told me I'd dry up and burn in hell flames if I talked so much as a word."

"And just who is the devil?" Murphy probed.

"Why, Satan," she told him unsmiling. "Didn't you know? He came up from hell to or-ganize the League of the Grateful Dead."

The bartender grinned and went back to toweling glasses.

"You're out the price of a double brandy, Murphy. She's hopped to the eyes."

"Go on," the reporter told her patiently. "You said you went to him two months ago to bring Bill back to life. Who's Bill?"

"My baby," she said simply. The flesh had grown strangely taut across her cheeks. "He died six months ago. And Satan told me if I gave him all my earnings for two months, he'd bring Bill back to life. That's why I went on the street. But he never. I guess we were such small fry he wouldn't mess with us."

Murphy stared at her, hard. The girl's lips were twisted as though she was crying but there were no tears in her eyes. Her cat green eyes, themselves, had lost their hardness and their glitter and were sunk deep in her head. He had to rap sharply on the bar to recall her wandering attention.

"You say that Satan murdered these two men?"

She nodded, with an effort.

"That's right. First he brought them back to life, and then he let them die again because they threatened that they'd talk just like I'm doing."

"Brought them back to life?" the bartender scoffed.

"Yes," the girl told him slowly. "He could empty all the graves in town if he wanted to. He's bringing Max Boderman, the rich banker, back to life tonight at Maplewood Cemetery. They say at the Club that his widow is paying half a million dollars for the resurrection." Her voice trailed off in a whisper.

The bartender reached for the phone.

"Better let me call a squad, Murph. The dame is not only hopped, she's nuts."

The reporter stopped him. He pointed to the girl but made no attempt to touch her.

"Turn on those ceiling lights, Jerry," he ordered curtly.

The bartender switched on the brighter lights and stood staring at the girl, his eyes bulging from his head.

THE GIRL STILL perched on the stool, one arm on the bar. But in the glare of the full light her whole figure seemed shrunken and shriveled. Her dress gaped loosely from her body. Her skin had turned a sickly brown. As they watched, it tightened across her cheekbones until it cracked like parchment. With an effort she turned her shrunken, faded eyes up to the clock and shuddered. Her voice was faint and seemed to come from far away.

"He said I'd die by eight o'clock if I talked. Satan said—"

Accustomed as he was to scenes of violence and sudden death, the reporter turned away briefly, gagged. The girl was dying, drying up as she sat there. Her words had stuck in her throat

as the flesh of her neck contracted visibly to a taut, dried thickness no larger than a small man's wrist. Then, as he watched, her eyes dissolved, dropped back inside her skull and disappeared. But the burning cigarette still dangled from her grinning teeth and smoke began to issue from the empty sockets where her eyes had been.

The bartender, staring wide-eyed, began to whimper and make strange noises in his throat. Murphy leaned across the bar and shook him.

"Snap out of it, Jerry. This is murder."

"But she's dead," the bartender whimpered. "She's dead. She turned into a mummy right before our eyes."

The reporter stood up on the rail and slapped him sharply.

"Snap out of it, Jerry!" he ordered. "You'll go nuts if you don't!" He discovered that he himself was shouting and fought hard for self-control.

His stomach retching, he backed off his stool, his eyes still on the girl and fumbled for his overcoat.

"You call the police. I'll phone the paper from the cab stand." He paused, fought his queasy stomach. "Then I'm going out to Maplewood Cemetery to watch Satan resurrect Max Boderman." One searching hand swept the bottle from which he had been drinking from the bar. The glass neck chattered against his teeth, briefly. Then he corked the bottle and dropped it in his pocket. His face was white but determined. "This is more than a story. Hell's loose in this man's town!"

The reporter forced himself to check the contents of the dead girl's purse. It held nothing but a motley assortment of make-up and odds and ends that gave no clue to her identity. Then he turned up the collar of his coat and strode out of the bar.

But the bartender didn't even see him go. He was still staring at the grinning mummy on the stool. A big man, his plump, smooth-shaven jowls shook like jelly. Then, as the still contracting skin of what five minutes before had been a living woman caused a bony, brown, mummified arm to slide along the polished bar, its outstretched fingers pointing toward him, he screamed. He was still screaming and smashing at the "thing" with bottles from the back bar when the police from the Chicago Avenue Station arrived.

CHAPTER TWO

THE DEVIL LAUGHS

At twenty-four hundred north, the western limits of Chicago are 72nd Street or Harlem Avenue. That's where the car line stops. Beyond that stretch, there are only a few cheap real estate developments, a few small suburban towns, then prairie. In between, several cemeteries blossom white and pink with their old-fashioned tombstones, stark white crosses, and squat, expensive mausoleums. Of these cemeteries, the largest and oldest is Maplewood.

Bounded on one side by the Chicago, Milwaukee and St. Paul tracks, on the others by two highways and the little unincorporated town of Prairie Grove, Maplewood slept—its dead wrapped warm under fragrant evergreen grave coverings and a three-foot blanket of snow.

Two yellow eyes that groped through the blinding snow and sleet grew to be a cab that skidded to a stop before the heavy wrought iron gates that separate the living from the dead.

"Four-sixty, Bud," the driver pulled his flag.

Murphy passed a five up through the glass partition, changed his mind and made it ten.

"Wait for me," Murphy repeated to the cabby.

The cab driver scrubbed at a side window with his glove, peered through the snow at the gates.

"You can't get in there no more tonight, Bud. They lock them gates at five o'clock."

"Wait for me," Murphy repeated.

He turned up the collar of his coat, pulled his hat down over his eyes, and stepped out of the cab, slamming the door behind him. The snow came to his knees and, ten steps away, the cab had vanished behind a stinging curtain of white.

"But it's nice to know it's there," Murphy smiled wryly to himself. "If I have gone nuts he can drive me right on out to Elgin. If I haven't—" He shrugged and shook the wrought iron gates.

The gates clanked eerily but didn't give. Murphy ran his gloved fingers down the center bars and found they were looped with a chain, in turn fastened by a stout steel padlock. There was, however, if he remembered correctly, a second, smaller gate that opened directly from the platform of the now obselete and seldom used Maplewood Station. There was a chance it might be open.

The reporter braced himself against the wind and plowed through the snow along the fence. At the corner of the fence he stopped and looked back. Loud on the rushing wind, the cemetery bell had begun to toll a requiem for the dead. Yet there was no light inside the lodge house or the office. Murphy stood, irresolute, listening to the bell while the short hairs on his neckline stiffened.

"What the hell," he reassured himself, "it's just the wind, that's all. Every phenomenon has got to have some natural explanation."

Still, it seemed strange that the bell should have started to toll. He turned the corner grimly. The wind was stronger here and he had to pull himself along the fence hand over hand. The gate he had remembered was both unlocked and open. And the snow on the path that led inside had been freshly trampled by many feet.

"So," Murphy said.

He crouched in the shelter of the ancient station and finished the whiskey in the bottle in his pocket. It tasted good but failed to warm him. When he had phoned the office regarding the girl on the stool, they had claimed that he was drunk. He almost wished he was.

FAR INSIDE THE cemetery a yellow light showed through the curtain of snow, went out, then showed again. Murphy moved toward it cautiously, wading from tombstone to tombstone where the bare shrubbery and trees failed to hide his progress from any possible outposts whom Satan might have stationed. The bell still tolled.

"Three mummified corpses and a resurrection," he muttered to himself. "What the hell? No wonder the office thought I had an edge on."

The yellow light grew brighter, turned out to be a pressure lantern standing in the low, stone doorway of a mausoleum. Its intermittent periods of darkness were caused by the passage of a score or more of heavily muffled figures who tramped a narrow circle around the mausoleum.

The reporter edged as close to the circle as he dared, stopped finally behind a huge stone cross. In the light from the lantern he studied the faces of the figures as they passed, and was surprised to find he knew as many of them as he did. Most of them were prominent business men and women whom he had interviewed at one time or another. But all had a strange unearthiness about their faces; an eager rapture he had never seen before. They seemed to be waiting for something—or for someone.

He tabulated their names mentally as they circled the expensive white marble Boderman mausoleum, stamping their feet and beating their arms against their bodies in an effort to be warm.

There was Boderman's widow wrapped in a sable coat that brushed her heels. She looked frightened. There was Judge Taggart, the retired Federal judge. And Marc Long, the merchant. Sam Green, the banker. Pete Harris the labor leader. Grenfal the lawyer. There was Petey Nichols, the gunman who had dropped suddenly of a heart attack in the lobby of the—

Murphy's mind stopped short in its tabulation. The grim, cold hand of fear clutched at his heart until he gasped for breath. He knew with a sudden, sickening sense of horror what had made their faces seem so strange. But for Max Boderman's widow, they were dead—had been dead, some of them, for half a year. He,

Tim Murphy, himself, had written the obit on most of them, had seen them lowered into the ground and had heard the thump of clods of earth upon their coffins. He leaned back on the cross and fought for sanity. He was mad. This thing couldn't be. Or could it? He had seen a living woman turn into a mummy right before his eyes—was seeing living dead tramp in a circle around the mausoleum of a man whom the girl had said that Satan meant to resurrect. He forced his eyes back to the circle.

As he watched, a puff of smoke rose from the snow before the mausoleum, turned into a red, blinding glare that forced his eyes to blink. When he opened them the flare had faded and a man stood where the smoke and flame had been. He was a man of medium size, well built, with a jet black mustache and a small goatee that looked like they were painted on the ivory pallor of his face.

Murphy realized he was breathing in huge, labored gasps.

"Satan, I'll bet you." He grinned involuntarily.

"That's right," a bland voice whispered in his ear. "That's right. He Satan. Supposing you come meet."

The reporter felt something prod him sharply in the back and knew without looking that it was a gun. He turned to see the usually smug, now evil and distorted face of Satan's Oriental secretary not six inches from his eyes.

"Why—" he hesitated.

The snout of the gun dug viciously in his spine.

"You come meet," the Oriental hissed. "Satan not like spies."

The gun insistent in his back, Murphy plowed in silence through the snow toward the circle of men and women clustered around the man who had appeared in smoke and flame. Satan was laughing. Murphy could hear him laugh, an unpleasant, tinkling little laugh that cut at his nerves with icy razor blades of fear.

• • •

DOCTOR MEREDITH WAS sober. There were three reasons for that. The first was that he had no money. The second was that in the only bar in which Tim Murphy had guaranteed his credit, a burly Irish cop had replaced the slavering bartender who claimed the dried and fragile mummy he had been discovered pounding into dust with whiskey bottles had walked into his bar alive. The third and most substantial reason he was sober was that Tim had not as yet come home to be imposed upon.

A tall, gaunt man with sad smiling eyes, Meredith had once been the top man in his line. His skill and his fees had been fabulous. And then the post-operative deaths had started. One, two, three, four, five, in orderly succession. Then there had been a lapse of almost two months before they began again. After the tenth death, Doctor Meredith had laid down his scalpel and vowed he had scrubbed for his last operation. And he had. A highly sensitive, cultured man, he had gone to hell fast.

It had taken him fifteen years to climb to the pinnacle of his fame as a surgeon. Ten months from the day he had laid down his scalpel, Doctor Agnew, who had been his assistant, had cut him dead on the street. Two months following that, Tim Murphy had picked him out of a Clark Street gutter and given him a home. For that Jim Meredith was grateful.

His long white fingers beat a tattoo on the frosted window of the apartment as the Doctor stared out at the night. His eyes were bloodshot and his nerves were screaming for a drink. Then the clock on the mantel struck twelve.

Meredith stared at it reflectively. If he could find a hock shop open he could hock it and perhaps buy half a pint. That the clock belonged to Murphy didn't even enter his consideration. He had fallen too low for that.

He picked up the clock and was weighing it in his hand when Murphy's key turned in the door. Murphy closed the door behind him and stood leaning up against it. His face was lined and haggard, his eyes deep pools of puzzled horror.

"You look," Jim Meredith told him, unabashed, "as though you'd seen the devil."

"I did," Murphy answered briefly. "And no need to hock the clock. I've brought you a quart of whiskey."

He tugged an unopened bottle from the pocket of his overcoat and set it on the table. The derelict reached for it, stopped, came around the table.

"You look all in, boy. Let me help you off with that coat."

"No," Murphy backed away. "Don't touch me, Doc. I don't know what the devil's done to me. But he did tell me I'd die if I talked. And I've got to talk to someone before I phone the paper."

As he talked he stripped off his snow-sodden overcoat and tossed it in a corner. Then followed it with his hat and shoes. He took his money, cigarettes, and notes from his pocket, piled them on the table and stripped to his shorts and shirt.

"You can't—catch—death, can you, Doc?" he asked.

"N-no," the once-great surgeon smiled. "I wouldn't say that death was catching. Why?"

"Because I've been rubbing shoulders with it for the last two hours," Murphy told him curtly. "I've been interviewing men and women I saw buried. I've been talking to the devil."

Meredith smiled politely.

"And damn it, don't smile at me." Murphy rapped. "Crack open that bottle and pour us both a drink—a big one. I'll be back as soon as I wash."

THE SURGEON DID as he was told. His fingers were trembling so he could hardly hold the glass but he waited for his drink until Murphy had finished splashing in the bathroom.

"How long," the reporter asked him as he sat down at the table, still dressed in only shirt and shorts, "would it take to turn a guy into a mummy, Doc?"

The surgeon sniffed at his drink, savored the bouquet reflectively, then gulped it.

"Perhaps," he coughed, "two years. Perhaps two thousand, dependent on the condition of the soil. Why?"

"Then you haven't read the papers?" Murphy asked.

"No," Meredith admitted, "not the last few days, I haven't."

"The devil can do it in no time at all," Murphy told him. "I saw a woman turned into a mummy in five minutes by the clock. I saw her dry up and die right before my eyes as if by magic. Now look, Doc. Pour us both another drink and listen to me."

Impelled by the urgency in his voice the older man obeyed.

"Yes—?"

Swiftly, graphically, Murphy told him what had happened in the bar.

"Impossible," the surgeon said.

"I saw it happen," Murphy shook his head. "And I saw more. I saw the devil bring a dead man back to life tonight." He sorted through the papers on the table. "I've written down the names of a dozen dead men and women whom I talked to. And if anything happens to me—"

Meredith smiled.

"It won't. Nothing more than a headache. But you certainly have gotten yourself a peach on, boy. I envy you."

"That's what my city editor told me," the reporter said dryly. He tossed Satan's red card on the table. "But if anything happens to me, that's the guy. He told me tonight I was going to die. And somehow I believe him."

Meredith sat staring at the scarlet card printed in gold that began, "WANTED—CORPSES."

"I met him tonight out at Maplewood Cemetery," Murphy told him. "His secretary, a slant-eyed chap by the name of Yoshama, prodded me up to Max Boderman's tomb with a gun."

As he talked the air in the room grew electric.

"I saw the devil lay his hands on Max, saw Max sit up in his coffin." The reporter's voice rose shrilly and broke. "So help me God, I did."

"Steady, boy," the surgeon told him. He poured a water glass half full of Scotch. "Drink that."

The reporter gulped it, stretched his forearms on the table and cradled his head for a moment. When he looked up his eyes were calmer.

"I'm letting it get me, Doc. And I mustn't. I've got to make someone believe me. The devil's come up from hell and he's right here in Chicago."

The derelict surgeon regarded the man who had befriended him. He wasn't drunk. And he wasn't mad. Jim Meredith would stake what little honor he had left on that.

"Go on, boy," he said quietly.

The reporter fished a cigarette from the crumpled pack on the table, lit it, and drew the smoke deep into his lungs.

"I don't know just exactly what his game is," he began. "But he's making millions at it. He charged Max Boderman's widow a half a million dollars tonight for bringing Max back to life."

"And it *was* Boderman you saw?" the surgeon asked.

"I THOUGHT OF that." Murphy looked up at him sharply. "But it wasn't a switch as far as I could tell. His widow recognized him and after a few hysterical shrieks she fell into his arms."

"But not even the devil could bring a dead man back to life." The surgeon shook his head. "The thing is mad."

"Or I am," Murphy said grimly. "I tell you I saw it, Doc. And I talked with Judge Taggart, and Sam Green, and Grenfal."

"But they've been dead for weeks, months."

"So have the two men whose mummies were found on the streets today," Murphy said grimly. "I—" he hesitated. "Would you mind getting me a drink of water, Doc? I guess I must have caught cold out there. I feel like I'm burning up." He gulped the glass of water greedily, sucked deeply at his cigarette, continued. "They were brought back to life, then allowed to die again because they threatened to talk, just like the girl did, just like I'm talking now."

The surgeon sat eyeing him sharply. His friend seemed somehow older, more haggard than he had ever seen him.

"Did he give you anything out there, Murph, make you drink anything, or inject anything sub-travenously?"

"No. Not a thing," Murphy told him. He grinned wryly through lips the skin of which seemed taut. "All I had to do was kneel in the snow with dead men and women all around me while Satan said Black Mass." His voice seemed faint and far away. "He promised us everything here on earth our hearts desire. And in return all those living dead men and women had to prom-ise him—" His voice trailed off inaudible.

Meredith got slowly to his feet, stared with clinically professional eyes at the other man's face.

"You're not well, Tim."

"No," the reporter admitted frankly. "No. I'm not." Revulsion filled his face. "I don't feel any pain, but I'm dying. I—I can feel my insides dissolving, drying up. I—I don't know how the hell he's done it, but he has."

He spoke dispassionately, calmly, drugged by the sleepy torpor of death. He was a dead man and he faced the fact. He had watched another die as he himself was dying.

Meredith stood in silence, his eyes on the other man's face. There was nothing he could do. There was nothing that anyone could do. He had watched death's stealthy approach too many times not to know. But this death was obscene.

The reporter's shrinking lips framed a word. But he never spoke it. The word evaporated in his throat as the liquid and the tissue of his glands and organs dissolved and shrunk into atomic matter in the painless hell flame that was eating at his vitals.

Then Murphy's eyes began to run, dripped down, a gelatinous mass, inside his skull. He was dead. Only the smoke-plumed cigarette stuck to

his withered upper lip was still alive. What once had been a man was but a leering mummy with cracked, dried parchment for a face.

Meredith slopped some whiskey in his glass with shaking fingers, raised it to his lips, then set it down untouched.

"No," he shook his head. "I don't need that. Murphy was my friend." He picked up Mur-phy's notes from the table and stared at them through blood-shot eyes. There was something vaguely familiar that the names of the living dead had in common—but what it was, his drink-sodden mind was unable to recall. "Mur-phy was my friend," he repeated. "I'll find the devil who killed him."

The dead man shifted slightly in his chair as the flesh on his bones contracted. The night wind howled cold and mocking at the window like a laugh—a devil's laugh straight out of hell.

CHAPTER THREE

PLEASE TO MEET SATAN

The girl at the switchboard was new. She stared dubiously at the unshined shoes, the unpressed suit, and the beard-stubbled chin of the man be-fore the desk.

"Yes—?"

"Doctor James Meredith," he told her. "To see Doctor Agnew."

She raised an eyebrow slightly.

"You have an appointment?"

"No," he admitted. "I haven't. But I know he always operates on Thursdays and I had hoped I'd find him here."

The girl had been about to order him out of the lobby, but the obviously cultured voice ema-nating from the derelict's bearded lips gave her pause. She consulted a list on her desk.

"Doctor Agnew will be here today," she ad-mitted. "He's scheduled to operate at eight."

Meredith looked at the clock on the wall. It was seven.

"Thank you," he told her. "I'll wait."

His worn shoes scuffing on the tile, he crossed the corridor of the hospital foyer and seated himself in a large, over-stuffed chair just to the right of a door that bore a small brass plate announcing that it was For Doctors Only.

From time to time a surgeon with an early morning schedule passed him. Most of them didn't even recognize him. The few who did merely nodded.

He opened the paper he had brought and stared thoughtfully at the headline. It was terse and grim with understatement. It read: TERROR GRIPS CITY.

The sub-head read in almost as many points: Tim Murphy Ace Reporter of *Morning Reformer* is fourth mummified body to be found!

There followed a description of the finding of the reporter's underwear-clad mummy following an anonymous phone call. There had been no one else in the apartment but there had been a whiskey bottle on the table with two glasses. The whiskey was being analyzed. A homeless derelict known to have been befriended by Murphy was being sought for questioning. It was believed, however, that he could throw little light on the situation. The best medical minds in the city after an exhaustive examination of the three mummified bodies previously found admitted themselves to be baffled.

A new and insidious terror had grown up over-night. Nor was that terror modified by the fact that two of the mummies found, while listed by the department of health as "deceased" some weeks previously, were said by sworn testimony to have been seen alive but a few minutes before their dried and mummified bodies had been discovered. As yet, their families had not been located for questioning.

This was contradicted, in turn, by an A.P. dispatch from Los Angeles. The widow of one of the men had been located there and swore there must be some mistake in the identity of the body. For, despite the fact that she and her multi-millionaire husband had been estranged for some time over another woman, she had been with her husband on the night that he had died in Mercy Hospital. The death certificate had been signed by Doctor Agnew.

MEREDITH FOLDED HIS paper neatly and slipped it back into his pocket. He wondered grimly if it might not have been best for him to take Tim Murphy's scribbled notes directly to his paper first, decided that it wouldn't. Tim's notes consisted mainly of a dozen scrawled names of men and women known to be dead. He, Jim Meredith, had the story, he believed, but he wanted to be certain of his facts before he talked.

He sat rubbing the worn welts of his shoes together and listening to the conversation in the doctor's lounge. It was, as was natural, mainly of the gruesome terror and tragedy headlined by the morning papers.

A voice he recognized as Ben Winton's, the noted pathologist, scoffed at the whole affair.

"But damn it, you know as well as I do," Winton snorted, "the thing's impossible. It's mad. Certainly. Some chemicals can burn up flesh and tissue like that." He snapped his fingers. "After all, in the chemical composition of the body we find sixty-six percent water, three percent nitrogen, two percent hydrogen, six and seven-tenths percent oxygen—all vulnerable elements easily done away with by an opposing chemical process. But the papers claim that two of those men were dead, climbed back up out of their graves and walked around for several weeks before they dropped dead—mummies."

"But not Murphy, the reporter," Glendive the genealogist protested. "Nor the mummy of the girl they picked up in that North Clark Street bar. Both of them were known to be alive at eight o'clock last night."

Someone else said something that Meredith couldn't catch. Then he saw Agnew coming in the front door of the hospital and got slowly to his feet as the other surgeon who had once been his assistant paused at the desk for his mail.

Prosperity, he decided, agreed with Bill Agnew. His former assistant, who had taken over his practice when the series of unexplainable deaths had driven him to drink, was plumper, less ferret-like about the features. He wore an expensive broadcloth overcoat lined with fur. His silver mounted bag was of pin seal.

Jim Meredith ran his hands down the sides of his own greasy top-coat. Despite his own fall, he didn't envy Agnew. The man was a fair surgeon, but he was money-mad. And not even his prosperity could conceal nor heal the twisted and deformed right leg that had left its indelible stamp of bitterness on the mind of the man. Agnew was always conscious of it, thrusting himself forward as if to hide it by making it all the more obvious.

"Hello, Bill," Meredith greeted him.

Doctor Agnew paused, pretended to wipe the steam from the Oxford glasses he affected, although Meredith knew that he had seen him when he first came in the door.

"Oh. Oh it's you, Meredith," he said finally.

"Yes," Meredith admitted. "It's me."

Agnew cleared his throat impatiently, frowned, and reached for his wallet.

"Well? How much this time?"

"This isn't a touch," his former superior assured him. "You've read the morning papers?"

"I have."

"Well, Murphy was my friend."

THE OTHER MAN looked puzzled, then his thin lips twisted. "What am I supposed to do, cry?"

"No," Meredith said quietly. "I just wish that you'd make it possible, Bill, for me to look at the hospital records."

"I don't understand."

"Judge Taggart died here at Mercy, didn't he?" Meredith asked him. "And Grenfal the lawyer? And Marc Long? And Pete Harris?"

Agnew puzzled his brow in thought.

"Some of those names are familiar," he admitted. "Perhaps they did. What about it? Mercy is one of the largest hospitals in the city. A lot of people die here. A lot of people die in every hospital. Just what is it that you want?"

"To have you make it possible for me to look at the records." Meredith smiled wryly. "I believe I've been dropped from the staff."

"Yes," Agnew nodded, "you have. And you can't blame the board, Jim. Frankly, the way you've let yourself go to pieces—"

"I know, I know," the older man interrupted wearily. "But if you'll just okay me to the girl at the desk and see that I have access to the death records for half an hour, that's all I ask."

For a moment the other man seemed about to refuse, then he shrugged.

"All right. But it sounds as insane to me as some of the other things that you've done." He stepped across the corridor to the desk. "This is Doctor Meredith," he introduced him. "He formerly was on the staff here and I'll appreciate it as a personal favor if you give him access to any of the hospital records he may care to see."

The girl behind the counter beamed. Her smile alone was proof of the former assistant's standing.

"Yes, Doctor Agnew. Just as you say, sir."

Agnew smiled in his superior fashion, turned to Meredith.

"Certain a few dollars wouldn't help you?"

The night before Meredith would have taken them and been grateful. Now he shook his head, flushed slightly.

"No. Thank you." He paused, eyed the other man intently. "But you might tell me this, Bill. What did you ever do with that saline anesthetic that we were working on?"

Agnew looked puzzled.

"I don't recall it, Jim. Why?"

"No reason," Meredith told him. "Just wondered." He turned his back abruptly, faced the desk. "And now if I may, miss, I'd like to look at those records. The case records and death certificates of certain names I'll give you. Men and women who have died here."

For a moment the ferret-faced surgeon glared at the threadbare back of the man who had once been his superior, then he turned on his heel and stamped across the corridor into the door that was marked—For Doctors Only.

• • •

WHEN SHE FOUND out that he had been *the* Doctor Meredith, the record clerk couldn't do enough for the shabby man, who for the best part of an hour had sat poring over the case records of men and women long since supposed to be dead.

"You saved my mother's life," she told him. "You trepanned for a blood clot."

Jim Meredith smiled wearily.

"That was a long time ago, before I lost my skill." He folded up the papers on which he had been writing and put them in his pocket. "But thank you. You've been kind."

He slipped into his top-coat as a fresh-faced young intern banged into the office.

"Four-sixteen just died," he told the clerk.

"Mrs. Boderman?" she asked.

"That's right." The intern grinned. "And boy. Would I like to inherit those millions."

Meredith frowned, puzzled.

"You don't by any chance mean Max Boderman's widow?"

"That's the one," the intern told him. "She came in an emergency last night. It seems she smashed that big imported car of hers right smack into a culvert out on the Maplewood road."

Meredith closed his eyes. In his day he had been considered an over-conscientious surgeon who refused to cut until every detail of the diagnosis checked with all known facts. And in the case on which he was working, Max Boderman's widow had worried him. Her death had clarified a lot. He was ready now to face Tim Murphy's editor. If he wasn't locked up as insane, he believed he could point out the devil. Proving it would be up to the police.

He bowed, thanked the record clerk again, and left the office. Through the thin partition he could hear the intern ask—

"And who was that bum?"

"Why that," the record clerk told him, "was Doctor Meredith. *The* Doctor Meredith."

The intern's muffled "Gee!" was solace to his soul. Perhaps Tim Murphy had been right. Perhaps he could come back. Perhaps he hadn't been responsible for those ten deaths. Perhaps—

The bite of the icy wind that rushed up Michigan Avenue to greet him as the door of the hospital closed behind him cut short his thoughts. It sank its icy fingers through his threadbare clothes and tore at his tortured nerves. What he needed, he decided, was a drink.

He counted the change in his pocket. He had exactly fifteen cents and he had picked that off the table on which Tim Murphy had died. He braced his body against the wind and walked out to the curb. The traffic light was against him. He stood huddled against a lamp post waiting for it to change.

"Taxi, mister?"

A cab drew up beside him and he shook his head.

"Better get in and ride, mister," the driver insisted.

"No thank you," Meredith refused. "I—"

He looked up to find himself staring into the muzzle of a gun held by the slim yellow fingers of a smiling Oriental who sat on the rear seat of the cab.

"I think perhaps you had better ride," the Oriental smiled. "Satan would like to see you."

Meredith licked his lips. The smiling Oriental was a killer. It showed in the glittering pin points of his iris, in the cruel, thin lips.

"But I don't know Satan," he protested.

The Oriental's yellow fingers whitened on the trigger of his gun.

"That is an oversight we mean to remedy. Step into the cab. You will please to meet Satan."

Meredith did as he was told. There was nothing else he could do.

CHAPTER FOUR

DEAD MEN DON'T TALK

The room was as impressive as the man. Semi-dark, it was lighted by four red flares, one in each corner. Each flare gave off an insidious, yet somehow pleasant, smell of sulphur. The walls were draped in thick black folds of heavy silk. The only furniture was the chair and desk at which Satan sat and a chair for the consultant. A fifth red beam of light shone through the glass-topped desk and etched Satan's ivory face in bas-relief against the gloom behind him.

"So," Satan smiled, "you are Doctor Meredith."

"I am," Meredith admitted.

Satan waved the waiting Oriental from the office.

"You may leave us, Yoshama. I hardly think that Doctor Meredith will attempt any violence."

The Oriental backed to the door, bowed from the room.

Meredith sat studying the face of the man before him. It was vaguely familiar. It once had been a strong face but both the eyes and the ivory pallor of the skin gave evidence to trained eyes that the man was addicted to drugs.

"You wanted to see me?" Meredith asked finally.

Satan smiled.

"Yes. It has been brought to my attention that you have developed an overwhelming curiosity concerning certain of my subjects who belong to the League of the Grateful Dead."

"Can't we drop the fol-de-rol?" Meredith asked. "You're not impressing me at all. I know you're a fake. And I believe I know the man who is behind you."

Satan merely smiled his languid smile.

"No one is behind the devil. I have chosen this means and form of returning to earth for certain reasons of my own." He paused. "But we digress. I want those notes and names that your friend Mr. Murphy so unfortunately wrote down last night at Maplewood Cemetery while I was resurrecting a certain Mr. Max Boderman from the dead."

Meredith took the notes from his pocket and laid them on the desk.

"Also what data you collected at Mercy Hospital this morning," Satan insisted.

Meredith added his own notes to the small pile of papers on the desk.

"I can remember the names," he smiled. "And when I leave here I'm going to the *Morning Reformer* first, and then to the police."

"The police?" Satan smiled. "I see you are still laboring under a grave misapprehension, Doctor Meredith. You still believe I am a fake, a charlatan."

"I know you are."

Satan shook his head.

"I am sorry, for your sake, but I am real. And when you leave this office, you won't talk. The police will merely be more mystified when a fifth mummified corpse is found." He chuckled. "You have no idea of the disciplinary effect of those four corpses on the members of my League of the Grateful Dead."

"They aren't dead. It's a racket," Meredith said grimly.

Satan smiled.

"There have been complaints?"

"No," Meredith admitted. "Dead men can't talk. You kill them before they can—kill them as you killed Tim Murphy, killed that woman in that Clark Street bar."

"That's right," Satan agreed. "As I am going to kill you in just a moment." He paused, opened a humidor on his desk, selected a cigarette and lighted it. As an after-thought, he waved his long thin fingers to the box.

Meredith took one.

"Thank you."

Satan extended the still burning lighter in his hand, an amused smile on his face. Meredith leaned forward, the cigarette between his lips. But before he could light it, the door to the office opened.

"Is the police again," the Oriental hissed. "They will not believe you are not here."

A frown of annoyance crossed Satan's face. He gathered the scattered papers on his desk into a mound.

"Burn these in one of the flares," he ordered. "I had hoped we could postpone this, but it seems we can't." Ignoring Meredith completely, he sat stroking his small black goatee. Then he smiled at the heavy, impatient rapping on the door. "So the police want to question Satan. All right. But I am afraid they will be surprised."

THE CORRIDORS OF the South State Street Central Bureau swarmed with camera men and leg men. A palpable fake though he was, they were covering the biggest story Chicago had ever known. Satan had been arrested.

Inside the commissioner's office, Commissioner Craig sighed wearily.

"Why will you persist that you are Satan? You're a faker and you know it."

The man who claimed that he was Satan smiled.

"Yes?"

The commissioner spat out his cigar.

"All right. We'll wait until your fingerprints come back from Washington. Until then we'll hold you on an open charge."

Satan shrugged.

"And now you." The commissioner turned to Meredith. "What were you doing there inside this charlatan's office."

"I was forced there at the point of a gun," Meredith told him truthfully.

"By whom?"

Meredith pointed to the sober-faced Oriental. "By that man there. I believe Yoshama is his name."

"Is that right?" the commissioner asked the Oriental.

"No, sir," Yoshama lied. He pointed to Meredith. "He come in answer to advertisement. He say he lose good friend named Murphy, would much like to meet his spirit."

The commissioner covered his face with his hands for a moment, then exploded.

"Now look here, damn it," he stormed. "I'm getting tired of all this run-a-round." He leveled a finger at Satan. "Just what kind of a racket are you running?"

"No racket," Satan told him. "If you would ever care to consult me professionally, I'll be pleased to talk to you. But under the circumstances I am afraid I must refuse. As you yourself suggested, why don't we wait until my fingerprints come back from Washington?"

The commissioner looked around the grim, stern faces in his office. Most of the more influential civic leaders had gathered there at his request.

"Is the editor of the *Morning Reformer* here?"

A wiry little white-haired man stepped forward.

"Here I am, sir."

"Murphy, the fourth mummified corpse that we found, worked for you. Is that right?"

"That's right."

"And you say that he phoned you last night that he saw the dame in that Clark Street bar turned into a mummy?"

"He did."

"And that he was on his way out to Maplewood Cemetery to watch Satan here resurrect the body of Max Boderman?"

"That's what he said. I figured he was high."

The commissioner nodded.

"I still do. But we can tell better on that score when the squad I've sent out to Maplewood call in their report. If Boderman's body is still in his tomb, then Murphy was drunk."

"But he wasn't drunk," Meredith protested. "I talked to him when he came back." He pointed a finger at Satan. "And as I've already told you, Tim said that he not only saw Satan there resurrect Max Boderman but he had talked to at least a dozen men and women whom you have listed on your files as dead."

The commissioner smiled skeptically.

"I believe you were once quite a well-known surgeon, Doctor. Can you explain a dead man coming back to life?"

"In this instance, yes, I think I can," Meredith admitted. He scribbled a phone number and a name on a piece of paper. "But before I begin my explanation I'd like to have you call that number and ask that man to be here."

The commissioner pursed his lips.

"WHY NOT?" HE decided finally. "The more the merrier. The whole town is going to have hysterics unless we crack this case." He handed the paper to an assistant. "Send out a squad car and bring this fellow in."

The assistant left the office.

"Might I ask the name of the man for whom you're sending?" the white-haired editor of the *Morning Reformer* asked.

"Doctor Agnew of Mercy Hospital," the commissioner told him. He stared hard at Meredith. "But just where does Doctor Agnew come in?"

Meredith smiled grimly.

"If I'm right, he's the devil."

The man who claimed to be Satan laughed thinly.

"How amusing. I seem to have a competitor."

"You, shut up," the commissioner ordered. He turned back to Meredith. "And you say you know how those guys and that dame were turned into mummies, Doctor Meredith?"

"I think I do."

The commissioner wiped the perspiration from his forehead.

"Thank God for that. Another of them mummified corpses popping up, and I'll have hysterics myself." He looked at the man who claimed to be Satan. "I was beginning to believe you were the devil."

"I am," the other told him smiling.

A lieutenant fought his way into the office through a mob of howling reporters. His eyes were puzzled. His face was pale. He looked at the man who claimed to be Satan and then looked away.

"Washington has just reported on those fingerprints, sir," he saluted.

"Yes—?" the commissioner looked up.

The lieutenant stared hard at the man who claimed to be Satan, huge drops of perspiration beading his forehead. He forced his eyes back to his chief.

"And Washington wants to know what the joke is, sir. They say that according to the fingerprints we sent them, he's ten men—and that all ten of those men are dead!"

The silence grew inside the office until the beating of their hearts pounded in the eardrums of the straining men like strange and somehow obscene tom-toms.

White-faced, the lieutenant laid a sheaf of telephoto pictures on the desk.

"According to the whorls of his left thumb, he is Mace Manders the magician who was electrocuted at Stateville two years ago for the murder of his wife. According to the whorls of his right thumb, he's Johnny Green, the bandit, who was shot last year by a squad from the Woodlawn station. According to the whorls of his left forefinger—"

The man who claimed that he was Satan laughed an unpleasant, tinkling little laugh.

"Perhaps now you will believe me." He picked up his hat from the commissioner's desk and shaped it on his head. "Satan is not one, but many people." He stretched out his hand and a belch of smoke and crimson flame flared in the doorway. "If you want me for any further questioning, gentlemen, I'd suggest that you go to hell!"

He had the door already open when the commissioner came to his senses.

"Stop him! Shoot him! Stop that man!" he bellowed.

The lieutenant leveled his gun.

"Stop!" he ordered.

Satan smiled, turned his back deliberately and walked out of the door into the hall.

"Stop!" the lieutenant ordered—then fired.

Six steel-jacketed bullets picked curiously at the cloth of Satan's well-tailored and departing back. But that was all they did do—that, and scatter the reporters who scrambled cursing for safety. Satan didn't even turn his head, just kept on walking down the hall.

"So sorry," Yoshama beamed. He closed the door behind them.

For a moment there was only silence in the room and the pungent smell of gun smoke. The commissioner broke it with an oath. His superstitious, Irish face was florid.

"By God!" he swore. "By God! *He was the devil!*"

CHAPTER FIVE

LEAGUE OF THE GRATEFUL DEAD!

Despite the fact that it was three o'clock in the morning and bitter cold, the corners of State and Madison were as crowded as they had ever been at noon. Men and women avoided each other's eyes as they milled in a mass for safety. The thing was mad, impossible—still, there was no explanation but the fact that it was so. Hell was loose in the streets of Chicago and the devil roamed the by-ways.

Twelve blocks down the street, past VanBuren, in a cheap South State Street bar, Doctor Meredith stared with solemn eyes at the headlines of the paper in which he had just invested the last three cents he had. A glass of five-cent beer sat on the bar in front of him—untouched.

The paper made no exaggerations. It merely stated fact. Since disappearing from the police commissioner's office in a harmless fusillade of lead, Satan had not been seen. . . . Contradictory witnesses testified he had disappeared into the ground—stepped into a cab—walked briskly north on State Street. . . . A mysterious fire had developed in the suite of offices that he had used in the Braddock Building. . . . The corpse of Max Boderman, said to be resurrected, was not in its tomb. . . . According to the infallible fingerprint department of the F.B.I. the prints sent them by the C.P.D. were those of ten men who had been executed in the State of Illinois within the last two years. . . . A ragged derelict, once one of the city's most respected surgeons, had made wild and unsupported accusations against a prominent citizen whom the paper allowed to remain unnamed. . . . The derelict, believed to be insane from drink, had disappeared. . . . It was known to be a racket of some kind. . . . It was known to be the truth. . . . Several noted clergymen were holding special services in an effort to re-establish the city on a normal spiritual keel. . . . The thing couldn't be. . . . It could be. . . . Responsible citizens were beginning to report to the police that they had recently seen men and women on the streets who were known to that department to be dead. . . . The grief-stricken families of the men and women specified had sworn that it wasn't so.

"And it all boils down," Meredith told his glass of flat, stale beer, "to the fact that no one knows a damn. No one even suspects the truth but me, and they say I'm mad."

"You say something?" the barkeep demanded.

"No, just thinking aloud," Meredith shook his head.

"Then drink your beer and get out," the barkeep ordered. "You bums make me sick. You come in here and soak up a night's warm lodging on a nickel beer."

Meredith walked to the door and stood staring out into the night. It had begun to snow again and the curbs had piled high with the drift. He wondered what he ought to do. Perhaps he was crazy. Perhaps the man was Satan.

He fished in his pockets for a cigarette, found one in his coat pocket, put it between his lips and fumbled for a match.

His hand stopped halfway to his pocket. He took the cigarette from between his lips and stared at it. It was an expensive Turkish brand. It was the one that Satan had given him in his office. His eyes grew suddenly cold.

"Well, I'll be damned," he said. "I will be damned."

He put the cigarette carefully back into his pocket. Then he strode out into the night, his shoulders squared. He knew where he was going—and he knew what he had to do.

• • •

THE BUILDING ITSELF was attractive and comparatively new. It had been built in the boom of '29 as a hotel, sold in the slump of the early '30's to Doctor Meredith for a private hospital, and at his mental collapse had been absorbed in the general debris of his estate. Later, an undisclosed syndicate had bought it as a residence club house, and as such it was now used.

A liveried doorman stood at the door, but few members came or went. Those who did went out the back way and at night. The neighbors were normally curious, but no more. It was obviously a rich man's club and as such held little place or interest in their own busy, narrow lives.

Outside the heavily curtained first floor windows, a lone watcher crouched behind a tree for meager shelter from the wind and snow. From time to time he raised his eyes to contemplate the bright white light that shone through the skylight window on the top and seventh floor in what once had been an operating room.

Inside the heavily curtained windows of the club house, the air was thick with smoke and conversation. The lounge was filled with old men, young men, rich men, poor men; colorful with red-lipped youthful girls whose eyes were too bright; drab with pursed-lipped, prim old ladies; tempered with well-dressed matrons, and all had one bond in common.

Most of them were living dead. Most of them had died, been buried, and were resurrected. All were in debt to Satan. All had sold him their souls for life. All belonged to the League of the Grateful Dead.

The League rules themselves were simple. There were only three of them. They were:

1: Thou shalt Eat, Drink, and be Merry for thou hast been dead and buried and now thou shalt live forever.
2: Thou shalt converse with no one but a fellow member of the League concerning thy resurrection under penalty of returning to the grave.

3: Thou shalt remember thou hast sold thy soul to thy master who is Satan. When he speaks *thou shalt obey*.

ON THE SECOND floor of the club house Yoshama the Oriental rapped softly on a paneled office door.

"Come in," the voice of Satan called.

Yoshama turned the door knob then stepped politely to one side.

"Please to proceed," he bowed.

The florid faced, white-haired man in the doorway nodded curtly, took his younger, golden-haired companion by the arm and walked into the office.

It was similar to the office where Satan had held his consultations in the Loop but even more elaborate. Purported hell flames flared against the entire background of the wall. The air was heavy with incense.

"Yes, Mr. Green—?" Satan asked. "Yoshama says you want to see me."

The dead banker nodded glumly.

"I do."

Satan indicated two snow white chairs with legs of gleaming human thigh bones, seats of interlaced human ribs, and backs of tibias webbed with human clavicles, each corner tibia posted with a human skull.

The resurrected banker sat down heavily.

"I want to get out of here," he said grimly.

Satan raised his neatly arched black eyebrows.

"That is possible—for a price."

"But we've given you almost everything we have," the golden-haired girl protested. She began to cry. "Oh, if I'd only known that it was going to be like this I never would have come to you the night Sam died. I'd have let him stay in his grave."

Satan shrugged.

"If it is Mr. Green's desire it can be arranged that he return to his grave." He smoothed out the pages of an early morning extra that featured a picture of the four mummified corpses. "I have sent three of our League members who grew garrulous down to hell within the last two days."

"No. Not like that," the banker shuddered. "I don't want to die. I want to live. But I want to leave this awful place—this club house. How much for Gwendolyn and me to leave here?"

"Money," Satan mused, "is the root of all evil, and I am evil." He considered. "Suppose we say the customary plastic surgical operation that I insist upon whenever a member leaves, your promise to report to me once every month, and five hundred—" He stopped short in the middle of his sentence, listening.

"Yes, Master—?" Yoshama asked him tersely.

Satan pointed to the wall.

"I thought I heard something just outside the window there, something that sounded like leather scraping on rungs of steel."

"Is perhaps somebody climbing up fire escape." The Oriental smiled evilly. A long, thin, glittering knife appeared in his hand. "You please to excuse me, Master."

Satan listened thoughtfully for a moment, then shook his head.

"No, Yoshama." He rose from the chair behind his desk, nodded curtly to the man and girl in front of it. "You two will leave now. We will discuss the matter later."

The elderly man got up wearily from the gruesome chair on which he sat and helped his still weeping companion to the door.

"Yes, Master," he said quietly.

Yoshama closed the door behind them, pulled a switch that killed the crimson hell flame, and parting an asbestos curtain on the wall, looked out and up through a window.

"Is man," he announced in a whisper. "One man. Is almost up to fourth floor now and climbing higher."

Satan lighted a cigarette, smiled thinly.

"He is welcome, Yoshama. Being Satan, I am intuitive. It must be the one man in all this city whom we might have reason to expect." He placed one long ivory finger to his forehead in mock psychic thought. "Yes. I should say it is the once-great Doctor Meredith who has grown over-anxious to become a member of the League of the Grateful Dead."

He chuckled evilly, without mirth. Yoshama ran his thumb nail the length of his glittering knife blade, chuckled with him.

FROM WHERE HE clung to the last steel rungs of the spidery fire escape, slippery with ice and sleet, the crawling lights of cars on the street below looked like toys. And the wind was stronger here. Jim Meredith braced his weight against the ladder and blew on the tips of his gloveless fingers to warm them.

It would, he thought, be so easy to just let go. He put the thought from his mind. He was the one man in Chicago who knew who the devil really was. It was up to him, for Tim Murphy's sake, if nothing else, to prove it—kill him if he could. He clutched at the icy steel rungs with his bleeding fingers.

"Up we go," he grunted.

With the last of his strength he pulled himself over the bulge of the roof. He lay there in the snow for minutes, breathing hard.

The skylight window, only feet away, lighted the snow around it. Too tired to stand, he crawled across the flat roof through the snow to where he could look inside. It once had been his own private operating room. It was as he remembered it with no new equipment added. Only the scrub nurse, the third nurse busily picking bloody sponges from the floor, and the anesthetist were new. They were, he decided grimly, probably members of the League of the Grateful Dead.

The corners of the room, lighted only by the powerful dome light over the operating table, lay in shadows. He stared long at the operating surgeon's back. He was performing a difficult operation on an elderly white-haired patient, and was bungling every move. The devil was attempting, probably had attempted hundreds of operations, that only six or seven surgeons in the world were qualified to do.

Meredith got slowly to his feet and peered

through the blinding snow to locate the kiosk of the trap door that he remembered led down through the roof. It was piled high with the icy drift but was unlocked. Painfully, with bleeding fingertips, the once-great surgeon picked the ice and snow away. It was then he found the bar. It was of steel, thumb thick, and two feet long. A pry bar, forgotten by some worker, it was a murderous bludgeon in the hands of a determined man.

The surgeon laid it down again where he could find it and tugged gently at the door. It opened slowly, outward. Then he picked up the bar again, stepped into the darkened stairwell and closed the door behind him.

The familiar odor of antiseptics filled his nostrils. He smiled wryly. He was only a few steps from his own operating room. He had come back as Tim Murphy had prophesied. But not in the manner Tim had meant. He had come to take life, not to save it.

"For God's sake hand me that adrenaline syringe," he heard a thin voice say. "Quick. The old goat's dying on the table."

"He's gone," a male voice Meredith decided must be the anesthetist's answered. "I can't feel any pulse at all."

"Well, take him away, then," the thin voice said impatiently. "And send up another case." Meredith could visualize the thin lips smacking.

Meredith waited where he was until he heard a swinging door sway shut and the soft suck of the rubber tires of a stretcher on tile fade down the hall. Then he stepped out of the stairwell, stared with hard, cold eyes at the door of the operating room presided over by the bloody butcher who posed as a human being.

"Wish me luck, Tim," he said quietly.

Grasping the bar firmly he strode across the hall and in through the swinging doors.

The surgeon looked up, smiled.

"Well, so you got here," he said thinly. "You're just in time. I'll take you next. I guess I'll do a trephine on you in an attempt to find your brains."

Meredith stood where he was, the bar tensed

in his hands, his muscles poised to spring. Then two figures stepped out of the shadowy corners of the room.

"Drop that bar!" a sibilant Oriental voice hissed in his ear. "Drop that bar or else you are a dead man!"

Meredith gritted his teeth against the pain as the sharp point of an eager knife sank experimentally for a good half-inch into the thin flesh between his ribs.

Then the soft voice of Satan chuckled.

"Your English composition is very poor, Yoshama. Doctor Meredith is a dead man whether or not he drops that bar."

CHAPTER SIX

THE DEAD DIE ONCE

Meredith hadn't a chance, and he knew it. But he resolved to die hard. With a surgeon's knowledge of anatomy, he knew that the slanting thrust of the knife blade where it was started would be painful, but not necessarily fatal. At least not immediately. The Oriental was expecting him to draw away. But he didn't.

Meredith literally spitted himself on the knife as he lunged, sideways, felt the blade slip into his flesh and twist from Yoshama's hand. Then the swinging steel bar in his own right hand curved in a vicious arc and he heard a satisfying crunch of bone as the Oriental's skull caved in.

"Stop him! Stop him!" the white-faced surgeon behind the operating table screamed.

Panting on one knee in the corner where the force of his blow had sent him, Meredith thought desperately. A wire ran around the baseboard of the operating room. If he could break that wire, plunge the room into darkness—he hooked the curved end of his bar in the wire and yanked. The wire snapped in two, its insulation frazzled. But the lights still burned.

"Ripping out the outside telephone wire won't do you any good," Satan smiled. "We don't need to call for help."

He walked slowly, warily, an automatic in his hand, toward the panting figure crouching on one knee. He didn't dare to fire for fear of hitting his compatriot in evil. Before he could, Meredith again did the unexpected. He ducked in under Satan's guard and swung the short steel bar at the terror-stricken surgeon's head.

It missed its mark by a hair's breadth as the screaming surgeon jerked back his head and the bar slid off his shoulder to fracture his upper arm just above the elbow.

That was the last that Meredith remembered. The whole back of his skull exploded and Yoshama's dead face came up from the floor to meet him.

When he recovered consciousness he was surprised that he wasn't dead. He hadn't expected to open his eyes again. He looked around him blearily.

He was still in the operating room, lying in the shadows in one corner. In the full glare of the dome light Bill Agnew sat on the operating table on which he had but recently killed a man while the anesthetist set his fractured arm, arranged it in a splint, and bound it to his body.

Jim Meredith smiled grimly. It was at least a compound fracture. He'd done that much. Bill Agnew wouldn't operate for months, if ever.

The man who claimed to be Satan was the first to notice that the man on the floor had come to. He walked over and kicked him in the teeth.

"You die hard, don't you?" he said.

Meredith spit out a mouthful of blood.

"Yes," he admitted, "I do. Perhaps," he added quietly, "it's because I've been dying for the last two years." He looked at the man on the table. "You did that to me, Bill."

His former assistant scowled.

"Just you wait until Breen, here, finishes fixing my arm. Then I'll fix you." He toyed with the scalpel in his hand.

"No," the man on the floor shook his head. "You can't do anything more to me than you already have."

But for the dome light over the operating table the rest of the room was in darkness. Meredith moved uneasily. He seemed to be lying on something sharp. He found it was the ripped end of the phone wire and hunched himself up to a sitting position against the wall. The knife was still in his wound. He drew it out and mopped ineffectually at the oozing blood with his hand.

"Knowing what I know now, though," he continued, "if I had that phone at your unfractured elbow for just five minutes, and could talk to the Commissioner of Police, I believe I could send both you and Satan, there, back to hell where you belong—via the electric chair!"

DOCTOR AGNEW SLASHED viciously at the cord of the useless phone with the scalpel in his hand, then hurled the heavy instrument at the man who had been his superior. It struck Meredith on the temple, fell, the mouth-piece one way and the receiver another while the severed cord lashed across his eyes like a whip.

"Certainly you may have it," he taunted. "Go on and call the police. They wouldn't believe you if you could." He chuckled obscenely despite the pain of his fractured arm. "The great Doctor Meredith." His face sobered. "But what caused you to suspect me? That new saline anesthesia on which we were working when your patients started to die?"

"That's right," Meredith agreed. He hunched himself back to a sitting position, his hands behind him. "I dropped it as too dangerous. But you added several new ingredients, didn't you, broke it down into a powerful gas, piped the gas into tiny vials and put them into cigarettes? All your victims had to do was light them. The heat dissolved the gelatine and they sucked the gas down into their lungs with the smoke. In five minutes they were dead . . . mummies, all the juices in their bodies burned into atomic matter."

"It was really very simple," his former assistant boasted. "That is, once you know the ingredients and principle." He warmed to his subject. "I went back to the early Egyptians, took—"

"If you please, Doctor Agnew," the anesthetist protested. "Sit still. I want to be certain that this splint is supporting your fracture correctly."

"It had better," Satan warned. "Doctor Agnew is a very important member of our League of the Grateful Dead." He chuckled. "He makes young men out of old men—sometimes."

"That one tonight was too old," Agnew shrugged. "He died on the table." He looked over at Meredith in the corner. "But just you wait until I start on you. You'll wish you died two years ago—" He stopped abruptly. "What was that?"

"What was what?" Satan asked.

"I thought I heard a woman's voice," the thin-lipped surgeon told him. "Probably one of our little coryphees down stairs that's drunker than usual."

"Probably," Meredith agreed coldly. "And if I had one last dying wish," he spoke distinctly, "it would be that the police could only know the type of place that you're running in my old hospital."

"Wistful thinking," Agnew chortled.

"Perhaps," Meredith agreed. "But I do wish that Commissioner Craig could be listening in on this little conversation here before you kill me." He looked at the man who claimed he was Satan. "The Commissioner actually half believes you are the devil—after that shooting in his office this afternoon."

"Merely a bullet proof vest and a lot of nerve," Satan chuckled. He nudged Doctor Agnew. "You should have seen them when the fingerprint report came back from Washington. It was worth the pain I suffered when you grafted on those fingertips just to see the expression on their faces."

Meredith sat up more erect.

"Who are you, really?"

"Mace Manders the magician," Satan boasted. "Sure they electrocuted me. But Doc here brought me back to life with methylene blue, gave me a nice new devilish face, and nine dead men's fingertips."

"You figured out this racket?"

"He did not," Agnew boasted. "I did."

"No, Bill," Meredith shook his head. "You're not smart enough to figure out a thing as big as this is."

"NO?" AGNEW JEERED. "I was smart enough to kill ten patients of yours by always managing to leave a sponge inside the wound and fishing it out before you found it when we did an exploratory or a post."

"So," the gaunt man on the floor breathed quietly. He closed his eyes, a wave of relief sweeping over him. "So that was how it was done." He raised his voice. "And some of them died right here in my old operating room where we are now."

Satan kicked him again.

"We can hear you. You don't need to shout."

Meredith sat doubled in pain for a moment, then managed to sit back erect, the wound in his side throbbing madly, the pain stabbing deep into him.

"I—I suppose," he said, "you two have made millions."

"Millions," his former assistant boasted. "And I've had all the experimental material that I needed. It's been a surgeon's dream."

"But how in hell, Bill," Meredith demanded, "do you bring the dead to life?"

Both Doctor Agnew and Satan chuckled like school boys. Then Doctor Agnew grinned his twisted smile.

"You compliment me, Doctor. I don't. They merely think they've been dead, that's all."

"It is simple," Satan boasted. "When a patient worthy of our attention goes to Mercy Hospital, Doctor Agnew merely drugs them into a cataleptic state and signs their death certificate. Then before the undertaker goes to work, Yoshama calls on the dead man's sweetheart or his wife, and tells her I can bring the dead to life—and I do."

"But all your members of the League of the Grateful Dead aren't rich," the man on the floor protested.

"That," Agnew told him, "is where we are smart. We take in an assortment of various types to staff our place and to entertain our paying guests. Some of them believe they have been dead—the others have sold their souls to Satan, here, to bring their loved ones back." Doctor Agnew's thin face was sharp with triumph. "And you are the man who said I was a fool, Jim—said I was money-mad. Well, I have it. And I'll have more. I've got a perfect racket."

Meredith shook his head.

"No, Bill. No racket is ever perfect. No matter how smart you are, there's always someone who out-thinks you." His battered lips formed the semblance of a grin. "You don't know it, Bill, but you're going to burn for murder. That's a promise."

"Kick him," Agnew ordered.

Satan did. In the mouth.

Meredith spit out a mouthful of blood, continued calmly.

"For example. You think you're so secure. What would you do if the police should raid this place and find two dozen men and women who they believe are dead?"

"They wouldn't find them," Agnew boasted. "Our doorman is a lookout. And at the first sign of the police, our 'guests' know what to do. They merely file into the cellar and from there into an unused portion of the little known merchandise tunnel that has honey-combed the ground beneath the streets of downtown Chicago for years."

"But we won't be raided," Satan stated with assurance. "Our 'guests' are afraid to talk. They believe I can send them to hell—and I can."

The anesthetist stepped back from the table.

"There. I think that will do it, Doctor Agnew."

The thin-faced surgeon slid down from the operating table.

"Pour me a drink, a stiff one," he ordered.

His younger assistant did so. The surgeon lifted the glass in a toast.

"To your long and lingering death, Doctor Meredith." He gulped his drink and threw the glass on the floor. "All right, put him on the table," he ordered. He smiled thinly. "I won't bother to scrub. I don't *think* that he'll die of infection."

THE OTHER TWO men laughed as they lifted the limp and unresisting figure of the bloody, once-great surgeon from his corner to the table.

"First"— Agnew probed none too gently with his dirty scalpel at the bleeding wound in Meredith's ribs—"we'll see how his reflexes are."

He turned the scalpel in his hand.

"Next, we'll see—"

The sharp bark of a service revolver spat at him from the swinging doors and the scalpel flew from his hand.

"What the hell!" he demanded, stopped short, his thin face blanching as the swinging doors swung open simultaneously with the frantic flashing of a red light on the wall—and a squad of grim-faced Chicago plainclothesmen walked into the room, guns in hand.

"Up with them. And up with them fast!" the lieutenant who had fired the first shot ordered. "The whole building is surrounded and you haven't got a chance."

Satan chose to disbelieve him. His arm jerked up and down, his gun spitting in his hand.

The big lieutenant staggered—then fired again.

Satan tried to raise his gun, but couldn't. He was dead, shot through the heart. He toppled to the floor, a crumpled, motionless heap.

The anesthetist chose to run. The phone cord tangled in his feet and tripped him. He lay where he fell, whimpering for mercy.

Doctor Agnew stood staring at the corner where Doctor Meredith had been lying. The phone he had flung from him in anger was connected roughly to the outgoing end of the severed wire along the baseboard.

The big lieutenant grinned, felt of his shoulder where one of Satan's wild bullets had burned a flesh wound. He nodded toward the phone on the floor.

"Clever, eh? The big Doc on the table there out-thought you. I don't know how he got you to throw him the phone, but you did. So he connects it to the outgoing line and we've been on our way ever since."

Doctor Agnew didn't answer. And they saw then why he didn't. One of Satan's wild bullets was embedded in his temple. His nervous system was completely paralyzed, and Dr. Bill Agnew was dying on his feet.

Eager hands lifted Jim Meredith from the table.

"We come up the outside fire escape," a red-faced detective explained. "And mighty glad to get here when we got here, Doctor."

"The relief was mutual," Meredith smiled. His eyes were on the face of his former assistant.

"He's going to die, Doc?" the lieutenant asked, plugging a wad of cotton packing against the wound in his own shoulder.

"No. Not just yet," Doctor Meredith told him. He seemed another man. Despite his bleed-

ing wound, his unshaven, battered features, and his bloody, ragged clothes, he fully looked the great and famous surgeon that he was. They all looked at him with respect in their eyes.

"No. Not just yet," he repeated. "There are several little items like the pretended resurrection of Max Boderman and the murder of his widow still to be explained. Besides, we'll want him to go to trial, spread the whole story in the papers, so that the countless men and women upon whom he has imposed will know the truth. I'll see to it that he's able to take the stand."

The lieutenant looked dubiously at the once great surgeon's battered lips and trembling hands.

"But can you save him, Doc?" he asked.

"Why of course," Doctor Meredith said simply. He held out a shaking hand and it ceased to tremble. "Of course I can save him. Tim would want me to. I'll save him. Tim would want me to. I'll save him for the chair. I promise you that, Lieutenant."

And he did. Tim Murphy had been right. For Doctor James Meredith did come back.

LOVE CHILD

GARRY KILWORTH

GARRY KILWORTH (1941–) was born in York, England, but traveled extensively in his early years, since his father was a pilot in the Royal Air Force, as he himself was for seventeen years. He attended King's College in London, graduating with a degree in English with honors.

In 1974, he won a short-story competition sponsored by Gollancz and the *Sunday Times* with "Let's Go to Golgotha"; he subsequently wrote more than a hundred fantasy, science fiction, historical, and general fiction stories, as well as seventy novels in the same categories; in 1980, he began to write children's books, also on science fiction, fantasy, and supernatural themes, winning numerous awards for them.

His fiction has received four nominations for World Fantasy Awards. In 1985, he was nominated for Best Collection for *The Songbirds of Pain;* in 1988, his nomination was in the Best Short Story category for "Hogfoot Right and Bird-Hands"; in 1992, *The Ragthorn,* written in collaboration with Robert Holdstock, was the winner for Best Novella; and in 1994 he was nominated for Best Collection again for *Hogfoot Right and Bird-Hands.* In 2008, his novel *Rogue Officer* won the Charles Whiting Award for Literature.

"Love Child" was first published in the *15th Fontana Book of Great Horror Stories,* edited by Mary Danby (London: Fontana, 1982).

GARRY KILWORTH

LOVE CHILD

THE STEAM TRAIN came to a halt with a great deal of respiratory noise. Burnett stepped from the first-class compartment on to the platform at Kuala Lumpur totally unprepared for architecture that was more suited to an Eastern temple than a railway station in the 1950s. Had there been a reclining Thai Buddha beneath one of the arabesque archways, or a jade eye in the centre of the main cupola, it would not have been out of place. That was what Burnett loved about the East: the cultural surprises it continually produced from its bulging pockets.

The third-class passengers from the open trucks were beginning to swarm over the platform, carrying trussed chickens and cardboard luggage fastened with string. He motioned for porters to retrieve his own luggage from the train, taking only one item himself: his Smithfield twelve-bore in its cowhide case.

Burnett took a tri-shaw to the Stamford Hotel, through street crowds that periodically closed in upon the transport until the clangour of bells and taxi horns cleaved the way for another few yards. In K.L. the pedestrians compose a single, large, amorphic lifeform that moves like an amoeba, pulsating under the hot sun. Wares were constantly thrust into Burnett's face during the frequent pauses for clearance. He ignored the traders, staring steadfastly at a point in the sky just above the horizon, as if this were his destination and nothing must be allowed to turn his attention from it, not for one second. He knew that a single word, even a sharp "No," was all the key they required to gain access to the pockets of his white suit. If he spoke or altered his gaze he would find himself

with a pineapple or a carving he did not require. His problem was, he was weak. He pitied them their poverty, and they, being poor and desperate, could sense that lack of strength in his character. "Please," they would say, once they had his eyes. "My children need food." And guilt would guide his hand to his wallet. They knew him through his aspect and his demeanour. But there were too many of them. He could not feed them all. They would leave him as destitute as themselves. It was an impossible situation. So he avoided their faces, all of them, and fought a desperate battle within himself. In Singapore he was known as "Old Stoneface," but the expatriates who thought they knew him were less aware

538

of his real feelings than the Malayan strangers who whispered their entreaties to him now.

STAMFORD HOTEL WAS situated at the top of a rise, and the tri-shaw man had to stand on the pedals in order to force the vehicle up the slope. Burnett fingered his pigskin luggage on the seat beside him, having transferred his guilt to concern over its weight and bulk. The Chinese grunted and heaved as he forced the pedals down, sweat trickling under the holes in his ragged vest. He looked emaciated; but then they all did, these morose little men of the Orient, with their stick-thin legs poking from khaki shorts three sizes too large for them.

At the hotel Burnett over-tipped the man and watched him touting for business as a middle-aged Japanese matron with the bearing of an empress came down the marble steps from the main entrance. Then a porter was there, reaching for the pigskin suitcases, and Burnett transferred his attention, and, once again, his sympathy.

His first-floor room was cool, having a high ceiling with two large fans whirling gently at half speed. After removing his jacket and placing it carefully on a hanger, Burnett made a local telephone call. Then he made a second call to room service, for a jug of ice-water. The porter had offered to unpack the suitcases but Burnett had declined; he did not like anyone touching the clothes he was going to wear. While he waited for the ice-water he removed a bottle of Scotch from his hand luggage. There followed a moment's reflection. There was something about this whole business which was very disturbing. Not his adultery and the subsequent result—that was physical. No, there was something else: an unpleasant sensation of not being in control, of being *drawn*, as it were, to this place. Yes, he had made the decision to come himself, but were there other influences beyond the obvious . . . ? God, this is idiotic, he thought. I'm master of my own destiny.

KAM JALAN ARRIVED fractionally after the water but raised his hand at the offer of a drink.

"No thank you, sir," he said in a respectful tone. "It is against my religion to touch alcohol."

Burnett regarded the Indo-Malay steadily. What religion was he? Hindu? Buddhist?

"Fine," he said, swilling the ice cubes around his glass. "I got your wire."

Kam Jalan nodded deferentially. "Yes, sir, but there is a small problem. It seems she is no longer in Kuala Lumpur."

Burnett was sitting on the edge of his bed. He leaned forward and pointed to a green wicker chair. Kam Jalan sat down, but stiffly, with his backbone as straight as a pole. The hairless skin was taut across his skull, and an over-active thyroid gland made his eyes protrude, revealing the whole of the iris. Until a year ago he had been the housing agent for the British Council, Burnett's employers, but he had since retired and moved to Kuala Lumpur. It seemed to Burnett that the old man had lost some of his previous regard for him. Kam Jalan's manner was distant—almost unfriendly.

Burnett asked, "But she is pregnant?" He paused, wondering how much of himself he needed to show to his former employee. "You see," he said at last, "my wife . . . we are unable to have children of our own."

Kam Jalan cleared his throat. His hands played nervously with a small cap that he wore to protect his baldness from the sun.

"I must respectfully ask you, sir, whether the girl will be well treated."

"I beg your pardon?"

"The girl, Siana Nath."

Burnett was about to rebuke the old man, was on the point of correcting his manners, when something stopped him. He sat for a moment wondering whether a lie would be acceptable, even if it were an obvious untruth. Sometimes they just wanted to avoid the responsibility, these people. A flying beetle hit the overhead fan and ricocheted across the room like a bullet. It struck the wall and landed upside down by Burnett's toe, kicking its legs and buzzing furiously. Burnett moved his feet. Kam Jalan reached out and turned the beetle right side up. He then looked up expectantly.

"I'm not in love with her," said Burnett quickly. "That must be obvious. But she will be provided for . . . Is that acceptable?"

Kam Jalan nodded. "It is as I thought. In that case I will take you to the village." He pointed to the beetle, now skittering across the tiles. "He will recover soon and before long fly into the blades again. How many times he does it will make no difference. There is no learning in a beetle."

A silence descended between them now. Burnett took one or two sips of whisky but found he was not enjoying it under the placid gaze of his companion. Then he realized the man had something more to say. Something important. He waited attentively.

"Do you intend," said Kam Jalan slowly, "to adopt the child?" His staring eyes were disconcerting, and Burnett looked away as he digested this unexpected question. Outwardly, he knew, he looked calm. Inside there was a maelstrom of emotions.

A shadow passed over Burnett's soul. He dismissed it, almost instantly.

"Certainly. The child is mine." He paused. "How many months?"

"I am told eight."

Burnett nodded, almost with relief. "The child is mine."

"Good," said Kam Jalan.

Burnett stood up and walked towards the window.

"Not good, Jalan. Not good at all. You see, I come from a family . . . not wealthy, but very respectable. Do you understand?" He turned to receive an answering nod, then his attention was on the bright redness of the flamboyant trees that cushioned the balcony from beneath and around. "They would not approve of . . . such a child. Fortunately my wife is a very understanding woman. Of course, she did not endorse the liaison, but that's over. She is willing . . . no, she is *desirous* of raising the child. We realize, too, that Siana Nath will want to visit, to see the baby from time to time—I understand that. Money does not quench a mother's natural yearning for her child. But there will be complications . . . "

Kam Jalan nodded again. "Yes," he said, "she will have the same problem. This is why she ran away from Singapore—then from Kuala Lumpur. The village where she has gone is not her home. Merely the home of a sympathetic friend."

Burnett was completely taken aback. That he would be unacceptable . . . the thought had not even crossed his mind. He hoped his surprise had not been recognized for what it was. Without turning around, he said, "We shall have to live in Singapore, probably for the rest of our lives."

"That is a long time. Things change."

"Not in my world. But don't let me give you the idea that this life doesn't appeal to me. I love it." He paused, then added, "Very much. I am a born colonial, you see." He did not add that the attraction was in the relatively small number of expatriates and exiles. He felt secure amongst a small band of people. It was like being in a little English village, without the disadvantages of geographical isolation. He was part of a community, an island of whites, in a sea of natives.

Kam Jalan coughed politely. Burnett reluctantly turned away from the cloud of blossom before his eyes and said, "Will tomorrow at six o'clock be too early to start?"

"No, sir. That will be fine. Shall I hire a Land Rover? It will *be* necessary to have four-wheel drive. The monsoons . . ."

"Jalan, thank you. I do appreciate this."

"You are very welcome, sir."

Kam Jalan gave an abrupt bow before opening the door.

• • •

THAT NIGHT, UNDER the mosquito net, Burnett listened to the whining of his small enemies and the scuttle of cockroaches across the floor. I suppose, he thought, people like Jalan would be angry if I killed a mosquito. And how they could believe a soul was trapped inside such a disgusting creature as a cockroach was beyond him. Primitives! He fell asleep with the jungles of Rousseau crawling into his bed, the loathsome waxy leaves finding out his mouth and ears and nose.

From the moment he entered the rain forest Burnett had the feeling that he was being watched.

Had the real rain forest been less frightening it would not have surprised Burnett. The following morning, however, his nightmare became tangible, and for the first time in his life he compromised his fears. Nothing would have induced him to step from the Land Rover into the thick undergrowth on the side of the track. There were eyes . . . creatures, everywhere, half-hidden by the leaves and tall ferns.

Silently, knowingly, it seemed, they watched him travel through their domain. He was uncomfortable in the extreme. The feeling of gross insecurity mingled with that strange sense of being manipulated. Had he come of his own free will? Of course he had, he decided. This mood would soon pass. He looked upwards, as the trees closed in overhead and he recalled stories of things that fell from branches.

Burnett gripped his shotgun until his fingers began to hurt.

At the end of the track, some seven miles into the forest, the sky suddenly opened up before them and they were in the kampong, the Malay village. He was safe, relatively safe, for a time. Children, and one or two women, came running up to the vehicle shouting and laughing, but soon a lean man with a regal bearing appeared and called them away. Kam Jalan climbed from the Land Rover and went to hold a long conver-

sation with him. Burnett kept his eyes moving over the scene. He was uneasy in these alien surroundings.

One of the tributaries of the Panang River flowed by the kampong, and Burnett stared into its grey waters from his perch on the Land Rover. Finally, Kam Jalan finished speaking with the headman and returned to the vehicle. His wrinkled forehead gleamed as he looked into Burnett's face.

"I am afraid, sir, that there is some bad news."

"She's gone?"

Kam Jalan shook his head. "Much, much worse. I am sorry to say she has died." He gestured at the growth behind them. "There are many illnesses one can catch in this place. The doctor tried to save her and failed. It is a sad thing. They buried her last week."

The girl was dead. That was not such a terrible thing if one considered it inevitable. He was not unfeeling, but early death was a common occurrence amongst the natives.

"The doctor . . . did he save the child?"

Kam Jalan seemed to hesitate, just for an instant, then he shook his head again. "He is not the doctor you think. A native. He uses magic, not medicine."

"A witchdoctor?"

Kam Jalan seemed confused. "Not for witches, sir, for people. But the magic is bad. It comes from evil spirits."

Burnett felt hollow inside. All this way. And now this. The child was dead. He was an ordinary man again.

"I see." Black magic. They had tried to save her life with the help of the devil. Kam Jalan was obviously thinking of the same thing, for he muttered in a disturbed tone: "It is not religious."

"I'm afraid it is," said Burnett, "but not the sort of religion you and I practise. Well, we'd better get back to K.L."

"The headman has asked that we stay. He is anxious that you avail yourself of his hospitality." Kam Jalan's voice was apologetic.

Burnett frowned. "For how long?"

"One or two days."

"Impossible," said Burnett. "I have to get back to Singapore."

"He was insistent, sir, that you stay. You are the father of the unborn child. It is a decent thing to do, to pay your respects. Their law is very strict on such things."

"Tribal laws, surely?" said Burnett stiffly. Suddenly the atmosphere of the village had become very oppressive. He felt entangled and helpless. Something was not right.

"But for them it is important. There is to be a ceremony. They would be very angry if we left before that."

Burnett thought, uncomfortably, of the local murders he had read about in the *Straits Times*. Bodies mutilated by knives. Every one of these natives carried a parang, the Malayan equivalent of a machete. Then there was this black magic business. Even some of the expatriates, those who had lived in the jungle, would not state, emphatically, that it was so much bunk, and none of them ever laughed about it. Burnett remembered tales of men who vomited live fish, or spiders, or snakes, until they collapsed and died, simply because they had upset a local sorcerer.

"We'll stay, then," he said. "But just until the ceremony is over. Then we leave."

"Yes, Mr. Burnett. The headman has asked that we stay at his house. He does not sleep in an attap hut like the others, but in a solid wooden structure. It is a great honour."

"Well, I'd rather we weren't so honoured, but I don't want to appear ill-mannered or unfriendly."

Burnett inspected the village, accompanied by the solemn headman, with Kam Jalan to interpret for them. He even met the witchdoctor (if that is what the man was) who seemed quite an ordinary youth. Burnett had expected a wizened old sage, with—well, frankly, with the trappings of such people: skulls, rags and lank, smelly hair. Instead, he was presented with this young man, hardly out of his adolescence, wearing a colourful kain sarong and smiling like an idiot.

The villagers themselves seemed a sullen lot, which was unusual for Malays. They regarded him steadily as he passed, and then they returned to their chores, but he noticed that even then their attention was not with their tasks. They were watchful, their brown eyes darting this way and that, as if they were waiting for something to appear.

IN THE EVENING he retired to the headman's hut and sat in the light of an oil lamp to discuss Siana. In the prison of the yellow glow the mood of the conversation began, perceptibly, to change. Burnett could hear the forest moving, hear its multitude of creatures calling. It came home to him forcibly that this was not Kuala Lumpur. Nor was it a hotel. Instead of cockroaches, the floor might be crawling with spiders the size of soup plates. What was there to keep them out? Out of politeness he had left the unloaded shotgun in the Land Rover.

The headman's voice lowered to a serious murmur which later fell even further to a mesmerizing drone, and Burnett had to fight to keep his eyes open. Also the smell of the burning oil, thick in his nostrils, was pulling at the wild pig they had eaten for lunch. It had been a long day and he was exhausted. He rocked slowly on his buttocks, listening, listening. Kam Jalan's softly-voiced translation crept in between him and complete unconsciousness.

" . . . when a woman dies in late pregnancy," Kam Jalan was whispering, "the sorcerer waits until three days after the burial, then exhumes the corpse by night. The dead mother offers her unborn child to him, that he might use his magic to make it live again. He takes the child and seals it in a jar of fluid, a potion, until it takes on the squat form of a *logi* and develops the strength of several men . . . "

Burnett's eyes were suddenly wide. He gripped Kam Jalan's arm.

"What are you saying? That Siana's baby is . . . has been stolen?"

"Not stolen, sir, for the mother is said to have offered the child after her death."

"How, if she was dead? How?"

Kam Jalan shrugged in the light of the lamp.

"I am not the sorcerer. I do not know the ways. These are just tales, sir, to impress us. I regret the translation. It was stupid of me not to remember we were talking of Siana, your lover. Stupid of me . . ." But Burnett could see by his expression that it had been deliberate. Still, he was shaken.

He was revolted but he could do nothing. The headman's eyes were on him, staring intently. This is insane, he thought. To remove the foetus and bottle it was a disgusting practice, even for primitives.

"Where is the . . . object now?" he managed to ask.

"Why 'object,' if it is alive? It is now the property of the sorcerer. He uses it as a slave, to rob from other villages, sending it into their huts at night . . ."

"My child? He uses my dead child to do that?" cried Burnett.

Kam Jalan held up his hand. "Please, do not shout. These people are most sensitive. You do not need to believe all this. It is a story told to us by the headman. Often these people do not know the difference between the fantastic and what is real. You and I are civilized men. These people are superstitious . . ."

"This is ridiculous . . ."

"Of course it is ridiculous. You must not mind what I say . . ."

When the lamp was finally extinguished, Burnett's thoughts were a turmoil of distrust and anguish. Later, in the middle of the night, he awoke from a fitful sleep to hear someone dragging a heavy weight around inside the hut. Then there was silence, and he knew he was being watched. For a long time he lay there unable to move, until sleep overtook him.

The following morning Burnett woke abruptly to find himself alone. An unnatural peace had descended upon the village. With a thick head he staggered to the doorway and looked out. The rains had fallen during the night, leaving the river swollen and congested with flotsam. The village looked deserted. Then he saw them, crowded around the chicken coops on the far side of the open ground.

He made his way to where they stood, gesticulating grimly at something lying on the ground. On reaching them he looked for Kam Jalan and attracted the man's attention. No one was talking much, but there was something very wrong—he could see it in their faces.

"What's the problem, Jalan?" he asked.

Kam Jalan pointed towards a heap of brown and red lumps by the wire: the bodies of the chickens. Then Burnett saw the smaller pile. He felt uneasy.

"Something has torn the heads from the chickens," said Kam Jalan. He picked one up and flicked at the wattle.

"What kind of animal would do that?"

"No animal," replied Kam Jalan enigmatically.

Burnett looked quickly at his face, but it was impassive.

Kam Jalan asked: "Did you hear the noise? In the hut last night?"

"Yes, was that you?"

"No, it was the same creature that did this." He looked directly into Burnett's eyes. "The *logi*."

"*Logi?* I don't understand," said Burnett.

Kam Jalan answered with a nod of his head.

"You do. You do. You understand. The *logi* is the baby of Siana. The time for pretending between us is past. You should face the truth."

Nearby, the river gurgled through tangled branches of natural dams.

"It was in our room? My child?"

"Your *son*."

Burnett tried to arrange his thoughts in perspective. His problem was in finding a motive. What did Kam Jalan and these villagers want from him? The scenario was elaborate and costly. They must have set it up with a definite purpose in mind. He knew he was to be the victim—but why? His fears, he was aware, were necessary if he were to save himself. He needed to be alert, primed for action. That meant humouring them and waiting until the opportunity arose for escape. He carefully resisted the strong temptation to look towards the Land Rover. Was it still there? Was the shotgun still on the seat?

He said, "Whoever was in our room, it must have been adult. That was no child moving around."

"You don't understand, sir. The *logi* is small, but very, very heavy. Compressed. It has the weight of a fully grown man."

Burnett looked towards the edge of the jungle, thinking he saw something move. "Where is it now? In there?"

"It hides during the day."

Kam Jalan was silent for a moment. Then he said, "They want you to do something for them."

Was this it? The whole village was present, watching him. He looked around at the faces, the expectant expressions.

"Yes?"

"They want you to shoot the *logi*, tonight." The words came out in a rush now. "You have a shotgun. It will be easy for you. Something went wrong, you see—with the magic. The sorcerer is young and a little inexperienced, and the *logi* runs wild. It should be the slave but it does not respond to commands. The whole village is in fear of it . . ."

"Why . . . ?" The thought was repulsive. To murder. A baby? A pink-skinned little boy? Even if it was smaller than usual. "Why don't they kill it themselves?"

Kam Jalan's answer filled Burnett with apprehension.

"We cannot catch it. Now you have arrived it will come to you. It knows you . . ."

Burnett felt weak, and his head was beginning to spin from too much sun and too little food. "It can't know me."

Kam Jalan smiled. "You are forgetting, sir, they have taught it who you are. They have

taught it your name. It knows how to call you. Last night it came to you. Watched you fall asleep. It sees. It hears. Darkness is no barrier to the eyes of a *logi*."

"Why didn't you kill it? Last night."

"I?" Kam Jalan looked affronted. "I take the life of nothing. Not even the smallest fly. It is against my religion. *You* must kill it." He paused. "The ceremony today is for you, not Siana. It is the dance of the hunter's moon."

So, he would stay, it seemed. But one thing was certain. He would not kill—certainly not his own child. What sort of man did these people take him for?

The ceremony was indeed no solemn occasion. They laughed, they performed acrobatics, they showered praises on Burnett's head. At least, Kam Jalan interpreted their shouting and prancing as honouring Burnett's prowess as a hunter. They stalked imaginary beasts and slew them with a gusto and bravado probably never displayed beyond the village clearing. The feasting and dancing lasted until evening, then, when the rain came down as a wall of water, they slunk away to their huts, exhausted.

AS DARKNESS FELL, Burnett walked across the kampong to the edge of the jungle. If his child was there he wanted to see it. Nothing. Not even the stirrings of animals or birds. But on the slow walk back to the huts he knew he was being accompanied.

Burnett went to the headman's hut. There the occupants made him sit in the centre of the wooden floor, and the polished leather case containing his shotgun was brought to him. Kam Jalan refused to touch the weapon, but the headman's son was eager to remove it from its nest of red felt and hold it in his thin arms. Reluctantly, it seemed, reverently, he parted with it, placing it carefully in Burnett's hands. Burnett removed two cartridges from his breast pocket and, aware of the seriousness of the occasion, broke the breech of the Smithfield and loaded it. They left him alone, with the gun across his knees.

Light left the hut swiftly, as if it had been sucked up into the atmosphere by a suddenly created vacuum. With the darkness came the uneasy suspicion that perhaps, just perhaps, he was being tricked.

A board creaked in the doorway.

Burnett slowly raised the shotgun until the barrels were pointing through the open doorway into the night. He could see the stars, but all else was blackness. Then came a shuffling sound and heavy breathing, like a man labouring during a climb.

"Who's there?" said Burnett.

There was no answer, except the loud croaking of a frog. His finger tightened on the trigger. Something was in the hut, crouched in a corner. Burnett relaxed and stood up. He walked slowly to the door, then out into the night, inviting the visitor to follow him back to the Land Rover. He sat in the vehicle for a few minutes until he felt it move with the weight of someone climbing into the rear. He was afraid, but it was a controlled fear. The supernatural was a terrifying abstract if dwelt upon, but this was his own flesh and blood, not some strange monster conjured up by evil forces.

THE WET SMELLS of the jungle came to him strongly as he sat considering what he should do next. Kam Jalan had the keys to the Land Rover. Burnett could oblige the villagers, and they would then let him leave. The other alternative was to force Kam Jalan at gunpoint to take him back to Kuala Lumpur.

"I'm not going to kill you, you know," he said, into the blackness around him. There was no answer.

Burnett made a decision. He jumped out and ran to the main hut and, as he had expected, found the villagers crowded within.

"Kam Jalan," he called into them, "drive me to Kuala Lumpur now, or I will open fire on these people. You shall be the first."

The Indo-Malay stepped from the huddled group and bowed sharply. He switched on an electric torch and led the way back to the Land Rover. Burnett was nervous, expecting at any moment to receive a parang in the back.

"Just a minute," he said. "My things."

"Sir?"

"My gun case . . . and holdall."

Kam Jalan shouted something, and a few minutes later two or three figures skulked past them in the dark. Burnett pressed the barrels to the back of Kam Jalan's neck.

"Remember, if they try anything . . . "

"They will not do so," said Kam Jalan sullenly.

"They had better not, or you'll lose your head."

Half an hour later Burnett was bouncing on the Land Rover seat as Kam Jalan drove them recklessly along the potholed track back to Kuala Lumpur. The rain was falling in great swathes of wind and water, but Burnett was determined to reach K.L. by midnight. He was elated at his success. He had never considered himself to be strong-willed or adventurous, and tonight he had proved something to himself.

"The suspension . . . " said Kam Jalan.

"Keep going."

The windscreen wipers laboured to keep the windshield clear of the flood.

They reached the hotel at twelve-twenty. The monsoon had ceased and Burnett jumped out of the vehicle, still carrying the gun. Nervously, he searched the back of the vehicle, but after several minutes found nothing. His holdall and gun case were there, and several pieces of equipment, including a box of tools, but certainly no child, supernatural or otherwise. He felt cheated. Had he imagined being followed from the edge of the village to the huts? And then again to the vehicle? What about the movement of the Land Rover on its springs? Perhaps the child had climbed out again, while he had been fetching Kam Jalan.

Well, it wasn't here now.

"Bring my things," he ordered Kam Jalan.

Disappointed, he climbed the steps and made his way to his room. There he stripped and went into the shower. He took his bottle of whisky in with him.

Once he was clean he felt refreshed. Wrapping a towel around him he returned to the bedroom. Kam Jalan had placed the gun case and the holdall on the bed.

"Damn the man," said Burnett irritably. He had expected him to wait.

The bed suddenly creaked.

Burnett looked down. What? There was something most . . . the holdall was creating a depression in the bed far too deep for the weight of a bag of personal effects.

It moved, very slightly. Afraid, yet at the same time fascinated, Burnett crossed to the bed and stared down at the case.

The top had been left unfastened. Slowly the opening began to part, and Burnett cried out as the holdall fell, over on to its side.

The *logi* was not like a small, pink-skinned baby after all. It was the colour of fungi that squat in deep caves, and it tumbled from the holdall as ungainly as a leaden toad, to roll clumsily on to the linen bedspread.

The bed sagged to form a pit in which the grotesque *logi* sat and regarded Burnett with a lugubrious expression. Its head tilted to one side as Burnett cried out again, loudly. It was not the repulsive, wrinkled skin of the creature which motivated the shout, nor the lidless eyes with mucus crusting their rims, but the familiar, the caricatured resemblance to Burnett's own features. There was the sound of a bullfrog again, only this time, his senses sharpened by his fear, Burnett recognized the word the Malays had taught it. He reached out for his shotgun, leaning against the wall, as the *logi* crawled rapidly towards the edge of the bed. The creature dropped suddenly on to his bare foot, crushing it. It dug its hard little fingers lovingly into the pulpy flesh.

"*Bapa*," it croaked happily. "Father, Father . . . "

Burnett's head was awash with pain. He steadied himself against the wall and grasped the gun. They stared at each other for a full minute, then Burnett allowed the gun to slip between his fingers. It clattered on to the floor. The *logi* pulled the weapon to itself and cradled the present in its arms.

CORPSES ON PARADE
EDITH AND EJLER JACOBSON

EJLER JAKOBSSON (1911–1986) was born in Finland, moved to the United States in 1926, and received his B.A. from Columbia University in 1935. He met his future wife in the same year, and she also received a B.A. from Barnard College in 1935. As a husband-and-wife team, they began writing for the pulp magazines immediately after graduation.

In addition to horror stories, they created a series detective for one of the most prestigious pulps, *Dime Detective,* in 1939. Nate Perry, known in the underworld as "the Bleeder" because he was a hemophiliac, found himself in numerous impossible situations but always managed to evade the single scratch that would mean his death. In the novella *The City Condemned to Hell,* they also created Dr. Skull, who battled the eponymous villain of *The Octopus,* a pulp magazine that lasted a single issue (February/March 1939). Dr. Skull then took on another villain whose diabolical schemes also lasted for a single issue in *The Scorpion* (April/May 1939), as recounted in "Satan's Incubator." The two Dr. Skull stories, written under the pseudonym Randall Craig, had been credited to Norvell Page until Bob Weinberg, one of the country's leading pulp experts, uncovered the author's true identity.

Ejler Jacobson also worked as an editor of such science fiction magazines as *Astonishing Stories, Super Science Stories, Galaxy,* and *If,* succeeding Frederik Pohl as editor of the latter two.

"Corpses on Parade" was first published in the April 1938 issue of *Dime Detective.*

EDITH AND EJLER JACOBSON

CORPSES ON PARADE

PUTRESCENT MASSES OF DECAYED FLESH, THEY WALKED THE STREETS OF NEW YORK—THE VICTIMS OF THE ROTTING DEATH. WAS BONNY, MY BELOVED, DESTINED TO BE OF THEIR NUMBER? COULD I, ALONE, OUTWIT THE MONSTERS THAT HAD TERRORIZED THE WORLD'S LARGEST CITY? I WOULD DIE TRYING....

CHAPTER ONE

DUES PAYABLE TO DEATH

THEY BURIED ANDY Carter on one of those bleak February mornings when the sun forgets to shine. He had a big turn-out; and I wasn't surprised to see every society editor in town at St. Anne's, dressed in mourning, with note-books and pencils constantly in hand, jotting down the notables present.

I guessed at the paragraph they'd give me: "Barry Amsterdam, New York's play-boy and thrill-seeker Number One, was grieving at the loss of his erstwhile playmate, the fabulously wealthy heir to the Carter utility millions, whose untimely death—" and so forth.

I only hoped they'd leave it at that. Because I *knew,* and so did others, that Andy Carter hadn't died of pneumonia. He had died of whatever it was that had made him a ghost-faced stranger the last time I'd seen him alive.

Or could you call that—life? That cringing shadow of a man who'd whimper as he pulled his hand from my clasp, refused to answer the natural questions a best friend would ask?

We didn't speak of it to each other, we who were the monied fraction of New York, but it was there, behind every bland mask of a face at the fashionable funeral. Andy Carter had died of stark, grisly terror!

"YOU LOOK LIKE the prelude to several long drinks Barry, my boy," said a slow voice at my elbow. It was Duke Livingstone, city editor of the *Chronicle,* and in times past, friend enough to squash some of my snappier high-jinks before they reached the headlines. Tall and baldish, with eyes like an owl's, and a mouth that was sometimes like a kid's and sometimes like a professor's. He was humorous; he had to be. A grimmer man might have gone crazy, knowing the things he knew about people and their short-comings.

"I feel like the tail end of a bad life," I told him. "And what brings you here? Poor old Andy wasn't that important."

Duke put a long finger against his thin nose and wagged it. "Poor old Andy," he said, "died without explaining a few things that might be interesting to the press. For instance, what happened to the Carter money? Andy didn't live long enough to spend four million—"

"Duke, skip it," I urged. "Skip it as an editor, anyway. Don't hurt the Carters any more than you can help it."

Duke's owlish eyes followed my gaze to a brave erect little figure, black-veiled, at the front of St. Anne's. "And that's another thing," he drawled. "I have a hunch Bonny Carter knows more about her brother's death than any of us. Don't worry. I won't interrupt her grief—yet. You're a little sunk on her, aren't you?"

Sure. I was sunk on her. Until Andy's—well, we called it illness—we'd been talking Armonk every night of the week. Duke knew it, so I didn't bother telling him. And I guess he knew I didn't want him around, just then, because he vanished, like the good fellow he was.

There was something about Bonny Carter, even in the stark shock of sudden loss, that made a man think of the way spring felt when he was a kid. She was—well, perfect. Violet eyes, tawny hair, flawless skin; that was only a part of it. You could feel something underneath that, a kind of beautiful purity that made you want to help her and protect her.

I don't know what she saw in me, except that I loved her; but I knew, from the way she reached out her hands to me the minute she saw me, that if anyone could comfort her in this tragedy, it was I. I swore silently to myself that I'd live up to her trust in me. God, how little we know our own follies! In spite of myself, through my very efforts to save her, I was to add to her sorrows!

"Barry," she whispered, "has he gone? That newspaperman, I mean?"

I held her fingertips, reverently. "Yes, he's gone," I said. "I asked him to. Duke's not a bad sort."

"No, he isn't. But I'm wary of reporters." She was a little breathless, and it was not the breathlessness that comes from tears. Her glance darted about unhappily, and then she beckoned me into a side aisle.

"I have to talk to you before we go to the cemetery," she said. "Barry, I don't know what I'll be like afterward. I've been so worried! We don't have a cent, Mother and I, and we don't know what's happened to it. Andy's club was awfully decent about paying for the funeral. But the living should pay for their own dead."

I tried to tell her that it would be all right, that the sweetest thing she could do for me would be to let me take care of her and her mother forever. But she retreated from me in a kind of appalled daze—and then I saw a look in those violet eyes that made me wish I'd died before I saw it.

It was the same look that had been on Andy's face the last time I saw him alive . . . a look that made you think terror, like a huge cancer, was amok in a living being, feeding on it and slowly causing its death.

She wasn't looking at me. She was looking at the pall-bearers, six black figures, moving with Andy's coffin down the aisle. Was it the candle-light, or the tragic occasion that made them seem what they were, that sad sextet? Or was it—my mind recoiled toward sanity from the thought—that same expression of panic gone hopeless that turned those faces, so familiar to cameramen around the town's hot-spots, into death's-heads of despair?

I DIDN'T SEE Bonny at the cemetery, nor after the burial, for the very good reason that the burial ended in a near-riot. I remembered thinking, then, that life had turned into a crazy caricature of death. I didn't know, you see, that I was as yet only in the hinterland of a horror that would blacken my world, later. . . .

It was just after the first spadeful had been flung against the coffin. Grant Anders, the lead-ing pall-bearer, stood very straight and gaunt at the edge of the grave, his loose black coat flapping in the February wind like the wing-humming of the Grim Reaper. Grant's fam-ily had come over on the *Mayflower;* he was an old classmate of mine. I thought that he was not looking too well.

Suddenly high, mirthless laughter pierced the reverent silence. It was Grant's voice. There was a sharp cracking sound. Grant faltered, and then plunged into the open grave, his dead fin-gers still linked around a smoking revolver.

I suppose I must have taken charge in the panic that followed, because when Sergeant Connor put a heavy hand on my shoulder, it seemed I had pushed eight men away from the body, and was engaged in slapping a middle-aged matron out of hysteria.

"I'm a friend of the Carters," I explained. "I know all these people. I tried to keep them from running wild."

"Ye've been doin' a bit of runnin' wild yer-self, m'boy," said the sergeant, not unsympa-thetically. "However, I'm glad ye let no one touch the body." He beckoned to a comrade in brass-and-blue, and they hoisted poor Grant out of the pit. "Suicide," they observed pithily.

Grant had been a great one for thrills when I knew him, and he was willing to pay for them whenever they offered. Consequently, he'd usu-ally carried at least a century on him, generally more.

Yet, when we examined his pockets in that vain half-blind search for motive that follows ev-ery tremendously wrong human act, we found— a nickel, two pennies, a clean handkerchief, and one slip of paper in the otherwise empty wallet. It was a notice, from the Quadrangle Club that dues, amounting to ninety dollars quarterly, were payable on the first of February.

I thought dully, and it was a thought that clicked on an empty cartridge, that members of the Quadrangle Club seemed to be showing a singular mortality. First Andy—now Grant An-ders. I was occupied with a resentment against Kitty Anders. Grant had married her on a dare, and it worked out as such marriages usually do. Grant had been good sport enough to stick it, but I was sure Kitty, with her erratic expensive tastes, had brought my former classmate to this pitiable end.

What a difference there is in women! I thanked God for the sweet sanity of my Bonny— little realizing that when I saw her next, she would seem far from sane.

I gave the sergeant my name, address and twenty dollars for being helpful. The funeral guests were gone; and what was left of Andy and Grant was in hands fit to deal with remains. Suddenly, after all the excitement, I began to feel a little sick—and more than anything in the world, I wanted to see Bonny.

NEITHER SHE NOR her mother were at the town apartment when I got back to Manhattan. I floundered into an easy chair, and gritted my teeth over a Scotch and soda. At ten-minute intervals, I phoned the Carters. By five in the afternoon, they were still out. I had just about decided to go over there and wait for them, when Suki, my man-servant, announced a visitor.

It was the city editor of the *Chronicle*. He helped himself to a Corona, and asked for a drink, and then his mouth that was humorous as a kid's came out with a bombshell.

He said, "Kitty Anders has just jumped out of the window." And then he sighed, and blew the kind of contented smoke rings you see in bedroom slipper ads.

When it penetrated, I shouted, "You're crazy! Or else everyone else is!"

"I always knew about everyone else," Duke answered. "You learn about them in my racket. Now, lad, I've done you a turn or two in our time. You knew the Anders better than I did. Would you say Kitty was the sort of woman who'd kill herself out of grief at the loss of a husband?"

I laughed, not happily. "Hardly. She's dead then?"

Duke nodded. "Most messily dead. It's a shame. She was a pretty woman. Say, didn't I tell you earlier you needed a drink? Keeps a man's stomach down. Swallow one, and I'll take you over for a look at the corpse. There's some kind of cop who says you know the answer."

I damned Sergeant Connor in my private thoughts, and went to the Anders' apartment on East Seventy-third in a press car. I'd avoided that apartment since Grant's marriage—it was gaudy, and there seemed to be a price tag on everything, screaming expense. I dreaded, too, the habitual reek of over-applied Oriental perfumes that had been a perfect expression of Kitty.

I needn't have. No hint of bottled flowers was in that air. Instead, a sultry foulness, faint but undeniable, hit us the moment we entered. Duke's long nose wrinkled in distaste. I wasn't imagining it.

In the bedroom, surrounded by gewgaws she would never enjoy again, lay Kitty Anders, and for salon she had the coroner, the press and the law. And now I placed that odor of corruption; it proceeded from the dead woman's decently shrouded body.

I said, "She's been dead for days!" and the coroner looked at me curiously and shook his head. . . .

"Take yerself a look," said Sergeant Connor, pulling the sheet from Kitty's face. I looked—and something in me froze. I'm not a coward; I've been in some tough spots in my time and laughed afterward, but this was different. In the first place, with the removal of the sheet, the stench became almost overpowering—as though Kitty had been pregnant with death before she died!

And on the dead face was that unnameable expression of hopeless despair that I had seen on too many faces that day. That was it—she had carried death within her like an unborn evil—I turned away, half-sick with a fear I dared not name to myself.

"Ye wouldn't know what makes the poor girl smell so horrible, would ye?" asked the sergeant.

I said, "The living don't smell like that, nor fresh corpses. . . ."

The coroner straightened, and looked at me. He was haggard and perplexed. "Of course not. But we have sworn testimony that Mrs. Anders was alive this morning, that she shouted a warning to passers-by before she jumped . . ." he shrugged, and went into the next room. Duke followed him, hoping, I suppose, to get a more complete report. The sergeant was busy with Kitty's effects.

I don't know what kept me in that tomb-smelling room, unless it were fear of the haunting uncertainty of the thing. Some malign fate seemed amok among my friends; tomorrow, unless I learned its source of power, it might strike nearer home. . . .

No one else had seen the small white thing clutched by those stiff white fingers. No one saw me as I stooped to wrest the thing from their clasp.

The fingers were soft to the bone, pulpy as though maggot-ridden. I forced myself to delve there . . . and the woman's hand turned to putty in mine, like a squashed putrescent fruit! I was a man; I didn't get sick on the spot. That would come later.

In her hand had been a membership card to the Quadrangle Club.

CHAPTER TWO

ONE TICKET TO HELL

"Snap out of it," Duke kept telling me, on the way back. "You're white, Barry. Well, do you know any more than I do? The sarge seemed to think you might. I'd like to get it into a six o'clock extra."

I didn't answer, because I was swallowing to keep my stomach where it belonged. Besides, what was there to say? Duke had a nose; he knew as much as I did.

Was it true, or was my imagination playing tricks on my memory? That last time Andy had retreated from me, at the Antler Bar, hadn't I thought, "What ghastly shaving lotion the lad uses!" For there *had* been a super-abundance of scent about him, a scent with sickly-rancid undertones. . . . God, it was true! Whatever they died of, these ill-fated things, they'd been dying of it for a long time before! Some loathsome disease, that rotted all of them, heart and brain last. . . . I swallowed, harder than ever, and managed to talk. "Looks like the dissolution of the upper classes. The snootiest club in town is really getting something to turn its nose." And I showed him the rumpled card I'd torn from those rotted fingers.

"Shut up," Duke said sharply. "You're letting it get you. Come back with me while I put the *Chronicle* to bed. She'll run an article on the Quadrangle Club that ought to stop the slaughter. You might have two cents to put in."

I said, "No," because I remembered, with tightening heart muscles, that I hadn't located Bonny all day. And she had told me that morning that she owed the cost of Andy's funeral to—the Quadrangle Club! No wonder she had looked as though doom were a little way off, watching her helpless struggle with malevolent and unfathomable eyes! It was enough to drive a man mad, that sinister shadow whose substance I could not perceive!

There was no need to phone. I knew, when I saw the mink coat and black hat on a couch in the foyer, that I had a most welcome guest. I heard the automatic playing the Pathetique symphony.

Bonny crouched, head buried in her elbows, in a big chair. Her small, black-robed body swayed mournfully to the third movement. God, I was glad to see her—and not to—to smell her!

She was pure, thank God, and untainted. Still had the same faint toilet water scent about her, woodsy with lavendar . . . she winced when I put my hands on her shoulders.

"Bonny, where have you been all day?" I asked anxiously.

She turned to me a white face in which the violet eyes looked like great bruises. "Dodging reporters," she answered. "Barry, I have to stay here tonight."

"You can't," I answered, with a sharpness that was as much reproof to myself as to her. "There aren't enough rooms. And—" I added, laughing feebly—"no chaperone."

"Chaperone!" She laughed with me, but it was a high, uncomfortable laugh that made my flesh creep. "Bitter music," she commented, and then: "What do I need with a chaperone? I want protection, just for tonight."

I shook her, for she was still laughing in that bitter, almost hysterical way, but it had no effect. "Bonny, you've got to tell me! What are you afraid of?"

She shuddered. "Everything—even you.

You've been wicked in your time, haven't you, Barry? Awfully wicked . . . but I love you."

That wasn't like Bonny. I'd told her all about myself, and the low-lights of my past, and she'd been pretty magnanimous about it. She wasn't one to rake up old ashes. Suddenly I hated that poignant music; like a crossed child, I snatched the record. I heard the needle whine once, and then the third movement of the symphony was in a hundred fragments on the floor.

"I felt that way—once," Bonny told me. She had stopped laughing. Her voice was flat, hopeless. "Now it doesn't matter. Can I stay tonight, Barry? It may be the last time I'll ever be near you. . . ."

I shouted, "For God's sake, talk straight! If you'd only tell me what's terrifying you—you can't stay here. Think, Bonny. We buried Andy this morning. You don't want to go to hell tonight, do you?"

She had resumed her rocking back and forth, in the cradle of her own arms. "Andy this morning," she crooned. "Tomorrow—Kitty. And the day after—who knows? Maybe Bonny. Poor Kitty. Poor Bonny."

I couldn't bear the picture her insane sing-song conjured in my mind. Bonny with her tawny hair to die like Kitty! I slapped my sweetheart, hard. She whimpered—and laughed!

I remember pleading and haranguing alternately, but nothing shook Bonny from her mad mood. I shot questions about the Quadrangle Club at her, but she kept crooning and laughing to herself, in the ghastly mockery of a lullaby. Finally I said, "I'm calling up your mother. She'll spank you for this."

"Mother's gone," said Bonny. "Poor Mother!" A telephone call to the Carters' proved she was right, for the time being, anyway.

I'd had enough skirting on the edge of nerve-strangling mystery. I could think of only one man who might know something—a very little something—and if I pooled my knowledge with his, we might together find a ray of blessed light.

"Suki," I shouted, forgetting that there were still human ears left not deafened by madness.

"Take care of Miss Carter. Don't let anyone in. I'll be back in an hour." I handed the boy my gun. He blinked, and nodded. Suki was a good boy, loyal and intelligent.

Bonny laughed as I walked out into the night.

DUKE WASN'T AT the office when I got there. They told me he'd gone to check some material for a special article on the Quadrangle Club, featured for front page release in the morning. I groaned, fell into Duke's swivel chair, and waited.

There wasn't much humor in Duke's face when he came in, at eleven-thirty. He took one look at me, and said, "When did you eat last?"

"I don't know. Maybe this morning."

"Let's step across the street. I won't say what I have to say to a guy with an empty stomach."

I didn't like the ham and eggs. I wouldn't have liked nectar and ambrosia, at that point. But Duke sat over me sternly, making me gulp the stuff down anyhow, and he only relaxed over my half-finished cup of coffee.

"I've been over to the Quadrangle Club," he said harshly. "An umpty layout; big brownstone front, thick curtains, and a stuffed butler at the door. Couldn't get in, though. God knows how they've kept the cops out after today's highjinks. They sponsored the funeral, didn't they? Well, you need a ticket from the Social Register to crash. I didn't want to waste time."

I said I'd heard all that before. The Quadrangle Club had been one of those things in the background all my life, like the Horse Show.

"My lad," said Duke, his face one long grimace from the bald spot on his brow to the cleft in his narrow chin; "do you know whom I saw in the lobby, just past the butler?"

"No. You look as though it might have been a ghost."

"Correct," said Duke. "It was Andy Carter."

There are points beyond which the mind cannot go, discrepancies of evidence which only the insane may enter and live. I knew, as soon as Duke told me that *I believed him.* And I know, too, that something snapped in my brain. It had to. I started moving, and moving fast.

First, I drove through every red light on the route to my own apartment. I wasn't surprised to find Suki blubbering and frantic, and Bonny gone. That was part of the grotesquely hideous nightmare.

"Miss Carter get telephone call. I not can stop her. She say—" Suki paused, and there was stark fear in his face—"her brother want her, she go. Is not Miss Carter's brother dead this morning?"

Dead! Kitty Anders must have been dead a week before she stopped moving about in the land of the living! What was to keep a corpse from rising then, if the dead forgot to die?

It was only after I got to the Quadrangle Club that the horror stopped. I put one finger on the doorbell and kept it there. The door opened to the width of a man's arm. Something bright flared astoundingly in my face, and blinded me. I didn't see or feel whatever it was that smashed down on my skull and sent me into oblivion with a burst of shooting stars.

I FELT MY head going round and round, just before I opened my eyes, I expected to wake up in hell, but they'd canceled that trip, apparently, because I was in my own bed, with Suki's worried brown face bending over me, and Duke Livingstone's back between me and the window.

Duke's mouth puckered as he turned. "Still with us?" he said. "When I found you in the gutter, you looked as though you had been done in for good." He paused and then exploded: "Nerts. What a set-up! The cops won't even touch it!"

My mouth was dry, and there was a weight on top of my head, where I'd been cracked, that seemed a truckload. I said, "I'm not so sure," and reached for the phone. Sergeant Connor told me cheerily that everything was under control.

"Then why the hell don't you raid that place?" I told him.

The sergeant answered, his cheer consider-

ably shaken, "Now, me boy, we can't raid a respectable private club because of a coincidence."

"A damned peculiar coincidence!"

His voice dropped to a whisper. "We got orders—not to touch it!" When I expostulated, there was a soft click. . . .

"Barry, there's only one way." Duke's voice was weary, as though he'd been up every night for a million years. "You've got that ticket I haven't got. You're a Social Register lad. Get in touch with the Quadrangle Club, and apply for membership."

It was a ticket, all right. A ticket to hell. But maybe I'd find Bonny in hell. . . . A brisk secretarial voice at the other end of the wire told me I would be investigated, and if I furnished the customary references, my membership would be considered. . . .

Duke's article on the front page of the *Chronicle* that morning was one of those brave damfool things that only cub reporters and veteran editors have the nerve to do. He told his story simply, starting with Andy's funeral. There was Grant's suicide, and Kitty's. He stated flatly that Kitty hadn't killed herself for Grant's sake. "The popular young matron," said he, "was anything but a faithful and loving wife."

He hauled over the Quadrangle Club, briefly mentioning its history as a tony haven for the best people of the Eighties; and he posed the question, reasonably enough. "Why has the ha-cha generation of blue-bloods joined the brownstone tradition? Can it be that behind those venerable portals there is a stimulus for those jaded appetites; a pleasure so exhaustive that its ending leaves nothing but self-loathing and desire for death?"

Duke grinned at me when I looked up at him, like a small boy who has made an offensive precocious remark and expects to be told how bright he is.

I said, "Nice work, Duke. I'm glad you left your latest hunches about the Carters out of it. That was decent."

"A newspaperman is never decent. I left that out because I may not have proof."

"Proof!" I howled. "You can't prove anything. The *Chronicle*'s going to run into the biggest libel suit in history."

Duke smiled his sad, crooked smile. "Maybe. But it won't go to trial tomorrow. And by the time we get our day in court, I'm gambling we'll have proof enough to halt the whole blamed mess."

I was finishing the second cup of black coffee. "And where would you be getting it?" I said.

Duke didn't answer, just kept looking at me.

"I know," I said. "You think I'm going to get it for you. God, I hope I can! I hope I can find Bonny—" I didn't dodge his whimsical blow to the chin. It was his way of bucking me up.

"You'll find her," he assured me. "If there's anyone who can crack the story, it's you. If you want an expense account on the *Chronicle* . . ."

I said, "No. I'm on my own."

"Got to be going," said Duke. "Think it over, Barry. A big paper has resources. Files of information, contacts . . . it can send you inside places you couldn't crack yourself. It's a help."

I agreed with him. It was the brightest ray of light I'd seen yet. Duke gave me a press card, informing the police that Barry Amsterdam was working for the *New York Chronicle*, and left me to my own devices.

CHAPTER THREE

DOOM CRACKS ITS WHIP

Judge Rainey told me that afternoon in his office, "If I hadn't known your uncle, Barry, I'd throw you out! What do you mean, I'm blocking a police investigation! Why would I do a thing like that? Why, I don't even belong to the damned club!"

"But," I insisted, "you're the only political force in town that could. The others don't come from your kind of family."

The Judge, a big man with a magnificent silver head, forgot that he'd known my uncle. He threw me out. . . .

It seemed hopeless, hopeless. It might be three weeks before I'd pass that brownstone front myself, and in the meantime, Bonny . . . I felt dry in the throat every time I thought of Bonny. It was like the thirst of a dying man lost in the Sahara.

Something made me look up as I walked through the front lobby of the office building. Something indescribably vile . . . and familiar. An odor of the charnel-house . . .

A woman, swathed to the eyebrows in silver fox, had just passed me. I recognized her at once as Judge Rainey's young and beautiful second wife. I ran after her, and grabbed her arm. She turned, and . . .

I—I had known Thea Rainey as one of the town's huskier young glamor girls, seen her cantering an hour after dawn, heard her throaty alive laugh . . . and now I saw her with the cancer of death almost victorious in her wasted frame!

"Barry Amsterdam," she said, and then she laughed—but what a laugh! The ghost of her youth, chuckling in hell . . . and, God help her, she stank. Under the heaviness of her perfume, there was a rank odor of decaying flesh. . . .

I had dropped her arm, but she retrieved mine. I shuddered at the touch, and she knew it, and licked her lips.

"They'll get you too," she whispered. "You're a nice lad, Barry. Once—you didn't know it, did you?—I fancied I loved you. They'll bring you to me in death, Barry . . . they'll let me kiss you. . . ."

I went back to Thea's apartment with her. It took every ounce of stomach I had, but I went. She promised she'd talk, if we were alone . . . she even seemed to know where Bonny was. . . .

Her butler served us sandwiches and highballs. She touched neither. When I had pleaded with her for agonizing minutes, she rose. Her chalky face assumed an expression of terrible despair.

"You want to know what they do to us?" she whispered, tensely, crazily. "I'll show you!" Before I could stop her, she had zipped her dress open from throat to hem. She stepped out of it. I cried, "Stop!" but she didn't stop. She stepped out of her slip, and I saw the white diaphragm below her brassiere, gleaming un-cleanly . . . she tore off the brassiere, and the silk shorts. In hideous nudity, she advanced one step toward me. Her breasts, her hips, seemed half-decomposed . . . and the smell! It was like the fumes that might arise from a city's garbage lying for hours under an August sun. . . .

And then I was engulfed in a putrefac-tion that had been the beauty of Thea Rainey. Her arm, white as the underside of a fish belly, twined about my neck, she pressed her naked body to me, she darted her face close to mine.

I felt the kiss of loathsome death, and when I would have withdrawn, she pressed closer. Then—I've read about lips melting in an em-brace, but I'll never read it again without being sick. For that was exactly what Thea's lips did. They squashed, with the same hideous *plosh* of rotten fruit that had marked the disintegration of Kitty's hand. . . .

I didn't turn to look. I ran. My mouth felt ghoulishly filthy, as though I were a cannibal epicure. I ran right to the *Chronicle* office.

"Duke," I said, "I know why the police won't touch it. It's not Rainey. It's Rainey's wife. . . ."

And then I was suddenly very sick.

THEA RAINEY'S FUNERAL was held next day at St. Anne's. Society was there; but it was a weirdly changed society from the polite group that had met two days before at Andy Carter's funeral. In fifty hours, the upper crust of Manhattan had been transformed to a cower-ing half-idiocy . . . no one mentioned the haste of the burial. We were thinking of other things. Each of us seemed menaced by some unholy de-struction. We did not speak to each other.

More, by two score, were the faces that wore an expression of hopeless despair. And we knew, we who had escaped so far, that they were the doomed . . . they told us nothing, though they had been our friends, and our loved ones.

There was a great wreath of flowers from the Quadrangle Club. But its roses and lilies were not enough to combat the mingled odor of strong perfumes that rose from those who had come to honor the dead. Perfumes that covered a vague but unmistakeable odor of decay. Thea Rainey had been embalmed cleverly; they had drained her blood and replaced the broken fea-tures with wax. But for her friends, the dying, no such service had been rendered.

I didn't go to the burial. I needed fresh air. I walked aimlessly about town that forenoon. I wasn't quite sane, I think. A dozen times, I fol-lowed some woman simply because she had red hair . . . but she was never Bonny.

Bonny! Had the thing touched her yet, the filthy disease that a doctor, in Thea's case, had despairingly named heart disease? Why hadn't she been at the funeral? Was she stolen, or killed?

I saw the last cars of Thea's cortège winding southward on Park. Dully I watched them; they were bound for a cemetery in Brooklyn.

But the last—was that a glimpse of tawny hair I caught behind the curtained window— made a U-turn, and headed north. North! They had buried Andy in Westchester . . . and Bonny had said she was going to—her brother!

I taxied to my garage, took my car, and stamped on the accelerator. It wasn't clever, half-blinded with dread as I was; for by the time I'd located Sergeant Connor, and had him ex-plain me out of traffic court in Yonkers, it was three-thirty. I was at Hawthorne by five . . . and when I came to the cemetery night was on me. Night without a moon . . .

The gates were locked, so I clambered over the wall. In the darkness the tombstones were a glimmering reproach to one who would discover their secrets. I crept along stealthily to Andy's grave. Once I saw a swinging lantern, and I ducked behind a monument, hugging the dank cold earth that was nourished on death.

But there were no lights where we had left Andy. *There was a pile of fresh earth where his stone had been, and the grave-pit yawned wide open*. With the cold sweat pouring down my face, I peered from behind the dirt-pile. . . .

Two hooded figures stood on either side of the unlidded coffin. And lying within, her pale hands crossed over the embalming sheet, her violet eyes alive with mad fear, was Bonny!

They were lifting the lid, ready to put it into place. . . . I jumped toward the nearest figure, caught him in a frantic half-Nelson, and pushed. Like a frightened ghost, the other figure leapt away.

"Barry, you don't know what you're doing!" shrieked Bonny. I didn't listen. I kept pushing. Beneath the black robe, I felt that familiar puttiness.

Bonny stood up in the coffin, her hair falling over her shoulders, pure as a dream of heaven in her white dead-dress. "Barry, let me die. . . . This isn't a hard death! It's over so soon . . . not like the others. . . . Let me save you, Barry!"

DIMLY, THROUGH THE wild hate that throbbed in my brain, I knew that she was giving her life for my salvation. I didn't want that, God, no! I pushed, a little harder . . . and the brain of the hooded thing splashed out of the rotted skull. I dropped the body. It fell with a soft whoosh against the coffin. When I snatched off the hood, I saw no face, only battered brain and bone. . . .

Bonny screamed. I turned, and saw the other hooded thing reaching down on me with the butt end of a revolver. No time to duck . . . I took it.

Later, I would remember, as though in a dream, that a black devil had carried Bonny away. But it would be no dream, because when I awoke, just before dawn, I was to find myself lying, cold and aching, across an open coffin in an open grave.

When I got back to town that morning, Suki handed me a single thing that had come by mail. It was a neat little invitation, black on white, asking me to attend my initiation at the Quadrangle Club that night, with the polite reminder, "Formal," in a lower left-hand corner. I looked at it till the letters danced—and fell into a drugged sleep of nervous exhaustion.

I awoke toward evening. Suki had laid out my soup and fish. I felt fresher, freer to think for the first time in days. That card . . . they'd rushed it, I thought . . . and I wondered if there were not some connection between last night's episode at the grave, and this morning's invitation. Either last night I had blundered on too much, or else . . . and another thought made me pause . . . or else the whole thing had been deliberate, that glimpse I'd caught of Bonny, luring me to witness a witless scene in a graveyard.

Too many horrors had forced themselves on my awareness in the immediate past. As I dressed, I thought how incredible it should be that I was going to the Quadrangle Club to unearth the grisliest of imaginable horrors . . . the Quadrangle Club, that had been for fifty years a guarded haven of wealth and prestige. It was almost insane, but then, my world had been insane for days.

Even as I drove over, the thought persisted that I was going on a fool's errand. I wondered why . . . somewhere at the back of my head a gap persisted, something I should have known, that eluded my dulled senses.

I pulled myself together, and went through the brownstone portals.

Old-generation tone. Cut-glass chandeliers, and the gentlemen taking their port in the card room. That was the Quadrangle Club. I recognized most of the members of my own set, the moderns and their would-be modern mammas and papas.

But we were stiff and strange with each other. Incense burned almost overpoweringly everywhere, but it was not enough to hide that other smell. . . . Half the faces were chalky and tragic, the other half like polite masks over real terror. Nowhere did I see Bonny.

"So you've joined too, Barry," Mona Wells said to me. She was a charming kid, lithe and dark and vibrant, recently married to a friend of mine, Martin Wells. But here, for a reason I could not fathom, her brown eyes were pools of sorrow.

I said, "Where's Mart? Haven't seen him around for a while."

The wine-glass in her fingers cracked at the stem. Her eyes grew mad. "Martin's been ill," she whispered. Then, "He shot himself at seven this evening. I left him lying in his blood."

"My God, Mona! What are you doing at—a party?"

"Party!" Her voice was the voice of an animal being tortured. "It was my invitation to join. . . ."

When I tried to follow her, she lost herself among the guests.

IT WAS ALL I could do to keep from running berserk among the guests, shaking them like rats to get the information I wanted. They were all people in whose families there had been recent tragedy—like Mona. Had Martin told her before he died? Was that why he died? And where was Bonny? Did she know . . . too much, too?

Music came from the dim hallway, and in the glittering drawing-room, guests were dancing. What a dance that was! Like the slow waltz of decaying corpses, who had entered hell in evening dress!

I stood and watched vainly among them for a girl with tawny hair. I felt a light tap on my shoulder, and there stood the portly butler, with Mona Wells, white and shaken, at his side.

"Mr. Amsterdam, if you please, I've received word that the initiation is to begin. Won't you come upstairs for your interview?"

We followed him up the winding old-fashioned staircase, Mona still refusing to look at me. At the end of a corridor, the butler swung open a door, and deferentially waited for me to enter. "In here, sir . . ." I paused, for the room was in darkness. Then I shrugged my shoulders. Nothing much was left to lose. . . . I passed the obsequious figure and went into darkness.

I heard the click of a lock behind me, and footsteps fading down the hall.

I found a wall by groping, and leaned against it. A voice, muffled as though it came through a filtered microphone, said, "That will do nicely, Barry Amsterdam. You may stand as you are."

I answered, "Who the hell are you?" My voice sounded grim, as though it were echoing from wall to wall of that small room, as though the room were a catacomb. . . .

"I am Justice, if you like a name." The voice, I told myself, in spite of the stiffness of those short hairs at my nape, must be human. Again that pestering gap! It was a joke. . . . I said as much.

"This is not a joke," the voice went on. "Justice has long been due to you and your kind— parasites, despoilers, fatteners on the land! There is in each of your lives, or in the lives of those you pretend to love, some crime too ugly for public knowledge. But Justice knows!"

Of course it was a human voice! Damnably human! That pestering thought at the back of my head was beginning to click . . . in a moment, I'd have my finger on it. I said, "What is this? Blackmail?"

As though it had not heard me, the muffled voice continued, "And you, Barry Amsterdam . . . we have waited for you a long, long time! Too long you have escaped the fate you merit, but you will not escape now."

The thing had clicked. *I knew the name of the man behind that voice.* It had been so evident, all along, that I'd missed it! Exultantly I realized that at last I was one step ahead of him, because I knew who he was, and he didn't know I knew it. I couldn't blurt it out now. It might have been my death sentence.

To keep my voice steady, I yelled, "So what?"

"You will mail to the Quadrangle Club in the morning a check for one hundred thousand dollars. You will shun the society of friends. You will do our bidding, come at our call, and respond out of your generosity to any further call for funds."

"The hell I will!"

"You will do these things, or else the death that rots before it kills will come to Bonny Carter."

I shouted, "You dirty perverted murderer!" I wanted to hit something, hard, but you can't hit at a voice.

"We are glad to accommodate with proof," the voice slurred on. Then I *had* to grab at the wall, because the floor started tilting under me, like one of those crazy things at Coney Island. I felt myself slipping, gently, to a lower level in the building where there was light.

CHAPTER FOUR

THE SCENT OF BURNING FLESH

I blinked a little. I was in a sort of cage, constructed by driving iron bars in a semicircle from floor to ceiling of a stone-walled room. The back wall of the cage was the section of the floor that had just swung down. At a height of ten feet there was a gap in the rails, through which I had fallen; and a sort of gate in front of me, latched on the outside.

The room beyond my cage was large and rectangular and had a platform extending across the far end. A big machine, something like a gigantic searchlight, occupied the left side of it. Wide cracks of light in the long wall to my left indicated a shut door.

There was a chair just in front of the camera-thing, a wooden chair, with leather straps about the legs and back. I peered, trying to find a sign of life in the purplish dimness.

Far to the left, in the shadows, two figures gleamed, luminously white. I cried out in sheer horror at the sight of them . . . they were women, nude, bound upright to stone pillars.

One of them was Bonny. Bands of adhesive covered her mouth.

Had I found her—too late? I went crazy mad, tried to force the steel bars that kept me from her, shouted insane challenges to the thing that had done this to us.

Two black-robed figures stepped from behind the machine. One of them stood guard over the helpless women; it was hooded, and I recognized it as the thing that had spirited Bonny out of her brother's coffin, that had taunted me a few minutes ago in the dark room.

I was cold with despair, because I *knew* who he was. I *knew*, but my knowledge had come too late—I could do nothing. And Bonny in deadly danger . . .

The other figure was not hooded—it was the club's butler! He descended from the platform and walked toward me, coming to a stop just out of reach of my arms. His robe fell open a little and I caught a glimpse of the heavy automatic that nestled in its holster under his shoulder. God! I thought. If I could only get my hands on that gun for thirty seconds!

The butler said, "Sir, the master wishes you to witness an exhibition. He trusts it will bring you around to his way of thinking." He retreated, and while my heart went berserk in my throat, I saw him unbind one of the struggling nude figures, and strap her to the plain wooden chair.

Not Bonny, thank God! The girl facing that evil-looking machine was Mona Wells. Like a demon lecturer explaining his lantern slides, the butler continued suavely, "Mrs. Wells has also refused to accede to our wishes. She has one more chance before we accomplish her end—a little prematurely, to be sure."

Mona shrieked in horror, "I won't do it! You can't make me, you murdering fiends! You got Martin, didn't you? Well, you can send me after him!"

As though it were a step in a routine, the butler opened that door on the left wall . . . light flooded the chamber. There, behind a network of iron bars, like the door to a prison, their foul white faces mad with hatred of the fiend who had destroyed them, stood the legion of the cursed—the rotting! Beyond them, I saw the sad but still-human faces of the others.

"Mrs. Wells," said the butler, "will do nicely for your education, Mr. Amsterdam." He stepped behind the machine. I heard a whirring sound, and there was a sudden, blinding flash of light accompanied by the sickening smell of burnt flesh. Mona shrieked again. God, I'll hear those shrieks in a dream the night before I die!

It had happened! That was all it took; a whirring sound, a flash of light, and you—started to rot! I joined her shrieks. Over and over again I screamed at the hooded monster and the inhuman butler: "You damned swine! You damned swine!"

Mona's voice died to a whine, and became silent. She slumped in her bonds. The butler undid her straps and led her back to the pillar and tied her up again. Her head slumped forward on her chest—she was unconscious. I hoped that she was dead.

The butler glanced at her once and then came over and stood near my cage—a little nearer than before. I could have almost reached out and touched him. A sudden inspiration flashed through my mind. It was a slim and desperate chance . . . but it *might* work! If only I could get him one step closer . . .

The rotting corpses who once were my friends were silent now behind their bars—silent with hopeless terror and despair.

THE HOODED FIGURE turned toward me. An unholy chuckle escaped from under the hood. "Do you see your friends now, Barry Amsterdam? Do you see them as they are? As you will be soon? Their bodies are rotting now even as their souls rotted long ago. It is Justice and they are afraid of Justice. They are afraid of me! Those who have not yet felt the power of my—for want of a better name, shall we call it Radium X-Ray?—treatment, know that their time to face it will surely come.

"They don't know me, Barry Amsterdam, these sons and daughters of the four hundred. I am only one of the forty million. But they are afraid of me! They know that they are safe only so long as they obey me. They cannot escape, for no matter where they go, I can follow them—because they don't know who I am. I can sit beside them on the train or drink with them at their houses, and they will not know that Justice has overtaken them. They will never know—until it is too late and their souls are roasting in hell!"

He stopped suddenly and gestured toward Bonny. "Perhaps another demonstration will convince you, Barry Amsterdam, that it is better to submit to me. She no longer has any money, so she can no longer obey my commands. It is time for her to meet the death her rotten soul deserves."

It had come! I could wait no longer. The single card I held must be played—a slim, last, desperate hope. . . .

I shouted:

"No one else may know you now . . . but I know you—Duke Livingstone!"

The hooded figure uttered a roar of rage and sprang toward his fiendish machine. The butler, his face white with sudden fear, took an involuntary step toward me—started to draw his pistol.

This was what I had hoped for! At the same moment I had shouted Duke Livingstone's name, I thrust my arms through the bars of my cage. My hands clasped behind the butler's neck and with the strength of a madman, I jerked his head toward me. There was the sodden crunch of flesh and bone meeting hard iron and the butler's form went slack in my arms.

Duke Livingstone had halted momentarily in astonishment at my sudden action, and that hesitation was all I needed. Holding the unconscious butler against the bars with one arm, my other hand darted to his half-drawn automatic. I fired two quick shots.

Duke spun heavily, reeled back a half-dozen paces, and slumped to the floor. I fired three more shots into his twitching body. It jerked convulsively and then was still. . . .

As the echoes of the shots died away there was absolute silence for a few seconds. I heard a high-pitched voice scream. "The butler has the keys!" and then all hell broke loose. Shrieking imprecations and crying for me to free them so that they might tear their former tormentors to pieces, the mob of living corpses beat frantically at the iron bars of their prison, while the yet untainted were almost hysterical with joy.

I found the keys, but before freeing the others I released Bonny and held my coat about her head as we hurried from that hellish room so that she could not see the sickening and ghoulish fate of Duke Livingstone and the butler. . . .

"I SUPPOSE IT drove him crazy," I explained to the reduced group of friends who had survived. "He was always saying that it got him, knowing the things he knew about people."

"He was a devil!" moaned Jane Anders, Grant's sister. "He got Judge Rainey's wife, to keep the police off us. He played husband against wife, mother against child. He was a ghoul!"

"We mustn't talk about it," Bonny whispered. "Barry, take me home."

She nestled against me in the car. "Barry, I tried to save you. That's why, yesterday, when I caught a glimpse of you from the car, I showed myself, hoping you'd follow me. If you couldn't rescue me at once, I thought at least you'd see that the mess was far too loathsome for you to bother with."

My arm wound tighter about her. "You thought that would keep me away! Bonny, didn't you know I loved you?" I thought for a moment of the inanity of women, and of the courage of this one. "But Bonny," I said, "why did you leave my apartment the night I left you with Suki?"

She shuddered slightly. "Duke Livingstone called and told me Andy was alive, that he'd seen him. He seemed to think I knew more about it than he did, so I didn't think anything was wrong, till I found myself his prisoner. He kept me gagged most of the time. . . ."

I swore softly at the dead. . . . "If I'd only realized what I should have realized a little earlier! I might at least have saved poor Mona Wells.

It kept bothering me, what the tie-up was between the Quadrangle Club and the horrors. I was helpless before it dawned on me that Duke was the tie-up. He had to be the man. It was he who'd suggested it to me in the first place. If it hadn't been for Duke, there just wouldn't have been a tie-up—either in my mind or in the newspapers. I wonder why he didn't try to keep it a secret?"

"Duke wanted his scheme to have publicity, because, I imagine, he was about ready to close operations in New York. With Thea Rainey dead, he couldn't stave off an investigation much longer. And when the investigation started, he'd be out from under. Then he meant to give the horror as much front page space as possible, so that when he started operations elsewhere under the same disguise, people would be afraid of him.

"He meant to use you, Barry, either as a victim or an ally. If you'd been frightened off at the graveyard—if you hadn't come to the Club—you'd have been his chief character witness at an investigation. But you came, Barry—and you saved all of us who were left to save."

I had been nodding as she explained, and suddenly I felt that my head wasn't going to nod any more at my volition. I was really faint. I pulled up to a curb, explained, and let Bonny take the wheel.

"Dearest, what's the matter?" she asked anxiously.

I said, "That darned clout on the head I took last night. Wonder if I should have it X-rayed."

"No!" She almost shrieked at me. "Don't—even—think of that word again!"

I HAD IT X-rayed, nevertheless, but there wasn't anything wrong except a bump. Bonny doesn't know about that. Our home life is about as harmonious as things human can be, but—I hope and pray neither of us needs an X-ray again! Because I still remember the look in Bonny's violet eyes, when I mentioned the word. . . .

WHERE THERE'S A WILL

RICHARD AND CHRISTIAN MATHESON

RICHARD (BURTON) MATHESON (1926–) was born in Allendale, New Jersey, then moved to Brooklyn, New York. He joined the army in World War II, serving in the infantry. He received a B.A. in journalism from the University of Missouri and then moved to California, where he became a prolific writer of short stories, novels, and screenplays.

His work has frequently served as the basis for television and theatrically released films, including *Duel* (1971), Steven Spielberg's first film, a made-for-TV movie about a sadistic trucker who terrorizes an innocent driver; *The Night Stalker* (1972), which won an Edgar Award for Best Teleplay; and episodes of numerous series, including *The Alfred Hitchcock Hour, Night Gallery,* and some of *The Twilight Zone*'s most memorable programs. Feature films based on his work include his own screenplay for *The Shrinking Man* (1956, filmed as *The Incredible Shrinking Man* in 1957), *Hell House* (1971, filmed as *The Legend of Hell House* in 1973), and, most famously, *I Am Legend* (1954, filmed as *The Last Man on Earth* in 1964, *The Omega Man* in 1971, *I Am Legend* in 2007, and which inspired George A. Romero's *Night of the Living Dead* in 1968).

His son, (Richard) Christian Matheson (1953–), has become one of the stars of the horror genre, producing the novel *Created By* (1993), the short-story collections *Scars and Other Distinguishing Marks* (1987) and *Dystopia* (2000), and a short-story and teleplay collaboration with his father, *Pride* (2002). Among his numerous credits for television series are as story editor for episodes of *Quincy, M.E.* and *The A-Team,* and as writer of scores of episodes for such series as *Amazing Stories, The A-Team, Knight Rider, The Incredible Hulk,* and *Three's Company.*

"Where There's a Will" was originally published in *Dark Forces: New Stories of Suspense and Supernatural Horror,* edited by Kirby McCauley (New York: Viking, 1980).

RICHARD AND CHRISTIAN MATHESON

WHERE THERE'S A WILL

HE AWOKE.

It was dark and cold. Silent.

I'm thirsty, he thought. He yawned and sat up; fell back with a cry of pain. He'd hit his head on something. He rubbed at the pulsing tissue of his brow, feeling the ache spread back to his hairline.

Slowly, he began to sit up again but hit his head once more. He was jammed between the mattress and something overhead. He raised his hands to feel it. It was soft and pliable, its texture yielding beneath the push of his fingers. He felt along its surface. It extended as far as he could reach. He swallowed anxiously and shivered.

What in God's name was it?

He began to roll to his left and stopped with a gasp. The surface was blocking him there, as well. He reached to his right and his heart beat faster. It was on the other side, as well. He was surrounded on four sides. His heart compressed like a smashed soft-drink can, the blood spurting a hundred times faster.

Within seconds, he sensed that he was dressed. He felt trousers, a coat, a shirt and tie, a belt. There were shoes on his feet.

He slid his right hand to his trouser pocket and reached in. He palmed a cold, metal square and pulled his hand from the pocket, bringing it to his face. Fingers trembling, he hinged the top open and spun the wheel with his thumb. A few sparks glinted but no flame. Another turn and it lit.

He looked down at the orange cast of his body and shivered again. In the light of the flame, he could see all around himself.

He wanted to scream at what he saw.

He was in a casket.

He dropped the lighter and the flame striped the air with a yellow tracer before going out. He was in total darkness, once more. He could see nothing. All he heard was his terrified breathing as it lurched forward, jumping from his throat.

How long had he been here? Minutes? Hours? Days?

His hopes lunged at the possibility of a nightmare; that he was only dreaming, his sleeping mind caught in some kind of twisted vision. But he knew it wasn't so. He knew, horribly enough, exactly what had happened.

They had put him in the one place he was terrified of. The one place he had made the fatal mistake of speaking about to them. They couldn't have selected a better torture. Not if they'd thought about it for a hundred years.

God, did they loathe him that much? To do *this* to him?

He started shaking helplessly, then caught himself. He wouldn't let them do it. Take his life and his business all at once? No, goddamn them, *no!*

He searched hurriedly for the lighter. That was their mistake, he thought. Stupid bastards. They'd probably thought it was a final, fitting irony: A gold-engraved thank you for making the corporation what it was. On the lighter were the words:

TO CHARLIE

WHERE THERE'S A WILL . . .

"Right," he muttered. He'd beat the lousy sons of bitches. They weren't going to murder him and steal the business he owned and built. There *was* a will.

His.

He closed his fingers around the lighter and, holding it with a white-knuckled fist, lifted it above the heaving of his chest. The wheel ground against the flint as he spun it back with his thumb. The flame caught and he quieted his breathing as he surveyed what space he had in the coffin.

Only inches on all four sides.

How much air could there be in so small a space, he wondered? He clicked off the lighter. Don't burn it up, he told himself. Work in the dark.

Immediately, his hands shot up and he tried to push the lid up. He pressed as hard as he could, his forearms straining. The lid remained fixed. He closed both hands into tightly balled fists and pounded them against the lid until he was coated with perspiration, his hair moist.

He reached down to his left trouser pocket and pulled out a chain with two keys attached. They had placed those with him, too. *Stupid bastards.* Did they really think he'd be so terrified he couldn't *think?* Another amusing joke on their part. A way to lock up his life completely. He wouldn't need the keys to his car and to the office again so why not put them in the casket with him?

Wrong, he thought. He *would* use them again.

Bringing the keys above his face, he began to pick at the lining with the sharp edge of one key. He tore through the threads and began to rip apart the lining. He pulled at it with his fingers until it popped free from its fastenings. Working quickly, he pulled the downy stuffing, tugging it free and placing it at his sides. He tried not to breathe too hard. The air had to be preserved.

He flicked on the lighter and looking at the cleared area, above, knocked against it with the knuckles of his free hand. He sighed with relief. It was oak not metal. Another mistake on their part. He smiled with contempt. It was easy to see why he had always been so far ahead of them.

"Stupid bastards," he muttered, as he stared at the thick wood. Gripping the keys together firmly, he began to dig their serrated edges against the oak. The flame of the lighter shook as he watched small pieces of the lid being chewed off by the gouging of the keys. Fragment after fragment fell. The lighter kept going out and he had to spin the flint over and over, repeating each move, until his hands felt numb. Fearing that he would use up the air, he turned the lighter off again, and continued to chisel at the wood, splinters of it falling on his neck and chin.

His arm began to ache.

He was losing strength. Wood no longer coming off as steadily. He laid the keys on his chest and flicked on the lighter again. He could see only a tattered path of wood where he had dug but it was only inches long. It's not enough, he thought. It's not enough.

He slumped and took a deep breath, stopping halfway through. The air was thinning. He reached up and pounded against the lid.

"Open this thing, goddammit," he shouted, the veins in his neck rising beneath the skin. *"Open this thing and let me out!"*

I'll die if I don't do something more, he thought.

They'll win.

His face began to tighten. He had never given up before. Never. And they weren't going to win. There was no way to stop him once he made up his mind.

He'd show those bastards what willpower was.

Quickly, he took the lighter in his right hand and turned the wheel several times. The flame rose like a streamer, fluttering back and forth before his eyes. Steadying his left arm with his right, he held the flame to the casket wood and began to scorch the ripped grain.

He breathed in short, shallow breaths, smelling the butane and wood odor as it filled the casket. The lid started to speckle with tiny sparks as he ran the flame along the gouge. He held it to one spot for several moments then slid it to another spot. The wood made faint crackling sounds.

Suddenly, a flame formed on the surface of

the wood. He coughed as the burning oak began to produce grey pulpy smoke. The air in the casket continued to thin and he felt his lungs working harder. What air was available tasted like gummy smoke, as if he were lying in a horizontal smokestack. He felt as though he might faint and his body began to lose feeling.

Desperately, he struggled to remove his shirt, ripping several of the buttons off. He tore away part of the shirt and wrapped it around his right hand and wrist. A section of the lid was beginning to char and had become brittle. He slammed his swathed fist and forearm against the smoking wood and it crumbled down on him, glowing embers falling on his face and neck. His arms scrambled frantically to slap them out. Several burned his chest and palms and he cried out in pain.

Now a portion of the lid had become a glowing skeleton of wood, the heat radiating downward at his face. He squirmed away from it, turning his head to avoid the falling pieces of wood. The casket was filled with smoke and he could breathe only the choking, burning smell of it. He coughed, his throat hot and raw. Fine-powder ash filled his mouth and nose as he pounded at the lid with his wrapped fist. Come on, he thought. Come on.

"Come on!" he screamed.

The section of lid gave suddenly and fell around him. He slapped at his face, neck and chest but the hot particles sizzled on his skin and he had to bear the pain as he tried to smother them.

The embers began to darken, one by one and now he smelled something new and strange. He searched for the lighter at his side, found it, and flicked it on.

He shuddered at what he saw.

Moist, root-laden soil packed firmly overhead.

Reaching up, he ran his fingers across it. In the flickering light, he saw burrowing insects and the whiteness of earthworms, dangling inches from his face. He drew down as far as he could, pulling his face from their wriggling movements.

Unexpectedly, one of the larvae pulled free and dropped. It fell to his face and its jelly-like casing stuck to his upper lip. His mind erupted with revulsion and he thrust both hands upward, digging at the soil. He shook his head wildly as the larva were thrown off. He continued to dig, the dirt falling in on him. It poured into his nose and he could barely breathe. It stuck to his lips and slipped into his mouth. He closed his eyes tightly but could feel it clumping on the lids. He held his breath as he pistoned his hands upward and forward like a maniacal digging machine. He eased his body up, a little at a time, letting the dirt collect under him. His lungs were laboring, hungry for air. He didn't dare open his eyes. His fingers became raw from digging, nails bent backward on several fingers, breaking off. He couldn't even feel the pain or the running blood but knew the dirt was being stained by its flow. The pain in his arms and lungs grew worse with each passing second until shearing agony filled his body. He continued to press himself upward, pulling his feet and knees closer to his chest. He began to wrestle himself into a kind of spasmed crouch, hands above his head, upper arms gathered around his face. He clawed fiercely at the dirt which gave way with each shoveling gouge of his fingers. Keep going, he told himself. *Keep going.* He refused to lose control. Refused to stop and die in the earth. He bit down hard, his teeth nearly breaking from the tension of his jaws. *Keep going,* he thought. *Keep going!* He pushed up harder and harder, dirt cascading over his body, gathering in his hair and on his shoulders. Filth surrounded him. His lungs felt ready to burst. It seemed like minutes since he'd taken a breath. He wanted to scream from his need for air but couldn't. His fingernails began to sting and throb, exposed cuticles and nerves rubbing against the granules of dirt. His mouth opened in pain and was filled with dirt, covering his tongue and gathering in his throat. His gag reflex jumped and he began retching, vomit and dirt mixing as it exploded from his mouth. His head began to empty of life as he felt himself breathing in more dirt, dying of asphyxiation. The clogging dirt began to fill his air passages, the beat of his heart doubled. *I'm losing!* he thought in anguish.

Suddenly, one finger thrust up through the crust of earth. Unthinkingly, he moved his hand like a trowel and drove it through to the surface. Now, his arms went crazy, pulling and punching at the dirt until an opening expanded. He kept thrashing at the opening, his entire system glutted with dirt. His chest felt as if it would tear down the middle.

Then his arms were poking themselves out of the grave and within several seconds he had managed to pull his upper body from the ground. He kept pulling, hooking his shredded fingers into the earth and sliding his legs from the hole. They yanked out and he lay on the ground completely, trying to fill his lungs with gulps of air. But no air could get through the dirt which had collected in his windpipe and mouth. He writhed on the ground, turning on his back and side until he'd finally raised himself to a forward kneel and began hacking phlegm-covered mud from his air passages. Black saliva ran down his chin as he continued to throw up violently, dirt falling from his mouth to the ground. When most of it was out he began to gasp, as oxygen rushed into his body, cool air filling his body with life.

I've *won*, he thought. I've beaten the bastards, *beaten* them! He began to laugh in victorious rage until his eyes pried open and he looked around, rubbing at his blood-covered lids. He heard the sound of traffic, and blinding lights glared at him. They crisscrossed on his face, rushing at him from left and right. He winced, struck dumb by their glare, then realized where he was.

The cemetery by the highway.

Cars and trucks roared back and forth, tires humming. He breathed a sigh at being near life again; near movement and people. A grunting smile raised his lips.

Looking to his right, he saw a gas-station sign high on a metal pole several hundred yards up the highway.

Struggling to his feet, he ran.

As he did, he made a plan. He would go to the station, wash up in the rest room, then borrow a dime and call for a limo from the company to come and get him. No. Better a cab. That way he could fool those sons of bitches. Catch them by surprise. They undoubtedly assumed he was long gone by now. Well, he had beat them. He knew it as he picked up the pace of his run. Nobody could stop you when you really wanted something, he told himself, glancing back in the direction of the grave he had just escaped.

He ran into the station from the back and made his way to the bathroom. He didn't want anyone to see his dirtied, bloodied state.

There was a pay phone in the bathroom and he locked the door before plowing into his pocket for change. He found two pennies and a quarter and deposited the silver coin. They'd even provided him with money, he thought; the stupid bastards.

He dialed his wife.

She answered and screamed when he told her what had happened. She screamed and screamed. What a hideous joke, she said. Whoever was doing this was making a hideous joke. She hung up before he could stop her. He dropped the phone and turned to face the bathroom mirror.

He couldn't even scream. He could only stare in silence.

Staring back at him was a face that was missing sections of flesh. Its skin was grey, and withered yellow bone showed through.

Then he remembered what else his wife had said and began to weep. His shock began to turn to hopeless fatalism.

It had been over seven months, she'd said.

Seven months.

He looked at himself in the mirror again, and realized there was nowhere he could go.

And, somehow all he could think about was the engraving on his lighter.

THE DEAD

MICHAEL SWANWICK

THE POWERFUL PROSE of the fantasy and science fiction by Michael Swanwick (1950–) has earned the Philadelphia-based author numerous prizes and accolades. After his first two books, *In the Drift* (1985), a speculation about the results of a greater Three Mile Island meltdown, and *Vacuum Flowers* (1987), in which people from Earth tour an inhabited solar system, his next five novels have all been honored. *Stations of the Tide* (1991), in which a planet of magicians and conjurers is threatened both by tidal waves (which recur every two centuries) and an evil genius who wants to control them, won the Nebula and was nominated for John W. Campbell and Arthur C. Clarke awards; *The Iron Dragon's Daughter* (1993), a fantasy set in a world in which the laws of magic and technology coexist, was nominated for Arthur C. Clarke, *Locus,* and World Fantasy awards; *Jack Faust* (1997), a retelling of Goethe's Faust legend in which Jack Faust is given the gift of technology, was nominated for British Science Fiction Association, Hugo, and *Locus* awards; *Bones of the Earth* (2002), which features time travel and the return of dinosaurs to Earth, was nominated for Nebula, Hugo, *Locus,* and John W. Campbell awards; and *The Dragons of Babel* (2008), set in the same milieu as *The Iron Dragon's Daughter,* was a *Locus* nominee. His short stories have won five Hugos ("The Very Pulse of the Machine," 1998; "Scherzo with Tyrannosaur," 1999; "The Dog Said Bow-Wow," 2001; "Slow Life," 2002; and "Legions in Time," 2003) as well as two Nebula nominations.

"The Dead" was originally published in *Starlight 1*, edited by Patrick Nielsen Hayden (New York: Tor, 1996).

MICHAEL SWANWICK

THE DEAD

THREE BOY ZOMBIES in matching red jackets bussed our table, bringing water, lighting candles, brushing away the crumbs between courses. Their eyes were dark, attentive, lifeless; their hands and faces so white as to be faintly luminous in the hushed light. I thought it in bad taste, but "This is Manhattan," Courtney said. "A certain studied offensiveness is fashionable here."

The blond brought menus and waited for our order.

We both ordered pheasant. "An excellent choice," the boy said in a clear, emotionless voice. He went away and came back a minute later with the freshly strangled birds, holding them up for our approval. He couldn't have been more than eleven when he died and his skin was of that sort connoisseurs call "milk glass," smooth, without blemish, and all but translucent. He must have cost a fortune.

As the boy was turning away, I impulsively touched his shoulder. He turned back. "What's your name, son?" I asked.

"Timothy." He might have been telling me the *spécialité de maison*. The boy waited a breath to see if more was expected of him, then left.

Courtney gazed after him. "How lovely he would look," she murmured, "nude. Standing in the moonlight by a cliff. Definitely a cliff. Perhaps the very one where he met his death."

"He wouldn't look very lovely if he'd fallen off a cliff."

"Oh, don't be unpleasant."

The wine steward brought our bottle. "Château La Tour '17." I raised an eyebrow. The steward had the sort of old and complex face that Rembrandt would have enjoyed painting. He poured with pulseless ease and then dissolved into the gloom. "Good lord, Courtney, you *seduced* me on cheaper."

She flushed, not happily. Courtney had a better career going than I. She outpowered me. We both knew who was smarter, better connected, more likely to end up in a corner office with the historically significant antique desk. The only edge I had was that I was a male in a seller's market. It was enough.

"This is a business dinner, Donald," she said, "nothing more."

I favored her with an expression of polite disbelief I knew from experience she'd find infuriating. And, digging into my pheasant, murmured, "Of course." We didn't say much of consequence until dessert, when I finally asked, "So what's Loeb-Soffner up to these days?"

"Structuring a corporate expansion. Jim's putting together the financial side of the package, and I'm doing personnel. You're being headhunted, Donald." She favored me with that feral little flash of teeth she made when she saw something she wanted. Courtney wasn't a beautiful woman, far from it. But there was that fierceness to her, that sense of something primal being held under tight and precarious control that made her hot as hot to me. "You're talented, you're thuggish, and you're not too tightly

568

nailed to your present position. Those are all qualities we're looking for."

She dumped her purse on the table, took out a single folded sheet of paper. "These are the terms I'm offering." She placed it by my plate, attacked her torte with gusto.

I unfolded the paper. "This is a lateral transfer."

"Unlimited opportunity for advancement," she said with her mouth full, "if you've got the stuff."

"Mmm." I did a line-by-line of the benefits, all comparable to what I was getting now. My current salary to the dollar—Ms. Soffner was showing off. And the stock options. "This can't be right. Not for a lateral."

There was that grin again, like a glimpse of shark in murky waters. "I knew you'd like it. We're going over the top with the options because we need your answer right away—tonight preferably. Tomorrow at the latest. No negotiations. We have to put the package together fast. There's going to be a shitstorm of publicity when this comes out. We want to have everything nailed down, present the fundies and bleeding hearts with a *fait accompli*."

"My God, Courtney, what kind of monster do you have hold of now?"

"The biggest one in the world. Bigger than Apple. Bigger than Home Virtual. Bigger than HIVac-IV," she said with relish. "Have you ever heard of Koestler Biological?"

I put my fork down.

"Koestler? You're peddling corpses now?"

"Please. Postanthropic biological resources." She said it lightly, with just the right touch of irony. Still, I thought I detected a certain discomfort with the nature of her client's product.

"There's no money in it." I waved a hand toward our attentive waitstaff. "These guys must be—what?—maybe two percent of the annual turnover? Zombies are luxury goods: servants, reactor cleanups, Hollywood stunt deaths, exotic services"—we both knew what I meant—"a few hundred a year, maybe, tops. There's not the demand. The revulsion factor is too great."

"There's been a technological breakthrough." Courtney leaned forward. "They can install the infrasystem and controllers and offer the product for the factory-floor cost of a new subcompact. That's way below the economic threshold for blue-collar labor.

"Look at it from the viewpoint of a typical factory owner. He's already downsized to the bone and labor costs are bleeding him dry. How can he compete in a dwindling consumer market? Now let's imagine he buys into the program." She took out her Montblanc and began scribbling figures on the tablecloth. "No benefits. No liability suits. No sick pay. No pilferage. We're talking about cutting labor costs by at least two-thirds. Minimum! That's irresistible, I don't care how big your revulsion factor is. We project we can move five hundred thousand units in the first year."

"Five hundred thousand," I said. "That's crazy. Where the hell are you going to get the raw material for—?"

"Africa."

"Oh, God, Courtney." I was struck wordless by the cynicism it took to even consider turning the sub-Saharan tragedy to a profit, by the sheer, raw evil of channeling hard currency to the pocket Hitlers who ran the camps. Courtney only smiled and gave that quick little flip of her head that meant she was accessing the time on an optic chip.

"I think you're ready," she said, "to talk with Koestler."

At her gesture, the zombie boys erected projector lamps about us, fussed with the settings, turned them on. Interference patterns moiréd, clashed, meshed. Walls of darkness erected themselves about us. Courtney took out her flat and set it up on the table. Three taps of her nailed fingers and the round and hairless face of Marvin Koestler appeared on the screen. "Ah, Courtney!" he said in a pleased voice. "You're in—New York, yes? The San Moritz. With Donald." The slightest pause with each accessed bit of information. "Did you have the antelope medallions?" When we shook our heads, he kissed his fingertips. "Magnificent! They're ever so lightly braised and then smothered in buffalo mozzarella. Nobody makes them better. I had the same dish in Florence the other day, and there was simply no comparison."

I cleared my throat. "Is that where you are? Italy?"

"Let's leave out where I am." He made a dismissive gesture, as if it were a trifle. But Courtney's face darkened. Corporate kidnapping being the growth industry it is, I'd gaffed badly. "The question is—what do you think of my offer?"

"It's . . . interesting. For a lateral."

"It's the start-up costs. We're leveraged up to our asses as it is. You'll make out better this way in the long run." He favored me with a sudden grin that went mean around the edges. Very much the financial buccaneer. Then he leaned forward, lowered his voice, maintained firm eye contact. Classic people-handling techniques. "You're not sold. You know you can trust Courtney to have checked out the finances. Still, you think: It won't work. To work, the product has to be irresistible, and it's not. It can't be."

"Yes, sir," I said. "Succinctly put."

He nodded to Courtney. "Let's sell this young man." And to me, "My stretch is downstairs."

He winked out.

KOESTLER WAS WAITING for us in the limo, a ghostly pink presence. His holo, rather, a genial if somewhat coarse-grained ghost afloat in golden light. He waved an expansive and insubstantial arm to take in the interior of the car and said, "Make yourselves at home."

The chauffeur wore combat-grade photo-multipliers. They gave him a buggish, inhuman look. I wasn't sure if he was dead or not. "Take us to Heaven," Koestler said.

The doorman stepped out into the street, looked both ways, nodded to the chauffeur. Robot guns tracked our progress down the block.

"Courtney tells me you're getting the raw materials from Africa."

"Distasteful, but necessary. To begin with.

We have to sell the idea first—no reason to make things rough on ourselves. Down the line, though, I don't see why we can't go domestic. Something along the lines of a reverse mortgage, perhaps, life insurance that pays off while you're still alive. It'd be a step towards getting the poor off our backs at last. Fuck 'em. They've been getting a goddamn free ride for too long; the least they can do is to die and provide us with servants."

I was pretty sure Koestler was joking. But I smiled and ducked my head, so I'd be covered in either case. "What's Heaven?" I asked, to move the conversation onto safer territory.

"A proving ground," Koestler said with great satisfaction, "for the future. Have you ever witnessed bare-knuckles fisticuffs?"

"No."

"Ah, now there's a sport for gentlemen! The sweet science at its sweetest. No rounds, no rules, no holds barred. It gives you the real measure of a man—not just of his strength but his character. How he handles himself, whether he keeps cool under pressure—how he stands up to pain. Security won't let me go to the clubs in person, but I've made arrangements."

HEAVEN WAS A converted movie theater in a run-down neighborhood in Queens. The chauffeur got out, disappeared briefly around the back, and returned with two zombie body-guards. It was like a conjurer's trick. "You had these guys stashed in the *trunk*?" I asked as he opened the door for us.

"It's a new world," Courtney said. "Get used to it."

The place was mobbed. Two, maybe three hundred seats, standing room only. A mixed crowd, blacks and Irish and Koreans mostly, but with a smattering of uptown customers as well. You didn't have to be poor to need the occasional taste of vicarious potency. Nobody paid us any particular notice. We'd come in just as the fighters were being presented.

"Weighing two-five-oh, in black trunks with

a red stripe," the ref was bawling, "tha gang-bang *gang*sta, tha bare-knuckle *brawla*, tha man with tha—"

Courtney and I went up a scummy set of back stairs. Bodyguard-us-bodyguard, as if we were a combat patrol out of some twentieth-century jungle war. A scrawny, potbellied old geezer with a damp cigar in his mouth unlocked the door to our box. Sticky floor, bad seats, a good view down on the ring. Gray plastic matting, billowing smoke.

Koestler was there, in a shiny new hologram shell. It reminded me of those plaster Madonnas in painted bathtubs that Catholics set out in their yards. "Your permanent box?" I asked.

"All of this is for your sake, Donald—you and a few others. We're pitting our product one-on-one against some of the local talent. By arrangement with the management. What you're going to see will settle your doubts once and for all."

"You'll like this," Courtney said. "I've been here five nights straight. Counting tonight." The bell rang, starting the fight. She leaned forward avidly, hooking her elbows on the railing.

The zombie was gray-skinned and modestly muscled, for a fighter. But it held up its hands alertly, was light on its feet, and had strangely calm and knowing eyes.

Its opponent was a real bruiser, a big black guy with classic African features twisted slightly out of true so that his mouth curled up in a kind of sneer on one side. He had gang scars on his chest and even uglier marks on his back that didn't look deliberate but like something he'd earned on the streets. His eyes burned with an intensity just this side of madness.

He came forward cautiously but not fearfully, and made a couple of quick jabs to get the measure of his opponent. They were blocked and countered.

They circled each other, looking for an opening.

For a minute or so, nothing much happened. Then the gangster feinted at the zombie's head, drawing up its guard. He drove through that opening with a slam to the zombie's nuts that made me wince.

No reaction.

The dead fighter responded with a flurry of punches, and got in a glancing blow to its opponent's cheek. They separated, engaged, circled around.

Then the big guy exploded in a combination of killer blows, connecting so solidly it seemed they would splinter every rib in the dead fighter's body. It brought the crowd to their feet, roaring their approval.

The zombie didn't even stagger.

A strange look came into the gangster's eyes, then, as the zombie counterattacked, driving him back into the ropes. I could only imagine what it must be like for a man who had always lived by his strength and his ability to absorb punishment to realize that he was facing an opponent to whom pain meant nothing. Fights were lost and won by flinches and hesitations. You won by keeping your head. You lost by getting rattled.

Despite his best blows, the zombie stayed methodical, serene, calm, relentless. That was its nature.

It must have been devastating.

The fight went on and on. It was a strange and alienating experience for me. After a while I couldn't stay focused on it. My thoughts kept slipping into a zone where I found myself studying the line of Courtney's jaw, thinking about later tonight. She liked her sex just a little bit sick. There was always a feeling, fucking her, that there was something truly repulsive that she *really* wanted to do but lacked the courage to bring up on her own.

So there was always this urge to get her to do something she didn't like. She was resistant; I never dared try more than one new thing per date. But I could always talk her into that one thing. Because when she was aroused, she got pliant. She could be talked into anything. She could be made to beg for it.

Courtney would've been amazed to learn that I was not proud of what I did with her—quite the opposite, in fact. But I was as obsessed with her as she was with whatever it was that obsessed her.

Suddenly Courtney was on her feet, yelling. The hologram showed Koestler on his feet as well. The big guy was on the ropes, being pummeled. Blood and spittle flew from his face with each blow. Then he was down; he'd never even had a chance. He must've known early on that it was hopeless, that he wasn't going to win, but he'd refused to take a fall. He had to be pounded into the ground. He went down raging, proud and uncomplaining. I had to admire that.

But he lost anyway.

That, I realized, was the message I was meant to take away from this. Not just that the product was robust. But that only those who backed it were going to win. I could see, even if the audience couldn't, that it was the end of an era. A man's body wasn't worth a damn anymore. There wasn't anything it could do that technology couldn't handle better. The number of losers in the world had just doubled, tripled, reached maximum. What the fools below were cheering for was the death of their futures.

I got up and cheered too.

IN THE STRETCH afterwards, Koestler said, "You've seen the light. You're a believer now."

"I haven't necessarily decided yet."

"Don't bullshit me," Koestler said. "I've done my homework, Mr. Nichols. Your current position is not exactly secure. Morton-Western is going down the tubes. The entire service sector is going down the tubes. Face it, the old economic order is as good as fucking gone. Of course you're going to take my offer. You don't have any other choice."

The fax outed sets of contracts. "A Certain Product," it said here and there. Corpses were never mentioned.

But when I opened my jacket to get a pen, Koestler said, "Wait. I've got a factory. Three thousand positions under me. I've got a moti-

vated workforce. They'd walk through fire to keep their jobs. Pilferage is at zero. Sick time practically the same. Give me one advantage your product has over my current workforce. Sell me on it. I'll give you thirty seconds."

I wasn't in sales and the job had been explicitly promised me already. But by reaching for the pen, I had admitted I wanted the position. And we all knew whose hand carried the whip.

"They can be catheterized," I said—"no toilet breaks."

For a long instant Koestler just stared at me blankly. Then he exploded with laughter. "By God, that's a new one! You have a great future ahead of you, Donald. Welcome aboard."

He winked out.

We drove on in silence for a while, aimless, directionless. At last Courtney leaned forward and touched the chauffeur's shoulder.

"Take me home," she said.

RIDING THROUGH MANHATTAN I suffered from a waking hallucination that we were driving through a city of corpses. Gray faces, listless motions. Everyone looked dead in the headlights and sodium vapor streetlamps. Passing by the Children's Museum I saw a mother with a stroller through the glass doors. Two small children by her side. They all three stood motionless, gazing forward at nothing. We passed by a stop-and-go where zombies stood out on the sidewalk drinking forties in paper bags. Through upper-story windows I could see the sad rainbow trace of virtuals playing to empty eyes. There were zombies in the park, zombies smoking blunts, zombies driving taxies, zombies sitting on stoops and hanging out on street corners, all of them waiting for the years to pass and the flesh to fall from their bones.

I felt like the last man alive.

COURTNEY WAS STILL wired and sweaty from the fight. The pheromones came off her in great waves as I followed her down the hall to her apartment. She stank of lust. I found myself thinking of how she got just before orgasm, so desperate, so desirable. It was different after she came, she would fall into a state of calm assurance; the same sort of calm assurance she showed in her business life, the aplomb she sought so wildly during the act itself.

And when that desperation left her, so would I. Because even I could recognize that it was her desperation that drew me to her, that made me do the things she needed me to do. In all the years I'd known her, we'd never once had breakfast together.

I wished there was some way I could deal her out of the equation. I wished that her desperation were a liquid that I could drink down to the dregs. I wished I could drop her in a wine press and squeeze her dry.

At her apartment, Courtney unlocked her door and in one complicated movement twisted through and stood facing me from the inside. "Well," she said. "All in all, a productive evening. Good night, Donald."

"Good night? Aren't you going to invite me inside?"

"No."

"What do you mean, no?" She was beginning to piss me off. A blind man could've told she was in heat from across the street. A chimpanzee could've talked his way into her pants. "What kind of idiot game are you playing now?"

"You know what no means, Donald. You're not stupid."

"No I'm not, and neither are you. We both know the score. Now let me in, goddamnit."

"Enjoy your present," she said, and closed the door.

I FOUND COURTNEY'S present back in my suite. I was still seething from her treatment of me and stalked into the room, letting the door slam behind me. So that I was standing in near-total darkness. The only light was what little seeped through the draped windows at the far end of the room. I was just reaching for the light switch when there was a motion in the darkness.

'Jackers! I thought, and all in a panic lurched for the light switch, hoping to achieve I don't know what. Credit-jackers always work in trios, one to torture the security codes out of you, one to phone the numbers out of your accounts and into a fiscal trapdoor, a third to stand guard. Was turning the lights on supposed to make them scurry for darkness, like roaches? Nevertheless, I almost tripped over my own feet in my haste to reach the switch. But of course it was nothing like what I'd feared.

It was a woman.

She stood by the window in a white silk dress that could neither compete with nor distract from her ethereal beauty, her porcelain skin. When the lights came on, she turned toward me, eyes widening, lips parting slightly. Her breasts swayed ever so slightly as she gracefully raised a bare arm to offer me a lily. "Hello, Donald," she said huskily. "I'm yours for the night." She was absolutely beautiful.

And dead, of course.

NOT TWENTY MINUTES later I was hammering on Courtney's door. She came to the door in a Pierre Cardin dressing gown and from the way she was still cinching the sash and the disarray of her hair I gathered she hadn't been expecting me.

"I'm not alone," she said.

"I didn't come here for the dubious pleasures of your fair white body." I pushed my way into the room. But couldn't help remembering that beautiful body of hers, not so exquisite as the dead whore's, and now the thoughts were inextricably mingled in my head, death and Courtney, sex and corpses, a Gordian knot I might never be able to untangle.

"You didn't like my surprise?" She was smiling openly now, amused.

"No, I fucking did not!"

I took a step toward her. I was shaking. I couldn't stop fisting and unfisting my hands.

She fell back a step. But that confident, oddly expectant look didn't leave her face. "Bruno," she said lightly. "Would you come in here?"

A motion at the periphery of vision. Bruno stepped out of the shadows of her bedroom. He was a muscular brute, pumped, ripped, and as black as the fighter I'd seen go down earlier that night. He stood behind Courtney, totally naked, with slim hips and wide shoulders and the finest skin I'd ever seen.

And dead.

I saw it all in a flash.

"Oh, for God's sake, Courtney!" I said, disgusted. "I can't believe you. That you'd actually . . . That thing's just an obedient body. There's nothing there—no passion, no connection, just . . . physical presence."

Courtney made a kind of chewing motion through her smile, weighing the implications of what she was about to say. Nastiness won.

"We have equity now," she said.

I lost it then. I stepped forward, raising a hand, and I swear to God I intended to bounce the bitch's head off the back wall. But she didn't flinch—she didn't even look afraid. She merely moved aside, saying, "In the body, Bruno. He has to look good in a business suit."

A dead fist smashed into my ribs so hard I thought for an instant my heart had stopped. Then Bruno punched me in my stomach. I doubled over, gasping. Two, three, four more blows. I was on the ground now, rolling over, helpless and weeping with rage.

"That's enough, baby. Now put out the trash."

Bruno dumped me in the hallway.

I glared up at Courtney through my tears.

She was not at all beautiful now. Not in the least. You're getting older, I wanted to tell her. But instead I heard my voice, angry and astonished, saying, "You . . . you goddamn, fucking necrophile!"

"Cultivate a taste for it," Courtney said. Oh, she was purring! I doubted she'd ever find life quite this good again. "Half a million Brunos are about to come on the market. You're going to find it a lot more difficult to pick up *living* women in not so very long."

I SENT AWAY the dead whore. Then I took a long shower that didn't really make me feel any better. Naked, I walked into my unlit suite and opened the curtains. For a long time I stared out over the glory and darkness that was Manhattan.

I was afraid, more afraid than I'd ever been in my life.

The slums below me stretched to infinity. They were a vast necropolis, a never-ending city of the dead. I thought of the millions out there who were never going to hold down a job again. I thought of how they must hate me—me and my kind—and how helpless they were before us. And yet. There were so many of them and so few of us. If they were to all rise up at once, they'd be like a tsunami, irresistible. And if there was so much as a spark of life left in them, then that was exactly what they would do.

That was one possibility. There was one other, and that was that nothing would happen. Nothing at all.

God help me, but I didn't know which one scared me more.

THE SONG OF THE SLAVES

MANLY WADE WELLMAN

MANLY WADE WELLMAN (1903–1986) was born in Kamundongo, Portuguese West Africa (now Angola), the son of a physician at a British medical outpost. His family moved to Washington, D.C., when he was a child, and he eventually graduated with a B.A. in English from what is now Wichita State University, then received a bachelor of laws degree from Columbia. He worked as a reporter for two Wichita newspapers, the *Beacon* and the *Eagle*, then moved to New York in 1939 to become the assistant director of the FPA's Folklore Project.

He began writing, mainly in the horror field, in the 1920s, and by the 1930s was selling stories to the leading pulps in the genre: *Weird Tales, Wonder Stories*, and *Astounding Stories*. He had three series running simultaneously in *Weird Tales:* Silver John, also known as John the Balladeer, the backwoods minstrel with a silver-stringed guitar; John Thunstone, the New York playboy and adventurer who was also a psychic detective; and Judge Keith Hilary Persuivant, an elderly occult detective, which he wrote under the pseudonym Gans T. Fields.

Wellman also wrote for the comic books, producing the first Captain Marvel issue for Fawcett Publishers. When DC Comics sued Fawcett for plagiarizing their Superman character, Wellman testified against Fawcett, and DC won the case after three years of litigation.

"The Song of the Slaves" was originally published in the March 1940 issue of *Weird Tales*.

MANLY WADE WELLMAN

THE SONG OF THE SLAVES

GENDER PAUSED AT the top of the
bald rise, mopped his streaming red forehead
beneath the wide hat-brim, and gazed backward
at his forty-nine captives. Naked and black, they
shuffled upward from the narrow, ancient slave
trail through the jungle. Forty-nine men, seized
by Gender's own hand and collared to a single
long chain, destined for his own plantation
across the sea . . . Gender grinned in his lean,
drooping mustache, a mirthless grin of greedy
triumph.

For years he had dreamed and planned for
this adventure, as other men dream and plan for
European tours, holy pilgrimages, or returns to
beloved birthplaces. He had told himself that
it was intensely practical and profitable. Slaves
passed through so many hands—the raider, the
caravaner, the seashore factor, the slaver captain,
the dealer in New Orleans or Havana or at home
in Charleston. Each greedy hand clutched a rich
profit, and all profits must come eventually from
the price paid by the planter. But he, Gender,
had come to Africa himself, in his own ship;
with a dozen staunch ruffians from Benguela
he had penetrated the Bihé-Bailundu country,
had sacked a village and taken these forty-nine
upstanding natives between dark and dawn. A
single neck-shackle on his long chain remained

576

empty, and he might fill even that before he came to his ship. By the Lord, he was making money this way, fairly coining it—and money was worth the making, to a Charleston planter in 1853.

So he reasoned, and so he actually believed, but the real joy to him was hidden in the darkest nook of his heart. He had conceived the raider-plan because of a nature that fed on savagery and mastery. A man less fierce and cruel might have been satisfied with hunting lions or elephants, but Gender must hunt men. As a matter of fact, the money made or saved by the journey would be little, if it was anything. The satisfaction would be tremendous. He would broaden his thick chest each day as he gazed out over his lands and saw there his slaves hoeing seashore cotton or pruning indigo; his forty-nine slaves, caught and shipped and trained by his own big, hard hands, more indicative of assured conquest than all the horned or fanged heads that ever passed through the shops of all the taxidermists.

Something hummed in his ears, like a rhythmic swarm of bees. Men were murmuring a song under their breath. It was the long string of pinch-faced slaves. Gender stared at them, and mouthed one of the curses he always kept at tongue's end.

"Silva!" he called.

The lanky Portuguese who strode free at the head of the file turned aside and stood before Gender. "*Patrao?*" he inquired respectfully, smiling teeth gleaming in his walnut face.

"What are those men singing?" demanded Gender. "I didn't think they had anything to sing about."

"A slave song, *patrao*." Silva's tapering hand, with the silver bracelet at its wrist, made a graceful gesture of dismissal. "It is nothing. One of the things that natives make up and sing as they go."

Gender struck his boot with his coiled whip of hippopotamus hide. The afternoon sun, sliding down toward the shaggy jungle-tops, kindled harsh pale lights in his narrow blue eyes. "How does the song go?" he persisted.

The two fell into step beside the caravan as, urged by a dozen red-capped drivers, it shambled along the trail. "It is only a slave song, *patrao*," said Silva once again. "It means something like this: 'Though you carry me away in chains, I am free when I die. Back will I come to bewitch and kill you.'"

Gender's heavy body seemed to swell, and his eyes grew narrower and paler. "So they sing that, hmm?" He swore again. "Listen to that!"

The unhappy procession had taken up a brief, staccato refrain:

"Hailowa—Genda! Haipana—Genda!"

"Genda, that's my name," snarled the planter. "They're singing about me, aren't they?"

Silva made another fluid gesture, but Gender flourished his whip under the nose of the Portuguese. "Don't you try to shrug me off. I'm not a child, to be talked around like this. What are they singing about me?"

"Nothing of consequence, *patrao*," Silva made haste to reassure him. "It might be to say: 'I will bewitch Gender, I will kill Gender.'"

"They threaten me, do they?" Gender's broad face took on a deeper flush. He ran at the line of chained black men. With all the strength of his arm he slashed and swung with the whip. The song broke up into wretched howls of pain.

"I'll give you a music lesson!" he raged, and flogged his way up and down the procession until he swayed and dripped sweat with the exertion.

But as he turned away, it struck up again:

"Hailowa—Genda! Haipana—Genda!"

Whirling back, he resumed the rain of blows. Silva, rushing up to second him, also whipped the slaves and execrated them in their own tongue. But when both were tired, the flayed captives began to sing once more, softly but stubbornly, the same chant.

"Let them whine," panted Gender at last. "A song never killed anybody."

Silva grinned nervously. "Of course not, *patrao*. That is only an idiotic native belief."

"You mean, they think that a song will kill?"

"That, and more. They say that if they

sing together, think together of one hate, all their thoughts and hates will become a solid strength—will strike and punish for them."

"Nonsense!" exploded Gender.

But when they made camp that night, Gender slept only in troubled snatches, and his dreams were of a song that grew deeper, heavier, until it became visible as a dark, dense cloud that overwhelmed him.

The ship that Gender had engaged for the expedition lay in a swampy estuary, far from any coastal town, and the dawn by which he loaded his goods aboard was strangely fiery and forbidding. Dunlapp, the old slaver-captain that commanded for him, met him in the cabin.

"All ready, sir?" he asked Gender. "We can sail with the tide. Plenty of room in the hold for that handful you brought. I'll tell the men to strike off those irons."

"On the contrary," said Gender, "tell the men to put manacles on the hands of each slave."

Dunlapp gazed in astonishment at his employer. "But that's bad for blacks, Mr. Gender. They get sick in chains, won't eat their food. Sometimes they die."

"I pay you well, Captain," Gender rumbled, "but not to advise me. Listen to those heathen."

Dunlapp listened. A moan of music wafted in to them.

"They've sung that cursed song about me all the way to the coast," Gender told him. "They know I hate it—I've whipped them day after day—but they keep it up. No chains come off until they hush their noise."

Dunlapp bowed acquiescence and walked out to give orders. Later, as they put out to sea, he rejoined Gender on the after deck.

"They do seem stubborn about their singing," he observed.

"I've heard it said," Gender replied, "that they sing together because they think many voices and hearts give power to hate, or to other feelings." He scowled. "Pagan fantasy!"

Dunlapp stared overside, at white gulls just above the wavetips. "There may be a tithe of

truth in that belief, Mr. Gender; sometimes there is in the faith of wild people. Hark ye, I've seen a good fifteen hundred Mohammedans praying at once, in the Barbary countries. When they bowed down, the touch of all those heads to the ground banged like the fall of a heavy rock. And when they straightened, the motion of their garments made a swish like the gust of a gale. I couldn't help but think that their prayer had force."

"More heathen foolishness," snapped Gender, and his lips drew tight.

"Well, in Christian lands we have examples, sir," Dunlapp pursued. "For instance, a mob will grow angry and burn or hang someone. Would a single man do that? Would any single man of the mob do it? No, but together their hate and resolution becomes—"

"Not the same thing at all," ruled Gender harshly. "Suppose we change the subject."

On the following afternoon, a white sail crept above the horizon behind them. At the masthead gleamed a little blotch of color. Captain Dunlapp squinted through a telescope, and barked a sailorly oath.

"A British ship-of-war," he announced, "and coming after us."

"Well?" said Gender.

"Don't you understand, sir? England is sworn to stamp out the slave trade. If they catch us with this cargo, it'll be the end of us." A little later, he groaned apprehensively. "They're overtaking us. There's their signal, for us to lay to and wait for them. Shall we do it, sir?"

Gender shook his head violently. "Not we! Show them our heels, Captain."

"They'll catch us. They are sailing three feet to our two."

"Not before dark," said Gender. "When dark comes, we'll contrive to lessen our embarrassment."

And so the slaver fled, with the Britisher in pursuit. Within an hour, the sun was at the horizon, and Gender smiled grimly in his mustache.

"It'll be dark within minutes," he said to

Dunlapp. "As soon as you feel they can't make out our actions by glass, get those slaves on deck."

In the dusk the forty-nine naked prisoners stood in a line along the bulwark. For all their chained necks and wrists, they neither stood nor gazed in a servile manner. One of them began to sing and the others joined, in the song of the slave trail:

"Hailowa—Genda! Haipana—Genda!"

"Sing on," Gender snapped briefly, and moved to the end of the line that was near the bow. Here dangled the one empty collar, and he seized it in his hand. Bending over the bulwark, he clamped it shut upon something—the ring of a heavy spare anchor, that swung there upon a swivel-hook. Again he turned, and eyed the line of dark singers.

"Have a bath to cool your spirits," he jeered, and spun the handle of the swivel-hook.

The anchor fell. The nearest slave jerked over with it, and the next and the next. Others saw, screamed, and tried to brace themselves against doom; but their comrades that had already gone overside were too much weight for them. Quickly, one after another, the captives whipped from the deck and splashed into the sea. Gender leaned over and watched the last of them as he sank.

"Gad, sir!" exclaimed Dunlapp hoarsely.

Gender faced him almost threateningly.

"What else to do, hmm? You yourself said that we could hope for no mercy from the British."

The night passed by, and by the first grey light the British ship was revealed almost upon them. A megaphoned voice hailed them; then a shot hurtled across their bows. At Gender's smug nod, Dunlapp ordered his men to lay to. A boat put out from the pursuer, and shortly a British officer and four marines swung themselves aboard.

Bowing in mock reverence, Gender bade the party search. They did so, and remounted the deck crestfallen.

"Now, sir," Gender addressed the officer, "don't you think that you owe me an apology?"

The Englishman turned pale. He was a lean, sharp-featured man with strong, white teeth. "I can't pay what I owe you," he said with deadly softness. "I find no slaves, but I smell them. They were aboard this vessel within the past twelve hours."

"And where are they now?" teased Gender.

"We both know where they are," was the reply. "If I could prove in a court of law what I know in my heart, you would sail back to England with me. Most of the way you would hang from my yards by your thumbs."

"You wear out your welcome, sir," Gender told him.

"I am going. But I have provided myself with your name and that of your home city. From here I go to Madeira, where I will cross a packet bound west for Savannah. That packet will bear with it a letter to a friend of mine in Charleston, and your neighbors shall hear what happened on this ship of yours."

"You will stun slave-owners with a story of slaves?" inquired Gender, with what he considered silky good-humor.

"It is one thing to put men to work in cotton fields, another to tear them from their homes, crowd them chained aboard a stinking ship, and drown them to escape merited punishment." The officer spat on the deck. "Good day, butcher. I say, all Charleston shall hear of you."

Gender's plantation occupied a great, bluff-rimmed island at the mouth of a river, looking out toward the Atlantic. Ordinarily that island would be called beautiful, even by those most exacting followers of Chateaubriand and Rousseau; but, on his first night at home again, Gender hated the fields, the house, the environs of fresh and salt water.

His home, on a seaward jut, resounded to his grumbled curses as he called for supper and ate heavily but without relish. Once he vowed, in a voice that quivered with rage, never to go to Charleston again.

At that, he would do well to stay away for a time. The British officer had been as good as his promise, and all the town had heard of Gender's journey to Africa and what he had done there. With a perverse squeamishness beyond Gender's understanding, the hearers were filled with disgust instead of admiration. Captain Hogue had refused to drink with him at the Jefferson House. His oldest friend, Mr. Lloyd Davis of Davis Township, had crossed the street to avoid meeting him. Even the Reverend Doctor Lockin had turned coldly away as he passed, and it was said that a sermon was forthcoming at Doctor Lockin's church attacking despoilers and abductors of defenseless people.

What was the matter with everybody? savagely demanded Gender of himself; these men who snubbed and avoided him were slaveholders. Some of them, it was quite possible, even held slaves fresh from raided villages under the Equator. Unfair! . . . Yet he could not but feel the animosity of many hearts, chafing and weighing upon his spirit.

"Brutus," he addressed the slave that cleared the table, "do you believe that hate can take form?"

"Hate, Marsa?" The sooty face was solemnly respectful.

"Yes. Hate, of many people together." Gender knew he should not confide too much in a slave, and chose his words carefully. "Suppose a lot of people hated the same thing, maybe they sang a song about it—"

"Oh, yes, Marsa." Brutus nodded. "I heah 'bout dat, from ole gran-pappy when I was little. He bin in Affiky, he says many times dey sing somebody to deff."

"Sing somebody to death?" repeated Gender. "How?"

"Dey sing dat dey kill him. Afta while, maybe plenty days, he die—"

"Shut up, you black rascal." Gender sprang from his chair and clutched at a bottle. "You've heard about this somewhere, and you dare to taunt me!"

Brutus darted from the room, mortally frightened. Gender almost pursued, but thought better and tramped into his parlor. The big, brown-paneled room seemed to give back a heavier echo of his feet. The windows were filled with the early darkness, and a hanging lamp threw rays into the corners.

On the center table lay some mail, a folded newspaper and a letter. Gender poured whisky from a decanter, stirred in spring water and dropped into a chair. First he opened the letter.

"Stirling Manor," said the return address at the top of the page. Gender's heart twitched. Evelyn Stirling, he had hopes of her . . . but this was written in a masculine hand, strong and hasty.

Sir:

Circumstances that have come to my knowledge compel me, as a matter of duty, to command that you discontinue your attention to my daughter.

Gender's eyes took on the pale tint of rage. One more result of the Britisher's letter, he made no doubt.

I have desired her to hold no further communication with you, and I have been sufficiently explicit to convince her how unworthy you are of her esteem and attention. It is hardly necessary for me to give you the reasons which have induced me to form this judgement, and I add only that nothing you can say or do will alter it.

    Your obedient servant,
    JUDGE FORRESTER STIRLING.

Gender hastily swigged a portion of his drink, and crushed the paper in his hand. So that was the judge's interfering way—it sounded as though he had copied it from a complete letter-writer for heavy fathers. He, Gender, began to form a reply in his mind:

Sir:

Your unfeeling and arbitrary letter admits of but one response. As a gentleman grossly misused, I demand satisfaction on the field of honor. Arrangements I place in the hands of . . .

By what friend should he forward that challenge? It seemed that he was mighty short of friends just now. He sipped more whisky and water, and tore the wrappings of the newspaper.

It was a Massachusetts publication, and toward the bottom of the first page was a heavy cross of ink, to call attention to one item. A poem, evidently, in four-line stanzas. Its title signified nothing—"The Witnesses." Author, Henry W. Longfellow; Gender identified him vaguely as a scrawler of Abolitionist doggerel. Why was this poem recommended to a southern planter?

> *In Ocean's wide domains,*
> *Half buried in the sands,*
> *Lie skeletons in chains,*
> *With shackled feet and hands.*

Once again the reader swore, but the oath quavered on his lips. His eye moved to a stanza farther down the column:

> *These are the bones of Slaves;*
> *They gleam from the abyss;*
> *They cry, from yawning waves . . .*

But it seemed to Gender that he heard, rather than read, what that cry was.

He sprang to his feet, paper and glass falling from his hands. His thin lips drew apart, his ears strained. The sound was faint, but unmistakable—many voices singing.

The Negroes in his cabins? But no Negro on his plantation would know that song. The chanting refrain began:

"Hailowa—Genda! Haipana—Genda!"

The planter's lean mustache bristled tigerishly. This would surely be the refined extremity of his persecution, this chanting of a weird song under his window-sill. It was louder now. *I will bewitch, I will kill*—but who would know that fierce mockery of him?

The crew of his ship, of course; they had heard it on the writhing lips of the captives, at the very moment of their destruction. And when the ship docked in Charleston, with no profit to show, Gender had been none too kindly in paying them off.

Those unsavory mariners must have been piqued. They had followed him, then, were setting up this vicious serenade.

Gender stepped quickly around the table and toward the window. He flung up the sash with a violence that almost shattered the glass, and leaned savagely out.

On that instant the song stopped, and Gender could see only the seaward slope of his land, down to the lip of the bluff that overhung the water. Beyond that stretched an expanse of waves, patchily agleam under a great buckskin-colored moon, that even now stirred the murmurous tide at the foot of the bluff. Here were no trees, no brush even, to hide pranksters. The singers, now silent, must be in a boat under the shelter of the bluff.

Gender strode from the room, fairly tore open a door, and made heavy haste toward the sea. He paused, on the lip of the bluff. Nothing was to be seen, beneath him or farther out. The mockers, if they had been here, had already fled. He growled, glared and tramped back to his house. He entered the parlor once more, drew down the sash and sought his chair again. Choosing another glass, he began once more to mix whisky and water. But he stopped in the middle of his pouring.

There it was again, the song he knew; and closer.

He rose, took a step in the direction of the window, then thought better of it. He had warned his visitors by one sortie, and they had hidden. Why not let them come close, and suffer the violence he ached to pour out on some living thing?

He moved, not to the window, but to a mantelpiece opposite. From a box of dark, polished wood he lifted a pistol, then another. They were duelling weapons, handsomely made, with hair-triggers; and Gender was a dead shot. With orderly swiftness he poured in glazed powder from a flask, rammed down two leaden bullets, and laid percussion caps upon the touchholes. Returning, he placed the weapons on his center table, then stood on tiptoe to extinguish the hanging lamp. A single light remained in the room, a candle by the door, and this he carried to the window, placing it on a bracket there. Moving into the gloomy center of the parlor, he sat in his chair and took a pistol in either hand.

The song was louder now, lifted by many voices:

"Hailowa—Genda! Haipana—Genda!"

Undoubtedly the choristers had come to land by now, had gained the top of the bluff. They could be seen, Gender was sure, from the window. He felt perspiration on his jowl, and lifted a sleeve to blot it. Trying to scare him, hmm? Singing about witchcraft and killing? Well, he'd show them who was the killer.

The singing had drawn close, was just outside. Odd how the sailors, or whoever they were, had learned that chant so well! It recalled to his mind the slave trail, the jungle, the long procession of crooning prisoners. But here was no time for idle reverie on vanished scenes. Silence had fallen again, and he could only divine the presence, just outside, of many creatures.

Scratch-scratch-scratch; it sounded like the stealthy creeping of a snake over rough lumber. That scratching resounded from the window where something stole into view in the candlelight. Gender fixed his eyes there, and his pistols lifted their muzzles.

The palm of a hand, as grey as a fish, laid itself on the glass. It was wet; Gender could see the trickle of water descending along the pane. Something clinked, almost musically. Another hand moved into position beside it, and between the two swung links of chain.

This was an elaborately devilish joke, thought Gender, in an ecstasy of rage. Even the chains, to lend reality . . . and as he stared he knew, in a split moment of terror that stirred his flesh on his bones, that it was no joke after all.

A face had moved into the range of the candlelight, pressing close to the pane between the two palms.

It was darker than those palms, of a dirty, slaty deadness of color. But it was not dead, not with those dull, intent eyes that moved slowly in their blistery sockets . . . not dead, though it was foully wet, and its thick lips hung slackly open, and seaweed lay plastered upon the cheeks, even though the flat nostrils showed crumbled and gnawed away, as if by fish. The eyes quested here and there across the floor and walls of the parlor. They came to rest, gazing full into the face of Gender.

He felt as though stale sea-water had trickled upon him, but his right hand abode steady as a gun-rest. He took aim and fired.

The glass crashed loudly, and fell in shattering flakes to the floor beneath the sill.

Gender was on his feet, moving forward, dropping the empty pistol on the table and whipping the loaded one into his right hand. Two leaping strides took him almost to the window, before he reeled backward.

The face had not fallen. It stared at him, a scant yard away. Between the dull, living eyes showed a round black hole, where the bullet had gone in. But the thing stood unflinchingly, somehow serenely. Its two wet hands moved slowly, methodically, to pluck away the jagged remains of the glass.

Gender rocked where he stood, unable for the moment to command his body to retreat. The shoulders beneath the face heightened. They were bare and wet and deadly dusky, and they clinked the collar-shackle beneath the lax chin. Two hands stole into the room, their fish-colored palms opening toward Gender.

He screamed, and at last he ran. As he turned his back, the singing began yet again, loud and horribly jaunty—not at all as the miserable slaves had sung it. He gained the seaward door, drew it open, and looked full into a gathering of black, wet figures, with chains festooned among them, awaiting him. Again he screamed, and tried to push the door shut.

He could not. A hand was braced against the edge of the panel—many hands. The wood fringed itself with gleaming black fingers. Gender let go the knob, whirled to flee into the house. Something caught the back of his coat, something he dared not identify. In struggling loose, he spun through the doorway and into the moonlit open.

Figures surrounded him, black, naked, wet figures; dead as to sunken faces and flaccid muscles, but horribly alive as to eyes and trembling hands and slack mouths that formed the strange primitive words of the song; separate, yet strung together with a great chain and collar-shackles, like an awful fish on the gigantic line of some demon-angler. All this Gender saw in a rocking, moon-washed moment, while he choked and retched at a dreadful odor of death, thick as fog.

Still he tried to run, but they were moving around him in a weaving crescent, cutting off his retreat toward the plantation. Hands extended toward him, manacled and dripping. His only will was to escape the touch of those sodden fingers, and one way was open—the way to the sea.

He ran toward the brink of the bluff. From its top he would leap, dive and swim away. But they pursued, overtook, surrounded him. He re-membered that he held a loaded pistol, and fired into their black midst. It had no effect. He might have known that it would have no effect.

Something was clutching for him. A great, inhuman talon? No, it was an open collar of metal, with a length of chain to it, a collar that had once clamped to an anchor, dragging down to the ocean's depths a line of shackled men. It gaped at him, held forth by many dripping hands. He tried to dodge, but it darted around his throat, shut with a ringing snap. Was it cold . . . or scalding hot? He knew, with horror vividly etching the knowledge into his heart, that he was one at last with the great chained procession.

"*Hailowa—Genda! Haipana—Genda!*"

He found his voice. "No, no!" he pleaded. "No, in the name of—"

But he could not say the name of God. And the throng suddenly moved explosively, concertedly, to the edge of the bluff.

A single wailing cry from all those dead throats, and they dived into the waves below.

Gender did not feel the clutch and jerk of the chain that dragged him along. He did not even feel the water as it closed over his head.

THE OUTSIDER

H. P. LOVECRAFT

ONE OF THE greatest of all pulp fiction horror writers, H(oward) P(hillips) Lovecraft (1890–1937) was born in Providence, Rhode Island, where he lived virtually all his life. Always frail, he was reclusive and had little formal education, but he read extensively, with particular emphasis on the sciences. He wrote monthly articles on astronomy for the *Providence Tribune* at the age of sixteen, then attempted fiction; his first published story was "The Alchemist," written in 1908 but not published until 1916. He wrote fiction for other small magazines, living in near poverty, earning his living by ghostwriting and editing the work of others, until he finally sold "Dagon" to the top fantasy pulp magazine in America, *Weird Tales,* in 1923. He became a regular contributor to that magazine until his death, with only a handful of his sixty stories appearing in other pulps.

He was neglected as a serious writer throughout his life, with only one volume being published while he was alive: *The Shadow over Innsmouth* (1936). After his early death, two admirers, August Derleth and Donald Wandrei, attempted to sell his work to commercial publishers. When they were unsuccessful, they created their own firm, Arkham House, for the sole purpose of collecting and publishing Lovecraft's stories, poems, and letters, beginning with the cornerstone work, *The Outsider and Others* (1939), and continuing with *Beyond the Wall of Sleep* (1943). Arkham House remains active as the leading specialty publisher of horror fiction.

"The Outsider" was originally published in the April 1926 issue of *Weird Tales.*

H. P. LOVECRAFT

THE OUTSIDER

UNHAPPY IS HE to whom the memories of childhood bring only fear and sadness. Wretched is he who looks back upon lone hours in vast and dismal chambers with brown hangings and maddening rows of antique books or upon awed watches in twilight groves of grotesque, gigantic, and vine-encumbered trees that silently wave twisted branches far aloft. Such a lot the gods gave to me—to me, the dazed, the disappointed; the barren, the broken. And yet I am strangely content and cling desperately to those sere memories, when my mind momentarily threatens to reach beyond to *the other*.

I know not where I was born, save that the castle was infinitely old and infinitely horrible, full of dark passages and having high ceilings where the eye could find only cobwebs and shadows. The stones in the crumbling corridors seemed always hideously damp, and there was an accursed smell everywhere, as of the piled-up corpses of dead generations. It was never light, so that I used sometimes to light candles and gaze steadily at them for relief, nor was there any sun outdoors, since the terrible trees grew high above the topmost accessible tower. There was one black tower which reached above the trees into the unknown outer sky, but that was partly ruined and could not be ascended save by a well-nigh impossible climb up the sheer wall, stone by stone.

I must have lived years in this place, but I can not measure the time. Beings must have cared for my needs, yet I can not recall any person except myself, or anything alive but the noiseless rats and bats and spiders. I think that whoever nursed me must have been shockingly aged, since my first conception of a living person was that of something mockingly like myself, yet distorted, shriveled and decaying like the castle. To me there was nothing grotesque in the bones and skeletons that strewed some of the stone crypts deep down among the foundations. I fantastically associated these things with everyday events, and thought them more natural than the colored pictures of living beings which I found in many of the moldy books. From such books I learned all that I know. No teacher urged or guided me, and I do not recall hearing any human voice in all those years—not even my own; for although I had read of speech, I had never thought to try to speak aloud. My aspect was a matter equally unthought of, for there were no mirrors in the castle, and I merely regarded myself by instinct as akin to the youthful figures I saw drawn and painted in the books. I felt conscious of youth because I remembered so little.

Outside, across the putrid moat and under the dark mute trees, I would often lie and dream for hours about what I read in the books; and would longingly picture myself amidst gay crowds in the sunny world beyond the endless forest. Once I tried to escape from the forest, but as I went farther from the castle the shade grew denser and the air more filled with brooding fear; so that I ran frantically back lest I lose my way in a labyrinth of nighted silence.

So through endless twilights I dreamed and waited, though I knew not what I waited for.

Then in the shadowy solitude my longing for light grew so frantic that I could rest no more, and I lifted entreating hands to the single black ruined tower that reached above the forest into the unknown outer sky. And at last I resolved to scale that tower, fall though I might; since it were better to glimpse the sky and perish, than to live without ever beholding day.

In the dank twilight I climbed the worn and aged stone stairs till I reached the level where they ceased, and thereafter clung perilously to small footholds leading upward. Ghastly and terrible was that dead, stairless cylinder of rock; black, ruined, and deserted, and sinister with startled bats whose wings made no noise. But more ghastly and terrible still was the slowness of my progress; for climb as I might, the darkness overhead grew no thinner, and a new chill as of haunted and venerable mold assailed me. I shivered as I wondered why I did not reach the light, and would have looked down had I dared. I fancied that night had come suddenly upon me, and vainly groped with one free hand for a window embrasure, that I might peer out and above, and try to judge the height I had attained.

All at once, after an infinity of awesome, sightless crawling up that concave and desperate precipice, I felt my head touch a solid thing, and knew I must have gained the roof, or at least some kind of floor. In the darkness I raised my free hand and tested the barrier, finding it stone and immovable. Then came a deadly circuit of the tower, clinging to whatever holds the slimy wall could give; till finally my testing hand found the barrier yielding, and I turned upward again, pushing the slab or door with my head as I used both hands in my fearful ascent. There was no light revealed above, and as my hands went higher I knew that my climb was for the nonce ended; since the slab was the trap-door of an aperture leading to a level stone surface of greater circumference than the lower tower, no doubt the floor of some lofty and capacious observation chamber. I crawled through carefully, and tried to prevent the heavy slab from falling back into place, but failed in the latter attempt. As I lay exhausted on the stone floor I heard the eery echoes of its fall, but hoped when necessary to pry it up again.

Believing I was now at a prodigious height, far above the accursed branches of the wood, I dragged myself up from the floor and fumbled about for windows, that I might look for the first time upon the sky, and the moon and stars of which I had read. But on every hand I was disappointed; since all that I found were vast shelves of marble, bearing odious oblong boxes of disturbing size. More and more I reflected, and wondered what hoary secrets might abide in this high apartment so many eons cut off from the castle below. Then unexpectedly my hands came upon a doorway, where hung a portal of stone, rough with strange chiseling. Trying it, I found it locked; but with a supreme burst of strength I overcame all obstacles and dragged it open inward. As I did so there came to me the purest ecstasy I have ever known; for shining tranquilly through an ornate grating of iron, and down a short stone passageway of steps that ascended from the newly found doorway, was the radiant full moon, which I had never before seen save in dreams and in vague visions I dared not call memories.

Fancying now that I had attained the very pinnacle of the castle, I commenced to rush up the few steps beyond the door; but the sudden veiling of the moon by a cloud caused me to stumble, and I felt my way more slowly in the dark. It was still very dark when I reached the grating—which I tried carefully and found unlocked, but which I did not open for fear of falling from the amazing height to which I had climbed. Then the moon came out.

Most demoniacal of all shocks is that of the abysmally unexpected and grotesquely unbelievable. Nothing I had before undergone could compare in terror with what I now saw; with the bizarre marvels that sight implied. The sight itself was as simple as it was stupefying, for it was merely this: instead of a dizzying prospect of treetops seen from a lofty eminence, there stretched around me on the level through the grating nothing less than *the solid ground*, decked and diversified by marble slabs and columns, and overshadowed by an ancient stone church, whose ruined spire gleamed spectrally in the moonlight.

Half unconscious, I opened the grating and staggered out upon the white gravel path that stretched away in two directions. My mind, stunned and chaotic as it was, still held the frantic craving for light; and not even the fantastic wonder which had happened could stay my course. I neither knew nor cared whether my experience was insanity, dreaming, or magic; but was determined to gaze on brilliance and gayety at any cost. I knew not who I was or what I was, or what my surroundings might be; though as I continued to stumble along I became conscious of a kind of fearsome latent memory that made my progress not wholly fortuitous. I passed under an arch out of that region of slabs and columns, and wandered through the open country; sometimes following the visible road, but sometimes leaving it curiously to tread across meadows where only occasional ruins bespoke the ancient presence of a forgotten road. Once I swam across a swift river where crumbling, mossy masonry told of a bridge long vanished.

Over two hours must have passed before I reached what seemed to be my goal, a venerable ivied castle in a thickly wooded park, maddeningly familiar, yet full of perplexing strangeness to me. I saw that the moat was filled in, and that some of the well-known towers were demolished; whilst new wings existed to confuse the beholder. But what I observed with chief interest and delight were the open windows—gorgeously ablaze with light and sending forth sound of the gayest revelry. Advancing to one of these I looked in and saw an oddly dressed company, indeed; making merry, and speaking brightly to one another. I had never, seemingly, heard human speech before and could guess only vaguely what was said. Some of the faces seemed to hold expressions that brought up incredibly remote recollections, others were utterly alien.

I now stepped through the low window into

the brilliantly lighted room, stepping as I did so from my single bright moment of hope to my blackest convulsion of despair and realization. The nightmare was quick to come, for as I entered, there occurred immediately one of the most terrifying demonstrations I had ever conceived. Scarcely had I crossed the sill when there descended upon the whole company a sudden and unheralded fear of hideous intensity, distorting every face and evoking the most horrible screams from nearly every throat. Flight was universal, and in the clamor and panic several fell in a swoon and were dragged away by their madly fleeing companions. Many covered their eyes with their hands, and plunged blindly and awkwardly in their race to escape, overturning furniture and stumbling against the walls before they managed to reach one of the many doors.

The cries were shocking; and as I stood in the brilliant apartment alone and dazed, listening to their vanishing echoes, I trembled at the thought of what might be lurking near me unseen. At a casual inspection the room seemed deserted, but when I moved toward one of the alcoves I thought I detected a presence there—a hint of motion beyond the golden-arched doorway leading to another and somewhat similar room. As I approached the arch I began to perceive the presence more clearly; and then, with the first and last sound I ever uttered—a ghastly ululation that revolted me almost as poignantly as its noxious cause—I beheld in full, frightful vividness the inconceivable, indescribable, and unmentionable monstrosity which had by its simple appearance changed a merry company to a herd of delirious fugitives.

I can not even hint what it was like, for it was a compound of all that is unclean, uncanny, unwelcome, abnormal, and detestable. It was the ghoulish shade of decay, antiquity, and desolation; the putrid, dripping eidolon of unwholesome revelation, the awful baring of that which the merciful earth should always hide. God knows it was not of this world—or no longer of this world—yet to my horror I saw in its eaten-away and bone-revealing outlines a leering, abhorrent travesty on the human shape; and in its moldy, disintegrating apparel an unspeakable quality that chilled me even more.

I was almost paralyzed, but not too much so to make a feeble effort toward flight; a backward stumble which failed to break the spell in which the nameless, voiceless monster held me. My eyes, bewitched by the glassy orbs which stared loathsomely into them, refused to close, though they were mercifully blurred, and showed the terrible object but indistinctly after the first shock. I tried to raise my hand to shut out the sight, yet so stunned were my nerves that my arm could not fully obey my will. The attempt, however, was enough to disturb my balance; so that I had to stagger forward several steps to avoid falling. As I did so I became suddenly and agonizingly aware of the *nearness* of the carrion thing, whose hideous hollow breathing I half fancied I could hear. Nearly mad, I found myself yet able to throw out a hand to ward off the fetid apparition which pressed so close; when in one cataclysmic second of cosmic nightmarishness and hellish accident *my fingers touched the rotting outstretched paw of the monster beneath the golden arch.*

I did not shriek, but all the fiendish ghouls that ride the night-wind shrieked for me as in that same second they crashed down upon my mind a single and fleeting avalanche of soul-annihilating memory. I knew in that second all that had been; I remembered beyond the frightful castle and the trees; and recognized the altered edifice in which I now stood; I recognized, most terrible of all, the unholy abomination that stood leering before me as I withdrew my sullied fingers from its own.

But in the cosmos there is balm as well as bitterness, and that balm is nepenthe. In the supreme horror of that second I forgot what had horrified me, and the burst of black memory vanished in a chaos of echoing images. In a dream I fled from that haunted and accursed pile, and ran swiftly and silently in the moonlight. When I returned to the churchyard place of marble and went down the steps I found the stone trap-door immovable; but I was not sorry, for I had hated the antique castle and the trees. Now I ride with the mocking and friendly ghouls on the night wind, and play by day amongst the catacombs of Nephren-Ka in the sealed and unknown valley of Hadoth by the Nile. I know that light is not for me, save that of the moon over the rock tombs of Neb, nor any gayety save the unnamed feasts of Nitokris beneath the Great Pyramid; yet in my new wildness and freedom I almost welcome the bitterness of alienage.

For although nepenthe has calmed me, I know always that I am an outsider; stranger in this century and among those who are still men. This I have known ever since I stretched out my fingers to the abomination within that great gilded frame; stretched out my fingers and touched *a cold and unyielding surface of polished glass.*

EAT ME

ROBERT McCAMMON

BORN AND RAISED in Birmingham, Alabama, Robert McCammon (1952–) graduated from the University of Alabama with a B.A. in journalism. Notoriously reticent about his life, McCammon continues to live in Birmingham with his wife, Sally Sanders.

His first novel, *Baal* (1978), about a satanic child of incalculable evil, set the tone for his future fiction, which is about battles against every form of horror, from the subtle terror of *Bethany's Sin* (1980), to zombies in *The Night Boat* (1980), to vampires in *They Thirst* (1981), and werewolves in *The Wolf's Hour* (1989), a *New York Times* bestseller that was nominated for the Bram Stoker Award as Best Novel. Other Bram Stoker Awards include *Swan Song* (1987), cowinner (with Stephen King's *Misery*), Best Novel; "The Deep End" (1987), winner, Best Short Story; *Stinger* (1988), nominee, Best Novel; "Eat Me" (1989), winner, Best Short Story; *Blue World* (1990), nominee, Best Short Story Collection; *Mine* (1990), winner, Best Novel; and *Boy's Life* (1991), winner, Best Novel. Soon after this unprecedented series of successes, he announced his retirement from horror writing, but returned with *Speaks the Nightbird* (2002), the first of a series of historical novels in which Matthew Corbett battles various forces of evil. Further books in the popular series are *The Queen of Bedlam* (2007) and *Mister Slaughter* (2010). In 2008, McCammon was given the 2008 Grand Master Award by the World Horror Convention.

"Eat Me" was originally published in *Book of the Dead,* edited by John Skipp and Craig Spector (New York: Bantam, 1989).

ROBERT McCAMMON

EAT ME

A QUESTION GNAWED, day and night, at Jim Crisp. He pondered it as he walked the streets, while a dark rain fell and rats chattered at his feet; he mulled over it as he sat in his apartment, staring at the static on the television screen hour after hour. The question haunted him as he sat in the cemetery on Fourteenth Street, surrounded by empty graves. And this burning question was: when did love die?

Thinking took effort. It made his brain hurt, but it seemed to Jim that thinking was his last link with life. He used to be an accountant, a long time ago. He'd worked with a firm downtown for over twenty years, had never been married, hadn't dated much either. Numbers, logic, the rituals of mathematics had been the center of his life; now logic itself had gone insane, and no one kept records anymore. He had a terrible sensation of not belonging in this world, of being suspended in a nightmare that would stretch to the boundaries of eternity. He had no need for sleep any longer; something inside him had burst a while back, and he'd lost the ten or twelve pounds of fat that had gathered around his middle over the years. His body was lean now, so light sometimes a strong wind knocked him off his feet. The smell came and went, but Jim had a caseload of English Leather in his apartment and he took baths in the stuff.

The open maw of time frightened him. Days without number lay ahead. What was there to do, when there was nothing to be done? No one called the roll, no one punched the time-clock,

no one set the deadlines. This warped freedom gave a sense of power to others; to Jim it was the most confining of prisons, because all the symbols of order—stoplights, calendars, clocks—were still there, still working, yet they had no purpose or sense, and they reminded him too much of what had been before.

As he walked, aimlessly, through the city's streets he saw others moving past, some as peaceful as sleepwalkers, some raging in the grip of private tortures. Jim came to a corner and stopped, instinctively obeying the DON'T WALK sign; a high squealing noise caught his attention, and he looked to his left.

Rats were scurrying wildly over one of the lowest forms of humanity, a half-decayed corpse that had recently awakened and pulled itself from the grave. The thing crawled on the wet pavement, struggling on one thin arm and two sticklike legs. The rats were chewing it to pieces, and as the thing reached Jim, its skeletal face lifted and the single dim coal of an eye found him. From its mouth came a rattling noise, stifled when several rats squeezed themselves between the gray lips in search of softer flesh. Jim hurried on, not waiting for the light to change. He thought the thing had said *Whhhyyy?* and for that question he had no answer.

He felt shame in the coil of his entrails. When did love die? Had it perished at the same time as this living death of human flesh had begun, or had it already died and decayed long before? He went on, through the somber streets where the buildings brooded like tombstones, and he felt crushed beneath the weight of loneliness.

Jim remembered beauty: a yellow flower, the scent of a woman's perfume, the warm sheen of a woman's hair. Remembering was another bar in the prison of bones; the power of memory taunted him unmercifully. He remembered walking on his lunch hour, sighting a pretty girl and following her for a block or two, enraptured by fantasies. He had always been searching for love, for someone to be joined with, and had never realized it so vitally before now, when the gray city was full of rats and the restless dead.

Someone with a cavity where its face had been stumbled past, arms waving blindly. What once had been a child ran by him, and left the scent of rot in its wake. Jim lowered his head, and when a gust of hot wind hit him he lost his balance and would have slammed into a concrete wall if he hadn't grabbed hold of a bolted-down mailbox. He kept going, deeper into the city, on pavement he'd never walked when he was alive.

At the intersection of two unfamiliar streets he thought he heard music: the crackle of a guitar, the low grunting of a drumbeat. He turned against the wind, fighting the gusts that threatened to hurl him into the air, and followed the sound. Two blocks ahead a strobe light flashed in a cavernous entrance. A sign that read THE COURTYARD had been broken out, and across the front of the building was scrawled BONEYARD in black spray paint. Figures moved within the entrance: dancers, gyrating in the flash of the strobes.

The thunder of the music repulsed him—the soft grace of Brahms remained his lullaby, not the raucous crudity of Grave Rock—but the activity, the movement, the heat of energy drew him closer. He scratched a maddening itch on the dry flesh at the back of his neck and stood on the threshold while the music and the glare blew around him. The Courtyard, he thought, glancing at the old sign. It was the name of a place that might once have served white wine and polite jazz music—a singles bar, maybe, where the lonely went to meet the lonely. The Boneyard it

was now, all right: a realm of dancing skeletons. This was not his kind of place, but still . . . the noise, lights, and gyrations spoke of another kind of loneliness. It was a singles bar for the living dead, and it beckoned him in.

Jim crossed the threshold, and with one desiccated hand he smoothed down his remaining bits of black hair.

And now he knew what hell must be like: a smoky, rot-smelling pandemonium. Some of the things writhing on the dance floor were missing arms and legs, and one thin figure in the midst of a whirl lost its hand; the withered flesh skidded across the linoleum, was crushed underfoot as its owner scrabbled after it, and then its owner was likewise pummeled down into a twitching mass. On the bandstand were two guitar players, a drummer, and a legless thing hammering at an electric organ. Jim avoided the dance floor, moving through the crowd toward the blue-neon bar. The drums' pounding offended him, in an obscene way; it reminded him too much of how his heartbeat used to feel before it clenched and ceased.

This was a place his mother—God rest her soul—would have warned him to avoid. He had never been one for nightlife, and looking into the decayed faces of some of these people was a preview of torments that lay ahead—but he didn't want to leave. The drumbeat was so loud it destroyed all thinking, and for a while he could pretend it was indeed his own heart returned to scarlet life; and that, he realized, was why the Boneyard was full from wall to wall. This was a mockery of life, yes, but it was the best to be had.

The bar's neon lit up the rotting faces like blue-shadowed Halloween masks. One of them, down to shreds of flesh clinging to yellow bone, shouted something unintelligible and drank from a bottle of beer; the liquid streamed through the fissure in his throat and down over his violet shirt and gold chains. Flies swarmed around the bar, drawn to the reek, and Jim watched as the customers pressed forward. They reached into their pockets and changepurses and offered freshly-killed rats, roaches, spiders, and centipedes to the bartender, who placed the objects in a large glass jar that had replaced the cash register. Such was the currency of the Dead World, and a particularly juicy rat bought two bottles of Miller Lite. Other people were laughing and hollering—gasping, brittle sounds that held no semblance of humanity. A fight broke out near the dance floor, and a twisted arm thunked to the linoleum to the delighted roar of the onlookers.

"I know you!" A woman's face thrust forward into Jim's. She had tatters of gray hair, and she wore heavy makeup over sunken cheeks, her forehead swollen and cracked by some horrible inner pressure. Her glittery dress danced with light, but smelled of gravedirt. "Buy me a drink!" she said, grasping his arm. A flap of flesh at her throat fluttered, and Jim realized her throat had been slashed. "Buy me a drink!" she insisted.

"No," Jim said, trying to break free. "No, I'm sorry."

"You're the one who killed me!" she screamed. Her grip tightened, about to snap Jim's forearm. "Yes you are! You killed me, didn't you?" And she picked up an empty beer bottle off the bar, her face contorted with rage, and started to smash it against his skull.

But before the blow could fall a man lifted her off her feet and pulled her away from Jim; her fingernails flayed to the bones of Jim's arm. She was still screaming, fighting to pull away, and the man, who wore a T-shirt with *Boneyard* painted across it, said, "She's a fresh one. Sorry, mac," before he hauled her toward the entrance. The woman's scream got shriller, and Jim saw her forehead burst open and ooze like a stomped snail. He shuddered, backing into a dark corner—and there he bumped into another body.

"Excuse me," he said. Started to move away. Glanced at whom he'd collided with.

And saw her.

She was trembling, her skinny arms wrapped around her chest. She still had most of her long brown hair, but in places it had diminished to the texture of spiderwebs and her scalp showed. Still, it was lovely hair. It looked almost healthy. Her pale blue eyes were liquid and terrified, and her face might have been pretty once. She had lost most of her nose, and gray-rimmed craters pitted her right cheek. She was wearing sensible clothes: a skirt and blouse and a sweater buttoned to the throat. Her clothes were dirty, but they matched. She looked like a librarian, he decided. She didn't belong in the Boneyard—but, then, where did anyone belong anymore?

He was about to move away when he noticed something else that caught a glint of frenzied light.

Around her neck, just peeking over the collar of her sweater, was a silver chain, and on that chain hung a tiny cloisonné heart.

It was a fragile thing, like a bit of bone china, but it held the power to freeze Jim before he took another step.

"That's . . . that's very pretty," he said. He nodded at the heart.

Instantly her hand covered it. Parts of her fingers had rotted off, like his own.

He looked into her eyes; she stared—or at least pretended to—right past him. She shook like a frightened deer. Jim paused, waiting for a break in the thunder, nervously casting his gaze to the floor. He caught a whiff of decay, and whether it was from himself or her he didn't know; what did it matter? He shivered too, not knowing what else to say but wanting to say something, anything, to make a connection. He sensed that at any moment the girl—whose age might be anywhere from twenty to forty, since Death both tightened and wrinkled at the same time—might bolt past him and be lost in the crowd. He thrust his hands into his pockets, not wanting her to see the exposed fingerbones. "This is the first time I've been here," he said. "I don't go out much."

She didn't answer. Maybe her tongue is gone, he thought. Or her throat. Maybe she was insane, which could be a real possibility. She pressed back against the wall, and Jim saw how very thin she was, skin stretched over frail bones. Dried up on the inside, he thought. Just like me.

"My name is Jim," he told her. "What's yours?"

Again, no reply. I'm no good at this! he agonized. Singles bars had never been his "scene," as the saying went. No, his world had always been his books, his job, his classical records, his cramped little apartment that now seemed like a four-walled crypt. There was no use in standing here, trying to make conversation with a dead girl. He had dared to eat the peach, as Eliot's Prufrock lamented, and found it rotten.

"Brenda," she said, so suddenly it almost startled him. She kept her hand over the heart, her other arm across her sagging breasts. Her head was lowered, her hair hanging over the cratered cheek.

"Brenda," Jim repeated; he heard his voice tremble. "That's a nice name."

She shrugged, still pressed into the corner as if trying to squeeze through a chink in the bricks.

Another moment of decision presented itself. It was a moment in which Jim could turn and walk three paces away, into the howling mass at the bar, and release Brenda from her corner; or a moment in which Brenda could tell him to go away, or curse him to his face, or scream with haunted dementia and that would be the end of it. The moment passed, and none of those things happened. There was just the drumbeat, pounding across the club, pounding like a counterfeit heart, and the roaches ran their race on the bar and the dancers continued to fling bits of flesh off their bodies like autumn leaves.

He felt he had to say something. "I was just walking. I didn't mean to come here." Maybe she nodded. Maybe; he couldn't tell for sure, and the light played tricks. "I didn't have anywhere else to go," he added.

She spoke, in a whispery voice that he had to strain to hear: "Me neither."

Jim shifted his weight—what weight he had left. "Would you . . . like to dance?" he asked, for want of anything better.

"Oh, no!" She looked up quickly. "No, I can't dance! I mean . . . I used to dance, sometimes, but . . . I can't dance anymore."

Jim understood what she meant; her bones were brittle, just as his own were. They were both as fragile as husks, and to get out on that dance floor would tear them both to pieces. "Good," he said. "I can't dance either."

She nodded, with an expression of relief. There was an instant in which Jim saw how pretty she must have been before all this happened—not pretty in a flashy way, but pretty as homespun lace—and it made his brain ache. "This is a loud place," he said. "Too loud."

"I've . . . never been here before." Brenda removed her hand from the necklace, and again both arms protected her chest. "I knew this place was here, but . . ." She shrugged her thin shoulders. "I don't know."

"You're . . ." lonely, he almost said. As lonely as I am. ". . . alone?" he asked.

"I have friends," she answered, too fast.

"I don't," he said, and her gaze lingered on his face for a few seconds before she looked away. "I mean, not in this place," he amended. "I don't know anybody here, except you." He paused, and then he had to ask the question: "Why did you come here tonight?"

She almost spoke, but she closed her mouth before the words got out. I know why, Jim thought. Because you're searching, just like I am. You went out walking, and maybe you came in here because you couldn't stand to be alone another second. I can look at you, and hear you screaming. "Would you like to go out?" he asked. "Walking, I mean. Right now, so we can talk?"

"I don't know you," she said, uneasily.

"I don't know you, either. But I'd like to."

"I'm . . ." Her hand fluttered up to the cavity where her nose had been. "Ugly," she finished.

"You're not ugly. Anyway, I'm no handsome prince." He smiled, which stretched the flesh on his face. Brenda might have smiled, a little bit; again, it was hard to tell. "I'm not a crazy," Jim reassured her. "I'm not on drugs, and I'm not looking for somebody to hurt. I just thought . . . you might like to have some company."

Brenda didn't answer for a moment. Her fingers played with the cloisonné heart. "All right," she said finally. "But not too far. Just around the block."

"Just around the block," he agreed, trying to keep his excitement from showing too much. He took her arm—she didn't seem to mind his fleshless fingers—and carefully guided her through the crowd. She felt light, like a dry-rotted stick, and he thought that even he, with his shrunken muscles, might be able to lift her over his head.

Outside, they walked away from the blast of the Boneyard. The wind was getting stronger, and they soon were holding to each other to keep from being swept away. "A storm's coming," Brenda said, and Jim nodded. The storms were fast and ferocious, and their winds made the buildings shake. But Jim and Brenda kept walking, first around the block and then, at Brenda's direction, southward. Their bodies were bent like question marks; overhead, clouds masked the moon and blue streaks of electricity began to lance across the sky.

Brenda was not a talker, but she was a good listener. Jim told her about himself, about the job he used to have, about how he'd always dreamed that someday he'd have his own firm. He told her about a trip he once took, as a young man, to Lake Michigan, and how cold he recalled the water to be. He told her about a park he visited once, and how he remembered the sound of happy laughter and the smell of flowers. "I miss how it used to be," he said, before he could stop himself, because in the Dead World voicing such regrets was a punishable crime. "I miss beauty," he went on. "I miss . . . love."

She took his hand, bone against bone, and said, "This is where I live."

It was a plain brownstone building, many of the windows broken out by the windstorms. Jim didn't ask to go to Brenda's apartment; he expected to be turned away on the front steps. But Brenda still had hold of his hand, and now she was leading him up those steps and through the glassless door.

Her apartment, on the fourth floor, was even smaller than Jim's. The walls were a somber gray, but the lights revealed a treasure—pots of flowers set around the room and out on the fire escape. "They're silk," Brenda explained, before he could ask. "But they look real, don't they?"

"They look . . . wonderful." He saw a stereo and speakers on a table, and near the equipment was a collection of records. He bent down, his knees creaking, and began to examine her taste in music. Another shock greeted him: Beethoven . . . Chopin . . . Mozart . . . Vivaldi . . . Strauss. And, yes, even Brahms. "Oh!" he said, and that was all he could say.

"I found most of those," she said. "Would you like to listen to them?"

"Yes. Please."

She put on the Chopin, and as the piano chords swelled, so did the wind, whistling in the hall and making the windows tremble.

And then she began to talk about herself: She had been a secretary, in a refrigeration plant across the river. Had never married, though she'd been engaged once. Her hobby was making silk flowers, when she could find the material. She missed ice cream most of all, she said. And summer—what had happened to summer, like it used to be? All the days and nights seemed to bleed together now, and nothing made any of them different. Except the storms, of course, and those could be dangerous.

By the end of the third record, they were sitting side by side on her sofa. The wind had gotten very strong outside; the rain came and went, but the wind and lightning remained.

"I like talking to you," she told him. "I feel like . . . I've known you for a long, long time."

"I do too. I'm glad I came into that place tonight." He watched the storm and heard the wind shriek. "I don't know how I'm going to get home."

"You . . . don't have to go," Brenda said, very quietly. "I'd like for you to stay."

He stared at her, unbelieving. The back of his

neck itched fiercely, and the itch was spreading to his shoulders and arms, but he couldn't move.

"I don't want to be alone," she continued. "I'm always alone. It's just that . . . I miss touching. Is that wrong, to miss touching?"

"No. I don't think so."

She leaned forward, her lips almost brushing his, her eyes almost pleading. "Eat me," she whispered.

Jim sat very still. Eat me: the only way left to feel pleasure in the Dead World. He wanted it, too; he needed it, so badly. "Eat me," he whispered back to her, and he began to unbutton her sweater.

Her nude body was riddled with craters, her breasts sunken into her chest. His own was sallow and emaciated, and between his thighs his penis was a gray, useless piece of flesh. She reached for him, he knelt beside her body, and as she urged "Eat me, eat me," his tongue played circles on her cold skin; then his teeth went to work, and he bit away the first chunk. She moaned and shivered, lifted her head and tongued his arm. Her teeth took a piece of flesh from him, and the ecstasy arrowed along his spinal cord like an electric shock.

They clung to each other, shuddering, their teeth working on arms and legs, throat, chest, face. Faster and faster still, as the wind crashed and Beethoven thundered; gobbets of flesh fell to the carpet, and those gobbets were quickly snatched up and consumed. Jim felt himself shrinking, being transformed from one into two; the incandescent moment had enfolded him, and if there had been tears to cry, he might have wept with joy. Here was love, and here was a lover who both claimed him and gave her all.

Brenda's teeth closed on the back of Jim's neck, crunching through the dry flesh. Her eyes closed in rapture as Jim ate the rest of the fingers on her left hand—and suddenly there was a new sensation, a scurrying around her lips. The love wound on Jim's neck was erupting small yellow roaches, like gold coins spilling from a bag, and Jim's itching subsided. He cried out, his face burrowing into Brenda's abdominal cavity.

Their bodies entwined, the flesh being gnawed away, their shrunken stomachs bulging. Brenda bit off his ear, chewed, and swallowed it; fresh passion coursed through Jim, and he nibbled away her lips—they *did* taste like slightly overripe peaches—and ran his tongue across her teeth. They kissed deeply, biting pieces of their tongues off. Jim drew back and lowered his face to her thighs. He began to eat her, while she gripped his shoulders and screamed.

Brenda arched her body. Jim's sexual organs were there, the testicles like dark, dried fruit. She opened her mouth wide, extended her chewed tongue and bared her teeth; her cheekless, chinless face strained upward—and Jim cried out over even the wail of the wind, his body convulsing.

They continued to feast on each other, like knowing lovers. Jim's body was hollowed out, most of the flesh gone from his face and chest. Brenda's lungs and heart were gone, consumed, and the bones of her arms and legs were fully revealed. Their stomachs swelled. And when they were near explosion, Jim and Brenda lay on the carpet, cradling each other with skeletal arms, lying on bits of flesh like the petals of strange flowers. They were one now, each into the other—and what more could love be than this?

"I love you," Jim said, with his mangled tongue. Brenda made a noise of assent, unable to speak, and took a last love bite from beneath his arm before she snuggled close.

The Beethoven record ended; the next one dropped onto the turntable, and a lilting Strauss waltz began.

Jim felt the building shake. He lifted his head, one eye remaining and that one sated with pleasure, and saw the fire escape trembling. One of the potted plants was suddenly picked up by the wind. "Brenda," he said—and then the plant crashed through the glass and the stormwind came in, whipping around the walls. Another window blew in, and as the next hot wave of wind came, it got into the hollows of the two dried bodies and raised them off the floor like reed-ribbed kites. Brenda made a gasping noise, her arms locked around Jim's spinal cord and his handless arms thrust into her ribcage. The wind hurled them against the wall, snapping bones like matchsticks as the waltz continued to play on for a few seconds before the stereo and table went over. There was no pain, though, and no reason to fear. They were together, in this Dead World where love was a curseword, and together they would face the storm.

The wind churned, threw them one way and then the other—and as it withdrew from Brenda's apartment it took the two bodies with it, into the charged air over the city's roofs.

They flew, buffeted higher and higher, bone locked to bone. The city disappeared beneath them, and they went up into the clouds where the blue lightning danced.

They knew great joy, and at the upper limits of the clouds where the lightning was hottest, they thought they could see the stars.

When the storm passed, a boy on the north side of the city found a strange object on the roof of his apartment building, near the pigeon roost. It looked like a charred-black construction of bones, melded together so you couldn't tell where one bone ended and the other began. And in that mass of bones was a silver chain, with a small ornament. A heart, he saw it was. A white heart, hanging there in the tangle of someone's bones.

He was old enough to realize that someone—two people, maybe—had escaped the Dead World last night. Lucky stiffs, he thought.

He reached in for the dangling heart, and it fell to ashes at his touch.

DEADMAN'S ROAD

JOE R. LANSDALE

THE ECLECTIC WRITINGS of Joe R.(ichard Harold) Lansdale (1951–) have made him a cult favorite in such genres as horror, mystery, adventure, science fiction, Western, comic books, and splatterpunk for more than four decades. More than most authors of his time, Lansdale has produced work for small publishers, often in limited quantities aimed at collectors, mostly in the form of chapbooks and short-story collections. Beginning as mainly a writer of paperback originals in various genres, he has gone on to become recognized as one of the most dependable and popular authors in the mystery field, as well as in horror and comics, and the winner of countless awards.

Generally regarded as his finest work is the crime novel *The Bottoms* (2000), winner of the Edgar Allan Poe Award, a nominee for the Dashiell Hammett and Macavity awards, and a *New York Times* Notable Book of the Year, an honor also given to the second novel in his Hap and Leonard mystery series, which features the exploits of an unlikely pair of East Texas crime fighters, one a blue-collar white man and the other a gay black man. He has been nominated for a Bram Stoker Award an astounding sixteen times, winning seven, and was named a grand master at the World Horror Convention. He has contributed scripts to several television series, including *Superman: The Animated Series,* and *The New Batman Adventures.* His novella *Bubba Ho-Tep* was the basis for the 2002 cult horror film of the same title, in which Elvis Presley and John F. Kennedy are in an old-age home battling an Egyptian mummy.

Lansdale has been engaged in martial arts for more than thirty years, is credited with having invented the form known as Shen Chuan, and has been elected to the Martial Arts Hall of Fame.

"Deadman's Road" was originally published in the February/March 2007 issue of *Weird Tales.*

JOE R. LANSDALE

DEADMAN'S ROAD

THE EVENING SUN had rolled down and blown out in a bloody wad, and the white, full moon had rolled up like an enormous ball of tightly wrapped twine. As he rode, the Reverend Jebidiah Rains watched it glow above the tall pines. All about it stars were sprinkled white-hot in the dead-black heavens.

The trail he rode on was a thin one, and the trees on either side of it crept toward the path as if they might block the way, and close up behind him. The weary horse on which he was riding moved forward with its head down, and Jebidiah, too weak to fight it, let his mount droop and take its lead. Jebidiah was too tired to know much at that moment, but he knew one thing. He was a man of the Lord and he hated God, hated the sonofabitch with all his heart.

And he knew God knew and didn't care, because he knew Jebidiah was his messenger. Not one of the New Testament, but one of the Old Testament, harsh and mean and certain, vengeful and without compromise; a man who would have shot a leg out from under Moses and spat in the face of the Holy Ghost and scalped him, tossing his celestial hair to the wild four winds.

It was not a legacy Jebidiah would have preferred, being the bad man messenger of God, but it was his, and he had earned it through sin, and no matter how hard he tried to lay it down and leave it be, he could not. He knew that to give in and abandon his God-given curse, was to burn in hell forever, and to continue was to do as the Lord prescribed, no matter what his feelings toward his mean master might be. His Lord was not a forgiving Lord, nor was he one who cared for your love. All he cared for was obedience, servitude and humiliation. It was why God had invented the human race. Amusement.

As he thought on these matters, the trail turned and widened, and off to one side, amongst tree stumps, was a fairly large clearing, and in its center was a small log house, and out to the side a somewhat larger log barn. In the curtained window of the cabin was a light that burned orange behind the flour-sack curtains. Jebidiah, feeling tired and hungry and thirsty and weary of soul, made for it.

Stopping a short distance from the cabin, Jebidiah leaned forward on his horse and called out, "Hello, the cabin."

He waited for a time, called again, and was halfway through calling when the door opened, and a man about five-foot two with a large droopy hat, holding a rifle, stuck himself part of the way out of the cabin, said, "Who is it calling? You got a voice like a bullfrog."

"Reverend Jebidiah Rains."

"You ain't come to preach none, have you?"

"No, sir. I find it does no good. I'm here to beg for a place in your barn, a night under its roof. Something for my horse, something for myself if it's available. Most anything, as long as water is involved."

"Well," said the man, "this seems to be the gathering place tonight. Done got two others, and we just sat asses down to eat. I got enough you want it, some hot beans and some old bread."

"I would be most obliged, sir," Jebidiah said.

"Oblige all you want. In the meantime, climb down from that nag, put it in the barn and come in and chow. They call me Old Timer, but I ain't that old. It's 'cause most of my teeth are gone and I'm crippled in a foot a horse stepped on. There's a lantern just inside the barn door. Light that up, and put it out when you finish, come on back to the house."

WHEN JEBIDIAH FINISHED grooming and feeding his horse with grain in the barn,

watering him, he came into the cabin, made a show of pushing his long black coat back so that it revealed his ivory-handled .44 cartridge-converted revolvers. They were set so that they leaned forward in their holsters, strapped close to the hips, not draped low like punks wore them. Jebidiah liked to wear them close to the natural swing of his hands. When he pulled them it was a movement quick as the flick of a hummingbird's wings, the hammers clicking from the cock of his thumb, the guns barking, spewing lead with amazing accuracy. He had practiced enough to drive a cork into a bottle at about a hundred paces, and he could do it in bad light. He chose to reveal his guns that way to show he was ready for any attempted ambush. He reached up and pushed his wide-brimmed black hat back on his head, showing black hair gone gray-tipped. He thought having his hat tipped made him look casual. It did not. His eyes always seemed aflame in an angry face.

Inside, the cabin was bright with kerosene lamp light, and the kerosene smelled, and there were curls of black smoke twisting about, mixing with gray smoke from the pipe of Old Timer, and the cigarette of a young man with a badge pinned to his shirt. Beside him, sitting on a chopping log by the fireplace, which was too hot for the time of year, but was being used to heat up a pot of beans, was a middle-aged man with a slight paunch and a face that looked like it attracted thrown objects. He had his hat pushed up a bit, and a shock of wheat-colored, sweaty hair hung on his forehead. There was a cigarette in his mouth, half of it ash. He twisted on the chopping log, and Jebidiah saw that his hands were manacled together.

"I heard you say you was a preacher," said the manacled man, as he tossed the last of his smoke into the fireplace. "This here sure ain't God's country."

"Worse thing is," said Jebidiah, "it's exactly God's country."

The manacled man gave out with a snort, and grinned.

"Preacher," said the younger man, "my name is Jim Taylor. I'm a deputy for Sheriff Spradley, out of Nacogdoches. I'm taking this man there for a trial, and most likely a hanging. He killed a fella for a rifle and a horse. I see you tote guns, old style guns, but good ones. Way you tote them, I'm suspecting you know how to use them."

"I've been known to hit what I aim at," Jebidiah said, and sat in a rickety chair at an equally rickety table. Old Timer put some tin plates on the table, scratched his ass with a long wooden spoon, then grabbed a rag and used it as a pot holder, lifted the hot bean pot to the table. He popped the lid off the pot, used the ass-scratching spoon to scoop a heap of beans onto plates. He brought over some wooden cups and poured them full from a pitcher of water.

"Thing is," the deputy said, "I could use some help. I don't know I can get back safe with this fella, havin' not slept good in a day or two. Was wondering, you and Old Timer here could watch my back till morning? Wouldn't even mind if you rode along with me tomorrow, as sort of a backup. I could use a gun hand. Sheriff might even give you a dollar for it."

Old Timer, as if this conversation had not been going on, brought over a bowl with some moldy biscuits in it, placed them on the table. "Made them a week ago. They've gotten a bit ripe, but you can scratch around the mold. I'll warn you though, they're tough enough you could toss one hard and kill a chicken on the run. So mind your teeth."

"That how you lost yours, Old Timer?" the manacled man said.

"Probably part of them," Old Timer said.

"What you say, preacher?" the deputy said. "You let me get some sleep?"

"My problem lies in the fact that I need sleep," Jebidiah said. "I've been busy, and I'm what could be referred to as tuckered."

"Guess I'm the only one that feels spry," said the manacled man.

"No," said Old Timer. "I feel right fresh myself."

"Then it's you and me, Old Timer," the manacled man said, and grinned, as if this meant something.

"You give me cause, fella, I'll blow a hole in you and tell God you got in a nest of termites."

The manacled man gave his snort of a laugh again. He seemed to be having a good old time.

"Me and Old Timer can work shifts," Jebidiah said. "That okay with you, Old Timer?"

"Peachy," Old Timer said, and took another plate from the table and filled it with beans. He gave this one to the manacled man, who said, lifting his bound hands to take it, "What do I eat it with?"

"Your mouth. Ain't got no extra spoons. And I ain't giving you a knife."

The manacled man thought on this for a moment, grinned, lifted the plate and put his face close to the edge of it, sort of poured the beans toward his mouth. He lowered the plate and chewed. "Reckon they taste scorched with or without a spoon."

Jebidiah reached inside his coat, took out and opened up a pocket knife, used it to spear one of the biscuits, and to scrape the beans toward him.

"You come to the table, young fella," Old Timer said to the deputy. "I'll get my shotgun, he makes a move that ain't eatin', I'll blast him and the beans inside him into that fireplace there."

OLD TIMER SAT with a double barrel shotgun resting on his leg, pointed in the general direction of the manacled man. The deputy told all that his prisoner had done while he ate. Murdered women and children, shot a dog and a horse, and just for the hell of it, shot a cat off a fence, and set fire to an outhouse with a woman in it. He had also raped women, stuck a stick up a sheriff's ass, and killed him, and most likely shot other animals that might have been some good to somebody. Overall, he was tough on human beings, and equally as tough on livestock.

"I never did like animals," the manacled man said. "Carry fleas. And that woman in the outhouse stunk to high heaven. She ought to eat better. She needed burning."

"Shut up," the deputy said. "This fella," and he nodded toward the prisoner, "his name is Bill Barrett, and he's the worst of the worst. Thing is, well, I'm not just tired, I'm a little wounded. He and I had a tussle. I hadn't surprised him, wouldn't be here today. I got a bullet graze in my hip. We had quite a dust up. I finally got him down by putting a gun barrel to his noggin half a dozen times or so. I'm not hurt so bad, but I lost blood for a couple days. Weakened me. You'd ride along with me, Reverend, I'd appreciate it."

"I'll consider it," Jebidiah said. "But I'm about my business."

"Who you gonna preach to along here, 'sides us?" the deputy said.

"Don't even think about it," Old Timer said. "Just thinking about that Jesus foolishness makes my ass tired. Preaching makes me want to kill the preacher and cut my own throat. Being at a preachin' is like being tied down in a nest of red bitin' ants."

"At this point in my life," Jebidiah said, "I agree."

There was a moment of silence in response to Jebidiah, then the deputy turned his attention to Old Timer. "What's the fastest route to Nacogdoches?"

"Well now," Old Timer said, "you can keep going like you been going, following the road out front. And in time you'll run into a road, say thirty miles from here, and it goes left. That should take you right near Nacogdoches, which is another ten miles, though you'll have to make a turn somewhere up in there near the end of the trip. Ain't exactly sure where unless I'm looking at it. Whole trip, traveling at an even pace ought to take you two day."

"You could go with us," the deputy said. "Make sure I find that road."

"Could," said Old Timer, "but I won't. I don't ride so good anymore. My balls ache I ride a horse for too long. Last time I rode a pretty

good piece, I had to squat over a pan of warm water and salt, soak my taters for an hour or so just so they'd fit back in my pants."

"My balls ache just listening to you," the prisoner said. "Thing is, though, them swollen up like that, was probably the first time in your life you had man-sized balls, you old fart. You should have left them swollen."

Old Timer cocked back the hammers on the double barrel. "This here could go off."

Bill just grinned, leaned his back against the fireplace, then jumped forward. For a moment, it looked as if Old Timer might cut him in half, but he realized what had happened.

"Oh yeah," Old Timer said. "That there's hot, stupid. Why they call it a fireplace."

Bill readjusted himself, so that his back wasn't against the stones. He said, "I'm gonna cut this deputy's pecker off, come back here, make you fry it up and eat it."

"You're gonna shit and fall back in it," Old Timer said. "That's all you're gonna do."

When things had calmed down again, the deputy said to Old Timer, "There's no faster route?"

Old Timer thought for a moment. "None you'd want to take."

"What's that mean?" the deputy said.

Old Timer slowly lowered the hammers on the shotgun, smiling at Bill all the while. When he had them lowered, he turned his head, looked at the deputy. "Well, there's Deadman's Road."

"What's wrong with that?" the deputy asked.

"All manner of things. Used to be called Cemetery Road. Couple years back that changed."

Jebidiah's interest was aroused. "Tell us about it, Old Timer."

"Now I ain't one to believe in hogwash, but there's a story about the road, and I got it from someone you might say was the horse's mouth."

"A ghost story, that's choice," said Bill.

"How much time would the road cut off going to Nacogdoches?" the deputy asked.

"Near a day," Old Timer said.

"Damn. Then that's the way I got to go," the deputy said.

"Turn off for it ain't far from here, but I wouldn't recommend it," Old Timer said. "I ain't much for Jesus, but I believe in haints, things like that. Living out here in this thicket, you see some strange things. There's gods ain't got nothing to do with Jesus or Moses, or any of that bunch. There's older gods than that. Indians talk about them."

"I'm not afraid of any Indian gods," the deputy said.

"Maybe not," Old Timer said, "but these gods, even the Indians ain't fond of them. They ain't their gods. These gods are older than the Indian folk their ownselfs. Indians try not to stir them up. They worship their own."

"And why would this road be different than any other?" Jebidiah asked. "What does it have to do with ancient gods?"

Old Timer grinned. "You're just wanting to challenge it, ain't you, Reverend? Prove how strong your god is. You weren't no preacher, you'd be a gunfighter, I reckon. Or, maybe you are just that. A gunfighter preacher."

"I'm not that fond of my god," Jebidiah said, "but I have been given a duty. Drive out evil. Evil as my god sees it. If these gods are evil, and they're in my path, then I have to confront them."

"They're evil, all right," Old Timer said.

"Tell us about them," Jebidiah said.

"GIL GIMET WAS a bee keeper," Old Timer said. "He raised honey, and lived off of Deadman's Road. Known then as Cemetery Road. That's 'cause there was a graveyard down there. It had some old Spanish graves in it, some said Conquistadores who tromped through here but didn't tromp out. I know there was some Indians buried there, early Christian Indians, I reckon. Certainly there were stones and crosses up and Indian names on the crosses. Maybe mixed breeds. Lots of intermarrying around here. Any-

way, there were all manner people buried up there. The dead ground don't care what color you are when you go in, 'cause in the end, we're all gonna be the color of dirt."

"Hell," Bill said. "You're already the color of dirt. And you smell like some pretty old dirt at that."

"You gonna keep on, mister," Old Timer said, "and you're gonna wind up having the undertaker wipe your ass." Old Timer cocked back the hammers on the shotgun again. "This here gun could go off accidently. Could happen, and who here is gonna argue it didn't?"

"Not me," the deputy said. "It would be easier on me you were dead, Bill."

Bill looked at the Reverend. "Yeah, but that wouldn't set right with the Reverend, would it, Reverend?"

"Actually, I wouldn't care one way or another. I'm not a man of peace, and I'm not a forgiver, even if what you did wasn't done to me. I think we're all rich and deep in sin. Maybe none of us are worthy of forgiveness."

Bill sunk a little at his seat. No one was even remotely on his side. Old Timer continued with his story.

"This here bee keeper, Gimet, he wasn't known as much of a man. Mean-hearted is how he was thunk of. I knowed him, and I didn't like him. I seen him snatch up a little dog once and cut the tail off of it with his knife, just 'cause he thought it was funny. Boy who owned the dog tried to fight back, and Gimet, he cut the boy on the arm. No one did nothin' about it. Ain't no real law in these parts, you see, and wasn't nobody brave enough to do nothin'. Me included. And he did lots of other mean things, even killed a couple of men, and claimed self-defense. Might have been, but Gimet was always into something, and whatever he was into always turned out with someone dead, or hurt, or humiliated."

"Bill here sounds like he could be Gimet's brother," the deputy said.

"Oh, no," Old Timer said, shaking his head.

"This here scum-licker ain't a bump on the mean old ass of Gimet. Gimet lived in a little shack off Cemetery Road. He raised bees, and brought in honey to sell at the community up the road. Guess you could even call it a town. Schow is the way the place is known, on account of a fella used to live up there was named Schow. He died and got ate up by pigs. Right there in his own pen, just keeled over slopping the hogs, and then they slopped him, all over that place. A store got built on top of where Schow got et up, and that's how the place come by the name. Gimet took his honey in there to the store and sold it, and even though he was a turd, he had some of the best honey you ever smacked your mouth around. Wish I had me some now. It was dark and rich, and sweeter than any sugar. Think that's one reason he got away with things. People don't like killing and such, but they damn sure like their honey."

"This story got a point?" Bill said.

"You don't like the way I'm telling it," Old Timer said, "why don't you think about how that rope's gonna fit around your neck. That ought to keep your thoughts occupied, right smart."

Bill made a grunting noise, turned on his block of wood, as if to show he wasn't interested.

"Well, now, honey or not, sweet tooth, or not, everything has an end to it. And thing was he took to a little gal, Mary Lynn Twoshoe. She was a part Indian gal, a real looker, hair black as the bottom of a well, eyes the same color, and she was just as fine in the features as them pictures you see of them stage actresses. She wasn't five feet tall, and that hair of hers went all the way down her back. Her daddy was dead. The pox got him. And her mama wasn't too well off, being sickly, and all. She made brooms out of straw and branches she trimmed down. Sold a few of them, raised a little garden and a hog. When all this happened, Mary Lynn was probably thirteen, maybe fourteen. Wasn't no older than that."

"If you're gonna tell a tale," Bill said, "least don't wander all over the place."

"So, you're interested?" Old Timer said.

"What else I got to do?" Bill said.

"Go on," Jebidiah said. "Tell us about Mary Lynn."

Old Timer nodded. "Gimet took to her. Seen her around, bringing the brooms her mama made into the store. He waited on her, grabbed her, and just threwed her across his saddle kickin' and screamin', like he'd bought a sack of flour and was ridin' it to the house. Mack Collins, store owner, came out and tried to stop him. Well, he said something to him. About how he shouldn't do it, least that's the way I heard it. He didn't push much, and I can't blame him. Didn't do good to cross Gimet. Anyway, Gimet just said back to Mack, 'Give her mama a big jar of honey. Tell her that's for her daughter. I'll even make her another jar or two, if the meat here's as sweet as I'm expecting.'

"With that, he slapped Mary Lynn on the ass and rode off with her."

"Sounds like my kind of guy," Bill said.

"I have become irritated with you now," Jebidiah said. "Might I suggest you shut your mouth before I pistol whip you."

Bill glared at Jebidiah, but the Reverend's gaze was as dead and menacing as the barrels of Old Timer's shotgun.

"Rest of the story is kind of grim," Old Timer said. "Gimet took her off to his house, and had his way with her. So many times he damn near killed her, and then he turned her loose, or got so drunk she was able to get loose. Time she walked down Cemetery Road, made it back to town, well, she was bleeding so bad from having been used so rough, she collapsed. She lived a day and died from loss of blood. Her mother, out of her sick bed, rode a mule out there to the cemetery on Cemetery Road. I told you she was Indian, and she knew some Indian ways, and she knew about them old gods that wasn't none of the gods of her people, but she still knew about them.

"She knew some signs to draw in cemetery dirt. I don't know the whole of it, but she did some things, and she did it on some old grave out there, and the last thing she did was she cut her own throat, died right there, her blood running on top of that grave and them pictures she drawed in the dirt."

"Don't see how that done her no good," the deputy said.

"Maybe it didn't, but folks think it did," Old Timer said. "Community that had been pushed around by Gimet, finally had enough, went out there in mass to hang his ass, shoot him, whatever it took. Got to his cabin they found Gimet dead outside his shack. His eyes had been torn out, or blown out is how they looked. Skin was peeled off his head, just leaving the skull and a few hairs. His chest was ripped open, and his insides was gone, exceptin' the bones in there. And them bees of his had nested in the hole in his chest, had done gone about making honey. Was buzzing out of that hole, his mouth, empty eyes, nose, or where his nose used to be. I figure they'd rolled him over, tore off his pants, they'd have been coming out of his asshole."

"How come you weren't out there with them?" Bill said. "How come this is all stuff you heard?"

"Because I was a coward when it come to Gimet," Old Timer said. "That's why. Told myself wouldn't never be a coward again, no matter what. I should have been with them. Didn't matter no how. He was done good and dead, them bees all in him. What was done then is the crowd got kind of loco, tore off his clothes, hooked his feet up to a horse and dragged him through a blackberry patch, them bees just burstin' out and hummin' all around him. All that ain't right, but I think I'd been with them, knowing who he was and all the things he'd done, I might have been loco too. They dumped him out on the cemetery to let him rot, took that girl's mother home to be buried some place better. Wasn't no more than a few nights later that folks started seeing Gimet. They said he walked at night, when the moon was at least half, or full, like it is now. Number of folks seen him, said he loped alongside the road, following their horses, grabbing hold of the tail if he could, trying to pull horse and rider down, or pull himself up on the

back of their mounts. Said them bees was still in him. Bees black as flies, and angry whirling all about him, and coming from inside him. Worse, there was a larger number of folks took that road that wasn't never seen again. It was figured Gimet got them."

"Horse shit," the deputy said. "No disrespect, Old Timer. You've treated me all right, that's for sure. But a ghost chasing folks down. I don't buy that."

"Don't have to buy it," Old Timer said. "I ain't trying to sell it to you none. Don't have to believe it. And I don't think it's no ghost anyway. I think that girl's mother, she done something to let them old gods out for a while, sicced them on that bastard, used her own life as a sacrifice, that's what I think. And them gods, them things from somewhere else, they ripped him up like that. Them bees is part of that too. They ain't no regular honey bee. They're some other kind of bees. Some kind of fitting death for a bee raiser, is my guess."

"That's silly," the deputy said.

"I don't know," Jebidiah said. "The Indian woman may only have succeeded in killing him in this life. She may not have understood all that she did. Didn't know she was giving him an opportunity to live again . . . Or maybe that is the curse. Though there are plenty others have to suffer for it."

"Like the folks didn't do nothing when Gimet was alive," Old Timer said. "Folks like me that let what went on go on."

Jebidiah nodded. "Maybe."

The deputy looked at Jebidiah. "Not you too, Reverend. You should know better than that. There ain't but one true god, and ain't none of that hoodoo business got a drop of truth to it."

"If there's one god," Jebidiah said, "there can be many. They are at war with one another, that's how it works, or so I think. I've seen some things that have shook my faith in the one true god, the one I'm servant to. And what is our god but hoodoo? It's all hoodoo, my friend."

"Okay. What things have you seen, Reverend?" the deputy asked.

"No use describing it to you, young man," Jebidiah said. "You wouldn't believe me. But I've recently come from Mud Creek. It had an infestation of a sort. That town burned down, and I had a hand in it."

"Mud Creek," Old Timer said. "I been there."

"Only thing there now," Jebidiah said, "is some charred wood."

"Ain't the first time it's burned down," Old Timer said. "Some fool always rebuilds it, and with it always comes some kind of ugliness. I'll tell you straight. I don't doubt your word at all, Reverend."

"Thing is," the deputy said, "I don't believe in no haints. That's the shortest road, and it's the road I'm gonna take."

"I wouldn't," Old Timer said.

"Thanks for the advice. But no one goes with me or does, that's the road I'm taking, provided it cuts a day off my trip."

"I'm going with you," Jebidiah said. "My job is striking at evil. Not to walk around it."

"I'd go during the day," Old Timer said. "Ain't no one seen Gimet in the day, or when the moon is thin or not at all. But way it is now, it's full, and will be again tomorrow night. I'd ride hard tomorrow, you're determined to go. Get there as soon as you can, before dark."

"I'm for getting there," the deputy said. "I'm for getting back to Nacogdoches, and getting this bastard in a cell."

"I'll go with you," Jebidiah said. "But I want to be there at night. I want to take Deadman's Road at that time. I want to see if Gimet is there. And if he is, send him to his final death. Defy those dark gods the girl's mother called up. Defy them and loose my god on him. What I'd suggest is you get some rest, deputy. Old Timer here can watch a bit, then I'll take over. That way we all get some rest. We can chain this fellow to a tree outside, we have to. We should both get slept up to the gills, then leave here mid-day, after a good dinner, head out for Deadman's Road. Long as we're there by nightfall."

"That ought to bring you right on it," Old Timer said. "You take Deadman's Road. When you get to the fork, where the road ends, you go right. Ain't no one ever seen Gimet beyond that spot, or in front of where the road begins. He's tied to that stretch, way I heard it."

"Good enough," the deputy said. "I find this all foolish, but if I can get some rest, and have you ride along with me, Reverend, then I'm game. And I'll be fine with getting there at night."

NEXT MORNING THEY slept late, and had an early lunch. Beans and hard biscuits again, a bit of stewed squirrel. Old Timer had shot the rodent that morning while Jebidiah watched Bill sit on his ass, his hands chained around a tree in the front yard. Inside the cabin, the deputy had continued to sleep.

But now they all sat outside eating, except for Bill.

"What about me?" Bill asked, tugging at his chained hands.

"When we finish," Old Timer said. "Don't know if any of the squirrel will be left, but we got them biscuits for you. I can promise you some of them. I might even let you rub one of them around in my plate, sop up some squirrel gravy."

"Those biscuits are awful," Bill said.

"Ain't they," Old Timer said.

Bill turned his attention to Jebidiah. "Preacher, you ought to just go on and leave me and the boy here alone. Ain't smart for you to ride along, 'cause I get loose, ain't just the deputy that's gonna pay. I'll put you on the list."

"After what I've seen in this life," Jebidiah said, "you are nothing to me. An insect . . . So, add me to your list."

"Let's feed him," the deputy said, nodding at Bill, "and get to moving. I'm feeling rested and want to get this ball started."

THE MOON HAD begun to rise when they rode in sight of Deadman's Road. The white cross road sign was sticking up beside the road. Trees and brush had grown up around it, and between the limbs and the shadows, the crudely painted words on the sign were halfway readable in the waning light. The wind had picked up and was grabbing at leaves, plucking them from the ground, tumbling them about, tearing them from trees and tossing them across the narrow, clay road with a sound like mice scuttling in straw.

"Fall always depresses me," the deputy said, halting his horse, taking a swig from his canteen.

"Life is a cycle," Jebidiah said. "You're born, you suffer, then you're punished."

The deputy turned in his saddle to look at Jebidiah. "You ain't much on that resurrection and reward, are you?"

"No, I'm not."

"I don't know about you," the deputy said, "but I wish we hadn't gotten here so late. I'd rather have gone through in the day."

"Thought you weren't a believer in spooks?" Bill said, and made with his now familiar snort. "You said it didn't matter to you."

The deputy didn't look at Bill when he spoke. "I wasn't here then. Place has a look I don't like. And I don't enjoy temptin' things. Even if I don't believe in them."

"That's the silliest thing I ever heard," Bill said.

"Wanted me with you," Jebidiah said. "You had to wait."

"You mean to see something, don't you, preacher?" Bill said.

"If there is something to see," Jebidiah said.

"You believe Old Timer's story?" the deputy said. "I mean, really?"

"Perhaps."

Jebidiah clucked to his horse and took the lead.

WHEN THEY TURNED onto Deadman's Road, Jebidiah paused and removed a small, fat bible from his saddlebag.

The deputy paused too, forcing Bill to pause

as well. "You ain't as ornery as I thought," the deputy said. "You want the peace of the bible just like anyone else."

"There is no peace in this book," Jebidiah said. "That's a real confusion. Bible isn't anything but a book of terror, and that's how God is: Terrible. But the book has power. And we might need it."

"I don't know what to think about you, Reverend," the deputy said.

"Ain't nothin' you can think about a man that's gone loco," Bill said. "I don't want to stay with no man that's loco."

"You get an idea to run, Bill, I can shoot you off your horse," the deputy said. "Close range with my revolver, far range with my rifle. You don't want to try it."

"It's still a long way to Nacogdoches," Bill said.

THE ROAD WAS narrow and of red clay. It stretched far ahead like a band of blood, turned sharply to the right around a wooded curve where it was as dark as the bottom of Jonah's whale. The blowing leaves seemed especially intense on the road, scrapping dryly about, winding in the air like giant hornets. The trees, which grew thick, bent in the wind, from right to left. This naturally led the trio to take to the left side of the road.

The farther they went down the road, the darker it became. By the time they got to the curve, the woods were so thick, and the thunderous skies had grown so dark, the moon was barely visible; its light was as weak as a sick baby's grip.

When they had traveled for some time, the deputy said, obviously feeling good about it, "There ain't nothing out here 'sides what you would expect. A possum maybe. The wind."

"Good for you, then," Jebidiah said. "Good for us all."

"You sound disappointed to me," the deputy said.

"My line of work isn't far from yours, Deputy. I look for bad guys of a sort, and try and send them to hell . . . Or in some cases, back to hell."

And then, almost simultaneous with a flash of lightning, something crossed the road not far in front of them.

"What the hell was that?" Bill said, coming out of what had been a near stupor.

"It looked like a man," the deputy said.

"Could have been," Jebidiah said. "Could have been."

"What do you think it was?"

"You don't want to know."

"I do."

"Gimet," Jebidiah said.

THE SKY LET the moon loose for a moment, and its light spread through the trees and across the road. In the light there were insects, a large wad of them, buzzing about in the air.

"Bees," Bill said. "Damn if them ain't bees. And at night. That ain't right."

"You an expert on bees?" the deputy asked.

"He's right," Jebidiah said. "And look, they're gone now."

"Flew off," the deputy said.

"No . . . no they didn't," Bill said. "I was watching, and they didn't fly nowhere. They're just gone. One moment they were there, then they was gone, and that's all there is to it. They're like ghosts."

"You done gone crazy," the deputy said.

"They are not insects of this earth," Jebidiah said. "They are familiars."

"What?" Bill said.

"They assist evil, or evil beings," Jebidiah said. "In this case, Gimet. They're like a witch's black cat familiar. Familiars take on animal shapes, insects, that sort of thing."

"That's ridiculous," the deputy said. "That don't make no kind of sense at all."

"Whatever you say," Jebidiah said, "but I would keep my eyes alert, and my senses raw. Wouldn't hurt to keep your revolvers loose in their holsters. You could well need them.

Though, come to think of it, your revolvers won't be much use."

"What the hell does that mean?" Bill said.

Jebidiah didn't answer. He continued to urge his horse on, something that was becoming a bit more difficult as they went. All of the horses snorted and turned their heads left and right, tugged at their bits; their ears went back and their eyes went wide.

"Holy hell," Bill said, "what's that?"

Jebidiah and the deputy turned to look at him. Bill was turned in the saddle, looking back. They looked too, just in time to see something that looked pale blue in the moonlight, dive into the brush on the other side of the road. Black dots followed, swarmed in the moonlight, then darted into the bushes behind the pale, blue thing like a load of buckshot.

"What was that?" the deputy said. His voice sounded as if it had been pistol whipped.

"Already told you," Jebidiah said.

"That couldn't have been nothing human," the deputy said.

"Don't you get it," Bill said, "that's what the preacher is trying to tell you. It's Gimet, and he ain't nowhere alive. His skin was blue. And he's all messed up. I seen more than you did. I got a good look. And them bees. We ought to break out and ride hard."

"Do as you choose," the Reverend said. "I don't intend to."

"And why not?" Bill said.

"That isn't my job."

"Well, I ain't got no job. Deputy, ain't you supposed to make sure I get to Nacogdoches to get hung? Ain't that your job?"

"It is."

"Then we ought to ride on, not bother with this fool. He wants to fight some grave crawler, then let him. Ain't nothing we ought to get into."

"We made a pact to ride together," the deputy said. "So we will."

"I didn't make no pact," Bill said.

"Your word, your needs, they're nothing to me," the deputy said.

At that moment, something began to move through the woods on their left. Something moving quick and heavy, not bothering with stealth. Jebidiah looked in the direction of the sounds, saw someone, or something, moving through the underbrush, snapping limbs aside like they were rotten sticks. He could hear the buzz of the bees, loud and angry. Without really meaning to, he urged the horse to a trot. The deputy and Bill joined in with their own mounts, keeping pace with the Reverend's horse.

They came to a place off the side of the road where the brush thinned, and out in the distance they could see what looked like bursting white waves, frozen against the dark. But they soon realized it was tombstones. And there were crosses. A graveyard. The graveyard Old Timer had told them about. The sky had cleared now, the wind had ceased to blow hard. They had a fine view of the cemetery, and as they watched, the thing that had been in the brush moved out of it and went up the little rise where the graves were, climbed up on one of the stones and sat. A black cloud formed around its head, and the sound of buzzing could be heard all the way out to the road. The thing sat there like a king on a throne. Even from that distance it was easy to see it was nude, and male, and his skin was gray— blue in the moonlight—and the head looked misshapen. Moon glow slipped through cracks in the back of the horror's head and poked out of fresh cracks at the front of its skull and speared out of the empty eye sockets. The bee's nest, visible through the wound in its chest, was nestled between the ribs. It pulsed with a yellow-honey glow. From time to time, little black dots moved around the glow and flew up and were temporarily pinned in the moonlight above the creature's head.

"Jesus," said the deputy.

"Jesus won't help a bit," Jebidiah said.

"It's Gimet, ain't it? He . . . it . . . really is dead," the deputy said.

"Undead," Jebidiah said. "I believe he's toying with us. Waiting for when he plans to strike."

"Strike?" Bill said. "Why?"

"Because that is his purpose," Jebidiah said, "as it is mine to strike back. Gird your loins, men, you will soon be fighting for your life."

"How about we just ride like hell?" Bill said.

In that moment, Jebidiah's words became prophetic. The thing was gone from the grave stone. Shadows had gathered at the edge of the woods, balled up, become solid, and when the shadows leaped from the even darker shadows of the trees, it was the shape of the thing they had seen on the stone, cool blue in the moonlight, a disaster of a face, and the teeth . . . They were long and sharp. Gimet leaped in such a way that his back foot hit the rear of Jebidiah's animal, allowing him to spring over the deputy's horse, to land hard and heavy on Bill. Bill let out a howl and was knocked off his mount. When he hit the road, his hat flying, Gimet grabbed him by his bushy head of straw-colored hair and dragged him off as easily as if he were a kitten. Gimet went into the trees, tugging Bill after him. Gimet blended with the darkness there. The last of Bill was a scream, the raising of his cuffed hands, the cuffs catching the moonlight for a quick blink of silver, then there was a rustle of leaves and a slapping of branches, and Bill was gone.

"My God," the deputy said. "My God. Did you see that thing?"

Jebidiah dismounted, moved to the edge of the road, leading his horse, his gun drawn. The deputy did not dismount. He pulled his pistol and held it, his hands trembling. "Did you see that?" he said again, and again.

"My eyes are as good as your own," Jebidiah said. "I saw it. We'll have to go in and get him."

"Get him?" the deputy said. "Why in the name of everything that's holy would we do that? Why would we want to be near that thing? He's probably done what he's done already . . . Damn, Reverend. Bill, he's a killer. This is just as good as I might want. I say while the old boy is doing whatever he's doing to that bastard, we ride like the goddamn wind, get on out on the far end of this road where it forks. Gimet is supposed to be only able to go on this stretch, ain't he?"

"That's what Old Timer said. You do as you want. I'm going in after him."

"Why? You don't even know him."

"It's not about him," Jebidiah said.

"Ah, hell. I ain't gonna be shamed." The deputy swung down from his horse, pointed at the place where Gimet had disappeared with Bill. "Can we get the horses through there?"

"Think we will have to go around a bit. I discern a path over there."

"Discern?"

"Recognize. Come on, time is wasting."

THEY WENT BACK up the road a pace, found a trail that led through the trees. The moon was strong now as all the clouds that had covered it had rolled away like wind blown pollen. The air smelled fresh, but as they moved forward, that changed. There was a stench in the air, a putrid smell both sweet and sour, and it floated up and spoiled the freshness.

"Something dead," the deputy said.

"Something long dead," Jebidiah said.

Finally the brush grew so thick they had to tie the horses, leave them. They pushed their way through briars and limbs.

"There ain't no path," the deputy said. "You don't know he come through this way."

Jebidiah reached out and plucked a piece of cloth from a limb, held it up so that the moon dropped rays on it. "This is part of Bill's shirt. Am I right?"

The deputy nodded. "But how could Gimet get through here? How could he get Bill through here?"

"What we pursue has little interest in the things that bother man. Limbs, briars. It's nothing to the living dead."

They went on for a while. Vines got in their way. The vines were wet. They were long thick vines, and sticky, and finally they realized they were not vines at all, but guts, strewn about and draped like decorations.

"Fresh," the deputy said. "Bill, I reckon."

"You reckon right," Jebidiah said.

They pushed on a little farther, and the trail widened, making the going easier. They found more pieces of Bill as they went along. The stomach. Fingers. Pants with one leg in them. A heart, which looked as if it had been bitten into and sucked on. Jebidiah was curious enough to pick it up and examine it. Finished, he tossed it in the dirt, wiped his hands on Bill's pants, the one with the leg still in it, said, "Gimet just saved you a lot of bother and the State of Texas the trouble of a hanging."

"Heavens," the deputy said, watching Jebidiah wipe blood on the leg-filled pants.

Jebidiah looked up at the deputy. "He won't mind I get blood on his pants," Jebidiah said. "He's got more important things to worry about, like dancing in the fires of hell. And by the way, yonder sports his head."

Jebidiah pointed. The deputy looked. Bill's head had been pushed onto a broken limb of a tree, the sharp end of the limb being forced through the rear of the skull and out the left eye. The spinal cord dangled from the back of the head like a bell rope.

The deputy puked in the bushes. "Oh, God. I don't want no more of this."

"Go back. I won't think the less of you, 'cause I don't think that much of you to begin with. Take his head for evidence and ride on, just leave me my horse."

The deputy adjusted his hat. "Don't need the head . . . And if it comes to it, you'll be glad I'm here. I ain't no weak sister."

"Don't talk me to death on the matter. Show me what you got, boy."

The trail was slick with Bill's blood. They went along it and up a rise, guns drawn. At the top of the hill they saw a field, grown up, and not far away, a sagging shack with a fallen down chimney.

They went that direction, came to the shack's door. Jebidiah kicked it with the toe of his boot and it sagged open. Once inside, Jebidiah struck a match and waved it about. Nothing but cobwebs and dust.

"Must have been Gimet's place," Jebidiah

said. Jebidiah moved the match before him until he found a lantern full of coal oil. He lit it and placed the lantern on the table.

"Should we do that?" the deputy asked. "Have a light. Won't he find us?"

"In case you have forgotten, that's the idea."

Out the back window, which had long lost its grease paper covering, they could see tombstones and wooden crosses in the distance. "Another view of the graveyard," Jebidiah said. "That would be where the girl's mother killed herself."

No sooner had Jebidiah said that than he saw a shadowy shape move on the hill, flitting between stones and crosses. The shape moved quickly and awkwardly.

"Move to the center of the room," Jebidiah said.

The deputy did as he was told, and Jebidiah moved the lamp there as well. He sat it in the center of the floor, found a bench and dragged it next to the lantern. Then he reached in his coat pocket and took out the bible. He dropped to one knee and held the bible close to the lantern light and tore out certain pages. He wadded them up, and began placing them all around the bench on the floor, placing the crumpled pages about six feet out from the bench and in a circle with each wad two feet apart.

The deputy said nothing. He sat on the bench and watched Jebidiah's curious work. Jebidiah sat on the bench beside the deputy, rested one of his pistols on his knee. "You got a .44, don't you?"

"Yeah. I got a converted cartridge pistol, just like you."

"Give me your revolver."

The deputy complied.

Jebidiah opened the cylinders and let the bullets fall out on the floor.

"What in hell are you doing?"

Jebidiah didn't answer. He dug into his gun belt and came up with six silver-tipped bullets, loaded the weapon and gave it back to the deputy.

"Silver," Jebidiah said. "Sometimes it wards off evil."

"Sometimes?"

"Be quiet now. And wait."

"I feel like a staked goat," the deputy said.

After a while, Jebidiah rose from the bench and looked out the window. Then he sat down promptly and blew out the lantern.

SOMEWHERE IN THE distance a night bird called. Crickets sawed and a large frog bleated. They sat there on the bench, near each other, facing in opposite directions, their silver-loaded pistols on their knees. Neither spoke.

Suddenly the bird ceased to call and the crickets went silent, and no more was heard from the frog. Jebidiah whispered to the deputy.

"He comes."

The deputy shivered slightly, took a deep breath. Jebidiah realized he too was breathing deeply.

"Be silent, and be alert," Jebidiah said.

"All right," said the deputy, and he locked his eyes on the open window at the back of the shack. Jebidiah faced the door, which stood halfway open and sagging on its rusty hinges.

For a long time there was nothing. Not a sound. Then Jebidiah saw a shadow move at the doorway and heard the door creak slightly as it moved. He could see a hand on what appeared to be an impossibly long arm, reaching out to grab at the edge of the door. The hand clutched there for a long time, not moving. Then, it was gone, taking its shadow with it.

Time crawled by.

"It's at the window," the deputy said, and his voice was so soft it took Jebidiah a moment to decipher the words. Jebidiah turned carefully for a look.

It sat on the window sill, crouched there like a bird of prey, a halo of bees circling around its head. The hive pulsed and glowed in its chest, and in that glow they could see more bees, so thick they appeared to be a sort of humming smoke. Gimet's head sprouted a few sprigs of hair, like withering grass fighting its way through stone. A slight turn of its head allowed the moon to flow through the back of its cracked skull and out of its empty eyes. Then the head turned and the face was full of shadows again. The room was silent except for the sound of buzzing bees.

"Courage," Jebidiah said, his mouth close to the deputy's ear. "Keep your place."

The thing climbed into the room quickly, like a spider dropping from a limb, and when it hit the floor, it stayed low, allowing the darkness to lay over it like a cloak.

Jebidiah had turned completely on the bench now, facing the window. He heard a scratching sound against the floor. He narrowed his eyes, saw what looked like a shadow, but was in fact the thing coming out from under the table.

Jebidiah felt the deputy move, perhaps to bolt. He grabbed his arm and held him.

"Courage," he said.

The thing kept crawling. It came within three feet of the circle made by the crumpled bible pages.

The way the moonlight spilled through the window and onto the floor near the circle Jebidiah had made, it gave Gimet a kind of eerie glow, his satellite bees circling his head. In that moment, every aspect of the thing locked itself in Jebidiah's mind. The empty eyes, the sharp, wet teeth, the long, cracked nails, blackened from grime, clacking against the wooden floor. As it moved to cross between two wads of scripture, the pages burst into flames and a line of crackling blue fulmination moved between the wadded pages and made the circle light up fully, all the way around, like Ezekiel's wheel.

Gimet gave out with a hoarse cry, scuttled back, clacking nails and knees against the floor. When he moved, he moved so quickly there seemed to be missing spaces between one moment and the next. The buzzing of Gimet's bees was ferocious.

Jebidiah grabbed the lantern, struck a match and lit it. Gimet was scuttling along the wall like a cockroach, racing to the edge of the window.

Jebidiah leaped forward, tossed the lit lantern, hit the beast full in the back as it fled through the window. The lantern burst into flames and soaked Gimet's back, causing a wave of fire to climb from the thing's waist to the top of its head, scorching a horde of bees, dropping them from the sky like exhausted meteors.

Jebidiah drew his revolver, snapped off a shot. There was a howl of agony, and then the thing was gone.

Jebidiah raced out of the protective circle and the deputy followed. They stood at the open window, watched as Gimet, flame-wrapped, streaked through the night in the direction of the graveyard.

"I panicked a little," Jebidiah said. "I should have been more resolute. Now he's escaped."

"I never even got off a shot," the deputy said. "God, but you're fast. What a draw."

"Look, you stay here if you like. I'm going after him. But I tell you now, the circle of power has played out."

The deputy glanced back at it. The pages had burned out and there was nothing now but a black ring on the floor.

"What in hell caused them to catch fire in the first place?"

"Evil," Jebidiah said. "When he got close, the pages broke into flames. Gave us the protection of God. Unfortunately, as with most of God's blessings, it doesn't last long."

"I stay here, you'd have to put down more pages."

"I'll be taking the bible with me. I might need it."

"Then I guess I'll be sticking."

THEY CLIMBED OUT the window and moved up the hill. They could smell the odor of fire and rotted flesh in the air. The night was as cool and silent as the graves on the hill.

Moments later they moved amongst the stones and wooden crosses, until they came to a long wide hole in the earth. Jebidiah could see that there was a burrow at one end of the grave that dipped down deeper into the ground.

Jebidiah paused there. "He's made this old grave his den. Dug it out and dug deeper."

"How do you know?" the deputy asked.

"Experience . . . And it smells of smoke and burned skin. He crawled down there to hide. I think we surprised him a little."

Jebidiah looked up at the sky. There was the faintest streak of pink on the horizon. "He's running out of daylight, and soon he'll be out of moon. For a while."

"He damn sure surprised me. Why don't we let him hide? You could come back when the moon isn't full, or even half full. Back in the daylight, get him then."

"I'm here now. And it's my job."

"That's one hell of a job you got, mister."

"I'm going to climb down for a better look."

"Help yourself."

Jebidiah struck a match and dropped himself into the grave, moved the match around at the mouth of the burrow, got down on his knees and stuck the match and his head into the opening.

"Very large," he said, pulling his head out. "I can smell him. I'm going to have to go in."

"What about me?"

"You keep guard at the lip of the grave," Jebidiah said, standing. "He may have another hole somewhere, he could come out behind you for all I know. He could come out of that hole even as we speak."

"That's wonderful."

Jebidiah dropped the now dead match on the ground. "I will tell you this. I can't guarantee success. I lose, he'll come for you, you can bet on that, and you better shoot those silvers as straight as William Tell's arrows."

"I'm not really that good a shot."

"I'm sorry," Jebidiah said, and struck another match along the length of his pants seam, then with his free hand, drew one of his revolvers. He got down on his hands and knees again, stuck the match in the hole and looked around. When the match was near done, he blew it out.

"Ain't you gonna need some light?" the deputy said. "A match ain't nothin'."

"I'll have it." Jebidiah removed the remains of the bible from his pocket, tore it in half along the spine, pushed one half in his coat, pushed the other half before him, into the darkness of the burrow. The moment it entered the hole, it flamed.

"Ain't your pocket gonna catch inside that hole?" the deputy asked.

"As long as I hold it or it's on my person, it won't harm me. But the minute I let go of it, and the aura of evil touches it, it'll blaze. I got to hurry, boy."

With that, Jebidiah wiggled inside the burrow.

IN THE BURROW, Jebidiah used the tip of his pistol to push the bible pages forward. They glowed brightly, but Jebidiah knew the light would be brief. It would burn longer than writing paper, but still, it would not last long.

After a goodly distance, Jebidiah discovered the burrow dropped off. He found himself inside a fairly large cavern. He could hear the sound of bats, and smell bat guano, which in fact, greased his path as he slid along on his elbows until he could stand inside the higher cavern and look about. The last flames of the bible burned themselves out with a puff of blue light and a sound like an old man breathing his last.

Jebidiah listened in the dark for a long moment. He could hear the bats squeaking, moving about. The fact that they had given up the night sky let Jebidiah know daylight was not far off.

Jebidiah's ears caught a sound, rocks shifting against the cave floor. Something was moving in the darkness, and he didn't think it was the bats. It scuttled, and Jebidiah felt certain it was close to the floor, and by the sound of it, moving his way at a creeping pace. The hair on the back of Jebidiah's neck bristled like porcupine quills. He felt his flesh bump up and crawl. The air became stiffer with the stench of burnt and rotting flesh.

Jebidiah's knees trembled. He reached cautiously inside his coat pocket, produced a match, struck it on his pants leg, held it up.

At that very moment, the thing stood up and was brightly lit in the glow of the match, the bees circling its skin-stripped skull. It snarled and darted forward. Jebidiah felt its rotten claws on his shirt front as he fired the revolver. The blaze from the bullet gave a brief, bright flare and was gone. At the same time, the match was knocked out of his hand and Jebidiah was knocked backwards, onto his back, the thing's claws at his throat. The monster's bees stung him. The stings felt like red-hot pokers entering his flesh. He stuck the revolver into the creature's body and fired. Once. Twice. Three times. A fourth.

Then the hammer clicked empty. He realized he had already fired two other shots. Six dead silver soldiers were in his cylinders, and the thing still had hold of him.

He tried to draw his other gun, but before he could, the thing released him, and Jebidiah could hear it crawling away in the dark. The bats fluttered and screeched.

Confused, Jebidiah drew the pistol, managed to get to his feet. He waited, listening, his fresh revolver pointing into the darkness.

Jebidiah found another match, struck it.

The thing lay with its back draped over a rise of rock. Jebidiah eased toward it. The silver loads had torn into the hive. It oozed a dark, odiferous trail of death and decaying honey. Bees began to drop to the cavern floor. The hive in Gimet's chest sizzled and pulsed like a large, black knot. Gimet opened his mouth, snarled, but otherwise didn't move.

Couldn't move.

Jebidiah, guided by the last wisps of his match, raised the pistol, stuck it against the black knot, and pulled the trigger. The knot exploded. Gimet let out with a shriek so sharp and loud it startled the bats to flight, drove them out of the cave, through the burrow, out into the remains of the night.

Gimet's claw-like hands dug hard at the stones around him, then he was still and Jebidiah's match went out.

JEBIDIAH FOUND THE remains of the bible in his pocket, and as he removed it, tossed it on the ground, it burst into flames. Using the two pistol barrels like large tweezers, he lifted the burning pages and dropped them into Gimet's open chest. The body caught on fire immediately, crackled and popped dryly, and was soon nothing more than a blaze. It lit the cavern up bright as day.

Jebidiah watched the corpse being consumed by the biblical fire for a moment, then headed toward the burrow, bent down, squirmed through it, came up in the grave.

He looked for the deputy and didn't see him. He climbed out of the grave and looked around. Jebidiah smiled. If the deputy had lasted until the bats charged out, that was most likely the last straw, and he had bolted.

Jebidiah looked back at the open grave. Smoke wisped out of the hole and out of the grave and climbed up to the sky. The moon was fading and the pink on the horizon was widening.

Gimet was truly dead now. The road was safe. His job was done.

At least for one brief moment.

Jebidiah walked down the hill, found his horse tied in the brush near the road where he had left it. The deputy's horse was gone, of course, the deputy most likely having already finished out Deadman's Road at a high gallop, on his way to Nacogdoches, perhaps to have a long drink of whisky and turn in his badge.

PIGEONS FROM HELL

ROBERT E. HOWARD

ROBERT E. HOWARD (1906–1936) wrote in numerous genres, including horror, detective, Western, boxing, and historical fiction, but his most famous creation, Conan, has become an iconic figure in the world of adventure fiction and film. Born in Texas, Howard had numerous odd jobs, all of which he hated, knowing he was born to be a writer. He produced reams of stories and poems while still a teenager and made his first sale to one of the greatest of all pulp magazines, *Weird Tales*, which published "Spear and Fang" in its July 1925 issue. He is also known today for his fantastic adventure series about the vengeful Solomon Kane, an Elizabethan Puritan swashbuckler in Africa; the barbarian King Kull, who thrived in ancient Atlantis; Bran Mak Morn, the king of the Caledonian Picts, an ancient Scottish tribe that fought the Romans; and, most memorably, Conan, the barbarian who lived in Cimmeria during the Hyborian Age, about twelve thousand years ago. Even as a young man, Conan was a large, heavily muscled wandering warrior who loved food, drink, women, and battle. His powerful sword was as invincible as he was, and he was always ready to fight. Barbarism, he proclaimed, was the natural state of being. He fought against hordes of enemies, monsters, and sorcery with a fearlessness that suggested an almost suicidal disregard for his own life. This may reflect the author's own view of the world. A lifelong depressive, Howard was inordinately close to his mother. When her tuberculosis reached its final stage, a nurse told him that she would never again be conscious; he put a gun in his mouth and killed himself at the age of thirty, by which time he had written an astounding number of books (more than fifty) and short stories (more than two hundred), mostly unpublished during his lifetime. Although Howard died young, Conan lives in the pages of the stories he wrote and the two films about Conan, notably *Conan the Barbarian* (1982), which made a star of bodybuilder Arnold Schwarzenegger, the future governor of California, who also starred in the sequel, *Conan the Destroyer* (1984).

"Pigeons from Hell" was first published in the November 1951 issue of *Weird Tales.*

ROBERT E. HOWARD

PIGEONS FROM HELL

I.

THE WHISTLER IN THE DARK

GRISWELL AWOKE SUDDENLY, every nerve tingling with a premonition of imminent peril. He stared about wildly, unable at first to remember where he was, or what he was doing there. Moonlight filtered in through the dusty windows, and the great empty room with its lofty ceiling and gaping black fireplace was spectral and unfamiliar. Then as he emerged from the clinging cobwebs of his recent sleep, he remembered where he was and how he came to be there. He twisted his head and stared at his companion, sleeping on the floor near him. John Branner was but a vaguely bulking shape in the darkness that the moon scarcely grayed.

Griswell tried to remember what had awakened him. There was no sound in the house, no sound outside except the mournful hoot of an owl, far away in the piny woods. Now he had captured the elusive memory. It was a dream, a nightmare so filled with dim terror that it had frightened him awake. Recollection flooded back, vividly etching the abominable vision.

Or was it a dream? Certainly it must have been, but it had blended so curiously with recent actual events that it was difficult to know where reality left off and fantasy began.

Dreaming, he had seemed to relive his past few waking hours, in accurate detail. The dream had begun, abruptly, as he and John Branner came in sight of the house where they now lay. They had come rattling and bouncing over the stumpy, uneven old road that led through the pinelands, he and John Branner, wandering far afield from their New England home, in search of vacation pleasure. They had sighted the old house with its balustraded galleries rising amidst a wilderness of weeds and bushes, just as the sun was setting behind it. It dominated their fancy, rearing black and stark and gaunt against the low lurid rampart of sunset, barred by the black pines.

They were tired, sick of bumping and pounding all day over woodland roads. The old deserted house stimulated their imagination with its suggestion of antebellum splendor and ultimate decay. They left the automobile beside the rutty road, and as they went up the winding walk of crumbling bricks, almost lost in the tangle of rank growth, pigeons rose from the balustrades in a fluttering, feathery crowd and swept away with a low thunder of beating wings.

The oaken door sagged on broken hinges. Dust lay thick on the floor of the wide, dim hallway, on the broad steps of the stair that mounted up from the hall. They turned into a door opposite the landing, and entered a large room, empty, dusty, with cobwebs shining thickly in the corners. Dust lay thick over the ashes in the great fireplace.

They discussed gathering wood and building a fire, but decided against it. As the sun sank, darkness came quickly, the thick, black, absolute darkness of the pinelands. They knew that rattlesnakes and copperheads haunted Southern forests, and they did not care to go groping for firewood in the dark. They ate frugally from tins, then rolled in their blankets fully clad before the empty fireplace, and went instantly to sleep.

This, in part, was what Griswell had dreamed. He saw again the gaunt house looming stark against the crimson sunset; saw the flight of the pigeons as he and Branner came up the shattered walk. He saw the dim room in which they presently lay, and he saw the two forms that were himself and his companion, lying wrapped in their blankets on the dusty floor. Then from that point his dream altered subtly, passed out of the realm of the commonplace and became tinged with fear. He was looking into a vague, shadowy chamber, lit by the gray light of the moon which streamed in from some obscure source. For there was no window in that room. But in the gray light he saw three silent shapes that hung suspended in a row, and their stillness and their outlines woke chill horror in his soul. There was no sound, no word, but he sensed a Presence of fear and lunacy crouching in a dark corner. . . . Abruptly he was back in the dusty, high-ceilinged room, before the great fireplace.

He was lying in his blankets, staring tensely through the dim door and across the shadowy hall, to where a beam of moonlight fell across the balustraded stair, some seven steps up from the landing. And there was something on the stair, a bent, misshapen, shadowy thing that never moved fully into the beam of light. But a dim yellow blur that might have been a face was turned toward him, as if *something* crouched on the stair, regarding him and his companion. Fright crept chilly through his veins, and it was then that he awoke—if indeed he had been asleep.

He blinked his eyes. The beam of moonlight fell across the stair just as he had dreamed it did; but no figure lurked there. Yet his flesh still crawled from the fear the dream or vision had roused in him; his legs felt as if they had been plunged in ice-water. He made an involuntary movement to awaken his companion, when a sudden sound paralyzed him.

It was the sound of whistling on the floor above. Eery and sweet it rose, not carrying any tune, but piping shrill and melodious. Such a sound in a supposedly deserted house was alarming enough; but it was more than the fear of a physical invader that held Griswell frozen. He could not himself have defined the horror that gripped him. But Branner's blankets rustled, and Griswell saw he was sitting upright. His figure bulked dimly in the soft darkness, the head turned toward the stair as if the man were listening intently. More sweetly and more subtly evil rose that weird whistling.

"John!" whispered Griswell from dry lips. He had meant to shout—to tell Branner that there was somebody upstairs, somebody who could mean them no good; that they must leave the house at once. But his voice died dryly in his throat.

Branner had risen. His boots clumped on the floor as he moved toward the door. He stalked leisurely into the hall and made for the lower landing, merging with the shadows that clustered black about the stair.

Griswell lay incapable of movement, his mind a whirl of bewilderment. Who was that whistling upstairs? Why was Branner going up those stairs? Griswell saw him pass the spot where the moonlight rested, saw his head tilted back as if he were looking at something Griswell could not see, above and beyond the stair. But his face was like that of a sleepwalker. He moved across the bar of moonlight and vanished from Griswell's view, even as the latter tried to shout to him to come back. A ghastly whisper was the only result of his effort.

The whistling sank to a lower note, died out. Griswell heard the stairs creaking under Branner's measured tread. Now he had reached the hallway above, for Griswell heard the clump of his feet moving along it. Suddenly the footfalls halted, and the whole night seemed to hold its breath. Then an awful scream split the stillness, and Griswell started up, echoing the cry.

The strange paralysis that had held him was broken. He took a step toward the door, then checked himself. The footfalls were resumed. Branner was coming back. He was not running. The tread was even more deliberate and measured than before. Now the stairs began to creak again. A groping hand, moving along the balustrade, came into the bar of moonlight; then another, and a ghastly thrill went through Griswell as he saw that the other hand gripped a hatchet—a hatchet which dripped blackly. *Was that Branner who was coming down that stair?*

Yes! The figure had moved into the bar of moonlight now, and Griswell recognized it. Then he saw Branner's face, and a shriek burst from Griswell's lips. Branner's face was bloodless, corpse-like; gouts of blood dripped darkly down it; his eyes were glassy and set, and blood oozed from the great gash *which cleft the crown of his head!*

GRISWELL NEVER REMEMBERED exactly how he got out of that accursed house. Afterward he retained a mad, confused impression of smashing his way through a dusty cobwebbed window, of stumbling blindly across the weed-choked lawn, gibbering his frantic horror. He saw the black wall of the pines, and the moon floating in a blood-red mist in which there was neither sanity nor reason.

Some shred of sanity returned to him as he saw the automobile beside the road. In a world gone suddenly mad, that was an object reflecting prosaic reality; but even as he reached for the door, a dry chilling whir sounded in his ears, and he recoiled from the swaying undulating shape that arched up from its scaly coils on the driver's seat and hissed sibilantly at him, darting a forked tongue in the moonlight.

With a sob of horror he turned and fled down the road, as a man runs in a nightmare. He ran without purpose or reason. His numbed brain was incapable of conscious thought. He merely obeyed the blind primitive urge to run—run—run until he fell exhausted.

The black walls of the pines flowed endlessly past him; so he was seized with the illusion that he was getting nowhere. But presently a sound penetrated the fog of his terror—the steady, inexorable patter of feet behind him. Turning his head, he saw *something* loping after him—wolf or dog, he could not tell which, but its eyes glowed like balls of green fire. With a gasp he increased his speed, reeled around a bend in the road, and heard a horse snort; saw it rear and heard its rider curse; saw the gleam of blue steel in the man's lifted hand.

He staggered and fell, catching at the rider's stirrup.

"For God's sake, help me!" he panted. "The thing! It killed Branner—it's coming after me! *Look!*"

Twin balls of fire gleamed in the fringe of bushes at the turn of the road. The rider swore again, and on the heels of his profanity came the smashing report of his six-shooter—again and yet again. The fire-sparks vanished, and the rider, jerking his stirrup free from Griswell's grasp, spurred his horse at the bend. Griswell staggered up, shaking in every limb. The rider was out of sight only a moment; then he came galloping back.

"Took to the brush. Timber wolf, I reckon, though I never heard of one chasin' a man before. Do you know what it was?"

Griswell could only shake his head weakly.

The rider, etched in the moonlight, looked down at him, smoking pistol still lifted in his right hand. He was a compactly-built man of medium height, and his broad-brimmed planter's hat and his boots marked him as a native of the country as definitely as Griswell's garb stamped him as a stranger.

"What's all this about, anyway?"

"I don't know," Griswell answered helplessly. "My name's Griswell. John Branner—my friend who was traveling with me—we stopped at a deserted house back down the road to spend the night. Something—" At the memory he was choked by a rush of horror. "My God!" he screamed. "I must be mad! *Something* came and looked over the balustrade of the stair—something with a yellow face! I thought I dreamed it, but it must have been real. Then somebody began whistling upstairs, and Branner rose and went up the stairs walking like a man in his sleep, or hypnotized. I heard him scream—or someone screamed; then he came down the stairs again with a bloody hatchet in his hand—and my God, sir, he was *dead!* His head had been split open. I saw brains and clotted blood oozing down his face, and his face was that of a dead man. *But he came down the stairs!* As God is my witness, John Branner was murdered in that dark upper hallway, and then his dead body came stalking down the stairs with a hatchet in its hand—to kill me!"

The rider made no reply; he sat his horse like a statue, outlined against the stars, and Griswell could not read his expression, his face shadowed by his hat-brim.

"You think I'm mad," he said hopelessly. "Perhaps I am."

"I don't know what to think," answered the rider. "If it was any house but the old Blassenville Manor—well, we'll see. My name's Buckner. I'm sheriff of this county. Took a prisoner over to the county-seat in the next county and was ridin' back late."

He swung off his horse and stood beside Griswell, shorter than the lanky New Englander, but much harder knit. There was a natural manner of decision and certainty about him, and it was easy to believe that he would be a dangerous man in any sort of a fight.

"Are you afraid to go back to the house?" he asked, and Griswell shuddered, but shook his head, the dogged tenacity of Puritan ancestors asserting itself.

"The thought of facing that horror again turns me sick. But poor Branner—" He choked again. "We must find his body. My God!" he cried, unmanned by the abysmal horror of the thing; "*what* will we find? If a dead man walks, what—"

"We'll see." The sheriff caught the reins in the crook of his left elbow and began filling the empty chambers of his big blue pistol as they walked along.

As they made the turn Griswell's blood was ice at the thought of what they might see lumbering up the road with a bloody, grinning death-mask, but they saw only the house looming spectrally among the pines, down the road. A strong shudder shook Griswell.

"God, how *evil* that house looks, against those black pines! It looked sinister from the very first—when we went up the broken walk and saw those pigeons fly up from the porch—"

"Pigeons?" Buckner cast him a quick glance. "You saw the pigeons?"

"Why, yes! Scores of them perching on the porch railing."

They strode on for a moment in silence, before Buckner said abruptly: "I've lived in this country all my life. I've passed the old Blassenville place a thousand times, I reckon, at all hours of the day and night. But I never saw a pigeon anywhere around it, or anywhere else in these woods."

"There were scores of them," repeated Griswell, bewildered.

"I've seen men who swore they'd seen a flock of pigeons perched along the balusters just at sundown," said Buckner slowly. "Negroes, all of them except one man. A tramp. He was buildin' a fire in the yard, aimin' to camp there that night. I passed along there about dark, and he told me about the pigeons. I came back by there the next mornin'. The ashes of his fire were there, and his tin cup, and skillet where he'd fried pork, and his blankets looked like they'd been slept in. Nobody ever saw him again. That was twelve years ago. The blacks say they can see the pigeons, but no black would pass along this road between sundown and sunup. They say the pigeons are the souls of the Blassenvilles, let out of hell at sunset. The Negroes say the red glare in the west is the light from hell, because then the gates of hell are open, and the Blassenvilles fly out."

"Who were the Blassenvilles?" asked Griswell, shivering.

"They owned all this land here. French-English family. Came here from the West Indies before the Louisiana Purchase. The Civil War ruined them, like it did so many. Some were killed in the War; most of the others died out. Nobody's lived in the Manor since 1890 when Miss Elizabeth Blassenville, the last of the line, fled from the old house one night like it was a plague spot, and never came back to it—this your auto?"

They halted beside the car, and Griswell stared morbidly at the grim house. Its dusty panes were empty and blank; but they did not seem blind to him. It seemed to him that ghastly eyes were fixed hungrily on him through those darkened panes. Buckner repeated his question.

"Yes. Be careful. There's a snake on the seat—or there was."

"Not there now," grunted Buckner, tying his horse and pulling an electric torch out of the saddle-bag. "Well, let's have a look."

He strode up the broken brick walk as matter-of-factly as if he were paying a social call on friends. Griswell followed close at his heels, his heart pounding suffocatingly. A scent of decay and moldering vegetation blew on the faint wind, and Griswell grew faint with nausea, that rose from a frantic abhorrence of these black woods, these ancient plantation houses that hid forgotten secrets of slavery and bloody pride and mysterious intrigues. He had thought of the South as a sunny, lazy land washed by soft breezes laden with spice and warm blossoms, where life ran tranquilly to the rhythm of black folk singing in sunbathed cottonfields. But now he had discovered another, unsuspected side—a dark, brooding, fear-haunted side, and the discovery repelled him.

The oaken door sagged as it had before. The blackness of the interior was intensified by the beam of Buckner's light playing on the sill. That beam sliced through the darkness of the hallway and roved up the stair, and Griswell held his breath, clenching his fists. But no shape of lunacy leered down at them. Buckner went in, walking light as a cat, torch in one hand, gun in the other.

As he swung his light into the room across from the stairway, Griswell cried out—and cried out again, almost fainting with the intolerable sickness at what he saw. A trail of blood drops led across the floor, crossing the blankets Branner had occupied, which lay between the door and those in which Griswell had lain. And Griswell's blankets had a terrible occupant. John Branner lay there, face down, his cleft head revealed in merciless clarity in the steady light. His outstretched hand still gripped the haft of a hatchet, and the blade was imbedded deep in the blanket and the floor beneath, just where Griswell's head had lain when he slept there.

A momentary rush of blackness engulfed Griswell. He was not aware that he staggered, or that Buckner caught him. When he could see and hear again, he was violently sick and hung his head against the mantel, retching miserably.

Buckner turned the light full on him, making him blink. Buckner's voice came from behind the blinding radiance, the man himself unseen.

"Griswell, you've told me a yarn that's hard to believe. I saw something chasin' you, but it might have been a timber wolf, or a mad dog.

"If you're holdin' back anything, you better spill it. What you told me won't hold up in any court. You're bound to be accused of killin' your partner. I'll have to arrest you. If you'll give me the straight goods now, it'll make it easier. Now, didn't you kill this fellow, Branner?

"Wasn't it something like this: you quarreled, he grabbed a hatchet and swung at you, but you dodged and then let *him* have it?"

Griswell sank down and hid his face in his hands, his head swimming.

"Great God, man, I didn't murder John! Why, we've been friends ever since we were children in school together. I've told you the truth. I don't blame you for not believing me. But God help me, it is the truth!"

The light swung back to the gory head again, and Griswell closed his eyes.

He heard Buckner grunt.

"I believe this hatchet in his hand is the one he was killed with. Blood and brains plastered on the blade, and hairs stickin' to it—hairs exactly the same color as his. This makes it tough for you, Griswell."

"How so?" the New Englander asked dully.

"Knocks any plea of self-defense in the head. Branner couldn't have swung at you with this hatchet after you split his skull with it. You must have pulled the ax out of his head, stuck it into the floor and clamped his fingers on it to make it look like he'd attacked you. And it would have been damned clever—if you'd used another hatchet."

"But I didn't kill him," groaned Griswell. "I have no intention of pleading self-defense."

"That's what puzzles me," Buckner admitted frankly, straightening. "What murderer would rig up such a crazy story as you've told me, to prove his innocence? Average killer would have told a logical yarn, at least. Hmmm! Blood drops leadin' from the door. The body was dragged—no, couldn't have been dragged. The floor isn't smeared. You must have carried it here, after killin' him in some other place. But in that case, why isn't there any blood on your clothes? Of course you could have changed clothes and washed your hands. But the fellow hasn't been dead long."

"He walked downstairs and across the room," said Griswell hopelessly. "He came to kill me. I knew he was coming to kill me when I saw him lurching down the stair. He struck where I would have been, if I hadn't awakened. That window—I burst out at it. You see it's broken."

"I see. But if he walked then, why isn't he walkin' now?"

"I don't know! I'm too sick to think straight. I've been fearing that he'd rise up from the floor where he lies and come at me again. When I heard that wolf running up the road after me, I thought it was John chasing me—John, running through the night with his bloody ax and his bloody head, and his death-grin!"

His teeth chattered as he lived that horror over again.

Buckner let his light play across the floor.

"The blood drops lead into the hall. Come on. We'll follow them."

Griswell cringed. "They lead upstairs."

Buckner's eyes were fixed hard on him.

"Are you afraid to go upstairs, with me?"

Griswell's face was gray.

"Yes. But I'm going, with you or without you. The thing that killed poor John may still be hiding up there."

"Stay behind me," ordered Buckner. "If anything jumps us, I'll take care of it. But for your own sake, I warn you that I shoot quicker than a cat jumps, and I don't often miss. If you've got any ideas of layin' me out from behind, forget them."

"Don't be a fool!" Resentment got the better of his apprehension, and this outburst seemed to reassure Buckner more than any of his protestations of innocence.

"I want to be fair," he said quietly. "I haven't indicted and condemned you in my mind already. If only half of what you're tellin' me is the truth, you've been through a hell of an experience, and I don't want to be too hard on you. But you can see how hard it is for me to believe all you've told me."

Griswell wearily motioned for him to lead the way, unspeaking. They went out into the hall, paused at the landing. A thin string of crimson drops, distinct in the thick dust, led up the steps.

"Man's tracks in the dust," grunted Buckner. "Go slow. I've got to be sure of what I see, because we're obliteratin' them as we go up. Hmmm! One set goin' up, one comin' down. Same man. Not your tracks. Branner was a bigger man than you are. Blood drops all the way—blood on the bannisters like a man had laid his bloody hand there—a smear of stuff that looks—*brains*. Now what—"

"He walked down the stair, a dead man," shuddered Griswell. "Groping with one hand—the other gripping the hatchet that killed him."

"Or was carried," muttered the sheriff. "But if somebody carried him—*where are the tracks?*"

They came out into the upper hallway, a vast, empty space of dust and shadows where time-crusted windows repelled the moonlight and the ring of Buckner's torch seemed inadequate. Griswell trembled like a leaf. Here, in darkness and horror, John Branner had died.

"Somebody whistled up here," he muttered. "John came, as if he were being called."

Buckner's eyes were blazing strangely in the light.

"The footprints lead down the hall," he muttered. "Same as on the stair—one set going, one coming. Same prints—*Judas!*"

Behind him Griswell stifled a cry, for he had seen what prompted Buckner's exclamation. A few feet from the head of the stair Branner's footprints stopped abruptly, then returned, treading almost in the other tracks. And where the trail halted there was a great splash of blood on the dusty floor—and other tracks met it—tracks of bare feet, narrow but with splayed toes. They too receded in a second line from the spot.

Buckner bent over them, swearing.

"The tracks meet! And where they meet there's blood and brains on the floor! Branner must have been killed on that spot—with a blow from a hatchet. Bare feet coming out of the darkness to meet shod feet—then both turned away again; the shod feet went downstairs, the bare feet went back down the hall." He directed his light down the hall. The footprints faded into darkness, beyond the reach of the beam. On either hand the closed doors of chambers were cryptic portals of mystery.

"Suppose your crazy tale *was* true," Buckner muttered, half to himself. "These aren't your tracks. They look like a woman's. Suppose somebody did whistle, and Branner went upstairs to investigate. Suppose somebody met him here in the dark and split his head. The signs and tracks would have been, in that case, just as they really are. But if that's so, why isn't Branner lyin' here where he was killed? Could he have lived long

enough to take the hatchet away from whoever killed him, and stagger downstairs with it?"

"No, no!" Recollection gagged Griswell. "I *saw* him on the stair. He was dead. No man could live a minute after receiving such a wound."

"I believe it," muttered Buckner. "But—it's madness! Or else it's *too* clever—yet, what sane man would think up and work out such an elaborate and utterly insane plan to escape punishment for murder, when a simple plea of self-defense would have been so much more effective? No court would recognize that story. Well, let's follow these other tracks. They lead down the hall—here, what's this?"

With an icy clutch at his soul, Griswell saw the light was beginning to grow dim.

"This battery is new," muttered Buckner, and for the first time Griswell caught an edge of fear in his voice. "Come on—out of here quick!"

The light had faded to a faint red glow. The darkness seemed straining into them, creeping with black cat-feet. Buckner retreated, pushing Griswell stumbling behind him as he walked backward, pistol cocked and lifted, down the dark hall. In the growing darkness Griswell heard what sounded like the stealthy opening of a door. And suddenly the blackness about them was vibrant with menace. Griswell knew Buckner sensed it as well as he, for the sheriff's hard body was tense and taut as a stalking panther's.

But without haste he worked his way to the stair and backed down it, Griswell preceding him, and fighting the panic that urged him to scream and burst into mad flight. A ghastly thought brought icy sweat out on his flesh. *Suppose the dead man were creeping up the stair behind them in the dark, face frozen in the death-grin, blood-caked hatchet lifted to strike?*

This possibility so overpowered him that he was scarcely aware when his feet struck the level of the lower hallway, and he was only then aware that the light had grown brighter as they descended, until it now gleamed with its full power—but when Buckner turned it back up the stairway, it failed to illuminate the darkness that hung like a tangible fog at the head of the stair.

"The damn thing was conjured," muttered Buckner. "Nothin' else. It couldn't act like that naturally."

"Turn the light into the room," begged Griswell. "See if John—if John is—"

He could not put the ghastly thought into words, but Buckner understood.

He swung the beam around, and Griswell had never dreamed that the sight of the gory body of a murdered man could bring such relief.

"He's still there," grunted Buckner. "If he walked after he was killed, he hasn't walked since. But that thing—"

Again he turned the light up the stair, and stood chewing his lip and scowling. Three times he half lifted his gun. Griswell read his mind. The sheriff was tempted to plunge back up that stair, take his chance with the unknown. But common sense held him back.

"I wouldn't have a chance in the dark," he muttered. "And I've got a hunch the light would go out again."

He turned and faced Griswell squarely.

"There's no use dodgin' the question. There's somethin' hellish in this house, and I believe I have an inklin' of what it is. I don't believe you killed Branner. Whatever killed him is up there—now. There's a lot about your yarn that don't sound sane; but there's nothin' sane about a flashlight goin' out like this one did. I don't believe that thing upstairs is human. I never met anything I was afraid to tackle in the dark before, but I'm not goin' up there until daylight. It's not long until dawn. We'll wait for it out there on that gallery."

The stars were already paling when they came out on the broad porch. Buckner seated himself on the balustrade, facing the door, his pistol dangling in his fingers. Griswell sat down near him and leaned back against a crumbling pillar. He shut his eyes, grateful for the faint breeze that seemed to cool his throbbing brain. He experienced a dull sense of unreality. He was a stranger in a strange land, a land that had become suddenly imbued with black horror. The shadow of the noose hovered above him, and

in that dark house lay John Branner, with his butchered head—like the figments of a dream these facts spun and eddied in his brain until all merged in a gray twilight as sleep came uninvited to his weary soul.

He awoke to a cold white dawn and full memory of the horrors of the night. Mists curled about the stems of the pines, crawled in smoky wisps up the broken walk. Buckner was shaking him.

"Wake up! It's daylight."

Griswell rose, wincing at the stiffness of his limbs. His face was gray and old.

"I'm ready. Let's go upstairs."

"I've already been!" Buckner's eyes burned in the early dawn. "I didn't wake you up. I went as soon as it was light. I found nothin'."

"The tracks of the bare feet—"

"Gone!"

"Gone?"

"Yes, gone! The dust had been disturbed all over the hall, from the point where Branner's tracks ended; swept into corners. No chance of trackin' anything there now. Something obliterated those tracks while we sat here, and I didn't hear a sound. I've gone through the whole house. Not a sign of anything."

Griswell shuddered at the thought of himself sleeping alone on the porch while Buckner conducted his exploration.

"What shall we do?" he asked listlessly. "With those tracks gone there goes my only chance of proving my story."

"We'll take Branner's body into the county-seat," answered Buckner. "Let me do the talkin'. If the authorities knew the facts as they appear, they'd insist on you being confined and indicted. I don't believe you killed Branner—but neither a district attorney, judge nor jury would believe what you told me, or what happened to us last night. I'm handlin' this thing my own way. I'm not goin' to arrest you until I've exhausted every other possibility.

"Say nothin' about what's happened here, when we get to town. I'll simply tell the district attorney that John Branner was killed by a party or parties unknown, and that I'm workin' on the case.

"Are you game to come back with me to this house and spend the night here, sleepin' in that room as you and Branner slept last night?"

Griswell went white, but answered as stoutly as his ancestors might have expressed their determination to hold their cabins in the teeth of the Pequots: "I'll do it."

"Let's go then; help me pack the body out to your auto."

Griswell's soul revolted at the sight of John Branner's bloodless face in the chill white dawn, and the feel of his clammy flesh. The gray fog wrapped wispy tentacles about their feet as they carried their grisly burden across the lawn.

II.

THE SNAKE'S BROTHER

Again the shadows were lengthening over the pinelands, and again two men came bumping along the old road in a car with a New England license plate.

Buckner was driving. Griswell's nerves were too shattered for him to trust himself at the wheel. He looked gaunt and haggard, and his face was still pallid. The strain of the day spent at the county-seat was added to the horror that still rode his soul like the shadow of a black-winged vulture. He had not slept, had not tasted what he had eaten.

"I told you I'd tell you about the Blassen-villes," said Buckner. "They were proud folks, haughty, and pretty damn ruthless when they wanted their way. They didn't treat their slaves as well as the other planters did—got their ideas in the West Indies, I reckon. There was a streak of cruelty in them—especially Miss Celia, the last one of the family to come to these parts. That was long after the slaves had been freed, but she used to whip her mulatto maid just like she was a slave, the old folks say. . . . The Ne-

groes said when a Blassenville died, the devil was always waitin' for him out in the black pines.

"Well, after the Civil War they died off pretty fast, livin' in poverty on the plantation which was allowed to go to ruin. Finally only four girls were left, sisters, livin' in the old house and ekin' out a bare livin', with a few blacks livin' in the old slave huts and workin' the fields on the share. They kept to themselves, bein' proud, and ashamed of their poverty. Folks wouldn't see them for months at a time. When they needed supplies they sent a Negro to town after them.

"But folks knew about it when Miss Celia came to live with them. She came from somewhere in the West Indies, where the whole family originally had its roots—a fine, handsome woman, they say, in the early thirties. But she didn't mix with folks any more than the girls did. She brought a mulatto maid with her, and the Blassenville cruelty cropped out in her treatment of this maid. I knew an old man years ago, who swore he saw Miss Celia tie this girl up to a tree, stark naked, and whip her with a horsewhip. Nobody was surprised when she disappeared. Everybody figured she'd run away, of course.

"Well, one day in the spring of 1890 Miss Elizabeth, the youngest girl, came in to town for the first time in maybe a year. She came after supplies. Said the blacks had all left the place. Talked a little more, too, a bit wild. Said Miss Celia had gone, without leaving any word. Said her sisters thought she'd gone back to the West Indies, but she believed her aunt *was still in the house*. She didn't say what she meant. Just got her supplies and pulled out for the Manor.

"A month went past, and a black came into town and said that Miss Elizabeth was livin' at the Manor alone. Said her three sisters weren't there any more, that they'd left one by one without givin' any word or explanation. She didn't know where they'd gone, and was afraid to stay there alone, but didn't know where else to go. She'd never known anything but the Manor, and had neither relatives nor friends. But she was in mortal terror of *something*. The black said she locked herself in her room at night and kept candles burnin' all night. . . .

"It was a stormy spring night when Miss Elizabeth came tearin' into town on the one horse she owned, nearly dead from fright. She fell from her horse in the square; when she could talk she said she'd found a secret room in the Manor that had been forgotten for a hundred years. And she said that there she found her three sisters, dead, and hangin' by their necks from the ceilin'. She said *something* chased her and nearly brained her with an ax as she ran out the front door, but somehow she got to the horse and got away. She was nearly crazy with fear, and didn't know what it was that chased her—said it looked like a woman with a yellow face.

"About a hundred men rode out there, right away. They searched the house from top to bottom, but they didn't find any secret room, or the remains of the sisters. But they did find a hatchet stickin' in the doorjamb downstairs, with some of Miss Elizabeth's hairs stuck on it, just as she'd said. She wouldn't go back there and show them how to find the secret door; almost went crazy when they suggested it.

"When she was able to travel, the people made up some money and loaned it to her—she was still too proud to accept charity—and she went to California. She never came back, but later it was learned, when she sent back to repay the money they'd loaned her, that she'd married out there.

"Nobody ever bought the house. It stood there just as she'd left it, and as the years passed folks stole all the furnishings out of it, poor white trash, I reckon. A Negro wouldn't go about it. But they came after sun-up and left long before sun-down."

"What did the people think about Miss Elizabeth's story?" asked Griswell.

"Well, most folks thought she'd gone a little crazy, livin' in that old house alone. But some people believed that mulatto girl, Joan, didn't run away, after all. They believed she'd hidden in the woods, and glutted her hatred of the Blassenvilles by murderin' Miss Celia and the three girls. They beat up the woods with bloodhounds, but never found a trace of her. If there was a secret room in the house, she might have been hidin' there—if there was anything to that theory."

"She couldn't have been hiding there all these years," muttered Griswell. "Anyway, the thing in the house now isn't human."

Buckner wrenched the wheel around and turned into a dim trace that left the main road and meandered off through the pines.

"Where are you going?"

"There's an old Negro that lives off this way a few miles. I want to talk to him. We're up against something that takes more than white man's sense. The black people know more than we do about some things. This old man is nearly a hundred years old. His master educated him when he was a boy, and after he was freed he traveled more extensively than most white men do. They say he's a voodoo man."

Griswell shivered at the phrase, staring uneasily at the green forest walls that shut them in. The scent of the pines was mingled with the odors of unfamiliar plants and blossoms. But underlying all was a reek of rot and decay. Again a sick abhorrence of these dark mysterious woodlands almost overpowered him.

"Voodoo!" he muttered. "I'd forgotten about that—I never could think of black magic in connection with the South. To me witchcraft was always associated with old crooked streets in waterfront towns, overhung by gabled roofs that were old when they were hanging witches in Salem; dark musty alleys where black cats and other things might steal at night. Witchcraft always meant the old towns of New England, to me—but all this is more terrible than any New England legend—these somber pines, old deserted houses, lost plantations, mysterious black people, old tales of madness and horror—God, what frightful, ancient terrors there are on this continent fools call 'young'!"

"Here's old Jacob's hut," announced Buckner, bringing the automobile to a halt.

Griswell saw a clearing and a small cabin squatting under the shadows of the huge trees. The pines gave way to oaks and cypresses, bearded with gray trailing moss, and behind the cabin lay the edge of a swamp that ran away under the dimness of the trees, choked with rank vegetation. A thin wisp of blue smoke curled up from the stick-and-mud chimney.

He followed Buckner to the tiny stoop, where the sheriff pushed open the leather-hinged door and strode in. Griswell blinked in the comparative dimness of the interior. A single small window let in a little daylight. An old Negro crouched beside the hearth, watching a pot stew over the open fire. He looked up as they entered, but did not rise. He seemed incredibly old. His face was a mass of wrinkles, and his eyes, dark and vital, were filmed momentarily at times as if his mind wandered.

Buckner motioned Griswell to sit down in a string-bottomed chair, and himself took a rudely-made bench near the hearth, facing the old man.

"Jacob," he said bluntly, "the time's come for you to talk. I know you know the secret of Blassenville Manor. I've never questioned you about it, because it wasn't in my line. But a man was murdered there last night, and this man here may hang for it, unless you tell me what haunts that old house of the Blassenvilles."

The old man's eyes gleamed, then grew misty as if clouds of extreme age drifted across his brittle mind.

"The Blassenvilles," he murmured, and his voice was mellow and rich, his speech not the patois of the piny woods darky. "They were proud people, sirs—proud and cruel. Some died in the war, some were killed in duels—the menfolks, sirs. Some died in the Manor—the old Manor—" His voice trailed off into unintelligible mumblings.

"What of the Manor?" asked Buckner patiently.

"Miss Celia was the proudest of them all," the old man muttered. "The proudest and the cruelest. The black people hated her; Joan most

of all. Joan had white blood in her, and she was proud, too. Miss Celia whipped her like a slave."

"What is the secret of Blassenville Manor?" persisted Buckner.

The film faded from the old man's eyes; they were dark as moonlit wells.

"What secret, sir? I do not understand."

"Yes, you do. For years that old house has stood there with its mystery. You know the key to its riddle."

The old man stirred the stew. He seemed perfectly rational now.

"Sir, life is sweet, even to an old black man."

"You mean somebody would kill you if you told me?"

But the old man was mumbling again, his eyes clouded.

"Not somebody. No human. No human being. The black gods of the swamps. My secret is inviolate, guarded by the Big Serpent, the god above all gods. He would send a little brother to kiss me with his cold lips—a little brother with a white crescent moon on his head. I sold my soul to the Big Serpent when he made me maker of *zuvembies*—"

Buckner stiffened.

"I heard that word once before," he said softly, "from the lips of a dying black man, when I was a child. What does it mean?"

Fear filled the eyes of old Jacob.

"What have I said? No—no! I said nothing."

"*Zuvembies*," prompted Buckner.

"*Zuvembies*," mechanically repeated the old man, his eyes vacant. "A *zuvembie* was once a woman—on the Slave Coast they know of them. The drums that whisper by night in the hills of Haiti tell of them. The makers of *zuvembies* are honored of the people of Damballah. It is death to speak of it to a white man—it is one of the Snake God's forbidden secrets."

"You speak of the *zuvembies*," said Buckner softly.

"I must not speak of it," mumbled the old man, and Griswell realized that he was thinking aloud, too far gone in his dotage to be aware that he was speaking at all. "No white man must know that I danced in the Black Ceremony of the voodoo, and was made a maker of *zombies* and *zuvembies*. The Big Snake punishes loose tongues with death."

"A *zuvembie* is a woman?" prompted Buckner.

"*Was* a woman," the old Negro muttered. "*She* knew I was a maker of *zuvembies*—she came and stood in my hut and asked for the awful brew—the brew of ground snake-bones, and the blood of vampire bats, and the dew from a nighthawk's wings, and other elements unnamable. She had danced in the Black Ceremony—she was ripe to become a *zuvembie*—the Black Brew was all that was needed—the other was beautiful—I could not refuse her."

"Who?" demanded Buckner tensely, but the old man's head was sunk on his withered breast, and he did not reply. He seemed to slumber as he sat. Buckner shook him. "You gave a brew to make a woman a *zuvembie*—what is a *zuvembie?*"

The old man stirred resentfully and muttered drowsily.

"A *zuvembie* is no longer human. It knows neither relatives nor friends. It is one with the people of the Black World. It commands the natural demons—owls, bats, snakes and werewolves, and can fetch darkness to blot out a little light. It can be slain by lead or steel, but unless it is slain thus, it lives for ever, and it eats no such food as humans eat. It dwells like a bat in a cave or an old house. Time means naught to the *zuvembie;* an hour, a day, a year, all is one. It cannot speak human words, nor think as a human thinks, but it can hypnotize the living by the sound of its voice, and when it slays a man, it can command his lifeless body until the flesh is cold. As long as the blood flows, the corpse is its slave. Its pleasure lies in the slaughter of human beings."

"And why should one become a *zuvembie?*" asked Buckner softly.

"Hate," whispered the old man. "Hate! Revenge!"

"Was her name Joan?" murmured Buckner.

It was as if the name penetrated the fogs of senility that clouded the voodoo-man's mind. He shook himself and the film faded from his eyes, leaving them hard and gleaming as wet black marble.

"Joan?" he said slowly. "I have not heard that name for the span of a generation. I seem to have been sleeping, gentlemen; I do not remember—I ask your pardon. Old men fall asleep before the fire, like old dogs. You asked me of Blassenville Manor? Sir, if I were to tell you why I cannot answer you, you would deem it mere superstition. Yet the white man's God be my witness—"

As he spoke he was reaching across the hearth for a piece of firewood, groping among the heaps of sticks there. And his voice broke in a scream, as he jerked back his arm convulsively. And a horrible, thrashing, trailing *thing* came with it. Around the voodoo-man's arm a mottled length of that shape was wrapped, and a wicked wedge-shaped head struck again in silent fury.

The old man fell on the hearth, screaming, upsetting the simmering pot and scattering the embers, and then Buckner caught up a billet of firewood and crushed that flat head. Cursing, he kicked aside the knotting, twisting trunk, glaring briefly at the mangled head. Old Jacob had ceased screaming and writhing; he lay still, staring glassily upward.

"Dead?" whispered Griswell.

"Dead as Judas Iscariot," snapped Buckner, frowning at the twitching reptile. "That infernal snake crammed enough poison into his veins to kill a dozen men his age. But I think it was the shock and fright that killed him."

"What shall we do?" asked Griswell, shivering.

"Leave the body on that bunk. Nothin' can hurt it, if we bolt the door so the wild hogs can't get in, or any cat. We'll carry it into town tomorrow. We've got work to do tonight. Let's get goin'."

Griswell shrank from touching the corpse, but he helped Buckner lift it on the rude bunk, and then stumbled hastily out of the hut. The sun was hovering above the horizon, visible in dazzling red flame through the black stems of the trees.

They climbed into the car in silence, and went bumping back along the stumpy trail.

"He said the Big Snake would send one of his brothers," muttered Griswell.

"Nonsense!" snorted Buckner. "Snakes like warmth, and that swamp is full of them. It crawled in and coiled up among that firewood. Old Jacob disturbed it, and it bit him. Nothin' supernatural about that." After a short silence he said, in a different voice, "That was the first time I ever saw a rattler strike without singin'; and the first time I ever saw a snake *with a white crescent moon on its head.*"

They were turning in to the main road before either spoke again.

"You think that the mulatto Joan has skulked in the house all these years?" Griswell asked.

"You heard what old Jacob said," answered Buckner grimly. "Time means nothin' to a *zu-vembie.*"

As they made the last turn in the road, Griswell braced himself against the sight of Blassenville Manor looming black against the red sunset. When it came into view he bit his lip to keep from shrieking. The suggestion of cryptic horror came back in all its power.

"Look!" he whispered from dry lips as they came to a halt beside the road. Buckner grunted.

From the balustrades of the gallery rose a whirling cloud of pigeons that swept away into the sunset, black against the lurid glare. . . .

III.

THE CALL OF ZUVEMBIE

Both men sat rigid for a few moments after the pigeons had flown.

"Well, I've seen them at last," muttered Buckner.

"Only the doomed see them perhaps," whispered Griswell. "That tramp saw them—"

"Well, we'll see," returned the Southerner

tranquilly, as he climbed out of the car, but Griswell noticed him unconsciously hitch forward his scabbarded gun.

The oaken door sagged on broken hinges. Their feet echoed on the broken brick walk. The blind windows reflected the sunset in sheets of flame. As they came into the broad hall Griswell saw the string of black marks that ran across the floor and into the chamber, marking the path of a dead man.

Buckner had brought blankets out of the automobile. He spread them before the fireplace.

"I'll lie next to the door," he said. "You lie where you did last night."

"Shall we light a fire in the grate?" asked Griswell, dreading the thought of the blackness that would cloak the woods when the brief twilight had died.

"No. You've got a flashlight and so have I. We'll lie here in the dark and see what happens. Can you use that gun I gave you?"

"I suppose so. I never fired a revolver, but I know how it's done."

"Well, leave the shootin' to me, if possible." The sheriff seated himself cross-legged on his blankets and emptied the cylinder of his big blue Colt, inspecting each cartridge with a critical eye before he replaced it.

Griswell prowled nervously back and forth, begrudging the slow fading of the light as a miser begrudges the waning of his gold. He leaned with one hand against the mantelpiece, staring down into the dust-covered ashes. The fire that produced those ashes must have been built by Elizabeth Blassenville, more than forty years before. The thought was depressing. Idly he stirred the dusty ashes with his toe. Something came to view among the charred debris—a bit of paper, stained and yellowed. Still idly he bent and drew it out of the ashes. It was a note-book with moldering cardboard backs.

"What have you found?" asked Buckner, squinting down the gleaming barrel of his gun.

"Nothing but an old note-book. Looks like a diary. The pages are covered with writing—but the ink is so faded, and the paper is in such a state of decay that I can't tell much about it. How do you suppose it came in the fireplace, without being burned up?"

"Thrown in long after the fire was out," surmised Buckner. "Probably found and tossed in the fireplace by somebody who was in here stealin' furniture. Likely somebody who couldn't read."

Griswell fluttered the crumbling leaves listlessly, straining his eyes in the fading light over the yellowed scrawls. Then he stiffened.

"Here's an entry that's legible! Listen!" He read:

" 'I know someone is in the house besides myself. I can hear someone prowling about at night when the sun has set and the pines are black outside. Often in the night I hear it fumbling at my door. *Who* is it? Is it one of my sisters? Is it Aunt Celia? If it is either of these, why does she steal so subtly about the house? Why does she tug at my door, and glide away when I call to her? Shall I open the door and go out to her? No, no! I dare not! I am afraid. Oh God, what shall I do? I dare not stay here—but where am I to go?' "

"By God!" ejaculated Buckner. "That must be Elizabeth Blassenville's diary! Go on!"

"I can't make out the rest of the page," answered Griswell. "But a few pages further on I can make out some lines." He read:

" 'Why did the Negroes all run away when Aunt Celia disappeared? My sisters are dead. I know they are dead. I seem to sense that they died horribly, in fear and agony. But why? *Why?* If someone murdered Aunt Celia, why should that person murder my poor sisters? They were always kind to the black people. Joan—' " He paused, scowling futilely.

"A piece of the page is torn out. Here's another entry under another date—at least I judge it's a date; I can't make it out for sure.

" '—the awful thing that the old Negress hinted at? She named Jacob Blount, and Joan, but she would not speak plainly; perhaps she feared to—' Part of it gone here; then: 'No, no! How can it be? *She* is dead—or gone away. Yet—

she was born and raised in the West Indies, and from hints she let fall in the past, I know she delved into the mysteries of the voodoo. I believe she even danced in one of their horrible ceremonies—how could she have been such a beast? And this—this horror. God, can such things be? I know not what to think. If it is *she* who roams the house at night, who fumbles at my door, who *whistles* so weirdly and sweetly—no, no, I must be going mad. If I stay here alone I shall die as hideously as my sisters must have died. Of that I am convinced.' "

THE INCOHERENT CHRONICLE ended as abruptly as it had begun. Griswell was so engrossed in deciphering the scraps that he was not aware that darkness had stolen upon them, hardly aware that Buckner was holding his electric torch for him to read by. Waking from his abstraction he started and darted a quick glance at the black hallway.

"What do you make of it?"

"What I've suspected all the time," answered Buckner. "That mulatto maid Joan turned *zuvembie* to avenge herself on Miss Celia. Probably hated the whole family as much as she did her mistress. She'd taken part in voodoo ceremonies on her native island until she was 'ripe,' as old Jacob said. All she needed was the Black Brew—he supplied that. She killed Miss Celia and the three older girls, and would have gotten Elizabeth but for chance. She's been lurkin' in this old house all these years, like a snake in a ruin."

"But why should she murder a stranger?"

"You heard what old Jacob said," reminded Buckner. "A *zuvembie* finds satisfaction in the slaughter of humans. She called Branner up the stair and split his head and stuck the hatchet in his hand, and sent him downstairs to murder you. No court will ever believe that, but if we can produce her body, that will be evidence enough to prove your innocence. My word will be taken, that she murdered Branner. Jacob said a *zuvembie* could be killed . . . in reporting this affair I don't have to be too accurate in detail."

"She came and peered over the balustrade of the stair at us," muttered Griswell. "But why didn't we find her tracks on the stair?"

"Maybe you dreamed it. Maybe a *zuvembie* can project her spirit—hell! why try to rationalize something that's outside the bounds of rationality? Let's begin our watch."

"Don't turn out the light!" exclaimed Griswell involuntarily. Then he added: "Of course. Turn it out. We must be in the dark as"—he gagged a bit—"as Branner and I were."

But fear like a physical sickness assailed him when the room was plunged in darkness. He lay trembling and his heart beat so heavily he felt as if he would suffocate.

"The West Indies must be the plague spot of the world," muttered Buckner, a blur on his blankets. "I've heard of *zombies*. Never knew before what a *zuvembie* was. Evidently some drug concocted by the voodoo-men to induce madness in women. That doesn't explain the other things, though: the hypnotic powers, the abnormal longevity, the ability to control corpses—no, a *zuvembie* can't be merely a mad-woman. It's a monster, something more and less than a human being, created by the magic that spawns in black swamps and jungles—well, we'll see."

His voice ceased, and in the silence Griswell heard the pounding of his own heart. Outside in the black woods a wolf howled eerily, and owls hooted. Then silence fell again like a black fog.

Griswell forced himself to lie still on his blankets. Time seemed at a standstill. He felt as if he were choking. The suspense was growing unendurable; the effort he made to control his crumbling nerves bathed his limbs in sweat. He clenched his teeth until his jaws ached and almost locked, and the nails of his fingers bit deeply into his palms.

He did not know what he was expecting. The fiend would strike again—but how? Would it be a horrible, sweet whistling, bare feet stealing down the creaking steps, or a sudden hatchet-stroke in the dark? Would it choose him or Buckner? *Was Buckner already dead?* He could see nothing in the blackness, but he heard the man's steady breathing. The Southerner must have nerves of steel. Or was that Buckner breathing beside him, separated by a narrow strip of darkness? Had the fiend already struck in silence, and taken the sheriff's place, there to lie in ghoulish glee until it was ready to strike?—a thousand hideous fancies assailed Griswell tooth and claw.

He began to feel that he would go mad if he did not leap to his feet, screaming, and burst frenziedly out of that accursed house—not even the fear of the gallows could keep him lying there in the darkness any longer—the rhythm of Buckner's breathing was suddenly broken, and Griswell felt as if a bucket of ice-water had been poured over him. From somewhere above them rose a sound of weird, sweet whistling. . . .

Griswell's control snapped, plunging his brain into darkness deeper than the physical blackness which engulfed him. There was a period of absolute blankness, in which a realization of *motion* was his first sensation of awakening consciousness. He was running, madly, stumbling over an incredibly rough road. All was darkness about him, and he ran blindly. Vaguely he realized that he must have bolted from the house, and fled for perhaps miles before his overwrought brain began to function. He did not care; dying on the gallows for a murder he never committed did not terrify him half as much as the thought of returning to that house of horror. He was overpowered by the urge to run—run—run as he was running now, blindly, until he reached the end of his endurance. The mist had not yet fully lifted from his brain, but he was aware of a dull wonder that he could not see the stars through the black branches. He wished vaguely that he could see where he was going. He believed he must be climbing a hill, and that was strange, for he knew there were no hills within miles of the Manor. Then above and ahead of him a dim glow began.

He scrambled toward it, over ledge-like projections that were more and more taking on a disquieting symmetry. Then he was horror-stricken to realize that a sound was impacting on his ears—*a weird mocking whistle.* The sound swept the mists away. Why, what was this? *Where was he?* Awakening and realization came like the stunning stroke of a butcher's maul. He was not fleeing along a road, or climbing a hill; he was mounting a stair. He was still in Blassenville Manor! *And he was climbing the stair!*

An inhuman scream burst from his lips. Above it the mad whistling rose in a ghoulish piping of demoniac triumph. He tried to stop—to turn back—even to fling himself over the balustrade. His shrieking rang unbearably in his own ears. But his will-power was shattered to bits. It did not exist. He had no will. He had dropped his flashlight, and he had forgotten the gun in his pocket. He could not command his own body. His legs, moving stiffly, worked like pieces of mechanism detached from his brain, obeying an outside will. Clumping methodically they carried him shrieking up the stair toward the witch-fire glow shimmering above him.

"Buckner!" he screamed. "Buckner! Help, for God's sake!"

His voice strangled in his throat. He had reached the upper landing. He was tottering down the hallway. The whistling sank and ceased, but its impulsion still drove him on. He could not see from what source the dim glow came. It seemed to emanate from no central focus. But he saw a vague figure shambling toward him. It looked like a woman, but no human woman ever walked with that skulking gait, and no human woman ever had that face of horror, that leering yellow blur of lunacy—he tried to scream at the sight of that face, at the glint of keen steel in the uplifted claw-like hand—but his tongue was frozen.

Then something crashed deafeningly behind him; the shadows were split by a tongue of flame which lit a hideous figure falling backward. Hard on the heels of the report rang an inhuman squawk.

In the darkness that followed the flash Griswell fell to his knees and covered his face with his hands. He did not hear Buckner's voice. The Southerner's hand on his shoulder shook him out of his swoon.

A light in his eyes blinded him. He blinked, shaded his eyes, looked up into Buckner's face, bending at the rim of the circle of light. The sheriff was pale.

"Are you hurt? God, man, are you hurt? There's a butcher knife there on the floor—"

"I'm not hurt," mumbled Griswell. "You fired just in time—the fiend! Where is it? Where did it go?"

"Listen!"

Somewhere in the house there sounded a sickening flopping and flapping as of something that thrashed and struggled in its death convulsions.

"Jacob was right," said Buckner grimly. "Lead can kill them. I hit her, all right. Didn't dare use my flashlight, but there was enough light. When that whistlin' started you almost walked over me gettin' out. I knew you were hypnotized, or whatever it is. I followed you up the stairs. I was right behind you, but crouchin' low so she wouldn't see me, and maybe get away again. I almost waited too long before I fired—but the sight of her almost paralyzed me. Look!"

He flashed his light down the hall, and now it shone bright and clear. And it shone on an aperture gaping in the wall where no door had showed before.

"The secret panel Miss Elizabeth found!" Buckner snapped. "Come on!"

He ran across the hallway and Griswell followed him dazedly. The flopping and thrashing came from beyond that mysterious door, and now the sounds had ceased.

The light revealed a narrow, tunnel-like corridor that evidently led through one of the thick walls. Buckner plunged into it without hesitation.

"Maybe it couldn't think like a human," he muttered, shining his light ahead of him. "But it had sense enough to erase its tracks last night so we couldn't trail it to that point in the wall and maybe find the secret panel. There's a room ahead—the secret room of the Blassenvilles!"

And Griswell cried out: "My God! It's the windowless chamber I saw in my dream, with the three bodies hanging—ahhhhh!"

Buckner's light playing about the circular chamber became suddenly motionless. In that wide ring of light three figures appeared, three dried, shriveled, mummy-like shapes, still clad in the moldering garments of the last century. Their slippers were clear of the floor as they hung by their withered necks from chains suspended from the ceiling.

"The three Blassenville sisters!" muttered Buckner. "Miss Elizabeth wasn't crazy, after all."

"Look!" Griswell could barely make his voice intelligible. "There—over there in the corner!"

The light moved, halted.

"Was that thing a woman once?" whispered Griswell. "God, look at that face, even in death. Look at those claw-like hands, with black talons like those of a beast. Yes, it was human, though—even the rags of an old ballroom gown. Why should a mulatto maid wear such a dress, I wonder?"

"This has been her lair for over forty years," muttered Buckner, brooding over the grinning grisly thing sprawling in the corner. "This clears you, Griswell—a crazy woman with a hatchet—that's all the authorities need to know. God, what a revenge!—what a foul revenge! Yet what a bestial nature she must have had, in the beginnin', to delve into voodoo as she must have done—"

"The mulatto woman?" whispered Griswell, dimly sensing a horror that overshadowed all the rest of the terror.

Buckner shook his head. "We misunderstood old Jacob's maunderin's, and the things Miss Elizabeth wrote—*she* must have known, but family pride sealed her lips. Griswell, I understand now; the mulatto woman had her revenge, but not as we'd supposed. She didn't drink the Black Brew old Jacob fixed for her. It was for somebody else, to be given secretly in her food, or coffee, no doubt. Then Joan ran away, leavin' the seeds of the hell she'd sowed to grow."

"That—that's not the mulatto woman?" whispered Griswell.

"When I saw her out there in the hallway I knew she was no mulatto. And those distorted features still reflect a family likeness. I've seen her portrait, and I can't be mistaken. There lies the creature that was once Celia Blassenville."

LIVE PEOPLE DON'T UNDERSTAND

SCOTT EDELMAN

SCOTT EDELMAN (1955–) has spent much of his professional life editing various magazines, mainly in the science fiction genre, including *Science Fiction Age* (1992–2000), which he founded; *Sci Fi Magazine* (2002–present), the official publication of the Syfy Channel; *Science Fiction Weekly* (2000–present), the online periodical of the Syfy Channel; and *Last Wave* (1983–1986), a semiprofessional magazine that he also founded. At his peak of involvement, he read ten thousand stories a year. His work on various science fiction publications earned him four Hugo nominations as Best Editor.

While his editorial chores prevented him from doing much writing, he has had more than seventy-five science fiction, horror, and fantasy short stories published in such magazines as *The Twilight Zone, Science Fiction Review*, and *Fantasy Book*. He has been nominated for four Bram Stoker Awards in the category of Short Story and Long Fiction. Among his books are a novel, *The Gift* (1990), which was nominated for a Lambda Award, and *These Words Are Haunted* (2001), a collection of horror stories. He has also written for such comic books as *Captain America, Captain Marvel*, and *Omega the Unknown*, and he created *The Scarecrow* for Marvel. Among his television writings were several episodes of *Tales from the Darkside*.

"Live People Don't Understand" was first published in the fall 2009 issue of *Space and Time*.

SCOTT EDELMAN

LIVE PEOPLE DON'T UNDERSTAND

Everybody knows in their bones that something is eternal, and that something has to do with humans.

— *OUR TOWN*, ACT III

EMILY REMEMBERED WHAT it was like to be alive.

In fact, at first, she had forgotten that she was dead. She lay in a coffin, the confines of which she could not yet bring herself to see, and thought herself newly risen from a nap. Gazing upward, she wondered why the familiar ceiling above, the one under which she had shared a marriage bed with her husband George, had been replaced by stars.

Adding to her puzzle, she sensed other sleepers stretched out nearby. Their presence made her uncomfortable. It had been difficult enough for her to grow accustomed to being a wife, to sleeping with another beside her—she remembered her nervousness on her wedding night and smiled—but to have strangers nearby her as well was more than should be asked of her. Their closeness here did not make sense, but then, dreams on waking often lost their sense, and so she did not let herself worry much about her confusion. She trusted that she would understand soon enough. But then she remembered those who should have been nearby, and all those feelings faded, to be replaced by a greater loneliness than she had ever felt in her life.

If she asked, perhaps these strangers would tell her why George was not at her side—the two of them had yet to spend a night apart, which is exactly as it was supposed to be—and where her newborn baby had gone. She had just had the baby, hadn't she? George, Jr., was four by now, and could cope without her there every moment, but the little one . . . it must be hungry without Emily there to share her milk. She couldn't even remember whether she'd had a boy or a girl—how could that be?—but she knew that she had to find her baby.

She had to find her George.

"Wake up," she shouted. It rattled her to do so, because she was not a person accustomed to shouting. "Oh, you must wake up and talk to me. Where am I? What is this place? Help me, won't you? Help me understand. One moment I was at home in my bed in Grover's Corners, and the next I'm waking from a nap . . . where? Hello? You can't fool me. You're out there, you can hear me, I know it. Stop trying to pretend that you're still asleep. It just won't work, not when I need you so badly."

"Hush," came an old woman's voice to her left. Or at least Emily thought her to be old. The voice sounded vaguely familiar, but Emily could not place it, because the woman's throat was drier and raspier than she remembered it.

"I can't," said Emily. "I won't. Really now, I don't see how you can ask me to be still, not when there are so many unanswered questions."

634

"Nonetheless, just hush," insisted the woman, and as she continued to speak, Emily realized who she was. "You'll get used to unanswered questions. Soon enough, they'll no longer bother you so much."

"Really now, you shouldn't be talking that way, Mrs. Soames," said Emily, ill at ease at talking so sternly to an elder. "It is Mrs. Soames, isn't it? Forgive me for saying so, but there's no need for you to be so rude."

"There's no need to be anything any longer," said Mrs. Soames. "Which is precisely my point. Just settle down and let me be."

"How can you sleep away the day that way?" said Emily. She did not pause to consider what forces could have possibly brought them together at this time. "It's Emily, Mrs. Soames. Remember how much you enjoyed my wedding? You always loved a good party. I remember that about you. How can you just lie there when there is so much out there to live for?"

A rich burst of laughter came from somewhere off to Emily's right. The sound startled her, but gave her no offense. She did not feel that her emotions were being mocked, and remembering back to another who would chuckle with a wisdom Emily had not yet earned, she realized who it was who lay so close beside her, and felt loved and embraced.

"Mrs. Gibbs?" she whispered, stunned to see her mother-in-law there, and yet pleased by her presence.

"Can't you get her to keep quiet?" said Mrs. Soames.

"Don't be so hard on Emily," said Mrs. Gibbs, as the woman's laughter died down. "She's only a child. The two of us had plenty of time to make our peace with what would come here. But she was at the beginning of things. Besides, don't you remember how you felt when you first got here, even with all that preparation? Don't you remember what it was like when you first took your place?"

Emily listened, and listened hard, for the answer meant everything, but there was only a long silence, as if Mrs. Soames was having difficulty remembering how to speak, let alone the moments of her arrival in this place, whatever this place was.

"Vaguely," Mrs. Soames finally said. "Yes. Yes, I *do* remember. Only . . . I don't think I want to remember."

"Well, there you go," said Mrs. Gibbs. "But you weren't always like that, let me tell you. She's young yet, in more ways than one. She can't help but remember."

Emily waited for Mrs. Soames and Mrs. Gibbs to address her again, instead of just bantering amongst themselves, but instead, their conversation petered out, and they fell to silence. Emily called out to them again.

"I think I know where I am," said Emily, astonished. "I'm still dreaming, aren't I?"

"No, dear," said Mrs. Gibbs, her voice sleepy. "All that happened before, up until the time you found yourself here, that was the dream, dear. Let it go."

"I can't." Anguished, she began to cry, but no tears came. She thought to touch her face to find out how it could possibly be that the weeping failed to dampen her cheeks, but her arms would not move, no matter how hard she tried. Struggling like that, the truth of her situation came upon her with a suddenness that was sickening. "I'm dead, aren't I?"

"No need to say it that way," said Mrs. Gibbs. "It's really not so bad. The experience can become quite pleasant after a while, actually. Now you rest, girl."

"Please," said Mrs. Soames.

"I can't!" she said, feeling herself grow hysterical. How ridiculous was that, to be dead and hysterical? She refused to be either. George wouldn't want her to be either. "Don't you see? I'll never be able to let go!"

"Enough," said Mrs. Soames. "Someone's coming! Behave!"

"What if it's a thief?" said Emily, made fearful by the sound of unsteady footsteps trudging up the hill. George was supposed to protect her from such things, but now her only comfort was in two old women, and what could they do? "What if he's here to rob us?"

"Don't be silly, girl," said Mrs. Gibbs. "You have nothing more which anyone would wish to steal."

There was so much more that Emily needed to say right then, but before she could respond further, she sensed her poor dear husband above. George was there, right at the edges of the newly turned dirt of her grave. She was shocked by how much death had distracted her, for until that moment, she had not been aware of his approach. He seemed different to her, though, than when she had seen him last.

"Mrs. Gibbs," she said. "What's happened to your son? He's so . . . old."

"*Tempus fugit,* dear," she said. "You'll learn that soon enough."

"Could I really have been asleep so long?" said Emily. "It must have been years. But he's here! He still remembers us, Mrs. Gibbs."

"That isn't always a good thing, dear. No, not at all. And he's here to see you, not me. Listen."

"Emily," George moaned. He dropped to his knees directly above Emily's head. As he sobbed, she wished she could touch his lined cheek to comfort him, but she could do nothing. "I'm sorry, I'm so sorry."

"You needn't apologize, George. Not you."

She could feel a wrenching in his heart, could feel his essence seeking her out but not being able to find her. Their two hearts had once beat as one, destined for each other from the very start, but now, his lone heart was barely a heart at all. She pleaded for a way to break the barrier that kept them apart, but it was useless. Though he was alive to her, she was dead in all ways to him. His fingers bunched in the wet dirt, pawing it like a soggy blanket that he hoped to pull from across her face.

"No one should have to die in such a horrible way," he said, gasping. "I cannot change that, so I will myself to forget it. But I can't do that either, Emily, no matter how hard I try. Do you forgive me after all these years, Emily? Could you?"

He wanted an answer from her, one that she, in turn, wanted to give, and he listened for words she could not make him hear. But she would forgive him anything, could not recall having ever wavered from such a thought, in part because she knew that he could not possibly do anything that it would actually be necessary for her to forgive, not in a thousand lifetimes. Not George.

The urgency of his yearning was overpowering, though, and it came back to her then, not all of it, not the details, just enough to know what had delivered her to her final resting place. Her mother had told her during those few times when she'd tried to impart the lesson of womanhood to her, that some women were not built for childbirth. How unfortunate for Emily to have to learn that first hand. But at least . . . at least their baby lived. She had that much to be thankful for. At least she had seen that much before she vanished from her first world and was forced to take her place in the next one.

"Don't blame yourself, George," said Emily. "You need to be strong for our child."

Emily wondered how old their littlest one would be, considering the sprinkling of gray in George's hair, and wanted to ask him, but he would not have heard, had heard none of it up until then. Feeling his pleas unanswered, he fell forward, and sobbed into the dirt, his cheek pressed so close to her that she could almost feel his breath.

"I shouldn't have done it," he said. "I know that. I even knew it then. But I was a coward. And I'll keep paying for that until the day I die."

George stood suddenly, and shook off his raw emotions as easily as he slapped the dirt off his knees. She felt her window on him closing down to be replaced by the face that he let the world see.

"I'll try to forget you," he said, a coldness to his voice. "With enough time, perhaps I could do that. But I doubt I'll ever be able to forget what I did. Goodbye, Emily."

He ran off too quickly, stumbling as he had when he'd arrived. Emily could not hold on to him, so she held on to his words.

"What did he mean?" asked Emily. "He was your son, Mrs. Gibbs. Is your son. Help me understand."

"Better not to know," said Mrs. Gibbs. "Let him just go. Let it all go."

"Should I?" said Emily. "Really? But you know. I can tell. You've figured it out. Why won't you tell me?"

"Because I care about you, dear. You'll be much happier that way."

"Then I'll have to ask Mrs. Soames to help. Mrs. Soames!"

No matter how Emily whined, she could not rouse the woman. She had slipped off to her final sleep. Only Mrs. Gibbs was left, perhaps invigorated by the visit from her son. Emily had no choice but to badger her mother-in-law further.

"But you must tell me what he was talking about," said Emily. "You must! Why was he asking for my forgiveness? He's your son, you know him best. I don't remember him ever doing anything I'd need to forgive! Do you?"

There was a sudden silence, and in that space, months seemed to pass.

"Mrs. Gibbs!"

"Dear?"

"George, Mrs. Gibbs. Tell me about George." Mrs. Gibbs sighed.

"It's much better that way," said Mrs. Gibbs, "to not remember. I'd rather not think about my son, if you don't mind. And you should do the same."

"No! I could never do that. This is my life—"

"*Was* your life, dear."

"—and I can't let it go as if none of it happened. I need to remember. How sad he was up there! What could have happened to make him so sad? Don't you care? You're his mother!"

With no seeming provocation, Mrs. Soames spoke up.

"If you really must know—" she began.

"Hush!" said Mrs. Gibbs. "Now I'll say it. Hush! Don't tell her any more! It will only bring more pain. She's here to learn to put the pain away, not to pick it up again."

"Tell me what?" said Emily. "I have to know."

"You *can* go back, you know," said Mrs. Soames. "You can go back and see how it was. How it used to be. Others have done it before."

"It isn't a good idea, though," said Mrs. Gibbs softly.

"I'm going to do it anyway!" shouted Emily. "I have to do it! I have to know again, to feel."

"Feelings are overrated, dear," said Mrs. Gibbs. "You'll learn that soon enough, whatever you do. So you might as well take the easy way. Walk around the pain, don't walk through it. That's always the better way."

"I don't care!"

"Oh, give up," said Mrs. Soames. "You're not going to talk her out of it. She's a tough one, all right. The sooner she gets it out of her system, the sooner we'll all manage to get some rest."

"I can see that you're right, Mrs. Soames," said Mrs. Gibbs. "I guess you knew better all along. So go, dear. You won't be able to change anything, you know. That much will always be true. But you'll be able to see. And it will hurt, dear, it will hurt a great deal. Knowing what you know now, how you'll end up, how there's no permanent way back, well, it won't be pretty. Are you sure you want to do this?"

"As long as I can see my Georgie again, see what it's like to be alive, that's all that matters."

"You're braver than I ever was," said Mrs. Gibbs. "And a great deal more foolish. But I knew that when you became a Gibbs, Emily. No matter. I suspect that you'll feel quite differently when you come back."

"If I can see my George, I'm not coming back. I'm never—"

Before another syllable could pass through her stiff lips, the stars above Emily were replaced by her husband's eyes. There was no strength in them as he looked down at her. She saw only fear.

"What's wrong?" she asked. He was young again, his hair dark, his face smooth. And she was young again herself. She could feel her baby struggling within her to be born. All seemed well with the child—her experience with George, Jr., had taught her so—and there should have been no reason for her husband to be afraid.

"I don't know," he said.

She remembered having done this all before, remembered herself asking, and him answering, just that way the last time, but now, there was a difference. This time, the surface of things revealed the truth beneath. When in response to her questions about his demeanor, he'd said, "I don't know," she could tell that he was lying. She *knew.*

Emily was stunned by this revelation. George had never lied to her before. But then, shifting her head on the sweat-soaked pillow, she corrected herself. Her worldview was not the same as it had been mere moments before. She now knew that she had only *believed* that George had never lied to her before. Mrs. Gibbs had been right in telling her that she would see things she did not wish to see. And what was worse, though she could watch events unfold, she found that she could not change her words, could not respond using the new information she had earned.

"But everything will be all right, won't it, George?" she said. "The baby—our baby will be all right, won't it? Tell me that the baby will be all right, George."

She already knew what he would say, but still, Emily was distressed when George could find no other words than the words he had spoken before.

"I don't know," he repeated.

Emily lay in the bedroom in which she'd expected to be when she instead woke to find herself in her grave. She could see all the possessions that once were hers, and the happiness at seeing them brought tears welling up, but because she could change nothing about this scene, they were tears from the pain of childbirth that her new self only interpreted as joyous. She was happy to feel them wet her cheeks as they could not do before, to know life again, but that joy did not stay long, for she could also see the bedroom as if from above, as if she'd lifted the top off a doll's house to peer down. And so when George turned his back on her in her pain, Emily could

see that his action was not entirely motivated because he was overcome with grief, though that is what her earthly self would have thought, *had* thought years before. With the eyes in her body, she could see George reaching to the end table for a glass of water, but with God's eyes, with the sight she had been given, she could see through him and around him and beyond him to the other side, watch helplessly as he slipped a small vial from his shirt pocket and tilted its clear contents into her drink.

"Here," he said, his voice leaden, and this time she knew that it was not so in a tone of concern. "This should make you feel better."

He held the glass to her lips, and as the liquid touched her tongue, the emotions that barreled through her grew even more grotesquely twin. Her living self, the one that knew of nothing but the living, and thought the dead were impossibly far away, was relieved to feel George's left hand at the back of her head, comforting her, urging her to drink deeply. She was loved. She was protected. Her new self, the one with the blinders of life burned away, saw things with sudden clarity as they really were, saw into George, and could see the panic there in him. She knew him then as a wife should never know her husband. He did not want this child, had not even wanted their first child, was not entirely sure that he had ever really wanted her at all. He had always felt himself trapped by his snap decision to stay in Grover's Corners. It had all become too much for him.

And so with trembling fingers he held the poison to her lips. He planned to tell his family and friends that she had died in childbirth. They would be surprised, but would not disbelieve. After all, such things were not so unusual. It was known to happen from time to time, just as her mother had warned her.

But she'd never figured it would happen to her.

And truth to tell, it hadn't happened. But only he would ever know. George, and now, most unexpectedly, Emily as well.

She drank deeply, and soon felt the movements of her baby slow, and realized that she had been wrong, that it, too, had died, and as she began to sleep for what was meant to be the final time, she looked into her husband's eyes and thought, with knowledge of the grave and with complete sincerity, "Poor, poor George."

And then her husband was gone, her baby was gone, and she was back on the hill under an open sky, where she was meant to be boiled down to her essence in preparation for the world to come.

"I'm going back," she said, to no one in particular. The stars had no answer, but at least one of her neighbors did.

"Is that you, Emily? Still worrying away at the world, I see. Don't you remember? You've already been back."

"Not the way I plan to go back now. You don't know about George, what he's done. I've got to go back for real."

"You can't do that, dear."

"Don't patronize me, Mrs. Gibbs."

"I'm not, dear. It's only that no one has ever gone back that way before."

"I'll do it. Just watch me."

"You know it will only mean more pain. You've learned that much already, haven't you?"

"It doesn't matter," said Emily. "I've got to see my George, see him now, see him and say more to him than the shallow things I said before. After what he's done, I've got to tell him something. Live people don't understand."

"They never will, dear," said Mrs. Gibbs.

"I can't let myself believe that. George will be different. George will understand. I'll make him understand."

"You can't *make* the living do anything."

"It doesn't matter. George will listen to me. I know he will."

"Oh, my boy will listen all right. But you're not the pretty girl you once were. If you go before him as you are now, and he sees you again, like this, he'll have to listen. You'll certainly get his attention. The true question is, will he *hear*?"

"I'll make him hear," said Emily, with the confidence possessed only by the newly dead. "You watch."

"I don't believe I will, dear. It's terribly tiring staying awake like this for you. I believe I'll rest for a while. And don't worry about the likes of us, dear. We'll still be here when you get back."

Emily listened for the sound of her mother-in-law sleeping, and the sounds of all the others around her who made up the history of Grover's Corners, but there was nothing—no breathing, no snoring, no hint that there was any life there. And in truth, there was not. But Emily refused to sleep the sleep of the dead, not when George was out there, his double crime still a fresh wound in her mind.

All of the strength that had been missing before, when George had wailed above her, coursed through her explosively now. Her hands, which had been tied by invisible bonds, now pushed against and through the flimsy wooden roof of her coffin. Carrying her will before her like a torch, she pierced the dirt above like a swimmer surfacing after a dive, and found herself on the hillside, looking down at the few distant lights of the town she so loved. She wished she could feel the wind against her face, but could not. Her torn and leathery skin was beyond that now. She looked down at her headstone, at the dates beneath her name that insulted her with their brevity.

"I was so young," she said.

"We all were," said Mrs. Gibbs with a final yawn, before turning back to sleep. "Now go do whatever it is you think you have to do."

Emily walked down the gravel roadway up which she had been carried. She remembered that now, remembered it all, though when it had occurred she had still been taking her first brief nap. Along the way she passed so many sleepers, and as she saw them, she felt their presence in a way she never had when as a child she played hide-and-seek among the tombstones. How could she have missed them? She wanted to call out to them all to join her, to return to their loved ones as she was doing, but she knew they would not listen. Unlike Mrs. Gibbs and Mrs. Soames, they were long gone, and would not have responded no matter how loudly Emily called. The part that belonged to the living had been completely burned away, so that all that remained was the eternal.

What she and George had was eternal, too. She would never forget that. And once she reminded George of that fact, he would be unable to forget it either.

She thudded noisily through the home that she and George had once lived in together. Her heart sank to see the clutter that he had allowed to overgrow the place she used to keep so clean. The piles were high and the dust was thick. It was late, and he was surely to bed, and that is where she found him. She sensed no others in the house. Her baby was dead, but where was George, Jr.? Perhaps he was spending the night with a cousin, which was just as well. She wouldn't have wanted him to hear what was to come.

Their half-full marriage bed looked bleak, and even though George was in the bed alone, he was curled as far away as possible from the side Emily had once occupied. He teetered at the edge of the mattress. Emily could not help but pause before the site where she had died. George, as if in his sleep sensing her there, turned fitfully. She spoke his name, but words were not enough to wake him. Her lungs did not seem to house the strength of her limbs, and so her words were but a whisper.

She leaned over to touch a shoulder, and his eyes snapped open.

"Emily," he said. His eyes were still full of fear, but it was not solely of Emily. It was of everything, as if there was no longer a part of the world that did not torment him. And he looked so old! Even older than when she had last seen him. Now his hair was completely white, and his skin was so wrinkled as to match the face she remembered on his grandfather. No wonder George, Jr., was not here; he was long gone to a life of his own.

How much time had passed in slumber? How much life had been lost?

"I'm so sorry, Emily," he said.

"I know that, George," she said, leaving her fingers pressed against him. He did not move, just lay there and studied her with eyes near tears.

"I cannot stop dreaming of you," he said. "Even when I'm awake, I dream of you. How can I ever make you understand, Emily? I can barely understand myself. I was so afraid. I thought I knew how to make my fear go away. But after what I did to you, after what I did to the baby, it only became worse."

"I know that all already, George. I've been given that gift. And that's why I'm here. That's why I've come back. To tell you that there's no reason to be afraid. No reason at all."

He smiled then, and sighed. From the strength of that sigh, it seemed to have been the first one he had allowed himself in a long while.

"Do you really mean that?" he said.

"Yes. Yes, I do, George. Life is wonderful, you see. I want to make sure you understand that."

"I do. I know that now, Emily."

"I'm glad," she said. "I love you, George."

"And I love you, too, Emily," he said, lapsing into sobs. "I'm sorry I never realized that until it was too late."

"It's never too late," said Emily.

And then she killed him.

GEORGE REMEMBERED WHAT it was like to be alive, but the stars above did not surprise him. He was not for a moment fooled that he still remained in such a state. There was no more life in him, and he knew how, and he knew why. He shuddered there in the grave beside his wife.

"It was all so terrible, wasn't it?" he said. "And silly. And pointless. How did we ever bear it, Emily? Emily?"

She was sleeping more deeply now, having done what she needed to do. There was no George out there whose presence in the world of the living kept calling her back.

His cry beside her woke her from her slumber.

"But it was wonderful, too, at times," she said, her voice still soft with the dreams of what would come. "Only we hardly ever knew it."

"If only we could have."

"I don't think that's possible, George, not for live people. That peace and that beauty was beyond us. I love you, George. Now you go back to sleep. Go back to sleep until we are made ready to meet again."

"I can't, Emily. There's something . . . I sense that there's still something out there."

"Don't be silly, George. It's time to wean yourself of all that."

"Wait! Listen!"

There was a shuffling on the rough road coming up the hill toward them, the hill beyond which the town of Grover's Corners had grown nearer to the graveyard. A middle-aged man stood over them, stooped with sorrow, his face achingly familiar to George.

"Why, it's like looking in a mirror," said George. "It's George, Jr., come to visit us. And look at him. How long have I been here?"

"He's far too old to be called junior any more, George. And he's not here to visit us, darling. He's here to visit himself."

"He seems so sad."

"That's because he still thinks of us from time to time. He thinks he lost us both too soon. How sweet."

George looked up at his son and felt the guilt that only the newly dead know.

"I don't want anyone to feel such sadness because of me, Emily. It reminds me of the way I couldn't help but feel about you. Couldn't we— shouldn't we—do something?"

"No, George. It's not the same with children. At least not with our child. His pain is different. It's not our place."

"Are you sure?" said George. "I feel it. I feel it right now. I have that choice. I could come back and free him from that burden. I know I could."

George's fingers twitched as his son shed tears by the tombstone above them. But before he could lift his arm toward the surface, Emily roused herself from her great slumber and snaked her hand through the mud to lace her fingers through his.

"No, George," she whispered with a yawn. "Let him be. He may be blind, but soon enough, he'll see. Soon enough, one by one, all of them will."

While George was focused on his wife's eternal touch, he realized that his son had stolen away. He did not know how much time had passed. He realized that he had been sleeping. By now, George might even have joined them through the natural coursing of time, though he did not sense his son in the ground nearby.

He called once more to Emily, but this time she did not answer. She had already been weaned of this world for once and always, as he soon would be, too. He looked forward to that moment.

As he felt himself drift back to sleep, maybe for the last time, he studied the swimming stars above. Someone had once told him about stars, how it took the light from them millions of years to get to Earth. It didn't seem possible, even with the promise of what was to come, that time could stretch on that long.

He could no longer feel Emily's fingers wrapped in his own, but he knew in his heart that they were still there. Millions of years. They were hurtling towards him. As the light raced above and the living raced below, George was ready to spend that time exactly where he was.

THE HOUSE IN THE MAGNOLIAS

AUGUST DERLETH AND MARK SCHORER

AUGUST (WILLIAM) DERLETH (1909–1971) was born in Sauk City, Wisconsin, where he remained his entire life. He received an M.A. from the University of Wisconsin in 1930, by which time he had already begun to sell horror stories to *Weird Tales* (the first appearing in 1926) and other pulp magazines. During his lifetime, he wrote more than three thousand stories and articles, and published more than a hundred books, including detective stories (featuring Judge Peck and an American Sherlock Holmes clone, Solar Pons), supernatural stories, and what he regarded as his serious fiction: a very lengthy series of books, stories, poems, journals, etc., about life in his small town, which he renamed Sac Prairie.

Derleth's boyhood friend and frequent collaborator, Mark Schorer (1908–1977), was born in the same town and attended the same university. He published his first novel, *A House Too Old* (1935), about Wisconsin life, while still a graduate student. He went on to a distinguished career as a scholar, critic, writer, and educator, holding positions at Dartmouth, Harvard, and the University of California (Berkeley). He won three Guggenheim scholarships and a Fulbright professorship to the University of Pisa. In addition to writing for the pulps, he sold many short stories to such magazines as *The New Yorker, Esquire,* and *The Atlantic Monthly,* but his most important work was his biography, *Sinclair Lewis: An American Life* (1961). He was elected to the American Academy of Arts and Sciences.

"The House in the Magnolias" was first published in the June 1932 edition of *Strange Tales;* it was first collected in *Colonel Markesan and Less Pleasant People* by August Derleth and Mark Schorer (Sauk City, Wisconsin: Arkham House, 1966).

AUGUST DERLETH AND MARK SCHORER

THE HOUSE IN THE MAGNOLIAS

IF YOU HAD seen the magnolias, you would understand without further explanation from me why I went back to the house. My friends in New Orleans realized that it was just such a place as an artist like myself would light upon for his subject. Their objections to my going there were not based on notions that the house and its surroundings were not fit subjects for really excellent landscape paintings. No, they agreed with me there. Where they disagreed . . . But I had better fill in the background for you before I get too far ahead in my story.

I had been in New Orleans a month, and still had found no subject in that old city that really satisfied me. But, motoring one day out into the country with Sherman Jordan, a young poet with whom I was living during my stay in the city, we found ourselves about four miles out of New Orleans, driving along a little-used road over which the willows leaned low. The road broadened unexpectedly, and the willows gave way to a row of sycamores, and then, in the evening dusk, I saw the house in the magnolias for the first time.

It was not far from the road, and yet not too close. A great veranda with tall pillars stretched its length in front. The house itself was of white wood, built in the typical rambling Southern plantation style. Vines covered great portions of its sides, and the whole building was literally buried in magnolias—magnolias such as I have never seen before, in every shade and hue. They were fully opened, and even from the road I could see the heavy waxen artificiality of those nearest.

"There's my picture!" I exclaimed eagerly. "Stop the car, old man."

But Sherman Jordan showed no inclination to stop. He glanced quickly at his watch and said by way of explanation: "It's almost six; we've got to get back for our dinner engagement." He drove on without a second glance at the house.

I was disappointed. "It would have taken only a minute," I reproached him.

I must have looked glum, for just as we were driving into New Orleans, he turned and said: "I'm sorry; I didn't think it was so important." I felt suddenly, inexplicably, that he was not sorry, that he had gone past the house deliberately.

I said: "Oh, it doesn't make any difference. I can come out tomorrow."

He was silent for a moment. Then he said:

"Do you really think it would be such a good picture?"

"I do," I said, and at the same instant I thought that he didn't want me to paint that house. "Will you drive me out tomorrow morning?" I added.

"I can't," he said shortly. "I've promised Stan Leslie I'd go boating with him. But you can have the car, if you really insist on painting that house."

I said nothing.

As we left the car he turned and said almost sharply: "Still, I think you might find better subjects if you tried."

A cutting reply about my wasted month in New Orleans was on the tip of my tongue, but I held it back. I could not understand my friend's utter lack of enthusiasm. I could not chalk it up to an inartistic eye, for I knew Sherman Jordan could be depended on for good taste. As I went upstairs to dress, there remained in my mind the picture of that lovely old house, surrounded by rich magnolias, marked off by the swaying sycamore trees.

My eagerness had not abated when I stepped from Jordan's car next morning, opened the gate, and went up the path under the sycamores to the house in the magnolias. As I mounted the steps, walked across the veranda, and lifted the knocker on the closed door, I thought of painting a close-up of magnolias. I was turning this idea over in my mind when the door opened suddenly, noiselessly. And old woman stood there, apparently a Negress, dressed plainly in starched white. Her face held me. It was peculiarly ashy—really gray—unhealthy. I thought: "The woman is ill." Her eyes stared at me; they were like deep black pools, bottomless, inscrutable, and yet at the same time oddly dull. I felt momentarily uncomfortable.

"Is the master in?" I asked.

The woman did not answer, though she continued to stare at me. For a moment I thought that perhaps she was deaf. I spoke loudly, and very distinctly, repeating: "Is your master in? May I see your master?"

A faint shadow fell across the floor of the hall behind the servant, and in an instant, a second woman appeared. "What is it?" she asked sharply, in a deep, velvety voice. The woman was so astonishingly attractive that for a moment I could not speak for admiration. She was almost as tall as I was, and very shapely. Her hair was black and drawn back loosely from her face. Her complexion was swarthy, almost olive, with a high color in cheeks and lips. In her ears were golden rings. Her eyes, which were black, shone from dark surrounding shadows. She wore a purple dress that fell almost to the floor. Her face as she looked at me was imperious; behind her dark eyes were smoldering fires.

She waved the servant aside and turned to me, repeating her question: "What is it, please?"

With my eyes on her face, I said: "I am John Stuard. I paint. Yesterday, driving past your place here, I was so attracted by the house that I felt I must come and ask your permission to use it as a subject for a landscape."

"Will you come in?" she asked, less sharply.

She stepped to one side. I muttered my thanks and went past her into the hall. Behind me I could feel the woman's alert eyes boring into me. I turned, and she gestured for me to precede her into the drawing room leading off the hall. I went ahead. In the drawing room we sat down.

"You are from New Orleans?" she asked. She leaned a little forward, her somber eyes taking in my face. She was sitting in shadow, and I directly in the light from the half-opened window.

"No," I replied. "I live in Chicago. I am only visiting in New Orleans." She looked at me a moment before replying. "Perhaps it can be arranged for you to paint the house. It will not take long? How many days, please?"

"A week, perhaps ten days. It is quite difficult."

She appeared suddenly annoyed. She was just about to say something when some distant sound caught her ear, and she jerked her head up, looking intently into a corner of the ceiling, as if listening. I heard nothing. Presently she turned again. "I thought it might be for only a day or two," she said, biting her lower lip.

I began to explain when I heard the old servant shuffle toward the door that led out to the veranda. The woman before me looked up quickly. Then she called out in a low persuasive voice: "Go back to the kitchen, Matilda."

Looking through the open drawing room doors, I saw the servant stop in her tracks, turn automatically, and shuffle past the door down the hall, walking listlessly, stiffly.

"Is the woman ill?" I asked solicitously.

"*Non, non,*" she said quickly. Then she said abruptly: "You do not know my name; I am Rosamunda Marsina."

Belatedly, I said: "I am glad to know you. You live here alone?"

There was a pause before she answered me. "The servant," she said, smiling lightly. She looked a little troubled. I felt that I should not have asked.

To cover my embarrassment, I said: "You have a nice plantation."

She shook her head quickly. "It is not mine. It belongs to Miss Abby, my aunt Abby. She is a Haitian."

"Oh, I see," I said, smiling; "She lives in Haiti?"

"No, she does not live in Haiti. She did live there. She came from there some years ago."

I nodded, but I did not quite understand. Looking about me, I could see that everything was scrupulously clean and well taken care of, and this was certainly a large house for a single servant to keep so well. I had seen from a glance at Miss Marsina's hands that she had no share in the labors of the household.

Miss Marsina bent forward again. "Tell me, say, I give you permission to paint the house— you would stay—in the city?"

My eyes dropped confusedly before hers, and at her question my face fell, for my disappointment was evident to her. I had hoped she would ask me to live in the house for the time that I painted it. Once more I started an explanation

to Rosamunda Marsina, suggesting that I might find some place in the neighborhood where I could get a room for the time, but throughout my explanation, I openly, shamelessly hinted at an invitation from her to stay here.

My speech seemed to have its effect. "Perhaps I could give you a room for that time," she said reluctantly.

I accepted her invitation at once. She fidgeted a little nervously, and asked: "When do you wish to begin painting?"

"I should like to start sketching tomorrow. The painting I shall have to do mostly late in the afternoon. I want to get the half-light in which I first saw the house—"

She interrupted me abruptly. "There will be some conditions to staying here—a request I must make of you, perhaps two." I nodded. "I am not a very sociable creature," she went on. "I do not like many people about. I must ask you not to bring any friends out with you, even for short visits. And I would rather, too, that you didn't mention your work out here unless necessary—it might reach the ears of Aunt Abby; perhaps she would not like it."

I saw nothing strange in her request, nothing strange in this mysteriously beautiful woman. "I shouldn't think of bringing anyone, Miss Marsina," I said. "I feel I am presuming as it is."

She stopped me with a quick, abrupt "*Non,*" and a slightly upraised hand. Then she smiled. "I shall expect you tomorrow then."

Both of us got up and walked to the door. I said, "Good-by," almost automatically. Then I started walking down the path, away from the house, feeling Rosamunda Marsina's eyes on me. Suddenly I heard running footsteps, light footsteps, and turned to meet Miss Marsina.

"One thing more, Mr. Stuard," she said hurriedly, talking in a low voice as if afraid of being overheard. "Tomorrow—is it necessary for you to bring your car? Cars disturb me." She looked pathetically at me.

"I shall not bring the car," I said.

She nodded, quickly, shortly, and ran back into the house without pausing. Looking back from the road, I saw her standing at the open window of the drawing room, watching me.

I found Rosamunda Marsina waiting for me next morning. She seemed a little agitated; I wondered whether anything had gone wrong.

"Shall I bring in the equipment and my easel?" I asked.

"Matilda can bring it to your room," she said. "Come with me. I am going to put you on the ground floor."

She turned and led the way into the house and down the hall. Opening a door not far beyond the drawing room she stretched out her arm and indicated the charming old chamber which I was to occupy, a room with great heavy mahogany bureau and four-poster, with a desk, and windows opening directly on the garden at the side of the house.

"It's lovely," I murmured.

She looked at me with her dark eyes, not as sharp today as they had been the day before. They were limpid and soft, tender, I thought. Then abruptly I caught a flash of something I was not meant to see; it was present only for a moment, and her eyes veiled it again—unmistakable fear!

She could not have known that I had seen, for she said: "You must not venture off the grounds, and not behind the house. And you will not go to any of the other floors?"

I said: "No, certainly not."

Matilda shuffled into the room, and without a word or a glance at us, put the equipment down near the bed. She departed with the same dragging footsteps.

"A curious woman," I said.

Rosamunda Marsina laughed a little uncertainly. "Yes; she is very old. She came here with my aunt."

"Oh," I said. "Your aunt is *here*, then?"

She looked at me, shot a quick startled glance at me. "Didn't I tell you?" she asked. "I thought I told you yesterday—yes, she is here. That is why I have made so many requests of you; it is because I don't want her to know you are here." Her voice betrayed her agitation, though her face remained immobile.

"She can hardly help seeing me some time, I'm afraid."

"*Non, non*—not if you do as I say." Once again fear crept into her eyes. She spoke quickly in a low voice. "She is a near-invalid. She has a club foot, and never leaves the back rooms of the second floor because it is so difficult for her to move." Rosamunda Marsina's hand was trembling. I took it in my own.

"If she would object to my being here, perhaps I had better go to one of your neighbors," I volunteered.

She closed her eyes for a moment; then flashed them open and looked at me calmly, saying impetuously: "I want you to stay. My aunt must not matter—even though she does. You must stay now; I want you to stay. She is not really my aunt, I don't think. She brought me from Haiti when I was just a little girl. I cannot remember anything. She is much darker than I am; she is not a Creole."

Again I had an uncomfortable feeling that something was wrong in the house, and for a moment I had the impression that Rosamunda Marsina was begging me to stay. "Thank you," I said; "I'll stay."

She smiled at me with her lovely dark lips and left the room, closing the door softly behind her.

That night the first strange thing happened. Rosamunda Marsina's suggestive attitude, the vague fear that haunted her eyes, the sudden inexplicable agitation of her voice—these things had prepared me. Perhaps if I had gone to sleep at once, I would have known nothing. As I lay there, half asleep, I heard a distinct sound of someone walking on the floor above me, in some room farther back than my own. I thought of Miss Marsina's aunt Abby at once, but recollected that the woman was a cripple and a near-invalid, and would not be likely to be up and about, especially not at this hour. Yet the footsteps were slow and dragging, and were accompanied by the sound of a cane tapping slowly at regular intervals against the floor. I sat up in bed to listen. Listening, I could tell that it was only one foot that dragged. Abruptly, the footsteps stopped. Miss Abby had gotten out of her bed somehow, and had walked perhaps to the wall of the room from the bed. I heard guttural sounds suddenly, and then the dragging footsteps retreating. The woman talking to herself, I thought.

Then, above the dragging footsteps, I heard a disturbing shuffling which seemed to come from somewhere below, followed by sounds as of doors closing somewhere. In a moment, all was quiet again; but only for a moment—for suddenly there came a thin, reed-like wail of terror, followed at once by a shrill scream. I sat up abruptly. A window went up with a bang, and a harsh, guttural voice sounded from above. The voice from above had a magic effect, for silence, broken only by the sudden shuffling of feet, fell immediately.

I had got out of bed, and made my way to the door leading into the hall. I had seen on my first visit that the house lacked artificial light, and had brought an electric candle along. This I took up as I went toward the door. I had it in my hand as I opened the door. The first thing its light found was the white face of Rosamunda Marsina.

"Someone called . . . I thought," I stammered.

She was agitated; even the comparatively dim illumination from the electric candle revealed her emotion. "*Non, non*—there was nothing," she said quickly. "You are mistaken, Mr. Stuard." Then, noticing the amazement which must have shown on my face, she added, uncertainly: "Perhaps the servants called out—but it is nothing; nothing is wrong."

As she said this, she gestured with her hands. She was wearing a long black gown with wide sleeves. As she raised her hands, the sleeves fell back along her arms. I think I must have started at what I saw there—at any rate, Rosamunda Marsina dropped her arms at once, shot a sharp glance at me through half-closed eyes, and walked swiftly away, saying, "Good night, Mr. Stuard." For on the white of her arms, I saw the distinct impressions of two large hands—hands which must have grasped her most cruelly, and only a short while before. Then, so suddenly as to leave me gasping, it came to me that Rosamunda Marsina had been waiting for me in the hall, waiting to see what I would do—and, I felt sure, sending me back into my room against her will!

I slept comparatively little that night.

In the morning I wanted to say something to my hostess, but I had hardly come from my room before she herself spoke. She came to me at the breakfast table, and said: "You must have had a powerful dream last night, Mr. Stuard. There was nothing wrong as you thought—nor did the servants call out!"

At once I understood that she was not talking for me. Her face was white and strained, her voice unnaturally loud. As quickly, I answered in an equal raised voice. "I'm sorry. I should have warned you that I am often troubled by bad dreams."

Miss Marsina lost her tensity at once. She shot me a grateful glance, and left the room immediately. But I sat in silence, waiting for a sound I felt must come. I had not long to wait— a few moments passed—then, from upstairs, came the soft sound of a door closing. Someone had been listening, waiting to hear what Rosamunda Marsina would say to me, what I would answer!

From that moment I knew that I would get no more painting done until I knew what mystery surrounded the house and Miss Marsina.

I sketched my landscape that morning, and my hostess stood watching me. I liked her lovely dark face peering over my shoulder as I worked, but both of us were a little uneasy, and I could not do my best work. There was about her an air of restraint which interposed itself mysteriously the moment she tried to enjoy herself. She seemed a little frightened, too, and more than once I caught her eyes straying furtively to the second-floor windows.

The second night in the house was a hot, sultry night; a storm was brooding low on the horizon when I went to bed, but it must have passed over, for when I woke up somewhere between one and two in the morning, the moon was shining. I could not rest, and got out of bed. For a few moments I stood at the window, drinking in the sweet smell of the magnolias. Then, acting on a sudden impulse, I bent and crawled through the open window. I dropped to the ground silently and began to walk toward the rear of the house unconsciously, forgetting my promise to Miss Marsina. I remembered it suddenly, and stopped. Then I heard a slight sound above me. I stepped quickly into the shadow of a bush, just at the corner of the house, where I could see both the side and rear of the house.

Then I looked up. There at the window of the corner room I saw a bloodless face pressed against the glass; it was a dark, ugly face, and the moonlight struck it full.

It was withdrawn as I looked, but not before I had got an impression of malefic power. Could it have been the face of Aunt Abby? According to what Rosamunda Marsina had said, that would be her room. And what was she looking at? Over the bushes behind the house, beyond the trees— it would be something in the fields. I turned. Should I risk trying to see, risk her spotting me as I went along the lane?

Keeping to the shadows, I moved along under the low-hanging trees, looking toward the fields. Then suddenly I saw what Miss Abby must have seen. There were men in the fields, a number of them. I pressed myself against the trunk of a giant sycamore and watched them. They were Negroes, and they were working in the fields. Moreover, they were probably under orders, Miss Abby's orders. I understood abruptly that her watching them was to see that they did their work. But Negroes that worked at night!

Back in my room once more, I was still more thoroughly mystified. Did they work every night? It was true that I had seen no workers anywhere on the plantation during the day just passed, but then, I had not left the front of the house, and from there little of the plantation could be seen. I thought that next day surely I

would mention this to Rosamunda Marsina, and the incidents of the night before, too.

Then I thought of something else. All the while that I had stood watching the Negroes, no word had passed among them. That was surely the height of the unusual.

But on the second day, I found that I had to go into New Orleans for some painting materials I had not supposed I would need, and for some clothes, also, and thus lost the opportunity to speak to Rosamunda Marsina before evening.

In the city, I went immediately to Sherman Jordan's apartment. Despite the fact that I had promised Rosamunda Marsina that I would say as little about my stay with her as possible, I told my friend of my whereabouts.

"I knew pretty well you were out there," he said. His voice was not particularly cordial. I said nothing. "I daresay you are completely entranced by the beautiful Creole who lives there?"

"How did you know?" I asked.

He shrugged his shoulders, giving me a queer look. "There are stories about," he said.

"About Miss Marsina?" I felt suddenly angry.

"Not especially. Just stories about that place. Nothing definite. If you haven't noticed anything, perhaps it's just idle gossip." But Jordan's attitude showed that he did not believe the stories about the house in the magnolias to be just "idle gossip."

And I *had* noticed something, but instantly I resolved to say nothing to Jordan. "What stories?" I asked.

He did not appear to have heard my question. "They're from Haiti, aren't they?"

I nodded. "Yes. The old woman is a Haitian. The girl is not." Was he getting at something?

"Haiti—a strange, fascinating place." He stood looking out of the window. He turned suddenly. "I'd like to beg you to drop that work out there, John, but I know it wouldn't be of much use asking that, now you've started. There's something not right about that place, because strange stories don't grow out of thin air."

"If there's anything wrong out there, I'm going to find out."

He shrugged his shoulders. His smile was not convincing. "Of course," he said. Then: "You know, there's an old proverb in Creole patois—'*Quand to mange avec diab' tenin to cuillere longue.*'"

"I don't understand Creole patois," I said, somewhat irritated.

"Literally, it is: 'When you sup with the devil, be sure you have a long spoon.'"

"I don't follow you," I said.

He smiled again. "Oh, it's just another warning."

I had no desire to listen longer to anything so indefinite and vague; so I changed the subject. I don't think anything he could have told me would have influenced me; I would have gone back to that house and Rosamunda Marsina no matter what was lurking there. But I expected nothing so strange, so horrible, as that which I did discover.

I returned to the house that evening, and again put off saying anything to Rosamunda. But she herself afforded me an unlooked for opening before I went to bed that night. She had come down from upstairs, and I could see at once that there was something she wanted to tell me.

"I think it's only fair to tell you," she said, "that your door will be locked tonight, after you have gone to bed."

"Why?" I asked, trying not to betray my astonishment.

"It is because it is not desirable that you walk around at night."

This hurt me a little, suggesting as it did that perhaps I might make use of the darkness to spy out the house. I said: "Rosamunda, there are stories about this house, aren't there?"

I was sorry at once, for she looked suddenly very frightened. "What do you mean?" she asked.

"I have heard things in New Orleans," I said slowly.

She mastered herself a little, asking: "What?"

"Oh, nothing definite," I replied. "Some people think that there is something wrong out here."

"Something wrong? What?"

"I don't know."

"Have you seen anything wrong?"

"No . . ." I hesitated, and she caught my dubious tone.

"Do you suspect anything?" she asked.

"I don't know," I said.

She looked at me a little coldly. Already I was beginning to repent my having spoken to her about the house. Also, she had suspected at once that I had broken my promise to her and had talked about the house. I had not foreseen that, and cursed myself for a fool. I had succeeded only in creating an atmosphere of tension.

That night I was awakened by a sharp cry of terror, which was cut off abruptly even before I was fully awake. I was out of bed instantly, standing in the middle of the room, listening. Once I fancied I heard the sound of Rosamunda's voice, a low, earnest sound, as if she were pleading with someone. Then, silence. How long I waited, I do not know. At last I took up my electric candle and made for the door. Then I remembered that it would be locked—as Rosamunda had told me. Yet I reached out and turned the knob, and the door was not locked!

I looked cautiously out into the hall. But I had time to see only one thing: a bloodless face, convulsed with hatred, staring into mine—the same face I had seen against the window of the second floor—and above it, a heavy cane upraised. Then the cane descended, catching me a glancing blow on the side of the head. I went down like a log.

How long I lay there I do not know; it could not have been long, for it was still dark when I came to—and found Rosamunda's frightened eyes watching my face anxiously, felt her delicate fingers on my forehead. I struggled to sit up, but she held me quiet.

"Be still," she murmured. Then she asked quickly: "You are not badly hurt?"

"No," I whispered. "It was just enough to put me out."

"Oh, it was my fault. If I had locked the door it would not have happened."

"Nonsense," I said quickly. "If I hadn't been so curious . . . if I hadn't heard your voice . . ."

"I am glad you thought of me, John." It was the first time she had used my Christian name, and I felt more pleasure than I cared to admit. But before I could express my sentiment, she said swiftly: "In the morning you must go."

"What? Go away—and not come back?"

She nodded. "If you do not go away, both of us will suffer. I should not have let you come, let you stay."

Boldly I said: "I'm not going until I can take you with me."

She looked closely at me; then bent quickly and kissed me. For a moment I held her in my arms; then she pushed me gently away. "Listen," she said. "In the morning you must go with your baggage. Go anywhere—back to New Orleans. But at sundown, come back to me. You must not be seen by Aunt Abby. I will wait for you in the magnolias just below the veranda."

I stood up, steadying myself against the doorframe. "I'll come back, Rosamunda," I said.

She nodded and fled down the hall. I went back into my room and packed my things.

In the morning I departed ostentatiously, making it certain that the older woman, Abby, had seen me go. But in the evening I was back. I never left the vicinity, and was within sight of the house all day. How could I leave there—when Rosamunda might be in danger? I approached the house that evening effectively screened by low trees and the magnolias.

Rosamunda was standing before the veranda, almost hidden in the bushes. She was agitated, standing there twisting her handkerchief in her hands. She ran forward a little as I came up. "Now I must tell you," she breathed. "I must tell someone—you. You must help me." She was obviously distraught.

I said: "I'll do anything I can for you, Rosamunda."

She began to talk now, rapidly. "We came from Haiti, John. That is a strange island, an island of weird, curious things. Sometimes it is called the magic island. And it is. Do you believe in magic things?"

I did have a knowledge of magic beliefs, some old legends I had picked up in the Indian country, and quite a collection of tales I had heard from levee Negroes. I nodded, saying: "I know very little of it, but I think it can be."

"You have never been to Haiti?"

"No," I replied.

She paused, turned and looked a little fearfully at the house; then spoke again. "There are many strange beliefs in Haiti," she said, talking slowly, yet betraying an eagerness to finish. Then she looked deep into my eyes and asked: "Do you know what a zombi is?"

I had heard weird half-hinted stories of animated cadavers seen in Haiti, whispered tales of age-old Negro magic used to raise the dead of the black island. Vaguely, I knew what she meant. Yet I said: "No."

"It is a dead man," she went on hurriedly, "a dead man who has been brought out of his grave and made to live again and to work!"

"But such a thing cannot be," I protested, suddenly horrified at an idea that began to form in my mind, a terrible suggestion which I sought to banish quickly. It would not go. I listened for Rosamunda's hushed and tense voice.

"Believe me, John Stuard—they do exist!"

"No, no," I said.

She stopped me abruptly. "You are making it hard for me."

"I'm sorry," I said. "I will believe you." But inwardly I protested; surely such a thing could not be! Yet I could not banish from my mind the memory of strangely silent figures working the fields at night.

Rosamunda spoke swiftly, her words coming in an agonized rush. "That woman—Abby—she knew how to raise these people from their graves. When we came to New Orleans, we came alone. Just the two of us. She was in a hurry to get out of Haiti; I now think she was wanted in Port au Prince. I do not know. I was only a little girl, but I can remember these things. Every year they come more and more distinctly to me. Soon after we were here, the slaves came."

I cut in: "What slaves?"

"They are in the cellars—many of them. All Negroes. We keep them in the cellars all day; only at night Abby sends them out to work. I have been so afraid you might find them, for you heard them screaming—and you might have seen them in the fields at night."

"But surely you don't mean—you can't mean . . ."

"I do. *They are dead!*"

"But, Rosamunda . . . !"

"Please, let me tell you what I know." I nodded, and she went on. "I was quite old when Matilda came. She was the last of them. All along up to her, the slaves came, one after the other. I never saw them come. One day they were just here; that is all. But many nights Abby was gone—and soon after, slaves would come. Abby always took care of them herself, making sweet bread and water for them. They ate nothing more. After Matilda came, something happened. Aunt Abby hurt herself, and couldn't leave the house. She wouldn't have a doctor, and since then she could leave her room only with great difficulty. She had a speaking tube put into her rooms; it ran down into the cellars, so that she could direct the men—those poor dead men—into the fields. They were taught to come back as soon as light showed in the eastern sky. Only Abby could direct them, but I could tell Matilda what to do. Over Matilda Abby had no power—it often happens that way.

"After she came, there were no more slaves. I was quite grown then, and I came on a newspaper one day that told of a series of grave robbings that had been climaxed by the recent snatching of the body of a colored woman, Matilda Martin. That was right after Matilda came. Since then, I have known. At first it was horrible for me to live here, but there was no place for me to go. I have been living with these dead men and Abby, John, and I cannot go on—and I cannot leave these poor dead ones behind me. I want to go away with you, but they must be sent back to the graves from which she took them."

Looking at her frightened yet determined face, I knew that she would go away with me. I did not want the house, nor the magnolias; I wanted Rosamunda Marsina. "There is a way, then, to send them back?" I asked, still only half believing her shocking story.

She nodded eagerly. "They must be given salt—any food with salt—and they will know they are dead, and will find their way back to their graves."

"And Miss Abby?" I said.

She looked at me. "She is too strong; we can do nothing if she knows."

"What shall we do?" I asked.

Rosamunda's eyes went suddenly cold. She said: "Matilda can be directed to Abby. Only I can direct her. Matilda hates Abby as I do. Abby is a fiend—she has robbed these dead of their peace. If I go from here, she must not be able to follow—else she will hound us until we are dead, and after that . . . I don't want to think what might happen then."

An idea came to me, and at first I wanted to brush it aside. But it was persistent—and it *was* a way out. "Rosamunda," I said, "send Matilda up to Abby."

Rosamunda looked at me. She nodded. "I was thinking that way," she said. "But it must be before she has the salt, because once she has tasted salt there is nothing left for her but to find her grave."

Then she shot a frightened glance at the windows of the second floor. She clutched my arm. "Quick," she murmured. "They will be coming from the cellars soon. We must be ready for them. They never refuse food, never. I have made some little pistachio candies, with salt. We must give the candies to them."

She led the way, almost running into the house. I came silently after her. Below me I could hear the shuffling of many feet, and above, the dragging footsteps of Miss Abby, moving away from her speaking tube. Rosamunda snatched up the little plate of candy and preceded me to the back door.

Then suddenly the cellar doors opened, and a file of staring men shuffled slowly out, looking neither to right nor to left, seeing us, yet not seeing us. Rosamunda stepped boldly forward, holding out the plate. The foremost of them took a piece of the salted candy, and went on, munching it. Their black faces were expressionless. When the Negroes had all taken of the candy, Rosamunda turned to reenter the house. "Come quickly," she said. "Soon they will know." I hesitated, and saw—and my doubts were swept away, leaving my mind in chaos.

The little group had stopped abruptly, huddled together. Then, one by one, they began to wail terribly into the night, and even as I watched, they began to move off, hurriedly now, running across the fields toward their distant graves, a line of terrible, tragic figures against the sky.

I felt Rosamunda shuddering against me, and slipped my arm gently around her. "Listen!" she said, her voice trembling. Above us I could hear suddenly the angry snarling voice of Miss Abby. At the same time the sound of wood beating wood came to us: Abby was pounding the walls with her cane.

Matilda stood in the kitchen, and Rosamunda went up to her at once, addressing her in a soft, persuasive voice. "Above there is Abby, Matilda. Long ago she took you away from where you were—took you to be her slave. You have not liked her, Matilda, you have hated her. Go up to her now. She is yours. When you come down, there will be candy on the table for you."

Matilda nodded slowly; then she turned and began to shuffle heavily into the hall toward the stairs. Upstairs, silence had fallen.

Both of us ran from the kitchen, snatching up two small carpet-bags which Rosamunda had put into the corridor, and which she pointed out to me as we went. We jumped from the veranda and ran down the path. Behind us rose suddenly into the night the shrill screaming of a woman in deadly terror. It was shut off abruptly, horribly. Rosamunda was shuddering. We turned to run. We had gone only a little way down the deserted road when we heard the nearby sound of a woman wailing. That was Matilda. Rosamunda hesitated, I with her, pressed close in the shadow of an overhanging sycamore. We looked back. A shadowy figure was running across the fields; in the house a lamp was burning low in the kitchen. And yet, was it a lamp? The light suddenly flared up. I turned Rosamunda about before she had time to see what I had seen. Matilda had turned over the lamp. The house was burning.

Rosamunda was whimpering a little, the strain beginning to tell. "We'll have to go away. When they find Abby dead, they'll want me."

I said, "Yes Rosamunda," but I knew we would not have to go away, unless that fire did not burn. We hurried on to New Orleans, and went to Jordan's apartment.

Next day it was discovered that the house in the magnolias had burned to the ground, Miss Abby with it. The Creole woman, Rosamunda Marsina, had spent the night with her fiance in the apartment of Sherman Jordan—so said the papers. Jordan had seen to that. Rosamunda and I were married soon after and went out to rebuild that house.

Since then, I have tried often to dismiss the events of that horrible night as a chaotic dream, a thing half imagined, half real. But certain things forbade any such interpretation, no matter how much I longed to believe that both Rosamunda and I had been deceived by too vivid belief in Haitian legends.

There were especially those other things in the papers that day—the day the burning of the house was chronicled—things I kept carefully from Rosamunda's eyes. They were isolated stories of new graveyard outrages—that is what the papers called them, but I know better—*the finding of putrefied remains in half-opened graves of Negroes whose bodies had been stolen long years ago—and the curious detail that the graves had been half dug by bare fingers, as if dead hands were seeking the empty coffins below.*

HOME DELIVERY

STEPHEN KING

THE MOST FAMOUS and beloved writer in America, Stephen (Edwin) King (1947–), was born in Portland, Maine, and graduated from the University of Maine with a B.A. in English. Unable to find a position as a high school teacher, he sold some stories to various publications, including *Playboy*. Heavily influenced by H. P. Lovecraft and the macabre stories published by EC Comics, he directed his energies to horror and supernatural fiction. His first book, *Carrie* (1973), about a girl with psychic powers, was thrown into a wastebasket and famously rescued by his wife, Tabitha, who encouraged him to polish and submit it. It received a very modest advance but had great success as a paperback and a career was launched—a career of such spectacular magnitude that King was the most consistently successful writer in America for two decades and remains the most popular author of horror fiction in history. In 2003, he was given the National Book Foundation's medal for Distinguished Contribution to American Letters. In addition to writing numerous novels and short stories, King has written screenplays and nonfiction, proving himself an expert in macabre fiction and film. More than one hundred films and television programs have been made from his work, most notably *Carrie* (1976), *The Shining* (1980), *Stand by Me* (1986, based on the novella "The Body"), *Misery* (1990), *The Shawshank Redemption* (1994, based on the short story "Rita Hayworth and Shawshank Redemption"), and *The Green Mile* (1999).

"Home Delivery" was originally published in *Book of the Dead*, edited by John Skipp and Craig Spector (New York: Bantam, 1989).

STEPHEN KING

HOME DELIVERY

CONSIDERING THAT IT was probably the end of the world, Maddie Pace thought she was doing a good job. *Hell* of a good job. She thought that she just might be coping with the End of Everything better than anyone else on earth. And she was *positive* she was coping better than any other *pregnant* woman on earth.

Coping.

Maddie Pace, of all people.

Maddie Pace, who sometimes couldn't sleep if, after a visit from Reverend Peebles, she spied a dust-bunny under the dining room table—just the thought that Reverend Peebles *might* have seen that dust-bunny could be enough to keep her awake until two in the morning.

Maddie Pace, who, as Maddie Sullivan, used to drive her fiancé Jack crazy when she froze over a menu, debating entrées sometimes for as long as half an hour.

"Maddie, why don't you just flip a coin?" he'd asked her once after she had managed to narrow it down to a choice between the braised veal and the lamb chops . . . and then could get no further. "I've had five bottles of this goddam German beer already, and if you don't make up y'mind pretty damn quick, there's gonna be a drunk lobsterman under the table before we ever get any food *on* it!"

So she had smiled nervously, ordered the braised veal . . . and then lay awake until well past midnight, wondering if the chops might not have been better.

She'd had no trouble coping with Jack's pro-posal, however; she accepted it and him quickly, and with tremendous relief. Following the death of her father, Maddie and her mother had lived an aimless, cloudy sort of life on Deer Isle, off the coast of Maine. "If I wasn't around to tell them women where to squat and lean against the wheel," George Sullivan had been fond of saying while in his cups and among his friends at Buster's Tavern or in the back room of Daggett's Barber Shop, "I don't know what the hell they'd do."

When he died of a massive coronary, Maddie was nineteen and minding the town library weekday evenings at a salary of $41.50 a week. Her mother was minding the house—or had been, that was, when George reminded her (sometimes with a good, hard shot to the ear) that she had a house that needed minding.

He was right.

They didn't speak of it because it embarrassed them, but he was right and both of them knew it. Without George around to tell them where to squat and lean to the wheel, they didn't know what the hell to do. Money wasn't the problem; George had believed passionately in insurance, and when he dropped down dead during the tiebreaker frame of the League Bowl-Offs at Big Duke's Big Ten in Yarmouth, his wife had come into better than a hundred thousand dollars. And island life was cheap, if you owned your own home and kept your garden weeded and knew how to put up your own vegetables come fall. The *problem* was having nothing to focus on. The *problem* was how the center seemed to have dropped out of their lives when George went facedown in his Island Amoco bowling shirt just over the foul line of lane nineteen in Big Duke's (and goddam if he hadn't picked up the spare they needed to win, too). With George gone their lives had become an eerie sort of blur.

It's like being lost in a heavy fog, Maddie thought sometimes. Only instead of looking for the road, or a house, or the village, or just some landmark like that lightning-struck pine in the Altons' woodlot, I am looking for the wheel. If I can ever find the wheel, maybe I can tell *myself* to squat and lean my shoulder to it.

At last she found her wheel; it turned out to be Jack Pace. Women marry their fathers and men their mothers, some say, and while such a broad statement can hardly be true all of the time, it was true in Maddie's case. Her father had been looked upon by his peers with fear and admiration—"Don't fool with George Sullivan, chummy," they'd say. "He's one hefty son of a bitch and he'd just as soon knock the nose off your face as fart downwind."

It was true at home, too. He'd been domineering and sometimes physically abusive . . . but he'd also known things to want and work for, like the Ford pickup, the chain saw, or those two acres that bounded their place on the left. Pop Cook's land. George Sullivan had been known to refer to Pop Cook (out of his cups as well as in them) as one stinky old bastid, but there was some good hardwood left on those two acres. Pop didn't know it because he had gone to living on the mainland when his arthritis really got going and crippled him up bad, and George let it be known on the island that what that bastid Pop Cook didn't know wouldn't hurt him none, and furthermore, he would kill the man or woman that let light into the darkness of Pop's ignorance. No one did, and eventually the Sullivans got the land. And the wood, of course. The hardwood was logged off for the two wood stoves that heated the house in three years, but the land would remain. That was what George said and they believed him, believed *in* him, and

they worked, all three of them. He said you got to put your shoulder to this wheel and *push* the bitch, you got to push ha'ad because she don't move easy. So that was what they did.

In those days Maddie's mother had kept a roadside stand, and there were always plenty of tourists who bought the vegetables she grew— the ones George *told* her to grow, of course, and even though they were never exactly what her mother called "the Gotrocks family," they made out. Even in years when lobstering was bad, they made out.

Jack Pace could be domineering when Maddie's indecision finally forced him to be, and she suspected that, loving as he was in their courtship, he might get around to the physical part— the twisted arm when supper was cold, the occasional slap or downright paddling—in time; when the bloom was off the rose, so as to speak. She saw the similarities . . . but she loved him. And needed him.

"I'm not going to be a lobsterman all my life, Maddie," he told her the week before they married, and she believed him. A year before, when he had asked her out for the first time (she'd had no trouble coping then, either—had said yes almost before all the words could get out of his mouth, and she had blushed to the roots of her hair at the sound of her own naked eagerness), he would have said, "I *ain't* going to be a lobsterman all my life." A small change . . . but all the difference in the world. He had been going to night school three evenings a week, taking the ferry over and back. He would be dog tired after a day of pulling pots, but he'd go just the same, pausing only long enough to shower off the powerful smells of lobster and brine and to gulp two No-Doz with hot coffee. After a while, when she saw he really meant to stick to it, Maddie began putting up hot soup for him to drink on the ferry ride over. Otherwise, he would have had no supper at all.

She remembered agonizing over the canned soups in the store—there were so *many!* Would he want tomato? Some people didn't like tomato soup. In fact, some people *hated* tomato soup, even if you made it with milk instead of water. Vegetable soup? Turkey? Cream of chicken? Her helpless eyes roved the shelf display for nearly ten minutes before Charlene Nedeau asked if she could help her with something—only Charlene said it in a sarcastic way, and Maddie guessed she would tell all her friends at high school tomorrow and they would giggle about it—about *her*—in the Girls' Room, because Charlene knew what was wrong; the same thing that was always wrong. It was just Maddie Sullivan, unable to make up her mind over so simple a thing as a can of *soup*. How she had ever been able to decide to accept Jack Pace's proposal was a wonder and a marvel to all of them . . . but of course they didn't know how, once you found the wheel, you had to have someone to tell you when to stoop and where exactly to lean against it.

Maddie had left the store with no soup and a throbbing headache.

When she worked up nerve enough to ask Jack what his favorite soup was, he had said: "Chicken noodle. Kind that comes in the can."

Were there any others he specially liked?

The answer was no, just chicken noodle— the kind that came in the can. That was all the soup Jack Pace needed in his life, and all the answer (on that one particular subject, at least) that Maddie needed in hers. Light of step and cheerful of heart, Maddie climbed the warped wooden steps of the store the next day and bought the four cans of chicken noodle soup that were on the shelf. When she asked Bob Nedeau if he had any more, he said he had a whole damn *case* of the stuff out back.

She bought the entire case and left him so flabbergasted that he actually carried the carton out to the truck for her and forgot all about asking why she had wanted all that chicken soup— a lapse for which his wife Margaret and his daughter Charlene took him sharply to task that evening.

"You just better believe it," Jack had said that time not long before the wedding—she never forgot. "More than a lobsterman. My dad says I'm full of shit. He says if it was good enough

for his old man, and his old man's old man, and all the way back to the friggin' Garden of Eden to hear *him* tell it, if it was good enough for all of *them*, it ought to be good enough for me. But it ain't—*isn't*, I mean—and I'm going to do better." His eye fell on her, and it was a loving eye, but it was a stern eye, too. "More than a lob- sterman is what I mean to be, and more than a lobsterman's wife is what I intend for you to be. You're going to have a house on the mainland."

"Yes, Jack."

"And I'm not going to have any friggin' Chevrolet." He took a deep breath. "I'm going to have an *Oldsmobile*." He looked at her, as if daring her to refute him. She did no such thing, of course; she said yes, Jack, for the third or fourth time that evening. She had said it to him thousands of times over the year they had spent courting, and she confidently expected to say it *millions* of times before death ended their mar- riage by taking one of them—or, hopefully, both of them together.

"More than a friggin' lobsterman, no matter what my old man says. I'm going to do it, and do you know who's going to help me?"

"Yes," Maddie had said. "Me."

"You," he responded with a grin, sweeping her into his arms, "are damned tooting."

So they were wed.

Jack knew what he wanted, and he would tell her how to help him get it and that was just the way she wanted things to be.

Then Jack died.

Then, not more than four months after, while she was still wearing weeds, dead folks started to come out of their graves and walk around. If you got too close, they bit you and you died for a little while and then *you* got up and started walking around, too.

Then, Russia and America came very, very close to blowing the whole world to smither- eens, both of them accusing the other of caus- ing the phenomenon of the walking dead. "How close?" Maddie heard one news correspondent from CNN ask about a month after dead people started to get up and walk around, first in Florida, then in Murmansk, then in Leningrad and Minsk, then in Elmira, Illinois; Rio de Janeiro; Biterad, Germany; New Delhi, India; and a small Australian hamlet on the edge of the Outback.

(This hamlet went by the colorful name of Wet Noggin, and before the news got out of there, most of Wet Noggin's populace consisted of shambling dead folks and starving dogs. Maddie had watched most of these developments on the Pulsifers' TV. Jack had hated their satellite dish—maybe because they could not yet afford one themselves—but now, with Jack dead, none of that mattered.)

In answer to his own rhetorical question about how close the two countries had come to blowing the earth to smithereens, the commentator had said, "We'll never know, but that may be just as well. My guess is within a hair's breadth."

Then, at the last possible second, a British astronomer had discovered the satellite—the apparently *living* satellite—which became known as Star Wormwood.

Not one of ours, not one of theirs. Someone else's. Someone or something from the great big darkness Out There.

Well, they had swapped one nightmare for another, Maddie supposed, because *then*—the last *then* before the TV (even all the channels the Pulsifers' satellite dish could pull in) stopped showing anything but snow—the walking dead folks stopped only biting people if they came too close.

The dead folks started *trying* to get close.

The dead folks, it seemed, had discovered they *liked* what they were biting.

BEFORE ALL THE weird things started happening, Maddie discovered she was what her mother had always called "preg," a curt word that was like the sound you made when you had a throatful of snot and had to rasp some of it up (or at least that was how Maddie had always thought it sounded). She and Jack had moved

to Genneseault Island, a nearby island simply called Jenny Island by those who lived there.

She had had one of her agonizing interior debates when she had missed her time of the month twice, and after four sleepless nights she had made a decision . . . and an appointment with Dr. McElwain on the mainland. Looking back, she was glad. If she had waited to see if she was going to miss a third period, Jack would not even have had one month of joy . . . and she would have missed the concerns and little kindnesses he had showered upon her.

Looking back—now that she was *coping*—her indecision seemed ludicrous, but her deeper heart knew that going to have the test had taken tremendous courage. She had wanted to be sick in the mornings so she could be surer; she had longed for nausea. She made the appointment when Jack was out dragging pots, and she went while he was out, but there was no such thing as *sneaking* over to the mainland on the ferry. Too many people saw you. Someone would mention casually to Jack that he or she had seen his wife on *The Gull* t'other day, and then Jack would want to know who and why and where, and if she'd made a mistake, Jack would look at her like she was a goose.

But it had been true, she was with child (and never mind that word that sounded like someone with a bad cold trying to rake snot off the sides of his throat), and Jack Pace had had exactly twenty-seven days of joy and looking forward before a bad swell had caught him and knocked him over the side of *My Lady-Love,* the lobster boat he had inherited from his uncle Mike. Jack could swim, and he had popped to the surface like a cork, Dave Eamons had told her miserably, but just as he did, another heavy swell came, slewing the boat directly into Jack, and although Dave would say no more, Maddie had been born and brought up an island girl, and she knew: could, in fact, *hear* the hollow thud as the boat with its treacherous name smashed her husband's head, leaving blood and hair and bone and brain for the next swell to wash away from the boat's worn side.

Dressed in a heavy hooded parka and down-filled pants and boots, Jack Pace had sunk like a stone. They had buried an empty casket in the little cemetery at the north end of Jenny Island, and the Reverend Peebles (on Jenny you had your choice when it came to religion: you could be a Methodist, or if that didn't suit you, you could be a Methodist) had presided over this empty coffin, as he had so many others, and at the age of twenty-two Maddie had found herself a widow with an almost half-cooked bun in her oven and no one to tell her where the wheel was, let alone when to put her shoulder to it.

She thought she would go back to Deer Isle, back to her mother, to wait for her time, but she knew her mother was as lost—maybe even *more* lost—than she was herself, and held off.

"Maddie," Jack told her again and again, "the only thing you can ever decide on is not to decide."

Nor was her mother any better. They talked on the phone and Maddie waited and hoped for her mother to tell her to come home, but Mrs. Sullivan could tell no one over the age of ten anything. "Maybe you ought to come on back over here," she had said once in a tentative way, and Maddie couldn't tell if that meant *please come home* or *please don't take me up on an offer which was really just made for form's sake*, and she spent sleepless nights trying to decide and succeeding in doing only that thing of which Jack had accused her: deciding not to decide.

Then the weirdness started, and that was a mercy, because there was only the one small graveyard on Jenny (and so many of the graves filled with those empty coffins—a thing which had once seemed pitiful to her now seemed another blessing, a grace) and there were two on Deer Isle, bigger ones, and it seemed so much safer to stay on Jenny and wait.

She would wait and see if the world lived or died.

If it lived, she would wait for the baby.

That seemed like enough.

• • •

AND NOW SHE was, after a life of passive obedience and vague resolves that passed like dreams an hour or two after getting out of bed, finally *coping*. She knew that part of this was nothing more than the effect of being slammed with one massive shock after another, beginning with the death of her husband and ending with one of the last broadcasts the Pulsifers' TV had picked up—a horrified young boy who had been pressed into service as an INS reporter, saying that it seemed certain that the president of the United States, the first lady, the secretary of state, the honorable senator from Oregon (which honorable senator the gibbering boy reporter didn't say), and the emir of Kuwait had been eaten alive in the White House ballroom by zombies.

"I want to repeat," the young reporter said, the fire-spots of his acne standing out on his forehead and chin like stigmata. His mouth and cheeks had begun to twitch; the microphone in his hand shook spastically. "I want to repeat that a bunch of dead people have just lunched up on the president and his wife and a whole lot of other political hotshots who were at the White House to eat poached salmon and cherries jubilee. Go, Yale! Boola-boola! Boola-fuckin-boola!" And then the young reporter with the fiery pimples had lost control of his face entirely, and he was screaming, only his screams were disguised as laughter, and he went on yelling *Go, Yale! Boola-boola!* while Maddie and the Pulsifers sat in dismayed silence until the young man was suddenly swallowed by an ad for Boxcar Willie records, which were not available in any store, you could only get them if you dialed the 800 number on your screen, operators were standing by. One of little Cheyne Pulsifer's crayons was on the end table beside the place where Maddie was sitting, and she took down the number before Mr. Pulsifer got up and turned off the TV without a single word.

Maddie told them good night and thanked them for sharing their TV and their Jiffy Pop.

"Are you sure you're all right, Maddie dear?" Candi Pulsifer asked her for the fifth time that night, and Maddie said she was fine for the fifth time that night (and she was, she was *coping* for the first time in her life, and that really *was* fine, just as fine as paint), and Candi told her again that she could have that upstairs room that used to be Brian's anytime she wanted, and Maddie had declined her with the most graceful thanks she could find, and was at last allowed to escape. She had walked the windy half mile back to her own house and was in her own kitchen before she realized that she still had the scrap of paper on which she had jotted the 800 number in one hand. She dialed it, and there was nothing. No recorded voice telling her all circuits were currently busy or that number was out of service; no wailing siren sound that indicated a line interruption (had Jack told her that was what that sound meant? she tried to remember and couldn't, and really, it didn't matter a bit, did it?), no clicks and boops, no static. Just smooth silence.

That was when Maddie knew—knew for sure.

She hung up the telephone slowly and thoughtfully.

The end of the world had come. It was no longer in doubt. When you could no longer call the 800 number and order the Boxcar Willie records that were not available in any store, when there were for the first time in her living memory no Operators Standing By, the end of the world was a foregone conclusion.

She felt her rounding stomach as she stood there by the phone on the wall in the kitchen and said it out loud for the first time, unaware that she had spoken: "It will have to be a home delivery. But that's all right, as long as you remember, Maddie. There isn't any other way, not now. It will have to be a home delivery."

She waited for fear and none came.

"I can cope with this just fine," she said, and this time she heard herself and was comforted by the sureness of her own words.

A baby.

When the baby came, the end of the world would itself end.

"Eden," she said, and smiled. Her smile was sweet, the smile of a madonna. It didn't matter how many rotting dead people (maybe Boxcar Willy among them) were shambling around on the face of the world.

She would have a baby, she would have a home delivery, and the possibility of Eden would remain.

THE FIRST NEWS had come out of a small Florida town on the Tamiami Trail. The name of this town was not as colorful as Wet Noggin, but it was still pretty good: Thumper. Thumper, Florida. It was reported in one of those lurid tabloids that fill the racks by the checkout aisles in supermarkets and discount drugstores. DEAD COME TO LIFE IN SMALL FLORIDA TOWN! the headline of *Inside View* read. And the subhead: *Horror Movie Comes to Life!* The subhead referred to a movie called *Night of the Living Dead,* which Maddie had never seen. It also mentioned another movie she had never seen. The title of this piece of cinema was *Macumba Love.* The article was accompanied by three photos. One was a still from *Night of the Living Dead,* showing what appeared to be a bunch of escapees from a lunatic asylum standing outside an isolated farmhouse at night. One was a still from *Macumba Love,* showing a woman with a great lot of blond hair and a small bit of bikini-top holding in breasts the size of prize-winning gourds. The woman was holding up her hands and screaming at what appeared to be a black man in a mask. The third purported to be a picture taken in Thumper, Florida. It was a blurred, grainy shot of a human whose sex was impossible to define. It was walking up the middle of a business street in a small town. The figure was described as being "wrapped in the cerements of the grave," but it could have been someone in a dirty sheet.

No big deal. Bigfoot Rapes Girl Scouts last week, the dead people coming back to life this week, the dwarf mass murderer next week.

No big deal until they started to come out everywhere. No big deal until the first news film ("You may want to ask your children to leave the room," Dan Rather introduced gravely) showed up on network TV, creatures with naked bone showing through their dried skin, traffic accident victims, the morticians' concealing makeup sloughed away either in the dark passivity of the earth or in the clawing climb to escape it so that the ripped faces and bashed-in skulls showed, women with their hair teased into dirt-clogged beehives in which worms and beetles still squirmed and crawled, their faces alternately vacuous and informed with a kind of calculating, idiotic intelligence; no big deal until the first horrible stills in an issue of *People* magazine that had been sealed in shrink-wrap like girly magazines, an issue with an orange sticker that read *Not for Sale to Minors!*

Then it was a big deal.

When you saw a decaying man still dressed in the mud-streaked remnants of the Brooks Brothers suit in which he had been buried tearing at the breast of a screaming woman in a T-shirt that read *Property of the Houston Oilers,* you suddenly realized it might be a very big deal indeed.

Then the accusations and the saber rattling had started, and for three weeks the entire world had been diverted from the creatures escaping their graves like grotesque moths escaping diseased cocoons by the spectacle of the two great nuclear powers on what appeared to be an undiveritable collision course.

There were no zombies in the United States, Tass declared: This was a self-serving lie to camouflage an unforgivable act of chemical warfare against the Union of Soviet Socialist Republics. Reprisals would follow if the dead comrades coming out of their graves did not fall down decently dead within ten days. All U.S. diplomatic people were expelled from the mother country and most of her satellites.

The president (who would not long after become a Zombie Blue Plate Special himself) responded by becoming a pot (which he had come to resemble, having put on at least fifty pounds

since his second-term election) calling a kettle black. The U.S. government, he told the American people, had incontrovertible evidence that the only walking dead people in the USSR had been set loose deliberately, and while the premier might stand there with his bare face hanging out and claim there were over eight thousand lively corpses striding around Russia in search of the ultimate collectivism, *we* had definite proof that there were less than forty. It was the *Russians* who had committed an act—a *heinous* act—of chemical warfare, bringing loyal Americans back to life with no urge to consume anything but other loyal Americans, and if these Americans—some of whom had been good Democrats—did not lie down decently dead within the next *five* days, the USSR was going to be one large slag pit.

The president expelled all Soviet diplomatic people . . . with one exception. This was a young fellow who was teaching him how to play chess (and who was not at all averse to the occasional grope under the table).

Norad was at Defcon-2 when the satellite was spotted. Or the spaceship. Or the creature. Or whatever in hell's name it was. An amateur astronomer from Hinchly-on-Strope in the west of England spotted it first, and this fellow, who had a deviated septum, fallen arches, and balls the size of acorns (he was also going bald, and his expanding pate showcased his really horrible case of psoriasis admirably), probably saved the world from nuclear holocaust.

The missile silos were open all over the world as telescopes in California and Siberia trained on Star Wormwood; they closed only following the horror of Salyut/Eagle-I, which was launched with a crew of six Russians, three Americans, and one Briton only three days following the discovery of Star Wormwood by Humphrey Dagbolt, the amateur astronomer with the deviated septum, et al. He was, of course, the Briton.

And he paid.

They *all* paid.

• • •

THE FINAL SIXTY-ONE seconds of received transmission from the *Gorbachev/ Truman* were considered too horrible for release by all three governments involved, and so no formal release was ever made. It didn't matter, of course; nearly twenty thousand ham operators had been monitoring the craft, and it seemed that at least nineteen thousand of them had been running tape decks when the craft had been— well, was there really any other word for it?— invaded.

Russian voice: Worms! It appears to be a massive ball of—
American voice: Christ! Look out! It's coming for us!
Dagbolt: Some sort of extrusion is occurring. The port-side window is—
Russian voice: Breach! Breach! Suits!
(Indecipherable gabble.)
American voice: —and appears to be eating its way in—
Female Russian voice (Olga Katinya): Oh stop it stop the eyes—
(Sound of an explosion.)
Dagbolt: Explosive decompression has occurred. I see three—no, four—dead—and there are worms . . . everywhere there are worms—
American voice: Faceplate! Faceplate! *Faceplate!*
(Screaming.)
Russian voice: Where is my mamma? Where—
(Screams. Sounds like a toothless old man sucking up mashed potatoes.)
Dagbolt: The cabin is full of worms—what appears to be worms, at any rate—which is to say that they really *are* worms, one realizes— they have extruded themselves from the main satellite—what we took to be—which is to say, one means—the cabin is full of floating body parts. These space-worms apparently excrete some sort of aci—
(Booster rockets fired at this point; duration of the burn is seven point two seconds. This may or may not have been an attempt to escape or possibly to ram the central object. In either case, the maneuver did not work.

It seems likely that the chambers themselves were clogged with worms and Captain Vassily Task—or whichever officer was then in charge—believed an explosion of the fuel tanks themselves to be imminent as a result of the clog. Hence the shutdown.)
American voice: Oh my Christ they're in my head, they're eating my fuckin br—
(Static.)
Dagbolt: I am retreating to the aft storage compartment. At the present moment, this seems the most prudent of my severely limited choices. I believe the others are all dead. Pity. Brave bunch. Even that fat Russian who kept rooting around in his nose. But in another sense I don't think—
(Static.)
Dagbolt: —dead at all because the Russian woman—or rather, the Russian woman's severed head, one means to say—just floated past me, and her eyes were open. She was looking at me from inside her—
(Static.)
Dagbolt: —keep you—
(Explosion. Static.)
Dagbolt: Is it possible for a severed penis to have an orgasm? I th—
(Static.)
Dagbolt: —around me. I repeat, all around me. Squirming things. They—I say, does anyone know if—
(Dagbolt, screaming and cursing, then just screaming. Sound of toothless old man again.)

Transmission ends.
   The *Gorbachev/Truman* exploded three seconds later. The extrusion from the rough ball nicknamed Star Wormwood had been observed from better than three hundred telescopes earthside during the short and rather pitiful conflict. As the final sixty-one seconds of transmission began, the craft began to be obscured by something that certainly *looked* like worms. By the end of the final transmission, the craft itself could not be seen at all—only the squirming mass of things that had attached themselves to

it. Moments after the final explosion, a weather satellite snapped a single picture of floating debris, some of which was almost certainly chunks of the worm-things. A severed human leg clad in a Russian space suit floating among them was a good deal easier to identify.

And in a way, none of it even mattered. The scientists and political leaders of both countries knew exactly where Star Wormwood was located: above the expanding hole in earth's ozone layer. It was sending something down from there, and it was not Flowers by Wire.

MISSILES CAME NEXT.

Star Wormwood jigged easily out of their way and then returned to its place over the hole.

More dead people got up and walked.

Now they were all biting.

The final effort to destroy the thing was made by the United States. At a cost of just under six hundred million dollars, four SDI "defensive weapons" satellites had been hoisted into orbit by the previous administration. The president of the current—and last—administration informed the Soviet premier of his intentions to use the SDI missiles, and got an enthusiastic approval (the Russian premier failed to note the fact that seven years before he had called these missiles "infernal engines of war and hate forged in the factories of hell").

It might even have worked . . . except not a single missile from a single SDI orbiter fired. Each satellite was equipped with six two-megaton warheads. Every goddamn one malfunctioned.

So much for modern technology.

MADDIE SUPPOSED THE horrible deaths of those brave men (and one woman) in space really hadn't been the last shock; there was the business of the one little graveyard right here on Jenny. But that didn't seem to count so much because, after all, she had not been there.

With the end of the world now clearly at hand and the island cut off—*thankfully* cut off, in the opinion of the island's residents—from the rest of the world, old ways had reasserted themselves with a kind of unspoken but inarguable force. By then they all knew what was going to happen; it was only a question of when. That, and being ready when it did.

Women were excluded.

IT WAS BOB Daggett, of course, who drew up the watch roster. That was only right, since Bob had been head selectman on Jenny since Hector was a pup. The day after the death of the president (the thought of him and the first lady wandering witlessly through the streets of Washington, D.C., gnawing on human arms and legs like people eating chicken legs at a picnic was not mentioned; it was a little too much to bear, even if the bastid and his big old blond wife *were* Democrats). Bob Daggett called the first men-only Town Meeting on Jenny since someplace before the Civil War. So Maddie wasn't there, but she heard. Dave Eamons told her all she needed to know.

"You men all know the situation," Bob said. He had always been a pretty hard fellow, but right then he looked as yellow as a man with jaundice, and people remembered his daughter, the one on the island, was only one of four. The other three were other places . . . which was to say, on the mainland.

But hell, if it came down to that, they *all* had folks on the mainland.

"We got one boneyard here on the island," Bob continued, "and nothin' ain't happened yet, but that don't mean nothin' *will*. Nothin' ain't happened yet lots of places . . . but it seems like once it starts, nothin' turns to somethin' pretty goddam quick."

There was a rumble of assent from the men gathered in the basement of the Methodist church. There were about seventy of them, ranging in age from Johnny Crane, who had just turned eighteen, to Bob's great-uncle Frank, who was eighty, had a glass eye, and chewed tobacco. There was no spittoon in the church basement and Frank Daggett knew it well enough, so he'd brought an empty mayonnaise jar to spit his juice into. He did so now.

"Git down to where the cheese binds, Bobby," he said. "You ain't got no office to run for, and time's a-wastin'."

There was another rumble of agreement, and Bob Daggett blushed. Somehow his great-uncle always managed to make him look like an ineffectual fool, and if there was anything in the world he hated worse than looking like an ineffectual fool, it was being called Bobby. He owned property, for Chrissake! He *supported* the old fart, for Chrissake.

But these were not things he could say. Frank's eyes were like pieces of flint.

"Okay," he said curtly. "Here it is. We want twelve men to a watch. I'm gonna set a roster in just a couple minutes. Four-hour shifts."

"I can stand watch a helluva lot longer'n four hours!" Matt Arsenault spoke up, and Davey told Maddie that Bob said after the meeting that no frog setting on a welfare lily pad like Matt Arsenault would have had the nerve enough to speak up like that if his great-uncle hadn't called him Bobby, like he was a kid instead of a man three months shy of his fiftieth birthday, in front of all the island men.

"Maybe so," Bob said, "but we got enough men to go around, and nobody's gonna fall asleep on sentry duty."

"I ain't gonna—"

"I didn't say *you*," Bob said, but the way his eyes rested on Matt Arsenault suggested that he *might* have meant him. "This is no kid's game. Sit down and shut up."

Matt Arsenault opened his mouth to say something more, then looked around at the other men—including old Frank Daggett—and wisely sat down again.

"If you got a rifle, bring it when it's your trick," Bob continued. He felt a little better with Frère Jacques out of the way. "Unless it's a twenty-two. If you got no rifle bigger'n that, or none at all, come and get one here."

"I didn't know Reverend Peebles kept a supply of 'em handy," Cal Partridge said, and there was a ripple of laughter.

"He don't now, but he's gonna," Bob said, "because every man jack of you with more than one rifle bigger than a twenty-two is gonna bring it here." He looked at Peebles. "Okay if we keep 'em in the rectory, Tom?"

Peebles nodded, dry-washing his hands in a distraught way.

"Shit on that," Orrin Campbell said. "I got a wife and two kids at home. Am I s'posed to leave 'em with nothin if a bunch of cawpses come for an early Thanksgiving dinner while I'm on watch?"

"If we do our job at the boneyard, none will," Bob replied stonily. "Some of you got handguns. We don't want none of those. Figure out which women can shoot and which can't, and give 'em the pistols. We'll put 'em together in bunches."

"They can play Beano," old Frank cackled, and Bob smiled, too. That was more like it, by the Christ.

"Nights, we're gonna want trucks posted around so we got plenty of light." He looked over at Sonny Dotson, who ran Island Amoco, the only gas station on Jenny—Sonny's main business wasn't gassing cars and trucks—shit, there was no place much on the island to drive, and you could get your go ten cents cheaper on the mainland—but filling up lobster boats and the motorboats he ran out of his jackleg marina in the summer. "You gonna supply the gas, Sonny?"

"Am I gonna get cash slips?"

"You're gonna get your ass saved," Bob said. "When things get back to normal—if they ever do—I guess you'll get what you got coming."

Sonny looked around, saw only hard eyes, and shrugged. He looked a bit sullen, but in truth he looked more confused than anything, Davey told Maddie the next day.

"Ain't got n'more'n four hunnert gallons of gas," he said. "Mostly diesel."

"There's five generators on the island," Burt Dorfman said (when Burt spoke everyone listened; as the only Jew on the island, he was regarded as a creature both quixotic and fearsome, like an oracle that works about half the time). "They all run on diesel. I can rig lights if I have to."

Low murmurs. If Burt said he could, he could. He was an electrician, and a damned good one . . . for a Jew, anyway.

"We're gonna light that place up like a friggin' stage," Bob said.

Andy Kinsolving stood up. "I heard on the news that sometimes you can shoot one of them . . . things . . . in the head and it'll stay down, and sometimes it won't."

"We got chain saws," Bob said stonily, "and what won't stay dead . . . why, we can make sure it won't move too far alive."

And, except for making out the duty roster, that was pretty much that.

SIX DAYS AND nights passed and the sentries posted around the island graveyard were starting to feel a wee bit silly ("I dunno if I'm standin' guard or pullin' my pud," Orrin Campbell said one afternoon as a dozen men stood around a small cemetery where the most exciting thing happening was a caterpillar spinning a cocoon while a spider watched it and waited for the moment to pounce) when it happened . . . and when it happened, it happened fast.

Dave told Maddie that he heard a sound like the wind wailing in the chimney on a gusty night . . . and then the gravestone marking the final resting place of Mr. and Mrs. Fournier's boy Michael, who had died of leukemia at seventeen—bad go, that had been, him being their only get and them being such nice people and all—fell over. Then a shredded hand with a moss-caked Yarmouth Academy class ring on one finger rose out of the ground, shoving

through the tough grass. The third finger had been torn off in the process.

The ground heaved like (like the belly of a pregnant woman getting ready to drop her load, Dave almost said, and hastily reconsidered), well, like the way a big wave heaves up on its way into a close cove, and then the boy himself sat up, only he wasn't nothing you could really recognize, not after almost two years in the ground. There was little pieces of wood sticking to him, Davey said, and pieces of blue cloth.

Later inspection proved these to be shreds of satin from the coffin in which the boy had been buried away.

("Thank Christ Richie Fournier dint have that trick," Bill Pulsifer said later, and they had all nodded shakily—many of them were still wiping their mouths, because almost all of them had puked at some point or other during that hellacious half hour . . . these were not things Dave Eamons could tell Maddie, but Maddie guessed more than Dave ever guessed she guessed.)

Gunfire tore Michael Fournier to shreds before he could do more than sit up; other shots, fired in wild panic, blew chips off his marble gravestone, and it was a goddam wonder someone on one side hadn't shot someone on one of the others, but they got off lucky. Bud Meechum found a hole torn in the sleeve of his shirt the next day, but liked to think that might have been nothing more than a thorn—there had been raspberry bushes on his side of the boneyard. Maybe that was really all it was, although the black smudges on the hole made him think that maybe it had been a thorn with a pretty large caliber.

The Fournier kid fell back, most of him lying still, other parts of him still twitching.

But by then the whole graveyard seemed to be rippling, as if an earthquake was going on there—but *only* there, no place else.

Just about an hour before dusk, this had happened.

Burt Dorfman had rigged up a siren to a tractor battery, and Bob Daggett flipped the switch. Within twenty minutes, most of the men in town were at the island cemetery.

Goddam good thing, too, because a few of the deaders almost got away. Old Frank Daggett, still two hours away from the heart attack that would carry him off after it was all over and the moon had risen, organized the men into a pair of angled flanks so they wouldn't shoot each other, and for the final ten minutes the Jenny boneyard sounded like Bull Run. By the end of the festivities, the powder smoke was so thick that some men choked on it. No one puked on it, because no one had anything left to puke up. The sour smell of vomit was almost heavier than the smell of gunsmoke . . . it was sharper, too, and lingered longer.

AND STILL SOME of them wriggled and squirmed like snakes with broken backs . . . the fresher ones, for the most part.

"Burt," Frank Daggett said. "You got them chain saws?"

"I got 'em," Burt said, and then a long, buzzing sound came out of his mouth, a sound like a cicada burrowing its way into tree bark, as he dry-heaved. He could not take his eyes from the squirming corpses, the overturned gravestones, the yawning pits from which the dead had come. "In the truck."

"Gassed up?" Blue veins stood out on Frank's ancient, hairless skull.

"Yeah." Burt's hand was over his mouth. "I'm sorry."

"Work y'fuckin gut all you want," Frank said briskly. "But get them saws while you do. And you . . . you . . . you . . . you . . ."

The last "you" was his grandnephew Bob.

"I can't, Uncle Frank," Bob said sickly. He looked around and saw at least twenty men lying in the tall grass. They had swooned. Most of them had seen their own relatives rise out of the ground. Buck Harkness over there lying by an aspen tree had been part of the cross fire that

had cut his late wife to ribbons before he fainted when her decayed brains exploded from the back of her head in a grisly gray fan. "I can't. I c—"

Frank's hand, twisted with arthritis but as hard as stone, cracked across his face.

"You can and you will, chummy," he said grimly.

Bob went with the rest of the men.

Frank Daggett watched them grimly and rubbed his chest.

"I WAS NEARBY when Frank spoke to Bob," Dave told Maddie. He wasn't sure if he should be telling her this—or any of it, for that matter, with her almost halfway to foaling time—but he was still too impressed with the old man's grim and quiet courage to forbear. "This was after . . . you know . . . we cleaned the mess up."

Maddie only nodded.

"I'll stop," Dave said, "if you can't bear it, Maddie."

"I can bear it," she said quietly, and Dave looked at her quickly, curiously, but she had averted her eyes before he could see the secret in them.

DAVEY DIDN'T KNOW the secret because no one on Jenny knew. That was the way Maddie wanted it, and the way she intended to keep it. There had been a time when she had, in the blue darkness of her shock, pretended to be *coping*. And then something happened that *made* her cope. Four days before the island cemetery vomited up its corpses, Maddie Pace was faced with a simple choice: cope or die.

She had been sitting in the living room, drinking a glass of the blueberry wine she and Jack had put up during August of the previous year—a time that now seemed impossibly distant—and doing something so trite it was laughable: She was Knitting Little Things (the second bootee of a pair this evening). But what else *was* there to do? It seemed that no one would be going across to the mall on the mainland for a long time.

Something had thumped the window.

A bat, she thought, looking up. Her needles paused in her hands, though. It seemed that something was moving out there in the windy dark. The oil lamp was turned up high and kicking too much reflection off the panes to be sure. She reached to turn it down and the thump came again. The panes shivered. She heard a little pattering of dried putty falling on the sash. Jack was going to reglaze all the windows this fall, she thought stupidly, and then: Maybe that's what he came back for. Because it was Jack. She knew that. Before Jack, no one from Jenny had drowned for nearly three years. Whatever was making them return apparently couldn't re-animate whatever was left of their bodies. But Jack . . .

Jack was still fresh.

She sat, poised, head cocked to one side, knitting in her hands. A little pink bootee. She had already made a blue set. All of a sudden it seemed she could hear so *much*. The wind. The faint thunder of surf on Cricket's Ledge. The house making little groaning sounds, like an elderly woman making herself comfortable in bed. The tick of the clock in the hallway.

It was Jack. She knew it.

"Jack?" she said, and the window burst inward and what came in was not really Jack but a skeleton with a few moldering strings of flesh hanging from it.

His compass was still around his neck. It had grown a beard of moss.

THE WIND BLEW the curtains out in a cloud as he sprawled, then got up on his hands and knees and looked at her from black sockets in which barnacles had grown.

He made grunting sounds. His fleshless mouth opened and the teeth chomped down. He was hungry . . . but this time chicken noodle soup would not serve. Not even the kind that came in the can.

Gray stuff hung and swung beyond those dark barnacle-crusted holes, and she realized she was looking at whatever remained of Jack's brain. She sat where she was, frozen, as he got up and came toward her, leaving black kelpy tracks on the carpet, fingers reaching. He stank of salt and fathoms. His hands stretched. His teeth champed mechanically up and down. Maddie saw he was wearing the remains of the black-and-red-checked shirt she had bought him at L.L. Bean's last Christmas. It had cost the earth, but he had said again and again how warm it was, and look how well it had lasted, even underwater all this time, even—

The cold cobwebs of bone which were all that remained of his fingers touched her throat before the baby kicked in her stomach—for the first time—and her shocked horror, which she had believed to be calmness, fled, and she drove one of the knitting needles into the thing's eye.

Making horrid, thick, draggling noises that sounded like the suck of a swill pump, he staggered backward, clawing at the needle, while the half-made pink bootee swung in front of the cavity where his nose had been. She watched as a sea slug squirmed from that nasal cavity and onto the bootee, leaving a trail of slime behind it.

Jack fell over the end table she'd gotten at a yard sale just after they had been married—she hadn't been able to make her mind up about it, had been in agonies about it, until Jack finally said either she was going to buy it for their living room or he was going to give the biddy running the sale twice what she was asking for the goddam thing and then bust it up into firewood with—

—with the—

He struck the floor and there was a brittle, cracking sound as his febrile, fragile form broke in two. The right hand tore the knitting needle, slimed with decaying brain tissue, from his eye socket and tossed it aside. His top half crawled toward her. His teeth gnashed steadily together.

She thought he was trying to grin, and then the baby kicked again and she thought: *You buy it, Maddie, for Christ's sake! I'm tired! Want to go home and get m'dinner! You want it, buy it! If you don't, I'll give that old bat twice what she wants and bust it up for firewood with my—*

Cold, dank hand clutching her ankle; polluted teeth poised to bite. To kill her and kill the baby.

She tore loose, leaving him with only her slipper, which he tried to chew and then spat out.

When she came back from the entry, he was crawling mindlessly into the kitchen—at least the top half of him was—with the compass dragging on the tiles. He looked up at the sound of her, and there seemed to be some idiot question in those black eye sockets before she brought the ax whistling down, cleaving his skull as he had threatened to cleave the end table.

His head fell in two pieces, brains dribbling across the tile like spoiled oatmeal, brains that squirmed with slugs and gelatinous sea worms, brains that smelled like a woodchuck exploded with gassy decay in a high-summer meadow.

Still his hands clashed and clittered on the kitchen tiles, making a sound like beetles.

She chopped . . . she chopped . . . she chopped.

At last there was no more movement.

A sharp pain rippled across her midsection and for a moment she was gripped by terrible panic: *Is it a miscarriage? Am I going to have a miscarriage?* But the pain left . . . and the baby kicked again, more strongly than before.

She went back into the living room, carrying an ax that now smelled like tripe.

His legs had somehow managed to stand.

"Jack, I loved you so much," she said, and brought the ax down in a whistling arc that split him at the pelvis, sliced the carpet, and drove deep into the solid oak floor beneath.

The legs, separated, trembled wildly . . . and then lay still.

She carried him down to the cellar piece by piece, wearing her oven gloves and wrapping each piece with the insulating blankets Jack had kept in the shed and which she had never thrown away—he and the crew threw them over the pots on cold days so the lobsters wouldn't freeze.

Once a severed hand tried to close over her wrist . . . then loosened.

That was all.

There was an unused cistern, polluted, which Jack had been meaning to fill in. Maddie Pace slid the heavy concrete cover aside so that its shadow lay on the earthen floor like a partial eclipse and then threw the pieces of him down, listening to the splashes, then worked the heavy cover back in place.

"Rest in peace," she whispered, and an interior voice whispered back that her husband was resting in *pieces*, and then she began to cry, and her cries turned to hysterical shrieks, and she pulled at her hair and tore at her breasts until they were bloody, and she thought, I am insane, this is what it's like to be in—

But before the thought could be completed, she had fallen down in a faint that became a deep sleep, and the next morning she felt all right.

She would never tell, though.

Never.

SHE UNDERSTOOD, OF course, that Dave knew nothing of this, and Dave would say nothing at all if she pressed. She kept her ears open, and she knew what he meant, and what they had apparently done. The dead folks and the . . . the *parts* of dead folks that wouldn't . . . wouldn't be still . . . had been chain-sawed like her father had chain-sawed the hardwood on Pop Cook's two acres after he had gotten the deed registered, and then those parts—some *still* squirming, hands with no arms attached to them clutching mindlessly, feet divorced from their legs digging at the bullet-chewed earth of the graveyard as if trying to run away—had been doused with diesel fuel and set afire. She had seen the pyre from the house.

Later, Jenny's one fire truck had turned its hose on the dying blaze, although there wasn't much chance of the fire spreading, with a brisk easterly blowing the sparks off Jenny's seaward edge.

When there was nothing left but a stinking,

tallowy lump (and still there were occasional bulges in this mass, like twitches in a tired muscle), Matt Arsenault fired up his old D-9 Caterpillar—above the nicked steel blade and under his faded pillowtick engineer's cap, Matt's face had been as white as cottage cheese—and plowed the whole hellacious mess under.

The moon was coming up when Frank took Bob Daggett, Dave Eamons, and Cal Partridge aside.

"I'm havin a goddam heart attack," he said.

"Now, Uncle Frank—"

"Never mind Uncle Frank this 'n' that," the old man said. "I ain't got time, and I ain't wrong. Seen half my friends go the same way. Beats hell out of getting whacked with the cancer-stick. Quicker. But when I go down, I intend to *stay* down. Cal, stick that rifle of yours in my left ear. Muzzle's gonna get some wax on it, but it won't be there after you pull the trigger. Dave, when I raise my left arm, you sock your thirty-thirty into my armpit, and see that you do it right smart. And Bobby, you put yours right over my heart. I'm gonna say the Lawd's Prayer, and when I hit amen, you three fellows are gonna pull your triggers."

"Uncle Frank—" Bob managed. He was reeling on his heels.

"I told you not to start in on that," Frank said. "And don't you *dare* faint on me, you friggin' pantywaist. If I'm goin' down, I mean to *stay* down. Now get over here."

Bob did.

Frank looked around at the three men, their faces as white as Matt Arsenault's had been when he drove the dozer over men and women he had known since he was a kid in short pants and Buster Browns.

"I ain't got long," Frank said, "and I only got enough jizzum left to get m'arm up once, so don't you fuck up on me. And remember, I'd 'a' done the same for any of you. If that don't help, ask y'selves if *you'd* want to end up like those we just took care of."

"Go on," Bob said hoarsely. "I love you, Uncle Frank."

"You ain't the man your father was, Bobby Daggett, but I love you, too," Frank said calmly, and then, with a cry of pain, he threw his left hand up over his head like a guy in New York who has to have a cab in a rip of a hurry, and started in: "Our father who art in heaven—*Christ*, that hurts!—hallow'd be Thy name—oh, son of a *gun*, I—Thy kingdom come, Thy will be done, on earth as it . . . as it . . ."

Frank's upraised left arm was wavering wildly now. Dave Eamons, with his rifle socked into the old geezer's armpit, watched it as carefully as a logger would watch a big tree that looked like it meant to fall the wrong way. Every man on the island was watching now. Big beads of sweat had formed on the old man's pallid face. His lips had pulled back from the even, yellowish white of his Roebuckers, and Dave had been able to smell the Polident on his breath.

". . . as it is in heaven!" the old man jerked out. "Lead us not into temptation butdeliverus-fromevilohshitonitforeverandeverAMEN!"

All three of them fired, and both Cal Partridge and Bob Daggett fainted, but Frank never did try to get up and walk.

Frank Daggett intended to *stay* dead, and that was just what he did.

ONCE DAVE STARTED that story he had to go on with it, and so he cursed himself for ever starting. He'd been right the first time; it was no story for a pregnant woman.

But Maddie had kissed him and told him she thought he had done wonderfully, and Dave went out, feeling a little dazed, as if he had just been kissed on the cheek by a woman he had never met before.

As, in a way, he had.

She watched him go down the path to the dirt track that was one of Jenny's two roads and turn left. He was weaving a little in the moonlight, weaving with tiredness, she thought, but reeling with shock, as well. Her heart went out to him . . . to all of them. She had wanted to tell Dave she loved him and kiss him squarely on the mouth instead of just skimming his cheek with her lips, but he might have taken the wrong meaning from something like that, even though he was bone-weary and she was almost five months pregnant.

But she *did* love him, loved *all* of them, because they had gone through a hell she could only imagine dimly, and by going through that hell they had made the island safe for her.

Safe for her baby.

"It will be a home delivery," she said softly as Dave went out of sight behind the dark hulk of the Pulsifers' satellite dish. Her eyes rose to the moon. "It will be a home delivery . . . and it will be fine."

DANCE OF THE DAMNED

ARTHUR J. BURKS

BORN IN WATERVILLE, Washington, Arthur J. Burks (1898–1974) had two primary careers: the military, and as a prolific pulp writer. After he served in World War I, he was promoted to aide to General Smedley D. Butler in 1924; he resigned in 1928 to become a full-time writer, but rejoined the marines when World War II broke out, supervising the basic training of nearly one-third of all marines engaged in the war, and retiring as a lieutenant colonel. Although he had started writing at the age of twenty while a lieutenant, it was in the 1930s that he earned the title "the Speed Merchant of the Pulps," producing between one and two million words a year for more than a decade. Unlike other hyperprolific authors, like Walter B. Gibson and Lester Dent, who wrote novels about the Shadow and Doc Savage, respectively, Burks rarely wrote novels and had few series characters, keeping to original short stories in virtually every genre, notably horror, mystery, aviation, science fiction, adventure, fantasy, and romance (under the pseudonym Esther Critchfield). He wrote about what it was like to write at such a furious pace for *Writer's Digest*, noting that he once had eleven stories in a single magazine under eleven different names. He had the reputation among other pulp writers (and editors) of being able to select any inanimate object in a room and write a thrilling story about it. Many of his stories were less plot-driven than those of his contemporaries, using instead a sense of mood to create terror.

"Dance of the Damned" was first published in the August/September 1936 issue of *Horror Stories*.

ARTHUR J. BURKS

DANCE OF
THE DAMNED

WILL SIX PEOPLE, WHO COULD HAVE
RETURNED FROM THE DARK LIMBO OF
DEATH, REMAIN THERE THROUGHOUT ALL
ETERNITY BECAUSE OF ME? THE WIND WILL
WHINE THAT QUESTION OVER MY GRAVE—
RUFFLING THE DUST IN SUMMER, WHIRL-
ING THE SNOW IN WINTER...TO THE END
OF TIME....

I KNEW IT was all wrong from the beginning; but it was a story the editor wanted. Bette
Carver was there to get the women's angle of the
macabre show. Bette was another reason I knew
it was all wrong. It wouldn't do her sensitive nature any good, to spend half the night in such a
dismal atmosphere. Imagine it! A deserted beach
club, where during hot summer months young
people made merry, turned over, in the icy grip
of winter, to a desolate roistering, a wild celebration of scores of deaths.

It was like this: Two years ago the *Cyclonic* had gone down off the Jersey Coast, with all on board. It had been returning from Bermuda with a holiday crowd, men and women able to afford the luxury of summer tan in mid-winter.

Nobody ever knew what happened, really. There was just a brief SOS after a blaze in the eastern sky and then, the queer message. Scarcely even a trace of the *Cyclonic* remained— except a piece of hatch-cover that came floating ashore, with bloodstains on it, stains of fire, and here and there a trace of a woman's hair.

It was pretty terrible, and neither Bette nor I relished the job of visiting that bit of flotsam to gather "atmosphere."

Bette shuddered.

"Heavens, Alex!" she said. "The mere sight of it gives me the creeps! If that piece of timber could speak! Think of the terrible way those poor people died—I can almost hear their screams. . . ."

"They were pretty good sports, Bette—" I said—"that *Cyclonic* crowd. Remember the last radio message the public got from her?"

Bette nodded. "It was so strange and hysterical," she said. "It must have been sent by a radio operator out of his head with terror. It said: '*Make merry for us, for we die!*'"

She gasped and turned on me.

"That's why Lola Garrick is giving this ghastly show tonight," she said. "Her mother went down on the *Cyclonic!* Her mother loved her pleasures. It's Lola's gesture of defiance. . . . Alex—the names of her guests—Let's get back and look them over."

I WAS GLAD enough to get away from that piece of the *Cyclonic* which bore mute testimony to a ghastly sea tragedy. The place was horrible. The huge piece of timber, filled with rusty nails and bolts, was half buried in the snow and sand. Grim ice stretched out from the beach for hundreds of yards to sullen grey water. I kept thinking of the drowned, coming up under the ice, bumping coldly and soggily along. . . .

I put my arm around Bette's shoulders. She was trembling like a leaf, and I knew it was not with the cold. She was frightened. The dismal atmosphere had done it. Snow was driving down, blowing almost parallel with the ground. It scurried along the boardwalk like clouds mashed flat against the wood. The night was eerie, freezing cold.

Bette's head came just to my armpit, so I had to bend to help her along. I had fallen in love with Bette, in spite of the fact that a newspaper office is no place for love to bloom in—it's too close to the grim facts of life, with all the sentimental trimmings cut away.

We went back to the clubhouse, and had scarcely put our heavy wraps away when I noticed how the windows rattled. There were roaring fires at either end of the big room, in pot-bellied stoves put in for this dance. I stared at the windows, on which driving snow was etching queer white shapes. Bette followed my glance, and shivered again.

"Ghostly!" she said. "And ghastly! The snow figures on the panes make me think of the drowned. White ghosts looking in! What do *they* think of this merriment?"

A band was playing. It was cold in here, even with the fires going; but the band was perspiring, and now and again its members stared at the windows, which rattled in their casements.

Lola Garrick was running the show. Her cheeks were flushed a rosy red. She was calling for a funereal waltz, with the lights turned down. I didn't like it. Bette kept on trembling. Her lips shook when she looked at me, as though she were about to cry.

Said Lola Garrick: "My mother went down on the *Cyclonic,* off this coast. Some relative of each of you went down with her. It was a pleasure cruise. Their pleasure was interrupted by death in the cold seas. What more fitting than that we go on where our relatives left off? They'd all have approved. They loved life and gaiety, they rebelled at the suggestion of death. So, *make merry for them, for they died!*"

She had paraphrased the words of the grim

quotation, the last radio message from the *Cyclonic*.

"We might as well dance, dear," I said.

The band swung into its tune, a slow, measured waltz that made me think of a military funeral, with the escort marching in solemn tread.

Bette's whole body was shaking as I held her.

"Look!" she said. "There's Harrison Graves; his wife was on that boat—with some other man—according to gossip. And Pierce Paget. His sister was on the *Cyclonic*. Cora Patterson, too, with a husband who she didn't know was on the *Cyclonic* until the passenger list was published. Every person here lost someone on that boat, just as Lola said. It's horrible, this celebration!"

I agreed with her. I shivered with the thought. I was acutely conscious of the fact that outside on the beach, which because of the ice extending a quarter mile from shore, the only relic of the *Cyclonic* was all but buried in the snow and sand and ice. I remembered how the wind had whistled through its cracks. I could hear the sound now. It seemed to come right into the brightly lighted dancing space with us, bringing an eerie refrain: *"Make merry for us, for we die!"*

ONLY, THE WINDY refrain, which I heard in my heart, was not a command, but a ghastly warning. All imagination—but I couldn't help it to save myself.

"The derelict," whispered Bette, against my chest, "I can hear it whispering, crying out against all this!"

Strange that she had the same idea, as though our frightened hearts were somehow in tune. That fact should have warmed my soul, because it proved a sort of lover's telepathy between us—but it didn't. It made my growing fear of weird consequences a black stone resting in my breast. I held Bette more tightly against me.

"Whatever happens," I said, "we're together. Nothing will happen to you while my arms are around you."

She shivered. "I'm afraid, just the same. I wish I hadn't come."

"Let's beat it," I answered.

"And let the editor down? Imagine how this will look, pictures and all, in the Sunday supplement. Look at these people, dressed as pirates, sailors. . . ."

We were interrupted by a sound that caused the musicians to stop in the middle of a bar and their horrified eyes to turn on the windows. All the dancers stopped, lifted their heads to listen. There was a strange, roaring sound, over our heads. I looked up to see the roof of the clubhouse shaking. Then I looked at the windows once more.

Lola Garrick began to laugh, a bit shakily.

"It's nothing," she cried. "What are you all keyed up about? It's been snowing for two days and nights, and the snow is heavy on the roof. The heat in here has warmed the roof, that's all, and the snow is sliding off. You all saw a sheet of it drop past the window. . . ."

"Like a winding-sheet," said a pasty faced man who was dancing with Lola's sister. "A shroud in the wind!"

"That's the spirit!" shouted Lola. "Make light of it! There's lots of fun to be had in this world, even yet. I wouldn't be surprised if our people on the *Cyclonic*, wherever they are now, were having a dance of their own. . . ."

That got under my skin. I was thinking of just such a dance—of the drowned trying to make shore, under the ice, bumping their heads against the underside of the ice, staring up at it with frosty eyes. That was the sort of dance *they* were having!

But the band didn't go on, and the dancers stood where they were. The sounds on the roof hadn't stopped yet. They were just different. I stared at the shaking ceiling above me. Very plainly, I could hear footsteps up there, heavy shoes crunching the snow—and after the footfalls, which went angling across the roof, the snow slid down, over the edge, past the windows.

Someone was up there, then, *making* the snow slide off!

That wouldn't have seemed strange under any other circumstance, but as matters stood, at least in my mind, the presence of something on the roof took on horrible significance. I thought of a frosted Neptune, coming out of the icy deep to preside over these ghastly festivities.

"Lola," I called, "who's up there? Who's missing from your party? Has the owner of this club sent someone to keep the roof clear?"

She laughed, a bit shakily.

"I had an express understanding with the owner," she said, "that he was to come nowhere near the place. As a matter of fact he turned everything over to me, and is getting drunk in New York tonight."

"Then, your guests . . ."

She must have memorized the roster, for she called off the names right away, and not one was missing. I could check her, for my paper had received the list in advance. Whoever was out there on the roof was a stranger, an unwanted guest.

We all listened. . . . The footsteps had stopped almost directly above the point where Bette and I stood. The wind whistled over the roof. It carried fine snow with it, which scurried under the eaves, over the comb of the roof, all about the clubhouse, like the scampering of little feet shod with ice.

In that instant the whole show took on a horrible significance.

These people were not the relatives of the victims of the *Cyclonic*! How had I ever got that idea? They were the victims themselves. . . .

Bette turned to me.

"They *are* the *Cyclonic* victims," she said— and I hadn't spoken aloud, either.

The dancers looked like corpses. The band was ghastly under the yellow shaded lights.

AND THEN THE footsteps began again; we heard them move to the edge of the slanting roof. Then, a thudding sound on the walk outside, and we knew that the unknown had dropped off. The steps approached the door. It seemed to me that the wind outside became

wilder, fiercer, as the visitor approached the door.

Then, the door, strong and heavy though it was, shook as though hammered by a high wind. The band was still silent. The dancers still stood in their places, looking at one another.

The door burst open. I whirled. For a minute or two I did not miss Bette. I was held spellbound by the apparition in the doorway.

Neptune, with frosted, blazing eyes, with icicles in his beard, his feet shrouded in snow. His breath steamed forth. Little eddies of wind-driven snow came in with him, to form white, still whirlpools on the door at his feet. He laughed, and his laughter was the sound of the wind.

He lifted his right hand, pointing—at one Hedda Murtin. I felt that he was a ghastly judge, passing sentence.

"You are first," said the apparition, his voice a guttural rasp, "to *make merry with those who die!*"

Nobody made a move to stop Hedda as she walked slowly, white-faced, right hand clutching her throat, to face the apparition. Standing for a second before him, she screamed, then turned and fled past him, vanished into the night. The apparition laughed and whirled around, going out after her, slamming the door. The door shook in its casements for a long time.

I whirled to Lola Garrick for an explanation, but she had disappeared.

Peter Fraym, Hedda's escort, yelled wildly, and dashed out of the door after them. He was gone fifteen minutes or so. Then he came back, stuck his head in at the door—and his eyes were wide and wild. He beckoned to me. I went with him, wondering at his strange terror-haunted manner.

He took me to the derelict where Hedda Murtin sprawled there, supine, under the box-like thing which, I had been told, was a hatch-cover from the *Cyclonic*.

It looked to me as though she had been in the water, all over, with her clothes on. But it didn't matter now. She was frozen stiff, and her clothes were a coating of ice about her dead body.

CHAPTER TWO

"I HAD A FRIEND . . ."

Peter Fraym knelt beside Hedda, tried to take her in his arms. Horror flowed over my whole body in cold waves. I stared out toward the sullen sea beyond the ice sheets, and saw traceries of fine snow rolling into, over, and past two pairs of footprints—two pairs, one of a man, one of a woman, leading out to the edge of the ice. Only one pair, the woman's, came back! There seemed to be no sense to it. But as I looked I thought I saw, out there at the edge, a black shadow come up on the ice, out of the sea, like a seal coming up to look. But I must have been wrong, for when I looked again it wasn't there.

Peter Fraym was trying to get Hedda to speak to him, and his voice was utterly heartbroken. He clutched her with frantic arms, and her clothing crackled because it was frozen. Her icy face was against his.

Finally it began to penetrate to his shocked brain, I suppose; the fact that Hedda, by some strange freak of the night, the storm and the party, was dead.

"You can't come back to me, Hedda," he said wildly. "Then I'll come to you!"

He jumped to his feet, still looking down at her. He ran his cold hands swiftly through all his pockets. Hunting a suicide weapon, I thought, and I was ready to grab him if he brought forth anything that would serve. But he didn't.

He whirled, finally, looked out to sea—for the first time connecting it with the condition of Hedda's garments. Then, I was sure, he saw what was left of the footprints, the trio of sets, leading out to the sea and back.

He looked at me and laughed: "It'll be a good story for your paper, Alex!" he chattered.

Then Fraym was away like a shot. I watched him start, and things were moving in my brain, like maggots. Hell was here, hell of some kind, and Bette was back there in the clubhouse in the midst of it. Lola Garrick was back there, too, maybe knowing more about it all than any of us had guessed. I wondered what, really, was behind the whole party.

Then I saw my duty and followed it. I couldn't allow Fraym, though I scarcely knew him, to go off like that. I started after him, knowing I could outrun him easily, even with the start he had.

"Fraym! Fraym!" I shouted. The wind caught the name right off my lips and hurled it into the night and the storm.

Fraym laughed without looking back, and drew away from me. I saw the sullen water at the edge of the ice spout up, as though it were shaping arms to receive the man who had lost his sweetheart. I suppose he got the same idea, and that the arms might be those of Hedda, for he flung out his own arms, as though he couldn't wait to embrace her, and shouted hoarsely into the wind:

"I'm coming, Hedda! Coming, coming!"

He speeded away. I almost broke my neck trying to catch him, but it was no use. The ice was getting mushy, and I knew that if I paused it would go out under me, letting me into deep water. I had to go back soon or I wouldn't go back at all. Only movement kept me atop the ice, as it kept Fraym.

Then he seemed to drop into a hole, and water splashed up through the hole in whitish spume, as though to throw tentacles around him. He laughed as he vanished through into the ice, and the spume arms disappeared.

I didn't make the mistake of stopping, turning, going back. To have done so would have sent me after Fraym. No, I didn't do that. I kept on running, but cutting a circle to the left, so as not to lose speed, so as to spread my weight over the ice.

And then, shortly, it was firm under me, and I had a grim job to do, one I didn't like, one that would send the pseudo-merrymakers into hysterics, I was sure. I had to take Hedda back to the clubhouse.

I didn't see anything around the half-buried derelict as I approached it, but I felt that something—something unearthly and abysmally evil—was there. I hated to go back. I had never dreaded anything as much in my life.

I picked out the white mound, in the dark under the rough planks, and kept my eyes on it, until I reached the spot where I must stoop to gather the dead woman in my arms.

I got a shock when I stood over the spot. Hedda wasn't there. It didn't look to me as though she had ever been there. There was no depression where her body had been—nothing!

AND NOW THE snow, drifting with the wind, had obliterated all footprints save those I had made on my return from the edge of the ice. From the clubhouse came the strains of eerie music; the band was playing again.

I started toward the lighted building, hurrying, breaking into a headlong run, feeling that icy menace of some sort followed me from the beach, eager to fasten cold fingers in the back of my neck.

But before I reached the door it opened.

I saw a familiar figure there . . . the figure of icy Neptune, entering the place again—for another victim?

I raced harder. The door slammed ahead of me. When I got to it I tried to swing it open, but it wouldn't budge. I kicked. I yelled. I screamed, but nothing happened. The laughter of guests came from inside, and the moaning of saxophones.

Then, all at once, those sounds stopped.

The door opened in my face. A monstrous figure, looking horrible against the light to one who came out of the dark, fairly rolled over me, like a two-footed Juggernaut. Neptune again, carrying a woman in his arms.

The woman was screaming. I saw, in the brief moment before the door closed and night pos-

sessed the world again, that the woman was Leslie Franks. She'd lost a philandering father on the *Cyclonic,* I remembered.

I grabbed for her. A hand that might have been a giant's hand, coated with ice, drove into my face. It drove sanity from me. I felt myself sinking into utter blankness. I felt the ground under my back. I had been perspiring with my exertions, and knew that I would freeze in a matter of minutes if I didn't keep moving.

But I couldn't make a move, because my muscles seemed to be paralyzed. Nor could I shout. But I fought with all my will to regain complete consciousness before I froze.

When I finally staggered erect, my feet were numb, my fingers were numb. Even my brain seemed numb.

I looked wildly around, but could see no one, anywhere, though far out, at the edge of the ice, I thought I saw a black shadow, going into the sea, bearing a victim—a victim that flung white arms wide, to meet the white arms of the sea, then to vanish. I heard an elfin scream come down the wind, and knew that Leslie Franks was gone, too. That made three.

I banged at the door, and this time managed to open it.

I stepped through. All eyes in the place were on me, filled with stark horror. Gasps of relief went up when I was recognized. I looked wildly around for Bette and Lola Garrick, and saw neither one.

Something had to be done about all this. I lifted my right hand, a gesture which must have reminded them all, as it reminded me, of the outstretched, commanding arm of Neptune, bidding his victims come to him, crawling, almost, like whipped curs, to die.

"Something is horribly wrong." My voice sounded like the cawing of a crow. "Hedda Murtin is dead. I saw her. Then she was carried away. I didn't see her go. Something just got her. Peter Fraym went into the sea, to find her. And now, you all saw another one go: Leslie Franks. . . ."

They just stared at me, unbelieving. I could

see they didn't believe. Lola Garrick still wasn't around anywhere, but a man came out of the men's cloak room, and cried out:

"What is there to worry about, you fools? Lola is pulling a gag, that's all. I don't know what sort of a story this newspaper reporter is trying to cook up to make nasty headlines for his tabloid, but don't fall for his guff. . . ."

They began to laugh again. For a moment I had my doubts. Maybe I was all wrong. Bette's fear, the whistling of the wind around the derelict, all had caused my imagination to work overtime, perhaps. Anyway, I'd give Lola the benefit of the doubt, because I *wanted* to. I couldn't believe that three people were dead, at the hands of a monster that went into the sea, and then came out again at will.

But where was Bette?

I had to find her. I raced for the rear part of the clubhouse, where there was a women's waiting room, and other rooms used for purposes about which I knew nothing. I knew Bette was probably in one of them, gathering items for the story she must write.

I hammered on one door, beyond which I heard rustling, and whispers.

The rustling and whispers did not stop, but none paid heed to my hammering. I called Bette's name, over and over again:

"Bette! *Bette!*"

THE WALLS OF the room threw the name back in my face with the force of a blow. And then a hand on my shoulder spun me around. I looked into the sneering face of the man who had just told the crowd that all this was a gag of Lola's, to entertain them.

"Women have rooms of their own to get away from men, especially men without manners," he said. "Beat it. Nobody would stand for you going in there!"

I swung at him. I was frothing at the mouth with terror for Bette, and with anger at this upstart whom I did not know. He drew his head

back. I scarcely noticed the movement, so easy and casual was it. But I missed him clean, almost as though my fist had passed right through him. In the next instant I was down on the floor.

His hand, palm foremost, had shot into my face, almost snapping my head from my shoulders. He stepped over me and was gone. Dizzy, sick, I crawled to my feet, eager to go on with the fight, to smash down this man who dared interfere in my search for Bette.

If anybody had noticed it, none gave a sign. But, down against the floor, I had heard words, coming under the crack in the door—words in Bette's sweet voice:

"Yes, I had a friend on the *Cyclonic*. I might have married him, if he had come back. . . ."

And cold chills raced up and down my spine as I stared at the heavy panels of that door. It wasn't that I was jealous of a man who had been part of Bette's life before my own advent . . . but that her words definitely stamped her as being as one with the others here, who had lost friends or relatives on the *Cyclonic*.

One by one, those friends were horribly dying.

Bette was automatically in line, and her turn might be next.

As though in answer to this thought another voice came through the panels of the door I had been forbidden to pass:

"You are next! *Make merry for us, for we die!*"

It was the voice of Neptune.

The scream that answered it was Bette's.

I stepped back, hurled myself at the forbidden door.

CHAPTER THREE

ICEBOX HORROR

Sometimes pictures flash across the human mind faster than any words could possibly paint them. Such pictures came to me as I flung myself at that door, beyond which I was positive that ghastly things were happening: the entrance of Neptune to the clubhouse; the death of Hedda Murtin and of Peter Fraym; the vanishing of Leslie Franks; the white armed spume reaching up from the far edge of the ice for its victims. It all ran together in a complete, horribly detailed picture before my shoulder even touched that door.

Beyond it I was sure that Bette struggled in the arms of whatever kind of man it was who had spirited Leslie Franks away, after knocking me down in the snow at the clubhouse door.

The door wasn't locked. It was almost as though a grim listener beyond it had timed everything to the split second. I had tried the door and had not been able to open it. Now, as my shoulder struck it, it gave inward with a bang that shook the clubhouse, and I sprawled on the floor on my face.

The door slammed shut again, as though dragged back by a spring, shaking the clubhouse with its reverberation.

I rolled over on my back.

Neptune stood before the window, with Bette in his arms. His face was split in a grin. The window was open, and snow came curling into the room. My eyes took in the hanging cloaks of the women, each of which seemed to be hiding some additional horror. I tried to get to my feet.

Neptune shot out his right foot, driving me back. I grabbed for it and missed. I mouthed threats, prayers, oaths. Bette seemed to be unconscious. Her arms flung wide—the creature carried her with an arm about her middle, so that she hung like an empty sack. But though I couldn't see her face, I was sure it was Bette.

The apparition—whatever it was—went through the window. I got to my feet and rushed after him—but it was no use. Neptune was gone. I hurled myself through the window, raced after a shadow that seemed to be fleet as the wind, out onto the ice for the second time that night.

And ended my chase hopeless, helpless.

The ice, or the night, or the snow, or the sea, or all of them together, had swallowed Neptune and Bette Carver. . . .

"Alex! Alex!" the call came to my ears from the window from which I had vaulted, and the voice was Bette's voice! My brain spun. I was crazy, that was plain—but I could not mistake Bette's voice. I raced back, my panting breath rasping from my lungs so harshly I could taste my own blood.

I went back through the window, and Bette met me. Her hair was all mussed up. She wore someone's ermine coat which scarcely covered her. Below it her legs were bare, as were her feet. The V in the throat showed an entrancing expanse of lovely skin. Bette blushed.

"There's nothing on underneath, Alex," she whispered. "I'll explain. It's wild, impossible, but here it is: I came in here. The lights went out, and a woman grabbed me. She whispered, so I didn't recognize her voice. She said that I, like all the others who had friends or relatives on the *Cyclonic*, would die tonight, that the spirit of the storm would slay me—would come and take me away. Well, Alex, I'm not the sort to take that kind of thing without a comeback. I conked the dame. I couldn't stand her chuckling laughter. I conked her, like I said, and put my clothes on her. I didn't have time to put hers on myself, before the Neptune monster came and grabbed up the girl he thought was me. Then you came. . . ."

"He went out with that other woman, whoever she was," I said hoarsely, "and the sea got them—at least got the woman. I'd have gone into the sea after you, if you hadn't yelled in time. I was mad, desperate. Bette—what in God's name is happening here?"

"Well, the lights came on just as Neptune came in, stayed on while you were here, and I spent a lot of time in the dark. But while I was scrabbling around, trying to figure what it was all about, I ran into something. I put my hand on a human face, that seemed to be frozen. The body's here somewhere, Alex, among these cloaks, or behind them."

That was a queer twist, and no mistake. I could see no sense in it, but I had to find out things.

Bette buttoned the cloak around her, and we got busy. I made sure that there were no hidden panels or closets on the right side of the room, and Bette and I began swiftly, feverishly, to take down all the cloaks on the coat racks, and pile them against the right wall. As we did so the music of the band kept coming from the dancing floor, and the shrill, hysterical laughter of the dancers, some of whom were destined, certainly, to die before morning.

We cleared four racks of cloaks, moving the racks against the pile of them when we had finished. I was beginning to think Bette had been imagining things, when we reached the wall behind the racks. There was a square door, newly formed. I stared at Bette. She looked at me, and her face would never be whiter. There were wooden buttons holding the door in place.

"That's it!" said Bette hoarsely. "That door was open, and I pushed my hand into it, and touched a cold, dead face! It was open because I was supposed to be pushed into it. . . ."

I FLIPPED THE fastenings, pulled out the door, looked into the black aperture beyond. It was an icebox. The inside of it was thick with frost. Its bottom was covered with chipped ice. There was plenty of room still unused in it. But that which *was* used, was used in ghastly fashion.

Lying almost under my eyes was Hedda Murtin! Lying beside her was Peter Fraym, whom I had last seen plunging into the sea beyond the ice. Lying next to Peter, on the other side, was Leslie Franks. The three dead ones were all accounted for. No mistaking the fact that they were dead. They had been dead when they were put in here.

And there was room for every one of the merrymakers in this ghastly clubhouse. But why were relatives of the victims of the *Cyclonic* being chosen? I had madness to deal with, I knew that. But even a madman has some sort of motive for what he does. And where did Lola Garrick fit into the horror?

"There's just one thing to do, Bette," I whispered. "We've got to get the other guests together, tell them what has happened, call the police and stop this horror."

She agreed. We went to the door. It was locked—tightly. No icebox door could have been more secure. And the window was useless. If we went out that way, we wouldn't be able to get back through the outer door, not with what we knew now. The person who had trapped us here would attend to that. We might, of course, jump from the window and save ourselves. But I couldn't think of that, and knew Bette wouldn't hear of it. We couldn't leave and let those others—even though they were strangers—die as the first three had died.

We banged on the door. Nobody outside paid us the slightest attention! That was queer, for I, beyond these same panels, had heard voices in this room. Our banging and clattering should be heard, even above the wild laughter, and the macabre music of the band. But nobody came to answer.

I whirled to look at Bette. Something had to be done. We had to find the way to do it. Bette glanced back at the door of that grisly ice chest. She gave a choked scream, for now that door was closed!

My heart almost stopped beating, but I forced myself to go to the door, open it again, and peer in. Neither Bette nor I could be sure that we hadn't automatically closed that door ourselves, to hide the cold faces of the dead. That's the only explanation I have now, after all this time, for not even a ghost could have come in by the window—the only other mode of ingress—and shut that door without our hearing him.

We looked into the box, and horror was piled upon horror. The box had, now, a fourth occupant.

That occupant was Lola Garrick, garbed in the clothing which had been Bette's!

I stared at Bette.

"But for quick thinking, sweetheart," I said, "and mountains of courage, you would be there instead of Lola. She *meant* for you to be there! She was hoist on her own petard. Nor does that end the horrors, for someone who also knew, had to put her there. A monster still roams the beach, and we've got to find him. Understand? Can you stand the cold for a little while? Are you afraid to go out into the dark for just a few minutes?"

She shook her head. I needn't, really, have asked.

WE WENT OUT through that ghastly window which, but for Bette's courage, might have been her exit from life. And even in the midst of the horror, Bette was enough of a woman to whisper to me:

"Even if *he* hadn't been lost on the *Cyclonic,* it would have been nobody but you, from the first moment I saw you."

Maybe she was sincere about it; women are peculiar creatures. Maybe she said it to buck me up, after the manner of brave women. Certainly, after her whisper, I could have moved mountains for her sake. I could have throttled tigers for her approval.

Most of my fear left me. No, it didn't leave me, never would, but I was somehow able to rise above it.

Bette and I went to that outer door where I had run into catastrophe before.

I thought we would have trouble getting in, but we didn't. I simply opened the door and led Bette in. I was afraid to release my grip on her wrist, lest the horror in the night whisk her away from me.

The merrymakers now were people from another world. It didn't take half a dozen questions for me to find out several things: every person here was afraid to go out into the dark. The telephone lines were all down or otherwise out of order, so that none could be advised of the horror here. The whole crowd was hopeless, helpless, like people on a sinking ship who know there can be no rescue, and only death can answer their cries.

And they made merry because they could not make decisions. They had started making merry to Lola's command, and did not seem to be able to stop. They were automatons, lacking only the ice and death to make them fit subjects for that box where the four already dead were resting.

"Who's missing," I cried, "besides Hedda, Leslie, Peter and Lola?"

Bette had to answer that for me. She did it by looking over the white faces, then checking her list, a swift, almost automatic appraisal.

"Burton Trask and Clara Holland, his fiancée."

I looked back at the crowd again, which was swaying, unconscious that they swayed, to the music.

"How did they go?" I demanded.

"*He* came and took Clara. Burton followed. None came back."

"I know where to find them," I said grimly.

And then I did something that must have shocked everybody. I walked up to Drew Kedick, who stood with his right arm about the waist of Greta Harms, and knocked him flat with a blow to the mouth.

CHAPTER FOUR

"IN THE NAME OF SCIENCE!"

Thank God, the blow had the desired effect, at least in part. There was a quick, questioning mutter from the other men. The orchestra stopped in the middle of a tune, and rose to its feet as one man.

Four men left their dancing partners to charge me. I stepped into them, fighting the best I knew how, talking as I fought:

"I had to do something to wake you people up. You all act as though you were hypnotized, just because of some strange goings-on, because of the night, the storm, and the occasion. The whole thing is macabre, unnatural, and it's had my goat as much as yours. But listen. . . ."

They drew back a little.

I stopped, panting, to tell them what I had seen and experienced outside. Drawing a breath, I ended with this:

"It isn't believable, yet all we have to do to see that every word is true, is to go into the women's cloak room, and look into the box behind where the cloak racks stood. There were four dead people in there when Bette Carver and I had a look. By this time there are six. I don't know why they're there, any more than you do. I'm completely certain that there's no supernatural reason. There's a mad one, perhaps, but one that is understandable and reasonable. But of this I am sure: unless we men do something about it, every person here will be dead before morning!"

One of the men finally managed to speak up.

"What is your suggestion?"

"Outside," I said, taking a deep breath, "is a man. We've all seen him in the fabled costume of Neptune, but he's a human being—a madman, perhaps—but a human being none the less. A crank, maybe, drawn here by the fact that this party has already had some publicity in papers in Jersey and New York. By sheer showmanship which has paralyzed us all, he has managed to destroy six of our number. He'll get the others if we don't come alive and use our heads. This party, save as a stunt, has no real connection with the ill-fated *Cyclonic*. There is no bridge between the living and the dead.

"This fellow has used the snow, and the night, and the derelict, out there, as props for his little act. He knows that we're all in an almost hysterical state of nervous excitement—and he's making the most of it. He's gambling that we won't react as normal human beings would react under normal circumstances—and he's winning. . . . Six of us are dead. . . .

"Here's my plan: The monster is a man, whom men can handle. Maybe some of the rest of us will be killed, getting him. But all of us will if we don't. I don't understand the things I saw outside—the people I saw go into the sea, only to reappear in that icebox I've told you about. Some of it may have been illusion, caused by the fear of the unknown which has mastered the rest of you. We'll find out about that later. Now, we have just one thing to do: find this Neptune monster and destroy him! Who's with me?"

A dozen of them came sheepishly forward, and I realized I had gone a long way toward cutting the horror trimmings off the Lola Garrick party. I saw approval of me in the eyes of Bette Carver, and felt I was on the right track.

"Are there any weapons among you?" I next asked. "I've got a pistol. We may need more. The man outside may have accomplices."

The question produced four or five weapons of different makes, and we were ready.

I gave last instructions to the women, before we went out into the night.

"Miss Carver, here, has seen the monster close at hand. He's just a man. She will be in charge here until we come back. If he slips past us, and comes in to take further toll, this is what you must do. Throw your arms around one another and hold fast, understand? If anyone of you tries to heed the call of Neptune, the others will hang onto her for dear life. Being only a man, after all, he can't drag you all out and duck you into the sea."

Then, at the head of the men, whose courage seemed to be coming back, we sallied forth from the door.

OUT IN THE driving snow their teeth began to chatter at once. I gave crisp orders.

"The secret lies out on the ice, I think," I said. "Now, at intervals of fifteen paces, we'll march out as far as we dare go. Don't bunch up, or your weight will send some of you through the ice. Listen for orders. When, and if, we flush our quarry, shoot first and ask questions afterwards."

It was a queer outfit that went out onto the ice. I scarcely knew, myself, why we did it, following a hunch more than anything else.

Fifty yards from shore, though, the conviction that I was right became stronger. The wind had piled drifts of varying heights, here and there on the ice. A man, a dozen men, could have hidden behind some of them. What better vantage place for the madman than those drifts, in which he could play hide-and-seek with his victims? He'd already ducked behind one or two, and I had seen him, and thought he had gone into the sea. The white arms which I had thought to be arms of salty spume had been swirling snow instead, kicked up by his body and that of his victim.

Then, when I had gone back, convinced that he had vanished into the sea, he had dipped his unconscious victims into some blowhole and allowed them to freeze. . . .

We marched out. My eyes searched the drifts of snow. In spite of my warning the men, from very fear, began to draw together, and I had to snap at them sharply, to make them keep their proper intervals.

Weapons were held at ready; we advanced slowly. Icy wind bit at our necks, hands, and faces. To stand still for two minutes was to feel the lethargy of death by freezing, creep into limbs and veins. We had to make this fast, or go back to get warmed up before going on.

Closer and closer to the edge.

The ice was cracking warningly now, and the men were scared. So was I, and glad Bette could not know it. And then, when I was about to issue the command for the return, we flushed our quarry. He stood out plainly against the snow. Neptune himself.

I fired every round in my pistol, aiming straight for his back. His arms shot high in the air. His scream, like that of a wheeling bird of prey, keened across the wastes of snow and water.

Other pistols spoke, almost with mine, and Neptune crashed down on the ice, which crackled under his weight.

"Quickly," I yelled, "take off your belts and fasten them together. I'm going after him."

They worked fast, all right, and in a matter of seconds, holding onto a chain of leather belts, I ventured out on the treacherous ice toward our "monster." Cold water came up around my ankles as the ice gave, but I knew, if the belts did not break, that the others would drag me back to

the clubhouse before I froze. I got my fingers in the neck of our quarry.

They began pulling me and gradually, dragging the monster, they got me to the beach.

There, on firm ground, with the "monster" dead in our hands, we gathered him up, and his dripping blood froze as it hit the snow at our feet.

"Into the clubhouse," I said, chattering with the cold. "We've got to lay the ghost right now, once and for all."

They shuddered as they gathered up Neptune for his last ride.

We went in at the door, dropped him on the floor. There was no mistaking him, for he was the same person who had taken Hedda Murtin away, and had caused the deaths of the others.

I spoke to the women.

"You can stop holding onto one another now. This ends the horror, I think. Maybe it would be just as well if you all went into another room. You too, Bette."

We went trooping into a room—*not* the room of the cloaks and the racks. I stooped and began pulling off Neptune's disguise. The others, breathing hard, stood around to watch and listen. Bette bent over the corpse of the unknown.

I saw his face. It looked familiar. I ripped off his tunic. There were six bullet holes through his chest, from the rear.

But the studious face was unmarred.

I looked at Bette questioningly. She nodded her head. She, too, knew the face of the man at her feet. His name was Bigelow Hutton, who had advanced a theory, some months ago, that human beings could be preserved, in a condition of suspended animation, for a period of years, decades—even centuries.

THE WORLD OF science had laughed at him. Hutton had answered by claiming that he had kept monkeys, dogs, cats, chickens, alive in that manner for weeks.

Scientists had called the man—in polite, scientific language, of course—a liar.

Bette and I had the story, then. Lola Garrick had been unfortunate indeed, in selecting this location for her party—for Bigelow Hutton lived within four or five miles of this particular strip of beach.

I could almost read his dead mind:

"I'll *prove* to the world that it can be done. I can't get volunteers to submit to my tests—so I'll take them where I find them. The setting is perfect!"

He must have connived with Lola Garrick, must have persuaded her to help him try the thing out here. Lola herself had fallen his victim by accident, or because Bette Carver hadn't been as hypnotized by fear as the others.

Bette and I, between us, explained it to the guests. I ended with this:

"Fortunately we snapped out of it in time. Six are dead. We've slain Hutton before he could do anything with the rest of us. Unquestionably he was mad. . . ."

And so it was left at that. Physicians were called in, as soon as possible, to examine the six who were dead. They were indubitably dead, and nothing could be done about it, they said.

But they kept looking at me. . . .

Bette . . . well, I caught her looking at me, many times. I knew that down the years, whenever I looked at myself in the mirror, whenever I lived over this horror in dreams, I would ask myself:

"Could he have returned the dead to life, if you hadn't slain him?"

Doctors said no . . . but I saw by their faces that they were not sure. And that's what will eat my heart out until the grave closes over me. Was I, indirectly, responsible for the death of those six, by killing Hutton before he could attempt to resurrect them?

I don't know. I'll never know. I just know this, and it, too, eats at my heart: Bette Carver loves me from the depths of her soul. I am sure, too, that until the unanswerable question is answered, she will never cease to suffer—and to doubt.

The wind across that desolate beach, even in mid-summer, keeps ringing in my ears, filled with my own doubts, fears, and questions . . . as it will sing and whine over my grave, ruffling the dust in summer, swirling the snow in winter . . . to the end of time.

Dec. 29, 1935

AFFIDAVIT

I hereby certify that, with Ed Bodin as witness, I visited that section of the Jersey Coast immediately adjacent to the area of the Black Tom explosion, and that while half freezing in a blizzard, conceived and prepared the story, setting forth the details of the plot to my witness, while both of us huddled under a shattered wooden hulk which had drifted ashore before the intense cold had frozen the ocean itself to a distance of several hundred yards from the beach.

(Signed) ARTHUR J. BURKS.

Subscribed and sworn to before me this 24th day of January, 1936.

EDWARD F. DONOVAN
Notary Public.

THEODORE ROSCOE

AS WAS TRUE for many of the most popular pulp fiction writers of the Golden Age of these garish and lurid publications, Theodore Roscoe (1906–1992) produced work in a variety of genres: hard-boiled for *Detective Fiction Weekly* and *Flynn's Detective Fiction*, as well as the cult classic novel *I'll Grind Their Bones* (1936); Foreign Legion for *Argosy* and *Adventure;* boxing for *Fight Stories;* aviation for *Air Stories;* and horror for *Weird Tales*, among many other genres and magazines, but he is probably best-known for his adventure stories set in such exotic locales as Timbuktu, Tangier, Morocco, and Saigon, which were a mainstay of the contributions to *Argosy.* Born in Rochester, New York, he was the son of former missionaries in India, which undoubtedly provided him with his lifelong curiosity and enthusiasm for travel.

One of his trips took him to Port-au-Prince, Haiti, to look into the frequently heard rumors of zombies, voodoo ceremonies, and other weird activities. He found ample evidence that these strange tales were true: goats hanging from trees, beheaded chickens, and shops that sold ouanga (a small bag containing the items needed to cast spells, both good and bad—parrot feathers, goat hairs, pebbles, spice, frog legs, perhaps a chicken head). The tales of the dead brought back to life to work as slaves in the sugar fields were rampant on the island and served as the inspiration for stories and two *Argosy* serials, *A Grave Must Be Deep* and *Z Is for Zombie.*

Z Is for Zombie was originally published in the February 13–March 6, 1937 issues of *Argosy;* it was published in book form by Starmont House (Mercer Island, Washington: 1989).

THEODORE ROSCOE

Z IS FOR ZOMBIE

CHAPTER I

THE TAFFY-HAIRED MAN

THE TAFFY-HAIRED MAN said, "Get out of here! *'Raus mit!*" His voice was slow, husky, a male imitation of Garbo's.

Ranier stood up to return the stare. There seemed to be four taffy-haired men, four faces spread fan-wise like a handful of playing cards. The doorway behind them was a blur; and the four faces scowled, then swam together, came into focus as a single astonishment to see if anyone else could be hearing this. But the café was otherwise unpopulated; Hyacinth Lucien, Haitian proprietor of the place, had gone out back to milk a goat. Ranier had been keeping his own council; drinking, here, in solitude. He turned to give the man who had interrupted him from the

doorway a challenging, "Says you!" but the pale German never gave him a chance.

It was over before Ranier could refocus his glare. A cruel blow glancing off the side of his jaw. A hand snatching him by the lapel, yanking him off balance, propelling him in a body-twist through the door. Shoved, he went stumbling across a dark verandah, caromed off a post, floundered backwards into night, and turned his lame foot on loose gravel.

THE SPRAWL MUST have knocked him out. He wondered afterwards if his head had struck a knuckle of coral, for he came to wandering lamely in wet fog around the side of the ramshackle building. He felt as if he'd been walking in his sleep. What with liquor and that blow and this wool-thick mist in night, it was hard to

"Dead!" she cried.
"Dead for fourteen years!"

chart his bearings. . . . This was the Blue Kitty Café. A goat's bleat came from somewhere in the rear, and a Negroid voice scolding in thick-lipped syllables. That would be Hyacinth.

Lamplight, pumpkin-yellow, flowed from an open window near by; Ranier saw his sea cap was lying in mud under the sill. When he stooped to retrieve it he saw the German sitting at table within, back to the window. The man was scrib-bling on an envelope. Ranier puzzled a moment at the shoebrush head, then remembered!

"Slugged me, by heaven! Now he's drinking my drinks! *My* drinks!"

In his haste to reach the front door and re-turn to the fray, he fell again, It didn't sober him any. Fury always blinded him, and he had to lie flat for a couple of minutes, waiting for his head to clear. Scraping mud from his knees, he ground his teeth together, outraged. The gall of

that Dutchman! The damned gall! Hitting you before you could ask the reason why! Wanted the whole café to himself, did he? Only one remedy for that sort of swine. A crack on the jaw!

Ranier recrossed the verandah and stood, fists clenched, in the doorway, glaring savagely at the usurper. Flies swooped through the tor-pid lamplight of the room; there was no sound but that. The taffy-haired man seemed unaware of Ranier's return. Slumped at table in mid-room, shoulders sluggish against the back of his chair, stomach half-under the table, left hand in pocket, right hand on table fixed around a glass, his chin on chest and his eyes three quarters closed, the pale man stared down his nose in rev-erie and did not so much as give Ranier a glance.

Ranier scowled darkly.

Fellow must think he could toss people around, take a comfortable posture and forget about it. Well, Ranier would refresh his memory. He snorted; stepped forward.

Still the figure at table refused to move. The bottle at his elbow was half-emptied during the few minutes Ranier had been outside; an inch of oily white liquid was in the clutched glass. Huh! A punch in the nose would rouse him lively enough. Ranier hiccoughed a warning of hostilities to begin again; he limped into the room another step, fixing his man with a fighting glare.

Was something wrong with the bird? Walked in here to start trouble, then passed out? The man's features were dull with that expression of blond Teutonic pokerishness; they had hardened into a stupid blank. White as chalk. Like the face of a statue with real hair and glass eyes.

Ranier stalled near the threshold to consider this phenomenon, angrily balked—you couldn't hit a man who refused to look at you!—then was conscious of familiarity in that face. He knew he'd seen that extraordinary pallor before. This Dutchman was one of the cruise passengers from the ship. All right, that would make another reason for pasting him in the jaw.

Ranier's lips thinned back. He'd wanted for a long time to take a sock at one of these bulldozing tourists. One of these small-timers who had three drinks and thought themselves Napoleon. Nobody could give Ranier a bum's rush and get away with it. Ready or not, the Dutchman had it coming. The man must be drunk—

Drunk.

Thought stayed Ranier's intended onslaught; held him at sudden standstill. Something in his spirit sank like a stone while a slow flush crawled up his throat and cheekbones. When the flush reached his forehead resentment against the taffy-haired man had turned to resentment against himself. He, himself, was drunk. Going to make a spectacle of himself, stage a loutish row because some lout had tapped him on the chin. Violating the only rule he had left not to violate—to hold his liquor like a gentleman.

A sickening weariness came over him, a headache, and a pucker of quince in his mouth. He spat dryly, walked across the room, and limped into an alcove off the bar, looking across his shoulder at the German in disgust. Something was abnormal about that Kraut. Queer.

In the alcove by himself, his drinks restored by the black Hyacinth who had reappeared with goat's milk and diplomacy only after the crisis was dispersed, Ranier found himself watching the taffy-haired man without wanting to, nor quite knowing why he watched.

FROM THE ALCOVE where he sat, he could watch the whole room in the back-bar mirror without himself being seen. He shifted his chair to watch the man better. It wasn't the man's slumped attitude of reverie, or the bleak whiteness of his face. The fellow had, so much as Ranier could now remember him, never been particularly animated on shipboard; Ranier had decided that the man's healthless pallor was functional. But the eyes looked bad. Glassy. Why should he walk in here and throw out the first person he saw? Ranier choked on a swallow of *aguardiente*.

Probably that Dutch pugnacity had come from liquor. Ranier fingered soreness under his cap, wondering how long he'd been unconscious and how many drinks his assailant had had to fold up during the interim. The room was stifling, and the German had put down a lot of that *aguardiente*, by the looks. Half a bottle. Enough to make anybody glassy-eyed if you weren't used to the stuff.

Ranier, who'd been putting down a lot of that *aguardiente* himself, poured himself another drink. Now his anger had faded; he felt only curiosity at his antagonist's conduct. The shabby adobe-walled room was airless in the hot yellow light of oil lamps; it smelled like everything else in Haiti, first cousin to a chicken coop. No breeze from the beach. A lazy sluffing of surf outside; inside a somnolent mosquito drone. Ranier turned his interest from the face in the mirror to the tide going down in his liquor glass.

"I'm drunk," he decided, lowering the tide. This Caribbean mouthwash did things to a fellow. Made a man stare the way that pale bird at the table was staring. Made another man's nerves think something was wrong. Ranier gulped half a glass, still watching the back-bar mirror. Trouble was, instead of deadening his sensibilities, alcohol always sharpened them. His mind could shut off, but the nerve-ends under his skin couldn't. They felt things. Way they were feeling queer atmosphere, right now.

John Ranier muttered, "To hell with it," and drained his glass.

He meant the taffy-haired man who had thrown him out of the door, then gone into a trance. He meant the Blue Kitty Café, the island of Haiti, tropical cruises, the ship out in the bay waiting to sail, the fact he was ship's doctor sitting here in this waterside hole, imagining something uncanny was the matter with that fool across the room.

He pushed the smudged white sea cap back on his rumpled dark head; ran slim brown fingers over his jaw, and regarded the surgeon's stripe on the unlaundered cuff of his uniform.

"To hell with it all."

HE MEANT THE M.D. certificate in his cramped ship's quarters; the five years he'd spent between New York harbor and Caribbean ports with this down-at-the-helm steamship line, dispensing seasick pills to nauseated ladies, adhesive tape to the crew, tomato juice to soused tourists who wanted to see the world through the bottom of a gin glass.

And what's Dr. Ranier doing now? Dispensing seasick pills and tomato juice! Don't tell me! Not the Dr. Ranier who was going to be the greatest surgeon of his day! Not the young, brisk, clever Dr. Ranier who ran that big glass and chromium office on Park Avenue, and did all those positively-miraculous-my-dear operations on pinguid millionaires? Not Dr. *John* Ranier who was wounded with the Rainbow Division

when he was sixteen, "came back and made good," social position, stock market, elegant practice, engaged to Helen Goddard of Goddard Steel and Coal—not *the* Dr. Ranier.

John Ranier put down a dry glass. "To hell with everything."

He meant *the* Dr. Ranier. The stripling who'd gone out to fight the war to end war, and came back decorated with a limp. Who'd fought through medical school to save the world from cancer and ended up doing wonderful operations on wonderful millionaires. Who'd been listed in the best stocks and at the oldest clubs and doffed his shiny tophat to shiny Helen Goddard who'd accepted his shiny ring. "Oh, John, I love you so." At least until the Depression. "But you couldn't expect me to go to that five-room house in Newark, John."—"I'll have to do seven million tonsillectomys and ten million trepannings before we can afford anything better."— "Honestly, John! Be the wife of a small town doctor?"

"And nuts to you, too," said John Ranier to John Ranier, grinning expressionlessly at the bottom of his glass. Four more of these *aguardientes* and his head would be pleasantly like the fog. He'd forget *the* Dr. Ranier who'd lost everything in a market crash and learned the price of everything and the value of nothing. Four more *aguardientes* and he'd even forget he'd been marked down low enough to consider brawling in a bar room with a taffy-haired Dutchman who—

Ranier drowsed.

Later, when it was important, he could not remember just what it was that jolted his attention back to the taffy-haired man. When it was important, he could not remember at just what moment the tourist party from the ship entered the café to join the Dutchman at his table and start ordering drinks. He was certain everything was all right with the taffy-haired man when those people from the cruise walked in; he could have sworn he heard the man grunt "*Ja*" and "*Jawohl*" in the opening conversation.

But later he couldn't remember. He'd paid little notice to the incoming crowd, except to mark them as tourists from the ship and hope they'd clear out soon with their ugly-natured friend.

Then, all at once, he was watching that white face in the mirror, again. He was aware that the man had not spoken for the past quarter hour. The taffy-haired man had not altered his posture or expression—chin on chest, glass in fist—his table companions were engaged in commonplace discussion among themselves— but some instinct, some galvanic tension in the atmosphere told Ranier there had been a change.

Were the others aware of it, too? Did those people now sitting at that table know something was queer? Cords tightened in Ranier's neck-nape. Something *was* the matter with that taffy-haired man!

He sat so still.

He looked so white.

He seemed dead—but wasn't.

CHAPTER II

A BLADE IN THE BACK

There were eight at the table, counting the man in question, and John Ranier was destined to remember them—the café as the stage, his encounter with the taffy-haired man as prologue. The table was almost centered in the room, end-wise to the bar and broadside to the door. It was long and rectangular, imitation Mission oak, outcast of some white planter's dining room; its company of chairs as chance-assorted as the tourists sitting in them.

The taffy-haired man slumped at the far end of the table, looking down its length toward the bar, which stretched across Ranier's end of the room. His back was toward the open window that admitted clammy tatters of fog, as if white curtains tacked to the outside kept blowing in over the sill.

At the Dutchman's left was the tourist named Mr. Brown. There was always a Mr. Brown on these $100 cruises. This Mr. Brown wore plus fours, golf jacket and camera case on a loaf-of-bread figure; the face of a damp but genial pie; eyes like blue huckleberries behind horn-rimmed spectacles; chuckly mouth. His name was Al, and at a moment's introduction he would call you "Fella." Composograph figure of all the fraternal orders in Ohio. As Ranier observed him first he was kissing a cigar almost as plump as himself and chuckling smoke at the slat-thin Roman-nosed individual at his side.

The man with the Caesar nose was a Professor Philemon Schlitz, narrow and nervous with a face four inches wide and pince-nez glasses which flaunted a prissy black ribbon. He wore a Ph.D. on his name and a sun helmet somebody'd told him to buy in Cape Haitian, the effect being that of an old maid school teacher playing Frank Buck. Not only an entomologist, he was a walking glossary of limericks; liable to veer from a discussion on dragon flies to come up giggling with, "Did you hear the one, 'There was a young lady from Sweden—'" or "'There was an old man from Siam—'" Everybody on the cruise liked him.

Nobody liked the man next to him—Angelo Carpetsi, swarthy New York Italian youth who'd been seasick on the way down and remained sour ever since. Coat on arm, he displayed a pink silk shirt, high-waisted trousers, trick suspenders. His eyes were feline, sleek, and he wore a Dance Palace haircut with sideburns. Ranier had found him taciturn and disagreeable, but had been amused at his cabin-mate who now bulked large beside him—Mr. Coolidge.

The name didn't fit a Brooklyn truck driver sweating in gaudy tourist attire. Mr. Joseph Coolidge, beetle-browed, grinning, cropped and cauliflowered, resembled a Tanganyika gorilla on a holiday. First night at sea he'd gone trampling and swinging his arms after every woman on the boat, and failing there, he'd resorted to bellowing rum-battles in all the Haitian ports of call. Both Coolidge and Carpetsi were more the Havana-cruise calibre, and Ranier had wondered what brought them on this Haiti excursion anyway.

ON THE OTHER side of the board, at the right of the taffy-haired man and across from Mr. Brown, was the woman called Daisy. Ranier had often wondered what became of those Baby Peggy prodigies when they grew too old for Hollywood; this blonde was the answer. Eyes big as black-eyed susans, the petals wide, as if they observed the world in a transport of childish wonder from under the floppy brim of a picture hat. Peroxide hair. Much powder, more paint, flabby cheeks, hard mouth, and that Kiddy Koop stare. Ten to one she'd roll those bulgy eyes (did they come from exophthalmic goiter?) and mew, "Itsy bitsy" and "Ooo, it's cute." The type that ought to be in a pasture, Ranier thought. Five years old from the neck up; from the neck down, all bosom and behind.

She was traveling with the man who sat beside her and across from the oily Carpetsi—an Irishman named Kavanaugh. A man who looked to be successful in his line and in taking care of himself. Jaw lean, nose sharp, eyes that could pick winners at Belmont. Women went for the dash of gray at the temples, the belted waterproof coat and snapped hat brim, the quality of hard confidence. There was intolerance in the way he addressed a remark, cocking his thumb and pointing his finger at a listener, as if to say, "This means you!" But why did these smart operators who knew their way around always travel with some blond pin-cushion who blubbered baby-talk? A dozen times he'd ordered the woman to shut up—aiming his pistol-barrel finger in exasperation—to let them hear what the Haitian gentleman, who was with them, had to say.

Monsieur Marcelline, this was; and unlike his countryman behind the bar, Marcelline was as smartly tailored as any of his white superiors at table, and nearly as condescending. His tone

was suave, his manner urbane. He'd boarded the cruise ship, Ranier recalled, at Cape Haitian with a second class ticket for passage around the island to Jacmel. Second class because his complexion was only a little darker than Spanish, maple-walnut with a few lavender pimples, known in the Haitian spectrum as *griffone*.

Languidly fanning himself with a new Panama, Marcelline was speaking good English with a Haitian-French accent, advising the white tourists in their plans.

"Everything I believe is ready, *monsieur*," to Kavanaugh. "There is a new coastal highway from here to our capital, and once we are on it we may travel at high speed. *Mais oui.*"

"A night drive ought to be interesting." Kavanaugh spoke in a flat-keyed voice with just a fine shade of boredom. "If we're delayed too long I suppose we can stop at some inn along the way. I'd like to make it by midnight; at all events we've got to be in Port-au-Prince by tomorrow morning. That's flat. You're sure there won't be any hitch."

"The starting time is at your discretion, *monsieur.*"

"And I hope, monsoor has some idea of where he's going," the Daisy woman gave her Irish escort a look, surprising Ranier with a voice that sounded like a lumberjack talking through a doll. "I don't like this night air."

John Ranier deduced the party had decided to abandon the cruise boat and motor along the coast to Port-au-Prince where they could spend time buying souvenirs made in New Jersey in the quaint marts of the Haitian capital, and pick up the ship when it came along. Mr. Kavanaugh was engineering the shore excursion, and Monsieur Marcelline had been recruited to do the arranging, hire the car, go as guide.

It was the taffy-haired man who was curious. His quarter-open eyes trained down the table in that glassy stare. Like camera lenses under motionless lids. As if the eyeballs were taking a long-exposure photograph. But his table companions didn't seem to notice anything. Only

John Ranier, watching the face in the mirror, felt his neck-hairs stiffening.

YET NOTHING HAD happened at that table since the tourist party came in. Ten minutes ago Marcelline had left the café on an errand, returning shortly to announce the car was outside waiting, and if they delayed a little longer the fog might lift. There was some concern about driving over mountain roads in fog.

Dense vapor which had rolled along the peninsular coast at early evening had thickened, burying the Gulf of Gonaives in blowing cotton. Coastline, headlands, bay and immediate foreshore were obscured in night-white blanketing, formless and opaque. A big German liner heading down the gulf for Port-au-Prince had vanished with the horizon, leaving in its wake a far, faint echo, like the moo of a lost cow groping its way through invisibility. Out in the bay the cruise steamer riding at anchor was a cluster of yellow gangway lights, pinpricks afloat in mist; and down beach the town was smothered. Mud streets, shanties, clay walls and palm-tops snared in drifting cobwebs. Outlines dissolved. Thinning, streaming, straggling, churning, the fog eddied around Hyacinth Lucien's Blue Kitty Café, curling up to the door, blowing in white curtains through the window at the taffy-haired man's back.

And something was wrong with that man!

Glaring at that face reflected in the bar mirror, Ranier gripped the edge of his alcove table, made as if to rise, shook his head, sat back with a frown. Anything was wrong, the man's tourist companions would know it, wouldn't they? Ranier tried to shrug off a feeling of undercurrents in the room. Hyacinth Lucien, behind the bar, swatting cockroaches with a chimpanzee hand. Bugs humming around the lamps. Somewhere out in the fog-hung town a gramophone was playing a Caribbean rumba, a tropical minor-key chant, the smoky snake-hipped rhythm quickened by the sifty time-beat of the *ouira* and the monotone *toky-tok-tok* of mahogany sticks.

For the last ten minutes not a flicker had crossed the taffy-haired man's face.

His table companions seemed to have forgotten him, their faces turned to the Haitian, Marcelline. Watching, listening, Ranier had a distinct impression that unseen wires had tightened in the room; a nervous emendation from that table, as if clocks inside those people had been wound up faster. Plump Mr. Brown was smoking vigorously. The boy, Carpetsi, kept turning his head to look out of the door at the fog. The blonde was fiddling with a powder puff as if it were a hot cake. Everybody was talking faster, louder. He stiffened in his chair, catching the words "dead man."

"Is it true the natives believe a dead man can be brought back to life?" Professor Philemon Schlitz was asking in a high-pitched voice. "I mean to say, this fantastic nonsense the guides were telling us in Cape Haitian about witch doctors who dig up bodies and reanimate them with magic so they walk about and—what do you call the things—?"

Marcelline throated an alto laugh. "*Monsieur* speaks of our Voovoo? *Alors,* there are mysteries, or, perhaps one should say, superstitions. Haiti, you comprehend, is not quite the United States. Especially in the mountains and coastal districts like this where the natives are, I am unhappy to say, somewhat primitive. *Par example,* the matter of bullfrogs. Few Haitians are not afraid of the frog, *monsieur.* Toads are agents of the Devil. Bullfrogs? Demons, *monsieur.* I give you my word, if you dropped a live bullfrog through the skylight of the government buildings—pouf!—every soldier in the place, including Monsieur the President, would jump out the windows."

A TIME WAS coming, although he didn't know it then, when John Ranier was to remember that speech. A time was coming when he was to remember every detail of that scene. The professor's piping query; Marcelline's alto laugh and answer. The professor adjusted his pince-nez nervously, leaning up the table towards his informant.

"But what about these dead people flitting about and all that? Those creatures you read about in books—eh?—gombies?"

"Z, *monsieur*," the Haitian corrected suavely. "Z as in *zombie*. Corpses resurrected, brought to life for magical purposes. One hears the rites are performed by that band of outlawed sorcerers known as the *Culte des morts*. The Society of the Dead, you would say. There are stories, then. Rumors of dead men who leave their graves to walk the jungles on silent feet—"

"Dave," the woman named Daisy snapped at Kavanaugh, "do we have to sit and listen to this? Frogs and live dead people—!"

"Madam will perhaps also hear the drums on the mountain," Marcelline went on blandly, "the *Rada* drums calling the people to some midnight dance, some *bamboche* to ward off evil. You see," he apologized with his shoulders, "we are Africans, we Haitians, after all. In the fog the drums will be beating, for the village people fear the white mists. It is said that on nights like this the dead walk best, and it might interest you to know there will be few Haitians lurking around the local cemeteries on such a—"

"Dave," the woman named Daisy said decisively, "I'll be so nervous tonight I could scream."

Kavanaugh's hard flat voice said critically, "You wanted to come, didn't you? You wanted to come on this shore party? And it won't hurt you, anyhow, if these shines believe all this hocus-pocus. So what?"

"Well, I could take less of it, myself," the guttural belonged to Angelo Carpetsi. "This place is givin' me goose pimples."

"*You* got goose pimples?" from Coolidge. "I got hen's eggs. Whaddya say, Kavanaugh, let's get under way. I'm a mass of nerves."

"We got to wait for the fog," suggested the plump Mr. Brown.

"The fog won't hurt," Kavanaugh said, "and I wish to God you people would quit stewing. It's quarter of eight, now. Okay with Marcelline, and everything's set, we can start at eight."

"Everything," Marcelline said in his darky alto, "is ready."

John Ranier set down his glass with a little bang, tugged his cap down over one eye, slammed back his chair, limped out of the alcove and pointed a finger at the taffy-haired man.

"That man is dying!"

In the hot, close room he might have touched off a bombshell. He had a glimpse of everything happening at once; chairs going back, people leaping up. Mr. Brown's shellrim spectacles big as moons behind the smoke of his cigar. The professor standing in astonishment, his left hand somehow in a beer glass. Carpetsi in a half crouch backing slowly from the table; Mr. Coolidge standing on spread legs, elbows bent, hands open like a wrestler's; the woman with her powder puff mashed to her lips. Kavanaugh twisted to face him, jaw pointed, hands jammed deep in the pockets of his trench coat. Marcelline bent and half turned, as if from a blow.

Out in the night the gramophone's haunting monody, and behind the bar a crash as Hyacinth Lucien lost control of a pan of bottles. Only the taffy-haired man at table's head hadn't moved.

Kavanaugh's flat voice started, "What the devil's—" when the googoo-eyed woman dropped the powder puff and screamed, her words running together in one long soprano screech.

"Ohmygoditsblood!"

John Ranier saw she was staring at a sticky dark liquor that had crept from under the taffy-haired man's chair to touch the toes of her big-bowed shoes. Everyone piled around the table to see. Everyone but the Dutchman who slumped in reverie with quarter-open eyes, hand fixed to a wine glass, shoulders glued to the back of his chair. Glued, Ranier saw, by a thin inch-small slit where a knife had gone through the cane chair-back into flesh. Blood wiggled in a syrup-like stream down the chair-back; dripped in Chinese torture-drops to the floor. But the knife was not there.

John Ranier moved his eyes in disbelief. Fog floated in silent curtains through the window ten feet away, but a thrown knife would have struck with a whack, and stuck. John Ranier knew the technique of knives. John Ranier knew cold steel had gone through that chair in one quick, expert stab; been yanked out deftly and with no more commotion than a butcher-blade through butter. John Ranier could recognize craftsmanship with a blade. That knife-wielder had touched the right vertebra to paralyze his man.

BUT WHAT WIZARDISH operator had done the thing? He'd been watching this room in the mirror for at least half an hour. That incision through chair and spine looked less than twenty minutes old. Yet for the past half hour not a soul in the room had walked behind the stabbed man's chair.

You could hear the stabbed man's faint, paralytic breathing.

You could hear the faint, paralytic breathing of everyone in the room.

It was Kavanaugh, breaking from amazement with an oath, who caught the sitter by the armpits, swung him up from the red-backed chair. The taffy head lolled and the man's shoes scraped the floor.

The Irishman's voice began to crash, "Don't stand around pop-eyed, you fools! Haarman's been badly hurt; we can't wait to find out how. We've got to get him to a doctor!"

John Ranier moved forward. "I'm a doctor."

Supporting the limp body, Kavanaugh looked over its shoulder with a hard-eyed stare. "Get out of the way," he told Ranier in a brittle voice. "You're drunk."

Anger hazed across Ranier's vision. "The words may be right, but I don't like your tone. I've had something to drink. Not enough to keep me from seeing that man will die if his bleeding isn't stopped."

He blocked Kavanaugh's way to the door. A quick impression the others were crowding up on three sides; Brown's pie-face gone to crust; Carpetsi's Italian eyes unpredictable; Coolidge lumbering close with the expression of a menacing Airedale.

Ranier directed, "I'll pack that wound, and someone better call the police. He was stabbed right here at your table. One of you must have the knife. One of you must have done it!"

Kavanaugh's lips were a pair of scissors, shearing out: "One of *us* must have done it? For all we know, you may have done it, yourself."

Ranier stared.

Marcelline's face swayed forward, glistening in lamplight, complexion gone from maple-walnut to vanilla. Under the rim of his Panama his eyes were circles of terror. He was pointing a finger at the window. His mouth flew wide and went, "Waaaaaaaah!"

CHAPTER III

CALL FOR DR. EBERHARDT!

Hyacinth Lucien's Blue Kitty Café was no glittering emporium at the corner of any Broadway and Forty-second Street, but a lamplit thatch-roofed obstruction on a fan of beach some distance from a fog-drowned Haitian village. Small Haitian villages are not lighted at night; the pedestrian walks the mud lanes armed with a small flashlight, a winkering beam against pitfalls of geography and the spirit; the sailor who knows his way about would never go venturing ashore without his pocket torch. Ranier's flashlight was in his hand before he crossed the doorsill.

Fog foamed up against the building's front, noiseless, turgid, heavy with the breath of tropic vegetation, the dead fish smell of a warm-water beach. Seaward the vapors had packed like cotton wadding, and conch shells were blowing. Inland, the night was blind as a cataracted eye. Ranier's mind, raw with that Haitian's scream in its nerve centers, calculated the distance to the wharf and the time it would take to row out to the anchored steamer, while his eyes followed the flashlight beam into mist. A searchlight couldn't have penetrated the whiteness, whatever Marcelline had seen would be evaporated.

"A face!" the Haitian was bleating. "It looked

dead—straight at me through the window—eyes—eyes like the shark—waaaaaah—!"

Ranier plunged out across the verandah; started around the corner of the building. Voices clamored after him. Oaths. Shouting. The blond woman had fainted, plopped to the floor. Kavanaugh, trying to catch her, had dropped the Dutchman's body, *thump!* Ranier was relieved to discover no man among the party had followed him out of the café. His shins collided with an unseen bench, and he sidejumped, dancing, the pain clearing his head. He thought, "Great Lord, I couldn't have—!" then sprang back from a looming shadow, swerving the startled flashlight.

Angles of polished metal reflected through the mist—a big black sedan parked under a tree. Must be the car Marcelline had hired for the shore party; a gawky, antiquated seven-passenger Winton, high-roofed as a hearse, with a squeeze-bulb horn at the driver's seat and pre-Prohibition brass-rimmed headlamps.

Ranier stepped to the car; switched on the lamps. Cones of weak light spread out in the billowing steam, illuminating a scant area of ground at the side of the building. Hurriedly Ranier scouted the approach to that yellow-lit side window. Tracks! He swore under his breath. His own tracks straying past the window where he'd limped in somnambulistic daze. And—he scanned them in excitement—the tracks of someone who had walked around the big sedan and stood facing that side window, looking in, stationed almost where Ranier was standing now. He could see the prints clearly in the soggy earth. Too clearly!

For that second set of prints had gone no farther; had come to a stop within six feet of the sill. Then whoever had stood there had retraced his steps around the car, skirted the tree and entered the café by the front door. These tracks had been made, then, by Marcelline when he'd fetched the car a while ago.

Ranier made a frantic and swift inspection with his flashlight. The soft loam near the window would have recorded the prints of a cat.

And there were no other prints. Marcelline's had stopped six feet from the sill; and, as he'd feared, his own tracks were glaringly under the window that had been open at the stabbed man's back. And the only ones there!

For five seconds John Ranier stood tense in the fog, listening. Voices babbled in the café; he could see into the lighted room, but, screened in vapor as he was, those inside could not see him. If Marcelline, looking out, had spied something, then it must have been nearer the window. What could the Haitian have seen? No prints to show what it might have been. Nothing.

WHEELING, RANIER SENT his light in fast looping circles about the sideyard. Toward the building's rear a chicken run, a mass of glistening green banana plantain, the dripping boles of cocoanut palms. Stinkweed and ilex. Nothing had disturbed this boscage. In the steamy heaviness not a leaf stirred.

Hedging the yard, a dense thicket of tall, pole-straight bamboo, too closely wedged for a snake to worm through. From previous visits he could remember a sheer limestone embankment walling up behind the bamboo, steep mountainside beyond. Anything might fade off undetected in this fog but there'd certainly be tracks. Only approach to the café was the donkey road along the beach, and the only tracks there were those imprinted earlier in the evening and by the Winton.

Ranier explored the chicken run; hurried to the rear yard. Goat-pens and garbage. Nothing there. He groped his way along the waterfront side of the building, fumbling through a smell of dead fish toward the verandah. His *own* tracks under that window! If he could only remember! If he could only remember what he'd been doing in that blank interval between the time the German threw him off the verandah and he struck his head, and the moment his mind cleared there in that side yard. Out on his feet, of course. Wandering semi-conscious. Blotto from that head-crack and alcohol. And he couldn't have—

He thought, "Or could I—?" Then pulled himself up, snarling aloud, "Don't be a fool, you left that sailor's-knife in your cabin aboardship, and the man was talking when that tourist crowd came in!" One of them did it. One of that crowd yelling in there did it, but the police—ten to one!—would try to fasten it on him. Steered, of course, by the guilty party.

Inside the café the voices were exploding like a package of firecrackers. "Give him air!"—"I tell you, *messieurs*, I saw a face!"—"Sit down! Sit down!"—"Look here, Brown, you was sitting at his left!"—"I tell you, I never left my chair for a—!" "I'm goin' back to the ship and tell the—!" "Right through his back! Right through his doggone back!"—"It was a dead face at the window, *messieurs*! *Ah, Sacré Nom de Dieu!* A dead face—!"

"The devil it was," Ranier had to say, stepping through the door. "Nothing out there in the soup. If Marcelline saw anything, I'm afraid he imagined it."

His glance scorned the bulgy woman reviving with dramatic energy in a corner; fixed coldly on the body on the floor. Mr. Kavanaugh, Mr. Brown and Mr. Coolidge were kneeling over the wounded man, struggling to remove his coat. Carpetsi cowered near the door, his sable eyes glowing fear in his olive face. In the background, Monsieur Marcelline mopped almost Aryan features with an unsanitary handkerchief, gasping incoherencies. The thin professor of entomology walked as if caged, wringing womanish hands.

John Ranier snapped, "Hyacinth! Bring water!" at the goggle-eyed Negro behind the bar; crossed the floor, shucking his white coat. He was thinking as he rolled up his sleeves, "The Dutchman hasn't a chance in hell. Lost about three quarts of blood. Whoever nailed him with this bunch at table, then sat tight while he was bleeding to death, is a cool customer." It made his neck ache. He was aware of Carpetsi's scared black eyes on his face.

"What you gonna do about it, Doc?"

"Try to stop that hemorrhage." He was about to add, "And you go call the police!" but his lips made a dry, thin line instead. After all, it was none of his business. If one of this bunch wanted to knock off a fellow-tourist in a mosquito-port in Haiti, what was that to John Ranier? Let the ship's captain worry, or the Secretary of State, or whoever it was had jurisdiction over crazy American tourists on foreign soil. The *Garde d'Haiti* would come soon enough. Stick to his own racket—doctor. Seasick pills and tomato juice for nauseated tourists.

But the man on the floor wanted something more than pills and tomato juice. John Ranier observed coolly, looking down, "He'll have to have a transfusion!" and he didn't care much, remembering that clip on the chin. Maybe the bird had clipped somebody else on this trip; got what was coming to him.

He said in a professional tone, "He'll have to go to some local doctor and go fast. Too far to row him out to the ship, and personally I'm not prepared."

"That's what I told you in the first place." Kavanaugh's tone was flat, metallic, authoritative. The Irishman regarded Ranier steadily with cold blue eyes that disliked Ranier's face and told him so. The stare implied Ranier was in need of a shave and clean linen; implied Ranier was a small time ship's doctor unable to manage a practice ashore, probably an alcoholic incompetent. The cold eyes scanned the shoddy sea cap, the soiled uniform; settled on John Ranier's foot. "That's what I said in the first place. He'll have to go to a doctor. You're too lurching drunk to be of—"

Quick crimson flamed in Ranier's cheek. "Lurching, am I? It just happens, mister, that instep was shot out by a Boche machine gun in '18. And by saying I wasn't prepared, I meant I hadn't come ashore prepared to give a transfusion to a man stabbed in the back by a murderer!"

Breath made a sucking noise through the Irishman's teeth. There was a sputter from the blonde; a bitten-off oath from Mr. Coolidge. John Ranier met a battery of angry glares with a shrug. They didn't like that word "murderer," it seemed. He'd pay this smart harp, too, for mentioning his bad foot.

BUT THE FLUSH cooled from his face as his temper relaxed. What did it matter if they thought him an incompetent pill-disher relegated to a ship? Nothing mattered when nothing was worth doing because nothing was worth anything. If anything was worth the trouble, right now, it was getting rid of this knifing affair before the police lost the point in a game of questions and answers.

He said to Kavanaugh with professional brusqueness, "This hardly seems the time to bicker, does it? If you wouldn't mind lending me a clean handkerchief, and I'll donate my shirt. All of you gentlemen. You there, Professor, if you'll rescue that basin from Hyacinth before he slops it all. Mr. Brown, will you lift his head? We can lay him on the table—"

The wound proved interesting.

Ranier managed a compress with skilled hands while his mind revolved on the puzzle of how a man could have been stabbed like this at a crowded table. Powerful blow to drive a blade so deep; knife double-edged, razor-honed, and must have been buried to the hilt. Short-circuited a vertebra to cut off the brain telegraph, ossifying the body to stone.

Slumped there full of *aguardiente,* the Dutchman mightn't have made a sound, anyway, and this toadstabber had gone in like a bullet, paralyzed him stiffer than *rigor mortis.* By the looks, it wouldn't be long before *rigor mortis,* either.

"He'll be with the angels by midnight," Ranier observed with forced geniality, looking up at the blond woman as he tied a bandage. "I don't suppose you're carrying any iodine or mercurochrome in your handbag?"

Lips compressed, she shook her head. He wondered what she was carrying in that bead bag gripped in her hands. Her hands, he noticed, were a lot older than her face. Looked, somehow, like her lips—compressed, defensive. It would take a lot to open her lips or that bag if she didn't

want them opened. But a bloody knife would have leaked a stain through the bead-mesh; and even if she had been sitting at the Dutchman's end of the table, a little nearer than Brown who'd been at his other side, she couldn't have done it. No woman could reach around behind a man's chair and drive in a knife like that. Or could one?

But her build looked flabby as the mumps, and that blade had been powered with muscle.

"No antiseptics among you?" Ranier's dried smile traveled to Brown—that moon face sweating like icebox butter. He'd seen men sweat like that before. From strain. And anybody was entitled to go yellowish when the man at his elbow has just been quietly stabbed.

Or had Brown put that glad hand of his around behind this Dutchman's chair? Then thrown the knife out of the window? Ten feet to the sill, though, and certainly such a toss would have been seen. No knife out there in the mud.

"Great Maker!" the fat man blurted. "He was sitting right next to me. Right there at the head of the table. It might've been me. *Me—!*"

"I'd like something to pour on this stab wound," Ranier interrupted the outcry. "You wouldn't have some American whisky in your coat, Mr. Brown. Any of you? Then I'm afraid I'll have to use this impure Haitian stuff. God knows what's in it."

Kavanaugh moved around the table. "God knows there's plenty of it in *you!*" he snapped at Ranier. "You realize if the man dies from this delay you'll be held responsible?"

"You mean one of *you* will be held responsible. Fellow's almost certain to die of tetanus in this country, even if he does survive hemorrhage." Turning his back on the Irishman's showy belligerence, he put an ear to the wounded man's chest. Not much blood left in that faint-tapping pump. He studied the Dutchman's white, unconscious face. "Transfusion or not, I don't think he'll live out the night. We can move him as soon as the bleeding stops." He looked around curiously. "He was going with you on a motor tour, wasn't he?"

"At my invitation," Kavanaugh said harshly.

"Or, rather, he asked if he could join us. Professor Schlitz wanted to come, and since Haarman was sharing the professor's stateroom—"

The thin man's mouth opened in a high-pitched outburst that dislodged the pince-nez from his nose. "I didn't do it. He was my cabin-mate, but I didn't do it! No, no, no! I hardly conversed with the man at any time on the cruise. I never saw him before until the first night on board. Why did I beg to come on this shore excursion? I'm an insectologist—yes!—my first vacation in years—from Upsala College—I don't know him—I didn't do it—" Sinking to the edge of a chair, he mopped his narrow face, staring wildly. "You don't think I did it, do you?"

"I didn't ask who did," Ranier reminded coolly.

Brown panted out, "None of us knew him before this cruise. In fact, I never seen any of these people until the cruise, myself. I—we—" He swallowed, looked about apprehensively.

RANIER TOOK A bottle of rum from the table, shook his head doubtfully; shifted the wounded man's position, poured the liquor into the crimson-soaked bandage. From the corner of his eye he noticed an interesting expression on the face of Mr. Coolidge. Doorknob ears, gold-plated teeth, squinty eyes, the face followed Ranier's every move with the brute concentration of a mastiff watching a cat that might jump. The squinty eyes caught Ranier's surveillance. The big man sidled up, and put a hand the size of a ballplayer's mitt gently on John Ranier's shoulder.

"You don't think one of *us* knifed this guy in hot blood, do you, pal? You wouldn't be thinkin' nothin' like that? It would get on my nerves."

"Certainly not, Mr. Coolidge." Ranier didn't look around. "You can see for yourself; Mr. Haarman tried to commit suicide."

The fingers on his shoulder tightened viciously. "Don't get funny, Sawbones. This dinge Marcelline says he seen a face out there in the fog. A face, get it? There's th' mug who dunked a knife in Haarman. Pitched it through the window at him, see?"

"And it jumped back out of the window, Mr. Coolidge."

Ranier was whirled to face the man's brilliant teeth. "Listen, quack! If you're gonna start a story that one of my friends here was playin' mumbledy-peg with Haarman, I'll slap your damn—"

Kavanaugh shouted, "Shut up, Coolidge!" catching the big man's elbow, jerking him aside. "We'll talk to the right authorities when we see them."

"Authorities will never catch he who used knife." It was Marcelline's voice, mediumistic in his blue-shadowed throat. The Creole was crystal-gazing at the door where the fog creamed, his features gray as stale fudge. "It was a dead face I saw, *messieurs. Mort de bon Dieu!* A face all streaming hair—sightless eyes—"

John Ranier pointed the empty rum bottle angrily. "Rot! There wasn't anybody out there nor anywhere near the café. The knife that stabbed Mr. Haarman must be somewhere right here in this room!"

SOMEWHERE RIGHT HERE in the room, perhaps nestling under somebody's sport coat or cuddling up a sleeve, waiting, watching, biding its time, measuring the distance to John Ranier's own spinal cord. He didn't fancy that. It didn't mix with *aguardiente,* and his digestion was beginning to feel it. He suppressed a hiccup, shifting his position so that his back was toward nobody in the vicinity, and found himself confronted by Mr. Kavanaugh who was facing him combatively, feet apart, eyes directed from under slanted hat brim, levelling that finger at Ranier in the manner of a "You Buy Liberty Bonds" poster.

Mr. Kavanaugh did not say, "Buy Liberty Bonds." He said flatly, "The knife ought to be around, Dr. Ranier, but it seems that it isn't. While you were outside just now, we made a search. Mr. Brown, Mr. Coolidge and Mr. Carpetsi permitted me to go through their apparel; and Professor Schlitz allowed us to search him. Since Marcelline was sitting at the far end of the table, he is obviously eliminated. I'll stand personally responsible for Miss May, here; she's quite unarmed. And since we're all going to be under suspicion in this mess, I allowed my friends to frisk me. Is that right, Brown?"

The plump tourist gulped, "That's a fact. There ain't so much as a penknife on any of us."

Kavanaugh aimed his finger at John Ranier's chin. "No, we didn't find any knives. What we did find out may interest you. Our friend the bartender there," he tossed his chin obliquely to indicate the bar, "our friend the bartender crashed through with the information that *you* were in the café here when Mr. Haarman first came in. The bartender says he was out in back, but he heard you havin' a quarrel. That was a half hour or so before the rest of us got here. The bartender says you went outside in front for a while, and then you came back in and sneaked into that alcove, there, where nobody could see you. Interested?"

"No," Ranier said. "Hyacinth was partly right. Mr. Haarman swaggered in here like a boiled owl and took a pass at me. Matter of fact, got pretty ugly. Shoved me out on the verandah. I didn't sneak back into that alcove, but walked there to avoid further annoyance and mind my own business. Haarman sat right here where he was sitting when you came in. He was all right when you met him here, wasn't he?"

Kavanaugh said in a hard voice, "He looked bad when we got here."

"He looked a hell of a lot worse after you'd been here a while," Ranier countered evenly. "And he looks rotten, now. But I'm not interested. It's none of my affair which one of you stabbed Mr. Haarman. As ship's doctor, I'm responsible to you people only when you're aboard; but I'll be called as a witness and expected to make a report on this case, and I'm going to make one."

He didn't tell the tall man his stomach felt

gone because he'd hunted through the wounded man's clothing under pretense of physical examination, and the knife wasn't concealed on Haarman, either. It made his diaphragm contract when he turned his back on Kavanaugh; bent over the table to inspect the bandaging. When he rounded on the Irishman again, he was holding two rumpled envelopes in his hand. One of the envelopes was smeared as if by red ink.

"These letters were in Haarman's hip pocket. He doesn't seem to have a wallet, but there's fifty *gourds* change in his trousers. I'll turn these letters over for Haarman's identification when I go aboard ship."

LIFTING THE STAINED envelope toward the light, he read the typewritten address, postmarked ten days before in New York—*Leo Haarman—Murray Hill Hotel.* He was about to tuck the letter in his pocket when his eye caught a name scrawled in pencil across one blood-stained corner, some jotted figures. The pencilled name was "Eberhardt"; and the jotted figures looked like stock market quotations—"4,000,000 m.—1,000,000 $." Hastily, and without reading these cryptic jottings to his audience, he stowed the letters in his tunic.

"You'll witness my taking them. I'll turn them over to the captain when I go aboard. Meantime," he told Kavanaugh, "I've done all I can for Mr. Haarman. One who did this job can rest assured the assassination's a success. He won't survive this phlebotomy, if you know what I mean."

The blond woman said hoarsely, "Ohmygod—ohmygod—!" closing her goitrous eyes as if she knew what he meant; and John Ranier turned for a last inspection of the Dutchman's pulse. Packing had stopped the hemorrhage, but the man was probably bleeding internally. Ranier picked up the almost lifeless hand. Dangerous to move him with the count that slow. Almost out. He stooped over the dying man's wrist, suddenly curious about a scar, brown and faded, on the man's damp palm.

Cut by a knife a long time ago, the scar looked like a brand. As if someone had branded that palm with the letter Z. Ranier moved stony eyes to the Dutchman's death-mask face. Violence in the past had marked his palm; had that deadly pallor of Haarman's—no whiter now than it had been on shipboard—come from fear or tuberculosis?

He pinched the man's index finger between his own thumb and forefinger. You could sometimes detect tuberculosis by a splayed condition of the finger-tips.

He said, without looking up, "I think this man was a con—" meaning to say "a consumptive"; but the sentence was rudely short-circuited by a hand collaring his neck-nape; wrenching him about-face from the table.

It was Kavanaugh's hand, and the Irishman behind it looked mad. Slanted hat brim and out-thrust jaw; eyelids almost closed, and the pupils glinting like nail-heads centered in the iris.

"What do you care what he was? Don't you think you've stalled around here long enough? Trying to let the man die? We're getting him out of here now—right now!" the tall man gritted out, releasing his hold on Ranier to flash a hand into his waterproof, extract a wallet, snap out a card.

"My name and address if you happen to think you want to bring any charges. David C. Kavanaugh, Caribbean-American Sugar Company, New York. Get this, Ranier. I'm due on important business in Port-au-Prince tomorrow. I'd arranged to drive overland tonight and these tourists—Haarman included—were going with me for the ride. You can check all this with the purser on the ship, but you're not going to muff this murder affair any longer."

He jabbed his finger at the doorway. "If you're smart you'll hike out of here and report what's happened to the ship's captain. You can also report you were in here stewed when this happened and in no condition to handle an emergency case. If you don't report at all— I guess we'll know who did this job. If you do go back, tell your skipper I took charge. I'll see

these people are under proper surveillance, and we'll all go together to the police; but first I'm takin' Haarman to a hospital, and the whole crowd's going with me."

He trained his finger at Marcelline. "*You!* Go out an' start that car! You—" at the black man saucer-eyed behind the bar—"where's the nearest hospital in this mud hole? The nearest doctor?"

"*Hôpital Médecin?*" Hyacinth Lucien ogled the body on the table; groaned. The man's black face shone like a dancing shoe while his fingers dabbled prayerfully with a little cloth packet of castor-beans, hair, rooster feathers and toenail parings—an *ouanga* charm suspended under his throat. "But there is one hospital, *monsieur,* five miles on the road that runs north from the village. Half way up the *morne.* The doctor, a white man, has been there many years. The name is Dr. Eberhardt."

Kavanaugh started for the door. "Brown— Carpetsi—Coolidge! For God's sake, don't just stand! Let's get Haarman under way! Daisy, go out and get into that car. Professor, you go with her!" Over the shoulder at Ranier, "Are you going, or not? Somebody ought to row out to that barge and bring back the captain. She was posted to sail at nine, and you won't have much time, either. We'll be waiting at this hospital— Dr. Eberhardt's. Get it?"

John Ranier nodded calmly. He was thinking: "Eberhardt? Eberhardt?" wondering where he'd heard the name before. There was a commotion at the table as Brown struggled with Haarman's inert shoulders, and Coolidge and Carpetsi wrestled with the Dutchman's soggy legs.

Then Kavanaugh was shouting again. "I told you to start the car, Marcelline! What in hell are you waiting for?"

Ranier looked up to discover that something had happened to the well-dressed Haitian's urbanity. Posed in the doorway, Monsieur Marcelline was peering out at the night, his lower lip hanging, body bowed forward, one hand cupped behind an ear. The sclerotics of his eyes were yellow butterplates beneath the brim of his Panama; his voice a ventriloquial squeak from the pit of his stomach.

"Listen—!"

FAR OUT IN night, echoes muffled in fog, a pulse had started beating. A pulse almost as faint as the heart beat of the man who was dying on that café table. When the wind stirred the fog to cloudy churning, the sound loudened; when the breeze petered out and the fog hung in the torpor of yeast, there was scarcely more than a tremor in the night.

Tumpy-bum-bum—Tumpy-bum-bum—

"Drums!" Marcelline whispered. "Drums of Damballa! Drums to ward off the un-dead dead who walk the jungles on silent feet! Drums to ward off *zombies*—*!*"

"Dave," the woman called Daisy screamed, "I'm going to scream!"

"You fool!" Kavanaugh's palm went stiff-armed into Marcelline's shoulder, catapulting the Haitian across the doorsill. "Get out there and drive that car! Come on, the rest of you! We're taking Haarman to the hospital!"

A floundering rush as Carpetsi, Coolidge and Brown, hats awry, faces sweat-oiled, hustled Haarman's sagging body out of the door. Kavanaugh's sharp commands rapping out through the mist. Doors banging on the Winton. Cough of an engine breaking into a rhythmic chugging. With that uproar outside, the café seemed empty as a hall.

In quick stealth Ranier dropped to one knee, sped a glance under the long table. The knife he had expected to find jabbed into the underside of the table, tucked under one of the chairs, somewhere on the floor, wasn't there. A last hurried scrutiny of the room; blank adobe walls, two lizards on the ceiling, Hyacinth Lucien rooted like a black cigar-store Indian behind the bar, the room's mirrored picture in that dim back-bar looking glass. No place for a knife to hide. Nothing.

He swerved; went swiftly to the door.

Out on the fog-smothered road the clumsy sedan was backing to turn around. Gears clashing. Saffron eyes wheeling in mist. A glimpse of scared faces crowded behind glass. Daisy's voice falsetto, demanding, "Dave Kavanaugh, if you're jamming me into this car with a murderer—!" A window cranking down, and Kavanaugh's face glaring out at Ranier.

"I advise you to bring back that captain! Don't forget! Dr. Eberhardt's—"

Eberhardt!

Something clicked in the foreground of John Ranier's memory. That was the name jotted on the envelope from Haarman's hip pocket. Along with that notation—four million m, one million dollar-sign. Had Haarman, himself, scribbled that cryptogram? An untutored German might write a million dollars like that. A million dollars! Eberhardt! Name too unusual for coincidence—

Sea-ward the fog gave echo to a deep-throated, funneling *rhooooooom!* The call hung trembling in the waterlogged air. Half hour to sailing time! John Ranier cried to Kavanaugh, "I'll get to the ship! See you later!"

The Winton lunged by his vision, going into second with a clashy roar. Mud spouted in brown streaks from the wheels. Kavanaugh jerked his head. A clot of mire spatted Ranier across the mouth as the Winton's rear end rocked by, sending him back in a recoil. Then he flung himself forward as if launched from a springboard. Head lowered, arms stretched; threw himself through flying mud at the ruby tail light of the sedan, catching with sure hands the spare-tire frame.

Not for nothing had John Ranier spent a boyhood on the streets of a city clogged with taxicabs. As the Winton spurted into high, he was sitting in the spare tire, back wedged as if in a life preserver, neck bent, arms hooked around the rim, knees pulled up, heels skimming the road. Fog whirled in the car's wake, and the doorway of Hyacinth Lucien's Blue Kitty Café was a banana-yellow adrift in mist, diminishing down the beach.

Nobody in the car was looking back, so John

Ranier was the only one to see Hyacinth Lucien's shadow flick out of the café door and go racing off towards jungle and invisibility.

CHAPTER IV

THE GIRL AT EBERHARDT'S

Haitian roads were never surfaced for joy-riding. This one following the beach was little better than a wagon track, deep water-filled ruts and unexpected potholes threatening any minute to overturn the skidding sedan. On one side, banks of foliage and sharp palmetto lashed at the fenders; on the other, the beach sloped down-grade into blackness and combing surf. The headlights gave glimpses of phosphorescent water slopping along the sand under the fog. Decaying marine life smelled dank green.

John Ranier, clinging to the spare tire of a 1919 Winton—a sedan occupied by a dying man and his murderer—told himself he was a fool. *Aguardiente* and that hieroglyphic notation had gotten him into this—the name Eberhardt plus the one million, dollar-sign. That fatal suggestion of money! A million dollars! Anybody ought to know by this time there wasn't that much money in the world, and those figures penciled on that envelope probably meant no more than the jotted name. Haarman, before coming ashore tonight, had doubtless asked the ship's captain the name of the local doctor; written it down. As for the figures, people were always scribbling. As for the *aguardiente*—that was bad. Bad.

If he could only see through that blind-spot where he'd been wandering while outside that open window. Hyacinth might tell the police that quarrel story; Kavanaugh certainly would. That settled it, right there. He'd have to stick with this surprise party to clear himself, as much for his own peace of mind as anything. Not that he could've stabbed Haarman, but—you could do strange things while you were unconscious.

But a minute later he was regretting the decision, cursing himself for a fool. He spat a mouthful of wet sand as the Winton took a curve, and clung to his scanty perch with numb arms. Puddle water, gravel, dead fish, seashells all blew up between his knees, and his troublesome foot throbbed. Why the devil had he obeyed an impulse to grab this car? Footprints under a window weren't circumstantial evidence to anything. Thing to do was drop off in the village and go straight to the *Gendarmerie*.

The superstitious Haitian at the wheel was driving like a maniac. . . .

If big money was behind this fandango Ranier figured he was a double sucker for sticking in his oar. Whoever had poked that knife into Mr. Haarman, then vanished the blade under the noses of his table companions back there in that café, was not only a magician but a chap who meant business. A killer familiar with his stuff. Someone in this sedan was laughing with a knife up his sleeve, while his other sleeve was probably supporting his victim.

It was as good a theory as any other possible one.

Ranier cranked his bent neck to look up at the sedan's rear window. Curtain was down. He could visualize the jam in there; Haarman doubled up on the rear cushions; the others crouching together, shoulders colliding as the car bounced over the ruts, eyes glaring at each other. He could hear nothing but the streaming wind, the spinning whine of the tires above the roar of the exhaust. Clutching his sea cap, he waited hopefully for a chance to drop off—the hell with this. But the Winton wasn't slowing down.

He could see nothing of the Gulf of Gonaives, and he wondered if the bay was still there. No sign of the cruise ship's gangway lights. Either the vessel had wheeled in the tide, or she was already standing out to sea. The Old Man wasn't the skipper to hold up sailing for late arrivals. He couldn't have made the ship, anyway, with a mile's row to her anchorage, but he might have had sense enough to keep clear of this sedan.

So he hung on. Weaving like an ark in a storm, the clumsy car swerved on a break-neck curve, wheeled through a cloud of mud, hit a stretch of gravel, roared across the loose planks of a bridge.

THE VILLAGE WAS gone before John Ranier realized they were beyond it. Crooked windows yellow with misty candlelight; pale adobe walls leaning at crazy angles; thatched roofs. Loose-hipped Negroes lounging in dim doorways, watching the car go by with the whites of their eyes. Dark storefronts gray-shuttered against the fog, their slatternly galleries overhanging the wooden sidewalks, kinky-headed Negresses looking down. Mules lined up at a hitching rail. *Bureau de Poste.* A weed-grown *parc* where the statue of Toussaint L'Ouverture clapped a cockaded hat to breast and sadly regarded the village's neglect and decay. The arched doorway of a *brasserie* where Haitians in straw sombreros looked up from marble-topped tables to gape at a white man hanging to a spare tire. *"Blanc!"* John Ranier caught snatches of outcry. *"Cochon! Tiens la—"* Black shadows and shanties huddled like toadstools.

In the weaving mist everything steamed, dripped. Palm-fronds were islands suspended in watery upper currents and patches of candleshine came through cracked shutters and seemed to float. Some scared pickaninnies huddled around the cinnamon smudge of a bonfire. An enormous Mammy with a kerosene can perched on her turban, a rooster under her arm, hugged against a Mother Goose picket fence and shook her fist and Creole imprecations after the speeding car. Swaying recklessly on a turn, the fender at Ranier's elbow scraped the hub of a two-wheeled cart, and Ranier cursed almost as frantically as the crone who shrieked from the driver's seat. *Bankety-bank-bank-bank* across a second bridge. A fleeting glimpse into the blue-walled courtyard of a building marked *Gendarmerie* where a black soldier in faded brown canvas leaned yawning on his rifle. A vine-covered railway shed and *wham-slam* across the glistening metals of a grade crossing; then the car was tunneling white night on open road, jungle sweeping by on both sides.

John Ranier set his teeth. Anyone should know better than to give a Haitian the wheel of a car. That fellow Marcelline would kill them all, and Mr. Haarman, who wanted gentle handling, must certainly be already dead from that bumping along the beach.

Improved highway was worse. The tires hummed on new macadam, axles screeching with strain at every curve. Cramped in a hoop of rubber, John Ranier could see nothing of the road save the little patch illuminated by the tail light, shiny and wet, a streak of black silk that whistled rearward under his heels and slipped aft into formless vapor.

The road climbed and wound. Now the village window-lights were a cluster of luminous oranges adrift to the left and below in pooling haze; gone. Where the devil was that black Barney Oldfield driving them? Five miles north to the hospital, Hyacinth Lucien had said. But Haitians were as careless with time and distance as they were with the speedometer of a car; five miles on a road in Haiti could be fifty to a white man, especially when the map was obscured in wool-thick mist and you were going sixty miles an hour on a spare tire. John Ranier suffered a certainty the Winton had left the road and was racing off into the sky. Monsieur Marcelline had missed a curve in the night and was steering for the moon. Lucky no celestial pedestrians were afoot on this cloudy highway; their fate would have been the same as that skunk's back there, no more than a brief acrid whiff in the nostrils. *Creeeeee*—another hairpin turn like that and the hack would lose a wheel. Presently they should sight the north star, for Ranier saw they'd just passed the Pleiades.

He marked the constellation clearly as it whizzed aft in blank space, a little cluster of twinkles above the road on an invisible hill, like candles burning on some cosmic birthday cake. Ranier wondered what the captain of the cruise ship would say when he explained his absence by claiming he'd whizzed by the Pleiades on a worn-out Firestone tire. "Drunk again!" probably. And, "You're fired." That red-jowled navigator would never believe the entrance to the famous constellation was a ghostly roadside arch marked "Cemetery" and the Pleiades were not stars but candles keeping vigil in a lonesome Haitian graveyard.

THE ROAD DIPPED, climbed, swerved. Blackness swept in behind the car, rushed by on both sides. Night mixed with fog and ceiling zero, all landmarks vanished. Ranier could guess the forest without seeing it; could sense the cliffs of timber massed on either side of the road, walls of vine, underbrush, close-packed trunks looming blacker than the darkness. He'd been smart, all right. If this relic didn't leap an unnoticed precipice he'd end up in mountain wilderness, miles from anywhere in Caribbean jungle with a party of panic-stricken tourists, a dead man and a homicidal expert who made butcher knives disappear in thin air. These Haitian limberlosts would be duck soup for anyone with criminal talent, and that glimpse of the village below with its yawning *Gendarmerie* had not been any reassurance. In a republic which beat goatskin drums to ward off wandering dead men, the law might be equally phantasmal. Haarman's assassin had certainly picked his spot.

Or was Haarman's assassin a her? That peroxide blonde didn't look capable of anything worse than kissing a Pekingese or gobbling four pounds of bonbons in a lace bed littered with pink ribbons and tabloids. Still, these faded violets were the tantrum type. There'd been that blood-letting in Philadelphia—back in the old ambulance-interne days. Dame looked soft as a bag of marshmallows, and cut her husband's throat from ear to ear. And Daisy had been seated nearest this case—

Brown next nearest, yet the Ohio real estate man (somewhere on the cruise he'd dropped remarks about Columbus and real estate) looked more overweight than dangerous, too. Golf knickers and dumpling cheeks didn't go with knives;

and murderers, of course, seldom looked the part. But Mr. Brown didn't seem the sort to stab his fellow-man in the back.

Nor did Professor Schlitz appear capable of any violence greater than sticking a bug on a hatpin. Too jittery for this cool-blooded job. Spent his life classifying butterflies and lecturing on mosquitoes at some obscure college, reciting limericks for relaxation. Those pince-nez spectacled eyes weren't the eyes of a killer. If they'd reflected the truth—

Carpetsi, on the other hand, fitted the part. Something oily and unsavory about the Broadway boy, and truth wasn't in his Latin eyeballs. But courage wasn't, either, and he'd been sitting too far down the table. While Mr. Coolidge of the cauliflowered ears, Mack truck jaw and monkey brow—a specimen who looked willing to choke his grandmother to death if the price was right—had been seated even farther away.

That left Marcelline and Kavanaugh. Inside the café, the dusky Haitian had sat at table's head, quite beyond knife-reach; he'd gone outside once to fetch the car, park it near the door and stand gazing into the window at Haarman's chair. Nothing in that. Six feet from the window his tracks had halted, and it was another ten feet inside to that fatal chair. You couldn't stab a man sitting sixteen feet away. But you might see blood on his chair-back, and you might walk into the room afterwards and talk about something else. The *Garde d'Haiti*, when and if they came, would do well to cross examine Monsieur Marcelline.

And they might find an Irishman in the woodpile. If anyone in this tourist batch looked competent to engineer someone's demise, the narrow-lipped Kavanaugh did. He'd admittedly organized the shore party, and Mr. Haarman had joined the ride on Mr. Kavanaugh's invitation. The man had a cold, direct eye and a cool alibi, and by midnight would probably be in touch with a lawyer. There was a ruthless self-assurance in this sugar company executive which made him appear quite capable of severing another's spinal cord with nicety and aplomb. Mentally, John Ranier shook his head. Characters under suspicion always turned out to be innocent, didn't they? At least it was that way in mystery plays. Only this wasn't any mystery play, and Kavanaugh, two chairs down the table from Haarman, hadn't left his seat throughout the evening.

Hyacinth Lucien had served a last round of drinks, Ranier remembered, then retired to his bottle-washing behind the bar. He couldn't possibly have juggled a knife and a tray of rum-glasses at the same time. There it was. No one could have done it. Someone had. When had that blade whisked in and out of the Dutchman's back? Hard to tell, because he'd begun that paralytic stare in the forepart of the evening, before the others came in. What had been the matter with him then? Why had he thrown Ranier out?

John Ranier decided with an oath as the Winton's tires screeled on a curve, that he didn't give a damn who stabbed that Dutchman—that he'd let his imagination get away with him—and that he'd drop out the minute this joy-ride slowed to forty an hour.

HIS DECISION TO drop out, right then, was taken out of his hands. *Screeee—am!* Jammed brakes gave out a stench of burning grease as the car took a side road on two wheels; *thump!* A sudden halt flung John Ranier from his perch and left him sitting upright on a roadway that was certainly not paved with clouds. There could be no doubt about it; the car and John Ranier were on solid ground.

Twelve feet beyond him the sedan smoked to a halt; voices broke loose in the night. Too dazed for action other than spitting a dislodged tooth, John Ranier sat on burning posterior while his vision cleared. Black shrubbery hedged the driveway where he'd come to earth; there was the vegetal sultriness, the close-hemmed feeling of jungle around. The sedan had stopped before a screened verandah that fronted a long, two-story frame building, the wings of which stretched off into misting darkness. Headlights

of the car streamed through murk to finger through the verandah screen and circle the front door with a wan luminescence.

John Ranier saw the building was painted white, and unlike the average country place in Haiti showed evidence of being in repair. A planter's villa from the old days, judging by the gingerbread and gargoyles running around the upper gallery. Great sablier trees extended moss-bearded limbs above the gallery rail, and in the drifting scud, opalescent with ghostly rays diffused from the car lights, the dark roof-line seemed to swim along in the night.

He saw a light in an upper window, as if someone were studying late.

He saw there was a pale lamp burning in the reception hall.

He saw a neat, black-lettered sign on the front door—*Ludwig Eberhardt, Docteur en Médecine.*

He saw the doors burst open on the Winton; Kavanaugh leaped to the ground, raced to the verandah, and started an urgent pounding on the door. Excitement shrilled from the car; the knocks echoed off into the drugged mountain stillness; it seemed a long three minutes before Ranier saw the door come open.

A girl was standing there. A slim girl, cool in a white linen dressing robe, with a gray tabby cat hugged in her arms. The car lights brushed gleams from tumbled, brown-gold hair, caught the blue of wide eyes in a cool tanned face, the carmine red of lips parted a little in surprise.

John Ranier scarcely heard Kavanaugh's rapping, authoritative outburst. "Let us in! Quickly! Been an accident! Man out here's dying—"

John Ranier saw the girl standing there in the door-frame facing Kavanaugh, and *aguardiente* or not, his heart skipped four beats and left him icy sober. Suddenly he knew that whether he wanted to or no, he wasn't going to leave that girl facing Mr. Kavanaugh and Daisy, Professor Schlitz and Monsieur Marcelline, Mr. Brown, Mr. Coolidge and Mr. Carpetsi with the remains of Mr. Haarman on this lonely mountainside in Haiti.

CHAPTER V

SOMETHING TERRIBLE—

Canvas shoes made no sound on gravel as they moved John Rainer across the driveway, and melted, unobserved, in the shadowy brush. In a bed of rank tropical fern, he crouched, listening, eyes on the sedan, the house. One thing was plausible. If anyone in that party was secreting a knife, he'd get rid of it before police were summoned; the nooks and crannies of that 1919 Winton would be logical for the hiding of cutlery. Ranier told himself he'd feel better when he located that knife, and his first move would be to search the sedan.

Then he heard Kavanaugh's shouting. "Hurry it, can't you? The man's bleeding to death! For God's sake, Daisy, get out of the way, and if you're going to faint again, get into the house where the young lady can look after you! Hold his head, Professor! Brown, you and Carpetsi help carry him. Coolidge, stay out there in the car with Marcelline. The girl says there's no telephone here, and you may have to drive back to the village for the police—"

Ranier muttered under his breath, parting the ferns before his face for a better view. She was holding open the screen to admit the scramble that charged across the driveway carrying Haarman; but Kavanaugh's tall shoulders, in front of her, blocked Ranier's sight.

Emitting a babble of sticky sobs, the Daisy woman was first to reach the verandah where, feminine-fashion, she lost no time in having a nervous breakdown. Ranier could hear the girl's voice low in quick sympathy as she put an arm around the weeping Broadway belle and led her into the dim hall. A stampede of feet on the verandah as Schlitz, Carpetsi and Brown blundered Haarman's body to the door, leaving in their track a spotty, winding trail, as if they'd been carrying between them a cake of drippy ice.

From somewhere in a back hall the girl's voice called: "This room. In here—"

Kavanaugh shouted back at the car: "Do as I told you, you two! We'll be in the emergency room with Haarman. I'll talk to this doctor. Ten minutes at the longest—"

"Take your time," Coolidge called. "We'll be on the job."

The door slammed. In the mountain's stillness only the muffled chugging of the car. Then the engine was cut off, the headlamps switched out; the silence was absolute. Ranier listened. He could hear no sound from the house. He peered in the direction of the car. In swimming blackness, Winton and its two remaining passengers might have been absorbed. A match broke this illusion; a brief blue-red splutter which showed Mr. Coolidge standing on the running board lighting a cigarette, his eyes under jaunty cap brim fixedly regarding the villa's front. He moved his head casually to speak down to Marcelline whose face was thrust from the driver's seat. There was a conversational murmur too subdued for Ranier to catch; the match died; there was only the spark of a cigarette some dozen paces away.

Ranier turned his attention to the hazed silhouette of the house. Except for the hall lamp and that yellow upper window, the villa remained in darkness, which meant Haarman had been hustled to some room at the back. No chance to go knife-hunting with those two watchdogs waiting in the sedan, but he might get a look at what was happening in Dr. Eberhardt's. Carefully he started through the ferns. Fog curled around him; invisible tentacles of moisture fingering his face. His movements whispered in the watery underbrush. A marshy odor, heavy with the scent of jungle plants; the air too torpid for breathing. Like picking your way along the weed-grown bottom of an aquarium. It was dark going with a feeling there might be snakes.

UNREASONABLY, HE FELT a lot better when he skirted the trunk of a sablier, lofted like an apparition in the night, and put the wing of the verandah between himself and the spark of Coolidge's cigarette. Looking back from the corner of the villa, he could see nothing. The side of the villa sprawled along a slope where the scrub had been cleared and there seemed to be a lawn.

Feeling his way along the dark sidewall, he moved swiftly under a row of black windows that were probably hospital rooms. When he paused to consider a black obstruction that was only a thick-trunked, lily-padded vine, he thought he could detect an odor of formaldehyde. The thick breath of a sick room. Smell of leprosy? What sort of place would this Dr. Eberhardt be running here?

Voices!

John Ranier flattened himself against the wall.

—"Lay him on his back. The pressure stops, sometimes, the bleeding. A knife, you say? How terrible! In a moment this hot water will be on, and the doctor should be here from his laboratory. If one of you would just start removing those bandages—" The girl's voice. Drifting around . . . the corner of the building from somewhere at the rear. Hurried, yet controlled, with a faint throat-huskiness shading into the least foreign accent. Somehow John Ranier knew her voice would be like that.

Daisy's voice: "Ohmygod, it's awful. That terrible road up the mountain. This awful country. I thought we'd never get here alive. I thought we'd go off the road. I want to get out of here. I—I—I—"

Brown's voice: "Y'see we was all in this café havin' a few drinks before we started to drive to Port-au-Prince, and poor Haarman just sittin' there with his back to a window, and—"

Kavanaugh's voice: "Save it for the police, Brown. And can't you hurry Dr. Eberhardt, miss? If this man dies—"

The voices came more distinctly as Ranier stole along the sidewalk; at the corner of the building he stopped with a gasp. Light washed through the screen of a window at the back, spread out fan-wise in the fog-drift. The window was broad and open; by standing away a lit-

tle and craning his neck, Ranier, concealed in a clump of Poinsettias, had an unobstructed view of the brightly lighted room. Two hurricane lamps with nickel reflectors shed a glare from white-washed walls that made faces bent over an operating table look greenish and unnatural. Brown, Carpetsi and Schlitz were fumbling with Haarman, who lay face up on the cushioned table, which was in the middle of the room. Kavanaugh, his coat open, belts dangling, stood with a cigarette in a doorway to a corridor. Daisy, her hat on her knees, hair in haystack disarray over cornflower eyes, sniveled make-up and tears into a handkerchief and worked a rocking chair in a corner. The sleeves of her linen robe rolled to the elbow, the slim girl stood at the taps of a washstand at the side, her back to the room, talking over her shoulder above the pour of running water.

To Ranier, familiar with the scrupulous tile of Bellevue and asceptic glass of Johns Hopkins, the room looked hopelessly inadequate and third rate—combination war-time dressing station, country doctor's office and old-fashioned apothecary shop. A shelf laden with a barber-shop assortment of colored bottles. Tin cabinet of surgical instruments. The outmoded operating table a cross between a dentist's chair and an ironing board. Moths blundered around the lamps and some dead insects clung to the window screen. Dr. Eberhardt's hospital was evidently not up with the Mayo Brothers.

But there was nothing wrong with the way that girl handled herself. Ranier liked the practiced way she scoured her hands; shook back her gold-glinted hair. Nurse's training. Lining up the case for the doctor. Not her first emergency; and a girl had stuffing to take up nursing in one of these tropic backwaters. Ranier liked that. He liked the firm brown look of sun-tanned arms, and the slim curves revealed by the tight-drawn robe. He didn't like the way Kavanaugh stood smoking, looking at her.

"Can't you ring for that doctor again?"

She nodded; reached for a push-button like a doorbell set in the wall. "He always comes at once when I ring it. If he is working hard, though, sometimes he does not hear the first time. He will come."

Schlitz turned from the table, unclasping his pince-nez. His eyes looked pink in a pinched face. "The bandages are undone. My God," his voice shook with appeal, "who would have thought this terrible consequence would have resulted from our planned shore excursion. Poor Mr. Haarman! Stabbed! Why," his voice shrilled as if it had just occurred to him, "with no more compunction than one might impale a Lepidoptera—"

"We'll all be murdered!" the sobs burst from Daisy. "I just knew something dreadful would happen when—"

Brown's voice chattered, "Honest to God, Kavanaugh—"

"Miss," Kavanaugh snapped at the girl, "will you ring for that doctor, again? Are you sure he's in?"

Her hand was on the call bell. "I was upstairs in my room asleep when you came," Ranier heard her tell Kavanaugh. "I saw a light under his door as I ran downstairs. I do not think he would go out and leave the laboratory light."

"*Nnnnnnyuh!*" The groan was a sound that startled the room.

Carpetsi leapt back from the table, white-lipped. "The guy's comin' around—"

"He ain't dead yet!" Brown gasped. Ranier had a glimpse of the pudgy man's face, pop-eyed. "He's still alive!"

Kavanaugh lashed out from the corridor doorway, "Miss, if you could get whoever's running this place down here, this man might have a chance!" and only the girl seemed to retain her presence of mind, darting from the washbowl to slip past the Irishman at the door.

"I will get Dr. Eberhardt," she said breathlessly. "The bell, sometimes it does not work if the battery is down. One moment, please."

Ranier, looking into the room from his station in the shrub, had a queer impression that when the girl's white shadow slipped into the corridor and disappeared from view on a whis-

per of running feet, another shadow entered the room. Something intangible, not to be seen but felt. Something that crossed Kavanaugh's face as he walked forward to gaze down on the operating table and its patient. Something that made Carpetsi stare at Brown, Brown glare at Schlitz, the professor peer about and wring his hands. Now the girl was gone they didn't like being left together alone. There was only the nervous squeaking of the woman's rocking chair; the pour of water from the basin taps.

Then, from deep within the house, the girl's voice screamed.

"Oh—come, somebody! Come quickly! Something terrible has happened to my uncle the doctor!"

CHAPTER VI

DEATH OF A DEAD MAN

He could hear feet pounding through the house as he skirted the dark wing, and he raced with no thought for a broken instep to beat them to the front. He knew her scream had come from that lighted upper room.

Coolidge shouted, "Hey!" from the direction of the car when he broke through the ferns and ran plunging along the line of the verandah. John Ranier didn't stop. Taking the verandah in two strides, he slammed through the front door, stumbled into the pale-lit reception hall. He saw the stairway, the balcony above, the girl's stricken face looking down from the upper-hall gloom; and he was on the fourth step going up when the others came out of the back corridor and ran shouting into the hall.

Kavanaugh saw him and yelled, "What th'— where the hell did *you* come from?" Schlitz, Brown, Carpetsi and Daisy were banging along behind Kavanaugh; at the same time Coolidge and Marcelline charged in from the front.

Coolidge bawled. "It's the doc from th' ship! He just run around from behind th' house!"

The hall filled with uproar. Ranier ignored

the crash of boots coming behind him, bending every sinew to mount the staircase and be first to reach the girl. "What's happened here? What's wrong?"

Her frightened eyes reminded him she had never seen him before and his unexpected appearance must be alarming. He must look like a maniac. Muddied, disheveled, sea cap askew. Face oil-smoked from that spare-tire ride, abrasions on his palms and the seat half out of his pants from that jounce in the road. He caught her arm.

"It's all right! I'm from the ship like the rest of these people! I came with them here—I'm the ship's doctor! Where's Dr. Eberhardt?"

She gasped, "He is not there—something terrible must have happened—" pointing down the balcony to a wide-open door. Lamplight streamed yellow from the door and some papers blew over the doorsill and scurried out on the balcony carpet.

Ranier started for the door, conscious of tumult coming up the stairs, oaths, puffs of winded breath, steps clattering like cavalry. The girl was close behind him. He heard her voice catch on a sob, appealing for quiet. "Oh—please. There are some very sick patients downstairs. We must not wake them— The laboratory—this is Dr. Eberhardt's laboratory."

Ranier halted on the threshold; stared into the lighted room. He was aware of the girl beside him; aware of her fear-darkened eyes and tremulous breathing. Kavanaugh was on the other side, features sharp, eyes cold steel under his downsnapped hat brim; and a coolness under his shoulder blades told him Marcelline and Coolidge were crowding up behind. He had to shake off a feeling he was surrounded; center his attention on this room.

"The doctor is not here," the girl breathed. "Something must have happened to him. Something has happened here—"

SOMETHING HAD HAPPENED in the room, all right. There might have been an explosion in this laboratory. The window that looked out on the gallery and driveway below was open, the screen out. The breeze that rippled a gray, dissolving curtain of fog over the sill, stirred a thresh of scattered note-papers, fever charts, record blanks and loose leaves across the floor. On the left-hand wall, shelved with a drugstore array of colored bottles, a score of bottles had been uncorked and overturned, dripping glisteny cascades of acid, powders and chemicals. A case of books—Ranier recognized Lister, Semmelweis, Pinel, Thorwaldsen's *Tropical Diseases* and Ringold's *Anatomy*—dumped its contents to join the mess, and surgical instruments were everywhere.

Near the door at his elbow an old fashioned roll-top desk might have experienced a hurricane, inkwell upended, pigeon-holes in disorder.

Along the right-hand wall a lab table was strewn with all manner of topsy-turvy, a scramble of test tubes, mortars, rubber hose, chemical jars, microscope lying on its side, glass cannisters overturned spilling glutinous messes of bacteriological culture. At one end of the table a big glass tank filled with live frogs gave off shimmering greenish light-rays as the amphibians—there must have been two thousand of them—sped, dived and darted in crazed schools against the glass. In that corner a human skeleton dangled like a marionette; turned slowly in the breeze with a faint clinking of hinged bones, and grinned at the green maelstrom in the aquarium.

"Hell!" Ranier said.

"He was up here by himself all evening," the girl whispered. "He was in here when I went to bed at eight o'clock because I am alone on call tonight with the patients. He was so very busy, so much to do with no one to assist—" Her voice choked. "He was experimenting—something so important he works on—a theory he could revive dead cells with adrenaline. Tonight he was to finish, to make the vital discovery. He told me not to call him unless for emergency. He said he would go out only if the case was extreme."

"Revive dead cells?" Ranier echoed. "Experimenting with—"

She whispered, "He has worked for years. I thought he was in here when I went down to answer the door. Look! His laboratory in ruins! What has done this? Where is Dr. Eberhardt? Never does he go out without leaving a written message to tell me where he goes. Always he leaves a note for me. On that—"

She was pointing at a white enamel table in the center of the tumbled room. Pointing at a small metal standard, on one corner of the table, a lead base with a thin five-inch spike such as housewives use for pinning a stack of milk bills and notes to the ice man. There was no little note pinned to this spike. A plump green bullfrog had been impaled on the standard. The frog's mouth was open like a purse, its eyes bulging. It worked its hind legs feebly. It was still alive.

But John Ranier wasn't looking at the frog. He was looking at a glass bowl set in the center of the table. There was a Bunsen burner flaming under the bowl, and the clear liquid in the bowl simmered and bubbled and gave off a pungence of something cooking. The odor filled the room. A faint flavor of boiled beef. John Ranier didn't like that center-piece. There were, in that bubbling bowl, two human hands. In the boiling water they swam and dodged about and rapped red knuckles on the glass as if they were alive.

NOBODY COULD SPEAK. Then the girl, staring at the opened window where the fog surged, whispered: "We must find Dr. Eberhardt! We must!"

John Ranier said huskily, "That bullfrog's still alive. This couldn't've happened very long ago. What time did you say he—"

Kavanaugh snarled, "It must've happened before we came! Otherwise we'd have heard the noise!" His fingers gripped Ranier's arm, shook. "You were outside there just now! Did you see anybody on that gallery out there? Did you see anybody around?"

"I was at the back of the house." Ranier wrenched away. "Why?"

"We didn't hear nothing at the front,"

Coolidge put in hoarsely. "Out in the car me and Marcelline—"

Marcelline blurted, "Regard! A frog there! *Sacré nom de Dieu!* It is the Voodoo! That frog—"

Everybody was pushing in. "Say," Brown's voice aghast, "ain't them somebody's hands there in that bowl?"

"Hands! A skeleton!" Daisy's scream soared soprano above mounting babble. "Ohmygod! Ohmygod! Ohmy—"

"Kavanaugh," Coolidge implored, "I think me and Marcelline better get started while my nerves hold out. We'll take Brown with us. It's a long way in the dark. This Eberhardt doctor ain't around, an' if we're goin' for the cops—"

Buzzzzzzzzzzzzzz!

Everybody heard it. Stood rooted. Stared.

Buzzzzzzzzzzzzzz!

There it was again, drilling the baited silence. Coming from a panel in the wall above the laboratory table. A short, insistent drone that lit a tiny red light-bulb in the panel.

Buzzzzzzzzzzzzzz!

The small bulb glowing again, on red, off red, like a firefly.

"Why—" the girl at Ranier's elbow gasped convulsively. "Why—that is the call bell from the emergency room. That is the buzzer from the room where we left the wounded man!"

"*Whaaat?*" It was Kavanaugh who whirled, eyes glowing. Face shocked for the first time that night. "By God, who—we left Haarman down there alone!"

A sensation of cold seemed to flow under John Ranier's scalp. Swept in the rush for the stairs, he tried to fight back fear; a seventh-sense feeling that unknown quantities had invaded the shadows around him and something diabolic and occult was loose in the fog-hung Haitian night. A man stabbed in the back and his table companions do not see it. Cryptic figures and the name Dr. Eberhardt scrawled on an envelope from the stabbed man's pocket. A Dr. Eberhardt's hospital near the scene of the crime, a lonely mountain villa and a beautiful girl. Dr.

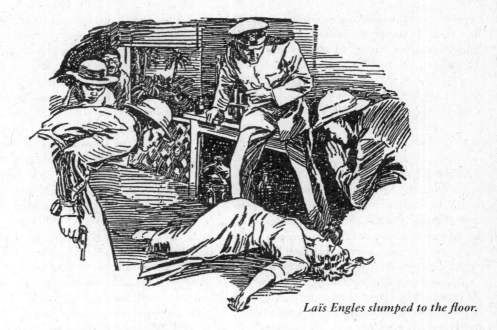

Laïs Engles slumped to the floor.

Eberhardt missing, his laboratory wrecked. A frog jammed on a spike.

Those three drones from the buzzer seemed the final terror. Three calls from a room where a man lay dying on an operating table, and alone. Who had pushed that bell to start them downstairs in stampede? John Ranier seemed to run in a cold wind. He could see the tuck was out of Kavanaugh, now. All the hardness was gone from the Irishman's face and his skin was niveous, cheekbones glistening as if under the icy spray of the morgue.

The girl's fear sickened him. Somehow—he didn't know how—his arm was about her waist as they followed Kavanaugh down the hall to the back corridor: he could feel her tenseness as they ran. *Thump, thump, thump,* the others were coming.

Then they were panting in the doorway of the emergency room, Kavanaugh holding them back, glaring. John Ranier saw the room was as they had left it. Only Haarman was there, on the operating table. The man's knees were drawn up as if in spasm, his left hand was clenched on his chest, his right arm hung limp, palm open. His face stared at the ceiling, an unseeing glassy stare. His mouth was open and his tongue showed.

"He's dead," Ranier said. "He must've just died."

It was the girl who gave the low-pitched, breathless cry.

"No— No— No—!"

Everybody looked at the girl. All color had fled from her face. Her eyes were wide, white-circled, appalled. She stood rigid, one hand clutched in the gold-brown thicket of her hair, the other pointing at Haarman's corpse on the operating table.

"What's the matter?" Ranier asked.

"That man!" the girl's voice was barely audible, a gray whisper in her convulsed throat. "His face—the scar on his right hand—I did not notice when they first brought him in tonight—I know that man! His name is Adolph Perl! Adolph Perl!" Her voice rose on the wings of terror. *"He couldn't have died just now! He died fourteen years ago in this very room! He died here in Haiti—Dr. Eberhardt buried him in the graveyard down the mountain—fourteen years ago—"*

Fog creamed and curled against the window

screen, opaque, wraith-like, silent. Not quite silent. Somewhere far out in the smothered night there was a low, sullen throbbing of wooden drums.

CHAPTER VII

THE GIRL'S STORY

The room had stopped breathing. In the corridor, the halls, the the stair-bannisters, upper rooms, dark passageways behind, all the normal night-sounds of a house asleep, all the nocturnal squeakings of floor-crack, of hinges straining in release, of timbers expanding after heat of the day, had stopped. Every clock, dripping faucet, mouse, might have died. The villa held its breath. Something in the air had quit. It seemed to Ranier as if the night itself was held in the grip of shock, like a great crouching beast muscle-locked in an ictus. Only its pulse was going, a low, dulled throb from the abeyant dark, no louder than the tapping of a fainted man's heart.

Nobody moved. In the shadowless glare of the hurricane lamps, the room with its bottles and operating table was stark; the body on the operating table, the people in the doorway like dressed figures in stone. But the girl with her right hand caught in her hair, her left hand extended in that awful attitude of pointing, was shivering. An imperceptible trembling that shook her lips, quivered down the soft curve of her throat, shook the slim lines of her figure, down the brown unstockinged ankles to her white tennis shoes. In the white of her face her eyes, glowing at the body on the table, were almost black. Ranier had never seen such eyes. Wider. Wider. The room dwindled in his own vision, other faces blurring into background. It was as if only the two alone were there—the staring girl, the contorted dead man in mid-room. And the girl was shivering and shivering. He must put a stop to this. He must break that shock before it broke the girl.

He hardly knew he moved. He hardly knew he moved through that immense silence, stepped to the operating table, consulted the taffy-haired man's lifeless pulse, pulled a blood-stained coat over the dead face. He hardly knew he walked, then, to the girl; caught her wrists to her sides, spun her rigid body in an about-face from the table, and commanded angrily, "Stop it! Stop it!"

His voice broke the spell; cut the overtaut nerves of tension; smashed the ice in the air. Figures came to life around him as if released; everybody seemed to yell at once. Kavanaugh was shouting at the girl, "What do you mean? What do you mean by saying Haarman died here in Haiti fourteen years ago?"

It was communicated to Ranier's sensitized skin that the Irishman's assurance had returned, and he had to admire the man's grit. Panic reacted in the others, but the tall, self-sure man had recovered his steely personality and was pointing that domineering finger again. His tone implied, "What the devil do you mean, trying to scare Dave Kavanaugh?"

"She made a mistake," Ranier said grimly across his shoulder. "Of course you did," he spoke directly to the trembling girl. "This Mr. Haarman came down on the cruise ship with us from New York. Someone stabbed him in that café down in the village, and he died a few minutes ago while we were upstairs in that laboratory. He must have revived in one of those spasms of strength that come sometimes just before death; staggered over to push that call button on the wall; then pulled himself back up on the operating table. Effort that finished him. You can see he's not been dead three minutes. You've mistaken him for somebody else."

The girl's eyes moved in dilated fascination to the lifeless shape on the table, and he could feel her wrists grow rigid in his grip.

She whispered, "I am not mistaken. It is he. Adolph Perl. He died here fourteen years ago. I saw him die."

SOMEBODY SWORE AND somebody made a sound like a whinny, and the look on the girl's face put an ache in the roots of John Ranier's hair.

Kavanaugh, who had walked to the operating table, spun furiously. "Well, he's dead, all right, all right. . . . What is this, an insane asylum? Girl tryin' to tell us Haarman is a guy she saw die once before!"

"She's mistaken him for someone she once knew," Ranier insisted.

"I am not mistaken. That scar on his palm. Shaped like the English letter Z." Her low voice reminded Ranier of the other-worldish murmuring of a person talking out of sleep. "That scar, it was cut in his hand by an Indian in Para, Brazil. The face I would know anywhere. Thinner, older, but the face of Adolph Perl. It was the last summer of the War, I met him. He was mate on my uncle's schooner, and then we were four years lost up the Amazon—"

Kavanaugh stared at the girl from under stretched eyelids. "The Amazon River in South America? Two seconds ago you said he died here in Haiti!"

"It was on our way back to Europe. Adolph Perl died when the schooner came ashore in Haiti. That was in 1922. And it is Adolph Perl, here now—on the very operating table where he—"

She put her face in her hands and began to cry softly; and an alto from the doorway moaned, "*Zombie!*" and nothing of this was real but the echo of those drums far off in the night. Even Kavanaugh became unreal, his cheekbones sultry, his eyes blue sparks, cocking his thumb like a trigger and aiming his finger at the stunned audience in the doorway, bawling suddenly:

"Well, what are you standing there for? You don't believe this nutty girl, do you? You realize there'll be a murder charge here, and all of us held up under one hell of an investigation? Haarman's dead and we've got to get a move on. Brown!"

The fleshy man designated by Kavanaugh's finger made a timid step forward. His spectacles looked owlish, and his lips made the sound of "Wh" twice.

"Snap out of it," Kavanaugh told him. "When you get to the village down below, call the American consul at Port-au-Prince on the phone. Tell him what's happened here, and to hop in a car and get here fast. Use my name, understand?"

"Whuh—when I get to the village?"

"Marcelline will drive the car. Coolidge, you go, too. While Brown's phoning, you get out those police. And bring 'em back on the jump." He whipped back his cuff to inspect a strap watch. "It's nine-thirty. Don't forget, all three of you are in this under suspicion. Try any funny stuff and it'll be just too bad. If you aren't back by ten, I'll swear out warrants for your arrest."

Angelo Carpetsi whimpered, "I'll go with them, Mr. Kavanaugh."

"Like hell," the Italian was corrected harshly. "You'll stick here with the rest of us till the cops come. Okay, you three. Go!"

They went. Pug-nosed Mr. Coolidge with his nerves, plump Mr. Brown and bugeyed Monsieur Marcelline. There was something in the sound of their fast departing heels that left no doubt about their being grateful to leave. Distantly the doors of the Winton were heard to bang; followed by the hammering of an engine, the squeal of a car bending a driveway on precarious wheels, zooming off down a mountain road in night.

John Ranier was thinking: "Now I've only got to watch the blond mess, the Professor, the Dago and Kavanaugh. Find Eberhardt and do something about this girl—"

Kavanaugh cut into his thoughts with:

"So now, ladies and gentlemen—" slurring the "gentlemen" as his eyes went coldly at Ranier—"the Haitian police will be here soon, and meanwhile we can wait right here where it's cozy and we can keep an eye on each other. And maybe the girl can tell us what's become of the doctor who runs this establishment, and explain this crazy nonsense about Mr. Haarman!"

If the Irishman's tone chewed a brittle suggestion of threat through his teeth, the girl at Ranier's side did not notice it.

"There were five of them who died," she whispered. "Five who died besides Adolph Perl. It was here they were stricken by the mauve death from Brazil, and here on this coast they were buried. And that man on the operating table was buried in the cemetery three miles down the road—"

CEMETERY THREE MILES down the road? Sweat beads bunched on John Ranier's forehead as he recalled the little cluster of candle-lit gravemounds constellating the fog-cloaked mountainside. He couldn't help a side-glance at the body on the operating table; a glance that moved hastily to Kavanaugh's scowling face, to the faces hovering in the doorway—Professor Schlitz's fear-cartooned features ridiculous in a sun helmet; the blond woman a portrait of misery scribbled in rouge and powder; Angelo Carpetsi's terrified black eyes. An hour ago they'd been bored American tourists seeing the Caribbean littoral through the bottom of a grog-bottle; now they were peopling a nightmare in which a member of their party had been slain by an invisible knife, only to be identified by a nurse in this jungle-locked retreat as a man who had died four years after the World War.

He looked sharply at the girl. Whispering through her fingers, her voice had been barely louder than the fog-muffled thumpings that were as counted heart beats from the white-washed night. She must have sensed the thought behind his scrutiny, for she dropped her hands from her marble-white face, let them fall inertly to her sides.

She whispered, "*Nein,* I am not mad. How it can be, I do not know, but it is the same man. I would have known him anywhere—anywhere—"

"But it *can't* be the same man," Ranier assured her, "People don't die twice, Miss—Miss—"

"My name is Laïs Engles. I came to the Americas from Griefswald, Germany—on a schooner with that man. It was the last year of the War, and I was six years old. My mother was dead and my father had been killed in the Battle of Jutland—it was my uncle, Captain Friederich, who took me on his schooner because the orphan asylums of Germany were crowded—there was no place for me to go. Adolph Perl—*he*—was mate of that schooner!"

Brushing past Ranier to confront the girl, Kavanaugh snarled: "If you've got to spin us a yarn, Miss What's-your-name, you might keep it straight while you're spinning it. While back you called Dr. Eberhardt your uncle; now it's some Kraut skipper during the War!"

"Captain Friederich was my real uncle. Dr. Eberhardt, who raised me here in his hospital after Captain Friederich died—him I call Unkle Doktor." Fingers clenched, she turned to send a dilated stare at the body on the operating table.

"That was in 1918, but I remember as if it were yesterday. My uncle's schooner was the *Kronprinz Albrecht,* very fast and with hidden engines. A blockade runner, like the famous *Emden,* it was to sail through the British fleet, cross the Atlantic, travel up the Amazon on a secret mission for the Kaiser's government. Do you understand? It was camouflaged as a tramp ship flying the flag of Holland; no one to suspect it was the German Navy. Another reason for taking me—a child on board would put the vessel above suspicion. And the crew were hand-picked volunteers." Her eyes shone strangely and she pushed a hand across her forehead. "Do you think I could forget this man—this man who was mate of that schooner?"

Kavanaugh's lip curled. "This happened when you were six years old?"

"So you think I would not remember? The long Atlantic voyage? The day we sailed into the Amazon at Para, where the mate—Adolph Perl—went ashore and got in a fight with an Indian who slashed that scar in his hand? *Nein,*" her eyes, fixed on that frowsty operating table, grew. "I remember well. My uncle, Captain Friederich, confined him for three weeks in irons because of that fight. Brazil had declared war on Germany, and it was dangerous for us to attract attention. That is how I could never mistake that scar—"

Ranier looked at the body that was stark under the hurricane lamps. Flies were walking on the coat that covered the taffy-haired man's face, and his hanging arm looked stiffer than it had a few moments ago. Already the dead hand had discolored a little. He jerked his eyes from the Z-cut scar to surprise a venomous expression on the face of Mr. Kavanaugh. Scorn fought with unbelief across the Irishman's hard-chiseled features; his eyes were twinkling at the girl under fanning lids; and, as was usual in domineering types, the man's doubt crystallized into anger.

He lashed at the girl, "Even if Haarman was the man you think was the mate of that schooner—which he wasn't!—just what would a German ship be doing, exploring up the Amazon in war time?"

She whispered, "Germany was desperate. All the world was leagued against her. The Kaiser wanted a secret pact with Chile, one of the few countries that was neutral. In the mountains of Chile were nitrates for explosives. Our mission was to reach Chile somewhere in the headwaters of the Amazon, to bribe the Chilean diplomats to declare war on our side against Brazil and Peru. From Para we sailed up the Amazon, across the interior of South America, deep in the vast river wilderness through a thousand miles of jungle, such a voyage as no schooner had made before. But we did not reach Chile. In those miles and miles of floating wilderness we became lost. How could I mistake anyone who was in that little handful of German sailors?"

Kavanaugh said harshly, "The mythical expedition gets lost in the Amazon and turns up in Haiti. Two times two makes six!"

But the girl's voice went on, low, appalled: "We were four years lost on the Amazon. Unexplored tributaries. Yellow channels everywhere. I think it was on the Rio Madeira tributary my uncle lost the way, deep in the heart of South America. Our schooner went aground and we camped in the jungle for months, waiting for floods to float her. Brazil was enemy country and we dared send no message for help. Our wireless went to pieces, too. From Berlin we had no word of news, and the sailors of the *Kronprinz Albrecht* almost forgot Germany or such a place as Europe. The primitive Indians of the Rio Madeira had never heard of the War; only Captain Friederich and Colonel Otto, the Prussian envoy in charge of the mission, refused to turn back. They had promised the Imperial High Command to reach Chile, a mission that might save their Fatherland. They were German officers of the old school. Adolph Perl—the mate—was a German of the old school. *Nein*, we pushed on until the schooner was rotting to pieces, the crew starving, only a few of us remained. Our gear was rusted, clocks stopped for lack of oil, time was lost track of. There was an old woman who had come with us from Germany to look after me—Old Gramma Sou. She used to tell me stories of Germany, and Adolph Perl, the mate, would stand listening. '*Herr Gott!*' he used to say. 'If only I could see the girls on the *Unter den Linden* again.' How many, many times have I thought of it!"

LISTENING TO THE girl's haunted voice as it spoke just then, John Ranier could almost forget this was a hospital in Haiti and she was talking of a cruise passenger who'd been murdered, stabbed that night in a waterfront café a few miles away. He could almost forget this strange bright room with its sinister fog-curtained window, its company of frightened tourists, its undertone echo of Negroid drums. He was seeing a river in far-off South America, a vast brown flood slipping through endless green, a tattered schooner manned by desperate men, a little German girl with yellow pigtails and round blue eyes. What incredible distances the vibrations of the War had traveled. She'd been six, and he sixteen—a boy in the muds of France, crawling through barbed wire with a smashed foot—a child with pigtails in the lost jungles of Brazil—

"After four years hunting for a way to Chile, my uncle had to turn back for supplies, for engine oil. We found our way to a place called Porto Velho. There were a few English and Americans there; a little camp in the jungle, building a railroad to Bolivia, they said. How they stared at us—all that was left of us. We thought them soldiers, but they were not soldiers. They said the War was over long ago. Can you imagine the feelings of Captain Friederich and his men? It was 1922—all those terrible miles of journey, those months in the jungle for nothing. I will never forget how Adolph Perl raved and cursed. How, when the schooner returned to Para, my uncle wept on learning Germany lay beaten, the Kaiser's government was no more; and in answer to his cable to Berlin came an order from an admiral he had never heard of. It was thought our ship had gone down long ago. So the *Kronprinz Albrecht* was ordered back to Germany at once, still under secret orders, and we started up the Caribbean. But a terrible storm drove us close to Haiti, drove us into this Gulf of Gonaives; our ship ran up on the beach of the village below. Fourteen years ago, that was. That night I first saw Dr. Eberhardt. That night—" her voice shook—"that night came the mauve death."

"The mauve death?" Ranier questioned hollowly. "What was that?"

"So Dr. Eberhardt called it," she murmured huskily. "A rare tropical disease with symptoms like beri-beri. Terribly contagious, it is, and kills within two hours of infection. The—the skin turns violet. Our—our schooner had brought it from the jungles of Brazil."

She pulled her linen robe tighter as if the room were suddenly cold; and John Ranier, watching her closely, felt a slow malignant dread begin to creep up his spine. Had sight of that wizardish laboratory upstairs, and the added shock of this emergency case, deranged the girl's mind? Carried her back to some terrible childhood experience which a stunned mind was translating into the present? Shock did queer things to people. Inspired hallucinations. But the girl looked sane—terrified, not deranged—

"*Verstehen-zie?*" she panted. "That awful germ, that mauve death must have been carried by our schooner, for Dr. Eberhardt said it had never before been in Haiti, and the night of the storm with our schooner on the beach, the disease broke out among us. I was then ten years old, and never could I forget that night. I could not! The darkness. The strange island. Bonfires on the beach. The Haitians crowding to see the ship. We came ashore in a lifeboat—all that was left of our pitiful expedition—with what luggage we could save. Dr. Eberhardt was among the Negroes; ran up to see if he could help. When he discovered we were Germans, he spoke to us delighted—but, *nein!* He stared suddenly at Colonel Otto and cried, '*Lieber Gott!* you must get out of this crowd at once; you must all come at once to my hospital!'"

Ranier said thickly, "But Miss Engles—" and she lifted a hand in protest, whispering, "Please! I must tell you! I must tell you what happened that night to us—to *that* man! Dr. Eberhardt— he brought us here to this hospital, and Colonel Otto was dead before we got here. My uncle, Captain Friederich, was next to die—an hour later. Then Old Gramma Sou, my nurse, whom I had grown to love as my mother. Nothing could save them. Dr. Eberhardt could not save them. 'It is the mauve death,' he told me that night. 'It is the mauve death that strikes like the lightning and spreads like the wind. You must be a brave little girl, my child. Some of your friends will never leave Haiti alive.'"

She stopped to draw a shuddery breath, and Kavanaugh's voice quarreled: "So this Eberhardt was in Haiti at that time, was he?"

"He has spent his life here in Haiti," her lips gripped back a sob. "Dr. Eberhardt is a great man, a scientist. He came here before the War, and when the fighting broke across Europe he refused to go back to Germany. His life is devoted to medicine, to his experiments, to his work among the Negroes. That night he was terrified for fear the mauve death would spread, and he fought to stop the contagion, knowing plague and panic would destroy all his work. It was terrible! Terrible! The American Marines were in Haiti at the time, and there was a marine sergeant at the hospital. Dr. Eberhardt sent him down to the beach with orders to burn the schooner. *Ja*, the American soldier burned our schooner that night, and gave his life to do it. The plague took him, too. He returned to the hospital—died!"

FISTS CLENCHED, EYES wide, she moved so suddenly at Kavanaugh that the Irishman, startled, sidestepped into Ranier. Off-balanced by his lame foot, Ranier swung against Professor Schlitz, and the thin insectologist shrieked as if tagged by a ghost. The white, morguish room dizzied in John Ranier's vision as he heard the girl's low-pitched words flung at Kavanaugh:

"Do you think I could forget one detail of that horrible night? Mistake anyone who was there? *Nein,* I remember every detail. How Colonel Otto, when he died, asked to be buried in his Potsdam uniform. Old Gramma Sou dying in the taffeta dress she had saved from the schooner— the dress she had brought from Berlin to wear at the embassy in Chile. Captain Friederich dying with 'God save the Fatherland!' on his lips. That marine sergeant—his name was O'Grady. A huge man over six feet tall, he was, and he fell to his face out there on the verandah, his cheeks all lavender, and he had a red moustache. Dying. Dying and singing a wild American song!

"How could I forget that brave man or any one of those brave Germans who gave their lives for the Fatherland four years too late, killed by the plague they had brought from Brazil. My uncle, Captain Friederich, blamed himself because the mission to Chile had failed; *ja,* he thought that was why Germany had lost the war. He cursed the death that was striking him down in Haiti, the death that would prevent him from carrying out his government's last order. He called Dr. Eberhardt that night. 'You must carry on for us!' he told the doctor. 'If the mate, Adolph Perl, dies also, *you* must carry on!' He

told Dr. Eberhardt the story of the secret mission. He gave Dr. Eberhardt a suitcase of papers, something of great value to Germany that should have been delivered to the diplomats in Chile. Now Captain Friederich had been ordered to return that suitcase to Berlin. Dying he begged the doctor to look after me, but first he made him promise to take charge of the suitcase; Dr. Eberhardt must swear as a German to return that valuable case to the German government. And Adolph Perl was weeping. Weeping that night. 'I will not die,' he cried. 'I will carry on for the Fatherland!' It was right out there in the hall. I was listening at a door, and I overheard."

Her fingers, pointing at the door, brought cries of fear from the tourists dummified in the frame. "Out there in the hall," she repeated. "Fourteen years ago. Colonel Otto, Captain Friederich, Old Gramma Sou—dead! And that American Marine on the verandah—fourth to die. And an Anglican missionary from a little village down the coast was fifth. An Anglican missionary who had stopped in to pray for the dying, and in two hours he, with them, was dead. *Ja,* it was a fatal disease, that mauve death. Dr. Eberhardt locked all the doors, let nobody enter after that. If word got loose there was a plague in the hospital, the Haitians would have rioted and murdered all the whites. Those of us from the schooner—all that had survived—we waited to be next. There were only three of us left. A sailor named Hans Blücher—myself—the mate, Adolph Perl. We waited for death to take us. In this very room we waited."

Turning slowly, fearfully, the girl pointed at the fog-blurred window across the room. "Dr. Eberhardt and the house-boy, Polypheme, they were in the stable back there behind the hospital. We could hear them sawing and hammering. Building coffins. I wept in fear, because I was little and it was late at night and I did not understand. I only knew the bodies were in a row out there in the front hall, waiting. And Hans Blücher, the sailor, wept too. And Adolph Perl, the mate, walked up and down cursing. I can see it now, as I saw it then.

"Hans Blücher said he was feeling sick, and he crept out into the corridor. We sat in this room together, Adolph Perl and I. We waited. Hans did not come back. In a minute Adolph Perl said, 'I am going after that man!' and went out into the corridor. I waited alone. The pounding of the coffins went on and on, like those drums you hear beating on the mountain tonight. After a while Adolph Perl returned. 'Hans Blücher has fled the hospital,' he told me. 'The scoundrel has run away.' Then Adolph Perl began to stagger and cough. He put his hand to his throat—his scarred hand. '*Heilegegott!*' he screamed. 'I have caught it from going out there. Now I, too, am going to die!' He climbed up on that operating table—that very table where you see him now—and lay there gasping—"

THERE WAS A sensation of frost forming on John Ranier's temples; it was too late at night for this sort of thing. Something in the girl's voice convinced him she was speaking truth, and her breathless words, whispering out of memory, described a scene more real than present actuality. The dread in her eyes, fixed now on Haarman's stiffening body, was no pretense. There was sanity in the white struggle of her lips to go on, as if the words were being dragged from her throat at great effort of will.

"Adolph Perl lay where you see him now, and Dr. Eberhardt ran in from the corridor, very angry. 'Who left the front door open?' And Adolph Perl lifted his hand, the hand with the scar. 'Blücher ran away!' he swore. 'I saw him running for the jungle. He was afraid he would get the contagion. Now I have caught the mauve death from going out there in the hall.' He was weeping, coughing, and he described the symptoms the others had suffered. He begged Dr. Eberhardt to take him out in the hall. 'Lay me between Captain Friederich and Colonel Otto. I want to die between my officers!'

"Dr. Eberhardt carried Adolph Perl into the hall and put him on the floor between the dead officers. Adolph Perl lay writhing. Then he lay still. Dr. Eberhardt looked down at him and groaned, 'He is dead. We must bury them quickly and secretly.' The doctor had been giving me injections, and he gave me another and told me, 'You are not going to die. You must help me now and not cry out or the Haitians will hear you. We must turn out all the lights so the Negroes will not see us.' The coffins were there in the hall. The lights were turned out. Moonlight came through. Dr. Eberhardt put all the bodies in the big yellow rough-boxes in a row. He said the bodies must be buried at once and he told me to take a last look at my friends; then he ran outside to help Polypheme hitch up the wagon. I was afraid to wait there in the hall alone, and I ran upstairs to the laboratory and hid. When the wagon came, I crept downstairs again. I had to help nail on the wooden lids. It was terrible, nailing on those lids. Dr. Eberhardt had covered all the faces with handkerchiefs in the dark, and—I am telling you this because—because—"

Hand to forehead, she stared at the operating table. "Because there was a streak of moonlight," she whispered, "and it fell across Adolph Perl's hand as we nailed up the coffin, and the last thing I saw was that brown, Z-shaped scar. Then I watched Polypheme and the doctor load the wagon. There were six coffins. 'We must hurry,' Dr. Eberhardt said. 'We must distribute them at different cemeteries along the coast so the natives will not see a lot of new graves together and suspect anything.' I remember how he climbed up on the wagon and wrote the names on the coffins with a pencil. How he held me on his lap. How we started off in the moonlight, Polypheme whipping the horses—"

Once more the girl was shivering. Lips colorless; face marble; eyes shining, narcotic. She cried, "Adolph Perl was buried that night. In the cemetery down the road—near the village. I saw it. I saw Dr. Eberhardt dig the grave. White with exhaustion, he was, but he dug every one of those graves, choosing sandy soil to make it easy for the shovel, digging, digging, while Polypheme held the lantern. *Ja*, then Polypheme would fill them, and the wagon would go on. We put Old Gramma Sou in the graveyard east of here, and the American Marine sergeant in the soldiers' cemetery beyond. The missionary in his own churchyard; then Colonel Otto at Bois Legone; and my uncle, Captain Frederich, last, at a place high on the *morne* overlooking the coast. But Adolph Perl was buried in the graveyard three miles below here, *ja*—I saw him buried—you can see the marker. He died of the mauve death that night, and I saw him buried— *and this man you have brought here tonight,*" she finished with a sob, "*is that same Adolph Perl!*"

"Ohmygod!"

Miss Daisy May was on the floor again.

CHAPTER VIII

THE WEBBED FOOT

And the girl, herself, might have fallen if John Ranier hadn't caught her in time. She swayed, and he steadied her, wondering about his own knees and doubting his sanity. He was imagining this. He'd had one drink too many down there at Hyacinth Lucien's, and *aguardiente* had gone to his brain. But the girl's slim body quivering against him was real enough, as the past, the dark scenes her husky-throated words had conjured to his vision were gone, and he was conscious of the present, tonight, Haiti outside, jungle and mountain close around, a villa smothered under breathless fog. White walls of a make-shift hospital room, and moths flitting under lamps. Kavanaugh's shoulder beside him, that fainted female on the floor, Carpetsi's pistachio-tinged face sweating, and Professor Schlitz's pince-nez, silly with fear.

It was a charade, a spell cast by the muffled *tumpy-bum-bum* that pulsed from the fogbank beyond the window screen and came into the room like a dead march for the body on the shabby operating table. The fogbank was a ghost looking in, and there were ghosts in the room that couldn't be seen. Ranier could feel their fingers in his hair. He knew he ought to

do something about it, but he could only stand there, muddied, disreputable, sea cap aslant, supporting a slim girl in white linen with gold lights in her hair and blue terror in her eyes; could only stand there glaring from the girl to the dead man in mid-room, the cruise passenger named Haarman who'd been stabbed to death tonight—a man this girl had seen buried fourteen years ago!

It was the insectologist who broke that cataleptic charade. Eyes popping the glasses from his nose. Voice climbing a ladder in his throat to a windy peak of falsetto.

"You hear what she says? You hear what this girl says?" waving his hands. "That man Haarman—she knew him during the war—she saw him die in Haiti in 1922! But he got on our boat from New York—! Was sharing my stateroom on this cruise! He told me he'd never been to sea before. Said he was German—yes!—but born in America—in the artichoke business in New York City. Artichokes!" the professor screeched. "He told me that! And he said he was taking this cruise for his health! His *health!* My God! How pale he always was! So horribly *pale!* His *health!*"

"And always walkin' around by himself!" Carpetsi said, staring frantically at the table and rabidly biting at a hangnail on his finger. "He'd never come into the bar, or—"

"And he'd always walk the deck in carpet slippers," the professor shrilled, as if the fact held some evil significance. "Carpet slippers! You'd be standing at the rail and he'd go by and you'd hardly hear him. As if—as if—"

"Who stabbed him in that café? No knife or nothin'! Marcelline said there was a face, didn't he? Didn't Marcelline say—"

"Those *zombie* things! The guides in Cape Haitian mentioned them, too. Dead men brought to life, and—"

A whimper broke from the Italian boy, jumping him around in the doorway. "Holy Jees, I'm gettin' out of here!" And then Kavanaugh's voice was crashing with the authority of gunfire, hammering, "Stand still, you fool! All of you, shut up! Nobody's going to leave." Striding across the floor, he jerked Carpetsi back from the corridor, shoved the thin man aside, blocked the exit. "Nobody's getting out of here, see? At least, not until those three fools come back with the police!"

FEET PLANTED APART, body bowed a little at the middle, the Irishman let his eyes circle the room with an uncompromising glare that came to rest on John Ranier and the girl at his side. Kavanaugh aimed his finger at Laïs Engles. "Get this!" he told her in a grating tone. "There's a murder been pulled off tonight, and no crackbrained ghost story is going to run me out of here before I'm cleared. I don't know you, see? and I don't know your reason for dishing out this yarn. Much obliged for an interesting tale to take up the time. Thanks. But I don't believe any of it."

"It's true," she whispered.

"Sure." Kavanaugh grinned. "This guy from New York was a German naval officer up the Amazon. He told us he never went to sea before and his name's Haarman, but he was a mate on a blockade runner, named Perl."

"I know him."

"He died of a stab-wound after we brought him here tonight, but he's the same man who died in this hospital fourteen years ago!"

"I saw him buried."

Kavanaugh sneered, "Oh, sure. Some of these black island witch doctors raised him from the dead and he goes up to New York and runs an artichoke business, and then he takes this Caribbean cruise back to Haiti for his health. But all this time he's a living dead man, eh? He's one of these *zombies*—"

"I don't know." She put her face in her hands. "I don't know—"

"I suppose this Dr. Eberhardt who runs this hospital would remember all about this German expedition who died of th' plague from Brazil? I suppose Dr. Eberhardt would recognize this guy?"

"Dr. Eberhardt only saw him that one night, but I am sure—"

"And where *is* Dr. Eberhardt?" Kavanaugh demanded. "Why isn't he here?"

"I don't know."

"Well, I know," the tall Irishman rasped. "Maybe there's such a thing as corpses coming back to life and going into the vegetable trade after fourteen years in the grave, but not in my bailiwick! I know Mr. Haarman got on this cruise ship in New York City ten days ago. I know he had a few drinks with me on deck and told me about his business in New York. I know he asked me if he could join a motor ride from here to Port-au-Prince, and chipped in his share for the automobile. I know he was alive back there in that damned dirty café where we were going to start out, and I know somebody stabbed him. I don't know why he was stabbed or who did it or how, but I know it's murder and he died in this hospital of yours for the first time in his life, see? If you think you can throw a scare in me with all this *zombie* rubbish, you're wrong."

He turned a thin smile at John Ranier. "And what does our ship's doctor think?"

John Ranier thought: "The man's talking sense, but he doesn't see this girl believes her own words."

He said slowly: "I'm sure Miss Engles has had a shock. Whatever happened tonight upstairs in Dr. Eberhardt's laboratory frightened her, and her imagination is overwrought." He touched the girl's arm. "There are such things as close resemblances. Many people look alike. After all, you haven't seen the man, Adolph Perl, in fourteen years, and you were a child when you last saw him. As for the scar on Mr. Haarman's hand, why that may be coincidence, too."

"The thing isn't worth bothering about," was Kavanaugh's harsh comment. "Telling us Mr. Haarman is a German naval officer she saw buried in 1922. She hasn't the slightest bit of proof—"

The girl's head came up, her wide dark eyes met the man's scoffing stare. "I have proof."

"Just because you saw that scar—"

"There is more than the scar."

Kavanaugh said in a low fury, "Listen, Mr. Haarman was never in Haiti before and you never saw him before and he isn't anybody named Adolph Perl and you know it!"

"Very well," her tone was weak with strain. "If the man is not Adolph Perl there is proof. In South America the sailors on my uncle's ship went barefooted. The left foot of Adolph Perl fascinated me as a child. The crew nick-named him the Duck. The toes of Adolph Perl were joined by a membrane. Perl had a webbed foot—"

Every eye in the room was drawn by that same icy magnetism. That body on the operating table. The dead man's shoes. High-laced brown shoes, thick-soled, awkward in the out-spread, loose-ankle posture of death. John Ranier heard Kavanaugh's half-throttled oath. Professor Schlitz made a gargling sound. Even the Daisy woman roused to her feet at this climax to cling on Carpetsi's sleeve and stare with eyes like doughnuts, whimpering.

The girl's white lips murmured, "If the left foot is webbed—"

John Ranier walked to the table, unlaced and juggled off the shoe, pulled off the sock; expecting, naturally, to find the left foot of Mr. Haarman was not webbed.

It was webbed.

CHAPTER IX

BE HE ALIVE OR BE HE DEAD

They ran. They fled that anamorphosis, went into the corridor as if that grotesque bare foot had kicked them wholesale through the door. John Ranier went with them because he could see no reason to remain behind with a Mr. Haarman whose naked pedal extremity showed an eczematous heel, a pallid callus-scabbed sole, a fallen arch, five dead toes pointed at the ceiling and that batwing-like membrane between the toes. Mr. Haarman, dead with a webbed foot,

did not invite companionship. The case, Ranier felt, was beyond a ship doctor's chirurgery. It might even have baffled a chiropodist.

Half way down the corridor he discovered Mr. Haarman's left shoe was in his hand, and the *bang!* it gave when he dropped it brought Kavanaugh around as if he'd fired a gun. The girl cried, "Oh!" running with her fingers across her mouth; and at the corridor's turn he could not help looking back, half expecting to see Mr. Haarman in the doorway, coming after his shoe.

Always to Ranier there'd been something of the eerie about a hospital at night, something beyond the calculations of *materia medica*. There could be a "witching hour" in medicine when the most hard-boiled and scientific practitioner sat back with folded hands to wait. For what? For something not in the book. Something outside the realm of test-tube, nostrum and pledget. Something that stirred through the hushed hallways or entered a dim-lit ward, barely moving the window curtains, to choose a patient for the "turn." The Unseen impulse that stemmed the tide of a hopeless hemorrhage to rescue the moribund for another day. The Caprice that stole into an adjoining room to beckon bony-fingered at a simple tonsillectomy case, and whisper, "You—"

It was there. In Dr. Eberhardt's hospital, cloaked in mountain isolation and fog. But it was more than the mystery of death or healing behind quiet doors; more than the nocturnal silence of whitewashed walls, the shadows restless under dimmed vigil lamps, the drugged air heavy with sick-room exhalations, germicides. There was, in this shadowy corridor, something invisible and malign.

The front hall was no improvement. The stairway at the side cast a bone-like pattern of bannister-shadows on the opposite wall. The pneumonia pallor of the night-lamp did not reach the upper balcony. Infected by the panic, the gray tabby sped from somewhere and streaked across the hall like a frightened thought. Miss Daisy May jumped the cat with a wail. Mr. Angelo Carpetsi helter-skeltered along the bone-shadowed wall, hooked his suspenders on an unsuspected knob and yanked open a closet door. An umbrella, a sun helmet and a black frock coat that might have been Dr. Eberhardt but wasn't, tumbled out of the wall-cupboard to tangle with Professor Schlitz's feet. Professor Schlitz said nothing, but proceeded to go through the front door at a pace undignified for a Ph.D. from Upsala. Seen from behind, he appeared to evaporate in the dark mists of the verandah, a process that was too much for him, for after a half second's contemplation of the fog outside, the professor wheeled and sprang back into the hall, panting like a spaniel. Where to go when a man with a webbed foot, fourteen years dead, was after you?

Kavanaugh barked, "Upstairs! Quick!" steering the blond woman around the newel post and dragging her up the steps.

Ranier found himself supporting the slim girl's elbow, and heard himself telling her, "There's nothing to be afraid of!" But he didn't mean it. There was a white blanch to her lips that could not have been there without reason, and she moved in a resistless way, impelled by his hand, as if too frightened to follow her own responses.

THEN THEY WERE in the laboratory because the lighted room—despite that unappetizing odor of cookery!—was better than any of a number of dark doors off the upper hall. They stood. Angelo Carpetsi with his back to the door as if holding it against an assault of haunts. Kavanaugh fanning the Daisy woman whose haystack head was buried in his shoulder, threatening to swoon at any moment. Professor Schlitz handkerchiefing his temples. Laïs Engles trembling. John Ranier fighting a conflict with the muscles in his stomach. You could not have heard a pin drop, but there was only the gurgly bubbling of water boiling in the glass bowl on the white table.

John Ranier walked to the table and turned off the Bunsen flame under the bowl. Two evil objects settled to the bottom of the bowl, and he saw the bullfrog on the near-by spike was dead, and the only sound then was not born of the room, but a faint undertone echo that might have traveled miles through the fog-hushed outer night to enter by the vapour-curtained window and throb in the stifled air. Had the tempo of those mountain drums quickened, or was that the rapid pounding of his own blood?

A shocking thought occurred to him. He said to Laïs Engles, "Those aren't—Dr. Eberhardt's hands?"

She shook her head violently.

But whose-ever they were (he couldn't look at the bowl) they'd want some explaining. So would that pilloried frog. What cannibalistic machination had been in progress up here, and what bizarre violence had disrupted it? That disordered desk; those spilled bottles of Prussic acid, cyanide, strychnine, ammonia; that scattered lab table. He wondered stupidly at the big glass tank swimming with frogs, at the skeleton looking on. The green whirligig in the tank might have been the visual expression of his own thoughts. What sort of experimenter was this old Dr. Eberhardt who had disappeared in this Chamber of Horrors? And how might this have to do with a Leo Haarman, taffy-haired Teutonic artichoke dealer, dead downstairs with membranes between his toes?

He took a turn about the crazy room, limping noticeably as he always did when excited, his thoughts stumbling in his head. Three problems, now. Who stabbed Haarman? How could Haarman be the mate of that Amazon expedition recounted by the girl—a German sailor who died in 1922? And where was Dr. Eberhardt? He paused at the window to pull fresh air into his lungs. Fog and darkness outside. Darkness and fog in his mind. He swung from the window to put a question to the girl, and saw Mr. Kavanaugh push the blond woman from his shoulder to confront the room with sudden decisiveness.

Kavanaugh's mouth was going angrily. "Now then, now then, what the devil are we running for?" as if someone's insubordination had caused a stampede. The Irishman's eyes were contemptuous. They circled the room with scorn. Narrowed at a bottle upright on one of the vandalized shelves.

He snapped, "Scotch!" Walked to the shelf, uncapped the bottle, and drank off an inch of Sandy Macdonald without coughing. He handed the bottle to the blond woman, and snapped, "Drink!" The blond woman tilted her picture hat and drank off an inch. Angelo Carpetsi snatched the bottle, drank, sputtered; passed it to Professor Schlitz who declined with a shudder. Kavanaugh took the bottle and returned it to the shelf. His hard flat cheeks had congested a little. He cocked his thumb and aimed his imperative finger at the door.

"You don't have to hold up that door, Carpetsi; nothing's coming after you. Haarman's dead down there! Dead, understand? He isn't any hoodoo named Adolph Perl, and he didn't croak any fourteen years ago!"

Professor Schlitz moaned out, "The girl said—"

"Never mind," the Irishman cut him off, "what the girl said!" Hands thrust in pockets, he wheeled, regarded Laïs Engles with a direct stare. "Doesn't it strike you as a coincidence that Dr. Eberhardt, the only person in Haiti who could verify this Adolph Perl yarn of yours, isn't here?"

She gasped, "Yes! Oh, God—What has happened to him? What has happened to Unkle Doktor? That creature you brought here tonight—"

JOHN RANIER STEPPED to the girl, took her by the arm roughly. "Look here, Miss Engles. Forget that—that man downstairs. You're mistaken about him somehow. We've got to locate Dr. Eberhardt, whatever we do! It looks as if there's been a fight in his laboratory here. There's mud on that window sill. Somebody came in." He controlled his tone. "Do you know if Dr. Eberhardt had any enemies?"

"Enemies? I—"

"Anyone," Ranier persisted, "who might break in on him, want to do him any harm?"

She sobbed, "He was kind, good to everyone. Established a free clinic. Gave vaccinations. All he wanted was to be left alone. The natives love him who know him. But they are people most superstitious. *Ja*, there are enemies on the island—"

"Who?"

"The *hougans*—those witch doctors who say he has robbed them of their business, who warn the ignorant blacks against him. There is that ugly Hyacinth Lucien who runs the café down in the village. He is a *bocor* who practises sorcery and sells charms to the deluded Negroes. Several times in the past he has threatened—"

"Hyacinth? He was there in his café all evening, Miss Engles. Anyone else? Did Dr. Eberhardt ever mention anyone? Someone not a native—who might have a reason—"

"*Nein—nein—*" She was crying in her throat, forcing the words through tears. "Who could want to harm Dr. Eberhardt?"

"Listen," Ranier demanded. All at once his tongue felt queer. An electrical taste, transmitting the thought telegraphed from his mind. As if his spinning brain cells, joining in collision, had caused a spark, a definite flash across his mental vision. A hunch that numbed his tongue. He said loudly, "That night fourteen years ago! When you and Adolph Perl and another sailor were waiting down there in the emergency room! All the others had died of that plague, you said, and you three were the only ones left. You and the mate and—?"

"And a sailor named Hans Blücher—"

"That's the one I mean," Ranier flashed. "What became of *him*?"

"That night he ran away. Adolph Perl went after him and said he saw him run from the hospital. He ran away to escape the contagion."

Angelo Carpetsi had edged around the rolltop desk to peep at the bowl which was still simmering on the center table. Temporary courage which had been inspired in the Italian by Kavanaugh's gritty assurance, a shot of Scotch and the door closed on the hall, now left the pink-shirted boy with a loud yell. He whirled on his heels, his complexion pasty as spaghetti. His black eyes glittered at Kavanaugh, at the girl, at Ranier.

"What the hell!" he yelled. "Are we gonna stand around an' talk? Are we gonna stand around here an' talk—with that *thing* downstairs? Don'tcha see what's in that bowl, there? Are we gonna *stand* here?" His voice close to hysteria, he hooked frantic fingers on Kavanaugh's sleeve. "It's your fault!" he shouted. "You sent the car away! You wouldn't let me go with Brown an' Coolidge! You wouldn't let me go! I wanna get outa here! Outa here—"

John Ranier was not sorry to see Kavanaugh's knuckles whip up under Carpetsi's jaw, closing the Italian's mouth with a crack that drove him to the wall and left him speechless. The pink-shirted boy had interrupted a thought, and thinking was getting difficult in this nightmare. What had he been asking the girl—

"That sailor who ran away that night. Blücher. Where did he go?"

"I don't know." The girl pressed her forehead and gave Ranier a dazed look. "Nobody knows. Why do you question me about Hans Blücher? In Haiti he was never seen again. Fearing he would spread the contagion, the doctor was very angry he ran off. That was not all. Hans Blücher was gone in the night, and with him the suitcase Captain Friederich had asked Dr. Eberhardt to send to Germany. Police were called, but Hans Blücher was never caught."

Ranier leaned at her, staring. "You mean—this Blücher ran off with that case belonging to the German government? The devil! Why didn't you tell us that before?" Turning his back on the girl, he paced down the laboratory to the open window, kicking at loose note-papers in his path. Wisps of moisture floated in from the night to finger his face while he stood looking out, his mind racing. Fragmentary thoughts, scenes, went topsy-turvy through his head. Haarman's plaster-cast face in that café. Down there on an operating table, that webbed foot bared. The

girl's story knotted in the tangle. Thoughts like live wires whipping about, contacting at some point, creating that flash. Good God, it would be incredible, but—

BACK TOWARD THE room, he slipped a hand into his breast pocket; fished out the letters he'd discovered on Haarman earlier that night. Ignoring the inexplicable notations pencilled on the stained envelope of one, he thumbed open and read the missives under the pretense of leaning from the window for air. Contents told him nothing. A dry cleaner's bill for one white linen suit (it would want more than dry cleaning now!). A circular and note from a travel bureau advising Mr. Haarman that the Adlon in Berlin was a splendid hotel and the Hamburg-American ships were *non-pareil*. Wait! Another thought sparked as he returned the letters to his pocket. Had Haarman been considering Europe, then (frightened, perhaps?) veered to the Caribbean?

He rounded from the window, lips compressed; then, before he could open them to frame the question in his mind, he was interrupted by an oath from Kavanaugh. The Irishman, who'd been stooped in a rubbish-strewn corner, picked a book out of the litter, swung about, elbowed the girl aside and confronted Ranier, narrow-eyed.

"Look here, Dr. Ranier, don't you think we've chattered long enough with this girl? Seems to me the thing to do would be search the hospital for this Dr. Eberhardt who runs the place. Why gabble about this Blücher guy when her story's nutty anyhow?"

"Suppose," Ranier said, "the dead man downstairs were Hans Blücher instead of Adolph Perl."

"Yes, and suppose," Kavanaugh's brows came together, "he's only a murdered man named Haarman!"

"This girl thinks he isn't. At the same time we know he can't be the German mate she says she saw buried in 1922. But," Ranier faced the Irishman's skepticism, "he *could* be somebody who knew that Perl fellow; someone made up, say, to resemble him. Suppose that Blücher, who skipped out that night, shipped up to the States and wanted to disguise himself. Why? The suitcase, let's say documents belonging to the German government; maybe he took 'em to sell to a foreign country. He figures the *Wilhelmstrasse* will be after him to get the stuff back. So he takes the identity of a man who's likely dead and at any event won't be known in the U.S.A. or described by the German secret service. He could assume the name of Haarman and the appearance of Adolph Perl. The scar would be easy enough. The toes a matter of grafted skin. Then, after fourteen years, he comes back to Haiti—"

"On a cruise?"

"How do I know? Maybe to silence Dr. Eberhardt and Miss Engles who're the only ones who would know about the stuff he stole? I'm only guessing. Trying to show this girl how Haarman, who seems to look like an Adolph Perl, might be the other sailor who—"

"That could not be!" Laïs Engles cried. "It is Adolph Perl downstairs. Never Hans Blücher disguised to look like him. The scar, the web foot, the face might be disguised. But never the build or color of the eyes." Her dark gaze swerved at those near the door. "Adolph Perl is the man you brought here tonight. Thick-set, heavy shoulders, blue eyes. Hans Blücher was very bony, very thin, taller, with brown eyes. Like you."

Her pointing finger brought a squeal from Professor Schlitz and a stifled oath of disappointment from Ranier. He groped despairingly, "You said there was something valuable in that suitcase—papers, you thought. Didn't you ever know what it contained?"

"Only that it was to have been delivered that time in Chile. Captain Friederich told Dr. Eberhardt what it was. Worth much to Germany. That is all I overheard. Dr. Eberhardt would know."

"And Dr. Eberhardt," Kavanaugh interposed bitingly, "still isn't here! Neither are those damfool black police! So I think it's time to cut all this comedy and get down to facts!" He pivoted

at John Ranier; ordered, "Put up your hands!" so unexpectedly that Ranier recoiled backwards, jarred into the laboratory skeleton. The bones clinkled.

Mr. Kavanaugh seemed to copy the skeleton's grin. Mr. Kavanaugh's shoulders were pulled forward, his neck shortened into his trench coat collar, chin jutting, hat-brim down almost to the bridge of his long hard nose. Mr. Kavanaugh's Irish eyes weren't smiling, but were points of hard blue coral sharpening themselves on Ranier's face. Mr. Kavanaugh had transferred the volume he'd salvaged from the floor to his left hand; but he was not pointing that bossy right-hand forefinger this time.

There was a Colt automatic in Mr. Kavanaugh's right hand.

CHAPTER X

ZOMBIES!

John Ranier looked in surprise at the gun and was almost glad to see it there. It was blue-steel, snub-nosed, business like. It looked quick, hard and compact, like the man who aimed it. But its menace was real, a definite focal point for fear, something that brought actuality into this creep-walled, fog-windowed place atmosphered with a whisper of Haitian drums and a wizardish hint of resurrection. It put the cards on the table. An Irishman was something you could get your teeth in.

Ranier lifted his arms. Somehow Kavanaugh's explosive gesture had flicked to his mind that scene in the waterfront café, when he'd picked up Haarman's hand and said, "This man was a con—" meaning to say "consumptive"; and Kavanaugh had interrupted with the same unexpected violence in his voice.

That hard voice had flatted again, commanding, "Come here. Walk towards me and keep your hands up."

"Dave Kavanaugh," the stout blonde screamed, "what are you doing?"

Mr. Kavanaugh banished query and woman with an impatient sideglance; stepped close to John Ranier, ran a quick hand over his coat, ribs, side pockets, hip. "All right, step back and relax," he directed. "You haven't got a gun. Just don't forget, from now on, that I have. That goes for everyone else in this nut factory!"

"I thought we were using knives tonight," Ranier said dryly, meeting those feral Irish eyes. "Where did your artillery come in?"

"Unpacked it from my traveling bag when we motored out here in the Winton. Had an idea I might be able to use it, and it won't be any mysterious mauve death if I do." He waved the gun threateningly. "Stand over there by the girl, will you, Dr. Ranier? You're both under arrest!"

It was an ultimatum as unexpected as the gun; brought an oath from Ranier, an exclamation from the waxworks figure of Professor Schlitz, a gargle from the blonde, a gasp from Angelo Carpetsi. "Say!" jaw hanging limp. "You're gonna arrest them two?"

"Under arrest!" Laïs Engles murmured in a lethargic way, her eyes uncomprehending on the gun.

"Yeah," Kavanaugh informed. "As an American citizen waitin' the protection of this foreign government, I'm taking some law in my hands."

She put her hands to her breast, her eyes bewildered. "I—I do not understand—"

"Then you will," Kavanaugh advised acidly. "Here's a man stabbed in the back and we bring him to your hospital for First Aid, and you let him die. You say you're a nurse for the Dr. Eberhardt who runs this place, but when we call for the doctor you don't know where he is. You tell us you've always lived here with this Dr. Eberhardt; he always leaves word where he goes; then you show us this laboratory smashed to hell. The doc is gone; you don't know how or when it happened—although you sleep on the same floor—and you don't know what's become of him. Is that enough?"

"But I—"

"It's enough," Kavanaugh promised through his teeth, "but it isn't all. We run back downstairs and find Haarman's bled to death. Do you start looking for Dr. Eberhardt, send out a call for help, yell for the servants as one might naturally expect—"

"But there are no servants," the girl shook her head in protest. "There are only the sleeping patients here; they would know nothing. The old house-boy, Polypheme, went to the village early this evening with the car and will not be back until—"

Kavanaugh lifted his left palm peremptorily. "Save it. Eberhardt's not here, anyway, and you then stall us with a wild bedtime story about Mr. Haarman being a guy you saw die fourteen years ago. A good trick, but it doesn't go down. Any more than Haarman's web foot proves he was once a German sailor called Adolph Perl, nicknamed the Duck."

JOHN RANIER LIMPED half a step at the man with the gun. "One minute, Kavanaugh! How would this girl know Haarman had a webbed foot unless—"

"Unless you told her?" The man's mouth quirked up the side of his face insinuatingly. "Unless you raced out here ahead of us and tipped her off. You're our ship's medico. Maybe on shipboard you spotted Haarman's phony toes. Tonight, after the stabbing, you scoot out here and wise up this girl. You were on hand when we pulled in with Haarman, weren't you?"

The implication was clear. Ranier said, staggered, "I rode out here on the back of the Winton. Got here the same time you did. As for Miss Engles, why would I tip her off about anything? I never saw her before in my—"

"Didn't you?" Kavanaugh's question came from a contemptuous smile. "You've been doctor on this cruise ship five years, I understand. Sailing around Haiti and making this port every two months or so. You wouldn't, conceivably, have called on your colleague in this God-forsaken spot; struck up a friendship with the beautiful, lonely nurse?"

The girl answered for Ranier, her accent

deep-throated, "I do not know this man!" pointing at John Ranier; and he felt a slow flush mount in his cheekbones. No, he'd never called on his colleague in this God-forsaken spot, as one physician on another. Never, in fact, heard of him until tonight. He hadn't struck up a friendship with the beautiful (Kavanaugh's sarcasm was uncalled for on that point) and lonely nurse. The only place he'd visited in this wretched port was the nearest bar. Swigging that damned *aguardiente*. Going to seed. Not that it mattered. Only if he'd been more clearheaded at the start of tonight's madness—

He heard Kavanaugh rasping, "Well, I'm holding the girl for your accomplice, Ranier, and I'm going to turn you over for the murder of Mr. Haarman and maybe Dr. Eberhardt."

Then he could feel the blood running down out of his face, and he was aware that the girl, stricken by the Irishman's malignant accusation, had pressed back to the wall, her hands behind her, shrinking from his nearness, her eyes repelling him with horror. Facing Kavanaugh, his lips went stiff with controlled fury.

"I don't know a damned thing about Eberhardt, or Haarman, either. How could *I* have stabbed Haarman back there in that café?"

Kavanaugh shrugged, bowing a little over his aimed gun. "I'm not saying you did. I'm saying I think you did."

"Why?"

"Why do I think you did?"

"Let's have it."

"I think you did," the Irishman's tone was mockingly judicious, "because you're the only one who was there in that café who could have done it. Logical?"

"I'm listening."

"Have some more." Kavanaugh might have been passing the jelly. "No one of our party at the table could've stabbed Haarman because the others at the table would've seen it. No one at the table went around behind his chair. Only other occupants of the dump were that black bartender and you. You don't accuse that coon of doing it, do you?"

"He couldn't—"

"That," Kavanaugh smiled, "leaves you."

JOHN RANIER DIDN'T smile. "Does it? I was sitting in an alcove off the bar, wasn't I? Mr. Haarman was in the middle of the room. How could *I* have stabbed the man?"

"Mr. Haarman was to meet the rest of us in the motoring party at the café, which was to have been our starting point. He went there a half hour ahead of us. You were there when he turned up. Admitted?"

"What do you mean admitted?" Ranier said, angered. He felt he would go cross-eyed staring at the gun which kept his fist from flying at the tall man's mocking teeth. There was a cat-with-mouse attitude about the Irishman that needed a stiff punching. Ranier could only open and shut his hands, glaring. "What do you mean admitted? I said so from the first, didn't I?"

Kavanaugh lifted an admonitory eyebrow. "You also admitted you and Haarman had had a little quarrel?"

"I told you about that, too. He'd been drinking. Ugly when he came into the café. Chucked me out of my chair. He took a pass at me, understand? I never put a hand on him. And what's that got to do with my stabbing the man when the rest of you were there."

"*Before* we got there," was the answer. Kavanaugh's eyes went slant-wise at the book he was holding in his left hand. His forehead wrinkled inquiringly. "You might've stabbed Haarman *before* the rest of us arrived. Eh?"

Ranier snapped, "That's a good one, since the man was chatting about the trip with you when you pulled up chairs at his table," but his forehead was wet in a sudden apprehension of the fox-look on the tall man's face, the smirk as he held out the book left-handed, indicating a page under his thumb.

"Haarman might've been stabbed before the rest of us got there," Kavanaugh was repeating softly. "He might've sat there in his chair talkin' to us and havin' a drink. Sure, just as if nothin' had happened. I'd never of thought it possible, till I seen this doctor's book lyin' open on the floor. Just the right paragraph, too. Haarman might have sat there dyin'—just like th' case on this page—*and not even known he'd been stabbed!*"

It was there in the pages of that medical book as it had been printed from the start of that evening in the back of Ranier's mind. Haarman *could* have been stabbed before the others came to the café; could have slumped there in his chair and gone on drinking and talking, never conscious of his fatal wound. There was that Austrian empress who was said to have continued a long walk after being stabbed by a shoemaker's awl, dropping dead without knowing of her wound—the many instances of soldiers going for hours without realizing they'd been hit.

Kavanaugh's voice was purring on: "That explains him talkin' to us when we met him. But he looked bad, sittin' there, all right. Ginned up, too. Never seen you creep up behind him. After he chucked you out, you come in behind him through the window, I suppose. Then went back out over the sill, threw away the shiveree, and walked in by the front door."

Ranier said huskily, "It doesn't hold water—"

Kavanaugh nodded agreeably, "Who's talking about water? I'm talking about blood."

"That's what I'm talking about," Ranier appealed to the room. "Cases of people being stabbed without knowing it apply to internal hemorrhage. Haarman's wound bled externally. That much blood, he'd certainly know it. Soaked his jacket across the shoulders. And if he was stabbed before you joined him there at that table, you'd have seen the stains when you took chairs beside him."

"The blood run down the back of his chair," Kavanaugh supplied smoothly. "Since none of us went around behind his chair we didn't see it. The coon who owns the joint didn't see you do it because he was out in back somewhere. All right, Haarman was still ticking when our party arrived. So what? So you see a chance to pin the job on one of us, or maybe blame it on these Voodoo ghosts. That jigaboo Marcelline plays into your hand by having visions and what-not. Also you realize we'll rush Haarman to the nearest hospital, which is Eberhardt's here. You stall around. Still Haarman keeps ticking. Then you tell us you're going to beat it out to the ship and fetch back the captain, but instead of that you take a short-cut, and you're already on hand at the hospital when we arrive. Didn't Coolidge see you tear from behind th' building when this nurse jerked that scream?"

"I tell you," Ranier's tongue felt thick, "I rode out here on the back of your car!"

"Unless, say, you cut up the mountain, an' got here first to forestall this Doc Eberhardt from giving Haarman a transfusion after you'd given him a blood-letting. Then let's say Eberhardt refused to lay off. There's a fight up here in this little museum of his. Was that how you ripped your Sunday pants? Your elbow, too? Look at th' cuts on your hands."

"I fell. I fell off the spare tire of that Winton!"

"Or," Kavanaugh said in his sweetened voice, "did this Doc Eberhardt knock you for a loop up here just before we came. Let's say he did. Then let's say you knocked him for a loop. Say the beautiful lonely nurse runs in. She sees Eberhardt out cold—dead, for the sake of argument. She sees you. I don't say it's love at first sight, y'understand; I say you've known her for some time. I say," Kavanaugh delivered the indictment in the bored tone of a District Attorney summing an obvious case for a stupid jury, "I say you and this girl are hand in glove together. At least, in part of this. Pretending you don't know each other. Huh! But you put Eberhardt out of the way, then cooked up this Adolph Perl gag to scare us off. The girl spins a fairy story about an expedition in Brazil when she was a kid, and Haarman comin' back to haunt her; and you play you're haywired by the whole set-up. Well, you can tell it to the bulls, if they ever get here."

• • •

KAVANAUGH FLIRTED THE gun impatiently; switched his address to the three tourists statue-struck behind him. "It's a pip, isn't it?" showing the book, before throwing it aside. "Poor Haarman was dyin' when we met up with him. Never knew it, either. I wonder what the cops will say when they see those footprints of Ranier's—the ones we saw when Marcelline turned the car around to start for the hospital— those tracks under that café window. Maybe I'm prejudiced," he whipped his aim back at Ranier, "but it seems to me my theory is a damn sight more reasonable than all this living-dead-man stuff!"

Consternation stalled Ranier's tongue. It was reasonable, all right. Reasonable enough to wring a cry from Carpetsi: "Why, th' dirty rat, you oughta let him have one from th' gun!" Reasonable enough to bring a whinny from Professor Schlitz: "Our ship's doctor! Great Scott! He might have murdered us all! I do believe he did stab poor Mr. Haarman!"

"He did," Kavanaugh sneered, "if you happen to be a Christian white man who doesn't believe in Voodoo and all this *zombie* hocus pocus. If—"

The Irishman did not conclude the remark. *Thump!* Sound of a door slammed somewhere in the lower part of the house took the words out of Kavanaugh's mouth; left him tense, beady-eyed, listening. Everybody turned to listen. No denying that below-floors report; unmistakably someone was in the house downstairs, had slammed a door.

A channel of cold air coursed down the back of John Ranier's neck, as if an unseen breeze had entered the room. Laïs Engles might have felt it, too, the way she shivered, staring wide-pupiled toward the hall; and Kavanaugh's face was frosty as he flung around at the girl, white but not so Christian. "Who's that? It's not Coolidge and Brown—we'd heard the car. Who slammed that door downstairs just now?"

Without replying, the girl made a swift move past the man, snatched open the laboratory door, sent a tremulous call out across the upper balcony glooms. "*Wer da?* Dr. Eberhardt—? Unkle Doktor—? Dr. Eberhardt, is that you—?"

The only answer was the gray cat arriving silently on the threshold, smiling up at the girl, then trotting into the room. Ranier looked at the cat, half-expecting to learn that this was Dr. Eberhardt.

Mouth ugly, eyes glittering, Kavanaugh caught the girl's wrist and twisted her back from the threshold. "Who's downstairs in this place?"

She gasped, "Only the patients. Four. A child with an amputated leg. A man confined in contagion with smallpox. A man dying of *dhangi* fever. A woman bed-ridden, dying of elephantiasis. They could not leave their beds." Her whisper lowered to hardly more than a movement of her lips. "That door—"

Kavanaugh's knuckles showed white from the grip on the gun. Stepping out on the balcony, he sped a quick glance down on the hall below, turned, confronted the laboratory with a grim eye.

"Wait up here! I'll be back in a minute, and I wouldn't worry about shooting the first one of you I caught trying to leave!"

He pulled the door after him; then his shoes made a hurried tattoo on the stairs. Then silence. Silence filled with the blond woman's alarmed breathing. In which Angelo Carpetsi's skin staled from olive to ptomaine-green while his tie sweat blue through his pink-striped collar. In which Laïs Engles stood rigid against the wall, her hands pressed to the plaster, eyes averted; and Professor Schlitz watched Ranier with the hypnotic stare of a bird confined with a cobra. Anger struggled with apprehension in Ranier's mind. These fools didn't have to be afraid of him; he was as lost in this jabberwok nightmare as they were. A bead of sweat guttered down the side of his nose, and he grimly considered an Anopheles mosquito that had buzzed out of the tainted air to sit on his hand. He pinched the head from the malarial insect, and stood in tension, waiting for sounds below. The gray cat polished itself against his shins.

TWO MINUTES. THREE minutes. What the devil was keeping that Irishman? What was going on in this mountain villa?

Had the ambulance party, rushing Haarman to this gloomy asylum, surprised some nefarious enterprise here in the hospital? At the thought, Ranier gave the girl at his side a glance of sudden mistrust. Maybe Kavanaugh had been right and that story of hers was a stall. Her manner was convincing enough, but he'd been fooled by one woman in his life—certainly a trained nurse couldn't believe in ghosts coming back from the grave. Her fear was masking something—something she was holding back? Well, the *Garde d'Haiti* ought to be here any minute now, and this guy Kavanaugh—

The door burst open, and Mr. Kavanaugh was back in the laboratory. Not the same Mr. Kavanaugh who had gone to explore downstairs. Somewhere during that prowl the Irishman had lost his self-possession. Mr. Kavanaugh's cheekbones showed the loss. His lips were pieces of chalk. Eyes glassy. Finger in collar, he seemed to sway in the doorway as if a deck were rocking under him.

"It's Haarman," his lips writhed in chalk-talk. "It's Haarman, and his shoe isn't there in the corridor where Ranier dropped it. He isn't in that room down there. The body— Haarman—he's gone!"

Then, before anyone had time to recoil from that shock, a motor-roar broke in the night outside. The sound grew. Tires skidding on loose gravel. A screech of brakes and wrenched springs as the car came into the driveway under the window. Kavanaugh blurted hoarsely, "The police!" and Ranier listened to boots pound across the verandah with something like Thanksgiving in his heart. Thanksgiving that changed to perspiration on his forehead. It was not the police!

He knew it was not the *Garde d'Haiti*, for that efficient and colorful *gendarme* patrol generally sauntered in pairs, and this new arrival came alone and at high speed.

The police would not have banged through the front door howling, "*M'sieu Docteur! Ma'mselle Laïs! Malheur! Malheur! Mortoo tomboo vient! Au secours!*"

Wild feet came stumbling up the stairs, bringing that frenzy in Creole; and Laïs Engles cried in answering dialect:

"*Polypheme! Ici! Ici! 'Vitement!*" She turned to those in the room. "It's Polypheme—the house-boy—back from the village! He—"

Then there came through the doorway the most terrified darky John Ranier had ever seen. A little old black man made of rags and licorice with eyes like saucers under the tatter-fringe brim of an enormous straw sombrero. Overwhelmed by the fifty-gallon brim, his face looked not much bigger than a raisin; one guessed he was lost under the hat and frightened by its omnipotence. He wore patchwork trousers and a sleeveless cotton jumper, the right half red, the left half blue, as if he'd sewed the garment from a moth-eaten Haitian flag; and there was a snowy goat-tuft on his chin. He resembled for all the world a black performing goat that had escaped a circus in full costume; and he performed in the laboratory doorway, rocking on hind legs, waving his forefeet at Laïs Engles, eyeballs like burnt matches rolling around in china saucers, mouth bleating, "Nnnnnyaaaaah!" Then, hat and all, he jumped the threshold; flung himself prostrate at the girl's feet.

She cried, "*Lever ou, tout suit!* Stand up, Polypheme! Speak English! Where is Dr. Eberhardt! What have you seen?"

He could stand before her doing a sort of jig, but the English was too much for him after a gibbered, "No see'm Dr. Eberhardt—Ah been village, come quick!" His linguistic ability blowing a fuse when it came to what he had seen.

Then Haitian and goat-bleats poured from his mouth, and even his native tongue seemed inadequate. He had to windmill his arms and roll his eyes. His goatee flickered, and the effort brought

*Ranier stared. The
little old lady—dead
for fourteen years—
looked much alive.*

globes of ink on his forehead. He pointed at the
ceiling, at the floor, at the fog-hung window; saw
the laboratory tank of bullfrogs and ended with
a caterwaul beyond translation.

But it needed no interpreter to make John
Ranier understand terror when he heard it. He
saw the fear in the little Haitian's eyes reflect in
the eyes of the girl. Saw her put hand to throat
as if in want of air, and gaze in white transfixion
at the window.

"What is it?" Ranier growled. "What does he
say?"

"He says," Laïs Engles whispered, "he has
just come from the village. A mob is gathering,
and the *Rada* drums are signals. Rumor has
started a *zombie* is loose—a dead man walking
in the fog. The blacks are angry, and Hyacinth
Lucien is spreading word Dr. Eberhardt is a sorcerer, a white magician who has raised this *zombie* from the dead. It was to warn the hospital
of danger that Polypheme left the village early.
On the way home he passed the graveyard. *Oh,
God!*"

She spread one hand against the wall for support, pressing the other to her forehead as if it
hurt. "He says—he says he saw near the road an
opened grave. An old lady sitting on a coffin. An
old lady who is dead. She wears a black bonnet

and a taffeta dress, and there is a live frog tied to
her wrist. She is the old lady, he says, who came
with me from Brazil. Who died in this hospital
fourteen years ago. *It is Old Gramma Sou—*"

CHAPTER XI

THE LADY AT THE GRAVE

If he survived to be ten thousand, Ranier knew,
the picture of that graveyard would be indelible
in his memory, although he never could quite
remember how he got there. Afterwards, it had
seemed like Kavanaugh's doing. Kavanaugh had
yelled like a Choctaw, "Come on!"

There was a tumble down the stairs, led by
the Irishman with the gun and followed by all
who did not wish to be left behind. A battle
to reach the night air. Ranier took time out to
sprint to the dark rear corridor and down the
corridor to the emergency room in the hopes
of finding Mr. Haarman, because Kavanaugh
must have been wrong and the dead man had to
be there—then wasn't. He could remember racing to join the others at the front; seeing what
looked like a small sedan.

From there to the cemetery everything

blurred. He stood on the running board, for all the seats were taken—Professor Schlitz squealing with the blonde swamping his lap; Kavanaugh and Carpetsi jammed together; Polypheme at the wheel with Laïs Engles—then no one had wanted to go. The small sedan hadn't wanted to go, either. Made in Detroit, it had suffered hard usage in this tropical environment, and tonight it was worn out. The fog had given it asthma, and its right eye was blind. It bucked spleenishly on leaving the driveway, shied at the turn, shimmied its front wheels when it hit the macadam, then shot on the downhill grade in spiteful abandon. Perhaps it would not have moved at all, if Kavanaugh hadn't muttered something virulent at the driver and flourished his automatic. All right, it would show them.

Ranier had traveled up the mountain on a spare tire; now he was racketing down it on a door. This Model T must have come from the same museum as the Winton, and there was the same sensation of zooming off into space. Night loomed in cliffs that scraped the running boards, and the fog streamed through the cracked windshield and under the wheels so there wasn't any visible road. The car's single eye, its battery dim, was useful solely in showing the curves when the wheels were on them and it was too late to do much about it. But it was no good worrying about accidents. The accidents had happened. If you were a ship's doctor accustomed to only normal miracles and suddenly confronted by vanishing knives and life after death, there wasn't much you could do but hang on.

Ranier hung on.

The woman in the back seat was shrieking like a dame on a roller-coaster as Kavanaugh fired oaths at break-neck turns and Carpetsi loudly remembered saints. Fog funneled by in rushing, fumid whorls; pearl-tinted in the path of the headlight; barrage-thick beyond, as if the night had been everywhere afire and doused, and now the charred blackness was smoking. At the steering wheel Polypheme was a pair of eyeballs, disembodied, with a faint blue shine of a cheekbone, and Ranier could see Laïs Engles'

hands, tight-nerved, deathly white, gripping the dashboard just above a dimmed grape-sized light-bulb.

IT WAS NO time to think about a dead man climbing down off an operating table, leaving the room to retrieve a shoe for his webbed left foot, and slamming the door in departure. Cardiac spasm did peculiar things; *rigor mortis* might cause a cadaver to salute a terrified morgue attendant, or quirk lifeless lips in a grin. But it never walked a dead man out of a hospital, or animated him throughout a Caribbean cruise after fourteen years in the ground.

It was no time, either, to recall the story a French consul in Port-au-Prince had once told him about the dead men they'd found working at the Hasco plant. Ranier recalled it. Hasco stands for Haitian American Sugar Company, and you can buy Hasco Rum today in any good liquor store in the States. You wouldn't expect the un-dead in a modern industrial plant under Yankee capital, but the rumor persisted that *zombies* had been seen there—John Ranier had laughed at the story.

It had been easy to laugh at the story told that time in the suburban country club at Kenscoff, where polite waiters served Planter's Punches under Japanese lanterns, and bored tourists capered to a Haitian orchestra butchering the "Black Bottom."

Zooming downhill through fog in this Model T stuffed with terrified tourists in a night alive with the threat of jungle drums, John Ranier didn't laugh. He heard the girl cry faintly, "Hurry, Polypheme—*Vite! Vite!* Oh, God— I've got to see—" and the fog seemed to be blowing in cold blank streams under his scalp. Blowing with the words, "Unreal! Unreal!"

No dead man could walk out of a door. If Haarman could saunter from that downstairs room after epidermal discoloration had set in, all the rules were off, and he might in truth have been buried four years after the War. It gave one's foundations no more substance than this mist at night. Better go back to elixirs, witch-burnings, wands. Accept the "touch-power" of Valentine Greatrakes, the miraculous beds of Cagliostro, and Perkins' tweezer-cure, Hippocrates and Galen were fools in tonight's fog; Pasteur, Jenner and Carrel had built on myths, and this old lady the house-boy claimed to have seen, might be there.

She was there!

A HAITIAN CEMETERY is, at best, a stage-set for ghosts, with broken masonry and jerrybuilt vaults and the helter-skelter parceling of the plots. The little mounds are heaped high with cockle shells; the moss grows green, and there are lizards; there might even be a granite angel with a broken nose. The tombstones have a way of leaning, like bones poked up out of the ground.

The Haitians know who tipped over those stones. They know who tilted that mound at an angle overnight; who blurred the letters once chiseled so deep in the marble. So their cemeteries hug the roads for comfort and burn their penny candles late. But neither candles nor the headlamp of a car were comforting in this particular mountain graveyard.

The headlamp's ray made a swerve across the road, streamed under the cemetery arch and diffused in a cone of misty luminescence that spread uphill in the murk, touching a gleam to wet marbles, creeping across the sleeping mounds. In the vaporous background, the vigil candles were outer moons in a void, each a sentinel to its own patch of earth, and beyond these yellow blurs, the jungle joined with the night in an impenetrable wall.

In the mist that unraveled above them, the dark mounds were smoking. Gray wooden crosses dripped. Vine-clad headstones showed patches of white through glistening creeper, and near the entrance arch one mound was distinguished by a little glass-windowed doghouse where mourners might peep at a wreath made of the departed's hair, a collection of the deceased's

belongings, a chromo of Saint Sulpice and a miniature of the departed looking holier than he was. The car-light streamed past this doleful reliquary and touched on something that would have cooled the thick-skinned hearts of Burke and Hare. That Scotch-Irish team of grave robbers would have run for their lives. Even the Model T jumped back.

She was sitting on an overturned coffin, her back propped against a tombstone at the head of an opened grave, regarding the pile of shoveled red sand heaped alongside, with solemn interest. She was frail, and old-fashioned, and the fog-shawl wrapped about her shoulders blew in tatters and wisps that floated away. Her black taffeta dress was the same stuff as the fog, delicate as cobweb, and the black kid gloves in her lap wanted mending. Some bright beads glinted from a crumbled reticule at her feet; and her shoes, styled of another period, high-buttoned like those of Mrs. Katzenjammer, were mossy from too long in the damp. But her granny's bonnet, fastened beneath her chin by an enormous bow, was almost jaunty. Her spectacles were bright. She looked spry. An old lady—the words occurred to Ranier with a taste of zinc in his mouth—well preserved.

Very well preserved. Approaching her on legs that moved through no volition of his own, John Ranier was sure she was alive. She was sitting there composing an elegy. She had come there with flowers and sat down to rest; come there out of the long ago, and was tired from the long walk. Ought to have chosen a better seat, though. That coffin-bottom was pretty well gone. In the darkness she'd mistaken it for a bench. She'd better go. That shawl of fog was draughty for frail shoulders, and the taffeta so thin it wore into holes and tatters as one watched.

There! She nodded at Ranier. Quaintly the bonnet nodded twice. Good evening, young man. Plain as could be. Then he saw the movement came from a fat green bullfrog tethered to her wrist by a length of string. When the frog jumped, her head moved. Tied by a hind leg, the frog made another restricted hop, and the old lady reproved her pet with a perky nod. Some flakes crumbled from the satin bow under her chin, and her glasses went awry. You wouldn't have expected Mother Goose in Haiti—

"Old Gramma Sou—!"

"Don't!" Ranier pulled the girl back, and she stood against him, hiding her face in his shoulder. Mindless, he stood in the headlamp's gray-yellow path, arm about the girl, while shadows charged by him, struggled together at the grave-edge. Professor Schlitz, after one appalled look, tottered backwards over two mounds, fell against the little doghouse near the entrance arch, ramming an elbow through one of the windows. Automatic hanging at his side, Kavanaugh went in a prowl around the opened grave, circling it twice, cursing in a harsh guttural monotone, coming at last to a stand beside the old lady in black. In the wet rays of the car light his face was marble. His eyes were cat-green. Inadvertently he touched the coffin with his boot toe, and the wood crumbled like punk. Oaths snarled from his teeth. Typically, the Irishman's fear appeared to translate itself into rage.

ANGELO CARPETSI WAS on hands and knees, staring down into the raw excavation. The blond woman stumbled up to Kavanaugh, holding her skirts up to one knee, slipping and sliding in the soft loam. Too late Ranier thought of footprints. That old lady, no matter how spry, could not have shoveled her way out without assistance. Someone else had been there. That length of string on her wrist looked new. The bullfrog could not break from the leash, although his desperate leaps reduced the glove holding him to leather fragments. It was better to think that someone had been there earlier tonight, someone who had arranged this necromantic old lady in that pose. Whoever it had been, the footprints would be blotted by this rush. Tightening his arm about Laïs Engles, Ranier could feel her shivers running up and down his own skin. His teeth jiggled. He heard glass jangle as the professor rebounded from the housed grave; heard

sounds something like words blurt from the Italian boy—"Empty—How'd that old woman—! Holy Mother—!" Heard Kavanaugh's tooth-ground oaths. Only the old lady sitting there in frayed taffeta remained composed.

The blond woman began to scream. She clutched Kavanaugh's sleeve, pulling him toward the car, screeching into his agate face. "Get me awaaaay!" her voice ascending as if in rage. "I've had enough of this! Enough of this, understand? That man murdered—! *This*—! I won't have it—! You've got to get me out of this—! You said there wouldn't be any danger—! Just a ride, you said, and you'd take care of ev—!"

She slipped to her plush knees, dragging him almost down on top of her, as his free hand smote across her mouth, stopping her outcry with an infuriated smack. "Get into the car!" He yanked her to her feet; shoved. "Get back into that car, by Judas, before I—" He sucked in his breath, green-lit eyeballs following her hysterical gallop through the archway; then wiped his lips on his wrist and wheeled to face the grave.

Carpetsi turned and rose from his knees with a corkscrew motion that brought him around to face Kavanaugh. Greasy hair slid in a raven's wing across his left eye. His right eye, black, glitterous, moved from side to side under a sickly lid. He whispered, "What the hell, Kavanaugh?" in a voice that seemed to come from a cramped stomach. Three times at Kavanaugh, as if the Irishman should have some answer.

Kavanaugh shook his head, panting, "I don't know how—I don't know how that body—"

Staring across the gold lights in Laïs Engles' hair, John Ranier growled, "Somebody did this! Somebody exhumed this—old lady! Yes, and propped her up against that tombstone—tied that live frog there!"

His own reaction now was anger. He'd let his imagination make him a fool. Heat dried pallidness on his forehead in an upsurge of rage against the vandals who had roused an old lady from her last sleep.

"Damn! Maybe I'm wrong, Kavanaugh, but

I'll bet the one who stole Haarman's body out of the hospital tonight is the same filthy rat responsible for *this!*"

"Stole Haarman's—" Kavanaugh's teeth came together with a click. "By Judas! Sure! Well, Ranier, how much do you know about that?"

"I don't know anything about it. I'm going to find out."

Carpetsi pushed hair from his left eye; stepped towards the Irishman. "This ain't no time to talk, Kavanaugh. I'm gettin'—"

"Shut up!" Flinging the command at the Italian from the side of his mouth, Kavanaugh kept his gaze focused on Ranier. "Just who do you think snatched Haarman's body?" His voice was harsh, threatening. "If you've got any ideas, let's have 'em. And about this!" He jerked his chin at the grave.

Ranier shook his head. "All I know is, that frog looks like one of the batch from the tank in Eberhardt's laboratory."

Carpetsi interrupted in a raw voice, "Kavanaugh! I'm goin'!"

"We'd all better go," Ranier snarled. "For the police."

"Like hell! After what that black goat in the car told us about the riot in the village?" Kavanaugh's mouth went up at one corner, baring teeth. "Those boogs would tear your beautiful nurse to pieces. Besides," he twisted at Carpetsi, "Coolidge and Brown went for those *gendarmes,* and they're due any minute. Pull yourself together, boy! I'll handle this! We're going back to the hospital, that's where. But first we're going to settle something."

SLIPPING THE AUTOMATIC into a pocket of his khaki waterproof, Kavanaugh stepped close to Ranier, stopped in front of him, glared down at Laïs Engles, his hard eyes fixed on the back of the girl's neck. "First," he repeated, aiming his finger at the girl, "we're going to settle something. She claims Haarman is a guy named Adolph Perl, a man she saw buried in

Haiti fourteen years ago. I don't know the game, see? I don't know the Hallowe'en racket! But as long as she's stickin' to her Haarman-Perl story, maybe she can show us *that* grave?"

Ranier gripped the girl's shoulder. "Miss Engles—"

Slowly she wheeled in his grasp. Gems of moisture glimmered in her hair, and her face was gardenia-white in the wreathing fog. Confronting that rectangular black pit and the frail watcher at the grave-side, she shut her eyes, swayed. Ranier held her firm.

"That Perl fellow, Miss Engles. We'd like to see *his* grave."

She whispered, "The tombstone—look at the tombstone—!" pointing.

Carpetsi uttered a strangled yelp, turning swiftly to see; and Kavanaugh's eyes swerved between wolfish slits, the pupils glinting yellow-green through quivering lashes. Aghast, John Ranier saw the girl's finger indicated the tombstone employed as a back-rest by that appalling old lady. The slab at the head of the opened grave. The old lady leaning against the edge of the slab gave a nod as if in confirmation, and settled against the stone a little more comfortably, her bonnet sliding down rakishly over her forehead.

The hazed headlamp of the car did not afford enough light for reading the weathered stone. Ranier snatched for his flashlight; sent a wan ray leaping across the excavation. The misty circle brought the slab into spectral relief, its legend clearly legible.

HIER RUHET IN GOTT
ADOLPH PERL
GEST. 3 JANUAR 1922
ICH HATTE EINST
EIN SCHONES VATERLAND

Professor Schlitz translated in a wizardish tremolo, "Here rests in God—Adolph Perl— Died third January, 1922—I once had a buh-beautiful Fatherland."

Laïs Engles cried, "I had that inscription put

on for him, myself. *That* is Adolph Perl's grave! The old lady—that is Old Gramma Sou, who was buried in the cemetery three miles from here!"

Her chin touched her breast sleepily, and she slowly went to the ground through Ranier's nerveless hands.

CHAPTER XII

DRUMS SPELL DISASTER

"By Heaven! if that *is* Perl's grave!"—"I told you, Kavanaugh!"—"What's this old woman doin' here when—?" "You can see it's just been dug up!"—"Where's Perl, then? He ain't here, is he? That means Haarman *was*—!" "If anybody thinks they can do this to me, Dave Kavanaugh—" "How *she* get here? If this dame was buried in some bone-orchard three miles away—?"

Voices. Voices banging, snarling, caterwauling in Ranier's ears, a pyrotechnic of words, sentences exploded unfinished, hanging fire in the air. Impossible to follow that play of expressions. Impossible to think. Fog seemed to swirl through Ranier's head as if doors had blown open in his frontal lobe, and his thoughts went scattering about his brain like the papers on the floor of that scrambled hospital laboratory. Voices were bats whisking through his brain-doors in erratic flight, and somewhere in his subconscious, drums were muttering.

He discovered his mouth was open, inhaling mould. He closed it, and dropped to one knee beside the girl. Chafed her wrists. Heard himself wheedling, "Take it easy! Take it easy!" in an insincere way. Like asking someone to have some ice cream in a catacomb. But it was hard to effect a bedside manner at the edge of a freshly-opened grave in a foggy cemetery; particularly when the rightful owner of the plot wasn't there, and the visitor sitting on the absentee's coffin was an old lady from a neighboring necropolis.

Bad enough to believe her above ground in her own graveyard without learning she was three miles from home. He'd thought Adolph Perl (if any) securely anchored in some burying ground nearer the village. What unearthly power had transported the old lady to this foreign field, dead with a live pet bullfrog? What was she doing at Perl's grave, and where was its original inheritor?

Kavanaugh was bawling in the direction of the car, "You get this, Daisy? Keep screamin' like that and you'll have everybody in Haiti down on top of us! The body that oughta be here ain't here, that's all. If you'll close that trap of yours and give me a chance to think—"

From the car Professor Schlitz's voice went piccolo. "*Perl's* grave! *Perl's?* Then Haarman is Perl— Of course he w-wouldn't be in his grave! It's precisely as the girl told us, don't you see? Don't you see?" The piccolo in his throat struck high G. "He was a *zombie!* In my stateroom! Dead tonight and walked off again. *Again!* Oh, my! He'll be roaming—!"

The insectologist's screech conjured visions of Mr. Haarman strolling down the night, vacant eyes staring, dead face expressionless, blood creeping from that hole in his back—perhaps carrying his shoe in a lifeless hand and walking on that exposed duck foot.

You could see things that way in the fog. Adolph Perl's grave empty. Haarman being Adolph Perl. As sensible as any of tonight's wizardries, with that café stabbing in broad lamplight; that cryptogram on Haarman's mail; Dr. Eberhardt's disappearance from a laboratory where hands cooked; Haarman's walk-out after death. The girl had said Haarman was Perl and Perl was missing from his grave and an old lady from another cemetery was here to pay her respects to the departed. It fitted with the girl's war story and the legends of Monsieur Marcelline. No denying that old lady, well preserved though she was, had been buried a long time—

Helping Laïs Engles to her feet, John Ranier shied a glance at the visitor across the excavation; would not have been surprised to see her stand up briskly, adjust bonnet and specs, bid them a hoarse good-bye, and lead her bullfrog off into shreds of mist.

Drawing the girl aside, he asked huskily, "Feel all right now?" At the sound of his voice, Kavanaugh and the Italian stopped shouting blurred words and looked toward him.

Laïs Engles shuddered. "Please—I will be—all right."

Ranier said dryly, "Don't look again, but—are you certain that's the—the old lady who was on the German expedition with—"

"Oh, it is—it is—!"

He said under his breath, "This is terrible!" Aloud: "Where's the cemetery the old lady came from?"

The girl whispered, "Beyond the hospital. Back up the road the way we came. About a mile the—the other side of the hospital."

"The other side of the hospital?" Kavanaugh shouted the word "other," shouldering forward. "Direction *away* from the town? Impossible!"

Ranier's tone was grim. "We're going there to look. Right now! We're going to the cemetery where the old lady, here, was buried."

"We ain't!" The snarl was surprising, coming from Angelo Carpetsi. The Italian boy's face was surprising. Pushing oily hair from his black eyes, he made a sudden lunge between Ranier and Kavanaugh, stood glaring from one to the other, his fog-drenched features glistening, wrenched. His pink silk shirt, pasted to his breast, pumped up and down. He cat-spat at Ranier, "You keep outa this!"

Ranier said through his teeth, "We're going to the cemetery where that old lady was buried!"

"We're goin' to find Brown an' Coolidge!" the Italian boy corrected. His eyes glittered. His face puckered like Mussolini's in the gnashing bombast of a speech. He pinched his finger-tips together and sawed the gesture up and down under Ranier's nose, spitting, "If you know what's good for you, quack, you'll keep your puss outa this! I say we're goin' to catch up with Coolidge and Brown!"

He wrenched around at Kavanaugh. "You've stalled long enough. Yeah. I know the racket. I'm

on to you, see? If it wasn't a stall, you'd be huntin' damn quick for Brown an' Coolidge an' that shine they went off with, instead of—"

Kavanaugh's eyes were barbarous as he plunged his hand into trench-coat pocket, shoved the bulge at Carpetsi and broke in with, "You greasy little wop, you've lost your head! I don't know any more about this than you do!"

"Yah?" The Italian boy was screaming now. "You're smart, ain't you, Kavanaugh? Too damn smart! Well, you ain't goin' to get away with it. I know you're in this with the ship's doc. You fixed it for this quack to be in that café when we started tonight. You're workin' this with him. Sure, you are!"

KAVANAUGH SQUINTED THROUGH the yellow-lit mist as if it were acrid and stung his eyes. Squinted from Carpetsi to Ranier while his sharp features registered wrathful amazement. "Can you beat that? He thinks," he scoffed at Ranier, "I'm hand in glove with *you!*"

"You betcha you are!" Carpetsi howled. "You're workin' together with this murderous sawbones, or you'd have knocked him off after Haarman was bumped. You dirty double-crosser, I suppose you think you're gonna smudge *me* out? Yah, it'll be me next. Me! All the while you're pretending you don't know a thing about this set-up in the graveyard, here—"

Kavanaugh put his face close to the Italian's; squalled, "It'll be you next, all right, if you don't close that yap! You'll have every boog in Haiti on our necks!"

"Let 'em come! Let 'em come!" Carpetsi's expression was close to rabies. His fingers scratched the air before Kavanaugh's face. "You can't put this over on me, you big mick! By God, I see the trick you're pullin'! I'm gonna spill your beans, Kavanaugh—"

Kavanaugh told him in a deadly voice, "You're going to shut up! You're going to shut up, Angelo, and go over and sit in the car. You'll shut up, or I'll shut you up!"

"Yaaah!" The Italian's face was the shade of liverwurst. "You'd knock me off now, if you dared, but you don't dare! Too many witnesses you'd have to dust off. I won't shut up! I'll spill your beans! If you think that stunt of sendin' off Brown and Coolidge—"

There was an interruption, then, that suspended the Italian's screeching in mid-air.

John Ranier, standing back with the girl, too dazed by Carpetsi's outburst at Kavanaugh to move, heard a shout from somewhere beyond the car. A full-lunged bellow that came from the darkness on the road, its source invisible in the mist.

"Hey, there! Who wants Coolidge?"

It spun Kavanaugh in a crouch. Sent Carpetsi reeling on his heels as if struck by a fist, combing wild fingers through his Dance Palace hair. Thrusting the girl sideways, Ranier glared in bewilderment toward the car under the cemetery arch where the blond woman had trilled a coloratura shriek and the professor was blatting, "Did you bring the police?"

Then boots came pounding under the fog-drizzled arch, crackled over the cockle shells of a grave mound, and Coolidge formed in the lighted area before the headlamp. It was not the same Coolidge who had gone for the police two hours ago in this nightmare. The man's appearance was that of a rhino flushed by big game hunters from a swamp. The tourist attire that had been incongruous on his Mack truck frame was plastered, shapeless with mud. His shoes were swollen with clay, pants mired to the knees, sleeves brown to the elbows.

Blinking in the misty light-bath, he faced the group at the grave-side and scowled from one to the next, stupidly. Gold gleams ricocheted from his teeth as his mouth pulled lungfuls of breath and his chest puffed like a blacksmith's bellows.

"I was leggin' it back to the hospital," he panted at Kavanaugh. "Seen you go by in th' flivver. Damn near run me down in th' fog, and you was by before I could yell. Got here fast as I could." Plucking off the cap he had hung on one doorknob ear, he mopped his face and forehead with the cap, rotary motion, panting, rolling his eyes. "There's been an accident, see? I'm a mass of nerves! Justa mass of nerves!"

KAVANAUGH SAID, "I'LL say there's been an accident!" pacing up to the big man in a way that made Ranier think of a terrier accosting a Great Dane. He shoved his pocketed gun into Coolidge's muddy midriff, and Coolidge looked down at the Irishman's nudging pocket, and scowled, and began to walk backwards. Kavanaugh followed him, walking forwards.

Coolidge blurted, "What the hell—!" as Kavanaugh walked him out of the headlamp's path, drove him stumbling away from the car, pushed him at a tangent toward the foot of the graveyard. In the fogged darkness, still walking, the two men were gray, half-melted shapes.

Clinging to John Ranier's arm, Laïs Engles peered into the vapour-screen where the men had dissolved to a merged shadow, and whispered, "What is happening? What is happening?"

Ranier said, "Wait and see."

He heard the Irishman's voice bang, "Tell your story, big boy, and tell it quick!" the bang lowering to a menacing rapidfire undertone, muffled words punctuated with oaths, too inaudible for listeners to catch. Coolidge replied in gushing whispers, evidently pleading. Their voices bleared to a smothered mumbling from which Ranier's ears caught fragments. Kavanaugh haggling, accusing. Coolidge groaning, panting, denying. Coolidge shouted, "Holy Jumping Judas!" and Ranier could see the white oval of his face as he stretched his neck to look past his inquisitor at the opened grave. Twice Kavanaugh caught the big man's lapel, seemed to be shaking him; several times the Irishman looked back, glinty-eyed. Ranier heard his own name spoken, Professor Schlitz's, the girl's.

It seemed to him the whispered inquisition was lasting a long time, but he stood at the foot of the grave with the girl, nerves tight, waiting because there was nothing else to do. Everything was ravelling off into mists, facts dissolving, swimming through his fingers before he could clench them on anything certain. Bad dreams were like this—figures formed; faded; changed features; cut illogical capers that in the dream seemed logical. Like one of those nightmares where you walked in jeopardy through a forest of unseen perils, only it wasn't a forest and you were falling through limitless space. But he wasn't falling through space. He was standing in a Haitian graveyard with a frightened girl. A frightened Italian was rooted near-by, making throat-sounds like whimpering. A frightened Negro, a frightened blonde and a frightened college professor were parked in a frightened Model T under the cemetery arch. Two frightened men were arguing in violent whispers off in the fog; and the only one present who wasn't frightened was the little old lady jaunty against the tombstone—uncaring because she was dead.

What had become of the Winton? Of Brown and the Haitian, Marcelline? But those would be easy answers compared to: What became of Haarman? Was he dead when he was killed? Was he Adolph Perl buried fourteen years ago, and if he wasn't why had Perl vanished from his grave? Simple answers compared to: How did this old lady travel three miles on those mossy shoes? Who brought her here and why? How the hell can I get this frightened girl out of this? Has that mob started from the village? Where's Eberhardt?

EBERHARDT! QUEER! THE name kept prowling through his subconsciousness with the insistence of those drum-beats tunneling the fog. He wondered if he'd spoken it aloud. No; that was Kavanaugh's voice. They were coming back into the light; the Irishman moving with swift, purposeful strides; the muddied Coolidge wiping his battered face on his cap.

"We're getting out of here," Kavanaugh came shouting, "right now! Everybody into the car!"

Angelo Carpetsi raised a whimper. "I ain't going."

"Don't be a fool," was Kavanaugh's tongue-lashing command. "Stay behind here in this bone-yard and the black mob that's coming from the village will tear you to mince. We're moving out! Quick!"

He strode at Ranier, pointing toward the road, talking with the up-pitched momentum of a radio announcer. "Smash up! The Winton! That damned coon Marcelline crashed the sedan in a swamp a mile this side of the village. Marcelline and Brown went on. Beat it on foot the rest of the way to get the police. Coolidge says the car's smashed to junk, and there's hell to pay down there. Gunshots in the village and drums going like express trains. There's a riot, all right. Marcelline told him to run back and warn the hospital. Coolidge says he passed this graveyard on the way up, but he didn't see anything because it was all he could do to keep his feet on the macadam."

"If I'd known what was here, I'd have never come back," the big man promised. "I'd have never come back after you passed me up the road in the flivver. I'm justa mass of nerves!"

Kavanaugh panted, "We'll be more than a mass of nerves if we don't get out of here!" And suddenly his hand was on Ranier's shoulder, his hard voice cracked, shaken, his manner conciliatory. "This is getting me, Ranier—sorry my nerves blew up a while ago. That goes for the girl, too. Lost my head the way the Italian kid lost his at me. Can't blame the boy, with things popping like they are. Now on, we got to stick together. Stand by me, will you?"

They were running for the car. Ranier, hand clasped over Laïs Engles' hand, nodded blankly at the Irishman beside him, and tried to remember something he had wanted to do. Kavanaugh reminded him.

"And you're right, Doc. We'll go to the graveyard where the girl says that old lady was buried. Try to find some clue—!"

Looking back from the Model T's running board, Ranier saw the old lady had assumed a more comfortable pose against Adolph Perl's headstone. Her glasses had dropped to her lap, bonnet tipped over her eyes, chin fallen to her breast. Wrapped in a cocoon of fog, she might have resumed her interrupted immortal doze. A cadence of low-boomed drums drifted through the cemetery vapours, and the old lady's chin sank further, as if lulled.

But she was not quite asleep. As the car charged off with pounding cylinders, Ranier saw her head nod perkily, twice—good-bye.

CHAPTER XIII

THE SECOND GRAVE

On the road the fog had thickened. Surging across the highway's surface as if the macadam were afire. Bushing up from the roadside. Rolling in white woolly bales before the headlight; boiling blackly astern. Where the road dodged between high embankments, the stagnated mist was the consistency of evaporating milk. Landscape, sky and night were blotted out. Jungles had dissolved to steam; solids turned into white, watery gas and set adrift. That a car from Detroit could stay on this nebulous Milky Way in Haiti was not the least of tonight's miracles.

But the car climbed and plowed through the vapour-blizzard with a disregard for safety that had its passengers howling. If it once slowed to forty it was not the driver's fault. The little black man at the wheel yanked the gas lever down to the last notch on its quadrant. Whatever those native drums had told him, he didn't like it. No need to wipe the steamed windshield. Under the brim of his giant sombrero, Polypheme's eyes were occult headlights that discovered a road the half-blind car couldn't see.

And once more Ranier was assailed by a sense of dream-like unreality. This race to escape an undertone muttering of drums. This desperate dash from cemetery to cemetery to inquire why an old lady, fourteen years underground, had tonight deserted her tomb. Skidding, rocking, slewing on unseen curves, threatening to fly

into fragments at every turn, the car boiled on through invisibility, and only the girl's fingers locked with Ranier's seemed real. He could not see the running board supporting him. He could only guess Mr. Coolidge was clinging on the opposite side, from occasional shouted references to nerves. Polypheme was a shadow with a pair of eyes, and the jam in the back seat a formless blur of shapes and outcries—groans from the professor, caterwauls from the blonde, howls by Carpetsi and oaths from Kavanaugh.

He could not see or hear the girl. Clutching the windshield post with his right hand, he locked his left hand with the girl's in reassuring pressure. She was there. In the front seat, and trembling, her invisible fingers icy cold. But he wasn't dreaming their frightened grip, and they were something human to hang on to when the car screeched on an unseen curve. It was strange as hell. Why hold the girl's hand? He hadn't held a woman's hand like that in all of five years. His grip wasn't fatherly, either. Why in the name of God should he try to reassure this girl? Who was she, after all? What was he doing in this nightmare, working up a protective instinct over a girl he'd never heard of three hours before, when he ought to concentrate on saving his own skin?

Ranier withdrew his fingers and fastened them on the door-frame. Was he going insane? A ship's passenger had been murdered; stabbed before his eyes! Body-snatchers were loose in the night, and a black mob was coming, and for all he knew—

Well, it was no time for romancing. For all he knew, the girl's lovely hand might have a part in this dirty business. Certainly when Kavanaugh had questioned her she'd held something back. Something concerning Dr. Eberhardt—that hospital?

As if summoned by his thought, the hospital loomed ghostly at the left of the road, and as the car raced past the entrance, Ranier had a glimpse of that lighted laboratory window shining Hallowe'en yellow through the black upper branches of the sablier tree. In the fog the place looked dismal as an owl-hoot. The car did not slow down, and the outsprawled villa was a misshapen shadow surrounded by the ghosts of trees, there and gone in the mist.

John Ranier looked back, wondering if Haarman's body were roaming that spectral place. Hell with that! Native Voodoo might dig up the dead, but it couldn't animate them, even on a night like this. Someone had stolen the Haarman cadaver for good reasons that weren't so good. To do away with the evidence? Hide the fact of homicide? You couldn't bring a murder charge when you couldn't produce the corpse.

Or had the taffy-haired tourist's body been appropriated for some darker purpose than concealment, some necrologic experiment conceived in this Haitian limberlost?

REMEMBERED WORDS PHRASED themselves through Ranier's mind. "He was experimenting—something so important he works on—a theory he could revive dead cells with adrenaline—tonight he was to finish, to make the vital discovery—" The girl's words, spoken when they'd found the wrecked hospital lab, the doctor absent. Dr. Eberhardt, again! Could this mysterious and as yet unseen physician be back of tonight's witcheries? Some half loony scientist, demented by years of isolation in this Caribbean backwater, bent on resurrectionism?

There was Eberhardt's name on that envelope from the murdered tourist's pocket. There was the girl's assertion the stabbed tourist was someone Eberhardt had buried fourteen years ago. There was that little old lady, another of that long-ago funeral party, transplanted to a robbed grave. There was the possibility that Eberhardt, missing in the night, had returned to the hospital, pilfered Haarman's body from the emergency room, slammed that downstairs door. What sort of doctor would walk off and leave dissected hands boiling over a Bunsen flame?

Ranier's imagination began to picture a dark figure chasing down the night with shovel and wheel barrow, hunting likely cemetery-subjects for experiments. The sort of creature who, in cone-shaped astrologer's hat and alchemist's robes, would conjure at midnight in a laboratory, a dabbler in mummy-dust and usnea (moss scraped from the head of a criminal who had been hanging for weeks on a gallows).

Whew! Ranier shook off a shiver. No moment to go woolgathering with that sort of material; better quit thinking until the next shock came along. Ten to one, he'd fall off this running board flying through nothingness, come to earth with a bang, and wake up back in the Blue Kitty Café, banging his chin on Hyacinth Lucien's floor.

But the ride went on. Climbing. Banking. Tunneling through jungles of vapour. Dipping through smothered undercuts. Taking unseen curves on two wheels. Uphill and down-dale through the dissolving, white-blanketed night; across an aerial trestle that had no more foundation than a rainbow, its girders merely shadows suspended in mist; between black rustling walls of timber that slashed invisible overhangs of foliage at Ranier's face; past the half-formed shapes of boulders, the half-seen trunks of great trees. Once the gray ghost of a donkey went by in the cloudy backwash like some waterlogged carcass seen from a ship's rail at night; and once there was a horse's skull on a post, like a rural mailbox at the roadside, a frowsty death's-head signalling Haitian Voodoo. In the momentary light of the headlamp, the eye holes steamed, and, as the car slewed past, the horse-teeth bit at the seat of Ranier's pants.

The ride went on; and the next shock came after the girl cried out of darkness, "Polypheme! Ici!" and the car skidded to a standstill with screeching brake-bands. Wiping mist from his vision, Ranier made out a rift in the jungle's wall, a little bay in the creaming forest, an open glade beyond the edge of the road. The fog was thinner in this clearing, as if held back on three sides by the close-packed trees, and the car light spread across the vale a moony illumination.

Grassy and sequestered, it might have been a picnic spot, save the knolls were mounds and the mossy rocks were tombstones and there were tilted wooden crosses and a scattering of late-burning candles.

No, it was not quite the place for jelly sandwiches. There was a path led in from the roadside, a sandy lane that picked its way among the mounds, and about twenty feet in from the road the path was blocked by a sand pile. There was an excavation. There was an uncovered coffin grounded alongside the excavation. There was a round-shouldered tombstone at the head of the excavation. From the roadside John Ranier could read the epitaph.

HIER RUHET IN GOTT
GROSSMUTTER SOU
GEST. 3 JANUAR 1922
ICH HATTE EINST
EIN SCHONES VATERLAND

But the figure sprawled beside the unlidded coffin was not resting in God. Neither was it Grandmother Sou.

Before he was half way up the path, Ranier knew who it was.

CHAPTER XIV

THE DEAD MARINE

Shatterpated, John Ranier stared down at the thing while the fibres of his skin twitched with repulsion and a cold passed through him and made his lamed foot ache. It was lying beside the empty coffin, an elbow negligently hooked over the coffin's cowling, its long legs outstretched in the weeds, one foot in the grave.

The mummified face under the faded campaign hat was distinguished from Tutankhamen's only by the wispy remains of a red moustache. One surmised it had not always been gaunt, for the uniform fitted loosely and the leather-faced leggings had sprung from the dwindled calves. The tunic was no more than a mustard colored gauze, a delicate garment spun by a khaki spider, and the bronze sharpshooter's medal was sewed to the breast pocket by cobwebs, and the webbed bullet belt, unhooked from its rusty buckle, had lost its cartridges.

John Ranier had seen that O.D. uniform before, that globe-and-anchor insignia above the hatband. He had seen it before, and in similar disrepair. Once he had stepped on it in the leaf-mould of Belleau Wood, and there'd been another in the wire at Cantigny. They seeded the earth from the home of Montezuma to the shores of Tripoli, these soldiers of the sea, but Ranier would have wagered this leatherneck was the first to rise from a grave after fourteen years, mascotted by a bullfrog. The frog was tied to the bullet belt by a length of grocery string, and it did not want to play mascot for a tough marine, a three striper of the breed that wouldn't stay down—

Ranier retreated, backing slowly down the path, step by step. Shadows retreated with him, gesturing maniacal motions with their arms, colliding and bumping in precipitate retreat, bombarding the rancid dusk with senseless cries.

Ranier was glad to get back to the road, let the fog pull the wool over his eyes. People stumbled and shouted around him, hugging the car for safety, darting wild glances off at the wallowing white night. Kavanaugh had his automatic clutched in his hand, and his long-jawed face seemed infuriated. Moving his head from side to side, he stood against the running board of the car like a captain defending a quarter deck against an expected rush of mutineers. When the insectologist made a leap to gain the back seat, the Irishman struck him aside with an elbow and a look of annoyance, snarling:

"Nobody's going yet! Nobody's going yet!"

The blond Daisy woman pushed back her picture hat, put her face in her hands, began to bawl. Angelo Carpetsi's teeth were audible in a flour-and-water face; and the big Mr. Coolidge walked up and down the road's edge, panting, "Holy Jumpin' Judas! Holy Jumpin' Judas!"

towelling his face on his cap, revolving ox-like eyes.

Unconsciously, Ranier had halted beside Laïs Engles who was standing in suspended animation, canvas shoes rooted in the myrtle at the bottom of the path, one hand to her throat, white face averted from that object in the weeds. He couldn't look at her. Not yet. He could only stand with fingers clenched in dry palms, his mind quivering, his ears only half aware of the uproar breaking around him like the clamor of a hundred skunk-panicked hens, his eyes held by that scene in the fog-hemmed glade.

Then Kavanaugh snapped, "Everybody wait!" in sudden decision, and, ramming pistol into pocket, sprinted up the path for another look. They could see him scouting around the rectangular crater, stooping to scrutinize the vacant longbox, peering gingerly at the mummy beside the box. He snatched back his cuff to examine his strap watch, then glared off toward the highway in the direction they had come. He struck a match on his shank, held a palm-cupped glimmer above the marble headstone, as if convinced the moony light from the car had played tricks with the epitaph; read the name on the stone aloud. Then he skirted the sand pile, kicking at the fresh-turned loam.

He called, "Footprints, but too smudged to make out. Might be one man or ten. You, Coolidge," aiming his forefinger, "come up here."

Grudgingly the big man ascended the path. Kavanaugh handed him a penny box of matches, and they knelt over the excavation; conferred in quarrelsome whispers while the Brooklyn truck driver scratched and held wax matches over the trench.

WATCHING THAT SHADOWPLAY, not looking at the girl, Ranier fumbled for her wrist, fastened his fingers around it, pulled her craftily to him so that their shoulders touched.

"Talk low. That's the marine?"

"Yes," she breathed.

"Who fired the plague ship from Brazil? Who died of the mauve death that night your German expedition landed in Haiti?"

"Yes."

"The mate, Adolph Perl, was buried first in that cemetery down by the village; the old lady we saw there tonight was buried here?"

"Yes— I—"

"This marine, those others who died that night together, they were all buried in different cemeteries by Dr. Eberhardt and Polypheme because the doctor didn't want a lot of new graves together, didn't want the Haitians to know there'd been the plague—?"

"Dr. Eberhardt feared a panic among the natives who were hostile to his work and—"

"Eberhardt and Polypheme," Ranier nodded toward the Negro huddled in the car, "buried those people? Polypheme would remember?"

"He drove the wagon with the rough-boxes. Filled the graves that night—fourteen years ago. He would remember that."

"Would he remember the people who were buried?"

"No—he—he did not know them. He did not see them that night before they died."

Ranier suggested in a low, grinding mutter, "But Dr. Eberhardt might have remembered them. Dr. Eberhardt tended them before they died, laid them out, managed that midnight funeral. Do you see what I'm driving at?"

He could feel her arm harden in his grasp. She whispered, "No."

"Listen," his eyes were directed straight ahead, but his murmur deflected at the girl, "you've got to tell me everything you know about Eberhardt and tell it quick. That tourist Haarman who was stabbed in the Blue Kitty Café and died in your hospital—that murdered man had an envelope in his pocket with Eberhardt's name scrawled on it and the figures, 'one million m, four million dollar sign.' Make anything of that?"

She shook her head.

"Haarman was stabbed this evening some time around seven-thirty. Was Dr. Eberhardt in his hospital at that hour?"

"I don't know. I go to bed at seven because I am on night duty with the patients. He was in his laboratory then."

"So he might've ducked out without you knowing it," Ranier deduced, rubbing the words off his lips with the back of his hand. "And some time in there his lab was scuttled. Where'd he usually spend his evenings?"

"Laboratory. Tonight he planned to stay in; let Polypheme take the car. He was very engrossed— experimenting—" Her voice trembled.

"Experimenting." Ranier nodded soddenly. "Adrenaline, you said, Reviving—trying to re- vive—dead cells. And a man who looks like a dead man comes to Haiti and is murdered. Then his body disappears. The body of the man he looks like is exhumed, missing. An old lady, dis- interred, is transferred to *that* grave and we find this marine at hers. All the while Eberhardt's missing. It doesn't rhyme. It's crazy as hell. But there's this much. Eberhardt's the only one in Haiti who might mistake Haarman for Perl; the only one, besides you, who knows the location of all these victims who were buried that night in 1922."

HER PAINFUL BREATHING came to a stop, and there was a momentary silence between them when she might not have been there. Her stricken inertia, impelled by his last statement, filled him with new uneasiness; and at the same time he became aware of Angelo Carpetsi's regard, noticed the Italian youth had sidled nearer in the fog to eye him covertly from where he stood beside the stalled car. But Carpetsi could not have heard much, what with the incoherent wailing of the blonde collapsed against a fender, and the falsetto obligato of Professor Schlitz demanding someone to tell him over and over again why he had ever quit the cruise steamer to go motor-touring at night down this baneful Haitian coast.

Detecting the Italian's baleful espionage, John Ranier kept his eyes fixed on the fog- blurred pair conferring in mid-graveyard, and tugged the girl's sleeve to back her along the road's edge into deeper shadow. The fog drank them in. Beyond the car light they were in that outer void, known by the sailors of Columbus to have been in these latitudes, where the night begins. The moony graveyard with its moony inhabitants, the parked car and the people there like a frenzied accident-crowd, were in another world. In the fogbank Ranier stopped just in time. Another step backwards and he might have gone over the Edge.

Standing with him, there, the girl was weep- ing. Tears of quicksilver moving in silence down the shine of her cheek. She was looking up at him, lips moving, and her husked words strug- gling against sobs, barely reached his ear.

"I know what you are thinking. I cannot help it—I did not want to tell you. Dr. Eberhardt— from that terrible night when all my friends died and left me homeless on this coast—has been a father to me. He saved me from the mauve death that night. Brought me up, taught me nursing— I was going to study medicine—some day take over his work. Oh, I cannot tell this of him— I cannot—!"

Ranier whispered, "You must! What are you trying to tell?"

"Last summer," she breathed. "Fever. He has been ill. Worked so hard, no rest, miles to see his patients, night after night with the sick, operations—fighting disease, ignorance, poverty among the mountain people—all by himself and no money to do it with and never stopping— locking himself in that laboratory. I've begged him to let up, and he would laugh. No time to let up in medicine, he would say. A doctor never lets up."

Ranier's lips twitched at the corners, husking, "Then you think—?" and she put an arm across her forehead as if to fend off the idea, shaking her head unhappily. "I cannot think. Tonight before supper he was—all right. But so worn, so white—ate nothing. Rushed up to his ex- periments on the verge of exhaustion. Lately— sometimes—he has done strange things—"

"What things?"

"Forgotten where he left his instruments. Misplaced prescriptions. Violent headaches, too."

Ranier thought, "Migraine," and averted his eyes from the pain reflected in the girl's. She was whispering miserably, "And he talks strangely about—about death. Serums to revive the dead—believes science will some day do it. Oh," her whisper broke, "it is horrible of me to imply—I was not going to tell you. But when I saw his laboratory tonight—his papers scattered, cultures spilled, those hands, that frog on the spike where he was always so careful to leave me a note where he has gone—*Lieber Gott!* but one night last summer when he was in a delirium of fever he wandered off without—we found him walking in that cemetery where—"

He breathed, "Wait!" and put a restraining hand on her arm with a false, "Don't be afraid, Miss Engles, the *Gardes* will be coming and everything'll be all right!" amplified for the benefit of Kavanaugh who was loping down the sandy path, followed by Mr. Coolidge.

SOME OF THE sand might have lodged in the Irishman's teeth. Addressing Ranier, he stood sucking in his cheeks with haggard breaths, his mica eyes shifting between Ranier and the girl. "We aren't waiting for any police," he gritted out. "Brown mayn't get to 'em until morning." His eyes burned, then, steadily at the girl. "Listen. That U. S. Marine up there is the mauve death victim you told us about?"

Ranier answered for her, "I was just checking on it. She says it's the same one—Sergeant O'Grady."

"It's a pip!" Kavanaugh exploded. "A pip! That grave was opened about three hours ago by the looks. Footprints all over the bottom, but try to make 'em out! Smeared. No go. Not a clue but that damned Greenback tied to his belt same as the one tied to the old lady. It's her grave according to that tombstone." Triggering his finger at the girl, "You're sure you saw the old woman buried in this spot?"

"I remember. Old Gramma Sou—"

"Who put up that slab for her?"

"I," Laïs Engles whispered. "For all of them—those Germans from my uncle's ship who died for their Fatherland. Each has the same—the little quotation. But the marine and the—the missionary who died with them, they were cared for by their own people. Dr. Eberhardt bought the stones for—mine."

Kavanaugh deflated his cheeks, and green cords bulged along his jawlines to match green highlights in his cheekbones. "Someone," he lifted his sand and gravel voice for all to hear, "dug up that Perl guy and the old dame and the leatherneck early this evening. They put the leatherneck here at the old lady's grave and dropped her off at Perl's. That's how it looks to me. And we got to find the body of that guy Perl."

He paused to let his words drift through the fog, sink in. "We got to find Perl," he went on in a flattened snarl, "because we can't get the answer on Haarman till we do. And we got to get the answer on Haarman or we'll all be up for his murder. My hunch is that Doc Ranier, here, was right. Find the bird who snatched the Perl stiff and we find the guy who killed Haarman—God knows how!—because, maybe, he looked like Perl. So we're going!"

"Going?" The fife-shrill screech was recognized as Professor Schlitz, trilling from the doubtful haven of the car. "Going? Going? Where are we going now?"

"To this marine's graveyard, you fool. And we're sticking together, don't forget that!" Making a pistol of his dexterous hand, the tall man cocked the thumb-trigger and levelled the finger-barrel at Laïs Engles' breast. "Let's have it, girl! Where was this non-com laid away?"

Clasping anguished hands, she shrank against Ranier as if afraid of the Irishman's pantomime. "It is not far—to the soldier's grave. A little way, on up the road. You will see the barracks of the marines."

"Holy Jumpin' Judas!" Coolidge unexpectedly roared. "Y'mean to say there's leathernecks somewhere up the pike? Marines? U.S. Marines?"

Kavanaugh lashed out, "Why the devil didn't you tell us there were some United States soldiers—"

"There are no soldiers there," Laïs Engles cried. "There are no soldiers who can help us. The marines were removed from Haiti when Herr Roosevelt became president in America. The Haitians did not want them, and the occupation was ended three years ago. The barracks you will see standing empty, deserted. There is a little graveyard back of the parade ground. No one has been there for three years."

Kavanaugh's greenish cheekbones glimmered, blistered with perspiration. He snarled, "Someone was there this evening! Someone who fetched this dead-head from that graveyard to this. We're going to have a look at this marine's grave. Maybe Perl's body is there!"

But the body of Adolph Perl was not in the little marine cemetery up the road where the little marine who was in the old lady's cemetery should have been.

CHAPTER XV

GOING TO JERUSALEM

Ghosts were there. Ghosts that trailed the rattletrap Model T driven by Polypheme of the incandescent eyes. Ghosts that rode in, and clung to, the car—an Irish sugar merchant, a Brooklyn mug, an authority on insects, a peroxide blonde, a swart Italian—the ghosts of tourists on a Caribbean cruise. The ghost of a girl with fear's dark light in her eyes; and the ghost of a surgeon who had died young of bitterness and become a frayed ship's doctor soaked in *aguardiente*. Live ghosts.

There were the ghosts of the World War, summoned by Laïs Engles' story to that foreign field—the sailors of the *Kronprinz Albrecht*, blockade runner that had ended its secret mission up the Amazon four years too late, and brought its ghostly survivors—shadelings of the Imperial Navy and the *Wilhelmstrasse*—here to die. Ghosts that refused to be laid.

There was the ghost who had slain Haarman; and the ghost of Haarman, web-footed, vanished in the night; and the ghost of unseen Dr. Eberhardt who might be foaming mad.

The night, itself, was a ghost, fuming and blowing, trailing its gauzy veils across field and road, stalking in moist white cerements through the jungle, blindfolded with eerie bandages, muffled in cotton, embracing with clammy half-liquid arms the earthy ghosts of black Haiti. You could hear its bloodless pulse when the car engine stopped, and in that moment when everyone waited for someone else to move. Pulsations faint as the first heart beats starting life in a chicken's egg.

Ranier stared at that abandoned marine barracks and knew they had found the headquarters of all loose banshees. Here was the spot. The house was haunted, and most of the spectres were home.

Set back from the road the low frame building, seen in fog, was like a carcass half consumed in a spider web, its framework showing in skeletal patches where the tar paper covering had been eaten away. The building—like American intervention—had not been favored by the tropics. Damp rot had spoiled its lumber. Its flesh-and-blood defenders had been withdrawn, and the spirits of Haiti had attacked the outpost, pried off the door to force an entry, and staved in the roof. The corral was overrun with weeds, outbuildings undermined and ambushed, the jungle closing in. You could see the spectral inmates passing and repassing behind the broken shutters, floating about the empty rooms; and when the car turned into the dooryard a horde of shadows fled around the corner, escaping into a boarded-up mess hall.

The ghosts here were American. Ghosts from the days of Benoit Batraville and Guillaume Sam and the Caco insurrections. Shades of Smedley Butler! Fog foaming across the weed-grown parade ground was the smoke of

Springfields in a soundless battle of wraiths; and Ranier almost listened for a faint bugle echo to summon phantom stalwarts of the Corps, red-skinned and roaring, the words of "*Mademoi-selle*" on their curse-baked lips, charging the fog with reckless bayonets.

Rounding the corner of that abandoned out-post in Haiti, he would have welcomed a few marines. Light from the one-eyed flivver didn't go very far in the surrounding fog. The girl in-dicated a footpath leading across the parade ground, and there was no telling what might greet them on that steamed-over field. You couldn't see five inches through the churning cream, and somebody's voice jittered, "Whoosh! Bats!"

BUT BATS HADN'T left those boot-tracks in the mud. Visitors had been on that path before them; heel-marked the way. But the spongy loam had bleared the prints so that it was impossible to guess whose or how many shoes had been up that path ahead of them.

Kavanaugh swore at the smudged tracks: "They been here and gone!" yanking out his .45 to snap off the safety catch. "Everybody to-gether, now. Where's the grave?"

"At the end of the path," the girl pointed, "across the field. You will see the crosses under a big silk-cotton tree."

Ranier hoped those early birds had gone. Or had one man left those splotched prints? Or was it a man? He cleared his throat, training the flashlight on the obscure footpath. "I'll go first. Come on." Swinging the girl into position behind him, he led off at a jog, and the others followed single file, invisible in the obliterating mist in a way that lifted the dog-hairs on Ra-nier's neck. He reached back to grasp Laïs En-gles' hand; marked Kavanaugh's muttery oaths behind the girl, the others bringing up the rear, Indian fashion. Nobody stayed behind at that haunted barracks.

Somewhere in mid-field the Irishman drew abreast of him, scouting the fogbanks ahead with wary gun. And a few paces farther in the clouds, he heard someone take a header in the weeds, Daisy May uncorking a scream and the profes-sor bawling like a calf, "Wait for me! Wait for me! I can't see!" The trotting line jarred down its length like a string of jolted freight cars, there was a scramble somewhere in the rear, then Coolidge's bellow, "S'all right, go ahead. I'm justa mass of nerves!"

The path bent a little uphill, shook itself out, stopped in a plot of trampled grass; and John Ranier reared up before an enormous phantom, the spirit of a gigantic gray tree formed sud-denly before his eyes. A vast-trunked, elephant-hided pillar, swooping skyward, its bearded upper limbs like the hanging gardens of Babylon drifting overhead, its gnarled outspread roots like tentacles feeding in the grass. Fog rolled in white surf through that forest of aerial limbs; swathed the trunk in groping pythons of steam. Man was small in the presence of that ancient jungle monarch. A search-light couldn't have discovered its top. But Ranier's flashlamp ex-plored the bottom. Microscopic at the feet of this forest Druid were the crosses.

Even in that hour of extremity Ranier found a burr in his throat for that expatriated little squad who hadn't gone home. They held the fort, even when the diplomats in Washington who'd sent them here had forgotten. Unremem-bered, they carried the flag, a weather-dimmed American flag someone had set in a flower pot under the tree. Their formation was military and their crosses erect, in line.

But the sergeant who should have been at the head of his company wasn't there. The white circle of the flashlight fell suddenly into a black hole; leaped out of the fresh-cut trench to a mound of smoking earth; discovered a cor-roded longbox; its lid ripped off, thrown side-ways across the dirt-pile. The flashlight shook as Ranier sent the scared ray torching to the head of the excavation, revealing the cross that stood there.

The German colonel was sitting beside the grave.

SERGEANT EDGAR O'GRADY
U.S.M.C.
WHEELING, W. VA.
DIED OF FEVER

No, the sergeant who should have been there was at the grave of the little old lady who was at the grave of Adolph Perl who looked like (he couldn't be!) Haarman. And it wasn't Adolph Perl at the grave of Sergeant O'Grady. Or anything that might be mistaken for an Adolph Perl.

At first Ranier thought there was nothing at that rifled grave. Then a sound from the unlidded coffin vitalized his hair. *Grumph!* Something slick and green looked over the coffin rim with terrified eyes; gave a leap to escape the white light-ray; flopped back on tethered legs. It was hobbled by a string to a rusty coffin nail, and John Ranier made a mental note never to eat frog's legs again. There was nothing more than that bullfrog in Sergeant O'Grady's coffin. There was, in that coffin, a handful of bones and a celluloid collar.

"The missionary!"

In the confused horror of the ensuing moment too many things happened at once. After-

wards, thinking back through the nightmare, Ranier could never quite sort the incidents in sequence. He could remember grabbing up a clod from the dirt-pile, breaking the earth in his fingers, shouting: "This sod wasn't turned an hour ago!" He could remember turning his horrified flashlight at the great, ghostly tree as if expecting it to embrace him with its arms. He could remember Coolidge lumbering forward with matches; Kavanaugh striding around the grave, glaring, gesturing his automatic. Daisy May was somewhere in the fog with Professor Schlitz, both wailing like babes in the wood, and Laïs Engles cried out through babbling pandemonium.

"—but the missionary was buried at Morne Cuyamel! At the crossroads a kilometer from here! In the churchyard of the Anglican mission at Morne Cuyamel—!"

"Zombies!" Polypheme howled. *"Cultedes morts! Zombies là!"*

Kavanaugh skirted the grave, ran past Ranier with a roar. "To the churchyard, then! Get back to the car, all of you! We'll go back to the grave of this missionary!"

Shadows raced about in the dark vapour, and Ranier wheeled on the girl with a low-voiced, "Wait! Don't leave my sight for a second! I've found out something here—something that's—" His voice stopped behind clenched teeth. The shadow before him was not the girl. His left hand swept out, gripped an arm. Silk tore in his steeled fingers.

"Doc!" Carpetsi's guttural words were oil-coated, seeping out of the mist. "For God's sake, don't spot me with that flashlight." He was there like a secret, gripping Ranier's lapel with his free hand. "Gotta talk to you—alone—make a chance—"

"Now," Ranier gritted. He could feel the Italian's body quivering. The answer was scarcely audible to his ear; choked syllables and a scent of garlic.

"No, no—careful—I know, see? I know who killed Haarman, and I know who's playin' Goin' to Jerusalem with these corpses. I'd be killed in a second if—"

The Italian's whisper was bitten off short. Interrupted by a sound of hammerblows somewhere in the distance. *Tonk-tonk-tonk!* Metallic concussions somewhere far in the fog's sceneless void.

Kavanaugh's voice squalled, "Shots!" Laïs Engles cried, "Up the mountain somewhere! Up on Morne Cuyamel where the Anglican mission—!"

Everybody was running.

CHAPTER XVI

EAR TO EAR

Everybody was running, phantoms across that fog-smothered parade ground, but there was nothing phantom about those reports which had echoed down through the smothered stillness. Three shots Ranier had counted. Gunfire on Morne Cuyamel where the Anglican missionary who occupied the sergeant's coffin had been buried. The sergeant was A.W.O.L. and that celluloid collar was occupying his place. But the bones of the missionary under that gi-

ant silk-cotton tree had told Ranier something that jelled the sweat on his forehead. When he learned Angelo Carpetsi's version he might know the answer to this jabberwok graveyard relay, and meantime he mustn't let Laïs Engles out of his sight.

In the dash for the car he caught up with the girl, but he had no chance to speak with the Italian. Tourists piled into the back like maniac firemen, aided by boots from the raging Kavanaugh and the howls of nerve-wracked Mr. Coolidge who knew everybody would be shot to hell before they got there. The firing on the *morne* had stopped with sinister abruptness, and there was no noise in the fogged dark now save the car's clatterly-bang, the yowling of the passengers and the drums you couldn't hear but knew were there.

Balancing on the swaying running board, Ranier interlaced his fingers with the girl's; put his lips close to her damp blowing hair. "Stick close when we get there—! Dangerous, now—! If shooting starts, they'll fire at the flashlight—! Drop to the ground—!"

"Oh, please." Her fingers squeezed his in appeal. He stooped his head to hear. Above the rushing opaque wind and the gasoline-smelling roar of the car he could catch but a fragment of her entreaty. "If it is Unkle Doktor—Dr. Eberhardt—please do not kill—"

Two-wheeling at sixty around a fogbanked curve, the car rocked like a ship; and Ranier, almost thrown from his narrow footing, lost the girl's voice. He muttered a word of assurance, something he did not feel, and concentrated on clinging to the invisible door. Foliage, sharp-thorned, lashed at his legs. Wet wind tore at his cap. There was a narrow underpass with a glimpse of railroad girders overhead where the fenders struck sparks from the concrete sidewall and Ranier only saved himself from being sand-papered off his perch by flinging his head and shoulders into the car.

That black gnome under the Pancho Villa sombrero was driving as if the Legions of Eblis were hugging his exhaust pipe. "Faster! Faster!"

That was Kavanaugh's shouting. If Polypheme failed to comprehend the Irishman's English, he understood the pistol-muzzle nudging his neck. Ranier weighed the advantages of being crash-piled on a hairpin turn or dying at the dank hands of some homicidal ghoul, and found neither to his exact taste. But it was no time to indulge twinged nerves. He could only hope the gunmen behind that fusillade had run out of ammunition, and he might discover from Carpetsi who it was. He hitched along the running board, cursing a corrugated stretch of macadam that loosened his teeth. Hands clutched his coat, pulling him inboard.

"Save me!" Professor Schlitz screeched. "Save me, Dr. Ranier! You're an officer from the ship! Don't let them go to this place! We'll all be murdered in our tracks! Murdered in our tracks!"

Ranier fought the insectologist off, cuffing, slapping. "Pull yourself together! Nobody's going to be hurt—!"

"Somebody's going to be hurt," Kavanaugh roared, "if they don't stop kicking me in the face! By God, Daisy, if you don't sit quiet I'll throw you out of the car!"

No chance to sneak a word with the Italian in that jammed uproar of hysteria and back-seat driving. He could glimpse Angelo Carpetsi's gray profile and glowing black eyes in the center of the crush, and those eyes radiated fear. Meeting his, they flashed a message of silence, an unmistakable warning to keep mum until an opportune time.

Ranier felt his way back to the windshield post, the Italian boy's whispered confession echoing in his mind. "I know who killed Haarman, and I know who's playin' Goin' to Jerusalem with these corpses—" Did the pink-shirted Dago really know? If so, why hadn't he told Kavanaugh, Brown, Coolidge; revealed the murderer back there in the café? Why that strange verbal flare-up with Kavanaugh back there in the graveyard near the village? And why the clandestine confession to him, Ranier, in the burying ground deserted by the U.S. Marines?

Did Angelo actually know anything, or was that another play in this underground game of vanishing corpses and scrambled graves?

SUDDEN APPLICATION OF the brakes put an end to these speculations. An end John Ranier could hardly have foreseen. Caromed off the front fender, he found himself in the road at the side of a low stone wall as unexpected on that jungled mountain as cocoanut palms would have been in Devonshire. Fog washed along the wall, obliterating lengths of its precise masonry, but when the white tide reached the iron gate it stopped, as if it realized its malarial breath did not belong there. The car's headlamp traveled through the gate which was standing ajar, and advanced across a grassy churchyard to the steps of a white mission house that was certainly, with its gothic door and pointed steeple, a copy of something north of England.

An infiltration of moonlight soaked the scene in a pale blue gloaming, and John Ranier stared at that church in the wildwood with his mouth open a little. It opened a little farther when he saw a mud-caked car, twin of Polypheme's job, parked in the rolling roadside smother beyond the gateway. The car was parked without lights, the driver's door hanging open, no owner in sight. Someone visiting the mission? No light in any window of the church, and its yard of tombstones still as death. Mosquitoes buzzed, augmenting the silence; foliage steamed and dripped. Everybody peered; listened. Even the drums were inaudible in that hundred-ton hush.

But gunfire had echoed in that moon-soaked stillness and its memory remained like soundless thunder in the air. Any moment now, and the rector in nightcap and gaiters should come fussing out of the church door to know the trouble. Had he come he would have learned it soon enough.

Ranier learned it when, instinctively keeping his head below the line of the wall, he limped to the gate; looked in. There was a faint flavor of gunpowder in the mist that floated around the gatepost. Ranier shocked back from the entry with a yell.

The grave was two mounds distant inside the gateway; and he was sitting, that German officer, with his back against a shoulder of the tombstone, in a pose John Ranier had seen before. There was a familiar arrangement, a patterned design to the layout—pile of fresh-spaded sand, raw-lipped excavation, uprooted coffin turned turtle among the peaceful neighboring graves— that displayed a consistent technique in the artist's veiled hand. The officer, himself, seemed familiar, almost expected in his shreds of a Potsdam uniform threadbare as gray moonshine, his tarnished buckles and moth-eaten tabs, mouldy boots outstretched in languor, green leather helmet like an inverted goblet lopped over one skullish ear. He was grinning like a Jolly Roger, and one might have believed him to be humming until one spied the cloud of midges that made black spots before his eyes. A German *Kommandant* on duty would not hum. The Iron Cross dangled from his skeleton throat, and stars on the bleached tunic collar proclaimed him a *Stabsoffizier* of high rank.

"Colonel Otto!"

But Laïs Engles' hand-smothered cry was not a necessary introduction. He had suspected the name of that death's head Hussar, even before his eyes discovered the tombstone legend which had nothing to do with the occupant of the lot. The headstone marking that violated grave was legible in misty moonlight; its epitaph singularly ominous.

REV. ARCHIBALD DAVIS
R.I.P.
DIED OF FEVER
3 JANUARY 1922

A Moment, Stranger, As You Pass By,
As You Are Now, So Once Was I.
As I Am Now, So You Will Be.
Prepare for Death, and Follow Me.

It was Coolidge who read the epitaph aloud, and it seemed nobody in the hugged crowd on that churchyard's threshold was willing to take that sombre advice. They weren't prepared for death, and the prospect of following the missionary left them cold. The blond woman uttered the sounds of a strangling parrot. Kavanaugh's oaths were sulphurous. Professor Schlitz came, saw and was conquered—that was one limerick he didn't like! He backed out of the gateway with nervous prostration on his scholarly visage; wheeling like a mare, and bolting for invisibility down the road.

Ranier said, "Hell! Hell!" and put out a sweaty arm to hold back the girl. He wasn't prepared for death, either. At least, not in the form it had taken in this magic-lantern churchyard scene. The artist had not signed this picture with a bullfrog, but the object affixed to the skeleton's hand was just as good.

RANIER STARED AT the automatic pistol in that knuckly fist of bones, and his blood ran thinner than the hint of powder-smoke in the air. The colonel was in no condition to have fired the weapon. But that pungence in the damp persisted; and the .45, balanced on his knee, was aimed into the trench beside him as if he'd lounged there idly pot-shooting at rats.

Ranier shuffled unwilling feet to the grave-edge, anxious to know what the bony marksman might have been sniping. Finding out, he damned his curiosity.

The Haitian *gendarme* had been shot through the head three times. On the sandy grave bottom he lay face up, mouth wide as a slice of watermelon, staring sightlessly at the obscured sky. A little landslide of sand had partly covered his legs, and there was a footprint clearly recorded on the breast of his khaki blouse. A glance at that shoe-shined black face told Ranier its wearer was dead. Horror bulging from those white-circled African eyes could only have been matched by the electric-light shock in his own.

"Murdered!" It was Kavanaugh at his elbow,

and the Irishman's eyes were hailstones. "A cop, by heaven! There'll be holy hell breakin' for this! That," he pointed at the skeletal sharpshooter at ease against the tombstone, "—that couldn'ta done it! Can you match this, Ranier? Can you match it?"

Ranier said thickly, "Those shots we heard— killed this *gendarme*. Not ten minutes ago. Grave-robber who did this—that *gendarme* must've driven up and come on him at work. He fired at the *Garde* before the fellow had a chance—!"

"Brown," Kavanaugh suggested hoarsely. "Brown and Marcelline got to the police in that village. That's how it was. They reached the headquarters down there, and the fool police captain telephoned some post up in this neck of the woods. God! They sent one man! *One* man!"

"His car's headed toward the hospital. Maybe you're right. He was passing the churchyard. Saw this infernal—" Bringing his teeth together on an oath, Ranier clipped off the speculation; pointed a shaky finger at the reasty human residue across the grave. "The gun!"

"I seen it."

"It's not the German's. He'd have carried a Lüger. It's," Ranier husked, "like yours. Colt .45."

The Irishman nodded, white-faced. "These body snatchers or who's doin' this, they knocked over this cop, dumped him into the ground and left the cannon in that skeleton's fist. Someone stepped on the cop, too."

Ranier circled the grave, dog-legged. It wanted some resolution to relieve that officer of his pistol. Dropping it into his side pocket, he told Kavanaugh, "I'll take it along; might be fingerprints. It's a U.S. Army gun. That marine sergeant's name on the butt. Get it?"

"What the hell—"

"Yes," John Ranier whispered fiercely, "what the hell." He scrubbed clamminess from his forehead with a shaky palm, his eyes dry and hot on the Irishman's haggard face. "I'll tell you what the hell. Somebody robbed the dead topkick of his gun; fetched it here. The bloody thing jammed on the third shot or it wouldn't have been discarded, you can bet on that. These ghouls are going to stop at nothing. Nothing. They—it—whatever it is, murdered Haarman. This *gendarme*. Any of us may be next. Adolph Perl, that old lady, the marine, the missionary, this German officer—do you see what's happening? Those people who died of that mauve death fourteen years ago, one after another they're being dug up. Know where we'll find the next—?"

KAVANAUGH INTERRUPTED, "WHAT I wanta know is why they're bein' spaded up like this and shifted around. What's anybody want with these corpses?"

"This thing isn't as mad as it looks, Kavanaugh. It's following some sort of plan, some devilish routine, but I've got a hunch there's something screwy with the routine. Listen. The next episode's going on right now, my life on it! In the cemetery where this Potsdam colonel ought to be." He called toward shadows hovering at the gate, "Miss Engles? We want to know where you saw this colonel buried."

"Bois Legone," her answer came faintly. "The little village half way up the mountain beyond here. There is a fork in the road and one takes the dirt road to the right. It is near the market place, a big cathedral—"

He brushed hairs of mist from his eyes; ordering, "Tell Polypheme to crank the car. And send Mr. Carpetsi in here, will you? Before we leave—Mr. Kavanaugh and I want a word with him."

Kavanaugh said from the side of his mouth, "The wop? What for?"

"He's got something to say. You might be interested."

A hippogrif's shadow formed at the gate, moved forward on squee-geeing wet shoes and came into focus as Mr. Coolidge, cap mopping a worried forehead, serious sobriety in his eyes. He puffed, "I heard you pagin' Carpetsi. He ain't in the car. He ain't there."

John Ranier didn't like the way he said it.

Kavanaugh demanded, aiming a finger, "What do you mean, he ain't there?"

"Angy ain't waitin' in the car," the big man informed glumly. "Couple minutes ago he told me he was a mass of nerves, and when I looked around to answer he wasn't nowhere in sight." His eyes slid sidewise from the tableau behind Ranier. "Don't say as I can blame him for takin' a run-out powder, or that louse-collector, either. See, they ducked in the fog. Angy's gone."

Kavanaugh bawled, "Get him!" thunderously; jabbing his gun-barrel finger into the big man's solar plexus to send him in an arm-swinging backwards stagger, dissolving into shadow as he went, out through the gate. "Bring back that ginzo! He can't have gone far in that soup out there. Get him!" He spat at Ranier, "So the slicker had something to spill, did he? Give you an idea what it was?"

Ranier's eyes strained at the curdled darkness of the road where Coolidge's boots could be heard galloping along invisible macadam. The big man was hallooing, "Hey, Angelo! Angy! They wantcha back here!" in a hide-and-go-seek quaver, striking futile safety matches that drowned in the surfed murk like sparks in a quiet ocean.

"He said he'd be killed if he told," Ranier muttered.

"He'll be killed if he doesn't," the Irishman proposed flatly. "I knew that spaghetti-swallower was keepin' something back. Yeah. This isn't the time, by all that's holy! for any of—hey, Coolidge!"

Boots on the road had stopped. Stopped as if the clattering truck driver had been snuffed out by a wand-touch in the mist, brogans and all.

"Coolidge?" Kavanaugh stretched his neck with a shout. "Are you there?"

About forty paces from the parked police car a match spluttered feebly, exhibiting the Coolidge face as a spoiled cabbage, disembodied and afloat in the toadstool-colored eddy. The match signalled frantically, and the big man's face, blue in distress, was screwed up like an infant's gathering breath for a colic howl.

"Where's Carpetsi?" Kavanaugh could have been heard in India. "Did you get him?"

The match expired to a spark that floated groundward. The face disappeared, and the howl came from Nothingness where it had been.

"He's been got!"

GOT! IT WAS a mild word for what had happened to Angelo Carpetsi.

A sickly euphemism flattering the thing that had overtaken the Italian youth out there in the glucose-thick woolpack of the road; the red butchery that had struck in silence, stealthily, without mercy, feeling its victim and tip-toeing off, unseen in invisible mantles of mist.

There had been no struggle. Nothing. Fifty feet down the roadway waited the shadow-shape of Polypheme's car, its myopic eye pouring light at the churchyard gate. Nearer, parked in the opposite direction, the blacked-in shade of the driverless police car. Not a pebble-throw distant, no more than a curtain-fog between, was the churchyard, moon-drugged with its own noisome mystery. And while Ranier and Kavanaugh had been stalking that moon-lit stage-set of death and tombstones, here in the dank darkness of the wings, obscured by ambient night, it had happened.

"He's been got!"

On the dewy black macadam Angelo Carpetsi, face up, stomach arched, fingers curling on the unyielding road-surface. Looking up into the flashlight's ray, the eyes already losing their Latin lustre. The agonized lips were lemon-color; the forehead, under a shock of polished hair, painted battleship gray. The shirtfront was dyed a deeper hue of pink; the high-waisted trousers mud-stained; and the patent leather shoes that had attempted escape were splayed as if the ankles had broken—had tangoed their last dance. Feebly they kicked for traction as the curled fingers strove to push up, but the road there was slippery. More slippery than any dance floor.

Ranier whispered, "Good God! It's an artery!"

and it seemed an hour, the minutes dragging by in chains, he stood there staring, fettered by the horror of the scene. The fog. The silence. The prostrate figure bleeding to its death. Coolidge squatting at the dying man's head, babbling like a child over a broken doll, lamely attempting to stem that arterial gusher with a handkerchief. The big man's hands were red mittens, his coat polkadotted maroon. As well have tried to cork a Holland dyke with a Dutch boy's thumb.

Ranier had to wait thirty seconds. Thirty seconds for his marrow to thaw. Was that murderer lurking off-side in the fog, watching, gloating at his handiwork, selecting his next subject? Better turn his back on that thought. That terrible spurting must have clocked a dozen minutes already on the bill, and it was slowing as if the power was being turned off. He saw there was nothing he could do; then he did it.

Thrust his flashlight into Kavanaugh's hand. Shouted at the girl, "The car! We're rushing him to the hospital!" Shed his jacket, peeled his shirt, ripped bandage out of the cotton sleeves. Drove the blubbering truck driver aside with a blow; attacked death with a shirt sleeve, blindly, mechanically going through the motions. Amazing Carpetsi had survived this long—amazing, in this red-fogged olla podrida of necrology and murder, any of them remained alive.

"Who did it! Who the hell?" That was Kavanaugh, pacing, juggling the flashlight, teeth bared, eyes feral, a panther caged by the fog.

"Ohmygod!" That was the fainting blonde.

"Holy Jumpin' Judas!" Coolidge, making faces at his hands.

"Crccccch!" The Model T streaking to a standstill beside the victim. The voice of Laïs Engles, "Hätte ich es doch gewusst! I saw him run off—!" The pulse thumping in the night. Whispering mist. Weaving light. Ranier's own voice speaking, unfamiliar, rusty, care-worn. "Lift him now. We're taking the flivver. Kavanaugh— you and the others in that gendarme's car. Better follow us to the hospital with—"

"Hospital, hell!" With a ferocious expletive the tall man swooped at something glinting in the road. Something that had been lying beneath Carpetsi's body. Something the Irishman snatched up, held in grassy fingers under the mist-drenched ray of the pocket torch. "Hospital, hell! Do you know whose glasses these are?"

There was blood on the black silk ribbon. The little gold nippers between the eyes had been crushed as if at some time underheel, and from the right lens a piece had been broken to leave a crescent of optical glass, a pixie scimitar of crystal, sharp-edged as a razor. Ruby gleams shimmered on the razor-edge.

"Aw," Coolidge mourned. "I never did trust that goof."

"Where—" Kavanaugh wrenched his head from left to right, lips flattened over his teeth. "Where is that college professor?"

The thin insectologist wasn't there. He gave no answer from the fog. In those mephitic vapours Professor Schlitz had gone, leaving behind his glasses. Had those glasses cut the throat of Angelo Carpetsi from ear to ear? He'd been going to tell who had played Going to Jerusalem with those corpses. He wouldn't talk, now. He was Going to Jerusalem, himself.

CHAPTER XVII

THE BENEVOLENT SPY

Nervous systems in human bodies are made to withstand a certain voltage. Push shock beyond that point, and the nerve-ends are burned out, the system electrocuted, reflexes may go in reverse. So coroners chuckle at their work, sophomores from divinity school shriek laughter shooting at other sophomores from divinity school in bombing planes, ladies giggle at funerals, and hangmen smile at the sight of hemp.

On that ambulance run to the hospital, starting from a churchyard where a ghost from the *Wilhelmstrasse* sat guard over a dead Haitian *gendarme* in an Anglican missionary's grave— racing through fog past a burial ground for U.S. Marines where the missionary usurped the coffin of a topkick—on past the woodsy cemetery in which the sergeant napped at the old lady's tomb—sixty an hour through a black steam-bath with Carpetsi's head, glaucous and dying, in his lap—on that midnight race alive with ghosts and the implacable threat of drums, John Ranier felt he'd reached the voltage limit.

Carpetsi's carotid severed by the professor's spectacles! Another gag like that and a man might begin to laugh. There is a point where Horror the Tragedian becomes Horror the Clown. Someone in this charivari of terrors must have a sense of humor.

Ranier discovered his lips curled up in a gibbous grin. Part of this joke was on him. Wanting escape from himself, from doctoring, from tourists and women, he'd come ashore tonight for a quiet bout at the bottle and landed splash in the middle of a devil's broth confected of medicine and tourists and himself with a frightened girl. A witch's brew of embalming fluid and blood (the line occurred to him), made in the shade, stirred with a spade.

Opening with the taffy-haired Mr. Haarman, German-American artichoke dealer, stabbed by an unseen knife in a lighted roomful of people. Reference to a Dr. Eberhardt in the victim's pocket and a cryptogram composed of boxcar figures. Mr. Haarman going (by chance?) to that same Dr. Eberhardt's hospital, locally at hand in Haiti.

Then Eberhardt's mysterious laboratory and more mysterious absence, and the bogey resemblance of the Haarman corpse to a web-footed German Navy man buried with a company of plague-victims in Haiti fourteen years before. The girl's war story of a lost Amazon expedition, a stolen suitcase, a homeless child on a burial party. Kavanaugh's accusations and his own self-suspicion dispelled by darker mystery—the dead Mr. Haarman's vanishment.

Then the menace of a Voodoo uprising; a cemetery chase, hare-and-hounds across fog-swathed graveyards; a series of resurrectionisms trademarked by little green frogs; a parade of the long-buried dead and an acrostic of mixed epitaphs, mounting to the murder of a Haitian *gendarme* within sight of a disinterred envoy from Unter den Linden, and this throat-cutting with a pair of pince-nez glasses.

Leading up to what? Ranier didn't know. The answer slumped beside him with its throat cut. Proof enough that Carpetsi had known the answer. Someone had known of the Italian boy's knowledge and thought it best to silence his gutturals for good. Ranier cursed himself for doubting the Italian's intentions, muffing a lead that might have ended this creeping hecatomb. Part of the answer he'd learned for himself in the marine cemetery under that monstrous-rooted tree. Learned from a handful of that richly-seeded earth, from the gnarled forest giant, from the missionary's misplaced remains. That had told him how. But, why? and who? Angelo Carpetsi, who might have told him, was dying.

BUT IT WAS no good crying over spilt blood. Nothing he could do. The wrist between his fingers had almost stopped ticking; when they reached the hospital he'd better give the girl the hypo, instead.

"Too late," he shouted above the wind-cry. "He's going fast. Tell that black boy to slow down before he jumps a cliff. And tell me again who was standing around the car when Carpetsi wandered off."

He could see the gray oval of her face turning to look back at him. Dark refractions of fear from her eyes. "I was there with the woman in the party—she was fainting. The college professor had run down the road. The big man, all mud, said he had better go after the thin one, it was dangerous to be alone on the road. He ran a little way after the Professor. It was then—I think—the Italian fled. In the fog I could not see. *Nein*, I did not expect—!"

Ranier put his face near the girl's. "You saw nothing else, heard nothing in the fog out there?"

"Nothing! The Herr Professor with the big man after him, *they* went south on the road. The poor Italian ran north—off by himself. In the mist they—they disappeared. I was looking at the churchyard, then."

The car skated on a curve, zigzagged wildly, decided to remain upright and let the girl go on.

"In a few moments the big man returned. He said the Herr Professor was gone and he did not dare remain alone in the fog. With the woman we waited at the gateway, watching you. *Aber,* I thought the professor and the Italian boy would come back—"

Ranier assured her grimly, "The Professor will come back. If anyone can land that insect-tologist, the Irishman can. How far from that Morne Cuyamel mission is Bois Legone—the place where you say the colonel was buried?"

Her answer drifted back, "Perhaps a kilo-meter." But five-eighths of a mile could be a thousand on this blindfolded coastal highway where murder was marching to the boom of Afro-Caribbean drums. Would Kavanaugh and Coolidge, the blonde propped howling between them, ever reach the next village? Driving off, back there, in the dead *gendarme's* car, the Irish-man's promise had been virulent.

"Don't worry, Ranier, we'll get him. That spindle-legged school teacher can't murder a guy in hot blood under *my* nose! We're goin' to Bois Legone and take a slant at what's happened there, and I'll call out every cop in the place. I'll get that killer for this if I have to burn down Haiti to do it! Wait at the hospital! Be with you in half an hour!"

Half an hour. Ranier calculated the distance in what was left of his mind. Measured it as three miles between the hospital and the English mission, an added kilometer to Bois Legone. Four miles. An empyreumatic four miles littered with the bones exhumed by someone, bloody-handed, bent on digging up the past. Someone celebrating a Satanic holiday with the femurs, clavicles and drum-sticks of those plague-victims buried by Dr. Eberhardt and a small German orphan on the night of January 3, 1922. Somebody looking for someone? Who? And for whom?

Yaaaaaahaaaaaa! The blatt of the automobile horn and a hare-brained swerve to avoid some visitation in the road, flung Ranier off the rear cushions, tangling with Carpetsi on the floor. But it was only a cow meandering in the mist; and another race-track curve, wrenching of metal and screeching brakes brought them alongside the verandah of the hospital, docked in the fog at Dr. Eberhardt's front steps.

If the doctor was in, the yellow upper window, the water-logged lower extensions of the villa gave no sign. In the pale entrance hall, spook-shadowed, silent, with its prowling staircase and dim second floor balcony, Ranier deposited his soggy burden on the settee near the hatrack and told the girl to wait with Polypheme. Damp-fingered, he took the gun that had belonged to Sergeant O'Grady from his pocket, and scouted the back hall, the emergency room. He found the bandage and cotton he wanted; scurried back to give them to the girl; mounted the stairway to the second floor, expecting anything to happen. But the laboratory was as he had last seen it save for the minor detail of the cat which was, when he entered the room, scrooched on the center table industriously eating the frog left impaled on the spike.

When he returned to the lower hall with a dressing and antiseptics, he found Carpetsi dead.

And Polypheme, looking like a worn-out um-brella, with a Winchester 30-30 in his hands.

Laïs Engles was gone.

A WITNESS TO that scene—the little Haitian Negro ambushed under that colossal straw hat with a rifle almost as long as he was tall; the haggard ship's doctor, heavy-handed with bottles and gauze and jammed automatic, stymied at the feet of a dead man, eyes fixed on the place where the girl had been—a witness might have had difficulty telling which man was most scared. The black man, the white man, the dead man—fear identical in the eye of each.

Rrrrrr-bong! *Rrrrrr*-bong! The wall clock,

itself, striking two in that appalled charade of silence, had to clear a nervous throat before speaking.

Then Ranier broke from lethargy with a roar, dropping things from his hands to make a lightning snatch at the black man's unexpected gun. "Where is she?" twisting the Winchester loose with a savagery that almost brought the houseboy's fingers away with the barrel. "I'll kill you if you've harmed a hair of her! Where's that girl? Where'd she go!"

The Negro's lower lip hung and jiggled while his butterplated eyes brayed silently at the fury on Ranier's face. Ranier shouted, "Miss Engles! Miss Engles!" and his voice choked out in the hospitalized silence, leaving a medicinal hush in the echoes' train. He swung back the rifle, golf-club posture, keeping his eye on Polypheme's palsied face.

"What've you done with her? By God, I'll bat your head off, you—!"

"Dr. Ranier—!"

He saw her, then, in a door that had opened down the hall. Towel on wrist, basin in hand, she ran quickly forward; seized his arm.

"*Was ist's?* What is wrong?"

He lowered the rifle shakily, expelling a breath of relief. She was all right, except for those woeful circles under her eyes, and now that he could see her there it occurred to him he'd been bellowing like a movie hero over the girl, too concerned about her presence or absence. This midnight Hallowe'en was getting him. Somebody walked around a corner and his nerves popped like roman candles. A flat feeling in his stomach angered him. Liquor dying in his digestion and the shock of the girl's disappearance had left him a little sick. Ranier found a second to marvel at his concern for her safety. He wondered, sardonically, what had happened to the hard-boiled ship's doctor who'd been impervious to everything.

He told Laïs Engles almost sullenly, "Don't do that. Walk off like that. Not in a place where anything can happen. Where'd the black boy get this rifle?"

"Unkle Doktor," she indicated an anteroom across the dim hall, "kept it in there. I told Polypheme to wait with the gun while I—" Her glance went to the settee, and her explanation concluded on a stifled, "Oh!"

"He's dead," Ranier bluntly agreed, giving Angelo Carpetsi a farewell scowl. Propping the Winchester against the bannisters, he stooped to collect the grave-robbed army automatic, bandage and a bottle of merthiolate from the floor. He stowed gun and medicaments into his pocket, then turned to take the basin and towel from the girl.

"The ginny can't use any first aid where *he's* gone." Ranier covered the staring face with the towel; confronted Laïs Engles in swift decision. "And we're leaving, too. I've got some things to do. Come on, we're checking out of here."

"*Nein.*" She moved backwards from his outreached hand.

Ranier protested harshly, "But you can't stay here. Nothing we can do for Angelo," he grated a short humorless laugh, "since people don't seem to stay buried in this country. And I'm not going to hang around here twiddling my thumbs waiting for Kavanaugh to come back. He may not come back. That village mob may come instead. I'm going up there to Bois Legone and taking you with me. I'll leave you at the *Gendarmerie* or the nearest white planter for protection."

"There is no *Gendarmerie*," the girl said, "at Bois Legone. Even if there was—I cannot go."

"You've got to. I want a look at the cemetery where that Prussian colonel was buried."

"Go, then. I will remain here."

"You can't," he snapped hotly. "I tell you, I've got to see that Bois Legone graveyard and see it quick. You think you could stay all by yourself in this howling madhouse?"

"Polypheme will be with me. We will have the rifle. It is not a madhouse." She drew herself up, and in the algid hall-light her face was marble carved in determination. "It is a hospital. Dr. Eberhardt is—is out; and there are the patients."

"Patients!" Ranier's eyebrows came together, eyes glaring.

"In the excitement—I forgot. Too long already I have left them unattended. There is smallpox here, a Negress dying, a child very sick."

Smallpox! A moribund Negress! A dying pickaninny! As if there wasn't enough hell in this murderous mumbo jumbo! He flipped an impatient hand.

"All right, I'll look at them. Right now. Then we'll leave Polypheme to tend them, and you'll go with me. Where are the beds?"

She said wearily, "*Nein*. Go. At two-thirty I must give an intravenous injection. *Ja*. I have done it before," she answered the unbelief on his face. "Other cases. When Dr. Eberhardt was overworked. So I will be on duty here."

"After all you've been through? Good God!"

"I am a nurse."

HE WANTED TO shake her. Make her listen to reason. Anger at heroics that seemed unreasonable saw-edged his speech. "Listen to me. I've got to go to that next cemetery because it's our only chance to catch up with the killer who's behind tonight's job. We've got to stop that murderer or it may mean our lives. This isn't any Voodoo racket. It's deeper. Something to do with that German war-time expedition to Brazil that you were with, that's plain. Those people who died fourteen years ago—Perl, the old lady, the rest of them—had something this ghoul is after. Whoever the devil is, he'd decapitate his own mother to get it. God knows where the next strike will hit."

Apprehension switched his eyes to the front door where a moist draught had opened the door a little. Tendrils of mist were clammy fingers curling around the inside knob, the gauzy and secret fingers of a wraith trying to force an entrance. Drum-beats walked in measured tread through the opening, padded softly down the hall in a monkish processional, unseen, and whispered off into dark recesses at the villa's back. The tremor beat under his hair.

He went on furiously, "Believe me, our lives aren't worth a nickel while this killer's on the rampage. And you're involved with that expedition. If it's Eberhardt—maybe mad, trying some crazy experiment—we've got to stop him. Brown and that fellow Marcelline—they never got to the police!—where are *they?* Kavanaugh, Coolidge, the blonde—I wouldn't trust any of them with the lights out—and this loco bug-expert on the loose! Add that outfit to a gang of body-snatchers—"

He stopped pacing, arrested by an idea. Turned at the girl in an excitement that lowered his voice to a slurred monotone. "Judas! I'm dumb. Why didn't I think of it before. Listen, Laïs!"

"*Ja*, I am listening."

"You know where those body-snatchers are, right now? Well, they weren't far ahead of us when we got to Morne Cuyamel. They were on their way to the colonel's cemetery at Bois Legone. Right now they're leaving Bois Legone, and I'd stake my life on it they're headed for *Captain Friederich's grave*. Sure! Wasn't that captain of your German expedition last to be buried? Well, they've gone right down the line so far. Get it? We can cut them off by going to that *last* grave before they get there. Where was that captain buried?"

She said tonelessly, "My uncle, Captain Friederich, was buried on the mountaintop above Bois Legone. A tiny cemetery there, overlooking the coast, on the main road to Port-au-Prince. You will know the entrance by stone urns which stand beside the road. My uncle's body lies in a mausoleum."

"A mausoleum!"

"It belonged to Dr. Eberhardt who bought it from a French planter. That night of 1922—the Herr Doktor gave it to me for my uncle's—"

Ranier blazed, "*That's* where we'll go! We'll head off the rats, by God! Give 'em a dose of that Winchester! Come on—!"

"Take the gun. I will stay. I am not afraid."

"Risk your life for a batch of niggers when—?"

"I cannot leave my patients."

Ranier's veined eyes squinted. "All right. I can't take the time to argue. You know this is a dangerous spot. I told you the only chance to stop this pogrom was to head off these jackals at your uncle's tomb," he warned roughly, "and that's where I'm going. It doesn't seem the moment to pull any of this Christian-duty stuff. You'd better save your own life and stick with me. It's madness to stay here!"

Direct, unwavering, the girl's eyes met his. "You are a doctor, *mein herr.* You know I must."

HE WAS A fool. He didn't need any little bird to tell him that. He knew it when he steered from the hospital driveway and headed the Model T for Bois Legone when any sane man would have skipped for the nearest timber patch and waited in hiding for the protection of daylight.

He was doubly certain of it when he stopped the flivver five hundred feet down the road, backed off the macadam shoulder into a screen of plantain, switched off the ignition and climbed to earth in the floating darkness. Save for that steady tremor in the night, silence. Smell of soggy loam, mould, closed flowers, vegetal decay. All of Haiti, at night, smelled like rotted floral pieces after a funeral. Around him the darkness foamed and coagulated and clung, the mist blacker than a steam of liquid stove-polish. He might have been a million leagues from Dr. Eberhardt's hospital. And he should have been, if he weren't nine kinds of a fool.

He groped his way along the road-edge. He wasn't seeking a nice, secure hiding place, either. He was limping back to that hospital, going to scout around the villa for a secret look at that German girl, a little sortie to check her actions once she thought him out of sight. That, at least, was his excuse to himself for returning. Trouble was, he knew it was an excuse.

John Ranier had probed too many subconscious motives from secretive neurotics to be able to hide his own inner motivations. Debunking himself had been one of his favorite amusements for the past five years, but in this emergency it was disconcerting to discover himself an idiot. John Ranier, his nerve-ends tuned to a million pricky needle-points of perception, knew he wasn't going back to spy on this girl at all, but to make sure she'd locked all the windows. He wasn't going back there to watch that girl, but to watch over that girl from some place of vantage for espionage on the villa, fearing for her safety.

At the last moment, before leaving her there, he'd gone the rounds to bolt-and-shutter all the windows, and found to his dismay there were neither shutters nor bolts on the emergency room. He'd lugged Angelo's mortal remains to a storeroom and out of her sight, and weakened to the point of visiting the sick beds and giving the Negress with elephantiasis a hypo, stalling, worrying. Worrying about those windows that couldn't be locked.

Then he'd kidded himself. Told himself he was staging a clever act, tricking the girl into believing he wanted her with him, kidding himself into thinking he actually wished to be rid of her.

Matter of fact, it was lucky for him she'd determined to stay behind. Damned lucky. Yet the minute he'd shut the door on her there in that stale hall a sick muscle had closed over his heart, and the sweat-beads of anxiety were still on his face.

Ranier perceived with sardonic grimness the War hadn't taught him what happened to gallants who went out of their way to stick their noses in danger zones. Even that charming experience with a coal baron's daughter had taught him nothing. And here was John Ranier playing Boy Scout over a woman he'd known less than seven hours, going to stand guard all night over a girl who might, herself, have a finger in this grisly Haitian pie, when he ought to be saving his own skin. He ought to have a rose in his teeth. What in God's name was that girl to him?

He hesitated to hunt for the road-edge,

warily shading the picayune ray of his flashlight as it sought the wet macadam. Scuffing his heels to keep them on the paving, he went on. He grinned to himself. "Sucker!" Suppose that girl did have a part in this wholesale body-snatching racket? And for that matter, suppose she didn't? Either way he was a fool. If she was part of the racket, he'd make a swell target for that Winchester he'd gallantly left with her. If she wasn't, what difference would it make? Tomorrow the police would come to the rescue, friends would take her away, and John Ranier would be a bum ship's doctor swinging over the horizon on his way to Nowhere. If she were attacked tonight what in God's name could he do about it. Rush cheering to the rescue with a jammed and rusty army automatic?

Even Don Quixote hadn't been such a fool. The romantic Spig had owned sense enough to pick windmills for adversaries. A clogged gun, in this hoodooed night, would be of less avail than Quixote's wooden lance, and he'd be jousting with adversaries something more than windmills, if past indications meant anything.

CHAPTER XVIII

THE SKULL

Ranier paused in the turbid darkness, peering, listening. Groped forwards like a blind man, feeling out the invisible road with uneasy shoes. Deserting that car amounted to cutting off his means of retreat, but if unknown eyes had been watching the hospital, ears listening at the walls, they'd think him on his way to Bois Legone. At least he had that much advantage. If he didn't know where his enemies were, they didn't know where he was.

Sweating, he halted again to listen. Limped a few paces forward. Stopped. Moved on. Those drums didn't seem any nearer, but every second the girl was alone in that fog-cloaked manse her life was in jeopardy. Provided, of course, she was

on the level. He quickened his blind-man's walk. Wait a second—

Ranier stopped with sucked breath. In the pitchy murk five inches before his eyes a black shape was waiting. He could almost see its face. His hair stood up. He heard a movement, a faint and sinewy creak, no louder than the sound of a stretched ligament in a flexed forearm.

He struck, left handed, before his galvanized right hand could thumb the switch of his pocket torch. Struck, and grabbed a hairy beard. The thing hit back, a hard little blow tapping him on the point of the chin. Hanging on, he swallowed a yell, and the flashlight came on, spearing its electric ray through the black.

"Hell!"

It wasn't Polypheme, although the caricature resemblance was remarkable. Ranier was hanging for dear life to the chin whiskers of a black billygoat. There was nothing funny about it.

The goat was dead, stiff-legged, front hoofs brittlely out-thrust, hind legs swinging at the height of a man's knees, clear of the ground. Ranier was clutching the animal's chin-tuft, and the animal was hanged by the neck from the fruited lower limb of a sapodilla tree that reached out over the road's edge.

Ranier let go hurriedly and backed away, keeping his light on the hanged goat. In the mist the dead animal revolved slowly and the rope creaked. Flesh contracted along Ranier's spine. He knew the meaning of this bugaboo; had seen such symbols in Haiti, before. A Voodoo warning! The goat had not been dead long. Earlier tonight it hadn't been there. That meant Negroes were in the neighborhood. Some skulking black *papaloi* had crept up in the night and marked the vicinity of Dr. Eberhardt's hospital with a high-sign.

He flicked off the torch with an oath; started down the roadside on a run, left hand outstretched, feeling his way along the sidewall of jungle foliage. A dozen strides beyond the sapodilla, he became aware of opalescence in the fog in front of him. Reflections lighting the mist. He halted, half turned as the mist brightened.

A car was coming up behind him. Coming from the direction of Bois Legone and at race-track speed.

Blades of light swept around a black bend in the night, went by him and dissolved in moving vapour clouds ahead. The road's smoking surface became visible. The sound of the engine broke through muffled silence with an abrupt roar. Before he could leap for cover the headlights were on him, picking him out of darkness with a pour of blinding light, yellow eyes racing at him out of the night. The car was on top of him with the suddenness of an express train rushing out of a blizzard. At him sixty miles an hour.

A tenth of a second he stood dazed in the onrushing light. Instinct jumped him away from the car's path. He saw the body of the car take form in the smother, the glistening plane of the windshield, the smudged shadow that was the driver's face behind the glass. At the same time the driver must have seen him. He heard the squeal of brakes, the uproar of a quickly throttled engine, the screech of tires skating on macadam.

He thought, "Kavanaugh!" as the car slewed, tilted, came at him sideways, made an oblique swerve to catch him full in the headlamps' glare. The car was still moving toward him, slowing down on the skid, ten feet from him, and he'd lifted a defensive elbow as if to ward it off, when the shooting started. *Spat-spat! Spat-spat-spat!*

He heard the shots in something like astonishment. Surprised at the ruthlessness of it; appalled at himself being the target. Flashes of blue-white flame spitting at him from the car. Glimpse of a wrist, a shadow-hand, an automatic reaching out of the driver's window. *Spat! Spat!* Quick daggers of fire poked at him. An invisible *zzzzzip!* tearing the lobe of his right ear. Instant pain.

Ranier fell. Plunged to the road with his head between his elbows, rolling across the macadam to escape those deadly headlights. *Spat! Spat-spat-spat!* Flame whiplashed from the car window, the reports deadened by the revving of the engine as gears went into neutral, bullets strik-

ing the road around Ranier's writhing body, glancing off the macadam, skittering off into the underbrush. He turned over twice and lay still in roadside weeds, auto lights blazing on his closed eyelids. All over now. The next bullet—

BUT THE CAR was turning. Backing and turning. Clash of meshing gears. Smell of oil-smoke from the exhaust. That gunman was leaving him for dead, wheeling in a reverse turn for a get-away. Light passed across John Ranier's squeezed eyelids; then darkness swept over him; sound of the car driving off. Ranier rolled over and sprang to his feet. Fading up the highway toward Bois Legone in the direction from which it had come was a misty, diminishing, red eyeball—the tail light of the fleeing sedan.

Oaths boiled to his lips as he watched the dwindling tail light scooting off into night. He began to swear blasphemously, viciously, hurling silent and scorching names after his departing assailant. Rage swelled in his throat, choking him. His temples burned. Fury mounted as he thought of himself standing unarmed and helpless in front of that murderously unexpected gun-blast; as he remembered the greedy sound of those bullets smacking the road around him, trying to hit him when he was down. Stand here and let that dirty hireling of the devil drive away?

John Ranier was running. Blindly. Crazily. Dashing for the flivver he'd parked up the road, and lighting his way with the pocket torch, aware of folly and uncaring. Cranking, flinging himself behind the agued wheel, slamming out of the undergrowth to the backfire explosions of a moon rocket, Ranier drove the Model T in white hot pursuit of the escaping gunman. He had forgotten his intended vigil over Dr. Eberhardt's ward. Forgotten the girl, the hospital, the storm gathering under the fog, the game of Going to Jerusalem. Rage melted the problem down to a simple basic. There was no involved mystery about the driver of that fleeing sedan. A human hand had triggered those gunshots. The question was only one of identity, and there was the answer racing off into night, wagging his tail light behind him. *Get him!*

ALONE, STEERING THE half-blind rattletrap through blowing cotton, apprehensive of mountain curves and chasms unmarked by guard rails, he would have been slowed to fifteen miles an hour after the first road-bend. Following a car made it easier. The car in the lead had good headlamps, and was making time. Ranier set his jaw, pulled down the gas lever, sloped his shoulders over the wheel and never took his eye from that red point of light marking the route before him.

The red point of light was a star climbing obliquely. A steep grade. It disappeared at the summit; reappeared as a meteor flying downhill. It dipped and vanished. A culvert. Described an arc and went out. A curve. Reappeared on the straightaway, dimming as it lengthened the lead. Cursing, Ranier drove the battered flivver to the limit of its endurance, following the convolutions of that red spark in nothingness ahead.

Somewhere they passed the cemetery where the U.S. Marine occupied the plot of Grossmutter Sou. A handful of candles there and gone in the murk. Farther on, the deserted marine barracks, the place where a missionary's celluloid collar turned up instead of a topkick's tunic. Moments later Ranier marked the Morne Cuyamel churchyard, fragmentary in fog, the Prussian colonel still lounging by the mission's headstone at the scene of a Haitian *gendarme*'s assassination.

Landmarks in the night. Like the unreal surprises in those old-fashioned scenic railways where the gondola rolled suddenly out of blackness into a briefly glimpsed horror-chamber labeled "Orpheus in Hades" or "Blue Beard Boiling His Wife," and women passengers screamed.

Ranier gave the churchyard scene a side-glance, and almost piled the flivver against the stone wall. When he steadied the shimmying front wheels back to mid-road, the tail light in the lead had disappeared. Rounding a quick road-bend, he picked it up again, this time so far in advance it was barely visible through the wrack.

Grimly he yanked the gas lever, goaded to frenzy by the thought of his assailant's escape. It was touch and go, racing a car through the packed fog on a dangerous mountain highway. Beyond Morne Cuyamel the Haitian coast might have been obliterated. The road climbed into a night that had no sky, no earth, no boundaries. Patches of jungle sailed by. Boulders adrift at the roadside. Around the next bend there could be anything or nothing. But Ranier held his eye to that scarlet bull's-eye in front of him and drove in pursuit like a madman, chasing the fugitive spark that stayed ahead of him, climbing, dipping, dodging like some malevolent star racing off through the Milky Way. Nothing phantom about that tail light, though. That car ahead was driven by someone real enough.

But drive as he would, Ranier couldn't close the gap between himself and the gunman's car. In the night's black swirl the tail light was growing smaller and smaller. Now, far ahead and above him, it was seen as a tiny pinprick soaring through invisibility. He shouted oaths, starting the Model T up a dizzy ascent. The car labored and slowed. *Tap-tap-tap!* Cylinders knocking, exhaust pipe glowing crimson under the floor boards. Single headlamp dimming as the engine struggled. Fog pressing in, churning over the hood in frothing rush, quick to take advantage of the failing headlight.

RANIER CURSED THE engineers who had made that grade. The road went up and up. Too steep for antiquated carburetors and spark-coils. Too black. Snorting, pounding, rattling every bolt, fluttering its rust-eaten fenders as if they were striving wings, the senile flivver would never achieve the top. Ranier thrust his head from the window and could no longer make out a red spark in the lead. Ahead steamed

Nothingness. Directly in front of the car's mist-hemmed, fainting light was a patch of macadam surrounded by Void. Where daylight might have showed mountain scenery sweeping to distant *massifs* or the far blue of the Gulf of Gonaives there was oblivion. Ahead of him, around him, behind him walls of fog. The car crawled.

He cursed the stalling motor, leaning far out of the window with his flashlight, trying to find the edge of the road. Finding it, he yanked in his head with a yell. That road's edge was closer than he had expected. His wheels were on it. The flashlight's ray, torching ahead of the front tires, had dropped out into space in a way that put a film of frost on John Ranier's forehead. That wasn't the nothingness of fog out there. It was the nothingness of nothing. The light had fallen over the road's rim and dropped to Infinity.

He stopped the car; peered. Wind passed across his face and brushed a rift through the vapour. Moonlight shafted through a hole in the cloudbanks and brought to momentary view the face of a cliff, a silvery alpine precipice that dropped a sheer two thousand feet in two seconds to a glimpse of beach below. Palm trees down there were no bigger than geraniums, a strand of sand no wider than a string of rice, the surf miniature as cream on a glass of beer. Staring down at that apparitional view, as if at a morsel of land seen from a balloon high in the stratosphere, Ranier felt the strength go out of his marrow. The pull of that abyss made him cry out. Another ten inches forwards on this fogged curve above that drop and the front wheel would have gone over.

Clouds boiled over the hole and he was gasping down at thunderheads with moonbows on their upper surfaces. A rush of rain slapped the windshield. Mist swarmed over the car. Night. The abyss vanished, but he could feel its awful magnetism there. His hands felt like leaves of lettuce, twisting the steering wheel away from the edge, driving the car at snail pace along the inside of the curve.

Putting his teeth together, he went on. If that gunman could make the grade, a look over a cliff-edge in Haiti wouldn't stop the chase. After what had happened earlier tonight, Ranier was certain his nerves would have calloused at a Chinese water-torture. Swearing helped. Slowly the numbness drained from his fingers. Anger, returning, warmed him like wine. Wine? He ran his tongue across gritty teeth. He would have traded his soul to Satan for a glass of *aguardiente*. And for a gun—

Two minutes later, engine picking up speed, the car gained the summit and hit a stretch of gravel. Here the fog had thinned to a consistency of cigarette smoke and streaks of moonlight showed roadway ahead, black-green escarpments of jungly timber on either side. Ranier yanked the gas, two-wheeled the flivver around a bend, jammed on the brakes with a snarl.

The road forked.

There was no sign of the car he had been hounding.

But there were other signs. A decaying signpost stood sentinel at the road-split, pointing its rickety arms in laconic direction. To the left the gravel went smoothly uphill into night. *Port-au-Prince. 105 Km.* To the right the road was a discarded washboard bending off through black trees. *Bois Legone. 1 Km.*

There were recent tire marks on the road to Port-au-Prince, and wheel-tracks as fresh on the muddy side road to Bois Legone. But something was hanging to the Bois Legone pointer on the signpost. Something that looked, in the lunar dimness, like a yellowed hornet's nest dangling on a string. Ranier saw it swaying under the signpost's wooden arm, revolving slowly on a breath of damp wind. He speared it with the ray of his flashlight the better to see.

It was an old ivory. A human skull hanging on a length of string that went through the eye-sockets. The wind wound it up slowly, and then it unwound. When it had stopped spinning it was grinning in the direction of the pointer above its polished head. Bois Legone.

Ranier drove his car up the washboard road through the black trees.

CHAPTER XIX

DAGGER IN THE DARK

Night, in that forest of mahogany, sablier, mapou and cedar, was an oppression of blackness only emphasized by the feeble cone of the car light and shafts of moon-ray that seeped through occasional rifts in the foliage overhead. The road was a tunnel, its walls shored up by the boles of giant trees, their upper limbs forming a roof that supported a sky of coal. Gourd vines dangled in loops and spirals, slapping the top of the car. A wormy mahogany that might have crashed of its own weight, lying prone at the roadside, its rotting bulk a feast for parasite fungi and huge toadstools, narrowed the path to the bare width of the car wheels. Ranier squeezed the old sedan between fallen trunks and wedges of timber that loomed like a canyon's side. Perfect spot for an ambush.

The road not even paved with good intentions. Washboard that became a brown paste. Muddy as a quagmire. The tires spun and slewed as the wheels fought for traction. The fog became a drizzle, turned to sooty rain, turned to fog, swarmed out from under the trees in clouds of stagnated steam. Then the car began to chug through breaks in the vapour, openings known to sailors as "fog dogs," where the moon could be seen as a blue-white globe caught in the inky forest-tops, and the trees, tiger-striped, glistening, assumed threatening shapes.

Ranier supposed this nightmare tour of Haiti in blackness, shadow and fog could go on for years. How long since he'd left that beach café to start this hare-and-hounds, this murder-chase across graveyards, through hospitals, uphill and down-dale across a Caribbean limberlost that had no compass, along the ledges of terrible chasms, into forest roads pointed out by skulls? Now the excitement of chasing a visible quarry was over, he suffered a letdown. His stomach and his mind began to turn. He was conscious of an ache in his bad foot and pain in his ear, but the bullet wound was nothing, the lobe had

stopped bleeding. Only it reminded him of that close call and that his unknown enemy was playing for keeps.

He fought off a reaction of cold fright, forcing his attention to fix itself on the road ahead, his mind grappling with the problem. One thing was certain. That gunman hadn't fired on him by mistake. He'd stood clearly exposed before the assassin's headlamps, and that gun had fired a direct fusillade that had only missed killing him by the grace of God. Which meant the would-be killer had been on an errand. Premeditated homicide, and out to get him.

Why? Because he'd rushed the dying Carpetsi to the hospital? Had the secret hand which cut the Italian's throat back there on the Morne Cuyamel road tried to slaughter him, Ranier, thinking the Dago on a last gasp might have talked? Then who, other than tonight's tourist party, knew him to want to kill him. If that gunman were one of the tourists—

There were Marcelline and Brown, reported as being at that village back down the coast. But the murder car had come from, and fled in, the direction of Bois Legone. Kavanaugh, the blond woman and Coolidge had left, or said they were leaving, for Bois Legone. Had one of them finished the others and doubled back to silence the ship's doctor?

Professor Schlitz, too; could the vanished thin man be behind this hecatomb? Or had it been Dr. Eberhardt, criminally insane, introducing himself with gunfire?

For the hundredth time since Haarman's impossible stabbing, identification as a man fourteen years dead and subsequent disappearance, John Ranier's brain whirled over the incidents of the past six hours, sorting, deciding, rejecting. Hard to think in a straight line and keep an eye peeled for sudden ambush at the same time. Concentration was difficult when every hair on your skin was crying, "Danger! Danger!" on a road like a spider's dream, and the puzzle turned on impossibilities to begin with.

• • •

PRYING INTO BLACKNESS ahead, his eyes glittered in febrile suspense, while his mind raced in a frantic hunt for answers. Four things he did know. He knew who Haarman was. He knew how those hopscotched bodies came to be at graves where they didn't belong. He knew there was more of method than madness in this morass of abominations; that a deep cunning rooted under the surface. And he knew Laïs Engles couldn't have fired the broadside which almost killed him twenty minutes ago.

But he didn't know how Haarman could have been stabbed in the back, unobserved; or whose fist had directed the blade. He didn't know how Haarman, scar-marked, web-footed, could be who he was; what had become of his body. Dr. Eberhardt's whereabouts and why remained unsolved. A motive for this welter of resurrectionism remained buried if its subjects didn't. He didn't know the whereabouts of the gunman who had almost murdered him. He didn't know at what moment this Haitian limbo would explode from the concussion of those angered devil-drums.

Was the girl safe?

He cursed himself now for having deserted her, and drove the old car bouncing, jolting, a wild race through the forest; his mind a whirl of confused intentions. To reach Bois Legone and summon some kind of help. To rouse the first house he saw, ask the way to a telephone, and call Port-au-Prince, the American consul, the *Garde d'Haiti*. To locate the Bois Legone cemetery and find out what had become of Mr. Kavanaugh, his girl friend and Mr. Coolidge.

The flivver bounced down a gully steep as a staircase, and he would have been through the mountain village without knowing it, if a brown cow hadn't appeared before his headlamp, forcing him to a jarring stop. Ranier flicked his flashlight; discovered he was in town. Not a streetlamp in the place, much less a telephone pole. Jackdaw fences and tin can shanties littered along a mud-rutted alley. Shabby brown walls, shuttered windows, silent doors locked against night. Two-thirty A.M. was not a likely hour in that Haitian community. The huts did not look asleep. There was an air of desertion about those soundless doorsteps that made Ranier wonder if the entire population had gone away. Some bony hounds, surprised by his flashlight, struggled up out of the gutter and crept off in hangdog silence, their starved tails between their legs.

Ranier cut the engine; listened. Not a leaf was stirring. Not a snore. Nothing but the persistent, far-wandering *tumpy-tump-tump* from the night, fog-swathed, tree-muffled in this forest fastness, something that might have been in a vein under his temple. His flashlight made a ghostly white circle, desperately running down the alley from door to door. Nobody home?

He wondered as he waded across the alley toward a hut if he might not be greeted by a blast of gunfire. Had the gunman, who'd tried to eliminate him back there near the hospital, chosen the road to Port-au-Prince or come to this world's end? A number of cars had ploughed the alley mire, and not so long ago, by the looks. Well, he'd have to chance it.

He pounded cautiously on a shuttered window. A scurry on the inside might have been a mouse; then silence. He slogged to the next hut and recklessly belabored the door with a gun-butt. As well have tried to rouse the Sphynx. A wan moon crept out of some black treetops, dragging tresses of greenish cloud, and floated slowly like the face of a drowned woman that had drifted out of weeds. Its rays were like the shafts of light at a pond-bottom, and the scene was done in shades of black, green-black, purple and silver; the buttressed masonry of a church at alley's end coming to view, its outlines watery and blurred as one of those little castles in a fish globe. Keeping in shadow, Ranier sloshed down the alley, shaping his course for the church. Somebody ought to be there.

Somebody was!

NOT IN THE church, but in a park to the left where the fog wreathed in orchid tints across untended grass and billowed around the base of a ghostly monument. A thick green hedge, shoulder high, rambled in ragged silhouette around two sides of the park; steep mountain swooped up behind; the church was a gray eminence standing by, and both church and park were fronted by an open square cluttered with deserted market stalls.

Ranier had emerged from the alley mouth and started across the square when he caught that shadowy movement in the park. He flattened against a stall, instantly alert. Around the base of that park monument, as noiseless in the mist as a swimming fish, came the shadow of a man. The shadow hesitated. Advanced into moonlight. Stood with hunched shoulders, intently watching the glooms where Ranier crouched. Ranier could not see the man's face, but the figure was familiar, the sun helmet a give-away.

Professor Schlitz!

And then John Ranier was staring in tripled astonishment, for the professor, evidently convinced he was unobserved, made a quick about-face, turned his back on the village square and went tip-toeing off across the park toward that silhouetted hedge, his torso bent, knees bowed, moving in the gingerly caution of someone stepping on eggs. Thefting toward the hedge as if, net in hand, he had sighted on that wall of foliage some rare and extraordinarily nervous butterfly.

Then, as if he himself were a collector and the insectologist of prize bug, Ranier dodged away from the vegetable booth and went after the professor. It was not until he had crossed the No Man's Land of the square that Ranier discovered the park monument was no Haitian national hero but the angel Gabriel, he had to look sideways at one slab that had remained standing in the granite celestial's lee. He couldn't have spied it from the square.

There was the headstone—

HIER RUHET IN GOTT
OBERST JOACHIM OTTO
GEST. 3 JANUAR 1922
ICH HATTE EINST
EIN SCHONES VATERLAND

There was the familiar pattern of opened grave, mound of steaming clods, broken long-box, something which had once been human spraddled in the trampled grass at graveside. Something which had once been human, but had never been a Colonel Joachim Otto.

Ranier only had time to recognize the Imperial German Navy in the cobwebby sea cap arranged at a jaunt across the skull's left eye. He muttered, "Captain Friederich!" and hastily shifted his attention to the shadow of Professor Schlitz stealing off into the fog. Moving without sound, Ranier trailed across the graveyard after his quarry. No time to wonder what had become of Kavanaugh and his party. No chance to worry about the night that crouched like a waiting, watching animal behind his back, or guess the meaning of the insectologist's presence in this vandalized cemetery. Another minute and the thin man would be in that hedge.

Ranier inhaled the word, "Now!"

The professor was about five feet from the bushy backwall, and Ranier some twenty paces behind the professor's unsuspecting coattails.

Ranier shouted, "Put them up, Schlitz! I've got you covered!"

The man whirled, throwing up frightened hands. He whinnied: "Oh my! Dr. Ranier—!"

Dog-legged, bristling, Ranier walked at him slowly, menacing with empty gun. "One move and I'll blow your head off! Caught with the goods, by Judas! I saw you sneak around from behind that monument where the grave is dug—"

He couldn't see the face under the sun helmet, but he could see the eyes. The thin man squeaked, "No, no! It was like that when I got here!"

Eighteen paces from the man. Ranier took another step at him, slow-motion, vigilant for a break. "What's the game, then? How'd you get here from Morne Cuyamel after you cut Carpetsi's throat?"

"I didn't!" Professor Schlitz squealed. "I didn't kill the Italian."

Fifteen paces from the man, fixing him with

unswerving eyes. "You didn't kill him, eh? Your eye-glasses. You shouldn't have left them under the body like that."

He could see the man writhe, lifting one foot and then the other like someone cornered and in a hurry to go somewhere. "Eye-glasses? Eye-glasses?" shrill as a piccolo on a sour key.

"You killed him," Ranier's words were slow as his next step forward, "because you heard him tell me, back there in the marine cemetery, he was going to spill the works. So you waited for him out there on the road at Morne Cuyamel and when he—"

The thin body squirmed, "But I—why—I *lost* my glasses in that marine graveyard. Yes, yes! Dropped them in the grass. Mr. Coolidge bumped into me on the path and in the darkness I dropped them."

"Keep up those hands, you!"

"Don't shoot!" the other gasped. "I didn't kill Mr. Carpetsi. Good God! You're making a mistake. I was hiding out on the road, crouched by the stone wall, when Carpetsi ran by. I'd been going to run away, but I was too frightened to move. A little while later I heard Mr. Coolidge call out. He'd found the Italian's body."

"Oh, sure. Suicide. Nobody did it. Nobody's doing any of this. Same as that body that dug itself up back there in the grass."

Hitching closer, Ranier had to stretch his lips in an ugly grin. Some motes of eerie moonlight drifted under the brim of that tourist sun helmet, illumining a false-face underneath; a professorial parody, bilious green, dripping perspiration. What struck Ranier funny was thought of his own face, bluffing above a scotched gun.

"I didn't do it," the false-face was chattering. "Then I saw you driving away with Carpetsi. Mr. Kavanaugh and the others were taking the dead *gendarme*'s car. I heard them say they were going to look for me, and I didn't know what to do. Then I remembered about you—"

"About me!" Ranier halted his advance.

"How you clung to the spare tire of our car on the way to the hospital. So I ran out of the bushes where I was hiding, and caught the spare tire of the *gendarme*'s car. Mr. Kavanaugh drove straight to this village. To this cemetery."

"You came up here with Kavanaugh?"

"They didn't see me," the false-face panted. "I dropped off in the market place, there. When they left the car and ran into the cemetery, here, I crept around by the church. I heard them shouting, then they ran back to the car and drove away, leaving me behind. I ran into the graveyard to see what was here."

"How long ago did they leave?"

"It couldn't have been half an hour. I tell you," excitement overcame fear in the thin man's windpipe, releasing his voice in a sudden blurt, "—I tell you, I've found out something. Something important. I should have run all the way to the hospital to tell you, but I feared I would never find the road, and then I thought—"

His blurting tapered into a strangely, wolf-like howl.

Nine paces from the man, facing him squarely and limping toward him, Ranier was caught completely by surprise when it happened. Caught by surprise, and, for a piece of a second, stunned to stone by the change that leapt across Professor Schlitz's face. Jekyll never altered to Hyde as swiftly as did the professor. The features under the foolish sun helmet screwed in a terrible paroxysm. Eyes crossed. Cheeks went out of shape. Lips flattened back and upper teeth popped out like sprouted fangs.

In that background of moonlight, fog and cemetery it would have chilled the veins of a witch. Uttering that half-throttled howl, the thin man flung out his hands and plunged straight at Ranier, charging from a standstill like a dummy thrown from a springboard. Ranier had only time to think, "Schizophrenia! Dual personality!" and fling the gun.

The weapon missed; sailed crashing into the hedge. Missed because the charging man lost his footing, tripped, fell. Hands reaching for Ranier, he stumbled and went down, his tongue flapped out, a plate of artificial teeth jarred from his

*Ranier stumbled out
of the boneyard, carrying
Schlitz.*

mouth. Sprawled in front of Ranier, his fingers just touching the toes of Ranier's frozen shoes. Shuddered violently, and then, as if the paroxysm had worn itself out, relaxed face down in the grass, fainted away.

Empty-handed, staring, John Ranier could have fainted away himself. His eyes swerved, shooting glances around that swivelled and swerved, shooting glances around that sleeping burial ground as if to see a thousand enemies there. Save for himself and the man at his feet there was no one in sight. Ants crawled on his skin as he glared at the spot where Professor Schlitz had been standing at bay. Five feet beyond the place where the professor had stood was the brambly black-green wall of hedge, fence-high, thick as a small dyke, a thorny if porous barricade against the forest's intrusion. Too high to jump, too dense for a cat to get through, it would have demanded scaling. But no one had gone over that wall. And no one could be hiding in the thin wisps of vapour straggling and uncoiling through moonshine.

John Ranier, shifting his glare to the unconscious body at his shoes, could have been no more thunderstruck if the granite Gabriel five graves distant in the gloom had flapped his stone wings and cracked the cemetery silence with a blast on his immortal horn. No more appalled if the unearthed residue of Captain Friederich had swooped to a stand beside that open grave, croaked, "I don't belong here!" and stalked off, creaking, through the mist!

"Professor!" Ranier gasped.

From the body in the grass came no answer. But a tomato-colored juice was spreading across the flattened shoulders. Ranier saw it had been no manic-depressive violence which had scrambled the man's features and inspired his reasonless rush. His snap diagnosis had been wrong.

Professor Schlitz had gone livid with pain, and his charge had been impelled by a blow from behind. Facing Ranier, standing there with his hands in the air, Professor Schlitz had been stabbed in the back!

CHAPTER XX

TO LAY A GHOST

The insectologist was not heavy. Clutching the man's grasshopper frame in his arms, Ranier raced across the cemetery, speeding over the flat white marble slabs as Eliza might have sped across the ice. The skull of a German sea captain grinned as he went by, and the angel Gabriel watched his departure with a lofty frown. The market place, a blur of empty vegetable bins. The alley of sleeping doorways. The Model T parked before the discontented cow.

Ranier deposited his burden on seat cushions, previously stained by Italian blood, then slammed the rear door, sprang to crank the engine. A witness to his actions would have guessed them to be the irrational maneuvers of a madman. Flinging into the driver's seat, he played with the gas lever, reviving the motor until the car shook on motionless wheels. Blue smoke bulged from the rear as he slowed the motor to a drone, then switched off the ignition, lights out. Shading his pocket torch under his hand, he climbed from front to back seat; fumbled hospital bandage, cotton, bottle of merthiolate from his pocket; set to work in the close gloom. A minute sufficed to stem the bleeding. Another to bandage the wound. He stooped to catch the man's snuffly breathing. That was all right. The savant from Upsala would live.

Opening and closing the tin door, Ranier's fingers made no sound. Two silent leaps to skirt the front fender, and he was disengaging the crank. Iron felt good in his fingers. He weighed the solid bar in his fist, grinning at the darkness, daring its next move. Once, in the old ambulance-riding days, he'd stitched the rhinocerous skull of a taxi driver cracked by a similar weapon. Crank in fist, he began to run.

"Damnation!"

The sound broke loose as he reached alley's end, jolting him to a stockstill. Somewhere in the vicinity of that night-drugged, mountain-

lost village a horse was running. Hell-bent for leather. Explosion of hoofbeats spattering out in the dark *Rat-a-pat! Rat-a-pat! Rat-a-pat! Rat-a-pat!* He hadn't expected that answer to his hoaxed departure, and he listened to galloping hoofs in raw dumbfoundment. Startling the nocturnal silence, the echoes might have issued from Sleepy Hollow. Any minute now and the Headless Horseman should go by.

But the hoofbeats were drifting away; fading off through the night—Ranier traced the direction with an oath! They went off somewhere behind the cemetery.

Ranier peered from the alley-mouth, wary of some ruse. Then, at a break-neck gallop of his own, he crossed the moon-shadowed market place; but instead of entering the graveyard as before, he ran around the front of the church, sprinting into the shadow of a buttressed wall, following a wing of old masonry that threatened to crumble under the ray of his flashlight.

A brass plate on an ancient door said God and the bishop were home, but he couldn't stop now to call on either of them.

Chasing the flashlight's ray, he discovered a monkish footpath that rambled behind the church, and this brought him to the rear of the neighboring cemetery.

Here he could follow the outside wall of the hedge, clawing through entanglements of plantain, berry and gourd vine which crammed the narrow aisle between hedge and forest. Moonlight couldn't get in there, but a horse had. A mile off in the night the hoofbeats were melting away, but the prints were left behind, a design of horseshoes stamped in the soft loam. Ranier spotted them with his pocket torch; sent the white circle playing up and down the hedge; swore. There was the gun he'd thrown at the professor. Sergeant O'Grady's automatic, imbedded in the bushy wall like a raisin in a sponge cake. Which meant the professor, when hit, had been standing on the cemetery side of the hedge at this point. And on this side a horse had stood, trod the leaf-mould, curvetted, galloped off through trees.

Dunced, open-mouthed in bewilderment, Ranier glared down at printed horseshoes there, while his memory somersaulted back through fog to a waterside café, a dank room jaundiced in lamplight, tourists at table, a taffy-haired man sitting back to an open window, stabbed in the spine. Ten feet from that window Haarman had been, there'd been tracks. Man-tracks—

Now, deep in the mountain forest, echoing from what sounded like a ridge, hoofbeats were expiring away. But even a horse couldn't reach five feet through a hedge of briar to stab an insectologist in the back!

WHEN RANIER REACHED the car, revived it with the crank, slammed into the driver's seat and kicked the gears, he was winded by something more than running. Professor Schlitz squawked to life as the wheels struck the uphill grade; in the rear-view mirror Ranier could see eyeballs, white-circled and frantic, glowing in the back seat dark as if a current in the sockets had been turned on. Ranier pulled his mouth sideways, keeping his own eyes on the road.

"Have a good sleep?"

His passenger struggled to bounce upright; opened his mouth; closed his mouth; clapped a horrified hand to the lower part of an ashy face; began to paw wildly at the cushions.

"I've—I've losh my teef!"

"In the graveyard," Ranier shouted. Another time and he could have chuckled. "Sorry. I didn't have time to look for them."

"Wha—wha happened?"

"You caught a knife back there in the cemetery. Remember?"

"Haaaaa—" Professor Schlitz grabbed his bandaged shoulder as if he feared somebody might steal it, exhaling in pain.

Ranier shouted above engine-roar, "Don't move that left arm any more than you can help. It's not fatal. Fleshy part of the shoulder; went through clean without severing any muscle. Just a slice under the skin, and tell me if it starts bleeding. You're a damn sight luckier than Angelo."

"I'm dying." White-rimmed eyeballs revolved in the man's contorted face. "Who did it, Doctor? *Who?*"

"The Devil!" Ranier grinned at the windshield. "I heard his hoofs."

"Hoofs?"

"Running away."

"Thash it!" The insectologist leaned forwards, clinging to the front seat. Under the simian concavity of his upper lip the man's toothless gums, pink in the gloom, yawped at Ranier's clipped ear. "Thash wha I was going to tell you about in the graveyard. I remember! Yesh! Hoofs! It was after Mr. Kavanaugh and his Aspasia and Misher Coolidge had driven away—p'raps fifeen minutes after."

His hot-potatoed words spluttered out above the thousand-tongued rattle of the car. "I'd been shtanding there wondering wha to do, right beside thash awful open grave, and shuddenly I was sure I heard a horsh walking behind the hedge. You know how a horsh walks? Yesh, I was sure! Nexsh minute I thought I heard a car shtop in the village, but I couldn't shee anything, so I shtarted for the hedge again. Great heavensh! I thought it was a *horsh!*"

"It was," Ranier snarled. "A horse hiding back there, and it stabbed you through the hedge. Make anything of that?"

"No!"

"So do I. Anyway, I did see the tracks. After I lugged you back to the car, it cut and ran."

"Where?" the professor gasped.

"How far can *you* see in this black fog?"

"I can't shee anything," the professor, chin hooked over Ranier's shoulder, was staring at the vacuum ahead of the windshield as if all the spectres of Tophet were concealed at the next turn. "Where are we?"

"On the dirt road leaving Bois Legone somewhere in Haiti. Can you pull yourself together and quit breathing in my ear long enough to answer a couple of questions?"

"Yesh," the man breathed in his ear. Breath that rose to a howling gale as the car missed a tree, swayed through clouds of brown puddle-water, hit a corrugated stretch of straightaway. "Why? Why did I ever leave Upshala and come on this gashly Haitian cruise?"

"Funny," Ranier shouted. "That was one of the questions."

"I'll never take another shabbatical year! Never! To think I wash going to Arizhona to shtudy the *Cimex lectularius!* Inshtead I come to Haiti to shtudy the grave worm! The grave worm!" Professor Schlitz repeated in the low C of a mouldy pipe organ. "The grave worm of Haiti is—"

RANIER WAS WILLING to dispense with the subject, pertinent as it was in that locality. Certainly the professor had come to a grave-worm-hunter's Paradise. Ranier cried hastily, "All right. All right. Then have you got any idea who tried to dent your spinal column back in that deserted village? Know anyone who might want to kill you?"

"I feel as if shomeone had," the insectologist wailed. "My God, aren't there already enough corpshes in thish miserable country? Who could want to kill *me?*"

"Mr. Coolidge, Mr. Kavanaugh, his Aspasia as you call her, Mr. Brown, Monsieur Marcelline, Dr. Eberhardt or his adopted niece or that Senegambian house-boy with the radio eyes. Or Hyacinth Lucien, or half a million Voo-dooed Haitians," Ranier ticked the possibilities hoarsely off his tongue. "Right now it looks as if your *bête noir* was a horse. I might want to kill you myself," he concluded bitingly, "if you don't come through with the truth."

At least it served to get that mouth out of his ear. Professor Schlitz flopped back on the rear cushions with a terrified snort. Twinged his shoulder. Caterwauled. Yelped as the car rocked around a curve, "Troof? I'll tell the troof! I schwear I will! What do you want to know?"

"Why you pulled a fade-away at Morne Cuy-amel," Ranier called back at the shrinking man. "How you got to this neck of the woods, Colonel Otto's grave, by yourself."

"I told you. I told you the troof. I came on the back of Misher Kavanaugh's automobile. He blamed me for Carpetsi's murder—I heard him shay I did it. Because my glashes were under the body. I don't know how they got under the body. I didn't kill the Italian. I never killed anything exshept a few *Stylopyga orientalis* and *Zeuzera pyrina* and *Stagmomantis carolina* speshimens and—"

"Naturally. Wanting to hide from Kavanaugh, you hooked a ride on his car."

"But I couldn't shtay behind! Not on thash road by that mission housh! Besides, I thought on the shpare tire—he'd never shink to look for me so closhe behind, and when he drove away—owwow—!"

"Keep off your left arm. What then?"

"There I hung," the insectologist described with a graphic groan. "What could I do? They didn't shee me. All the way up thash dreadful road, thinking every moment would be my lasht, the way Misher Kavanaugh drove. Like you're driving now! Oh my God—there'sh a shkull!"

He was leaning over Ranier's shoulder again, blowing in his ear, pointing a finger of dread at the windshield, at something discovered by the car light in the creamed night ahead. Ranier hadn't forgotten that semaphore-armed sign-post with its gewgaw decoration. Apprehension filled him as he saw it now. It confirmed a suspicion that he had, thirty minutes ago, chased a gunman to this road-fork in the mountains, and maybe what had happened afterwards in Bois Legone wasn't his imagination. So the mush-mouthed hunter of *Stagmomantis carolina* and grave worms, squawking over his shoulder, was real! Just when he'd decided the whole thing was a midsummer night's dream.

SIGNPOST AND SKULL streaked by. Car and professor screeched at the strain as Ranier took the fork, top speed, wrenched the front wheels out of a shimmy, missed a jay-walking pig, and raced up the graded gravel. On through the night. *Port-au-Prince. 105 Km.*

773

Well, the girl had said it was on this main road, and it wouldn't be long now.

Ranier shouted at the man behind him. "If that's your story, stick to it. You drove with Kavanaugh to Bois Legone. Then?"

"I told you how it wash. They didn't shee me, and Misher Kavanaugh drove shtraight to that village back there and parked in the market place. I wash terribly frightened. There washn't a soul in schight, and I wash afraid they'd shoot me. But Misher Kavanaugh and Misher Coolidge and thash woman, they climbed out and ran right into the shemetery."

"What'd you do?"

"I jumped off the car and ran and hid by the schurch. I could shee them, but they couldn't shee me."

"What'd they do?"

"They shtood," the professor swallowed a gurgle, "—they shtood looking at thash awful open grave—just like all those others we shaw. Misher Kavanaugh shair, 'By God, itch Captain Friederish's body here at the Kraut colonel'sh grave. Itch the girl'sh Dutch uncle!' He began to shwear, and Misher Coolidge looked schared and began to shwear. Mish May shtarted in shreaming and shwearing and cursing at Misher Kavanaugh—'Itch your fault! Itch your fault!'—calling him names. Never have I heard sush language from a lady! Never! I tell you, sh'sh a terrible woman! Yesh! Misher Kavanaugh just went black in the face. He told her to shut up or he'd give her shomething to bellyache about, and when she continued shreaming, he struck the woman in the nose and knocked her into the grave. To think I've been ten days on shipboard wish sush terrible—"

"Go on! He knocked her into the grave—"

Professor Schlitz pulled an elbow across his boneless upper lip. "But thash all. Only when Mish May climbed out of the hole, all wet sand and weeping, she had shomething in her hand. She shaid she found it down there. Misher Kavanaugh snatched it away from her. I heard him shay to Misher Coolidge, 'Well, thish proves he was here, all right!'"

"What?" Ranier, half listening, his attention bent on a zigzag treacherously fogged, pulled up sharply. His hand leapt from the wheel to snare his passenger's lapel. Dragging the man unceremoniously up and over, planting him upright in the seat at his side, he cross-questioned him fiercely, "Kavanaugh said that? Who was he referring to?"

"I don't know—owow! My shoulder. If I only had my teef—!"

"Never mind," Ranier yanked his companion's lapel, "the teeth. Try to remember!"

He released his hold just in time to grab the wheel for a precarious grade crossing. Railway metals swimming up off the road; *rumpety-bump!;* an alarm bell affixed to the warning, *Chemin-de-Fer,* whizzing by the window with a vaguely-heard dinging that was snuffed out astern before it was there, a tocsin as futile in this fog-swamped, drum-periled night as a banged dishpan in a hurricane at sea. Would a train be coming across Purgatory? As if locomotives were the danger in this chaos!

"Who'd Kavanaugh mean by *he?*"

But the professor, addled by pain and fright, didn't know. "Thash all Misher Kavanaugh shaid. And Misher Coolidge shaid, 'Didn't I tell you, Dave? Don't that prove I'm on the level?' Then Misher Kavanaugh shaid Misher Coolidge better be on the level and so had everybody else, or he'd soon put them sixsh feet under it. He waved his gun at Misher Coolidge while he shaid it, and then he shtarted running for the car. 'We got to catch up, and catch up quick!' he yelled. They all ran to the car and jumped in, and Misher Kavanaugh drove away like mad, leaving me there alone. For a while I was too shcared to move. Then I crept out into the shemetery, and thash when I thought I heard a horsh, and you came. Where," the thin man appealed, "is thish awful thing going to end? Murderers! Corpshes! Stabs—!"

HAILSTONES SHOWERING UP under the fenders drowned out the professor's concluding jeremiad. Ranier swore at an oily curve; banking through mist like an airplane. Trees swished by and, surprisingly, a steamroller somebody had brought from America and left to rust of loneliness in roadside weeds. He strained his throat above the crackle of newly-tarred highway, twisting his mouth sidewise to shout.

"What'd you say it was the blonde found in the grave that touched off Kavanaugh?"

The insectologist, who'd been crooning moans and petting his bandaged shoulder, stiffened violently upright, flung hand to mouth, palming a startled gasp. "Why—I didn't shay! Why—of coursh! Thash the important thing—the very thing I wash going to tell you just as I wash shtabbed! Mish May, in that grave back there— she found a hat!"

Rainer's attempt to take an S-curve with one hand and catch his companion's throat with the other almost capsized the car. Wheels and chassis screeched; Ranier was yelling, "*A hat? What kind of a hat?*" and Professor Schlitz's eyes were round gas globes in the dusk under his sun helmet, his mouth yammering between blown cheeks:

"A man'sh hat! All squashed and shtepped on, too! A Panama!"

Ranier cried across the steering wheel, "He's the one Kavanaugh meant, you fool! He must've been at Colonel Otto's grave before you got there. I knew all along that smooth Haitian never went for the police! That Panama belongs to *Marcelline!*"

"Yesh!" the professor wailed. "Marshell-ine—!" His mouth collapsed on a howl. Tarred gravel slashing the underside of the fenders made a hailstorm rataplan as Ranier, barking oaths, jammed on the brakes. Smoke poured from the emergency, gagging the air with a pungence of calcined grease. The Model T slid, vibrating; jerked convulsively; stopped in mid-career and choked silent, as if appalled.

Directly in the path of the headlamp, a man's legs were outsprawled, shoes carelessly exposed on the road. The body, doubled as if broken, was almost concealed in the rushes of a shallow ditch that drained the road's edge, and a great yellow tree, its vast girth protruding from the forest's wall, towered like a shade from Erebus summoned to stand sentinel over the dead man.

Ranier knew the body to be lifeless by the pigeon-toed posture of the shoes, even before his own pigeon-toed shoes reached the road. He limped past the headlamp for a better look. There was no use walking quietly. Two miles over the mountain they must have heard those tires eating up the tar, and now his footfalls made a peanut-brittle crunching loud enough to wake the dead. But the body in the weeds didn't waken. When Ranier halted, regretting his curiosity, there was only that otherworld hint of man, the noiseless smoulder of the fog, and the presence of the tree. The body had been skewered. Skewered by the splintered end of a bamboo pole, a sliver of which had gone through the ribs and punched out under the shoulder blades. Blue fists had a death-grip on the pike where it entered the chest, and the force which had driven that jab had broken the long pole at a dozen of its joints; shivered the light stiff wood so that it looked as if it had been struck by lightning.

Then, backing inadvertently from this grim-reaped harvest, Ranier walked against the tree, grazed his scalp on iron, whirled to direct his flashlight up the column of bark. At the height of a tall man's head, driven to the hilt, a knife had been stabbed into the tree. White cord fluttered from the iron handle. As if a frog or some other trademark had been dangled there to sign the job. Ranier's flashlight, hunting some token in the roadside weeds, found nothing but tracks. On the shoulder of the road, close to the mud-splashed body, a trail of horseshoes hoof-stamped in warm tar!

There was a gargled exclamation from Professor Schlitz.

"Shpeared! Shpeared like a bug! He was shtanding by the road, and shomebody went by like one of those horshmen in the *Lives of the Bengal Lancers.* Shpeared him on the pike; then left the knife in the tree as a warn—why, heav-ensh! Itch—"

Ranier steadied the flashlight's occult circle on the dead man's face. Speaking of the Devil!

"—*Itch Marshelline!*"

Ranier nodded. "Come on, we've got to get out of here."

"Whuh-where are we going?"

"Captain Friederich's mausoleum! Last stop! To lay a ghost!"

CHAPTER XXI

UNHOLY GROUND

The mausoleum looked naked through the creamy scud.

HIER RUHET IN GOTT
HAUPTMANN VICTOR FRIEDERICH
GEST. 3 JANUAR 1922
ICH HATTE EINST
EIN SCHONES VATERLAND

Approaching that black-lettered legend cut in stolid German capitals on the marble door, it came to Ranier that this might be his last stop, for a fact. The little white house was still. Too still. With the fog-drift smoking around its base, moonlight slanting across the peaked roof and falling in mile-long shafts down the cliff at its back, the little house gave the impression of a tomb afloat in space. On that lonely corner of the mountain it had come detached from its lugubrious surroundings, been set adrift. Ankle-deep in mist, Ranier wondered if he were on solid ground.

His shoes made no sound on the turf. Around him the graveyard, its one side fenced by the monolithic boles of Caribbean pine, its terrain littered by tumbled memorials, faded plaques and a flock of angels brooding over mounds, slept as a graveyard should. Or as a graveyard shouldn't, on a night in Haiti when all rules were reversed, the towns playing dead and the cemeteries playing Going to Jerusalem.

Skin twitching, acutely conscious that some-thing had gone wrong in a place where nothing should be right, Ranier halted, listened. Had that bullet-scratch on the ear made him deaf? In this silence, the turn of a leaf would have made a report. It couldn't be possible this half acre on a summit under the moon had been left out of the game. Nervously, he eyed the mausoleum. If the little white house saw him coming it gave no sign.

He was sorry, now, he'd left Professor Schlitz in the car parked at the entranceway urns; he could have welcomed even that companionship. Something should be here that wasn't. This grave-yard was dead. All at once Ranier knew why.

Those drum-beats which had followed him for the past six hours had stopped. Weren't coming. As if the pulse of Haiti had quit. Nerved to that ceaseless repetend, Ranier's senses had become adjusted to the tension, and now, released from strain, his nerves went to pieces as if too suddenly deprived of drugs.

He ran. Charged at the little white house with bursting lungs and fists clenched, forcing climax by assault. The silent door was waiting three inches ajar, a gouge in the marble where a crowbar might have pried the casement. Any minute now and something would come out of that door. Green hands. A knife-blade. Bullets. Ranier laughed as he strove to widen the breach, swing the massive barrier. There was a gush of stale air mixed from mould, old earth and mortar. A screech from hinges atrophied by disuse.

Then he was standing in the damp solitude of a tomb, jelled in a twilight that might have been left there since the third of January, 1922, eyes riveted at what lay on the floor.

What lay on the floor were an overturned coffin, an axe-split coffin lid, and about two hundred dry, disjointed human bones. There were, too, on the floor a mess of footprints and about a million beetles and something Ranier didn't notice until later. Right then he saw nothing but those two hundred odd human bones.

They weren't bones to Ranier, but fragments. Two hundred jumbled fragments of a puzzle he wanted more than anything in his life to solve.

• • •

HUMERUS. TIBIA. PELVIS. Clavicle. Long afterwards he was to wonder how he did it. Long afterwards—the memory sending a draught down his neck—he was to wonder how, in that cold-walled vault in a seance of blue-windowed moonshine, a thousand creeps in the silence close around him, graveyard at his back, mice-feet in his hair, his mind harried by the ghosts of mass-murder and unknown killers and vanished dead—how he could pit himself against that jigsaw of bones and beetles to reconstruct a man.

"Radius. Femur. Ulna. Scapula—" Naming the pieces as they came to hand. On his knees; panting; fingers flying over that scrap heap of human kindling in necrologic dexterity, sorting, collecting, fitting, matching. Rummaging for an elusive metacarpus. Picking the heap for a handy patella. Wishbone here. Shins there. Now the cuboid—

The great Vesalius, himself, would not have worked faster. Ranier's fingers ached and his eyes burned. Knuckles. Vertebrae. Now he needed the seventh cervicle. Harder to find than Adam's missing rib. The bones, straw-colored, marrowless, made a faint dry rattling as he sorted them in the gloom, and their problem was further involved with particles of cloth that turned to dust at the touch, snarls of faded wool yarn that might have been a sweater, scraps of leather, in the macaroni heap of the ribs a few tarnished brass buttons. Like a box of dominoes mixed with an old lady's sewing basket, then scattered across the floor.

Some of the bones had been snapped underheel; stepped on and splintered like that bamboo jousting pole through Monsieur Marcelline. It was a job to repair a fractured fibula with that picture in mind. Marcelline, dead on the Port-au-Prince road—what had his Panama been doing in that grave at Bois Legone? How came Marcelline to these backwoods when, presumably, he'd gone with Mr. Brown for police help down the coast? Where did that leave Brown?

Had the dumpling-faced tourist in plus fours met with some crimson come-uppance, too?

Faces, bodies, incidents, scenes raced in merry-go-round circles through Ranier's head while dried bones raced through his fingers. The merry-go-round whirled in fog through Nowhere, and its riders were living and dead. Some rode in half-seen secondhand Fords and one, headless, unidentified, on a horse. Some dropped by the wayside, and others disappeared in the murk, and the brass ring was an answer you snatched at, thought you had, and missed.

On this cloudy carousel a web-footed man named Haarman was stabbed (why?) and his body vanished. A Haitian *gendarme* appeared, shot through the head. A dance-hall Italian had his jugular hacked on a pair of glasses which belonged to a pundit of insectology, himself the victim of a knife. Murder, an unknown killer drunk with blood and success, impaled a fourth victim on a bamboo pole. You got on the merry-go-round; that was one way of getting off. Faster and faster went the ride. Graveyards flew by. You hung on, leering at emptied coffins, bodies propped on headstones they didn't own. Hanging on with you was an Irishman, diamond-eyed, snarly, socking his blond woman friend, pistolling a listener with a pointed finger, accusing you over a gun. (That killer, firing from an automobile, had had a gun!) Near by was a googoo-eyed Daisy, romping about in terror, assuring her Irish escort the fault was his. A man named Coolidge of mighty muscles and mangled nerves stood on the merry-go-round with muddied feet, grimacing, somehow in the show. They got on and off, like the man named Brown, and for a while you couldn't see them, but they might be there.

The ride started in a waterfront café run by a Negro who mixed Voodoo cocktails, and went off into unmapped spaces. In an outer circle of night nameless shadows moved; shapes cadaverous as the undernourished and grinning Holbein figures of Plague and Death pictured in old medical book wood-cuts. The shadowy presence of Resurrection Men tip-toeing on the outskirts with barrow and shovel. A faceless physician wearing pink rubber gloves and an invisible cloak, hiding behind a fogbank, a possible Knox in cahoots with Burkes and Hares.

Centered in the merry-go-round was a hospital where a frightened girl waited between closed doors with secrets in her eyes. You didn't trust her any more than you trusted any woman, but you feared for her safety. Her companions were dead leftovers from the War, and her uncle, a ship's captain dead fourteen years, had evacuated his mausoleum in a land where corpses learned to walk, and the walls around her were closing in. The walls closed in as the speed of the merry-go-round shrank its dimensions. The night with its outer band, its shadowy perils closed in. The people on the carousel, all that were left, Coolidge, Brown, the blonde, Kavanaugh (their whereabouts uncertain) closed in. A mob of black men silenced their drums to advance. The faceless doctor was there. A grave-worm expert called frantically for help but made no sound through bare gums; and a strange body, compost of German sailor, *zombie* and murdered tourist menaced the girl, muttering, "Adolph Perl! I am Adolph Perl!"; and the only way you could save her was by solving a jigsaw puzzle made of human joints, but the joints were scattered, scattered—

RANIER JERKED HIS chin from his chest in panic. Lord, what a dream! Whole nightmare in forty winks. He couldn't pass out now from that *aguardiente*. Scared out of exhaustion, he went at the bone pile in redoubled fury, cursing a seventeen-second nap where every watch-tick counted. On the edge of breakdown it was hard to know where hallucination ended and reality began. When the night, itself, was a fog. Reality a tomb in moonlight on the corner of a cemetery.

"Now the twelfth thoracic. First lumbar. Coccyx—"

Talking aloud to concentrate. Grabbing, joining, arranging with feverish haste that sepulchral design. Putting two and two together for an answer that wouldn't make four. Piece by piece he assembled the human spine. Tacked on the ribs. Joined shoulder blades, arms, fingers; then pelvis, thighs, thin white legs, bony feet.

It was almost done. A place for everything and everything in its place. Marionette ready for its strings. Or, in that moony tomb-light, a beheaded spectre drawn by swift chalk-strokes there on the floor, wanting only one final touch for identification. The head.

Queerly, in haste to accomplish the more difficult pattern, leaving the easy for the last, Ranier had ignored the skull. Come to think of it now, with the scrap heap straightened, the corners left to the beetles—he wheeled and glared in dismay—it wasn't there. All that fearsome artistry for nothing? Cursing, he went to his knees, clawed through splinters of coffin lid for that last jigsaw-fragment. It wasn't in the corners or under the chopped wood. A horrifying thought assailed him as his hands ransacked and couldn't find. Had the corpse, once gracing that framework, been minus a head when entombed? Sweat came through his collar.

"That would mean Dr. Eberhardt—uh!"

He found the skull gratefully. Behind the upsided coffin, wedged against the wall. Returned the stare it gave him with its cavernous eyes looking up at his flashlight. Then, staring, Ranier experienced a numbness of the face. That skull had been cracked, at some long-past date, like an Easter egg. The occipital bone fractured at a time when it wasn't a death's-head. Blunt instrument, fall, heavy blow from behind—it was written as if by a fine black pen in shaky hand across the base of the hollow gray globe; but it wasn't that. Nor was it the fact that this death's-head occupied an address registered for another.

It was something about that grin. Something freezy and unsociable in that white-jawed skull-smile that sent what his Scotch ancestors would have termed a "cauld grue" through Ranier's being. His downreaching hand started back as if those bony jaws had snapped. But they didn't snap. He looked in spite of himself. That skull was holding something between its teeth.

Locked in that merry grimace was a piece of faded broadcloth, as if it might be biting a handkerchief to stifle uncontrollable laughter from within. Jutting tongue-like from a corner of those jaws, a rag of shiny yellow material, such as a bulldog might tear from an oilskin raincoat. And chewed between the white teeth, looped out through the molars, lustrous, iridescent, unbelievable even in the Aladdin's lamp of his flashlight—a string of pearls!

Pearly teeth in that skull! Ranier's hand shook so in the act of picking the thing up that its lower jaw dropped loose. Bites of cloth fell to the floor. Pearls scattered, rolled like marbles around his shoes, as if a jewel box had spilled.

"Pearls!"

IT WASN'T AN oyster! It was a skull! A skull dropping chewed white pearls from its teeth! Petrified, confounded, Ranier glared at the skull in his hand; could not have been more thunderstruck had it opened its jaws and delivered Hamlet's soliloquy. His reflexes strained for release, as if he were standing with a live bomb. He must rid his fingers of the laughing thing, drop it, throw it. Then he saw, although it had been waiting before him all this time, his unfinished diagram on the floor. Summoning a final effort of will, he went to one knee; set the skull to its owner's bony shoulders, and reeled back, panting. The skeleton was restored.

A shadow fell across the mausoleum door. The terror-bugged eyes of Professor Schlitz looked in. The thin man pointed at the skeleton.

"Who'sh *there?*"

Eyes on the skeleton, Ranier blurted, "Holy—!"

The response, of course, was "Holy who?"

But the insectologist failed to give it. Somewhere in the night outside the sepulchre a succession of sharp gunshots broke the silence like blows on glass. The shots were far away. They were followed up by an undertone baying, a distant many-voiced clamor as of a myriad hounds suddenly sighting a trapped fox. The shots repeated, *crackety-crack-crack-crack!* and the baying grew.

"Look!" Professor Schlitz screamed.

Ranier leapt out into moonlight to see.

Through holes in the cloud-roof of a valley now visible below this cemetery height, at a lower and distant level in the night, a red smudge was glowing, a flush of fever developing through far-off haze. Sparks darting behind, and bringing to view, a fringe of miniature trees; and bedlam as one might hear it from a cloud high above an opened grating of Hades.

The drums were thudding again!

And on a ribbon of blue-black road perhaps a mile below the cemetery, seen where it emerged from fog and followed a cliff-edge into obscurity again, a horseman was riding. Midget in perspective, he broke out of vapour, raced through a drift of moonlight on a downhill gallop. No horseman such as Ranier had seen before! More like the creation of a scared child's imagination. For that figure bent in the saddle seemed a faceless blob-smear of yellow, a shapeless spook composed of something that gave off fish-scale flashes of moonshine, formless as a watery shadow blown through wind.

"It's the hospital on fire! He's heading there! We've got to save the girl—!"

CHAPTER XXII

SEIGE AT THE HOSPITAL

The Pikes Peak Handicap. The Italian Grand National. Oldfield's coast-to-coast grind. Campbell at Daytona. Galliéni's immortal taxi-dash to save Paris. All the Indianapolis heats, the hill-climbs, road tests, historic drives and record races of motordom were nothing, Ranier knew, to the drive he started then. Sixty miles an hour in a twelve-year-old Model T implies a steep downhill grade and the fastest ride in the world. Add the hazards of fog, unmarked curves, cliff-rims innocent of guard rails, uncertainties of moonlight and night, and a road that twists and winds in the quick-wrench convolutions of jiu-jitsu through a mountain maze of Caribbean forest, tropic jungle, canyon and coal-mine invisibility, and you have something more than a joyride.

Ranier had it. There were times when, the steering gear almost torn from his hands, he marveled that the chassis didn't rip from the wheels and jump the curve. Moments when the wheels soared over razorback bumps and his head cracked the roof. Bump, swerve, screech and bang on an unpaved stretch. Slewing a hair-pin downhill turn as if cracked on the end of an invisible whip. *Slam-bam* on the grade crossing. *Ziff-ziff-ziff* the trees went by. The fog cut to whistling mist-ribbons. The night streaming past like soup. *Swish!* a curve. *Zip!* an underpass. *Rrrrrrt!* the narrow span of a mountain bridge. *Hmmmmmm* on a downhill chute.

The car spurted and tipped on two wheels. Bounced and shook and jumped like a goat. Pieces broke away and were left behind, the right front fender shying off like a wing shot from a plane. Floorboards came loose under the clutch and things dropped from the dashboard and disappeared. The radiator cap went. The tires, any moment, would explode, the engine drop through, the car burst into a cloud of machinery, nuts and bolts.

Ranier took his chances without looking. Of that wild down-the-mountain spin, the road itself, he could afterwards remember nothing. He drove like a drunkard, leaving accidents to fate. The road was a vague streak fleeing under the headlamp; there was a steering wheel fastened to his hands; an impression on the eardrums of flying downhill. If he guided the mile-a-minute course it was with seventh-sense instinct and the corners of his eyes. His mind wasn't in it, but in a burning hospital where a girl might be trapped

in a snare of mystery and fire. His face watched through the windshield, but his eyes were glued for a horseman somewhere in the dark ahead, his attention nailed to a rosy smudge in blackness back of beyond.

The smudge moved around in the sky as the road dodged. On the cliff-edge where they'd spied the horseman it seemed leftward and below. An S-curve later it had moved to the right. At the last it was fixed dead ahead, a crimson mirage above red-stained forest-tops, blushing clouds toiling upward against night, fattening, merging, hanging in a pall. The red light spread in a widening haze. Where the clouds blushed deepest, gold sparks went up in spirals and scrolls, curling and whirling about like the roller-coaster skyline of an amusement park. On the wind a hint of wood-smoke, on the eardrums a sound as of nearing battle, an undertone long-roll pandemonium like a sustained cheering, but too low-pitched for applause.

"It's the Voodoo mob! They're attacking Dr. Eberhardt's hospital. If *she's* there—!"

Ranier didn't know he was crying out, for he'd forgotten there was anyone to listen. Professor Schlitz had long since given up trying to call attention to himself, his risked life and the speedometer. Bouncing on broken cushion-springs beside Ranier, he lounged in complete lackadaisy, thin legs outstretched, sun helmet rolling around his shoes, back slumped, face relaxed. What more could happen to an insectologist after a night of larking about graveyards with mummies, bones and back-stabbings? He'd lost his glasses and his teeth. Having abandoned hope for life, he retired into the superb detachment of some auto-race mechanic bored with the hazards of the hundredth lap; fainted.

HE DID NOT see what Ranier saw. That sudden swerve around a hill of darkness into unnatural light. A last quarter-mile stretch of road leaping visible in fire-glow. Trees red and black standing up in the night; the fog dispersed; landscape around; the sloped silhouette of a ridge ahead, and scarves of blue-scarlet flame leaping up from behind the ridge, their racket drowned by a Baalish tumult of shouts, poundings, gunshots, drum-thunder.

He did not see what Ranier saw on that otherwise deserted stretch of road between the curve and the ridge. A yellow, shapeless figure that might be a man, dismounting from a roan horse, grabbing the reins, leading the horse off the road into a forest in a tangent toward the flame-lit ridge. Ranier saw those roan hindquarters melt in the underbrush, and set his teeth. But the wheels under him could go no faster. Bolts clattered to the ground as he yanked the emergency at the roadside where the horseman had been. Professor Schlitz went under the dashboard, and the car shocked up short in a nest of ilex scrub. Ranier left them there.

He was following a path, a horse-tracked bridle trail that ambled through forest toward the crimson-lit ridge. The path ambled, but John Ranier didn't. Body stooped, he ran Indian fashion, powerfully, sullenly, spurred by scorched wind in his face, the roar of close battle in his eardrums.

He caught his man at the top of the rise where one could glimpse the burning hospital and the mob. The man was tying his horse to a trailside sapling. His excited hands botched the knot, and his head was turned toward the fire carnival on the slope below. Seen at close range, he was not a spectre, but a lumpish figure in a yellow oilskin raincoat that fell to his shoetops, his face and head almost hidden by the whaleboat brim of a shiny yellow sou'wester.

Ranier hit him from behind like a panther. Caught him in a headlock, throwing him helpless to his knees as a cowboy bulldogs a steer.

"*Donnerwetter!*" the voice exploded under Ranier's arm. "Who does this to Dr. Eberhardt!"

"Eberhardt!" Ranier wrenched the man in an arm-lock. "Where have *you* been all night?"

"Been? Been? *Gott in Himmel!* Where do you think I have been? Asleep in some bed? Sitting with folded hands? Then you do not know anything about quintuplets!"

.   .   .

"QUINTUPLETS!"

It was, of all that red phantasmagoria of demonism, death and madness, the strangest moment, the craziest impossibility of all. That word! Dropped like a spoonful of milk into that witch's goulash of mayhem and murder. Against that fog-and-firelight background where the shadows ran flitterjibbet through the mutilated shapes of tropical trees, and the tang of hot wood-smoke invaded a basic perfume of orchids and vegetal decay. That word, on a four o'clock dreary with vanished dead and obligato terror, above the battle yells of black men, the crackle of gunfire, the bedlam of jungle drums. *Quintuplets!*

An uncontrollable feeling of laughter came over John Ranier. Staring at a quaint little man in a yellow sou'wester and swaddly oilskins—the figure off a cod-liver oil bottle, for all the world—he saw a face as German as a cooken with funny-paper walrus moustaches and apples for cheeks and innocent confoundment in round blue eyes. And around that figure the vision conjured by the little man's word—a string of babies, five in a row, black mites as like as five peas in a pod. Babes in *that* wood! It made the sweat come out on his forehead and his stomach ache.

"You've been all night—to a delivery!"

The gnome was bewildered. "Why not? Why not? The woman's husband came for me at seven-forty-five. Of course I told Polypheme to take the car. So I must go in this husband's buggy. Fifteen miles north in the mountains, and I was not prepared. I had expected next week, diagnosed twins, not a litter! *Herr Gott!* Five of them. Nothing ready. I must boil water. Wash linen."

His voice rose, annoyed, pettish. He'd mislaid his present surroundings and become the absent-minded country doctor impatient with the annoyances of his practise, irritable after a sleepless all-night call.

"These ignorant Negroes. Quintuplets! At this time! Am I a laundress? A dishwasher? All that I must do. I am busy! I am a scientist, not a baby doctor! But, *ja,* I must leave my laboratory in the midst of a vital discovery and play stork for five little—!"

It was remarkable. So remarkable that Ranier, who wanted to reach that storm-swept hospital more than anything else in the world, could only stand with his mouth open, wordless, the sweat of fright on his face and hysterical laughter under his belt. It was the little yellow gnome who woke up first. Staggered back on the path as if realizing for the first time he'd never seen Ranier before. Became indignant, recalling he'd been attacked. Then frightened, his beaver eyes catching firelight, reminding him of his hospital.

"*Himmelkreuzdonnerwetter! Aber,* my hospital! My laboratory! What is the meaning of this mob down there! Who are *you—?*"

Then Ranier could break into action, grab, point, shout. "The girl. I left Laïs Engles in there! Quick! We've got to get her out before they—!"

"Laïs!" Dr. Eberhardt screamed. "*Mein Gott—!*"

Ranier was running. Dragging the gnome in oilskins at his heels. Helter-skelter through dense undergrowth, down-slope, racing for the blazing villa around which fog and smoke tumbled in turmoil and black figures danced ring-around-the-rosy like fiends around a bonfire in the Pit. The farther side of the villa was in darkness, but the near wing, as they drew closer, went up like tinder. A Vesuvius of gold flame jumped skyward. Surrounding grounds came to light under a blizzard of sparks, and Negroes were swarming everywhere, running, jumping, shadows flickering in and out through the blacker boles of trees.

"They've fired the hospital! It is the work of those *bocors,* those witch doctors! They have incited the natives!" The cod-liver-oil gnome behind Ranier was raging now. "To ruin my work! To capture Fräulein Engles. They will kill her! Sacrifice her! *Gott, Gott!* See, shooting—!"

"No—look!" Ranier cried out as he ran.

"It's not the mob's gunfire. They're armed with knives. It's in that upper window!"

IN THE WINDOW at the villa's front, overlooking the open gallery in the shadow of the big sablier tree above the driveway. The laboratory window! Its light was out, but another light was there. On and off, on and off, stabbing electric-blue spurts that jabbed out over the sill, flashing and gone with staccato explosions that spanked one-two-three above a bolero of pounded drums, an oratorio of howls, and crashings that sounded like axes on wood.

Axes on wood! Ox-bowing out toward the highway, the forest path gave a momentary glimpse of the hospital verandah where the mob was packed in mass-meeting fury. Flung stones smashed through the verandah screen, banging the inner wall, and dark shapes were bunched at the front door like firemen, fighting to chop an entry. But they weren't firemen. Ranier could distinguish their screams; see the flash of axe-heads at work; hear the punishing blows above the roar behind them and the *spank-spank-spank* from that upper window.

"She's up there! The girl and Polypheme with a rifle!" His throat prayed, "God! Hold on! Hold on!"

The little man screamed, "The door cannot last. If those Voodoo priests get their hands on a white girl—!"

The cry put wings to Ranier's feet. Yanking the other's arm, he jerked him into a thicket; fought, dragged, pulled him through dense-grown palms, shaping a course for the hospital's rear. Bronze smoke lolled around the incendiary wing, and in this acrid smother they broke from the jungle's wall, unseen by coal-skinned firebugs dodging in the haze.

The rear grounds where outbuildings and a barn were in shadow, seemed left to a squad of torch-bearers, arson-bent. Dancing savages doing an adagio to a roundelay of meaningless squalls, the glow from their flaming pine-knots putting a crimson polish to ebon muscles, gleaming on curved banana knives, shining on egg-shell eyes and mouths of piano-key teeth.

Ranier shouted, his voice masked under the din. "Window of the emergency room! In back!"

He'd be a long time grateful for his foresight in bolting all those shutters; a long time grateful for the memory of that one window which had no hurricane blinds or glass. The black torch-bearers, charging the barn, gave the chance for an open dash to that wing which was screened by Poinsettias. Ranier yelled at the gnome, and they made it. Smashing mosquito-wire with a fist, he boosted the little doctor over the sill; followed with a violence that left him breathless, dizzy in the inner dark.

The room, fitful with running wall-shadows and red reflections, trembled to the pounding of the villa's front; a rumpus of voices coming up the hall. The small man in sou'wester and oil-skins started for the corridor door—the door that in a long-ago dream had been slammed in passing by a dead man with a webbed foot. Ranier cried, "Dr. Eberhardt! Wait!" and fled around the shadowy operating table, fingers stretched toward a bottle-laden shelf.

Whang! The door was slammed again. Slammed open, this time, bursting inward to catch Dr. Eberhardt in the face, knock him kicking to the floor. Smoke rushed in from the corridor. And a coffee-browned Haitian pyromaniac, a Samson of a man with a stevedore's torso, vast flat feet, a torch in one Statue of Liberty fist and a banana-knife the size of a headsman's scimitar in the other. Torch uplifted, he paused on the threshold, glared at two white faces in agreeable surprise. Then he got another surprise.

CHAPTER XXIII

MIDNIGHT

Caught at the medicine cabinet behind the operating table, Ranier had spun at the intrusion of this ogre, not unarmed.

The black man had no time to comprehend

the bottle in John Ranier's hand. Like a flash Ranier threw. Squarely and truly at the giant's ace-of-spades nose. Smash! A tiny bomb-burst of shivered glass. A small bright explosion. Vitriol.

It brought the muscle-monument down plunging, squalling, blinded, thrashing with paws to face against the operating table, spinning in a carom against the medicine cabinet. There was a bull-in-china-shop collision as the dark Samson fell. A cascade of bottle-glass, powders and volatile fluids burying the colossus in a chemical bath. The machete was lost under the pile-up before Ranier had a chance to grab; and a howl from Dr. Eberhardt announced the arrival of a second adversary in the corridor door.

Ranier met the challenge with a projectile of carbolic. There was a scorched shriek in answer; the burnt face departed the doorway; a new crop arrived. Ranier screamed, "Let 'em have it! Let 'em have it!" thrusting bottles into the little doctor's hands. Flinging iodine from an uncorked jug, he charged the corridor, shouting, boring through a thresh of wildmen that fought like circus carnivores panicked in a runway. The jam fell back, battle yells changing to peals of anguish as poison bottles burst on mouths of teeth and eyes bleared with scalding chemical.

Shattering the emptied jug on a woolly top-knot, Ranier kicked, slugged and bit a path for the hall, and the gnome in oilskins was a following vengeance, scattering antiseptics on malingerers in the wake. Jubilant screams received them at the corridor's turn; became frantic howls at the touch of acid. But the dark crush storming through the chopped front doors kept coming, shoved forward by those behind. From wall to wall the hall at stairway's foot was packed with Haitian rabble, black-skinned, brown, lavender, high yellow; a subway-like riot of tar-brushed faces going Uptown under a display of machetes, pitchforks, clubs, *cocomacaque* bludgeons, butcher knives.

That hall was hot. Somewhere a furnace was going under forced draught. The steady monotone of flames shook the building with a menacing chant. Heat breathed through the sidewall opposite the staircase, surcharging the riot-rocked air with an autumnal wood-smoke. Upstairs the pump gun was chattering to a multisonous hubbub as of crockery breaking, wood being kindled; and through that upper smashing of breakage and gunnery and the lower bombination of the fire and the stormed hall, there threaded the jungle-tone of *Rada* drums and the roar of the crowd outside—wolf-howls, jackal screams, outbursts of song, mad shouts. The rifle cracked small in that hullaballoo, but its sound filled Ranier with a hope that powered his punished body with a reserve charge of dynamite.

"Hold on! Hold on, upstairs! We're coming—!"

A madman fighting madmen to reach the stairway. Punching, tackling, driving a wedge through a sea of torches, teeth, African baseball bats, giant razor blades. Somehow he reached the post. Somehow, the little doctor at heel, he was half-way up the stairs.

A dagger, missing both of them, lodged quivering in wallpaper beside Ranier's head. Black hands reached over the bannisters, pinning Dr. Eberhardt's oilskins to the steps with a pitchfork.

"Go on! Go on!" the yellow gnome screamed. "*Himmel!* do not wait for me!"

Ranier tore the man loose with an arm-sweep, the raincoat ripping on pitchfork tines. Reminded of a skull with a bit of oilskin in its teeth, he laughed savagely, boosting the little man up the steps ahead of him, four at a time. Turning to fling a venomous pint of ammonia at a ragged Cacao. Pursuing his climb with yells and a blood-thirsty sickle. Laughing fury at something he could see to combat, something he could hit with fists, something he could revenge on.

The black man fell downstairs, caterwauling, but his twin loomed wraith-like in the smoked murk at the stairhead, beckoning them up with a butcher knife, daring their ascent. Ranier wiped the grin from that smoky countenance with nitric acid. The enemy came down in a tumbling acrobatic, head under arm, knees to belly, bouncing by like a Roman chariot wheel with outthrust blade. Ranier spurred the descent, kicking lustily; had all his limbs at the stair-top. He yelled when he saw the balcony unpopulated, the laboratory door closed on the upper gloom. Yelled and attacked the panels with frantic fists, pounding, crying the girl's name.

"Open up! Let us in! For God's sake—!"

He was beating on the door, and a Cape Cod little figure crouched at the balcony rail pouring driblets of liquid fire on fiend-faces raging below. Tan smoke piled up the stairway; embers geysered from tossing pine-knots; in the demoniac bedlam, torchlight on his cheeks, whiskers as if fire, red coals for eyes, Dr. Eberhardt made a small Mephisto measuring out penalties on mutineers in a hell-well. Ranier tore his throat to be heard.

"Laïs! Miss Engles! It's Ranier and Dr. Eberhardt! For God's sake, Laïs, if you're in there—!"

"*M'sieu—!*"

IT WAS POLYPHEME. More goatish. More overwhelmed by the sombrero. Polypheme, gray as terror, who plucked back a bolt, turned a key, opened the door. Behind his electric-bulb eyes and crow-like shadow, the room was a cavern. Light flashed with sound in this blackness, filling the room with a thunder-crack and a bluish, instantaneous flash that showed John Ranier the girl.

She was standing by the window, pressed close to the wall beside the upright frame. Shooting at an angle and a little downward at enemies somewhere below the gallery under the fire-reddened foliage of the sablier tree. She had changed to a nurse's costume; a play of flickering crimson colored the smoke-haze in the window, illumined her profile, found bright gleams in looped hair under the nurse's cap. Her face, too, might have been starched. She fired again, giving Ranier a gun-flash glimpse of her white shadow-figure, tense marble face. But she looked calm, soldierly. Firing, ejecting the shell, drawing aim, firing; handling the Winchester with the workmanship of a man.

"Laïs—!" Ranier plunged through the door.

"Laïs! *Liebcs Fräulein! Ach, du lieber Gott in Himmel!*" The undersized gnome in yellow romped forward with open arms. "*Aber,* you are safe. We are in time—!"

Ranier slammed the door against the assault mounting the stairs; fought to fasten lock and bolt. He could hear the girl crying, "*Unkle Doktor! Unkle Doktor! Wir warten schon den ganzen die Nacht!* Oh, I thought you would never, never come! It is terrible! They broke in the contagion ward. I saw them kill the patients—terrible things have happened. Oh, God, where have you been—?"

"Been? Been?" It was the querulous voice Ranier had heard on that path in the forest. "Didn't you see my message? Where do you think I would go and stay all the night? That black Maman Celestine did not have twins, but five. I must wash. Scrub floors. Borrow a horse to get back. As if quintuplets are not enough, I am seized by this ruffian on the path—"

Ranier shouted, "John Ranier. Ship's doctor. S.S. *Cacique,* Atlantic-Caribbean Line." At the girl, "Have you seen those people—Brown, Kavanaugh, the big lug, the woman—?"

She cried, "No one! I have been trapped up here since—"

"People? People?" Dr. Eberhardt's voice rose shrill, that of a peevish child quarreling over a doll in an earthquake. "A ship's doctor! People! Laïs, why did you not get my message? You know I always leave one on the table, here, when I—"

There was a ping like a violin string snapping in the darkness; glass smashed on the wall to Ranier's right, releasing an aromatic smell. Polypheme, hiding in a corner, howled; and the Winchester flashed *bang-bang-bang!* in the girl's hands.

She cried, "Keep back, Unkle Doktor! Do not come near the window! They are throwing knives, rocks—!"

"My laboratory!" The small physician came back into the situation with a yell. In the gunflash Ranier saw him standing hands to forehead, wild-eyed. "My experiment! *Himmel herr Gott!* it is ruined. My cultures! And my papers, my writings, my documents, my records—!"

He was on the floor, pawing desperately in rubbish and blowing papers. Ranier shouted, "Records?" and the wailed reply was, "*Ja, ja, ja,* of all my life work, my case histories, the births, the deaths—!" and Ranier almost forgot to hold the door. Objects broke to pieces all around him, but pieces fitted a puzzle on his mind. Another answer! Death records!

He stood as if something had hit him; then something did. A stone from the window. A despairing cry from the girl:

"They come up the gallery! Dear God! they are climbing the tree!"

A CRASH ON the door behind him threw him to his knees. Wood quivered under a triphammer pounding, and a long sliver splintered out of the panels, admitting a thin axe-blade and a ribbon of scarlet light. The window! The door! No place for slackers. Somehow he pummeled Polypheme out of hiding; made the terrified little Negro understand about the desk. Wrenching at weight, they shoved the desk against the cracking portal while the girl sniped from the window, Dr. Eberhardt wailed, missles whined into the laboratory with the velocity of hornets, banging and bouncing on floor and shelves, shattering glass.

"The chemicals!" Ranier dodged to Dr. Eberhardt's side. "Quick, quick! Before they break in! Which bottles—"

"These shelves, these above the laboratory sink. But the potent ones were in the emergency room. A little acid here. *Gott in der Höhe!* Give it to the ungrateful, ignorant, witch-burning devils—!"

Here, there the little man raced, pillaging cabinets and cupboards, heaping ammunition on the center table. Precious little, and they'd need it from the sound. Ranier's heart sickened when he heard the girl cry after a shot, "The rifle—all the cartridges are gone!"

Promptly the door burst to pieces. Ranier swept Laïs Engles into a corner; yelled, "Dr. Eberhardt, take the window!" spun to peg a bottle at a face coming in from the hall balcony. Breaking glass, a screech from the window sill told him Dr. Eberhardt had simultaneously scored. From then on he was busy with his own sector of defense, fighting to hold the door.

They came, fled, reappeared. Attacked and counter-attacked. Ebony devil-masks, tar-barrel torsos framed against torch glare in the jagged door-jambs. Not the educated Haitian of the cities, but the mountaineers, peasants, huggermugger mobsters who can be summoned for any vandalism or riot—this crowd the black equivalent of European book-burners or American lynch gangs, without so far back to go. Like barbarians they charged; superstition-maddened, drum-maddened, primitives with the darkness of the Ivory Coast and Dahomey in their veins; souls untamed by four generations in coats and pants, undomesticated by life in the Caribbean jungles.

They'd kept their gods, Damballa, Papa Legba, Gbeji-Nibu, Ayida-Wedo. Kept them behind a thin lip-service of Christianity—as white men keep their dark gods—hidden in grass-roofed outhouses, secret temples, tucked in the blacker corners of their hearts. Kept them for just such a night as this when white men stabbed their brothers with invisible knives in waterfront cafés, when the dead left their graves to walk in cerements of fog.

"Damballa! Vini 'gider nous!"—"Papa Legba, connais moon par ou!"—"Damballa queddo! Lé-lé sang!"

Brayed from thick chocolate throats those invocations put an icicle up Ranier's spine. Damballa, guide us! Legba, know your worshippers! Damballa, this is the hour for blood!

Drums roaring, throats roaring, fire roaring behind them, they charged the doorway, battled to get over the barricade. John Ranier drove

them back. Drove them, scorched and yowling, back from the desk with throws of astringent liquid, jets of watery flame. Crouching at the table in mid-room, he uncorked the bottles with his teeth; hurled the contents as if the desk were an Argonne parapet, the bottles hand grenades. Behind him Laïs Engles sobbed over an empty gun; Polypheme was under the sink; Dr. Eberhardt bouncing in frenzy between table and window to hold his side of the fort.

The room shook to the crackle of glass, clang of thrown knives, snap of sticks, smash of crockery. There was a time while the overhead dimness was thicker with missiles than a remembered twilight over Belleau Wood. Sappers might have been under the floor. Smoke, turgid with the smell of burning varnish and fried wood, clouded the hall balcony, swirled in through the door. Puffs of chemical in colored tint and stifling acid fumes choked the doorframe. Another charge was coming.

"Damballa! Damballa Oueddo!"

Ranier met the assault with liquid fire. Showered the breach with uncorked bottles of flame. Nitric acid. Deadly sulphuric. Household ammonia. Try a drink of that! Here's an eye-opener! Something to remember us by!

A shower of hydrochloric cleared the doorway. Not the first time in history the primitive warrior was stopped by a judicious use of chemistry. But it couldn't last. The charge was coming again. Those assorted vials of concentrated pain were giving out. Heat burned the air to bronze. The floor was blistering, becoming untenable. A cry from Dr. Eberhardt's whiskers flung Ranier around to see the tree beyond the window monkey-jammed; Negroes shinning up the trunk, lizarding out on the gallery-touching limbs, hanging in the bright foliage like clusters of monstrous fruit.

He scoured the doorway with a throw of carbolic; pressed a last bottle into Laïs Engles' hand. A Negro had thumped down on the outside gallery, trotted to the window, put one leg and a shining steel machete over the sill. Scowling, he drove Dr. Eberhardt aside with a vengeful slash, swung in the other leg, dropped lightly into the room. His scowl watched Dr. Eberhardt and his teeth grinned.

His silhouette blocked the window, and his Congo presence filled the room with a lion-like breathing and a fetor of black grease. A dented top hat was tilted Ted Lewis fashion over his brows; around his naked shoulders a circlet of pig's-hoofs dangled; ragged pink trousers were belted by a dead snake from which hung an apron of gourd-rattles. Knife aloft, sweaty sinews glistening, he stood with his nostrils opening and shutting like gills while his rocking-horse eyeballs measured the scene as if it were a feast.

STARING AT THIS dreary master of ceremonies, Ranier couldn't believe Dr. Eberhardt's cry:

"Hyacinth Lucien! *Aber,* you *Schweinhund,* I will see you killed for this. When the police find out you are not a bartender, but a dirty *hougan* priest, a *bocor*—!"

The black man rumbled, "*Pas capab'! Gendarmes* too late. You bad witch doctor, *chauché, de culte des morts.* Dig *zombies;* raise dead. We know." His scowl saw Ranier; deepened to a thundercloud. Saw Laïs Engles and beamed delight. "You witch doctor, too. Talk with *zombie. Zombie* friend of *mademoiselle!*"

Running thumb across knife-blade, he crouched for the spring. John Ranier swung the girl behind him in sick suspense. The black man's feet were noiseless on the floor. Ranier broke from fascination to meet him half way. His fist started from his shoe-tops; flush on the point he caught that grinning jaw. He didn't miss because he couldn't. All the pent desperation, all the power in his being, the last ounce of dynamite went into the blow, as if that shining black jaw were the focal point of the whole night's evil.

Crack! It should have felled an ox. It did not so much as alter the black man's facial expression. The jaw never turned. Ranier felt as if he

had punched an anvil. The Negro was on him; the knife a guillotine poised to whack. It was coming down—

It stopped!

Stopped as if that upraised arm had jammed at the shoulder socket. A convulsion scribbled the minstrel face under the tophat. Eyes jerked sideways as if fish hooks had caught them. Breath gushed through the teeth, blubbering the black rubber lips. *Fffffffaaaaaaa!*

A backward leap for the window. Somersault over the sill. Dive off the gallery rail, crash in shrubbery below, scream to curdle the night. In a vertigo of astonishment, John Ranier was gaping at the vacuum where the champion had stood. Knife and executioner were gone!

Laïs Engles screamed, "Frogs!"

A bullfrog, making a green streak out of shadow, landed bellywhacker on a mat of firelight where those black feet had fled. The frog was followed by another. A third. Two more. Ranier saw the floor was alive with green mites. Bouncing and flipflopping, squat-tag over the heating boards, looking up at him with the bulged, indignant eyes of United States Senators routed from a Lilliputian election hall. An amphibian stampede escaping that aquarium smashed on the laboratory table.

A sentence went through his mind; Marcelline's alto words in a café setting nine hours or nine thousand years ago? "I give you my words, *messieurs,* if you dropped a live bullfrog through the skylight of our government buildings, every soldier in the place would jump out of the windows—"

Frogs! It went with "Quintuplets!" With Haarman's webbed foot, Professor Schlitz's spectacles, that cracked skull with a string of pearls in its teeth. He captured and held up one of the slippery creatures by a jumbo leg. Black faces looking in through the window screeched and vanished as if exorcised. Ranier spun to see dark savages mounting the doorway barricade. The leader gestured a meat-axe. He spied the thing in Ranier's clutch.

"Waaaaah!"

• • •

RANIER TIGHTENED HIS fingers, and the frog shot from his squeeze like a cake of wet green soap. The frog lit on the balcony; the balcony was cleared by magic. Dr. Eberhardt sailed a greenback out of the window. Chorused terror, a wild stampede in the branches of the sablier tree—

To his last day Ranier knew he would remember that escape from that abominable laboratory; that frog-fusillade across the smoking upper balcony; that charge behind a barrage of croaking swamp-mites. They carried the broken tank to the stairhead; Ranier threw. Fat frogs and lank. Frogs that went like green arrows through the smoke, sailed like speckled bats in the stifling haze. In the cinnamon smudge below an Ethiopian riot milled, clawed and fought to get through the front door and evacuate the hall. Where hydrochloric acid had failed, where bayonets would have failed and the Charge of the Light Brigade been barbecued, a plague of green amphibians turned the tide.

Ranier would always remember that. Old Testament deliverance in 1936. Himself, at the stairhead, pelting those black backs with bullfrogs. Dr. Eberhardt yanking greenbacks from the pockets of his yellow rainslicker and ten-word German oaths from his throat, hurling both with raging accuracy at terrified Negro skulls. Doctors gone back to witchcraft! Medicine failing, resorting to a remedy in Voodoo!

And he would always remember Laïs Engles flying down the stairway in her nurse's costume, fierce-eyed, hair a loose golden shawl, chin up to the last, racing to snatch a gray tabby from the smoke below, hugging the cat in her arms. And the sight of Polypheme, the house-boy, lavender with fear, slipping on a frog that was spread like a banana peel on the bottom step and floundering on greased heels across the hall. Like a roller-skater he hit the sidewall, head on, grabbing for equilibrium.

The night must disgorge another horror before they could get out of there. For the house-boy's grabbing hand caught a knob, and the knob yanked open a cupboard door. That closet in the wall! There had been a moment engraved on Ranier's memory when an Angelo Carpetsi hooked high-waisted suspenders on that same door in the wall, fetching to light an umbrella and sun helmet which might have been (and wasn't) Dr. Eberhardt.

What spilled from the cupboard this time— the door springing open like a jack-in-a-box at Polypheme's touch—was something that might have been (and at one time was) Mr. Haarman.

He had not been waiting for a street car. Not in that baking hotbox, with one shoe in his pocket and his webbed foot bare; his eyes two staring zeros, mouth agawp; hands stiff at his side and palms outward, the right palm showing a scar in remembrance of an Indian at Para, Brazil.

Ranier shouted, "Haarman!" and he came out of the cubicle, bowing. He bowed too far. Bowed off balance and toppled, mouth baked open, eyes front, throwing affectionate arms around Polypheme's neck to drag the squalling house-boy to the floor.

It cleared the last superstitious Haitian from the verandah outside and the last Haitian superstition from John Ranier's head.

The girl was crying, "He was alive, Unkle Doktor! Only dying when they brought him to the hospital tonight. You remember the *Kronprinz Albrecht*, the plague, the funerals? It is the mate who died—Adolph Perl—!"

Outside the mob was a fleeing elephant herd; a dragon-tongue of fire burst from the cupboard door. In that blast of incandescence Dr. Eberhardt bawled: "Adolph Perl! *Ja*, it is! How? *How?*"

Match flares of fire were exploding around the little man's rooted feet; Ranier saw in alarm that his own trouser-cuffs were smoking. He screamed, "I'll tell you how!" and kicked. Kicked out with his lame foot and gave that taffy-haired dead body a boot that made his bad foot ache!

CHAPTER XXIV

EN ROUTE

Five A.M.

Port-au-Prince—69 Km, said the sign.

Flat miles of coastal highway Ranier had not seen before. The road smooth as glimpses of obsidian gulf. The Model T settling into a rhythmic hum. The grayness thinning ahead where presently the city would be seen. The night charred black behind where a conflagration, long visible in the sky, had burned to carbon. Behind him in the car—Laïs Engles, Dr. Eberhardt, and Professor Schlitz . . .

It couldn't have happened. None of it could have happened. At the *Gendarmerie* in the fishing village five miles back the *Gardes* had not noticed a tall white man, a stout woman with blond hair, and a big man all mud going by since four o'clock in any car. *Non,* they had seen no fat American in short pants driving for Port-au-Prince. *Oui,* this was the only road, and cars go by with much frequence, but then there had been the fog. A fire? *Oui,* they had seen red sky and heard drumming on the mountain. "But such things are common in Haiti, *monsieur,* and on a night such as last—"

Besides, the telephone line to the west had not answered. Doubtless, Caco bandits had cut the wire. But yes, *monsieur* could telephone Port-au-Prince from here. *Monsieur* and his party were in distress? A pity they did not have time for breakfast, a jug of *clairin,* perhaps a glass of *aguardiente.*

Ranier had only had time for the *aguardiente* and two cryptic long-distance phone calls to the capital. One to the All America Cable office. One to general headquarters of the *Garde d'Haiti.*

It couldn't have happened, but here was Polypheme at the steering wheel beside him; a pale girl in nurse's costume and a little walrus in Cape Cod oilskins and an insectologist without his glasses in the back seat. Ranier had waited for calm while Dr. Eberhardt re-bandaged the professor's wound and hysteria died. In the gray light he could see his passengers, haggard, bewildered, sitting in limp exhaustion; the doctor's beaver eye had not been off him for a minute. The girl's quiet sobbing had stopped long ago. Hugging the cat, she watched him too.

RANIER TURNED TO face the back seat, and was saying: "To begin with—I was there in Hyacinth Lucien's café when this tourist came in. I suppose," narrowly, "you know the place, Doctor?"

"*Aber,* that swine will never run it again with his black neck broken from that jump like we saw!"

"He's out of it now," Ranier banished him grimly, "but Hyacinth had nothing to do with what happened there. He merely used that stabbing in his bar as propaganda to incite a race riot and burn your hospital. Probably been laying for you a long time for cutting into his witch doctoring racket. Getting back to the café—this tourist Haarman walked in and saw me a little tight. That must've been about quarter to seven last evening."

"Tight?" The old German snorted.

"Means a few drinks. Enough to put me on edge," Ranier described, "and at the same time make me wonder if what happened afterwards wasn't my imagination. Haarman ordered me out, and, when I didn't go, took a punch at me, getting me unawares. I went off the verandah and hit my head. Woke up wandering in a daze some minutes later, and saw Haarman sitting at my table inside.

"Haarman looked queer, then, but he'd always been deathly pale on the ship, and I figured he was one of those dipsomaniacs who think they can beat up the world when they're liquored up. He'd been drinking my *aguardiente,* I saw, and I suppose he'd had plenty before he came ashore." Ranier turned his glance on the insectologist. "He was oiled on shipboard yesterday afternoon, wasn't he, Professor?"

"In the ship's bar before dinner," the thin one remembered. "We were all there talking of the motor drive. He wash drinking heavily then."

"I'll bet. Who," Ranier narrowed his eyes at the wan face under the sun helmet, "bought him those drinks?"

"Carpetsi, moshtly. I bought him one." The man's toothless mouth puckered as if he might cry. "He'd ashked me to join the drive and I felt obligated. Obligated! Oh, my! I don't know why he ashked me. No, I don't."

Ranier said, "I do," grimly. "But we'll come to that. Well, Haarman was walking on his heels when he came to Hyacinth's café. The rest of you were to meet him there, is that right?"

"Yesh. He went there a half hour ahead of ush."

"Or, maybe, he was *sent* on ahead. I've an idea he got there early for reasons other than his own. Perhaps to see if the coast was clear. At any rate, he didn't like my company, and he wasn't diplomatic about asking me to leave. From the look in his eyes, I've a hunch he may have been doped. I could see his face in the back-bar mirror, and he seemed to pass out. Then some time after seven o'clock," Ranier directed his words to Dr. Eberhardt, "about the time you got your R.F.D. call, I should judge, this tourist party from the ship showed up at the café. I was a trifle woozy, myself, by that time—from that knock on the head, I guess—but these tourists walked in and ordered a round of drinks with Haarman. Professor Schlitz can check me if I'm wrong."

The professor groaned an affirmative to this, and Ranier waited for the wheels to take a curve before going on.

"From the alcove I could watch this bunch at table in the middle of the room. They'd all come down from New York together on the cruise, except Marcelline, who'd boarded ship at Cape Haitian. This Marcelline sat at the bar-end of the table; the others ranged along the side. A Mr. Brown from Ohio; the professor, here; an Italian named Carpetsi, now dead; a Mr. Coolidge.

"On the opposite side, a blond Broadway relic, and her Irish boy friend, Mr. Kavanaugh. Our Mr. Haarman was at the far end of the table, sitting with his back to an open window and about ten feet from the sill. Dense fog outside, and he was pretty fogged, himself, by then. He'd cooked his own goose by drinking that *aguardiente*. So there's the set-up; the victim anaesthetized, the café a good quiet place to put him on the spot, and the fog just suited their scheme."

Professor Schlitz cried, "*Their* scheme? Whosh?"

RANIER LEANED OVER the back of his seat to fire a cigarette, watching three faces in the match glare.

"The ones who maneuvered Haarman to that out of the way café," he shook out the match, "to kill him. The ones in that little tourist party who were in the know. Maybe most of them—maybe only a couple of them—I'm not sure which ones, but it won't be long before I find out.

"Anyway, this innocent little jaunt across Haiti by motor was to have been something more than a jaunt, and not so innocent. The original plan, the scheme behind this motor trip, was Haarman's. Kavanaugh claims he was driving to Port-au-Prince on business and wanted company. Whether Haarman and his crowd attached themselves to an innocent party remains to be seen. But the big idea was Haarman's game. He had helpers. They double-crossed him."

Ranier pointed his cigarette at the insectologist.

"This underground game of Haarman's calls for a gang. I knew there was more than one on the job from the first. You can't stab a man at table and nobody see it happen, sitting at close quarters like that. Prepared with alcohol, Haarman didn't know it when the knife went in; never made a squeak. But someone at your table had to know it. Someone must've seen it. Someone was holding out. Well, Carpetsi, for example, saw it. He was in on the scheme, one of the gang. He was going to squeal, later. That's why his throat was cut."

"The Italian boy," Laïs Engles cried.

"One of the gang," Ranier snapped. "There *was* a gang when the thing started. A gang that left New York together and sailed to Haiti, playing tourists on a Caribbean cruise. A gang headed by Haarman, who came to Haiti after something Haarman knew about. As I say, Haarman was double-crossed; knifed by one of his pals. You're lucky, Professor. I think the knife was originally intended for you."

The insectologist grabbed himself by the throat.

"Me?"

"I can only guess on this point. You were invited on the so-called motor tour as a fall guy. A blind. A dupe to make the drive look innocent. Besides, this scheme called for a stooge, somebody to be wounded to give the gang a chance to call on Dr. Eberhardt's hospital. Wait—" He apprehended an explosion of German from the gnome-face under the sou'wester. "I'll explain that when I come to it. The point is Professor Schlitz was picked—maybe I'm wrong—to be this accident-victim. It would look quite natural. Party of American tourists driving cross-country to see Haiti at night. A white man mysteriously injured in a waterfront dive. Rush to the nearest doctor. The gang, I believe, had planned this accident for Professor Schlitz. But something went wrong. Haarman, himself, got the works."

Ranier exhaled smoke. Then he continued:

"Why? I can only speculate again. Suppose that devil, Hyacinth, recognized Haarman when the crowd came into the café? Suppose Hyacinth recognized Haarman's scarred hand when he served him a drink, and Haarman's gang realized it? Or just suppose it was opportunity for a fast double-cross—Haarman was soused, sitting with his back to a window, fog handy—a good chance to knock him off and grab his major share of the profits—"

Ranier drew a sharp lungful of cigarette smoke; expelled it through his teeth. "I think

that's it. They wanted his share. Anyhow, this scheme that mushroomed out of Haarman's brain turned into a toadstool and killed him. His gang was tougher than he was. *He* was stabbed."

THE SPEEDING CAR hit a jolt in the road, and Dr. Eberhardt, bounced; exploded. "But all this is impossible! *Donnerwetter!* Impossible! How could this man you call Haarman be in that café last evening? How can he have a gang, as you say, and come on your ship from New York? How can he be alive in the first place? When he is one Adolph Perl! When he is a man who came to Haiti in 1922 and died of a plague, and I, myself, saw him in his coffin fourteen—"

Professor Schlitz shrilled, "Then he *wash* a living dead man—"

Ranier shouted above voices, wind and tires, "He was a living dead man, perhaps, but not the kind you think. A living dead man from the minute he trusted a gang with his dirty work, and put his back to that window in the café last night. This is what happened.

"Everybody at the table was chattering about the fog, the proposed motor drive. Marcelline, the guide—he wasn't a guide, by the way, but one of the gang—Marcelline went out to see about the Winton he'd hired. About ten minutes later he came back into the room. During that time, Haarman was stabbed."

"But I wash at the table," the insectologist gasped. "Nobody at the table made a move."

"No."

"Then how—"

Ranier made a red circle with his cigarette. "I'm a fool or I'd have guessed it at the time. Only I wasn't looking when it happened, and when Haarman did get my attention, I was seeing a reflection in the mirror behind that bar, so the angle there didn't give me a clue. You," he pointed the cigarette at the thin man, "didn't see it because your attention was probably snared in another direction. Afterwards I saw tracks outside the café, but they stopped six feet from the window. Haarman was stabbed through that window just the same."

"But if he sat ten feet from the sill on the in-shide—?"

"A long reach." Ranier shook his head. "But so has bamboo. Ever see these Haitians cutting down ripe cocoanuts? Then recall that splintered pole we found in Marcelline's ribs."

"Good God!"

"Good weapon. Stiff bamboo. Knife lashed to the tip. A quick jab; exit knife through window curtained with fog; enter murderer through door talking about the weather. He occupies the conversation, holding attention to his end of the table with a discourse on Voodoo. No one is more astonished to see Haarman unwell. In the ensuing hue and cry, he spies a face at the window. Maybe it was his conscience, but I doubt if Marcelline had any."

"*Marshelline!*" Not many hours before, the professor had mashed the name through his gums on a similar cry. "Marshelline shtabbed Misher Haarman?"

"His tracks outside. Who else left the café and went around by that window? Remember that thicket of bamboo out there? Afterwards he chucks the pole, hides the knife in the Winton—not the only tools he's stowed in that 'hired' car—and comes back into the room; no blood on *his* shirt. Two birds killed with one stone. The gang has cut Haarman out of his share of the spoils, and they've got their accident-victim. Now the secret machinery is under way, they've ditched its inventor, and they're going to run the machine for themselves. First stop: Dr. Eberhardt's hospital."

CHAPTER XXV

RANIER'S EXPLANATION

A road sign whizzed by the window. Ranier craned his head to read it in the coming daylight. *Port-au-Prince—53 Km.*

He picked up the story harshly. "But before the machine gets out of the café, there's a cog in the gears. That's me. They didn't know how much I'd seen, and they had to let me walk out and work on Haarman—they couldn't kill me with the Professor and Hyacinth Lucien looking on. Professor Schlitz was another cog—what to do with him? Well, they took him along to get him later—he could add to the confusion at the hospital, and that's what they wanted. Confusion. They got it when Miss Engles recognized Haarman. I don't suppose they counted on the girl being there."

Dr. Eberhardt hunched forward from the back seat. "Am I going mad? Still you talk about this man Haarman as if he had been alive! I tell you, he was a German sailor named Adolph Perl, who died—"

"Fourteen years ago. 1922. And was buried in a graveyard three miles down the road west of your hospital." Ranier nodded wearily. "Miss Engles identified him, too. By the scar on his hand, by the webbed foot she'd seen when he was a sailor on her uncle's War expedition up the Amazon. That was a cog in *my* machinery, when I heard that. I thought Miss Engles was lying."

He shifted his eyes to the white dimness of her face. For the past ten miles she hadn't stirred; had sat white and strained, cat in arms, her eyes unswerving on him as he talked. An expressionless headshake refused a cigarette. He told her huskily:

"And *you* were an unexpected wrench in this gang's machinery. I don't suppose they'd been told about that little girl who was on your uncle's secret expedition for Germany. If they were, you were probably described as a little girl because people forget children grow up. More likely the supposition was you'd been sent back to Germany long ago. You were a cog in the gears," Ranier gestured, "but not too dangerous a cog. This gang could use your story, as a matter of fact, to advantage. Make it seem like Haarman's a *zombie*. Cloak their machinery under a mask of Voodoo magic.

"It was all right, after all, because it scared the hell out of everybody, myself included, and the gang was plenty anxious to get rid of me when I turned up in the hospital. They had to work fast in that hospital."

"I do not understand. *Nein!* Why should anybody come to my hospital," Dr. Eberhardt panted. "Who are they? Why?"

"Haarman, stabbed in the back, dying, was used as an entreé. An excuse to get in. I think," Ranier guessed, "the idea was to get you, Dr. Eberhardt, busy in the emergency room. Keep you downstairs. The gang had been told about the layout of the hospital. Haarman knew the rooms; knew your desk was in the upstairs laboratory—"

"*Heilige Gott!* But he was Adolph Perl, I tell you!"

"He was dying, all right, in your emergency room last night. But Dr. Eberhardt was unexpectedly out on a call. The ones who killed Haarman didn't care. Remember, Professor, who carried Haarman into the hospital?"

"Brown and Carpetshi carried him in. Kavanaugh and hish blond woman and I followed after." The thin man rinsed sweat from his forehead; leaned back groaning. "We put him on the operating table."

"Leaving Coolidge and Marcelline outside in that Winton. And while the rest of you were inside, and I was around in back looking through the window, the laboratory upstairs was wrecked.

"Can you guess who shinned up the gallery and did the job? Well, I wouldn't put it past Coolidge, but we don't know yet. Marcelline was in it, that's certain. The lab wasn't just smashed up, either, but left as a set-up to make it look like the work of Haitian vandals. Dissected hands over that Bunsen flame. Frog left on that spike as a Voodoo sign. That's why Miss Engles didn't find her message from Dr. Eberhardt. One of those rats found it, saw the doctor was out, stole the note. But I didn't know what this gang was after until that battle with the mob hours afterwards. Dr. Eberhardt's records, that's what they were after. Dr. Eberhardt's *death records.*"

"*Himmel herr Gott!*" the little physician choked dramatically. "What for?"

Ranier lifted himself on an elbow to growl, "Haarman wasn't able to tell his crew of criminals where Adolph Perl was supposed to've been buried. That's what they had to know. They wanted to find the grave that belonged to Adolph Perl. And they knew you'd kept a record of it somewhere in your files."

"Perl's grave? Perl's grave? A dead man comes back to life and has to have my files robbed to find his own grave—?"

"I tell you, Coolidge *or* Marcelline, or both of them, ransacked your desk, wrecked the lab, stole the death records and got back to the car parked in the driveway. Down in the emergency room Miss Engles kept ringing for you. You didn't come. She ran upstairs to find out why you didn't answer; she saw the mess in the laboratory and screamed."

THE GIRL SAID to the gnome in German, her voice low, toneless, "I thought you had been abducted by the natives. I thought you had been killed."

Dr. Eberhardt panted, "I do not understand any of this. Shades of Kaiser Wilhelm! What does it mean?"

"Curiously enough," Ranier told him, giving him a hard stare, "the shades of Kaiser Wilhelm were in your hospital last evening, Doctor. In those death records, too; the ones stolen from your files. Of course, when the girl screamed upstairs and I dashed around to the front, Coolidge and Marcelline were there sitting in the car. They followed me into the hospital and played amazement at sight of that upstairs room. Meanwhile Haarman died on the operating table downstairs. Hemorrhage. The gang inherited his profits; had the death records in their possession; the machine was running smoothly except for my reappearance.

"Everything conspired to their advantage, though. Miss Engles was terrified, telling her astounding story about Haarman. Your absence, Dr. Eberhardt, played up the mystery. The fog outside made it perfect because it would keep the natives indoors with their heads under their pillows. Kavanaugh sent Coolidge, Brown and Marcelline back to the village to bring the police. Then he started a murder investigation on the Haarman stabbing.

"By that time I was certain one of the tourists killed Haarman, but I didn't know who and there seemed to be no motive. The mystery of the laboratory appeared to make it a Voodoo job, though. And Miss Engles' story had me down. We got up to the laboratory; Kavanaugh accused *me* of Haarman's murder. A door banged downstairs. The Irishman went down, came back, said Haarman's dead body had walked off. Well, we knew where the body walked off to—into that cupboard in the hall. But who put it there? I'd think Kavanaugh put it there—to further scramble the mystery and make us believe Haarman a *zombie*—but he was upstairs when that door banged. Unless—"

Fingers in his hair, Ranier stiffened up; glared at Laïs Engles. "By George! That cat!"

"*Meine Katze?*"

"She was downstairs in that room. *She* could have brushed the door. Or wind could have slammed it. Then Kavanaugh, running downstairs to see, could have hidden the body, and rushed back saying it was gone. So the *zombie* angle is established and we're addled out of our wits, providing it *was* a trick played by Kavanaugh. We don't know yet. We don't know."

Ranier glared at countryside passing the window, fields of millet, thatch-roofed huts, thick-leafed banana plantain gray in early light. Fog was lifting on the Gulf of Gonaives and soon there would be some sky. He waited for the tires to screech on a long flat curve; smoking impatiently. His listeners in the back seat were coming out of shadow like negatives forming on a film.

"We do know," he went on sternly, "what happened after that. Polypheme, driving back from the village to tell us Hyacinth was rounding up a mob, saw a dead body sitting by an open grave in the cemetery by that road. Adolph Perl's grave, as it turned out. The boys with the death records had located Perl's headstone. Who disinterred that coffin?

"We know Brown, Marcelline and Coolidge never reached the village *Gendarmerie.* Coolidge said Marcelline wrecked the Winton in the fog. Did he? Did he ditch the car to get rid of Coolidge and Brown, and open that grave by himself? Or did Coolidge help him with the shoveling, and Brown, too. Or was Brown, innocent, left dead in the jungle somewhere?

"I'm sure of one thing. There were pick-axes, spades and ropes under the seats of that Winton, and *Monsieur* Marcelline worked on that grave. And then, with everything running like hot oil, the machinery blew all to pieces. Smashed up right there in the light of those shaded lanterns in the fog. It was Adolph Perl's headstone, all right.

"But a little old lady in taffeta and bonnet was in his coffin!"

"*Was ist das? Was ist das?*" Dr. Eberhardt's puffed eyes blazed at Ranier, cheeks swelled, purpled. "You try to say an old lady was at the grave of Adolph Perl instead of—! *Who put her there?*"

Ranier shook his head.

"Nobody put her there. She was there."

"*Aber, nein!* I, myself, buried her—*ja,* with Polypheme's help, in a little cemetery the other side, at the east, of my hospital! Fräulein Laïs will tell you—"

"She did tell me," Ranier ground out. "She did say that, Dr. Eberhardt, *and so did your death records!* So did the headstone over the grave. When we found an old woman's body at that grave marked for Adolph Perl—I thought she'd been transferred. But she wasn't transferred. She was there last night when those ghouls exhumed that coffin. They didn't expect to find her in that coffin under Perl's headstone. You bet they didn't! And it smashed this secret machinery of theirs, this dirty underground machinery they'd stolen from Haarman—smashed it to hell!

"I'd like to've seen their faces, I tell you! If Haarman had been alive to engineer the thing himself, he'd have dropped dead. We thought we were crazy when we saw the old woman's body at Perl's headstone, but those rats who dug her out from under must've had twice the shock."

RANIER'S VOICE CRACKED in excitement, crying at his stunned audience.

"And if you think those grave-diggers had a shock, if you think *I* had a shock—I'm sorry, Miss Engles, it was horrible for you!—think of the blow it handed the rest of the gang, the ones who'd stayed there with us in the hospital, expecting everything was running smoothly and on schedule. What did *they* think? Carpetsi, for instance. Well, *he* thought he'd been double-crossed by this double-crossing mob. He thought his jackal pals who'd done that bit of digging had pulled a fast one, tricked up the grave with this old lady's corpse, hidden the body that should have been there, and pulled a sneak with the spoils. If Kavanaugh is in on this racket, that's what he thought, too. The Italian was all for chasing after Coolidge and Marcelline and Brown, right then. But his idea was wrong. His gang hadn't double-crossed him. They'd found Old Gramma Sou there in the first place.

"Now the machinery was off the track, if you understand me. Way off! Those grave-diggers didn't know what to do. They had to work fast, too. Marcelline probably clawed through the death records and found the location of the old lady's grave.

"That Haitian was clever. Fearing his own countrymen, knowing the Haitian penal code strictly forbids tampering with graves—knowing, too, the superstitious fear of his people—he leaves a frog tied to the exhumed body, enough to scare the police galley west. That's why he'd appropriated a jar of frogs from the laboratory. Good protection.

"The next step is to dig up Old Gramma Sou's grave—maybe the prize they're looking for is there, since she's (for reasons they can't fathom) *here*. Can you follow this, Miss Engles?"

The girl whispered, "I think so, but I do not understand."

"Let's follow the grave-diggers. Marcelline was one of them, if Coolidge and Brown were the others, I don't know. They raced, unseen in the fog, to the old lady's grave. Don't think they didn't work fast. If that soil hadn't been dry sand underneath we'd have caught up with them in a hurry. But what happens? Under the old lady's stone they find the body of the U.S. Marine. The machinery of their plan is wrecked again. Nothing for it, but they've got to open the grave of that marine. Foiled again. A celluloid collar. The missionary in the grave of the marine. So on to the grave of the missionary."

"Then they did not," Laïs Engles breathed, "move the bodies from one cemetery to another?"

"Angelo Carpetsi thought that was what they were doing. So did I, at first. God knows what the rest of this gang thought. There are two gangs working now, see? The ghouls, racing from cemetery to cemetery, following that list in the death records—that list who were buried fourteen years ago on that night of the plague. And there was that half of the gang which was pursuing the work of the ghouls, didn't know what was happening, couldn't figure the game any more than you and I were able to figure it."

Ranier paused for breath, then went on.

"Do you recall what happened at Adolph Perl's supposed grave? Coolidge turned up. Was he one of the grave-diggers, or did Marcelline really ditch that Winton and drive on, alone, in another car? Coolidge said the Winton was wrecked and he didn't know where Brown and Marcelline were. But what did he tell Kavanaugh when they walked off in the fog by themselves? Did he tell Kavanaugh to wait around a while, then hit for the old lady's cemetery and keep stalling on the mystery angle? Anyway, that's what happened, wasn't it? We beat it to the grave of Old Gramma Sou; saw the marine;

beat it to the grave of the marine; found the missionary—exactly as those diggers ahead of us had. But I hit on something at the marine's grave." Ranier made a white fist and considered the knuckles grimly. "I hit on something on that grave under the big tree where the missionary's bones were in that soldier's coffin—"

He paused for breath, mopping a glaze from his grimed face. Smoke hurt in his throat, and his tongue, dried, was reluctant to go on. A stiff glass of *aguardiente* would have been venison at this point—why had he ever left that café in the first place?

He resumed thickly: "That grave under the tree wasn't sand. It was wet earth loam, easy digging, a compost of leaf-mould, damp and absorbent soil. So there was little left of the coffin; not much left of the bones; hardly more than that clerical collar. See the point, Dr. Eberhardt? Those other bodies, buried in dry sand at an altitude generally dry, had—had almost mummified. Like those mummies you see in Mexico—at Guanawato, bodies turned to leather by atmospheric condition. But in that compost under the big tree, the leaf-droppings of a thousand-year-old forest giant—decay, yes. There was the proof. The missionary had been buried in the marine's grave *from the first*. The marine in the old lady's. The old lady in that one marked for Adolph Perl.

"Then while I was staggered with that discovery, more mystified than ever, we heard shots on Morne Cuyamel at the missionary's mismarked headstone. The ghouls, of course, had exhumed the body of Colonel Otto. And their wrecked machine hit another snag. A *gendarme*, driving by the mission house, saw them at work. They shot first." Ranier sighed.

"MURDER HAS A way of developing like cancer. After you've killed once, I suppose, another homicide or two makes little difference to the hangman. That secret machine Haarman had set in motion was fueled on a murder at its

inception. Those grave-robbers were desperate. They shot the Haitian *Garde* with a U.S. service automatic they'd found on the buried marine; planted it in the fist of your Colonel Otto; dumped the *gendarme* into the grave and lit out for Bois Legone—"

He punched out his cigarette on window-glass pale with a suggestion of day. "I'd like to know why nobody in the vicinity roused at that shooting. Loud in that fog as stones banged underwater. Doesn't anybody live in that Morne Cuyamel mission house?"

Dr. Eberhardt grunted, "The Reverend Waldo Claphouse. *Aber,* he is down with *dhangi* fever. The natives would not dare put their head out of doors near a cemetery. On a night of fog—"

"It was thick on that Morne Cuyamel road, all right. Thick enough for another murder. Angelo Carpetsi's. Convinced he was being double-crossed, the Italian gave me a whisper, told me he was going to talk. Somebody overheard him, and from then on he was marked for a tonsillectomy."

"On my eye-glashes!" Professor Schlitz gagged. "The glashes I losht when I fell down in that marine graveyard. Hish throat—my glashes—!"

"Somebody," explained Ranier, "picked 'em up. Piece broken from a lens. Good gag to leave behind. But it took a blade to cut a throat that might be talkative. If Angelo hadn't lost his nerve and tried to run away, if he'd stayed with me, there, he might not be a handful of ashes back in that hospital. But that Morne Cuyamel stage-set was too much for Carpetsi. Took a cue from the Professor's exit, and tried to exit himself. He did. Miss Engles says," he looked across his cigarette at Dr. Eberhardt, "she saw Mr. Coolidge start off in the fog after Professor Schlitz."

The girl said tightly, "That is what I saw."

Ranier speculated, "But couldn't he have changed direction without being seen? Everybody was staring at the graveyard. Couldn't he have sneaked a wide circle, steering clear of the car lights, and caught up, say, with Carpetsi? Perhaps it was Coolidge who picked up those pince-nez of yours, Professor. Left them under the body to frame you. But he used a razor-blade."

"You mean to shay—you mean Misher Coolidge cut—?"

"Jugular vein and carotid artery." He was staring at a little splash of sunlight, crimson over his head, that had come through the windshield.

He heard the insectologist protesting weakly, "But Misher Coolidge was Misher Carpetshi's friend. On the boat they—they were thick as fleas."

He suggested dryly, "Thicker, perhaps. But, Professor, you ought to know about fleas. If Coolidge didn't cut the Little Angel's throat, who did? Did you? No," he waved off a gum-spluttered denial hurriedly, "you wouldn't leave your spectacles, I imagine. That was a dumb at-tempt to throw suspicion on you. However, at the time I didn't know. Still don't. Maybe some-body else did it, somebody who was behind us all the time we were behind the grave-digging crew.

"We weren't far behind those ghouls, either, at Morne Cuyamel. Sand or not, all this shovel-ing had slowed them. I think I'd have overhauled them if I'd gone straight to Bois Legone, but Carpetsi was still alive, there was a chance to sew him up and a doctor can't let a man die. Miss Engles and I," he told Dr. Eberhardt, "rushed this Italian back to your hospital. I've an idea our gangster friends weren't sorry to see us go. They weren't sorry Professor Schlitz was gone, either. We were a problem, and this scheme of theirs, haywire as it was, was driving them crazy. Three murders, now, and still no prize in sight.

"So Coolidge, Kavanaugh and Miss Daisy May set out for Bois Legone to find out what ca-pers had been cut at Colonel Otto's tombstone. Incidentally, Professor Schlitz attached himself to their car—the car that murdered *gendarme* had driven up in. They find the grave at Bois Le-

gone is vandalized; Captain Friederich's body, there, where the colonel's should've been—"

LAÏS ENGLES PUT her face in her hands.
A hoarse roar from Dr. Eberhardt.

"You—you are crazy! I do not believe a word of this, *nein!* Fräulein Engles' uncle, the captain of that ship, we put him in a mausoleum high on the mountain. A mausoleum built by a French planter who was lost at sea before he could use it. I bought it, myself, when I first came to Haiti, and I gave it to Fräulein Engles for her—"

"Just the same," John Ranier said evenly, "Captain Friederich's body was in Bois Legone at Colonel Otto's grave."

"I shaw it," Professor Schlitz put in, drearily. "It wash there, all right. Wish a shea cap on itch head."

"Meanwhile," Ranier pursued, "the grave-digging detachment, scotched again, have gone up the mountain to that last cemetery. Kava-naugh, Coolidge and Miss May follow. What happened from there on is in the dark; all I can do is guess by the evidence, I know the work-ings of the machinery, not the engineers. I think Kavanaugh and party caught up, there, with the grave-diggers. If Kavanaugh wasn't one of the gang—he's dead. The blonde is dead, too. Or if Coolidge isn't in the gang, *he's* dead. I'm not worried about Mr. Coolidge, though. Carpetsi was his cabin-mate, his pal. Birds of a feather.

"Anyway they're up with the grave-crew. Can that be Brown and Marcelline? We haven't seen a sign of Mr. Brown all night. Who helped Marcelline shovel? At all events, Marcelline was sent as an emissary on horseback. My guess is, the Haitian guide had been leading the chase in the Winton which was never wrecked at all. But he returned to Bois Legone on a horse he'd picked up somewhere—cattle walk all over these damned roads. Why? *To pick up a hat he lost by accident while digging that Bois Legone job.* Fatal for the gang if that hat was found. For Marcel-line, anyway. He wanted that Panama.

"And somebody else was dispatched on an errand. Given a gun and the dead *gendarme*'s car. The errand being to stop *me* from any investigation I might be making on the sly. This gunman caught me on the road near the hospital."

"You were shot?" Laïs Engles gasped through her hands.

"Shot at. The fellow missed. I suppose I'll never know who it was." He described the chase through the fog. "Of course he took the fork going toward Port-au-Prince, to join his gang at the cemetery on the mountaintop. I went to Bois Legone, wrong choice. Lucky for Professor Schlitz, though. Marcelline, coming on a back trail, had reached Bois Legone and sneaked up on horseback behind a hedge that bordered the cemetery. And he stabbed the Professor through the hedge, just as the Professor was going to tell me about seeing that Panama hat. Stabbed him right in front of me. I didn't see how, in the fog. But the same weapon he'd used on Haarman, remember. Thinking he might need such a weapon, Marcelline had cut himself another pole and lashed his knife to the tip. The hedge spoiled his aim."

"My shoulder!" the insectologist, his wound suddenly remembered, exhaled a loud groan. Then straightened up to gasp, "In that case— who was the rider who killed Marshelline?"

"Marcelline," Ranier said through his teeth. "Hoist on his own petard, by God! Talk about justice. Racing back up the mountain, he came out on the main road for better speed, spurred to rejoin the gang. Horse hit that roadside ditch, full speed. Marcelline was thrown. Pole hit that big tree, jamming the knife up to the hilt. Other end, splintered, went through the Haitian like a lance. Score one for fate. And we're getting," Ranier promised, "to the end of that trail."

It was almost light in the sedan. He could see their faces; the girl's expression masking a fear that had never left it since a moment, there, in the hospital when he'd unlaced a dead man's shoe; the insectologist's, greenish, somehow like that of a magnified mantis on its stalk-thin neck; the purpled cheeks, marble eyes, sea-cow moustaches of Dr. Eberhardt in a mutiny of disbelief—he could see their faces, and he could see his own reflection, ugly with soot, black quills on his chin, hammocks under his eyes, blood on his ear, tousled, beaten, haggard, looking back at him from the rear window. The lips snarled back, showing teeth, and he was saying:

"Those curs found what they wanted in Captain Friederich's mausoleum. It had to be there. Their underground machinery was off the track, but it was following a certain course, and they finally guessed the reason. So did the gangsters following the grave-digging crew. So did I, as I told you, at that grave under the big tree. Listen, Dr. Eberhardt. Your death records were wrong."

"*Whaaat!*"

"That night you buried those six plague victims. January the third. 1922. Fourteen years ago. Those coffins lined up in the hall. You turned out the lights so the natives wouldn't see what you were doing. You sealed the coffins. Polypheme helped you carry them out to the car. Miss Engles told me you wrote the names in pencil on the roughboxes. You were working fast, in the dark, putting those bodies down from cemetery to cemetery—"

"*Ja, ja!* I buried them myself, I tell you. I—"

"You were one ahead each time on the list," Ranier said slowly. "Think. There was Adolph Perl, number one. The old lady, number two. The marine, Sergeant O'Grady, as three. Missionary, four. Colonel Otto, five. Captain Friederich, six. But you jumbled them in your haste, understand? You buried the old lady first. Number three in *her* plot. Number four at number three's. Colonel Otto at number four's. Captain Friederich at Colonel Otto's. And in Captain Friederich's mausoleum you put—"

"The coffin—*the coffin that had Adolph Perl's body in it!*" Dr. Eberhardt shouted.

"No," Ranier said.

• • •

THERE WAS A long, stunned pause.

"What is that you say?"

Slow ribbons of smoke drifted from Ranier's nostrils as he said, "Dr. Eberhardt, do you remember what happened that night fourteen years ago when you laid out those people who died of that plague?"

A flush of exasperation, anger, bafflement crimsoned the plump face under the yellow sou'wester.

"You do not make sense. Nothing tonight makes sense. Am I going mad? Do I hear this? Just now you tell me Adolph Perl—number one coffin—is put by mistake in the mausoleum of Captain Friederich—number six—*aber,* then you tell me—"

"I asked you if you recalled what happened that night you buried those people. Something disappeared, Miss Engles told me."

"A suitcase!" the red face blurted. "A suitcase of valuable—a dispatch case owned by the German government which I have returned to Berlin if Adolph Perl, the mate, should die. It was stolen. It was stolen by a sailor—"

"The sailor, Hans Blücher," Laïs Engles helped him in a breathless tone.

Ranier said roughly, "This Blücher ran out of the door. Perl went after him to bring him back. Perl came back alone, crawled up on the operating table, saying he was dying, he'd contracted the plague."

"That is so," the girl whispered.

"He asked Dr. Eberhardt to lay him in the hall so that he might die beside his officers. Dr. Eberhardt went out to the barn to fetch the coffins. You, Miss Engles, ran upstairs, hid for a while—"

The little doctor roared, "What? What is this about?"

"The body of Adolph Perl was not in that coffin in the mausoleum."

Laïs Engles sobbed, "But it was! It was! I saw it there when the lid was nailed on—saw his hand—the scar—"

Ranier leaned across the seat, eyes squinted, stern. "Dr. Eberhardt! You know what was in that suitcase owned by the *Wilhelmstrasse.* The case that secret mission intended for the Chilean diplomats in exchange for Chilean help—to buy explosives from Valparaiso. What was it?"

"Documents," the old man muttered. "Papers from the Kaiser."

"That's not all!" Rainer's tone was iron.

"*Nein,*" came the thick-throated whisper. "Also there were jewels. The neutral powers would not take paper money. Germany had no gold. There were jewels in the suitcase, heirlooms, the last hopeless donation of a beaten people. Four million marks' worth of jewels."

"Four million marks," Ranier said harshly, "equalled one million dollars. There were a million dollars' worth of jewels, gems wrapped in packets of oilskin, in Adolph Perl's coffin, but Adolph Perl's body wasn't. The body in that coffin was that of a smaller man, thinner, a scar painted on his hand—I'd guess with iodine from your laboratory—a body exchanged in the dark while the little girl was upstairs and you were out in the barn with Polypheme. That body had four million marks' worth of jewelry stuffed up its sleeves, its trouser-legs, under its sweater— Adolph Perl's clothing, incidentally—to make it look heavier and give it weight. I suppose it was too dark with the lights out to see the face, but you should've examined it more closely, there in the hall, Dr. Eberhardt. More closely, before nailing on the lid. That body had been smashed on the back of the head. I saw the fractured skull. It had *this* in its teeth."

With numb fingers he fumbled from his pocket a handful of pearls, a string of bitten cherry-sized globules that rolled about on his palm and shone skim-milk blue in the morning light.

"In the skull—" Dr. Eberhardt choked. "In its teeth—!"

"A man suffocating might bite his own arm," Ranier said huskily. "Hans Blücher woke up in that coffin. Hans Blücher was entombed alive."

CHAPTER XXVI

END OF THE TRAIL

It spoiled an orange sunrise that flamed with tropic flamboyance down the eastern *mornes,* painting a panorama of crinkly green-brown mountains, blazing blue gulf, the Jim Crow roofs of Port-au-Prince like litter on a beach, the tall masts of the wireless station incongruous on a skyline as luminous, exotic and gaudy as a macaw.

Haiti yawned by on a mule, going to market. Highways into town were clogged by circus parades of oxen, burros, dogs, goat-carts, trick bicycle riders, minstrels in bright costumes, jugglers balancing great baskets of fruit on cannon-ball heads, pickaninnies, turbanned crones, parrots and Nubians; cackling, mooing and shouting to create an impression of activity in a republic of sloth, a celebration to Morning after Night.

Ranier silently cursed slow traffic, his eye on the sprawled confusion of the waterfront where the Swastika-painted stacks of a great German touring liner overshadowed the town, placidly smoking in preparation for departure. She was, Ranier recognized, the ship which had moaned its way down the gulf last evening when the fog began. Other than a tangle of small fishing vessels, the only ship in port.

His own hooker wasn't due till noon, but he took the Model T from Polypheme and didn't spare the horse-power, racing for the municipal pier. Grim-jawed, tense, he drove; shifting his eyes but twice from those three black-and-white funnels, when he turned his head to answer two questions.

Laïs Engles asked in an odd, stiff voice, "Then—then Mr. Haarman *was Adolph Perl?*"

"Yes. The webbed foot settled it in my mind. Too rare an abnormality for coincidence. I had to assume he was the mate on your uncle's schooner; then figure out who it was you saw in that coffin, instead. Had to be the other sailor, of course. Blücher, panic-stricken in that quaran-

tined hospital, would naturally try to run for it. Natural enough for Adolph Perl to've gone after him, but it wasn't so natural for Perl to come back, the place a death-house as it was. No, he must've come back for something more than patriotism in a cause long since lost.

"We'll never know the truth of it, but Adolph Perl caught Blücher from behind, cracked him with a gun-butt probably, and my guess is he tucked Blücher into that cupboard, that same cupboard in the hall where he himself was stuffed fourteen years later. Then he played the big dying scene for Dr. Eberhardt, faking the symptoms and pulling a phony death-rattle. And Dr. Eberhardt took it for granted the man was dead."

"*Herr Gott!*" the old physician blurted. "How could I make such a mistake?"

"I can see how." Ranier's tone was without censure. "An epidemic bursting out on you like that, late at night, excitement, one death after another—and anybody'd be up in the air. You gave Adolph Perl a hasty once-over, maybe hurriedly felt for a pulse, in the darkness and all his acting deceived you.

"Besides, if that mauve death was as contagious as you say, you'd instinctively be pretty leery of close contact. Anyway, he wasn't dead, and when you hurried away to build him a coffin, as he knew you'd do, he got busy. The little girl had run somewhere to hide, the lights were out, it was a cinch to change clothes with the body in the cupboard, paint that artificial scar, smear up the face. A long chance of course, but a million dollars is a long shot anywhere. And it worked. Adolph Perl emptied that suitcase, stuffed the packets of jewelry into the clothes he'd put on Blücher, and fled.

"A perfect scheme in its way. German agents would be looking for Blücher, not Perl. He couldn't have passed a suitcase loaded with four million marks' worth of jewelry through the customs, either. So he'd buried his treasure; all he had to do was hide out till the uproar blew over, then come back to Haiti with a batch of grave-diggers, exhume the loot and smuggle it back to Germany. What I can't understand is why he waited fourteen years."

Dr. Eberhardt mopped a stricken forehead. "*Himmel!* To think that man, Blücher, was only unconscious when I nailed up the coffin. I was excited that night. Worn out. I feel as if I had murdered—"

"Not you," Ranier corrected, kindly. "Haarman—Perl—killed him."

"The *arachnid!*" the professor condemned learnedly. "The dirty *solpugid!*"

Laïs Engles breathed fiercely, "They must all be punished! Do you think we will catch them at the pier?" And Ranier turned his head the second time to smile at her thinly and answer by a shoulder-lift.

THEN, WITH THE ship's iron hull towering up alongside like a long dark cliff against the sun, midgets gazing down from a lofty focsle head, officers bright trifles on the bridge, tugs fussing under her nose, sailors standing by the lines—all the hustle, bustle and dock-halloo of sailing time, Ranier was certain he'd backed the wrong hunch.

Customs police met him at the pier gates with negative headshakes. *Gendarmes* greeted him with shrugs and empty hands. A line official accompanied the car down the long jetty to the gangway where tourist passengers were straggling up the roped incline, and a white-and-gold purser, passenger-list in hand, was examining the papers of a party anxious for cabin-space.

An ultramarine sky heated overhead, and the crowded pier, cramped between ship's hull and walls of a warehouse, was baking. Ranier fried in perspiration and impatience, waiting a word with this Nazi-moustached ship's purser who was tied up with red tape at the gangway's foot. The purser tried to speak bad French, and his prospective passengers were trying to speak bad German. Ranier gave the group a quick scrutiny.

The man of the party, French and elderly, stoop-shouldered in dark cutaway, pointed Vandyke beard and green sun glasses, was excitedly hunting for mislaid visas and demanding to know if German pursers thought Frenchmen were stowaways. The German was fussy about details. There were three women in the Frenchman's party, standing by in gloomy silence, all dressed in the sombre black of deep mourning, heavily veiled in tragedy, and the Frenchman wore the black arm-band of bereavement on his sleeve; but the ship's purser was a stickler for rules. Nobody could have escaped his eagle eye to stow away on board, tragic or no.

No, he finally found time to answer Ranier's question, there were no other new passengers embarking. Those who were going aboard were German tourists who had come on the cruise. *Ja,* all the tour people were now aboard, and so soon as he could straighten out the difficulty with this Frenchman and his party, the only newcomers so far, the liner would sail.

"Man and three women." Ranier shook his head glumly at Dr. Eberhardt, waiting in the shadow of the godowns. "Only ones going aboard from here. Guess I've missed the turn. But there are other ports in Haiti, and the *Garde d'Haiti*, this morning, is watching every one."

"*Cable pour m'sieu.*" A line official touched his arm.

Ranier ripped open the envelope, read sullenly, handed the missive to Professor Schlitz. The cable read:

Man Answering Your Description, Scar, Webbed Foot, Sentenced State Prison Auburn, N.Y. August 1922, Second Degree Murder Conviction, Killing in Utica, Under Name Gustaf Tropmann. Released Auburn January 1936.

"There's your spider for you, Professor. Another murder, soon as he could reach New York from Haiti. Auburn Prison. So that's why he was delayed. Explains his pallor on the cruise, too. I took a long chance and wirelessed a friend of mine in the New York police. At first I thought he was a consumptive, remember? I—"

He choked on a smoking oath.

Watching him, Laïs Engles gasped, "What is the matter?"

He'd been going to ask the professor to recall how, on pointing out Haarman's pallor to Kavanaugh, the Irishman had stopped him on the syllable "con." Had Kavanaugh known Haarman to be a convict?

JOHN RANIER NEVER voiced that speculation, or answered the girl's query. Brushing his three companions aside, he leapt away from the sheet-iron wharf-wall where they had been standing; went threshing across the pier like a small whirlwind, elbows going like pistons, boots kicking a path. Stevedores, porters, darky dock wallopers struggled to make elbow room. People saw the steely eyes, the purposeful jaws and ugly pallor of this man battling to reach the gangway, and trampled to get out of range. Somewhere sailors were yelling, the khaki *gendarmes* were running from the customs gate. Clamour broke loose in the sunshine.

The ship's purser, in voluble argument at the gangway's foot, did not notice Ranier's approach, but the Frenchman with the parted Vandyke and smoked glasses saw him coming, whirled in spry alarm, cried out to the three veiled women.

Ranier punched with everything he had, uppercutting the man's neat beard a blow that tore it loose by the roots. *Crack!* Vandyke and sun glasses went flying.

Everything whirligigged around him as his fingers found the man's throat and they locked together. He could hear himself squalling, "Kavanaugh! Kavanaugh!" while white faces shouted and boiled around them, police whistles shrilled, Germans bellowed down from the ship's upper decks, riot churned on the pier.

Kavanaugh's complexion was goose-color save where adhesive had peeled the skin from his jaws. His eyes squeezed shut and his tongue poked blue from his teeth. John Ranier would have choked him to death, gripping like a bulldog, if it hadn't thundered. Not exactly thunder.

A gun jabbed under his arm went *bonk!* The bullet scorched cloth under his armpit; hit the unmasked Irishman in the liver.

Kavanaugh died against him, and he had to fling the body off, leaping around just in time to catch a revolver by the barrel and deflect a second bullet into planking at his feet. Black cloth and a woman's funeral veil ripped in his clawing right hand; then he was waltzing furiously with a lady in black, an astonishing lady who breathed hoarse profanity on an odor of strong tobacco at his face, and kicked his shins like a soccer player.

With a violent wrench he wrested the gun from this enemy's grip; drove a knee into a corseted midriff; the astonishing widow went down, skirts tearing to the hip, exposing golf stockings and plus fours. Ranier removed hat and veil with a soccer-kick of his own, and Mr. Brown looked up at him with a dislocated grin and popping unconscious eyes.

Gendarmes were chasing a second black figure down the jetty. Afterwards he wondered whether she fainted or tripped on stretched hawser; but he saw her veil tear loose as she fell; saw that half-second glimpse of blowzy peroxide hair, shrieking baby-mouth, horrified googoo eyes; saw her plunge in a roil of pink underwear and skirts down between ship and pier.

An oily geyser spouted up the ship's side.

Somewhere Professor Schlitz was screaming, "Mish May! Mish May!"

Somewhere Laïs Engles screamed, "Look out!"

Another gun was banging; people were running past him, running from that third black figure in funeral weeds which was standing against a sheet-iron warehouse wall and firing indiscriminately at everything.

"Come and get it!"—(*Bang!*) "Come on, you dingy lugs, and get it!"—(*Bang-bang!*) "First guy that touches me is it!"—(*Bang-bang-bang!*)

It was strange. Strange to stand there frozen at that deserted gangway, staring at that black figure against the bright wall as if at the personification of death come to take him in broad daylight. A sort of magic had cleared the pier. In a twinkling the crowd had gone, the *douane* become deserted, the faces vanished from tier on tier of deck-rails in the ship's wall behind him. People were crouched behind cotton bales, salt bags, mounds of luggage, loading trucks, and he was left in the open like the Last Man, a dead Irishman and an unconscious fat man between himself and Death. Death waiting there in the sunshine, grotesque and clownish in appropriate mourning costume, black skirts, black veils, a tub-shaped black hat dowdily over the forehead. Death aiming an automatic pistol in one hairy big-knuckled hand.

"SO IT'S YOU?" Death was addressing him in a buttery chuckle. "Gummed the works for us after all, didn't you, Doc? Well, I missed you last night in the fog, but I ain't gonna miss you this time."

A big paw cleared the veils before the eyes, and the Coolidge face looked humorous in its masquerade; eyes like merry carbuncles, jaws grinning a gorilla display of gold-plated teeth. The countenance of a Mack truck decked in the feminine elegance of a Parisienne funeral-hearse, First Class. He winked at John Ranier over the levelled gun, his expression mischievous.

"I'm sorry," he said amiably, "because I kind of liked you, Doc." He paused to wipe suds from the corners of his lips. Said plaintively, "You hadn't oughta upset me just now when I'm a mass of nerves."

Ranier had a feeling of everything in suspended animation. His arm hung volitionless. There was a gun in that hand, but it would take a thousand years to aim and fire, and the gesture would mean suicide. Facing Mr. Coolidge in yellow sunlight, Mr. Coolidge like some huge urchin having fun in his aunt's bustle—facing that gold-toothed grin and hair-trigger gun, Ranier felt heavily depressed.

Everything, now, was over. Something inside him had finished.

Tomorrow he would be a bum ship's doctor dealing seasick pills and tomato juice to American tourists on an endless cruise. Tomorrow he'd be on his way from bar to bar, *aguardiente* to *aguardiente*, a little duller, a little grayer.

Funny, wasn't it? All night expended in an effort to prove there were no such phenomena as the "living" dead? He perceived he'd been chasing the wrong man. *He* was the *zombie*—

He said wryly, "I'm sorry, Mr. Coolidge, because I kind of liked you, too." Deliberately he raised the gun.

The revolver was heavy and his hand was slow. He could see his shabby cuff climbing past the lower buttons of his tunic. Years went by. When his wrist came even with the fourth button, the big man opposite him fired. Ranier heard the explosion, but he never saw the flash. Laïs Engles' scream was simultaneous with gun-roar, her movement fast as a shadow blown by wind. Like a shadow she was there, flying from obscurity near the gangway behind him to throw her arms about Ranier and bring him to his knees at the moment of Coolidge's shot.

Instantly the whole pier semed to blow up. Fire flashed and banged from the liner's bridge, from the foredeck, from portholes under the deserted railings. Spurts of flame from behind bales and crates near the cargo booms, from luggage-stacks on the jetty, from doors in the *douane*. A blizzard of bullets raked across the pier, beating against the sheet-iron warehouse wall. Germans are invariably good marksmen, and the *Garde d'Haiti* once took second place with their Olympic Games rifle team.

When the smoke finally cleared, the sheet-iron wall looked like a sieve.

Mr. Coolidge was a mass of nerves.

John Ranier sat on the gangway holding a slim girl in nurse's costume in his arms, cursing a scarlet blotch spreading under her crumpled collar.

THE GONG WAS going *damn-damn-damn-damn* to voice his thoughts, and the ambulance, hitting fifty, seemed to crawl. Somehow he drove Dr. Eberhardt, Professor Philemon Schlitz and a scared Negro interne to the front end of the swaying white compartment; then, outwardly cool, worked deftly with calm hands over the unconscious girl. By pretending this was Philadelphia, a traffic accident, he could ignore the white pain on her face and steady his touch.

"I've stopped the hemorrhage, Dr. Eberhardt. She's going to be okay."

"Gott sei dank!" The old man was wringing his dry sou'wester in dripping hands. "She will not—she will not die?"

Ranier gave him an upturned grin. "Not her. Bullets don't stop her kind. Bullets are for those rats back there on the pier."

Professor Schlitz burst out with: "But how did you recognishe them when you did? How did you know it was Misher Kavanaugh and—"

"The Mick put over his disguise all right," Ranier said. "Probably learned the art of make-up in prison shows at Auburn. They must've had those costumes in their luggage. But you can't change a habit overnight, even if you can change your face. Kavanaugh gave himself away. I recognized him when I saw him pull that habitual cocked-finger gesture of his at the ship's purser."

"The *Schweinhund!*" Dr. Eberhardt swore. "Dogs! They shot my little girl—my poor little girl—!"

John Ranier snarled, "Cheer yourself on this, Doctor. Think how those rats must've felt when they found Captain Friederich's mausoleum already opened when they got there—opened when the first gang of grave-robbers arrived. Hijacked, see?"

"What is that you say? What is that?" The old physician took his eyes from the unconscious girl; yelled.

"I say Marcelline and Brown, the grave-digging crew, found the tomb already opened when they got there from Bois Legone. Somebody'd beat them to it." Ranier lifted his voice above the ambulance gong. "Somebody'd been there ahead of them and rifled the coffin. Some job to explain to Kavanaugh, Coolidge and the blonde, when they arrived on the scene and wanted their share. I'll bet there was a row. But Kavanaugh and his gang never got those jewels at all."

"How do you know?" Professor Schlitz was half out of his leather seat. "How do you know those crooks didn't get the—"

"Because they didn't have the loot at the pier," Ranier told him. "I telephoned ahead to the *Garde d'Haiti* and told them to examine every last piece of baggage going aboard that German liner. That's what the argument was about at the gangway. But the pier officials didn't find the stuff at the customs gate, and told me so when we arrived at the pier. I thought I'd missed my guess. But—"

"But who got the jewels?" Dr. Eberhardt burst out. "Who robbed the mausoleum first?"

"A nice question." Ranier mocked a frown. "Kavanaugh, Coolidge and the dame didn't get them, and the grave-digging crew didn't get them. Must be someone else, then. Someone who guessed where they'd be from the way that game of Going to Jerusalem was progressing. Someone say, who didn't go from Morne Cuyamel to Bois Legone, but cut Bois Legone from the itinerary and jumped straight to that last cemetery on the list. Someone, say, who rode as far as the fork in the highway on the back of Kavanaugh's car, dropped off at the road fork and, maybe, picked up a stray horse. Then beat the grave-diggers to the mountaintop, broke into the tomb with a shovel or pick such as might be left lying around; smashed the coffin and got the goods."

"YOU," RANIER SWITCHED the pronoun, "then circled back to Bois Legone; ducked the horse somewhere, and waited around in that graveyard, knowing I'd turn up and *you'd* have an alibi story as well as protection. Marcelline was sent back to get his Panama, but he was also sent back to get *you* and when—"

The thin man's leap did not take Ranier by surprise. Truly and with ferocity he drove his fist to the man's boneless mouth, reducing Professor Schlitz to a heap on the ambulance floor.

John Ranier had never, in his surgical career, so astounded an audience or worked so miraculous an operation. A gastroenterostomy that produced from under the prone man's vest an amazing viscera of precious stones, strings of amethyst, pearl necklaces, a diamond tiara, loops

of azure light and vermillion brilliance, a handful of sapphires and a chain of topaz. Diadems, lockets, bracelets, brooches. Opals and three emeralds and moonstones. A tumor under the belt produced a flow of jade. Rubies were blood.

The ambulance was stopping under a vine-cooled arch, and Ranier saw the calm white facade of a quiet hospital. The professor could tell a pair of *gendarmes* leaning in the entry about his operation.

John Ranier straightened up to dump a million dollars' worth of jewelry into Dr. Eberhardt's stunned lap. He was thinking of Wilde's comment on the price of everything and the value of nothing. Which was true in some cases, but not in the case of four million marks' worth of jewels which the German government would pay plenty for; and not in this ambulance case.

He saw Laïs Engles was conscious, smiling gamely at him through white pain. He took her hand in his.

"You'll be all right," he promised gently, smiling down. "I'll have that piece of lead out of you before you know it, and I'm going to take care of you, myself. I've just done a million dollar job, and I'm appointing myself Dr. Eberhardt's new assistant. We'll start work rebuilding his hospital as soon as you're on your feet."

John Ranier knew he was grinning foolishly, unprofessionally, but he couldn't stop it. He'd found something worth doing, something he wanted to do. There was no such thing as a *zombie*, after all.

PERMISSIONS ACKNOWLEDGMENTS

"Bringing the Family" by Kevin J. Anderson. Originally published in *The Ultimate Zombie*, edited by Byron Preiss and John Betancourt (New York, Dell, 1993). Copyright © 1993 by Wordfire, Inc. Reprinted by permission of Kevin J. Anderson, president, Wordfire, Inc.

"Death and Suffrage" by Dale Bailey. Originally published in *The Magazine of Fantasy and Science Fiction*, February 2002. Copyright © 2002 by Dale Bailey. Reprinted by permission of the author.

"Ballet Nègre" by Charles Birkin. Originally published in *The Magazine of Fantasy and Science Fiction*, November 1967. Copyright © 1967 by Charles Birkin. Reprinted by permission of Amanda Toyne.

"They Bite" by Anthony Boucher. Originally published in *Unknown Worlds* magazine, June 1942. Copyright © 1942 by Anthony Boucher, copyright renewed by The Estate of William Anthony Parker White. Reprinted by permission of Curtis Brown, Ltd.

"Dance of the Damned" by Arthur J. Burks. Originally published in *Horror Stories* magazine, August/September 1936. Copyright © 1936 by Popular Publications, Inc., copyright renewed 1964 and assigned to Argosy Communications, Inc. All rights reserved. Reprinted by arrangement with Argosy Communications, Inc.

"It Helps If You Sing" by Ramsey Campbell. Originally published in *Book of the Dead*, edited by John Skipp and Craig Spector (New York, Bantam, 1989). Copyright © 1989 by Ramsey Campbell. Reprinted by permission of the author.

"The Old Man and the Dead" by Mort Castle. Originally published in *Book of the Dead 2: Still Dead*, edited by John Skipp and Craig Spector (New York, Bantam, 1992). Copyright © 1992 by Mort Castle. Reprinted by permission of the author.

"Mission to Margal" by Hugh B. Cave. Originally published in *The Mammoth Book of Zombies*, edited by Stephen Jones (London, Robinson Publishing, 1993). Copyright © 1993 by Hugh B. Cave. Reprinted by permission of the Estate of Hugh B. Cave and Milton J. Thomas.

"The Ghouls" by R. Chetwynd-Hayes. Originally published in *The Night Ghouls* (London, Fontana, 1975). Copyright © 1975 by R. Chetwynd-Hayes. Reprinted by permission of Linda Smith, Executrix of the Estate of R. Chetwynd-Hayes.

"The House in the Magnolias" by August Derleth and Mark Schorer. Originally published in *Strange Tales*, June 1932. From *Colonel Markesan and Less Pleasant People* (Sauk City, WI,

2007. Copyright © 2007 by Joe R. Lansdale. Reprinted by permission of the author.

"Mess Hall" by Richard Layman. Originally published in *Book of the Dead*, edited by John Skipp and Craig Spector (New York, Bantam, 1989). Copyright © 1989 by Richard Laymon. Reprinted by permission of the Estate of Richard Layman.

"The Outsider" by H. P. Lovecraft from *Dunwich Horror & Others*. Copyright © 1984 by Arkham House Publishers. Originally published in *Weird Tales*, April 1926. Reprinted by permission of April Derleth, Arkham House Publishers.

"Pickman's Model" by H. P. Lovecraft from *The Dunwich Horror & Others*. Copyright © 1984 by Arkham House Publishers. Originally published in *Weird Tales*, October 1927. Reprinted by permisison of April Derleth, Arkham House Publishers.

"Eat Me" by Robert McCammon. Originally published in *Book of the Dead*, edited by John Skipp and Craig Spector (New York, Bantam, 1989). Copyright © 1989 by The McCammon Corporation. Reprinted by permission of Robert McCammon care of Donald Maass Literary Agency.

"While Zombies Walked" by Thorp McClusky. Originally published in *Weird Tales*, September 1939. Copyright © 1939 by *Weird Tales*. Reprinted by permission of Weird Tales Ltd.

"The Taking of Mr. Bill" by Graham Masterton. Originally published in *The Mammoth Book of Zombies*, edited by Stephen Jones (London, Robinson Publishing, 1993). Copyright © 1993 by Graham Masterton. Reprinted by permission of the author.

"Where There's a Will" by Richard Matheson and Richard Christian Matheson. Originally published in *Dark Forces: New Stories of Suspense and Supernatural Horror*, edited by Kirby McCauley (New York, Viking, 1980). Copyright © 1980 by Richard Matheson and Richard Christian Matheson. Reprinted by permission of Don Congdon Associates, Inc.

"Feeding the Dead Inside" by Yvonne Navarro. Originally published in *Mondo Zombie*, edited by John Skipp (Baltimore, Cemetery Dance, 2006). Reprinted by permission of the author care of Fine Print Literary Management.

"The Corpse-Master" by Seabury Quinn. Originally published in *Weird Tales*, July 1929. Copyright © 1929 by *Weird Tales*. Reprinted by permission of Weird Tales Ltd.

"After Nightfall" by David A. Riley. Originally published in *Weird Window*, 1970. Copyright © 1970 by David A. Riley. Reprinted by permission of the author.

"Dead Men Working in the Cane Fields" by W. B. Seabrook. Originally published in *The Magic Island* (New York, Harcourt, Brace & World, 1929). Reprinted by permission of William Seabrook and the Watkins/Loomis Agency.

"Vengeance of the Living Dead" by Ralston Shields. Originally published in *Terror Tales* magazine, September 1940. Copyright © 1940 by Popular Publications, Inc., copyright renewed 1968 and assigned to Argosy Communications, Inc. All rights reserved. Reprinted by arrangement with Argosy Communications, Inc.

"Later" by Michael Marshall Smith. Originally published in *The Mammoth Book of Zombies*, edited by Stephen Jones (London, Robinson Publishing, 1993). Reprinted by permission of the author and the author's agent, Ralph M. Vicinanza.

"It" by Theodore Sturgeon. Originally published in *Unknown*, August 1940. Reprinted by permission of the Estate of Theodore Sturgeon care of Ralph M. Vicinanza Ltd.

"The Dead" by Michael Swanwick. Originally published in *Starlight 1*, edited by Patrick Nielsen Hayden (New York, Tor, 1996). Copyright © 1996 by Michael Swanwyck. Reprinted by permission of the author.

"Bodies and Heads" by Steve Rasnic Tem. Originally published in *Book of the Dead*, edited by John Skipp and Craig Spector (New York, Bantam, 1989). Copyright © 1989 by Steve Rasnic Tem. Reprinted by permission of the author.

"Marbh Bheo" by Peter Tremayne. Originally published in *The Mammoth Book of Zombies*, edited by Stephen Jones (London, Robinson Publishing, 1993). Copyright © 1993 by Peter Tremayne. Reprinted by permission of the author and Brandt & Hochman Literary Agents on behalf of the author.

"April Flowers, November Harvest" by Mary A. Turzillo. Originally published in *Midnight Zoo*, May 1993. Copyright © 1993 by Mary A. Turzillo. Reprinted by permission of the author.

"Treading the Maze" by Lisa Tuttle. Originally published in *The Magazine of Fantasy and Science Fiction*, November 1981. Copyright © 1981 by Lisa Tuttle. Reprinted by permission of the author.

"The Songs of the Slaves" by Manly Wade Wellman. Originally published in *Weird Tales*, March 1940. Copyright © 1940 by *Weird Tales*. Reprinted by permission of David A. Drake on the behalf of the Estate of Manly Wade Wellman.

"Jumbee" from *Jumbee and Other Uncanny Tales* by Henry S. Whitehead. Originally published in *Weird Tales*, September 1926. Reprinted by permission of April Derleth, Arkham House Publishers.

"The Cairnwell Horror" by Chet Williamson. Originally published in *Walls of Fear*, edited by Kathryn Cramer (New York, Morrow, 1990). Copyright © 1990 by Chet Williamson. Reprinted by permission of the author.

"Come One, Come All" by Gahan Wilson. Originally published in *Book of the Dead 2: Still Dead*, edited by John Skipp and Craig Spector (New York, Bantam, 1992). Copyright © 1992 by Gahan Wilson. Reprinted by permission of the author.

"The Crawling Madness" by Arthur Leo Zagat. Originally published in *Terror Tales* magazine, March 1935. Copyright © 1935 by Popular Publications, Inc., copyright renewed 1963 and assigned to Argosy Communications, Inc. All rights reserved. Reprinted by arrangement with Argosy Communications, Inc.

ALSO EDITED BY OTTO PENZLER

THE BLACK LIZARD BIG BOOK OF PULPS
The Best Crime Stories from the Pulps During Their Golden Age—The '20s, '30s, & '40s

Weighing in at over a thousand pages, containing more than fifty stories and two novels, this book is big, baby, bigger and more powerful than a freight train—a bullet couldn't pass through it. Here are the best stories and every major writer who ever appeared in celebrated pulps like *Black Mask*, *Dime Detective*, *Detective Fiction Weekly*, and more. These are the classic tales that created the genre and gave birth to hard-hitting detectives who smoke criminals like cheap cigars; sultry dames whose looks are as lethal as a dagger to the chest; and gin-soaked hideouts where conversations are just preludes to murder. This is crime fiction at its gritty best.

Crime Fiction

THE BLACK LIZARD BIG BOOK OF BLACK MASK STORIES

The Greatest Crime Fiction from the Legendary Magazine

An unstoppable anthology of crime stories culled from *Black Mask*, the magazine where the first hard-boiled detective story, which was written by Carroll John Daly, appeared. It was the slum in which Dashiell Hammett, Raymond Chandler, Horace McCoy, Cornell Woolrich, John D. MacDonald all got their start. It was the home of stories with titles like "Murder *Is* Bad Luck," "Ten Carats of Lead," "Diamonds Mean Death," and "Drop Dead Twice." Also here is *The Maltese Falcon* as it originally appeared in the magazine. Crime writing gets no better than this.

Crime Fiction

THE VAMPIRE ARCHIVES

*The Most Complete Volume of Vampire Tales
Ever Published*

The Vampire Archives is the biggest, hungriest, undeadliest collection of vampire stories, as well as the most comprehensive bibliography of vampire fiction ever assembled. Whether imagined by Bram Stoker or Anne Rice, vampires are part of the human lexicon and as old as blood itself. They are your neighbors, your friends, and they are always lurking. Now Otto Penzler has compiled the darkest, the scariest, and by far the most evil collection of vampire stories ever. With over eighty stories, including the works of Stephen King and D. H. Lawrence, alongside Lord Byron and Tanith Lee, not to mention Edgar Allan Poe and Harlan Ellison, it will drive a stake through the heart of any other collection out there.

Fiction

ALSO AVAILABLE IN MASS-MARKET VOLUMES:

BLOODSUCKERS
The Vampire Archives, Volume 1
Including stories by Stephen King, Dan Simmons, and
Bram Stoker

FANGS
The Vampire Archives, Volume 2
Including stories by Clive Barker, Anne Rice, and
Arthur Conan Doyle

COFFINS
The Vampire Archives, Volume 3
Including stories by Harlan Ellison, Robert Bloch, and
Edgar Allan Poe

THE BIG BOOK OF ADVENTURE STORIES

Everyone loves adventure, and Otto Penzler has collected the best adventure stories of all time into one awe-inspiring volume. With stories by Jack London, O. Henry, H. Rider Haggard, Alistair MacLean, Talbot Mundy, Cornell Woolrich, and many others, this wide-reaching and fascinating volume contains some of the best characters from the most thrilling adventure tales, including The Cisco Kid; Sheena, Queen of the Jungle; Bulldog Drummond; Tarzan; The Scarlet Pimpernel; Conan the Barbarian; Hopalong Cassidy; King Kong; Zorro; and The Spider. Divided into sections that embody the greatest themes of the genre—Sword and Sorcery; Megalomania Rules; Man vs. Nature; Island Paradise; Sand and Sun; Something Feels Funny; Go West, Young Man; Future Shock; I Spy; Yellow Peril; In Darkest Africa—it is destined to be the greatest collection of adventure stories ever compiled.

Fiction

AGENTS OF TREACHERY

*Never Before Published Spy Fiction from
Today's Most Exciting Writers*

For the first time ever, Otto Penzler has handpicked some of the most respected and bestselling thriller writers working today for a riveting collection of spy fiction. From first to last, this stellar collection signals mission accomplished. Featuring: Lee Child with an incredible look at the formation of a special ops team; James Grady writing about an Arab undercover FBI agent with an active cell; Joseph Finder riffing on a Boston architect who's convinced that his Persian neighbors are up to no good; John Lawton concocting a Len Deighton-esque story about British intelligence; Stephen Hunter thrilling us with a tale about a WWII brigade; and much more.

Spy Fiction